THE FAMINE CYCLE

THE COMPLETE SERIES

J.D.L. ROSELL

Cover illustration © 2024 by Ömer Burak Önal
Cover design by Rachel St. Clair of Claymore Covers
Chapter header image © 2024 by Rachel St. Clair of Claymore Covers
Interior illustrations and chapter backgrounds © 2021, 2022 by René Aigner
Interior design by J.D.L. Rosell
Maps by Kaitlyn Clark

ISBN 978-1-952868-48-1 (Trade paperback)
ISBN 978-1-952868-49-8 (Ebook)

Published by Rune & Requiem Press
runeandrequiempress.com

CONTENTS

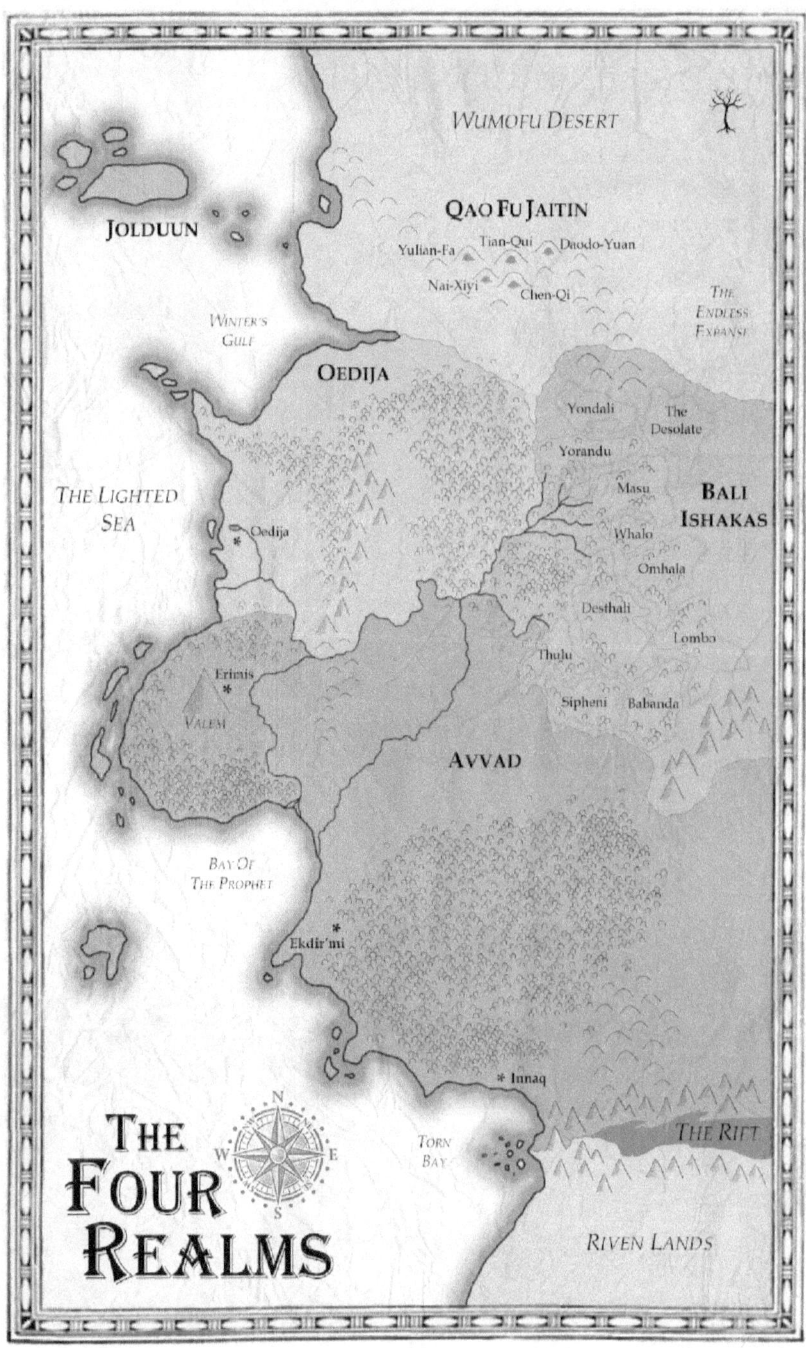

WUMOFU DESERT
JOLDUUN
QAO FU JAITIN
Yulian-Fa
Tian-Qui
Daodo-Yuan
Nai-Xiyi
Chen-Qi
THE ENDLESS EXPANSE
WINTER'S GULF
OEDIJA
Yondali
The Desolate
Yorandu
Masu
BALI ISHAKAS
THE LIGHTED SEA
Whalo
Omhala
Oedija
Desthali
Lomba
Thulu
Erimis
Sipheni
Babanda
VALEM
AVVAD
BAY OF THE PROPHET
Ekdir'mi
Innaq
N
THE RIFT
W
E
TORN BAY
THE
FOUR
REALMS
S
RIVEN LANDS

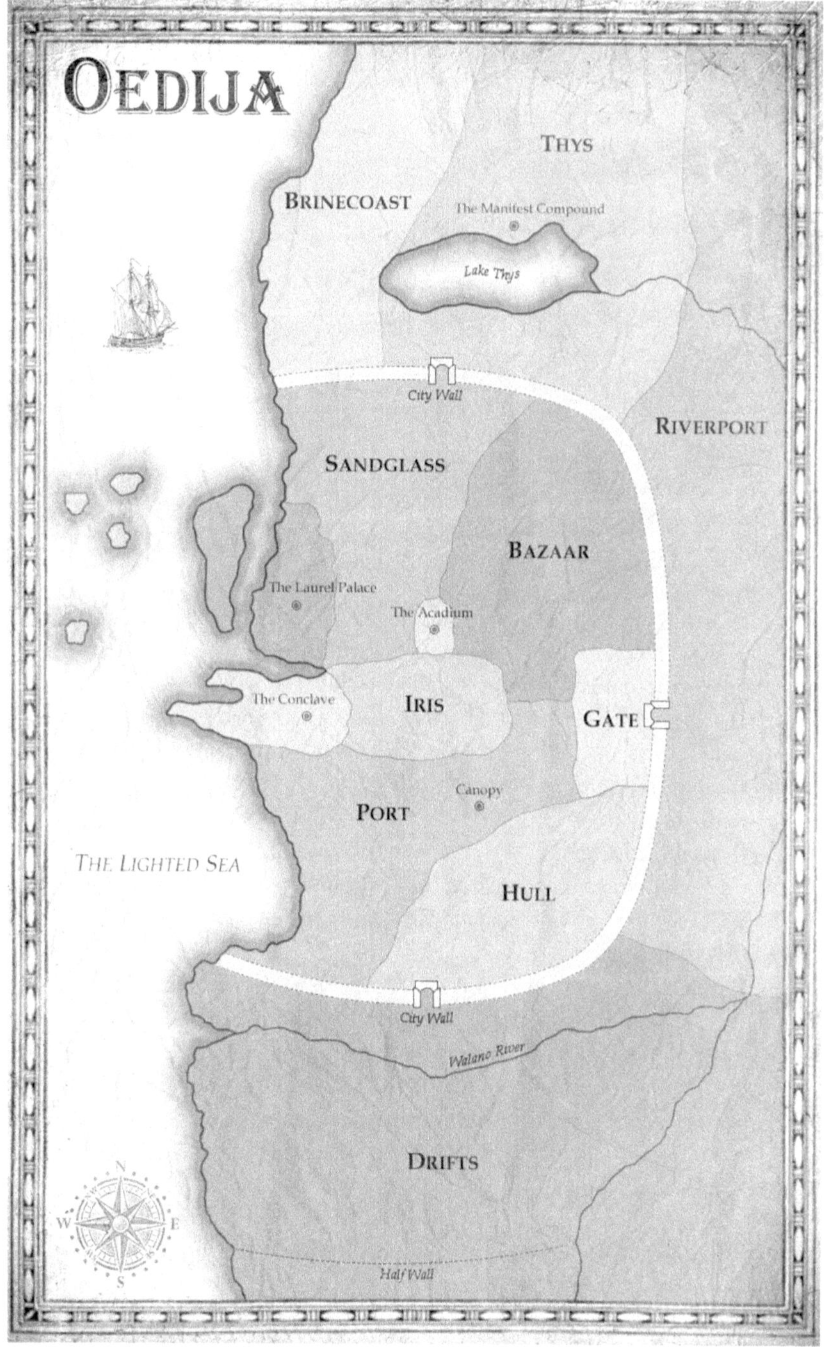

OEDIJA
THYS
BRINECOAST
The Manifest Compound
Lake Thys
City Wall
SANDGLASS
RIVERPORT
BAZAAR
The Laurel Palace
The Acadium
The Conclave
IRIS
GATE
Canopy
PORT
THE LIGHTED SEA
HULL
City Wall
Walano River
DRIFTS
Half Wall
N
W
E
S

INTRODUCTION

The idea for The Famine Cycle came to me in a dream.

I know, I know—it sounds too apocryphal to be true. But I swear by my good writing hands it's precisely how it happened.

It was the morning after my wife—then girlfriend—and I had moved to Seattle. I awoke in the bed of the Airbnb where we were staying with a notion lodged in my mind, almost a question:

What if a private investigator existed in a fantasy world?

At that point in my life, I'd never read anything like that, and it struck me as a novel idea. Even now, I've only run across the concept a few times in other books, and always with a different spin—yet it's a step too far to claim it's *entirely* original.

Still, the idea fascinated me and captured my imagination. As we began our life in a new city, I began formulating how Oedija, the city where most of the series takes place, would be set up.

Unsurprisingly, Oedija's shape isn't dissimilar from Seattle's, and many other aspects of our lives there—scraping by as early twenty-somethings with unfulfilling jobs while trying to follow our passions—also found their way into the story.

But before I could begin writing anything, I had to know my protago-nist. So I was fortunate when, after long months of trying to get in her head, Airene of Port finally spoke to me.

Another spurious story! you might exclaim. For this one, you would be closer to the mark. Airene's voice came less by inspiration than doggedly uncovering it over time. The first several attempts at writing her perspective were spectacular failures. In fact, writing as Talan—an important side character who headlines the novella *The Phantom Heist* (also included)—came much easier to start.

Still, as I kept putting myself in Airene's sandals, she began speaking to me. I often looked out the window during my hour-long bus commute and imagined how she would describe our surroundings, or what observation she would make of a passerby or fellow rider.

In fragmented whispers, our indomitable Finch came alive.

The rest of the world and story unfolded from there. Ancient Greece and Rome informed much of the setup of Oedija and the Four Realms as well as the mythology. The magic came from taking the different kinds of energy that exist in our world—kinetic, thermal, chemical, etc.—and giving them a mystical bend. The dragon god Famine has its backbone in the Chinese mythical creature Taotie.

I could pick out a hundred more inspirations—but who has time for that?

So I will end with this. This story and its cast of characters came from particular moments and places in my life, and those experiences are instilled in every page. Yet my hope is that it reaches far beyond anything you or I have experienced. That is transports you beyond our world to a fantastical—and sometimes terrifying—new realm.

May you enjoy the journey of The Famine Cycle trilogy and its ancillary stories, and come to know and love the bonds between our three Finches, their friends, and even their enemies as I have.

~ *J.D.L. Rosell*

WHISPERS OF RUIN

THE FAMINE CYCLE
BOOK I

PROLOGUE

I was not born a warden.

For much of my childhood, I showed little sign of the arcane. I didn't even show promise of rising above my station. The daughter of an indebted carpet merchant and an ailing shipwright, I was fortunate merely to attend the public scholarium and learn my letters. That I received high marks was of little import.

In Oedija, the Pearl of the Four Realms, social hierarchy was rigid. No man or woman became something that their parents were not.

Yet my nature rebelled, as did my brothers'. I made nothing of our similarities for much of my life. Our mother had passed on her stubbornness to us; it was inevitable that we should try to throw off her hypocritical yoke.

Now, I know this to be no coincidence. It was our fate. But I did not understand that then. The fire that filled me seemed all my own.

The passion that has consumed me flourished one day while passing through the markets. My ears caught a fragment of conversation, a hint of gossip, but of a kind that held dark depths. At five, I didn't understand what it meant for one patrician to sleep with another out of wedlock, as the washerwoman I eavesdropped upon had confided to another. Yet when I told my father of this, his eyes widened, and he bade me to not repeat it where I could be overheard. Punishment could be doled out for slander, he said. And because I loved him, I complied.

But in his reaction, I understood something I had not known before.

Secrets held power, a power others feared. Young and powerless, I yearned to claim it.

So began what would become my life's calling. By the time I was eight, I'd sought more dangerous tales than salacious scandals, opting instead for street-side scams and moneylender muggings. I would return home after long, dusty days and illustrate my hard-earned stories in colorful detail to my brothers for their amusement.

By the time I was twelve, I'd sold my first secret.

At fifteen, when adolescents settle on their occupation, I named myself a Finch after the Order of Verifiers, a long-disbanded branch of the government, to carry on their mission of exposing truth wherever deception obscured it. When I set to the work a year later, I found myself more often chasing profit than justice. But always, I told myself it was in the eventual pursuit of that noble goal.

But my calling had its limits. When I sought to uncover the secret most important to me and failed, my belief in my purpose faltered. I had honed my skills and developed my network, and for what?

What did any of this matter if I could not even find my eldest brother's murderer?

I was eleven when they found his body in a canal. His face was nothing like I remembered, bloated with death and prolonged exposure to saltwater. Yet it was the scars, thin and violet, that spiderwebbed from his eyes that haunted my memories most. They tantalized with the secrets they held. Even as young as I was, I sensed if I could understand their origin, I would know how my brother died.

A decade later, I received a hint more of the mystery. Yet in the end, answers eluded my grasp. The trail ran dry, the clues turned up cold. Not for all my prowess as a Finch could I track down the killer.

Despair, however, is a tempering flame. It was from this failure that my calling truly began to find its purpose. That I became discontented with blackmailing scoundrels and exposing ignominy, and I searched for a higher purpose.

I was not born a warden. I had no touch of magic. But when the three horns of the Laurel Palace sounded their mournful voices over Oedija, I set down the path to become one.

A warden who would reshape the face of the Four Realms.

A warden who, Eidola willing, would cage a god.

CHAPTER ONE
FEAST & FAMINE

The Festival of Radiance, a celebration as old as Oedija itself, is a reminder of the Hunger War that drove our ancestors across the Lighted Sea, in the days when the daemon god Famine slew the Foremost of our gods and nearly swallowed the world…

- The Traditions of the Eleven: Eïdolan worship in the demotism of Oedija; by Oracle Iason of deme Iris; 1164 SLP (Succeeding the Lighted Passage)

Perched on the edge of the rooftop, I searched for the smuggler.

It was the wrong time for a hunt. Forum Demos was packed as tightly as fish in barrels after a day's ample catch, a full third of Oedija's population gathered for the Despot's address. Expecting to spy one man among thirty-thousand was a fool's wish.

But though my back ached and my legs had gone numb from hanging off the eaves, I didn't let up.

I had no other choice.

"We should give in, Airene. We're never going to find him." Xaron stretched and yawned, then reached back for his cup of festival wine, nearly spilling it in the process. Though he dressed like a fop and possessed the athleticism of a gymnast, Xaron had the manners of a boar. His yellow coat and scarlet trousers sported many stains from the day's activities.

"We need the coin," I reminded him drily.

"But we won't find it today." Nomusa, our third accomplice, spoke up from my other side. "Zotikos will need to surrender the goods before we can pick up the coin from Maesos."

"Thanks for having my back." I gave her a long-suffering grimace.

She smiled back, a teasing curve to it. Her dark, olive skin and revealing robe accentuated her natural beauty. When we'd been younger, standing next to her had made me self-conscious of my own middling looks. But nine years of working and living together had cured that small jealousy. Her bared arms revealed the intricate, blue tatu that wound up to her elbows. They told the truths of her past, for those who could read them.

Xaron leaned into me, his breath sour with wine. "How much longer until we can convince you to leave it off? Radiance ends today, and with it goes the free wine."

I was hanging onto my resolve by a thread myself. But I forced myself to say, "Until we find him."

Xaron lapsed into morose silence and took another drink. Nomusa held her tongue. Not to be made a liar, I renewed the search, if half-heartedly. The dying light strained my eyes, promising an aching head that night.

The great amphitheater spread out below us. A quarter-mile of marbled tiers cascading down to a colonnaded dais, every tier was filled to overflowing, their occupants from all echelons of society. Patricians, citizens, honors, plebeians — this gathering was the closest that rich and poor came to being equals.

Amid that mass of humanity, Xaron, Nomusa, and I needed to spy one particular man from a rooftop at the back of the forum. But though the man would be wearing the colored robes of the mercantile class, I'd searched the tiny figures below for far too long. My eyes felt too large for their sockets. My head buzzed with festival wine. My vision swam.

It was as fruitless as a pyr hunt, and I knew it.

I kicked the blood back into my legs and stared up at the sky. Finches, each with tiny scrolls tied to their thin legs, flitted above, flecks of fast-moving colors in the sunset light. Even now, just before the largest gathering of the year, the messenger birds of Oedija received no rest. A gentle breeze, the last of the warm summer winds, blew against my face. Shouts, laughs, and shrieks from the orphans underneath our feet filled the air. No doubt many of the urchins had taken their fair share of the festival wine. Freely dispensed by the People's Conclave during the five days of the Festival of Radiance in a flagrant facade of generosity, this was the children's last chance to indulge and escape the misery of their daily lives.

A new voice broke through the other noises to rise over the tumult of the crowd, slowly quieting them. Squinting at the dais, I saw an oracle of the Eidolan faith, the religion of Oedija's ancestors, stood between the grand marble columns. The old man's voice was worn as pilled wool, yet loud enough to be heard all across the public square, thanks to the mystical aid of our present Hilarion.

"Our story begins long before our demotism and the Conclave," the oracle spoke, voice echoing through the now-quiet amphitheater. "Before the Tyrant Wardens took Oedija for their own, and set those attuned to the Pyrthae to rule over those who were not. Long even before the first Wreath occupied the Laurel Palace. We go back to just before the Lighted Passage, when our ancestors sailed from their blighted homeland in the west to a faraway land in the east — this land, settling the stones on which we now stand."

The oracle paused, then continued as if reluctant to do so. "The story begins with Famine. Some have called Famine a serpent, a great serpent. But he was no more a snake than a phoenix is a finch. Some have called him a dragon, yet this can still not do him justice. For when Famine opened his mouth wide, he could swallow the whole of Telae."

Famine. Despite the joviality of the festival below, the specter of the daemon god loomed large over the city these days. A drought promised forthcoming food shortages. Prices were already rising, and would only climb higher as stores ran low. With hunger would come strife. Robbery. Rioting. Perhaps even revolt, if things were as bad as the reports promised.

As much as I wished to give up my search, I couldn't. Without claiming the much-needed coin from the job, Nomusa, Xaron, and I might soon find ourselves among the starving.

Xaron stirred and pointed. "There! By the Pillar. Is that him?"

I followed his direction, peering at the immense column of gray stone that rose high into the sky above. One of the remnants of an older civilization, the Pillars and the others like it scattered across Oedija made for convenient landmarks. I picked out a man standing near its base in bright red robes, a stark contrast from the browns surrounding him. Next to him stood a man half a head taller than everyone else.

A thin smile found my lips. Zotikos, the man we'd been searching for, and his bodyguard were those two men; I was sure of it.

Nomusa leaned forward. "Can you see who he's meeting with?"

I reached into my satchel and pulled out my peering glass. Looking through it, I brought the man in red robes into focus. He was turned away from me, but his close-cropped, curly hair was the same as Zotikos's.

I lowered the glass and shook my head. "Too far to tell, and too many surround them. We'll have to move closer."

"Meeting by the Pillar." Xaron tutted. "You'd think criminals would know to be a little less obvious."

I shrugged. "I won't object to a straightforward venture for once."

"Don't speak too soon," Nomusa chided. "This job isn't over."

We made our slow way off the roof to the street below and endured the gibes of the orphans surrounding us. As our feet found the cobblestones, I muttered to Nomusa, "Is it just me, or are we getting too old for this?"

She drew me in with an arm around the waist. "You just need to practice Ixolo with me. Then you'll be as nimble as any street orphan."

"Or as naturally graceful as I." Xaron leaped the last several feet to the ground and stumbled as he landed.

I rolled my eyes. "Graceful as a three-legged mule. Hurry up."

As we pushed through the crowd, the stench of unwashed bodies filled my nose. From the dais, the oracle finished his story.

"Tyurn Sky-Sea knew we could not face Famine unarmed. So, giving all of his strength, he granted us his gift. Attuning the First Wardens to the Pyrthae, humanity gained the gift of magic. Wardens drew on the power of that spiritual realm and fought alongside the gods. Wielding the energetic elements like soldiers use swords and spears, they worked together to drive Famine and his horde from the world and, once again, bound him."

As he concluded, there was a spattering of applause, then silence — the quiet of anticipation. Soon, Despot Myron Wreath, purported ruler of Oedija, would take the stage for his annual Radiance address. All around me, folk murmured their hopes for him. They dreamed of a year of plenty and quiet streets.

But Myron could do little for them. Even if he still possessed the influence of his forebears, nothing could prevent the hunger soon to come. No amount of trade with the other nations of the Four Realms could change the fact that our granaries were near empty and our fields fallow. Each nation had to watch out for themselves now.

It wasn't long before I glimpsed our quarry again through the crowd. Zotikos turned around for a moment, a scowl on his face. His guard, a tall, broad man who wore a yet deeper frown, stood nearby scanning the crowd. The smuggler turned back, gesturing at someone before him.

Xaron whistled. "That's a big man he brought."

"Not a problem for you, though." I cast him a sidelong glance.

He grinned. "Not if you let me off my leash."

"You're lucky we don't muzzle you, too." Nomusa grabbed his arm. "Come on. Let's get this over with."

CHAPTER TWO

OF SMUGGLERS AND DESPOTS

By all measures, Myron Wreath has proven to be a moderate and even-tempered man. Aware of his powers' bounds, he has rarely, if ever, strayed into perilous waters. In his twenty-two year reign, he has done much to preserve the traditions and state of the nation, and despite his efforts having a negligent effect on decreasing belief in the Eidola, he has done well in improving the commercial state of Oedija…

I find that few, if any, are opposed to his reign for many years to come.

- A Modern Account of the Wreaths; by Acadian Helene, Master Historian; 1170 SLP

We pressed forward, the crowd thinning as we neared. The bodyguard's forbidding glare was enough to make people think twice about coming close. Leaning around those in front of me, I caught a glimpse of Zotikos's contact. My mouth went dry.

The man was an honor, his caste clear from his shaved head and tin spiral earrings. But despite being of the servile class, he wore robes at least as rich as the merchant's. His dark green eyes met Zotikos's with the poise of a patrician, a jovial gleam in them. But though unusual, none of this was surprising. It wasn't our first run-in with Low Consul Feiyan's right-hand man.

"Kako," Xaron breathed. "What's he doing here?"

I fought back a scowl. "What else? Dealing with smugglers is business as usual for Feiyan."

Nomusa shook her head. "We should have suspected she was behind this."

"She could just be an opportunistic buyer," I said sarcastically.

Nomusa raised an eyebrow. "Very likely, when he comes first thing to meet her righthand man after a long trip from the Bali highlands."

Xaron waved a hand. "Never mind that. Are we doing this or not?"

All three of us were nervous, that was plain. I couldn't help a wry grin. Nearly a decade in, and I still got butterflies before confrontations.

I glanced at the far-off dais. "Despot Myron's taking the stage. If he gives his usual performance, it should be a good distraction."

Confirming my words, the crowd roared as Despot Myron Wreath mounted the platform and waved regally to his people. At fifty years, he retained a broad frame, handsome features, and sharp eyes. He was a man you'd trust equally to lead an army and rein in a chamber full of bureaucrats — though, in truth, he did neither.

The Despot of Oedija boomed over the tumult. "My people! Thank you for this marvelous welcome!"

As a deafening wave of cheers swept over us, Xaron grinned at Nomusa and me and shouted, "Despot Myron, claiming the stage as usual!"

The cheers quieted, and the Ruling Wreath continued in his strong, rich voice. "We gather here to celebrate, as we do every year, the blessings that the Pyrthae grants us. The rains that fall from the heavens; the sun that warms and energizes; and, of course, our ancestors who take the form of pyr and move through and among us. Each one of us is touched by the radiance of the realm above." He gestured with a wide wave above him. "Let us never forget that."

A solemn murmur rippled through the crowd.

"Long, long ago," Myron continued, "our forebears encountered a catastrophe in the western lands. The Hunger War. The calamity was so profound that they deemed their lands too desolate to continue sowing. Thus, they abandoned them forever. A hard decision, indeed, and one that could have had terrible consequences. But they held to faith. With the Eidola lighting the way, they traveled the endless seas, braving starvation and storms for eleven full spans. Children grew languid and weak. Men and women faltered at the oars. But finally, they landed here, on Oedija's shores, and founded this great city. The Lighted Passage, as we now call it, was a great hardship to bear. But without our ancestors's courage, the prosperous Pearl of the Four Realms would never have existed."

There were some assents of approval, but joining them now was a susurrus of discontent. I didn't have to look far to know why. Though people were clad in their festival best, many of them were unwashed and underfed. Myron had overplayed his hand. Most did not feel the prosperity he claimed.

But the Despot seemed to understand their shifting mood. "I know we face trials now, many trials indeed. The gods and spirits of the land and sky have plagued us with pestilence and droughts, robbing us of our plentiful harvests. And Valem stirs, discontented, in the south, so that Avvad's fields are covered in ash, the rivers are muddied and polluted. The trade caravans that might alleviate Oedija's hunger encounter obstacles and delays. Yes, I know we have many trials to overcome."

As Myron paused, those who had protested were hushed with anticipation, waiting for his next words. *With hope,* I realized. They truly believed the Despot could say something that would change their situation. Desperate, they needed something to believe in and found none better than our nation's puppet ruler.

Myron's next words, however, were hard. "But turning to false religions is not the answer. Believing in false claims — in delusions — because you wish them to be true will do our future no favors."

The crowd was quickly becoming agitated now. Jeers and calls were hurled down at the dais. Laurel guards, with green leaves painted on their armor and carved into their helms, began to wade in at the edges of the crowd, spears and shields held at the ready. The less wise among the masses resisted, and spats broke out as guards dragged away the most vehement of the decriers.

I shared a look with Nomusa and Xaron. In my memory, unrest was unprecedented at Myron's addresses.

"But we need not dwell on our trials!" Myron boomed over the protests. "Today, we celebrate both the victories of the past and the present. And that is not all! For today, one of our own returns, who will one day wear the Evergreen Wreath in my stead. A day long from now, gods willing."

The crowd, who would have normally agreed, barely responded. Still, the Despot smiled benevolently up at us like we'd cried out his name.

"But I will let her speak for herself. My daughter, Asileia Wreath, future Despoina of Oedija!"

He swept his arm behind him, and his daughter came striding out from the eaves to join him. Asileia was a thin woman, taking after her mother, the daughter of a Qao Fu matriarch. She walked with such a sense of command that you could almost believe her an Oedijan ruler of old. As she strode forth, fine jewelry danced upon her and glittered brilliantly in the festival lights. She'd never had her father's sense of modesty when it came to demonstrating the inherited wealth of the royal family. But even more striking were the golden tatu that shone on her skin. At this distance, I couldn't tell if they were more extensive than when we'd last seen her. They gave her an otherworldly cast, making her seem like a pyr come into the flesh.

"That ought to be distraction enough," I noted to Xaron and Nomusa. "I'm going in. Wait for the signal."

Nomusa glanced at me. She knew that I spoke the reminder more for my sake than theirs. "We'll do our part. 'Thae's blessing, Aire."

I nodded and turned back to our quarries, who stared at the shimmering Asileia Wreath. Not giving myself another moment for doubt, I approached the trio.

The bodyguard spotted me immediately. I pretended to be peering toward the dais until I was within a dozen strides, then looked around with a smile. A smile wouldn't stop his fist from pounding me into the stones at the smuggler's command. But it might allow me a word or two first — all I needed.

Kako had followed the bodyguard's gaze. His face lit up as he gestured toward me. "Airene the Finch!" he shouted over Asileia's speech. "Excuse me, Zotikos, but here is an old friend come to visit. If I know her at all, I believe she'll have words for you as well."

"Kako," I greeted the honor stiffly as he approached. "How's your mistress?"

"Very well, thank you. Power suits her nicely." He gave me a coy smile.

I pointedly looked away.

Zotikos studied me with an open scowl. "An old friend, you say. What words do you have for me, girl?"

Little rankled me more than a man's casual scorn. My reply was cool and calm. "Many you won't wish to hear, Zotikos of Hull. And many you would not wish your wife to hear, either."

His lips curled in distaste. "A dirty pleb should speak no words to my wife. Leave us, wench. We have business to discuss."

His bodyguard turned toward me. My heart, already racing, began to gallop. But I continued to ignore the big man.

"As do we. If I were you, I'd send Feiyan's man away. You don't want an audience for what I'm about to say."

Kako watched with open amusement. "Never fear, my dear. I freely leave you to your fear-mongering. But remember the last time you meddled in Feiyan's business. I would think carefully before you interfere again."

With a subtle bow, the honor turned away and disappeared back into the crowd.

Relieved as I was to see Kako's back, the full attention of Zotikos and his henchman was no easier to bear. The merchant had reddened in the face as he turned back to me. But before he could speak, a collective gasp turned our heads.

"Yes!" Asileia was shouting. "The elder Eleven, the Eidola of old, have spoken to me. And as no other mortal has experienced, I have become—"

Her voice cut off as Despot Myron ripped Hilarion's hand away from her neck and slapped it to his own. "Thank you, Daughter," he said. As his low, powerful voice rolled over us, I could feel his rippling anger. "We are all happy to see you home."

Asileia stood for a moment, quivering with rage, then stalked off the dais.

Zotikos and his bodyguard turned back to me. "An ominous night for interruptions," he said coldly. "You spoil my business and threaten my wife. Who are you, Airene the Finch, and what do you wish to say?"

I didn't flinch. A Finch for nine years, I'd encountered more men like Zotikos than I cared to recount. And at the core of every one of them were the dark secrets they kept hidden from the world. Lies they whispered to themselves to obscure the truths that defined them.

But I knew how to unravel them.

"You've been keeping a secret, Zotikos. One that would break your family if it were revealed. Your wife might not care for honors, but I doubt she would excuse you… mishandling her handmaid during her evenings away." Despite the revulsion hollowing me, I pasted a knowing smile on my lips. "But it's up to you whether she hears of it or not."

The merchant's expression spasmed. His eyes darted from me to his impassive guard, then to the crowd around us.

"Liar!" he hissed, but the words caught in his throat. "It's all lies! You know nothing!"

"No doubt you wish to believe that. I, however, would not risk your reputation over a misplaced shipment from the Bali highlands."

Zotikos's eyes widened, then he gave a wild laugh. "Aha! So that's what this is about! You want a cut, do you? You think to threaten me so I'll just hand over the profits to you, you greedy strumpet? I know people, important people. I'll have you strung up for your slanderous words!"

I glanced at the bodyguard, who stared daggers into me, then pulled my gaze back to the smuggler. This was the critical moment. I had to hold firm. Swallowing hard, I prepared to lose a few teeth.

"That will not keep your family from falling apart, Zotikos. That will not keep business partners from looking at you twice and deals falling through. But all that can be prevented. Your secret will be safe with me. All you must do is return what you stole to those with whom you broke contract."

The river merchant stared at me balefully, his mouth pressed into a hard line. He was considering my offer. Soon, he would relent. He just needed one last twist of the knife.

"Think carefully, Zotikos. Everything you possess is on the line. Your dignity, your relationships, your fortunes — *everything*. And it can all be safe if you do the right thing."

I reached into my robes and seized the object concealed there. The bodyguard, no doubt suspecting a weapon, snaked his hand forward to grab my slender arm in a bruising grip. Pain raced through me, but I didn't struggle. I just had to wait a moment longer.

Xaron and Nomusa stepped into view behind the smuggler and his brute.

"I'd listen to her," Xaron said with a nonchalant air. "She won't let it rest until she's had her way."

"And you won't rest either," Nomusa said coldly. "This is the best way out for you, trust us."

Zotikos whirled. His bodyguard didn't release me as he eyed the newcomers warily.

"And who are you two?" the smuggler demanded.

I gestured toward them. "Zotikos, meet my fellow Finches. The other people who hold your fate in their hands."

"Finches?" His eyes narrowed. "Airene the Finch… Now I know why you sounded familiar. Filthy spies and thieves, the lot of you!"

"Can't dispute you there," Xaron said easily. "But it's hard to feel bad about it when we blackmail scum like you."

I could see we had him. If I had been alone, he might have forced down the fear of someone knowing his secret, assuring himself that his bodyguard could take care of it. But he couldn't stop three people from talking.

"Fine!" the river merchant snapped. "Fine. I'll give my investors their due. So long as you never speak of this to anyone." He eyed me shrewdly. "Which one of them put you up to this?"

I smiled thinly. "Best make sure you don't leave out anyone, just in case."

Zotikos bared his teeth in nearly a snarl, then gestured sharply to his bodyguard. The brute gave me one last bald glare, then released me and followed after his master.

Xaron grinned openly as he and Nomusa joined me. "That went well. As soon as you called us in with the lodestone, that is."

I rubbed at my prickling arm as my fingers brushed the concealed lodestone. Bonded through magnesis, one of the energetic elements, to a stone Xaron carried, each would move when the other was touched. It had been useful for faraway communication on many occasions, and served as a signal on this one.

"In the end," I conceded. "We'll have to follow up tomorrow evening to make sure he remembers what's at stake."

"I'd expect nothing less of the pig than to try and weasel his way out now." Nomusa stared at the retreating backs of the smuggler and his man, then turned her head aside with a small shake of disgust. "Come. There's a little of the festival left. We should give off this thankless work for a bit, find an untapped barrel, and celebrate."

I sighed, trying not to think of Zotikos's wife, and whether we did a greater injustice by keeping quiet or telling her. But it didn't matter. I wouldn't inform her of what scum her husband was unless Zotikos failed to deliver. A Finch was only as good as her word.

I followed after my companions to claim one last piece of Radiance.

CHAPTER THREE

CALL OF THE HORNS

Oedija — o, Oedija — my home of contradictions
The Pearl of Civilization, yet fearful even of its jester
The advocates of freedom propped up on the backs of slaves
A people who rule themselves by choosing others to rule them
A religion that died when the gods
Abandoned us to the Tyrant Wardens…

- High Poetry of Lowly Things; by Hilarion the Second; 1085 SLP

Several turns of the sandglass later, Nomusa, Xaron, and I stumbled back up the stairs of the derelict tower we called home. With wine-logged heads and sour stomachs, the climb to the top seemed never-ending.

As much for distraction as out of curiosity, I asked Nomusa, "Asileia truly said she was — what was it, 'the Hand of Clepsammia'?"

"So she claims. And supposedly, she has oracles following her around declaring the same thing."

"Two circles left," Xaron panted. "We're almost to Canopy."

"It's not that far," I chided him. "What happened to her governing the Peninsula?"

Nomusa shrugged. "How should I know? Myron made it seem like a good thing she'd returned. But he'd have to spin it that way."

"She was probably booted for burning her subjects alive," Xaron interjected.

I cast him a disdainful look. "Don't believe every rumor you hear. It's a long way from the Oedijan prefectures. Events are often inflated."

"But do you really doubt it? The woman mutilated herself. She cut off her ear markings and disavowed her mother's heritage. And now she's back when she's not supposed to be."

I shrugged. Being Qao Fu himself, Xaron was particularly offended that Asileia had severed the additional ear lobes of their people. It was typically a point of pride for the Qao Fu, and many — including Xaron — wore earrings through their ear markings. We didn't know why Asileia had removed hers, but it didn't much incline Xaron to like her.

We finally reached the top of the tower, the eleventh circle. The previous ten floors were filled with poor families or young men and women with nowhere else to go. At least in the loft atop it, we had the circle to ourselves. It was the best our bribes could afford. As Finches — hunters of secrets, misdeeds, or other knowledge that might turn a profit — we didn't have the most reliable income and couldn't risk trying for something more expensive.

Living on top of the tower was both a blessing and a curse. At the moment, with unsteady legs and a head already pounding from sour festival wine, I wondered what had possessed us to move here.

Yet as we pushed inside the door, Canopy was a welcome sight. Opposite the door, a great bay window, only a little cracked and grimy despite our negligence, afforded a stunning view of Oedija's cityscape. Along the right side, four small enclosures we'd fashioned into bedrooms, their ceilings open to the rest of the loft, huddled against each other. To the left lay the kitchen, cluttered with unwashed pots, and the pantry. I breathed in the faint stench of mildew and bird droppings, which wafted in from the finch cage on our balcony. The scents may not have been fair, but to me, they were the smell of home.

Saying their goodnights, Xaron and Nomusa closed themselves into their bedrooms. I wasn't ready for sleep yet. Despite my better judgment, I drew yet another cup of wine from the barrel that our last loftmate, Corin — who worked as a cartwoman rather than a Finch — had claimed for us, then moved to the bay window.

The festival lights glittered in the inner and outer demes of the city, as both inside and outside the wall the celebration continued. Bonfires, pyr lamps, and torches illuminated the city from below, while the green light of the radiant winds and the three moons, full as they were every Radiance, shone above. The gray Pillars rose ominously from the demes, the magic-forged columns shadowed specters in the darkness. Beyond the city wall, a gargantuan bonfire burned, so large I wondered for a moment if it were a city fire spreading.

But as I swirled my glass, my thoughts drifted. The sense of disquiet that had filled me of late, a cloud that followed wherever I went, rose in me once more. Amid the hunt earlier, it had dampened so I could almost forget about it. But it had always been there, simmering beneath the surface.

I feared to think what it meant.

Standing atop our derelict tower, staring over the glimmering city, I wondered what had come of my nine years of striving. Perhaps it had never been about the truth. Perhaps it was the power of it, of hunting down a story and claiming its essence for your own.

But the hunt could only thrill for so long. And it was hard to believe any of it mattered when, despite all the skills I had gathered, I still couldn't find my brother's murderer.

A sudden sound yanked me from my thoughts. It took me a moment to recognize it. Not since I was a child had I heard it, for it only sounded in the direst circumstances. It blared over the rooftops and poured into the reveling forums and silent alleys. It vibrated in my chest and shook all other thoughts away.

The shell horns of the Laurel Palace called over Oedija, solemn and forlorn.

Three warnings came by the horns. The first, for fire. The second, for war. And the third, for a death.

Fire was likely. With wood buildings common along the peripheries of the city, the bonfires of Radiance posed a grave danger if mismanaged. The fire that burned in deme Thys beyond the wall seemed a likely candidate.

War, beyond rare skirmishes, had not been known in recent history, not since the Concordance of the Four Realms. The Bali ishakas to the east quarreled among themselves. The Qao Fu jaitin to the northeast remained isolated, their power waning. The Avvadin Imperium to the south seemed content with conquering their southern neighbors along the Rift.

The horns sounded twice, then a third time. I had heard this call only once before. I'd been young then, and in my fear, I clutched to my father's robes and asked him if we were safe. He'd taken me into his arms and rocked me back and forth. *Three horns are nothing to fear, Little Songbird,* he'd murmured. *Three horns are nothing to fear.*

As the echo of the horns died away, the late festival-goers below pantomimed their distress. Some cried into their hands. Others clutched their heads and fell to their knees, heedless of the mud that caked the street. Some just stood staring up, as if asking the gods how this could happen.

I closed my eyes. The fading vibrations seemed to shake me awake after a troubling dream, filling in the gaps that had formed in me over the past two and a half years. The desire for knowledge ignited in me once more.

Three calls of the horns announced that Despot Myron Wreath, beloved monarch of Oedija, was dead.

Three horns made me remember what it was to be a Finch.

CHAPTER FOUR

CHANGING WINDS

The Bali ishakas, a people of plateaus
Who succeed in only tearing each other down
Living in a land of plenty, yet never wealthy
They sit under thorny trees, hoping for wisdom
Like children, their Shakas squabble among themselves,
Never seeing the tiger prowling at their backs

- High Poetry of Lowly Things; by Hilarion the Second; 1085 SLP

In the turns after the shell horns blew, I flitted through the streets, dredging up every contact I knew. Some of the lights from the festival still glowed, but many had been extinguished. People had fled to their homes, waiting to see what would come in the wake of the Despot's death.

I could not have slept if I'd tried. I didn't know what was behind Myron's death or what it meant. But I knew enough. This represented change, more change than Oedija had seen in a century. And with change came opportunities for those who seized them.

Most of my contacts were missing, but a few were still around. I squeezed them for information, shelling out copper cullets and nickel magnes for whispers. I clung to every word. Yet for all my efforts, I learned nothing more substantial than the shimmering radiant winds. All agreed that Despot Myron had died within the Laurel Palace — but as to the cause, none could speak. Some claimed it to be a natural death. Others claimed assassination by

Avvad, the neighboring empire to the south ever the object of suspicion. Still others believed Myron Wreath's own daughter to be responsible, since his untimely demise corresponded so closely with her return. But when I pushed for evidence or firsthand testimonials, my contacts became predictably coy.

Rumors of rumors — that was the best I could claim.

Gray dawn edged into the sky by the time I let off my search. Though I needed rest, I mostly stopped in order to reconvene with Xaron and Nomusa, who I assumed had left to dredge up whispers of their own. I'd bolted from Canopy without waiting for them, fire already coursing through my veins. I hoped that between the three of us, we could find a clear path forward.

Weary as my body was, my mind still turned. Inside me burned a thrill that I had not felt in a long time. It reminded me why I'd first become a Finch.

I slowly ascended the eleven circles of our derelict tower to Canopy. Reaching the door, I turned the handle. It was unlocked. Hesitating, I cracked it open and peered inside. A single pyr lamp lit the shadowed room. It was just enough to detect the silhouette sitting in a chair, a goblet held in its hand. Only when I saw the gleam of the figure's golden hair did I let out my breath.

Entering, I latched the door behind me and crossed the room. "Linos. What are you doing here? And don't tell me you've tapped our festival wine."

The boy glanced up from the chair with a grin, then took another drink from his goblet. "Blame Nomusa — she let me in and told me to make myself comfortable. And you know this isn't my first taste, Sasa. You're not Pata. You know what I am."

"A scoundrel? I've known that since you were born." I held out my hand. "Give it here. You'll do whatever you please on the streets, but here, you don't drink."

My younger brother slowly gave over the goblet, his sneering smile telling me what he thought of my rules. As I took it, I glimpsed his hand in the pyr light. His knuckles were red and scraped. I quickly turned away and set down the goblet. My hand had begun shaking so that I thought it would spill.

When I had control of myself again, I turned back. Studying his face closer, I saw purple bruises beginning to form along his jaw.

"You've been fighting again," I said as calmly as I could.

His smile slipped away. "Someone was ruining our festival fun. I took care of it."

"And what about when someone takes care of you?"

Linos snorted and turned toward the bay window. "That won't happen."

I looked him up and down. His clothes were dirty and torn. It might have been excusable when he was eight-years-old, but at fifteen, he should have been past this mischief. As a man, it carried far direr consequences.

"Why did you come here, Linos?" I asked softly. "You should go home, clean up, put on a change of clothes. You reek, you know that?"

"And let Mother harp on me? I'd rather not. Besides, can't I visit my sister?"

"I don't like seeing you like this. You know that."

"Why? Because you think you can protect me?" His eyes were bright with drink, I saw now. "You should know better. I don't need anyone's protection."

I didn't try arguing. Quarreling with Linos had never worked before. "At least eat something. Knowing you, you've had nothing but wine all day."

"You're getting as sour as Mother. I didn't come here for a free meal, Sasa. I came on business. Or don't you want to know about the smuggler's markets?"

"I'm done with smugglers for the moment. Something else has my attention."

Linos raised an eyebrow. "And what's that?"

I hesitated. Despite his delinquency, I trusted my brother. He was the only member of my family whom I saw regularly. We even worked together on occasion, though I cringed at how he learned his information. But he was neither wise nor reliable. If there was someone behind the Despot's disappearance and they caught wind of my hunt, it could put the entire venture at risk.

I found myself speaking anyway. "I'm trying to figure out what happened to Myron Wreath last night."

He stared at me for a moment before a slow grin spread across his face. "You can't be serious."

I gave him a flat stare. "As serious as ever."

His smile faltered. "Sasa, that's crazy. Even for you."

"How? I'm a Finch. Parsing fact from rumor is what I do best."

"But not something like *this*. This is way beyond you."

I felt my temper rising. "You think I should abandon it."

"Of course!"

Something in his voice cooled my anger. There was real concern there, as well as something else. I searched my younger brother's face. What could cause him to worry? I didn't know he was capable of it.

As quickly as it had come, it was gone. Linos rose with a smile, though he didn't meet my eyes. "If you want to waste your time, far be it from me to stop you. Just let me know if you want to hear about the Valemish arks — I hear the contraband inside them is fascinating."

"Don't get in any more fights," I said to his back.

He flashed me one last smile over his shoulder, then slipped through the door.

Locking it behind him, I walked to the bay window and stared out over the pale cityscape. Did Linos know something that I didn't? I wondered if I should have pressed him for it. But pressure rarely worked with Linos; that he preferred living on the streets like a vagabond to living under Mother's rules was evidence of that. If he wanted me to know something, he'd tell me in his own time. More likely, it was his boyish arrogance at play.

I turned away from the window and entered my bedchamber, hoping for sleep that I doubted would come.

CHAPTER FIVE

LOOSE ENDS

The Qao Fu jaitin, ever on the edge of ruin,
Skulking in caves like beasts hiding from hunters
Eating algae in place of bread and honey,
Too timid even to hunt down meat,
Too wise to enter the world at large…

- High Poetry of Lowly Things; by Hilarion the Second; 1085 SLP

I dreamed. Colors shifted within a fog, light refracting as if through glass. From that fog came a face, reptilian and malevolent. I looked up, and instead of the sky above me, the ground reflected back to me as if I stared at a mirror.

When I awoke, sunlight streamed in through the open ceiling. Groggy, I remembered the night's dream for a moment before all that had happened the night before returned to me.

Despot Myron was dead.

I sat bolt upright, heart pounding. From the noises outside my room, Nomusa and Xaron were up and about. Despite the late hour of the morning, evident from the bright sunlight on the ceiling, they were still here. Perhaps they'd been waiting to confer with me before they made a day of it.

Rising, I entered the main living space. Xaron had his feet kicked up on the back of our well-loved divan, idly playing with wisps of radiance between his fingers, weaving them in and out of each other and cursing as he broke the pattern. When we were alone, he didn't hide his greatest and most dangerous gift: that he was a warden, one of those touched by gods and given access to the energies of the Pyrthae. He was a fool ever to use it in my opinion. If discovered, he'd be hunted down and either killed or put into the Acadium, where he might as well be dead for all the freedom he'd be afforded.

Xaron looked up and flashed me a grin as I emerged, then narrowed his eyes again at the wisps of light twisting above his fingertips.

Nomusa was also before the window, moving smoothly from one form to the next in her people's martial art, Ixolo. Dressed in tight underwraps and glistening with sweat, she didn't even glance over at me.

An unpleasant realization slowly dawned on me.

When I hadn't shifted or spoken for a full minute, Xaron glanced at me again. "Something wrong?"

"What are you two doing here?" I tried to keep the edge of annoyance from my voice.

Nomusa and Xaron exchanged a look.

"Didn't I tell you?" he said to her smugly, then returned to his light weaving.

Nomusa just shook her head and continued her movements. She whipped herself into the air with a spin, then landed with splayed limbs like a prowling cat.

I finally found the words I'd been searching for. "You heard the horns. You know what's going on. But you're not out trying to find out anything. You're up here. *Practicing.*"

"And you were sleeping," Nomusa observed, barely out of breath despite her exertions.

The magic disappeared from Xaron's fingertips. "Look, Aire. The Despot's death is a shock and all that. But it isn't something we can do anything about."

"No?"

"No," Nomusa affirmed. "It's ridiculous even to consider investigating."

I looked from one to the other. The initial unpleasant surprise had faded, leaving me perplexed. "This is what we became Finches for. We'll never get another chance like this. How can you not want to know what's going on?"

"Many reasons." Xaron ticked them off on his hand. "One, it's dangerous. Two, it's pointless. Three, we're hungover."

"You're hungover," Nomusa corrected.

"There's just no profit to it," he continued, rising from the divan with a groan. "Besides, I have somewhere to be later, and I want to be fresh as a summer daisy."

"Again?" I said, exasperated. "And I assume you still won't tell us where you've been going this past season?"

"Perhaps a lady's house?" Nomusa asked, a smile quirking her lips.

"Perhaps," Xaron hedged as he strolled up to me and looked imploringly into my eyes. "Leave off this Myron business, Aire. No good can come of poking your nose into it. Besides, we have the Zotikos job to finish up."

"I'll leave off this job like you'll leave off channeling."

He chuckled. "Point taken."

I looked at him, then Nomusa. "I can't do this without you both. So, foolish as it is, I have to ask you to help."

Xaron hesitated, then dropped his gaze.

I sighed. I'd expected nothing less, but hoped for more. "I'll be back sometime later."

With that, I strode to the door, strapped on my sandals, and left.

I went slowly down the eleven circles of our tower, hoping one or both of my companions would come hurrying after me. But as I emerged from the tower onto the street, no one followed. I shook my head and started walking. Despite their lack of support, my resolve had not wavered. I would see what events had unfolded throughout the night. No matter their apathy.

I visited each of my contacts again as quickly as I could. Little had come in while I slept, but a few points of interest rose to the top.

Kyros Brighteyed, the Archmaster of the Acadium, and Tribune Vusumuzi, one of the highest officials of justice, had visited the Laurel Palace soon after the shell horns had blown. Theoretically, they hadn't yet left. It was particularly interesting because both were heavily involved with wardens and penning them in. It was also said that by way of the glowing gaze for which the Archmaster received his epithet, Kyros could see where channeling had recently occurred.

It could mean a warden had assassinated the Despot. Or one of the Imperium's bound pyrs, known as Silks, could be responsible. Or it could have nothing to do with channeling, and Vusumuzi and Kyros were just there to eliminate the chance that it did. Still, the implications were intriguing.

Feiyan, the Low Consul with whom I'd had misdealings in the past, had also visited the palace, but to confer with Asileia Wreath. Uneasily, I wondered what the Low Consul and the soon-to-be Despoina had to discuss. With those two women involved, it was best to assume the worst.

By two turns past noon, I'd gathered all the whispers I could, but still had no path forward. Still, I was committed to this hunt now. Now, I had to make sure Xaron and Nomusa were as well.

That meant tying up loose ends.

I found my way through Port to Maesos's shop. People had begun to return to the streets after a night spent in fear, and I walked past men and women peddling skewers of unknown meats from carts and stands, and traders spreading small trinkets from faraway places on rugs. Bali wood carvings from their trees rumored to grow as big around as Pillars and nearly as tall. Qao Fu silver workings with agate from their desert caves. Intricate bead workings and finely woven rugs from Avvad. All the Four Realms were present in Oedija. A Wreath might be dead, but life went on.

Arriving at the glassblower's door, I knocked and waited impatiently. Moments later, Maesos cautiously cracked open the door. Seeing me, a smile spread across his face, and he fully opened the door. "Airene! Glad to have one pleasant thing happen today. Don't be shy — come in!"

"I can only stay a moment," I warned him as I stepped inside the dark shop. The only light came from the glass pieces displayed on platforms across the room. It was Maesos's signature: incorporating pyrkin into his glassware in shifting designs that mesmerized his clientele. The old artisan had never had more success, though he did need to call in a Finch every once in a while to take care of problems that cropped up. Like a certain smuggler I'd stalked the day before.

"You heard the horns, of course," Maesos said as he wiped ashy hands on his dirty apron. As usual, his clothes were a mess and his hair singed. "Terrible thing. Myron Wreath always seemed a decent sort."

"Yes. I thought the same thing. Which is why his death is all the more surprising. Did you hear the Council declared it a natural death?"

"A natural death?" Maesos bellowed a laugh. "That old bull? I doubt it! What did they say he died of?"

"Foul humors of the heart. He's supposed to have dropped dead in the palace's banquet hall."

"A man of his size wouldn't let anyone stand in the way of his meal. I should know." He slapped his belly with a grin.

"That's actually what I wanted to talk about, more or less."

"Myron's gut?"

I gave him an indulgent smile. "About his unnatural death. This might be the job of a lifetime for me. If I prove it was an assassination and discover who was behind Myron's death..." I shook my head, unable to voice my hopes.

Maesos gave me a fond smile. "Oh, Airene. You haven't changed since you were a girl pretending to apprentice at my shop while you snuck around and took care of my competitors. That same fire still fills you after, what, ten years already?"

I grimaced at the memory. When, at my Calling, I had declared myself a Finch, I'd learned just how profitless naming yourself a Verifier of Truth was. Though I continued to believe myself a Finch incarnate, I had bowed to reality and become the clerk to a certain eccentric glassblower. Maesos, a recent widower then, had needed someone to attend to his accounts and the storefront while he devoted more time to his craft. Either he was desperate enough to take on a willful, inexperienced girl, or he saw something in me others did not, for he took me under his wing.

Though I'd lamented the necessity of helping the odd man and loathed the menial task of counting beads on an abacus, there was one place I truly excelled: undercutting Maesos's competitors. The glass smith finally became curious when his profits had doubled in the second season of my employment. When put to the question, I succumbed to his gentle urging and revealed the truth: that my evenings had been spent on excursions to the other glass shops in the surrounding demes, investigating their offerings for flaws, understanding their competitive advantages — and, where possible, digging up the dirty secrets of their practices.

Thus Maesos had become the first of my many clients.

"Ten years," I affirmed. "Ten long years."

The glass smith smiled. "If anyone deserves a break, it's you. Follow this dream, then. But you don't need me to tell you that."

"No. But you can still help me. Did that rat Zotikos come by here today?"

Maesos frowned. "No. Should he have?"

I sighed. "Let's just say he was warned. I should follow through and ensure he delivers it, but…"

His eyes lit up with understanding. "Leave it for later, Airene. It's not immediate. I was eager to get my hands on those new strains of pyrkin because I had one to show you — a strain said to dampen a warden's channeling."

I raised an eyebrow. "And you believed whoever told you that?"

He smiled sheepishly and shrugged. "Ridiculous, I know. But after that warden Iela tried to kill you three years past…" He shook his head. "It was my fault you got mixed up in all that. I owe you something."

I tried not to remember the face of the woman he'd named. I'd seen it often enough in my dreams.

"You don't owe me anything," I said firmly. "But if you're alright waiting…"

"Yes, yes." He waved me toward the door. "Best get on with it. I know how you are when you catch wind of a mystery."

It was my turn to smile sheepishly. He knew me all too well.

———

Two turns later, I found myself in a dirty back alley tavern.

The Ignorant Intellectual was far from my usual choice of drinking holes. Not only was it on the opposite side of the city in deme Bazaar, but its clientele were a rough sort. The place stank of cheap spirits and unclean patrons who hadn't made it to the chamberpots before heaving their guts. A goblet of wine rested before me, but I didn't dare drink from it, not trusting the dirty rag with which the bartender had wiped it. I suspected he'd sold me leftover festival wine. But then again, when I ordered "a chalice of unrequited intoxication," I wasn't looking for drink.

"You'll wear out your pretty teeth, grinding them like that."

I startled and looked around at the man standing next to me. "You know I hate when you do that."

Talan wore his usual half-smile as he slid down next to me. His dark, shoulder-length hair was barely restrained by a greasy leather strap. He wore a once cream-colored tunic underneath a sky-blue vest, and dark trousers tucked into worn boots. But cleanliness wasn't what I expected from the Guilder. One of the agents of Oedija's predominate crime syndicate, he had become a contact and a friend in the three years I'd known and worked with him.

He stole my goblet of wine and sniffed it, wrinkling his nose. "How does that barkeep ruin festival wine?"

"I assumed he would. But you know why I'm here."

"Yes, I suspect I do." He studied me critically. "But don't you think sniffing around the Despot's death is a bit extravagant, even for you?"

"Don't try to talk me out of it. I just want to know what you've heard."

His smirk didn't dissipate as he leaned back into the hard booth, hands folding behind his head. "I think you might require something more than talk. How about we take a walk instead?"

He rose smoothly and offered a hand to me. Perplexed, I took it and let him lead me out of the tavern.

"Where are we going?" I asked as we headed in the direction opposite from the way I'd come by.

The Guilder turned back with his usual half-smile. "Do you trust me?"

"Not in the slightest."

"Good." He turned and started down the alley.

Shaking my head, I followed.

After a series of back alleys, Talan finally stopped at the end of one opening into a forum. From the position of the Pillars looming above us, I knew we'd crossed from Bazaar into the neighboring deme Sandglass. The forum was laid out as a square, with a small moat separating a courtyard from the surrounding buildings, and delicate bridges crossing over. On the island formed by the canal stood a lonely edifice, a bluff, black pyramid barely illuminated by blazing braziers and twice as tall as the surrounding buildings.

"Interesting activities have been occurring here," Talan said softly. "Activities some might believe less than legal were they in a different line of work than myself."

"I assume you're referring to the arks? Linos mentioned something about smuggling items through them."

"Perhaps. More to the point, I refer to what I believe they harbor in the heart of the temples." His eyes bore into the dark stone as if he might see through it.

"And what's that?"

He flashed me a mischievous grin. "I can't tell you everything right away, can I? I know you, Airene. You're in this for the intrigue."

I smiled despite myself. "Come on, Talan. I'm in the middle of the biggest job of my career. I need to know if I'm wasting my time on more Avvadin conspiracies of yours."

The Guilder's smile slipped. "We'll find out soon enough. For you and I are going to investigate within."

I stared at him. "You're not serious."

He raised an eyebrow. "Am I not? Me, the most famous vault-breaker to come out of Erimis, isn't serious about breaking into a simple Valemish temple?"

"Yes. Because that same famed vault-breaker knows that a certain Finch isn't fond of house-breaks."

He cast me a wink. "We'll see who prevails."

I already knew. Since the last exception I'd made two years before, I'd held to my resolution. It'd be simple to resist this wild pyr chase as well.

I turned away. "Thanks for the brief diversion. But it's time to get back to the real work."

Talan halted me with a touch to my arm. His fingers burned with an inner fire, as they always did. I shivered, as I always did.

"Consider it," he implored.

As I met his eyes, they burned with something else, a fervor I couldn't understand. Even knowing his stories, his hate for the Valemish and Avvad was beyond what I could comprehend.

"I will," I lied, and I left him there in the dark alley.

CHAPTER SIX

CHANCE ENCOUNTERS

Avvad, oh mighty Imperium, warrior of the Four Realms
Volcanic Valem puffing up its backside
The leash of the Silks held in the hands of the Tefra
Priests too ugly to remove their masks
Fear, the yoke of its people, in the guise of belief
A cattle nation of conquerors the Kahin-Shah leads

- High Poetry of Lowly Things; by Hilarion the Second; 1085 SLP

Five long days passed.

I sat in a cafe by myself, sipping a cup of coffee, spirits low. Presumably, I waited for Xaron and Nomusa. Zipho, the owner of the cafe and a friend of ours, had a lead on a job for us and had asked us to meet at her cafe two turns past noon. After a morning of fruitless sniffing around, I'd arrived early and sat silently to drink my coffee.

I didn't want to abandon the hunt. I didn't want to consider other jobs. But with our purses rapidly lightening and food prices continuing to climb, I hardly had another choice. To make no mention of Nomusa and Xaron's continued resistance. Nomusa had tried bullying Maesos into letting us finish his job, but the loyal glassblower had stood firm even before her anger. Yet with the way things were going, I would have to track down Zotikos after all, if only for a little coin to continue my inquiries.

For five days, I'd scrambled for information. I'd tried to enter the Laurel Palace and been rebuffed. I'd tried to enter the Acadium to see

Archmaster Kyros and the Tribunal to see Tribune Vusumuzi, but been turned away at both gates. I'd thrown coins at hints of whispers and received less back.

The immediacy of the puzzle was rapidly dissipating. Myron had received a small, private funeral, at odds with the man who had always drawn a crowd. Plans for Asileia's Ascension were well underway and would commence the next day. Soon, she would be the Ruling Wreath. Whether or not she was behind her father's murder, I doubted she would be amenable to someone investigating it.

For all my efforts, I'd learned little. Feiyan had met with Asileia again and again, confirming my suspicions of a relationship between them. But what sort of relationship remained unclear. Valemish temples continued to be well-frequented, but whether the traffic was innocuous or not, I could not tell. Finally, whispers told of activity from within deme Thys. Xaron had said the Manifest had gathered a village there, and from what I heard, he wasn't wrong. Thousands of people were said to have set up in the encampments around the lake in the deme, and all were hoping for an impossible dream: to become attuned to the Pyrthae. But I didn't think a cult, even a growing cult lauding wardens, was likely to be behind killing Oedija's monarch.

I'd seen Talan yesterday during one of my long treks out for information. The Guilder had been less than empathetic and repeated his offer to accompany me into the heart of Sandglass's Valemish temple, pointing out I had no better leads. I found myself considering it before I returned to my senses. I wondered how desperate I'd be before I accepted, and feared I wasn't far off.

A quarter-turn after they were due to arrive, Nomusa and Xaron entered the cafe. I'd already finished my coffee.

"About time," I said drily as they approached my table.

"We're not that late," Nomusa objected. "And you can wait a little longer while we get drinks." She headed toward the bar that ran through the center of the room, behind which the portly Bali who owned the cafe, Zipho, bustled.

"Order mine too — you know what I like." Xaron sat down opposite me. "Learn anything interesting while you were out?"

I shrugged and recounted the day's learnings. "So not much," I summarized morosely.

He nodded with a sympathetic smile. For a moment, he looked as if he would say more. But he pressed his lips back together and remained silent.

"Let me guess," I said. "You think the hunt's dead in the water."

"I didn't say that. But I wouldn't be wrong if I had."

I shook my head. "I'm not done yet."

He shrugged and looked away.

An awkward silence fell. Despite my annoyance, I made a play at reconciliation. "And what did you do this morning?"

His gaze wandered to the ceiling. He didn't have to answer for me to know.

"Gone to your mysterious woman again?"

He finally met my eyes. "I've told you," he said with a touch of irritation, "it's not like that."

"Then what's it like? You haven't told us any details."

"I'll tell you. Eventually."

Nomusa approached the table and, seating herself, set Xaron's drink in front of him, a mug of coffee so sweetened with honey and milk as to be unrecognizable.

"What'd she say?" I asked.

"She was annoyingly vague." Nomusa took a sip of her coffee and made a face. "And distracted. I'd ask her for another drink if I thought it would be any better. You would think being the true Heir of our ishaka would count for more."

Normally, I would have rolled my eyes at Nomusa invoking her claim to royalty. Not that it was untrue. When she was a child, her father, Shaka of the Yorandu, had been killed with the rest of her family. Only her aunt and Nomusa had survived. Fearing for Nomusa's life, she had taken her to Oedija and cared for her until her death. Since then, Zipho, also of the Yorandu ishaka, had taken her under her wing and treated her in a uniquely Bali manner as both her rightful leader and an errant daughter.

But I was far from a joking mood. I couldn't think of who else Zipho would want us to meet other than a prospective client. With dread, I thought about how much harder it would be to drown out Nomusa and Xaron's objections to my fruitless pursuit when we had a paying job waiting in the wings.

She shrugged. "All I know is that we're meeting someone soon and were lucky they didn't arrive before us."

Just then, someone entered the cafe. All three of us looked around expectantly.

Xaron quickly turned back to the table, eyes wide. "Tribune," he muttered.

My heart hammered in my chest as I stared at the newcomer. The Bali man was dressed in the maroon robes of the Tribunal and stood scanning the cafe with a calm expression. His skin was dark and rich as newly rained earth. Though his robes hung thick about him, his thin face betrayed his spare frame. White gloves peeked out from beneath wide sleeves, and around his neck hung a bronze medallion composed of two half-circles connected by a thin lattice of silvery threads. The robes were sign enough of who he was, but the medallion legitimized his station as part of the Confessionary Tribunal, Oedija's judiciary branch of the government.

I leaned forward and spoke in a low voice. "That's not just any Tribune. That's Tribune Vusumuzi. He looked into Myron's death and is in charge of the Shepherds."

Zipho bustled over to the Tribune and made a big show of pouring him a drink, a performance at which Vusumuzi smiled politely.

"Did Zipho want us to meet *him*?" Nomusa whispered, incredulous.

My mouth had gone dry. This couldn't have come at a better time. After all my scrambling, here was someone with firsthand information on the murder. Why now, of all times, Zipho chose to introduce us was beyond me. But if the gods wanted to bless me with good luck, I wasn't going to object.

"They're coming," Xaron muttered as the pair approached. It took me a moment to understand the depth of his nervousness. Then it finally clicked. Tribune Vusumuzi, being in charge of the Shepherds, enforcers of the laws restricting wardens, would undoubtedly make a feral like Xaron uncomfortable.

The Tribune held a steaming cup as he stopped before our table. From behind his back, Zipho gestured impatiently for us to rise. We readily complied.

"Nomusa-sha," Zipho said, addressing Nomusa in the Bali manner, "please meet Tribune Yorandu Vusumuzi-sa. Honored Tribune, this is Eshalo Yorandu Nomusa-sha, true Heir to our ishaka."

Vusumuzi bowed and offered his arm. Nomusa gripped it at the forearm from above, while he gripped from below.

"Vusumuzi-sa," she said formally, "I am always delighted to meet a fellow of our ishaka. Have you been gone from it long? Zipho-ma has not given your family name."

"Please, call me Vusu, Nomusa-sha," the Tribune said as he withdrew his hand. "And as you may already suspect, I left our home a long time ago. The family I come from is no longer of consequence, as I am its last member." Though his words were firm, he smiled in a kindly manner.

"His tatu tell a different story," Zipho said conspiratorially. "He has only shown me once, but my eyes do not deceive. From the line of the old kings, he is."

I knew little of the history of the Bali chiefdoms, and nothing of the kingdom that had once united them. I glanced at the sleeves hiding his tatu. Nomusa's eyes showed she wished to see them as well but did not ask. Perhaps it would be considered rude.

"It is not entirely out of the realm of possibility," Vusu said with a smile. Then he turned to me. "And may I ask your name?"

That he addressed me directly threw me off balance for a moment. Typically, Bali spoke only to each other, even when others were present. Perhaps he had been so long in Oedija that he had adopted our manners.

"Airene," I said after a moment's pause. "Of Port."

He nodded slowly. "Very nice to meet you." He held out his palm face-up, and I hesitated before greeting him the Bali way. Even through his sleeve and glove, his skin felt feverishly warm. I withdrew quickly, studying him. Was he ill? It would explain his thinness. When I met his gaze, he smiled at me, and something about it seemed sad. It confused me, but I didn't let it show in my expression.

"And you?" Vusu said, looking past me to Xaron, who stood the farthest back of us all.

"Xaron of Port."

Vusu held out his hand, but Xaron looked aside as if distracted. Vusu let his arm drop but gave my friend a considering look. I wished Xaron had simply accepted the greeting. He risked drawing the Tribune's suspicion by not having done so.

Zipho watched the exchanges with more than a bit of her own puzzlement, but she quickly recovered her sheen of affability and turned to Nomusa. "I thought you all might be interested in talking."

With a nod, she returned to her counter to attend to the growing line of customers.

Vusu made no move to sit, so Nomusa, Xaron, and I remained standing. Silence fell as Vusu studied each of us. Despite the awkwardness, his gaze remained calm. I wondered what Zipho's reason for introducing us was. I didn't dare believe what I hoped for.

I broke the silence. "Tribune Vusumuzi, I'm sure you've been busy these past few days."

He smiled again. "No more than usual, I'm afraid. Myron's death is just the latest trial."

It seemed a flippant dismissal of the momentous event. Could Vusu not suspect anything of it? Could it be a natural death after all? My stomach sank.

Desperate to keep my hopes afloat, I said, "I would think the Despot's death is a greater challenge than most."

Vusu continued to wear his slight smile. "It is a piece falling on a board full of pieces, Airene of Port. But other designs continue forward."

"You see this as a game, then. I wonder who the players are."

The Tribune's eyes crinkled. "No one surprising for you if I'm not mistaken. Yes, I've heard of you three before. Finches, after the old Order of Verifiers."

I tried to repress a wince. Our work wasn't exactly illegal, but it couldn't be called sanctioned by the law either. And Xaron's abilities had sometimes been key to our success. Perhaps a pattern would be apparent to one who worked closely with wardens like Vusu.

"Yes," I replied shortly.

"Do not fear. I have no wish to interfere with your work. In fact, I believe it a worthier path than most. After all, at its heart is the pursuit of truth. And truth should always be unveiled, lest we all suffer the consequences of secrecy."

The Tribune was not at all what I'd expected. I wondered what Nomusa and Xaron made of him. "I appreciate you saying that. We try to uphold the Verifiers' mission as much as we can."

"And from what I've heard, you've done well."

I nodded, unsure of what else to say. I knew where I wanted to turn the conversation, but considering the Tribune's earlier dismissal of my inquiry, I didn't think I'd have much luck.

Vusu glanced at the sandglass Zipho had mounted on one wall, which told the time as two-and-a-half turns after noon.

"I fear I must go." He looked to each of us in turn, and I thought his gaze lingered uncomfortably on Xaron. "It was a pleasure meeting you, Airene, Nomusa-sha, Xaron. Do stop by my solar soon. I would like to speak further. Perhaps your talents might be useful in these tumultuous times."

Stunned, I muttered words of thanks, then each of us bowed. The Tribune nodded his acknowledgment and turned away, setting his mug on the counter untouched. Waving his farewell to Zipho, he turned out of the cafe.

A moment later, Zipho bustled up next to Nomusa, staring at the closing door. "That man! Half the time he comes in and forgets to eat or drink. No wonder he's withering away!"

Nomusa drew her close. "Zipho-ma, why did you introduce us to the Tribune? And don't think to play coy with me anymore!"

The cafe owner huffed. "I do not play coy, Nomusa-sha! A Tribune is a good man to know, is he not? Vusumuzi-sa has come here for some time, on and off. I would not have asked him to meet you, as I did not want to overstep my relationship with him."

Nomusa bowed her head in thanks.

"But then he asked about you," Zipho continued.

"He initiated this?" I interjected, forgetting myself.

Both Nomusa and Zipho scowled at me.

"Yes," Zipho replied stiffly, though she looked at Nomusa. "He asked about you two days ago. I was vague, but when he continued to be interested, I invited him here."

"You should have told us more directly," Nomusa rebuked her. "What if he were after us?"

Zipho scoffed. "Vusumuzi-sa is a good man."

"He's a Tribune. Still, I thank you. He could be a good man to know."

Making our pardons, we left Zipho's. I burned to ask what their impressions were of the Tribune, but I couldn't do it now, not out in the open. Vusu had known of us. Gratifying as that was, it was worrisome. We would not stand up to the scrutiny of the Tribunal.

But even so, we'd talked to the Tribune, and he wanted to speak further. It was another lead if I pursued it with patience. A man of contradictions such as Vusu was not to be trifled with lightly. But even with the risks, I would approach him. I couldn't stop now.

I halted abruptly in the street. Xaron and Nomusa turned back.

"Hunting again?" Nomusa asked in a neutral voice.

"Now?" Xaron objected. "We have to discuss what just happened."

"I have to know more if I'm going to speak further with the Tribune." I said it off-hand as if it were a given.

They stared at me, speechless.

"He was there," I continued hurriedly. "He saw the scene of Myron's death, and likely his body. If anyone would know if it was murder or not, it's him." I met each of their gazes. "Tomorrow I mean to go to his solar and ask him about it. And I mean to know as much as I can at that time."

Nomusa laughed scornfully and began walking away. Xaron lingered a moment, looking helplessly at me. "Good luck," he said, then followed after her.

As I watched them leave, loneliness settled in again. The three of us had usually worked together on inquiries. I doubted I could have remained a Finch for so long without them. But still, I couldn't give this up because they would not join in. I had to believe that once they saw evidence of a conspiracy, they'd cave. They would come around in the end.

Someone grabbed my arm.

I startled and spun away, disoriented. Everything came into clear focus as I recognized the honor grinning at me, his hand still extended from touching me. Kako.

"You," I hissed. Fear, cold and clammy, spread inside me.

"Me," Kako agreed easily. "Had you expected someone else?"

"What do you want?"

"You know what I want. Or should I say, what my mistress wants."

Whispers went both ways. Feiyan must have heard I'd been inquiring after her. She was the hawk watching for ripples on a pond, ready to dive at the first sign of prey — only she had a hundred eyes watching for her. I had been careless.

And carelessness could deliver Xaron straight into the Shepherds' hands.

"We had an agreement," Kako said, his tone pleasant, his eyes anything but. "You were not to investigate anything related to my mistress. In return, we would leave be your… secret."

Fear chilled me. I knew the secret he referred to. As a result of the incident three years ago when I'd narrowly avoided dying, Feiyan had gathered that either Xaron or Nomusa was a warden. Though she didn't know which of them was, I knew it would do little to protect any of us if Shepherds came knocking at Canopy's door.

Though I needed to appease him, I could give no more than a perfunctory bow. "I apologize. It was not your mistress I've been looking into. It's the woman she's been seen with."

The honor shook his head with a knowing smile. "No, no, Airene of Port. Do not attempt to deceive me with such thin lies. You knew precisely what you sniffed after. Yet, like a hungry mongrel, you could not help yourself. I understand this. We all have desires burning inside us, waiting for the opportune moment to sate them."

His gaze had gained an uncomfortable edge. I looked aside. "I will avoid her. You have my word."

The honor took a step closer. "And you will avoid whispers of Asileia Wreath as well," he said in a low voice. "Understood?"

"Yes."

He leaned back, his smile renewed. "Good. Now may you have a pleasant, uneventful day. Can't have too much normalcy in times like these."

He gave a mock bow as he spun off into the crowd. I watched the strange honor as he disappeared out of sight.

I turned and walked quickly toward Canopy. No doubt Feiyan would keep eyes on me still. I would be able to learn nothing more today. But no matter what I'd told Kako, I would not stop. That Feiyan protected Asileia was further confirmation that something was amiss here. I would have to step more carefully and speak more softly and continue on. Despite the risks.

Though I wondered what this hunt would cost me.

CHAPTER SEVEN

FINCH IN THE RAIN

Though the Wreaths were reinstated as the monarchs of Oedija, true power was reserved for the members of the People's Conclave. Yet one hundred and twenty-one Servants were far too many to act quickly in emergent situations. Thus the Demos Council was formed, eleven Low Consuls each elected through the support of ten fellow Servants. These Low Consuls have, in dire times, wielded supreme power. However, oftentimes the eleventh seat has lain undecided, disagreements remaining between the Servants who would determine it. Thus the Archon, representative of the Wreath in the Conclave, has acted as the deciding vote in tied decisions, and has brought back some measure of power to the Laurel Palace.

- Oedija: A History; by Acadian Helene, Master Historian; 1167 SLP

Nomusa and Xaron were surprised to see me return shortly after them. But as they sensed my mood, neither commented on it. The afternoon wound on and evening settled in, and soon, our usual routines found us.

Despite the impending famine, neither of my companions seemed avid to pursue another job. Nomusa eventually went out again, purportedly to stir up some leads, but I knew it was as likely she'd wind up in a tavern on the arm of a handsome man. Xaron, meanwhile, reclined on the divan and practiced his channeling.

Stuck inside for the day, I pretended to read the book open before me, *Tales of the Desolate*. A book of Bali tales pressed upon me by Nomusa when the Manifest cult started to rise in Oedija, it recounted legends surrounding the Zakale people, who, following twin warden brothers named Yama and Lophe, nearly conquered the whole of the Bali high-lands. When they failed, the rest of the ishakas exacted vengeance on them, expunging every man, woman, and child from existence, even to the name, for the Zakale became known as the Unnamed afterward. What Nomusa found fascinating was just as a serpent god had been at the center of the Zakale cult, so was a wyvern for the Manifest. Though if it was for the Manifest a god or a mere symbol, neither of us knew.

But my attention wandered from the pages. What to do about Feiyan was beyond me. I couldn't continue to ply my contacts without her know-ing. I didn't know who was reporting on me, or where she had eyes posted. Until I had a solution, I couldn't continue to investigate.

All the more infuriating because now I was surer than ever that there was actually something to investigate.

The door to Canopy roused me from my brooding thoughts. Corin, the last of our loftmates, entered and wearily bent to unstrap her sandals, no mean feat with her legs caked in mud. As a cartwoman, she ran back and forth along Oedija's streets, transporting those who could afford not to walk. She was one of the few women to take on such a laborious profession, but was built well for it. Outlanders, as the natives of the islands to the far northwest were called, were known for their strength and tall stature. Corin, however, was a force unto herself, both in body and mind. Working day and night, she sought to raise enough money to bring her sister, Kari, over to Oedija. Corin was a woman of few words, but as far as I understood, Kari was persecuted for some reason, and might be safer in Oedija. But in the two years Corin had been living in Canopy, she had not raised enough money to bring her over.

We greeted each other, but the cartwoman quickly retired to her room. I tried to return to my reading, yet found myself distracted by Xaron's channeling. Channeling ice, I'd learned from him, was no mean feat. It involved manipulating one of the elements, radiance, in an inverse manner. But it was from whom he'd learned it that irked me.

Nearly three years ago, a feral warden named Iela, who'd had a propensity for channeling ice, had come into our awareness after killing a patrician. When we had pursued her, she'd singled me out, and by a threat to my family, lured me from Canopy. Just before she was going to kill me, she'd boasted of her master experimenting on and killing my older brother, Thero, years before. Talan had saved me, but it was I who had killed her.

I shivered at the memory of plunging the knife into her neck. My stomach turned.

"Airene?"

I met Xaron's gaze, but my eyes flickered to the icicle he had willed into being. "I'm fine," I lied.

His eyes followed mine, then widened. In a moment, the icicle dissipated into shimmering mist. "'Thae below, Airene. I didn't even think about... well, you know."

"You shouldn't have to." I tried for a smile.

From his expression, I knew I'd failed. Xaron studied me as he leaned back into the divan, but he said nothing.

As much to escape the memories as to fill the silence, I found myself speaking. "Sometimes, I'm jealous of you."

He laughed. "I'm sure you are."

"No, really. When I was little, I wanted nothing more than to be a warden."

"Truly?"

I nodded. "For years, I pestered my mother and father, begging them to tell me why I wasn't attuned, and how people received the blessing of a god to become so. I wanted to know all about the Pyrthae and how wardens channeled its energy, and how it felt to work magic. Of course, they didn't have answers for me. I asked about it at our local temple, but the oracle knew little, and the few paltry books in its library held more myth than fact."

He smiled smugly. "They're writing about it secondhand. Of course they wouldn't know." His grin faltered. "It's funny. I was just the opposite of you when I was young. I hated that I was a warden."

That was hard to imagine. I couldn't picture Xaron not being a warden. It was too integral to who he was. "Really? Why?"

"My mother. And the extent of my... gift." He paused for a long moment. "My parents fled the Wumofu because of the Matriarchs' restrictions on channeling. My mother wished to utilize an energetic element not sanctioned for use within the jaitin, one based on formulae, and the Matriarchs refused her request to pursue them. But Mother's not one to take no for an answer. There's no hiding something like that among the Qao Fu caves, so we came to Oedija. For a while, she practiced in secret, despite the risk of death hanging over her and Father. She even became famous in some circles for her powerful distillations, though obviously no one knew she channeled to create them."

"How did that work? I thought wardens utilized energy, not formulae."

Xaron shrugged. "From what she said, distillations *do* have energy, just like fire and force. And because of this, she was able to use them as mediums for channeling incredible effects."

I shook my head. "I'll take your word for it. Still, that doesn't seem so bad a home to grow up in."

"Everything was different for me. Before I was born, Mother had an accident. An experiment had gone poorly, and she'd burned herself up both arms and across her torso. It changed her, my father says. From then on, she's been in pain. She gave up her concoctions and stopped using her powers. And she didn't want the same thing to happen to me. She decided playing with the elements was bound to burn you sooner or later."

"So no channeling."

"No channeling around her," he amended with a slight smile. "She tried not to let me start, but that didn't sit well with a curious child like me, especially not when my attunement was so strong."

My gaze wandered to his hands. Xaron had ten shifts, seen in the faint, ever-moving patterns along his fingertips. It meant he was as powerful a warden as they came. Such a strong attunement only emerged once a generation, even in a city the size of Oedija, at least according to what Xaron had told me. Not that he had much opportunity to use it.

"What does it feel like?" I asked, staring at his hands. "When you're channeling?"

He didn't answer, but shuffled a hand in his tunic and produced two copper cullets and three nickel magnes on the tips of his fingers. His brow creasing, he stared at them like a taskmaster at a tested pupil. After a moment, the coins began to float, lifting a cubit away before settling to hover a few inches above his fingertips.

It seemed a mere parlor trick, but I knew it was far more. It was access to a world parallel to our own, a plane beyond my understanding. The Pyrthae was said to be composed of the energetic elements, and home to pyr and the gods. I didn't know that I believed in spirits and divine beings, but it was hard to deny the existence of the Pyrthae when Xaron could access its power.

"It's like undamming a stream," he said softly, eyes watching the coins. "You always feel it there, pushing, almost pleading to be woven and formed."

"Where does it push?"

"Everywhere. But it starts here." He used his free hand to indicate his torso.

"The locus." The point through which wardens drew the Pyrthae's power. The drawings I'd seen in the temple library showed a man with his limbs splayed and a circle drawn around him, with the locus indicated at the middle point. The exact center of a human being.

Xaron nodded. "You have to dam it consciously at first, but it becomes second-nature."

"Sounds exhausting. I never knew you had to maintain it. Is that why you're constantly itching to channel?"

"Not exactly. If you could feel it, you'd know why. It's invigorating, sensing the power rush through you. Intoxicating."

"No wonder you can't control yourself," I teased.

He grinned sheepishly. "Exactly."

"Is there one element that is more invigorating than the others?"

"Yes and no. Each element has a unique feel. Radiance makes you warm and light-headed. Kinesis is the opposite — you become grounded in the physical and feel like you can do anything. Magnesis is subtler. There is a humming that flows through you, soothing and stirring at the same time." He smiled — from the humming of magnesis in him at that very moment, I imagined. "The effect is greater if you channel more, or if you don't know how to direct the energy. When I was young and first channeled, the energy didn't know where to go, and it filled all of me so I thought I would burst. Now, the flow knows: straight to the fingers and toes."

I shook my head. Strange that the most delicate parts of the human body could control so much power. "So you let it stream in and then… what?"

"You form it." He tapped his head with his free hand. "With your focus. What we call your mental energy."

"And that's it?"

He flashed me a wry grin. "In a sense. But it takes years of practice to channel reliably. I failed to control even kinesis for years, which usually comes easiest to people. The things I managed were by accident, like when my father woke me and I sent him flying across the room like he were a doll. But it's like music. You can hear how a song is supposed to go long before you can play it. And even people who have no training can feel the music, and know when it's right and wrong."

I stared at the gaps above his fingers, straining to see what held the coins up. But it was like the weight of the Pyrthae, ever pushing down on the air and us — a force you could feel, but couldn't see. I sat back, disappointed.

He saw and laughed. "Trying to see what causes magnesis is like trying to see how a singer sings. You can't see the mechanism. And what's more, you lack the faculties to emulate the effect."

I arched an eyebrow at him. "Someone's sounding scholarly today."

He blanched, then muttered, "You asked, didn't you?"

I studied him as he looked aside. It was a strange reaction to an innocent statement. Seeing nothing else for it, I shifted course. "So you just felt the energy pushing on your dam one day?"

He seemed to recover. "Well," he said, laughing so that the coins wobbled, "there wasn't a dam at first. To be honest, it's like wetting the bed when you're young — your body has to learn to prevent it. You build that self-control, that limit." He patted his navel. "And eventually, with the right training, it's only there when you need it."

I fished a coin from my purse and threw it, trying to take down one of his hovering coins. But even though it connected, the coin drifted back into place. Xaron had such a look of satisfaction I couldn't help but reach out and swat them away.

"Hey!" He laughed and rose to retrieve the coins.

Smiling, my eyes wandered by habit to the finch cage on the balcony. A drizzle had started outside, and the cage was indistinct, but I could just detect a finch pecking from the seed basket. On its leg, a bedraggled message flapped in the wind.

Xaron followed my gaze. "A finch?"

I was already rising. "I'll go see what it says."

Excitement bubbled up in me as I exited into the chill night and took the new arrival in hand. He shivered, and I cooed softly to him as I untied the message, then put him in the cage with the others until it was time to send him back.

Retreating inside, I squinted to make out the smudged lettering:

The Wolf is watching.

The note was unsigned. I stared at the script, trying to pry out more from those four words and understand what they meant, to make no mention of who had sent them. The script looked vaguely familiar, but wasn't immediately recognizable.

Xaron approached to examine it over my shoulder. "What's it say? I can't make it out."

"'The Wolf is watching.'"

"From who?"

"Don't know."

He stepped back, brow creased in thought. "Who have you sent queries to lately? Who might need to respond with a cryptic message, sending a bird out on the worst night for it? Who's in danger?"

His questions sieved my contacts until I recognized the floral script. "Nikias."

"The new Archon's steward?"

"The very same."

"I suppose he might know what's going on. But strange that he feels in danger."

A smile had found my lips. "Not so strange if you assume one thing."

Xaron groaned. "Let me guess. That the Despot was murdered."

"It makes the most sense. This afternoon—" I cut off mid-sentence, having been on the verge of telling about my earlier encounter with Kako.

But with the inquiry gaining momentum and Xaron finally showing interest, I didn't want to undermine it now. "This afternoon I learned that Feiyan has been meeting with Asileia a lot recently."

He raised an eyebrow. "I thought you'd already told us that."

"I heard it again, which is significant enough," I lied. "And what do you think Vusumuzi wants with us? Why seek us out now, when he must have heard we were Finches from Zipho a long time ago?"

"What are you getting at?"

I held up the message. "This isn't an ordinary message. It's short, unsigned, and in a code we don't have the cipher for. And it came in the rain — not a good time for finches to fly, but the best time for a bird to pass unseen. And the words — 'The Wolf is watching.' If this came from Nikias, that means someone is watching from inside the Laurel Palace — our Wolf, whoever that is."

"Not necessarily from within. They could be watching outside."

I shook my head. "He wouldn't be worried about interception if they were outside. It'd be simple enough to sneak out a bird."

Xaron shrugged. "Fair enough. So who is the Wolf?"

I thought for a moment. "If we narrow it down to people within the Laurel Palace, that makes it easier to guess. Asileia is the most obvious choice, but I wouldn't describe her as a wolf."

"Maybe that's the point. I wouldn't necessarily be specific about the person I was accusing if I were sneaking out a message."

"But it wouldn't make for much of a code then, would it? I think it has to cue someone in particular."

"What about one of her oracles? Or maybe Feiyan, since she's there so often now? She has some wolfishness to her."

"It could be any of them. Or it could be Jaxas, or First Laurel Lykos, or a hundred other people we don't know about. But I know one thing. If someone doesn't want word getting out from the palace, it tells us there's something more going on." I cocked a smile at Xaron. "You don't cover up an accident."

Finally, I saw it in his eyes. He believed. And he was curious, too, if Myron was murdered.

"Fine." Xaron exhaled noisily and looked out the bay window. "So how do we start narrowing down who it could be?"

I followed his gaze and stared out over Oedija, thinking. With the Festival of Radiance ended, the view had dimmed. Yet between the green radiant winds and the moons, a soft light still blanketed the rooftops.

Before I could answer, a knock came at the door. Three quick raps — a familiar signal.

Xaron cocked an eyebrow. "An appropriate time for your brother to visit. In the middle of the night while we discuss conspiracies against the realm."

I gave him a flat look, then crossed the loft to open the door. Linos sported his usual tousled, blond hair and soiled clothes. But instead of a confident smirk, he wore a serious expression. Despite the worry that rose in me, I knew I had to keep the conversation light. Linos was flighty. If something were wrong, I couldn't risk scaring him off.

"Back already?" I observed drily. "Two visits in half a span. I'd almost think you miss me."

"No such chance." His smile was quick and nervous. "Purely here on business."

"Business that I'll want no part of, I'm guessing."

He seemed to sense my true suspicions. "I'm not in trouble. I have information I think you'll want. Are you going to let me in?"

I stepped aside slowly, watching him as he entered. He had a slight limp to his step and shadows under his eyes, but seemed not much the worse for wear. Closing the door behind him, I drew him into a hug.

"Do you have to?" he complained as he extricated himself.

"I'm your Sasa, aren't I?" I grinned at his uncomfortable glance at Xaron. "Don't worry. He knows you're my Little Lion."

"I don't know why I help you," he muttered. "You want to hear this or not?"

"Let's have it. What do you have that could possibly intrigue me?"

Despite my light tone, apprehension filled me. His eyes flickered to the door before settling back on me.

His voice was lower when he spoke. "You're still looking into what happened with the Despot, right?"

My attention perked up. "Yes."

"Have you had any leads?"

I considered how truthfully to answer that. "Some. But nothing too promising."

"Then you haven't heard the First Laurel will be visiting the Valemish temple in Sandglass tonight?"

My heart began to pound. "Where did you hear that?"

His eyes were bright with excitement, but he shrugged. "I was hanging around the palace and overheard some guards talking about it."

I considered it. First Laurel Lykos was head of the Laurel Palace guard. If he was out visiting a Valemish temple in the middle of the night, I had to know why.

"When did you hear this?"

"A few turns ago? I came here as soon as I could."

"And he's going tonight?"

"Not long after dark falls, from what I heard."

I considered it. "What are you doing at the temple, Lykos?" I muttered. As I said his name, a realization jolted me. "'Thae below. The Wolf."

Linos stared at me. "Alright there, Sasa?"

I shook my head. "Never mind. Thanks for the tip. You don't know how much it means to me."

He barked a laugh, louder than normal. "You've done more than enough favors for me. Call us even."

"I wouldn't go that far. I'll be following up on that now. I'd offer for you to stay, but I know how you like our wine…"

"No, that's alright." He glanced behind me toward the bay window. "Actually, there was one other thing."

Impatience fluttered inside me. "What is it?"

"I might be going away for a while. A span, maybe." He didn't meet my eyes.

The thrill of the hunt faltered, and the usual worry edged in. "Why so long? Mother will throw a fit."

"Nah, she won't. I'm hardly there anymore." He lowered his gaze to the floor. "I just didn't want you to worry if, you know, you tried finding me."

I opened my mouth, then closed it. Linos didn't like when I worried about him, saying it reminded him too much of our mother. Instead, I contented myself with, "Thank you for telling me."

He nodded, then abruptly turned toward the door. As he opened it, he hesitated at the threshold. "Take care, Sasa."

"You too, Little Lion."

He nodded, then closed the door.

Before it clicked shut, I'd turned back toward Xaron. I had to believe Linos could take of himself. Besides, I had a job to pursue.

"You heard all that?" I said as I walked back to where he reclined on the divan.

He studied me. "I did. But I don't understand your conclusion. How do you know Lykos is the Wolf?"

"It might have been enough that he's watchful and head of the 'pack' of laurel guards. But I also remembered from my schooling days that Lykos means 'wolf' in the Lighted-tongue."

Xaron laughed and stood. "Simple as that! The things I never could have known. Figures a stuffy old man like Nikias would use the old Oedijan speech as a cipher."

"No time to waste; we have to go." I went to the door and began strapping on my sandals.

His smile faded. "I suppose so. But what about Nomusa?"

"No time to find which tavern she wound up at. Are you coming or not?"

Xaron groaned, then went to find his own sandals. "You'll get me killed one day."

I smiled grimly. Considering what we were about to do, I could only hope it wouldn't be today.

CHAPTER EIGHT

TEMPLE'S HEART

Two turns later, Xaron and I found ourselves entering the Ignorant Intellectual. With the night growing long, it was nearly deserted. A pair of drunks argued loudly in one corner, and a few others were scattered across the room in various stages of stupor. It was the last place I wanted to be, with the first real lead on my investigation quickly slipping through my hands. But even as I fidgeted with the strap of my satchel, I knew it was necessary.

When breaking into a Valemish temple, it paid to have a professional.

Talan took his time, half a turn passing before the Guilder emerged through the tavern door. His hair was untidier even than usual, and I wondered if I'd finally caught him sleeping.

"A later call than I've come to expect from you," he observed with a raised eyebrow. "What's the hurry?"

"We'll tell you on the way."

Ushering him out of the tavern, I set our course for Sandglass as I filled him in. He listened in silence until I finished, then observed, "Your brother is remarkably well-informed."

I glanced at him, but the night hid his expression. "What does that mean?"

"Nothing more than what I said. It was wise of you to call me. I assume you've never been to a Valemish sanctum before?"

"Never had reason to. Is that where Lykos will go?"

"More than likely. Depends on what he's after. But I suppose we'll find that out soon." With an enigmatic smile, he gestured us forward.

As we reached the temple forum, I peered out. The forum felt ominous with its stillness. All the bustle of daytime was gone, leaving the black igneous temple to loom alone in the night. The braziers mounted around its base only succeeded in casting flickering shadows along its dark sides. Ascending the stairs in secret to reach its single entrance — and exit — would be an impossible task. I suddenly saw the genius of its architecture. A structure of stone with only one way in or out had to be inconvenient, but it could act as a fortress if need be. My stomach churned.

Talan touched my arm lightly. "Men approach the temple."

I saw them almost as soon as he did, three figures crossing the small bridge over the moat. Their armor gleamed with the light of the braziers, but I couldn't see if the green leaves of the Laurel Palace were painted upon them. Yet from the shoulders of the middle man, a short cape whipped back and forth, throwing shadows across the courtyard with each step. I sent Linos a silent thanks. Only First Laurel Lykos, head of the guards of the Laurel Palace, would wear such a cape.

The three men paused in front of the temple, then climbed the stairs. At the top, Lykos hammered on the door, but waited no more than a moment before he pushed his way in. One guard followed him, while the other closed the door and took post outside.

Xaron cursed softly. "How are we supposed to sneak past now? We should have gone immediately."

Talan's smile didn't falter as he nodded at my satchel. "I think our lady Finch has something in mind."

"I do." Heart pounding, I reached inside the satchel and drew out two masks and medallions.

Xaron leaned forward, wide-eyed. "Tell me those aren't what I think they are."

Talan cupped one of the medallions, studying it. "I believe they are." He looked up slyly as he released it. "Tribunal medallions. Or at least, they're supposed to be."

"They're good enough forgeries to pass a cursory inspection." I held out a mask to Talan. "Up to you if you trust me."

Xaron looked outraged. "You two are entering without me?"

I winced. "Sorry, Xaron. But I only have two sets, and Talan needs to show me the way through."

"Let me go in your place then. As much as I'd hate to spend more time with him than I have to, I'm a house-breaker. This is what I do."

"No. I have to go. I need to see and hear exactly what they say. You know how I work."

"You seemed happy enough to let me risk my neck for other jobs," Xaron muttered as he slumped back against the wall.

Talan was turning the mask over in his hand, a tapestry of orange and yellow and shaped as a finch's face. "You kept these from the previous Carnival of Veils, didn't you?"

I shrugged. "Possibly."

"A bit strange for a Tribune to wear these in the season opposite the festival. You believe the guard will let us pass without showing our faces?"

"He'll have no choice. We outrank him."

He slipped the medallion over his neck. "This is an even more foolish disguise than the last time I broke into a temple."

"You've told me about that time, and I'm fairly certain this is better than entering a haunted vault as acolytes to dance away daemons."

He grinned. "Now that you mention it, you're right. That was far stupider."

I slipped on my own medallion and felt the weighty iron settle under my chiton. With any luck, just telling the guard we were Tribunes would admit us. After all, as a man of the Laurel Palace, he had no right to bar anyone from entrance to the temple. But it paid to be prepared.

Xaron put a hand on my arm as I started to strap the mask on. "Aire," he said urgently, "please. This is rash even for you."

I gently pried his fingers away. "I have to do this, Xaron. I have to find out what Lykos is up to."

He looked far from convinced, but he backed away, frowning, his eyes tight with worry.

"Besides," I continued, "you have to keep me safe. You still have your lodestone?"

He nodded glumly. "You want me to keep watch, don't you? To warn you if the guard comes after you."

"You stole the words from my lips. Can you do it?"

"You know I will." He pulled me into a quick embrace. "Be careful."

"I will."

Turning away, I adjusted my mask to sit more comfortably. The eye slits were narrow, and I couldn't see as much as I preferred. I'd just have to make do.

"You ready?" I said to Talan.

He'd also donned his mask, but I could see his eyes crinkling in a smile behind it. "A Guilder is always ready for trouble."

Xaron suddenly reached out and gripped Talan's arm. "Keep her safe, rogue," he said in a low, rough voice.

"I will." Talan met Xaron's gaze until he withdrew his hand.

"And I'll protect both of us," I said sarcastically. "Now come on before you two start hugging."

Talan and I stepped out from the alley and walked toward the bridge. Crossing the moat, we entered into the flickering light of the forum's braziers. The guard noticed us immediately, his head following our approach like a hound to the movements of a squirrel. My breath came shallow and my heart was loud in my ears as we approached the temple.

When we were twenty paces away, he cried, "Halt! Who goes there?"

Talan and I didn't break pace. By unspoken agreement, we reached the stairs and mounted them on either side.

"Halt, I say!" the guard commanded again, the edge of his voice growing sharper. "No one without the proper authority—"

"Does this suffice as 'the proper authority'?" I drew out my Tribune medallion and brought it into the light.

The guard's expression spasmed. His eyes darted from the medallion to my masked face and back. But though he looked uncertain, he didn't move aside.

"Pardon me, Tribunes," he said, eyes sliding between us. "But you're not dressed as usual. And why wear Carnival of Veils masks?"

"Why indeed would men go about in disguise?" Talan said drily. "We did not wish to be recognized, fool."

The laurel guard's jaw clenched. "Listen. I know you two can go wherever you please. But I've got orders to keep everyone out. If you would just wait half a turn or so, everyone can—"

I ignored him and moved forward, gripping the door handle behind him. The guard stepped into my way, preventing me from opening it. I met his eyes through the mask's eye slits and didn't look away. I willed him to believe the lie, willed myself to believe it.

Whatever he saw made him flinch and step aside. Repressing a sigh of relief, I walked forward and pulled open the door. "Tell no one of this," I warned. "Including your First Laurel."

With one last glare at the guard, Talan and I slipped through the door and pulled it shut behind.

My eyes took a moment to adjust to the gloomy interior. The sparse, square chamber was lit by flickering torches, and held nothing more than an offering tray in the same black stone as the rest of the temple. Three hallways branched out before us. The dark, igneous rock closed in on all sides, making them look like tunnels into the heart of a volcano. If only it could be as warm. I shivered in the cave-like chill, drawing my arms close around me.

Talan's warm touch on my arm was a welcome change. "We'd best move quickly."

I tried recalling what I knew of Valemish temples from my few past visits. "The middle passage should lead to the altar chamber, right?"

Talan nodded. "If the First Laurel wished to speak to the Kul of this temple, that would be the path he followed."

I knew little of the Valemish, but enough to know a Kul was the head priest of a temple, like an oracle for Eidolan sanctuaries. "Then that's the way we'll go," I decided.

We set off down the hallway. The corridor soon turned into a stairwell with barely enough room for two astride. At the end of the stairs, which went far enough down to take us below the level of the street, more passages and rooms branched off from the main hall. Keeping straight, the ceiling and walls began slowly widening, and ahead I could see the edges of lit braziers illuminating what looked to be a large, open room. The altar chamber neared. My heart, already beating hard, began to race.

When we were a short distance from the entrance, I stopped Talan with a touch. Voices echoed faintly from the chamber ahead.

"Is there a better way to sneak in?" I whispered to him.

He shook his head. "One entrance, open to the rest of the altar chamber. If they're in there, they'll see us enter. But if they're in the sanctum beyond it, we'll still be safe."

I weighed the risks in my head, then nodded. What was one more risk at this point?

We started moving forward again, slower now. Every creak of my sandals made me cringe. We stopped five paces from the entrance to listen again. The voices echoed across the chamber, which I could tell was large and cavernous. The words were still indistinct and soft. They had to be in the sanctum.

Talan was already moving past me, and I followed him through the wide archway. For a moment, all I could do was stare.

The altar chamber's ceiling rose high above, its heights lost in the darkness. Stained glass windows lined the walls sixty cubits up, backlit with torches and illustrating people and stories in vivid color. The stone pews encircling the center altar were austere, while the figures etched into the floor were carefully wrought. The plateau on which the altar rose was carved with figures reaching up, their bodies mangled, their faces contorted with pain. A ring of black coals around its base told of fires lit there many times before.

But all this was ornamentation next to the depiction of their god. Slowly, I recognized the patterns on the floor drawing a man's face half-morphed into a lizard, scowling up at those who dared to tread on him. Valem, ever watching from the Underearth he ruled, always demanded obedience from his followers.

I had moments to take it in before Talan pulled me toward the center of the chamber to crouch behind the altar's plateau. The voices echoed louder here, and I could just make out their words. I shared a nervous look with Talan and leaned around the stone to listen.

"Don't lie to me," a man's voice commanded, sharp and hoarse.

"Of course I won't," a second man said smoothly. "Everything I have claimed is the truth, or may Valem burn me where I stand."

I guessed the first man was Lykos, and the second the Kul. The priest's voice was deeper and full of velvet tones; I could imagine him preaching before a congregation. The First Laurel had the tone and directness of a soldier.

After a moment of silence, Lykos's harsh voice came again. "Let me ask a different way. I am not a Tribune. I am not responsible for punishing traitors conspiring with foreign enemies. I am here for one thing: the protection of the Wreaths."

"A concern we all share, most wholeheartedly, I assure you."

"Play your games and speak your false words, priest. But continue this farce, and you will find undermining the Despot's rule to be costly."

"The Despot's rule? But surely you mean the Despoina — is her Ascension not on the morrow?"

Lykos didn't immediately answer. "Of course," the First Laurel spoke again, voice tight with anger. "But it won't be in her name that the Tribunal comes here tomorrow morn."

Sandals shuffled on stone; metal rubbed and rattled. Lykos and his guard were leaving, and after revealing so little. Yet all the same, I took Talan's arm to pull him away.

Talan resisted, nodding toward the voices, expression disguised behind his finch mask. Blood hammered in my ears, but curiosity won out. I held my breath and listened again.

"Now wait, my good First Laurel. There's no need for this."

The footsteps ceased. "Tell me what you know," Lykos said, voice echoing louder. He had entered into the altar chamber. Fear prickled down my spine, but I remained next to Talan, pressing closer to the pained stone faces.

"Tell me," the First Laurel's voice snapped like a riding crop. "All of it."

"It is nothing more than revenue, good First Laurel, to support those who need it most," the Kul said, his voice pitched higher. "Why would we kill the venerable Myron? It can only destabilize the currency and commerce. Bad for business, wouldn't you say?"

Footsteps sounded again, and I flinched until I realized they were headed away from us. Talan's hand found my arm, hot with Pyrthaen energy, steadying and reassuring.

Lykos spoke so softly I could barely hear. "And what are you bringing into our city, priest? What is in those arks?"

"My good First Laurel, I am not at liberty to say. That is most sacred business—"

"I have seen the masks. Do not put me off with talk of sanctity. If you think I could believe you innocent, you are a fool."

Something twitched against my leg. Biting back a startled yell, I thrust my hand against it. As it settled over a smooth, round object, I remembered. *The lodestone.* Xaron was sending the signal.

"The guard is coming," I hissed to Talan.

"If he just entered, then we still have time. Listen."

"Very well," the Kul was saying, his voice simmering with anger. "Masks and robes are interred within, holy objects to us."

"The masks of the Tefra are far from holy things."

My breath caught. The Tefra, priestly wardens who fanatically served both their god and their nation, were responsible for the Avvadin Imperium's widespread military success. Silks, the pyrs they enslaved, were relentless in battle and impossible to kill.

I didn't like to think what it meant if Tefra had come to Oedija.

"And what about the robes?" Lykos continued.

"Garments for priests to wear," the Kul replied bitingly.

"Do not toy with me, priest. I tire of this farce. Show me one of these arks."

"Admit you into the sanctum's heart?" Outrage limned the priest's words. "Already you have defiled this temple. I cannot allow—"

"You do not dictate what you allow!" Lykos's voice cracked like a whip, silencing the Kul. "Show me to this ark, or I will find another priest without a wish to be wrapped in chains."

"Valem will burn you," the priest promised darkly. "This way."

Their footsteps faded as they entered deeper into the sanctum. I pulled at Talan's sleeve, but he was already rising. We walked on quick, quiet feet back the way we'd come and into the flickering light of the corridor. No sooner had we reached the entrance, however, than did we see a figure striding down the stairs.

Talan and I pulled back and locked eyes across the doorway. My mind grasped for what to do. The only way to flee was further into the temple, but I doubted we'd find refuge in the sanctum. Eventually, Lykos and his guards would find us. Not knowing what else to do, I pulled up my chiton and found the hilt of my dagger, then pulled it free.

Talan watched me. When I met his eyes, he shook his head, then motioned for me to back away. His eyes were flat and cold behind his mask.

I knew then what he intended. I didn't move, but shook my head sharply.

He pressed his lips tightly together, but curtly nodded, then motioned me back once more.

This time, I complied with relief. There was no avoiding conflict now, but at least the guard wouldn't die. I hoped.

The laurel guard stepped through the doorway moments later, sword bared. He almost walked past Talan, then startled and whirled toward him, raising his sword. "Back!" he barked. "And step into the light!"

Talan motioned with his hand. The sword in the guard's hand suddenly acquired a life of its own, spinning then slamming into the man's helmet with a dull ring.

The guard stumbled back. "Tyurn's balls!" he growled, staring at the sword, now floating in the air where he'd gripped it. "How—?"

"It will all be a dream soon," Talan reassured him, then flicked his wrist. The sword struck forward, the flat of it again connecting with the surprised guard's helmet with a loud ring. This time, the man fell to his knees and swayed, disoriented.

"Damn you," the laurel guard said thickly.

Talan stepped forward and, taking the sword in his hands, swung it at his head a third time. Finally, the soldier folded over and didn't rise.

I let out the breath I'd been holding and stepped forward, wincing as I stared down at the prone guard. His face was slack, and a trickle of blood ran down his cheek. "He'll live?"

"Hard to know with three blows to the skull." Talan set the sword down next to the guard's hand, positioned as if it had fallen from his grasp. "I'm more concerned that he'll remember a warden put him down."

"Maybe he'll think it was a dream." I flashed Talan a weak smile. "Come on. We'd best get out of here."

CHAPTER NINE

EYES IN THE DARK

Six demes lay inside the city
Four lay outside
Six sheltered by thick walls
Four left out to dry

Six, the inner city demes:
Iris, center of the eye
Sandglass, counters of the coins
Bazaar, bustling marketplace
Gate, entrance to the rest
Hull, site of old ship moored
Port, sea-trade near and far

Four, the outer city demes:
Brinecoast, salt stacks 'long the shore
Thys, lake large and vast
Riverport, trade up the Walano
Drifts, mix of mud and mines

All the demes are Oedija,
All the demes make up one.
And with the Conclave and the Wreaths,
The demes number eleven.

Gathering Xaron on our way out of the temple, we headed toward one of Talan's nearby hideouts. The walk was quiet, all of us watching for signs of pursuit or city guard patrols. If they held us for questioning, Lykos would as good as have us.

To stay out of sight, Talan led us through alleys and back-ways and over rooftops so even I had difficulty keeping track of our path. It was tense, laborious work, and by the time Talan stopped, I was panting, pain needling my sides.

I eyed the small, wooden door we'd stopped in front of, which was set into the corner of a moss-covered tenement building. "This is the place?"

He smirked. "Not up to your standards?"

"As much as I expected from *you*," Xaron muttered.

Talan opened the door, and after Xaron and I exchanged a skeptical look, we followed him inside. It was, if possible, even drearier within. The room was so small I could almost touch opposite walls. Rubble and dirt had accumulated in the corners, and a suspicious black mold grew on the planks. A musty scent hung heavy in the air. All that occupied it was a narrow cot and a lidded pot that assumedly contained pyrkin. Closing the door behind us, Talan confirmed my suspicions when he opened the pot, and a soft green light like sunlit moss filled the room.

I wanted to sink onto the cot and rest, but I wasn't about to risk it. "We're safe here? Except from lice, that is."

Talan didn't share my qualms, but sat down on the cot, perfectly at home in his grubby clothes. "Perhaps, if we went unobserved. Either way, we should stay here for the night. We'll find out by the morning whether or not we escaped attention."

"Stay here until morning?" Xaron exclaimed. "You have to be kidding."

Talan donned a mocking smile. "For you I am."

I blushed, but if there were hidden intent in Talan's statement, I chose to ignore it. "Don't you have a secret tunnel we can escape through?" I suggested sarcastically. "I thought the Underguild had a network all across Oedija. "

"They do. But my hiding holes aren't connected. That would ruin the whole point of having places to tuck away."

"You could have at least kept them up."

He raised an eyebrow. "I have over a dozen such hideouts. And I can't hire an honor to clean them. Far more important that my shirts aren't in one place than that they're clean."

"Ah, yes. One of the lessons from your famous heist." I cringed as I leaned against the wall. "A shame you didn't also learn not to gamble, or to mess about in Valemish business."

A smile curved his lips. "I'm a slow learner."

"I don't want to stay here longer than I have to," Xaron interjected. "What did you two learn in there anyway?"

"Lykos is suspicious of the Valemish," Talan said, his eyes closed.

"Or wants to make it seem so," I pointed out.

"It wasn't a show. If it were, they would not have come in the dead of night."

"Unless someone were trying to make his investigation look legitimate to cover his own tracks."

Xaron stared at me with a creased brow. "Can you two start at the beginning? What *actually* happened in there?"

I sighed, then briefly recounted what we'd witnessed. By the time I finished, Xaron's eyes were wide. "I suppose it means Myron was murdered, doesn't it?"

I hid a smile. "Probably. Though it could be unrelated, the timing is too suspicious. And what other reason would the head of the laurel guard have to investigate the Valemish? He isn't in charge of the safety of the demotism, only of the Wreaths and the Laurel Palace."

"Perhaps because war with Avvad endangers us all." Talan's eyes were slitted open, gleaming in the green light.

Xaron looked thoughtful. "So the masks, the robes… Does it mean Avvad is invading? That Tefra are coming to Oedija?"

"Perhaps they're already here," Talan said darkly.

I shook my head. "If they are, they've been keeping a low profile. No one has spoken of Tefra masks or priests with burned faces. But that's beside the point. Lykos is charged with the safety of the Wreaths. It's far more likely his investigation of the Valemish has to do directly with justice for Myron's murder."

"If he *was* murdered," Talan said with a smile.

"Why would Lykos suspect the Valemish?" Xaron wondered aloud.

Talan rose on an elbow. "The Valemish are an arm of Avvad, no matter how much they might plead otherwise. If the Molten God's priests are at work, it is at the behest of the Kahin-Shah."

"But the Kahin-Shah has seemed content with conquering the Riven Lands up till now," Xaron pointed out.

Talan shook his head. "Burak Aasjuqal is never content. It is a matter of when, not if, he turns to conquer the Four Realms."

"But the Kahin-Shah has not done so because trade and peace are profitable," I said. "That hasn't changed. So if Avvad is behind this, why now? I think we should look at who else might have profited greater."

Talan and Xaron looked at me expectantly. I smiled. They knew me well enough to sense a forthcoming proposal.

"Myron Wreath was well-loved, but he had little actual power. His death has caused unease in the city, but it hasn't destabilized the government and gained any advantage for Avvad commercially. If anything, it disadvantages Avvad in the short-run. There is, however, one person who greatly benefits from Myron's death."

"Does she happen to be holding her Ascension tomorrow?" Xaron piped in.

"Asileia Wreath does benefit, and is certainly mad enough," Talan said. "But that, too, serves the Kahin-Shah's purposes. If Oedija is unstable, then it makes it all the easier to conquer."

We sat in silence for several long moments. Hunger gripping the city was bad enough. Now it seemed Oedija was dry kindling, ready to set aflame at the first spark.

Xaron spoke into the lull. "There could be a third party that benefits."

Talan and I both looked to him. "Who?" I asked, brow furrowed.

He looked almost sheepish. "The Manifest."

"The serpent cult in Thys? They may be gaining followers lately, but I doubt that qualifies them for insurrection."

Xaron shook his head. "I don't know about that. Their compound has been growing more of late, and their Seekers, as they call them, become more zealous by the day. Their leaders, the Visage of the Wyvern and the Dishonored, speak of revolution, of empowering the common man and woman, of overthrowing those who would keep them down. They have a base of operations in the Wyvern's Claw, the amphitheater off the lake. And they have dangerous ideas about wardens, even by my standards." He shrugged. "You know I think magic shouldn't be outlawed and punished. But they… they think it should be unbridled."

Talan watched him through narrowed eyes. "You seem to know an awful lot about the Manifest."

Xaron shrugged and smiled, but the smile seemed strained. "You hear things."

I stared at him, wondering, but let the odd moment pass. "If it's the Manifest, this investigation of Lykos's is moot."

"As it would be if Asileia is to blame," Xaron countered.

I shook my head. "Not if it's deliberate deception. Think about it. If Asileia were responsible, she would need to pin it on someone else. Who better than Avvad?"

Talan leaned up against the wall. "So you're proposing that Asileia killed her father and is covering it up by setting Lykos on a false trail."

"Or they're in collaboration together, along with Feiyan. More likely than not, Feiyan is behind the deception. It's always been her forte."

Talan shrugged. "It's possible. But I think this the lesser of the two mysteries now. Perhaps these Tefra masks mean something else. Perhaps they seek to force the wardens of Oedija to join their ranks."

"Force them?" Xaron narrowed his eyes. "How could they do that?"

Talan met Xaron's gaze. "Considering we prefer not to speak, I haven't told you of my life in Erimis and the things I've seen." He glanced at me. "You remember the Damask Esir?"

"Of course. Elite soldiers controlled by pyr to serve the Kahin-Shah."

"The one Damask Esir I knew was also a warden."

Fear slowly rose in me at the thought. It meant Xaron was susceptible to being controlled by Avvad. Even Talan was vulnerable.

Xaron sighed. "Just what I needed — another thing to stop me from sleeping at night."

"You don't have any trouble sleeping — I've heard your snoring." I pushed away from the wall. "Speaking of sleeping, I suppose we'd best all grab a few turns' rest before the sun rises."

Xaron rose and stretched with a great yawn. "Good. I was just about to fall asleep where I stood."

Talan rose from the cot as we made our way to the door. Opening it, I stepped out into the night and scanned the area. Shadowy figures lingered in an alley opposite of us, but I doubted they were laurel guards or city watch as they slinked away.

I could tell Talan was uneasy as he stepped up next to me and watched the alley where the figures had disappeared. "Are you sure you shouldn't stay?" he asked in a low voice.

"I'm sure."

He shook his head. "Have it your way. But remember there are more dangers than Lykos in the city, especially now."

"We will." I took his hand and pressed it. "Thank you. You're always there when I need you."

Talan flashed me a small smile. Releasing my hand, his eyes flickered to Xaron, and he nodded at him.

I turned to Xaron, who didn't bother hiding his smirk.

"You sure you want to leave?" he muttered to me as we walked away.

I rolled my eyes and didn't bother to respond.

———

A drizzling rain fell on our way back, both a blessing and a curse for travel. Rain hid us from the city guard and drove them to take shelter. But rain was also miserable when we had a two-turn walk through the dark city streets.

We made it back to Crossing with little incident. It was only as we turned onto our street that a shadow materialized from an alley. I grabbed Xaron's arm and hissed, "Ahead!"

Xaron flinched and raised his hands, preparing to channel.

But when the face came into the light of the pyr lamps mounted on the corner, I relaxed. "You could have just walked with us, you know."

Talan stepped from the darkness. "I need to speak with you. Alone."

"Here we go," Xaron muttered under his breath.

Ignoring him, I studied the Guilder. His brow was drawn, and he wore no hint of his usual smile. "I'll meet you inside, Xaron."

"I'm sure you will." Xaron cast one last droll look back before disappearing inside the tower.

Talan motioned me toward the eaves of the tower door. I huddled next to him. "What is it?"

He leaned close, his voice soft. "You were watched on your way home."

Fear trickled down my spine. "Where? I didn't see eyes in the rafters."

"They were there all the same. I plucked those that I happened across, but I'm sure there were more."

I felt dizzy. "How do you know they watched me?"

"They tailed you across the whole of Iris. I did not intercede needlessly, I assure you."

"Thank you. You shouldn't have followed me, though. You have better things to do than protecting me."

A smile tugged at the corner of his lips. "But you need so much protection."

I flushed. "You can't always keep me safe. One night won't make a difference in the long run."

"This night could have." He paused. "Besides. I couldn't sleep in that room. It's horrible and smells like a cave."

I laughed softly. "Yes. It does."

Talan reached forward and took my wrist in his hand, his fingers brushing warm against my skin. "Is there someone who might have reason to watch you, Airene? Someone alerted to your hunt?"

I sighed and pulled my wrist away. The truth wouldn't stay buried forever. And it would be a relief to tell someone. "Feiyan," I admitted. "She sent Kako to threaten me yesterday."

Talan's eyes went as hard as flint. "Threatened you how?"

"Remember how she suspects Nomusa or Xaron of being a warden? Kako said she'd set the Shepherds on them if..." I sighed. "If I didn't stop investigating Myron's death."

"So that's why you believe Asileia to be behind it." Talan gathered a considering look. "It's a dangerous game you play."

"No more than you gamble everyday by being a Guilder."

"True," he acknowledged easily. "But I'm a warden and much more capable of protecting myself than you. And it is my own life I gamble with, not others."

I wanted to argue, but he was right. Guilt churned in my gut. "What else can I do, Talan? I have to follow this hunt to its end."

"Why? Why not leave it and keep yourself safe?"

"And let Feiyan win? And let Myron's murder be covered up by lies?" I shook my head. "You know I can't do that."

Talan wore a half-smile again. "And you're sure those are the reasons you're doing this?"

"What's that supposed to mean?"

"You know my story, Airene. I have held nothing back from you. You know I have seen my share of desperate people." He paused, eyes flickering back and forth between mine. "No hunt is worth your life."

I turned my head aside, unable to meet his gaze. It hurt to know what he thought of me — some poor, desperate woman clinging to an invented purpose because she had no other. It didn't help that I wondered if he was right.

As much out of need as to escape my thoughts, I found myself speaking. "Can I ask you a favor?"

"Of course."

"When Linos gave me the tip earlier about Lykos, he also told me he'd go missing for a while. He told me not to come looking for him, but with everything going on, I can't help but worry." I met his gaze. "I won't be breaking my promise, though, if you're the one who looks after him."

He nodded. "He's young, but he doesn't completely lack sense. I will find and watch over him all the same." He gave me an odd look. "But he isn't the one I was concerned about."

I sighed. "I'll think about what you said. That's as much as I can promise."

Talan took my hand, and I pressed his in return. Without a word, he released his grasp and turned away. I watched him disappear down an alley and lingered a moment longer before shaking my head and making my way inside.

As soon as I entered Canopy, Xaron and Nomusa turned toward me from near the bay window, nearly silhouettes in the dim light of the loft. I raised an eyebrow as I approached them. "Trying to spy on me?"

"Why'd you have to stand next to the tower?" Xaron complained.

Nomusa wasn't smiling. She had shadows under her eyes, accentuated by the low light. I wondered if she'd slept that night.

"Xaron had just started to fill me in on what you two were up to with Talan," she said, her words picked carefully. "Care to elaborate?"

Tired, hungry, and paranoid as I was, it took all my self-control not to snap at her. Instead, I took a breath and explained what had happened. Guilty as I felt, I held back my last conversation with Talan. I wasn't ready to risk the job yet by telling them about Feiyan's threats.

"You could have been killed," was all Nomusa said when I finished.

"But we weren't. And now we have further leads."

"Not much. What did you learn? That the First Laurel is investigating the Despot's murder? Hardly surprising. And can you really know what the Valemish are up to from this one conversation?"

I shook my head. Why Nomusa had such resistance to the inquiry, I couldn't explain. When we'd first become Finches, we'd dreamed of an opportunity like this. It seemed that those days were gone.

I stretched and yawned. "Time for bed. See you both tomorrow."

I rose and headed for my room. Before I could enter, Nomusa approached and folded me into an embrace. Surprised, I relented. Touch was common for her, but considering her stance toward the job, I hadn't expected any hugs forthcoming.

"I know I haven't been cooperative," she said softly in my ear. "And I can't say I agree with your inquiry. But... I've lost family twice, Aire. I don't want to lose you, too."

All of my pent-up annoyance with her suddenly dissipated. I held her tighter. "We've always taken risks, Nomu. Yes, these are greater than before. But I'd be denying the very thing I'm meant for if I didn't look into this."

Nomusa didn't answer for a long moment. "I know. But can you at least not take such foolish risks?"

I gently extricated myself from her. "We'll see."

She turned her gaze aside. We both heard the lie in the words.

CHAPTER TEN
ASCENSION

Asileia Wreath, unlike her father, has never seemed aware that the Despoina would have any limits to her authority. In this, she is like Zalfene Wreath, who, generations before, built the Half Wall and nearly began a war with Avvad. Reports of her activities as governor of the Oedijan peninsula are preliminary, but Asileia appears to use autocratic methods to enact laws with little consultation from her subjects, nor even agreement among the landed patricians…

Should she fail to learn wisdom, I fear for our nation when Asileia wears the Evergreen Wreath.

- A Modern Account of the Wreaths; by Acadian Helene, Master Historian; 1170 SLP

A bird awaited me when I woke.

Rising before Nomusa and Xaron — though after Corin — I went to the balcony, as was my habit. There waited an unfamiliar finch, impatiently hopping back and forth. Heart pounding, I took up the messenger bird and unwound the scroll from its leg. It bore no distinguishable seal, but I suspected who it was from as soon as I began reading.

My Honeycomb,

I have left you forlorn for far too long. We must be reunited, and at once, or I fear I shall expire from want. I miss the sweet nectar of your kiss; life here is far too bitter and growing more so every day.

Meet me at the place where, if I were so blessed to be the Wreath, I might first lay eyes upon you, and at the time this evening that she might least observe it.
Forever longing for your flower,
Your Aimless Bumblebee

I smiled at the floral, love-sick language. It was at odds with the stiff, formal man I knew Nikias to be, but Jaxas Wreath's steward was a surprising man. When it came to his own master, he was loyal to the bone. For all other matters in the Laurel Palace, however, his tongue was alarmingly loose.

On the whole, the message seemed thin on information and thick with alarm. If Nikias felt threatened, it didn't bode well for his continuing to provide information. Still, if he wanted to meet, that would have to be enough.

Xaron appeared in the balcony doorway and scowled at the dreary sky. "Any news?" he asked.

"Nikias sent another finch. He wants to meet."

His expression brightened. "Truly? When?"

"Tonight, if I'm reading the message correctly. In Forum Demos during Asileia's Ascension. Here, read it yourself."

Accepting the message, Xaron glanced it over and made a face. "Has he never written a love letter before? Laid it on a bit thick to be believable."

"And made it too obvious — I was quick to decipher it, and I'm sure others would be as well. Still, I don't see what choice we have but to meet him."

He handed me back the message. "How about *not* meeting him?"

I raised an eyebrow at him, then looked him up and down, noticing for the first time he was fully dressed. "Where are you headed?"

He gave me an uncertain smile. "Visiting my parents. Their health isn't well."

I snorted, knowing the lie for what it was. Though it did hurt that he didn't tell me where he went these mornings. "Very well. Keep your secrets."

"I'll see you tonight. Meet at Zipho's first? Four turns past noon?"

"Fine. See you then."

Once he'd left and the finch was sent, I returned inside. A thought occurred to me, one that made me sweat. If we met Nikias tonight, he'd expect to be paid. The steward wasn't a cheap informant. Most of my eyes and ears around the city took copper and nickel for payment. Nikias accepted nothing less than silver, and a hefty amount at that.

I chewed my lip as my eyes slid to the loose stone in the kitchen wall where we kept our shared Finch money, which comprised half of what we earned. I knew as well as Xaron and Nomusa how much was left there: thirty-three silver scions, fifty-nine nickel magnes, and a smattering of copper cullets. The steward likely wouldn't take less than fifteen scions. Considering the times, it was foolish to spend half of our money on one whisper.

Yet I knew what I would do. No matter how underhanded it seemed, this would be best for all of us. Discovering the Despot's murderer would bring more wealth than any of us would be able to spend.

The ring of rationalization was loud in my ears.

I slipped the false stone from the wall and set it softly on the floor. Glancing over my shoulder to make sure Nomusa's door was still closed, I took out the silver, a full fifteen pieces, and silently stashed them in my private purse, quieting them with slips of cloth between each coin. Replacing the stone, I swept away the dust from the floor below the cache.

As I rose, I heard the creak of an opening door. My heart caught in my throat. I sidestepped closer to the pantry and began pulling down food.

I glanced back as Nomusa emerged from her room. "Morning," I said with false cheeriness.

"Morning," she replied, walking toward me. "I'm starving."

"You always wake starving." My teasing sounded overdone to my own ears, my voice unnaturally high-pitched. I hoped Nomusa wouldn't notice.

She smiled blearily at me. "Ixolo burns fuel." She looked me up and down. "Leaving already?"

"I want to know what Oedija whispers before the Ascension tonight. Though Xaron beat both of us out, if you can believe it."

She pulled out bread from the pantry and began cutting it. "To his usual mysterious spot, is it?"

"So it seems."

I needed to leave. It somehow seemed the silver would give me away the longer I stayed. "We're meeting at Zipho's four turns after noon for the Ascension. I'll see you there?"

"Sure." Nomusa nodded at my hand. "But aren't you going to eat that mango first?"

I looked down at my hand. I hadn't even noticed what I'd grabbed. Letting out a nervous laugh, I replaced it on the shelf. "I'm not as hungry as I thought. See you later."

Nomusa watched me strangely as I headed toward the door. "Till then."

I put on a strained smile and turned away. Only as I exited did I remember I hadn't mentioned Nikias. But with my stomach turning, I didn't turn back, but fled down the stairs.

———

As promised, Nomusa, Xaron, and I met at Zipho's that afternoon. With guilt still coursing strong through me, and the mystery of Xaron's morning between us, it made for awkward conversation over coffee.

We made small talk as we pushed on to Forum Demos. Nomusa told us of her night, which consisted of a handsome man in a tavern who claimed to be a laurel guard. I smiled in response while my mind wandered. I had only just realized I'd have to pay Nikias in front of them, and I didn't have the first clue as to how I'd pull it off.

"Are we meeting Nikias first?" Xaron asked suddenly.

Startled from my thoughts, I guiltily looked at Nomusa. She wore a frown. "No one told me we were meeting Nikias," she said slowly.

Xaron glanced at me. "You didn't mention it this morning?"

"It slipped my mind," I lied.

An awkward silence fell between us.

"You may as well tell me about it now," Nomusa said flatly. "What did the message say?"

Xaron recounted the missive and my conclusions about what it meant. "We don't know exactly where he intends to meet, but I'm sure we'll sort it out."

"Do you have the message? I want to see the exact wording."

Silently, I handed it to her. Apprehension built inside me as she read. Sooner or later, her mind would turn to payment. I didn't know what I'd say if she asked about it.

"*Meet me at the place where, if I were so blessed to be the Wreath, I might first lay eyes upon you, and at the time this evening that she might least observe it,*" she read aloud. "He has a fondness for convoluted riddles, doesn't he? At least its meaning is obvious."

"Is it?" I asked, curious. "Where exactly is it?"

"The Pillar. It rises right before the dais. Impossible to miss."

Xaron groaned. "Not the Pillar again. A bad cipher and a poor meeting place... I'm beginning to question this whole venture."

"As am I," Nomusa said wryly.

I looked away, having nothing to say in response.

When we were still a mile away from Forum Demos, the crowds thickened. Sweat and the stench of humanity permeated the air. I kept one hand on my purse and a wary watch. No one celebrated ceremonies as much as cutpurses, and I wasn't about to line some urchin's pockets.

We passed the gated Acadium, its campus of towers the last landmark before the forum, and a welcome sight after our long, uncomfortable march. Seeing it made me wish again that I could have one conversation with Archmaster Kyros and hear what he knew of the Despot's death. At least I would soon speak to Tribune Vusumuzi. I'd learn what I needed, so long as I could find the patience to tease it out.

As we drew close to Forum Demos, a palpable excitement grew in the air, electrifying the shouts and hurrying our steps. To my surprise, I found that I'd caught it as well. Though a leaden weight still lingered in my stomach, my spirits lifted bit by bit. The sun began to set, and the glow of lights from Forum Demos appeared ahead. Pyr lamps, braziers, oil lanterns, even candles were suspended above the streets, a path of stars to light our way.

Then we reached Forum Demos itself, the sprawling half-mile of amphitheater packed full of people for the second time in a span. We made our way directly toward the Pillar. My anxiety increased with every step. Would I be able to slip the silver to Nikias? I didn't dare think of the ethics of it lest I lose my nerve.

As we reached the Pillar, I scanned the crowd for the steward, but he was just one in a sea of humanity. Xaron, a few inches taller than I was, rose on his toes, but fared no better. Nomusa was half-hearted in her search, her scowl deepening with every new person who shoved against her.

Finally, I saw him. I'd only met him a few times before, but I recognized the squinting eyes set in the scrunched face looking back and forth. Finely trimmed gray whiskers lined his jaw, and even in the midst of the crowd, he stood erect and proud in his patrician finery.

I pressed toward him without alerting Xaron and Nomusa. A desperate idea had occurred to me. I just had to hope the steward would comply.

Nikias turned and noticed me, then stood and waited. He didn't acknowledge me, for which I was thankful. No doubt both of us wished to escape as much notice as possible.

Nearing him, I withdrew the purse of silver from inside my chiton's pocket and clutched it tightly in my hand. As soon as I stood before him, I thrust it toward him.

The steward reflexively stepped back. "What is that?" he demanded, shouting to be heard.

"Take it!" I hissed, pressing it into his hand. "I'm paying in advance!" A glance over my shoulder showed Xaron and Nomusa heading our way.

Nikias's ample eyebrows drew down, but he accepted the purse and secreted it beneath his many-layered robes.

Just then, my companions joined us. "Nikias!" Xaron greeted him. "Good to see you! You should have told us you were such a stunning poet!"

The steward scowled. "As much as I would love to bandy words, I must return to my master's side soon."

My mouth felt dry as I leaned close, my companions leaning with me. "Tell us what you know of the Despot," I said as loud as I dared.

Nikias nodded sharply. "The official story is he died of foul humors of the heart due to the rich foods of the festival. But the honors tell another story."

"Go on."

Nikias spoke so low I could barely hear. "The Despot was murdered in his own rooms. Pushed from his balcony by the look of it."

"Pushed from his balcony?" I frowned. "How do you know? Was his body found below?"

Nikias's whiskers bristled as he leaned away. "No body has been found that I've heard of. But the Despot was gone without a trace! Not a spot of blood on the carpets, nor bed sheets, nor walls. The only thing out of sorts was that his balcony door was ajar, and a spattering of mud lay on the stone."

I glanced at the others. Xaron wore a skeptical look, while Nomusa seemed thoughtful. Turning back to Nikias, I asked, "How can we be sure he didn't disappear somehow? Perhaps he was kidnapped."

Nikias looked to the sky as if seeking consolation from the gods. "No one saw him leave, no one, out of the entire Laurel Palace. There's only one door to Myron's old chambers. He entered that night and never left."

"But someone else must have entered as well," Xaron objected. "Or are you saying the old boar threw himself to the rocks?"

Nikias ignored him. "There is more. An honor overheard the guards afterward. One said he heard arguing from inside, then a roar like a blazing forge. He and his fellow tried to enter but found it bolted from within. It was only after the First Laurel had arrived that they broke it open and found nothing inside."

The First Laurel had been the first to arrive. That cast a new light on Lykos. I'd assumed him innocent. Either there had been no other evidence on the scene, or he had disposed of it before others arrived. The roar could be explained by a tricky bit of chemistry or an enchanted object. Pyrthaen-lit braziers, for example, had a tendency to blaze up on occasion.

Or, of course, it could be from the magic of a rogue warden.

"Safe to say there were two people in that room," Xaron reasoned. "Unless the Despot was as crazy as his daughter."

"And if they had a way in," Nomusa interjected, "they would have had a way to secret out the Despot."

"It's impossible!" Nikias protested. "There are no secret passages to that room, I can assure you of that. And the balcony is as inaccessible. Not only is it watched by a dozen guards from a dozen different angles, and lit as brightly as the moons, but it is set over a sheer, slick cliff. Not even the most dexterous of gymnasts could manage it."

"Perhaps they didn't enter," I said, a thought coming to me. "Perhaps they hid in the room until the Despot returned."

"And then went where?" Nikias pressed. "Did they leap after their dark deed was finished?" He sniffed. "I hardly think even the most dedicated assassin would commit to that."

I shared a look with Xaron, and he shrugged. Nomusa seemed to have spoken her piece and remained silent as well.

"Is there anything more?" I asked Nikias. "What about Asileia Wreath? And Lykos — what has he been up to?"

"One at a time," he said irritably, eyes darting this way and that. "The palace has felt like the air before a storm, to borrow my master's words. People move with caution and speak softly, especially around our soon-to-be Despoina. As for her, I've seen with my own eyes that she has truly been touched by malevolent pyr."

It was hardly surprising to hear. Yet I couldn't let others draw conclusions for me. Too often in the past had others' assumptions led me astray. "What signs has she shown?"

"What hasn't she? She surrounds herself with those backwater oracles, who prattle in her ear that she's the 'Hand of Clepsammia' and other such rubbish. She speaks to herself in front of others. She sees things that are not there, while other times she's blind to people standing directly before her. But most of all…" Nikias hesitated.

"Don't stay silent now," I coaxed him.

His jaw flexed. "I cannot say more. It would betray my master's confidences, and that I would not do for silver or gold."

I leaned back, disappointed. He had given much already, but this seemed to be the crucial bit. What had Jaxas, Nikias's master, told him that was so important? It might be the key to knowing if Asileia was guilty or innocent.

"Then at least speak of the First Laurel," I pressed. "What has he done since the Despot's death?"

"How can I tell? He's hardly been in the palace. But others have said he's looking into the Despot's death, and Lykos has never given me reason to believe otherwise. I would not suspect him in your little game."

I nodded. It didn't exonerate him, but it was good to know Nikias's opinion.

Nikias glanced back toward the dais. "I must return. I cannot promise to speak again. The way things are looking under the Despoina, information may cost my life next time."

"Then you'd best avoid paying," I said with a forced smile. "Thank you as always, Nikias. May the Eidola watch over you."

"I had better pray someone will," the informant muttered as he turned and stalked through the unwashed crowd, shoulders raised like an alley mongrel.

"How much of that was lying at his master's behest?" Xaron murmured in my ear as we watched the steward disappear into the crowd.

I shrugged, glad that neither of my companions had inquired into the seeming lack of payment to Nikias. "You'll drive yourself madder than Asileia worrying about the truth. All we have to worry about is what fits."

"What *does* fit?" He ran a hand through his hair. "I still feel as if we've not discovered anything conclusive."

"We can discuss this later," Nomusa broke in. "Let's go to our usual perch."

We pushed back up through the crowd to the buildings lining the back of the forum, then clambered up the crates to the roof above, ignoring once more the jeering of the orphans. No sooner had we sat than an unnaturally amplified voice cut through the crowd.

"Hark!" Hilarion's high-pitched voice called. "Make way for our beloved Wreath!"

The procession streamed through the crowd like a great snake. Rank upon rank of trumpeters, dancers, and polished city watchmen marched through Forum Demos toward the dais.

After the common paraders came the foremost of Oedijan officials: the Servants of the People's Conclave. Signifying their connection to the people, they walked on foot, though their flawless, flowing robes sewn with an abundance of cloth and pinned with gems and silver spoiled the effect.

Behind the Servants walked the Low Consuls, the supreme leaders who ruled through the Conclave. As I spotted Feiyan walking among them, her chin held up proudly, I sent up a small prayer that she would trip over the hem of her robes. To my dismay, no gods or pyr paid me heed, and the snake of a woman passed by unimpeded.

Next came the Tribunes, swathed in burgundy robes, with the Shepherds walking among them. In aqua cowls and manacles hanging from their wrists and ankles, the warden enforcers of the Confessional Tribunal kept their gazes forward and held themselves in an unnaturally stiff manner. My stomach twisted upon seeing them, as it always did. There was something strange about Shepherds that I'd never quite been able to put my finger on.

The Acadians followed the Tribunes and Shepherds, Archmaster Kyros Brighteyed at their head. His telltale eyes could be seen glimmering even from this distance. After the Acadians rode the five Stratechons, elected leaders of the city watch and the militia taxoi when needed.

Finally, the royal palanquin passed by. Eight honors contorted their bodies to bear our new Despoina down the steps to the dais. Before her rode Hilarion, the middle-aged, warden jester looking distinctly uncomfortable atop his humorously small mule. His sackcloth clothing no doubt made his situation all the worse. A mocking crown of golden wheat was twined about his mostly bald pate. With the piteous sight he made, I could almost understand people becoming dismissive of wardens' powers, as Hilarion was meant to do.

Coming behind them rode Lykos, making for a stark contrast. He peered about with his wolfish eyes from atop a fine chestnut, polished bronze armor shining.

As the last of the parade followed, the Despoina was carried up to the brilliantly illuminated dais, and the canopy of her palanquin was pulled back. The gathered crowd collectively gasped — how godly she appeared! Her skin had been rubbed with golden pyrkin, and with her chiton cut to leave both breasts exposed, there was plenty of skin to glow. Had she been anyone but our Despoina-to-be, she would have been derided as a whore. But Asileia's nakedness cast an aura of power. She appeared brighter than the three moons and more wondrous than the radiant winds. I suspected she basked in all her contrived glory.

"I don't think Myron glowed like the sun during his Ascension," I said to Xaron and Nomusa.

"Myron wasn't mad," Nomusa surmised.

Hilarion's high tenor broke through the babbling of the audience once again. "Hail!" he called. "Hail, one and all! The Low Consuls of our nation!"

The ten Low Consuls of the Conclave processed to the front of the dais to stand beside the Despoina-to-be, looking like frail, mortal creatures next to a radiant goddess. One by one, Hilarion pressed his fingers to their throats, and each said their piece to muted effects from the crowd. True rulers of Oedija or not, the common people were not here for their speeches.

After they'd finished, High Tribune Photina stepped forward. Held aloft in her hands was the Evergreen Wreath. The crown was said to have been worn by the first Despot six hundred years before, and was still as vibrant a green as the day it was woven. The crowd rose in a sudden roar of cheers — and jeers, unless my ears were mistaken. My interest piqued, I fished out my peering glass and adjusted it to watch the proceedings.

Hilarion pressed his fingers to Asileia's golden throat as she stepped forward. "People of Oedija," her commanding alto boomed. "The demos of our demotism. I welcome you, and welcome your worship."

There was pocketed applause, but more loudly rose the murmurs.

"That wasn't what they expected, I'll warrant," Xaron muttered. "The mad hag."

"We gather here not just for ceremony," Asileia continued. "We gather not just because tradition demands it. We gather to witness the passing of this nation's leadership, and to witness a change more profound than the switching of the seasons. We gather to witness my donning of the Wreath."

This was something the people could get behind, and they started clapping. But true to her manner, Leia barreled through with barely a pause.

"Some claim I am to be a mere figurehead, as my father was, and his father was, and his mother before that. Little more than a statue on a throne." Her voice rose in anger. "Some claim that I will be meek as a lamb, shepherded by a band of old fools."

Murmurs gave a bubbling undercurrent to the speech. Something was stirring, though I couldn't tell precisely what.

"They are wrong!" The Despoina's voice crashed like cymbals in my ears. "And they will be shown to be wrong! This is my promise to you: change is coming. And it is coming tonight."

The bubbling became a swelling river, protests and assents sounding in equal measures. I shared a worried look with Nomusa and Xaron. None of us moved. If something were to happen, we had to be present for it.

"We are weak," Asileia sneered. "We bow under famine and hunger. Our army is little more than children playing with toys. We cower before another nation as if we were already their slaves. But we will cower no longer. I bow before no one. *No one!*"

People began crying out now, the noise reaching a zenith. I couldn't tell if protest or approval was winning out. Even still, the Despoina's voice crashed over them, like thunder over stormy seas.

"I am the Eidola's chosen, the Hand of Clepsammia! The oracles have spoken of my coming! And I will lead our nation to the glory it was fated to seize!"

And with that, a hush stole over the crowd. For some, it was heresy. For others, it was hopelessly grandiose. I knew it now to be mere madness.

Then, through the peering glass, I saw Asileia suddenly jerk back from Hilarion, her mouth parted in a scream. It echoed through the forum, then abruptly cut to a normal pitch. Heart pounding, I pieced the scene together from glimpses.

The Despoina, her robes engulfed in hungry flames, stumbling across the dais.

The Low Consuls scattering and scrambling to flee the platform.

Hilarion, still standing where the Despoina had left him, staring in horror at his hand.

"Kill him! Kill him!" Her scream echoed thinly up the forum. Focusing my glass on Asileia, I saw she pointed at someone. As I followed the line of her finger, I glimpsed Hilarion as a sword whipped a red line across his neck. The jester crumpled to the ground. But the attacker wasn't finished yet. The sword bit into the back of Hilarion's neck, spraying blood across the stage, and a third time as the sword pierced through his back.

I watched through my glass, trying to steady my shaking hands, as I identified the assailant. Lykos, gleaming armor spattered with blood, withdrew his blade and scanned the swell of faces as if searching for more victims. All the while, Shepherds swarmed the stage.

Asileia Wreath still screamed as honors rushed up to her and swung rags to dampen the flames licking across her golden skin. The noise of the crowd drowned out her words. I saw someone kneel by the dead body of Hilarion — Kyros Brighteyed, his gaze as hard as Lykos's had been.

"Great ancestors protect us all," Xaron muttered as he gripped my arm. "Did that just happen?"

I was too preoccupied to answer. As shock slipped away, suspicion replaced it. I panned my peering glass across the stage, studying the scene.

"Airene, we have to leave," Nomusa said, taking my other arm. "It isn't safe here."

I sighed and lowered the glass, then followed them off the rooftop to the chaotic streets below.

INTERLUDE I
JAXAS

Jaxas stood just beyond the doorway, head turned aside. From the corner of his eye, he could see the room lay in disarray. Mirror glass glittered across the carpeted floor. Curtains had been ripped down and torn apart. Pillow feathers were strewn about the bed.

She stood in the midst of the chaos, the goddess calm again after the storm. The Despoina had returned to her right mind.

"Leia?" Jaxas inquired cautiously. He didn't look at her. "Are you sure you wouldn't like me to call back the surgeon?"

A turn before, her skin had been reddened and boiled by the lancing flames of the late Hilarion. But Kallias the Sculptor had done his job well. As she stood naked in the middle of the room, he could see the Acadian surgeon had returned her flesh to its ashy bronze.

If only he could restore all she had lost.

"Leia?" he called softly once more.

"It is not the first time I've burned, Archon Jaxas." She distanced him with the new title she'd granted him. "You have not forgotten my mother's gift to me, have you?"

He had tried to forget many times, but Leia had never let him. She despised him for how he saw the best in her. Or how he imagined it.

"That disgusting skin hanging from my ears," she continued, merciless, though she seemed to be speaking to herself. "And she thought I would keep it — hah!"

Jaxas tried again to lead the conversation away. "You look well, but if it hurts too much to put on your robes, I can call the honors back—"

"You do not need to coddle me, Jaxas. Just because my father is dead does not mean I cannot take care of myself." She laughed mirthlessly.

"Then perhaps you will dismiss me."

"Come closer — I cannot hear you from over there."

He could feel her mocking smile, but it was his Despoina's explicit command. As little as he wanted to, he turned to the room and faced her. He had seen his cousin naked before, and not only as children, for their bathing times sometimes coincided. But never had she displayed herself like this before him. He took two obliging steps forward and halted.

Her lips curled. "Closer."

He took another step.

She laughed aloud at him again. "You always were skittish." Now she approached him, coming close enough to touch. She held herself tall and erect, as if her nudity were armor, as if the shame it spread through Jaxas were something to be proud of.

Leaning closer, she spoke in his ear, breath tickling his neck. "I know he's dead. Even though there was no body, I know it. Would you like to know how?"

He said nothing, dreading her words.

"Because, dear cousin, I killed him."

Jaxas stepped back, his heart racing. "You don't mean that," he said as calmly as he could manage. "You can't. I sat with you that night in your father's solar."

"Not with all of me." She smiled at his shock, his fear, his loathing. "I am the Eidola's chosen. The Hand of Clepsammia moves her spirit as readily as a pyr between the Pyrthae and the world of flesh. I killed him, if not with my worldly hands, than with my immortal ones."

"Leia, don't say such things. You're not in your right mind."

She laughed, and before its harsh sound, he couldn't bear to stay a moment longer. He turned from her chambers and fled.

Down the hall from her doors, he pressed himself against the cold stone. Her laughter had cut off as abruptly as it had come. No doubt she had lapsed back into one of her stupors — her visions, as she called them.

Jaxas closed his eyes and tried to still his spinning head. He didn't believe it. He couldn't. Not of her. But he'd heard it from her own lips. She believed she had killed him. Was delighted she had. Even if she hadn't done it, wasn't that bad enough?

He continued to flee, his footsteps falling faster and faster. His eyes burned, but he wiped away the few tears that came until his eyes were dry. This was the sign he'd been waiting so long for, he told himself. It was an impossible task before him, but he could not flinch from it any longer. She had shown too much of herself now. He could no longer tell himself that somewhere in her, beyond the cruel desires and feelings, there was some good part of her that would rise above the rest.

He came to an abrupt halt before a tall window that looked out over the bay. The night had hidden much of the sea from view, but in the crests of the waves, pyrkin came alive in green washes. He had always treasured living in the seaside palace. The orphaned cousin taken in at eight when his parents died of plague, he'd always known he was lucky to even be alive, much less be surrounded by plenty. Myron had cared for him as a father for a son, steady even when his wife succumbed to the same disease. And Asileia, having lost her mother, bonded close to Jaxas in her grief.

The peaceful sounds drifting up the cliffside could not calm him now. Asileia was not the girl he'd grown up with. To continue loving her, she who had once been a sister to him, would be living a lie.

Yet doubt haunted him. Even knowing what she was, even knowing what she believed herself capable of, he didn't know that he would be able to do what needed to be done. For the good of all. Eidola above, for Asileia's own sake.

Jaxas stared out over the quiet ocean, seeing little and understanding less.

CHAPTER ELEVEN

THE AUGUR

Master Eltris says there are many things to be seen in birds. She says they are attuned to the Pyrthae in ways that humans are not. All of us contain the energetic elements within us — radiance, kinesis, magnesis, and the like — but many animals possess these to a greater degree than we, and birds most of all. Master Eltris claims that birds are able to fly high among the cold winds because of a natural attunement to radiance and kinesis. And they navigate by magnesis, reading the magnetic fields that encompass Telae the way we would read a map.

In whisper finches, the Master Augur says, the most important of the energetic elements is present. It is this element that we humans possess that allows us to think in our heightened capacity, and to force our will on the world. Quintessence, she calls it, though she cannot tell me any more of it than that. If I ask, she quickly grows cross.

But I do not wish to study birds. I believe her to be a daft, wool-eared woman. Even if I did like her, I fear I have ruined my chances to become a master by being placed under her tutelage. Archmaster Kyros does not appear to care for her either. I am sure she would not be Master Augur had she not already long held the position. It's said she's as old as most of the buildings in the Acadium, even if she doesn't look it. I believe it when she talks sometimes, of things people shouldn't know of. The look she gets in her eye frightens me.

- Diary of an Acadian pupil, name and date unknown

It was well after dark when we reached our derelict tower and wearily climbed to the top. Once there, we gathered the last of the scraps in our household and made a meager meal, complete with goblets filled with the dregs of festival wine.

"Alright," Xaron said, collapsing into the old armchair and ripping off a bite of dried sausage. "What happened back there?"

I barely tasted the food I ate. "It's more proof that Asileia killed her father."

"How?" Nomusa demanded. "The Despoina was attacked by a warden. How else could those flames begin so suddenly?"

"Unless it was a performance. You couldn't see Hilarion's expression before Lykos cut him down. He stared at his hand like it had betrayed him."

"Perhaps it was an accident," Nomusa suggested.

Xaron shrugged. "Such things can happen even with an experienced warden. But one thing I do know is that Hilarion wasn't trying to kill her. His fingers were pressed to her throat. It would have been simple to do, if stupid, considering the forum was full of witnesses."

"Unless someone was trying to make a point," I murmured. "The Manifest… didn't you say they're for liberating wardens?"

Xaron's brow creased. "Yes. But didn't we just establish that Hilarion wasn't trying to kill her?"

"I still agree with that. But would it be possible that someone was framing him?"

"Shepherds were around the dais," Nomusa noted.

Xaron shook his head. "No Shepherds were close enough or at the right angle. It had to have been someone within a dozen feet, and even then they'd have to be a powerful warden." He paused, his eyes going wide. "Oh, Tyurn's tits…"

"What is it?"

Xaron looked between us, then sighed. "You know how I've been leaving most mornings for the past several months?"

"Hard to miss," I said drily.

"Well, I suppose I now have to tell you what I've been up to… and it wasn't visiting my parents, or seeing a special woman. I've been — well, receiving lessons from an Acadian."

Silence filled Canopy.

Nomusa recovered before I did. "You're even stupider than I thought."

He smiled sheepishly. "I'm sure that's not altogether surprising."

I was far from amused. "How could you, Xaron? If you're caught, you could be confined there for the rest of your life — if the Shepherds don't decide to kill you instead."

"I know the risks. I know it's a foolish thing to do. But it's all a long story. What's important is that in my time in the Acadium, I've learned a lot about another warden who was on stage with Asileia, one powerful enough to channel radiance at a great distance before it burst into flame. And one who might have the motivation to frame Hilarion."

It took all my self-control to rein in my impatience. "You've just told us you've been a fool for the past season. Now you're holding out on us. Who else could have done it?"

Nomusa's eyes widened. "Kyros Brighteyed. That's who you mean, isn't it?"

Xaron nodded. "I've heard things spoken about him, but I didn't know what to make of them. That he comes and goes at strange turns of the night. That he has become increasingly vocal about the need for Acadians to step up their role within Oedija. Even that he's been training Acadians to fight."

Fear struck through me, quick and cold. "To fight? What does he want, to become one of the Tyrant Wardens of old?"

"Or maybe he's the leader of the Manifest," Nomusa said darkly.

Xaron shrugged helplessly. "I can't say for sure. But Eltris can probably tell us more."

Nomusa and I shared a look. "Who is Eltris?" she inquired.

"She's, well, my mentor, I suppose."

"Mentor for channeling?" I guessed.

He nodded. "My mother never taught me anything beyond dampening my gift. I'm *shur*, a ten-shift warden, yet Eltris has shown me just how little I know." He lowered his gaze. "It may seem wrong to you. 'Thae above, it felt wrong to me at first. But learning about channeling can be for good as well as evil."

I didn't look at him, not wanting him to see the fear in my eyes. "Let's assume that Kyros did set up Hilarion. What would he gain from it? This can only incite anger against wardens."

"But if he's part of the Manifest, that may serve him well," Nomusa said thoughtfully. "People clearly support the cult's ideas. If he inflames relations between wardens and the demotism, it could propel their movement further."

"I have an idea." Xaron stood and stretched. "How about we go visit Eltris tomorrow morning. She can tell us more about Kyros, and I can stop feeling guilty about lying to you."

I hesitated. On the one hand, I didn't have a better explanation for what had happened at the Ascension. But I found it hard to accept that the Archmaster was leading an insurrection of wardens. It didn't explain what was happening with Asileia and Feiyan, nor with the Valemish. And I still found the Manifest the least of the threats that faced us. Cults were fragile, and surely all the more so with wardens involved.

"It seems risky to gossip about Kyros in his own domain," I hedged. "How can you be sure we won't be watched?"

"Eltris has mouthed off about him this long. I'm sure we'll be fine."

I looked at Nomusa, who shrugged. "May as well," she said. "We might find out something."

I sighed. If it could bring me closer to the Archmaster, one of the few who had seen the scene of Myron's disappearance, then I had to at least try. "We'll go then. But afterward, we stop by the Tribunal to speak to Vusu. It's past time we heard what he said."

Xaron looked uneasy. "You two can go. I'll pass. That Tribune makes my skin crawl."

I nodded with understanding. The branch of the demotism that backed the Shepherds wouldn't be a comfortable place for Xaron to enter.

"We have a long day tomorrow," Nomusa said, rising. "And you two didn't rest much last night. Let's try to sleep the night through for once?"

My heart was light as I went to my bed. Despite everything that had happened, I found a smile tugging at my lips. Perhaps they didn't know it, but both of them were finally on board with my hunt.

Things were starting to look up.

I woke to the taste of blood.

I turned onto my side and spat in my washing dish. Working my swollen tongue around my mouth, I suspected I'd bitten it during the night. I groaned and sat up.

The dream slowly came back to me.

An endless, red ocean had surrounded me. The viscous liquid clung to me as I broke the surface, but I'd enjoyed the feeling of being coated in it. It felt like having a second skin under which I could not be harmed.

Next to me, a man rose from the sea. I turned to him, smiling. But before I could see his face, I'd awoken.

I rubbed the dream-crust from my eyes, the logic of the images unraveling. I recognized it now as a scene stolen from the book Nomusa had lent me, *Tales of the Desolate*. Yama and Lophe and their Unnamed ishaka had conquered their neighbors and Nomusa's ancestors, the Yorandu. For some unexplained ritual, they had begun slaughtering their prisoners. The Twins had hung up the bodies as they slit their throats, draining them of blood into a large pit. Then they were said to have bathed in it. All in the name of their Serpent God.

I shook my head and rose from bed. Eidola above, I had to return that book of myths to Nomusa, or it seemed I'd go crazy.

Xaron and Nomusa rose soon after. As he usually did, Xaron made straight for the pantry and groaned. "No food."

"No time for that," I said impatiently. "We can get something on the way."

"Our money won't last long on stall food," Nomusa pointed out. "Especially since we're not taking paying jobs."

"We still need food!" Xaron objected. "Can't we get some on the way?"

"Fine. I'll draw a silver from the fund." Nomusa headed toward the loose stone in the wall.

My stomach lurched. "I'll get it!" I lunged from across the room, reaching the stone before her and pulling it out.

I could feel Nomusa staring at my back. "I didn't know you were so eager to buy groceries."

I kept the bag containing our stash as much out of sight as possible. "Someone has to keep a leash on Xaron."

He laughed. "It's true. I'd eat us out of this tower if I could."

Nomusa didn't say anything. The coin withdrawn, I tied up the bag again and replaced the stone, then stood and turned. "Ready?" I asked lightly.

Nomusa gave me a studying look, then nodded. As Xaron and I followed her out the door, I repressed a sigh of relief. For now, my lie remained undetected.

I doubted the reprieve would last long.

———

It was only a turn before noon by the time we arrived at the Acadium. As we approached the gates, Nomusa and I slowed, uncertain before the scrutiny of the guards. Xaron, however, urged us forward to the small gatehouse, where little more than his name had the gates swinging open. Masking my surprise, I followed him up the stone pathway to the buildings on the hill above.

My curiosity soared as I stared at the campus around me. The Acadium had been carved out slowly over the past century, the Conclave allotting bits and pieces as the years wore on and its population of wardens and scholars grew. As a result of this incremental development, the buildings demonstrated a clashing variety of architectures. The central forum at the top of the hill was a prime example, with what might have been a patrician's manor facing an adobe house barely fit to be a bakery. From our vantage point, I could see the campus continued in every direction in a similarly mismatched fashion, all the way to the far end, where a black tower rose high into the clear sky, only eclipsed in height by the gray Pillar before it. It had to be at least twice the height of our own derelict tower. I wondered if it, like the Conclave's dome and the Pillars, were relics from the Lighted years of Oedija, when wardens were revered rather than penned up like caged bears.

"The Archmaster's tower," Xaron said when he caught Nomusa and I staring. "You can see how someone would think themselves above others from up there."

Xaron led us past the forum and down the other side of the hill. We followed the paved road that wound through the campus for a while, glimpsing the numerous inhabitants of the Acadium. Acadians wore robes of gray, brown, and black, and distinguished themselves by colorful stoles indicating their discipline of study. Pupils were afforded no stoles, but hurried about in even more meager clothes to their tasks. Honors, too, walked the road, as well as a few common folk — laborers and merchants, by the look of them.

When we had gone halfway to Kyros's tower, Xaron turned off the main road into an alley with an uneven dirt path. Walking a little ways in, the buildings began to look increasingly desolate. Windows were boarded up. Debris lay scattered before doors. In the corners, wood rotted and stone had worn away. Peeking above the forgotten buildings was a squat stone tower, like a bent, old man among his starving grandchildren. It was before its gray, weathered door that Xaron stopped.

"Is this where she lives?" I asked in a low voice.

He nodded, then let out a long breath. "Brace yourselves."

As Nomusa and I exchanged a look, Xaron knocked twice. Several long moments passed. I glanced at Xaron, but he made no move to touch it again.

"Is she coming?" Nomusa asked drily.

No sooner had she spoken than the door cracked open. A pair of startling yellow eyes peered out from behind wisps of curly gray hair.

"Not today," the woman within said. "And not with them." She started closing the door.

"But—" Xaron objected.

"Not. Today." The door rapped shut.

Xaron stared at it in disbelief for a moment, then looked around sheepishly. "She gets like this. But usually, if I try again—"

"*Not. Today,*" Eltris repeated through the door.

"Friendly, isn't she?" Nomusa noted in a low voice.

"You may want to keep that to yourself," Xaron spoke aloud. "She has eerily keen hearing."

I stared at the door, wondering at the amber eyes behind it. "You've told us her name, but we know next to nothing of this Eltris."

Xaron shrugged. "Eltris is Eltris. She's the Master Augur in title, but no one pays much attention to her order." He glanced at the door again, and his eyes suddenly lit up, a wicked grin spreading across his face. "You see," he said loudly, "augury isn't a legitimate Pyrthaen discipline like the others here at the Acadium. It's not rigorous or really all that useful—"

The door opened again to reveal an old woman, bent and scowling like a forest crone. A frumpy, brown robe fell past her feet, battered pins barely holding it together. Master Augur Eltris glared at each of us, her frown deepening with each passing moment.

"If you must antagonize me," she said, disgust dripping from her words, "you'd best do it in here."

As Xaron followed her into the tower, he didn't bother to suppress a grin. I looked at Nomusa.

"We're already here," Nomusa said without enthusiasm. "May as well hear what the crone has to say."

"Xaron said she has good hearing," I reminded her before entering through the decrepit doorway.

It was dark within. The tower's arrow slits were boarded up, and the walls were lazily smeared with yellow pyrkin. A mess of books, papers, broken pens, and other implements sought to trip us with every step. Nomusa's mouth tightened as she looked over the mess. She had never been able to tolerate clutter.

Eltris stood at the base of a staircase that wound around the edge of the room. Her eyes caught the light, making them gleam like a cat's.

"Why are they here?" she demanded of Xaron.

"We need to talk to you, master. About Kyros."

I wondered if I even knew Xaron. There hadn't been a shred of sarcasm in his voice when he'd said "master."

The frumpy woman snorted. "I'm not a gossip. Their curiosity is not my concern."

"It should be," Xaron pressed. "If Kyros has been—"

"Can they channel?" She glanced at Nomusa, then stared at me for a long moment. Her eyes seemed to flash, but when I blinked, only the pyrkin light gleamed in them.

"No," she continued. "As I suspected. Scoria, the both of them."

"Scoria?" I asked.

Eltris snorted. "Those who can't channel are scoria."

I wondered if I should feel insulted. Before I could decide, the augur turned away to ascend the stairs. "If you are finished with this," she called over her shoulder, "we will attend to your training."

Xaron looked pleadingly at Nomusa and me before climbing the stairs himself. I was curious enough that I clambered up after him, though Nomusa looked more annoyed than before as she followed.

The second circle of the tower emerged in a wash of flickering light. The air hung hot and heavy, no doubt from the braziers lining the edge of the room and illuminating it in lieu of the boarded up windows. Their flames blazed too brightly to be natural. I stared at them, curious why I'd never seen such Pyrthaen creations before. The rest of the room was empty except for a large rug, faded and pilled, that ran the length and width of the tower.

Whistling suddenly filled the air. I looked up and saw a couple dozen finches in the eaves. To my amazement, I thought I detected the blue breast of a whisper finch among the mix, but I couldn't be sure. How an Acadian could afford one was beyond me. From all I'd heard, one could purchase a modest estate with the price such a rare bird would fetch.

Eltris had hobbled over to the far end of the carpet and stood facing us. Noticing me watching her birds, she nodded up at them. "My assistants."

I kept a straight face. "Their singing is lovely."

She snorted and turned her gaze to Xaron. "If you wanted to show off in front of these girls, you chose the wrong way. I'll put you on your back if I see one lapse of concentration."

"Yes, master." He took up a position opposite of the augur, closed his eyes, and rolled his shoulders, visibly relaxing his body.

I watched, bemused, as they proceeded to move slowly and deliberately, breathing deeply through their noses. All was silent except for the calling of the birds overhead. Nomusa had shed her look of annoyance and was watching with growing interest. "Not unlike Ixolo," she whispered to me.

"No talking," Eltris said without opening her eyes.

Nomusa frowned again, but she said nothing more.

After they performed the breathing exercises and movements for a quarter turn, the true training began. Eltris's first demand was that Xaron channel a radiant ray that she couldn't break. Setting his hands forward and screwing up his eyes, he attempted to do just that, projecting a beam of light toward Eltris. Before it reached the opposite side of the tower, however, the beam fractured and fell apart. I winced. Eltris hadn't even been looking when she dismantled his channeling, instead cooing softly to a bird that had alighted on her finger.

Xaron gritted his teeth and tried again. Twice more he shot the radiant ray at his teacher, and twice more she broke it apart. After his ray shattered a sixth time, Xaron threw up his hands. "Show me how to do it already!"

"You know how," Eltris snapped. "Knowledge is not enough. You must apply what you know."

"I don't know what to apply," he muttered sulkily.

I exchanged a glance with Nomusa. Xaron was as talented of a warden as I knew, yet Eltris countered his channeling with seemingly little effort. I wondered with no small amount of trepidation how powerful she must be.

Eltris sighed. "You think of channeling as ten separate streams, one for each of your shifts."

"I don't," he protested. "Not exactly. I have to weave the ten streams into one—"

"No. It is one channel, from when you draw it in through your locus to when you channel it through your fingers. One, all the way through." She nodded. "Keep the stream as one, and no one will be able to break it apart."

"Alright," Xaron said dubiously.

Once again, he raised his hands, and after a moment, channeled radiance. This time, the ray nearly reached Eltris before it spun apart.

"Better," she said grudgingly. "Try again."

By the time they had finished, the ray had touched Eltris twice. A smile tugged at the augur's lips for a moment, but it was gone as she moved to the next task. "Now we will switch, and you will break my channeling."

"I thought you said no one would be able to break my stream if I thought of it as one," Xaron objected.

The augur's expression soured. "That is for radiance. Now we are channeling kinesis."

"Ah, right." He glanced over at us. "Kinesis takes a form that is easily dispersed for those who know how. It lacks the natural integrity of radiance."

"You have the knowledge," Eltris said, a hint of approval in her tone. "Now apply it."

Without hesitation, the augur thrust out her hands. Around them, the air rippled, and pure force barreled across the room toward Xaron.

He didn't dodge out of the way, but tried his best to shred the wave. Though whatever he did seemed to lessen the impact, the wave still sent him sprawling, the old carpet doing little to cushion his fall. I stifled my laughter once again, and Nomusa struggled to do the same.

Xaron shot us dirty looks, but wordlessly returned to his feet and readied his stance. Eltris gave him no time to prepare before shooting the next wave over.

Again and again, Xaron was knocked down by his teacher. When Eltris was satisfied that Xaron wouldn't master kinetic shredding that day, she moved onto magnesis. "This should be simple enough for you. Raise the lodestone."

Xaron, beaten and bruised, started to smile. But from the smile creeping onto his master's lips, I had a feeling he'd have just as little success here as before. Xaron extended one hand and furrowed his brow at the small, black stone six paces before him. But instead of it rising into the air, it stayed where it was.

He dropped his hand. "You're stopping it!"

Eltris smirked openly and held up her hands. "You cannot disperse or shred magnesis. What, then, could I have done?"

"You—" Sweat beaded on his forehead, and he wiped it away distractedly. "You created a pull in the opposite direction. A like or greater field to counteract my own."

"Very good. Now, how do you undo my efforts?"

"Creating a pull greater than your own…"

I kept in a snort. That option didn't seem likely.

His eyes fell on the stone. "Or… I move your anchor."

The carpet suddenly rippled as something shot under it toward Xaron. He leaped out of the way just as it sailed out from underneath to clatter against the wall. A sheet of metal, I saw it was when it finally settled.

Eltris was frowning. "You could have pulled it more gently and spared my wall."

"Sorry." Xaron ran a hand through his hair, pulling it from its tail to fall about his face, as he grinned shamefacedly.

Eltris glanced over at Nomusa and me for a moment, then looked away. "Perhaps that is enough for today."

Xaron's expression fell. "Master, if I could…?"

"Quickly," the augur snapped.

"Perhaps we could make one more attempt at sparks," he rushed to say. "Since I seem to have the best feel for magnesis."

"Yes, you do seem inclined that way…" She nodded sharply. "We will make three attempts. Do you remember the positions from before?"

He nodded as eagerly as a child offered a honey-stick, then held up his hands less than a foot apart. His brow drew down, and his eyes focused on the air between them.

"Good," Eltris said after a few moments. "Your magnetic field is stable. Now expand it."

His jaw clenched, Xaron slowly drew his hands apart. After a moment though, he threw his hands up and hissed in frustration. I guessed that he'd let the magnetic field lapse, though my "scoria" eyes could see nothing of his magic.

Eltris's frown deepened. "Again."

This time, she held to the task so long that even I started to grow restless. When Xaron finally managed to sustain the magnetic field with his arms spread nearly as wide as they could go, I thought we were in the clear. But Eltris took him one step further.

"Place one end of it on this iron ore," she commanded, tossing him a grey-veined chunk of rock.

Xaron, a field assumedly still sustained between his hands, kneeled and placed one hand on the ore. After a few moments, he lifted it away and stood, grinning. I couldn't see it, but from the way he only held up one hand toward the ore, I guessed he now sustained the field between his hand and the rock.

Eltris allowed him a brief smile. "Good. Now kneel down again. You will need to make the field as strong as possible if you're to form a path."

"Right," Xaron said as he obeyed. Sweat dripped down his brow as he stared at the air between his hand and the piece of ore. I wondered if he could see the magnetic forces that lay between. A pang of envy went through me. I never much enjoyed the reminder of all I missed out on experiencing because I wasn't a warden.

"The air must be transformed into plasma for lightning to follow the path." Eltris walked to the cluttered perimeter of the room and withdrew from a pile of debris another piece of ore. Holding it in one hand, she placed her other hand on it and drew it back as suddenly as if she were drawing a bowstring. I jumped as sparks crackled between them, my heart thumping in surprise.

Eltris glanced over with a mean glint to her eyes. "Is this the show you came for?" she taunted Nomusa and me.

I didn't respond, but shared a rebellious look with Nomusa. Though, I was honest, the augur was not far wrong.

The frumpy tutor turned back to her mentee. "You saw how I did it?"

Xaron nodded, then reached out to pick up the ore.

"Don't hold it," Eltris snapped, and Xaron dropped the stone and jumped back. "If you don't know how to redistribute the energy, you'll shock yourself. Leave it on the ground for now."

He nodded, then kneeled to form his field again. We waited while he stared at the ore, his hand hovering above it. Another quarter-turn passed. As fascinating as channeling was, this practice session was becoming tedious. I started to pace, my mind falling away from the sights before me to mull over my inquiry into the Despot's killer. When would we speak of Kyros Brighteyed? I didn't want this trip to end up a waste of time.

Though I wasn't watching directly, I still noticed when Xaron produced a spark. A bright flash filled the room, and Xaron yelped and leaped back, staring at his hand. The Master Augur threw back her head and laughed.

"We'll make a warden of you yet!" she declared.

Xaron's grin was as wide as I'd ever seen it.

The smile died on Eltris's lips, though, as her eyes swept over Nomusa and me. "Why did you ask after Kyros?"

Caught off-guard, I searched for a response. Xaron's tongue was looser.

"We're hunting for the Despot's killer," he said, "and have a suspicion that—"

"Xaron!" Nomusa and I hissed together.

He looked between us. "We can trust her," he objected. "She knows far more damning things about me than this."

I bit back words that would have to be saved for later. For now, I had to try to salvage the mess Xaron had made. "It's true that we're curious about Myron Wreath's death," I said evenly. "And we know the Archmaster saw his rooms the night he was killed."

Eltris's eyes were sharp as a hawk's as she stared at me. "That might be true. But why ask me about rumors concerning Kyros?"

Xaron opened his mouth, but at my glare, he closed it again. Nomusa answered instead. "Better to know the man before we approach him."

The augur walked across the old, fraying carpet to stop a dozen paces away from us. "Tribune Vusumuzi also visited the Despot's chambers, it is said. Why not pay him a visit?"

I narrowed my eyes. It had to be a deflection from talking about Kyros, yet it was eerie how close it came to foretelling our plans. "Perhaps we intend to," I supplied.

Eltris looked at Xaron, studying him. I hid a wince, hoping he would stay strong beneath her gaze.

He cleared his throat. "So, master. Could you tell them what you've told me about Kyros?"

A mirthless smile spread across her lips as her gaze turned back to us. "I suppose I could. That's why you two came, after all. To hear the Archmaster has begun training wardens to use their gifts."

My pulse quickened. "Xaron did hint at it," I said, trying not to betray my excitement. "So it's true? He's teaching Acadians to fight?"

"Yes. Just as I'm teaching Xaron to."

I pursed my lips at that. This was all so that Xaron could fight? But it was a mystery for another time. "How long has he been doing so? And how many?"

"How should I know? I'm an old crone who stays in her tower all day. But I've heard the rumors since a full season ago."

"Why now?" Nomusa demanded. "He's been Archmaster for years. Has he been training Acadians from the beginning, or did something else bring it on?"

"Why did a drought strike this harvest when the past decade has been bountiful? Why is the Demos Council in a tighter deadlock than it ever has been before? Why did Asileia Wreath catch fire in the middle of her Ascension?" Eltris wore a grim smile. "The city is full of unanswerable riddles."

Uneasiness spread through me as I contemplated the augur. Despite what she claimed, she seemed to know far more than a recluse in a tower should. I wondered how much we could trust any of what she said.

"Can you tell us nothing more of Archmaster Kyros, master?" Xaron pleaded.

Eltris turned her head aside. "That will be all for our lessons today. It may be some time before I am ready for our next one. You may check in three days if I am ready."

Xaron's expression crumpled, but he gave a small bow. "Yes, master. I will come back then."

As Xaron led us out of Eltris's tower, I cast one last look back at the augur, but her gaze was turned aside. Yet I had the uncomfortable feeling of her eyes on our backs as we descended the tower stairs into the gloom below.

CHAPTER TWELVE

WITH EVERY GOOD TURN

HIGH TRIBUNE: Why have you come before us today, Verifier Jaxale?

VERIFIER: My reason is plain, High Tribune, yet it requires foundation to explain.

HIGH TRIBUNE: Go on then. We do not have all day.

VERIFIER: The Confessionary Tribunal was established as the sister branch of the Order of Verifiers, was it not? To accept the cases brought before it by both Finches and common citizens alike, and distribute justice as its Tribunes found wise?

HIGH TRIBUNE: Yes, in large part, that is our aim. But ours is the parent order, not the sister. We are not equals.

VERIFIER: Your words make many things clear. For often have I brought whispers that form a clear picture of corruption and yet been ignored. That you believe it your right to do so is, as I understand the Charters, a deviation from your mission.

HIGH TRIBUNE: Fortunately, that is for the Conclave to decide, not you. That is all, Verifier. Do not return unless you have something for me to consider. I do not appreciate my time being wasted.

- Verifier Jaxale before High Tribune Krynollon; 1067 SLP

After we navigated the mess of Eltris's tower and made it back into daylight, Nomusa exhaled. "What an insufferable hag."

"She can probably still hear you," Xaron pointed out. Despite his ultimate success during the training session, he seemed almost morose now.

I leaned closer and whispered, "We'll have to talk more about her later. For now, it's past time that we paid Vusu a visit."

Xaron shook his head. "I'll pass."

"Maybe you can ask around and see what people are saying about the Ascension."

He acquiesced with a nod.

"I'd ask you to buy food on your way back," Nomusa said. "But knowing you, it'd be all candied meat, and gone by the time you returned home."

"Can't fault you there." He smiled, recovering a bit of his old humor. "I'll gather whispers then. When will you be back at Canopy?"

"This evening, most likely," I said. "I might do some poking around myself after our meeting."

Nomusa shrugged. "The same for me. I need to check in on work that will actually make us money."

I gave her a small smile, choosing not to take it as a gibe.

"Then we'll have story time around the hearth." Xaron nodded toward the gate. "Now let's get out of here. No matter how many times I visit, this place still gives me the creeps."

———

We parted ways outside of the Acadium. For a time, I listened to the bustling stall owners calling out their goods and services as I thought over the augur's words.

"Does she know more than she's letting on?" I wondered aloud. "Or does she think she knows more than she does?"

"Your guess is as good as mine. What worries me more is her influence over Xaron."

I chewed my lip. "He would have told her anything she'd asked about if we hadn't stopped him."

"And he calls her 'master.'" Nomusa shook her head. "I don't see what we can do. But it makes me uneasy."

"One thing at a time, I suppose. We can figure it out after we meet with Vusu."

Not long after, we arrived at the Tribunal. Located in deme Iris halfway between the Conclave and the Laurel Palace, the Confessionary Tribunal was housed in a building with a white dome. Mirroring the symbol of their order, the dome was separated into two halves by a hand-width crack. Not nearly as large or grand as the Conclave, it still had an impressive number of wings extending out from the main body. Formerly an Eidolan temple, deific statues of patina-painted bronze and moss-covered marble remained scattered across the courtyard.

Queasy with anticipation, I approached one of the guards at the gate, a young man with dark, handsome eyes, with Nomusa following close behind. "We're here to see Tribune Vusumuzi," I told him.

He looked me over, then his eyes flickered to Nomusa. "Airene of Zipho's?" he addressed me.

I would have smiled at the moniker had I not been stunned to be greeted by name. "That's me."

"Right this way. Your friend may enter as well."

I repressed a cringe, knowing how Nomusa would take the unintended slight. A glance her way showed she already wore a cold expression. Not an auspicious beginning to a difficult conversation.

Opening the gates, the guard led us between the rows of laurel trees and ferns to doors of plated gold, an extravagance that even the Laurel Palace didn't boast. Inside, the building shimmered with gold and white pyr lamps and pyrkin spread in designs on the walls. Above us, the Eidola had been painstakingly painted and preserved. Tyurn Sky-Sea stood in the center of the fresco, his tell-tale shimmering cloak waving behind him, leaving the rest of his muscled figure bare. The other two of the Foremost — his wife, Yena Third-Eye, and their son, Caradon Night-Veil — curled along the sides of the dome around him, while the Resolute Seven were crowded around the edges. I picked out Clepsammia, her sandglass held in the palm of her hand and a bemused smile on her lips. Behind the rest of the Eidolan gods loomed the Jealous One, Odaon the Sun, burning with his hatred for the living.

The young guard led us across the room to a female clerk sitting behind a desk. "Pelagia will help you," the guard said, and with a small bow, he departed.

The clerk looked a bit older than Nomusa and me, and wore spectacles perched on the tip of her nose. As she studied us, the skin above her nose pinched in well-defined creases. "What do you need?" she asked bluntly.

"Hello," I said pleasantly. "We're here to see Tribune Vusumuzi."

Pelagia's expression didn't shift. "He told me to expect you."

I glanced at Nomusa. It was as if Vusu had expected us that very afternoon.

The clerk's eyes slid to Nomusa. "I don't know who you are."

"She and I work together," I said hastily as Nomusa's expression blackened. "The Tribune will be delighted to see her as well."

Pelagia sniffed. "We'll see about that, won't we?" she said, rising. "Follow me."

The clerk led us down the halls in silence, clutching a stack of papers to her chest. When we'd passed nearly a dozen doors, she stopped and gestured to an entrance much like the others. "He'll be in there. Knock before you enter."

I nodded. "Thank you."

The clerk gave us a strange look, then briskly walked back down the hall. When she was out of earshot, I turned to Nomusa. "What was that about?"

"Vusu must agree with the change in regime in my ishaka," Nomusa said, her tone flat.

I shook my head. "You're jumping to conclusions. Maybe he's just lived too long in Oedija. He is rather old. Or maybe he's just ornery."

A faint smile graced Nomusa's lips, but it quickly disappeared. "I shouldn't have come."

"No, this is best. Between the two of us, we'll get the answers we need."

She inclined her head, which was all I could hope for at this point. Bracing myself, I knocked.

"Come in," Vusu called from within.

I took a breath and opened the door. The solar was as underwhelming as the door, cramped and small for one with such authority as the Tribune. It had no windows, but was lit by a number of pyr lamps mounted on the walls. Likely it had been a priest's quarters back when it was an Eidolan temple. Opposite the entrance, a birdcage housed a white and black finch, a gently glowing blue patch nestled underneath its beak. I stared at it. What were the odds that I would see two whisper finches in one day?

"Fascinating, is she not?" Vusu rose from a small desk in the far corner. He smiled as he walked over and reached a finger through the bars to stroke the bird's feathers. "Disela is her name."

"Disela," I echoed, stepping closer to the cage. "What does it mean?"

The Tribune hesitated, then said softly, "Remembrance."

"Remembrance," the whisper finch repeated loudly. I stared in wonder. The bird hadn't stumbled over its pronunciation, but spoken it as clearly as any native Oedijan.

An uncomfortable silence fell over the room. Nomusa, standing near the doorway, still hadn't said a word. I looked about Vusu's solar as I thought of how to begin the conversation. The walls were bare save for one arras, a depiction of a dragon with its mouth gaping open. I recognized it at once: Famine, the daemon god, trapped inside his mask, as some of the myths claimed he had met his end.

I nodded at the banner. "A rather ominous hanging to stare at all day."

Vusu smiled faintly as he glanced at it. "I find it a good reminder. That there are threats lurking just beyond our awareness, waiting to consume our good works, should we let them."

Again, the strange answer put me at a loss for words. Nomusa was no help. Vusu at least looked at her now, but he still offered her no words.

Finally, he moved and drew two chairs out opposite to the one at his desk. "Please, sit," he said, gesturing toward them.

Once we were seated, he sat as well, maintaining an upright posture. "Nomusa-sha," he finally acknowledged her. That he used her royal honorific seemed a good sign. "I hope you're keeping well."

"Well enough." Her reply was far from warm.

He nodded politely, not seeming to notice. "But I suppose we are all busy these days. You saw what occurred at the Ascension?"

"Yes," I said. "A horrifying thing for Hilarion to attack the Despoina."

Vusu eyed me carefully. "You need not uphold pretenses around me, Airene. Unless you truly believe it was Hilarion who attacked Asileia."

My pulse quickened. Sensing an opportunity, I took a gamble. "No, I don't suppose we do. Nomusa and I believe someone framed him."

The Tribune smiled. "As shrewd as I'd hoped. I'm glad you stopped by my solar today."

"And why is that?" Nomusa asked flatly.

Vusu met her gaze. "Because, Nomusa-sha, things are stirring within this city that need to be uncovered. Things I had believed impossible until recent years." He paused to rub the bridge of his nose. "Forgive me. It has been a taxing span."

"No apology needed." I leaned forward. "What exactly are you referring to?"

"One particular issue. A recent matter that is on many of our minds."

I forced myself to remain still, waiting, hoping.

He looked at me, his dark eyes seeming like great chasms for a moment. "The death of the Despot was no accident," he said quietly. "And I mean to find out who is responsible."

My breath caught, though I tried not to let it show. "I suspected as much," I said as calmly as I could manage. "As it so happens, we've already been looking into it, to the extent of our reach. Though all we've had to go by were rumors and conjecture."

"Then we ought to rectify that." The Tribune smiled slightly. "Reach will no longer be a concern for you. Tribunes find very few barriers in their investigations. With my sanction, you will not struggle to gain an audience with anyone. But first, you will need a symbol for your new office."

My mind raced over the words, hearing but not comprehending.

Vusu reached behind him and opened a drawer. From it, he withdrew a dull, metal chain with a medallion swinging from the end of it. A symbol of two half-circles stared back at me, but unlike the Tribunal's symbol, they faced away from each other. Atop them, a chevron pointed toward the heavens so that the symbol resembled a bird.

"Is that…?" I started to ask, stunned.

"The symbol of the Order of Verifiers," Vusu confirmed. His eyes flickered to Nomusa, but he held the medallion out to me. "I cannot bestow a Tribune's medallion upon you, but this ought to work just as well. And it suits you, does it not?"

I took it slowly, cradling the heavy iron in my hand. The back of the medallion was uneven and rough. I ran my fingers along it. "Will people recognize it? It's been so long."

"I've sent missives to those whom it should concern, instructing that you should be able to go anywhere I would and speak to whomever I may. This includes the Conclave, the Laurel Palace, the Acadium, and anywhere else you might see fit."

I ran my fingers along the symbol, unable to believe what Vusu was telling me. A lingering question cast it all in doubt. "But… why would you trust me with this? Trust us," I amended quickly, hoping Nomusa hadn't noticed my misspeak. "This is only the second time we've met."

"Yes," he said, smiling gently. "But I know you better than that. The reputation you and your companions have managed to gather is quite the achievement for ones so young. I spoke to some of these former clients of yours, including Zipho, of course."

We'd only performed minor tasks for Zipho — cafes were in a less predatory line of work than some businesses — but it didn't surprise me to hear Zipho recommending us, if only for Nomusa's sake. Yet Vusu's trust still seemed premature.

I gently placed the medallion in my lap. "I am grateful, Vusu. But it's still somewhat hard for me to believe. This… it's exactly what we've been waiting for."

"I know. And, unless I'm mistaken, you are exactly what I've been waiting for."

"You," the whisper finch suddenly said from behind, "are exactly what I've been waiting for."

I startled and looked around at the bird, then glanced at Nomusa. She did not look as pleased, but stared stoically back at me. Inwardly, I sighed. It likely meant objections were forthcoming.

Looking back to Vusu, I asked, "Does Disela always do that?"

"Often enough that I spill my drink at least once a day. The honors are becoming terribly cross with me." He gestured to the medallion. "I hope this brings you aid enough. If you find any door still barred, come to me, and we will sort it out. Or come by for any other reason — you are always welcome."

It was a generous offer. I nodded politely, unsure of what else to say.

He began to rise, then hesitated and settled back down. "There is one more thing. You have no doubt heard of the Despoina's latest actions? Among the embassies?"

A flush gathered at my neck. Here he was entrusting us with a Verifier medallion, and we were already behind on events. I cursed Xaron silently for holding us up in the Acadium that morning. "I don't believe so," I said neutrally.

"It has only just occurred. Asileia Wreath has seen it fit to insult, threaten, and expel half the dignitaries among the embassies. The Qao Fu, the Bali, even Avvad have been subjected to her capricious moods."

"An eventful first day as Despoina," I noted.

"Indeed. Yet her demands of the Avvadin envoy are worse still. She says if the Kahin-Shah does not pay tribute, Oedija must respond with force."

Threats against Avvad. The sheer idiocy of such an act defied my comprehension. I clutched the Verifier medallion and stared at the floor, wondering how long our fragile city could withstand Asileia's whims.

"If I may make a suggestion for your first line of investigation," Vusu interrupted my thoughts. "Our new Archon, Jaxas Wreath, may be of assistance to you. I have spoken with him on several occasions, but I have the sense he has more to tell regarding his cousin's recent behavior."

Yet another point of intrigue. I nodded, and as he rose, I rose with him. Nomusa followed more slowly.

"I cannot thank you enough," I murmured. "I'll let you know as soon as I find out more."

"Do," he said with a smile, then bowed his head to his work as we left his solar.

———

Despite our earlier plans, Nomusa and I both returned to Canopy.

"He gave us a Verifier medallion." I'd said it half a dozen times, ran my hands over it constantly on the walk through Oedija, but it still didn't feel real. The medallion I wore on my neck was the same as the Finches of old had worn. I'd nearly attained what I'd always wished for, but never dreamed possible. To be a Verifier not just in mimicry, but in actuality.

And it had all but fallen in my lap.

"He gave *you* the medallion," Nomusa observed flatly.

I couldn't let her wounded pride fester. "I know he slighted you. I know it's strange the way he gave it to us. But just think for a moment. Think about what this can give us access to. You heard what he said. The Acadium, without Xaron needing permission from that strange augur."

"And I was so eager to return."

I ignored her sarcasm. "The Conclave, maybe even while it's in session."

"How intriguing, listening to a bunch of old fools prattle on about politics."

I knew she didn't want to hear it, but I couldn't contain myself. "Even the Laurel Palace. 'Thae above, we're supposed to go speak with the Archon himself."

Nomusa leaned in close. "Listen to me," she hissed. "You're not using your head. Look at this, *truly* look at it, and tell me you don't find the whole situation suspicious."

"Yes, it's unusual," I said with annoyance. "But it's simple to explain. The Tribune is looking into the Despot's death and has heard good things about our reputation. Why wouldn't he want our assistance?"

"For exactly the reason you stated in his solar. He doesn't know us."

"But he knows people who do. We don't always know the people we work with. Remember the first time we worked with Talan? We didn't know the first thing about him, but that turned out well in the end."

Nomusa shook her head. "You're still missing the flaws in your reasoning."

"And you're speaking from a bruised ego rather than logic," I snapped. "What other possible reason could Vusu have for giving us access? And how could it benefit him other than exactly as it seems?"

She fell quiet, though not in submission. She often withdrew when she was losing an argument. I snorted in disgust. We continued our long walk home in silence.

For a while, I brooded on Nomusa's stubbornness and the truth of her points. But slowly, unable to make sense of the windfall myself, I decided to accept it and think rather of the opportunities Vusu had just afforded us. We'd go to Jaxas first, if only to honor Vusu's suggestion. Then I had more than half a mind to look further into Kyros. Confirming our suspicions regarding his role during the Ascension would go a long way toward unraveling the conspiracy.

My plans had begun to circle by the time we reached Canopy. Letting Nomusa ascend before me, I debated how soon I could reasonably use the medallion. Would his messages be received today? Or would tomorrow be the earliest I could test it? My impatience was winning the argument, but I forced myself to keep climbing. First, we had to check in with Xaron.

As we ascended the last circle of the tower and came before our door, Nomusa stopped abruptly. "*Faresh*," she muttered.

Her tone instantly drew me from my thoughts. "What?" I asked, trying to look around her.

She leaned out of the way, and I stared. The lock to our door had been broken and now hung among splintered wood.

"It would be wiser not to enter," she murmured.

"And never return home?" I swallowed. "Whoever did this did it explicitly. It's a warning, not a trap." I had a bad feeling I knew who the warning was from, too.

After a moment's hesitation, Nomusa nodded and cautiously pressed the door open. We stepped inside.

My stomach twisted into knots as I took in the destruction. The legs of the tables ripped off. Shelves torn from the pantry. The divan shredded and fractured in half. Dishes lay shattered on the floor, clay shards joining the glass from the broken bay window. The wind whistled into Canopy, cold and incessant.

Xaron, alone among the wreckage, spun at our entrance, hands raised. I flinched, half-expecting flames to erupt from his hands, but he quickly lowered them again.

"Sorry," he said with a nervous laugh. He gestured to the wreckage about him. "I'm a bit jumpy."

Nomusa stepped carefully over the broken bits across the boards. "What happened?"

"It was already like this when I returned. Whoever it was had it in for us, though, didn't they?" He gestured to the kitchen.

I instantly saw what he meant. "Our savings."

He nodded. "Gone. I checked."

"Our personal stashes as well?" Nomusa demanded.

Xaron shrugged. "I only checked mine, but it was also taken."

Nomusa stalked over to her room and disappeared within.

I stared over it all, rooted to my spot by the door. Part of me had known something like this would happen. Yet I hadn't warned either of them. I hadn't let them decide for themselves if what I did was worth the risk. And Corin — she'd return to a ruined house, and all the savings she'd accumulated would be gone. What would she do, with everything she'd earned to bring her sister to Oedija dissipated?

"Airene?" Xaron asked, approaching from across the loft. Nomusa had emerged from her room, her deepened scowl confirming that her savings were gone as well.

I took a steadying breath, for the little good it did me. It was past time to end the lies.

"I have something to tell you both..."

CHAPTER THIRTEEN

MARKS

The Eidola, the gods of our people, number eleven in total, a number many hold to be holy — or among gamblers, lucky.

Foremost among the Eidola are three:

Tyurn Sky-Sea, World-Father and seed of the gods;

Yena Third-Eye, the World-Father's wife and the watcher of all things, of which she whispers into her husband's ear;

And Caradon Night-Veil, their eldest son, and the one who brings night to shield us from the day.

- The Traditions of the Eleven: Eidolan worship in the demotism of Oedija; by Oracle Iason of deme Iris; 1164 SLP

Nomusa left immediately after my confession, slamming the door behind her. With the latch broken, it swung uselessly back open. I stared after her. Perhaps I should have been more open before. Perhaps I should have told them all from the start. But would I have done differently, even now? I wasn't sure I wanted to know that answer.

Xaron remained in Canopy, staring out the bay window. After a long silence, he turned and met my gaze. I searched his face, but for once, his feelings were hidden from me.

Then he smiled slightly, which only served to reveal the sadness behind his eyes. "Let's get some food. I have enough coin for us to eat tonight at least."

"Alright," I agreed. He held back his true feelings, and I didn't enjoy the suspense. But he had the right to respond in his own time.

The day was turning golden as the sun fell behind the sea, and the buildings cast long shadows over the street as we exited the tower. "Can we pick up sweetmeats?" he asked hopefully.

I waved a hand. "If you want to eat like a child, that's your business. Either way, I'll pay for your meal. I owe you that much."

"You owe me at least ten silvers, actually."

His tone was teasing, but I still winced.

I bought our meals and was scandalized by the expense. The price was half again as expensive as it had been the last time I'd bought stall meat. With no savings and no paying jobs, I wasn't sure even the substantial progress we'd made on the Despot job would be enough to keep us from going hungry.

I returned, dejected, to the tower stoop to sit and eat with Xaron. After licking his first skewer clean, he finally spoke. "Why didn't you just tell us?"

I bit back the defensive words that first sprang to mind and instead responded as honestly as I could. "I thought you would stop the hunt."

"Really? Why?"

"You and Nomusa seemed hesitant. I thought you believed it a fool's errand."

Xaron laughed. "Most of what we do are fool's errands. Sure, this one is riskier than most. But that doesn't mean I wouldn't have supported you. You know that I suspected you'd paid Nikias Canopy funds without telling us? I knew that pompous weasel didn't tattle for free."

I hid my wince by chewing through another bite of goat. "You know how you've been distracted lately, and spending more and more time at the Acadium? I think I took that to mean you weren't invested in the hunt. That you didn't approve of it." I shrugged. "I guess I jumped to conclusions."

"I can understand that, and you should know I didn't intend it. But the rest..." He shook his head and studied the cobblestones. "Feiyan's threat was toward me, Airene, even though she doesn't yet realize it. I know it's affected all of us, but what she said nearly three years ago — that's aimed at me. I've seen what the Shepherds can do. Even with the training I've had so far, no way could I beat one if she set them on me."

I rested my hand on his arm. "It won't come to that."

He raised his gaze to meet mine. "How can you promise that? You won't give up the job."

His words wrenched a knife through my heart. I feared to speak. There was only one truth I could offer him, and it wasn't what he needed to hear.

He looked aside. "I'm not trying to guilt you; really, I'm not. In fact… I think you should keep going."

Hope and guilt twined together in my gut. "Truly?"

"It's the right thing to do. If the Despot really was murdered, he deserves justice." He flashed a smirk worthy of Talan. "And that's what we Finches deliver, isn't it?"

I squeezed his arm. "Xaron… Are you sure?"

He took my hand and pressed it in return. "I'm sure. Just one thing. Don't lie to me again. Please."

I bowed my head. "I promise."

We sat for a few moments holding hands in companionable, if guilty, silence.

"Do you want to go out tonight? And use that new medallion, I mean."

I glanced up and down the street. "I do, if only to listen around to the whispers on the street. Speaking of which, we never talked about if you learned anything."

"Oh, right." He slurped the juices off of his fingers, grinning when he noticed my grimace. "Can't waste the best part! Did you hear what the Despoina did to the Avvad diplomat?"

"Vusu told us," I admitted.

"Oh," Xaron said, deflated. "That's the biggest piece. But if you want the smaller details, I—"

"A strange sight," a voice said from next to us. "Airene of Port, relaxing before an inquiry has been pursued to its bitter end."

I'd halfway risen before I recognized who it was. Talan leaned against the tower wearing his usual half-smile, yet he was transformed in every other respect. His clothes were clean and tailored, though still in an Avvadin style of trousers, tunic, and jacket. His hair was free of sweat and oils and neatly pulled back in a tail. Gone was the greasy Guilder, replaced by an Avvadin man who could almost pass as respectable.

I sighed in relief. "You scared me. What are you doing here?"

"What *are* you doing here?" Xaron muttered.

Talan ignored him. "I have news. Uncertain news, to be sure, but as he's your brother…"

My gut wrenched. "Linos."

Xaron looked between us. "What's happened to Linos?"

Talan's gaze rested on me. "My orphans have seen him among the Seekers."

I blinked. "He's mixing with the Manifest?"

"More than that. He appears to have joined them."

My mind spun, trying to understand his revelation. Linos wasn't a fanatic. He longed for freedom and independence. Why he would surrender that to join a cult was more than I could comprehend.

Yet one thing at least was clear: I had to go after him.

"Explain on the way," I said to Talan.

He raised an eyebrow. "The Manifest compound is a poor place for a late-night visit."

I gave him a flat stare. "Whether or not he's there willingly, I need to go to him. I've already lost one brother. I don't intend to lose another."

Talan studied me for a moment before he nodded. "Your boldness never ceases to amaze me, Airene the Finch." He returned me a mocking bow. "Of course, I will come at your behest."

A fraction of the tension left my shoulders. "Thank you," I murmured. "Really."

He waved off my words, his eyes never leaving mine.

Xaron stepped forward. "I'm coming too."

We both looked at him. "I think not," Talan said calmly.

Xaron rounded on him. "And you believe you can stop me?" He shook his head. "If Linos is in trouble, I don't mean to stand by. 'Thae above, I'm the best house-breaker in Oedija."

Talan's mouth twitched. "You do believe that's true, don't you?"

Xaron scowled, and I rested a hand on his arm. "Thank you," I said, trying to instill all the gratitude I felt into the words. "Especially now of all times."

The frown broke into an embarrassed smile. "Of course I'll help, Aire. Nothing's changed between us. Besides, he's your little brother."

My little brother. Guilt poured afresh through me. Linos had told me he was going away. He'd told me not to worry. I should have read the sign for what it was. I should have protected my little brother, even from himself. Especially from himself.

"No point in wasting time," Talan said, turning on his heels. Xaron and I followed behind.

Deme Thys was a long way from Port, on the north side of Oedija beyond the city walls. It gave Talan ample time to explain what he'd learned of Linos.

"They saw him at one of the Manifest's gatherings," he began.

"They. Multiple orphans spotted him? But there are supposed to be thousands of Seekers."

"There are. But Linos was easy to spot, considering he was up on the stage of the Wyvern's Claw."

"The Wyvern's Claw," I repeated. My father had taken me to it once more than a decade ago, before it had stopped hosting plays.

"The old, wooden amphitheater north of Lake Thys," Talan

explained, taking my words for a question. "They think the name makes the rickety thing grander."

I dreaded my next question, but Xaron had no such qualms. "What was he doing on stage?"

Talan took a long moment to answer. "My orphans aren't precise with details, especially not speeches. But it sounded like he was being held up. As an example."

"I can't imagine Linos as much of an exemplar," I said with a thin smile. "Did he look well?"

"Hard to say. He wore gray robes, and did what the Visage commanded him to." Talan glanced at me, his expression hard to read in the dimming light of the evening. "But you know what the Manifest claim. That they can make wardens of ordinary folk."

"You don't believe that," I said, aghast.

"Of course not. But there are many things that wardens can do beyond what Xaron has displayed. Worse things. Take the Damask Esir."

"The elite soldiers of Avvad? What do they have to do with this?"

"They're not just elite soldiers, Airene, as you should know. They're disciplined and loyal to the death. Because they've been made to be by the priests of Valem. The Tefra yoked their minds to serve the Kahin-Shah, and in doing so, took away all will of their own."

His words filled me with foreboding. Despite myself, I pictured Linos in a cell, shadows standing around him. What had been done to him that he would obey anyone's commands? The boy I knew took orders from no one.

I lengthened my stride. "Then we have no time to lose."

Even as we increased our pace, darkness had fallen by the time we reached the northern city gate. Despite the turmoil following Myron's death, peacetime practices were still being followed, which meant the gates were open day and night between the inner and outer demes. The guards watched us with evident interest as we passed through, but perhaps it was because we were the only ones crossing at that time. I hoped so. The less we were observed this night, the better.

Once outside the walls, Talan told us the plan he'd concocted. It was straightforward and simple. Since the Manifest movement had recently inflated beyond any hopes of regulation, the entrances to its compound were loosely monitored. Entering would be little more than a matter of walking in.

Yet as we approached the compound, it became apparent we'd been misinformed. Tall wooden fences, nearly twice as tall as myself, extended in either direction, with torches mounted at regular intervals. There was no gate, only an opening in the wall, yet that entrance was guarded by no fewer than four Seekers, their faces cast in shadow. As we were within reach of the torchlight, I guessed they'd already spotted us.

Xaron leaned in close. "I could easily vault over that wall, as could he." He nodded toward Talan. "You, however, are a different story. You still want to go through the gate?"

"We all go through the gate. They've likely seen us by now, so it would look suspicious for us to stray." I plotted fast. "We're three people looking to become Seekers. We couldn't sneak away from our homes until nightfall without being immediately noticed. We all work at a glass shop." It was the trade I knew best from my early years in Maesos's employment.

"Fine," Talan said. "But I assure you both, there's nothing to fear. They are welcoming as far as cultists go, so long as you know what to say."

"And you have much experience with cultists?" I inquired with a raised eyebrow.

He gave me a sly smile. "More than you might think."

As we approached, one of the guards called out to us. "May the One grace you! Who of our brothers and sisters approaches so late at night?"

"May the One not pass over you," Talan replied. "We are three of those who have been lost among the Unknowing."

We walked up to the gate, stopping a dozen paces away. I shifted my feet nervously, hand itching to grasp the knife hidden beneath my chiton. I'd killed one person before and had no desire to do it again. Yet approaching the cultists at this hour put me on edge, in no small part because they stood between me and my brother.

"You speak as Seeker," another of the guards spoke, a man with a gentle voice. "Yet you lack the mark. I cannot allow you to pass without questions." The man nodded at Xaron and I. "You two. Are you initiated as well?"

I hesitated, unsure of the best thing to say.

"No, they are not," Talan spoke for us. "I apologize, but I told them it would be best that they let me speak. I did not want to offend my brethren without need."

"You need not fear that," the same guard as before responded. "We welcome all Seekers to see the Truth for themselves. But would it not have been better to come during the day? Storms are gathering on the horizon, and red men walk the streets come darkness."

His words incited a burning curiosity in me, but I didn't dare ask after them. Instead, I gave a bow and spoke, judging that they wanted to hear from more than Talan. "I apologize as well, good guards. We are but newly fled from our employer, a glass smith down in Port, and could only find the opportunity to come unnoticed during the night. Our friend was kind enough to wait to escort us. We understand it is difficult to admit us at such a turn of the night, but we have nowhere else to go. If you admit us now, I assure you, we will be as devoted as any of our new brethren."

There was a pause of appraisal before the cultist said softly, "A curious profession to produce someone with so honeyed a tongue."

Fear tightened in my gut.

Then the Seeker shrugged. "But who am I to question a woman's pretty words? We welcome all who seek the Truth here. And the seeking does not wait for the sun." At a nod, the shadows stepped aside and turned to form a tunnel for our passage. As they turned, the firelight finally illuminated their faces.

For a moment, the world seemed cast in glass. I stared at the patterns that played along their skin, violet lines spiderwebbing around their eyes, cascading out like ripples in a still pond. This was the first Seeker I'd seen, yet I knew that pattern. Fourteen long years ago, I had seen it inked onto a face I knew well, and had not seen it since. Now the pattern suddenly appeared before me again.

"Jaxale."

I felt a tugging at my arm, and noticed Talan there, a shadow across his face hiding his expression.

"Jaxale," he repeated, "are you ready to go?"

Slowly, I understood his attempt to hide my identity. I nodded mutely. He and Xaron led me forward, between the faces imprinted with the tatu of my long-dead brother.

"May you find what you seek," the cultist said, "and the One not pass over you. There is a gathering two nights hence, Seekers. If the One wills it, perhaps we will see you there."

"If the One wills it," Talan responded, then quickly pulled me through the gate.

I hardly knew myself as we walked through the Manifest compound. I couldn't make sense of what I'd seen. The compound, cast in a darkness alleviated by intermittent pyr lamps, only added to my confusion. What did this place have to do with Thero's death? What was the connection across fourteen years?

I let Talan lead me along the street, packed dirt wide enough for two carts to pass abreast. Shadowed tents lined either side, as similar to one another as stones in a river. Some few people moved along the road with us, but I heard many rustling within their makeshift homes, settling in as they lay down to sleep.

After a time, the tents lining our right were replaced by a series of shops, dissimilar from the tents only in that they stood taller than the squat homes and had wide entrances that were draped closed at the late hour. They did not look well-secured; it wouldn't take a determined thief to steal their wares. Further to our right and down a hill, I saw the dark canopy of a strip of forest. Beyond that, by the shore of Lake Thys, rose the Wyvern's Claw, two hundred cubits high, seeming a shadowy mountain in the darkness. The long talons, curved spires of wood that rose well above the last of the viewing platforms, were silhouetted against the moons. Even at this hour, torches burned along its walls, a risky venture near all that wood.

My two friends directed me down the road. Though I saw my surroundings, my thoughts circled around the Seeker tatu. One memory rose above the miasma of the others. Iela, the feral warden I had long ago killed in self-defense, had claimed her master was behind Thero's murder those fourteen years ago. She'd described the strange pattern of tatu on his face, the same as I'd seen on the Seekers' faces tonight. But what did it mean? That her master had been at his experiments for the past decade and a half? Or longer? But with what aim? And did it mean this master was also the architect behind the Manifest?

We went further into the compound before Talan directed us into a shadowed alley, where he and Xaron gently settled me down onto the wet ground. I sat, heedless of the mud that caked my chiton and soaked through my underwraps.

"Airene," Xaron said worriedly, "what's going on? You froze back there. And you haven't spoken since we entered."

Talan pressed my hand. "Airene," he said in a low voice, "did you notice something I did not?"

I worked my tongue around my dry mouth. "Thero."

Xaron's brow creased. "Your brother? What does he have to do with this?"

I kept my eyes on the ground. My vision was full of memories. "We found him after he'd been gone for three days. The guard pulled him from a moat. Another few minutes, and he might have been flushed out to sea. His features were bloated and purpled, so much so that I almost didn't recognize him. But there was still enough of his face to see the pattern inked into it. The same tatu those Seekers wear."

"Are you saying he was part of the Manifest? But he died fourteen years ago. The Manifest have only been around for a few months." Xaron paused, his brow creasing. "Haven't they?"

"I don't know."

Talan shook his head. "Perhaps we should not be here until we know more about who and what we face."

I rose to my feet. "No. We can't turn back now. Not only would it seem suspicious to the guards, but... I need to know. I need to find out what this means." I met each of their eyes in turn, and saw the same concern

CHAPTER FOURTEEN
SEEKERS

Next of the Eidola come the Resolute Seven:
Lavvash, goddess of thunders and the passions;
Hinaron, god of the humors and health;
Saxeus, god of the seas and storms;
Nadalene, goddess of the forests and growing things;
Mandeia, goddess of psyche and spirit;
Cendaur, god of beasts and birds;
And Clepsammia, goddess of time and fate.
Last is the Jealous One, Odaon, who is mounted in the sky as the burning sun,
longing to destroy all from his lonely, high place, but is only able to bring life to the world.

- The Traditions of the Eleven: Eidolan worship in the demotism of Oedija; by Oracle
Iason of deme Iris; 1164 SLP

As we reemerged onto the main road of the Manifest compound, I leaned toward Talan. "Where do we seek Linos first?"

He scanned the area around us, ensuring no one was close enough to hear. "The Wyvern's Claw. The place where their largest gatherings are held."

"Why there?" Xaron asked. "There won't be any gatherings at this time of night."

"From what I've heard, the most valuable members have their quarters within the amphitheater, including the Dishonored and the Visage of the reflected in both their expressions. "I need to find Linos before the same thing happens to him as happened to Thero."

I didn't need to say anything further. Talan nodded, and Xaron followed suit.

"Come," Talan said, then turned back toward the street.

I drew in a deep breath and followed. "I'm coming," I murmured to my brother's faraway ears. I just hoped I wasn't too late.

Wyvern. If Linos is important enough to parade on stage, then he's certainly important enough to hold back there."

"And we're just supposed to rely on your intuition," Xaron said sarcastically.

"Enough, Xaron," I snapped. "Talan hasn't led us wrong before. I trust his information and so should you."

Xaron's mouth worked for a moment, then pressed into a firm line.

We walked in silence toward the amphitheater. Continuing along the street until we reached the beginning of the path down the hill, we saw four more Seeker guards standing watch. Talan only just pulled us back into the shadows before they glanced our way.

"We must cross down the hill off the path. Step carefully. The terrain is slick and steep, and we can bring no lights. Especially not summoned ones." He glanced at Xaron at this last statement.

"I wouldn't do that," Xaron muttered.

I suppressed a sigh. "Let's go then."

The thin light from the moons and the shifting radiant winds helped us see as we approached the hill and began to pick our way down. But with the tent shops looming behind and thick foliage overhead, the paltry light was soon choked out, throwing us into near complete darkness. I could barely see my companions as we slipped and slid down the hill. Already caked with mud, I didn't bother trying to stay clean. My hands were scraped and cold, my sandaled feet much the same.

Halfway down, I grew tired of my chiton snagging on every stone and root, so I pulled it off and tucked it under a tree. "We'll return for it?" I asked Talan.

He nodded. "Best to leave no trace of our passage."

"Just a little further," Xaron muttered.

I followed his gaze to the Wyvern's Claw, no higher than a hundred paces past the tree line. Now level with the base of it, it loomed more than ever. It was a wonder that such a large building could be overtaken by a cult with so little protest from the Conclave. True, it had been in disrepair and infrequently used to host dramas or other public events in recent years. But now, I wondered what influence they possessed to be able to maintain such a claim.

We ghosted through the forest to the edge of the trees, then at a signal from Talan, we stole across the open ground. There was only one entrance to the Claw that Talan had been able to detect, the wide gate in front. No fewer than eight Seeker guards stood watch by it. Even though many of them were focused at the moment on a game of tiles, there were still more than enough of them to cause a racket if attacked.

Huddling next to the wall in one of the pools of shadow between the mounted torches, I gathered Talan and Xaron close. "Any ideas?"

Talan pointed up. "Were I on my own, I would enter there."

I followed his gaze and saw that thirty cubits above, the wall was shorter as it rose to its full height at the top of the stands. My mind boggled at the feat. "Thirty cubits? Is that possible, even for you?"

"It's definitely possible," Xaron declared. "I've nearly leaped that before."

"Have you?" Talan remarked drily,

"It doesn't matter," I cut in. "I can't get up that way, so we need a new plan."

Talan looked thoughtful for a moment. "Perhaps you could stay out here," he suggested quietly.

"Absolutely not." I'd wondered when one of them would suggest it. "He's my brother, and I've let him get caught up in this mess. I won't abandon him now."

"Even if it means endangering him further?" Talan shook his head. "Airene, I understand what it is like to leave your task in another's hands. But I assure you, I will do everything in my power to recover Linos."

"We both will," Xaron interjected.

I set my jaw. "There has to be a way. Just give me a moment to think of it."

"Every moment we wait is another moment we might be discovered," Talan pressed.

I swallowed down a sharp reply and said instead, "What if I show them the Finch medallion?"

Xaron blanched. "You've only just received it, Airene. You haven't checked if anyone has acknowledged it yet."

"They won't recognize it here." Talan's eyes were filled with pity, but his words were assured and cool.

I knew they were right, yet I found myself shaking my head. "I'm going," I repeated. "So instead of thinking up objections, help me figure out how I'm getting up there."

Talan and Xaron exchanged looks. I wondered if this would be the one issue that united them. But Talan glanced back at me and shrugged. "All we need is rope."

"And do you have one hiding in your trousers?" Xaron asked sarcastically.

"No. But the docks along Lake Thys should have plenty."

Relief flooded me. Despite my bold words, I hadn't been sure I would actually be able to enter. "Let's go retrieve one then."

"You stay. You'll only slow me down." With a slight smile, Talan turned and loped silently into the darkness.

Xaron and I stood waiting. The night air was chill here near the lake, and I shivered.

"He'll be alright, Linos," Xaron murmured. "He's a tough kid. Way tougher than I was at his age."

"He's probably still tougher than you." I managed a smile.

Xaron flashed me a tempered grin. "True. It's never been my strong suit."

We lapsed into silence, listening anxiously for any sound of movement. The last thing we wanted was for an errant patrol to find us.

When footsteps approached, we both tensed. It seemed too soon for Talan to return. Yet as the firelight revealed his lilting smile from the gloom, I breathed a sigh of relief.

He hefted the rope in hand. "There will be a disappointed captain at the docks, but we have our rope. Careful, though. It's slick with moss."

"Sure. You're certain you two can get up there?"

Xaron chuckled as he turned to face the wall. "I suppose you'll just have to see, won't you?"

Talan inclined his head, then gestured to the stands rising above. "Perhaps you can show me how it's done."

"I will," Xaron declared.

Crouching low and placing his hands on the ground, he heaved himself up into the air. The speed with which he ascended was astonishing. My jaw drifted open as I craned my head back to watch him jump not only to the lip of the stands but just over it, then disappear out of sight to land with a light thump.

"He's powerful," Talan admitted, "but he lacks refinement. And wisdom."

"Two things you have plenty of," I said sarcastically.

He smiled lopsidedly. "I'll throw down the rope once I have it secured." Without another word, he turned and, with less effort and more finesse, followed Xaron up.

I waited anxiously, peering at the dim ledge above. Soft scuffles echoed down. Just when I wondered if I should call up to them, something moved above, and the rope fell down with a hiss to swing before me.

Wasting no time, I grabbed it and began to climb. As Talan had warned, the rope was slick with moss, but it afforded just enough grip. I braced my feet against the wall and hauled myself up, hand over hand. My arms, unaccustomed to such work, began to burn halfway up, but I soon reached the top of the wall, where Xaron and Talan helped me over.

As I kneeled and shook out my arms, Talan hauled up the rope and coiled it. "Can't leave it around," he whispered, then held it out. "Take it. Just in case."

I accepted it, wondering uneasily what scenario he was planning for. Around the bend of the stairs, I could see the glow of the sentries' fire at the entrance. From the laughter that echoed up to us, they hadn't detected anything amiss. But all it would take was one mishap to bring them running.

"No point in waiting around," Xaron muttered, glancing down the stairs. "Which way?"

Talan pushed past him to the dark corridor beyond. "Only one way to go, unless you wish to say hello to our hosts."

I followed, shrugging. Xaron scowled, but came behind.

Talan led the way down the corridor, which skirted the edge of the amphitheater. Eventually, we would reach the large backstage building. Though we stepped lightly, the wooden walkways of the Claw defied silence. That I carried a heavy rope made walking quietly no easier. I winced with every creaking footstep, expecting guards to come pouring out on either side of us at any moment. But as none came, I dared to hope we were in the clear.

The corridor finally ended, and a door emerged from the gloom. Halting before it, Talan considered it for a moment.

"Between the two of you, surely we can open a lock," I teased quietly.

"Allow me," Xaron said snidely, stepping forward.

But before Xaron could get close, Talan placed two fingers inside the lock. A moment later, a small puff of air blew out of the hole, then a click sounded. Nudging it with his shoulder, the door swung open. Talan looked at Xaron with a raised eyebrow.

I shook my head and began to pass through, but Talan held out an arm and entered first. It shamed me, but I was glad he led the way.

Inside the room was even darker than outside. I peered around us, wondering who might be lying in wait in the shadowed corners. With a creak, Xaron shut the door behind us, leaving us in pitch black. Then a light flared to life next to me, white and pure. Talan held up a hand, and between his fingers, an orb like a star shone and unveiled the room around us. I blinked at the sudden sorcerous light, eyes adjusting, then studied the room. The room was sparsely decorated. A single table with two rickety chairs were tucked into a corner next to a cabinet. A covered pyr lamp was mounted near the door. Stepping around the room, I saw small signs of habitual use scattered about the place. Two cups with the dregs of liquid at the bottom. A cloak draped over the back of a chair. The floor free of dust.

"People pass through often," Talan observed quietly. Nodding toward the passageway beyond, he began to move on.

Following him, I found the archway led to a narrow corridor, with room for no more than one person to comfortably fit at a time. At the end of it, Talan's light illuminated a door. No light shone from underneath, indicating it was unoccupied, unless we'd stumbled upon sleeping quarters.

Talan glanced back with a raised eyebrow, and I nodded. Putting his hand to the keyhole, it only took another moment before this door, too, unlocked at his touch. He pushed it open, and Xaron and I followed him in.

This room was better furnished than the first. Setting down the coil of rope to ease my aching shoulder, I looked around. Opposite us, a door promised to continue our journey. Two windows faced out over Oedija, glittering city lights shining in. Before them, a small platform elevated a wicker wood chair. And hanging off one of the gnarled ends rising off the back of the chair was the leering mask of a dragon.

An uncomfortable feeling stirred in my gut. I glanced at Talan. "Do you know what that is?"

He shrugged. "The mask of the Visage of the Wyvern, perhaps. They say he always wears a white peplos and a mask with the aspect of a dragon. Explains his name, doesn't it?"

Though my anxiety had increased, I continued to look around. In the center of the room, a large map was spread across a table. Approaching it, I saw it was a careful rendering of the Four Realms. Several marks defaced it in dark ink. A crossed-out circle marked Oedija. Avvad had one circle over its capital, Erimis, though this circle remained open. The Qao Fu jaitin had no circles, but one lay out in the wasteland to the far northeast, encircling what seemed to be a poor sketching of a tree. The Bali plateaus had many open circles, nearly as many as there were ishakas. Littered across the map were figurines, crudely carved, but plain in their depictions. Soldiers. Horsemen. War machines. Even, I guessed, the Tefra and their enslaved pyr, Silks.

"Xaron, Talan," I called softly. "Come look at this."

They approached and stood around the table, studying it for several long moments. Xaron pointed at the circles. "It has all of the Four Realms marked. I'd guess these are plans for starting new cults, except for the circle deep in the Wumofu."

Talan shook his head. "The figurines tell the tale. Cultists do not concern themselves with armies and nations."

I lifted my gaze to look around once more. The unease that had haunted me since entering the Claw crystallized. The map. The wicker wood chair. The fortified position looking out over Oedija.

"This is a war room," I said quietly.

Talan suddenly raised his hand and went stiff, listening. Xaron stilled as well, brow drawn together. Finally, I heard it myself: footsteps echoing along the hall, making the floor vibrate.

My chest felt so tight I could barely breathe. "The next door," I whispered. "You have to unlock it."

Talan was already moving toward it, using his unlocking trick again. As soon as the click came, he pushed on the door, but it resisted him.

"Barred from the other side," he muttered.

"I could blow it off," Xaron suggested, his voice high with anxiety.

Talan shook his head. "They'll know we're here anyway, and it could trap us further. We make our stand here."

I didn't know what to make of the words. *Make our stand.* For a moment, I stood in indecision next to the barred door. What was I supposed to do to take a stand?

Talan noticed and took my arm. "Find cover. I'll make sure they notice me first. You just make sure to stay out of the way."

His chivalry finally roused my spirit. "I'll fight as much as I can," I promised him. Not waiting for an answer, I scanned the room for a hiding spot. Only two were readily apparent: crouched behind the map table and behind the wicker wood chair.

Xaron shifted in indecision next to me, eyes darting between the open and closed doors.

"Duck behind the chair," I advised him, giving him a push in that direction.

He looked glad to be told what to do and moved quickly behind it.

I went to my own position behind the map table and drew my knife. Crouching there, it suddenly felt much less covered than it had first seemed. I could only hope it would be enough. Talan moved to the corner just beyond the door and pressed against the wall, then extinguished his light.

Left in darkness, I stared at the only entrance to the room and waited. Waited, grinding my palm into my blade's grip. Waited, listening to the footsteps grow ever closer. Waited, knowing how helpless I was in a fight, knowing there were far too many Seeker guards in the compound. Fear, cold and craven, rose in me. I would have fled if I'd had a choice.

We'd left the door open, so I saw their light first, creeping down the hall. Then figures emerged from the darkness. The man who came first didn't look like a guard. Balding and thin, he wore spectacles over the violet tatu around his eyes. But it was the light projecting from his fingertips that amazed me most of all. Fear squeezed me harder, and breath came shallower. He was a warden.

The man stepped into the room, his brow drawn as he gazed around him. Two more figures loomed in the hallway beyond, light projecting from their own hands. Two more wardens.

Before the lead warden could glance his way, Talan struck.

CHAPTER FIFTEEN

IN RUINS

Daemon run far
Daemon jump high
Daemon breathe fire
Daemon drop sky

Daemon come find you
If you run
So don't call daemon 'round
Keep him hung

- Children's rhyme, origin unknown

Talan lashed out, a knife flashing in his hands as he stabbed into the man's gut. The Seeker warden shrieked and stumbled back, his light extinguishing as his hands fell to his stomach. From the light in the hallway beyond, I could see blood, black wetness in the gloom, staining his clothes.

The two Seekers in the hallway shouted and rushed forward, hands outstretched. From the lights in their hands, I saw one to be a Qao Fu female of middling years and the other a stout Oedijan youth. Spotting Talan, they both leveled their hands at him, and fire and force leaped toward him.

Talan dove, but was sent tumbling across the room by their assault. The two Seekers stalked after him, hemming him in with a barrage of magic. Talan dodged or blocked most of the blows, but a kinetic wave found its way through his defenses, slamming him back against a wall.

I couldn't crouch in fear forever. Forcing myself up, I crept around behind the two seeker wardens. The hilt of my knife felt so slick with sweat that I thought it would slip from my fingers. Gripping it tighter, I rose and charged.

The young man glanced back, his eyes widening. Fear struck me anew, yet I continued forward and raised the knife with a scream.

Something knocked hard into me from the side, sending me crashing into the wall. My head knocked against the wood, and stars sparked into my vision. As I staggered back to my feet, my body felt drunken and clumsy. I turned toward the direction of the attack, focusing my unsteady gaze. The balding man leaned against the wall, one bloody hand raised toward me. As I stared, another kinetic wave came barreling down on me.

I threw myself to the ground. As the wave passed, it beat me against the floor, knocking the wind out of me. But I'd avoided the worst of it. Gasping for air, I pushed myself up and dove behind the map table, hoping it would give some protection while I recovered.

A glance Talan's way showed that Xaron had joined the fray. Blinding light flashed from his fingertips as he contended with the middle-aged woman from behind the wicker wood chair. Talan engaged the young man. As I watched, he sent the Seeker flying backward with a powerful kinetic attack, a snarl on his lips.

"Watch the one in the corner!" I called to Talan, then threw myself toward the young man. He had hit the wall badly and was slow in rising. Not letting myself doubt or think, I stabbed at him.

My poorly aimed blow caught the Seeker in the shoulder and, biting in, glanced off bone. The young man howled with pain and anger, then punched his fist into my gut.

It hit with the force of a kicking horse. I crumpled, all breath and fight in me gone as pain spread throughout my body. I crawled away, knife lost, barely able to see for the darkness creeping up in my vision.

The young man stood over me, hand outstretched, when his head suddenly kicked back. As he slumped over, I saw dark liquid leaking from his eye. Or where his eye had been — all that was left now was a jagged, bloody hole.

"Take cover!" Talan roared as he leaped over the map table, scattering figures as he passed.

I fell to the ground at once, too weak from the Seeker's blow to go anywhere else. From beneath the table, I glimpsed Talan landing on the other side, then the Qao Fu woman's feet lifting as he hit her with a kinetic attack, slamming her into the opposite wall. Xaron's feet danced across the floor as he, too, channeled at the woman.

Something tickled my nose and throat, making my eyes water, and the back of my neck felt uncomfortably warm. I turned and noticed smoke billowing up from flames licking across the wood floor and walls. Pushing aside weakness, I rose, coughing as smoke filled my lungs with each shallow breath.

"Fire!" I gasped, though I wasn't sure anyone heard me.

"Back away from it!" Talan commanded.

I staggered toward the door. A glance at the first Seeker in the corner showed he was dead. The Qao Fu woman had similarly gone still, her head craned back at an unnatural angle and her body sprawled upon the floor. And I knew the youngest of the Seeker wardens was not likely to rise.

Now, we just had the flames to worry about.

"What do we do?" I asked, fear making my voice high and sharp.

Talan shook his head. "Run. There's nothing else we can do."

"But Linos might be in here!"

"Wait! Let me try to shred it!" Xaron swayed where he stood, but he held his hands toward the fire. The flames already rose nearly as tall as me, and smoke and heat poured out from them.

"Hurry!" Talan said sharply.

Xaron's eyes screwed up in concentration, arms trembling as he held them out. A moment passed. Two. Still, the fire continued to grow and consume.

Talan backed up to the doorway, pulling me with him. "We have to go!" he shouted.

"I can do this," Xaron said through gritted teeth. He hadn't moved, though the flames advanced across the room toward him.

"Xaron!" I pleaded.

Suddenly, the fire spluttered, then began to dissipate. As suddenly as they'd spread, the flames died out. Soon, all that was left behind were glowing embers and smoke hanging thick in the darkness.

"I did it." Xaron coughed, staring dazed into the smoke.

"You did," Talan admitted grudgingly. A light blazed to life in his hand again. "Now let's go."

Xaron shook his head, then staggered toward us, stumbling and nearly falling. I moved forward and steadied him, though I felt none too steady myself.

"Are you alright?" I asked him as we followed Talan through the doorway.

His eyes were vacant as he glanced at me. "Airene, I... I killed that woman."

My throat closed shut. All I could do was squeeze his arm and press forward.

We made it out of the corridor, then through the next room. The night air outside brought cool relief and fresh air to my fevered skin. But as shouts from the Seeker guards filled the air, I knew we couldn't stop to catch our breaths.

"Move quietly, but swiftly," Talan commanded over his shoulder as he slowed his pace to a fast walk. "Could be they don't know where to find us yet."

We obeyed, moving along the outside of the amphitheater. The wood creaked with each step, driving anxiety through my gut. The shouts faded in and out below. I didn't dare glance over the railing lest they see me.

The pounding of feet sounded ahead. Around Talan's form, I saw figures racing toward us. The foremost leveled his spear and charged, eyes wide with fear, mouth pulled back in a snarl. Talan didn't back down, but raised his hands. Kinesis barreled forward from his fingertips. The Seeker crashed into the others behind, collapsing them in a tumbled heap. Talan swiftly followed the first attack, hands jabbing forward again and again. Concentrated kinesis pounded like arrows into the guards, dealing death everywhere they landed.

Then Talan dropped to the floor. "Duck!" he bellowed.

I obeyed at once, hoping Xaron would do the same. As my knees hit the wooden planks, something hissed overhead with terrible speed. As wood splintered behind us, I grasped what it had been. The guards had brought crossbows.

Talan cursed and rose, channeling with a fury. The Seekers screamed and fell away. A second crossbowman tried to get in a wild shot and missed. Soon, the few guards still standing were fleeing back the way they came. Even then, Talan did not relent, but shot at their backs, felling a few more.

I gagged as the stench of burned flesh filled my nose, but held myself upright. I tried not to look at the dead guards as I stepped over their bodies. I could not help but count them. *Seven.* Seven more Talan had killed. I tried focusing, tried remembering how many guards had been at the entrance. Eight, I was fairly certain.

"One escaped," I told Talan. "He'll call for reinforcements."

"Then we'd better get the hell out of here." He glanced back. "When we reach the edge, I'll carry you over."

I nodded, though I felt far from certain about that prospect. Even for Talan, such a feat seemed a stretch. Yet with time pressing short, the rope back in the war room, and no idea what reinforcements might be coming, I had no choice but to agree.

We left the bodies behind, then the lip of the wall appeared ahead. Skirting to the end to make sure no one lay in wait, Talan turned back to me. "Ready?"

Repressing my fear, I nodded and stepped toward him. Bending, he scooped an arm under my legs and back. Barely giving me time to wrap my arms around his neck, he lifted me off my feet, stepped over the lip of the wall, and leaped.

I clung to him as the air rushed past, the torches blurred, and the dark ground reached up to swallow us. The impact of landing was so powerful and sudden that I nearly bit off my tongue. But though Talan bowed under the impact, he didn't let me fall, but set me back on my feet again.

"Thanks," I said breathlessly to him.

All he could do was grunt in response and move out of the way as Xaron leaped down to land beside us, his landing much softer.

Talan staggered forward a couple of steps, then shook his head and drew himself upright. "No time to waste. We have to get out of here."

Following him, we stumbled away from the Claw and back into the dark forest.

CHAPTER SIXTEEN

WORTH

The tale of Kyno, the man who wished to be a warden, is often told by parents to children to explain why Tyurn's gift should not be desired.

In the story, Kyno, a man with a wife and many children, wishes one day he had a warden's magic to make his life easier. If he were a warden, he reasons, he could use magic to carry the wood to his hearth and light a fire, and his home would ever after be warm. Magic could ease his aching back, and put food on the table. Magic, he thinks, could put to rest all his cares and concerns.

That night, he wakes to find his little finger flashing with sparks. Panicked, he thrusts his hand into a bucket of water. But rather than putting out the spark, a charge like lightning zips through him.

Dazed, Kyno reels and falls to the mud, rolling around like a pig to dampen his magic. But though his little finger stops sparking, it now begins thrusting out such forceful air that he's tossed about in the mud to and fro, becoming bruised and battered as a fish in a dry bucket.

Finally, exhausted and beaten, Kyno decides it's a dream and returns to his bed just as he is, mud-splattered and bruised.

But it is not a dream. When Kyno wakes, he finds his house burning down around him and his wife and children screaming for him to get out. But it is too late.

The story ends with Kyno looking at his little finger and saying, "If I had known all the trouble you'd cause, I never would have wished for you." Then he burns down with the house.

- Tales of Wardens: A brief study of Oedijan folk stories; by Acadian Helene, Master Historian; 1160 SLP

We were three shadows as we stole up the night-shrouded hill, all moving slowly from our wounds. I suspected that I had suffered the least. Though my muscles protested and my gut throbbed, nothing was broken, and I had not suffered any burns. I could not see much of my friends, but what little I did see horrified me. Xaron's face was dark with bruises, but he had at least recovered enough of his wits to climb his way up. Talan looked less battered, though his stony expression betrayed deeper wounds. Yet we had to press on, lest the Seeker guards who shouted from beyond the forest find us.

"Where are you taking us?" I asked Talan, keeping my voice soft.

"Another of my hiding spots." His head remained down as he picked a path through the dark woods. "As I said, you can never have too many."

Though the expression felt foreign in that moment, I smiled. At least he retained his sense of humor. But as I thought of what he had done back in the Claw, the smile quickly dissipated.

We labored our way up the rest of the hill. As we neared the end of the tree line and the tents appeared above us, Talan reached out to stop us. I flinched at his touch. His hand was still wet with blood.

He spoke as if he had not noticed my reaction. "Up ahead. Guards watch the forest. To reach my tent, we must pass by them." He looked at Xaron. "Are you ready to fight again? We must kill them quickly and quietly."

I seized Talan's arm, fighting back the discomfort at touching him. "No. No killing."

Talan looked at me, darkness hiding his expression. "Then what do you propose?"

I had no immediate answer. But if there was a way to avoid bloodshed, I had to find it. I cast my gaze along the line of tents, desperately hoping to see something. The guards, many more than we had seen before, were spaced a dozen feet apart, and each carried a torch. I could see no way to slip between them.

But then, maybe we didn't have to. "We need a diversion. Xaron can set one of the tents on fire with his trick from Eltris. Right, Xaron?"

He looked around at me, and even in the darkness, I saw hollowness in his eyes. "Yes," he said softly.

"Can you do it?"

He seemed to give himself a shake. "Yes," he said more firmly. "I can do it."

"Fine," Talan relented. "We'll try it your way."

Xaron looked between us, then nodded to himself and turned away. As he faded into the shadows, I started to follow him, but Talan stopped me with a touch. "We'll need to enter on the other side of the diversion," he reminded me. "It will be quicker for him to rejoin us when he's ready."

I nodded, though I suspected he was hedging his bets. No need to lose me if Xaron botched the job. I tried to have more confidence in my friend.

A minute passed, then two. I stared at the tents lining the hill above us. They had to be at least thirty paces away from the tree line, much farther than Xaron had been able to channel radiance in Eltris's tower. Doubt gnawed at me. I wondered if I had put too much pressure on him.

Just as I resolved to go check on him, calls of "Fire!" sounded down the line. Guards from along the tents rushed to the calls.

"Amateurs," Talan sneered softly as Xaron rejoined us. I half expected Xaron to be wearing a wide grin, but he was sober as he stopped alongside us. Talan nodded once in approval to him, then pointed. "We make for that gap. Right... now!"

He darted forward, keeping low, and Xaron and I followed on his heels. Breath hissed between my teeth as we ran up the last stretch of the hill. I expected to hear shouts of alarm, but as we passed between the tent shops, the guards still seemed focused on the fire half a dozen tents down. We slipped onto the street unnoticed.

Talan led us across the road and into a field of squat tents, then began a disorienting path through them. The further we went from the street, the deeper the darkness became around us, as clouds had choked out the moonlight. To keep us together, I grabbed hold of Talan's coat in one hand and took Xaron's hand in the other. "Stay close," I whispered to them.

It took an excruciatingly long time to arrive at Talan's tent. In the thick darkness, I didn't know how he could tell it apart from the others. It barely looked large enough for two people, much less three. Still, as he bent down and opened the flap, I ducked my way in.

It was even darker inside the tent. Xaron and I crouched in the far corner, our backs pressed against the heavy cloth, until Talan entered. Folding closed the flaps, he pulled off the lid to a jar of pyrkin, and a green glow like the radiant winds lifted the edges of darkness in the tent. A blanket spread across much of the dirt floor but didn't quite reach the edges. Other than the blanket and the pyrkin pot, the tent hosted only a small basket of clothes and a small pitcher of water we had narrowly avoided overturning.

Talan crawled to the pitcher and lifted it to his nose, sniffing, before he held it out to me. "It's not fresh, but it doesn't seem to have fouled yet."

I accepted it from him and drank from the spout. He was right that it was far from fresh, but after the long night, I was happy to drink water of any quality. After I finished, I handed it to Xaron, who also drank a hearty fill, then handed it back to Talan. The Guilder finished it off, then set it back in the corner.

For many long moments, we sat in silence. The quiet settled heavy and thick in my lungs until it felt like I couldn't breathe. Guilt pressed down on me so I thought I would drown.

"I'm sorry. I'm sorry for getting you both wrapped up in this."

Talan looked up. "Don't apologize. We knew what this might lead to."

"But we didn't even find Linos," I continued miserably. "He's still lost here, somewhere. And you two got hurt, and had to..." I trailed off, not wanting to face the truth of what had just happened.

"I killed them." His voice was flat and emotionless. "I killed them because they meant to kill us first."

I shook my head violently. "*I* killed them. If I hadn't rushed us into the compound and the Claw, none of this would have happened."

"Airene." Talan leaned across the tent to touch me in comfort, but I recoiled.

"And I can't stop seeing you kill them." I whispered the words, not daring to meet Talan's eyes. They were callous and unreasonable. Yet that didn't change the horror of what I'd seen, how I'd witnessed my friend transforming into a man I didn't know.

Talan withdrew his hand and studied me. "Airene. I killed them to protect you."

"I know. Don't you think I know that?"

"What I'm saying is that it's not your fault. It was me, not you. I need you to understand that."

"So what, I can see you as a killer?" I swallowed hard, the next words inevitable. "You slaughtered them. They didn't stand a chance. I heard their screams, their pain, their fear. I can't forget that."

Talan's gaze wandered to the canvas above us. For a moment, we watched the roof of the tent shift lazily from the breeze outside.

When he spoke, his voice was tight with bridled emotion. "Many people kill. Drunk patrons in tavern brawls. City watchmen on patrol. Tribunes ordering executions. I have killed many times for many reasons. You knew that. Why should witnessing it change anything?" His gaze lowered to meet mine. "Especially since you have killed for me."

I looked away, unable to deny it. Nearly three years before, I'd slain a warden who had been trying to kill Talan after he'd intervened on my behalf. I drew in a shuddering breath. Even if it didn't banish the ill feelings I had toward Talan, it did give me pause.

"You're right," I muttered. "And I'm sorry for that, too."

Talan shook his head, a small smile playing at his lips.

Not yet ready for levity, I turned to Xaron. "How are you doing? Those bruises look painful."

"I'm fine," he responded without looking up. His hair, dirty with mud and ash, hung about his face.

I sighed. I knew what plagued him. The same thing had haunted me for the last three years. But I didn't push him. Xaron rarely held his feelings back for long. He'd talk when he was ready.

Turning my gaze back to Talan, I forced myself to meet his eyes. "What did we learn from our excursion?"

He shrugged. "The Manifest have grand designs for Oedija and the Four Realms. If they can accomplish them."

"War." I breathed the word, unable to truly believe it. War had been a thing of the past for the Four Realms. Now only butchers like the Kahin-Shah indulged in it, and only then in faraway lands. I couldn't imagine purposefully orchestrating it and breaking the Concordance.

I focused my thoughts. "The figurines. I'd assumed they represented where forces currently were in the world. But thinking back, they weren't positioned as I would expect them to be. Avvad's armies were not near the Rift, but along our border. And I could have sworn there were Tefra and Silks positioned within Oedija city itself."

Talan's eyes gleamed strangely in the green light. "They could be projections, or intentions for what they seek to accomplish. Or perhaps things are not as they seem."

A shiver ran through me at the thought. I remembered again the mask hanging from the back of the wicker wood chair. "Who is the Visage of the Wyvern?" I murmured. "And the Dishonored who stands by him? What do they want?"

"Blood and power, it would seem. We can only truly know if we discover their identities."

"Find out who they are." I nodded. "They are at the center of it all. If we can stop those two, perhaps the movement will fall apart."

Talan inclined his head. "Perhaps."

"But Linos… What part could he play in this? In politics and war? Why bring him onto the Claw's stage? Why hold him among the elite Seekers?"

"My orphans will not be able to tell us that. They see and hear much, but understand little. To know, we must see your brother ourselves." He glanced thoughtfully aside. "The Seekers at the compound entrance. They mentioned a gathering in two nights. Perhaps that would be such an opportunity."

After the chaos of the night, I had nearly forgotten. I nodded. "That sounds like the perfect opportunity. But, Talan... I would understand if you don't want to be involved."

Talan's lips twisted into a wry smile. "Ah, Airene. When will you learn better? I am with you, now and always."

I smiled, chest warming. "I'm glad to hear it."

My smile faded as I glanced at Xaron. I doubted he'd feel the same way. He'd curled up on the ground, facing the tent's side so I couldn't see his face, but I suspected he was awake, reliving the moment when he'd killed the Qao Fu warden. I looked aside.

"Could all this have been worth it?" I asked softly of no one.

Talan smiled bitterly. "We'll soon find out, won't we?"

CHAPTER SEVENTEEN

BEYOND THE CLAW

Oedija is a society with four distinct classes: the honors, the underclass, the citizens, and the patricians.

At its foundation are the honors, or the Kalthuae, as they are named in the histories. A distinctly Oedijan caste, they are a people unpaid for their labors, but well-treated and respected for their service. Yet for all their good treatment, the rigidness of the caste, which deems that honors cannot marry outside of it nor possess any wealth of their own, puts many ill at ease.

- Oedija: A History; by Acadian Helene, Master Historian; 1167 SLP

We settled down to rest, but sleep evaded me. I lay between Xaron and Talan and struggled to keep still while my thoughts raced. Again and again, my actions seemed to make matters worse. Yet I couldn't tell where I'd stepped amiss. What more could I have done, only knowing what I did then? I forced my thoughts down a different path. No point in regretting the past. No amount of guilt would change anything.

I thought back to the Claw's map. I wondered what the circles meant and why Oedija's was crossed out. Perhaps the Manifest meant to assassinate the leaders of each nation. But though it fit for Oedija, and could apply to Avvad and the Bali, the circle for the Qao Fu was far beyond their jaitin. There had to be something I was missing.

A thought came upon me with such clarity that I nearly bolted upright. As if it had been placed in my head by the hand of a god, I had a plan.

One that could resolve both the puzzle of the Despot's disappearance and save my missing brother. One that could tear down the Manifest and restore stability to Oedija. Perhaps, in time, it could even help us weather an Avvadin invasion, if it truly were impending. I even had the means to take the first step.

I lay there for a long time, burning to begin. But we could not yet rise. We hadn't left a clean trail behind us from our foray into the Claw. Besides the battle and bodies, I'd left the rope in the war room and my chiton in the forest. The Seekers would be on high alert. If we were to have any chance of escaping the compound, we would need to wait for its occupants to be fully awake and bustling about their business. With an effort, I held myself still, coaxing my budding plans to blossom.

Many excruciating turns later, golden morning came wholly upon us. Outside, the compound was bustling with noise and life. I allowed myself to sit up, desperate energy staving off exhaustion, and moved to settle a hand on Talan. A moment before I touched him, I glimpsed the blood dried on his sleeve, and I hesitated.

"I'm already awake," he said without turning. "You need not touch me."

I startled guiltily, then steeled my resolve and touched his shoulder. "I don't hold it against you, truly. I'm thankful. I just… need a bit of time."

Talan shifted to look at me from the corner of his eye. "I understand. It took some while to look at myself after the first time."

His words twisted sharply inside me. I drew in a breath, trying to calm myself. "We'd best be going."

Talan nodded, then sat up without looking at me.

I withdrew my hand to wake Xaron. When I turned back to him, however, his eyes were open, staring at the ceiling of the tent. I studied him with growing concern. He had said little since leaving the Claw.

"Xaron?" I said hesitantly. "How are you feeling?"

He glanced briefly at me, then resumed staring at nothing. "I'm not going to fail again," he said calmly.

His words jarred me. That wasn't what I thought had been bothering him.

"I've been training with Eltris for the last two months," he continued. "Two months of intentionally learning how to use my talents to contend with other wardens. But last night, when it came time to use that knowledge, I lost my head. Someone who couldn't have been more than a four-shift and could only channel kinesis nearly had me."

Every thought that occurred to me promised only to make him feel worse. Yet I had to say something. "Xaron. No one expected you and

Talan to get attacked by wardens. Deep depths of the 'Thae, who could have expected that? It's not your fault."

Xaron jerked his head at Talan, who was bent over the small basket of clothes. "He was ready. He killed the rest of them, and easily. And he's a seven-shift. I'm *shur*, a ten-shift. I should be capable of more." He rose and muttered, "I will be."

I didn't like the thread of his thoughts, but all I could do was look helplessly at Talan.

He nodded at Xaron, a small smile on his lips. "You can. You are capable, Xaron, just inexperienced. Stay alive long enough, and you'll find where you stand."

I glowered at Talan.

He shrugged. "We are what need makes us. And now, we are escapees. We had best leave as soon as we are able. I have a change of dress for myself, but I will have to find clothes for you two. Give me half a turn, and I shall bring back some serviceable items."

I nodded grudgingly, and turned away as he dressed, despite his mocking invitation for me to watch. The truth was, I shied more from seeing his wounds than seeing him exposed. In the light of the morning, I had to witness what my rash decisions had inflicted upon my friends.

Talan soon dressed and left, warning us not to exit until he returned. Xaron and I sat in uncomfortable silence. I stewed over his earlier words until I found a safe question. "You never really explained how you met Eltris."

"Trying to get me to talk, are you?" He looked up. The pain in his eyes struck arrows through me.

Before I could answer, he nodded. "I suppose you deserve some explanation. It started about two months back, just after that job that involved the house-break."

I remembered it all too well. "With that merchant who sold those elixirs made of bat feces?"

He gave a hollow laugh. "Right. And you were so against the house-break you wouldn't even come."

"I stand by that."

"Anyway. After entering into his home, I didn't make it far before an old woman stopped me. I was so startled when she appeared that I channeled. To defend myself, I suppose."

"From what I've seen of Eltris, I don't think that would have ended well for you."

A ghost of a smile touched his lips. "I didn't attack, fortunately. Once Eltris convinced me she wasn't turning me in to the Shepherds — at least not at that moment — and she'd told me who she was, I decided it was worth hearing her out. She quickly made it clear what I could gain, first by chiding me for being inefficient at channeling kinesis, then promising she could improve my ability to channel tenfold."

I frowned. "Surely that sounded suspicious. For one, how did she find you? And why offer to teach you?"

Xaron shrugged. "She's a powerful warden, Airene. It's said that Kyros Brighteyed can see traces of channeling. I think she can see even more. I believe she can see the strength of a person's attunement, and maybe even the potential of those with loci closed to the Pyrthae."

Such an ability teased my imagination. I couldn't help but wonder what Eltris had seen in me. But it was foolish to dream of such things now.

"As for teaching me," Xaron continued, "I was intrigued, and agreed to meet her at a neutral location—"

"Intrigued? Xaron, that's a pretty flimsy reason to meet someone who could have called down the Shepherds on you. She could have been leading you into a trap."

"Yes, well..." He ran a hand through his tangled hair. "You can't understand, Airene. I have this gift, a strong one. I could be one of the best wardens this age has seen with training. Yet to have to keep it secret, to hardly use it, to stagnate... You can't know how that feels." He stared at his hands. "To not be able to use it when I need it most."

"I can. Of course I can. But you have to remember the risk. You could be locked up in the Acadium, or outright killed."

Xaron glanced sidelong at me, then looked away. "What you just said tells me you don't know. If you were forbidden from using your right hand again, how would you react?"

It wasn't the same, I wanted to argue, but the words died on my lips. His attunement wasn't just a tool. It was a part of him. I couldn't imagine Xaron not being a warden. But the feeling still burned in my gut that the risks he took weren't worth it.

I conceded as much as I could. "I understand where you're coming from. But that doesn't explain why you had to start meeting in the Acadium."

"She couldn't teach me properly outside of it. Small displays of chan- neling can go unnoticed outside the Acadium, but for extensive, ongoing training, it would be much riskier. After meeting a couple of times at the old river-port, I decided it was worth the risk. I trusted her." He bowed his head and stared at his hands. "For all the good that training has done me."

"Why now? You've channeled for all this time, yet she only now approaches you. It has a foul smell to me, Xaron."

He glanced up at me. "Oh, it does, does it? And what about your new medallion — that's not a mite convenient?"

I blinked, and a hand went to touch the medallion hanging under my clothes. "That's not the same. Vusu knew our reputation. But with Myron's disappearance, he only just now needed our help. It's a mutually beneficial agreement. It's nothing like your and Eltris's arrangement. What does she benefit from that?"

"Perhaps she needs me," Xaron said icily. "And only just now decided it was worth the risk."

"Needs you? And why would she need to teach you martial channeling? I'm liking this less and less. She's an Acadian master, Xaron. She should have turned you in as soon as you entered the grounds."

He gave me a scornful look. "She doesn't believe wardens should be locked up. She doesn't believe we should allow others to determine our lives, or sway how we use our abilities. Eltris believes that gifts such as ours should not go to waste among smoldering tomes, but be explored to their fullest capacity. So we can stand ready when we're needed."

His words struck a chill through my heart. "She believes like a Seeker then," I said quietly. "That the power of the Pyrthae should reign unbridled."

Xaron turned his head away in disgust. "I knew you wouldn't understand. Why do you think I never told you?"

"Oh no, I'm very sympathetic," I continued hotly. "I, too, wish for the great Tyrant Wardens of the past to rise and rule the polis again. It worked so well last time, didn't it?"

"You know that's not what she means."

"Well, it ought to be, because that's where we'll end up with if we stop regulating wardens."

He was silent for a moment. "And what about me?" he asked quietly. "Should I be locked up with everyone else?"

I gritted my teeth. "Of course not. You have more sense than to lord your power over others."

"But I don't use my gift for good exactly, do I? I break into people's houses. Last night, I used it to fight, to… kill." His voice shook, but he drew a breath and pressed on. "I'm not a shining example of the good warden. Yet you don't think I should be locked up. Shouldn't we give everyone in the Acadium the same chance? Shouldn't we let them be people and not criminals before they have the chance to decide?"

It felt as if another spoke through him. His master had ingrained her philosophies in him well. I shook my head. "No one gets a fair shot at life, not even patricians and Wreaths. We're all what need makes us, like Talan said. So you haven't had the chance to develop your channeling. At least you haven't been forced to serve an Acadian master carting books back and forth across the campus, studying a discipline you care little for. No one gets everything they want. Maybe the way things turn out is the best they can be."

I didn't believe the words even as I said them. They'd been repeated to me a thousand times in a thousand ways, but there was always something flawed in that argument. Was stability such a noble aspiration when the fate of so many was determined by where or to whom they were born? By mere chance?

Xaron stared at me like I'd become a stranger. "I thought you of all people would understand. Particularly while we take refuge in a cultist compound. Look around us, Airene. Oedija is changing. The world is changing. And if I don't adapt ahead of it... Then I can't protect the ones I care for."

Words failed me. I lowered my gaze and studied the edges of the worn rug. What a fool I'd been. All this time, he hadn't just been doing it for himself. And I'd been blind to it.

"I understand," I said softly. "Just... be careful. You're not the only one who wishes to protect your friends."

He looked like a thirsty man given water. He surprised me by pulling me into an awkward embrace in the small space. A moment later, he broke it off with a groan. "I forgot it hurt for a moment," he said, gingerly touching his side.

I winced. "We'll get you looked after just as soon as we get out of here."

He nodded. "Then we'll watch out for each other."

The only smile I could manage was small and sad. I knew how little I could protect the ones I loved. "Yes. We'll watch out for each other."

———

A quarter-turn later, Talan returned with clothes and a fresh pitcher of water. After rinsing off the soot — and blood — as much as we could, Xaron and I dressed, then left the tent. I peered around nervously, expecting Seeker guards to appear at every corner and apprehend us. The Manifest compound seemed to buzz without any unusual alarm, but I felt that a trap must be waiting.

Even once we'd joined the crowds on the main street, I felt only marginally better. People jostled us as they hurried past, most showing more urgency than we dared to. As we passed the blackened row where Xaron had set the tents on fire, the crowd thickened. Some people, perhaps the owners of the tents, gesticulated angrily at the Seeker guards standing silently before them. I bent my head and hurried Xaron and

Talan past them. One guard had escaped, and I didn't want to chance that our descriptions had been passed on to all of them.

Once we were safely past the destruction, my attention was drawn to a man in shabby robes as he stood on a stand, shouting to a half-moon of intent listeners. "We must not flinch before our fates, my fellow Seekers! We must not back away! No, we must run and embrace our destiny and become who we were always meant to be! We must accept the power of the One, and wield it in his name!"

Now that I had seen wardens truly were among the Manifest's flock, his proselytization was unsettling. Though I still doubted they could make wardens, for most, seeing a warden openly would be enough to inspire belief.

It had been enough for Linos, apparently.

We quickly approached the fence marking the end of the compound. I leaned toward Talan. "What do you have in mind? We can't just walk through."

"Look again, my Finch. During the day, the compound is open. All may come and go as they would."

"Even us?"

He shrugged. "We shall see how well information disseminates among their guards."

I held my breath as we passed through the opening. I didn't look at the Seeker guards, but kept my eyes forward, willing them not to see me. Around us, a small caravan of people also passed, disguising our approach.

"May the One grace you."

Dread filled me as I glanced over. A young guard, his face covered in the Manifest tatu, smiled slightly at me. I stared in return. For a moment, I thought it was Linos who smiled at me, but the fancy quickly passed.

I blinked and paused mid-step, realizing he expected a reply. "May you seek — may you find what you seek, and the One not pass over you." I thought that was more or less what Talan had said the night before.

The man only smiled at my blunder and waved me through. I hurriedly followed after my companions.

Outside the compound, we quickened our pace until the fence was out of sight, then ducked into an alley. Xaron wiped a hand across his brow but said nothing, his eyes still hard and pinched.

After we'd caught our breaths, Talan spoke. "I don't know what else we can do right now but wait for the gathering tomorrow night. I'll try to find a better way inside the Claw, but it's not a task for which my orphans are well suited, and the Seekers will be on higher alert now."

"Of course. Don't take unnecessary risks. But anything you can do, you know I'll appreciate."

He nodded.

I drew in a breath. "In the meantime, I have a plan to begin."

Xaron looked up with a spark of interest, but it was Talan who spoke, an eyebrow arched. "What plan?"

"A drastic one. But a measure our leaders should have taken long ago." At his doubtful look, I flashed him a smile. "It will take too long to explain, so you'll just have to trust me."

Talan snorted and stretched like a cat, then stepped toward the entrance of the alley. "I'll leave you with your secrets, then. Just remember not to take any risks that I would."

With one last lazy smile, he disappeared around the corner.

Xaron leaned closer. "What do you mean to do?" he asked quietly. "Or are you going to exclude me from your plans as well?"

I took his arm and led him out of the alley. "No, I won't leave you out. But I can't tell you where ears might overhear. So how about I just show you?"

He pulled me to a halt, and I complied, though not gracefully. "Airene," he said seriously. "Stop for a moment. Have you really thought this through? We just fought for our lives. We're injured. We're wearing borrowed, ill-fitting clothes and haven't had more than a few moments of sleep. And Nomusa isn't even with us — who knows where she is." He stared imploringly at me. "I know I'm prone to rashness, but don't you think this goes well beyond that?"

I was in no mood for a lecture. "And this coming from the man who trusted his life to an Acadian on a whim. Xaron, my brother is still trapped back there. The Manifest is—" I cut off abruptly and looked around. "This isn't the place to discuss this."

"Then let us go somewhere we can. Back to Canopy, or wherever else you think is best. But we need food and rest. We need to stop and think."

For a moment, I wavered. My decisions had gotten him injured last night. I owed him recuperation. Yet I found myself shaking my head, slowly but firmly. "There's no time. Not for my brother, not for us, and certainly not for Oedija."

Though it wrenched my heart, I pulled my arm from my friend's grip and turned away, then began walking down the street back toward the city. I walked alone.

Despite my firm words, I felt my energy flagging now that the immediate danger was over. Guilt and shame replaced fear now, spurring me past exhaustion and into desperation. I had few allies and fewer friends, and here I drove away one of my closest. Yet I didn't see how I could do any differently.

Footsteps pattered on the street behind me. As Xaron walked up beside me, my faltering hopes rose once again. I smiled over at him with genuine warmth, but all he could return was a shrug.

"I'll follow you, Airene, into the dark depths of the 'Thae. You know I will. Just don't get us lost down there."

"I won't." I wondered how much he would believe that when he saw where we were going.

Though my empty belly grumbled and my feet dragged, we pressed on through the morning, entering back into the inner city and walking through the demes. Xaron asked no more questions, but walked by my side, looking around warily as if he expected to be attacked at any moment. It wasn't an unreasonable suspicion. With my next step, Feiyan might finally make good on her promise to expose him to the Shepherds. It tore at me to do it, but it was a risk he had accepted, and a measure I had to take.

As our destination came into sight, Xaron's eyes widened. "You can't be serious." He looked down at himself, dazed. "I never dreamed I'd be walking up to the Laurel Palace looking like this."

I gripped him by the shoulder and kept him moving forward. "That's more like the Xaron I know. Don't worry. With the news I have for the Archon, he'll barely notice."

CHAPTER EIGHTEEN

UNSPOOLING

As the next closest kin to Myron's line, Jaxas Wreath remains an important figure in the royal line. Related through the sister of Gandyrion Wreath, Myron's father, the early deaths of many of the royal line have left him third in line to inherit the Evergreen Wreath. Little can be said about him, as he has been quiet in his actions. Yet what he has set his mind to, he has done well and with sound morality. Until Asileia's appointment as a governor, Jaxas was often seen by his cousin's side, assisting in her projects and tempering her worst impulses. Many times, he intervened for a whipping girl before Asileia's impudence took her punishment too far…

- A Modern Account of the Wreaths; by Acadian Helene, Master Historian; 1170 SLP

The Laurel Palace sat atop its many-tiered hill like a gilded dragon on its hoard of riches. There were enough columns and domes and towers to befit an Avvadin prince, with roofs and palisades of bronze and walls of white marble and limestone. The pillars before the double wooden doors loomed like a beast's maw, and a thousand eyes glittered with the windows reflecting the light of the morning sun.

I glanced down at myself. Xaron was right about one thing: we were far from adequately dressed. My hair felt a mess, and new cuts and bruises showed from beneath my ill-fitting and stained chiton. Xaron was in even worse shape, his tunic little more than a burlap sack. I suspected Talan had brought him such shabby clothes intentionally. Were I a guard at the palace gates, I would turn us away in a heartbeat. I could only hope Vusu's medallion would work as promised.

"Ready?" I muttered to Xaron as we approached the two men standing before the gates.

"This isn't what I thought I'd be doing this morning," Xaron murmured in reply. But he stayed by my side as we moved forward.

The laurel guards caught sight of us approaching from the bustle and watched with growing amusement. "Halt there," one of them said, the shorter of the two. "More plebs thinking to see the Despoina, eh?"

"I am Airene of Port." I paused, hardly believing what I was about to say. "I'm here to see Archon Jaxas Wreath."

I didn't need to see their eyes under their visors to sense their astonishment.

"Best not be foolish," the second guard said, his voice soft but firm. "You know we can't allow that."

I reached into the collar of my tunic and drew out the Verifier medallion. I was surprised to find my hand was shaking. Great forgotten gods, could I be so nervous to use it? At least my voice didn't quiver as I spoke. "My companion and I are of the new Order of Verifiers, sent by Tribune Vusumuzi to speak with the Archon about certain matters to which he is privy."

I held out the medallion. The heavy, metal circle slowly spun at the end of the chain, Finch symbol glinting in the sunshine.

The shorter guard drew it up in a gauntleted hand. "And I don't suppose we get to know of these certain matters, do we?" he asked sarcastically.

I met his shadowed gaze steadily, though the shaking in my hand caused the medallion to dance. "I don't suppose you do."

The taller one suddenly startled. "I think she's telling the truth. Missive came a couple days ago regarding it. The First Laurel told us to keep an eye out."

The guards exchanged a lingering look. Unease crept along my spine. Had Lykos made inquiries after our run-in with his guard in the Valemish temple? But even if he had, I didn't see how he'd discovered who I was. I set my jaw and held my ground.

"Ah, yes," the shorter guard said as he glanced at me. His expression was inscrutable as he released my medallion. "Come with us, then, both of you."

He nodded to his comrade and motioned back at guards on the other side of the gates, who began to crank the heavy metal doors open.

I glanced at Xaron, and he shrugged. It was as warm of a reception as we could have hoped for, and better than being thrown in the dungeons by far. Still, I couldn't help but feel we walked into a wolf's den as we followed the guards through the open gates.

It was a long walk up the hill. As we ascended the endless stairs, we passed tier after tier of manicured gardens, each level more ornate than any yard I had seen before. Trickling fountains, intricately carved statues, and striking plants drew the eye. But, tired and preoccupied, my interest failed me, and I dropped my gaze to the ground, striving to keep one foot in front of the other.

Finally, the high doors to the palace drew nearer, and none too soon. Between the steep hill, the long night, and half a day without food or drink, my head felt light and dizzy. I set my jaw and braced my legs while our escorts signaled for the doors to be opened, then followed behind as they admitted us.

The doors were opulent, but the massive atrium introduced a new meaning to the word. Gilded surfaces glittered in the light of a thousand pyr lamps. White marble and veined silver stone were waxed to brilliance. The effect was softened by plush Avvadin carpets, red as a Stratechon's cape, and laced with the Wreath's colors of green and gold. From this great hall extended many winding staircases. At least six were in sight, and an archway promised more just beyond it.

There were many bright and promising hallways and staircases to choose from, but the laurel guards selected the darkest one. As we headed toward the corridor, my sense of foreboding increased. I stopped at the threshold, self-preservation calling too strongly to continue.

"Come on now," the shorter guard said. "We wouldn't want to keep the Archon waiting." In the brightly lit room, I could see his mocking grin under his helm.

"Are you sure that's the right way?" I felt sure it wasn't, but I needed to keep them talking until I figured out what to do next.

"Oh yes, very sure. He and I are old friends. Knew each other when we were in our cribs, side by side, we did."

I bowed briefly. "You know, I think we can find our own way. Thank you for your escort." Motioning to Xaron, I turned on my heel.

A hand snaked out and held me fast.

"No one is allowed to roam the palace without an escort," the taller guard said anxiously. He had seized Xaron, and I worried he might do something rash from the black look he cast at the guard.

"Especially not you," the shorter guard said, who held me. "You have another appointment to keep."

I tried to break free. "Take your hands off me. What gives you the right?"

He laughed and tightened his grip. "Here in the palace, we have absolute right. It's best you remember that for your own health, girl."

"No need for that," the taller guard muttered. "Just doing our duty."

"If you'd like to continue to do your duty, you'll unhand me," Xaron said darkly.

They tried pulling us back into the dark corridor, but not hard enough to overcome our resistance. I knew their patience wouldn't hold out for long.

"Why arrest us?" I demanded. "What have we done wrong?"

The taller guard was about to speak, but his comrade cut him off with a glare. "Can't say. We're under strict orders. Now let's go — it'll be better for you if you come quietly."

I gritted my teeth and resisted, expecting a punishing blow at any moment. Yet before they could become violent, voices cascaded down a stairway to echo in the lofty entrance hall. I redoubled my efforts, pulling at my captured arm with my other. Anyone talking that loudly here promised to be exactly the sort of people the guards wouldn't want to make a scene in front of.

I knew what I had to do. Suffocating my pride, I drew in a breath, then shouted at the top of my lungs.

My scream cut off as sparks exploded in my vision. The back of my head smarted where the guard had hit me. I suddenly felt queasy.

"No more of that," the guard snarled in my ear. Before I could say another word, he clapped a gloved hand over my mouth and pulled me roughly back into the corridor. I struggled and bit at his hand, but all I received for my efforts was the taste of grimy leather. Darkness began to fall around me.

"What is the meaning of this?"

The guard abruptly released me, and I stumbled upright, dazed. As figures approached down the stairwell, I gathered my wits, caught my breath, and quickly brushed back my hair to look marginally less like a mad woman. Two people stood at the front of a procession of honors, gazing at me with expressions as opposite as their appearance. Lykos, the First Laurel, didn't wear a helm, revealing a balding pate and peppered beard. His steely gray eyes, catching me in an unblinking gaze, made my skin crawl.

The other I had not seen so close before. Archon Jaxas Wreath was as thin as a corpse, his eyes shadowed, cheeks sunken, and veins showing through his sallow skin. In contrast to Lykos, his gaze was calm and considering.

"I asked you a question," the Archon said, his voice soft, his gaze shifting between the two guards. "For what reason are these two held?"

The shorter guard shook me, though not as roughly as before. "Let's see it, then."

I drew out my Verifier medallion and held it out, hand shaking anew.

The Archon stepped forward and curled a hand under the medallion. As he examined it, a faint smile blossomed on his lips. "A Finch," he observed. "Surely I must speak with the first of the Order to reemerge in a century. Release her and her companion."

"Archon," the First Laurel spoke in his hoarse voice, "I do not mean to contradict, but—"

"I'm well aware of your suspicions, Lykos. I have always made it a point to listen to your briefings. But your reservations give me all the more reason to speak with her."

Lykos stared at me for several moments longer. He was a hard man to lock eyes with, but I managed it. Finally, he gave our captors a nod, and the guards unhanded Xaron and me.

"Come with me, if you please," the Archon said, then turned and walked down a much brighter hallway. The honors following in his wake streamed past us with many a curious glance.

I exchanged a look with Xaron, then we wordlessly followed, leaving Lykos and his guards behind.

CHAPTER NINETEEN

THE ARCHON

Since Asileia departed three years ago, Jaxas has flourished in his own right, though not always in ways that please those of Preservist inclinations. It is said that he garnered support for the Equalist measure to provide public granaries for times of famine, and he secured further rights for the women on the Lotus Ships, who were notoriously mistreated in their night work. He has, however, also fought to continue public funding for Eidolan temples, an effort older generations would most likely appreciate amidst the growing skepticism of the younger patricians.

Should he ever come into the Evergreen Wreath, Jaxas's rule might promise stability, but also significant changes. However, should Asileia produce an heir, he would be further supplanted from inheritance. Yet, loyal as he has shown himself to be to both Asileia and Oedija, I find it likely he will be content to serve at her side.

- A Modern Account of the Wreaths; by Acadian Helene, Master Historian; 1170 SLP

We caught up with the Archon, walking around the contingent of honors to follow at his heels. For such a frail-looking man, he moved swiftly.

"He came not a moment too soon," Xaron muttered. "I was about to send those two beyond the 'Thae if they hit you again."

"Your violent rashness is sweet." I glanced at the Archon. "Let me do the talking. That is, if you can rein in your impulsivity."

He flashed me a sly smile. "We'll see how I feel."

We continued at Jaxas Wreath's heels for a few more paces before he glanced back and slowed to fall into step beside us. "You need not act so formal," he said with his phantom smile. "After all, you did shriek to catch my attention."

I flushed at the memory. If it wasn't the most horrifying thing I'd done, it certainly ranked high among them. "My apologies, Archon. I didn't have rotting in a dungeon on my list of tasks for today, and that seemed the quickest way out."

"It's a small thing to apologize for. At the very least, I won't imprison you for it."

The Archon did not treat me as someone below him, but as an equal. I swallowed and decided to do the same. "I did not know if you would or not. The whispers I hear of you are thin and insubstantial. For such a prominent figure, you surround yourself in silence."

"A mysterious man — I like the sound of it." His eyes slowly scanned the rich decorations in the corridor surrounding us before settling back on me. "Perhaps it makes me quite the eligible bachelor as well."

"Oh, quite. Hardly another topic occurs among the women at the baths."

He laughed softly. "You have a glib tongue, Airene. I'm sure it serves you well as a Finch."

My pulse quickened as he used my name, even as I deduced who had told him. "Tribune Vusumuzi sent word."

"Indeed he did. But you had come to my attention before that." His gaze flitted between Xaron and me.

My tongue worked around my dry mouth. "Few people in deme Port gain much attention from the Laurel Palace."

"True. But few people assault laurel guards in Valemish temples within a span of the Despot's disappearance."

My heart thundered in my chest. Little point in denying it now. "Assault is a strong word," I murmured.

Jaxas laughed softly again. "I'm inclined to agree. He may not seem it, but Lykos can be dramatic when his hackles are raised. Which, as I'm sure you've guessed, is quite often."

I felt my knotted shoulders slowly relax. "Dramatic seems a curious word to assign the man."

"Yes, there's something about him, isn't there? Something metal behind the eyes."

We emerged from the hallway into a tiered garden, one layer falling away under another. White stone paths shone in the sunlight and curved under the slender limbs and bright green leaves of laurel and olive trees. Pyrkin shimmered over statues and in cascading fountains. The garden seemed a fractured, hazy rainbow. Its arches and columns extended into the distance.

The Archon started down one of the winding paths, and Xaron and I fell back into step with him, the honors never far behind.

"Fortunate that I came by," Jaxas observed. "It is unlikely I would have chanced upon you in the dungeons."

I caught a glimmer of mischief in his face and suspected he said more than his words. "Fortunate indeed."

"Vusu has spoken of your talents. If what he says is true, I have need of you and your associates, Airene." His gaze abruptly sharpened as he looked at Xaron and me. "What were you searching for?"

I was taken aback by the sudden question. "We came to speak with you," I said carefully.

He stopped walking. Behind us, the honors stuttered to a halt. As if just noticing them, the Archon waved a hand, and they shuffled back out of earshot. He returned his gaze to me, and his eyes, soft and sunken, seemed to burn with resolve.

"That night at the temple," he clarified. "What were you hoping to gain there?"

I forced myself to hold his gaze. "We'd heard rumors," I said slowly. "Of certain activities."

"Activities." He shook his head. "Airene, now is not the time to withhold. If I wanted you in chains, I would have let the guards take you."

The statement had enough truth in it to loosen my tongue, if only a bit. "I don't know what I hoped to gain. But a nighttime visit by the First Laurel to a Valemish temple so soon after the Despot's death was too promising an opportunity to let slip away."

"So you were tracking Lykos's movements? Following where he went?"

"Call it a happy accident. Like you saving us from the dungeons."

A smile ghosted upon his lips. "Except that was no happy accident. I have eyes in this palace, ones loyal only to me. Without their warning, I would have had little reason to go to the atrium, as there are a hundred more convenient routes to my usual spaces."

In that moment, Jaxas seemed to possess all the hardness of the First Laurel and none of the Despoina's fragility. I struggled to keep his gaze.

"I ask again, Airene," he continued. "Why did you follow Lykos to the Sandglass temple that night?"

I sensed the sharp blade of the guillotine hovering above my neck, and one wrong word could bring it crashing down. Yet I had to say something. "I had been investigating Myron's disappearance for the past half-span, as I didn't trust the reports of his natural death. Myron was too hale a man to die so suddenly, even at his age. Then the rushed private funeral, and the

Despoina's Ascension so soon after… It didn't settle well with me. Yet I'd had no leads in that time. None, until I heard of Lykos's planned excursion to the Sandglass temple that night."

It was a gambler's throw to admit it all. If I believed the rumors, Jaxas was the Despoina's pet, serving her in every capacity — even desires of the flesh, according to the more salacious tongues. But the Archon had not been the man I'd been expecting. Though weak in body, he possessed a strength of mind that brimmed from his shadowed eyes.

I studied his expression, hoping I had judged correctly, but I could not catch the emotions that flashed in it. Eagerness? Regret? My fate — and Xaron's — hung on the balance of his judgment.

A silence extended over us. Wind whistled through the arches and rustled the leaves. Water pattered in the fountains. Xaron fidgeted with his hands. I shifted my weight from one foot to the other, breath coming quick and shallow. All the while, I stared at Jaxas, waiting for an answer.

The Archon, whose gaze had dropped, looked up. "You are correct. Our official explanation doesn't suit the facts."

I blinked. Was that an admission?

Before I could speak, he continued. "We wanted to contain panic. To present a sense of normalcy during a time of transition. But I cannot ignore this any longer. I cannot turn aside from what has truly occurred. Which is why I brought you here. Yes, it was I, though Vusu orchestrated the meeting on my behalf. He expressed great confidence in your abilities. Now that I have met you myself, I find myself swayed to his belief." He turned to fully face me, the loose sleeves of his robes billowing slightly in the wind. "So I must now offer you a proposition, Airene Finch. Are you prepared to hear it?"

I turned to face him as well, the situation gaining a strange formality. "Yes, I am, Archon Jaxas," I said, feeling slightly faint.

"I call it a proposition, but it is not one I expect you to refuse. Do you still wish to hear it?"

I forced myself to maintain eye contact as his gaze vacillated between steel and sadness. "I believe I've already accepted it, Archon."

His shadow-smile returned for a brief moment. "Then for clarity's sake. As the first of the new Order of Verifiers, you, Airene of Port, are to investigate the murder of Myron Wreath, the late Despot of Oedija. You are to have whatever resources you require at your disposal for your search, and you are to look into anyone of suspicion, without being bound by rank or decency." He stared at me a moment longer. "Investigate anyone of suspicion. Do I make myself clear?"

"Yes, Archon," I murmured, though words were nearly stolen from me. It was so clear as to be confusing. *Anyone without bounds.* Including himself.

Including the cousin who was almost a sister, who wore the Evergreen Wreath.

The Archon nodded at Xaron. "Vusu spoke of you as well, Xaron, and of your third companion, Nomusa, who has preceded you here."

In an instant, the glow of success faded.

"Nomusa is here," I said, trying to make it sound like a statement rather than a question.

The Archon's eyebrow rose. "Yes. She was admitted for the same reasons you were, but as I was busy at the time, Low Consul Feiyan elected to entertain her on my behalf. They are still wandering the gardens last that I heard."

My heart hammered in my chest. How Nomusa had come here, and why she was meeting with Feiyan, were questions I could not begin to answer.

"We will encounter them soon, I expect," Jaxas continued. "But you are my concern for the moment, Xaron. I would confer the same responsibility and title upon you, if you will accept it."

Xaron startled, as if not expecting to be addressed. Or perhaps he was as distracted by the news of Nomusa as I was. "Ah, yes, Archon," he stumbled to say. "That is, I accept."

Jaxas nodded. "Good. Then it is settled."

But my thoughts were far from settled. Pushing Nomusa and Feiyan from mind, another burning question spilled from me. "Why now? It's been nearly a span since Myron's death. If you wished us to investigate this, why not summon us earlier? Why let us meander our own way here?"

Jaxas nodded slowly as if he'd been expecting the question. "There are things I know that you have yet to hear. The Manifest have secured the borders of Thys, and enforce it through their arms. Rumors have it that wardens are among their ranks, yet Vusu has ever counseled patience and delayed sending in the Shepherds. He wishes for stability, but I fear it was swift action that would have served us better. The Stratechons have raised taxoi to man the inner city walls, but too few and too late, and they lack the boldness we now need.

"As for our Despoina..." He paused and closed his eyes for a breath's count. "She has officially ejected the Avvadin diplomat and threatened war with the Imperium. And despite assurances from the Council and myself that we would never take such an action, the Kahin-Shah will take offense."

Fear crept up my spine. "Will two horns soon blow from the palace?"

He shook his head. "It will not come to that, I think. A concession of tax remittance is underway within the Conclave, and some agreement will be reached. Nevertheless..."

I wanted badly to believe politicking would suffice. But I had seen the map inside the Wyvern's Claw. I'd been attacked by the Seeker wardens, and the wounds they'd inflicted still pained me. War, it was beginning to seem, was an inevitability.

Jaxas shook his head again, as if trying to banish the ill tidings, then motioned the honors back to us. "We should formalize our agreement."

One of the honors produced three goblets on a platter, which he promptly filled with a bottle of wine and handed to us. Archon Jaxas held up his cup, and Xaron and I followed. Without a word, we drank, as was the old Oedijan way when deals of commerce were struck. Apparently, the same held true for agreements of subterfuge and justice.

He lowered his cup a moment later and dabbed at his lips with a cloth. "Rooms have already been prepared for you to stay within the palace. It is traditional for Verifiers to take up residency at the Aviary on the Conclave grounds, but sadly, it has fallen into disuse since the Order was dismantled. Until such a time as it can be refurbished, or the Council reaches out to take hold of you themselves, you may stay here on Wreath property at our expense."

I exchanged an astonished look with Xaron. It was a boon I hadn't dreamed of receiving, and one that we sorely needed. "Thank you, Archon. Words cannot express our appreciation."

He smiled thinly. "It is for my convenience as well as yours. I wish to have my Finches at my disposal. Besides, keeping you within Wreath boundaries limits the number of eyes and ears who know that I use you."

Once again, cold clarity reasserted itself. Now that the Archon had us, he wouldn't easily let go. We were in a cage still, if more comfortable than the palace's dungeons. And here I'd begun to think Jaxas Wreath was a kind man.

The Archon turned away to look out over the sea, and with a nod at Xaron, we stepped up next to him. Though he was surrounded by people, I had the sense that Jaxas was far away and alone. And as I contemplated his position, I remembered my own. An unforeseen windfall had appeared to me, it was true enough. But as long as Linos was in the hands of the Manifest and the mystery of Thero's death went unsolved, I had no right to any measure of elation.

"Do you believe in the Pyrthae?" the Archon asked suddenly. "That it exists?"

I raised an eyebrow as I looked up. "Of course. We see it in the sky above."

He waved a hand dismissively. "There are other explanations for the radiant winds than a haven for lost spirits. At another time, I might recommend texts on it. But even without skepticism, I find myself hesitant to believe in it. Believing in things immaterial… It can cause a great deal of trouble."

In my experience, such statements were often said by those troubled by things immaterial. But I knew when to hold my tongue.

He looked to me, expression soft as the high tide shore. "Bring me more than ghosts to fret over."

I nodded, unsure whether it was a command or a plea.

He turned back to the gardens. "Ah. The last of our Finches has returned to the roost."

I tried to hide my surprise as I looked around. Standing on the tier above us were two familiar figures. Nomusa stared down at us with a somber expression, while Low Consul Feiyan wore a self-possessed smile.

"The other two of our new Verifiers, I see," Feiyan said with calculated derision. "When the Archon is finished with you, I'd like a word. I believe we have a few matters to settle."

I didn't look at Feiyan, but at my friend standing beside her. Nomusa stared back, her expression flat and unreadable. She and I had worked together for nine years and lived together for nearly as long.

Yet I couldn't help but wonder if all our shared lies had finally caught up to us.

CHAPTER TWENTY

TRUTH'S COST

There is much discrepancy about the spirits of the Pyrthae and their origins, including whether or not anything resides within the realm at all, or indeed if it truly exists as a separate plane of existence parallel to our own Telae. Yet assuming spirits and their realm exists, there are a few things agreed upon.

The first is that there are lesser and greater spirits. In Oedija, we refer to the lesser spirits as pyr and the greater as gods, and believe a discrepancy in power exists between them. In some texts from the Age of Despots, there are mentions of a third being of spirit called Quintyr. How these beings differ is not clear, though influence and origin certainly appear to be important. Pyr, for example, can be of Pyrthaen or Telaen origin, such as our deceased ancestors, whereas Quintyr are said to be born only of the Pyrthae, and cannot reside outside of it. Gods, like pyr, are not restricted by origin, and there are tales in many lands of men and women performing heroic deeds and attaining divinity.

Those, however, can safely be dismissed as mere folk tales with little truth behind them.

- The Traditions of the Eleven: Eidolan worship in the demotism of Oedija; by Oracle Iason of deme Iris; 1164 SLP

A irene of Port," Feiyan said sweetly as she started down the stairs toward the Archon, Xaron, and myself. Nomusa followed in her wake.

"Feiyan," I said flatly, refusing to acknowledge her title or look at her. I didn't pull my gaze away from Nomusa. "What were you two discussing?" I addressed my loftmate.

Nomusa's mouth tightened. "What we were forced to."

"Yes, she was quite forthcoming." The Low Consul turned her smile on the Archon. "Perhaps we should speak later. I believe I can tell you many things you'll be interested to hear."

Jaxas gave her a stiff bow. "I would be happy to hear anything you might have to say."

I wondered briefly at their relationship. With both of them bonded tightly to the Despoina, they were bound to have regular interactions. And if this occasion was any sign, they weren't on the friendliest of terms. But that was a matter for another time. "Archon Jaxas, if would you excuse us, I'd like to talk over what we discussed with our associate."

He frowned, but after a moment's consideration, he nodded. "Of course. The Low Consul and I should converse before our Council meeting. We will speak more this evening. We each have more to say, I do not doubt."

I bowed deeply as I struggled for a response. I wasn't sure I should feel the depth of gratitude that I did for a man I barely trusted, much less express it. So I simply said, "Thank you, Archon."

As Jaxas nodded his dismissal, I took hold of Xaron and pulled him unceremoniously to the side. Nomusa frowned, but followed as we moved to another corner of the garden, sheltered from sight and sound by a laurel hedge and a glittering fountain.

As soon as we were alone, I rounded on Nomusa. "What did you tell her?"

Nomusa crossed her arms. "What I thought would keep us out of danger."

Xaron paled, but his expression remained determined as he asked in a low voice, "You didn't compromise us, did you?"

"How could it be I who compromised us?" Nomusa demanded in return. "Was it I who ignored her threats? One of us had to do something, or Feiyan would have done worse than sack Canopy."

I gritted my teeth, but held back my acid thoughts. "So you went to talk to her."

Her eyes blazed as she met my gaze. "Yes. I tracked Feiyan to the Laurel Palace, and her name gained me admittance. She was quite eager to speak with me."

"No doubt enjoying the opportunity to gloat," Xaron noted.

Annoyance crossed Nomusa's face, but she continued as if he hadn't interrupted. "She proposed that we make a mutually beneficial deal. In exchange for information, she would no longer antagonize us, nor turn in 'our feral,' as she called it."

My eyebrows shot up. "And that's it? You tell her a few whispers, and she lets us off the hook?"

"There was one additional condition. That we stop investigating the Despot's death, no matter the Archon's insistence on the matter."

I shook my head and rubbed at the bridge of my nose. My head was starting to ache. "Just what information was she so interested in anyway?"

The muscles in her jaw worked for a moment. "All that we've learned in our hunt," she admitted.

"*Our* hunt? You're talking about the hunt you impeded at every turn, and now throw away?"

"I'm trying to save us from your foolishness!" Nomusa hissed through clenched teeth.

"Easy, both of you," Xaron said, turning sideways to step between us. "Nomusa, what exactly did you reveal?"

Nomusa exhaled sharply. "I told her our suspicions and how we'd come to them insofar as they concerned the Despot. Of the Valemish, the Manifest. The Despoina herself."

I rolled my eyes. "Little wonder she wanted us to stop investigating."

"She always wanted that," Nomusa retorted. "Nothing I said changed that."

Xaron sighed and stepped back again. "At least we have a dialogue with our favorite hive queen and know she still doesn't intend to turn us in without provocation."

"Then I assume you won't do anything to provoke her? Like meet with the Archon this evening?" Nomusa's eyes bore into me.

I shook my head. "I'm still going."

"Let's go find our rooms before we talk about this further," Xaron interjected. "I'm sure one of Jaxas's honors can point us in the right direction."

I relented to Xaron taking command of the situation and was relieved when Nomusa did the same. As we followed after him, I studied my old friend. Anger still ran hot through me for her rash actions, but beneath it, there was a small strain of relief that she had acted in our best interests, misguided though the attempt may have been.

But when she glanced back at me, I turned away. If she expected an apology, she'd be waiting a long while.

CHAPTER TWENTY-ONE

THE HAND OF CLEPSAMMIA

Clepsammia is eighth of the Eidola, the daughter of Tyurn Sky-Sea by his infidelity with one of the deep-dwelling Sandwatchers. Nearly from birth, she was given Telae's Sandglass and put in charge of keeping the time of our world flowing at a steady grain. One of two deities born of another race, Clepsammia has ever been an outcast.

It is uncertain if it was her position or her origins that gives her such a unique insight into the streams of time. By turning her sandglass, she may visit any epoch of the world that has occurred or is still to come. Yet though she possesses unique knowledge, the Keeper of Time has in most of our stories contented herself with little more than the occasional enigmatic warning. Only in one tale did she do more, when she tried turning her father away from the mistake that would lead to his demise…

- The Traditions of the Eleven: Eidolan worship in the demotism of Oedija; by Oracle Iason of deme Iris; 1164 SLP

Two honors from Archon Jaxas's regiment led us to rooms on the opposite side of the palace. The hallways leading up to them were orderly, but not opulent like the main atrium we'd first entered. After informing us of the locations of various necessities, the two honors left us to our own devices. Though hunger gnawed at my stomach and weariness dragged at my limbs, it was the filth and the lingering memory of blood on my skin that sent me to the baths. Xaron, ravenous as usual, urged Nomusa to go with him to the feast hall, which left me on my own. That suited me fine; I needed time to think.

It was only once I was alone and walking down the hallway to the baths that I questioned my decision. Just a turn or so before, Lykos had tried to detain me and throw me in the dungeons. Even now that the Archon had claimed me as his own, a nagging paranoia persisted, especially when I passed between the guards scattered throughout the palace. Their eyes followed me with what seemed more than idle curiosity, and their words felt laced with secret venom. But for the moment at least, none laid a hand on me.

By the time I reached the baths, I was nearly shaking, though it could have as easily been from hunger and exhaustion as fear. I stripped off my ill-fitting clothes, keeping only the Verifier medallion with me, and relented to being oiled and scraped by an honor. Once she was finished, I slipped into the water. Though a roof sheltered the bathhouse from the elements, it was open on three sides, providing marvelous views of the sea and coastline, though it also admitted a chilling wind. No one else was at the baths at this turn of the day, so I had the view all to myself. Idly wiping the clinging oil from my skin, I stared out over the sea at the hazy horizon.

Somber thoughts accompanied me. Of Thero, and the lingering mystery of his death, and the dark master behind it. Of Linos, and my failure to retrieve him, and my fear that he'd meet the same fate. As I bobbed in the water, rubbing my hands over stinging cuts and bruises, I wondered if I'd given up too easily, if I shouldn't have pushed to infiltrate the Claw no matter the cost. The Verifier medallion, which I'd kept clasped over my neck, unable to trust parting with it, felt cold and heavy against my skin.

I closed my eyes and listened to the breeze rustling off the cliff and the lap of water on the edges of the pool. Slowly, my guilt's sharp edges dulled, and clarity returned. I couldn't have done anything more, not at that moment. I would have just gotten Xaron, Talan, and myself killed. What I'd done already had been foolish enough. To let the guilt hinder me now would only do my brother a greater disservice. I sighed slowly and let myself relax.

"Airene of Port. Or should I say, Verifier Airene."

I startled and spun around, arms crossed over my breasts. Nikias stood with hands clasped behind his back, dressed in all the finery of his station as steward to the Archon, and a severe expression to match.

"Hello, Nikias," I said drily. "Could you not wait until I'd dressed?"

His cheek twitched. "I come in regards to your dress. My master has had garments delivered to your rooms. I took the liberty to have some sent here as well as to dispose of your old clothes." He didn't bother hiding a sniff to show what he thought of their state.

That was a kindness I hadn't expected. "Thank you. Is there anything else?"

"As he conveyed before, my master will meet with you this evening to discuss your tasks. Your meeting will be at the Laurel Groves. Are you familiar with their location?"

"Vaguely." I knew where the royal gardens were, but as it was a place for patricians, Servants, and Wreaths, I'd never had occasion to visit.

"A carriage will await you at the sixth turn of the evening outside the palace doors. Be there promptly; my master is not to be kept waiting." Nikias bowed stiffly, then turned on his heel and left.

I let my arms fall. The calm of the bath had been disturbed, so I rose from the water and hurried to the changing room.

A peplos had been laid out for me, far finer and more elegant than anything I'd worn before. I ran a hand over the soft silk and marveled at the expense. It made me uncomfortable to think about donning it, especially since I rarely wore peploses, which exposed one shoulder and therefore eliminated the possibility of wearing a tunic beneath.

Even more discomforting was the jewelry laid out with it, an assortment of silver bracelets, rings, and earrings, altogether worth twice as much as what Feiyan had stolen from Canopy. I put on the peplos, but was loathe to touch the jewelry. Did the Archon honestly want his Verifiers dressed in such finery? Perhaps I was meant to serve a different function than I imagined, a puppet in a plot I had yet to discover. It was uncomfortable to consider Jaxas in this new light, but I knew too little of him to rule it out. Another possibility was that this was a test, though what its purpose might be, I could not tell. Whatever his reasons, I decided not to wear them, but took them in hand. Perhaps it would be an insult to the Archon, but I couldn't abide wearing jewelry that announced my arrival in every new room with its rattling.

I returned to my chamber and entered without inquiring after Xaron and Nomusa. Weariness, which had prickled at my consciousness during my whole stay in the palace, now seized hold of me. Closing and locking the door, I collapsed onto my bed with barely a cursory look around. The fine furnishings could wait to be appreciated until I awoke. With a vague hope that I wouldn't sleep too late for our appointment with Jaxas, I drifted off.

A knock woke me. Disoriented, I bolted upright and stared about the strange room in confusion.

The knock sounded again. "Airene," Nomusa's voice came through the door. "We have half a turn to be outside the palace doors."

"I'm up." I looked around blearily, trying to orient myself to my surroundings. Slowly, I remembered where I was, and the twists and turns in my fortunes that had brought me here.

"You might hurry," Nomusa said, annoyance clear in her voice.

"One moment!" I rose, groaning. Where before I'd been exhausted, now I was sore and stiff as well. Not to mention ravenous. It promised to be a long day yet. At least I was already dressed. I found a mirror resting on the bedside table and examined myself. I was clean, but my hair was a messy cloud around my head, as I hadn't bothered to arrange it after my bath. Fortunately, a comb had been provided, and I used it in an attempt to tame the tangled bush.

As I tailored myself back into a presentable condition, I tried working my mind around my plans again, but the hunger was too great. Too little time to do everything necessary, as usual. I threw down the comb in frustration and, strapping on my sandals and donning the Verifier medallion, I bolted out the door.

Xaron and Nomusa were waiting outside. As I stepped into the hall, Xaron yawned widely. "Morning," he said miserably. He was even more of a sight than myself, his face swollen and scabbed. Even stranger was that he'd been provided robes for the occasion in place of his usual coat and trousers, which made him squirm in discomfort.

"It's evening. And don't moan," Nomusa chastised him with a fleeing smile. As usual, she looked radiant, with her hair smartly done and a rich silver peplos clinging to her figure. She hadn't spurned the jewelry as I had, but wore it all, bracelets jingling on her wrists and rings clinking on her fingers.

"Come on, Airene," she said, turning away. "We'll be late."

"I'm famished. Is the dining hall near?"

"No. You'll just have to cope."

"I guess I can relinquish part of my stash," Xaron said grudgingly.

After I'd restored myself from the mound of food Xaron had stolen from the kitchens, him grumbling about losing his late-night meal the whole time, we hurried through the palace to the front doors. Xaron and I chatted of small things, not daring to touch on more pertinent topics. I much preferred Xaron in his current high spirits to the brooding man he'd been the night before.

As promised, Nikias had ordered a carriage to wait for us, with an honor holding the reins to a pair of mules. "If we might hurry, master and mistresses," the man said with a low bow. "We are past the time Steward Nikias instructed me to depart."

Nomusa glowered at me and climbed into the carriage, Xaron and I coming after. As soon as we were seated, the honor shook the reins, and the mules started clopping down the marble path.

We were quiet at first, and I stared out of the barred windows of the carriage. I'd never ridden in such high style, yet I hadn't hesitated to climb in and accept the privilege like a born patrician. It made me uneasy how quickly I was adapting to this new lifestyle.

"Why are we meeting Jaxas in the Laurel Groves?" Nomusa broke the silence, reluctance plain in her voice. She spoke softly enough that the clamor of the horse and carriage would mask her words from our driver.

I met her gaze. If she was willing to talk, I'd meet her halfway. "I don't know. He didn't say."

Xaron shrugged. "Something to do with the Despot job, no doubt."

"With Despot Myron's death?"

I nodded. "It's what he's hired us for. To get to the bottom of things."

Nomusa was quiet for a moment. "That will go against Feiyan's demands," she said quietly. "Xaron, are you prepared to accept that?"

Uncertainty flashed across his face, but I saw the man I'd glimpsed the night before return as he sharply nodded. "Yes," he said in a rough whisper. "I won't live in fear."

I clenched my jaw and turned my gaze out the window. I hated what necessity made us risk, but I couldn't think of any way around it.

"What did you find in Thys?" Nomusa pressed.

I spoke before Xaron had a chance to. "What did you tell Feiyan?"

She scowled, but it was Xaron who answered. "Let it go, Airene. She did what she thought was best. We can settle all that later. Right now, we have to work together. Or are you forgetting what's on the line?"

"No, I'm not," I answered coolly.

"Good. Then let me do the talking."

Xaron recounted the events of the night before with enough embellishment that it took all my self-control not to cut in. When it came to the violence, though, he was conspicuously brief. After he finished, Nomusa nodded, her expression thoughtful.

"That does seem serious," she admitted. "But the Manifest doesn't have the means to take over the city, much less start a war with Avvad."

"Perhaps not. But they must have significant resources to erect and support an encampment of that size in the midst of an oncoming famine." I paused, considering. "They've been shielded from all echelons of the government. Which means someone must be protecting them. One of the Stratechons, a First in the city guard, or someone in the Tribunal, possibly."

Xaron's eyes widened. "Jaxas said Vusu had counseled him not to send in Shepherds to the Manifest. But we saw wardens there. You don't think...?"

"No, I don't," I replied sharply. "We'd never have gotten as far as we have without Vusu. What possible reason could he have for aiding us if he's a Seeker?" I shook my head. "More likely it is someone from the Preservist faction among the Council. Jaxas said they'd also advocated for little to be done."

Nomusa leaned forward. "Unless the Preservists are more connected to Avvad than any of us suspected. All of them have ancestry from the Imperium."

"We can't assume that," I murmured, but there wasn't much heart to my words. It made too much sense to me to deny it. "But unless the Manifest and Avvad are somehow connected, I don't see why they'd want to foster them."

"Chaos," Xaron guessed. "Undermine the city's stability so that it makes it easier to conquer."

"Then what about the Despoina's strange behavior? And Feiyan's plotting and protectiveness? It seems too far a stretch to wind them in."

Xaron shrugged. "Asileia's crazy. What else is there to figure out?"

I suspected it was the truth as the Manifest loomed ever larger in my mind. But it wasn't an assumption we could safely make, not with our limited information. And it didn't solve one central question: if Asileia wasn't the master at the center of the Manifest, who was?

The carriage finally rumbled to a halt. I looked out to see we'd arrived at our destination. The Laurel Groves were known as a horticultural wonder of the Four Realms, and I saw they lived up to their name. Fountains, marble walkways, and manicured aisles wove together in dazzling arrangements. Flowers of orange, periwinkle, and violet emerged amid emerald green leaves and trees hanging with gold-limned moss. Laurel trees in the peak of their summer bloom filled the air with a wonderfully sweet scent and dotted the groves with white flowers like stars. As in the palace gardens, pyrkin was used to highlight effects, but on an entirely different scale. Where in the gardens everything was kept tightly in check, here a balance had established itself between the tidiness of architecture and the chaos of creation.

The approach of the Archon with his usual group of honors drew my attention. "I am glad to see you made it," he said as he arrived, sounding slightly out of breath. "We'll go on foot from here. If you'll come with me..." Jaxas Wreath's words trailed off, but he turned sharply on his heel and started back the way he'd come, sending his honors scattering before him.

My accomplices and I disembarked and hurried after him. Unlike earlier that day, I immediately walked by his side. "What are we here for, if I may ask, Archon?"

"Ah, so you haven't guessed?" His eyes gleamed with mischief. "And here I thought your wealth of information was endless."

I shrugged. "We're not seers."

Jaxas only chuckled softly.

"Archon, if I might speak of a subject that is of vital importance…" I trailed off. The request sounded too formal and stiff. I'd never get around to my point if I didn't state it bluntly.

I started again. "There's a danger to the city, and nothing is being done it about it that I can tell. I hope the information we have will change that."

Jaxas glanced at me, then at Xaron and Nomusa behind us. "I believe I know of what you speak," he said in a low voice. "We will talk of it later. But now, I must show you why I've brought you here."

I repressed an urge to share a skeptical look with Xaron and Nomusa. What could he have to show us in the Laurel Groves? "As you wish," I relented.

We turned the next corner to find a strange sight. Asileia Wreath lay under an olive tree, staring up through its leaves. She had never seemed a woman to be caught unawares, but as we approached, she didn't seem to notice our presence. Her oracles were a different story. Three in number, they crowded around her like vultures over carrion and gazed up at our party with jealous possessiveness. I ignored the sycophants and watched our Despoina. She could have been dead for all she moved or blinked. I wondered if the glass-thin sanity of our Ruling Wreath had finally cracked.

I rounded on the Archon. "Why didn't you tell us we were meeting the Despoina?"

Jaxas Wreath shrugged. "Surely you have many questions for her. Now is your time to ask."

I turned my gaze away from him and looked back to my friends. Nomusa stood with as haughty a posture as I'd ever seen her don. Xaron slouched and cast his eyes about nervously, looking as unsettled as I felt. I wanted to confer with them and ask what questions we should pose to her. But the Archon was already beckoning us forward.

"Come — it's not fit to keep the Ascended Wreath waiting." He and his retinue of honors pushed closer, leaving us no choice but to follow.

As we approached the Despoina, the situation became yet more bizarre. I expected her to shake off whatever stupor gripped her and resume her royal manner, but she didn't move. When we were a dozen paces away, the oracles finally moved to stand before her. They were cowled in dark brown robes, their faces hidden from view. All I could distinguish them by were their disparate sizes, with several cubits between the smallest and largest.

"You are not worthy," the middle one said.

"She is listening and is not to be disturbed," the largest one continued.

"Leave and never return," the smallest finished.

Jaxas ignored them all. "Leia," he said softly. "Leia, I've brought you guests, ones who won't hiss poison in your ear."

"You are not worthy," the first oracle repeated stubbornly.

I stood there, uncertain of what to say. Jaxas slowly peeled his eyes from Asileia to settle on the oracles. "Move from our way," he said quietly.

A pause. "You are not worthy," the first oracle said once more.

"I know," the Archon replied. The humility in his tone surprised me. "But we must speak to her all the same. Move and let me see her."

The oracles barely shifted, yet I sensed their unease. The middle one stepped aside first, the other two following after. They muttered something as we passed between them, but I couldn't hear the words.

Approaching the Despoina, Jaxas knelt next to her under the boughs of the olive tree. "Leia," he said softly. "We have guests. Some people I'd like you to talk to. Will you stand?"

The leader of our nation didn't bat an eye. Her lips barely parted, and a wordless moan escaped.

Jaxas closed his eyes for a moment. When he opened them, his gaze had grown hard as granite. "Leia. You must rise now."

Her eyelids fluttered, then closed. "Why do you bother me?" she said faintly. "I am trying to rest."

"With your eyes open?" The Archon's anger spilled forth in cutting words. "You don't need any more rest. You need to rise."

"Indeed?" Leia's eyes snapped fully open, and her face adopted the hard lines I'd initially expected. "Because my war to save our city from invading pyr is inconsequential? Because I don't stay up, day and night, guarding you and every other small mind in this polis from their grasping claws? And you wish me to pause my watch to do, what? Speak more with the Avvadin ambassador?" She squeezed her eyes shut again. "We have spoken enough. I will hear no more of his talk of commerce and *mutual benefit*. He is a weak man, a paragon of a nation in decline."

Jaxas opened and closed his mouth, his shadowed eyes smoldering. But I could see his anger was getting us nowhere. I'd long ago learned to trust my gut, even if it sometimes led me to strange places. Before he could speak, I boldly stepped forward and slipped down to the ground.

Asileia Wreath stared at me with slitted eyes. "And you are?"

I crossed my legs under my borrowed peplos, ignoring how dirty I was making the delicate fabric. "Trying to get comfortable."

Her hard expression didn't flicker. "You are not worthy to sit here."

So it wasn't just the oracles who thought so. "I'm sorry to disturb you, my Despoina. I have heard of your... hardships."

She stared at me a long moment, then her eyes slid back into her head. "You don't know the half of them."

"Then tell me. What is this war to save Oedija?"

She sat bolt upright so quickly I nearly scrambled away in surprise. "I am the Hand of Clepsammia," she declared so loudly it was almost a yell. "I will cast you down from your unholy throne, daemon! Begone, before I grow angry! Begone, before—!"

She stopped as suddenly as she started, going as rigid as a plank and eyes staring wide and straight ahead. I was hesitant to speak, but I had to make the most of this conversation. Jaxas might cut our talk short at any moment.

"Despoina Asileia, I need you to tell me—"

"I don't need to tell anyone anything. *I* am the Hand of Clepsammia."

I swallowed my pride. "Of course you are. As the Hand of Clepsammia, do the gods speak to you? Do they ask you to do anything for them?"

"I do what I wish. And what I wish is their will." Her eyelids fluttered. "But it is I who is in control."

"Was it your will or theirs to kill your father?"

The oracles hissed and stepped forward, only stopped by a sharp reprimand from Jaxas. Xaron chuckled inappropriately. Yet no one spoke against my accusation.

I kept my eyes on the Despoina. Slowly, she met my gaze and smiled. "Wasn't it marvelous? The first test of my power. There he went, gone without a trace."

I stared at her, searching her eyes, not daring to believe her words. I found nothing there but the certainty of madness.

I rose, thoughts tumbling about my mind like marbles in a cup. Glancing back, I saw the Archon staring at me with a strange twist to his expression. Nomusa wore begrudging respect, while Xaron's brow was knitted in consternation.

I turned back to Asileia, who still lay on the ground, and bowed. "Thank you for your time, my Despoina."

She had already resumed staring up through the trees and paid me no mind.

Jaxas Wreath took a deep breath. "If you'll give us a moment," he said in carefully measured tones, then turned to his cousin.

The honors, Xaron, Nomusa, and I shuffled back along the path until we were out of earshot, but still within line of sight. The oracles lingered behind until the Archon cast a withering look in their direction, then they walked over to stand next to us stiffly. The whole company watched the silent pantomime between Jaxas and Asileia, her ignoring him, him gently pleading.

"You misunderstand her," an oily voice said from next to me.

I looked over to see the largest of the brown-cowled oracles staring down at me. Under his hood, I found beady, glittering eyes staring from beneath peppered eyebrows and a prominent forehead.

"Pardon?" I asked politely.

"She is the savior of our city. You would do best not to question what she does in service of it."

"You are not worthy," the middle-sized oracle intoned.

I shrugged. "I'll take that into consideration."

The oracle nodded as if my reply was enough, then he and his fellows moved further away.

Xaron and Nomusa pressed in closer. "Did she admit what I think she did?" Xaron asked dubiously.

"Yes, we all heard it," Nomusa said impatiently. She nodded toward the oracles, who had turned their backs on us. "What I can't figure out is why they're still following her around."

"Lingering opportunists," I said with a shrug. "We've got bigger concerns than them."

But Nomusa still wore a thoughtful expression as she looked away.

Xaron glanced between us. "Are we not going to talk about what the Despoina confessed to?"

I smiled and put a hand on his arm. "Later will be soon enough."

After several more minutes, the Archon finished his piece to the Despoina and rejoined us. From his slumped shoulders and her continued position on the ground, the conversation had not gone well.

"We move on," the Archon said as he swept past us. His posture showed defeat, but his voice was still full of command. "You have another appointment to keep."

"Another appointment?" I glanced at Nomusa and saw my question echoed in her eyes. "With whom?"

"A ghost," the Archon said with the shadow of a smile. "One I'm sure you're eager to meet."

CHAPTER TWENTY-TWO

REMNANTS

If spirits do exist in the Pyrthae, they do not have much interaction with us of the material plane. At certain festivals, such as Oedija's Carnival of Veils, trickster pyr are said to appear and cause mischief, though little evidence supports that such pranks are truly of Pyrthaen origin. Some Eidolan sects believe that rituals can call forth pyr to provide aid or do harm to others, though again, I remain unconvinced that any perceived intervention isn't simply in the minds of the ritualists.

- The Traditions of the Eleven: Eidolan worship in the demotism of Oedija; by Oracle Iason of deme Iris; 1164 SLP

Jaxas kept us in suspense for the ride back up to the Laurel Palace. In our separate carriage, Nomusa, Xaron, and I quietly debated what the Despoina's subtle admission of guilt meant, but our next appointment begged speculation. I had my suspicions, and when I shared them, Nomusa and Xaron nodded along in agreement, apprehension and eagerness battling in their expressions.

When we reached the palace, we ascended the stairs to a grand hallway with a lofted ceiling and plush, red carpet over the stone. At the end of it lay a pair of large, wooden doors. Whereas everything else was gilded and glimmering, these doors were scratched and plain. A matronly honor waited by them, whom I understood to be a head of the palace staff. She informed us that the doors were a remnant from the Wardens' War, when the newly freed people of Oedija raided the palace and gutted it of all its value. All else in the palace had been restored, but this reminder of those dark times had been ordered to remain.

The Archon stopped before the doors. "These are the Ascended Wreath's official living quarters. Myron, however, preferred to have his chambers elsewhere." He shook his head. "He claimed it was too ostentatious for his liking, but I believe he always feared assassins in the dark. A poor irony, isn't it?"

Nomusa and I shared a look, while Xaron chuckled irreverently. Jaxas didn't comment, but led us down the hall to a smaller door. This one had figures carved into it. I recognized Tyurn Sky-Sea in the center of it, his star-crested mantle sweeping over the rest of the mural.

"Did Myron believe in the Eleven?" I asked, curious.

Jaxas nodded. "He believed we'd lost something when we abandoned the old ways and beliefs. The way his daughter behaved only served to reinforce this belief."

I tucked the fact away for later and stared at the doors, imagining what was beyond them.

The Archon sensed my eagerness, and he smiled faintly. "Chiri, please open the old Despot's chambers."

"Yes, Archon," the matronly honor said. Trepidation filled her voice, yet she complied, producing a ring of keys and turning an iron one in the lock. She gave a push, and the door swung slowly open.

My heart pounding, I stepped forward at Jaxas's inviting gesture. Nomusa and Xaron walked next to me, staring past the frame and into the room beyond. But as the door opened fully, my stomach lurched, hard and sudden. Bile burned the back of my throat. I swallowed hard to keep it down.

"Airene?" Xaron touched my bare shoulder. "Are you okay?"

His touch was unbearably hot. I gave a wordless cry and shrugged off his grip, taking a step back and breathing hard. As I stepped away, the pain ebbed, as did the fire from Xaron's touch.

He stared at me in astonishment, not daring to come closer. It was Nomusa who slowly approached next. "Aire?" she asked cautiously. "Are you well?"

My cheeks flushed as Jaxas, Chiri, and the other gathered honors stared at me. I swallowed hard once more before I trusted myself to speak. "I'm fine." I turned to our host, trying to pretend that nothing had happened. "Have the rooms been disturbed?"

Jaxas studied me carefully for a moment, then gestured to Chiri. "I'll let the matron of the palace speak."

Chiri looked less certain of my wellness. Still, she replied, "Not a man or woman has been permitted to enter since the first night."

"But someone entered that night?" I followed up quickly. My stomach still turned, unsettled.

The honor eyed me, sizing me up, or perhaps wondering if I was about to create a mess that she'd have to clean up. At a nod from the Archon, she continued. "The Archmaster Kyros, the Tribune Vusumuzi, and the First Laurel Lykos were the only ones to go within. I saw myself that they did not put anything amiss."

"You didn't enter yourself?" I asked Jaxas. "Nor the Despoina?"

He shook his head, eyes shadowed by the pyr lamp mounted behind his head.

"May we enter?" Nomusa spoke. "We won't learn much by standing in the doorway."

The honor looked scandalized by the suggestion, but Jaxas nodded. "Of course."

Xaron and Nomusa glanced at me, and I felt a new flush settling over me. Setting my jaw, I stepped determinedly forward, even as I tensed for the coming blow. I was not disappointed. My stomach thrashed again, and hot bitterness hit the back of my throat. But instead of recoiling, I barreled through the doorway. At once, the feeling faded, leaving my organs mangled and throbbing.

The Archon entered with us. "Are you well?" he murmured to me as Xaron and Nomusa spread out to look around.

I nodded. Though the danger of retching seemed to have passed, I didn't want to risk opening my mouth.

Seeking a distraction, I peered around the room. It was modest for a Wreath, only a few dozen paces across. Dominating the room was a four-poster canopy bed that looked fit to sleep a giant, its sheets and blankets undisturbed and tidy. The Despot had not yet been to bed the night of the three horns, it seemed. I tucked the thought away for later.

Other doors led off from the main chamber. I wondered if he'd gone to any of them when a breeze drew icy fingertips along my exposed shoulder. Glancing over, I saw the doors to the balcony were slightly ajar.

"Have those doors been open since his disappearance?" I asked Chiri, who had remained by the door.

"As I said," the honor stated, sounding more than a bit annoyed, "nothing has been disturbed since His Majesty's disappearance."

"Thanks," I said, not bothering to hide my sarcasm, then approached the balcony.

The balcony faced west over the sea, affording an excellent view of the brilliant sunset. Pink lined the horizon, and orange caught on the clouds above, then faded to a lighter blue etched with the green rivers of the radiant winds. This room was high up on a cliff and positioned over the sea, so the wind was cold and biting, and I had little in the way of shelter from it. As gooseflesh spread over my skin, I set discomfort aside and scanned the foreboding cliff below us and the sheer walls of the Laurel Palace to either side. Having seen Xaron and Talan at work before, I knew wardens were capable of incredible acrobatics. Yet ascending this wall seemed beyond even the most skilled warden. Even they had to have occasional handholds. Though the stories told of other abilities like walking the Pyrthae, I dismissed them as legend. If such things were possible, the restriction in the Four Realms on channeling likely meant such abilities were beyond any living warden's reach.

I discovered another barrier to entry when my gaze fell to the turrets on the island below. While a palace mounted on a cliff above the sea would ordinarily be vulnerable to naval attacks, the Laurel Palace was sheltered by a narrow island just off the shore. The guard towers built there would no doubt have eyes on the Despot's rooms at all times. Even if someone did manage to ascend the walls, they'd be spotted by half a dozen different men.

Unless, of course, those guards were no longer loyal to one they were supposed to protect.

Stepping back inside, I approached Jaxas. "Have you questioned the guards stationed that night? On the towers and outside the door?"

He frowned. "Yes. They reported seeing the Despot step out on the balcony for a moment, then step back within. Nothing else."

They were lying. The night of Asileia's Ascension, Nikias had told me that an honor had overheard the guards talk about arguing and a sound like snapping fire from within the room. More had transpired than the laurel guards had admitted to their Archon, or perhaps than Jaxas had admitted to us.

I closed my eyes, thinking it over. I heard the other three in the room gather closer, but they didn't speak, and I didn't look at them. Only when the pieces began to fall into place did I open my eyes again. My friends and the Archon stood waiting.

"I think we should close the doors," I said quietly, "and talk among ourselves."

The Archon studied me with an inscrutable look, then gestured to Chiri by the door. "Please, Chiri, if you could give us a moment alone."

The honor looked aghast. "In here, my Archon? There are restless pyr still astir."

"We'll be perfectly fine, I'm sure."

With one last disapproving look, Chiri pressed shut the doors.

Jaxas turned back to me. "What do you make of this?" he asked quietly.

"Much is uncertain. But we do know some things. Things that can't wait to be discussed any longer."

I stared at the Archon, and he met my gaze unflinchingly, as impassive as before. I continued. "What remains unknown is how the Despot was killed, if he even was killed."

Xaron's brow creased, but he remained silent. Nomusa looked less surprised. She, like I, must have worked it out as we looked around his quarters.

I gestured around us. "There don't appear to be any signs of struggle, which might mean any number of things. He might have been pushed from the balcony. Or maybe he was killed and his body smuggled out. For the moment, we'll set the matter aside. We can't draw conclusions until we know more."

Jaxas's facade cracked for a moment, a flicker of curiosity crossing his thin features. "Go on."

"About who might have done it, we know more, including some of the connections and motives behind the players." I shifted from one foot to the other, unable to completely contain my nervousness. The accusations I was about to level might have grave consequences if Jaxas wasn't the man I thought he was.

He seemed to sense my hesitancy. "I know this is a delicate matter, Airene. You have my word, you won't be punished on account of suspicions alone."

I noticed that didn't preclude consequences. Yet I found myself speaking nonetheless. "We have reason to suspect Archmaster Kyros Brighteyed in Myron's disappearance, as well as First Laurel Lykos. Not only were they both some of the first to enter the Despot's quarters, but they have also displayed suspicious behavior in the time since."

I told Jaxas of how I now saw Lykos's investigation into the Valemish temple as a sham, a show for a false trail. The loyalty I'd sensed in the First Laurel had to be loyalty to someone else, someone he thought he owed greater fealty to than the Wreaths. I also explained how while the laurel guards had reported one thing, the honors had heard them speak of another, and how the guards mounted on the island across must have seen something of what occurred on the balcony. The Archon didn't make any motion of agreement or disagreement but simply listened in silence.

Then I explained the Archmaster's involvement, including the disturbing rumors of Kyros gathering and training Acadians to use their attunement to fight. I also explained our interpretation of Hilarion's supposed assassination attempt at the Ascension, and how Kyros was the closest other warden, and how he might have set the man up.

At this point, Jaxas spoke just one word. "Why?"

I drew in a breath. I felt lightheaded with the implications of these revelations, but I'd said this much. There was only one way to proceed.

"Kyros must be associated with the Manifest, perhaps even the leader of it. It's said the Visage of the Wyvern claims to be a warden and has built his image to seem that way."

"Kyros as the Visage himself," Jaxas mused. He seemed thoughtful. "And do you have suspicions as to why he might do this?"

"Power," Xaron spoke up. "You don't have to listen to him for long to see a man like him chafes at chains."

The Archon glanced at Xaron, then looked back to me. "Then you believe Archmaster Kyros to be an enemy of the state. That he seeks to destabilize Oedija through the organization of a dissident movement, the assassination of our leader, and the re-militarization of wardens within the Acadium."

I hesitated, glancing at both Xaron and Nomusa. When I saw my own belief mirrored back to me, I nodded.

"And what of the Despoina?" he asked.

I saw in his minute expressions how closely he'd kept this question. How much he feared its answer.

I shook my head. "She wishes for power and significance and seeks to expand her position. But I do not believe her capable of her father's disappearance." I hesitated. "That is, I do not believe she has the ability to execute it as quietly and smoothly as it has been accomplished."

Jaxas nodded gravely as if he understood my unspoken sentiment. Nevertheless, relief shone in his eyes. "I will take these thoughts into consideration. Is there anything else? For Chiri's sake, I would not wish to overstay our welcome."

Xaron, Nomusa, and I shared a look. I almost asked for a moment to speak among ourselves, but before I could, Xaron forged ahead. "We do have one more thing to say, Archon. You have an enemy whom you've ignored for far too long."

Nomusa's eyes widened, mirroring my own reaction. But the Archon only wore a small, sad smile.

"Yes, I suspect I have," he murmured.

Xaron took it as a sign to continue. "The Manifest plan to overthrow the demotism. I saw the war map for myself, Archon. As you said, Kyros and his lackeys want to destabilize you and the Despoina, then take over when Avvad invades from the south."

A pregnant silence filled the room. "Then you are saying," Jaxas said calmly, "that not only have we ignored a threat within our nation, but a threat from without. And that we must deal with both immediately. Is that correct?"

Xaron still wore his determination as armor, but his eyes flickered to me. I said reluctantly, "We believe them to both be significant threats. The sooner they are dealt with, the better for all."

Jaxas nodded once more. "This, too, will be taken into consideration." As if we hadn't just announced the impending demise of Oedija, he gestured politely toward the doors. "You may take your leave now."

Xaron and Nomusa started to comply, and the Archon turned away, but I stayed where I was.

"And when can we expect your decision?" I asked. "A significant Manifest gathering is occurring tomorrow night. It might be best if a course of action was decided by then."

Jaxas glanced over his shoulder. "As far as I'm aware, when the Order was still intact, Verifiers of Truth did not determine the demotism's policy."

The rebuke was no more than I deserved. Even as a nominally appointed Verifier, why should I, not even a citizen in my own right, question the Archon? I flushed but didn't look away. I almost confessed the real motivation behind my urgency. But if I admitted my brother was held hostage, he might question my motives and conclusions. I held my tongue and curtly bowed.

The Archon barely seemed to notice as we exited, but stared out over the balcony into the coming twilight.

CHAPTER TWENTY-THREE

RUDE AWAKENING

It is uncanny, what happens to a warden's mind when they are forged into a Shepherd. Not even the honors are so servile as they. It is as if another occupies their mind, moves their limbs, governs their thoughts…

- Tribune Yalissa before the Demos Council; 1071 SLP

He won't do anything," Xaron muttered as we descended the staircase from the Despot's quarters and headed back to our rooms.

"We did all we could," Nomusa said firmly. "And we will continue to do all we can."

"This isn't over," I said, almost to myself.

By the time we reached the chambers, my stomach was rumbling again, and I convinced Xaron to go with me to the feast hall. Nomusa decided to retire early, claiming to have little appetite after the meeting. Xaron and I ate our fill of what remained from that night's dinner and chatted of menial things, even as my mind wandered back to the many problems weighing me down.

They pressed in closer when we returned to our rooms. As I lay down, I thought of Talan, who no doubt worked tirelessly to learn all he could of the Manifest and Linos's whereabouts. I hoped he would be able to get in contact if he learned anything. I also remembered with a start that Corin hadn't had word from the rest of us in days. I was failing as a friend as well as a sister. I turned on my side and clutched the blankets close, trying to banish the guilt and fears that hounded me.

They chased me into dreams, where fragments of the day and night before floated about me. The faces of the Seeker guards with their bright, violet tatu. The flashes of channeled radiance and waves of kinesis bursting around me. I suddenly found myself running, fleeing the broken memories.

"Flee," a boy's whisper sounded in my ear.

I jerked my head around, but I saw and felt nothing but mist.

The whisper came in my other ear. "Flee, Airene. He has his claws in you."

I whipped my head around, terror making the world around me pulse. Then I saw it. The creature emerged from the fog in hazy detail. The face of a lizard loomed dozens of cubits tall and looked as if it was made of smoke. Its mouth gaped as it swam through the dream toward me.

"He feeds," the boy's voice said, fear etched into his voice. "He comes."

"Who?" I yelled as I ran. My feet carried me nowhere. Abruptly, the ground was stolen from under me, and I ran on light and air. I glanced over my shoulder and saw the lizard's forked tongue dart out, tasting the air. Tasting for me.

"Flee, Airene," the whisper finch murmured. "Taozu comes."

The lizard's maw made the world black behind me. I ran, but not fast enough. I felt the mouth closing, the long, sharp teeth blocking escape—

I jerked awake, sweating and breathing hard. For a moment, I lay there with my heart racing. The dream had already started to fade, the logic of it unraveling as the day pressed in through the windows. I shook my head and rubbed at the aching in my temples. As if I didn't have enough to worry about when awake, my mind had to invent terrors in my sleep as well.

Pushing away the fragmenting memories of the dream, I rose and went to the huge closet in the room. I was relieved to find that Nikias had supplied chitons for my wardrobe. Selecting a dark green robe, I dressed and resolved to ask the steward about obtaining a tunic and trousers as well. I blinked as I realized again how swiftly I was adjusting to someone else providing for me. I shook my head and planned instead to buy them myself as soon as I could find a moment — and the coin — to do so.

Shouting from just outside my door jolted me from my thoughts. My heart began hammering once again. Had Lykos and his guards come for us? Jaxas had said he would protect us, but I didn't know whether he actually could or not. I pressed my ear to the door and listened to the shouting. Xaron's voice was distinct from the rest. Without strapping on sandals or fixing my tousled hair, I unlocked the door, wrenched it open, and spilled into the hallway.

If my heart had hammered before, now it thundered. Three cowled men in aqua robes stood before Xaron's open door, manacles trailing from their raised hands. My friend must have been just within, for I heard him shout, "I swear by all the gods, I'll attack if you come in here!"

I stared, unmoving. I'd had nightmares of this happening in Canopy. But with everything that had been occurring, I never thought they'd catch up to Xaron here. I saw how stupid I'd been now. We hadn't stopped investigating the Despoina, not from the way Feiyan saw it. And now she'd carried through on her threat.

"Hold!" I snapped, marching up to the three. The Shepherds looked around at me with shadowed eyes. If I'd hoped to cow them, I was disappointed, for I saw no fear in their eyes. They were hollow, emotionless pits that seemed to stare through me.

The Shepherd in the middle answered me. "Another Finch," he said with a thin smile.

"Stay back, Airene!" Xaron shouted from around the doorway.

The Shepherd continued as if he hadn't been interrupted. "But you do not sing as pretty of a song as this one. Stand back, foolish girl."

Suddenly, it felt as if I hit a wall. My body smarted from the impact, but I tried not to let it show. I knew one of them must have formed a wall from kinesis — the one closest to me, if his subtle gesture was any indication. They could easily do more if they had half a mind to.

My body trembled with fear, but I couldn't abandon him. "Xaron is a Verifier under the protection of Archon Jaxas Wreath. I don't know what you think he did, but you'd better take it up with the Archon if you're going to try arresting him."

The Shepherd laughed without mirth. "I don't need the Archon's permission to dispose of ferals."

I forced an astonished look. "Xaron? A warden? You must be japing." I jabbed my finger at the doorway. "I've lived with him for six years. I think I'd know if he was a feral."

"And you would tell us, I suppose?" There was a glint to the warden's eyes. "We have ways of knowing, I assure you, Finch."

I had as much effect as I'd expected. Yet despite the Shepherd's confidence, something held him back, for none of the enforcers moved into the room. From all I'd heard of their abilities and what I'd seen of Xaron's fighting, I didn't doubt that they could handily take him down. But they didn't know that. Perhaps they were proceeding cautiously, waiting for an opportunity to present itself, or hoping to convince Xaron to yield peacefully. Or perhaps they were waiting for permission from someone.

Whatever the truth, I knew I had to keep trying. "You take commands from Tribune Vusumuzi, do you not? It just so happens that we know each other well. How about we call him over and see what he thinks about Xaron being a warden?"

There — a glimmer of uncertainty in their postures. The two silent Shepherds exchanged glances, while the middle one continued to stare at me. "Tribune Vusumuzi need not weigh in on clear matters like these," he said.

Before I could respond, he spasmed. One of his eyelids twitched, then a corner of his mouth. The twitching spread. All along the Shepherd's body, his muscles jerked until he could barely stand upright. I watched in horrified fascination as he collapsed to the ground. His companions looked down at him, but made no move to provide aid.

I looked between the two still standing, wondering who to address next, and what had caused the reaction in the first. "Do either of you want to countermand Tribune Vusumuzi?" I asked them impetuously.

They didn't look at me, but stared into Xaron's room. Neither of them fell to the ground incapacitated, though the one closest to me negated his wall of kinesis. Emboldened, I took another step forward. The closest Shepherd's head snapped toward me.

"We await his judgment," he said in a hoarse whisper.

Just then, I heard footsteps hurrying down the hall.

"Hold!" Vusu's voice echoed from the corridor. Trailing after him was the clerk from the Tribunal, clutching a binder of vellum to her chest.

"Hold!" the Tribune repeated. His forehead shone with sweat, but he wasn't out of breath. Vusu stared calmly around him, eyes pausing on me for a moment before settling on one of the Shepherds. "Explain what is occurring."

The Shepherd closest to the Tribune pointed into the room. "We were told a feral had taken up residence in this room by the honor of a Low Consul. We came here to see if it was true. We know this man, Xaron, to be attuned to the Pyrthae. We were executing the detainment protocol when you arrived."

Vusu glanced at the collapsed Shepherd. "He tried to disobey again," he said, his words more a statement than a question.

"Yes," the same Shepherd answered.

The Tribune sighed and walked around the Shepherds to stand next to me, glancing into Xaron's room as he passed. "I apologize, Airene. But I must believe them. Your friend Xaron is a warden." He shook his head. "I know this must be distressing to you."

Frustration and despair washed through me. "You can't take Xaron away. Whatever else he is, he's a Verifier under Archon Jaxas's protection."

"I'm afraid that is beside the point here," the Tribune said almost gently. "Wardens are not allowed outside the Acadium's influence, nor even their compound, besides the masters. This is the way it has to be. For the good of all."

"You don't understand," I said, desperation tinging my words. "I need Xaron for the task you set before me. Things are going on here, things I can't even begin to tell you about, that could affect all of us." My mind whirled, searching for the answer. "At least discuss it with Jaxas. Perhaps you can work out a compromise."

Vusu glanced toward Xaron's doorway for a long moment. "Perhaps," he said slowly. "he could stay here for a day or so."

Hope surged inside me; I didn't dare speak.

"It does not seem your friend would go willingly, as matters stand," Vusu continued, "so it is small as far as concessions go. But I can promise you this much: no Shepherd or any person under Tribunal authority will seek to arrest Xaron for a day and a night."

It was a relief, if a small one. But even as I took Vusu at his word, a colder part of me wondered why he would grant us this favor. Even as Verifiers, who were we that he would bend the law for us? I didn't dare question him on it though. I couldn't afford to have him revoke the reprieve.

I bowed to the Tribune and turned back to the room. "Xaron, did you hear that?"

"Yes." His reply was terse. Evidently, he hadn't relaxed at the Tribune's words.

"Thank you." I bowed to Vusu again.

Vusu gave me a small smile. "I must keep Shepherds here to watch over him, but as I've said, they will not enter for at least a day. And you will know beforehand if they intend to."

He gave a small bow, then turned away. Not knowing what else to say, I stared at his retreating back down the hall, the clerk following once again on his heels.

CHAPTER TWENTY-FOUR

PREPARED

The underclass outnumber the honors. Composed of plebeians too poor to be considered citizens, they are miners, cooks, sailors, and more. The underclass are often the first to feel hardships of natural disasters like drought, for patricians keep their honors fed, while plebs must care for themselves.

- Oedija: A History; by Acadian Helene, Master Historian; 1167 SLP

Though Vusu had left, the Shepherds remained where they were, two standing and the third twitching on the ground. Turning my mind from one inscrutable mystery to another, I considered them. I'd never been in such close contact with Shepherds. Now, I saw the strangeness that people spoke of. They acted with inhuman rigidity, and seemed physically incapable of disobeying a command from their Tribune. And that was to say nothing of the way they spoke and stared with those empty eyes. It reminded me of Talan's theory, that Shepherds were yoked in much the same way that the Avvadin Imperium controlled their elite warriors, the Damask Esir — by using a pyr to forge a bond that compelled them to obedience.

That knowledge and what I'd just witnessed of their rigid loyalty were enough to renew my courage. I took a deep breath and started forward. The closest Shepherd immediately gave me a sharp look. "You should not enter," he said in his hoarse voice.

"But I will." I stepped around him, tense, but they let me pass through the doorway unimpeded.

As I entered the room, the sight of my friend almost brought laughter and tears at the same time. Xaron was clad in nothing but underwraps. His lithe muscles were still tensed with his hands slightly raised, no doubt ready at any moment to channel. His gaze was hard, but I could see the strain of maintaining his vigilance from the shiver that ran through his body.

I walked up slowly to him and placed my hands on his wrists, pushing his hands down. "You have to relax."

He resisted for a moment, his eyes never leaving the Shepherds in the doorway. "I can't," he said through clenched teeth. "I need to be ready." The shiver ran through him again. "Shepherds, Aire. They're actually here."

"I know," I said, guilt rising higher inside me. "But you need to stop channeling, Xaron. They can't disobey Vusu, and he gave his word that they won't enter until tomorrow."

Xaron held on for a moment longer, then sighed and let his arms fall. He didn't relax, however, until he slouched out of sight of the doorway. "Close the door. I don't want them staring at me with those dead eyes."

I obliged, turning back after the door was closed and locked.

"And, er… if you could grab my clothes…"

With a small smile, I handed him a white tunic with a vibrant yellow coat and tan trousers. It seemed Nikias had paid attention to Xaron's style as well as his measurements.

Looking away until he dressed, Xaron drew my attention back with a touch on the wrist. "What do I do, Aire?" he asked miserably. He glanced back at the window opposite of the door. "Try to escape while I might still have a chance?"

"They'll chase you down. Vusu's command won't protect you then." I shook my head. "We should at least wait until Vusu speaks with Jaxas. Perhaps something will come of it."

Xaron's expression was drawn, the doubt on his face a mirror to my own, yet I tried not to let it show. Perhaps all we could do now was think of other things and forget the things we couldn't change.

"Where is Nomusa?" I asked him.

He shrugged. "You think I know? I woke to those three banging on my door. Talk about a rude awakening."

"At least they knocked." I gave him a weak smile. "I suppose I'll have to go find her. And hunt down Jaxas as well. The sooner we get this sorted out, the better." I thought of a few other things we needed to sort out as well. With the Manifest gathering tonight, we couldn't afford any delays in our planning.

Xaron seemed to read my mind. "Go. I'll appreciate you talking to them, but don't worry on my account. You have plenty of other worries besides me."

"Of course I'm going to worry about you," I said, aghast. "Besides, you're only in this position because of me."

"I accepted that this might happen, remember? This isn't your fault. Stop trying to put all the responsibility on your shoulders, Airene. You can't control everything."

I smiled wanly. "But you know I still have to try." I pulled him into a sudden hug. He must have stolen a bath somewhere in the past couple days, for his hair smelled faintly of olives. "Everything will be okay," I whispered, as much to myself as him.

"I know."

I broke the embrace and stepped away. His warm touch lingered on my arms as he let go. I smiled and tried to fight back the sadness at leaving him there, the wolves howling at his door.

"I'll be back as soon as I can," I promised him.

"I'll be here. Unless I'm not." He gave me a rueful smile.

"You'd better be."

I turned and left, marching between the Shepherds without a sideways glance. Then, stopping by my room only to gather my sandals and a tie for my hair, I went off in search of an honor. Finding one outside of the dining hall, I convinced her to lead me to the Archon and followed her down the familiar path to the palace gardens. We headed to a copula that projected off the palace to hang over thin air. The Archon stood staring out over the sea, strong winds tousling his short, curly hair. At least my own messy tresses wouldn't look amiss.

Thanking the honor, I approached him. "Archon Jaxas."

"Airene. I've been waiting for you."

He gestured for me to come forward, and I approached cautiously to stand by his side. Perhaps it was the wind catching his voice, but he sounded strangely distant.

Jaxas continued to stare out over the sea in silence for a long moment. "Why did they come here?" he finally said.

It took me a second to understand whom he was referencing. "Our ancestors?"

He nodded absently. "Why leave instead of fight whatever threatened them? And the gods who were said to lead them — how could they so easily abandon their home?" He shook his head. "It makes me wonder. Are there some threats out there so great, so terrible, that nothing can stand before them?"

Perhaps it was the wind that drew my skin into gooseflesh. Or perhaps it was the memory of being chased by the giant beast from my dream, and the whisper finch telling me to flee. But superstition would gain us nothing now. "With all due respect, Archon, the threats that face us are not so grave as to call for that. We know more or less what they are. Now we must stand and fight."

"So you say." He finally looked at me, and I saw that his eyes were nearly as empty as the Shepherds'. "Yet how are we to fight with no army and no authority?"

Fear gripped me. I forced myself to ask the question, though I suspected I didn't want to hear the answer. "What did the Council say?"

His eyes fell to his hands, knuckles white from gripping the limestone banister. "As they said before. That the Manifest movement is unsustainable, and that it must soon buckle in on itself as its food and coin start to run dry. That raising the taxoi and attacking our own people would fan the flames, not dampen them, and might lead to a city-wide rebellion." His eyes slid over to meet mine. "And that you and your associates are to continue your investigations into the former Despot's death and present to the Council what you have discovered on the morrow."

My eyes narrowed as I studied the Archon. "What do they expect by then? That I'll give them a convenient suspect that they can present before the people and call the issue closed?"

"Not even that much. The Low Consuls much prefer keeping the truth of Myron Wreath's disappearance behind closed doors. All they want are reassurances that no further harm will come to the Despoina."

I shook my head in disgust. "And if I tell them the Manifest is behind it?"

"Then I am sure they will call you a liar and throw you out onto the streets, never to seek your services again. At best."

I considered the options before us. It hurt me to say the words, but I knew I had to. "Jaxas, I won't lie about this. There's far too much at stake for me to deceive the Council, no matter how much they delude themselves." I paused. "Your pardon, Archon. I did not mean to speak so harshly."

"You did," Jaxas observed drily, "as I mean to agree with you. And as you mean to help in any way you can, so do I seek to help Oedija."

I didn't mention the limits of his power. As the Archon, he was the representative for the Despoina in the Conclave. But the Laurel Palace had far less power than the Council. He could not call armies, could not command the city guard, and had no control over the Tribunal or Shepherds. All he had was influence, the limited resources of the Wreaths, and the laurel guards. Not nearly enough to dismantle the Manifest, much less deal with the Imperium.

I wanted to thank him, but all I could do was look away. I felt nearly as sick to my stomach as when I'd entered the Despot's quarters. "What do we do?"

His voice was surer than mine. "Only what we can."

The same thing I'd told Xaron, I noticed. It brought me back to another urgent matter. "Jaxas, have you spoken with Vusu? Something has happened."

He blinked at the abrupt change in topic. "Yes. We just met."

I turned to face the Archon fully. "And?"

He drew in a slow breath. "Verifier Airene, I cannot countermand the mission of the Shepherds, nor will I. I am sure your friend Xaron is not a criminal, nor a danger to our nation. But that doesn't change that he's a warden." He hesitated, then amended, "A feral warden. To make an exception for him would be to throw away a hundred years of institutions that protect against Tyrant Wardens rising again."

My heart pounded hard. "How long does he have before they take him?" I asked quietly.

"The day and night Vusu promised. Beyond that…" Jaxas shook his head. "I'm sorry. There's nothing more I can do."

A dozen arguments sprang to mind. I grasped at the least offensive of them. "Then don't let them kill him. Let him become an Acadian."

Jaxas shook his head again. "He's far too old to be introduced there, and if I read him correctly, far too willful. He would never submit to a cage, however gilded."

He had only met Xaron a couple of times, but he'd noted his disposition accurately. I gritted my teeth, the other arguments falling to pieces before me. No matter how sympathetic he might be, Jaxas wasn't going to budge. Xaron and I would have to make other arrangements.

"I know he's your friend, Airene," he said softly. "But there is nothing you can do for him now."

I didn't want to speak of it anymore. "Then let us do what we can. What do you intend to do about the Manifest gathering tonight?"

Jaxas considered me again for a long moment. "What I believe you intended to do no matter what I instructed. I will send you and Verifier Nomusa to be my eyes and ears there and report back what occurs."

Reconnaissance. Perilous forces were moving within and against our city, and all our leaders intended to do was watch and listen. I tried to push down my anger. Not only would it ill serve me, but I knew it was misdirected. Jaxas acted as much as he believed himself able. I could hardly expect others to be as rash as myself. The knowledge did little to lessen my frustration.

I gave a perfunctory bow. "Then we will make ready to leave this night. Where may I find your steward? I have requests to make of him."

Jaxas's eyes narrowed, but if he was suspicious of my capitulation, he didn't voice it. "At this time of day, he will likely be in the larders, scribbling in his ledger. But I should give you one last detail for your mission tonight. Another will go with you, someone who I think will be useful for navigating the Seeker compound. He will meet you in the atrium at the seventh turn of the evening."

I wondered who it was, but only nodded. Jaxas didn't seem willing to tell me, and I wasn't going to beg. "If I have your leave?" I requested stiffly.

The Archon sighed. "You may go."

I turned and walked away.

"And Verifier Airene?"

Reluctantly, I turned back. "Yes?"

His eyes bored into me. "Remember: only do what you can, and no more. I would not lose an asset so newly gained."

I clenched my jaw so hard my teeth hurt. All I could manage was a sharp nod before I left the gardens.

———

I found Nikias in the larders and requested a tunic and trousers from him, despite my earlier resolution to buy them myself. At this point, I wasn't even sure if I'd be allowed to leave the palace without permission, and with all I had to do, I didn't want to waste time trying. Nikias ungraciously complied and said the clothes would be found and brought to my room before I departed that evening, evidently having foreknowledge of our trip that night. I thanked him and left.

Despite worry gnawing away my own appetite, I knew Xaron would be starving. It was the least I could do to bring him food. Visiting the kitchens, I soon bore a platter of egg tarts, flatbread, spiced meats, and fruit to his room. The Shepherds were still standing before the door when I arrived, including the one who had earlier collapsed. I faintly made out Nomusa's voice from within. My heart in my throat, I maneuvered my way around the immovable Shepherds to open the door.

My friends spun around at my entrance, tensing until they recognized me. That didn't lighten their expressions, however.

"Where have you been?" Nomusa demanded. Her robes today were a deep turquoise with a low dip in her neckline. As before, silver jewelry glinted across her body.

"Doing what I can," I retorted, carrying the platter over to the bedside table and setting it down. "Which is apparently little more than an honor."

Xaron sat on the bed and reached over, his movements sharp and nervous. "At the moment, that's the best I can hope for," he said morosely.

I took a tart and studied my friend as I chewed. His mood had only worsened in my absence. What I had to tell him wasn't going to make him feel any better.

I sucked in a breath and dove into my conversation with Jaxas and our excursion that night. As predicted, Xaron's mood turned as black as the Lighted Sea in a storm.

"So you'll leave me here," he said flatly. "Alone."

"We don't have a choice," I replied in a low voice. I remembered how keen Eltris's hearing was and worried that the Shepherds' might be as sharp through some trick of channeling. "We have to get you help, Xaron. Finding Talan is our only chance."

Xaron snorted and bit savagely into a skewer of meat. "As if that will help," he muttered.

Ignoring him, I looked at Nomusa. "Do you at least agree?"

She considered for a moment. "Yes. We have to do what is expected of us, and we have to get you help. Airene and I won't be of any use here even if they do come."

"They won't until we return. Jaxas and Vusu both assured me." Still, I couldn't help but fear it was all a ruse. But even if it was, I saw little else that we could do. Xaron couldn't stay on guard all night.

He turned his head aside. "Then go. I'll be fine."

"But if they do come," I continued. "You still have your lodestone, don't you?"

"Of course."

"Give us a signal. Alright?"

Xaron nodded, though he didn't meet my eyes. I turned to the door, yet I couldn't help glancing back at Xaron, who watched us with hooded eyes from the bed. I couldn't find the right words to say, so I gave him an uncertain smile before leaving him in the room that had become his cell.

CHAPTER TWENTY-FIVE

THE GATHERING

Next are the citizens of Oedija, those who own a plot of land of at least twenty-five cubits on each side, and have resided within Oedijan borders for two consecutive years, or have family members who have resided here for eleven consecutive seasons. These are often successful artisans, merchants, as well as many of our public servants. They often have little significant family wealth, but live comfortably, elect their Servants, and vote on measures of law brought before the public.

- Oedija: A History; by Acadian Helene, Master Historian; 1167 SLP

The seventh turn of the evening took its time in arriving. Even with the necessary preparations that Nomusa and I undertook, it felt as if the beads in the sandglasses mounted in the palace halls fell ever slower, each turn lasting longer than the one before.

Finally, the seventh turn was announced with the long tolling of the bells. Both Nomusa and I were dressed in tunics and trousers, and she looked as common as I'd ever seen her. Knives were secreted against the small of our backs and lashed under our sleeves, though I knew they'd be small use against Seeker wardens. True to his word, Jaxas met us in the soaring chamber of the atrium soon after the toll. His usual line of honors trailed him, but it was the figure next to him that drew my attention. A thin, gangly boy with dark hair that hung in front of his eyes, he wore a frown like it was a shadow he couldn't shake.

"Verifiers Airene and Nomusa," the Archon said as they approached, "here is the accomplice I mentioned will be accompanying you. Meet the latest man to bear the name Hilarion."

I couldn't help but stare at the boy. He sulkily met my gaze, then turned his eyes aside.

"Archon," I said carefully, "what made you think his attendance is a good idea? He's still half a boy."

Jaxas acknowledged it with a dip of his head. "Of this, I am well aware. Yet you don't become the Despoina's Hilarion without having certain commendable qualities."

Studying the boy again, I thought it unlikely that those extended beyond his attunement to the Pyrthae. "Which is why he is by her side now, I suppose."

"Ah..." The Archon's eyes shifted. "She has been a bit... wary since her Ascension. But truly, I was not sure you had devised a reason for your attendance of the gathering. Hilarion provides the perfect excuse."

"A reason? Half of Brinecoast and Thys will be in attendance. It's true that guards checked my companions and me at the compound gate, but that was at night, and not during a gathering."

"Perhaps not. But consider: if the Manifest worship the idea of every man and woman channeling, and you bring them a warden, who do you think you'll get to talk to? Where might you gain access?"

I met Jaxas's gaze. We both knew what offering up Hilarion might mean for the boy. Nomusa's hardening eyes told me she guessed as well.

The Archon turned. "The guards will be watching for your return."

With that, he left, his entourage following after, leaving the morose boy alone with Nomusa and me. I addressed him. "Did he even ask if you wanted to come?"

I didn't expect him to answer, but Hilarion looked up sharply through his bangs. "That's the joke no one seems to get," he said darkly. "No one ever asks."

I exchanged a glance with Nomusa. Our long walk promised to be longer still.

———

As predicted, the journey to deme Thys was not wholly enjoyable. The events of the past span and my role in them weighed on me, and my Verifier medallion felt heavier with each step. It did not make it any easier that I was sore and tired as well. Yet I had to carry on — for Linos's sake, and Xaron's. Deep depths of the 'Thae, I had to go on for the polis itself now, as strange a thought as that was.

I led my small party to deme Bazaar. When he realized we weren't headed straight for the gate outside the city, Hilarion stopped. "Where are we going?"

"I'm thirsty," I lied. "We're visiting a favorite tavern of ours."

The boy scowled. "Fine," he muttered, following again. "As usual, no one values my time."

I turned away from him to hide my eye roll, and Nomusa smiled briefly. Neither expression went unnoticed, for when I glanced back at him, Hilarion's frown had deepened.

The tavern was far from my favorite, but I still felt easier as the Ignorant Intellectual came into sight. If anyone could help with the problems facing us, it was Talan.

"Wait out here," I instructed the boy. "You're too young for spirits."

He crossed his arms and leaned against the wall, heedless of the grime that dripped down it. As Nomusa and I entered, I wondered if he wouldn't just run away. What bound any Hilarion to stay loyal? This boy didn't have the dead look of the Shepherds. Strange that a jester should have more freedom than his enforcers.

The Intellectual was fuller and noisier than I'd seen it before, though the clientele was the same shady stock as usual. I slipped between two men to get to the bar, which was crowded with men calling for drinks. "Watch it," one of them snapped at us. A sharp look from Nomusa made him scowl and turn away. I tried flagging down the barkeep unsuccessfully for a few minutes until I finally reached over and tugged at his sleeve. The normally mild-mannered man looked around with irritation, though when he recognized me, some measure of it faded.

"Ah, you," he said, his eyes flitting to either side.

"Yes. I'll have my usual, please."

He stared at me for a long moment, ignoring all the other men shouting for his attention. I wondered if he hadn't heard me and was about to repeat myself when he responded. "I'm afraid we're out. Come back some other time."

I watched him as he turned to help others, uncomprehending. "A chalice!" I shouted stubbornly after him. "You know what it's filled with!"

He turned back with fire in his eyes. "I told you, we're out!" He resolutely ignored me as he began filling his patrons' drinks.

I knew a hopeless cause when I saw one. Pushing away from the bar, Nomusa and I forced our way back out of the tavern. Her eyes were full of questions, but Hilarion turned toward us as we exited. So I shook my head, mouthing to her, *Later*.

As we headed for the gate, I worked through what Talan's absence meant. Either he was unavailable as he'd never been before, or the barkeep no longer worked for him. Neither scenario boded well. I knew Talan could take care of himself, but he wasn't the most cautious of men. And when dealing with the Manifest, I worried he'd bitten off more than he could chew, especially after he'd killed their wardens and guards.

On the other hand, his meddling might have finally gotten him kicked out of the Underguild. Or his network could be eroding, just as mine seemed to be amid all these sudden changes. Even with a Guildmaster as his advocate, he was not insulated from punishment. Particularly if the Underguild was aligned with the Manifest.

I shook my head. Uncertainty haunted me at every turn. I didn't know how I would tell him of Xaron's plight. With no other choice, I carried on, hoping something would come to me, and soon.

We reached the Sandglass gate where a swell of people waited to exit the inner city. Pulled from my thoughts, I stared around in mute amazement. I had known the Manifest movement was large, but I hadn't realized it extended to this many people outside of the compound.

"*Faresh,*" Nomusa swore under her breath.

I glanced at her. "At least we won't need an excuse."

Hilarion scowled. "Then I'll return to the palace."

"No," I replied sharply. "The Archon sent you with us. Stay close by."

He shot me a black look, but he stayed with us as we wove through the crowd toward the gate.

It took well over a half a turn before the city guard waved us through. He and his comrades looked harried and irritable and didn't bother examining anyone passing by. Such laxness made me feel uneasy, even if it aided us for the moment.

Once through, I clung to Nomusa and Hilarion as Nomusa forged a path through the crowd. It was only when we broke free of the reek of the masses that I could properly breathe again. "I thought there were public baths for a reason," I muttered.

"You're one to talk," Nomusa said snidely.

I considered her for a moment. A chilliness lingered between us. The trust we had forged over nearly a decade would be long in mending. I repressed a sigh and touched her arm. "Come. Whatever performance the Visage and the Dishonored have planned will probably start soon."

Nomusa nodded, then led us back into the stream of people winding toward the Manifest compound.

As we walked, I found that my errant comment had resurfaced past thoughts. Who *were* the Visage and the Dishonored? I'd given little thought to the identity of the Visage other than my suspicions of Kyros Brighteyed, and none to the Dishonored. For Kyros, it would seem a tricky balance to strike. Surely someone would have noted his crossing into the compound. Or did he have another way of reaching the Claw? Perhaps a boat lay ready to take him across Lake Thys so that his comings and goings were kept secret. Or perhaps he had some mystical means of travel.

Then there was his second-in-command, the Dishonored. I wondered what that title was supposed to mean, and why I'd had so little report of him. Wisp, the keenest of my contacts, would likely be able to tell me something, but it had been a long time since I'd been able to track her down. Perhaps it was best that I saw for myself.

The crowds were thick and crushing around us. I tried not to breathe too deeply, the air ripe with the unwashed bodies of the underclass. We twisted, tumbled, and swirled among the people like kelp in a turbulent wave. I clung to Nomusa and Hilarion, holding fast despite the boy's flinch at my touch.

It felt like an eternity before the river of people flowed through the compound, then down the hillside to the Claw, easing and spreading out. The reprieve didn't last long, as we were funneled back together at the entrance to the Wyvern's Claw.

I was somewhat distracted from my misery as the amphitheater rose around us. It had been an impressive building at night, but by the illumination of evening light, I balked at its immensity. Tier upon tier ascended above us, with row stacked on row of benches in each section. I strained to make out the people in the upper tiers. How many could those stands seat? Thirty thousand? Forty? Fifty? Easily a quarter of the population of Oedija could fit in the wooden bleachers without rubbing elbows, to mention nothing of the amphitheater floor where my companions and I stood. It defied comprehension.

But why were all these people here? No doubt for some, idle curiosity was reason enough, to see a spectacle outside their usual routine. But for the others — did they, like Linos, harbor childish dreams of claiming a warden's power? But no; I had but to look around me to see the truth. Thin children holding to their famished mothers. Men with bent backs and hollow cheeks. Famine gnawed at the polis, and those people living in the peripheries were the first to feel it. Loyalty had been bought with simple promises. *Food. Shelter. Certainty.* These were what the common people strived for, as they had not the means to strive for anything more. And these were the very things that the Conclave had failed to provide.

I found myself staring up at the sky as it drained to a bruised blue. Above us, the eleven spires of the Claw curved overhead, leaning over to almost touch each other in the center, like the long, sharp nails of a leviathan trying to scratch free a piece of the sky. The Manifest had taken a dragon for its sigil, but it seemed a swarm of locusts would have been more suitable. I did not blame those who had joined as Seekers; I could not claim to know the right or wrong of any of their situations.

But I knew that, unchecked, their hunger would consume the polis, and all of us with it.

I held onto Nomusa and Hilarion as we continued forward. Midway through, the crush of the crowd stopped moving forward and pushed in even tighter around us. I fought for room to breathe, earning scowls and halfhearted curses. I reluctantly settled into my discomfort. This didn't promise to be a pleasant event.

Hilarion yanked his wrist away and rubbed it while Nomusa pulled me close. She spoke loudly, but I could still barely hear her over the clamor of crying children and loud talking. "What happened at the Intellectual?" she asked.

I explained as best as I could. "I don't know what else to do," I concluded.

Nomusa's brow drew down in consideration, but she made no reply.

The people around us began looking toward the stage, lively chatter giving way to muttering and staring. I could barely see the stage between the heads of the people in front of me. The platform beyond was unremarkable, though the two huge braziers that were mounted on either side and threw orange, flickering light over the stage floor filled me with nervous apprehension. Only then did I remember how precarious our safety was. One tipped torch, and the whole place would go up in flames. It did little to settle my already tattered nerves.

A roar cascaded from the stage, deafening and intoxicating. I gave a small cheer of my own to not look out of place, then cringed as lights flashed from hands around me. What caused them, I couldn't see.

The racket redoubled, and I strained to look past the seething mass of bodies to the stage. The dais erupted in light, and the crowd became deathly quiet. An ethereal light unmatched by a three-moon night emanated from the platform. A silhouetted figure stepped to the front.

"Brothers!" a pleasant baritone boomed over our heads, Pyrthaen-magnified. My pulse quickened. A warden, unbound by law, stood before us all and openly used their power.

"Sisters!" the man continued to shout. "Sons and daughters! Fathers, mothers, friends, and neighbors! We gather here not as individuals, but as a family! All of us are Seekers of the One who graces the sky above us!"

Cheering clapped like two bricks over my temples. A woman near me screamed and leaped up and down, eyes rolling into the back of her head like she were possessed. I felt my presence of mind slipping away in the crowd's emotions like a leaf in a swollen river.

"There are those who would not have us here," the man continued. "Those who would not see the common people become powerful. Well, what do we have to say to that?"

Jeers passed over like a storm, leaving me sweating with their dissatisfaction.

"No, they cannot keep us down. For we have the One's power inside of us, from the oldest gaffer to the youngest child. And it is emerging, isn't it? Soon, we will show them all who we truly are!"

When the cheers died down, the honey-voiced man continued. "Daemon-lovers, they call us. Worshippers of false gods. Cultists. But we know who we are. We are Seekers. We are the Manifest, wardens on the verge of expression. Soon, we will have our power. And with it, we will take back what is ours by right."

Silence stole over the amphitheater, tens of thousands of people hanging onto his every word. No Wreath had ever held such rapt attention. Between the heads of the people, I finally caught a glimpse of the speaker, a man swathed in robes of black. As the Visage was supposed to wear robes of white, this had to be the Dishonored. I did not see anyone holding a hand to his throat. Did that mean he was a warden himself?

"Now, we will hear from the man who led us here," the Dishonored continued. "The man who will lead us onward to our grand destiny. The man... but he is more than a man. He is half a god himself." The man fell to his knees and out of sight, yet his echoing whisper could still be heard. "The Visage of the Wyvern."

The crowd shifted, slender trees bending to a strong gust. They wondered if they, too, should kneel like the Dishonored. I clenched my teeth and hoped my pride wouldn't have to endure that.

But everyone stayed on their feet as a man in a white peplos slowly entered the stage. The brightness of his robes sharply contrasted with his skin, dark and rich like mossy earth. His face was covered with a red mask, no doubt the dragon mask I'd glimpsed in the war room.

The crowd leaned forward as he slowly stopped in the center of the stage. As he neared, the dark-robed prophet rose and stepped aside. We watched in silence as the masked man stood there, unmoving except for his head, swiveling to take us in.

Then came the fire.

CHAPTER TWENTY-SIX

THE VISAGE OF
THE WYVERN

Last are the patricians, the wealthy nobility that has persisted largely since the Lighted Passage landed on Oedijan shores. Though their political influence has waned in recent years with the rise of demotism, patricians are still the backers of most commercial ventures within the realm and own the vast majority of its wealth. On them falls the responsibility of raising the taxoi in times of war as well as leading and arming their militias against the enemy. With their significant social and commercial influence, patricians have often occupied much more than half of the seats on the Conclave, and almost all of the Demos Council.

- Oedija: A History; by Acadian Helene, Master Historian; 1167 SLP

The flames rose from the man in a spire, thin as a needle, then spun out in a thousand graceful ribbons, like ripples from a stone in a still pool. Cries of fear and panic rose as it spread closer to the crowd. I stared at the blazing cyclone, beautiful as the three full moons over a red sunset, mesmerizing as the green radiant winds painted across a midnight sky.

Then came the inferno.

Comets split off from the tornado and landed with splashes of flames on the wooden supports. The heat that washed over us was as intense as Maesos's furnace. Panic set in. People around us jostled and pushed back toward the entrance. I didn't resist the flow, but fought to keep myself from being flattened, losing Nomusa and Hilarion as the crowd swept me up. But it wasn't enough. The entrance was too small and the people too many. The flames were speeding everywhere, too fast to escape. The meaninglessness of it all, the cacophony of terror, made me want to collapse in despairing laughter.

Then came the storm.

It crashed around us like a thousand cymbals, booming like ten thousand drums. It screamed like war itself. The sky split as if it were made of porcelain. Quick as blinking, bolts of lightning pounded the ground outside the amphitheater. I ducked down with the rest, cowering, waiting for the next one to fall on my head.

"Am I so callous as this?" called a voice different from the first, a voice used to the reins of command. Somehow, it seemed familiar. "Would I kill you as frivolously as your Conclave would? As your Despoina would? As your Stratechons would?"

I risked a glance up just in time. All at once, the flames disappeared, falling away like torn strips of cloth, then dissipating into thin air. The intense heat died at once, and the cool night air crept back in. As the crowd stilled to look around in wonder, I stared with equal measures of awe and terror at the man on the stage. "Who are you?" I whispered.

"The Dragon!" shouted someone nearby. "The Dragon has come to save us!" Others took up the cry, passing it along until the amphitheater was echoing with the chant.

The Dragon. It was just another word for wyvern, yet my thoughts caught on it.

"No!" the masked man shouted, quieting the chant. "I am not the Dragon. I am he who comes before, who will usher in a new age. I am not the Dragon — *we* are the Dragon! We of the Manifest, deep in our cores, each have this power inside us! And what must you do?"

Confusion took over. The shouted answers made me laugh again. What could we do? Such power was impossible. No man should have magic like that at their fingertips. No Tyrant Warden had, nor any wardens before them. Not since the days of gods and pyr living among us had such strength existed. Nothing we did mattered; we were ants before this daemon-wrought man.

Yet even as I cowered at his power, I raged within at what he had brought to my city. A god's power he might wield, but he was still a man, with all a man's failings and flaws. Impossible as it seemed to match his might, I had to hope that this warden was fallible. *Somehow.* A smile twisted onto my face, a sliver of bitter humor growing inside me. Ridiculous to think anyone could overcome him after the display he'd just put on.

"You must rule yourselves!" the Visage finally answered his own question. "Follow me, and I will show you how. This night marks the first that we take back this city. This night, the men and women who call themselves

Low Consuls and Servants of the people will tremble, for the true citizens of Oedija rise!"

The Visage raised his arms, and the Claw lit as bright as the sun. "This night," he shouted, "each one of you will begin to become gods!"

I grinned mockingly as the crowd's cheers reached a zenith. It felt like the smile worn by a skull.

Amid the fading light, the leader of the Manifest motioned for silence. "But I do not make promises without proof. You believe without seeing. Yet how much stronger will you believe when you see one of our own has succeeded in harnessing his power?"

"Show him!" some called from the crowd. "Let us see Vessel!"

"Yes," the Visage said, gratification plain in his voice. "Yes, you know him. Some of you have seen him before. But for the rest of you..." The man in white robes extended his arm to the side. "Vessel! Attend me!"

As a slim figure in gray robes walked onto the stage, my rigid grin slid away. I couldn't see much at this distance, little more than a blond shock of hair atop an adolescent's head. But I still felt as if I'd taken a blow to the gut.

The Visage clasped the boy's shoulder as he came near. The boy didn't react, staring out over the Claw.

"This is Vessel," the Manifest leader declared. "The first of you to receive the One's grace. Vessel, show us your gift."

The boy raised a hand. From it, a plume of fire erupted and shot halfway across the amphitheater. But I wasn't watching the display. I couldn't tear my eyes away from the boy, from the fear that held my heart in a deathly grip.

The boy continued to channel radiance until the Visage said in a carrying whisper, "That is enough, Vessel." The boy obeyed immediately, cutting off the stream of flames and letting his hand fall back to his side. He was as rigidly obedient as a Shepherd. Hollow. Empty. Just as a proper vessel should be.

"You see?" the Visage said to us. "If this boy can become a warden, then any of us can. All you must do is submit yourself to the One. Submit, Seekers, and the One will work wonders through you."

The sound rose, bit by bit, as each took up the chant. First a tide, then a wave, then a tsunami flowing inexorably forward. "Dragon!" they called. "Dragon! Dragon!"

The Visage stood calmly, accepting it all, as the Dishonored joined him at his side. But I did not look at either of them. I could not peel my eyes away from the boy who stood with them. I could not help but fear that despite all my efforts, I was too late.

Too late to save my brother. Too late to save Linos.

But I didn't know for sure. And though doubt was a poor replacement for hope, I clung to it as the world reeled and tumbled around me.

———

I didn't look away from the stage until the Visage, the Dishonored, and Vessel had retreated into the eaves. Only then did I wade through the crowd to find a clear place outside the amphitheater's entrance. There I waited, stewing in my tumultuous thoughts, until I saw Nomusa dragging Hilarion in her wake. I waved and they made their way toward me.

For a few moments, we were silent as the hum of excited conversation emanated from the crowd flowing past us. Hilarion looked sulkily between us. "Can't I go back to the palace now?"

"No," I answered without looking at him. A glance at Nomusa showed my own fears reflected in her eyes. I hoped it wouldn't hold her back from what I'd resolved to do.

I motioned my two accomplices near. "Once the crowds thin out, we'll approach one of the Seeker guards."

"Why?" Hilarion asked, suspicious.

The Archon and I had shared an understanding. No doubt Jaxas Wreath had hid his intentions from the boy. "There's no time to explain," I said, bridling my impatience. "The Archon instructed you to do as I say."

"He didn't tell me to obey you," Hilarion argued. "He said to follow you here. I did that. Now it's time to go back to the palace."

He started to walk away, but Nomusa's hand snaked out and seized his wrist. "I wouldn't do that," she warned in a low voice.

The boy's eyes flashed. "Maybe you forget what I am."

Nomusa didn't loosen her grip. "And maybe you forget what happens to a rebellious Hilarion. Or didn't you attend the last Ascension?"

The boy's expression spasmed, and my gut twisted. But I knew we couldn't relent.

"Fine," he muttered. He wrested his arm from Nomusa's grasp and rubbed at his wrist. "But no more grabbing."

I nodded. "Come on. It looks like our opportunity has arrived."

Weaving through the thinning crowd, I led them over to the nearest guard, a woman with a broad face and a dark braid draped over a shoulder like a snake. Summoning all the underclass charm I could, I said cheerily, "Eleven blessings to you! If you could spare a moment—?"

"Move along," the Seeker snapped, barely looking around.

"Now, no need to—"

Her glare silenced me. "If I chatted with every pleb passing through here, this gate would still be jammed," she said. "Now move along."

I struggled to keep my expression pleasant. "I have a cousin here, Hilly, and he wants to join you. He's a war— that is, you know..."

That caught her attention. "Hand," she said to the boy.

Hilarion stepped forward and gave her his hand. After a moment of intense concentration, the guard threw it aside and scowled. "You would try and trick me? The One has clearly passed over him. Leave, before I have a mind to do worse."

"What?" I grabbed both of Hilarion's hands and understood at once. Hilarion only had his shifts on one hand, and he'd given the ordinary one to the guard. "He thinks he's a clever boy," I said apologetically and held out his other hand. "It's this one that shows his talent."

The guard eyed me suspiciously, but accepted it again. After a moment, she nodded sharply. "You should hope he isn't so cheeky with the Visage. It won't end well for him. Come, Hilly. I will show you the way. Move!" Seizing Hilarion by the wrist, she started to drag him through the crowd. I could tell the boy was tired of being towed around, but he was smart enough to go along with it. Or trusting enough. The pair moved quickly, the crowd parting for them, while Nomusa and I struggled to follow.

As they climbed the stairs to the next tier, the guard noticed us and turned back with a snarl. "Not you two fools! Just him. You did your duty bringing your cousin here. Now he's in the care of the Visage."

I thought fast. "It'd be best if we came with him. Hilly was so nervous coming here — you saw how he acted out. I'd hate to see how he'd behave if we weren't there."

"Save your air, woman. I've heard it all before. Come, boy." The guard turned back up the stairs.

"Wait!" I took the stairs two at a time after them, ignoring the guard's glare. "Let me explain! He has a condition. Falls to the ground in spells, see. I know how to hold him down so he doesn't hurt himself."

"I can hold a bucking invalid as well as any," the guard said drily. "What were you planning to do once you'd brought him here? Stay with him?" The Seeker laughed. "You're not half as special as to warrant that."

The guard turned and tugged Hilarion after her again, eliciting a muttered protest from the boy. They strode down the wooden corridor along the long curve of the amphitheater, the same way I'd travelled with Talan and Xaron two nights before.

I glanced back at Nomusa and saw she hadn't followed. "Come on!" I hissed at her. "They'll get away!"

Nomusa looked aside. "I'm not coming."

"What? What are you talking about?"

"This is going to get you killed. Me as well, if I were going with it. I won't do it, and you shouldn't either."

I didn't have time for her excuses. The guard and Hilarion were already disappearing out of sight. "Fine," I snapped. "I'll go by myself."

I turned away and ran after the pair, trying to push away fear and frustration. Though I couldn't blame Nomusa for not jumping off the brink with me, the surprise still felt as sharp as betrayal.

When I caught up with the guard and Hilarion, an edge had crept into my voice. "Fine! I'll admit it!" I called to them. "I want to see him, the Visage. I want to know him, know his might—"

"Get in his bed?" The guard gave a harsh laugh. "Not the first." She rounded on me again, all humor faded. "Listen, lady. If you don't walk back the way you came, we're going to have to settle this another way."

"And how's that?" I dared to ask.

She scowled and glanced back at the Claw's entrance, no doubt looking for reinforcements. But a glimpse behind showed no one had noticed us below, nor was anyone close enough to hear her shout over the remaining crowd.

The Seeker realized it too. "Fine," she snapped. "If you don't turn back before we reach the door at the other end, you may not leave here alive."

She continued to drag Hilarion on, and I set off after them. My throat was so dry that it was hard to swallow, but we were too close for me to give in now. I had to continue. I had to see Linos.

We reached the door, and the Seeker turned. "This is your last warning."

I crossed my arms, trying to appear more certain than I felt. "Open it. I'm not going anywhere."

"On your head." The guard knocked sharply, then leaned into the door to whisper an entry phrase. I held my breath as we waited, pushing away my doubts. Too late to turn back now.

The door opened, and a woman answered it. She was young, and might have looked comely had she cared for her appearance.

The guard spoke softly to her for a moment before pulling Hilarion forward and gesturing back to me. The woman at the door turned to study me. "Who are you?" she asked.

"Jaxale of Hull," I lied.

The woman looked about to speak, then stiffened with her mouth open. She held rigid for so long even the Seeker guard grew uncomfortable. "Honor Seda?" the guard prompted her, eyes wary.

I stared at the woman in confusion. The guard named her an honor, yet her name and features seemed Avvadin, and she lacked the shaved head and tin spiral earrings. The dissonance did nothing to ease my nerves.

The woman finally stirred. "He wishes to see you," she muttered. She stepped aside from the door, holding it open. "If you'll come with me. The boy as well."

Gooseflesh spread over my skin. The greater part of me wished to turn and flee. But as the woman led Hilarion within, the boy cast me an uneasy glance, and I knew I could do nothing but follow.

"Watch your step," the supposed honor warned us from the darkness. "If the boy wishes to channel any light, he may."

Hilarion immediately complied, a bright glow emanating from his fingertips. The sparse surroundings were revealed under the faint illumination, little changed since my recent visit. My breath came quick and shallow as we entered the hallway, approaching the door at the end. From beneath the door, light escaped from the room beyond. My heart pounded harder.

The woman Seda set a hand to the handle. "My master will see you now."

She opened the door, spilling light into the dim corridor and blinding me. I blinked and followed mutely forward. My heart threatened to escape my chest. My folly struck me in full force. But I couldn't turn back now.

The room bore scars from our battle with the Seeker wardens, wood splintered and blackened along the walls and floors, but the main elements were still intact. The map table stood with its red circles, the stage bore its wicker wood chair. But now, the chair was occupied by a man with dark skin in a white peplos. A red mask with the aspect of a dragon hung on the back of the chair. The man sat before the windows, back erect, eyes sharp and studying me. My breath hissed out as my eyes settled on him. The Visage of the Wyvern was unmasked.

And I knew him.

Recognition dulled my wits, and I could do nothing but stop in the doorway and stare at him. The Visage smiled sadly back, and I saw him as I'd known him before.

Tribune Vusumuzi.

"Please bring her closer, Seda," Vusu said with a motion. "Airene and I have much to discuss."

CHAPTER TWENTY-SEVEN

BEHIND THE MASK

You cannot pen us in. You cannot bind us to your will. We have the power of gods at our fingertips. Try to cow us with your hounds — we will strike them down. And you along with them.

- Augur Naldeia, Daemon, at her trial shortly before her execution; 1065 SLP

I stared at Vusu. He sat straight-backed on his throne. Clad in his sleeveless white peplos, his white gloves were gone, his arms and hands left bare, his tatu visible. They were the familiar vibrant blue of Nomusa's, but they extended far beyond hers, all the way up to his shoulders. They also moved before my eyes, slithering like a mass of worms along his skin. The whole of his arms composed his shifts. Even having witnessed his displays before, it was only now that I fully grasped the extent of his power. And the extent to which I'd deceived myself.

I looked away from Vusu to the stranger to his right. A man swathed in dark robes — the Dishonored, I assumed. His name suddenly made sense as I took in the shaved head and spiral earrings of an honor glimmering beneath his hood. The Dishonored nodded slowly to me, and in his blue-green speckled eyes, I sensed familiarity, as if this was not the first time we had met, though he was a stranger to me.

I thought the room otherwise empty, until Vusu, his dark eyes still on me, made a beckoning gesture. "Vessel," he said. "There is someone here I'd like you to see."

An adolescent boy stepped out from behind the throne. Gray robes clung to his thin frame, but even with the unfamiliar dress, he had the same mop of blond hair, the same nose he shared with myself and our mother.

Linos.

Many changes had been wrought upon my brother. I had to cling to the doorframe as I observed them. His blue eyes, ordinarily alive and intelligent, were dull amid the spiderweb of lavender tatu. The inked lines were jagged and erratic, not straight-edged like the designs Seekers painted onto themselves. Jagged as Thero's had been, fourteen long years before.

"What have they done to you?" I whispered.

"This must be a shock," Vusu said mildly, drawing my attention back. "I apologize for the falsities I perpetuated. But sometimes lies are necessary for the truth to be unveiled."

I didn't look at him, but continued staring at my brother. "Linos," I said, voice trembling. "Linos, look at me."

"He won't respond to that name anymore. He is Vessel now." Vusu glanced at my brother. "Vessel, tell your sister what you are."

"I am Vessel, empty in preparation for the One." His voice was monotone, eyes staring at the wall behind me.

The anger simmering beneath my fear caught fire. "Linos!" I snapped. "*Look at me!*"

Vusu held up a hand, and I flinched. I remembered the inferno that had come from those fingertips. "Calm yourself, Airene," he said softly.

His words only inflamed me further. "Why?" I demanded, glancing back at Linos, my heart rending a little more. "Why do this? He's a boy, just a boy."

Vusu shook his head. "You crave understanding in all things. To you, an unanswered question is as good as a festering wound. Soon enough, you will learn the necessity of it. But that will come in time. I have other work for you."

My emotions simmered so near the surface, I almost laughed. What else could I do when the world had become an absurdity? "You have work for me? You're too kind."

His eyes narrowed slightly, betraying his annoyance. It gave me more satisfaction than it should have. "You jest, but you will obey. Not willingly, I know all too well. Your loyalty to the realm is strong, if misguided." His gaze slid over to my brother. "But I believe your loyalty to your family is stronger, is it not?"

Rage almost stole words from me. I managed to choke out, "What do you want?"

His eyes studied me for a moment. "Consent. Fear. Admiration. The three pillars to a strong rule. The foundation for a necessary resistance. I need these, Airene, for the sake of all. And I will acquire them. With your aid."

"I don't understand."

"Then let me be clearer. You have been investigating Myron Wreath's disappearance. You need not wonder about that anymore. I am responsible."

The bald admission astonished me. For once, no further questions came to mind.

The false Tribune smiled thinly. "Perhaps you think you understand now. But full understanding will come later. What you must focus on now is the task I lay before you. While I am responsible for the Despot missing, you must interpret the evidence as if Asileia Wreath is responsible. I know there is ample evidence to frame her. Including her own admissions."

I listened, straining to understand what the man behind the Visage wanted, what he hoped to gain. But my anger burned away any reason still within me.

"Finally," Vusu continued, "you will leverage your burgeoning relationship with Archon Jaxas Wreath to summon a trial of the Despoina within the next span. There, you will present your case against Asileia Wreath and convince the High Tribune to convict her of Myron's death."

My fragmented thoughts struggled to put themselves together. "And if I refuse?"

Vusu shook his head, a sad smile on his face. "Of course you would ask. I knew you might need convincing to understand the depth of my convictions. Yet I wish you hadn't forced me to it." He looked slowly over at Linos. "Vessel. Demonstrate your obedience. Kill the boy."

My brother, still a moment before, whipped into motion. His hand shot out toward Hilarion, whom I'd nearly forgotten was present with us, and a plume of fire erupted from his fingertips. I stumbled back from the blast of heat and fell to the floor as the room filled with screams. Hilarion fell to the floor, writhing, as flames eagerly consumed his blackened body. I stared in horror, stomach churning.

"Do not toy with your prey, Vessel," Vusu said through the noise. "End it."

I looked back at my brother, his vacant eyes watching the tortured boy. "Linos," I said weakly.

Linos didn't make any sign he'd heard me. The air rippled around his fingertips, grew sharp, then whipped toward Hilarion with a crack. I closed my eyes and looked away, but I heard the snap of bone all the same. The screams ceased at once. But the hissing of hot fat, the stench of burned flesh, the crackle of the dying flames—

Next I knew, I was retching onto the floorboards. But it was the guilt washing over me that left me weak and shaking.

"Have I provided enough instruction?" Vusu asked quietly when I finished.

I wiped at my mouth with the back of my hand and, trembling, stood once more. "You're a monster," I whispered. Out of the corner of my eye, I saw Hilarion twisted on the floor, his neck like the bent stem of a trampled flower.

He gave a sudden laugh, a laugh full of sharp, broken glass. "You do not know monsters, Airene. My sins are many, but they pale to the evil of others." He shook his head. "But some must be sacrificed for any to survive."

I couldn't look at the boy's body. The Archon had been the one to bring him to me, but I had used him willingly. I had told him all would be fine. And now he was dead. "You do all this so you can rule. But a land of ashes is all that will remain."

Vusu smiled thinly. "Perhaps that is all I desire. But I would not presume to know what I want, Airene. False assumptions, as you should have learned, can draw people down dangerous paths."

I clenched my fists and stared at Vusu. The man had manipulated me at every turn. He had helped only to aid his own cause. He had taken Linos from me and turned his mind inside out. He had likely done the same to Thero all those long years ago, then killed him when he failed. Rage ran through me like wildfire. It was the only thing holding me upright, feeding me the strength that all my sorrow and misery and guilt threatened to leech away. I wanted to burn his carefully constructed plans to the ground.

"They won't flock to you," I said with forced calm. "Even if you discredit Despoina Asileia, Jaxas Wreath is next in line. He'll wear the Evergreen Wreath in her stead."

"Perhaps that would be true, but for one thing." His smile was paper thin. "They will not need to raise a new Despot. They will have their old one returned to them."

I remembered what I'd seen in the Despot's quarters. The empty room. The open balcony doors. The guards who reported seeing nothing, only hearing a loud noise like thunder. For a man who could raise an inferno and call down lightning, kidnapping the ruler of Oedija must have been simple.

"You didn't kill him," I said slowly. "You took him to be your puppet ruler."

Vusu nodded. "Partly correct, at least. But that is enough for now. You have your task set before you. I expect I'll have your compliance." He smiled thinly. "I will be there in attendance myself to ensure you have done as I have instructed."

My stomach suddenly roiled again. Clutching a hand to my gut and grimacing, I glanced at Linos. "Accuse the Despoina and take her to trial. And if I do that, you will set Linos free?"

Vusu almost looked as if he pitied me. "I fear you misunderstand me on purpose. No, I will not set Vessel free. He is mine now." He leaned forward on his wicker throne. "If you succeed, Vessel won't burn your family and friends before you. Your mother, father, sister. Corin. Xaron. Nomusa." He smiled thinly. "I have already taken two of your brothers. Do not force me to take the rest of those you love."

As his words sank in, I found something growing inside me, a festering desire like nothing I'd felt before. I didn't just want to stop Vusu to save Linos and the others, or keep Oedija safe from him. I wanted to see him hurt. I wanted to see him lost to despair. I wanted to know what he treasured most in life and crush it before him. I yearned for it. I burned. It was a hunger burrowing its way into my heart and hollowing it.

For now, I contained it. I held it in. There was nowhere for it to go. Not yet.

But I could not hold back a despairing question. "Why do this to us? To Thero? To Linos? To me?"

"Why you and your kin? It is a mystery I am still piecing together myself. Something grows in you, a seed..." He stared beyond me for a moment, as if remembering a distant memory. "We are all seeking to fill the holes riddling us. The lingering hungers that never fade." He shook his head. "The thirst I must slake will take a world, I imagine. But I must start somewhere."

Vusu looked away, sagging back against his wicker throne. His voice was suddenly weary. "I expect to see progress in the coming days. If she is not on trial within the span, I would not depend upon your loved ones' safety."

He flicked his finger again, and the Avvadin honor who had guided me in took me by the arm and led me back through the door. I looked back one last time at the people in that room. The Dishonored. Vusu. Linos.

"I'll save you," I whispered to my brother.

Even to my ears, the words rang false.

INTERLUDE II

EAZAL

Eazal descended the last of the stairs, licked his cracked lips, then passed through the doorway. The windowless chamber was dim, lit only by smokeless torches, with the low ceiling lost in shadows. It evoked the familiar, oppressive feeling the Subjugated were supposed to feel. The bag in his sweaty hands threatened to slip and spill the heavy coins across the dark stone floor. He tightened his grip, stood up straighter, and walked to the attending scribe's desk.

The scribe looked up from his scrolls. As he was cross-eyed, Eazal could only assume he was looking at him. "Here for a loan?" he asked in a bored, expectant voice.

Eazal tried to speak, coughed, tried again. "The opposite, actually. I'm here to pay mine off."

The scribe stared at him, his wandering eyes trailing to the sides. "Pay it off?"

"Yes." Eazal lifted the sack of coins and rested it on the desk with a clinking of metal. "Here is my debt, plus the agreed-upon interest."

"Pay it off," the scribe muttered. "You know, you just might be the first."

"What is, ah, the process for doing so?"

"I'm not sure. If you'll wait one moment…" The scribe's gaze strayed to the bag, but with his eyes, it could have been an accident. Eazal suspected otherwise. With the silver in that bag, the scribe would be able to leave his thankless position for good. It had to be tempting, even for one of the Subjugated. Yet the man left it on the desk as he turned and swept through a curtain at the back of the room.

Eazal shifted nervously as he waited for the scribe to return. To keep his mind busy, he thought through his commerce. When to deliver his last shipment of carpets to Riverport. When the next shipment was coming in. Where the guards would come from, who had recommended them, how much he could trust them…

But no matter how he tried to focus, his thoughts, as always, strayed back to his family.

When he'd returned to Oedija after his two-year exile, he had hoped at least to come back to a wife, a daughter, and a home untouched by lost time. Of the three, only the home remained, and that barely, for it had been stripped bare, and the whores squatting there had turned it into a brothel.

They didn't leave you, he reminded himself, not for the first time. *You left them. Your negligence. Your guilt.*

He had tried to make things right. He'd gone to his connections, begged and pleaded for a second chance. All had turned him down — all except for one, who relented when he finally reminded her of their past affections for one another. Despite her own dire straits, she financed him one ill-fated trip. Eazal had sent the caravan to Avvad, seeking to purchase fine carpets that would have secured his position once more as a merchant of middling capacity, and perhaps even have attracted the eye of the master merchants in the Ten-Tiered Bazaar.

But he had, once again, failed. Unexpected storms had caused delays, and highwaymen, who had increased with the droughts now common throughout the Four Realms, had carried off what little hadn't been ruined. Eazal was left bereft and friendless once more, estranged even from his last friend, and without a prayer of a second chance.

He had thought of returning to the profession that had landed him in trouble in the first place, but quickly dismissed it. His days of brewing tinctures were over. After the things he'd been party to, he couldn't return to being an apothecary without wondering if he was disabling — or killing — those who drank his potions. To make no mention that it might tip off those better left unaware of his return to Oedija.

Though it was the last place he'd wished to return to, he'd turned to the temple for aid. To his surprise, he had heard whispers of a service unheard of in the Violent Father's halls before: moneylending. A shameful practice perhaps, but Eazal had long since been disillusioned to the faith, and found few qualms if they handed money out to dishonored men like himself. So he'd walked up to the desk, to a scribe like the one who had disappeared through the curtain, and taken out a loan. A sizable loan. A loan large enough to finance a second caravan, this one making the trip successfully, and catapulting him back into respectability.

But that hadn't brought his wife and daughter back.

In time, they will forgive, he told himself. *Lost Mother willing, they will forgive.* But even as he submitted the prayer, he knew it fell on deaf ears.

After the last of the money he'd left them two years ago had run out, both his wife and daughter had been forced to take desperate measures. His wife had moved in with a widower, a former partner of Eazal's. They had lived together as if they were married for nearly the entire time he'd been absent. Even so, Eazal held onto a sliver of hope that she was not forever lost to him. His wife could not marry another man, and she would ever be in uncertainty; the widower might tire of her and cast her aside for a younger, prettier woman if he so desired. If she returned to him, Eazal told himself he would forgive her. After all, hadn't he had his own dalliances in the past? She would see reason. Eventually.

His daughter was in a more precarious position. She had spoken her vows to a sailor, one who took Valem's mandate of dominance far too literally. Eazal's throat tightened to think of it. Before his exile, he might have killed the man for harming his daughter, consequences be damned. But somewhere along that long, lonely walk through the wilds of the lands, caution — or cowardice — had seeded itself in him. He had precious little he could call his own, but at least he had something once more. He would wait and hope that his daughter would forgive him and return home.

His thoughts were interrupted when a woman entered the chamber. He stared at her for a moment, her size catching his eye, as she rose well above him and had the stolid look of a laborer. Even more, her skin was the pale color of sea froth on a stony shore. An outlander, here in one of Valem's temples. When she returned his gaze and approached, he flushed and looked away, cursing his inquisitive eyes.

"I am looking for the clerk," the woman said to him, her voice not as deep nor loud as Eazal had expected, though it did have an outlander accent.

He gave her a polite nod. "And I am waiting for him to return. He's just gone back to see if the Kul is available."

The outlander was silent for a moment. "The priest?" she asked finally.

Eazal nodded, realizing too late that "Kul" wouldn't be a familiar term to those outside of the Subjugated. She wasn't here for faith, but the same reason he was: debts owed, or soon repaid, in his case. He wondered what had driven her to such madness.

He and the woman waited in awkward silence until the scribe finally emerged from the curtains. A second person followed him out. A thrill of fear went through Eazal as he stared at the Kul. The skin around the large priest's eyes was still bubbled and red, though it had been years since the calderas of the Father had been burned into his flesh. Once a priest was made, he could never leave Valem's service; just as the scars lent the priest authority over his fellow man, it lashed him to the Father's chains for life. Chains — Eazal could not be rid of them soon enough.

"Sakin Faldul — how pleasant to see you return," the priest said. His size was intimidating, though not as large as the outlander woman. His voice was warm and rich with the sly manner of a shopkeeper. "I had just been wondering after you."

His skin crawled at hearing the false name he'd given the temple. It had been a necessary lie, even if it still made him uneasy. "Me, my Kul?"

"Of course you, my good man! And why not you? When you have such marvelous… talents."

Eazal shifted his foot before he could think about it. "Valem leaves such crumbs as he can spare, my Kul. I possess no more talent than any other."

"Such modesty!" The Kul's eyes gleamed, then slid over to the outlander. "Ah, and another welcome face. I will speak to you after, if you will wait a moment."

The woman's voice creased into a deeper frown. "You promised safe passage for my sister. But I've not had word that she sails."

"Because she does not sail," the Kul said, his tone as patient as an adult speaking to a child. "When you made your request, you did not mention her reasons for fleeing, nor the complications. That was… ungracious of you."

The tall woman grew very still. "You will still bring her?" she asked uncertainly.

The priest smiled broadly. "If you agree to our revised terms, I'm sure we can come to an understanding. But first, I must speak with this man. All depends on his answer. Come, Sakin Faldul. We will discuss your situation in private."

Eazal had listened with a growing unease, and wondered what depended on him as he followed the Kul behind the curtains. He glanced back one last time at the woman and saw his discomfort reflected in her eyes before the curtains obscured her from view.

"This way." The priest led him down a narrow hallway until they reached a small door, then opened it and gestured him inside. As with all the rooms in the temple, it was dark and cramped, with an altar of stone and a small rug before it. Eazal hoped that his knees, wearing out with age, wouldn't be made to endure supplication before the altar.

The priest closed the door behind them. "You have kept the prayers, have you not, Sakin Faldul?"

Eazal carefully considered his next words. The priests of Valem had always shown an eerie sense of the truth, and he didn't want to lie any more than he had to. "I keep them as well as I can."

The priest's eyes gleamed. "Worshipping with the sun's movement might be difficult when you are constantly traveling, wouldn't it be? Have to arrive to your destinations on time! No matter — the effort at subjugation is what is important. An effort that I expect will continue."

"Of course, my Kul." Eazal cleared his throat and gathered his courage. "If I may ask, did your scribe mention my purpose in coming?"

"Yes, he did." The priest nodded at the bag Eazal still clutched in his hand. "Is this your remittance, then?"

Eazal offered the purse. Strangely, despite the wealth it held, he felt eager to be rid of it. "One hundred silver scions, in addition to an interest of ten silver. And, if you please, an additional donation of ten silver to the temple to convey my gratitude."

"Too kind of you." The priest took the bag and hefted it experimentally. "It certainly has the feel of some hundred coins. I am happy to hear you have succeeded in your ventures."

"Thank you, my Kul." Every bone in his body begged to turn and walk away, but Eazal forced himself to stillness. Here in the temple, the Kul had to dismiss him before he could leave.

"However," the Kul said, "this payment is not what we are truly seeking. We are alone now, Sakin Faldul. It is time you are honest about the blessing Valem has given you."

He went rigid. He didn't dare contradict him, nor did he dare admit it. So he remained silent, staring at the priest as if in confusion.

The Kul smiled wider. "Show me your Branding, man. It is on your foot, is it not?"

His blood ran cold. There was little point in denying it. He wondered dully how the priest had found out.

"You wish me to show you now?" he asked, feigning dumbness in his reluctance. "To take off my boot and—?"

"Yes, all of it," the Kul said patiently. "I have it on good report, but I must see the truth for myself."

Slowly, Eazal leaned against the stone and pulled off his boot and sock, then held up his wrinkled foot awkwardly. The priest leaned down and peered closely at Eazal's toes. Finally, he nodded and straightened.

"It runs weakly in you, but I know Valem's signs when I see them. You have channeled before?"

"Yes. When the Brand first appeared."

"And it came to you when, exactly?"

He hesitated. He didn't want to speak of that night, and the other nights that had precipitated it. The despair that had swathed him in the darkness as he rocked back and forth in the bushes on the side of the road, with no comfort beyond a thin, ragged blanket and the occasional begged meal. He didn't want to speak of the curses he'd hurled at Valem for the misfortunes that had been heaped upon him. Nor did he wish to speak of that darkest moment, when he had stood at the edge of a cliff, his feet peeking out over a hundred-cubit drop.

When the blue-breasted bird had come to him.

How it had reached him out in the middle of nowhere, he could not comprehend, nor how it had spoken to him in a human voice. He had heard of whisper finches before, but he'd never visited houses wealthy enough to keep one. Nor did he understand the message that it had spoken to him in a boy's voice: *You are not alone, Eazal. I am here with you. I have not given up on you. I will not abandon you to yourself.* But despite the words, the bird had left soon after, leaving him more bitter than before. Someone — his wife, his daughter, a gloating competitor — must have sent the mocking message to deepen his misery. Yet how could they know where to find him? He himself had not known where he was.

His Branding had appeared that very same night. For the first time, Eazal had channeled. Just a bit, a small burst of sparks that sent his heart galloping and his boot smoking. But the flash of light had been enough for him to know. Valem had not left him to his fate. The Molten God still had uses for him.

Only he no longer knew if he believed it was Valem's hand at work. Eazal hadn't kept his prayers. He hadn't renewed his faith in the darkness of his travels, but lost it. If this was what happened to him when he kept faith, he had reasoned to himself, then what worse could happen if he broke it? Yet despite his renunciation, Valem's blessing remained. He wondered if Valem had ever had anything to do with it.

"Well?" the Kul prompted.

He'd been quiet for a long time. Sometimes that happened since his long sojourn; he lost track of the moment, like he often had during the countless turns of lonely walking. "When I was on the road," Eazal answered, then added belatedly, "my Kul."

"You do not flaunt it. That is good. You could hardly be accused of misusing His gift." The priest smiled thinly. "But I have a better application for it. A matter for which you, Sakin Faldul, are particularly well suited."

Fear trickled down his back. He moistened his lips. "What is this task, my Kul?"

"There is a woman with whom you're intimately familiar." The priest paused. "The one who exiled you from the city."

Eazal tensed. He had given a false name. He had said nothing of the circumstances that had led to him leaving Oedija, nothing of the three people, including the young woman that the priest referred to, who had brought his life crumbling down.

"I do not know of whom you speak," he finally replied.

The priest eyed him, his expression searching. "Do not test me. Eazal."

Eazal clenched his teeth. He shouldn't have returned. He'd known he shouldn't have. Yet even for the safety of his family, he couldn't keep away from Oedija.

"Of course you remember," the priest continued. "I am sure you thought of little but your revenge during your years away."

Eazal didn't reply this time, not trusting himself to lie further, and not knowing how much the man knew.

The Kul frowned. "I thought you would appreciate this opportunity, Eazal." He shook his head. "Whether you do or not, I must lay this task at your feet. For it is you who must accomplish it."

Foreboding pressed down on him, but Eazal forced himself to nod and say, "Yes, my Kul."

The frown eased slightly. "Since she wronged you those many years ago, she has pried into others' affairs, including those of our faith. Yet she was useful in other capacities, airing the foul laundry of others and accusing them of crimes they likely did not commit, and so we left her alone. But now, she is at the end of her usefulness. It would be best if she did not pry into our affairs again." The priest eyed him. "Do I make myself clear, Sakin Eazal?"

His mouth was dry. His stomach tossed and turned. "Why me?" he finally asked.

"Why you? Because of your history. It must seem motivated by purposes beyond political ones, and must not be explicitly associated with the faith. After your long absence from any Valemish temple, you qualify in this capacity. And it must not be done by a hired man; that, too, would excite too many questions. No, Sakin Eazal. You are the perfect candidate to carry out this unfortunate deed."

But Eazal was already shaking his head. He could only play this part so long. Even for his family. "With all due respect and obedience, my Kul. My debt was one of monetary value. This debt I've paid in full." His courage almost failed him under the priest's cold stare, but he forced himself to continue. "This request... I do not want to fulfill it, nor do I feel I am obligated. I cannot help you."

There was silence for a long moment. Eazal bowed his head, wondering if his words had been too hard, if he could have refused in another way.

"You are one of the Subjugated, Sakin Eazal," the priest said in a low voice. "It does not matter what you want or what you think you are due. In your time of need, when all others abandoned you, the faith saved you. Do you forget that so quickly? You owe us your life. The time has come to surrender it."

"No." Anger smoldered inside him as Eazal raised his head to meet the Kul's gaze. "No. I won't murder an innocent woman."

"Innocent?" The priest snorted. "She is far from that. Or do you forget what she did?"

"I haven't forgotten."

"Then you remember how she murdered that woman in the alley, do you? Stabbed her through the neck, as I recall. Had you not run, who's to say she would not have done the same to you?"

His resolve was thinning. "She was protecting herself," he muttered. "She had no choice."

The priest smiled thinly. "No. Perhaps not. But neither do you. Or do you forget the penalty in this city for being what you are?"

The anger washed away in a moment, replaced by fear. Eazal finally saw the trap. Being Branded might mean being blessed by Valem. But he didn't doubt the Kul would turn him in to the Shepherds if it served his purposes.

Still, he shook his head. He was not a brave man. But even a coward could stiffen his spine. "I won't kill anyone."

The Kul's expression became ugly. "You disappoint me greatly. Then you leave me no choice." He leaned in close. "It is not just you who will suffer, Eazal. Or did you think we didn't know your wife and daughter?"

The words broke him. His head fell, eyes stinging with tears. He'd been weak and returned when he knew he should not have, hoping to be with his family. But now, he'd endangered them once more.

He couldn't fail them again.

He sighed. "How am I to do it?"

CHAPTER TWENTY-EIGHT

THE WHISPER FINCH

VERIFIER: So have my convictions been formed.
HIGH TRIBUNE: Your convictions. That the leashing of Shepherds
puts too much power in the hands of the Tribunal. In my hands.
VERIFIER: Yours, High Tribune, and the Tribunes acting as their
handlers.
HIGH TRIBUNE: Thank you for your report, Verifier. As always,
you have been thorough in your investigations. However, I must
inform you that your fears in this case are misguided. No one
wishes for the return of the Tyrant Wardens, my Tribunes least of
all, which the improper use of the Shepherds could only facilitate.
VERIFIER: I am sure that is true now. But the truth I hoped to
convey is that an institution must be solid from its foundation.
This is a flaw that will one day be exploited.
HIGH TRIBUNE: That is enough. I trust you will find your own
way out.

- Verifier Jaxale before High Tribune Krynollon; 1067 SLP

I held on for Xaron.

The cracks were quickly spreading. As the honor Seda led me out of Vusu's war room and back into the amphitheater corridor, the pieces of myself threatened to fall apart. But I held together, clutching at my one remaining goal, the one atrocity I might be able to prevent.

What I could do to help Xaron, I had not the slightest clue. But I knew he was still alive. The lodestone in my pocket hadn't twitched that I'd felt. There was still hope. And as long as I had hope, I had to keep going.

Halfway down the amphitheater, Nomusa materialized from an alcove. "Airene," she said, relief and guilt warring in her eyes. "You made it out. You can't know how—"

She stopped, suddenly noticing the woman next to me. "Where's Linos? And Hilarion?"

Before I could answer, Seda bowed. "I leave you here," she murmured. "Do heed my master's words."

She turned and walked back the way we'd come.

Nomusa looked baffled as I resolutely stalked past her. "Airene, speak to me," she said, following. "What happened in there?"

Anger leaked through the fog of despair that had settled over me. "You would know if you had been there."

"You really expected that I would go in there with no idea of what dangers lay beyond?" she exclaimed, incredulous. "That I would risk my life on — what, a hunch? Where is Hilarion, Airene? Why did he not come out with you? And your brother—"

I rounded on her. "Vusu has him, Nomusa. He made Linos a warden, and he made him kill Hilarion. And now he's as empty as the Shepherds. There's no righting that." I swayed. The cracks inside me opened a little wider, and the hunger to make Vusu feel the pain I felt grew greater. But I was growing thin and tired. I had too little hope left. After what I'd seen him do, the power he'd wielded, the impossibility of harming him made the dream of vengeance impossible to sustain.

Nomusa put her hands on my shoulders. "Airene, look at me. You're not making any sense. What do you mean, he made Linos a warden? And that he killed..." She shook her head as if denying the words. "And what does Vusu have to do with this?"

I closed my eyes and drew in a shuddering breath. "Not here. We have to get out of the compound and back to Xaron. Vusu commands the Shepherds. He will break his word, if he hasn't already."

Nomusa's eyes widened. She seized me and dragged me toward the stairs. "No time to waste then."

The Seeker guards were surprised to see us descend from the Claw, but with the same laxness they'd shown the rest of the evening, told us not to linger at the next gathering and waved us through. We walked quickly up the hill and through the rest of the compound, not daring to go faster lest we attract the wrong sort of attention.

Once we were through the compound's gate, we ran. Even though defeat had exhausted me to the bone, somewhere in me I found the strength to press on. Nomusa easily kept pace beside me. We passed through deme Thys and had nearly reached the gate to the inner city when a shadowy figure emerged from an alley and made straight for us.

Nomusa cried out and leaped toward it, adopting one of her Ixolo stances, while I, panting and wild-eyed with confusion, reached for one of my hidden knives. But the shadow held up its hands, and a familiar voice said, "Wait! I've had enough violence tonight without fighting you two."

"Talan," I said with a relieved gasp. I released my knife and stumbled toward him. Before I knew what I was doing, I fell into him and wrapped my arms around his middle. The Guilder caught me and held me, surprising me by running a hand through my hair. His body was lithe and strong pressed against me, comforting in its surety.

"I've been watching for you," he murmured in my ear. "And I'm glad to see you safe. But your brother is not yet."

The momentary comfort dissipated. I pulled away. "No, he's not. I saw him. I stood in the same room as him."

Talan's eyebrows rose. "You did?"

"She has yet to explain it to me as well," Nomusa said drily.

I shook my head. "There's no time. Xaron is in trouble. Shepherds had him cornered in the Laurel Palace when we left. They may try seizing him at any moment now."

"You left him surrounded by Shepherds?"

I clenched my teeth. Both of them needed to know everything I did, yet there was no time, nor did I seem to have the wit capable of proper explanation. "Tribune Vusumuzi is the Visage," I said hurriedly. "He said before that they — the Shepherds, I mean — would wait until tomorrow morning to enter Xaron's room and arrest him. But now…"

The Guilder nodded, accepting the revelation with astonishing composure. "Then I'll go ahead and do what I can." He pressed my hand one last time, then turned away.

Though time pushed down hard on us, I stopped him. "How will I reach you again? The barkeep at the Intellectual wasn't compliant."

He paused, turning halfway back. "There is much I need to tell you as well. Guildmaster Hax is dead, as is Peralda." He shook his head. "The Underguild is tearing itself apart, and my network has suffered for it. I must expect that all of my hiding spots are compromised and that any of my contacts might turn on me."

I stared dumbly at Talan for a moment, the words washing over me. "Two Guildmasters, dead tonight?" I shook my head. "Another time. How will I contact you?"

"I will seek you out at the palace as soon as I'm able. Now, fly back there, my Finch." He flashed me his half-smile, then turned and ran back into the dark alley from which he'd emerged. He wasn't headed toward the gate; I wondered if he meant to scale the fifty feet of the city wall, or if he had other ways around.

Nomusa seized my arm and pulled me toward the gate. "He's right — we need to hurry. Come on."

I nodded and set off at a jog.

The city guards, as disinterested as they had been before the gathering, waved us through without a second glance. We broke into a faster trot when we turned out of sight. The palace wasn't far, but the distance seemed to stretch on. I pressed on, clinging to the hope that we weren't too late. I seized onto a desperate idea. If we could convince Jaxas that Vusu was the Visage, he might be able to overrule the commands that the Shepherds had been given. I dismissed it as quickly as it occurred to me. I could do nothing that endangered my friends and family further than I already had. And undermining Vusu's authority and exposing his true alignments would be going against his will. Vusu was right; he had known where to strike his dagger.

Finally, we made it to the palace gates. Panting, stitches stabbing my sides, I held up my Verifier medallion as we approached the laurel guards standing watch. I hoped they weren't the same men who had tried kidnapping Xaron and me earlier.

"We're Verifiers for the Archon," I said between breaths. "We need to get through."

The guards exchanged looks. "We were told to watch out for you—" one of them began.

"Save it," I cut him off. "A pair of you fools tried taking us yesterday. It didn't work then and it won't now. So how about you just let us in and save everyone the trouble?"

Surprisingly, the guards relented, and soon, Nomusa and I were passing through the gates and ascending the many stairs to the glittering palace above. "You're becoming as ill-tempered as me," Nomusa observed, as breathless as I'd ever heard her.

I couldn't answer. Air hissed between my teeth, and I felt faint. I took the stairs as fast as my leaden legs would allow. The guards at the doors admitted us, but called after, "You're too late! The action's already over!"

My heart wrenched at their words, and we pressed on faster still.

We sprinted through the atrium, then down the hall toward our rooms. As we approached the doors, I saw that the Shepherds no longer stood watch in the hall. My hopes plummeted further as I saw Xaron's door hanging open. But it was only as I entered his room that my hopes were crushed.

The bed still smoked, little more now than charred wood and ashes. The other furniture was pressed against the walls in crumpled heaps. Not even the broken window, a potential sign of escape, could relieve the stupor that claimed me. Even if Xaron had temporarily fled, I knew it wouldn't last long.

I sank to my knees, hardly noticing the hardness of the marble floor. My mind went numb, feeling as if I fell away from myself.

"Airene!" I heard Nomusa cry, but it came from far away. I could not find it in me to respond.

I did not lapse into unconsciousness as I wished; that would have been too great a relief. Instead, I stared at the latest of my long list of failures. My fate was sealed. I was chained to the path Vusu had set before me and could do nothing but stumble along it.

"He didn't give me the signal." I felt in my pocket and drew the lode-stone out, staring at the smooth, gray stone. Maybe he *had* given the signal. Maybe I'd been running, or jostled in the crowd, and hadn't noticed the lodestone twitch.

As I moved the lodestone in my hand, I noticed movement in the corner of my eye. Startling, I gained my feet and stared at the ashy corner of the room. A suspicion made me feel sick to my stomach, and I twitched the lodestone again.

The movement came again from the ashes.

Approaching, I bent over and swept the debris aside. There, laying among the ruins, was Xaron's matching lodestone. I took it in my hand and rose, staring from one to another in my hands. Much good they'd done him in the end. Closing my hands on them, I turned and left the ruined room.

"Airene," Nomusa said again, following. "We have to find him. You saw the window. Maybe—"

"It's over." My voice was leaden. "You know what the Shepherds are capable of, and what Xaron is. He doesn't stand a chance."

I didn't wait for an answer, but continued to my room. Without another word, I shut myself within.

———

I dreamed again of the whisper finch and the gargantuan lizard. *Flee*, the bird urged me. *He has his claws in you.* This time, I didn't run, but turned to face the huge creature looming out of the mist. I did not flinch as it reared and rushed forward, then closed its gaping mouth around me.

I was drenched in sweat when I awoke. The nightmare made all too much sense now. Even my dreaming mind had seen that the Visage of the Wyvern had been the threat looming over Oedija, and that I'd been dancing to his tune. I squeezed my eyes shut in the darkness of the palace room. Suddenly, the foreignness of the place closed in. I longed for something familiar, for my bed in Canopy, or even the room I had shared with my oldest sister, Sophene, as a child. Yet even if they had been available to me, I could not make myself stir and rise. I was drained, empty. Not even the hunger for revenge found sustenance.

"You are not alone, Airene."

Instincts of preservation found strength where nothing else could. I bolted upright, my hand clutching something. A knife, one of the two I'd hidden on myself earlier.

"Who's there?" I called out in a quavering voice. In the darkness, alleviated only by a sliver of light from a capped pot of pyrkin, I could not see the intruder.

"I am with you."

I spotted the speaker at the same time as I recognized the boy's voice. The whisper finch had perched on my window sill, shadowed but for the glowing patch of blue on its breast. Yet I sensed that its eyes were unerringly focused on me.

"You." I lowered the knife but didn't sheathe it. I felt dazed. "You spoke in my dreams."

"I have not given up on you," the whisper finch continued resolutely. "I will not abandon you to yourself."

I laughed hollowly and turned my head aside. But as I looked away, I glimpsed out of the corner of my eye something else standing with the bird. I looked back, blinking, but nothing was there. Yet I couldn't shake the feeling that I'd seen the faint outline of a boy cast in blue standing next to the bird.

"Who sent you? And how did you get in here?"

"It is too late to flee," the boy's voice said. "So we must turn and fight. Will you fight with me, Airene?"

A helpless rage sparked to life within me. "Why don't you answer my questions?" I demanded. "Who are you? How do you know my name and where to find me?"

I rose, leaving the knife on the bed. I would need both my hands to catch the bird. But the whisper finch sensed my intentions. As I approached, it took flight and settled on the top of the dressing cabinet on the opposite side of the room.

"Be ready, Airene," the bird said, continuing as if it had not been interrupted. "He has his claws in you. His change will come soon."

"Answer me!" Ridiculous as it was to demand this of a bird, I could not bear yet another mystery flitting beneath my nose.

"Be ready," the whisper finch warned me one last time. Then the blue patch disappeared from the top of the cabinet.

I advanced, straining to see where it had gone, but could not find it. Stalking over to the pot of pyrkin, I ripped off the cover and cast the light around me. Nothing. The bird had disappeared. If it had ever been there.

I sank onto my bed and leaned back on my hands when pain cut across one of them. Yelping, I looked down. The knife, unsheathed, had sliced into my palm. I stared down at the blood oozing from my hand, the yellow light of the pyrkin giving it a strange orange cast. It throbbed with the beat of my heart, trickling down my hand to drip onto my trousers.

The pain focused me. Ignoring my wound, I searched through the whisper finch's mysterious words. Perhaps it was right. I could not flee. Maybe it was time to turn and fight. Strange that I should find strength in the words of a bird sent by a stranger when all else had failed.

I picked up the knife and sheathed it, then settled back onto the bed, heedless of the blood I might spill on it. *Fight.* Chained to a path I might be, but I didn't have to go complacently. I would make Vusu struggle for every inch he took me down the road he'd planned for me. Even with my loved ones' lives at stake, I couldn't put aside this… duty, I supposed. Loyalty to Oedija, he'd called it. Maybe it was. With the foundations of our society cracking underneath us, to stand by and let it bury us all, my friends and family included, was something I could not allow myself to do.

I closed my eyes, but I did not sleep. Slowly, thoughts began to stir, unfold, bloom. The sandglass must have turned many times as I thought through and tempered my ideas into something that resembled a plan. Threads I had not considered suddenly wove into a net sturdy enough to cast. There were loose ends. There were weak lines. But it was a start. A way to begin to fight back.

When the glow of dawn crept in through the window, I rose and bound back my hair. I washed my face in the washbasin set out for me, then the blood that had crusted over my hand. I settled a chiton over the tunic and trousers I still wore from the night before. I painted the expected veneer over my hardened resolution.

I touched the Verifier medallion, still hanging from my neck, as it had since I'd received it from Vusu. He had given it to me so I would do his bidding. But I didn't think only of my gullibility. I remembered, too, the whisper finch in the night and the boy's words that had come from it. And I remembered the mission set long ago before the first Verifiers of Truth. They had been killed and ignored and finally cast aside. But they had not swayed from what they knew to be right.

I turned from the room and set out to spin my net.

CHAPTER TWENTY-NINE

TYING LOOSE ENDS

The isikhayha trees are singular, both in look and function. My time with them was brief, but poignant…

The sight of the trees was immediately enchanting. I was dazzled by the light emanating from rivulets of pyrkin down the isikhayha's sides in green and gold and tangerine. The trees were large and most oddly formed, for their trunks did not rise up in a single unit, but expanded into a web of smaller trunks that bound themselves into a great orb without any gaps between. I could not see if anything was bound inside the spheres. The trunks were lined with thorns both great and small. A man thrown against the tree would be impaled to his death, and indeed, I was informed that this was the punishment for some crimes, though no signs of gore lingered.

Above the sphere of trunks and thorns extends a canopy of branches, cascading up and out like a thick head of hair. The leaves are golden all year round and know no season, and are small and shaped like spearheads. The tops of their branches would likely reach through the oculus of the Conclave, were one to grow within it.

- An Oedijan's Account of the Bali Ishakas; by Manenes of Gate, an itinerant scholar; 1140 SLP

I opened the shop's door and stepped inside without invitation. The glass pieces displayed on pedestals glowed in many hues, casting the dim room in eerie, shifting light. Closing the door behind me, I turned into the hall to the workshop, where I heard the forge burning, and the grunts of a man at work.

Maesos didn't notice me enter. He sat working his jacks around a wad of orange-hot glass that I could already tell would become a vase. His bald pate dripped with sweat from the thick heat of the room, making his remaining curly hair hang limp and slack. The work apron over his yellowed tunic and trousers was riddled with ashy holes. Glancing over, Maesos didn't startle, but smiled up at me as he continued working his jacks around the molten glass.

"Maesos," I said, staying by the door and out of the oppressive heat. "It's good to see you."

He stole another look. "You look like you've spent all night in a forge. What are you up to, little Finch?"

I drew a breath. "I need your help."

His brows furrowed as he continued his work. "It wouldn't be concerning our Low Counsel, would it? I've been working out something for her should the occasion arise. A beautiful, ornamental orb that may or may not explode in a few days." He flashed me a boyish grin.

I returned him a begrudging smile. "Feiyan's not the problem. Not at the moment." I pushed down thoughts of Xaron and pressed on. "My younger brother, Linos, got caught up with the Manifest. And I need your help to save him."

Maesos's smile faded, and he worked silently for many moments longer. Withdrawing the blowpipe, he placed it on a pair of forked stands, then moved over to another furnace to withdraw a blowpipe that had been sitting with one end in it. "You feel responsible," he finally said as he moved back to his seat.

"Of course I do."

"You're not." He darted a look at me, one bushy eyebrow cocked. "Every man and woman leads their own life and makes their own decisions. You can't be with your brother at all times, Airene, nor should you. You have to make a living and find a bit of happiness for yourself."

I turned my head aside and stared into the corner, where a sliver of darkness had escaped the glow of pyrkin. *Happiness.* How far that was from my mind now.

"I didn't come here to talk about that."

"Fine." He rose and replaced the second blowpipe in the furnace. "What do you need my help for then? I'm an old man who makes ornaments and vases for a living. Hardly the kind of man you'd ask to rescue a boy from a cult."

"There's something happening to the city, Maesos. Something that I don't have time to explain. But there's going to be a coup, and wardens from the Manifest are behind it." Giving voice to the suspicions I'd held these past few days made it sound crazy even to me.

"Coup? Wardens trying to take hold of the polis?" He raised the fully formed vase for a closer look. "Eidola above, I've lived too long."

"I think you can help."

"Can I?" He bellowed a laugh as he rose and moved toward the far corner of the room, where he opened the door to a dark clay lehr for cooling. "And I thought I was the mad old gaffer!"

I gave him a slight smile. I'd thought he was the mad one as well. But with what I had in mind, I wasn't so sure any longer.

"In Zotikos's shipment, you were receiving a pyrkin strain rumored to dampen a warden's channeling, right?"

He placed the new vase in the lehr and shut the door. "Yes. So I was told. Pyrkin scraped from the trunk of an isikhayha, one of the Bali spirit trees."

"I didn't believe it could be true before. But now, I need it to be."

Sitting, he studied me. "What do you mean? Do you have something in mind?"

I sighed. "Only a plan for the desperate. If I asked you to make crossbow bolts with glass orbs affixed to the ends, could you do it?"

"I suppose so."

"Good. Then I have a visit to make. If I succeed, I expect I'll be back shortly."

Maesos shook his head with a resigned chuckle. "And here I thought I'd go to my grave a bored, happy man. Very well. I'll await your return."

Nodding grimly, I left his shop.

———

Few visitors strayed into Hull. Located in the southeastern corner of the inner city, it was so named for the skeleton of a beached ship that leaned over a dry branch of the Walano River. That image epitomized the whole of the deme. Lichen and vines ate away at the stone and wood of its buildings. Most seemed not to have seen fresh paint in my lifetime, and a few looked on the verge of collapse. It had not been as long as I preferred since my last trip. Yet here I was, a span later, visiting for the same errand as before.

I knew the way to the smuggler Zotikos's manor, having earlier wormed his secret from his serving staff with a few well-placed coins. Less than a turn after leaving Maesos's shop, I had arrived before the manor and stood facing it. It was not unimpressive, rising several stories high, but the merchant seemed to have fallen on hard times. No guard stood at the gate, and trees and bushes along the path to his door lay untrimmed. I marched through the gate and up to the door, then knocked loudly.

Several long minutes later, the door opened to reveal a tired-looking woman. "Yes? How may I help you?"

"I need to see your master. Please tell Zotikos that Airene the Finch has come to see that he completes his task this time."

The woman blinked at me. "Oh, my dear, I'm sorry. I've grown so used to answering my own door that I've forgotten how strange it must be. But if you need to see my husband, I can bring him here."

A flush crept up my neck. Zotikos's scorned wife was the last person I wanted to insult. "My apologies. But if you would do that, I'd be grateful."

"Of course." She smiled and began to turn away, letting the door close behind her.

Inspiration struck me then. "And please, if you'd return with him, I'd appreciate speaking with both of you."

The merchant's wife looked back with a quizzical look, but she nodded before closing the door.

I waited impatiently, thinking. If Zotikos's wife answered the door herself, times were hard indeed for their household. Perhaps Zotikos wouldn't even have that giant of a bodyguard he'd had before. That would make this much easier. But how had the smuggler been ruined so quickly? I doubted my interference could have had such a dire impact.

Minutes later, the door opened again, this time to reveal both Zotikos and his wife. Anger already smoldered in the smuggler's expression. "What are you doing here?" he snapped.

"Hello, Zotikos. What a lovely manor you have." I held back other insults for his wife's sake.

Her face grew pale even at that small slight, while her husband's purpled. "You come to my house and insult me," he said in a low, threatening voice. "I should have you thrown off my yard."

I gave him a knowing smile. "You won't do that though, will you, Zotikos? Even if you had a man to do so. After all, we have unfinished business to discuss. I held up my end of the bargain. It's time that you held up yours."

The merchant's angry gaze fell on his wife. "As I told you, it is merely business. You may leave us."

"But she asked me to..." Her nerve faltered as his glare intensified. "Very well. Excuse me, Airene the Finch." She bowed and swiftly departed.

I let the silence stretch between us as Zotikos glared at me. "I don't know who told you those filthy lies you threatened to tell my wife," he said in a low, harsh voice, "but rest assured they paid for it. I threw them all out — steward, cook, servants, and guards. All!"

"Even your tall, well-muscled admirer?"

"Even him," he snapped. "And now you come and tell my wife to stay while you insult me—"

"We had a bargain," I interrupted, my patience quickly fraying. "And you broke it. Yet, as despicable as I find you, I am still willing to uphold the deal. I will not speak of your injustices against your wife so long as you, here and now, deliver the shipment promised to the glassblower, Maesos."

Zotikos laughed bitterly. "So it was he who hired you. Well, too late for that. Now go away. You've done your worst."

He moved to slam the door in my face. Acting without thinking, I threw my shoulder against the door and opened it wide, then shoved the merchant back against the wall behind him to pin him there. The man's eyes bulged, and words failed him as he spluttered. He and I were of a height and build, but the contest was far from even. The merchant had grown too used to others doing his dirty work for him. Or perhaps, with blood pounding inside my skull, I was more dangerous than I realized.

"How about we strike a new bargain," I suggested with a sharp smile. "Go fetch the shipment yourself while I wait here, and I'll leave you alone."

"God-touched bitch," he spat. But I noticed that he didn't make any move to dislodge himself.

I pressed harder into his chest until he gasped. "Now!" I snarled.

"I can't!" he practically squealed. "I sold it!"

My stomach sank. "Liar."

"Sold it!" he repeated frantically, clutching weakly at my arm.

"Who? Who did you sell it to?"

"The Low Consul! Feiyan of Port!"

The fight went out of me. I released him and stepped back. *Feiyan.* Of course. My far-fetched plan hinged on the woman who had likely had Xaron killed.

"If you lied..." I left the threat hanging as I turned away and went quickly back to the street.

CHAPTER THIRTY

SPINNING

Yet seeing these isikhayha trees did not answer my question of what they protected their ishaka against. When I posed this question to the Shaka, she shook her head and did not answer in words I could understand, and though I sought a translation, none was provided. I must settle on speculation. With their plateaus largely peaceful and free from disturbance by both spirits and wardens, I must assume the isikhayhas protect against influences of the Pyrthae. Perhaps daemons are trapped within their spheres.

It is one mystery I am most happy to wonder at, and never discover.

- An Oedijan's Account of the Bali Ishakas; by Manenes of Gate, an itinerant scholar; 1140 SLP

It was well into the afternoon by the time the Laurel Palace came into sight. I had known no better place to return. Feiyan was as likely to be here as at the Conclave or her own manor, and Talan might be waiting nearby with news. Besides, after the day's hindrances, exhaustion and doubts weighed me down. But I kept going. As unlikely as my chances of success were, I had to try to stop Vusu.

As I approached the gates, a figure came out from an alcove toward me. My stomach fluttered with hope as I turned, expecting to greet Talan. Instead, I blinked in surprise. "Corin?"

"Airene." Canopy's last loftmate trudged over to stand before me. She looked the worse for wear, which was saying something, as her job usually kept her coated in dust and mud, and she smelled as if she hadn't bathed since the three horns had blown.

Even with everything else pressing on my mind, I suddenly realized how deeply I'd wronged her. "Corin, I can't say how sorry I am about everything." My gaze slipped from her face; looking her in the eyes had become unbearable. "I know you'd been saving up to bring your sister to Oedija. Now all your savings are gone. Because of me."

"It was not you who broke into Canopy."

I forced myself to meet her eyes. "But it's my fault, Corin. I brought Feiyan's henchmen down on us. She warned me, and I ignored it. And now we're both without our home." Unexpectedly, I felt a hot pressure on my eyes. After everything else, it seemed strange that this small ache would be the one to bring tears. Corin averted her gaze, clearly uncomfortable.

As I wiped at my eyes, an idea occurred to me that cheered me, if only slightly. "I'm staying at the Laurel Palace and have the Archon's ear. I'm sure you could stay with us. And after things calm down, if you still want to bring your sister here, maybe I could get Jaxas to finance her ship."

Corin's eyes widened, and she lifted her head to stare at me. I returned the look, puzzled. Had I said something to offend her? Perhaps it was her strange sense of honor, which compelled her to earn the coin necessary for her sister's passage without aid from anyone else.

"No," Corin said at length, looking away again. "I will find a way."

I let it lie for the moment. If we survived what was coming, there would be time to discuss it later. "At least stay at the Laurel Palace. I know you can't have money for another place to stay."

A long pause followed. Slowly, the cartwoman nodded. "Thank you," she whispered, the words seeming to cost her.

I reached forward to take her arm, but she drew back. I didn't understand what was going on with her, but the time I had for her troubles had dried up. "Come. I'll see if Nikias can't find you a room."

Corin kept three paces behind me as we approached the palace gates. The guards eyed us, but admitted us without complaint. I was glad to see my position as a Verifier was worth that much at least.

Passing through the palace doors, I found we had a greeting party. Nikias stood in the middle of the main hall with a pair of honors, hands folded behind his back, his expression severe.

"Nikias," I greeted him as we approached.

"Verifier Airene, you are late in reporting to the Archon. Your companion Nomusa has already given her account, but my master informs me that it is vastly incomplete. He has summoned you to his solar at once."

I was in no mood to bandy words with the prickly man. "Fine. You can take me to him in a moment. But I'll need a few things from you in return."

Nikias's eyes narrowed. "And those would be?"

"First, my friend here needs a room in the palace."

The steward scowled. "This is not an inn, Verifier Airene. We are not required to provide lodging for your every passing acquaintance."

"Just give her a room, Nikias. If you want to argue about it later, fine. But I have to report to Jaxas now, and I'd like to know that Corin is treated well before I go."

The steward sniffed, his mustache bristling. "Fine. Name your other requirements and be on your way."

"Bring Nomusa up to the Archon if you can. I want her to hear everything as well."

"Very good. Is that all?" His sarcasm was not lost on me.

"Nearly. Should you receive a report of a disreputable-looking Avvadin man hanging around the front of the palace, please notify me."

"I would be happy to act as your messenger finch," he snapped. "Now, if you please, do your duty and go to the Archon."

I glanced over at Corin. "They'll take you in now. Just ask if you need anything."

The big woman didn't nod or respond, but remained with her head bowed. I imagined it was shameful for her to be in this position, taken care of by not only me, her friend, but also served by honors. But Corin's pride was the last thing I could be concerned with now.

As an honor stepped forward and led Corin away, I turned back to the steward. "Take me to him."

Nikias motioned sharply to an honor. At her indication, I followed her up the stairs.

After many twists and turns through chambers and hallways, the honor and I arrived before a simple wooden door. The honor knocked lightly, then opened it and ushered me inside. The room I entered was bright, light streaming through a wall of windows, catching on the dust hovering around stacks of books and scrolls. Plates of fruit, meats, and bread were set out on a table in the middle of the room.

The Archon sat in one of the dark corners amid the books, his pen scribbling on a piece of parchment. He continued writing for several more moments, then slowly set the pen in its stand and lifted his gaze.

"Verifier Airene," he greeted me. He looked tired, and the shadows on his face made his appearance seem even more wasted than the day before.

"Archon." I gave him a brief bow.

Jaxas gestured to a seat adjacent to his writing desk. "Please, sit. Or we can step onto the balcony if you prefer. Even in the daytime, the view of Oedija is excellent."

"Sitting is welcome." My rumbling stomach begged for me to pick up some morsels, but I resolutely ignored my needs and sat.

Pushing the parchment before him aside, the Archon leaned forward, forming a steeple with his hands. "Nomusa gave an interesting report, but I'll need your account to fully understand it."

"Yes." My throat tightened as I thought over what I'd witnessed the previous night, and how I'd now have to relive it. "I'll help you make sense of it. But first, I have to ask. What happened with Xaron?"

"Ah, yes." Jaxas's eyes were hidden in the hollows of his skull. "The Shepherds invaded your friend's room sometime around the mid-turn of the night. A fight ensued. Some claimed to hear claps of thunder from the room. Others saw him fleeing the grounds with two Shepherds in pursuit."

I closed my eyes, emotion choking me. For a moment I couldn't speak. I drew in several shuddering breaths.

"I'm sorry, Airene," Jaxas said softly. "Even if he was a feral warden, I know he was your friend. Yet I do not know that anyone can escape a Shepherd."

I fought for control. "He understood the risks," I said, my voice shaky. "We all did."

He looked at me and slowly nodded.

A light tapping sounded at the door. I turned, grateful for the distraction. A moment later, Nomusa was escorted in. I halfway stood, suddenly uncertain. She paused at the sight of me, then rushed over and wrapped me in an embrace.

"You scared me last night," she whispered in my ear. "With everything that happened, and how you just seemed to drift away... And then you were gone this morning!" She abruptly pulled away and shook her head with a small smile. "I'm just glad you're all right."

I nodded, tears suddenly stinging my eyes. "But Xaron..."

"I know," she said simply. "But we can't lose hope. Maybe he escaped."

I shook my head, but didn't respond. There was no point in dwelling on it. I couldn't help Xaron. But I might still aid Oedija.

Turning, I met Jaxas's gaze. "I should give report."

Jaxas exchanged a look with Nomusa, then gestured for us to sit. "Please."

I did not give them the complete tale, though it was nearly so. I told of our approach to the Wyvern's Claw, the size of the crowds, and the laxness of the guards. I spoke then of the show the Dishonored and the Visage of the Wyvern put on, and how very close everyone there came to burning alive. Jaxas nodded, and Nomusa indicated she had covered as much.

After a moment's hesitation, I told them of Linos, though I did not yet admit to the Archon that he was my brother. Instead, I spoke of him as a credible case of the Manifest turning an ordinary person into a warden.

Jaxas's brow creased. "And how do you know that the attunement was not just buried within him, waiting to be expressed?"

I glanced at Nomusa, and at her nod, I felt a sliver of gratefulness. She hadn't already told him. I drew in a breath. "I know because... He's my brother."

The Archon was still for a long moment. "I am sorry, Airene," he said softly. "Though words can ill convey it, I truly am."

I didn't acknowledge it. I couldn't yet. Instead, I barreled on with my report, the details becoming lost in the blur of revelations that followed. When I unveiled the Visage's identity, Jaxas nodded, seemingly unsurprised.

"Tribune Vusumuzi," he murmured. "I never would have suspected the old man. He always struck me as kind, if resolute."

"His attunement is more powerful than I've ever seen. The whole of his arms moved with his shifts."

"I wish I had gone with you," Nomusa said quietly. "I would have liked to have seen his arms."

"To see his shifts?"

"No — his tatu. Zipho told us he'd shown her them before and that they were of the Yorandu, but it always seemed strange to me. He never showed deference to me beyond the formal address — not that he needed to," she amended quickly. "But Zipho and the few other Yorandu in Oedija all do speak to me that way. It just didn't fit."

"Well, now we know why," I said heavily.

"Almost. I suspect he's not Yorandu. But that raises the question: which ishaka is he from?"

That question might have fascinated Nomusa, but it was the furthest query from my mind.

"When you encountered him," Jaxas interjected, "did Vusumuzi say anything of note?"

I hesitated. Now I stood on the precipice, with deadly consequences either way I chose. I studied the thin, sickly Wreath sitting across from me and wondered once again why he had done as he had. The choice before me hinged on Jaxas being true to the realm.

I glanced at Nomusa, but she had no answers. If I were to trust Jaxas, trust him with my friends' and family's lives, I had to know the one thing holding me back.

"Why did you let us investigate Asileia Wreath?"

Shadowy emotions flitted across his face, so quick I couldn't identify them. "You know why," he said quietly. "Because, no matter what I might wish to believe about her, Leia will do anything to achieve her goals. No one — myself, her father — no one means as much to her as herself. I believed she was capable of killing her father if it served her goals, and I needed to know the truth of it." He sighed. "That she showed symptoms of insanity upon her return from the Peninsula only heightened my suspicions."

Jaxas looked away. I stared at him, realization settling in. He loved Asileia. Mad as she was, she was still his family. Yet rather than protect her, he had sought the truth behind her father's disappearance. No matter the cost.

How could I hold myself to anything less?

"Vusu instructed me to accuse Asileia of Myron's murder, then have her convicted in a trial. And if I don't comply, he'll kill my family and friends."

I glanced at Nomusa, and she stared back at me, her mouth slightly parted. She seemed more surprised than upset.

The Archon's expression was inscrutable. "It was risky for you to tell me this."

"Just as it was risky to bring on three strangers to an investigation that could break Oedija."

He bowed his head in acknowledgment. "I appreciate the trust you've placed in me, Airene. I swear to you, it is not misguided."

Nomusa's gaze had fallen to the floor. I hoped she had the same conviction as Jaxas did.

The Archon rose, folded his hands behind his back, and began to pace. "Vusu wishes to have Asileia pushed out of the way," he mused. "But that would leave me in line to be the next Despot."

"It would, if not for one other thing. Myron isn't dead. Vusu kidnapped him, to present him as soon as the Despoina is discredited. He means to send the whole system spiraling."

A small smile worked its way onto his lips. "I've been aiding your cause. If Leia is convicted by your testimony, it will cast suspicion on myself. After all, what better motivation would I have to take away the Evergreen Wreath from Leia than to wear it myself?"

That piece hadn't occurred to me yet, nor Nomusa, from her reaction.

"I must hear your report in its entirety," Jaxas continued. "What else did he say?"

I thought back. "It isn't so much what he said as what he did. He… he killed the boy Hilarion." I did not mention it was by my brother's hand that the deed was done.

The Wreath bowed his head and was quiet for several long moments. "I sent him with you," he said softly. "If you blame yourself for his fate, don't. His blood is on my hands."

"His blood is on Vusu's hands."

Jaxas inclined his head. "Anything else?"

I shook my head. "Nothing of significance." I didn't mention our brief encounter with Talan afterward. I had kept the Guilder secret thus far and had no intentions of revealing him now. He had always valued his anonymity, and I meant to honor that for as long as I could.

"I'd hoped to put off our decision until later." Jaxas continued to pace, the creases in his brow growing ever deeper.

"We have to deal with him here and now." I braced myself for the words. "And I think I have a way to do it. To make it seem like we are implementing his plan, but will in actuality foil him."

Both Nomusa and the Archon looked over in surprise.

"You do?" Nomusa asked skeptically.

"Don't hold us in suspense," Jaxas said with a faint smile.

I hesitated a moment. A plan to trap the most powerful warden in Oedija. I was even madder than I'd thought.

Taking a deep breath, I began to speak.

CHAPTER THIRTY-ONE

THE DEMOS COUNCIL

…And from the Conclave will be elected a Council of eleven Low Consuls, each elected by ten Servants, who will determine matters of expediency. To them are ceded powers of swift military action, response to disasters, the management of foreign entities, and criminal matters of the highest order. In matters of commerce and the wealth of the realm as well as laws of lesser haste, the Council is to cede responsibility to the greater Conclave…

- Charter II of the formation of the Demotism of Oedija; 1063 SLP

Afternoon was bleeding into evening by the time Nomusa and I departed from Jaxas's solar. We'd discussed, refined, and finally committed to my scheme. There were still many risks involved. There were still loose threads. Yet, together, we had begun weaving a web that might just be strong enough.

But there was much work to be done. Once we'd honed the details to as fine a point as we could, Nomusa and I took our leave of the Archon. We took with us his promise of setting up a meeting for later that evening, a meeting that I once would have fawned over attending: a meeting with the Demos Council and the other heads of Oedija's institutions. The ten Low Consuls would be there, as would the Stratechons, the High Tribune, and Archmaster Kyros. Significant as they all were, though, the conference was just another piece in the puzzle now.

As we descended the steps to return to our rooms, Nomusa touched my arm. "I know we've been avoiding this, but we have to find Xaron. Everything else has been set in motion. Now, we need to find out what happened to our friend."

I didn't answer for a moment. As desperately as I wished to know if Xaron had survived, fear that he had not was stronger. But fear was a poor excuse to do nothing for him if something could be done. "You're right. Where do we start?"

"Shepherds chasing after a feral warden would likely draw many eyes and ears. Perhaps we should ask in the usual places?"

I sighed. "We don't have the coin to pay them, remember? I barely have two magnes to rub together. The Archon's mercy is all that's keeping us fed and sheltered."

Nomusa drew out her purse, setting it jingling with a shake. "I have my own stores, as well as the bit I took to buy food for Canopy. We'll have enough for this."

My excuses exhausted, I nodded. "Then let's see what the city is whispering."

———

A few turns of plying our contacts yielded more intriguing results than I'd expected, if not in the direction we desired. As food costs continued to climb, disputes were breaking out among the agricultural guilds, which only made the situation worse when even less food was brought in than before. In even more worrisome news, ever since the night of the gathering — the Dragon's Dusk, some silver-tongued fool had named it — the Manifest was said to be stirring like a hornet's nest, the people within the compound seeming to have awakened with innumerable activities. They built bonfires; they built houses; they sowed the ground for fields and dug trenches. Vusu and his Seekers were fortifying their position. The Manifest was preparing for war.

Others whispered of the Despoina's absence from the public scene after her erratic behavior, but none could say what it meant. Some said she grieved her father's death. Softer, it was murmured that she hid from her guilt, though no one outright accused her of the deed. I smiled bitterly at that. It would make the web we spun all the more convincing to the common people. We heard, too, that to show their displeasure at Asileia's insult to the Avvadin emissary, many of the Valemish priests had mounted blazing braziers before their temple doors.

But of our immediate concern, we heard only enough to tantalize. A feral warden, it was said, had fled into the heart of Iris with Shepherds in close pursuit. If it was Xaron, the news wasn't good, for no one had seen the warden leave the deme, nor had they glimpsed the Shepherds again.

Having few leads, Nomusa and I wandered Iris aimlessly for a turn, but happened upon no further clues. My hopes lay solely with Talan, though it worried me that we had not heard from him since the night before.

Returning to the palace as the sun hung just over the sea, I hoped to see him waiting outside the grounds for us, but no such luck was to be found. We walked back up to the palace and to our bedchambers. There, Jaxas Wreath himself stood before our doors, while Nikias hovered nearby wearing a severely offended expression. The usual gaggle of honors lingered behind.

"Verifiers," the Archon said mildly as we approached. "I expected you to be more easily summoned. We must hurry; the meeting occurs within the turn and on Conclave grounds."

"Our apologies, Archon," I said with a slight bow. "We were looking into the fate of our accomplice."

"Ah." Jaxas's neutral expression clouded with conflicting emotions. "And do you have news of him?"

"Little of use," Nomusa said tartly.

"A shame." The Archon actually did sound regretful. "If you had found him, I had an idea to..." He shook his head. "But no need to rouse restless pyr. We must depart at once. It will not do to keep them waiting."

I nodded and forced the matter from my mind. "We're ready when you are, Archon."

Two carriages were waiting out front for us. Jaxas took the first one, while Nomusa and I slipped into the second. Before our driver took us after the Archon, his steward saw it fit to give us one last stern lecture. "It does not bode well to keep my master waiting, nor the other leaders of our nation. Be more timely in the future, Verifiers."

"We will, Nikias," I said wearily. "But it is you who delays us now."

With a scowl, the steward stepped back, and the driver set off.

Our carriage took us over the bridge that connected the Laurel Palace to the Conclave grounds, a graceful construction of white marble, with arches and columns supporting it over the chasm that fell to the sea seventy spans below. But it paled in comparison to the structure to which our carriage pulled up.

The Conclave's massive dome bloomed before us like a flower bulb on a godly scale, rising hundreds of feet high with shining bronze plating and white marble that still gleamed as if newly set and waxed. A sanctuary to the Eidola built by the original settlers of Oedija, it was said to have been forged partly by magic. Seeing the impossibly seamless curve of the dome, the agelessness of its stone, and how the bronze had not ceded to a green patina even after many long centuries, I found myself believing it.

We exited the carriages to rejoin the Archon. Jaxas noticed our awed expressions, and his mouth quirked in a slight smile. "Yes, it is impressive. I remember craning my head back the same way as you when I first came here as a boy."

I drew my gaze from the edifice to the Archon. "The Council is within?"

He nodded. "The Low Consuls don't meet within the main chamber, but we'll need to cross through it." He motioned to a few attending honors who had traveled on the back of his carriage, and they pulled open the doors to the building at the heart of Oedija's demotism.

I found myself once again slack-jawed as we entered through the two grand doors. The dome's tremendous height looked even higher from within, its peculiar and unnatural architecture made clear by the lack of supporting beams or columns on its smooth, curved ceiling. Ringed balconies spiraled down the dome, supporting gilded effigies of old heroes and yet more gods. At the top was a shining oculus that admitted the dying golden light of the day through it. Each ring down was trimmed with a dull gold, and where the sunlight hit it from the oculus or the many windows below, it glittered faintly. It was as wide across as it was high and dizzyingly massive.

While the ceiling curved up, the floor sloped down like an amphitheater, rows of seats layered and offset so that the speaker's platform below was visible. On the platform was mounted a podium and a gargantuan mounted bell. This, I realized, was where the Archon presided over Conclave sessions.

Late in the day as it was, I had not expected to see many people, but the Servants of the Conclave, elected officials from every deme of Oedija, still filled the soaring chamber with a susurrus of murmurs. At our entrance, many glanced up, their expressions mildly curious. As we passed, whispers died down and eyes cast aside, yet I had no doubt as to where their attention lay. I was surprised to find that my stomach fluttered with nervousness. I had always worked within the shadows of the polis's most powerful. Now I blanched at being the object of their attention. If I was forced to work long within the Conclave, I doubted I would enjoy it.

Jaxas led us down the many tiers to the small, shadowed space behind the speaker's platform. There, a small, humble door presented itself, hidden from view from the rest of the chamber. As we stopped before it, Jaxas again smiled at our surprise. "Yes, the Council meets within. Humility is often the best guise for hubris." He continued quieter, "Are you ready to begin?"

Studying the Archon, I wondered if he was asking it more of himself than us. I nodded. "We're ready."

Jaxas motioned to an attending honor, and she opened the door. With one last lingering look, the Archon led us inside.

The chamber looked to have been adapted from a cave. Its windows were little more than natural openings with no glass covering them, so the scent of salt and seaweed filled the room. As we entered, the Low Consuls of the Demos Council looked up. There were ten of them, all seated around a slab of stone smoothed so that its surface reflected like glass. Conversation ceased as we entered. I didn't meet their eyes, but dropped my gaze to the strange table and the goblets of wine set before each member.

There were ten of them, the Low Consuls, though there were supposed to be eleven. One of the seats remained empty due to political deadlock. Thus, it fell to Jaxas as the Archon to break tied votes. The Servants were the official representatives of Oedija's citizens, and the Ruling Wreath was given the glory. But the Low Consuls commanded all of Oedija's politics from the shadows.

I recognized their faces, both from the notices posted in the forums of each deme as well as from the recent Ascension. On one side of the stone slab sat the five members of the Preservist faction, the faction most closely aligned to Avvadin ancestry and policies. As their name implied, they sought most of all to preserve the state of the polis, holding change to be more detrimental than how matters were presently.

On the other side of the table was a more eclectic group. Three comprised the Equalist faction who, when they managed to draw a majority in the Conclave, passed legislation like basic protections for prostitutes and establishing public granaries. But the famine showed the holes in their accomplishments. Though the granaries existed, the Equalists had only managed to secure a fraction of the grain needed to supply them to stave off disasters. So it was that starvation was proceeding unchecked as the current drought progressed.

I couldn't help but suspect one particular Equalist in having a role in this duplicitous outcome. Feiyan stared at me with a small smile, her narrow eyes crinkled in consideration. Her peplos was unassuming, her only concession to frivolity a silver necklace adorned with glittering emeralds, but I knew better than to believe her humble. It was just as Jaxas said; humility was ambition's mask. I imagined Xaron, dead in a ditch somewhere in the city, and had to clench my teeth hard to hold back words I could only regret.

The Low Consuls weren't the only ones present. Around the edges of the cave-like room stood other notables of Oedija. Before one window were the five uniformed and white-haired Stratechons, their red lacerna

thrown over their shoulders. The half-cloaks distinguished their elite military status along with their laurel-crested breastplates.

Next to them stood High Tribune Photina, staring severely over the heads
of the others. She, like the Stratechons, often preferred Preservist policies. I
couldn't help but feel irrationally angry toward her. While it was true that the
Shepherds were under her command, she had little choice in the mandate
being carried out. Anyone who sought to change the way that wardens were
managed in Oedija would quickly lose their authority. Yet she was the head
of the institution that had likely killed my friend. I could not easily forget that.

The man who stood in contrast to that institution was under another
window. Kyros Brighteyed glared over the gathering, his sagging jowls
making his scowl even more pronounced. As my eyes slid over him, I
considered once again what to make of the Archmaster. If what Xaron
had said was true, that Kyros was training wardens to fight, we still had
good reason to be suspicious of him. As he met my gaze, his scowl did not
shift, and I saw that his eyes glowed eerily. I averted my gaze, wondering
what the Archmaster saw as he peered at me.

Orhan of Bazaar, the leader of the Preservists, spoke first. "Jaxas, how
good of you to join us." He smiled brilliantly, looking the picture of an
Avvadin patrician in his diamond-patterned, velvet robes.

"A good turn after you said you would," growled Berker of deme
Sandglass, Orhan's secondhand man, whose pockmarks were barely
disguised beneath his curly beard.

Daelya of Brinecoast, leader of the Equalists, snorted and leaned back
in her chair, her willowy body curving into it. "As if you keep any of your
promises."

Berker flushed as he leaned forward. "And what do you mean by that?"

"Berker," Orhan said with a laugh, placing a hand on the bigger man's
shoulder and pressing him back into his seat. "Peace, my good man. We're
here on serious business, not to quarrel with each other." He eyed Daelya
from across the table. "Isn't that correct, my dear?"

Daelya raised an eyebrow, but nodded silently.

Jaxas walked slowly to his own chair and sat. Nomusa and I remained
where we were by the door, seeing no obvious place for us.

"Low Consuls," the Archon said, raising a hand toward us, "this is
Verifier Airene and Verifier Nomusa."

All shifted their gazes toward us. My stomach fluttered, but I forced
calm onto my expression.

"Ah, the little Finches who have been causing such a disturbance,"
Orhan said with a smile. "You are most welcome."

"Very welcome," Feiyan reiterated. She, too, smiled at us, but it was tinged with frost. "And dressed so prettily for us — we appreciate the effort you put into your presentation."

I ignored her, keeping my focus on our task. "If you have heard of us," I began, "then you may have also heard of our purpose in being here." At a nod from Jaxas, I continued. "For the past span, since the first of Odaon, Nomusa and I have been looking into the murder of the late Despot Myron Wreath."

The Low Consuls shifted, as did the rest of the attendees. I felt the gaze of Kyros Brighteyed most keenly, but it was Orhan who spoke. "Murder, you say?" the Preservist leader observed, his head tilting. "But I do believe Despot Myron was declared to have died of natural causes."

"And yet here we are."

Orhan's mouth quirked. "So we are. Perhaps subterfuge isn't necessary before someone with such incisive perception. Very well, Verifier Airene. We will drop the pretenses within this room."

"L-looking into it?" stuttered Iason, a nervous, old man of Preservist inclinations. "What m-measures have you taken?"

I hesitated, but there was no path but forward. "We have investigated the possible motives and actors behind Myron's murder. Recently, we visited the Despot's chambers and spoke with the Despoina."

"You spoke with her?" Daelya leaned forward, her eyes alight with interest. "She hasn't been to a Council meeting since her Ascension."

"Though after what she did with the Imperium's ambassador, it's best that she stays away," Berker rumbled. "Does she mean to start a war we cannot win?"

I glanced at Jaxas and saw his head bowed and eyes obscured. I wondered if my remarks would hurt him, even knowing this plan. But before I could speak, Nomusa stepped up beside me. "Yes, we spoke to her. And what she told us was as good as an admission of guilt."

"Guilt?" Zehaar, a beautiful Avvadin woman of the Equalist faction, repeated with skepticism. "What precisely was said?"

"I asked her directly if she killed her father," I responded. "She said in return that it had been a test of her power, a test that had gone well, as the Despot had completely disappeared."

Murmurs started around the room. Jaxas dropped his head into his hands, so full of despair I doubted it was wholly an act. Zehaar looked about her, seeming to measure each reaction, the Archon's most of all. "I, for one, am not convinced," she declared. "Delusion seems her crime more than regicide. Why admit guilt if she truly were guilty?"

Orhan spoke up. "It's true that it is not a direct admission. If we were to proceed with a trial, I would be more comfortable if an explicit confession were brought forward."

"She admitted it." The Archon slowly raised his head from his hands, his face stiff as a waxen mask. "She told me in words as clear as you could want. 'I killed him,' she said the night of her Ascension. When she still appeared… sane."

The muttering around the room escalated to confused chatter. I shifted, trying to contain my nervous energy. *A trial* — it had come to this point without even our suggestion. The lines of our net were twisting fast now. I hoped they would hold.

Orhan sighed heavily, barely audible among the noise of the disbelieving Council. "Then we have the beginning of our proof," he spoke loudly. "Even if it is with heavy hearts, we had best proceed while the fire is still hot."

My gut clenched again as the rest of his faction nodded along. Daelya, however, shook her head. "No. I will not comply with this."

Berker was nearly trembling with rage. "An admission of guilt! Three witnesses on two separate occasions! And one of those the Archon of the Conclave, and practically her brother! Is that not enough for you?"

"We have all seen her." Daelya leaned forward, her expression hard. "We know how far gone she is. Do you truly think she is capable of it, of murdering her own father, then hiding it until now? No. I believe she is mad, and that she should not be punished further for it."

"She was not mad before that night," the Archon said softly to the stone table. "She was not mad."

"Perhaps her crime drove her to this point," Orhan offered. "In any case, such a confession can hardly be ignored. We have found no better explanation for Myron's death."

As the rest of the Low Consuls took up the debate, I studied the leader of the Preservists. That Orhan seemed convinced of the Despoina's guilt with so little information, and none of his faction spoke up to dispute it, was unsettling. Another game was being played here, I was sure of it.

"My fellow Consuls!" Feiyan suddenly stood, chair scuttling back across the stone floor. "Are we not forgetting something? A threat that is much more likely to be behind our Despot's death?"

"Don't tell me you're concerned about Avvad again," Esen sneered.

Feiyan stared at her flatly for a moment, then looked to the other members of the Council. "Not Avvad. I speak of the threat that we have allowed to fortify just outside of our city's walls. The enemy that has stolen the hearts of the underclass, even of honors, and fomented unrest among them in their aim to undermine the very foundation of our demotism." Her gaze turned smoothly to me. "The ones who harbor and train wardens as we turn our eyes aside."

"The Manifest?" Berker said in disbelief.

Even as anger flared in me at her clear reference to Xaron, the analytical part of my mind turned. Of all of the Low Consuls, I had suspected Feiyan as the most likely to be working with the Manifest. Yet here she was, openly speaking against them, and laying the Despot's supposed murder at their feet. In one swift speech, she'd become the one person on the Council I could be most certain was not aligned with Vusu.

As the clamor among the Council flared up again, Jaxas and I briefly met each others' eyes. The net would soon be cast. But for my family's sake, and for Linos, I knew it could not be aimed at Vusu and his Seekers.

Before I could intervene, Orhan clapped his hands. "We stray from our purpose here. Whether or not the Manifest is an issue is irrelevant to Asileia's guilt. With your permission, Archon, I propose we move this issue of putting the Despoina on trial to a vote. Simple majority."

"Granted," Jaxas Wreath said, perhaps a tad too quickly, though no one else seemed to notice.

"All in favor?" Orhan asked as he raised his hand.

As expected, the other four Preservists followed suit. Orhan frowned slightly that he did not have the majority he sought, but continued. "Opposed?"

Feiyan immediately raised her hand, and Daelya and Zehaar followed a moment later.

"Abstain?"

Verchlesa and Tychon, the two independent Low Consuls, predictably voted as such.

"Then with the eleventh seat as yet unfilled, it falls to the Archon to decide." Orhan shifted to look at him. "Well, Jaxas, what will it be?"

Jaxas didn't look up for a long time, steepled fingers playing one over the other. I thought I knew what held him back. Even a fake condemnation of his cousin must be difficult. It did not make me feel any easier about what he would do. I stared at him, willing him to look at me and honor his word, but he continued to watch his slowly moving fingers.

"Jaxas?" Orhan prompted. "Remember what you said of her confession. Remember your duty to your polis."

The Archon's swallow was visible even from where I stood. "We shall have the trial," he said quietly. "I vote in favor."

Orhan nodded solemnly and stood, and the rest rose with him. "Then it is decided. Prepare the Tribunal, Photina. We expect her trial in two days. No need to delay this any further than is necessary."

They filed out of the room while Nomusa and I stood by. The true rulers of the city, who would so easily throw a Wreath to the dogs if the situation called for it. Unease spread in me as I turned the possibilities over in my mind for why Orhan and his Preservists had done it. But I could think of no better explanation than the obvious. The Wreaths had always been mere figureheads, and a symbol that no longer served its purpose had to be cut away.

Kyros Brighteyed lingered a moment longer than the rest. It took all my resolve not to cringe away as he leaned his generous bulk in close. A faint aroma of sweat and sulfur hung around him.

"Tread carefully, Finch," he sneered softly. "I've heard of you sniffing around my Acadium. I know what you're about. And I'll be watching you."

My thoughts spun, but I kept my expression neutral. "I serve at the pleasure of the Archon."

"I'm sure you do." He shouldered past me to exit the room.

"What did Kyros say?" Nomusa whispered as she came up next to me, Jaxas just behind her.

"He's suspicious," I murmured. "Of what, I don't know."

"Then we'll remain cautious." Jaxas's depression seemed to have lifted, and he held his thin frame upright again. "I do not believe we can trust him."

"No," I agreed. "Not in this." Nomusa also nodded in agreement.

After we left the room, the three of us started our way up the Conclave's great chamber. Many of the people who had occupied it before had left. Other than the departing Low Consuls, only a few honors lingered, sweeping and wiping down the surfaces of the benches and tables before them.

So I was startled when, halfway up, Feiyan and her honor Kako stepped out from the eaves.

Feiyan wore a lazy smile. "You seem to be missing one of your number, Finches."

Fury immediately resurged in me. Before I could respond, Nomusa hissed, "You *fareshi* whore of a *kaluae*—"

"Nomusa," I cut her off. My own temples pounded with anger, but I kept my words measured and controlled. "What do you want, Feiyan?"

"Oh, many things." Her gaze wandered about the chamber, while Kako's remained hard upon me. Her eyes settled on the Archon. "Most of all, I wished the Despoina to be left alone, a security she has commanded that I ascertain." She shook her head slowly. "Yet I find that difficult to achieve when her closest confidantes betray her."

Jaxas flinched, but retained his composure. "We all know what she's capable of, Low Consul," he said quietly. "I cannot look away from the truth before me."

"You mean the truth you have constructed?" Feiyan's gaze slid over Nomusa, then settled on me. "If it has come down to manufactured truths, then perhaps I should no longer stay my hand. What do you think of the matter, Kako?"

"The same as you, mistress," the honor replied at her shoulder, not shifting his unnerving stare from me. "Our Despoina deserves to be protected at all costs."

"Precisely my thoughts," Feiyan said with another viper's smile. "You'll be hearing from me soon, I expect, Verifiers."

The Low Consul and her man began to turn away. Nomusa spoke to their backs. "You think to threaten us into silence when all of Oedija hangs in the balance? You'll ruin it all, Feiyan!"

Feiyan glanced over her shoulder. "Will I? Or is that your intention?"

As she stalked up the stairs, I stared after her, considering. Something about the conversation struck me as strange, yet I couldn't put my finger on it.

"*Fareshi* whore," Nomusa muttered. She was as stiff as an offended cat. "With what she did to Xaron…"

At her mention of him, it finally came to me. I seized Nomusa's arm and drew her close. "Does Feiyan think we're part of the Manifest?"

Jaxas's brow knit in consideration, while Nomusa's eyes widened. "Ah," she breathed. She glanced around. "We shouldn't discuss it here."

"No," I agreed. I looked at Jaxas. "Should we return to your solar?"

The Archon nodded. "Briefly. We have much that needs to be done."

He didn't need to tell me that. Though the web threatened to unravel at any moment, still we had to weave it.

CHAPTER THIRTY-TWO

PYRKIN

The sole interaction of spirits with the material plane that has credibility is the attunement of wardens. That some have the ability to channel magic is indisputable, and it can be seen at every public event due to the antics of the Wreaths' jester Hilarion. That some are born with this ability while others attain it later, too, has been proven time and again. That such an event might take place randomly certainly implies an interaction of some kind with Pyrthaen beings. But why, then, does it appear to be in the bloodlines of others?

I suspect that those who wield the Pyrthae's elements might be able to gain more insight into these mysteries. Yet, for the good of all, their magic is restrained, and even with knowledge lost or never recovered, I must agree that such a cost must be paid for peace so that the Tyrant Wardens never again return.

- The Traditions of the Eleven: Eidolan worship in the demotism of Oedija; by Oracle Iason of deme Iris; 1164 SLP

Having returned to the Laurel Palace, Jaxas, Nomusa, and I discussed Feiyan's suspicions. Why she thought we were part of the Manifest was obvious enough. We had been harboring a feral warden, Xaron. We had entered the Seeker compound not once, but twice, and I didn't doubt she was aware of both forays. If Feiyan happened to know the Visage's identity, she would be very suspicious of the fact that Vusu had been the one to recruit us as well as grant me the Verifier medallion.

The realization did little to make me like her more. But it did lead us to an uncomfortable conclusion: Feiyan was one of the few people we could trust not to be part of the Manifest. So I was forced to consider the unthinkable: to ask for her help. The chances of it yielding anything were close to none, but still we agreed that Nomusa and I would try before we parted ways. At the very least, I might recover Maesos's pyrkin. Perhaps it was a long shot that it would do anything to a warden's channeling. But it was our only chance of coming anywhere close to thwarting Vusu.

For his part, Jaxas agreed to continue the official preparations for the trial, including nudging the Council toward a conviction. I didn't think he'd need to do much in that respect, at least. In addition, he would try to determine if First Laurel Lykos had been duped by Vusu, just as we had, or if he was loyal to another. This information was particularly important to secure. The laurel guards wouldn't attend the trial unless specifically requested, as the Conclave had its own guards whom only the Low Consuls and Stratechons could command. Despite his determination, I sensed that Jaxas's conflicted feelings on the situation hadn't fully resolved. I understood them well. Our fake condemnation could result in very real consequences for those close to us. But there was little we could do but move forward. I could only hope Jaxas would stay strong.

Nomusa and I left his solar late that night and found our own beds. But as I lay there, still wearing my soiled tunic and trousers in case I had to rise quickly, sleep evaded me. My thoughts were too full of Linos and Xaron and how I'd failed them both. I saw images of the rest of my family killed the same way I'd doomed Hilarion: screaming and wreathed in flames cast by Linos's hand. Somehow, I clawed the pictures from my mind and settled into an uneasy slumber.

I rose early the next day and met Nomusa in the feast hall. While we ate, we discussed our plans once again and settled into our tasks. She would do what she could to find Talan and discover Xaron's fate. I would visit Feiyan and ensure everything was progressing well. That afternoon, we would meet again and try to sway what allies we knew we could rely upon.

Nomusa left before I did, for I first had to visit the palace aviary. I started composing a message to my family. Even if I'd had the time, I hesitated to visit them in person, fearing it would somehow make things worse. Since I didn't have the specific scent for their house here in the palace, I would have to send it to the public aviary in Riverport, the deme where they resided, which meant my words would have to be vague. In the end, I kept it brief, but asked them to leave their house for the next few days. I had little faith in my mother acting on my request, but still I made it, if only to ease my conscience. I doubted there was anywhere they could go where Vusu would not find them. But I had to do what I could.

I started to compose a letter to Vusu next, anxious to ensure he'd received news of the trial, but I stopped short of completion. If it was intercepted, Vusu might interpret it as an intentional betrayal. I burned the half-scrawled parchment in a nearby brazier and left the aviary. If he had as wide of a reach as he seemed to, he would hear of it soon enough. My small tasks done, I left the palace and headed toward Port.

A couple of turns later, I stood in front of the most substantial estate in Port. Feiyan's manor had a view over the bay and the port from which the deme gained its name. The docks were busy this time of day, commerce hardly slowing despite the brewing trouble. Trade had treated the Low Consul well. Though clearly larger than others, her home was not a patrician estate as of yet. A successful merchant, one might think. The limestone was well-treated, but lacked the decoration of old money. There was a fountain in its open-air garden, adorned with only a small statue. Rich, but not half as rich as the owner wanted to be.

I was admitted at the gates, but as I set up the stairs to the manor's doors, I was stopped by a waiting man. "Business?" he asked in a tone halfway between boredom and annoyance.

"I need to see your mistress."

"Feiyan? 'Fraid that can't happen. She's with a very important client, she is."

I gave him a studying stare. From the look of him, I guessed he didn't know how to tell anything but lies. "She'll make an exception for me. Why don't you go ask her?"

"Right. I'll just saunter up to the mistress and ask if she wants to see some dirty twat off the streets." He spat at my feet. "Guess I'm playing it too coy. Let me put it this way: If you don't have coin for me, you don't get past. Got it?"

I barely had enough in my purse for a meal, much less a bribe. "You seem a straightforward man. So let me be blunt with you." I drew out my Verifier medallion and held it up. "Employed by Feiyan or not, I can have you thrown in the dungeons. How's that for a bribe?"

The man's eye flickered from my face to the medallion. "You're not a Tribune. Ain't got the right symbol."

"No, it doesn't. But it does have the authority I claim." I slipped it back over my neck. "So either you can risk a cold cell, or you can let me through."

The man stared at me for several long moments, then turned away. "Stay here," he muttered, then walked into the house, closing the door behind him.

The ill-mannered guard kept me waiting long enough that I started plotting other ways in. But eventually he came back and ushered me inside with a short wave. "Come on, then. My mistress wants to hear what you have to sing after all."

I silently followed the guard within.

He led me through an atrium barely more impressive than the one in my family's house, then through the inner garden, and finally out to a courtyard with a view over the sea. There, a woman reclined on pillows piled on a stone bench. Most striking of all was that she lay stark naked. I quickly looked away. Nakedness outside of the baths was considered shameful to those who saw it. My face flushed at the insult.

"Not bad on the eyes, eh?" the door guard said with a leer at the woman. "But I think you came for the sight over here."

The guard led me around a series of pillars to where a familiar woman stood staring over the water. I tried not to let my teeth clench as I approached Feiyan on my own, the guard staying back to make eyes at the nude woman.

I stopped just short of the edge, standing behind her left shoulder. "Feiyan."

"Ah, the little Finch," the Low Consul said without turning. "I hope you enjoyed the sights on the way in."

I held my tongue.

"I'm not always inclined that way. Toward women, that is," Feiyan observed absently. "Sometimes, I have a man in her place. I find it a good reminder of what we are underneath it all. All the clothes, titles, privileges." She turned and smiled lazily at me. "Just flesh and bone, aren't we? Nothing that can't bruise or break."

I decided it was best to ignore her strange words. "We need to talk."

"So I hear. But it's odd. I thought I'd said all I needed to when I set those Shepherds on your friend. Xaron, wasn't that his name?" She chuckled. "I suppose it doesn't matter now. Though I must say, it was a good guess on my part. After I spoke with your other friend Nomusa, I thought it must be him. The Bali seemed too proud to remain in hiding her whole life."

My teeth clenched, and my fists bunched at my sides. As much as I might want to, pushing her off the balcony wouldn't help Xaron, but only make his death in vain.

"Let's say that's in the past," I managed to say.

Feiyan's eyes widened, her surprise seeming genuine. "How… magnanimous of you."

It took all my self-control to continue. "The Despoina's trial is tomorrow."

"Yes, even the cobblestones know. I should have suspected a Finch is good for no more than repeating the messages they are given."

"But the trial is not just about the Despoina's guilt or innocence. Someone in particular will be in attendance. Someone we have to stop for Oedija to remain whole."

Feiyan laughed, her voice shrill. "Oh, Airene. Stones don't shift because your star rose and fell, and fantasies do not become reality. Really, you seem as mad as Leia these days. But then, to have aligned yourself as you have, you'd have to be." She shook her head. "I think I've heard enough. You weren't nearly as entertaining as I'd—"

"Listen!" I hissed, stepping so close that our faces were barely a foot apart. "The Manifest is moving to take power, and you know it."

All humor fled the Low Consul's face, and she stared hard back at me. "You would know, wouldn't you?" she said softly.

"I know what you suspect, but you're wrong. I'm no Seeker, nor are Jaxas or Nomusa. We've had no part of them."

Her eyes widened in mockery. "No? Considering all you've done to wrongfully accuse Despoina Asileia, I find that hard to believe."

"Then let me explain." I drew in a deep breath, readying myself. "Their leader, the Visage of the Wyvern — he's the most powerful warden I've ever seen."

"I expect you would know, having seen much of him in the past span. Or have you not visited the compound twice since Myron was killed?"

"Myron was not killed. He was taken. And the Visage was behind it."

Feiyan studied me. "If you know so much, then perhaps you can explain just who the Visage is. Who is the man behind all of this? And what does he want?"

"I know as little as you why he does what he does. But as to who he is…" I braced myself for the words, knowing what they might cost me if I was wrong about Feiyan. "The Visage is Tribune Vusumuzi."

Feiyan's face went strangely still. "Ah. An interesting choice, I'll grant you that."

"He's the reason that Archon Jaxas pushed for a trial. Vusu wants the Despoina condemned for her father's murder to disrupt the polis. He himself will come to speak her final sentence. And when he appears, we aim to put an end to all of this."

Feiyan glanced over the water, which glittered in the morning sunlight. "If he is what you say he is," she said slowly, "then you have not a prayer of a chance of stopping him."

"I have a plan."

"Oh, good. Since your plans have worked so well in the past." She glanced back. "Forgive me if I do not beg for the details."

"You don't have to believe in it. You don't need to know anything about it. But I need your help if we're going to stop him. Fighters, weapons, gold — the Laurel Palace has some reserves, but it will arouse the wrong sort of suspicion if too much is used in one night."

She laughed again, but this time it was low with disbelief. "You don't tell me your plans, and yet you expect me to aid a hopeless cause and condemn myself in the process. Is this your poor attempt at revenge?"

I grabbed for her, hardly knowing what I was doing. All I knew was that I couldn't let her turn me down. But even as I gripped her arm, I was hauled backward. The door guard clucked his tongue as he wrenched my arm behind my back until I cried out.

"Now, now, it won't do to touch the mistress," he chastised in my ear, greasy locks brushing against my face.

"Feiyan!" I drove desperately on, struggling to twist my arm free. "You know what's at stake! You can't ignore what is happening!"

The Low Consul turned away. "Take her from my sight."

I wanted to rage at her, hit her, throw her off the cliff and watch her splatter across the stones below. She had hurt me, destroyed my home, and as good as killed Xaron. But no matter what bad blood remained between us, this wasn't about her or me. This was about the fate of the realm. This was about saving Linos.

"At least give me what Zotikos sold you!"

Feiyan stiffened, then turned back. "Wait, Gaoxo. Hold her there. Why would you want that contraband?"

I frantically thought of how much to reveal. "There are rare strains of pyrkin from the Bali highlands within it. I have need of one of them."

"Why? Don't play coy with me, Finch. It's long past time for that."

Her guard Gaoxo twisted my arm harder against my back for emphasis. "Tell the truth to the mistress, now."

"It dampens a warden's channeling!" I blurted. "We need it to ambush Vusu!"

Silence fell but for the whistling wind off the sea. Feiyan seemed frozen as she studied me. Then a slow smile spread across her face. "Someone has been telling you pyr stories, Airene. You will rest the fate of our realm on a few vials of pyrkin?"

I shrugged, the motion awkward with my arm held behind my back. "What choice do I have?"

The Low Consul shook her head. "Gaoxo, please escort the mad Finch from my manor. And give her some seed for her trouble."

"No!" I tried to wrench free, but the guard had too firm a grip. Ignoring my protests, he wheeled me around toward the entrance and took me away from his mistress.

Gaoxo was not gentle as he threw me down the entrance steps, and even less so when he peppered the stones around me with cullets and magnes. "The mistress's seed," he called down to me. "Eat up, little Finch. Oh, and here's a little water to wash it down." He spat in my face and grinned.

I wiped the wet globules from my cheek and stared back at him. "I'm not leaving till I get that shipment."

"No? Then you'll have an uncomfortable wait. Don't see a chamberpot around, do you?"

I stared defiantly back up at him. I had no real plan. No matter how I turned the matter, there was little I could do now that Feiyan had refused me. But I couldn't give in. This was the crux to the ambush. Without it, Vusu had as good as won. And Linos would remain in his clutches.

The door opened behind the guard, and he whirled in surprise. A man in serving robes emerged with a crate in his arms.

"What's this?" Gaoxo demanded. "The mistress told me to send her from the property."

"And she sent *me* with this gift," the manservant replied stiffly. He descended the stairs and stood before me. "Airene the Finch?"

I could only nod.

He held the crate forward, its contents clinking softly inside. "My mistress wishes you to have this. She sends words as well: 'Let the cockerels fight each other.' If you'll take it…"

I accepted the crate silently. *Let the cockerels fight each other.* So she meant to stand back and watch. From her, I could scarcely expect more. But with a healthy heaping of luck, it would be enough.

I hefted the heavy crate and began my long walk across the deme.

———

Maesos answered almost as soon as I knocked at his door — or kicked at it, as it so happened.

"You confronted Zotikos? I just heard the merchant had a run-in with a madwoman." He saw the crate in my arms and his eyes widened. "And you recovered it?"

"It's heavy," I offered, voice strained.

"Of course! Allow me…"

The old glassblower took the crate and ushered me to the back of his workshop. Securing the door behind me, I followed him, arms aching after the long walk from Feiyan's compound. I could still scarcely believe she'd relented, though how much the gesture would matter remained to be seen.

After he'd set down the crate, Maesos turned back toward me, holding his back and wincing. "I don't envy you carrying that from Hull."

"It wasn't in Hull."

I explained what had occurred in brief. At my facing Feiyan, he whistled softly. "Not an easy woman to face down, our Low Consul. But you did it."

"For all the good it will do us. Are you sure the tales tell true of this pyrkin? And if they do, why would its use not be more widespread?"

Maesos had bent over the crate and pried it open, revealing rows of vials packed with soft cloth to keep them from breaking. As he drew one out, I saw it shone with the soft blue-green of the shallow waters on the northern coast of the city. "I do not know if its properties are real, but I do trust my supplier. As I mentioned before, this is pyrkin from the Bali spirit trees, the isikhayha. It is a capital punishment to scrape the pyrkin that grows on its trunks, so few would risk it, even for such properties. And as far as I know, only the Thulu trees host this strain."

I stared at the vial as Maesos unstoppered it and wafted the scent to his nose. It was pungent enough that I could smell it from where I stood, the scent of moss after a fresh rain filling the room. It seemed to calm the roiling anxiety that had swirled inside me for the last few days. "It has some effect at least," I admitted. "Just smelling it settles my nerves."

He nodded encouragingly. "But to know if it will truly work, we must test it on a proper subject. But where to get such a warden, I do not know."

I thought morosely of Xaron and Talan. If only I knew where they were, this would all be much easier.

"Maybe I can ask an Acadian I know," I suggested without hope. I doubted Eltris would be willing, but I had no other option.

Maesos seemed to sense my hesitation. "Take a vial and do what you can," he said kindly. "In the meantime, I'll finish out these bolts. Just need to put in the pyrkin and affix the heads now."

I nodded. "I'll be back soon."

He raised an eyebrow. "So you said yesterday."

I shrugged and smiled, then turned to leave. But as soon as I'd turned away, Maesos suddenly gasped. I spun back around, expecting him to be hurt somehow, but he just stared at me with wide eyes.

"Airene! I almost forgot to tell you!"

"What? What is it?"

"Your Guilder friend came by here. Said he had a message for you, that you were to meet him as soon as you could down at the 'Children's Cave.' He said you'd know the one."

My heart pounded. "Did he say whether the news was good or bad?"

Maesos shrugged helplessly. "No. I would have asked, but he was gone almost as soon as he came. Seemed in a big hurry."

Talan at least was alive; my knees went weak with relief. But what of Xaron? Even though it was blazing hot in Maesos's furnace room, I clutched my arms at the sudden gooseflesh that rose off my skin. "Thank you, Maesos. I have to go, but I'll see you tomorrow at the Conclave gates when dawn breaks?"

The glassblower bobbed his head. "You will, my Finch." He grinned like a child. "I'll get this down pat, don't you worry. If I don't have three dozen of the bolts, I don't deserve to be called the finest glass smith in Oedija!"

"Let's not get ahead of ourselves," I said with a small smile of my own.

He waved his hand. "Go, go. You know where to find me."

I left his shop at a run.

CHAPTER THIRTY-THREE
WARDENS

…And so, despite the admirable courage and dedication shown by our self-named Finches, the Council has deemed it necessary to disband the Order of the Verifiers of Truth. This is for the good of all; for the commerce, so its monied families and factions are not cast needlessly into the dungeons; for the demotism, so its Servants are not frivo-lously run out of office; and for the Finches themselves, who have suffered, I am told, a startling number of deaths among their members…

- Archon Cameos, announcement of the dissolution of the Order of the Verifiers of Truth, 1067 SLP

My heart was in my throat as I departed for the far end of Port, questions of Xaron's survival and Talan's news spinning in my mind. Why he had chosen the Children's Cave as a hideaway became obvious enough as I thought about it. Though it was not much of a cave, barely thirty cubits deep, it was dug into the side of a cliff off of Oedija's main ports, and was infrequently visited by only the most daring of children. I had heard of it when I was first establishing myself as a Finch, and had even had a child take me to it once, but I was surprised that Talan knew of it as well.

Several turns later, I reached the cliffs where I thought I remembered it lay. Afternoon had arrived in full. Nomusa would already be back at the palace, impatiently waiting for me. If I had been thinking straight, I would have sent a finch from Maesos's shop to tell her to proceed without me. But at the moment, that was the least of my concerns. I had to know what had happened to Xaron.

Traversing along the top of the cliff, I searched for the cave's marker. It had been a red rag tied around a mounted stick when I'd visited nine years before, but I doubted it would be the same now. Gray boulders were piled around me, and uneven stones beneath my feet made the trek difficult, cutting at my exposed toes as I walked with haste. But I didn't see the red rag. Leaning against a boulder, I caught my breath and plotted how to find the new sign. I could try and hunt down a child in the area who might know, but it would take time, and time was something I had precious little of. Still, I couldn't leave without hearing what Talan had to say.

I started moving again, but instead of looking for the red rag, I searched for anything that seemed out of sorts. A new generation of kids visited the cave now, and they would have their own way of marking it. It wasn't long before I saw it: a small cairn piled on top of the largest boulder. I smiled to myself and made my way past the stone to peer down the cliffside.

Knowing where to descend was only half the battle. Now, I had to navigate the precarious hand- and footholds, timeworn and broken by the many children who had clambered over them. At least I could identify the path; scratches in the cliffside made it clear where I should place my hands and feet, so long as I could grab on. If I remembered correctly, the cave wasn't far down. Steadying myself with several deep breaths, I bent over the edge and slowly, carefully, let myself down.

It was a torturous quarter-turn as I crawled down the cliff. Sweat beaded my forehead and ran into my eyes, but I didn't dare let go of the stone to wipe it clear. My hands and forearms burned with the exertion, and the rest of my body protested as well. But finally, the mouth of the cave came into sight, and I pulled myself inside.

Within the shadowy mouth, a figure leaped to its feet. There was a pause, then, "Airene? Airene, is that you?"

I rushed forward at his voice. "Xaron!"

We met in a tight embrace. For a moment, all I could do was hold my friend and bury my face in his shoulder. Only his gasp of pain made me release him.

"Sorry. Are you alright?"

"Oh, it's not so bad." Xaron flashed a rueful grin. "After all, I made it out alive."

I shook my head in amazement. "How? Three Shepherds came after you."

His smile slipped away. "We killed them."

"You and Talan?"

He nodded. "Really, he killed two, and I got one before that. But that's still a lot more than most people can claim. Certainly more than my old feral friends. They didn't even manage to take down one."

"What matters is that you're alive." I took his hand and squeezed it, eyes burning. "No thanks to me."

"Airene, don't. I told you, I accepted the risks." He tried to pull me into another hug, but I pushed him away.

"It's not just that. Xaron, you barely escaped with your life. You've almost died twice in the past few days." I couldn't meet his eyes. "And I'm about to ask you to risk it again."

His face stiffened. I didn't need to see his eyes to know the conflict waging behind them. He nodded once, swallowed, nodded again. All I could do was watch him from the corner of my eye, hoping he would agree and hating myself for that hope.

He gave a third nod, and this time he spoke. "Yes." He cleared his throat and said louder, "Yes — of course I'll do it."

I didn't meet his eyes. "Thank you," I murmured.

"It's just who I am," he continued as if I hadn't spoken, his gaze traveling beyond me. "Or who I need to be."

I finally lifted my head. Not so long ago, he'd been my wine-guzzling, starry-eyed friend who happened to be able to channel. Now, he was becoming a warden like the stories of old. It was who I needed Xaron to be. Even if it wasn't what either of us wanted.

Pebbles and dust suddenly spattered the entrance of the cave. I startled and spun around. A moment later, a silhouette swung into the cave and sauntered toward Xaron and me. I didn't draw my knife. I'd know Talan Wraithsbane's swagger anywhere.

Despite my somber mood, I pulled him into an embrace as well. "Thank you," I whispered in his ear.

The Guilder chuckled softly as he folded his arms around me. "I wouldn't let the little man die," he replied, pitching his voice loud enough for Xaron to hear.

I pulled away at the reminder and glimpsed Xaron's scowl before he turned his head aside. A pang of guilt passed through me, and I let go and stepped back.

Talan's gaze passed between us, but his half-smile never faltered as he leaned against the cave wall. "You've saved me a few words I see. Now you know my news."

It was only then that I took in their shabby state. They didn't look as bad as the night we'd tried infiltrating the Claw, but between the cuts and burns and bruises, they weren't far off. "Tell me what happened."

Xaron ran a hand through his messy hair. "Not much to say. The

Shepherds came for me in the night. I was dozing at the time, so they had the element of surprise, but fortunately, I used what Eltris taught me this time. I turned aside their first few attacks and managed to flee out the window before they came to terms with what happened." He shrugged. "From there, it was cat-and-mouse. I headed toward Iris, keeping to the rooftops. If my life hadn't been in mortal danger, it might have been exhilarating — I've never channeled like that before. From there, I broke into a few manors and tried to shake them off my trail, but it didn't work. Those bastards were like hounds with the scent. No matter what I did, they just seemed to know where I was."

"Maybe they can sense channeling like Kyros," I guessed.

Talan shrugged, as did Xaron. Even though they were both wardens, they knew little more than I about the full range of possibilities of their magic.

"In any case," Xaron continued, "they were starting to catch up and got a few hits in. One kinetic wave clipped my leg and made me miss my landing on a rooftop." He straightened the leg with a grimace. "Still hurts, but at least it didn't break. That might have been it if Talan hadn't shown up."

The Guilder gave a mocking bow. "It's true," he said extravagantly. "I swooped in and saved the damsel."

I pushed him lightly in protest and looked at Xaron, expecting to see another scowl. Instead, a reluctant smile had taken hold. I couldn't have been more amazed had alchemists transformed lead into gold before my very eyes.

"Alright," I demanded. "What exactly happened out there?"

Xaron laughed softly. "Look. I'd still rather spend time with a full chamberpot than him. But when a man saves your life two times in three days, you can't hate him *that* much."

"It seems I still have much to teach you," Talan said with a smirk.

Xaron shook his head with a rueful smile of his own. "But anyway, we've told you what happened with us. It's time you tell us what you've been up to. Talan said Vusu could no longer be trusted, but beyond that, we're both in the dark."

I sighed and told them all I knew. The retelling was not as painful this time, but the sharp reminders of my shortcomings were far from pleasant.

At the end of my tale, Talan nodded slowly. "I'm not surprised."

Xaron rolled his eyes. "Of course you're not."

The Guilder continued as if he hadn't been interrupted. "I'm sorry, Airene. I should have caught sight of this."

I laid a hand on his arm. "No one could have anticipated this. Vusu must have a means of traveling unseen. Perhaps he uses a radiant illusion like you've used before, Xaron. He's certainly capable of far more than that." I shook my head. "The power he has... I fear for both of you."

"Fear for us?" Xaron blanched as he realized now what my earlier request had meant. "Gods. You mean to set us against *him?*"

Talan's brow knit, too, as he looked to me. I raised my hands. "Not as things are. But I have a weapon that might even the odds."

"And what would this weapon be?" Talan asked.

I gave him a coy smile. "Pyrkin."

"Pyrkin?" Xaron arched an eyebrow. "What, to make him easier to see?"

"Your faith in me is heart-warming," I noted drily. "Since our run-in with Iela nearly three years ago, Maesos has been seeking to acquire a certain strain of pyrkin, just in case we ever faced a warden again. Recently, he found the strain and paid to have it smuggled out of the Bali highlands. He claims it can suppress a warden's ability to channel."

"And you believe that old gaffer?"

I drew out the vial of pyrkin from my purse. Where my fingers touched the glass, the strange substance glowed a brighter green. "Not exactly. But, on the slim chance that it does work, I need to test it on both of you."

Talan sighed and held out a hand. "I'm sure I've touched worse."

"I'll bet you have," Xaron muttered, but he followed suit.

Breath coming quick with anticipation, I unstoppered it and again smelled its pleasant, mossy scent. Tilting it, I dotted a small amount on each of their fingertips where the skin moved with their shifts. "Now try to channel."

For a moment, nothing happened. Then, as one, they cried out and clutched at their hands. Talan hissed and wiped his hand madly on the side of the cave, skin tearing and leaving a bloody smear behind. Xaron tore off his shirt and used the ragged garment to scrub furiously at his fingertip, then threw the shirt to the cave floor.

I stared in amazement at the two panting men. "It worked," I breathed.

"It burns!" Xaron moaned, peering at his finger. "It *still* burns!"

Talan, meanwhile, had calmed and now stared at his bleeding finger. "I think that will do," he said mildly.

Something inside me unwound. This had been the crux of the plan. And it was real. I steadied myself on the cave wall. "This might work. We could actually win."

"What might work?" Xaron demanded. He held up his reddened finger to me. "What exactly did I do this for?"

I took a breath, then told them the plan that Nomusa, Jaxas, and I had devised. The web that would, if we had woven it carefully enough, ensnare Oedija's enemy and render him helpless.

The plan that would kill Vusu.

Talan had gone very still by the time I was done, while Xaron was quivering with nerves. "Are you sure about this?" my fellow Finch asked uncertainly.

I nodded. "We have no other choice."

"He won't fight alone," Talan observed quietly. "We've seen what he has at his disposal. The Seeker wardens. The Shepherds." He shook his head. "And I do not know what allies we might recruit."

Xaron suddenly straightened. "Eltris! Have you gone to Eltris yet?"

It was my turn to stare skeptically. "Before I'd heard from Talan, I was going to have her check this pyrkin. But no, I haven't gone to her."

He shook his head. "I've told you, Airene, she's a warden to match Kyros. If we could get her on our side, it would go a long way."

"I suppose I could check." I looked between the two of them. "You should both probably stay here, though."

"But when it comes time," Talan said in a low voice, "we'll be by your side."

"And to let you know when that time arrives, you might need this." Fishing in my pocket, I drew out Xaron's lodestone.

A grin spread across his face. "You recovered it!"

"I did. But you'd better keep a better hold of it this time."

His grin turned sheepish as he accepted it from me.

Stepping back, another thought creased my brow, and I turned to Talan. "There's no chance of aid from the Underguild, is there?"

Talan shook his head. "It seems that Kalindi is taking power and establishing himself as the sole Guildmaster," he said, anger sharp in his words. "Even if he is not in league with Vusu, I doubt he would be amenable to opposing him."

I sighed. "Then I'll have to seek out other allies." I glanced at Xaron. "Like your bird master."

"See? You have that much in common," he pointed out with a grin.

I wished I could linger, to joke and pretend like everything wasn't coming to a likely end. But the concerns of the trial hounded me onward. "Wish me luck. I'll see you both at the trial."

They nodded, then watched as I scrambled my way out of the cave and back up the cliffside.

———

A turn and a half later, I arrived at Eltris's tower. My Verifier medallion granted me access to the Acadium campus, and after a brief while wandering, I'd remembered the way to the Master Augur's den. I knocked rapidly on the tower door and waited for a response. With Eltris's sharp hearing, I expected she'd detect me wherever she was in the tower. But five minutes had passed before I stepped back and started to wonder if the recluse was at home.

"You here to see that crazy old bat?"

I turned to see a woman in Acadian robes addressing me. She had dark skin, not the earthy browns of the Bali, but the deep bronze of the Avvadin provinces in the southern reaches of the Four Realms. There was a presence about her, like she owned the ground she walked on, that set me on edge. Acadians were supposed to be sheep, but this woman was far more like the fox stalking them. Xaron had said that Kyros was training some within the Acadium to work battle magic. I wondered if this might be one of his pupils.

"I was just stopping by," I hedged.

The Acadian studied me. "Well, if you were trying to speak to Eltris, you're out of luck. She went missing two nights ago and hasn't been seen since." She nodded up at a window on the tower. "Someone even went in to check if she had just locked herself up inside, but they didn't find anything. She's just gone."

Chills ran up my spine. Xaron had made it clear that Eltris was set against the Manifest. If she'd gone missing, I suspected I knew what had become of her.

"That's… unfortunate. Thank you for telling me."

"Sure." The Acadian turned away, then spoke over her shoulder. "If you're going to ask after her, I'd be careful. Strange things are happening. I wouldn't trust anyone you don't have to."

As if I needed the reminder, much less from a stranger. I nodded. The Acadian returned the gesture, then sauntered off on her way.

I lingered a moment longer and looked up at the tower window. A mad thought went through my head to check on the augur myself. I didn't know that passing Acadian woman, nor if she could be trusted. The next moment, though, I dismissed the notion. While Xaron had a great deal of confidence in his mentor, I was not so sure Eltris was worth risking my neck.

I had just turned away when a voice demanded from behind me, "What are *you* doing here?"

I twisted around, a hand reaching for my knife before I recognized who it was. "Master Eltris."

"Let go of that, girl," Eltris snapped. "If you think that would be of any use in the Acadium, you're even more of a fool than I thought."

I quickly released the knife, cheeks growing hot. Somehow, the frumpy, short woman made me feel like a naughty pupil at my schoolhouse lessons. "Where did you come from?"

The Master Augur snorted. "You wouldn't understand if I told you. What are you doing here? Why hasn't Xaron come to me of late?"

I opened my mouth to speak, but hesitated, not knowing where to begin or how much to tell. "He's been busy," I said vaguely. "You've been suspicious of the Manifest, isn't that correct, master?"

"I'm asking the questions, girl. How about you finish answering them."

I reined in my patience and stepped closer to the augur, desperately hoping Xaron's trust wasn't misplaced. "The worst has come to pass," I said in a whisper. "The Visage of the Wyvern is a Tribune named Vusumuzi, and he has the city in a chokehold. He took Myron Wreath captive and is coercing me and others to hold a trial against the Despoina to disrupt Oedija's confidence in the Laurel Palace. But instead of him trapping us, we'll trap him when he shows up to the trial—"

"I've heard enough," Eltris cut me off. "And my answer's no to the question you're about to ask."

I stared at her, stunned. "What do you mean, you've heard enough?"

The Master Augur shook her head. "You're looking in the right direction, girl, but seeing all the wrong things. It's right there in front of you, all of it, yet you're completely blind to it."

Even with my fraying patience, I tried to make sense of her words. "You're saying I don't see the risks? I know what danger Vusu poses." I pitched my voice lower. "He's the most powerful warden I've ever seen."

I jumped back as Eltris suddenly barked with laughter. "But that's *all* you see!" she exclaimed. "What of the questions behind it, girl? *Why* has Vusu become so powerful? If he has always been this strong, why has he done nothing for so many years?"

I had guesses, but I sensed that wasn't what Eltris was looking for. So I remained quiet and tried not to glare.

Eltris studied me for a long moment, then shook her head in disgust. "You think the world is within these city walls. Girl, look beyond them to find the questions you need to ask."

"And those are?"

She stepped so close that I could smell her breath, sour and unwashed. It took all my willpower not to lean away. "Why, in the whole of Telae, are there only the Four Realms that are of any significance? Even you must have learned the world is a sphere, and that the Four Realms occupy only a small space on it. Why, then, do so few people populate it?"

I didn't understand how this was relevant, and Eltris seemed to see it in my eyes. "Fine!" she continued. "A more pointed query then. Why did our Oedijan ancestors embark on their Lighted Passage? What made them leave their homeland and sail across the vast sea to make landfall here? A whole nation uprooted in a single moment. Yet no one wonders why."

I opened my mouth to reply, but Eltris bulled over me. "And to the northeast! What of the Endless Expanse beyond the Wumofu Desert? Once an empire reigned there, a thousand years ago. Yet now their cities lie in ruin, their lands sand and dust, their lakes and rivers dried up. And their descendants live in caves on the edge of that desolation, as absorbed by their ignorance as you."

Ignorant. Of all the insults she could have hurled at me, this was the one that cut the deepest. "You speak of empires risen and fallen in ages past. But I'm concerned with keeping our own realm from splintering apart."

"As am I!" Eltris snapped. "So then, girl — where else are you to learn how to keep a realm from ripping asunder if not from the lessons of history?"

I had no response to that. Yet my frustration, brimming and threatening to take possession of me, didn't allow me to admit it.

"The lands beyond the sea to the west; the deserts to the east; to say nothing of the Rift and the Riven Lands beyond it to the south," Eltris continued more softly. "Girl, you can't see a storm coming by watching for rain at your feet. You look up and see the dark clouds covering the sky. Look up, and tell me: What is coming?"

It was suddenly too much. "Riddles," I said bitterly. "I beg for aid and all you offer are riddles."

Eltris looked as disgusted with me as I was with her. "Finches," she hissed. "And you're supposed to be a sharp lot." She turned away. "I've wasted too much time here. Leave me be."

"I don't suppose I'll see you at the trial," I shot back at her, a bitter edge to my words.

The Master Augur didn't bother to answer, her fingers tapping across her crossed arms.

I exhaled in frustration, not caring how it looked, and turned on my heel. She wasn't the only one who had wasted her time.

CHAPTER THIRTY-FOUR

LOYALTY

To secure the illusion, some privileges were granted to the Wreaths. First, they were returned possession of the Laurel Palace, their ancestral home, as well as the lands granted to it. Second, they were given a guard of their own to defend it, never to number more than three score. And third, they were to act as Oedija's nominal ambassador with foreign entities, though all matters of importance were to be approved by the Conclave or the Council.

- A Modern Account of the Wreaths; by Acadian Helene, Master Historian; 1170 SLP

Upon returning to the palace, I found an honor waiting to inform me that Nomusa and Jaxas were expecting me up in the Archon's solar. As I entered, they broke off their discussion and rose to their feet.

"Where have you been?" Nomusa demanded.

"Attempting to find us allies." I walked over to the center table, again laden with food, and helped myself. I'd barely taken the time to eat or drink that day. "And mostly failing," I spoke around a mouthful of a fragrant, aged cheese and a crispy wafer.

My companion crossed her arms. "You could have told us."

I raised an eyebrow. "Sorry. I was busy finding out Xaron is alive."

Nomusa's expression lifted instantly. "He is?" she exclaimed. "He survived?" She rushed over and wrapped me in my third embrace of the day, almost knocking the plate of food from my hands as she did. "He beat three Shepherds, Airene! Three!"

I gave a small laugh. I didn't mention Talan. Tomorrow would be soon enough to expose him. "Yes. I can't believe it either."

"He's hiding out, then?"

I nodded. "Somewhere safe. Don't worry, he's fine now. And he promised he'd come to the trial. But..." I extricated myself from her arms, and my eyes flickered to the Archon, who still sat in his chair. "Even with his help, we don't have nearly enough manpower to take down Vusu tomorrow."

Nomusa's smile faded and the lines across her forehead returned. "No. We don't. After I realized you wouldn't be showing up for a while, I set out on my own to search for allies. I looked into whether we could get a faction of the Underguild on our side, but they're all falling in line with that Kalindi. I even looked into hiring mercenaries," she said with a small laugh, "but I couldn't find anyone I could stomach, much less pay."

"I had similar success with Feiyan and Eltris."

Nomusa's eyebrows shot up. "Those are two people I hadn't expected you to ask."

I shrugged. "Who else is there? Surprisingly, Feiyan actually came through. I obtained the pyrkin we need." A small smile spread on my lips. "And it works. Xaron confirmed it."

"It works." Nomusa's eyes were wide as she considered the possibility.

Jaxas nodded slowly. "Then all this plotting may yet bear fruit."

I nodded, studying him. He'd shown little in the way of reactions thus far, even at the news of Xaron defeating three Shepherds.

Before I could speak, he inquired, "And what of this Eltris? She is the Master Augur, is she not?"

"Yes. And Xaron's tutor as well. But for all that, she would not pay me heed, but spoke in riddles around me. I would not count on her aid."

The Archon looked thoughtful for a moment. "My own inquiries have failed. I had the opportunity to spend some time with First Laurel Lykos, but I could not determine whether or not he is loyal to us or to Vusu. There is still time to give him our trust if we think it necessary, but I still hesitate to do so."

"Better it remains a secret then. The same with Kyros. They'll both be at the trial, so we'll find out their loyalties soon enough."

"But unless Lykos instructs it, the laurel guard will not be present," Jaxas pointed out.

I nodded wearily. So few allies, so many powerful enemies, and several other parties who might sway either way. I did not see how the trial could turn out well. Yet there was no other way forward. When I obtained the pyrkin bolts from Maesos, we would have no soldiers to shoot them. And even if we tried firing them ourselves, a foolhardy idea, we would arouse suspicion if crossbows went missing from the armory.

Silence reigned while I finished eating, then lingered afterward as we stared into the flickering flames of the hearth.

"What if," Jaxas said slowly, "we do not move against Vusu at the trial?"

My chest tightened. I had feared that someone would waver in their conviction. Until the moment came, I still did not know if I myself could stand firm. But I spoke despite my doubts. "We have to ensnare him at the trial. It's our only opportunity. And it's the turning point for the polis. After her trial, Asileia Wreath will be discredited, and Vusu will reveal that her father has miraculously risen from the grave." I rubbed at my temples. "If we let that happen uncontested, she may lose all her influence, and you and us with it."

Nomusa shifted, and I looked at her, expecting her to disagree. So I was surprised when she said, "I agree with Airene. This is the time to strike, if only because Vusu would not expect us to."

Jaxas shook his head. "You do not know that."

"No, we don't," I conceded. "But I think I know something of Vusu now. He's proud. He believes his plans infallible, and that he himself is untouchable. Of course he knows we plot against him. But he must think none of it will matter so long as he gets what he wants. That our resistance is as futile as a fly's to a spider."

"And maybe it will be," he murmured.

Despite his doubts, when we separated some minutes later, our plans remained in place. We bade each other a solemn good night, the weight of the morning already bearing down on us.

Upon reaching our rooms, we found someone waiting for us. "Corin," I said as we walked up to her. In the midst of everything else, I'd nearly forgotten she'd taken up residence in the palace. She wore now what I suspected were the palace's rudest garments, which was to say they were far finer than her usual cartwoman's clothes.

"I didn't know you'd come here," Nomusa observed mildly, making no other gesture of greeting. They had never been close, despite living together for several years.

The cartwoman nodded before looking back to me. "There is nothing for me to do here," she said softly as if afraid of being overheard. "Is there something you need me to do?"

Distracted as I was with everything else on my mind, the last thing I wanted was to come up with ways for Corin to feel useful. Still, I knew better than to turn away an ally when we had so few — and an idea had occurred to me. "You know, there is. Maesos — you remember the glass-blower? — he's forging a certain kind of crossbow bolt and means to meet us at the Conclave gates tomorrow morning. Could you help him cart his wares in?" I knew Maesos could manage it himself, but considering this was the heart of our trap, it wouldn't hurt to have two people on the task.

Corin hesitated only a moment before nodding. "I can do that."

I touched her briefly. "Thank you, Corin."

With that, we each slipped into our rooms. I stopped only to remove my sandals and hidden knives before I collapsed onto the bed. My thoughts and fears whirled in my mind, too many to concentrate on any particular one. I stopped trying. What would be, would be. Resignation swiftly carried me off to a deep, dreamless slumber.

———

I woke to scraping. Metal against metal. I sat up on an elbow, my groggy mind working to make sense of the sound. Something rattled in the door. A key turning in the lock. As comprehension set in, my heart began to hammer.

I whipped out of bed. In the darkness, I couldn't see where I'd discarded my knives, so I settled for the pyrkin pot, visible by the sliver of light escaping from beneath its lid. Taking it in both hands, I moved behind the door and raised it overhead, ready to smash it down on the first intruder to enter. The chill of the night mixed with my fear so that I began to shiver as I stood there, waiting.

The bolt settled. The door pushed open to reveal a figure. By the flicker of torchlight from outside the room, I saw a copper helm with a twist of leaves carved into it. A laurel guard. I held my breath, waiting for him to see me, but his eyes went first to the bed. He crept toward it without looking around.

The second man who entered, however, looked directly at me and star-tled. "Tyurn's balls—!"

I swung my pot as hard as I could into the slot of his helm. The clay shattered as it connected, spilling brilliant light down the front of the soldier's muscled breastplate and into his eyes. As he cried out and stum-bled back, the first guard looked around and spotted me in the sudden brightness. I recognized him: the man Talan had hit with his own sword in the Valemish temple.

He stalked back toward me. "You shouldn't have done that," he sneered, his short sword ringing as it left its scabbard.

I backed away, feeling at the cupboard behind me for other things to throw. But it was too late. A third guard dashed into the room and seized me, detaining both of my arms. "Enough of this," he growled in my ear as he bore me to the ground.

I tried to shout, but a gauntleted hand clapped over my mouth, filling it with the taste of sour leather. I tried biting through it, but only achieved an aching jaw for my efforts.

"You'll get your due soon," the squash-nosed guard chuckled as they hauled me bodily from the room. "'Thae above, you'll get it soon."

The guard I'd hit with the pot glowered down at me, his face dripping with yellow pyrkin, his skin fiery and red from the contact. His glare also promised vengeance.

They dragged me roughly down the hall. As we passed Nomusa and Corin's rooms, I heard nothing from behind their doors. I could give them no sign.

No one was coming to my aid.

Rage gave way to terror. And I'd thought I could save the polis. Bitterness mixed with the rest of my caustic feelings. I gave up my struggles, saving my strength for a moment when it might count.

I'd expected them to carry me down to the dungeons. They took me up instead. Desperate curiosity seized me, but I couldn't have asked where we headed if I'd wanted to. We arrived at the defaced doors of the Ruling Wreath, then continued down the hall to the chambers where the Despot had actually resided. My confusion only grew.

As soon as we were inside the doors, they threw me to the ground, the rich carpet only partially cushioning my fall. I drew in a ragged breath and clutched my hands over my middle. The same nauseating illness as my last visit washed over me.

As the sickness began to pass, I lifted my head to find a man waiting. He was silhouetted by the soft light of the moons with his back to me, but it was still simple to guess who he was.

"Lykos." I tried not to show how rattled I was, but my chattering teeth betrayed me.

The First Laurel turned, his steely eyes catching a glint of light before they were once again cast in shadow. "A story will be called on the streets tomorrow. Verifier Airene, overcome with guilt over her deceit of the Despoina, cast herself over the balusters of the Despot's old rooms to the sea below."

"I don't understand," I said through clenched teeth.

"Then let me make this clearer." Lykos approached to stand over me. "As the First Laurel, it is my duty to protect the wearer of the Evergreen Wreath from harm. You, along with the treacherous Archon Jaxas Wreath, mean to condemn the Despoina of a crime she did not commit."

I still didn't know where his loyalties lay. Perhaps he was telling the truth. Perhaps he was a dutiful guard. Or maybe he was in league with Vusu, and this was a test of my resolve before the trial tomorrow. As far fetched as that seemed, I had no idea of what lengths the traitor Tribune might go to.

So I kept my response neutral. "Neither you nor I know who killed Myron Wreath. That is why we must hold a trial."

"You may not know," the First Laurel said coldly. "But I do."

"Then tell me. Unless you would condemn yourself."

Lykos's eyes didn't shift. "You mean to lay your sins on me as well."

Opposition didn't seem likely to get me anywhere. I shifted tactics. "First Laurel Lykos, listen to me. Archon Jaxas brought me into his service three days ago. I don't know the circumstances around Myron Wreath's disappearance, nor who had a part in it. But I must act now. Things are happening—" I fumbled for the right words. "—a coup is underway, and plans are being set into motion. So I'm forced to do what I can with the tools that I have."

The First Laurel stared down at me. "Then you mean to condemn the Despoina because she makes for the most convenient scapegoat."

He was like a wolf with the scent, implacable in its hunt. "Lykos, please. I can't tell you what is going on without risking others' lives. But I can say that if you don't allow me to proceed with this trial, many people will die, and Oedija as we know it will collapse."

One of the guards snorted behind me. "Just listen to the wench, sir. Now she wants to save the city!"

"Quiet," Lykos said without raising his voice. His guards' chuckling abruptly ceased.

His gaze never left me. "You convinced the Council that the Despoina is responsible for her father's death. You devised an expedited trial for her guilt. Yet you expect me to believe that you're trying to save Oedija from an unknown threat."

"I know how it sounds. I know I look guilty. But if you just give me a chance to — to—" I could not think of a way to convince him without betraying my secrets. And I couldn't do that when I was still unsure of him. Not when I knew what Vusu would do if he discovered I'd betrayed him.

"She's guilty," the squash-nosed guard spoke up again. "Sir, you have to see—"

"I told you to be quiet."

A long silence filled the room, broken only by the creaking of the laurel guards' armor. I dropped my head and wrapped my arms tighter around me as I thought desperately of a plan. But my thoughts turned in circles around each other.

"On the one hand," the First Laurel said at length, "you could be scrambling to save your life." He paused. "What were you doing at the Valemish temple?"

I looked up at him, startled by the disjointed question. "I was informed of suspicious activities coming through the temple and thought there might be more to it. Perhaps even something connected to Myron Wreath vanishing. That you were there was a coincidence."

His cold eyes gave no sign as to whether or not he bought my story. "But you do not believe them responsible. Who, then?"

I dropped my gaze again. "The Despoina," I whispered.

Lykos barked a harsh laugh. "It seems my interrogation has come to a close."

I didn't know if it was desperation or the strange sickness that burned in the back of my throat that compelled, but I threw my head back and stared up at him in defiance. "Lykos, I can't tell you who I am truly concerned about. But ask yourself: Who benefits from a city in chaos? Who would wish for the downfall of the Wreaths?"

The guards shifted, looking at each other, but Lykos remained still. For a moment, as he stared down at me, I thought I had gotten through to him. He would realize the truth of what I had been trying to tell him. This misunderstanding would be set behind us, and he would join us in fighting Vusu at the trial in the morning.

His next words put an end to hope. "Take her to the balcony."

I didn't struggle as the guards grabbed my arms, dragged me over to the balcony doors, and wrenched them open. The biting sea wind cut through my clothes, yet it was nothing compared to the cold fear that had frozen my limbs. I had failed. And now I would die for it.

"Why kill me?" What little self-possession I still had was swept away with the wind. "What does it gain?"

He stepped out beside me and my captors. "You are to be a key witness in the trial. Get rid of you, and I reduce the chances of its success. I defend my Despoina from false accusations."

"Please." Unbidden tears stung my eyes. "I'm just trying to do the right thing. I'm trying to save my friends and family. Please. Please don't do this." The words came tumbling from my mouth, one after another, barely considered. Only one secret did I hold back.

For a moment, I thought I saw doubt in his eyes. The next, the guards pulled me away, pushing me against the railing, rough stone scrapping against my exposed midriff. The pain awoke my survival instinct again. I suddenly kicked to life.

"I have to be there!" I cried through numb lips. I tried not to stare over the edge at the black waters below as they forced me to bend over it. "I have to stop him!"

Lykos brought his face close to mine. "Him. Who do you seek to stop?"

I clamped my mouth shut, afraid the truth would spill from me as those first traitorous words had. Blood flooded my mouth as I bit my the inside of my cheek.

Lykos shook me hard. "Tell me!"

Tears were frozen on my nose. I clenched my teeth and remained silent.

The First Laurel stared at me for a long moment, then straightened and nodded. His guards began heaving me up, bracing their legs to get the leverage to force me over the railing.

Reckless rage overtook me. A scream ripping from my throat, I pulled at their hands and braced against the stone to kick back. They grunted and stumbled, but kept their holds.

"Please!" I screamed. "I swear by the Eleven, by the 'Thae, by whatever gods you want, I'm doing what's right!"

A fist slammed into my stomach and knocked the breath from me. Pain mixed with the sickness, and I curled up on the ground as the guards let go.

"Tell me," Lykos said as he stood over me.

Scraped skin burned with pain. Deeper pains lanced with fire. "I've said all I can," I whispered.

The guards grabbed my arms, and the fist came again. As agony spread through my gut, I spat up on the stone. One guard let out a disgusted grunt, but neither hesitated in hauling me back toward the railing. I couldn't catch my breath. Cold had penetrated me to the bone. Pressure built in my head like it would burst. The world pitched, and suddenly I was halfway over the baluster. I felt the weakness of fear come over me, and I went limp.

"Tell me, Finch!" Lykos shouted from behind me. "Tell me!"

I let my head hang as the craven part of me scuttled forward, whispering: *Tell him. What harm can it do? Tell him.* But I shut my eyes, bit my tongue, and held my confession back.

"Release her."

I waited for the long, weightless fall. Instead, they pulled me back and dropped me on the stone floor of the balcony.

Shock numbed my mind. All I could do was pant for several long breaths before I looked up at the First Laurel.

"I had to know." His hard eyes glinted with the purple light of the cloud moon. "Had to know if you would keep your word to the last.

Archon Jaxas is no fool, but..." He looked away. "Cover her and escort her back to her room."

The squashed-nosed guard stared in astonishment at his superior, while the other fetched a blanket from Myron's old bed and draped it over my shoulders. I drew it around myself, but continued to stare at Lykos from a huddle on the ground.

"You knew?" I whispered. "You knew the whole time?"

He nodded curtly. "The Archon told me this afternoon. I swore him to silence until I determined for myself whether or not I believed him and would aid in your sham trial."

Sudden clarity came over me. I had held back the truth, unable to trust Lykos after too long of a suspicion. But all he had done was to protect the Despoina; his loyalty was with the Wreaths and always had been. As Asileia was not guilty, neither was he. And by holding back the plan, I had convinced him that I was worth trusting.

I stood slowly, staying upright through sheer force of will. "The ambush. The crossbow bolts." I forced myself to meet Lykos's gaze, though after what I had just suffered at his hands, I wanted to cringe away. "I need men to fire them."

He returned my stare. Fragile as I felt, it was almost enough to make me break. Finally, he nodded. "You will have them."

The guards stepped up to either side of me, but I ignored them, pretending like they hadn't nearly thrown me off the balcony. It was worth forgiving and forgetting all of it if the laurel guards would fight on our side tomorrow. It was what I had to repeat to myself to keep walking steadily toward the door.

"Verifier Airene," Lykos said from behind me. "I... apologize. But I had to know you could be trusted."

I stopped and took a deep breath, forcing down my fear and anger. "We both want what's best for Oedija. The only apology I need is crossbows and swords tomorrow."

Then, chin up, shoulders back, ignoring the pain and weakness cascading through my body, I walked to my room, not looking back once at the laurel guards who followed.

CHAPTER THIRTY-FIVE

ON TRIAL

HIGH TRIBUNE: After careful review of the testimonies from all parties, it is with a heavy heart that the Confessionary Tribunal finds Zalfene Wreath, Despoina to Oedija, guilty of crimes against the Charters, the demotism, and the institutions which hold us true, by acts of aggression against foreign states, conspiracy, and murder.

- The Trial of Zalfene Wreath, from the records of the Confessionary Tribunal; 1087 SLP

The glow of dawn stole through the window and pressed on my eyelids, waking me from an uneasy stupor. The trial would begin a few turns after dawn, and I was to meet Maesos and Corin at the Conclave gates before. Yet for the moment, I couldn't force myself to move. Aches and wounds pained me all across my body. Scrapes and cuts covered my skin, while bruises ran deeper. The worst of the pain was in my abdomen, and not just from laurel guards' fists. Twice now the illness had come upon me when entering the Despot's quarters; I couldn't consider it a coincidence. But as to what caused it, I hadn't the faintest idea.

But strange ailments weren't my primary concern. The trial had come, and with it, a reckoning. For my family and friends, for Linos — 'Thae above, for the realm. I had managed to gather allies through, quite literally, blood, sweat, and tears. But it was still all too likely that none of it would come to fruition.

Yet one thing I knew for certain: staying abed would not delay the inevitable.

I rose slowly, trying to ignore the fresh pain that washed over me, and pulled out a clean chiton. Despite my tunic and trousers being stained with blood and dirt, I pulled the flower-embroidered robe over them. I smiled grimly to myself. The irony of my clothes was apt on the day our polis's own festering wounds would be revealed.

When I exited my room, I did so slowly. A moment later, I realized I watched for guards, the craven part of me expecting them to be lying in wait. Cursing myself to courage, I adopted a normal pace and visited the kitchens. There, I nibbled on a loaf of flatbread. It was all I could manage — my stomach was still halfway ill, and even the palace's rich coffee didn't have its usual appeal.

Upon my return, I found Nomusa waiting outside my room.

"There you are," she said impatiently. "I've been waiting… What happened?" Her eyes darted over my face and body.

I forced myself not to cover my arms, where cuts and bruises were plainly visible. "Negotiations. About which I need to have a word or two with Jaxas. But at least we have the laurel guards on our side."

"You have to stop telling stories halfway through. From the beginning, Aire."

"I'll tell you on the way. We're already late for Corin and Maesos."

I caught her up on the details. By the time I finished, she wore so fierce a scowl I was sure even the First Laurel would flinch to see it.

"Once this is over," she promised darkly. She raised her fist, shaking off a long flowing sleeve as she did, showing she wore steel punching rings across her knuckles.

"Won't be much good against a sword," I noted drily.

"We'll see about that." She hid them again and shook her head. "I can't believe I didn't hear any of it. I can't believe I wasn't there."

"It turned out for the best, though, didn't it?"

She nodded grudgingly. "I suppose."

I smiled weakly. "You'll be okay working with Lykos?"

She shrugged. "We'll see. At least Vusu is still more of a *fareshi* bastard than him."

"That he is," I said quietly, recalling to mind Linos's scarred face.

We went to the stables where, to my surprise, a carriage was quickly brought out for us. Jaxas's own had already left. Climbing in, we bumped down the road to the Conclave bridge. I stared out over the railing to the moody sea. Thick clouds, dark enough to be thunderheads, loomed along the horizon. The monsoons were still a month away, but those clouds promised tumultuous weather.

I startled as someone ran up alongside the carriage into view. As I recognized her, I cried for the driver to stop and threw open the door.

"Corin!" I would have drawn her into a hug had she not been sweating like hard-ridden horse. "Aren't you supposed to be with Maesos?"

She shook her head, beads of sweat flicking from her hair. "Conclave guards won't let him through. Suspicious of his wares." She motioned behind us. "I came in through the palace gates. They remembered me with you from before."

A pit formed in my stomach, and I grimaced. "I need those bolts, Corin. Could you bring the cart through the palace gates?"

Corin shrugged. "Conclave guards are at the end of the bridge. But I brought what I could."

Only then did I notice the strange way she'd been holding a hand to her tunic. Reaching under with her free hand, she produced four crossbow bolts with glass orbs at the tips. I accepted them, staring at the green pyrkin shimmering inside the glass.

"Thank you, Corin," I said softly. "Could you bring in more the same way?"

The cartwoman nodded.

I smiled and reached out to grasp her shoulder, but Corin edged away. I withdrew, frowning, wondering why she was even more leery of touch than usual lately. Putting it from my mind, I climbed back into the carriage and faced her again. "We'll see you when you return."

She nodded again and took off at a jog back the way she'd come. Nomusa shook her head, but said nothing as our carriage took off rumbling again. I clutched the crossbow bolts in my hands, then thought to tuck them beneath my robes. I'd have to find out a way to pass them to Lykos as soon as I could.

Soon after, we pulled up in front of the Conclave. The courtyard was already full of people milling about. As I dismounted, awkwardly holding the quarrels underneath my chiton, I looked out over the shaved heads of honors and the glittering helms of guards, hoping to see Lykos. Then I heard it: a distant rumble, like the ocean was rushing to the shore, only coming from the direction of the city. Turning, I looked across the topiaries, fountains, and statues littered across the marble courtyard and saw beyond the black iron gate the movement of a crowd. I doubted they had gathered in support of our Despoina. But were they Seekers, or was this coming from the spite of the starving, neglected population at large?

Nomusa and I approached the Conclave doors to be admitted by the guards. As I looked to see if the crests on their helms were the sun-and-dome of the Conclave or the leaves of the Laurel Palace, I noticed the aqua cowls next to them. Two Shepherds waited, a man with a narrow face and teeth that protruded over his lip, and a woman with features soft and round. Both had the same dead eyes as the Shepherds I'd seen before.

"Verifier Airene," the male Shepherd said as we stopped before them. "Tribune Vusumuzi sends his regards."

Fear crept over me. I had known the Shepherds would likely remain within Vusu's control, but it was still unnerving to witness it — and even more as the female Shepherd's eyes fell to my hand, still clutching the crossbow bolts beneath my robes.

Not knowing how to respond, I ignored them and spoke to the guards. "I am Verifier Airene and this is Verifier Nomusa. We are to be admitted by Archon Jaxas's orders."

I saw now that the guards were a mix of Conclave and laurel guards. At least it seemed that Lykos had succeeded in bringing his guards into attendance. Part of me couldn't help but wonder if they would stay true.

"Into the dark depths of the 'Thae you go, eh, Verifier?" one of the laurel guards japed.

I wished I could somehow pass them the quarrels. Instead, I just nodded as he and his companions heaved open the doors to the Conclave, then entered after Nomusa.

We were not the first inside. Many Servants of the Conclave were seated on the stone benches, and honors stood inside the eaves, waiting with refreshments. I might have seized a glass of wine had I not already had my hands full. Nomusa, unburdened, accepted one and quickly drank down half its contents.

Sighing, I scanned the room. The Council was present except for Feiyan. I doubted she'd show up, knowing as she did what was coming. The Stratechons, too, were in attendance, as was Archmaster Kyros. His eyes met mine from across the room, but I quickly looked away. It drove needles of worry through me not to know which side he'd join. Jaxas, too, was in attendance, speaking to a knot of Servants. But one person was not yet there.

I leaned close to Nomusa and whispered in her ear. "He hasn't arrived yet."

She nodded, scanning the room herself. "But he will come."

I didn't know if I hoped Vusu would or not.

But first, there were preparations to be finished. Holding the bolts to my belly, I spotted the closest laurel guard. It would have been more reassuring to hand them to Lykos directly, but we'd look suspicious enough as it was.

Making our way through the crowd, I moved to stand before him — or rather, *her*, as I discovered as I neared. She had a strong jaw for a woman and bore her half-plate as easily as her male fellows. Her gaze was impassive as she looked me up and down, then nodded toward a relatively isolated alcove. Even among all those people, I couldn't help a spike of anxiety at being so near the laurel guard. But I forced down my fear and followed her into the shadows.

Another pair already in the cove glanced our way, then returned to their conversations. The laurel guard paused when we were in the far corner and met my gaze again, eyes shadowed. "Verifier Airene. I trust you have something for us?"

"Yes." With a glance to either side, I awkwardly worked the bolts out from the neckline of my chiton, Nomusa standing at my shoulder to block us as much as she could from view. The pyrkin orbs at the end of the quarrels flashed green as they emerged, then settled to a soft, mossy glow again. I held them out to the guard, and she accepted them wordlessly and slid them into a quiver resting at her hip, the pyrkin orbs hidden.

Not knowing what else to say, I nodded to her, then turned away with Nomusa.

"They'd better stay true," Nomusa muttered as we emerged from the alcove.

"They will." I spoke as much to my own doubts as hers.

Scanning the room again, we set our sights to our next quarry, who was walking down the stairs to the front of the room. Low Consul Orhan of Bazaar and his faction sat in the foremost rows of the chamber, chattering amicably among themselves. As we stopped before them, the portly man looked up, the very picture of pleasantness. "Ah, the Verifiers who made all this possible. What a happy occasion this must be for you. A true apotheosis of your career."

I kept my expression impassive. There was little point in acknowledging the absurdity that we both knew it to be. "Yes, of course, Low Consul."

"Of course, we're all grateful as well," Orhan continued, gesturing to his compatriots. "We never could have accomplished what you so swiftly have."

"You almost sound as if you wished for it," Nomusa stated, her tone just shy of impetuous.

"Perhaps we do, perhaps we do." He winked at me.

It was as good as an admittance of guilt. Yet, soon, it might not matter. Even if the Preservists had worked to bring the imperial rule of Avvad to Oedija, Vusu could overturn all their plans in a moment.

Orhan's grin grew wider at my expression. "But that's enough chatter for now. The trial will begin soon. After will be soon enough to discuss other matters."

I bowed silently, Nomusa following, then we turned away from the faction. How little he knew how uncertain that "after" was.

———

"Despoina Asileia Wreath, please approach the dais."

The High Tribune's warbling voice echoed throughout the massive domed chamber. Nomusa and I watched from among the colonnades lining the right side of room, standing with the honors, clerks, and guards. I scanned those present once again. All one hundred and eleven Servants and Low Consuls were attending as far as I could tell — except for Feiyan. Vusu, too, was still missing. Worry was beginning to gnaw at me. Had he discovered our deception? Yet there was nothing I could do but wait.

As she complied with High Tribune Photina's order, the Despoina was more composed than the last time I'd seen her. Her dress was a muted blue, and she wore little in the way of jewelry. No twigs adorned her hair besides the Evergreen Wreath. Her eyes stared about with distant scorn, vague enough that I suspected she was as deluded as ever.

Leia stopped short of the podium and turned to face those gathered. Her gaze lifted above them to the statues of the Eidola on the wall — looking to those she deemed her peers, I didn't doubt.

"Despoina Asileia," the High Tribune began, "the charges placed before you are grave. You are accused of the murder of your father, the former Despot Myron Wreath, by your own hand or by your orchestration. How do you plead?"

The Despoina's lips curled in a sneer. "You cannot touch me."

The High Tribune leaned forward. "I ask again, Asileia Wreath. How do you plead?"

Leia raised her chin. "Guilty."

The room erupted into astonished whispers.

"Guilty," the Despoina repeated, her voice cutting through the murmurs, "of taking my rightful place as the Hand of Clepsammia, the arbiter of retribution's divine will. You cannot unseat me from my destiny."

"Indeed," the High Tribune acknowledged drily amid a second round of murmurs. "Then we'll proceed with the witnesses. You are dismissed."

Even from where I was, I saw anger flash in Asileia's eyes. Yet she obeyed and left the dais, if stiffly.

"If only it was the last we'd hear from her," Nomusa muttered.

Perhaps it would be, when Vusu came. *If* he came. I kept the black thought to myself.

I quickly grew familiar with the tediousness of trials. Witnesses summoned forth, one after another, beginning with Lykos and his reports from the watch the night of the three horns. Intriguing as it should have been to hear his perspective, I learned little, and was reminded when looking at him of sharp memories of the night prior. I shoved them down, ignored my aching body, and tried to pay attention as the First Laurel took nearly a turn of the sandglass to read through the testimonies.

Then the High Tribune called out for Tribune Vusumuzi to provide witness. After a ponderous pause, she noted with irritation that he had failed to attend. For a moment, there was a stir in the Conclave at the absence of this key witness. Anxiety that he had discovered our trap stirred in me anew. Fear, cold and sharp, cut through me at the thought of what might even now be happening to my family, to Xaron, to Talan. But I had to hold on to hope. I didn't have another choice at this point.

The Council soon decided to proceed with the trial in spite of Vusu's absence, with an assurance that if he appeared, time would be made for his witness. Then Kyros Brighteyed rose and gave his testimony. I listened carefully to the Archmaster. He reported seeing "Pyrthaen residue" in the Despot's chambers, which he claimed was an aftereffect either of a pyr's presence or a warden's channeling. I rubbed my temples. I knew all too well who had channeled in Myron's bedchamber. I learned nothing new from his testimony. And though I'd hoped to discover which way Kyros's loyalties leaned, it seemed as indeterminate as before by the time he left the dais.

As the former steward of the Laurel Palace spoke next, I glanced at the laurel guards stationed around the chamber. Interspersed between sets of Conclave guards, they numbered nearly two dozen. Most had crossbows leaning at their feet or strapped to their backs. If Corin could sneak in more pyrkin bolts, we stood a good chance of hitting Vusu. Yet a glance back showed no sign of the cartwoman or Maesos, much less Vusu himself.

"Verifier Airene of Port!"

I startled and met the gaze of High Tribune Photina, who, having just belted my name, stared at me with growing impatience. It was my turn. Taking a deep breath, I slowly made my way down the stairs to the podium.

I felt disconnected from my body as I began to speak, forgetting my words almost as soon as I said them. But I must have made a convincing case, for I evoked a reaction that echoed all the way up to the highest circles of the chamber. At my recollection of the Despoina's earlier admission of guilt, the outraged muttering rose all the way to the oculus. I left the dais with no accusations of my own — there was no need when Asileia had condemned herself. I couldn't help but notice Jaxas staring down at his sandals and felt a pang of pity for the Archon.

The end of the trial was growing nearer; we could all feel it. Anticipation and fear pulsed in me as the High Tribune called Jaxas to the dais. I couldn't hear the Archon's words through the buzz of my thoughts, couldn't concentrate on the reactions of the gathered Servants from my gaze constantly flitting to the doors. My heart raced. Sweat trickled down my hairline. My mouth went dry.

Yet for all my agonizing, I still wasn't prepared for his arrival.

My gaze had settled back on Jaxas and his hollow eyes when the air behind him rippled, then tore open. I stared, disbelieving. A crack, incandescent and jagged, grew wider with each passing moment, ripping apart the fabric of the world. Around me, Servants and honors gasped, and guards fumbled for their weapons with panicked shouts. The crack opened into a tear; brilliant light spilled forth from it. A wave of heat washed over us, turning the cool chamber into a hot midsummer day. My gut suddenly kicked and throbbed, and I bent double with agony. But I couldn't look away.

A figure appeared within the tear, silhouetted against the blinding light. At first, it looked upside down, then slowly righted itself as it came closer. *A daemon* — it had to be a daemon come among us. My numb mind could invent no other explanation. The dark figure grew larger within the gash until it blocked the whole of the light behind it.

Then it stepped through.

I could tell it was Vusu as he emerged and moved away from the light. He wore the red mask of the Visage and the same white peplos as he had at the gathering. His arms were bared, his blue tatu dim compared to the brilliant light behind him, but with a glow of their own as they slithered across his skin.

Then another figure emerged from the rift. As the thin boy with blond hair in gray robes walked up to stand at Vusu's shoulder, my heart wrenched, more painful than my heaving stomach and throbbing head. Linos stared forward, not looking to either side, seeming as empty as he had in the Claw. *Still Vessel.* The bitter realization curled through me.

As Vusu and Linos cleared the rift, it began to retreat and close, like a patch of frost before a flame's heat. Vusu stepped toward Jaxas, who had staggered to the side of the dais as he stared, open-mouthed, at the intruders. The former Tribune raised his hands up as if in surrender, his gaze traveling across the chamber. Following it, I saw him looking at the guards' leveled crossbows. From the tips of four of them emanated the green glow of the pyrkin bolts. My heart was in my throat. Vusu was Bali.

Would he recognize what it meant that they pointed pyrkin-headed quarrels at him?

My hand fell to the pocket where the lodestone lay. Twitching it hard three times, I signaled Xaron. Hopefully he and Talan were not far. I didn't know how long we'd have.

"What is this? Who are you?" the High Tribune demanded, her voice cracking and betraying her. As if to hide her fear, she turned toward the doors. "Shepherds! Apprehend this feral!"

"I do not blame you for not recognizing me, Photina." Vusu's voice filled the chamber, magically magnified so that it dwarfed hers. "I am much more now than you've seen me before. I represent not only myself, but a people. A cause. A new reign of power." He gestured to the back, where the Shepherds stood, unmoving. "The Shepherds know this. They will not harken to your call."

"You don't represent the people," Jaxas said, his voice tiny compared to Vusu's, yet still carrying through the chamber. "The Servants are the voices of the people. They were chosen by them. They were selected by fair and representative elections."

"Elected by who?" Vusu strode across the stage, his tatu seeming to shine brighter with each passing moment. "The citizens of Oedija. A fraction of the true population, set above the rest by the fortunes of their ancestors. What of the common people? What of the honors, paid not in coin, but in scorn?"

"It is their honor to serve!" one Servant cried from the crowd. "Just as it is our duty to serve by ruling!"

"Have you given them any other choice? Slavery does not seem so honorable when you wear the chains."

Vusu paced back the other way. I watched him, teeth clenched hard. I longed for Lykos to give a command to fire and be done with this. I burned with hate as I stared at him, and all the more when my eyes fell on my brother behind him. Linos hadn't shifted and seemed little more than a statue.

More Servants stood, some objecting and shaking their fists, but most stayed seated and silent. They had seen the power of this warden who could tear apart the very fabric of the world. They could feel the thickening tension in the air and feared to be caught in the midst of it.

Vusu raised his hands. "I did not come to discuss political philosophy with you," he said, his voice carrying over the rising shouts. "I came for a purpose."

He turned to the Despoina, seated at the edge of the dais. From where I stood, I couldn't see her expression, but she didn't shift as he approached and laid a hand on her shoulder. Jaxas convulsed visibly, but he didn't try to intervene.

"Photina," Vusu said to the High Tribune below him, "after my years of service to you and our cause, I ask only one favor of you."

Photina suddenly seemed to recognize who he was. "Vusumuzi? You, a feral?" She shook her long mane in disbelief. "But how could you—?"

"Do this one thing for me," Vusu interrupted. "Condemn Asileia Wreath for the crimes of which she is accused."

The Despoina finally flinched under his hand, but he kept a tight grip. I wondered if he channeled radiance to burn her, for her face twisted in pain.

"I cannot," the High Tribune said uncertainly, then continued more confidently, "I *will* not. You cannot make demands of—"

She never finished her thought. Vusu raised his hand and, like an over-ripe melon dropped to the floor, the High Tribune's head burst open. People scattered all about her, splattered with red and gray gore. Some curled under the benches in numb shock or sobbing helplessness. Others retched on the floor. But most remained where they were, terrified of drawing Vusu's ire. Around me, those nearest the doors began pressing toward the exit. I fought against the tide to remain where I stood, unable to look away from the bloody mess that was the High Tribune's cadaver. Only now did I fully comprehend the depth of my folly.

Vusu inspected his white garment and wiped at a red spot absently. His voice projected above the pandemonium. "I am sure I can speak for the High Tribune when I declare the Despoina of Oedija, Asileia Wreath, guilty of murdering her father—"

Through the noise, a string snapped. A bolt cut through the air, then produced a sharp crack as it pierced its target.

Right through the center of Vusu's mask.

CHAPTER THIRTY-SIX

CRACKED VISAGE

Short has been the puppet reign of the Wreaths, and for the greater part of it, they have played their role well. The first to accept the arrangement, the doddering Amanon Wreath, wanted any semblance of power he could manage, and was content with the mirage supported by a trough of wine a night. His daughter, Zalfene Wreath, was not so hazy-eyed. Her construction of the Half Wall, which was intended to encircle and protect even the outer demes, is now infamous for nearly provoking war with the Avvadin Imperium.

Other Wreaths followed, each swinging toward one end of the spectrum or the other, each struggling to accept that imagined power was not real power...

- A Modern Account of the Wreaths; by Acadian Helene, Master Historian; 1170 SLP

I stared at the pierced mask, breath freezing in my lungs. The bolt had entered just above the open maw. Pyrkin spilled out of the dragon's mouth like emerald fire, streaming down the fangs, down the jowls — and finally settled on the hand that held it, outstretched and away from his face.

"Well," Vusu said as he straightened. The resonance had faded from his voice. He held the mask before him and turned it back and forth as pyrkin crawled down his bare arm in green rivulets. "I can see my authority is not yet respected."

Somehow, he had pulled off his mask and used it to stop the bolt. I stared in numb wonder at his speed, but held my breath for another reason. Glancing at Lykos, I found him staring at me. I gave him the barest shake of my head, though I didn't know if he'd pay me heed. We had to wait and see if it took effect before we attacked, lest we find ourselves sorely outmatched. Whether or not he comprehended my line of thought, the First Laurel didn't order the attack.

"Airene of Port."

Those who had not already fled around me stepped away. I stood motionless at the top of the Conclave tiers, feeling the gaze of everyone remaining on me. But Vusu's shadowed eyes, staring up from the dais below, were the hardest to bear.

Even knowing that Vusu's power was draining away, I found it hard to respond. "Vusu," I said, unable to keep a tremble from my voice.

"Airene," he repeated with his head tilted. "Didn't I tell you the consequences of disobedience?"

My face burned. I didn't know the cost of seeming in league with Vusu should I survive this. But this wasn't only about surviving. "I didn't disobey," I said, speaking louder and regaining a measure of composure.

"No? Then your man, the glass smith — Maesos, I believe his name was. He wasn't coming here with more of these—" Vusu held up the mask, now teeming with pyrkin. "—meant for me?"

A pit formed in my stomach as I stared at the pyrkin now reaching his shoulder. It didn't faze him. Yet neither had it bothered Talan and Xaron, not until they had tried to channel. There was still hope.

"Did you mean to illuminate me up as a festival lantern? You should not have bothered, Airene. For the sake of everyone present." He held up his palm, casual, yet his slightest gesture held more menace than the leveled spears of a hundred soldiers. All around me, Servants, honors, and guards instinctively took cover. It took every ounce of my resolve to keep my feet rooted in place.

I licked my lips, closed my eyes, and took a deep breath. None of them slowed my racing heart. When I opened my eyes, Vusu still stared at me with a slight frown, like an uncle who had hoped for more from his promising niece.

I found myself rising to his challenge. "You say you're for the people, yet you set yourself above all others. You say everyone might learn to channel if they trust in your leadership, yet I've seen the cost of your power." My gaze lingered on Linos, but he had finally moved, tilting back his head to stare at the bright oculus above, where light poured in as the sun neared its zenith. Sunlight gleamed in his golden hair.

My eyes burned, and I fought to speak as my throat closed. "You say you wish to save this city, yet all you bring is destruction."

Vusu's expression didn't shift. "So it must seem. But you do not know all."

"Then why?" My anger made the words come out almost at a shout. "Why do any of this?"

Pyrkin crawled up his chin, yet Vusu didn't move to wipe it off. "We all have holes we must fill. We all have hungers for which we will give up all else." He shook his head and stiffened his upraised arm. "The cycle must be broken. No matter the sacrifice."

His fingertips, then his whole hand, began to glow with building radiance. My breath caught. I stared dumbly at him. I had failed. And now I would die for it.

The pyrkin crawling over him flared green. Vusu gave a pained yelp, staring at the pyrkin along his arm with wide eyes.

"What is this?" His gaze traveled up, latching onto me. "It cannot be... pyrkin from the Thulu isikhayha?"

For a moment, I was too stunned to do anything but return his stare. The realization that our moment had come brought me back. I looked to Lykos. The First Laurel made the barest movement of his hand.

Then came the chaos.

Twenty crossbow locks snapped forward. Twenty sharp points aimed for the usurper's heart. They would strike true; they had to. He had no magic to stop them.

Yet before the missiles could reach him, a wall of flames leaped up before Vusu. Linos stood with his hand outstretched and his empty eyes locked onto where Vusu had disappeared from sight. He channeled to protect the man he believed to be his master.

Fear for Linos roused me from my despair. "Don't hurt him!" I cried out. But my words were lost as the Conclave filled with the clamor of battle. As Conclave and laurel guards both surged toward Vusu and Linos with spears, swords, and shields, the crowd of Servants, honors, and notables of Oedija clawed to escape. I tried to follow the guards down, but was pushed back into the eaves and crushed against the wall. Nomusa had been lost in the din. Through the roiling mass of bodies, I caught a glimpse of spears leveling as they charged onto the platform.

"No!" I cried out, shoving with all my strength to form a path. I pushed against patrician and citizen alike, not looking back to see whom I knocked down, whose teeth my shoulder scraped against. My eyes were fixed on my brother. As Linos channeled to protect Vusu, three spearheads thrusted toward him. I rushed down the curved stairs, though I was too far away to do anything but watch.

As the guards struck forward, Vusu's voice rose briefly above the noise, and my brother snapped into action. As if he'd known they were there all along, he spun and slithered between two of the thrusting spears as he grabbed the third, sending it flying from the guard's hand with a rippling kinetic push. The other two spears were already stabbing forth again, but Linos leaped above them, the gray tail of his robe trailing behind. As he came back down, the guards set their spears to gut him. They never found the chance. Waves rippled from his feet, and the guards fell back screaming, their skin reddening with blisters.

Someone shoved into me, nearly knocking me to the floor. When I gained my feet, I saw that Linos had quieted the guards' screams and turned to engage others. Those were my allies he'd killed, but I couldn't help relief flooding through me at seeing him alive.

I closed my eyes. Linos would fight until he was dead, or Vusu was — I knew it to be true. He was more Vessel than my brother now. But somehow, I had to stop him, or the guards would surely kill him. I had to stop his channeling. Maybe then, he could be subdued without being hurt.

But to do that, I needed one of Maesos's pyrkin bolts.

As I turned to my new hunt, four aqua-cowled, manacled figures leaped through the middle of the chamber. Cursing, I scrambled back for cover again, cowering behind a column and watching the scene unfold. My cowardice saved my life. The Shepherds brought death with them, throwing waves of fire and force around them, breaking apart centuries-old stone and killing men and women by the handful. I felt the heat of the blasts wash over me. Guards fell from the nooks where they'd concealed themselves. The rafters around the oculus, stocked with a dozen laurel guards, crumbled circle by circle as concentrated waves of kinesis erupted from the Shepherds' hands. Men came tumbling down to hit the ground with sickening squelches. One fell close enough to me that I felt his blood spray against my skin as he split open. I wiped the droplets from my face, numb with shock.

Other guards were up on the balconies above and behind me; they fared little better. One Shepherd had leaped up and left waves of flames in his wake, rousting out any crossbowman cranking their weapons behind the benches and sending them flailing and screaming over the railings. Another Shepherd pulled at the air, and swords, spears, and even armored guards came flying past him. It was as deadly a use of magnesis as I'd seen, far beyond Talan and Xaron's simple tricks.

Despite the odds, the guards continued to fight. I heard First Laurel Lykos shout from across the chamber, and the cheer of men rallying for a charge. One Shepherd took a bolt in the arm, then a second in the neck, sending him tumbling to the ground. Yet at least half of the guards must have been killed already. I couldn't tell which way the battle swayed.

"Enough!"

Another voice broke through the fray, mighty and amplified with Pyrthaen power. Wincing at the brutal wave of sound, I turned and saw Archmaster Kyros standing amid the chaos, untouched. His eyes shone bright as he glared about him. At his shoulders stood two Acadians, one a terrified young man, the other the woman who had spoken to me outside of Eltris's tower. I watched anxiously. Their entrance into the fray would turn the tide. But which way?

"End this!" Kyros commanded of his Acadians. Raising his hands, he turned himself to face the balconies, then sent out a wave of kinesis unmatched by anything else I'd seen. The balconies were blocked from my view, so I couldn't see if it was at soldiers or Shepherds that he aimed. The chamber shook as the wave connected, and dust and debris spilled anew from the balcony. Then a body tumbled to the ground, aqua-cowled and still. Hope hammered in my chest again. He'd killed a Shepherd. Kyros was on our side.

As the two young Acadians leaped up to engage another Shepherd, I turned back to the dais. There, Linos killed a guard with a sharp scythe of kinesis to the man's throat. My heart wrenched, fear and guilt driving through me. With only one Shepherd left fighting and Vusu still covered in pyrkin, the Acadians would soon turn to engage Linos. I was running out of time to save him.

Purpose steeling my will, I crouched low and darted out into the melee, questing for the place I'd last seen a guard with one of the special bolts loaded. Orange fire spat overhead, and smoke choked me at every breath. Twice I laid myself flat to avoid debris flying overhead. I was coughing from the dust by the time I reached where I thought the guard had been. The man was dead, his head split open by a broken piece of marble. Trying not to look at his ruined corpse, I checked the quiver at his hip, but found nothing but normal bolts. I took the quiver anyway, but found the man's crossbow had a cracked wing. Useless. I threw it back to the ground in frustration.

"Help." A man crushed by a collapsed column moaned from nearby. I clenched my teeth and dodged around him. He was beyond my help, but I could still save my brother. Misplaced guilt could wait.

The next two guards didn't hold a pyrkin bolt either, but I found a crossbow still whole. As I looked around, my fingers fumbled over the unfamiliar device. I didn't even know how to load a quarrel. Did I pull back on the string, putting my foot in the brace? Or was it something to do with the levers on the top and bottom? I cursed myself for not asking earlier. My eyes strayed to the faintly moving bodies around me. Soldiers, honors, Servants — their wounds leveled them to a single caste now, a bloody mire on the Conclave floor.

I slumped back against the last row of benches, crossbow falling into my lap. Everywhere, my body hurt. Any hope of saving Linos was fast fading. Even if the guards hadn't fired all their pyrkin quarrels, they wouldn't have survived long in this fight without shattering. The Acadians would finish off the last Shepherd soon. There was nothing I could do.

Why not flee?

I tried pushing away the cowardly thought, but it renewed itself at each fresh scream and bone-rattling blast rocking the stone. It was all I could do to remain where I was. I had little to offer in this fight. But I still had to try.

Then it came to me. Vusu was the one who held my brother captive. Perhaps I didn't need to restrain Linos's powers.

All I needed to do was kill Vusu.

I risked looking toward the dais. Though Vusu's powers were restrained, he was far from impotent. As I watched, a pair of guards advanced, taking advantage of Linos's distraction to attack what appeared to be a powerless old man. As one, they stabbed forth their spears in a move that should have trapped him. But with speed I'd thought impossible without channeling, Vusu narrowly dodged one spearhead and wrapped the other in the length of his white peplos. Though the guard ripped it away, Vusu danced forth with the vigor of a much younger man. Coming close, he kicked the guard's leg out from under him. As the man crumpled, the other stabbed at Vusu's back, yet somehow he spun and knocked it wide. With barely a glance around, Vusu's foot found the first guard's helm and kicked, forcing the man to stumble back or break his neck.

Tearing my eyes away, I stripped off my chiton and shielded myself from the debris as best I could as I set to figuring out the crossbow. With mindless desperation, I put one foot into the stirrup that hung off it and tried pulling at the string. It cut into my fingers, and I let it thrum back into position, panting, my fingers now slick with blood. I tried the other lever and noticed a satisfying tug of resistance. I'd found the right lever at least. Bracing myself, I pulled with all my strength and clicked it into place.

Loading a quarrel, I hefted the weapon slowly, careful of the two levers. Its power paled in comparison to the magic surging around me, but I was fully aware of how easily I could end a life with it.

Just as I set it, the grand double doors to the Conclave burst open once more. I crouched again, hope sinking. Four more Shepherds entered, crossing the chamber in great bounds and casting death around them.

"Come on, then!" Kyros Brighteyed boomed. A wave of kinetic energy cascaded overhead to crash into the wall, sending dust and debris flying.

Cowering among the benches, I faintly noticed two more shadows flit over the oculus. My ears were ringing, and the clamor surrounding me was muffled like I had a blanket pressed against my head. Yet I still heard Vusu's strained call, "Kill them, quickly!"

Cradling the crossbow, I ghosted to the end of the aisle and peered out, and my heart soared.

Xaron and Talan had arrived at last.

The next moment, hope turned back to fear as a Shepherd leaped toward them. My friends immediately reacted, attacking in synchrony. As Xaron channeled a flare of radiance and drew the Shepherd's attention, Talan cut through the air with a bright violet arc of light. It left no mark, but the Shepherd shrieked, then tumbled to the ground, unmoving but for a dim, silver wisp rising from her body.

"Hah!" Kyros projected from behind me. "The augur's pupil fights well! But more of them approach, wardens. End the Tribune quickly!"

Talan and Xaron exchanged a glance. Talan nodded toward the dais, while he turned to another Shepherd. Xaron complied at once, leaping across the chamber in two huge bounds. But before he could reach Vusu, a Shepherd leaped from nowhere to engage him.

I feared for my friends, but I couldn't help them. I could only do one thing to help turn the battle. I looked beyond Xaron furiously exchanging blows with the opposing warden to the dais beyond. With the Shepherds fighting for their own lives, Vusu had only Linos still protecting him from the guards, and my brother looked to be nearing the limits of his fledgling power. He swayed as two spearmen thrust at him, yet knocked aside their spears just in time to avoid being gutted.

Vusu fared little better. A spear had stabbed through his thigh and left a trail of bright blood down his leg. Pyrkin still smeared his chest and arms in green, but they had grown faint and thin. His peplos had been abandoned, leaving him shrunken in his underwraps.

Hefting my crossbow, I crept down the edges of the benches, knowing I would have to be close to be able to hit him. But as I neared the dais, a challenger stepped out to meet Vusu, and my stomach sank once more.

Nomusa had abandoned her long, flowing chiton to reveal dark, tight-fitting clothes beneath. Punching rings gleamed on her fingers, and she clutched a knife in one hand. She walked forward with a hunting cat's grace. I exhaled in frustration and lowered my crossbow. I couldn't risk a shot with Nomusa so near. I could only hope her Ixolo training would be enough.

Nomusa lunged, her feet sliding forward as she lashed out with her knife. But though Vusu was injured and no doubt wearied, he'd had many more years of practice than her. As he bent out of the way of her blow, he caught Nomusa's arm and twisted her to the ground. Their movements came fast and flurried as they tumbled and turned and lashed about the platform. They were like two hard winds twining, a storm forming between them, as they fought up the length of the dais.

Nomusa suddenly caught Vusu in a hold and flung him to the benches. But as she leaped down after him, Vusu gained his feet just in time to avoid her follow-up blow. Their deadly dance continued. Neither seemed to be slowing, but I feared it was only a matter of time.

Vusu leaped onto the dais again. As Nomusa tried to follow him, he served her a hard kick to the chest and sent her flailing back to the stone floor. Nomusa tried cradling her fall and succeeded only in twisting one arm painfully beneath her. She tried rising, but could barely move.

My time had come. I sighted the crossbow, leveling my shot — and yet another rose against Vusu.

First Laurel Lykos staggered up the dais stairs to the leader of the Manifest. The soldier's helm was gone, and red lines streamed down from his steel-gray hair. Yet as he raised his sword overhead, he did not tremble, nor did his hard eyes leave his foe.

Vusu kneeled on the platform, breathing hard and clutching his wounded leg. His exertions were finally catching up to him. Yet as the Visage of the Wyvern looked up and met Lykos's eyes, I knew he had not given in.

Before Lykos's blow could fall, Vusu spoke again with a resonance that trembled through me. "Taozu! I will give what you ask!"

Lykos swung his sword, but it was too late. Fire, red and yellow and orange, coiled around Vusu as he rose to his feet once again. As the blade entered the flames, it melted into globules of metal that splattered the floor around them. The inferno extended, reaching out for the First Laurel, and as tongues of fire stole up his arms, even his iron resolve broke. He threw himself to the ground, screaming and batting helplessly at his arms as his men rushed to aid him.

Vusu rose from the fire and turned his gaze across the room. "Fools," he said in a whisper that carried. "Now see what you have wrought."

CHAPTER THIRTY-SEVEN
SACRIFICE

Praise be the wardens,
The hands of the Quintyr,
Who work the will of the gods,
Who forge great cities of stone and fire,
Who heal ills of mind and body,
Who keep at bay the daemons

Praise be the wardens,
They who save us all…

- Scroll fragment; origin unknown; estimated 256 SLP

I raised my crossbow uncertainly. Now that he had regained his channeling, I doubted any shot of mine would help. Before I could decide to shoot, a third person stepped up in challenge.

"Let us test your mettle then, Vusu!" Archmaster Kyros bellowed, raising his hands toward the dais.

Vusu turned with his own hands raised, and their magic collided in a storm. Though they stood barely two dozen feet apart, with Vusu on the dais and Kyros on the floor below him, the wall of their contending power spanned the room and shot up to eat away the ceiling. Fire and lightning and force warred against each other, and it was clear which side was the stronger. Though Kyros threw all his will into the fight, Vusu eclipsed him. His sorcery bore down on the Archmaster, shrinking his wall. Kyros wore a snarl, but exhaustion was overtaking his fury. His loose skin stretched tight under the strain, and his limbs trembled under the weight of power.

A gap opened in the wall of magic, and a tongue of lightning flicked through and almost gently touched Kyros. He flew back, his channeling abruptly cutting off, and crashed into a bench. I only knew he was alive from his pained cursing.

Vusu ceased his own channeling for a moment, swaying. Even with the resurgence of his power, he was tiring. But it was only a moment before he gathered himself and raised a hand toward Kyros. I gripped my crossbow tightly, but still, I waited. I couldn't waste my shot. Once again, I could do nothing but watch.

"Vusu!"

The Visage of the Wyvern glanced up, and I followed his gaze. Talan and Xaron stood on the only unbroken balcony remaining in the Conclave.

Xaron, who had spoken, continued. "You have no more pets to protect you. You have no more allies. Submit, so no more have to die here."

Glancing around, I saw he was nearly correct. No Shepherds remained, though it had come at a cost. Few guards were alive, and I saw only the female of the two Acadians still standing. Only Linos, alone amid the corpses on the dais, remained by Vusu's side.

Vusu lowered his hand and shook his head. "You do not understand what is at stake here. You cannot, not with that augur having whispered in your ear." He looked around. "I do not relish what I've done. Yet to stop now would be to render their sacrifices void. I must carry this through, all the way." His eyes went skyward now. "For all of our sakes."

Sparks flew between Xaron's hands. *Lightning.* Xaron had finally summoned it after all his training and meant to use it against Vusu. My breath caught.

Xaron yelled and threw the lightning bolt forward. Vusu's hands shot up. As the lightning reached the usurper, it burst and scattered in rivulets around him. Vusu smiled. Sparks about his hands gave warning a split second before lightning, greater than what Xaron had summoned, burst toward my friends.

Xaron and Talan threw themselves to the sides, and the lightning burst where they'd been, shattering stone. In the shower of debris, I couldn't see what had become of them.

"No!" I drew up my crossbow again, even though it was too late. Reckless hate ran through me. I'd take my shot, the one I'd waited so long for. I'd pay him back for all he'd done to me.

But as I leveled it, Vusu convulsed and dropped to his knees.

"Not now!" Vusu croaked, his hands scrabbling over the dais. He seemed to speak to the ground. "You cannot defy me now!"

I didn't wait to interpret what his words meant. I took him into my sight, tightened my grip.

Then I fired.

As I pressed the bottom lever, the crossbow kicked back into my face. The spring gouged my cheek. I dropped the weapon and clutched at my wound, but ignored both as I looked up to see if I'd aimed true.

Vusu, still on his knees, sat up slowly. A hand traced over the quarrel lodged between his ribs. Blood trickled out from around the wound. His eyes rose and found me. A strange smile twisted his face.

"All this," he rasped, "and it is you who have doomed us."

Cold fear crept over me, but I thrust it aside. "Talan! Xaron!" I called. "Finish him now!"

I saw figures move out of the corner of my eye. Yet they did not surge forward.

Vusu shook his head slowly. "Vessel!" he wheezed.

My brother immediately approached, stepping over the corpses. Blood ran down him in a dozen wounds, yet his dead eyes did not show any pain.

Terror seized me. Dropping my crossbow, I ran forward. "Linos, stop!" I shouted. "Don't go to him!"

Linos glanced over at me and hesitated for a half a moment until Vusu commanded him again. "Vessel!"

"Don't go, Linos!" I ran to the stairs of the dais like I'd never run before, heedless of the rubble and bodies I had to step on and around. I slipped on blood and went down hard on one knee, but I barely felt it as I rose and continued my mad dash forward.

Part of me registered that Talan and Xaron had emerged from the ruins and leaped across the chamber to fling radiance and kinesis down on the prone Visage. Yet even with a crossbow bolt in his side, Vusu found the strength to disperse and shred the magic before it reached him. I ran forward, heedless of their attacks. My sights were set on Linos.

But my brother had reached Vusu and stretched a hand toward him. As Vusu touched his arm, my brother stiffened. A moment later, he spasmed and fell to the ground.

"No!" I screamed, crossing the last dozen paces. Vusu looked around at me, his face wan. All strength had faded, leaving him old and shriveled, even as Xaron's and Talan's magic continued to rain down to no effect. In his hand had appeared a knife.

"Taozu," he spoke in a whisper that carried, "I give to you your sacrifice."

He cut the blade across Linos's arm.

I screamed as I ran forward. My brother's empty gaze fell to the blood leaking from his arm.

The air above them rippled.

I didn't stop, even as I recognized what was happening. As he had entered the Conclave, so Vusu meant to leave. Reality tore open once again, but in a different guise than before. Reptilian jaws, the size of a carriage and shining with ethereal light, lined with teeth as long as a man, bit through the world. As the maw formed, the air bent around it.

Despite myself, I slowed before the head of the giant creature. I felt as if I were back in my nightmares, facing the beast that had pursued me back into wakefulness.

The daemon beast, or at least the head of it, bent toward Vusu and Linos as if it meant to swallow them. I stumbled forward again. I didn't know what I'd do. I didn't think of the consequences. I just couldn't let Linos slip away from me once more.

The Pyrthaen creation's jaws closed over them. I crossed the last few feet between us and dove. My hand shot through one of the beast's lips, its light-made skin giving no resistance, then closed on an ankle — *Vusu's*, I saw a moment later. I didn't let go. Debris tore at me as I hit the floor. Breath was crushed from my lungs. As I looked up, wheezing for air, I saw the Visage's eyes widen with surprise.

The jaws closed. The world ripped away.

Then — nothing.

Everything had ceased. All sound. All movement. All color, breath, heartbeat. Yet I existed. I was nothing *but* awareness, pure and true. I thought and felt without senses interceding. I was in a land beyond living.

Not knowing how, I opened myself to the dizzying reality around me. Senses flooded back in, sharp and bright. I saw, yet what I saw didn't make sense. The world had doubled. Above me, a broken earth pressed in close. The world I'd left behind, I recognized it. Cracked slabs of stone seemed to form from nowhere just above me and fall up to crash into what had once been the floor of the Conclave, but now formed my ceiling. I saw my friends moving as slowly as swimmers through molasses through that upside-down world, running toward the spot where Vusu, Linos, and I had vanished.

The mirror world, the one in which I stood, shifted and swirled in defiance of the natural laws and order. I stood before the dais in the second Conclave, yet it was not the same. Though my senses were painfully keen, what I perceived seemed a misty veneer, like this world was a flickering candle that could, at any moment, blow out. Colors refused to remain their proper hue. Light bent and twisted, swirling in curves and spirals. An incessant wind whipped around me, deafening what hearing came back to me. My feet stayed planted to the stone floor, but I felt I might lift away from it if I didn't keep myself rooted.

I looked down at my body. All the pains I had borne in the real world had disappeared, as had the heaviness of the sky bearing down on me. I felt light and free. I looked at my hands, and like the world around me, my skin shone and was as thin and transparent as newly formed ice. Wonder at the creature I'd become filled me.

But then I remembered why I was here. *Linos.*

I looked up, and standing first before me was Vusu. Like me, he was a hazy shadow of himself. No quarrel bled in his side, nor did he bear any other wounds from the battle. Yet he alone seemed solid in this world, moored like a stone in a river. His eyes were bright in his earthy skin as he stared at me.

Beside him stood my brother, shining with a gray light. It should have been him I looked to, but it was the beast that loomed behind them that finally drew my gaze.

I had heard stories all my life of the thing that towered over them. A legend gone from the world, restrained by the Eidola long ago, his appetite never to be sated again. A daemon I had always believed to be little more than fairy tale and myth, one to scare children into obedience, or to explain the world's cruelty. Now I knew the stories were true. Now I knew that everything that was occurring in Oedija was insignificant in comparison.

I craned my head back, but even as I gazed upon the monster, I could not fully comprehend it. I could not understand how it was possible, or why this was happening now. Yet I also could not deny it.

Famine had returned.

CHAPTER THIRTY-EIGHT
FAMINE

So with Aida of the Green as Sacrifice, the gods bound Famine, restraining his power and keeping at bay his endless hunger. And to ensure he stayed there until the end of Telae and Pyrthae, they threw him deep into the roots stoneward, where the days crawl into eternities, and his power would not touch any world again.

- The Seeds of Famine, a translation from the Lighted-tongue; by Oracle Kalene of deme Hull; 881 SLP

I stared up into Famine's black, slitted eyes as they glared down from a hundred cubits high. His great maw hung open, unhinged like a snake about to swallow its prey, and its throat was a black, depthless cavern that fell away behind the crumbling Conclave wall. Scales, each as large as a laurel guard's shield, shifted in the fickle light of the Pyrthae, morphing into scarlet, blue, and aubergine in turns. His snout, tapered like a mountain slope, was curled into a snarl above bared, white incisors as thick as columns and as sharp as spears. A violet, forked tongue flicked over his teeth, tasting as if in anticipation of seizing its prey.

I was frozen in place before Famine. I had followed Vusu and Linos on a whim, and now I stood helpless before the daemon god who sought to swallow the world. Yet for the moment, he made no move toward me, but watched me with eyes black as a moonless night.

"Airene!" Vusu's voice brought me back to myself as it cut through the incessant wind of the Pyrthae. "You should not have followed! You will draw another of his seeds!"

I didn't understand, but at his voice, anger flared up in me again. As Famine continued to watch, motionless but for his whipping tongue and a slight sway, my fear was overrun by fury.

"You were a fool to think you'd get away!" I yelled back.

His hollow eyes were dark pits in the bright world. "You don't understand. What I do, I do for the good of all. For the continuance of all."

It was too much. A scream ripped from my throat, and I found myself charging at him. It was as if a daemon had taken possession of my body and drove it forward. My rage was a blaze out of my control, threatening to consume me. Above us, Famine shook his head back and forth. Terror, rising in me and setting my legs to trembling, almost won over as the great eyes peered down at me with narrowed interest. But if the god was going to kill me, I'd make sure he'd kill his servant as well.

Vusu didn't move as I ran at him. "He will take away far more than your life," his whisper cut through to me, speaking as if to my thoughts.

The words fell on deaf ears. Caught in my red anger, I flung myself at him. The sky's weight lifted from me so that I moved forward in a blur. Above, a shadow like a cliff fell over me. Famine descended, the daemon god's mouth gaping open, swallowing the sky and the Conclave walls alike as he came. I gritted my teeth and braced myself for the last rending even as I crashed into my enemy.

Something pierced my spine, then entered through to my belly. My legs went numb; pain shot through the rest of my body. My rage burned hotter. Vusu, whom I'd sent sprawling, pushed at me, but I wrapped my arms around him. He didn't resist, but his shadowed eyes suddenly widened.

Something slammed into my side and carried me off of him, suspending me for far longer than nature's laws should have allowed. I felt short arms wrap about me and glimpsed gray hair whipping out from beneath a hood.

"I'll kill you!" I howled into the Pyrthae's gale, struggling against whoever had enwrapped me. But the world had begun pulling away, my body becoming heavier. My gaze fell on the gray figure behind the dark one. Thrashing against the figure who held me still, I willed myself toward my brother.

"Linos!" I yelled. "Linos, grab hold of me!"

My brother didn't move. His features were indistinct, barely recognizable. Still, I clawed my way forward. Above, Famine rose for another strike.

"Stop resisting!" the figure who held me snapped. "We must leave! Now!"

"No! Not without Linos!" He was almost within my grasp. I lunged for

him, and my translucent fingers seized his wrist. I took hold of my brother.
I didn't let go.

Famine roared. The deafening wave of it vibrated the world, shaking
me so that I threatened to come apart. But I held myself together, and
clung to Linos, even as the figure who had me from behind tried dragging
me away. Famine surged down again, his maw trying to swallow us once
more, but we had begun rising. The floor left as we fell into the sky. I
closed my eyes as vertigo rocked my sight back and forth.

I slammed into stone.

Groaning, I pushed at the arms that held me with my free hand. My
head pounded, and pain flooded my body. My gut heaved. The anger that
had filled me in the Pyrthae drained away, leaving me weak and shaking. I
rolled over and let loose the little contents of my stomach on the ground
next to me. When I was finished, I lay my cheek on the stone. It was hard,
but slightly warm. *From the battle*, I realized.

"Aire! Come back to us!"

Their voices called to me as they crowded around. They touched and
held me, helping me sit back up as my paltry strength returned. But I
looked first at the wrist still clutched in my hand. Linos sprawled out on
the floor next to me. A weary smile stole over my lips. I'd done it. I'd
brought him back.

Then I looked up at the people around me. Nomusa, one of her eyes
swelled shut and her brow creased with concern, gently caressed my head
like I were a child. Xaron had an arm around me, squeezing me in too
tight of a hug. Talan kneeled before me, gripping my free hand gently in
his warm grasp and wearing a half-cocked smile. It was all I could do to
stare blankly around at them. My friends, here to hold me and check on
me. Even as Linos lay senseless next to me, even after I'd stared a daemon
god in the eyes, I found comfort in it.

Above loomed two more friendly faces. Corin, clothes even dirtier than
before, loosely held a bundle of crossbow bolts with glowing glass balls at
their tips. Next to her stood Maesos, the glassblower's face crinkled into a
smile.

It was only then that I turned to see who had drawn me back to the
real world, though I suspected I already knew. Eltris stared back with a
sour expression and crossed arms. Her short, gray hair as messy as an
untrimmed bush, and her robes were ragged with holes. I shook my head
in disbelief. The Master Augur had come to our aid after all, and in the
most spectacular of ways.

At my look, she broke off her glare to scan the scene around us. "You
made a mess of this," the augur observed, though I didn't know to whom.

She pointed at one spot among the destruction. "Xaron, was that black mark your bolt of lightning?"

Xaron winced. "Yes, master. I missed my target."

The augur harrumphed and began pacing the wreckage. I looked uneasily around as well. The stones had ceased to rain down from the ceiling, but from the precarious look of the fractured dome, it wasn't likely to hold for long. Bodies littered the ground all about us. I held to Linos, not trusting to let him go. Though his chest rose and fell, I didn't know what would happen when he woke. I couldn't bear to lose my brother again.

"That place…" I said at length. "Was it the Pyrthae?"

Eltris snorted. "The least part of it, but yes."

I shook my head as thoughts tumbled around in it. Stories told of wardens traveling to the home of spirits and gods, but I had never dreamed it might actually be possible. Especially not for me.

Then I remembered what I'd seen. "Famine. He's real. He's returned."

Eltris held my gaze amid the shocked expressions of my friends. "He's not returned completely yet," she said shortly. "But he will soon. Vusu has been weakened. He will not hold him for much longer." Her eyes slid down to Linos.

I shook my head. "I don't understand."

"I understand even less," Xaron muttered.

"Of course you don't," the Master Augur snapped. "Nor will you until I have the time to tell you." She looked around at the ruined Conclave. "Vusu has held Famine in his power for many years now. Ever since he laid siege to the united ishakas under the guise of Yama, in fact."

I scrambled to keep up. "Yama? From the Bali legend?"

"That was over a century ago," Nomusa said in disbelief. "You can't expect us to believe that."

"Believe what you will," Eltris replied shortly. "But open your ears to this: Though Vusu has gained great power from the Quintyr, he has ceded as much to him. And no warden has ever held him back forever."

Even amid the flurry of things I didn't understand, my mind quested back to the last strange thing Eltris had said to me in front of her tower. "You said there was a reason behind all the great disasters across the world. Was Famine the cause of them? The fall of empires? The destruction of the lands?"

The augur's face twisted into a mocking smile. "You solve my riddle after you've seen its answer. How insightful of you."

Annoyance flared in me anew. "You could have just told me instead of talking around it."

"You wouldn't have listened, girl. And don't expect me to believe otherwise."

Her words cooled my anger as quickly as it had risen. I sagged forth, not wanting to admit she was right, so I said nothing. I ran a hand along Linos's arm. His skin felt feverishly warm.

"I hate to rush such spectacular revelations," Talan cut in, "but we may wish to preserve our lives first. Shall we find the door?"

"Finally, a person with some sense." Eltris turned away, then turned back. "But put that Bali pyrkin on the boy first. No sense in risking it."

I startled at the suggestion and looked at him, chewing my lip. Linos still had a vague, empty look in his eyes. I suddenly realized I hadn't even addressed him since bringing him back. Unwittingly, I was treating him just as he appeared: a human statue.

I took both of his hands. "Linos," I said softly, trying to catch his eye. "Linos, look at me."

He didn't respond, but stared up at the broken dome, unseeing.

"Don't wait for the sky to fall," Eltris said drily.

"Which doesn't seem too far fetched now," Xaron muttered.

I took a deep breath. "All right. We'll do it."

Corin drew out a quarrel and broke the glass tip on a flat piece of stone. Then Nomusa stepped in, brushing aside the glass and scooping up the pyrkin with her good hand to spread it over Linos's hands and arms. "I think that should do," she said softly, wiping her hand clean.

Eltris nodded sharply, then stalked over the wreckage toward the entrance.

Talan and Nomusa lifted me and Linos to our feet. My brother could walk, it seemed, but there was no will behind it. The task fell to Talan to lead him to the entrance. Nomusa stayed by me, but I wasn't sure who supported whom. The wounds she had sustained from Vusu clearly ailed her, and her arm was braced against her in a makeshift sling. Xaron, who was more injured than I'd first noticed, limped next to us, while Corin and Maesos followed behind.

It was slow going for our crew, and after much effort and scraped hands and knees, we reached the door. Despite our haste, I paused to look back. The Conclave lay in waste. Half-burnt corpses littered the floors. Columns had been severed in half, and the great dome above was rent open. All of this had come about because of one man.

But now I knew Vusu wasn't just a man. He was a legend returned, backed by the power of a bound god. I couldn't doubt the sacrifices we'd made to stop him this time. Nor hesitate at the sacrifices still to come.

I felt a warm hand rest gently on my arm. "Airene?" Talan said softly.

I nodded and took a step forward, and we exited into the bright, noisy world.

CHAPTER THIRTY-NINE

ALL THAT SHATTERS

\- High Poetry of Lowly Things; by Hilarion the Second;
1085 SLP

As soon as we emerged, we were assaulted by questions. Guards, Servants, and patricians demanded answers of us. Just as I resolved to shove past them, Jaxas Wreath and his usual retinue of honors pushed their way through to us. Putting a proprietary hand on my shoulder, he led me and my companions away from the bustle, his honors clearing the way.

When we'd reached a more isolated part of the courtyard between two leaning laurel trees, he drew me away from the others. "Are you well?" he inquired gently.

"As well as could be expected." I glanced at Linos. The truth was, I felt better with each passing moment. Why that should be after all I'd put my body through, I couldn't say. Though who knew what to expect after visiting the Pyrthae. My head still spun at all I had just experienced.

"I worried when only Archmaster Kyros and his Aeadian emerged. But I could compel no one to enter within, not even after all had fallen silent."

He glanced back as well, drawing his arm away, his gaze lingering on the shattered Conclave dome. "I do not think our plan was wise," he said softly, and though his mouth quirked at the understatement, his eyes were sad.

"No. Perhaps not."

He stared at the ruined building for a long moment. "But we shouldn't speak here. Mobs are said to be ravaging the city. We should retreat to the safety of the palace before we discuss our next steps."

I nodded, dazed that I should be included in such deliberations. Though after the battle and the Pyrthae, it felt a very ordinary kind of awe. "Shouldn't the Low Consuls be present?"

"They are gathering at the palace as well, but I would hear your account first. I will see to them afterward." He looked at me again. "But we should get you into a carriage. You have much to think over, I'm sure."

"More than enough." Never had such an understatement been uttered.

Jaxas sent two honors back toward the crowd. "I won't pester you during the ride over," he said to me. "Your report can wait until you see me in my solar."

I gave him my thanks. As the carriages arrived through the noisy crowd, he climbed into his carriage, while my companions and I piled into the second. When it became clear that we numbered too many, Corin opted to take Maesos back to his shop, then meet us back at the Laurel Palace. I worried for her, but none of us could stay safe for long, and the glassblower couldn't be expected to stay away from his shop.

Eltris, too, was determined to part ways. "I have many things to attend to, girl," she snapped at me as Xaron and I tried to convince her to come.

"Greater things than telling our Archon of the threat we face?" I asked, incredulous.

She snorted. "You still have little idea of what that is. This is only the beginning, and someone must keep the watch." She glanced warily at Linos. "Keep an eye on that gray boy. And keep pyrkin spread on his shifts."

Without a word of explanation, the Master Augur stalked off toward the ruins of the Conclave. The rest of us exchanged glances, but we knew trying to stop her would be pointless.

So it was that Nomusa, Xaron, Talan, Linos, and I headed to the Laurel Palace in the carriage. Along the way, they urged me to tell them what had happened after I'd leaped into the rift with Vusu and Linos. Glancing at my brother, I gave them a brief account, but refused to dive into the specifics, saying they should wait until we met with Jaxas. The little I hinted at was enough to make their jaws drop.

Truly, though, even I didn't know what to make of what I'd experienced. Famine, the dragon god of old, had loomed above me. I had not believed the gods were real, not after they had been absent from the world for so long. Pyr had been hard enough to buy into. Now I found myself forced to consider the possibility that everything I thought to be legend and folk tale might just be real.

After I finished, my friends caught me up on their own stories. Xaron and Talan had intended to reach the battle sooner, but had been delayed by a handful of Shepherds standing guard. Once again, it defied my understanding how they could have taken on so many of the Tribunal's enforcers. "How are you doing it?" I pressed.

Xaron nodded at Talan. "It's him. I don't know how he does it, but he channels something that makes them collapse and… frees them, I suppose. Though mostly they die from it."

I looked to Talan with a questioning look. "Frees them?"

Talan quirked a smile. "Perhaps I'll explain more thoroughly another time. For now, let us say that I have a means of severing the connection that allows Vusu to control them. The process is often fatal, as the Acadian's apprentice observed."

Xaron and Talan had come a long way in their relationship, but the gibe still made Xaron scowl. I smiled. At least some things hadn't changed.

We arrived at the palace and made the long, weary walk up the stairs to the doors. Nikias greeted us there, the steward looking more anxious and sympathetic than I had ever seen him, though with far more fortitude than most after such an unimaginable situation.

"Come, come," he said as he bustled us up to Jaxas's solar. He eyed Linos strangely, but only said, "The Archon is waiting, as is food and drink. And the baths will be ready for you when you're done with your discussion."

We thanked him and ascended the stairs to find things arranged just as the steward had said. I had not expected to be able to eat, but at the sight and smell of the good food, I found myself wanting to heap as much on my plate as Xaron did.

But first, I went to my brother, bringing him a plate of flatbread and roasted lamb. "Linos, I brought you something."

Limos looked down at the food. Without taking the plate, he grabbed the lamb and shoved it into his mouth, heedless of the pyrkin that still dripped from his fingers. Hopefully it wasn't dangerous to ingest. I sighed. At least he still had that much will to live.

I left him with the plate and a cup of water in the corner of the solar as I returned to heap my own plate full and sit with the others around the hearth. As soon as I sat, Jaxas leaned forward and asked in a quiet voice, "That is your brother?"

I nodded. "We recovered him from Vusu."

The Archon glanced uneasily at the corner where Linos sat. "I don't think he should be here."

I stared at him, astonished. "Why not? He'll do nothing once he's done eating, I assure you. He'll be no trouble."

"Yes. But Airene, he is a warden. And he just fought for Vusu."

Cold fear crept down my spine. Suddenly, I felt it had been a terrible mistake to bring him here to the palace, where he was so utterly within Jaxas's power. "It was not his choosing. He was made this way."

"No warden chooses it," he said gently. His eyes flickered to Xaron and Talan. I wondered if he feared their reactions, since he now knew they were both wardens as well. Yet he'd invited them to his solar, and without any guards. Surely he didn't mean them ill.

"He fought for the Betrayer," the Archon continued. "Even if it was not his will, it does not change the danger he poses. What if Vusu were to seize hold of him again and try to kill all of us here?"

"His hands are covered with the pyrkin that brought Vusu to heel," I pointed out, fear sharpening my words. "He can't channel, I promise you."

Jaxas shook his head. "I wish I could say otherwise, Airene. But he must be kept away from where he can be a danger. I know these times call for extraordinary measures, so I will not exact what our laws would demand. But I would have him at least kept in the Acadium, where he might gain the help he sorely needs."

His thoughts echoed my own. Little as I wanted to, I knew I could not deny Jaxas this. "Fine," I agreed miserably. "But not yet. Let me stay with him a little while longer."

Jaxas hesitated, then nodded. "Very well. He can stay while you tell us what you saw."

I drew in a shaky breath and glanced at my brother. I felt guilty for the suspicion I bore for him myself. If Vusu could command him to kill, could he also use him to listen in on us? Yet I couldn't bear to send Linos away yet. I had to treasure what little time I had with him.

Without further hesitation, I launched into my story. I wondered if the Archon would believe me. If I hadn't experienced it myself, I knew I would have trouble swallowing the tale. As I reached the point where I leaped into the rift, I watched Jaxas for a reaction, but he kept his expression carefully composed. Even telling of Famine looming above me in the Pyrthae was only enough to produce slight twitches. The others were less restrained, and Xaron openly gaped.

When I finished, silence reigned over the solar for a long breath. Jaxas rose to stand by the window. Outside, the day was bright and cheery, a strange contrast to all we'd experienced.

Without turning around, Jaxas spoke. "I knew there was more that I didn't understand. But I did not suspect it would be… this." He shook his head, his expression hidden from me. "In light of all that has happened, what I have to say seems inconsequential. But I think we may find it necessary to formalize it sooner rather than later."

His words piqued my interest. "What do you mean?"

Jaxas turned to show a wry smile. "This evening, I will propose to the Conclave — whoever remains of it — that the Order of Verifiers be reinstituted. Not just as attendants to the Wreaths, but as a legitimate branch of the government. You will be named First Verifier and lead it, with Nomusa as your Second, should that arrangement suit you. If the measure passes, and I think it will, no one will be beyond your access, no matter how isolated or powerful. And you will find the truth that our polis so desperately needs."

I looked down at the tiled floor. Once, such an honor would have been everything I could want. Yet now, the offer felt hollow. I had barely recovered my brother, and then not even whole. We had stopped Vusu, but only for the moment, and at great cost. And now we faced a threat beyond any of our imaginings.

"I failed," I said softly. "I didn't know who was behind all of this until it was far too late. How can you expect me to find the truth now?"

"None of us knew the truth. But you drew closer to it than any other."

Not any other — Eltris knew far more than any of us had. Yet Jaxas didn't know that, and so he turned to me. But not only because of that, I realized. He trusted me. It was enough to make the difference.

"If you insist. But I have two conditions before I accept."

The Archon nodded gravely, though his eyes flickered to Linos. "Name them, and I will do whatever is within my power to ensure they are fulfilled."

I took a deep breath. "First, if I'm to be named First Verifier, Nomusa should be given the same title. She deserves it, and works better when she's the one directing others."

I glanced at her and was glad to see she shone with gratitude.

Jaxas looked between us, a faint smile on his lips. "I can tell she is well suited to authority. One might almost think she were born to it."

I startled and shared a look with Nomusa, wondering how much the Archon knew of her background.

"My second condition," I hurried on, "is that Xaron also be named a Verifier, and Talan be given access to the same resources, though he will not be a Verifier in name."

The Archon nodded. "I expected you would want to take care of your friends. But you must understand, wardens must abide by different rules."

Xaron tensed, while Talan's gaze grew hard. Yet as Jaxas turned to Xaron, he did not seem to notice. "While I am not able to make you a Verifier, Xaron, I hope you will accept a different position. Now that it is openly known that you are a warden, you must have a title that will protect you, yet still grant you a generous amount of freedom. I believe I have that solution."

Xaron stared at the Archon, his fluttering fingers betraying his anxiety. "And that is?"

"The Despoina is in need of a new Hilarion." His brow drew down, no doubt remembering what had become of the previous two. "I thought you might be the man for the task."

The look of astonishment and dread on Xaron's face would have been enough to make me laugh at another time.

Nomusa had no such qualms. "Oh, he'll be perfect for it," she said through her chuckles.

Talan's smirk showed he agreed.

Xaron tried to ease his frown, to little avail. "I thank you, Archon," he said stiffly. "I guess I have no choice but to accept."

Jaxas smiled faintly. "Do not fear. The Despoina hasn't been in much of a jesting mood of late. I doubt you'll be made to do flips and festival tricks."

"I had better not," he muttered.

Jaxas turned then to Talan. "As for you, Guilder Talan. Or perhaps it is former Guilder now."

It would have made me laugh to see the astonishment on Talan's face had it not made me fearful myself. How the Archon knew so much about each of us, I had not the slightest clue. It hardly seemed he needed an Order of Verifiers to learn all the secrets he wished.

"I am afraid the greatest gift I can offer you is freedom at this point," Jaxas continued. "As I have no other legitimate positions that wardens may occupy, you must either join the Acadians or face the Shepherds' justice. However, considering your service to the polis, I will not subject you to those today. You may resume your life outside the law as it was before, at least until such a time as I cannot ignore it."

Talan bowed his head. "It is more than I expected, and quite sufficient for me." He smiled wryly. "I prefer freedom to wearing a jester's bells."

Xaron scowled. "Just wait a span," he muttered. "We'll see how you feel then."

I didn't feel quite as sanguine about it. It rankled me to leave Talan without resources. Yet he had survived this long on his own. I had to hope he would remain capable of it, even devoid of his link to the Underguild.

Jaxas looked back to me and Nomusa. "Well then. If you two will accept, the position of First Verifier is extended to you, provided the Council agrees to reinstate the Order."

I looked at my friend once again, and she nodded. "It looks like we'll do it," I said.

"Then I will inform you of the results when I have them, though I do not expect much resistance." He looked between Nomusa and I. "There is one last thing on that matter. As of old, you and those you name as your Verifiers will be granted a place of residence on the Conclave grounds. You may have noticed us passing it as we came across the bridge, an odd-looking building situated near the cliffside."

I shook my head, but Nomusa said, "I saw it. It looks like a place pyr would go to die again."

"Yes, its maintenance has fallen off in recent times," the Archon admitted. "But as soon as the measure is passed to establish the Order, I will have renovations begin at once. I expect it won't be long before it is suitable for you to reside in."

The mention of living quarters made me realize I had forgotten someone again. "Corin. I need her to be named a Finch, too."

That raised the Archon's eyebrow. "The cartwoman? I do not think we can justify a cartwoman in that role to the Council."

The reminder jolted me for a moment. If matters proceeded as they were supposed to, then we wouldn't have to answer to Jaxas, but to the Council. Which included Feiyan. And Orhan and his Preservists. Fear was becoming far too familiar a companion of mine lately.

I bit my lip. We'd already left Corin out after Canopy was ransacked. I couldn't do it again. "On the contrary — a cartwoman is the perfect Finch. She'll be the least suspected, and a cartwoman hears all sorts of conversations when people think they aren't listening." I braced myself for my next words. "Besides, I believe as First Verifier, I would have the right to appoint any to be a Verifier that I — and Nomusa — see fit."

The Archon met my gaze. "Yes, I believe that is true. My apologies for not seeing the value in such an arrangement. And of course, I will not infringe on an institution whose power is derived from the Conclave. Now, if that's settled..." He came over and sat in his chair again. "I believe that is all of immediate concern. You all have gone through many trials. It's high time you took care of yourselves. Go; rest, eat, and drink. Oedija will stand for at least one more day without any of you keeping watch."

The four of us shared weary smiles around at that. We all looked as if we needed the rest.

"We'll try," I promised with a small smile.

The Archon nodded, then gave us his dismissal. As one, we rose to leave, though Xaron stopped long enough to grab one more skewer of lamb, while I coaxed Linos to leave the plate of juices he'd been lapping up behind. Jaxas watched as we left, his eyes unshifting as he studied my brother.

Uneasy, I hurried Linos away.

ATTUNED

The door had barely closed behind us before Talan murmured, "He makes extravagant promises."

I met his dark eyes, holding Linos's hand as I led him down the stairs. Even after the long days of fighting, they hadn't lost their shrewdness. Nor their mocking laughter.

"He does what he can," I said. "It's all we can ask of him."

"On the contrary. I could ask for a great deal more."

"Then what do you suggest? That we strike out on our own?" I looked him over. "You're already ragged and filthy. Leave you on your own for a span, and we won't recognize you from any other vagrant in the alleys."

He snorted. "I'll manage. Even if it comes to that."

I glanced at Nomusa. From the look she returned me, she knew what I had in mind. When she shrugged, I looked back to Talan. "Become a Verifier."

"Now hold on," Nomusa said with mocking seriousness. "I'd have to agree to that."

"Which you would." He gave her with a lazy smile before rolling his gaze back to me. "But you heard the Archon. He would never allow it."

I found it hard to believe Jaxas would turn him in after everything that had happened. But no matter what I thought, Talan would never trust him. "Then we'll make you a Verifier in everything but name. You'll have money, access, anything you need."

He was shaking his head before I'd finished. "Neither the Conclave nor the Laurel Palace will be able to protect me from Kalindi. And make no mistake — the Guildmaster will be after me once he's secured his hold on power. He never was one to leave loose ends, and I will be sure to make myself far more than frayed string."

"Don't be a fool," I warned him. "You don't jab a tiger outside of its cage."

"Nor do you let it roam free."

I shook my head. There was no dissuading Talan once he had his mind set. "I suppose we need someone watching the Underguild. Just be careful."

"Airene." His eyes were serious as they held mine. "Only a man with nothing to lose throws it all away. And I have something yet to hope for."

I looked away, hiding my rising flush. In another time and place, when a city wasn't falling apart around us, when my scarred brother wasn't following behind me mindlessly, perhaps it would have been the spark that ignited whatever lay between us. But here and now, it couldn't be.

Pushing down my disappointment, I turned to the others. "You heard our orders from the Archon. Who's ready for a round of drinks?"

Xaron, who had been distant during the conversation, suddenly lit up with a grin. "I thought you'd never ask!"

———

It could hardly be called a celebration, but the time that Xaron, Nomusa, Talan, and I spent drinking wine that afternoon in the feast hall was enough for me. Even with all the concerns weighing down on us, and my brother sitting silently next to me with an unshifting, blank expression, we managed to speak of lighter topics. Like if Xaron was required to be drunk all the time as Hilarion. Or how Nomusa was supposed to find a good man to warm her bed when the city was in chaos. And how Talan was as likely to be sleeping in a sty as a bed if he didn't accede to becoming a Verifier. None of us forgot what we'd been through and what was to come. But for the moment, we were able to laugh at our hardships. And laughter gave us the strength to carry on.

In the early evening, the Acadians came for Linos. As I watched them lead him away, I wondered guiltily if I should have escorted him there myself. The streets were dangerous; violent mobs roamed the demes, to make no mention of Seeker wardens and Shepherds under Vusu's sway. But I wouldn't be able to protect him any more than the Acadians, and one of the Acadians who came was the hard-eyed woman who had fought by our side in the Conclave. If she couldn't protect him, no one could.

After he was gone, the rest of us went our separate ways. I held Talan for a long while before I let him go back out into the city, though I first attempted to elicit an oath from him to stay safe. He pressed my hand and left without another word. He never was one to make false promises.

Xaron, restless even when injured, went to see the quarters afforded him as the latest Hilarion, while Nomusa sought a bath. Though she implored me to come with her, I begged off and retired to my room. Exhaustion deeper than any I'd experienced yet coursed through me, and I wanted nothing more than to rest.

Yet, when I was alone in my room, sleep fled before the memories that flooded my head. I stared up at the ceiling, remembering what it had been like in the Pyrthae. I imagined the room as it would be there, mirrored above and below, but shifting and incandescent. I wondered if I would ever enter that ethereal place again. I wondered what it meant that part of me wanted to.

But it was the memory of Famine, and of my brother and Vusu standing before the daemon god, that haunted me most. I shivered and clutched my arms around me. I did not expect to shake the cold, yet my fingers felt oddly warm. Soon, the cold had fled, and warmth spread throughout my body. The afternoon's wine was settling in, I supposed. I was glad for its comfort.

A knock at the door startled me from my trance. Heart hammering, I rose and cautiously opened the door.

A female honor stood on the other side. "Verifier Airene?"

"Yes?"

"Someone waits for you at the front gates. Corin, she says her name is." The honor bowed briefly. "I am sorry, but they will not admit her, though she claims to have been granted access before. Security has increased, considering..."

I sighed. The rest of us had been reveling while Corin had, as usual, been doing thankless labor. And dangerous work, considering the state of the city. I glanced down at myself, still in my dirty and torn trousers and tunic. No doubt my hair was a mess, and I didn't smell clean. But they were frivolous concerns, and Corin no doubt suffered a worse state.

"I'll go now, if you'll take me to her," I told her.

The honor accompanied me down to a side gate in the northeast corner of the Wreath grounds. There, Corin waited for me, fidgeting with her hands and scuffing her feet. She wasn't usually prone to nervousness, but I didn't have to wonder what had upset her. In addition to everything we'd heard of riots and Seekers, plumes of smoke rose over the buildings in the distance. I wondered morosely if the shell horns would warn of widespread fires soon.

As I walked through the gate, I greeted Corin. Instead of approaching, she motioned me apart from the guards and down the narrow street leading away from the palace grounds. I followed her, my apprehension growing.

"Corin, is something wrong?"

She didn't stop and turn toward me until we were out of earshot of the guards, and even then, she didn't meet my eyes. "Maesos. He's hurt."

My mouth went dry. "What happened?" I demanded. "Where is he?"

"Thieves. They stole his cart and hurt him." She gestured down the street. "I took him to an abandoned house nearby."

"An abandoned house? Why didn't you—?" I shook my head. "Never mind. Is he hurt badly? Can he move? We need to get him back here. I'm sure we could have one of the palace healers attend to him."

"He hurt his leg. I couldn't move him alone."

"Then we need to get a cart, or a carriage—"

"No time," she cut me off. "We can help him together. Only one leg is injured. But we should hurry. The thieves might return."

I tried making sense of the situation. Corin wasn't acting herself, nor did her words add up. Whatever had occurred had clearly rattled her. I feared greater still for Maesos.

"Fine. We'll go now, and you can explain more on the way."

We set off at a jog back into the city. The streets were eerily empty, the people shuttered up in their homes, waiting out the riots. Distant shouts and screams told of the mobs' movements. With any luck, they'd stay far away from us. As we traveled, I asked between panting breaths about the details of their attack. Maesos, the old fool, had apparently tried protecting his wares when a group of young men had waylaid them, and they'd hurt his leg in vengeance. Corin had stood by; unarmed against their knives, she'd known she couldn't resist. After they'd left, she'd dragged the glassblower into a nearby house, which she'd found with the door open, and left him there to go fetch me.

As we turned into a narrow street of Sandglass, though, an uneasy feeling gripped me. The rows of houses on either side looked more decrepit than most neighborhoods in the deme. Nothing stirred behind the boarded-up windows. I couldn't decide if they were signs of safety or danger.

I glanced at Corin. "Why were you over here? This isn't on the way to Port."

She glanced up and down the street, perhaps worrying about the gang of boys returning. As she spoke, her words tumbled together, her accent more pronounced than usual. "We came here when they wouldn't let us through the Conclave gates. Thought it would be out of the way." She stopped and gestured to a house. "This is where he is."

Catching my breath, I looked up with apprehension. Crowded in close to the other buildings, the abandoned house was a dull sandy color, flat-roofed, with narrow windows. It didn't look inviting.

"Let's go get him then."

I started toward it when Corin grabbed my arm. "Airene."

I jerked to a halt. Her grip was tight enough to hurt. "What is it? You're hurting me."

She held my arm a moment longer, then released it. "Don't go in," she whispered.

I rubbed my arm where she'd gripped me. "Don't go in? But you just said Maesos is hurt and needs our help."

"I lied."

I stared, uncomprehending, as her words sank in. I looked up and down the street. I saw nothing, but I had the distinct feeling that something lurked just beyond the shadows.

"What do you mean, you lied? Corin, I need to know what you're talking about. Right now."

She raised her gaze, finally meeting my eyes. "They have her," she said in a strangled voice. "They said they could bring her over from the islands, but they took her captive. And now, if you don't enter the house, they'll…"

My mind whirled. "Who was taken captive? And who did it?" The first part clicked into place. "Does someone have your sister, Corin?"

She nodded slowly.

"Who has her? Who?" I felt as if walls were closing in around me. Was it Feiyan? The Underguild? Or one of Vusu's henchmen, come to finish me off?

"The Valemish."

I stared at her. "The Valemish. You're sure?"

"Yes. Their priest threatened my sister. The Kul."

I scrambled to understand. Why would the Valemish wish me harm? Could they have found out I'd entered one of their temples and held a grudge for it? Was it to do with my association with Talan? Both seemed too flimsy of reasons to orchestrate such a betrayal.

But their motivation wasn't my immediate concern. It slowly dawned on me how difficult it would be to get out of this bind. If they had Corin's sister, and she failed to do as they'd asked — having me enter the house alone — then her sister would be killed. And for all I knew, if we tried leaving without entering, hidden watchers might stop us anyway.

Frustration flooded me as I stared at my friend. The Valemish might be the ones threatening us, but it was Corin who had landed us in this situation. She should have come to her friends before trusting the Valemish. Yet, as angry and betrayed as I felt, I could not fault her for being blind when it came to her family.

I drew in a shaky breath. After what I'd witnessed in the Conclave, I didn't think I could feel real fear again. But at least then, I hadn't faced my enemies alone.

One last desperate thought gave me pause. *The lodestone.* Perhaps I could signal Xaron, and he would come to my aid. But then I remembered the lodestone had been in the chiton I'd shed in the Conclave. Now, it was lost among the ashes. And even if I could have signaled Xaron, he wouldn't have known where to go.

I sighed, then squared my shoulders. "I'm entering."

Corin's eyes widened. "But—"

"We can't risk your sister getting hurt. And I don't see another path out. This is the only way to keep her safe, and for us to survive." *Or at least have a chance of it*, came my bitter thought.

Corin started to speak, then looked aside. I did the same. There was nothing really left to say.

Facing the house, its squalor took on a sinister air. Before I could lose my courage, I strode forward and pressed against the door, already hanging partly open. I hoped for a moment it wouldn't give, but it swung open to my touch with a loud creak that made me wince. Whoever waited within knew I was coming now. I continued forward all the same.

The entrance was tight and narrow with little room to do anything but kick off the mud from my sandals. I could see little, as the only light came from behind me.

"Maesos?" I called in. They knew I was coming already, but perhaps by playing my part, I might gain some edge. "Maesos, where are you?"

I moved into the atrium. It was tall, at least two stories high, if still narrow. The darkness was lifted slightly by a narrow slit of light from a high, boarded window. As I stepped in and strained to peer into every dark corner, I saw movement out of the corner of my eye. Blood hammered in my ears as I spun around. A man stepped free from the shadows.

"Who are you?" I demanded, voice quavering. My hand strayed to the knife tucked against the small of my back. Every part of me screamed to flee, yet I stayed. For Corin and her sister, and for my own sake, I had to stand firm.

The man took a slow step forward, moving into the slit of light. As his face became visible, I flinched in recognition.

"Eazal," I said, disbelieving. "The apothecary."

"Airene of Port." The man spoke in a cracked, deep voice. He was Avvadin, evident from his bronze skin, green eyes, and the cloth wrapped about his head. He wore a simple tunic and trousers in place of more traditional robes, though he looked clean and respectable. His hands were clasped behind his back.

Anger quickly filled me as I considered him. Three years before, Eazal might have helped me solve the mystery of Thero's death. Instead, he had fled the city, taking whatever he knew of my brother's murderer with him. Though I'd now paid Vusu back in part, his wrongs were far from righted. And but for Eazal, we might have uncovered Vusu's plans years before they came to fruition.

But for him, Linos might still be whole.

"I'm surprised you returned, Eazal," I said coldly.

The apothecary tried on a smile, but it slipped away. He looked as if he might become ill. "I'm not here over old wrongs, Airene. Believe me when I tell you that."

I gripped my hidden knife tightly. "But perhaps I am. I can't forget what you've cost me."

Eazal stared at me, buried emotion glimmering in his eyes. *Guilt? Regret?* He glanced away before I could tell.

"Perhaps it is best this way," he said softly. "After all, I cannot turn aside from my purpose, either. The Kul commands that I do this. Demands it. My last sacrifice to Valem."

His words sent ice through my veins. I had shot Vusu with a crossbow. I had come face-to-face with a daemon god. Yet here, in this dark shack of a house, I'd died at the hands of a man I'd inadvertently forced into exile. I was so afraid I almost laughed.

"Debts are owed," he said softly, and his hands came around. In one of them, a sharp knife gleamed as he crossed another narrow strip of light between us. The other he raised to his mouth, and I caught the glow of pyrkin before he closed it and swallowed. He coughed, then straightened. The sweat on his face shone as he stepped through the last patch of light between us. "I'm sorry, Airene."

As I wondered what he'd swallowed, my gut suddenly wrenched. Fire spread from it, more visceral than anger or fear. Despite the man stalking toward me, I felt my attention drawn inward.

"They used you to sow chaos," he continued. He was twelve paces off, eleven. "But now that you've served your purpose, you're expendable. As am I."

The heat spread, burning through my veins. The tips of my fingers itched with the feverish warmth. I ran them along the rough leather hilt of the knife. I narrowed my eyes and blinked off the sudden beads of sweat, trying to concentrate. I didn't draw the blade. I had one chance to strike, and I meant to make the most of it.

He sighed, slowing six dark paces off, as if reluctant to take the final steps. "This is how it ends."

"No." My head felt light like I were intoxicated. The fire inside me had burned away the anger, leaving a strange, disconnected clairvoyance. "This doesn't have to be how it ends, Eazal. We can settle this another way."

He took one more step, then another. "No, we can't. Not anymore."

Raising the dagger, he dashed forward with impossible speed. My mind in a fog and my vision hazy, I drew out my own knife and slashed wildly before me. As I flailed, I felt everything I'd held inside suddenly pouring out. All my helpless rage, my crippling fear, the guilt for all the things I did and did not do. All my failures and my successes. I struck blindly, and as I did, I felt something inside me break free. Heat flooded through me anew. My body did not feel like my own. My gut untwisted, and pain fled before the stream of fire that poured through me.

My fingertips no longer itched, but burned as they pulled at the stream and spread it forth. Flashes of light burst from my hands, blinding me. Vibrations built to a tremendous force, shaking and rattling my body. Sparks shimmered over my skin. From my feet, flames and force spread out in waves, disintegrating my sandals and blasting the dirt floor.

Suspended in the light and warmth, I stared in wonder at the energy flowing from me. I knew what it meant. Yet I couldn't yet put words to it.

Eazal had fallen back, cowering against the wall, as he stared at me with wide eyes. "You, Branded?"

The fear in his voice finally broke through my dumb wonder. "I'm not!" I cried.

But my hands and feet proved me wrong. Power continued to pour forth, ever greater with each passing moment. The circle of destruction around me was spreading. The knife in my hand melted before my eyes.

Before the impossible display, Eazal fled. Flinging the knife to the ground behind him, he cast back one more look, then disappeared out of sight. I felt little relief at his departure. I stared at my body, horror piercing through the calm aura that had until that point enthralled me.

"How is this happening?" I whispered. I'd always wished this day would come when I was a child. But now that it was here, I was terrified that it would never stop. "How?" I cried out.

The flames at my fingertips flared.

As if a dam had broken, fire burst forth to paint the walls and sear the floor. My skin blistered; my feet scorched. The house around me went up in flames. I watched, helpless to stop any of it.

Then, as suddenly as it had begun, the stream of energy stopped. All around me, flames died down, leaving the walls black and smoking. Exhausted beyond anything I'd experienced before, I collapsed to the floor and into the darkness beyond it.

Next that I knew, I was in Corin's arms, jostled with every step. My senses were dim. I saw she carried me along the street in her arms. Her panting sobs were loud in my ears. But though I saw and heard, my awareness ended there. I had no more command over my body than if I were asleep. I barely felt my limbs except for the pain slowly creeping at the edges of my mind. Trapped, my focus retreated within, where the ebb and flow of the energy still pulsed, like a glimmering light I could not look away from. I strained for its warmth like a drunkard at a wineskin. It was intoxicating, power undiluted. And I longed for more.

I did not think anything could draw me away from it, yet a sound cut through my stupor. It was a sound I had heard only a few times before. It was the sound that had set me on the path that had led me to this point.

The shell horns of the Laurel Palace, loud and long and mournful, blew once more.

The first horn sounded, and some part of me wondered if the fire had started with me. Then the second horn blew. I waited, expecting a third to come, if only because it had before.

But none ever did.

Three horns is nothing to fear, Father had once said. But he had not spoken of two. No one alive had heard just two horns call. Yet all knew what it portended.

I closed my eyes. Dread drew me away from the kindling magic inside me. *War.* We were going to war. But with whom?

The horns' call propelled our nation toward a cliff, beyond which Vusu and his daemon god waited, Famine stretching his mouth open to swallow us all.

War had come to Oedija. But war was only the beginning.

ECHOES OF CHAOS

THE FAMINE CYCLE
BOOK II

PROLOGUE

He watched the great serpent coil tighter around the ailing man.

Azhi had long grown used to waiting. Perhaps he'd been a boy when he died, but two centuries had turned his mind ancient beyond any elder. Patience was the measure of his existence, more constant than the flow of time, more persistent than a cancer.

But the time for waiting was coming to an end.

The serpent twitched for a moment, then turned toward him. Azhi kept miles between them, but as the beast's eye turned on him, fear carved into his core. The leviathan was black as a moonless midnight, black as an endless chasm. Black as a hunger that could never be sated.

He shivered and turned away. The Corrupted couldn't reach him, not while he was still bound. But his bonds were fraying. Taozu had never been contained for so long by a man — nor could he have been, if not by his own choice. When the moment came for him to break free, Azhi had no doubt it would also be of his choosing.

Changing his form into force, Azhi flew back over the city. Oedija was mirrored above and below him, the towers of the Laurel Palace stretching toward each other. Only the Pillars touched, and these melded together, crossing the boundaries of the higher, lower, and material planes.

As Taozu reemerged, these cities would shift, changing to suit the great serpent. But only if he remained uncontested.

Azhi had learned many lessons in the Wumofu during his childhood long, long ago. *When the serpent coils,* his father had said, *back away. It has claimed that sand for itself.*

So Azhi would move far away, and leave Oedija's defenses to the last god to claim it. But only so he could bring back that which could seal Taozu once more.

Azhi flew up into the city hanging above, keeping within Oedija's walls. He swept through the streets, searching amid the shadowed forms for the spark that he had started. For the man who had grown to trust him through his constant guidance and companionship.

He found him curled up in the churned mud of an alley, head bowed, hiding his tears and shame. His headwrap had unwound slightly, letting loose thin, brown hair in tufts. His body was spare, but lithe. A man still in possession of his strength, even if he did not know it. A man far from his end.

Ascending again and leaving the man behind, Azhi broke through the illusion of the city and arced through the cloudy emptiness above it. When he descended, he found himself in a tower. Birds flew below him in the rafters, and a woman, bent with age but still moving with vigor, fed one from her hand.

As he entered, her keen, golden eyes found him. The smile she'd shared with the finch transformed into a scowl.

"You need her again?" she scoffed. She spoke, but it was the reverberations of her thoughts that sounded clear in his mind.

Yes.

"Fine. But mind you take care of her."

Azhi drifted down to where the bird waited. She watched him approach, her blue crest seeming to glow brighter as he neared.

Then, as gently as the woman held her own bird, Azhi coaxed the whisper finch to admit him.

The world lurched, then righted itself. Abruptly, Azhi found himself clutching wood with clawed feet. He twitched a wing, then the other, cocked his head, and blinked.

"You'd think you'd be used to it," the woman called from below.

Azhi flapped his wings experimentally, then threw himself off and glided down. He flew once around the woman, then settled on a window sill. The window was boarded up but had a gap just large enough for a small bird to pass through.

"He's breaking free," Azhi said, his voice coming out as a boy's. Always, it was startling to hear it unchanged from the twelve years he had been when he died.

"We always knew he would."

"I shall have to leave soon. Now you must be the watcher."

"So I have always been. Where do you go?"

Azhi turned his bird's head out the window and glimpsed gray sky outside. "To where hope rests."

The woman snorted and released the finch. "Hope. Does it still exist? But never mind. Dead or not, we'll still try." She waved a hand. "Go. But bring my bird back whole."

Azhi just cocked his avian head, then turned and leaped from the window.

As he flew over the city, the wind lifted his light body, sending it far aloft. Chill as it was with the coming monsoons, the whisper finch wasn't bothered. This was what it had been made for.

As he neared the wall, he turned and dove, heading for the familiar alley. Breaking his dive short as he drew close, he flapped his wings and settled on the roof above the man. He'd stopped sobbing now and rested his head against the wall behind him.

His eyes turned up, then widened as he saw the whisper finch's glowing crest. "You again," he whispered.

"Hello, Eazal. My friend."

The man didn't smile, but only bowed his head again. "Why don't you leave me alone? I want to be alone."

Azhi considered him for a long moment. Perhaps he was wrong. Perhaps he was too broken for this task. But he had to make use of what tools he had.

"But did you think Valem Branded you for nothing?" he suggested softly. "Did you think he held no purpose for you?"

Eazal threw his head back and laughed, the sound sharp and devoid of mirth. "Oh, I know Valem's purpose for me, or at least those who claim him. I failed in that as well."

"You have not served it yet," Azhi soothed. "But first, we must keep you alive. Come; follow me. I will lead you from the city. Then I will show you what you were meant to do."

The man turned his head back to Azhi, eyes narrowed, mouth drawn. "Why should I care?" he asked, the words choked. "I've failed them. Over and over, I've failed them. How could I ever do enough?"

Azhi knew to whom he referred. "You could save them, and this city, and the whole of the Four Realms. But you must trust me. I saved you once, on the cliff. Do you remember?"

"Yes. And I've lived to regret it."

"But you lived, and you have time to right those regrets. Come, Eazal. Your purpose doesn't end here. You're destined for something greater."

Though his connection to the Pyrthae was tenuous, Azhi felt a glimmer of a sensation at his words, as if someone had smiled in approval. He ignored it, and ignored, too, the shiver that ran through his bird's body.

Eazal slowly rose to his feet and looked at him. "I don't believe you. I don't think I'm meant for anything. But... I don't know what else to do."

Azhi flew forward and alighted on his shoulder. "Then come," he whispered in the man's ear. "I will show you the path."

CHAPTER ONE

TRUTH IN DREAMS

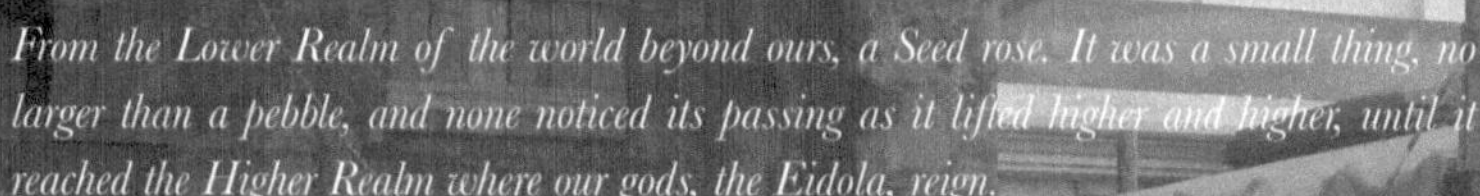

From the Lower Realm of the world beyond ours, a Seed rose. It was a small thing, no larger than a pebble, and none noticed its passing as it lifted higher and higher, until it reached the Higher Realm where our gods, the Eidola, reign.

Tyurn Sky-Sea, Ruler of All Realms, Lord of All, was strong in arm and limb. He was master of the stormy sea and the violent sky and could be harmed by neither. But his quintessence was fallible, the fabric of his mind loosely woven, and his actions had ever been erratic.

The Seed, upon arriving in the Higher Realm, sensed this weakness in the Foremost of Gods and sought to exploit it. Creeping in as Tyurn Sky-Sea slept, it fed him dreams of glory and plenty and filled him with pride, slowly whittling his mind to its own purpose.

— The Seeds of Famine, a translation from the Lighted-tongue; by Oracle Kalene of deme Hull; 881 SLP

I drifted between dreams.

From one scene to another, I was swept along, each image as devoid of meaning as the next. I watched, unable to do anything, unwilling to even if I could.

A man, broad in stature, with thick gray hair just beginning to bald, sat hunched in a cell, knees drawn up to his chest. Fallen from grace, he seemed, a different person than the one he was supposed to be.

A gust of wind whipped the man into sand, and another took his place. This man was clad in a tattered robe that looked to have once been white.

He swayed as he walked into a shadowed room, then sunk to his knees on a worn reed mat. His eyes, dark as the heart of a monsoon storm, told of pain. Yet though the shaft of a quarrel was lodged in his side, it didn't seem the source of his torment.

Another turn — now a gray woman, eyes preternaturally wide, smile twisted and bitter, gazed down on me as she floated above the ruins of a city.

Another turn — now the face of a boy, still as snow on a distant mountain peak, stared up from a bed. Phantoms moved in a haze around him, but he didn't notice. He had eyes for nothing but what he saw above. I felt I must lay next to him, and as I did, I lifted my gaze to see what he saw.

The great maw, an endless abyss lined with long, sharp teeth, descended. It didn't come quickly, yet I couldn't move to escape. I grasped the boy's hand as slowly, inexorably, the jaws closed over us—

I sat up, gasping. Darkness blinded me. For a moment, still caught halfway in the dream, I thought myself in the terrible beast's mouth. Then I felt a bed beneath me, and the thick covers that had fallen away as I sat up. My skin, sticky with sweat, grew rough with chills as the cool air washed over me.

Night. I was in a bed, unclothed, and it was night. No beast had hold of me. I was safe.

Wasn't I?

"Airene?" An accented voice, drowsy with sleep, spoke from the darkness next to me.

I flinched, as much from recognition as surprise. "Corin?"

In the darkness, barely lifted by the faint light from the windows across the room, I heard her movements rather than saw them: the rustling of clothes, the creaking of a chair. "Yes," she said. "I am here."

"Here?"

"The Laurel Palace."

I clutched the blankets closer. Memories from what seemed a long time ago assaulted me, one after another. Despite the covers, the chill seeped in deeper. My teeth began to chatter.

"Are you well?" Another creak of the chair as she rose.

"Yes," I said quickly. "I'm fine. Just caught a chill, nothing more."

Corin made a sound that might have been agreement or doubt, then the chair creaked as she sat. I stared at her outlined figure until I was sure she was settled, then eased myself back down.

"What happened?" I asked quietly.

Another protest from the chair as she shifted. But Corin gave no answer.

My heart thumped harder at her silence. "Did you... see me? See what I did?"

"Yes."

I thought it must have been a dream. What I imagined that I remembered was impossible. Or if not impossible, then so unlikely and rare that it could only be called that.

"Are you sure? Perhaps a candle spilled. Perhaps it was something that Eazal did—"

"No. It was you, Airene. I saw."

I shrank away from her words. The cold struck deep through me once again. *It can't be*, I told myself again. *It can't be true.*

I couldn't have channeled.

But I didn't challenge Corin. Though the events afterward were hazy, I recalled all too clearly the moment it had happened. It had felt like a completion, a sating of a desire I'd never known I had. A warming of cold parts of me I hadn't known were frozen. I remembered the opening to it, the drawing of it, and the expulsion, all occurring so naturally that it had seemed impossible for it to be the first time.

But I recalled, too, the fire burning and scorching as it swept over me. Yet as I ran my hands over myself, I didn't feel raw flesh or angry boils but smooth, unbroken skin. I sat back again. If I'd imagined that part, how much of the rest did I misremember?

"The Archon visited you," Corin spoke again. "While you slept."

I couldn't think about Jaxas at the moment. Not with everything else I had on my mind. "What about Xaron and Nomusa? And Talan?"

"Yes. They have come often, though the Guilder only once."

I took a steadying breath. If my memories didn't lie, and if I were found out, everything I had worked for, everything I strived to do, would be compromised. My very life could be forfeit.

So why did I feel giddy with anticipation?

I'm a warden.

I held the words in my mind. It was too strange a thought to believe. For Xaron and Talan, it was natural to call them wardens — it was who they were. But me? It couldn't possibly apply to me.

I'm a warden.

I'd channeled fire and force. Radiance and kinesis. I'd nearly burned a building down. Unless it was the most vivid dream I'd yet had, it was true. And Corin claimed to have seen it as well. Burns or no, it was true.

I was a warden.

A sudden vertigo swept over me. I felt as if I couldn't take a proper breath. But with Corin present, I fought back for control. With each breath, I slowed my pulse. Yet other memories from before I'd channeled intruded, quickening it again.

Corin had betrayed me. She'd lied to lure me into a house in Sandglass. She'd served me up to the whims of the Valemish. True, she'd confessed at the last moment, and warned me of what waited within. But it didn't change that I'd been forced to enter and face down my would-be assassin. Even with her warning, even with Eazal's obvious reluctance for his task, I'd have died if my attunement hadn't manifested at that moment.

Caustic words burned on my tongue, but I held them back. She'd done it for her sister. Even if she'd been a daemon-struck fool to put her sister's life in the hands of the Valemish, I understood why Corin had acted as she had. But understanding didn't fix what had broken. Trust couldn't mend in a day. If it ever could.

I broke the long silence. "Where are they now, Xaron and Nomusa?"

"Xaron is Hilarion." Corin shrugged, barely visible in the darkness. "He follows the Archon and the Despoina."

"I'm sure he's pleased about that." I smiled at the thought of Xaron in the jester's sackcloth clothes. It didn't seem every Hilarion wore them, but I hoped Xaron would be forced to put them on. His sensibilities of fashion would be driven mad. But more importantly, Xaron being Hilarion meant he was safe from the Shepherds. Though I wasn't sure how many Shepherds remained within Tribunal control now.

"And Nomusa?"

"We... do not speak."

A wry grin found my lips. At least that much hadn't changed. "She's visited though?"

"Everyday."

Everyday. Only then did I realize I'd overlooked a critical fact. "This isn't the same night as Despoina Asileia's trial, is it?"

"No. It's the third night."

I lay still. *Three days.* I'd lost three days. Who knew what changes had come over Oedija. How much Vusu had recovered his strength.

How much Famine had gained in power.

I sat up again. "I need clothes."

"Why?" Corin sounded alarmed. "It is night. Time for rest."

"There's no time to lie around. Where are my clothes, Corin?"

"Airene." Corin had stood, but hadn't moved toward me. "You've lain as if dead for three days. You've had little more than broth. You need rest."

Ignoring her, I swung my legs out from under the covers. A fire had lit inside me. Weakness wasn't going to put me off, nor any shame of nakedness. "If you won't bring me clothes, I'll get them myself."

I stood, or tried to. The ground lurched, sending me tumbling, and I fell hard on my hands and knees. As I tried to rise, something wrenched in my gut. I found myself heaving, little more than a dribble coming up.

Corin was helping me up a moment later, and I didn't resist as she settled me back into the bed. "You need to rest," she said again, reprimand in her voice.

I was suddenly too weary to respond. My seizing gut had woken a terrible ache that made me want to curl up into myself. "Is there more broth?" I asked, stopping just short of mewling. "I'm starving."

"I'll see if there is some in the kitchens. But only if you stay here."

I nodded against the pillow. "Yes. I will."

Corin paused a moment longer, not seeming to trust my word. But she left the room all the same. The door creaked as she pulled it closed, then there was a small clatter as she turned a key. I pressed my lips together, considering. Whether she'd locked it to ensure that I stayed or to protect me from those without, I couldn't say.

The thoughts that had wracked me now seemed too vast to consider. Sleep crept up at the edges of my mind. I didn't resist. Before Corin had returned, I fell free from the world once more.

———

I woke a second time to sunlight creeping in through the windows. Groaning and stretching, I gazed blearily around the room. Corin didn't stir from the chair where she sat, head lolling against the wall. She couldn't be comfortable, yet I saw no signs that she'd sought to make the situation more bearable. On a table beside the bed sat a bowl of broth, fat congealed over the surface.

Hunger suddenly assaulted me so that my hands shook as I seized the bowl and began to quickly spoon the cool broth down.

My noisy eating woke Corin. She said nothing as she cracked open an eye and saw me bent over the bowl. A faint smile crossed her face. "You're awake."

"Mhm." I didn't pause eating but carved out the fat by the spoonful. It filmed my throat as it went down, but starved as I was, I didn't mind.

She rose and stretched with a yawn. "Your visitors will likely come soon. You wish to dress?"

I nodded and set the bowl aside as I finished. "And maybe have some more food," I said hopefully. "Something solid. I think I can hold it down now."

Corin complied, moving lethargically across the room to bring me a chiton and underwraps from the dressing closet. As I took the clothes, she turned to the door and unlocked it.

"Corin," I said to her back. "Thanks."

She turned around and gave me a weak smile. I returned it as best as I could. Perhaps things between us couldn't return to being the same. But I hoped they would. Corin had always been the steady rock in Canopy. I felt slightly unmoored without being able to rely on her.

Corin left, and I stood to dress. My body still felt tired and trembling, but when I eased onto my legs, they held. I marveled at the weakness that made standing an accomplishment.

Corin hadn't returned by the time I finished dressing, nor anyone else arrived. My mind began to wander. I checked my skin for burns and confirmed what I'd suspected: not a blemish marked my body. I shook my head in disbelief and resolved to ask Corin if I'd had any wounds when she'd taken me from the house. I could ponder the mystery once I knew more.

I lowered myself back onto the bed and examined my fingertips. The skin seemed as it had before. No matter how I searched, I didn't see any sign of movement on the prints there.

I lowered my hands and tried to keep the panic at bay. Perhaps one's shifts didn't appear immediately. Perhaps it took channeling at least twice before they showed. But now, I couldn't help but wonder if Corin and I hadn't both imagined it. Maybe I wasn't attuned.

Maybe I wasn't a warden.

No. I wouldn't accept that. I would prove what I knew myself to be. Because, though I'd rarely allowed myself to admit it, I'd always wished to understand what Xaron and Talan felt when they channeled. I wanted the power of the Pyrthae at my fingertips, achingly so.

Unwilling to give in, I closed my eyes and tried to channel. I dredged up the vague memories of that first occasion four days before, and even dimmer remembrances from how Xaron and wardens in my books had described the experience. The locus, located at the center of the body around the navel, was where the link was supposed to form. But no matter how I concentrated on the spot, no matter how I clenched my gut or gritted my teeth, I couldn't open any such connection.

Relaxing my muscles, I sagged forward. When I'd channeled the first time, the energy had pushed out without any effort on my part. Why were things different now?

I left off the attempts and lay back down on my bed. My head hurt, and the queasiness had returned with a vengeance. I sighed and let myself go limp. Sleep edged against my awareness.

Three soft knocks came at the door.

I bolted back upright and stared toward the entryway. My heart thundered in my chest, and fear made chicken-flesh of my skin. I hadn't realized how badly recent events had shaken me. In that moment of mute terror, I'd expected that knock to signal Shepherds calling at the door.

The knock came again. "Airene?" a muffled voice spoke through. "Corin said you were awake. We thought we'd come check on you."

Xaron. I exhaled in relief as I recognized his voice. "Come in," I called, hating the way my words warbled.

A key turned in the lock, and the door swung slowly open. Xaron entered first, tiptoeing as if fearing to intrude. He looked much the same as before, with sharp, handsome features and narrow, brown eyes that darted about nervously. But there was one significant change. Gone were the colorful coats and trousers he'd always worn, replaced now by a long, drab tunic of coarse sackcloth, belted together by a short length of rope. His sandals, too, were lashed to his feet with rope that must chafe, and his dark, silken hair was bound back by a piece of twine thread with dried corn husk, a crown fit for a jester. He donned a grin at my smile, though no doubt he knew what made me laugh.

"It's good to see you up," he said as he approached.

Before I could answer, another familiar figure entered behind him. Jaxas Wreath was as thin as before, his face hollowed, and his dark eyes nearly lost in shadows. The Archon's spare frame shrunk into the opulent robes and heavy stoles that hung about his neck. Of the two of us, he looked the likelier candidate to have barely eaten in the last three days. Yet I knew that hidden within him was a strength of mind as I'd never seen before.

"First Verifier Airene." A ghost of a smile lightened the formal words. "Are you feeling better?"

I bowed my head, the most respectful acknowledgment I could manage. "I can stand for a minute or two and am hungry enough for a feast." I cocked a smile. "I'd say I'm on the mend."

The Archon returned a wan smile of his own as he entered further into the room. He kept his distance, as if fearing I might pass ill humors to him. "The hunger is to be expected. You've been unconscious for several days."

I met Jaxas's sharp gaze and wondered uncomfortably how much he knew about my bout of illness. I remembered all too well how he'd turned Talan aside for being a warden. Xaron had been forced to become the new Hilarion in order to stay around. If I were in the same situation, I doubted he could devise a similar arrangement. I certainly couldn't be kept as First Verifier.

Xaron, who had kneeled by my bedside, took my hands in his. "I would have been here," he said gravely. "But a certain taskmaster has kept me very busy."

"I've asked you to tumble once," Jaxas said with an amused twist to his lips. "But I'm afraid I must ask another favor. If you could give us the room for a moment, I would have a private word with Airene."

Xaron's expression spasmed, but he nodded sharply and rose. "Of course. I'll be right outside."

With a perfunctory bow to the Archon, he turned out of the door and closed it behind.

Jaxas moved no closer. "It must be quite the malady to have rendered you unconscious for nearly three full days. Do you remember what happened?"

I studied his face, which had creased with seeming concern. Did he honestly believe me sick? Or was he giving me a convenient excuse? Or was it the terrible third possibility: that he knew the truth, and handed me the rope to hang myself? Why I felt Jaxas might wish to trap me, I couldn't say. I had plotted with him to take down Vusu. But even so, I'd only known the man for a handful of days. Anything might have happened in the days I'd lain unconscious.

But as long as he didn't speak of my channeling, I had no intentions of mentioning it.

"Not much," I said. "Everything is a bit blurry. But Corin has been able to help fill things in."

One thin eyebrow raised high. "Indeed. And yet she was so forgetful when I asked her of it."

I repressed the need to swallow. This wasn't what I wanted to be doing right now. My stomach felt as if it ate itself with my hunger. Had he come to interrogate me now because he knew I was vulnerable? No matter how I wished to see the best of Jaxas, ruthlessness was bred into him. He had acted as my benefactor, but even still, he was a Wreath through and through.

"It was a confusing time for us all," I said carefully. "And she didn't have the complete picture."

Jaxas inclined his head. "Of course. Perhaps you can fill in the gaps for me as well."

I considered refusing. After all, even though he boarded me in the Laurel Palace, I didn't have to report to him anymore. It was to the Conclave that Nomusa and I now owed our allegiance, so long as they reinstated the Order of Verifiers. But Jaxas had given us Finches a chance when few others would. Even if it had been Vusu's machinations that first brought us to his employ, I owed Jaxas much.

So I spoke what I could: a lie laced with truth. I said that Corin had brought me to help Maesos, who had been robbed and injured. I said that Maesos wasn't there when I arrived, and instead, someone who meant to kill me lay waiting. Of Corin's betrayal, I mentioned nothing, nor of what happened after the encounter with Eazal.

Jaxas barely blinked through the telling. "I see," he said as I finished. "And what of the fire?"

My mouth went dry. "Fire?"

"It must have been a deep slumber you fell into. For you had burns up and down your body not three days ago."

It had become hard to breathe. I wondered if I should admit the truth now. But as the words formed on my lips, an idea came to mind. I jumped at it, no matter how unbelievable it seemed.

"Yes, I've been puzzled by that since Corin told me," I said, wrinkling my brow. "The only thing I can think of was my trip into the Pyrthae. With so few people having gone there, it makes sense we wouldn't know what happens when they do visit. Maybe it healed me."

"Ah." His even tone betrayed no sign of what he thought of my theory.

"But if something strange had to happen to me," I hurried on, "I'm glad it was healing. I have a feeling that a lot of work lies ahead."

"Yes. I think the Council will keep you busy."

Something in his tone struck me as curious. Before I could speculate, Jaxas suddenly slumped into a chair. I watched in surprise as the Archon put his head in his hands and rubbed at his eyes.

"This is too exhausting," he said, his words muffled by his hands. "I'm sorry, Airene. I didn't come here to pitch barbed questions. These past three days… I almost envy you being able to sleep them away."

Guilt flickered in me. "Regardless of what happened, you should take care of yourself. You look even thinner than before."

He looked up with a smile twisted on his lips. "An accurate observation, if lacking your usual tactfulness. But your concerns should not lie with me. I fear we've only slowed Vusu and his Seekers. And if you can believe it, the Manifest is the least of my worries." He held my gaze. "Avvad marches north."

Only then did I remember the horns. They'd called as if in a dream, two long blows from the shell horns mounted atop the Laurel Palace. One signaled a fire spreading in the city; three the death of the reigning Wreath.

Two were called for war.

"Avvad marches north," I repeated. Many variations of those words had been uttered before, but always as an eventuality. Not something that would ever happen in our lifetimes. It was like a boulder positioned above that we'd said would never fall, but now barreled down upon us.

"Birds arrived the day of the trial, telling of the gathering of their troops from the southern provinces and the marshaling of their resources. The object of their conquest is all too clear from our spies' reports. They are still several spans from even setting march toward us, but I convinced Low Consul Daelya that we should sound the horns as soon as possible, to prepare the people for what is to come."

Several spans to gather and prepare, then several more to march. I had little experience with armies, but I knew it took time and resources to move that many soldiers. "They'll be here by the first of the monsoons," I guessed.

Jaxas smiled wryly. "And I hope their troops feel the brunt of what the rains have to offer. So long as drought doesn't steal them away."

We sat quietly, contemplating all that this meant. One thing hung between us unsaid. Even if the Manifest did not threaten us from the north, Oedija couldn't withstand the might of the Avvadin Imperium.

"Why?" I muttered, almost to myself. "Why now?"

"You know as well as I do." He sank back against his elbows. "We are vulnerable. Our trade is weak and unprofitable. And Leia has insulted the Kahin-Shah on numerous occasions. But truthfully, it is mostly because Burak Aasjuqal is a conqueror. Ever since he took the imperial reins twelve years ago, he has cast a greedy eye north, seeking to claim the Pearl of the Four Realms."

But my thoughts had turned in another direction. "But the Kahin-Shah isn't our primary concern. He can't be. Don't tell me you've forgotten."

Jaxas stared at his hands for a long moment. "I haven't forgotten," he murmured. "Nor will I. But what can I do, Airene? What can any of us do against such a force? Against… a god, or whatever he is?"

His despair only served to strengthen my resolve. "Whatever is in our power. Famine must be stopped. No cost will be too great, no price higher than the one he'll extract."

"No cost too great." The Archon shook his head. "You say that now. But will you still believe it when the time comes for the sacrifice?"

Before I could respond, Jaxas rose. "I'm afraid I have many things to be about. But I'm sure I'll see you up and walking soon."

With his imminent departure, a nagging thought became urgent. "Jaxas, my family — do you know if anything has happened to them? Vusu threatened them before the trial. I think he might retaliate."

"You need not fear that. I sent them to one of the provincial Wreath estates as soon after the trial as I could. Your mother didn't go easily, but wine, good food, and care for your father convinced her in the end."

I couldn't help a bemused smile. "That sounds like my mother. Thank you. It's far more generous than I deserve."

Jaxas didn't return the smile. "I cannot pretend I did it only for your peace of mind. To have you compromised by threats against your family would be… untenable."

My smile slipped. I should have expected nothing less of a Wreath. "I understand. Whatever the reason, I'm glad they're safe."

The Archon nodded and turned away. "Come see me when you're up. Though once you talk with Nomusa, I'm sure you'll have even less occasion to than before."

I wondered at that. "I know we won't report to you anymore, Jaxas. But I hope we'll continue to work together."

"With so few eyes on the true enemy, we'd be fools not to."

Unsmiling, he turned and swept from the room.

A moment later, Xaron slipped back in. He wore a happy grin that, paired with his clothes, should have made me laugh. But my thoughts were so heavy that not even the sight of him as Hilarion could lift them.

"Oh, cheer up," he said as he sat on the bed next to me. "He's gone now. No need for the long face."

I tried for levity. "That's not what has me down. I was just thinking how sorry I am that you're a fool now."

His grin redoubled. "Fitting, isn't it? You'd never believe the freedom it affords me! I can channel nearly whenever I want, so long as I'm not making people nervous."

Knowing well how often he'd yearned for that liberation, I smiled. "Like a dream come true."

"But you," he continued, his brow furrowing. "What happened to you, Airene? Corin just kept saying that you should tell us yourself. Her story to Jaxas doesn't add up. What were you doing in Sandglass searching for Maesos?"

I hesitated. I wanted to tell Xaron the truth, but I wasn't sure he'd see Corin's betrayal the same way I had. Part of me wondered if it would be better to lie.

But no. We couldn't start keeping secrets from each other again. We'd already seen how well that played out when this whole hunt began.

So I told him. Of Corin's betrayal, and Eazal's attempted assassination, and my channeling — or my dream of it. Holding up my hands, I showed him how no shifts moved.

"Can I have imagined the whole thing?" I asked tentatively. "Am I that desperate to be a warden?"

Despite all I'd told him, he looked pleased. "I never knew you wished for it so badly. But no, I don't think you imagined it. Corin saw the flames coming from you, didn't she? And after what she did, I doubt she'd lie again. Besides, I saw your burns when she brought you back, and now look! They're healed, and it's only been three days." He shook his head. "I have no idea how you did that. Though you're not the first — that Acadian, Kallias the Sculptor, is said to heal as well. As for your shifts, back when I was living in the wardens' commune, a woman who went by Hel came by her attunement late in life, the same as you. It took her a long while to be able to channel on command, or even for her shifts to show up."

It was almost too much to hope for. Yet hope I did. "You believe me?" I asked tentatively.

"Of course! Did you think I wouldn't?"

I pulled him into an embrace. "Thank you," I murmured. "You don't know how much that means to me."

His lips curled into a smile as he pulled back. "Oh, I think I do."

A knock came at the door. I immediately stiffened and pulled away. *You're safe*, I chastised myself. *No one is coming for you.* But my heart continued to pound all the same.

Xaron cast a worried glance at me, yet he only called, "Who is it?"

"I brought food," Corin responded from without.

Xaron's expression blackened as the key turned in the lock. I put a hand on his arm. "Don't say anything," I warned him.

He gave me a mutinous look but remained quiet as Corin entered, a huge platter of food balanced in one hand. I stared in astonishment at the array of dishes. Fresh bread, both flat and in loaves; skewered and spiced goat, fish, and mutton; golden grapes, mangoes, and nectarines; and in the center, a generous bowl of soup.

"Who are we feeding, a taxos?" I said over the grumbling of my stomach.

Corin started to smile, but a glance at Xaron wiped it away. She set the platter on the waiting table near the wardrobe. "I can bring dishes to you," she offered quietly.

"No, I'll come over there." I pulled Xaron with me. His arm was tense beneath my grip, but I settled him in a chair next to me and gestured for Corin to do the same. "Eat with me. There's no way I can finish all of this."

She hesitated, then shook her head. Her eyes darted toward Xaron again. "No, thank you. But I'll return later."

"Not too soon," Xaron called snidely as she slipped out the door.

"Stop that," I chastised him half-heartedly as I dove into the meal.

Xaron spoke around a mouthful of bread. "Stop what?"

"Treating her like that."

He stared at me, his mouth falling open to reveal half-chewed food. "She could have gotten you killed, Airene. She lied to you and intentionally led you into a trap. How can you expect me to be civil?" He shook his head. "She can't stay in the room with you."

"What will you do? Throw her out?" I gave him a wry smile. "You're forgetting something, Xaron. She saved me after her betrayal. And she only betrayed me because the Valemish hold her sister captive."

"The Valemish *still* hold her sister captive. You can't trust her, Airene."

"But I do, Xaron. Even if it's broken somewhat, I still trust her. She was torn between two loyalties and slipped up. I don't think she'll do it again."

Until I'd spoken, I hadn't fully realized how I felt. But the words rang true.

He threw up his hands. "There's no reason to believe that! Besides, why take the risk? You can be friends from afar. Just don't let her stay near you."

"I know you're just trying to protect me. But I have to give her another chance. If others don't deserve second chances, why do I?"

His expression softened, and he squeezed my hand, though the gesture was spoiled by the grease filming his hand. I laughed and pulled my hand away to wipe it on a cloth.

"You did your best, Airene," he said seriously. "No one could have done anything more, considering what we're up against. Linos will be fine — you'll see."

I pretended to be absorbed in my meal so I wouldn't have to meet his eyes.

Xaron rose, looking longingly at the rest of our feast. "Much as I hate to, I should return to my duties."

I raised an eyebrow, hoping it hid my disappointment. "What? Taking a tumble for the Despoina?"

"Ha-ha. Actually…" It was his turn to hesitate. "It's not my Hilarion responsibilities exactly."

"You have my attention, if that's what you were after."

He ran a hand through his hair, untucking a tuft from his corn-husk crown. "No secrets," he mumbled. "I'm not even sure why I'm so awkward saying it. May as well get it over with. You remember that group of Acadians? The one Kyros had been training?"

My eyes narrowed. "Yes."

"Well. I've joined them."

I hesitated, sorting through the rush of feelings. "Do you think that's a good idea? You're sailing uncertain tides as it is."

"It's our only option, Airene. With Vusu having taken most of the Shepherds and commanding who knows how many other wardens, the only place to find reliable wardens is at the Acadium."

I shrugged, not finding an adequate response. Training to use his channeling to fight certainly wasn't what Hilarion was supposed to do, and I didn't like the idea of him violating the rules of his position. But he was right. In times like these, we couldn't let what was expected stop us from doing what was necessary.

"I wish I could join you." The words were out of my mouth before I considered them.

He raised an eyebrow. "You?"

I glanced sharply at him. "Why not? If I'm a warden—" I cut off abruptly, realizing how loud I'd been speaking. "If I'm a warden," I continued softer, "then I should use my gift to fight Vusu directly, not hide behind the rest of you."

Xaron looked stricken. "But Airene, you're early in your attunement. Your shifts aren't even appearing. This isn't something that can be rushed. You have no idea how dangerous it is. If you try to channel before you can control it—"

"I'll just have to manage." I waved wearily to the door. "I don't want to keep you from what you need to do."

He suddenly seemed reluctant to leave. "Airene, promise you won't bite off more than you can chew."

"Will you train me then?"

His swallow was visible. "I suppose," he muttered. "Though you should go to Eltris for that."

"Eltris?" I laughed low and bitter. "I doubt she would give me the time of day. Even if my shifts do show up, there's no way I'll be a ten-shift. What's the word for that again?"

"*Shur.*"

"You were a special case. From her manner, I don't think she often teaches."

He donned a small smile. "You're probably right about that."

I rose and pulled him up as well. "Thanks for visiting. But we both have things to do."

"The only thing you should be doing is resting," he said seriously. "Airene, I know the world is ending. But you should take it easy."

I rolled my eyes. "A compelling argument. Can you be in your quarters later this evening? I want to see what luxuries Hilarion is afforded."

"I'm probably the best-rewarded jester in the whole of the Four Realms." He pulled me into a tight embrace and spoke in my ear. "Please. Give yourself the time you need to recover."

"I will."

We both knew it was a lie.

As soon as Xaron left, I hastily finished my meal, putting away two more skewers, a loaf of bread, and two mangoes. Then, groaning from my distended belly, I pulled on my sandals, which someone had stored in the closet. I didn't have a mirror, though from the way everyone reacted to me, I doubted I wanted to see how I looked. My one concession to decorum was to run a hand through my tangled hair, hoping the greasiness wouldn't be too noticeable.

Though exhaustion assaulted me all the more with a full belly, I resolutely walked to the door. But before I could leave, I suddenly noticed something. A familiar weight was missing from around my neck. I touched my chest, even though I knew I wouldn't find it there.

My Verifier medallion was missing.

I thought furiously. Had my channeling somehow affected it? But the medallion hung on a chain — it would have taken a powerful fire to burn it off. The likelier option was someone had removed it. But who had done it, and where had they taken it? Without it, I wasn't sure that I could wander the Laurel Palace, or go anywhere else for that matter.

But I couldn't stay in my room. There was too much to do. Though my stomach protested, my legs wobbled, and my head felt stuffed full of wool, I yanked open the door. Everyone else seemed to have a key to my quarters, yet no one had thought to leave me one, so I left it unlocked. I didn't own anything of value anyway.

I looked to either side down the halls, striving to remain upright. At every moment, exhaustion assailed my weary body. Three days of sleep had never been so tiring. It took me far too long to recognize the hall as the same that I'd stayed in before, my current room two doors down from my former.

I started walking, then stumbled to a halt. Where was I heading? I knew I had duties. As one of the First Verifiers of a recently established order, the Conclave would no doubt expect things of me. But until I spoke with Nomusa, what my duties were wasn't clear.

But I knew I had an even more critical task. The greatest of our enemies was still largely undetected, and I knew far too little about him. I had to understand what Famine was to know how to fight him. And to fight Vusu as well.

Eltris was the obvious choice for such information. I doubted she would tell me any more than she wished, but it was a start. I nodded to myself and set off down the hallway again. To Eltris's tower then.

"First Verifier Airene?"

I spun, hand going to the small of my back where my knife used to be. The unbalanced turn almost sent me sprawling. As I righted myself, I saw a female honor watching me with evident sympathy.

I was disoriented by more than surprise. My first reaction had been to reach for my missing knife. When had violence leaped to the forefront of my instincts? But I shook away my alarm and tried on a smile. "Yes?"

The honor smiled uncertainly back. "I am sorry I surprised you, First Verifier."

"Not at all." My smile was swiftly transforming into a grimace. "Were you seeking something?"

She bowed quickly. She was younger than me, I saw then, and had pretty green eyes. "Yes, First Verifier Airene. First Verifier Nomusa has been sending me to see if you were awake."

"Has she?" I knew how busy she must be, but I couldn't help a stab of annoyance that she wasn't coming to check in on me herself.

The honor nodded. "Yes, mistress First Verifier, every two turns. If I found you up, I was to give you a message."

I crossed my arms. "I'd better hear it then."

"You are to meet her in the gardens. So long as you are able." From the honor's expression, she felt doubtful of that.

"I'll manage," I said drily. "She's there now?"

"Yes. Would you like me to accompany you?"

"No need. I'm sure you have other responsibilities to be about."

She bowed again and parted with another wary smile. I turned in the opposite direction and, like a soldier after a long march, began to make my way to the gardens.

CHAPTER TWO

THE ORDER OF VERIFIERS

It began with a hunger.

Tyurn Sky-Sea stared over his dominion. He loved his worlds — the Higher and Lower Realms of the Pyrthae as well as the material world of Telae. But that day, instead of feeling pride, he felt an emptier feeling.

The Lord of All longed for more.

He saw starvation. He saw the craven overcoming the brave, the petty disdaining the proud. Tyurn Sky-Sea looked and knew there must be more he could give.

'There can be,' a whisper sounded in his ear. 'If you but listen to me.'

The Ruler of All Realms knew himself impervious to charms and glamours, and thus he believed this voice came of himself. Intrigued, he asked it, 'What do you mean?'

'You wish for more than you have,' the whisper said. 'You crave it. Your dominion is flawed, and you wish to perfect it. Yet you, King of Many, do not know the way.'

'No, I do not,' said Tyurn Sky-Sea, troubled, for there was little he did not know.

'Am I not Lord of All?' he questioned the voice. Had the doubt come from anyone but himself, he would have thundered his denial.

'If you were Lord of All, how could you and your subjects ever lack for anything? But I, born of your desire, know how you may live up to that name, King of Many. It is simple, what you must do. Then all the lands will grow rich and bountiful.'

It rankled the pride of Tyurn Sky-Sea to be less than the master of everything. Thus, he said at once, 'And what is it I must do?'

Thus the Seed spoke to Tyurn Sky-Sea, and the Ruler of All Realms went forth and did as it said.

I walked the gardens for a long, painful time. Plodding along one winding path after another in the mile-long courtyard, sheltered under rows of columns on either side, I forced my leaden legs forward and managed to remain upright.

As I passed a willow tree, I suddenly stopped. My ear always keen for whispered words, the hushed conversation alerted me to someone on the other side of the tree, secreted within the foliage. I peered through the gently swaying branches. Two figures stood on the other side, their features hidden beyond the red and pale yellow of their robes. Quieting my breath, I stepped through the willow branches, trying to come near enough to make out their words.

But no sooner had I stepped under the tree than my foot found a branch and cracked it. The figure wearing pale yellow whirled around, and I recognized Nomusa even before she spoke. She was dressed as I hadn't often seen her, with her chiton plain and no jewelry adorning her neck or wrists. Her hair was in simple plaits against her head, though still executed with her usual tidiness. Humility seemed to be what she sought to present to the world, and she captured it perfectly.

Her surprise faded as she recognized me in turn, only to be replaced by an expression I couldn't read. "Airene!" she said too loudly to be natural. "You're awake! How are you feeling?"

I stepped through the sweeping leaves. The figure in red was already quickly walking away, a hood masking his or her face. Before I could say anything, Nomusa stepped up and embraced me. I returned it, curiosity biting deep.

As we pulled apart, I wore a smile. Considering everything else we had to discuss, Nomusa could keep her secret for the moment. "I'm fine now, though my belly is still trying to eat itself," I said truthfully.

She laughed heartily and pulled me into another hug. "I'm glad to see you up. We've all been so worried." She abruptly pulled me away again. "What happened? What Corin said made no sense."

I studied her. While I'd been asleep, Nomusa had undergone a metamorphosis. Instead of the reluctant, skeptical partner, she once again seemed alive and invested. It was like having her back from our early days of Finching, the friend I had long missed.

"I'll have to tell you later," I said. "I can't have anyone overhearing."

"If they do as poor a job spying on us as you did earlier, I think we'll be fine."

A wry grin worked its way onto my face. "I'm far from my best right now."

She looped her arm in mine. "I suppose your tale can wait. I have plenty to catch you up on."

She began walking us back through the gardens the way we'd come — the opposite of the direction the figure in red had taken, I noticed. But I said nothing of it, wondering if Nomusa would speak of the hooded stranger herself. And if she didn't, what that might mean.

"How about we sit while we talk?" I suggested.

"I would, but… Since you're up, you really should go before the Council. They've been asking for you every time I see them, and my usual meeting with them is in just over a turn."

I groaned. "I should have stayed in bed."

Nomusa looked me up and down and pursed her lips. "Yes, you should have."

"Come on. I'm not that bad off."

She snorted lightly and continued to pull me along. "I suppose I'll begin with what's most pertinent. It's official, Airene."

I looked sharply at her, guessing what she meant. "They actually went for it?"

"They did. The Council approved the mandate two days ago. The Order of Verifiers is once again an official branch of the Oedijan demotism."

I had thought I was over that particular victory, particularly as I knew it came with strings attached. But despite my apprehension, a glow of pride warmed my chest, and I had to hold back a grin.

"But though we're Verifiers now, you still have to be confirmed as my fellow First Verifier," Nomusa quickly followed up.

The warmth dissipated. "By the Council?" Half of the Low Consuls were Preservists under Orhan's thumb. Considering their close alignment with the Valemish and their ancestral home in Avvad, it seemed a safe bet that they were privy to Eazal's attempted assassination of me. Probably they were the orchestrators of it. I doubted any of them would support me gaining power. I'd need the full support of the other five Low Consuls to pass. If I could manage that, I at least could count on Jaxas casting the deciding vote in my favor.

"Did any of the Preservists confirm you?" I queried.

Nomusa's brow furrowed. "Actually, yes. All of them did."

I stared. "And you don't suspect this is a trap?"

"I know it is." She gave me a nervous smile. "I haven't told you of the agreement binding us."

"Best tear off the bandage."

She raised a finger. "First, we must make a full account of our activities and the coin we spend. We have a clerk to help with that portion, at least, to whom we'll report each day for the Aviary ledgers."

"The Aviary? It's ready to reside in then?"

"Of sorts." Nomusa grimaced. "It still reeks of finch droppings — they'd been using the whole place to keep birds, you know, not just the tower. And the furniture is minimal. Still, there are some comforts — we have a cook and an honor who comes by daily to tidy up."

I wondered if the honor would also take the time to rifle through our belongings and report anything of interest to the Council. "I can live in most conditions. After all, I've stayed one night with Talan. Not like that," I hastily amended.

Nomusa smiled coyly. "I'm sure it wasn't."

"You're hopeless." I abruptly switched the topic. "Do we have a collective allowance, or is it individual?"

"Both. Fifteen silvers a day for the whole Order, though we'll raise eyebrows if we individually spend more than five."

I felt even weaker in the knees than I had before. Fifteen silvers had been half our collective savings before the shell horns had blown. To be afforded that amount in a single day was staggering. "We could buy off Nikias every day," I marveled.

Nomusa's frown told me she hadn't forgotten my earlier contentious bribe. "We could. But once we bring on more Finches, it will be spent quickly."

"More Finches?" I was baffled. "But we can't initiate Xaron and Talan."

"I wouldn't want to hire those lazy sops anyway. But of course we'll gather more, Airene. With a war coming, and the Manifest stirring trouble, and corruption in our own government, we're going to need more than the two of us to keep tabs on it all."

"But who could we trust?"

She watched me carefully. "Things are going to be different, Airene. We'll likely have to give people responsibilities even if we don't fully trust them. You need to be ready for that, because that day is coming soon."

I turned my gaze away. After all the treachery we had recently undergone, I was far from sure I was ready. But all I said was, "Very well."

We exited the palace. With the monsoons soon arriving, the sky was thick with clouds, yet the muggy heat of summer still clung on. Given the state I was in, I dreaded the walk down to the Conclave and looked longingly at a carriage waiting on the marble road below the stairs. Instead of turning our path to avoid it, however, Nomusa pulled me toward it.

"What are you doing?" I hissed.

"Catching our ride down." She glanced at me, amusement glinting in her eyes. "Who did you suppose this carriage was waiting for?"

Without stopping for an answer, Nomusa greeted the driver familiarly and took his hand to step up into it. As the driver turned to me, I mutely accepted his aid as well and entered. It was a relief to sit again, especially on cushioned seats, though the cramped quarters were stuffy and hot.

"Do you regularly use a carriage now?" I asked Nomusa.

She smiled faintly. "Another of our privileges. Though our special treatment from the Laurel Palace may end if things continue the way they do."

"Tension between the Council and the Despoina?"

"Between the Council and the Archon. Jaxas has been vocal about confronting our foes now that we know who they are. He's drawn the ire of Orhan and his lackeys for it."

Anger stirred in my gut, more insistent than hunger for the moment. "Of course," I muttered furiously. "You'd think that having lived here as long as they have, they'd feel more loyalty."

"You never forget your homeland." Her eyes had a distant look, and I knew she was thinking of her own home ishaka a thousand miles away.

"What do they want us to do anyway? The Council, I mean."

Nomusa drew away from her contemplation. "Ah, now we're at the crux of it. We're to investigate corruption."

"Corruption?"

She nodded. "They — the Preservists and Verchlesa, as it is — are interested in understanding what led to the Despot being taken and the rise of the Manifest unimpeded, and who was behind it."

I stretched my cramped legs. "Ironic, isn't it?"

"Of course. But what better way to keep ahead of charges of corruption than pointing the finger at others?"

"Maybe they hope we'll go after Jaxas. Since he was affiliated with Vusu and all."

"Or maybe that we'll try and take down the Tribunal." Nomusa snorted. "As if we would be that much of fools."

Despair clawed at my chest. "Is nothing being done then?"

"Some things are. They can't completely ignore an oncoming army, so the Council has put out an order for the taxoi to be raised again. When Avvad marches, we'll have the semblance of an army... though if they'll fight for Avvad or Oedija remains to be seen. Particularly when we may not be able to feed them."

"Have the droughts become that bad?"

"They're only the beginning. The more immediate problem is bringing what little harvest there has been into the city. The Council is negotiating with the Underguild for passage, but Kalindi's demands have been unten-able, to say the least."

I winced. "The Council is negotiating with the Underguild for food now? That's more desperate than I'd hoped for."

Nomusa shook her head. "Since Kalindi overtook the Underguild, he has used far more aggressive tactics than we've yet seen from the syndicate. Crime has increased on the streets for many reasons, but most of the murders seem to be traced back to him. His most significant attempt at control has been to seize many of the shipments of grains and other foods before they pass through the city gates and hold them ransom."

The Underguild was extorting the demotism itself. I'd missed more in three days than I could have imagined possible. Yet still, I knew I hadn't heard the heart of what I needed to. "But what of the real danger? What are they doing about Famine?"

Nomusa pushed the curtain aside from the window to peer out. "Nothing," she said softly. "Nothing at all."

"They know, don't they? That Famine is real and rising again?"

She didn't meet my gaze. "Jaxas told them what you'd seen and implored that they remember what they saw at the trial, the Pyrthaen serpent swallowing Vusu and Linos and all. But the Low Consuls weren't convinced. They said it was an illusion, that it must be a simple conjuring for a warden of Vusu's strength."

I trembled, hot anger coursing through me. "But you corroborated him at least, right? You told them what I saw?"

Her hesitation spoke volumes. "The Order is still in its infancy—"

"You know he's real! I saw him! I went into the Pyrthae and saw him, Nomusa!" I noticed my voice was loud enough for the driver to hear, but I found it hard to care. Why should I hide the truth from anyone? They would all know far too soon.

"I know," Nomusa said hurriedly. "I know what you saw. But that doesn't change the fact that we need to seem credible as an organization right now. And no matter how true it is, claiming that a daemon god has risen from the legends is not a good way to establish our name."

I reined in my anger. It wasn't fair to put the blame on Nomusa. Even if she should have done more. "Then target Vusu," I suggested. "They saw what he is capable of. Surely that at least can stir them to action."

"You'd think. But he hasn't been seen since Asileia's trial, and you know what they say: When the pyr doesn't appear—"

"—It isn't here, I know," I finished the saying with irritation. "But he's had three days to recover now. If he can heal like Kallias the Sculptor, then he's already at work again."

Nomusa gave me an odd look. "I never took you for a believer in that sort of thing."

I flushed despite myself. "Vusu has the power of a daemon god behind him. I don't think regeneration is outside the realm of possibility."

She shrugged. "But maybe he won't recover. Maybe that quarrel you put in him will kill him. After all, even wardens aren't immune to corruption of the flesh."

"You don't know that," I pointed out heavily. Her words were tempting, and I wanted to believe them. But I felt the wrongness of them in my gut. Vusu still loomed large, and as long as he was a danger, Famine would be as well.

Standing before the god in the Pyrthae, I'd sensed far more than what my material senses could tell me. I'd felt the hunger that drove him, endless and ever-sharp, cutting at him every moment that he couldn't sate it. It was a craving far greater than what any addicted asher felt while waiting for his next hit of silvertongue. And his hunger wasn't for flesh. More I couldn't understand, but remembering that feeling of a predator casually studying me as prey struck icy fear through me anew.

The carriage rolled up before the Conclave. For a moment, it was all I could do to stare at the changes wrought over it. The broad dome of bronze and white marble was broken like an egg's shell, half of it torn away during our struggle with Vusu. Everywhere it had cracked and crumbled, time was catching up with the grand edifice, green and gray patina spreading out from the rents.

As Nomusa exited, I tore my eyes away and followed. As I lowered myself, my legs nearly collapsed under me. I bitterly wondered if my hunger was yet the depth of Famine's. A smile twisted onto my lips as I took Nomusa's offered arm, and we walked toward the tall double doors, now riddled with wide fractures.

It was only as the Conclave guards studied us that I realized I'd forgotten to mention something. "Nomusa," I muttered, "I don't have my Verifier medallion. Someone must have taken it while I slept."

"I took it," she responded briskly. "At the behest of the Council. Until you're confirmed, they didn't want you flashing it about."

"I never flashed it about," I protested, but was relieved nonetheless. If it was missing, best that there was a chance of getting it back. Even if it came at a cost.

The guards barely delayed us as they greeted Nomusa warmly. I kept my face carefully composed. It didn't surprise me that Nomusa had already made friends with the guards, particularly since one of the pair hadn't been hard on the eyes.

As the handsome guard cracked open the door, we slipped inside.

Amusement was replaced by silent awe. Much of the great chamber had been swept of debris, yet the signs of the fight were still written on the walls. A thick layer of dust began a dozen cubits up where it seemed the cleaners couldn't reach. All but the most massive blocks had been cleared away. Now that I thought about it, I was astounded that the Servants and Low Consuls were continuing to use the building at all. It didn't look stable with the many crevices in its pillars, walls, and floors, not to mention the cracked dome above.

Yet I followed Nomusa around the edge toward the Archon's platform. The giant bell that had been mounted there to call everyone to attention had split up the middle, and the offending rock, twice my size, lay nearby. Banishing silly thoughts of omens, I focused my attention on the small door behind the platform as we stopped ten paces short of it.

Nomusa paused. "You're sure you want to do this now?"

"We're already here," I said wearily. "And you said it was a shoo-in, didn't you?"

"We'll see," she answered, with less confidence than I'd hoped for.

Nomusa turned to the guards waiting on either side of the door. "I am First Verifier Nomusa. Will you admit me and my companion, Airene of Port, so that she may become First Verifier alongside me?"

A male honor appeared from the shadows of a nearby column. "They are in conference at the moment and requested that they remained undisturbed. If you will wait, they should be done within the turn."

Nomusa's nostrils flared, but she only turned on her heel and marched for the dais. I followed and gratefully sat next to her on the edge, resting my protesting legs and leaning back on my arms.

We waited in silence. Both of us knew the things we had to tell each other must be spoken in secret. Yet now that we paused, I felt the pressure of my news once more. I wriggled my fingers on the stone, wondering if my shifts had appeared yet, wondering if I'd be able to channel if I attempted it. But I didn't dare try. Though I hoped I would be able to control it, my memories of the first instance inspired little confidence.

My gaze wandered over to the Archon's bell again — but for a moment, my eyes saw not what was, but what had been. Asileia Wreath stood upon the dais, her chin uplifted. She scattered into mist as a hole ripped through the fabric of the world. Teeth, iridescently white, erupted from nowhere. And from between them stepped a shadow. The shadow paused, then turned its head toward me, revealing Vusu's face. *"After all this,"* he said slowly, *"and it is you who have doomed us."*

A touch on the arm startled me out of the reverie.

"Airene?" Nomusa asked, concern plain in her voice. "Are you alright?"

"Fine," I said faintly. I stared at where I'd seen the vision, but it had become only ruined stones again. I shook my head. No amount of sleep could cure madness, but I had to hope that was the only remedy I needed.

The Council's small door finally cracked open. "Is she here yet?" an irritable man's voice called out. *Berker*, I recognized with a twist of disgust; Orhan's righthand man, and as staunch a Preservist as they came.

The male honor hurried forth from the shadows. "Yes, Low Consul. First Verifier Nomusa has come, and she has brought the other you wished to see."

"That's putting it strongly," Berker growled. He revealed his pock-marked face as he opened the door further. "Well?" he barked. "Are you coming or not?"

"She has only just risen from her sickbed," Nomusa rebuked him as we rose and walked to the door. "Have some patience for once, Berker."

"Have care, Finch." The large man didn't move from the doorway. "You serve at our leisure."

"We serve the people and the demotism," Nomusa said smoothly. "Now, I'm sure your fellow members of the Council would appreciate if you didn't waste any more of their time with juvenile antics."

The man's heavy jowls became yet more pronounced as he scowled, but he relented, turning and stalking back inside. Sharing an amused look with me, Nomusa led the way in.

The Council's meeting chamber was much as I remembered it, and I couldn't detect any changes from the battle that had waged outside its doors. It still seemed more a cave than a room, with the unshaped walls and ceiling melding into each other, and small, uncovered windows opened toward the shore. The winds were strong off the sea today, as they tended to become in the spans before the monsoons arrived, and the scent of salt was heavy in the air.

In the middle of the room, seated around the glass-smooth slab of gray stone that served as a table, were the nine other Low Consuls. As before, the Preservists sat on one side, while the Equalists and the two independent Low Consuls sat opposite. I did my best not to look at Feiyan, but I couldn't help but notice her small smirk as she studied me. Jaxas, too, was present, though he stood by the windows apart from the rest.

"Airene of Port," Orhan greeted me warmly. As usual, he was immaculately groomed and decorated, his remaining gray hair finely curled, and he wore a robe of crimson lined with gold. "I am glad to see you up and walking. I heard you took frightfully ill after the events following the Despoina's trial." He didn't stand, nor did any of the others, but it was hardly surprising. As they were Low Consuls and I was presently little more than a plebeian in their eyes, decorum didn't call for it.

I, on the other hand, was obligated to bow. "Low Consuls. I apologize for my earlier absence. As you said, I had taken ill and have only just risen."

"You need not have rushed," Orhan said pleasantly.

I studied him, wondering how much he meant by that.

Zehaar of the Equalists took a turn next. "We have many matters to attend to, so I suggest we quickly resolve this quaint formality," she said briskly. "Airene was elected as First Verifier by Jaxas before her illness, and was, as we have discussed at length, behind the counterplot to Vusumuzi's plans. Her accomplishments speak for themselves."

Berker snorted, but it was Orhan who spoke. "Indeed, they do. Which is why I am quite skeptical of her appointment."

I looked sharply at the portly Avvadin man, but at a warning glance from Nomusa, held my tongue.

"After all," he continued, "she was, as you say, responsible for that whole bloody debacle. If not for her, Photina would still be alive, as would many Servants and other stewards of the demotism. Your First of the laurel guard, Jaxas, would also be alive. The rabble that wanders our streets every evening, these so-called 'dusk mobs,' would not terrorize our streets and markets. And if you failed to notice, we do not even know the location of our Despot, nor have we received any demands for ransom — if, indeed, he is alive. Only First Verifier Nomusa's report causes us to believe so, and she claims to know this secondhand by Airene's account."

Jaxas turned toward the Low Consuls and stood over them. The gray light behind him limned his robes and cast his face in shadow.

"It is dangerous to assume you know how things might have gone otherwise, Orhan," he said quietly. "Vusu is set on power. With or without Airene's intervention, it would have come to blood."

"You say one thing and contradict yourself in the same breath," Orhan noted with a smile.

Daelya, head of the Equalist faction, leaned forward, her dark brow drawn. "Enough. Speak plainly your position, Orhan, as well as the rest of you who seem to take issue. What's your complaint?"

Esen, the only woman among the Preservist Low Consuls, spoke now, wearing her usual severe expression. "We know too little of her, and what we do know is contentious."

"I can vouch for her," Jaxas offered. "It was enough for Nomusa's appointment."

"Except she had Feiyan's backing as well," Esen countered.

Despite my earlier resolution, I looked in amazement first at Nomusa, then Feiyan. The Qao Fu woman wore an even smugger expression than before, while Nomusa shifted with discomfort.

"I'm afraid I can't speak as well for Airene as I could for her companion," Feiyan said in a tone so full of sorrow a playwright would have applauded her performance. "She has been troublesome and tiresome in all my dealings with her. True, she has some talent for sniffing out trouble. But I cannot see her in a leadership position in the Order of Verifiers."

"Feiyan," Daelya said with undisguised exasperation, "I know you have some personal vendetta against the woman. But try to prevent it from coloring your professional opinion."

Feiyan looked so affronted I had to fight back a smile. At least one of the Low Consuls appeared to lean in my favor. Still, as I needed at least five to win the appointment, my odds were not looking good.

"Low Consuls," Nomusa spoke up. "If you need someone to attest to her competency, you need look no further. As I told you before, she and I have worked together for the last nine years. In all that time, never once has she been less than trustworthy and dependable, and has often been the primary investigator in our cases."

"If that's so, why are you presently the First?" Berker smirked through his scraggly beard.

Nomusa ignored him. "Airene is entirely capable of acting as First Verifier beside me. It would be a grave mistake not to appoint her so."

"This is taking far too long," Zehaar snapped. "It is past time we put this to a vote."

But Orhan leaned forward, wearing an expression that filled me with foreboding. "But what of what Vusumuzi said?" he asked softly. "He all but named you his accomplice, Airene. I would like to hear an adequate explanation if one can be provided."

I stared at him. I'd forgotten that brief interaction, forgotten even the words Vusu had said to me. Had they actually been incriminating, or just allusive enough to arouse suspicion? Forming a defense without knowing seemed all but impossible.

So I told the truth, or as much as I could. "He insinuated that we worked together because he believed it to be so. I allowed Vusu to think that he and I were accomplices in discrediting the Despoina so that we might ambush him."

"Vusu, she calls him," Berker sneers. "She implicates herself through her familiarity!"

I flushed, but before I could speak, Jaxas stepped forward. "Vote as you must. Just don't maintain this mummery any longer."

Orhan smiled, the mockery in it plain to see. "Very well, Jaxas. There's no need to be testy. If you wouldn't mind?"

Jaxas's eyes flickered to me for a second, then looked down. "All in favor of appointing Airene of Port to be First Verifier alongside Nomusa in the new Order of Verifiers?"

Daelya raised her hand, then Zehaar. Verchlesa and Tychon, to my relief, followed suit. But though I scanned the assembled members of the Demos Council, no more hands rose. Feiyan sat back with arms crossed, a small smile playing on her lips. Fury and frustration clashed so that my vision blurred and my head grew light. I reached out for the wall to steady my balance and set my jaw. I wouldn't collapse in front of that spiteful woman.

Jaxas's disappointment laced his words as he said, "All opposed?"

As expected, all five of the Preservists' hands shot up. I glared at Feiyan, expecting hers to rise as well. But still, she sat unmoving.

Jaxas's frown deepened. "Abstain?"

Feiyan shifted, but only to rest her hands on the table. "You know," she said slowly, her eyes still on me, "I'm still quite uncertain."

"Then abstain," Orhan advised pleasantly. "After all, that is what the option is for. And you seemed more than willing to practice it when you didn't attend the Despoina's trial."

Feiyan ignored the gibe but continued to look at me with a small smile. "But for such an important vote, I feel it is my duty to choose one way or the other. If only I knew the proper course."

My eyes challenged her, daring her to be so petty as to ruin me over our rocky past. She was more than capable of it, I knew well enough. Yet I couldn't pull my gaze away.

"Stop this at once!" Berker barked. "Which way will it be, Feiyan?"

She moistened her lips, raptor eyes still on me. "I vote in favor. Let us leave it to the Archon to decide."

Berker's face went red, while Orhan's smile slipped a bit. I didn't know how to react. Why had she suddenly acquiesced? I doubted she'd found a conscience. It was just as hard to believe she was not as petty as I'd thought. Which could only mean my appointment somehow played to her hand.

"I vote in favor," Jaxas said at once. "So it's decided. Congratulations, First Verifier Airene, on your new appointment."

Nomusa put an arm across my shoulders and pulled me close. I let my gaze drift from Feiyan to my fellow First Verifier and shared a smile with her. At Nomusa's whispered prompting, I murmured a thank you, then was ushered from the room. I only glimpsed Jaxas's broadening smile before Nomusa pulled me from the Council room and out into the main chamber of the Conclave.

"Airene!" She seized my hands as soon as the door closed, heedless of the honor and guards standing nearby. "You managed it!"

"Barely." My head felt woozy again, and my legs threatened to give way. "I thought you said it would be simple."

"I thought it would be. But you know Feiyan — she loves getting a rise out of you."

I shook my head. "That was more than enough excitement for one day. I need a large meal and a long nap."

"Very well, my fellow First Verifier. But there's something else you should accept first." She reached inside her neckline and drew out not one chain, but two, hidden beneath her dress. I was surprised at the eagerness with which I reached for the medallion hanging from her hand.

Grinning, Nomusa handed me one of the Verifier medallions. I immediately slipped it on. As it settled on my neck, the solid weight of the iron was reassuring. I didn't hide it under my robes, though. Even if it had first been given to me by Vusu, I would now wear it openly and proudly.

"That's better," she said approvingly as she led me out of the Conclave. "Now, time to enjoy the fine, new quarters our position affords."

VISITORS IN THE DARK

...But though Tyurn Sky-Sea sought to assuage his kin, Clepsammia, Goddess of Fate, stepped forward and announced in a quiet, carrying voice:

'Ruin will this Seed of Bounty bring. The fields, now abundant and green, will turn fallow and yellow. The rivers will dry into desert canyons. Your people will starve and curse your name, Father. Famine, this kin of daemons will bring, and famine will be the harvest you reap.'

But Tyurn Sky-Sea would not listen. Though his daughter had never spoken an untrue word, his hope for the Seed was too great, its whispers of power and plenty too intoxicating to deny...

- The Seeds of Famine, a translation from the Lighted-tongue; by Oracle Kalene of deme Hull; 881 SLP

I had missed the Aviary on the carriage ride. Now, as we crossed the Conclave grounds, our new home came into sharper focus. It was a misshapen thing, three stories high at its tallest point, that clung to the slippery stones along the top of the cliff like an ancient lizard. Its sloped roof was covered in dark green moss and the cracks in its walls were lined with black mold. It didn't promise the rest and retreat I'd hoped for.

Yet I caught glimpses of its former grandeur as well. Fluted columns adorned the front of the atrium, and its pediments had once been etched with great care, even if the carvings were now worn and obscured by moss and vines. From its right side rose the tower where, Nomusa informed me, some of the Conclave's many finches were kept, which were now at our disposal.

The neglected building was starting to grow on me by the time we reached it, all the more from my exhaustion. My energy waned with each passing moment; I felt I could sleep on a bed of stone. But Nomusa, full of enthusiasm, insisted that she give me the tour immediately.

"Here's the atrium, which doubles as a feast hall," she said as we entered. Two long tables that each seated ten were in similar condition as the rest of the building. Pointing to the back corner, Nomusa continued, "Off that hallway are the kitchens. Never fear, those have been thoroughly scrubbed out."

"What a relief."

"Through here," Nomusa said as she led us off to the right down a narrow hallway, "are the bedchambers. Ten on this floor, twelve on the second."

"Where are the stairs up?"

"Off the finch tower."

I shook my head. "That doesn't make sense."

"I didn't design it, did I? Come on — you still haven't seen the tower."

The tower was much as I'd expected: tall and filled with small birds of every color and pattern. The stench of droppings was so strong my eyes watered. No doubt the place hadn't seen much cleaning since its abandonment. I spotted nearly forty finches at a glance. Nets draped at regular intervals throughout the tower, allowing a swift hand to capture birds at any level from the stairs that wound around the edges.

"I've seen the tower. Now can I see my room?"

"Of course." Nomusa smirked and started up the stairs.

I didn't follow. "Why up there? I saw plenty of room down here."

"The ones further up have more air flow and less mold. So, unless you want to be breathing that stuff in all night..."

With a heavy sigh, I followed her up.

She spared me at least by turning into the first room. "This one will do, if you don't mind the smell of bird dung."

"Let's see how it is at the end of the hall."

"You'll be right across from me then. I can't wait to shout conversations across the hall."

"I can't wait to hear one of those Conclave guards who will no doubt visit," I muttered.

Nomusa only smiled coyly.

We turned into the last room on the left, and I finally saw the state of my new room. There was nothing in the way of furniture, only a rotted frame that seemed unlikely to support a mattress. It was hard to believe there was less mold up here than the chambers below, for it spread across every surface. The open windows, with no glass or shutters to keep out the coming cold of the monsoons, had only worsened the situation, bringing in the wet winds from the sea.

"I know where our first fifteen silvers are going to," I observed.

Nomusa laughed. "It's not so bad, really. I didn't know which one you'd want, so I was having Hyrol — he's the honor who comes by — clean the main areas. But we can have him attend to your room first." She gestured behind her. "I've got a bed and a relatively clean room if you want a nap. Just don't sleep there all night."

I wrapped her in a hug. "You have no idea how much this means to me."

"From the look of you, I think I do. Now go ahead. When you wake, you'll have food and a bed. And I hope you'll be in a more talkative mood. I won't wait for your secret forever."

Nodding, I swayed into Nomusa's room and collapsed onto her bed. Almost as soon as I closed my eyes, I fell into a heavy sleep.

———

My eyelids fluttered open. The dim light told of evening fast falling, yet my exhaustion had barely lessened. My hunger was sharp enough, however, that I rose and slowly descended to the atrium. To my relief, Nomusa had been true to her word, and the pleasant aromas of fresh food greeted me upon entering the room. Recently baked flatbread, ripe mango and soft cheese, a long, smoked fish — all waited on a covered platter on one of the long tables. I set to clearing the platter out in a manner that would have made Xaron proud.

I groaned as I thought of Xaron and my promise to find him this evening. The hunger dulled as I set into my third portion, but little energy came with its retreat. Even sitting up and eating was a chore. My Hilarion would have to wait for another night for me to visit.

Besides, if I could move about, I had more important tasks. If I were to retain my position, I had to show the Council I took being First Verifier seriously and make headway on their investigation of corruption, as much as that was possible. And even though Vusu hadn't been sighted, the Manifest remained a constant threat. Most of all, I needed to learn more about the true enemy lurking behind all the others. A visit to the Acadium seemed in order come morning.

When I couldn't manage another bite, I returned upstairs. In my haste to find food, I'd barely glanced at my room, and so hadn't noticed the scrubbed walls, ceiling, and floors, as well as the mattress and night table, complete with a pot of yellow pyrkin, that now decorated it. The mattress sagged in the middle and the blankets looked well used, but clean. I resolved to thank Hyrol at the first opportunity as I settled into it. Though I still needed to do something about the open windows. Even wrapped in the two blankets the honor had provided, a faint chill seeped through.

But though the sun had fallen and light faded from the sky, sleep eluded me. In its place whirled thoughts my exhaustion had kept at bay. Slowly, tentatively, I focused on my navel, on the spot where I'd felt the Pyrthae's power flow into me, and imagined it opening. First as a flower; then a fountain spilling forth; then a shaft of light through a window in a dusty room. Nothing worked. I remained as closed off to the Pyrthae as if I'd never become a warden.

If I even was one now.

For the first time since waking from my long slumber, I wondered how I'd have become attuned. I thought I'd channeled when Eazal attacked me. But it was said a god had to open you to the Pyrthae, and I was sure I would have remembered if one had come calling. Could this fluke have resulted from my journey into the Pyrthae, a parody of the theory I'd suggested to Jaxas? I didn't want to consider it, but the possibility suddenly seemed likely. No one traveled through the realm of spirits that I knew of — no one save Vusu and Eltris. But they were both wardens, and I—

I was not.

I breathed out heavily. That was all this had been: the rare effect of a strange experience. I wasn't a warden after all.

Something scuffled across the room. I sat bolt upright and stared at the dark corner. Likely it was a rat, or perhaps an escaped finch from the tower. But after what I'd done to Vusu, it was as likely knives in the dark sent to finish the job Eazal had started. Unarmed and exhausted, I stood little chance against them.

A patch of faintly glowing blue emerged from the darkness.

I guessed what I was at once. *A whisper finch.* The rare bird had perched on the foot of my bed. I stared mutely at it, my fading terror having driven all thoughts from mind.

"They will come for him," it said, the familiar, boyish voice strangely contrasting the avian body. "You must warn him before they do. They fear the knowledge he'll bring to Oedija."

Cold struck through me. "Who?" I asked urgently. "Who comes for whom? Why do you speak in riddles? If you mean to help me, speak plainly."

"I cannot," the whisper finch murmured. "They hear all that passes through these tongues."

"Who hears?" I demanded. "Vusu? Famine? How can you help if I don't know what you mean?"

The bird fluttered into the air to land on the nightstand, its small body limned in the faint light of the pyrkin pot. With an incline of its head, it seemed to beckon me closer. Apprehensive, I set my ear next to it. The whisper was so soft I could barely detect it.

"They will come for him the night he arrives."

The whisper finch suddenly moved, and I jerked back. But rather than lunging forward, it had toppled backward from the night table and hit the floor with a soft thud.

I stared at it for a long moment, unmoving, as the blue patch of light slowly began to fade. As the shock of the moment faded, I slowly brought my will to bear and reached out toward it. A finger brushed the soft feathers that made up the blue spot on its breast. It didn't move, and I felt no stirring of life.

Slowly, I withdrew my hand. Questions rose in my mind, driving away all hope for sleep. Why had it died? At the very least, it confirmed a suspicion I'd long held: that this bird was a messenger for someone else, not the speaker itself. But who was behind it? I'd had too much assistance from the boy who spoke through the birds to believe he meant me ill, even if his counsel had always been shrouded in enigma. But what form did my helper take? A patrician boy with far too much knowledge? A pyr? A god?

I sighed and leaned my head back against the wall. Of his message, I could divine little more. *They will come for him the night he arrives.* It was too little information to know whom he meant. "They" could refer to the Manifest, Avvad, or the Underguild, or perhaps another unknown party altogether. But who would they come for? The Underguild might go after Talan. Or perhaps it meant Shepherds hunting Xaron. But those were both more important to me than they would be to some random boy. More likely it meant someone more public — Myron perhaps, or Jaxas. There were too many players for me to know for certain.

They fear the knowledge he brings to Oedija. What knowledge could be feared? And who feared it? Who could bring such knowledge? At the very least, they sounded like someone not of Oedija. Was it someone coming from Avvad? Or perhaps an immigrant from the Bali or Qao Fu?

Some of his words at least seemed clear. The last "they" it had spoken of, the one who heard what came from whisper finch tongues — it had to be Vusu and Famine; such power must be beyond anyone else. I pulled the worn blankets tighter about me. How much could the daemon god and his follower hear? Just what whisper finches spoke? Or far more?

So deep was I in my thoughts that I only noticed the scraping outside my window a moment before a figure peered in. I shouted and grabbed the pot of pyrkin from my night table, holding it aloft. The intruder's face was shadowed in the fading light, but I recognized the chuckle as he folded the rest of the way in.

"You ought to shutter your windows. Vagrants could climb in at all turns of the night." The man glanced around the room, then down, quickly finding the fading glow of the dead whisper finch. "Or invaluable birds can die."

"Talan." I set down the pot and rose from the bed to wrap him in an embrace.

Talan pulled me close and rested his chin on my head. He smelled of smoke and sour wine, but also the earthy smell that was solely his own. "Hello, little Finch," he murmured in my hair. "You might wish to bathe."

I pushed him away, unable to keep my scandalized expression completely hidden. It only provoked another laugh.

I couldn't help smiling back. "Speak for yourself. Where have you been?"

"Busy," he said with his usual half-smirk. "I'm sorry I couldn't visit you more often, but Kalindi is tightening his grip. His spies are everywhere around the Conclave and palace. I had to—" He cut off abruptly. "But never mind that. How are you? Are you feeling better? And what of this dead whisper finch at my feet?"

"I'm alive — it's about all I can ask for. As for the bird, I'll tell you in a bit. If you wouldn't mind us sitting…"

He immediately settled me onto the bed and sat next to me. We leaned against the wall and, at my insistence, he pulled the blankets over both of us. I was distinctly aware of his warmth nestled against me.

"I have something to tell you."

He cast a quizzical look at me. "I think you have a great many things to tell me. Like why Corin has been allowed to remain by your side after she betrayed you."

My stomach sank. "How'd you figure that out?"

"It wasn't difficult to reason. She summoned you in a rush, lured you from the palace to an undisclosed location on an excuse that proved to be false, where you were almost murdered."

His eyes flashed with such anger I had to stop myself from flinching.

"She betrayed me," I admitted. "But she had very good reason to."

"What? Her sister being held by the Valemish?"

I shook my head. "It's unsettling how much you know."

"It's my job to know, and your job to act on that knowledge. So. What will you do about her?"

"I don't know. But that's not what I wanted to tell you."

His eyebrows shot up. "No? You have my attention now."

"There's one thing you can't have already guessed." I drew in a deep breath and let it out slowly. "When Eazal attacked me, I… channeled."

He stiffened. "Is this a jape?" he asked quietly.

"I'm serious, Talan. I channeled. I felt myself open, then fire and pure force came out from my feet and hands—"

"You weren't touched by one of the Buyujinn," he interrupted. "You weren't a warden before. How can you be now?"

"I don't know!" I was starting to grow annoyed. "But I know what I experienced. Do you believe me?"

For a moment, he looked away and said nothing. Nearly a minute passed before he sighed. "Yes. I believe you. Though I don't understand."

Considering all we'd encountered, I marveled that this was what baffled him. "I'm not the first to have become a warden late in life."

"No," he agreed. "There are two of us in this room that have had that pleasure."

I'd almost forgotten his own origins as a warden. He'd been able to channel all the three years I'd known him, so I'd never thought of Talan as anything other than a warden. "A Buyujinn, isn't that what you called her? The one who opened you to the Pyrthae?"

He nodded. "She was one of the many faces of the Lost Mother. I distinctly remember what it was like when she opened me." He looked askance at me. "Did you feel a presence when you channeled? Did anyone speak to you?"

"No one but the apothecary."

Talan was silent again. "Perhaps there are more ways of becoming a warden than I knew."

I didn't want to say my next words, but I was tired of doubting. "What if it was a fluke from visiting the Pyrthae?"

He slowly met my eyes, but I turned my gaze aside. I didn't want him to see the depth of my longing.

"I don't know," he said at length. "It's possible. I know much, but of the plane of pyr and gods, I'm as ignorant as a child."

It had been too much to hope that he'd know more. "What of Pyrthaen-blessed birds?"

He cocked his head. "I suppose you're referring to the dead whisper finch on your floor."

"It passed me a message, one I can't understand. Someone is coming for a man the night that he arrives in Oedija, someone who fears some knowledge the man has. And I'm supposed to warn him."

Talan studied me for a moment. His eyes were hooded from the way the thin light hit his face. When he spoke, his tone was measured, but I could feel something pressing behind the words. "You don't know who sent the bird?"

I hesitated. "It was a boy's voice, as it has been before."

"Before?"

I told him of the two occasions the whisper finch had visited me in my room in the Laurel Palace, and how they had seemed more like conversations than messages, though that wasn't supposed to be possible through whisper finches.

"I don't know who the boy is," I confessed. "But he's been helpful."

"Riddles aren't of much help," Talan noted drily. "And that seems to be all he gives you. Airene, this is a dangerous game to play — as a gambler, I'd know. Whisper finches deliver messages from other people. They repeat what they've been told. They can't carry on conversations. That someone knows where to find you is bad enough. But if they can waste whisper finches on a whim, killing them after their message… They must possess a fortune." His hooded eyes found mine. "If you dwell on this boy's message, you're playing his game. And I should think you've had enough of playing others' games."

That stung. Guilt and humiliation flooded me as I remembered how thoroughly Vusu had duped me. I turned my head aside. "You're right. It's foolish to put stock into the words of a bird, even a whisper finch. I'll forget what it said."

He placed a hand on my arm. Despite the roughness of his words, his touch was warm and comforting. "I'm sorry," he murmured. "I didn't mean to hurt you."

"Don't. You don't need to apologize for being right."

I glanced back at him. Though he wore his usual half-smile, behind the teasing mockery, something more bubbled to the surface. Heat spread through my chest in anticipation. I turned toward him, my own hand reaching out and touching his side. I found myself almost trembling as I tilted my head up toward his.

Abruptly, he pulled the covers off his legs and rose. The chill of the room siphoned away the warmth in an instant.

"I have much to do tonight still," he said, not meeting my eyes. "What I did to enter here will soon be discovered."

"Fine. I know you're busy."

He seemed not to notice my change in tone, but turned to the window. As he mounted a foot to the sill, he paused. "Don't try channeling, Airene. It can be dangerous if you don't know what you're doing."

"You didn't have a tutor when you learned," I said icily.

"I was lucky. I don't want your safety to rely on luck."

"None of us are safe, lucky or not."

We stared at each other through the gloom.

"I'm only abiding by the rules you set for us," he muttered. "I didn't stop because… Well. You know how I feel for you."

His words shook me from my annoyance. All I could think to say was, "Oh."

He turned away. "I'll return as often as I can."

I gathered my wits again. For the moment, it seemed best to pretend nothing had happened. "Where are you staying?"

"I can't say. Don't visit my old hiding holes though — they're all compromised now that Kalindi is in power. I'll find you."

Without another word, he disappeared through the window.

I listened to him scramble down and watched the empty space he'd left behind. When all had gone silent outside again but for the steady ebb of the waves against the cliffs below, I settled down with a sigh. Feelings tangled in my stomach so that I was almost relieved he was gone, but for the loneliness that crept in.

I expected the night's encounters to keep me awake. But soon, my thoughts slowed their spiral and dragged me down into another dreamless slumber.

CHAPTER FOUR

THE ACADIUM

For eleven seasons, the lands of Telae saw bounty like had never been known before. The harvests were abundant; the wells and springs were full of clean water; the plagues and wars that had pestered the lands retreated into memory. All was well, and the people thanked the Lord of All for it, praying that it would continue for another eleven seasons to come.

Tyurn Sky-Sea looked down upon his people and listened to their praise and was satisfied. Here he had wrought something truly worthy of his name.

In the turning of the seasons, the Seed had taken root in his ear and sprouted a single tendril trailing down his back like a snake from the trunk of a tree. Again, it implored, 'More. You want more.'

And Tyurn Sky-Sea, Ruler of All Realms, found that he did.

- The Seeds of Famine, a translation from the Lighted-tongue; by Oracle Kalene of deme Hull; 881 SLP

When I awoke the next morning, I felt almost myself again. Though it was an overcast day, an omen for the coming storms, my mood remained buoyant. Finally, I could move without feeling as if my bones were made of iron and my stomach an empty pit I couldn't fill.

I'd neglected to take off my chiton the night before, but lacking any other clothes, I smoothed it out as best I could. With any luck, I'd be able to send Hyrol over to the Laurel Palace and retrieve the clothes that had been stored there, though I wasn't sure they were mine to claim. Perhaps he could find me some trousers and tunics as well. It felt strange going so long without them underneath my robes.

Going downstairs to the atrium, I found a surprise waiting for me. Corin stood as I entered. Despite myself, I couldn't help uneasiness rising in me. Talan's words stirred in my mind, as did Xaron's reprimand. Ignoring them, I approached my old loftmate.

"Sorry I didn't tell you where I was yesterday," I began. "Everything's been a blur."

The large woman shook her head. "I knew where you'd go."

"Where are you sleeping now? Did they keep you up at the Laurel Palace last night?"

Another shake of her head. "Here," she said simply.

I wondered what Nomusa thought about that. "We'll get you a proper room tonight. As soon as I find Hyrol, that is." I glanced around the room. "Has anything come for breakfast?"

"No."

I sighed and went back into the kitchens. As Nomusa had said, they'd been scrubbed and looked well-kept. Our cook, Sizani, was a Bali woman from a different ishaka than Nomusa. She reminded me of Zipho with her brisk, business-like manner, though she had a warmer smile than the cafe owner. We chatted about small things as she served hot flatbread with some fruit and cheese from the dark pantry. Corin and I ate in silence in the kitchens while she worked, then left.

"What will you be doing today?" I asked Corin as we exited the Aviary. There was a spring in my step. It felt good to have strength in my legs again.

Corin shrugged, not looking at me. "I don't know."

Suddenly, I remembered her mission. "Gods, Corin. I can't believe I haven't asked. Have you heard anything more about your sister?"

Misery softened her stony countenance. "No."

"We'll find where she is. Then we'll get her back." Baseless promises, but I couldn't help uttering them. I doubted I'd have time to find her sister. I hadn't even visited Linos yet. Though that, at least, would be amended soon.

When Corin didn't answer, I continued. "I'm going to the Acadium today. You're welcome to join me, but I understand if you have other things to do."

"I'll come with," she said at once. "It's not safe to wander alone."

I frowned. "Is it so bad out there?"

Her dark look told me all I needed to know.

As we approached the Conclave gates, a noise like stormy waves crashing against cliffs rose louder and louder. We left another of the many groves spread throughout the Conclave grounds, and it suddenly washed over us, stunning me for a moment. A mass of humanity crowded against the walls and gates, shouting and protesting and screaming. Dirty faces, ragged clothes, haunted expressions — to a one, they looked every bit as much the rabble that Orhan claimed they were. Yet I knew what drove them. Fear and hunger, the blights of civilization, had seized hold of Oedija.

I turned my gaze aside and tried pushing down the guilt. Here I was, pampered with good food whenever I requested it and kept apart from the terrors that befell the rest of the city. Yet I was just another of the common people who'd had a stroke of good luck. Why did I deserve to eat when they couldn't?

Corin drew me away. "There's another exit," she said as we left the main gates behind. "They don't know of it yet."

The sounds of protest dimmed behind us, and I felt my guilt ebb. I didn't try to cling to it. Guilt, I'd discovered before, would ill serve anyone. All I could do was my part.

The side gate was guarded by two Conclave soldiers from the inside and was as devoid of protestors as Corin had promised.

"You sure you two want to go out there?" one of them asked at our request to leave, a grizzled veteran with a scar running along his forehead.

"Yes, we're sure," I replied.

"Have a care then. Women like yourselves are easy prey for those dusk mobs."

I ignored the unintended slight, focusing on the unfamiliar term, which I'd heard Orhan use earlier. "Dusk mobs?"

The man stared at me with even more concern. "You don't even know of them? 'Thae above, woman, where have you been? Yes, the dusk mobs — with all those dirty plebs mopping up any bystander unfortunate enough to be in their way. The ones that have been breaking into shops, tearing down stands, terrorizing any markets still foolish enough to open. The mobs have all but put a standstill to honest work in Oedija."

"Is it so bad?"

The guard's companion snorted. "Let's just say it's not good. You at least have some protection on you?"

I was starting to regret not hunting out a kitchen knife in Sizani's kitchen. But Corin nodded. "Plenty," she asserted.

The two men looked up at her, both of them shorter than the big outlander woman.

"Maybe they'll be alright," the veteran muttered. "Well, on with you then." His eye finally caught my medallion, which had been partially obscured in the folds of my chiton, and they widened slightly. "Ah, my apologies, Verifier. I had only seen your superior coming and going here."

"First Verifier," I corrected him. A warmth of pride flushed my chest at the sudden respect. "First Verifier Nomusa is my accomplice, not my superior. Now, if you'll open the gates…"

Any superiority I felt quickly vanished out on the streets. With the guards' warnings heavy on my mind, Corin and I walked quickly along the cobblestones toward the Acadium. It wasn't terribly far from the Conclave, but with tension pounding in my temples and hungry eyes watching us from the shadows, the journey seemed much longer.

"Should we keep to the main roads or back alleys?" I looked up and down the promenade. Few folk walked it at the moment. I didn't want to find out why.

Corin shrugged. I might have thought her unconcerned but for the occasional glance she cast around us. "I haven't been out much."

I chewed my lip. "Let's take the backways. I don't trust being seen out in the open when the road's empty."

I didn't know this part of Oedija well, but by glimpsing the high points of the Pillars between buildings, we progressed slowly toward the Acadium. But when twice we were forced to turn around in dead-end alleys, frustration and fear began to mount. Though we passed many people crouched in the alleys who watched us, and more than a few begged for money, we hadn't come across any who seemed to mean us harm.

As we ran into a third dead end, I cursed under my breath and began to turn around. But a voice came from behind us. "That's far enough, hanims. We'll be having whatever's on you now."

Heart in my throat, I whirled to see five young men stalking toward us. They were ragged and dirty and had a sharper hunger in their eyes than those we'd passed in the alleys. In their hands were makeshift weapons: knives of varying shapes, a club with long nails sticking out haphazardly, a mop handle with a knife bound to the end of it. Yet poorly armed as they were, they severely outnumbered us.

Fury fueled by fear flared up in me. If only I knew how to channel, if only I was a warden, these men wouldn't pose a problem. As it was, there was only one solution.

I unthreaded my coin purse slowly. The five silvers inside clinked softly together, even padded with cloth as they were. Each clink shot rage through me. Here I was once again, helpless. I'd stood down the most powerful warden of our age. Yet soon after, I'd been nearly killed by a middle-aged apothecary, and now I was being robbed by five common youths. Only then did I realize it wasn't me who had stood up to Vusu. It was my allies surrounding me that had been my strength. Without them, I was nothing.

"Don't take all day," the one with the club snapped, his bloodshot eyes bulging. As I saw his white fingertips, fear shot through me. This one was an asher, one who indulged in silvertongue, a drug smuggled up from Avvad. When ingested, the stimulant often made its user manic and unpredictable.

I quickly tossed my purse to the youth who had spoken first, who adeptly caught it. He looked like he'd have been handsome in other circumstances and possessed a calm authority. Hopefully he would keep the asher in line. Corin followed a moment later with her own purse, not bothering to hide her scowl.

The boy peered inside mine, and a delighted grin spread across his face. "What a find! Thank you, hanims." He gave a mocking bow. "Now we'll take our leave. But what's that hanging from your neck?"

My hand went protectively to the Verifier medallion. "You don't want this."

"No? But I think I'll be the judge of that." The youth sauntered over and, despite my attempt to dodge, he hooked the chain with a finger and drew me closer. Against my better judgement, I held on for a moment longer. But I was still too weak to resist as he wrenched it from my grasp and yanked it off my neck.

I seethed with fury as he studied it, a thoughtful expression on his dirty features. "Iron, or I don't know my weights," he said with evident disappointment. "And a crude carving. What's it for?"

"Something you'll be hunted for having," I said, threat creeping into my voice.

The youth tossed it back to me suddenly, and I only just managed to snag the chain before it could hit the dust. "It looks too similar to the Tribunal circle for my liking," he dismissed it. "You a Tribune?"

"No." He deserved no more explanation, and I gave him none.

The amusement had faded from the boy's expression. Behind him, the asher glared at us, the muscles of his face spasming. A rabid dog barely restrained, that one. Fear dampened my outrage.

"Hide it next time," the boy advised. "That way no one will be tempted. And I would cool your anger, hanim. With some other thief, it might get you killed."

Without another word, he turned and walked away. The asher watched us from over his shoulder, but he and the others followed their leader away. I kept my expression stony until they disappeared around the corner.

When they were gone, I let out a breath. I could always find more coin.

And having frequented the streets of Oedija my whole life, it wasn't my first mugging. That we'd survived without harm should have been a relief. But it was a poor salve for the helplessness burning inside me.

I started up the alley. "Best not wait for that asher to return. It's time we were inside the Acadium's walls."

A moment later, I noticed Corin hadn't followed. Turning back, I found her rooted in the same spot. "Corin? You coming?"

"Every time." Her voice was tight and strained as a taut rope. "Every time I save coins, they are stolen from me."

Guilt welled up in me. I knew what she was saving her coins for. And I'd been responsible for the first time she'd lost all her savings as well. "I'll find a way to help you, Corin. I swear it."

She cast me a bitter look, then came down the alley and slid past me. Repressing a sigh, I followed.

We kept a warier eye out now. Having no coin to steal put us in a more dangerous position than before, not less. After all, anyone who went to the trouble of robbing us wouldn't be pleased to come away with nothing but an iron medallion. And there were men with thirsts for uglier things than silver. Pushing the thought from my mind, I kept a watch out for the Pillars and pressed on.

Finally, we emerged from an alley to see the walls of the Acadium rising before us. I hurried toward the compound, Corin on my heels. Pulling the medallion out from the folds of my chiton, I let it fall between my breasts as we approached the guards.

But even as their eyes skirted over the medallion, they didn't immediately let us in. "One of the new Verifiers, are you?" one of the guards asked, a woman with braided hair the color of autumn blushing vines. With hair that red, she had to be an outlander like Corin. "Wondered when you lot would come by."

"To come steal Acadium secrets," her companion muttered, a gaunt-faced man.

Though it struck me as strange, I thought it best not to ask. "Your secrets are safe, never fear. But if you would admit us, we're in a bit of a hurry."

"Would love to," the woman said sarcastically. "But I should warn you: I can't guarantee you coming out."

At my narrowed eyes, the man rolled his eyes. "She means the mobs. They come by the gates every few turns to yell about daemons and such."

The woman snorted. "Like these Acadians would hurt anyone. They're sheep for our Shepherds, just the way it should be."

"Thanks for the warning." I couldn't completely hide my exasperation. "Now, the gate..."

As they cranked it open and we started up the hill within, I mulled over their words. I'd heard all of these attitudes about wardens before, but it took on a different feel now. After all, *I* might be a warden. All those ridiculous beliefs could apply to me as well.

"So that's what people think of wardens?" I whispered to Corin. "That they're daemons or sheep?"

She shrugged. "Many believe my people savages. That we do not know which end of a spoon to use. People believe honors to be little more than livestock, not really people. This is not so different."

I opened my mouth, then closed it. Put like that, it was hard to complain, even if it still didn't sit well.

Ascending the initial rise into the Acadium's campus, we navigated our way through its varied buildings. I considered altering our course to seek out Linos, but quickly dismissed the thought. Much as I wished to see my brother, this errand was more pressing. There would be time enough later for him once this was all over. Besides, as much as I might wish otherwise, there was nothing I could do to help him.

Moving along the cobbled road that cut through the center of the Acadium, I made my way toward the place where an old, decrepit tower squatted. As Eltris's home came into view, it once again struck me as the ugly cousin among a homely family. In front of its dingy door, an Acadian apprentice waited, identifiable by his plain brown robes.

"Greetings," he said in a bored voice. "Do you seek Eltris as well?"

I cocked an eyebrow. "We're not the first?"

"Hardly. The Master Augur is very popular lately. But you won't want to wait around. She hasn't graced her tower in three days." The pupil, little older than Linos, sighed and leaned against the mossy tower. "And guess who's left with lookout duty?"

I frowned. I didn't know where else I'd find the augur. As usual, Eltris thought of no one but herself.

Muttering a farewell, I led Corin back down the alley to the main thoroughfare that ran through the Acadium. Reaching the cobblestones, I hesitated for a moment and looked to my right, where a black tower rose from the far end of the campus. Setting my jaw, I headed toward it.

Corin fell in beside me. "Where do we go?"

"To find someone who might know where Eltris is."

As she fell silent again, I studied our destination. The tower wasn't as tall as the Pillar that rose just before it, but it soared far above the rest of the city. Made of seamless black stone, its construction reminded me of the Conclave. Another of the magic-forged buildings from our ancestors, perhaps, or from the people they'd conquered a thousand years ago. As was tradition, the Archmaster of the Acadium had claimed it as his own.

As we neared the tower, more Acadians appeared around us. They wore robes of the cheapest dyes, dark blues and cloud grays and clay browns. Acadians had always shown a sense of frugality, though whether it was forced on them or if they adopted it themselves, I didn't know. Despite the meanness of their clothes, the streets smelled cleaner than elsewhere in Oedija, and the passersby wore kindlier expressions. Considering our earlier encounter, friendliness was a welcome change.

Yet a sense of unease crept up on me. My palms grew clammy and my mouth dry. It took me a moment to understand why. If I were a warden, would the Acadians around me be able to tell? Eltris had seemed to know who could channel, as did Vusu. Kyros was said to be able to detect traces of channeling. What if other wardens possessed similar abilities? Innocuous glances suddenly seemed suspicious. I avoided their eyes, finally understanding the hunted feeling Xaron and Talan always carried with them.

It only intensified as we reached the base of Kyros's tower. Two Acadians and two guards stood by the tower door. One of the guards, a woman of middling years, stared at us as we approached.

"Name and business?" she barked.

"Airene — First Verifier Airene," I corrected myself. "Here to speak with Archmaster Kyros."

"Verifier, you say?" one of the Acadians spoke. He wore a more genial expression than the guard. "How intriguing! But the Order of Verifiers has not existed for over a century."

"Actually, Master Nikanor, it was just re-established a few days ago," the second guard said, a young man who wore an obliging smile. "We were warned you might show up, First Verifier."

His words sent a thrill of alarm through me, but I kept my voice calm. "You make it sound quite ominous."

The guard's grin widened. "That depends. Do 'digging up old bones' and 'stirring up a pot of trouble' sound ominous to you?"

I bowed mockingly. "It seems my reputation proceeds me."

"Fortunately for you, the Archmaster didn't prohibit your entrance. We can escort you up if you're willing."

The second Acadian, who had been watching the exchange with an irritated expression, suddenly outburst, "They get to go right in? But I've been waiting here for ages!"

"And you'll continue to wait!" the female guard snapped. "As for you, Verifier, I won't hold this door forever. Best get yourself inside."

I glanced at Corin. "My companion ought to come as well."

The woman's face took on an alarming shade of red. "Don't have orders for that, do we? Just you inside, no one else!"

The young man shook his head and hauled the door open to the tower. "I apologize, First Verifier. This way, if you please."

"You don't have to wait for me," I told Corin.

The former cartwoman shook her head. "I'll wait."

I gave her a grateful smile before following the young guard in. A dark, squat atrium waited beyond, lit by faintly glowing pyr lamps whose cultures seemed about to die out. The guard led me to a staircase that spiraled up the middle of the room.

"The Archmaster waits in his quarters at the top. Unfortunately, I cannot guarantee he'll grant you an audience until we knock. His health has been erratic." There was apology in the guard's voice.

It was a good thing I hadn't tried to come here yesterday as I'd intended. From the height of the tower, I doubted I'd have managed it. I was skeptical of even doing so today. "Nothing for it, I suppose."

And so we climbed. After the eighth circle, my feet were dragging. After the fourteenth, my legs were leaden. When we reached the twentieth, I finally begged for a break and sat panting on the landing just by the stairs. The guard looked away politely, but I detected a small smile on his lips.

The one recompense for my labors was a series of fascinating sights. One level hosted an apothecary's laboratory, every surface glowing in iridescent hues. Another was full of nothing but mirrors of every shape and size, some so large they stretched to the ceiling. The floor where I rested was on one of the more ordinary floors, with little more than a kitchenette that looked cold and disused, and wood piled in the corner.

"The Archmaster's chambers are two circles further." The guard spoke in a soft tone now, as if afraid of being overheard. "Whenever you are rested, we can proceed."

Twenty-two circles in total. Our ancestors had always had a fondness for multiples of eleven. The derelict tower where our abandoned Canopy was located had risen eleven itself.

"I'm ready," I said, not eager to be thought weak by the handsome young man.

Rising on jittery legs, we ascended the last few stairs. The final flight rose to a door, the room beyond walled off. An honor waited for us, a woman a decade older than myself by the faint lines on her face.

"First Verifier Airene comes to beg an audience of the Archmaster," the guard told the honor. "Is he taking visitors?"

The honor shook her head. "I regret to say the Archmaster is still taking his rest. He sustained many wounds and needs time to recover."

My stomach sank. All this way for nothing. But no sooner had disappointment set in than a voice boomed from within, "Admit her!"

The honor looked embarrassed. "Pardon me, First Verifier. It seems I was mistaken. Please, come in."

Skeptical but relieved, I left my escort in the stairwell and entered. Kyros's quarters were not as lavish as I had expected, though they were by no means austere. Books were messily arranged on bookshelves lining the walls, alternating with ancient-looking tapestries. Thick carpets layered the floor. A few oddities were present as well. The room was lit by levitating pyr lamps, the same as I'd seen at Asileia's Ascension, that were somehow maintained through magnesis. And along one wall, a series of items were encased in glass that didn't seem to warrant such a display, like a glass orb that contained nothing within it, and a dagger of white wood that looked fit for little more than play between children.

The Archmaster himself lay prone on a four-poster bed in the middle of the room, tucked under a sea of thick comforters. The room was cold enough that my skin rose in chills, but under those heavy blankets, it had to be hot and uncomfortable. I wondered if Kyros Brighteyed had taken some strange ill from channeling too much. After all, he'd contended with Vusu and lost.

"Leave us," Kyros said firmly to the honor. "And bring Isidora."

I wondered who she was and worried that he already looked forward to his next appointment. I set my jaw and stood still with forced patience.

As soon as the woman had left, the Archmaster studied me. "So. You survived your trip into the Pyrthae."

His eyes didn't glow as they usually did, but were a dun dark brown. Still, they carried all the sharp temper he'd displayed before. I shifted uncomfortably under that gaze. If there was an Acadian capable of knowing wardens at a glance, it was Kyros.

"Yes." I offered nothing further.

"Well?" he prompted testily. "Has anything strange happened to you?"

"What qualifies as strange after one has visited the Pyrthae?"

Kyros suddenly slammed a hand on the frame of the bed with a resounding crack. "Damned depths, woman! Now is not the time to tiptoe around the truth like you're afraid of shattering the crockery! You've been abed for three days. Why?"

I held my tongue. Before, I had intended merely to pry what information I could from the man and leave him to his recovery. But now that he'd forced a confrontation, I wondered if I should aim higher. After all, Kyros had held Vusu at bay for a time. And he'd trained some Acadians to fight, two of whom I'd seen in action at the battle within the Conclave. He could prove to be a valuable ally.

And he could teach me to channel. To fight against Vusu and Famine myself, and not expect my allies to do all the work.

But he could also ruin me. I didn't know him, and I certainly didn't trust him. He might have fought Vusu, but that didn't necessarily put us on the same side. I needed my position as First Verifier more than I needed to learn to be a warden right now. Much as it pained me to admit it, Xaron was right. I couldn't progress fast enough for it to make much of a difference. If I was to fight against the daemon god and his servant, it would have be as I'd always done before: plots and lies, webs and whispers.

"Well?" the Archmaster demanded. "Out with it!"

"I've been ill. I was unconscious most of that time, and weak when I was awake. When I could finally rise, I was ravenous." I shrugged. "That's all."

"And what did you see there? Did you see what Eltris claims?" His scowl twisted into a mocking grin. "Did you see Famine?"

A scowl hardened my own features. "I did."

He snorted. "So you're as much a fool as she is. If that's all you have to say to me, leave me be. I, unlike you, have suffered serious wounds and need my rest. Onala!"

I didn't move, even as I heard the door open behind me. "I'm not finished yet, Archmaster. I have questions to ask you in return."

"Do you?" A vein pulsed in his forehead. "Very well, *Verifier*. Put me to your questions."

"What do you know of the daemon god Famine?"

He responded as I thought he would, spluttering a harsh laugh. "It was a trick, girl! An illusion by Vusumuzi! You cannot imagine the things a warden as powerful as him can do. The things he could make *you* do." His eyes glimmered with a maliciousness it was hard to imagine.

I tried not to let it faze me. "Where might I discover more about Famine? Is there a library that might have texts on him?"

The Archmaster suddenly fell into a bout of coughs. "A library!" he exclaimed as soon as he could speak. "Oh, yes, we have a library *full* of legends and myths. In fact, try Tomes — I'm sure you'll find all kinds of useless bilge there to keep you happy."

I took his jest as permission. "Who should I see to find these tomes?"

"Tomes is a section of the library, foolish girl! Go there and tell them I sent you." The Archmaster's lips found a sickly grin. "That ought to give that ancient hag the shock to finally keel her over."

His bitter humor grated on my nerves, but I managed to hold my temper in check. "I doubt she'll take me at my word. I'll need a token of approval. Your seal would do, I assume."

"My seal? Do you think me a king? You need no seal. When you reach her, she'll allow you in."

I was just about to protest further when something gave me pause. It was like a thought unbidden, something half-remembered slipping across my mind. Only I recognized the thought was not my own.

Suddenly gripped by curiosity, I reached after whatever had touched my mind, only to recoil. Pain flared in my head as I attempted to follow. I winced and put a hand to my temple.

As the pain ebbed, I found Kyros watching me with sudden interest. A smirk slowly spread across his face. My heart pounded in my chest, and I pulled my hand away from my temple.

"So," he said at length. "That's how it is. I wonder how."

"Thank you for your aid," I rushed to say. "There is one other thing I wished to ask you about."

"There is one other thing you *should* ask me about." Kyros grinned openly now, his eyes laughing.

I pretended not to notice. "Before the Despoina's trial, you were training wardens. Training them to use their magic to fight as Shepherds do."

The humor swiftly drained from the Archmaster's face. "I don't know what you heard," he snapped, his foul temper suddenly returned. "But I would never do such a thing."

"Of course not," I said smoothly. "After all, such a crime would certainly condemn you to death. It might dismantle the Acadium as we know it. If the head suffers corruption, the rest of the body likely holds it as well. I merely wished to verify it. That's what I do, isn't it?"

"Get out." He spoke the command softly, then repeated it louder. "Get out! Damned if I know why I let you in."

"Thank you, Archmaster." I turned smoothly and left the room, passing by the stricken honor Onala to descend the stairs.

Two circles down, I paused and caught my breath. My heart raced, and regret coursed through me. I'd prodded Kyros where he was vulnerable, picking at his flagrant disobedience of the law, which could ruin him and the Acadium if exposed. But *why* had I done it? Had it been to claim back some measure of control as he smirked and guessed at my secrets? I suspected he hadn't been bluffing; Kyros didn't seem fond of subtleties, nor one to put on a false face. If he smiled the way he had, he knew something that I wished he didn't. And at the moment, there was only one secret I desperately wanted to guard.

Despite myself, a private elation sparked to life. If Kyros believed me a warden, then I couldn't have imagined it. And that wasn't the only proof. When he'd spoken of not needing a seal or message from him, I'd felt something strange passing through my mind. It must have been channeling; how else could my sensing it tip Kyros off? But if it were channeling, it was nothing like the magic I'd experienced thus far.

My thoughts were interrupted by the sound of footsteps coming up the stairs. I quickly moved to the next circle down and stepped aside just in time to see someone rise from the stairwell. I was surprised to find that I recognized her: the Acadian woman who had fought against Vusu and his Shepherds at Asileia's trial. One of Kyros's trained wardens. The very ones I'd implied I'd rat out if the Archmaster revealed my secret.

The woman smiled as she recognized me. "First Verifier Airene. How good to see you." Despite the speed with which she'd ascended, she didn't pant or shine with perspiration. She wasn't a great beauty, yet there was something undeniably attractive to her, a surety and natural grace in the way she moved that couldn't be falsified.

"Yes, I am she," I said. "And you must be Isidora."

The Acadian made a face. "I'll bet you heard that from Kyros. He loves to irk me by using my full name. Please, call me Isi."

"Very well, Isi."

There was an awkward pause as I tried to think of a way to excuse myself. But my mind was too full to make smooth conversation. For the Acadian's part, she seemed to sense something was off.

"I think I understand," she said after a moment. "He's already told you."

I blinked. "Who has told me what?"

It was Isi's turn to be confused. "But why would you—? Ah. Of course. You were at the Despoina's trial."

"Yes, I was."

The air grew yet more uncomfortable between us. Now we both knew I could ruin her with that secret. But who had she thought would have told me? Kyros? It didn't seem likely, but I couldn't imagine who else she'd be talking about.

Isi smiled, and it was tinged with something I couldn't understand. Sympathy?

"I know it can be a shock, Airene, wardens using their channeling for more than tricks or tools. But what Kyros and I did, what our fallen brother did, was what our gifts were meant for. The initial wardens were called to defend and protect, as I'm sure you know. We were only doing our best by Oedija, just as you continue to do. And I would think that with —" She paused. "But if he has not discussed it with you, I shouldn't intrude."

Amid my confusion, I couldn't find a response. At length, the Acadian nodded to me and continued her ascent up, seeming as self-possessed as before. She thought she had my measure, and that their secret was safe. That grated on me more than anything.

Stewing silently, I made my long way down, feeling as if I only understood half of what I'd heard in this damned tower.

CHAPTER FIVE

TOMES

In the twelfth season, the world's fortunes began to turn.

The pyr changed first. Spirits of harvest and benevolent ancestors, who had always been helpers to humans, suddenly played mean-spirited tricks. Tools went missing. Crops spoiled. Calves sickened and died. As the holy men and women were called upon to placate them, the pyr ignored their pleas and continued their mischief.

Then worse things began to occur. Trees that had borne bountiful fruit the seasons before wilted with blight. The breath of frail babes faltered and ceased. Wine became vinegar as it was drunk. All that had been given began to be taken away twofold, and the name of Tyurn Sky-Sea became a curse on his people's lips.

The Lord of All stared down in horror and rage. 'What have you done?' he cried to the Seed.

'What have I done?' the Seed replied. 'Was it not you who gave all this to your people? Then is it not you who is turning it to ash?'

'What do I do?' the Lord of All begged of the Seed.

'Do not fear. I will help,' the Seed soothed him. 'All you must do is lend me your power, and I will put all aright.'

Tyurn Sky-Sea had lost much in eleven seasons. He did not feel the Seed pressing his roots deeper inside him.

'Set things right,' he said to the Seed, and gave yet more of himself away.

— The Seeds of Famine, a translation from the Lighted-tongue; by Oracle Kalene of deme Hull; 881 SLP

As promised, Corin waited for me outside of Kyros's tower. I marveled at her patience. No doubt long hours of waiting for the next person needing a cart had developed it, but it came so naturally to Corin that it had to be in her blood.

Despite my sour mood, I flashed her a small smile as I came down the tower stairs. "If you wouldn't mind, there's a couple more things I'd like to do here."

Her face as impassive as before, she nodded. "It's not safe to return on your own. I'll stay with you."

And I'll help you recover your sister, I promised her silently, hoping I could.

Corin scanned the grounds. "Where to first?"

I hesitated. I knew what I ought to do. My brother had lain here in the Acadium for four days without seeing anyone he knew. To go to him would be the right thing to do. But I couldn't force myself to say the words. A wall of guilt held them back. Guilt at having failed him. Guilt that I didn't want to witness what I'd let him become.

"The library," I finally said. "I guess we'll have to ask directions."

The friendlier of the two Acadians, both of whom still lingered nearby, looked over with a smile. "I can help you with that…"

The old man pointed us in the library's direction, and Corin and I thanked him before making our way across the Acadium once more. The nonsensical winding paths between the eclectic buildings were almost beginning to grow familiar. Following the directions, we wove between edifices and around Acadians leisurely carrying on with their business. In contrast to the city outside, there seemed almost a lightness to the air. The Acadium was not yet starving. I wondered how things would change when they were.

Nearing the library, the crowds started to thin. It brought a small smile to my lips. Acadians were supposed to be studious by nature. But when the only thing they had in common was their attunement to the Pyrthae, it didn't surprise me to see so few interested in the art of reading. With ancient texts, reading became a tedious chore, and one I little looked forward to.

I almost didn't believe when we'd arrived at the library. Had the Acadian not warned us it rose only a story high, I would have passed it by for one of the grander buildings on campus. Still, it had a certain stateliness to it, with two fountains set in long, rectangular mirror pools extending toward the entrance stairs, and squat, stolid columns that were more functional than beautiful. Though I thought it couldn't be more straightforward, etched along the pediment were letters announcing 'library' in the Lighted-tongue of Oedija's ancestors.

We entered through the weathered front doors into a dark, tall-ceilinged foyer. The air was chill and smelled of stale parchment and dust. The room was gently lit by a chandelier of pyr lamps and sconces mounted on walls. All around us, orderly lines of shelves ran to the surrounding walls, blocking from view what I assumed were yet more shelves. Every available space was filled with books.

My earlier derision evaporated as I stared around me. Never before had I seen the promise of so much knowledge. It seemed unimaginable that so many books could have been written in the world, much less collected here in one place. My mouth hung open until I caught myself.

Footsteps echoed through the airy room as a portly boy hurried toward us. "Hello!" he huffed as he stopped a few paces away. "May I help you?"

For a moment, I forgot what I'd come for. "Ah, yes. I'm looking for books on old Eidolan legends. I was told Tomes might hold the ones I'd want."

"Tomes?" The boy, who I assumed was an apprentice of some kind, seemed surprised. "Hardly anyone but the Master Historian goes down there now. And I'm afraid you'll need permission from the Master Librarian."

"I believe I already have it."

The boy seemed even more confused. "Yes, if you say so, Mistress…?"

"Airene." I didn't correct him on my title. Somehow, it seemed petty to lord it over a child.

"Mistress Airene," the boy repeated, then turned to Corin. "And if you could tell me your name?"

Corin looked startled at being addressed. The woman was remarkably skilled at going uncommented for long periods of time, particularly for a woman of her size.

"Corin," she muttered.

"Mistress Airene and Mistress Corin — a pleasure meeting both of you." He bowed deeply. "I am Pupil Platon."

"Pleasure to meet you as well, Platon." I bowed politely in return.

Platon beamed. "If you'll please wait here, I'll just confirm with Master Hagne that everything is in order." The apprentice grinned at us again before turning and jogging back the way he'd come.

As he left, Corin muttered, "Mistress Corin…"

I hid a smile.

The boy returned a short time later. "She wasn't pleased," he said cheerily, "but she said you were permitted, so long as you followed the rules."

"The rules?"

"I'll tell you as we go, if you please. Now if you're ready, mistresses…"

Walking now instead of running, Platon chattered as he led the way. I found his words washing over me while I marveled at the sights around us. As we approached the chandelier, the ground fell away, revealing floor upon floor faintly lit by pyr lamps below. My eyes widened as I counted five floors before the light became too faint to make out any further. If each level had as many books as this one did, the sheer amount of knowledge contained in these walls was astounding.

It was also intimidating. What I needed to know about Famine was not likely to be common knowledge, if it existed at all. Not to mention I didn't know what kind of text would be most helpful. Ancient histories, mythic stories, religious texts, perhaps even merchant ledgers might hold the secrets I needed. I was searching for a needle in a granary. My stomach sank at the prospect of the turns of work that lay before me, particularly when we had less than six spans before Avvad's armies began sieging the city.

My mood soured as we descended, my already sore legs protesting the many stairs. Platon apologized over and over, explaining that ancient texts were kept as far from the elements as possible to aid in their preservation. I nodded distractedly as I debated whether I should bother going through with this or not. Perhaps all I needed was to track down Eltris. It could be that the augur held the answers to all the mysteries surrounding Famine.

Though, when I thought of it further, I wondered if she did. For all she seemed to know, Eltris hadn't been able to stop Vusu or Famine. She couldn't save Linos. The Master Augur knew much, but she wasn't omniscient. And I couldn't rely on an unreliable woman in times like these.

We descended five floors before the pupil stopped. "Here they are, mistresses!" Platon announced cheerily, spreading his arms at the shelves before us. "The most ancient Eidolan legends from the quills of the finest historians and storytellers the Four Realms has known."

I stepped forward, leaning in close to the books to squint at their titles. Many were so layered with dust they were impossible to make out. I reached out to clean the spine.

Platon danced forward, smiling nervously. "Ah, Mistress, do be careful. Remember Master Hagne's rules, which I just told you?"

I hadn't listened to his rules, but I didn't want the young Acadian pupil to know that. Smiling apologetically, I withdrew my hand and kept studying the spines, looking for promising titles in legible print. Most of the words were in the Oedijan sea-tongue, but of such an old dialect they might as well have been in the Lighted-tongue. The education my mother and father had given me at home hadn't touched on ancient languages, and the five years I'd attended a public scholarium were scarcely sufficient to read in the older forms of the sea-tongue. This wouldn't be an easy search.

"May I help?" Platon asked after a time. He seemed eager for our task to be over, no doubt anxious we might break another of his mistress's rules.

"Look for titles on the Lighted Passage. Or anything relating to Famine."

The boy bobbed his head and hurried down the aisle. "Go slow, Platon," he muttered to himself as he searched. "Pretend like you're swimming to the book. Slow and even, handling them gentle as lambs."

I tried to block out his words as I squinted at the swimming letters. In such dim light, the ancient script was all but impossible to read. At my prompting, Platon fetched a pyr lamp, but it only helped marginally, particularly as the pyr lamps were kept dim as a rule. Platon explained that the cultures were pruned to reduce risk of light damage to the books. Corin stood at the end of the aisle waiting for us. Unable to read even the modern sea-tongue, a library was probably the last place she wanted to be. I tried to ignore the squirming in my stomach and kept searching.

By the end of two turns, Platon and I had gathered between us three books: *The Legend of the Lighted Passage; Daemonic Tales: Encounters with Malevolent Pyr;* and *The Seeds of Famine.* Of the three, the last sounded the most promising. Not only was it the oldest, but it was also a translation of a much older text, one the author claimed to be written in 18 SLP, not two decades after the Lighted Passage.

Though my eyes ached and my neck was stiff, I opened *The Seeds of Famine* onto one of the book stands near the end of the shelves which, as Platon explained, kept the book from opening flat and ruining the spine. Then I started to read.

From the Lower Realm of the world beyond ours, a Seed rose. It was a small thing, no larger than a pebble, and none noticed its passing as it lifted higher and higher, until it reached—

"Is it helpful?" Platon appeared at my shoulder and looked curiously at the yellowed pages before me. "Remember, keep it on the book stand and turn it slowly. Like handling—"

"—A lamb, I remember." I tried shutting out the pupil and continued scanning the cramped script.

…Until it reached the Higher Realm where our gods, the Eidola, reign. Tyurn Sky-Sea, Ruler of All Realms, Lord of All, was strong—

"This is probably the oldest book I've ever handled," the boy mused.

"You're not handling it, I am. Now please, will you be quiet?"

Though his interruptions were worsening my headache, I immediately regretted the sharp words. Turning back, I winced at the pupil's expression.

"I'm sorry, Platon," I said softly. "I didn't mean to snap at you. I just need to concentrate."

The hurt vanished immediately. "It's alright. You're probably uncomfortable down here. I was pretty uncomfortable the first few times I came down here. It's dark and musty, and you have to move so slowly..."

I sighed and leaned my head against my hands, kneading my eyes with my palms. I'd get no peace with the boy here. And somehow, being around him brought Linos to mind. "We'd better go. I'm assuming I can't take these with me?"

The pupil looked scandalized. "Of course not! You'd ruin them! Meaning no offense, Mistress Airene, but any kind of exposure at their age would be bad for them. Particularly moisture. But I can reserve them for you here!"

I pushed away from the table. "Do that. Then we'll get out of here. I've had enough of squinting at squirming lines in the dark for one day."

Once Platon had secured my three finds in a cubby at the end of a shelf, we made our way back up to the ground floor. My legs, already sore from my long ascent up Kyros's tower, protested with every step, but all I could do was grimace and carry on. There was no way I was complaining about getting tired in front of Corin, not to mention the boy, who practically skipped up the stairs with boundless energy.

When we reached the main doors again, the boy turned. "I'll see you soon? When you come back to read those books?"

"I imagine you will."

Platon beamed. He had a way of smiling that made him seem much younger than the thirteen years I'd initially thought him. "I'll see you then, Mistress Airene!"

"Just one thing before we go. Do you knowing where the healing ward is?"

———

After the pupil's directions got us lost, Corin and I eventually received adequate instruction to find our destination. The healing ward — called the Ward, appropriately enough — was on the opposite side of the campus in a long building built of gray stone. It easily stretched five hundred cubits in either direction and rose three stories high. From the look of it, the Ward could house hundreds of the ill, perhaps even a thousand, if not very comfortably.

Nervously, I led Corin through the front door. A clerk waited at a small desk before us, watching unsmiling as we stopped and looked around. From the hall beyond the desk, I heard the murmur of voices, punctuated by screams.

Wincing as another shriek pierced the air, I approached the clerk. "I'm looking for Linos of Port."

"Are you? And what's your interest in Linos of Port?" The clerk studied me with an arched brow.

"I'm his sister. Airene of Port."

The clerk nodded and began to flip through a book splotched with ink, chewing absentmindedly on the end of her pen as she did. Finally, she jabbed a finger at a scribbled line. "Here he is. Ward three, bed sixty-four."

Muttering the clerk's directions to myself, I led Corin through hallway after hallway, every one of them lined with doors. I wondered if this building had been built with this intention, for it seemed to suit the needs of a healing ward perfectly. Most patients occupied their own rooms. All spoke of the healers of the Acadium and how crucial they were in times of plague. But for regular use, with access to the Acadium restricted, I wondered who was actually able to seek assistance. Perhaps only patricians and the other notables of Oedija could secure access.

It wasn't clear from those I saw. Some of their robes were cleaner and of finer material, but the fineness of a garment's weave didn't matter much when a person was in the thrall of foul humors. I turned my gaze aside from angry red boils and chest-wracking coughs. Though healers were everywhere, it seemed unlikely that some of those around us would make it out alive.

We passed through another archway, then '64' was on a door ahead of us, engraved in a wooden plaque. The door was shut. Nervously, I approached it and laid a hand on the plaque. It was cool to the touch. I hesitated a moment longer, conscious of Corin watching and waiting behind me, then knocked softly on the door. When I didn't hear a response, I slowly opened it.

Linos lay on a bed within, staring up at the ceiling with wide, unshifting eyes. He didn't look over as we entered and shut the door quietly behind us. Barely two spans had passed since his last visit to Canopy, but as I looked down on him, I felt my little brother had aged far more. The first growth of blond stubble had appeared over his lip. Someone had washed his face and arms, which lay over the unadorned blankets covering him. He wore a rough brown robe different from the gray one I'd last seen him in. He looked thin, though no more than before.

As my chest grew tight, I searched for distractions. Opening the drapes to allow in more light, I tucked the blankets under him as I had when he'd been a child. Anxious to know he'd been treated well, I sent Corin for a healer. A healer's assistant came instead with a long-suffering look, but upon hearing I was kin, he patiently recounted Linos's care. There was not much to speak of. Kallias the Sculptor had visited twice, but neither session had shown progress. Beyond that, Linos had barely stirred, though he took care of his needs when prompted. "It's as if he needs reminding how to live," the assistant mused.

I dismissed him, unable to hide my sour expression.

Once he'd left, I spoke to Corin without looking at her. "Could you give us a moment?"

Without a word, she left the room, pulling the door closed behind her.

I turned back to Linos. His expression hadn't shifted. But for his chest steadily moving up and down, I might have thought him dead. I stepped closer and reached toward him. My hand shook as it settled on the exposed skin of his arm.

Pain split through my skull and brought me to my knees. I was barely aware I'd fallen. I felt myself flayed open, layer by layer exposed like a body under a knife, each spike of pain precise and efficient.

Something was doing this cutting, something foreign and daemonic. Suddenly, I became aware of it, the thing that was pulling apart the deepest parts of myself and laying them bare.

Defiant rage filled me. I gathered the shreds of myself and pushed against the invading presence. At first, my resistance accomplished little. Then, measure by measure, I began to force it out. I became aware of my body again and wrenched my hand away from my brother's skin. As soon as contact was broken, the looming presence fell away, leaving my head aching and my body shivering.

I clutched my arms tightly around myself and rose shakily to my feet. My head felt stuffed full of fleece, my thoughts sluggish as molasses. But I forced myself to see beyond the pain and look down on my brother.

He stared up at me, grinning.

A small, startled noise rose in my throat before I could stop it. "Linos?" I managed to gasp.

"So you are another of his seeds." It was my brother speaking, yet somehow, I knew the words were not his. They came out harsh, biting. My brother had taken pride in his rich baritone since his voice had dropped the prior year. He'd never spoken this way before.

I forced myself to keep his gaze. "What do you mean?"

A mocking grin twisted his face. "You know what I mean. Are you not a First Verifier now? Surely you can figure this out."

I clenched my jaw and forced myself to face the truth. This was not Linos I spoke with, but the one who had taken his place. *Vessel.*

"What have you done to my brother?" My words shook with repressed emotion.

"I *am* your brother. Now, at least." Linos's eyes glimmered. "He has his claws in you, Airene. He wishes to know you further."

"Who do you speak of? Vusu? Famine?"

"You seek answers, to understand what has happened, what *is* happening. He can help you. You must go to him. No one else can tell you all you need to know."

I wanted to shake my brother, to drive out whatever daemon possessed him. I wanted to unhear his words that wormed their way into my head. But, once again, I could do nothing.

"I'm going now, Linos," I said in as steady a voice as I could. "I'll come see you later when you're feeling better."

Finally, those bright blue eyes closed, and his head fell back against the pillow. For a moment, I dared to hope he was returning to his rest, unmarred by daemons.

Then slow laughter rasped from his throat, wave after wave spasming his body.

Clenching my fists so tightly my nails drew blood, I fumbled for the door's latch and fled the room.

CHAPTER SIX

QUINTESSENCE

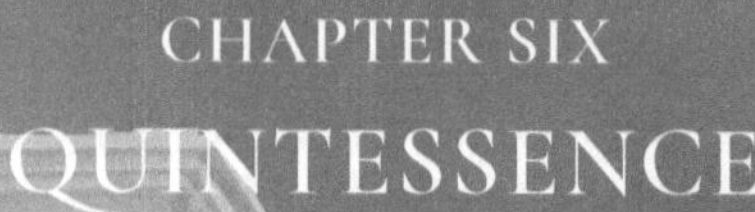

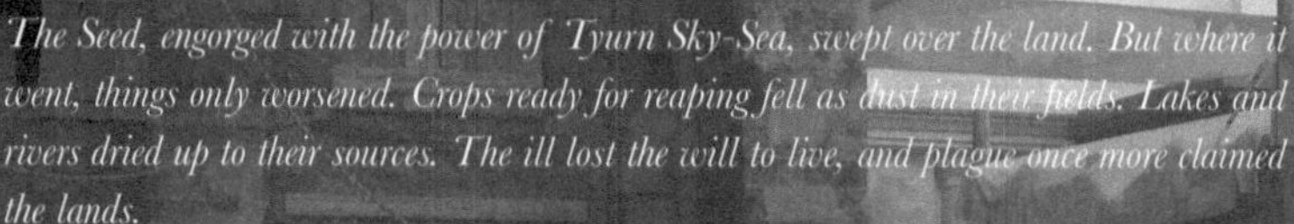

The Seed, engorged with the power of Tyurn Sky-Sea, swept over the land. But where it went, things only worsened. Crops ready for reaping fell as dust in their fields. Lakes and rivers dried up to their sources. The ill lost the will to live, and plague once more claimed the lands.

Clepsammia appeared before her father and saw what he had become. Tyurn Sky-Sea, once as large as a mountain and as strong as a giant, had shrunk to a starved, sickly man. He could not lift his head to greet his daughter, nor even recognize her as she neared.

The Goddess of Fate clasped her father's hands, kneeling by his bed. But her voice was iron, forged hard in grief's fires, as she spoke. 'Father! You must rise from your bed! Come see what your pride has brought to those you swore to protect. Did I not warn you that this would come to pass? This Seed that grows is not of harvest, but famine. You have brought an end to all realms, oh Lord of All!'

Tyurn Sky-Sea roused at her words. But even as his anger and pride stirred, he looked over Telae and found his daughter had spoken true. All that his dreams of plenty had brought was ruin.

'What can I do, Daughter?' he asked, all hope dead in his breast. 'I have doomed us all!'

But Clepsammia, Maiden of the Sands, wore a sad, knowing smile, for all knowledge of what was and is to come was hers. 'Not yet, Father. For there is yet one thing you can still do…'

- The Seeds of Famine, a translation from the Lighted-tongue; by Oracle Kalene of deme Hull; 331 SLP

We walked the Acadium campus in silence as my mind buzzed. Now more than ever, I needed answers. Linos's words — *Or Vessel's*, I thought bitterly — had made my questions burn brighter. What did they mean? And could the figure he referred to be anyone other than Vusu or Famine?

And then there was what had happened when I'd touched him. I gingerly rubbed at my temples as we exited the Acadium gates. The pain had dulled to an ache, but my mind still felt raw and vandalized. Who or what that had been, I still didn't know. It bore an echo of the ravenous hunger I'd felt radiating from Famine when I'd stood before him in the Pyrthae, but it hadn't possessed the same depth or vastness. And I'd contended with its will and broken free. Whatever that daemon was, it wasn't Famine himself. A dark part of me wondered if it actually was Linos who had attacked me. But I had another theory. And until I consulted Talan about it, I'd cling to it and believe my brother still held on somewhere inside his body.

Corin stopped in the street just out of earshot of the Acadium guards. "Be wary," she cautioned in a low voice. "We are still in danger."

"I know that," I said, rousing from my thoughts. "I'd be hard-pressed to forget our mugging."

She gave me an expressionless look, then turned and left down a side road.

I bit back my words and followed. She didn't deserve my irony, not after she'd waited patiently with me all day. Even if much of it was done from guilt, it didn't change that she'd been a steady friend to me when Nomusa, Xaron, and Talan couldn't be.

"Look, Corin—" I began.

"You've had a long day," she interrupted without turning around. "We've not eaten since morning. And you were recently ill. I'm not offended."

I hesitated, more convinced than before that she was. "Still, I'm sorry. I appreciate you being here today."

She didn't turn, but nodded once. I would have to be content with that, it seemed.

"We should pass through the Laurel Palace," she said after traveling a while along the road. "It's a shorter path out in the open."

I nodded my agreement. "As long as my medallion still opens the way, I'll take any shortcuts."

———

The laurel guards let us through the gates at a flash of my medallion. Three-quarters of a turn after, we finished crossing the bridge and stood before the Aviary.

"I suppose we need to get a room outfitted for you," I mused as we approached the building. I went a few steps further before I noticed Corin had stopped. I turned back, trepidation rising in me. "Corin?"

"I'm leaving." Her gaze traveled over my head.

I sighed. "I wasn't lying when I said I'd try to find your sister."

"I know."

We were both still for a moment. "Where will you go?" I asked softly. "What will you do?"

The big woman shook her head. "I'll find her."

Corin had come on her own to Oedija, so I knew she didn't have any relations here, nor other friends that I knew of. She had no place to go. Even with her iron will, she needed a place to sleep. And no matter what had happened between us, she was still my friend.

"Seek out Maesos," I said. "He'll give you a place to stay as long as you need one. Though he may have you cart his wares around a bit."

She considered this for a long moment before nodding. "It is a good plan. Thank you."

"It's the least I can do."

By impulse, I stepped forward and pulled Corin into a tight hug. "You'll find her," I muttered into her rough tunic. "Just take care of yourself until you do."

The former cartwoman hesitated, then loosely put an arm around me until I stepped away. Without another word, she nodded, then turned in the direction of the Conclave gate. I watched her go. Not a coin to her name, but she boldly moved forward. If only I could be so decisive in my actions. I delayed even visiting my sick brother. Shaking my head, I turned and entered back into the Aviary.

But I'd only just stepped into my room when restlessness seized me. Now that I had a moment to myself, I wondered what I was doing, returning to the Aviary before the day was done. There was still a turn or two of light left. Yet here I was, back in my room. Was I so afraid of wandering the streets now? Did I think I would be mugged again or worse? Or had it been my encounters with Linos, Isidora, and Kyros that drove me to take shelter?

None of it was an excuse. Though I was tired and sore, I couldn't rest. Not until I'd done all I could. Groaning, I rose and went to seek Nomusa. Surely she would have some Finch task for me.

But the cook didn't know where she was, though she did point with exasperation to the feast she'd made for just me and Nomusa that lay untouched on the foyer tables. I relented and gorged myself on the fine foods. Guilty or not, I still needed to eat.

Full and sleepy, I wandered out of the Aviary, but stopped from indecision at the stoop. Nomusa could be at the Conclave. Or perhaps she was up at the Laurel Palace meeting another mysterious contact. Or a dozen other places that she now frequented but I didn't know about. I rubbed my aching head. Hunting her down would be nigh impossible. She and I would have to start consulting each other if we were to coordinate as First Verifiers.

My headache reminded me of another person I ought to seek out. Rising with a groan, I set off for the Laurel Palace. If I ran into Nomusa along the way, all the better.

I made the long trip back up the hill atop which the Laurel Palace sprawled, then asked the first honor I passed where Hilarion's quarters lay. At her directions, my eyebrows rose. Xaron had not jested when he said Hilarion was afforded fine rooms. But joy for my friend was hard in coming as I mounted yet another spiral staircase to ascend Hilarion's tower. My legs burned and air wheezed in my lungs as I mounted the last of the steps to reach the door at the top. Too tired even to knock, I was startled as the door swung open to reveal my friend's grinning face framed by a black cloud of unkempt hair.

"How did you know?" I said between pants.

"How could I not? I heard your huffing and puffing the whole way up!" He treated me to another teasing grin as he motioned me inside.

I gratefully sank into a chair and accepted the glass of wine he poured me, then examined the rooms he'd been afforded. Hilarion's quarters were composed of multiple chambers. The one we sat in had no bed, and two other doors led off to either side. It was a waiting room like no other I'd seen. The implements of decades of Hilarions decorated the walls and tables, awaiting their next opportunity to entertain. Marionettes hung from hooks. A strange wheel contraption leaned in one corner. What looked to be an unactivated magnetic pyr lamp was tucked against the doorframe. Silk streamers in every different color flowed down another wall. All was situated to remind the guest that the person who occupied these chambers was a fool, and all he possessed was for enjoyment alone.

Xaron settled himself into the chair next to me, sipping on a glass of wine as well, though he'd poured from a different bottle than mine. I discovered why as I sipped my own. A smoky port — Xaron drank lighter wines with tones of fruit, not the strong stuff I preferred. I smiled in satisfaction.

"The decorations are a bit tawdry, but they'll do for now," Xaron said amicably. "Glad you were able to make it up here."

I gave him a wry grin. "If I hadn't already ascended another tower today, perhaps it wouldn't have been so difficult."

He raised an eyebrow. "Not many towers around here. Which one did you go up?"

I told him of my visit to the Archmaster. Xaron's brow furrowed further with each sentence.

"Then he seemed to send her a message," I continued, "though he did nothing but lie in his bed. I think he channeled. After he said I wouldn't need his seal of approval, I felt… something. In my mind."

Xaron stared at me, a wild look in his eyes, before composing himself. "Right," he muttered. "I almost forgot you were a warden now."

A flush of pride warmed my chest. I tried to ignore it as I pressed, "But what was it? Was it channeling? And if so, what kind? All I know are the three energetic elements — radiance, kinesis, and magnesis. But are there more?"

Xaron hesitated. "Possibly. My mother has a way of channeling completely different from anything I know. Had," he corrected himself with a sour expression. "I suppose she doesn't use her gifts anymore."

"What way of channeling?"

"She was an apothecary, if you remember. But she wouldn't just concoct alchemical solutions. She studied their reactions, then mimicked them. She discovered how to channel the energy from those reactions, something she called 'catalysm'."

He ran a hand through his loose hair. "I was so young when she had her accident, it's hard to piece together what I saw. You know how when you combine two opposing solutions, they might have a reaction? Like… like yeast with honey. If you leave them in warm water, they foam, or when combined with flour, cause bread to rise."

"Of course."

"That reaction has an energy of its own. Yeast doesn't have a strong one, but there are plenty stronger. And my mother discovered all of them." He grimaced. "Hence, her accident."

I still wasn't sure I understood. "So catalysm might be a fourth energetic element. But even if it is, it doesn't explain what Kyros did to pass that message to the Master Librarian. I doubt it had to do with leavening bread."

Xaron grinned. "Humor me a little longer. As I was getting to, the energetic elements are thought to all be found in our bodies."

I frowned. "Radiance and kinesis I can understand. But magnesis?"

"Wouldn't you like to think lightning flows through our veins? But think for a moment. Did you ever rub your clothes against a rug when you were young, then touch something metal, or another person?"

"Of course. I used to tickle Linos on Mother's carpets, then force him to touch the faux silver vase in the foyer. He'd yelp like a hurt puppy." I smiled sadly at the memory.

Xaron smiled sympathetically. "And when he touched the metal, you saw the spark that formed? Or have you ever felt the shock that goes through you? Well, that feeling is not far from the buzzing feeling of magnesis when you channel it."

"Alright. Say I buy all that. What are you getting at?"

"If it's true, if all the elements are present within us, then perhaps the mind has an energy as well. The soul, or spirit — or quintessence, as oracles would call it."

"An energy of the mind." The thought didn't perplex me as much as it once had. With both Kyros and Linos, there had been another presence touching my mind. And I'd interacted with them using my own. But that didn't mean it was an energy. Did it?

"You've got me questioning everything I thought I knew," I confessed.

He shook his head. "You're telling me. Eltris says I don't know half of what wardens are capable of. And seeing what Vusu could do — traveling into the Pyrthae, summoning Famine — I know it must be true."

"And there's always more to learn."

My thoughts having turned to it, I told him of my visit to the Acadium library. Xaron wrinkled his nose. "I don't suppose you've met the Master Librarian yet."

"No, I haven't." I squinted at him. "Why?"

"Oh, I'll just let you find out for yourself."

I let the cryptic answer slide and told him of Linos and our encounter.

"You're proving quintessence exists in one day." Xaron looked impressed. "But I'm sorry to hear of your brother."

"It's nothing more than I expected," I said dully. I wondered how I'd break the news to my family, whenever I saw them next. I rubbed my eyes. A problem for another time.

Another thought came to me. "Oh, I forgot to mention. I ran into Kyros's Acadian battle warden on his tower's stairs. A woman named Isidora."

Xaron spasmed and spilled his wine. "Did you?" he commented, his causal manner ruined as he jumped up and fetched a rag to mop up the wine.

I narrowed my eyes. "Are you hiding something?"

For a moment, he pretended to be absorbed in his cleaning. Then he sighed, threw aside the stained rag, and settled back in his chair. "Not exactly. Just that the group of Acadians who have been learning battle magic… We've been training under Isi."

Isi. So he was familiar with her enough to call her by her shortname. Just as he called me by mine. "I see."

He looked ready to say more when the door burst open. I rose with fists clenched, but it was Nomusa standing in the doorway. She looked as ready to attack someone as I.

"There you are!" She strode up to us with a scowl on her face. "Good thing you asked an honor for directions or I never would have found you. Had you heard?"

I took a breath to loosen my chest. "'Thae above, Nomusa. Don't barge in like that."

"Had you heard?" she demanded again. "Either of you. Do you know who's coming here?"

"Just tell us already," Xaron said, his bewilderment matching my own.

"Charatta Yorandu Komo." She spoke the name like a curse.

Only one part of it had any meaning to me. "Yorandu. They're from your ishaka."

"Not just from my ishaka. Komo is that usurper's son." Nomusa spat on the floor, heedless that it now belonged to Xaron. "The *Shaka's* son."

The significance finally dawned on me. The son of the man who killed her parents, who exiled her from her homeland and birthright — he was coming to Oedija.

"Nomusa, I hadn't heard anything," I said honestly. "I'd have told you if I had."

But Xaron flushed pink. "I… may have heard of this. One of Komo's emissaries arrived a couple of days ago telling us he was coming."

I winced as Nomusa rounded on him. "You heard," she said in a low voice, "that the son of the man who killed my parents was coming here and didn't think to tell me?"

"I was barely paying attention!" Xaron protested, but Nomusa just hissed, stalked over to a chair, and slumped down.

Willing my sore legs into motion, I walked over and sat next to her, gently placing a hand on her shoulder. She was shaking with emotion — rage, no doubt, but I suspected grief as well. Nomusa had never really gotten over losing her homeland and family in one stroke, even a decade later.

"Tell me about his coming," I implored her softly. I hoped a report might draw her from her misery.

She drew in a shuddering breath. "He's to arrive here four days from now, come at the behest of the Despoina. Apparently Oedija and Yorandu have been in communication since well before the Night of the Three Horns. The urgency of Oedija's situation has accelerated the schedule for their plans."

"Which are?"

A bitter smile curled her lips. "What else can we offer that false prince but the Despoina's hand?"

I considered this. I'd never heard Nomusa plotting to take back her ishaka, but such significant ties to Oedija would certainly complicate ever making such a plan. By joining our royal family with their rulers, we obligated ourselves to come to their aid in war, just as they did for us.

I was torn. I knew what I should say to Nomusa as a friend. But Oedija needed every ally we could get. Unable to deny one over the other, I held my tongue.

Nomusa turned her gaze on me, eyes glistening. "Don't think for a moment that I don't know we need allies. I've been attending the Council meetings. I know just how ill-prepared we are to face the threats before us. The Stratechons might be gathering the taxoi, but did you know they still have no definitive plans for dealing with the Manifest or Avvad?" She shook her head. "We need warriors. I just… Why did it have to be *them?*"

"I know." There was nothing else I could say. I intertwined my arm with hers and leaned into her side.

Xaron settled down on her other side and silently wrapped his arm around her, his hand resting on my shoulder. For a moment, it was almost as if we were all back in Canopy, scraping by as unconfirmed Finches. Aching nostalgia filled me to my bones.

But a thought turned the feeling cold. If I could return things back to the way they were, would I? It would take away all the pain and death and uncertainty closing in on us. But with it would go the achievements and dreams of a lifetime. Becoming a Verifier. Becoming a warden.

I was glad I didn't have to make that choice.

Nomusa straightened and gently pried us off. "You never mentioned what you had to tell me before," she said to me. "It seemed important."

I shared a look with Xaron.

Nomusa wasn't oblivious. "What? Does he already know?"

"I told him as soon as I awoke," I confessed. "But you'll understand why."

The telling came easier now that I was more certain. When I finished, Nomusa didn't seem shocked or fearful, but studied me with a narrowed gaze. "You're sure?" she asked softly. "Your fingerprints shift?"

"Fairly sure. Encounters today make me more so. And no shifts have appeared yet, but as Xaron explained to me, they may take some time to show."

"A span, a season." Xaron shrugged. "If Airene channeled, she must be a warden."

But Nomusa didn't look convinced. "You went into the Pyrthae. Maybe what you experienced was a strange result from it. Like an afterimage from looking too closely at the sun."

"Channeling isn't the same thing as staring at the sun," I noted drily. "But I have other reasons to believe it's not just in my head." I recounted for her the instance in Kyros's bedchambers.

When I finished, Nomusa observed, "So you're not sure it was channeling, what you felt?"

My tongue was growing harder to restrain. "No. I'm not sure."

She looked as if she wanted to say more, but shook her head and rose. "Keep an eye on matters, I suppose. The last thing we need is for you to catch fire. In the meantime, I have plenty to keep you busy. Speaking of which…"

I rose, trying to master myself. Now was not the time to be bickering among ourselves. Even if Nomusa *was* being obstinate and skeptical. Masking my annoyance, I wrapped Xaron in a hug and murmured in his ear, "Maybe we can both pay Isi a visit soon."

The shrug he gave could have been agreement or refusal. I let it slide, and after Nomusa had said her own farewells, I followed her out the door.

————

As we walked down the Laurel grounds and across the bridge back to the Aviary, I kept the conversation far from Komo by prying information from Nomusa. Speaking in hushed tones and keeping a watchful eye out for those who drew too near, I tried to catch up on everything she knew of the Manifest, Avvad, and the Valemish.

Of Vusu and the Manifest, little deviated from the hasty summary she'd given me before. The Seekers continued to reinforce their compound and maintained a steady flow of food for their followers. Shadows had been seen flitting about rooftops at night in the northern inner demes. Seeker wardens, Nomusa guessed, and not very skilled ones for so many to be seen — unless they wished to be seen. Still, it was another danger to fear at night. *If only shutters could keep out assassins*, I thought drily.

Of Avvad, she had even less to say. They marshaled their forces from the provinces and gathered their supplies into wagons. All seemed on schedule for six spans, as before. One additional thing had been noted, however: they'd sent birds to the Bali ishakas, reportedly to request aid. Nomusa and I both knew Kahin-Shah Burak's real message: stand with Avvad, or be the next to fall. We'd see if the ploy worked.

The Valemish were said to have largely been contained within their temples. Posting the city guard before them was a bigger concession than had been expected of the Council, yet it did little to impede the flow of people in and out of the temples.

The worst of the news concerned food. The public granaries had been giving out the little grain they'd managed to properly store, but the estimates Nomusa had heard at Council meetings reported only enough for two spans more, three if the food was rationed severely. But even those estimates were generous, as they assumed that the foodstuff the Underguild held hostage would somehow be negotiated back.

"A poor time for a drought," I noted sourly over the wind billowing over the bridge.

"You think it is coincidental timing?" Nomusa shook her head. "I don't believe everything that augur Eltris says. But I do think she might have a point about the disasters throughout our history. Perhaps... perhaps the Serpent God is behind this as well."

I was surprised I hadn't seen it, and even more so that Nomusa had. "I wasn't sure you believed me. About Famine, and his return."

"I didn't want to. And I don't like thinking about it." She shook her head. "What can we do against a god? It seems futile to even think about it. We have enough problems without daemons and legends coming to life."

I thought of Linos at that, wondering if I could muster the energy to recount the incident again.

"Airene?"

I sighed. "I know what you mean. But I saw him. Maybe that's why I can't help but worry about him and little else."

"Maybe."

We fell into silence, listening to the sea crashing against the cliffs below us and the wind whistling in our ears. The evening was gloomy and blue, fitting for our somber mood.

Only as we stepped off the bridge did Nomusa speak again. "I suppose we should discuss your responsibilities."

I raised an eyebrow. "Don't you mean *our* responsibilities?"

"I'm already established in certain arenas. The Council knows and trusts me far more than you. You have the Preservists and Feiyan against you. If you try interceding in their politics, they might vote against what you support just out of spite."

It wasn't a responsibility I envied, yet I couldn't help but feel put off. After all, no matter how quarrelsome the Low Consuls might be, it was within the Council chamber that nearly every important decision for the realm was made. To be excluded was a sore blow.

"I'm also growing more familiar with the Conclave every day," Nomusa continued. "It would be best if I head up that arena as well."

"Considering our responsibilities are to rout out corruption in the demotism, that seems to leave little for me to do."

She smiled thinly. "Not by a long stretch. What I was thinking is that you'd be responsible for calling at patrician homes. After all, corruption takes many forms, and we've scarcely begun to consider them all. Financial backing is what I wonder about now. The Seekers are getting significant money reserves from somewhere. Who's giving it to them, and why? We've barely even considered the question until now."

Before the night of Myron's disappearance, it would have been an opportunity I looked forward to. Now, I just thought of all the time it would take away from my true aims. But I was a First Verifier. Futile though this task might seem, I had to help Nomusa preserve our position for the time when we would most need it.

"Then I'll track their investors down," I answered gamely.

Nomusa glanced at me. "There's another task you could take on."

My enthusiasm proved to be short-lived. I sighed. "Out with it."

"Hiring other Verifiers to pick up your inevitable slack."

I smiled sheepishly. "You see right through me."

She smiled in return, but only briefly. "But do remember to take this seriously. Being Verifiers for the Conclave is different than it was for Jaxas. The Council needs to see progress on their directive, and soon, or they'll disband the Order as quickly as they resurrected it. But this is what we always wanted, isn't it? To be at the heart of things, cutting to the secrets that matter most? To change the course of Oedija?"

Her resolve inflamed my own. "Yes," I said quietly. "That's what we wanted."

She exhaled like she'd been holding her breath. "Good. Now maybe we'd better rest before yet another long day."

We'd arrived at the Aviary and, after a hasty meal, we both went to our rooms. I briefly debated sending a finch to my family and decided it could wait until tomorrow. I'd already faced that issue once today and couldn't force myself to revisit it. Besides, I wasn't exactly sure which estate Jaxas had sent them to, or if I had the scents needed to direct a finch there. I sighed and put it from my mind as I undressed and settled into bed.

As I drifted off, I thought of another message I'd have liked to send. Talan's visit the night before had been far too brief, and I wanted to see him again. But he'd refused to say where he stayed, and I doubted a finch would be able to safely reach him anyway. I'd pry his location from him the next time he came, along with the answer to my question about Linos.

Sleepily, I imagined reaching out to him, grasping after his shadow as it flitted across the city. I followed it through the courtyard of the Conclave and onto the streets, but always it kept ahead of me. Still, I felt I could find its source, if I could only gain a proper vantage point.

I looked up, and only then saw that Oedija loomed above me as well as around. The world had doubled, half of it hanging precariously overhead. But I was seeking Talan. I drew my gaze away and continued my search, first running, then soaring as I gained speed. My feet left the ground.

I swept through Iris; when I didn't find him there, I sought him in the demes beyond. As I quested further, focusing on my task became harder, and I had to thrust more of myself into my search. I felt stretched, thinned, but I didn't dare slow. If I slowed, I might never find him.

Then I felt him: a warmth in the cold night. Nearing, I saw his bright flame appear amidst the dun bodies that filled the city. Not recognizing the place in Hull where he was, I approached, curious as a moth.

But as I neared, I saw Talan did not burn alone. Another flame, curiously detached, like it burned at the end of a long wick, hovered next to him. This second flame rose into the mirror world above. An impulse to sever the long flame seized me, and I felt the edges of myself sharpening. The anger came so suddenly and strongly that I barely had the strength to hold it at bay.

Then I felt another gaze upon me. I turned from the two flames and was near blinded by the inferno rising silently behind me. It swept forward, a wildfire in full bloom, and closed in around me. It drank from the fury that oozed from me, and from my fear as well, as I comprehended the vastness of this entity.

I gathered myself close and searched for an opening, but any escape was fast closing. All around was a sphere of writhing flames, each tendril yearning to burn me into itself. I stiffened my resolve and dared them to try.

The walls of fire began to close.

"Stop!"

The word reverberated through me, though the voice that had called it sounded weak. The inferno faltered, then retreated to form a gap, as if fearing the voice. In the center of the gap, a small black figure floated, unbothered by the flames that licked its feet. I stared in wonder at this being who could not be burned.

"You are mine still," the figure said, the same booming resonance in its reedy voice. *"Your seed does not yet lie fallow."*

The flames pulsed, as if daring the newcomer to try.

"Return to me!" the black figure hissed, spreading its arms.

But the conflagration didn't obey. Instead, it surged toward me, flames reaching its blistering arms forward.

Another figure, gray with streaming shadows about it, suddenly appeared between me and the great fire. It seemed the flames would consume it as well as me, but at the last moment, the fire surged to a halt.

"Return to me!" the black figure commanded again, voice stronger yet.

Caught between the figures of gray and black, the inferno gathered into itself. Then slowly, reluctantly, the great fire began to retreat. It flowed along itself toward the dark figure, then slithered inside it in glowing streams. The rivulets streamed over its arms like the retreating waves of the Lighted Sea over a rocky shore. The figure's pain washed over me, one wave after another, until the inferno was a glowing sphere inside its middle.

Then the shadowed figure turned its gaze upon me. *"You would doom us all,"* it said. Then it disappeared.

The gray figure, still floating before me, slowly turned around. I stared in mute wonder at its strangeness. She resembled a woman, but her features were so strangely disproportionate I knew she couldn't be human. Her eyes were angled sharply and opened wide, with irises black and silver. Her hair streamed about her head, silver against the gray of her body, moving as if they were a thousand tiny adders. Her robes hung in tatters, revealing gray skin beneath, and streamed in eleven long tails below her.

The strange woman drifted closer, then opened her hands. In one, I saw she held a sandglass, small and without a frame, little more than two glass bulbs fused together. Sand dripped down in it, the stream unnaturally slow to fall. Her other hand was empty.

This empty hand she extended toward me as she stopped before me. Her gesture was unmistakeable. I hesitated only a moment. She had saved me. She couldn't mean me harm.

I took her hand.

Suddenly, I was thrown swiftly down. The ground rushed toward me, closer and closer, then the blinding crush—

I sat up, gasping for air. Sweat beaded my skin, and a feverish heat radiated from me. All I could do was pant and let the memory of the dream stir in my mind. *A dream.* Surely that was all it had been.

I pulled the blankets off, needing my hot skin to be exposed to the cool air, when I heard a strange crackle. Something flaked beneath my fingers. For a moment, I stood statue-still; then I reached one shaking hand over to the pyrkin pot on my bedside table and lifted the lid. Yellow light flooded the room, revealing two black marks upon my blankets. My hand rested in one. The other, I was sure, was where my other hand had been lying.

I stared for a moment, breath caught in my throat. *Radiance* — the word echoed in my mind. I had channeled radiance.

Relief washed over me.

I should have worried that I might have burned down the room, and perhaps the whole Aviary. But the doubts that had gnawed at me for the last two days were finally dispelled. Shifts or not, I knew I was a warden.

I'd channeled radiance.

And I could have killed Nomusa. The thought chilled my excitement. If I couldn't control my channeling, how could I keep my friends safe? I clenched my fists around the ashy blankets, feeling the black flakes crumble against my palms. I had to learn to control this. I'd endangered my friends far too often already. How could I put them at risk from myself?

Then, out of nowhere, words crashed into my mind, splitting it wide open.

COME TO ME!

The thought burst in uninvited, chopping through me like an axe. Vaguely, I was aware of falling back against my bed, arms flailing out to either side, limp as a corpse. I felt the parts of myself scatter all around me, and it was beyond me to put them back together.

Fragmented, I sank into darkness.

CHAPTER SEVEN

THE GOOD PUPIL

Tyurn Sky-Sea listened to his daughter's words and knew them for wisdom.

'Very well,' he agreed with a heavy heart. 'If the fault is mine, the price is also mine to pay. Thank you, Daughter, most true to my heart.'

Clepsammia, the Hand of Destiny, said nothing, but only smiled a sad smile.

Tyurn Sky-Sea looked at the world below, the world he so loved, and made his decision. He would give of all his remaining strength to grant those he had failed the power to protect themselves.

From among humans, he chose eleven of the noblest, bravest, cleverest, and wisest. Foremost among these was Agmon who would become known as Brandheart, already a famed general in his own right.

To the eleven, the Ruler of All Realms said:

'I, Tyurn Sky-Sea, Lord of All that walks, swims, or soars, do admit to you, my lost children, that I have committed a grave sin. And so I will repay you with power only a god has before wielded, that you might defend yourselves against my error.'

And so he made these eleven humans the First Wardens, and the First Wardens awoke to their newborn divinity.

The Seeds of Famine, a translation from the Lighted-tongue; by Oracle Kalene of deme Hull; 881 SLP

P ain like nothing I'd felt before greeted me when I awoke. I gingerly touched my temples, opening my eyes to slits. Even that small amount of light evoked a fresh round of agony. My mother had sometimes complained of migraines as if there were no greater pain. Now I understood why.

Groaning, I forced myself to sit up. My stomach roiled, queasy and unsettled. For a moment, I thought I wouldn't hold down whatever remained of last night's dinner. I felt miserably sorry for myself as I put my legs off the side of the bed. Why today, of all days, did my mother have to be proven right?

Then the memory of last night rushed back in.

Come to me.

I would have sprang to my feet if I could have. As it was, I hunched against the misery and slowly began dressing. Somehow, I now recognized who had spoken the command. Even though I couldn't explain it, I had no doubt it was Eltris who had reached out to me. She'd summoned me to her.

And I'd fallen unconscious.

Strapping on my sandals, I wondered if it had been her that struck me unconscious, or the events that had come before. The dream had been strangely vivid. Could it have been more than a dream? Caught in its throes, I'd ignored all the strange aspects of the world. The city mirrored above... I'd imagined flying through the Pyrthae, I suddenly realized. But of Talan and the long flame with him, the dark figure that tamed the firestorm, the strange, gray woman who had protected me... It had to be nonsense made up by my imagination.

Unless I'd truly visited the Pyrthae again.

Madness. I pushed away the thought and slowly eased onto my feet. My aching head made my limbs shaky and weak, and every movement jarred. My neck felt so stiff it was difficult to turn it from side to side. I knew my hair was a mess, but I could only summon enough care to grab a cloth band to bind it back. My Verifier medallion hung heavy around my neck.

Just before I left my room, I noticed two things waiting for me on the floor by the door. Cursing how far away they were, I bent slowly to retrieve them. One was a knife half a cubit long, nestled into a plain leather sheath that was connected to a series of leather bands. The other was a folded piece of parchment. I picked them both up and opened the note.

Remember to report to our clerk Galene as to your expenses the day before and retrieve today's allowance. If she isn't waiting for you in the atrium, you can find her in the clerks' chambers off the Conclave.

Wear this knife always. It won't be comfortable, but it won't be in danger of slipping down.

Don't entrust yourself to a cartman. There have been reports of them delivering patricians and clerks of the law into the hands of brigands and Guilders. Your feet will carry you safer.

And who's sleeping late now?

~ Nomusa

Her reminder was timely; I'd completely forgotten about reporting to our clerk, though I'd noticed the distinct lack of silver among Nomusa's gifts. I tried reining in my impatience at the delay. Eltris had called me, and I'd already wasted a night in answering her. And now, it wasn't only about learning what I could of Famine. I glanced back at the twin sears on my blanket. Best to hide evidence of my channeling, as much as I could — the last thing I needed was Hyrol's suspicion, especially if he did turn out to be someone's agent.

After I'd stuffed the blanket under my bed, the best hiding spot I could manage until after dark, I followed Nomusa's advice and unbound my chiton to strap on the knife. Little good it would do me under my robe, I thought sourly. Once again, I yearned for a tunic and trousers, even if I didn't often walk about in them alone. *But why not?* I wondered. Wasn't the situation dire enough that I should do what was practical, not what was expected of me? Corin regularly wore such pedestrian clothes, after all.

And why stop there, I thought as my hair fell in my face for a third time. *Why not shear my hair short as well?* But in the end, once the knife was securely against my back, the leather rough against my skin, I tied my chiton on again and bound my unruly hair back in a tail. Appearances still mattered to an extent, at least to my mind. For now, I'd preserve them.

The headache still assaulted me as I descended the stairs through the finch tower, the birds' chirps a dozen needles stabbing repeatedly into my skull. But as I entered the atrium, I found my nausea easing and my habitual hunger returning so that I resolved to break my fast.

Then I saw someone waited for me. The woman was clearly a Conclave clerk, not only in dress but in manner. She'd seated herself in the middle of one of the long tables and spread out her work's materials around her. A small strongbox, a ledger neatly arranged, an inkwell and pen sitting at the ready. Her hands were folded before her and her eyes on me, as if she'd been doing nothing but waiting for me to descend.

"First Verifier Airene," the clerk said briskly. "Please be seated. We have the Aviary finances from the past day to discuss." She gestured to the chair opposite her.

"Galene, I presume?"

The woman gave a curt nod. "Of course. Now if you would, we can settle these accounts straightaway."

"I've only just risen. If you'll permit me a moment for my body's needs."

I couldn't keep the annoyance from my voice. Even if my head didn't feel as if smiths were busily pounding away at it, the woman's disregard for my time pulled at my frayed patience.

Her lips thinned. "Very well. I will be waiting."

I took my time. Once I'd returned from my morning necessities, I snuck back in through the kitchen and made a small meal of what Sizani had prepared. Bread, fruit, and cheese, my mainstay these past few days, continued to be what was served. Torn between haste and a petty desire to make the clerk wait, I let my disturbed stomach set the pace, then returned to the atrium.

Galane's narrowed eyes let me know the delay hadn't escaped her notice. "If you are ready," she said coldly.

I sat. "I am."

She straightened the ledger before her, though it had seemed straight to me before, then dipped her pen in the inkwell. "I believe, First Verifier, you were given an allowance of five silver scions yesterday. If you would tell me how much of it you spent and on what, we can soon be finished here."

"I didn't spend any of it."

She raised an eyebrow. "Then you have no need of an allowance today."

"No, I do. I don't have it anymore."

"I'm afraid I don't understand."

Though I'd been playing coy at first, now I found the truth hard to admit. "I was robbed. All of it was stolen on my way to the Acadium."

As she noted this in her ledger, Galene's expression plainly spoke her disbelief. "I see," she said as she finished the entry. "I would advise that you be more careful today."

I nodded regretfully. "It is a bad habit of mine, making friends with thieves."

She made no comment, but made another note in her ledger. Then, setting her pen neatly in its stand after dabbing the end with a cloth, she shifted to the strongbox and, turning a key in its lock, opened it. I heard the faint rustling of coins within as she moved it.

"Five silver scions, as is your allowance." She withdrew the coins and set them in a neat stack before me.

I took them. "Do you have a purse as well? I'm afraid mine was taken."

Galene stared at me as if I'd asked her for gold. "I do not carry purses with me, First Verifier. I am not a street peddler."

I found it hard not to roll my eyes. "I'll manage then. If that's all..." I rose to my feet more swiftly than was comfortable. The food had helped my aching head, but the world still tilted violently in my vision.

The clerk watched me. I wondered if she thought me sick from too much wine; I knew I must be displaying some of the signs. Perhaps that was what she thought I'd spent the coin on. "I will see you tomorrow, First Verifier Airene," she said, judgment plain in her voice.

I didn't acknowledge her as I left. With silver in hand, I had what I needed from her.

By the time I'd crossed the bridge and exited the Laurel grounds, my headache had eased, and I increased my pace. Even though a fair number of people wandered the streets, I remembered keenly my robbery from the day before. No need to be on Oedija's streets any longer than I had to. Keeping to the main roads, I managed to make it to the Acadium gates without any incidents, only stopping briefly at one of the few peddler's stands to buy a small purse. The woman's eyes went wide as I handed her a silver to change, and I wondered if she would have enough small coins to do it. But a minute later, I walked away with nickel, silver, and copper all softly clinking in my purse, tucked safely beneath the neck of my chiton.

Entering through the Acadium gates, I headed directly for Eltris's tower. Reaching it, I found no Acadian apprentice waiting today. I wondered why as I knocked loudly three times at her door.

There was no answer. I waited less than a minute before I tried again. "Eltris!" I called in. "Eltris, are you in there?"

When she still didn't answer, doubts finally surfaced. Maybe it hadn't been Eltris who had called me after all. Maybe someone had tricked me. Or maybe, still caught in the midst of my strange dreams, I'd imagined it.

I rubbed my eyes, temporarily relieving the pressure building in my skull, then stared up the tower. Was she even here? Perhaps she was up on the second floor and couldn't hear my calls. For a moment, I had the mad idea to climb the tower and enter through a window. Instead, I sighed and turned away. If Eltris was there, she wasn't ready to talk. And I had too many other things to do to wait around.

I'd taken only a few steps away when I heard the creak of the door opening behind me. I whirled to see a scowling woman standing in the tower doorway, curly gray hair springing from her head, a frumpy brown robe hanging from her stout, short frame.

"Eltris," I greeted her, trying to hide my surprise. "So you are here."

The Master Augur wasn't as polite. "So you finally decided to come."

"Finally?" My mind spun as I reconciled her words. "Your call — I didn't imagine it?"

"No, you didn't. And I waited all night for you to figure that out."

My shock was quickly giving way to irritation. "You could have sent a finch, like any ordinary person, instead of… whatever you did."

The augur stared at me, her yellow eyes piercing. "No, I couldn't. Not with the danger you were putting us all in."

Before I could ask what she meant, she turned back into her tower. Only the open door gave me any indication to follow.

Apprehensive but too curious to turn away, I entered the dim tower. From the little light, the entry room was as much a disaster as before, like a rat's nest built up over decades. Eltris already limped up the stairs, so I didn't linger, but followed her to the second floor.

Though the boarded windows blocked out the daylight, smokeless braziers filled the room with an intense light. Above, finches sang and flitted among the rafters. A worn rug extended across the stone of the tower floor.

As I looked around, Eltris walked to the opposite side of the room, then turned to face me. "Now," she said without preamble, "channel."

I blinked. "What?"

The Master Augur glared at me, her hands twitching at her sides. "You're a warden now, if you hadn't figured it out. And new wardens are dangerous — as you reminded me last night. So I must teach you to channel. Now—" She gestured impatiently. "—go on!"

"Master Eltris, what do you mean about last night? Was I… was that channeling?"

"Yes. Unguided, unwise, and dangerous channeling, for you and the rest of us. So, though I have much else to do, I will at least show you enough not to get us killed."

"But why was it so dangerous?" I insisted. "Was I in the Pyrthae?"

Eltris stared at me with disgust. "Can you not even recognize that? Then you also must not know who almost claimed you."

A horrible suspicion arose in me at her words. Suddenly, the vast sphere of fire and the shadow within it made all too much sense. "Famine found me. He was going to consume me, burn me away to nothing." I tried to remember the fuzzy details. "But the shadow that commanded him — that was Vusu, wasn't it? He stopped Famine from attacking me."

The augur sniffed. "You're not entirely devoid of intelligence, then."

My questions were insistent enough to ignore the gibe. "But why? Why would he do that? I thought he'd want to kill me after I put a quarrel in his side."

"You're the Finch," Eltris said, lips curling. "You should tell me. Now, if you're done wasting my time with your suspicions, show me how much you can channel."

I knew better than to push my luck, even if the questions still needled me. And, if I were honest, a large part of me yearned to know what Eltris could teach me.

But I could only shake my head. "That's the problem. I don't know how."

She snorted. "Of course you know how. If you're a warden, you can channel."

"But it just happened on its own the first time. I felt my locus opening up and then—"

"Don't use such words," Eltris cut me off. "Not until you know what you are talking about. Tell me of the sensations and where you felt them when you channeled."

I tried to remember. "It felt like an area in the middle of my stomach opened up. Not like a hole exactly; more like a molten stream pressed in and through me into the rest of my body, that I couldn't help but release."

She nodded sharply. "And before that?"

I closed my eyes and put myself back in the moment. "I grew hot, feverish. It made me sweat and itch. I didn't think much of it at the time, though, as I was distracted."

"Distracted?"

I hesitated, then cracked my eyes open and replied honestly. "Someone was trying to kill me."

The augur stared hard at me for a long moment. Then, "Anything else?"

Only Eltris wouldn't question attempted murder. "No," I said with a touch of amusement. "Nothing else that I remember."

"Very well. We must make you hot again then." The augur suddenly raised her hands toward me. A moment later, heat like I'd never felt before pressed in around me. I gasped at the sudden change in temperature and staggered. It was hotter than anything I remembered, hotter than any steam room or sunny summer day. Only the day I'd channeled had been hotter. My headache, which had been fading, filled my head to bursting.

But I knew what Eltris was trying to do. Fighting through the discomfort, I willed myself to open to the fire and force that had poured from me before. As heat washed over me, I pushed away images of my skin blackening and my eyes drying in my skull and tried to channel radiance.

Nothing came.

"It's not working!" I cried out. "How do I make it work?"

As abruptly as the heat had inundated me, it ceased. I gasped as cool air rushed back against my skin and clutched my arms around me, shivering.

"As I suspected," Eltris said calmly. "You're not fully attuned to the Pyrthae."

"Not fully attuned?" I asked through chattering teeth, a pit forming in my gut.

"Oh, you are a warden, there's no doubt to that. But when first attuned, the locus is not yet developed, and thus won't open on command. Only through repeated accidental channeling does the locus form enough to be controlled."

My worry eased, but only slightly. "So all those accidents — the fire, the dreaming. All of that has to happen again before I can control this? But what if I—?"

"I'm not finished!" Eltris interrupted. "If I'm to train you, you must be silent when I speak. All my pupils have called me 'master' during training, and I don't intend for our relationship to be any different."

I swallowed down the bitter draught, as I knew I had to. "Yes, master."

"Good. Yes, more accidents will happen before you achieve control. But there are some things you can do to limit the damage. Most important will be to practice the exercises I'm about to show you, as they will help give you some measure of control over your channeling when it does come over you." Eltris gestured impatiently. "When you're ready…"

Sweat still coated my skin, chills wracked my body, and my headache pounded inside my skull. But I couldn't waste time with weakness. "I'm ready."

We began with me lying down and breathing through my belly, then tightening my gut. This, Eltris said, was to increase awareness and control over the area where the locus formed. Through controlling the locus, I could begin to channel at will, or stop channeling. She continued to instruct me in building awareness in my arms and hands, then legs and feet, as I would need command over every part of my body to gain complete control.

We kept at it until the Acadium bell tolled, signaling just under a turn had come and gone since I'd arrived. Eltris nodded and bade me to rise.

"Practice this as you lie down to sleep each night. Build awareness throughout your body. Over time, you will learn restraint, and it may prevent the worst of the accidents. So long as they don't come on too strongly."

I wished she'd left the last part unsaid. "Thank you, master."

"But these exercises won't prevent what you did last night. How did the dream come upon you? What were you thinking about?"

I couldn't prevent a flush rising up my neck. "Nothing, really. I was just thinking about… a friend. About how it would be nice to see them."

"Don't think of the Pyrthae. Don't think of channeling. Don't think of daemons or Famine or Vusu. And in particular, don't think about myste-rious men."

I stared at the batty old woman, thinking I must have misheard her. But though her mouth was still set in a frown, the corners of it twitched.

Fully blushing now, I said quickly, "I'll try. But I don't know that I can control what I think before I sleep. My mind drifts as I relax."

"Then don't relax," Eltris retorted, all traces of humor gone. "If you must think of anything at all, think of mundane things. But if you are to be safe, you must clear your mind completely. If your mind is a blank slate when you sleep, it will not stray into dangerous waters. Now sit, legs crossed, back straight. You will practice clearing your mind."

Whereas the awareness exercises had been relaxing, clearing my mind proved aggravating. I'd never noticed how many thoughts drifted through until I tried keeping them all out. My frustration mounted as, time and again, I could maintain no more than a few seconds of complete blankness. If I couldn't manage to clear my mind now, I held little hope I'd be able to do so in the darkness of my room, when my fears and worries had an easy time worming their way in.

"It isn't possible." I opened my eyes and looked up at Eltris, who stood over me.

The augur scowled. "Not for the feeble-minded. But you must do it. I've warned you what will happen otherwise."

"But I don't understand how dreaming can lead me into the Pyrthae. Is…?" I hesitated to ask the question, anticipating the augur's chastisement, but there was no help for it. "Is it quintessence I'm channeling?"

Rather than chastising, Eltris scrutinized me for a long moment. "Quintessence, you call it," she muttered. "A suitable name, I suppose."

"What is it exactly? Xaron seemed to think it was the mind, or perhaps the soul."

"No one knows for certain."

I waited for her to explain. I wanted to stand, but was afraid the movement would prevent whatever explanation was forthcoming.

She looked away from me, craning her head back to peer at the finches flitting above. "Quintessence is the rarest and most precious of the Pyrthaen elements. It does not work in the same way as the others. While the abundant energies like radiance, kinesis, and magnesis exist as the fundamental components of the Pyrthae — like water, earth, and air in our plane — quintessence is congregated into entities and seems to be an animating force. In sufficient quantities, it enables control over the other energetic elements."

I opened my mouth to ask the dozen questions racing through my mind, but Eltris continued before I could speak.

"Just as the elements reside within your body, so does quintessence. Perhaps it is what makes us conscious and aware, the substance of our mind. Or perhaps it is, as many of the religions would tell us, our immortal souls." Eltris's lips curled, showing what she thought of the idea. "Whatever it may be, it is the element that enables us to channel — the conduit by which we control the flow of energy, the hammer by which we forge it."

She stopped and stared down at me, seeming to expect an answer.

I nodded hesitantly. "I think I understand. But I don't get how this connects to me dreaming my way into the Pyrthae."

For once, she didn't mock me, but nodded. "Quintessence isn't just used for forming the other elements. As an energetic element itself, it can also be channeled."

Confusion turned my thoughts upside down. "But if quintessence is what our minds are made of, how can we channel it? Wouldn't it mean there is… less of us? That we're giving a part of ourselves away?"

"I say 'channeling,' but it is more like the use of a tool than the flow of energy. Instead of expelling something like fire or force, you use the hammer itself for whatever your ends might be."

"And one of those uses is entering the Pyrthae."

"Yes. Among many others."

"Like passing messages between minds?" I guessed. "Or seeing traces of channeling after the fact?"

She narrowed her eyes, the calm teacher dissipating. "Perhaps. But those don't concern you. For you shouldn't channel quintessence at all."

I raised an eyebrow. "And why's that?"

As she looked up again at the rafters, I could tell her patience was reaching an end. But she almost managed to keep her voice even as she explained, "Channeling quintessence draws dangers that using the other elements does not. When a warden channels magnesis, for example, they draw the energy into our world from the Pyrthae. No part of them leaves Telae, our realm — they are simply allowing Pyrthaen elements in. But when a warden channels quintessence, a part of them enters the Pyrthae. Only by doing so can our minds escape the confines of our bodies." Her gaze returned to me, sharpening. "As you did last night."

I nodded, the thought making my skin clammy and chilled. "I think I understand. When I entered the Pyrthae, Famine could find me."

Eltris eyed me shrewdly. "As I said, quintessence is the most precious of the elements, and the more you possess, the more power you wield. And it is also what Famine has an insatiable appetite for."

Cold, sharp and sudden as the kiss of the monsoon winds, bit through me. "So that's what he wants. Quintessence."

"Yes. Famine, as all the Quintyr, is oriented toward one aim. His particular obsession is the consumption of quintessence."

"But if it's quintessence he's after, why does he destroy everything in his path?"

Again, that considering look came into Eltris's eyes. I was drawing close to her limit, I knew. But I hadn't reached it yet. "In the Pyrthae, quintessence is rare. But here in Telae, everything alive possesses quintessence. Grass, trees, birds, fish — and in the greatest measure, humans."

I felt so faint I was sure I'd have collapsed if I were standing. "So that's why he wants to return to our world. To Telae."

She wore a bitter smile. "Finally, you understand. And you know why it's so important that you don't stray into the Pyrthae."

The augur turned and walked toward the stairs. Unwilling, I rose, stretched out my stiff limbs, and followed behind. There were so many more questions I had, so many she might be able to answer. But one nagged more insistently than the rest.

I decided to push my luck. "Master, if I could ask one more thing. I understand why it's dangerous for me to channel quintessence. But you said I endanger everyone by doing so."

Eltris didn't turn until she stood by the top of the stairs. I stopped just before them facing her. But I saw from her stiffened jaw and creased brow that I was to be disappointed.

"Practice your exercises and refrain from channeling quintessence," she said shortly. "That's all you need concern yourself with. Now, leave me to my work. I'll follow up with you when I have the time."

I knew I was treading dangerous waters now. But I couldn't leave it there. "Three days. I'll call again in three days, and we can make time then. Master."

Anger flashed in her eyes. For a moment, I thought she'd refuse simply out of spite. "Five," she finally said. "Five days. The second turn after noon."

It was much further away than I'd hoped for. But any promise of her spilling more of her secrets was better than nothing. To say nothing of exploring more of my new magic.

"Fine." I gave her a small bow and turned down the stairs, feeling her gaze follow me into the gloom.

CHAPTER EIGHT

ALLEY WHISPERS

The Seed, even ripped from its source, had gained enough power to assume its own form. Rootless, it roamed the skies, brooding.

'If famine I bring,' it thought, 'then Famine I will be named.'

The daemon Famine thought long and hard as he flew, and finally saw the sacrifice of Tyurn Sky-Sea spelling his own destruction. Though he had not been able to prevent it, he suspected he might be able to use the gift to his advantage.

So Famine sowed seeds of his own among those Tyurn sought to protect, poisoning them and hoping to turn them to his own purposes.

— The Seeds of Famine, a translation from the Lighted-tongue, by Oracle Kalene of deme Hull, 881 SLP

A somber mood claimed me as I set foot again on the cobblestones of the Acadium's main street. Though I'd finally spoken with Eltris and learned more than I thought the batty old woman would ever let on, the knowledge hadn't heartened me. In some ways, knowing Famine's motivations didn't change anything. I'd always known he desired an end to our world. But to know he'd grow more powerful with each soul he consumed brought a creeping chill to my skin, as if a sudden shadow had fallen on me on a sunny day.

And as I thought on it further, I realized I had more questions than ever before. If Eltris was correct about my dream — and I sensed she was — Vusu and the strange woman had stopped Famine from consuming me. And after the trial, the Master Augur had said he'd bound the daemon god to him. The little I knew didn't add up. What was Vusu's hold on Famine? Something allowed him to yoke and harness the power of the god. Perhaps that only went to show that Famine wasn't a god; he was a Quintyr, as Eltris had insisted, though I scarcely knew what that meant.

Most pressing of my questions, however, was why Famine hadn't broken through to Telae, and when and how he would. For I had no doubt he would eventually. He had come many times before, if Eltris had spoken true. And the Master Augur had said after the trial that Vusu wouldn't be able to hold him back for long. I had assumed Famine was returning as soon as I laid eyes on him in the Pyrthae. Now, I felt the trickle of sand counting down each moment until he did.

My headache pounded anew, and my body had grown sore. I wanted to curl up on the ground and sleep. But I kept walking. Even if I could have slept, even if I wouldn't have been afraid of falling into the Pyrthae, I still had work to do, and no time to put it off.

I made for the Acadium exit, forgoing both Tomes and my brother. My head already felt crammed full with what I'd learned from Eltris, and I knew I wouldn't have the focus or attention to decipher the old texts. As for Linos… I could do nothing for him. Until I knew how to rid him of the daemon that claimed him, it would do little good for me to rouse it. Eltris might know how. But I knew my hopes were better entrusted to Talan.

One thing heartened me at least. Though I hadn't channeled or even come close to it, I clutched fiercely to the hope the augur had instilled in me. I would channel, and I would learn to control it. I had no other choice. And from the buoyant elation that filled me, I knew I'd have it no other way.

Exiting the Acadium gates, any lingering excitement quickly dissipated. I was headed for Port and had to cross Iris to get there. What might have been a nostalgic walk back to my decade-long home presently had me looking over my shoulder and checking every passing alley. But dangerous though my path might be, I knew I couldn't put it off any longer. It had been too long since I'd acted the proper Finch.

The day was overcast, and the close press of buildings left many back streets poorly illuminated. Even here in Iris, filthy men watched my progress from shadowed alleys. My hand twitched, ready to seize my hidden dagger, for all the good it might do me. I kept to the main roads and hoped my luck would hold out.

For this journey at least, it did. As I turned a corner, the homey, wooden sign of Zipho's emerged in front of her cafe. A smile found my lips. It had been too long since I'd seen the matronly cafe owner. I doubted even Nomusa had the time to make it out here. Hopefully, the troubles that had seen the rest of the city had left her store untouched.

But as I entered within, I found it was a vain hope. Less than half of her usual clientele was present, and those who were looked up suspiciously as I entered. I averted my gaze and approached the counter.

"Airene!" Zipho came bustling into view from the other side of the tree that grew through the middle of the shop. "Where have you been? And Nomusa — that *fanla* has not been by in half a span! Now is no time to take a break." She gave me a reproachful look before coming around the counter to pull me into a big hug.

I returned it with a startled grin. "Sorry, Zipho," I said as I extricated myself. "We've been busy."

"Sit. I will brew you a cup of coffee thick as mud, just the way you like it, and you will tell me what has happened."

I did as she instructed, knowing there was no way around it. Besides, it felt good to sit, and even better when she brought me a steaming cup of coffee. I took the clay mug in hand and breathed it in. Scents of chocolate and licorice filled my nose. Almost from the first sip my incessant headache began to recede.

Zipho settled down in the chair opposite of me. "Now. What have you to say for your absence?"

I debated how much of the truth to reveal, then told her as much as I thought she'd believe. I spoke of Vusu's betrayal, and Myron's abduction, and Asileia's relative innocence. But of Famine, and my visit to the Pyrthae, I said nothing. Nothing, too, did I mention of the Preservists and the Valemish plotting with Avvad. I had little more evidence than suspicions and couldn't see how sowing discontent among Oedija's population would help us now.

Zipho nodded along for much of it, clearly having heard some of these things as rumors. But at the mention of Vusu, she muttered, "If that man shows up here..." But she let the threat hang unfinished. We both knew how empty it was.

I drank down the last of my coffee and stood, slipping a coin from my purse and sliding it subtly under my mug. I knew she wouldn't take my coin outright, and as no other customer had come in during our chat, I suspected she'd soon need it.

"Thank you, Zipho," I said. "That was just what I needed."

The matronly woman rose as well. "You are welcome anytime. But make sure you send Nomusa my way!" She continued in a lower voice. "Just because she's a queen doesn't mean she can ignore a lowly cafe owner."

I smiled and turned out of the cafe. My smile grew wider when I heard Zipho's astonished call as she discovered the silver coin I'd left for her.

Even the thought that I'd have to report it to that abysmal clerk Galene didn't dim my pleasure.

The gentle drizzle that had begun outside, however, did dampen my mood. I shivered and resolved to sort out clothes or a cloak from a seamstress. The monsoons would arrive in full all too soon.

I didn't go far from the cafe, but turned into the alley next to it. Before, the alley had been empty of Oedija's vagrants, as the ground here tended to grow muddy during the monsoons. But now, no fewer than five figures huddled down against the light rain, pulling ragged garments around themselves. I stood at the entrance to the alley, squinting at the faces of the vagrants to see if I recognized any of them.

"I wondered when you would come."

I spun around to see a slight woman with her features hidden under a hood leaning against the wall next to me. How she'd managed to come up silently behind me with her limp, I didn't know.

"Hello, Wisp," I greeted her.

Wisp didn't respond, but turned away. It was no more than I'd come to expect from her. My primary informant for over a year now, she had quickly managed to gather a network of informants so extensive and reliable that the rumors she passed along were as good as fact. Yet that knowledge came with a price; a price, I hoped, that wouldn't be inflated by the uncertain times.

"We shall go somewhere more private," Wisp said over her shoulder as she began to walk away.

I followed as she led us to an alley so narrow I doubted I could enter without my shoulders brushing either wall. I eyed it skeptically, but Wisp, narrower of stature than me, easily slid in. Once again, I followed, though grudgingly. Like most of the backways around Oedija, the alley smelled of piss, and it reeked all the worse for the cramped quarters.

Wisp turned back halfway down. "You will watch my back and I yours," she said flatly. "Now. What do you wish to know?"

I kept my eyes behind her. "All that you know. It's been long since we last saw each other."

"Yes. But I suspect there is much you could tell me that I don't know." She cocked her head. "Perhaps we can lower your price for a bit of information of your own."

"Perhaps." I wondered uneasily what knowledge she wished to know. My fingers were suddenly uncomfortably hot and itchy. I distracted myself by slipping out fifteen magnes and holding them out, palm down. "Why don't you start?"

She accepted the coins and secreted them away. "What first?"

"The Manifest."

Wisp flashed a rare smile, as if she'd been expecting the request. "Of them, I hear rumors and shadows. But there are some few facts I can share."

She told me of the Seekers' activities, which were much the same as before, if more detailed than Nomusa provided — of building more permanent housing, and training the common folk for war, and the beginnings of cultivation, despite it being late in the season and with droughts in the fields all around Oedija.

Then she touched on more pertinent things, like how the Seeker wardens displayed themselves openly, with violet tatu inked along their exposed arms and around their eyes, similar to how Vusu himself appeared. They seemed to have taken leadership positions among the Seekers, commanding them in martial and domestic affairs alike. I wondered how such a structure would fare. Wardens were no better leaders than any other person, and some would no doubt prove to be poor at the role. The inefficiency such a hierarchy would produce, as well as perhaps the resentment among the populace, might work to our advantage. Even so, I acknowledged it was a thin hope. There would have to be significant internal strife for it to be of use.

Making the Seeker compound even stranger were the demographics joining it. Even more than commonfolk, honors left their ancestral positions to join the movement. It was hardly surprising considering how many were treated little better than slaves, and some a good deal worse. Yet I wondered why, after a thousand years, honors chose now to cast off their societal chains. Perhaps they sensed the weakening state of the realm. Or perhaps Ariston the Dishonored was the spark to set their desire for freedom ablaze. I tucked the information away for later consideration.

"Of their leader," Wisp continued with a gleam in her shadowed eyes, "all I know is what he is not. He is not among the common followers of the Manifest. He is not seen by anyone but the Seeker wardens, Ariston the Dishonored, and his personal honor, Seda. By their movements, it is rumored he remains entrenched in a room deep in the Wyvern's Claw."

A grim smile forced its way onto my lips. I was not proud of the vindictive satisfaction I felt at the likelihood that Vusu lay suffering, but neither could I deny it. From Wisp's sly look, I thought she knew, or at least suspected, my part in his current condition.

I changed the topic to ask of the Valemish next, but found the rumors were less satisfying. There were movements among the temples and between them, but nothing suspicious beyond that. What might be hidden on the people who traveled between the temples, Wisp couldn't tell me. Only when she hesitated and glanced behind her did my interest pique.

"You've heard rumors," I guessed.

Wisp nodded reluctantly. "I do not like telling anything but fact."

"I won't tell anyone if you don't."

I caught a dubious glance from beneath her hood before she lowered her eyes. "Those who sleep the streets speak of disappearances. Of phantoms in the night who come to claim victims. Of corpses left behind, stripped of their skin and souls."

It sounded ridiculous, but I knew better than to laugh. I'd heard Talan speak of such things before. *Ikoz*, he'd called them in the ash-tongue — Silks, in the sea-tongue. Pyr bound to the will of the Avvadin Imperium, they were so named for the bands of shimmering cloth wrapped around their invisible, ethereal bodies that chained them to service.

As if Oedija needed another danger on her streets.

"Thank you, Wisp," I said, glancing over my shoulder before pulling out my purse. "If you hear anything more, tell me first. I'll make it worth your while." I slipped out two scions and held them out.

With a gleam in her eye, the informant snatched the coins from my hand and turned to walk abruptly down the alley.

But as she limped away, a farfetched idea suddenly occurred to me. "Wisp. One other thing."

She halted with a lurch and half-turned back, head cocked to one side.

I could scarcely believe what I was about to say. But I had to do my part for the Order, if only for Nomusa's sake. "Wisp, I'm now First Verifier to the new Order of Verifiers. I'm sure you already know this."

She gave a curt nod.

"As First Verifier, I'm obligated to recruit others to our cause, those whom I deem competent and dependable. We're seeking how the Manifest came to form, and how former Tribune Vusumuzi was able to finance his movement—"

"No." Wisp turned away and continued her dogged walk down the alley.

A reluctant smile pulled at my lips. It was no more brusque than I'd expected.

"I'll take that as you'll consider it!" I called after her before turning the other way.

As I walked back north, I mulled over Wisp's news. But try as I might, I couldn't put the pieces before me into a pattern. They seemed just a collection of whispers and facts, movements of people and spirits and countries all outside of my control. I could tell the Council what I'd heard, of Silks rumored to be on the streets, but with the Preservist faction's stranglehold on the Demos Council, no good could come of it.

Even less could be done of the movement of honors into Thys. Or, if action was taken, it wouldn't be anything I'd want to be part of. I couldn't condone locking up honors as if they were Avvadin slaves, nor disciplining them with the whip as the imperials to the south were said to.

And of Seeker wardens openly displaying themselves, even that flagrant display of magic could bring no response. Several Shepherds had died during Asileia's trial, while others had joined with Vusu. Only a handful were left in Tribunal control from how Nomusa told it. The Acadians training to fight were not officially condoned and were probably still fledging in their abilities. Even witnessing Isidora's display when fighting the Shepherds, I found it hard to believe many Acadians capable of martial ability. I hoped I'd be proven wrong.

I sighed. Once again, all I learned led me nowhere. And yet I could do nothing but seek to gather more scraps in the hopes they eventually might amount to something.

Despite my promise to Nomusa, I didn't call on patricians, but returned to the Acadium to seek out the library. There, three ancient texts awaited me. For all the good reading them would do me.

The same guards who had greeted me that morning eyed me skeptically as I re-entered, but I ignored them. They'd grow used to seeing me soon enough.

As before, the pupil Platon eagerly accompanied me down into Tomes. With my wits fully about me this visit, I firmly issued him away to read in peace. Only after he'd repeated the Master Librarian's rules three times did I convince him to retreat to the other end of the shelves, where he paced and talked to himself. After a time, I was able to shut out his murmurs and muddle through the ancient words in the first book I'd selected, *The Seeds of Famine.*

What I learned both fascinated and perplexed me. According to the old book, Famine had first come from "the Lower Realm," some part of what I assumed was the Pyrthae, then tricked the Eidolan god Tyurn Sky-Sea into giving it his power. Only when Clepsammia, Goddess of Fate and Tyurn's daughter, showed her father the truth did Tyurn free himself of Famine's influence, then die giving birth to the First Wardens. Only once he was free did Famine come to know himself. And once he did, he set out to poison Tyurn's Gift.

I leaned back and rubbed at my sore neck. How much of it was truth, and how much fancy? On the one hand, the original composition was soon after the Lighted Passage. But that didn't mean it was soon after the events inscribed. Famine I'd seen with my own eyes and knew him to be real. But the Eidolan gods — were they supposed to be real as well? Of them, only Tyurn was said to have died in the Famine War. So if they existed, where had they hid for over a thousand years?

But some of them had to still exist. After all, wardens were supposedly attuned to the Pyrthae by the gods. And unless my own attunement was a strange accident, a god had done so for me. So perhaps the Eidola were not completely myth, as I'd always supposed.

As I pored over the words, Platon came over begging to return upstairs. I was happy to oblige, particularly as, from the way he danced, I suspected he needed to relieve himself. Besides, my headache had returned, and my eyes felt gritty from staring at the cramped words for so long.

"How long has it been?" I asked as I returned the book to its cubby.

"It must have been three turns at least! You stared at that book for forever! Begging your pardon, mistress."

Consulting the sandglass mounted next to the library entrance, I found the pupil had overestimated; only two turns had passed. Still, I'd read enough. Evening was quickly approaching, and I had to return to the Aviary before night fell. Besides, if I was being honest, part of me was eager to practice Eltris's exercises and make another attempt at channeling. Despite what she'd cautioned, I figured it'd come sooner or later. Better to channel when I intended to than when I didn't — or so I told myself.

I waved goodbye to Platon as he bolted for a chamberpot. On the library steps, I briefly considered visiting Ward before turning toward the Acadium gates. I'd be returning here everyday, most likely. There'd be other opportunities to visit Linos. But I couldn't completely fool myself as to my reasons for avoiding it as I walked quickly toward the exit.

It was shorter to take the back ways to the Laurel Palace so I could cross the bridge back over to Conclave grounds, and for a moment, I was tempted. But remembering my robbery, any desire for a shortcut immediately dissipated. I strode along the main road, looking to either side. The few people still on the streets looked as suspicious of me as I was of them.

It wasn't long before I heard them.

They swept onto the street behind me like a flood, thrusting torches and clubs into the air and screaming like daemon-masked, drunken revelers at the Carnival of Veils. So suddenly they filled the street with noise that I couldn't believe they were truly there for a moment. As they passed, they overturned the few carts and stands left on the stones, tore down hangings and signs before shops, and banged against the boarded-up windows.

I didn't have to see much to know I'd stumbled in the way of a dusk mob.

Anywhere seemed safer than before that angry mass of humanity, so despite my earlier reservations, I fled into the closest alley. I shared it with nearly a dozen others, all of whom seemed set to squat there for the night.

"Never seen a dusk mob?" one bent woman mocked me from the base of the alley wall. She spat at my feet.

Heart hammering against my ribs, I ignored her and watched the passing crowd. They looked dirty and poor for the most part, and predominantly male. But what unified them most was the rage painted on their faces. I cringed back from it. Their fury seemed almost palpable to me, a noxious air suffocating me as they passed. The only other time I had felt such a depth of hate had been before Famine himself.

Enthralled by the dusk mob, I startled when someone grabbed my arm.

Fear and fury coursing through me, I turned and lashed out, striking my captor with quick blows to the nose then the leg. I didn't even look at his face until after he'd cursed and sprang back, one hand to his face. I didn't recognize his features, shadowed as they were under a hood.

Not caring about propriety, I hauled up my chiton and ripped free the knife Nomusa had given me, then held it before me in what I hoped was a menacing manner. My lips pulled back in a snarl.

"Stay away from me!" I hissed.

The man glowered at me. Blood trickled between the fingers of the hand held to his nose, while the other had disappeared inside his coat. "They didn't mention you were a feral minx," he snarled, his voice turned nasal.

"They?" I demanded.

A blue glow emanated out from the sleeve of his upraised arm. My blood went cold. I didn't need to see the full tatu to know it was an unblinking eye. The mark of the Underguild.

"Tyurn's balls," I said faintly.

The man leered at me. "Now you understand. Be glad the Undermaster wishes to extend you an offer, or I would cut you down where you stand."

The Undermaster — Kalindi, I suspected it referred to, from what Talan had told me. It seemed the Underguild's usurper had taken on a new title.

I glanced at the vagrants who shared the alley with us, but they were backing away, fear plain on their faces. Looking back at the Guilder, I didn't lower the knife.

"Go ahead," I said. "Tell me Kalindi's offer."

The man's eyes narrowed. "The *Undermaster*," he said with emphasis, "knows of your association with the traitor Talan Wraithsbane. He doesn't hold this against you. But he does ask one thing in return for his forgiveness."

It took an effort to hide my sneer. "And what's that?"

"It's simple, really. Tell us where he is."

I almost laughed. Strange as how our friendship had developed, my loyalty to Talan was as strong as to Xaron, Nomusa, and my family. There was no chance that I'd confess his location even if I'd known it. But flat refusal could bring the ire of the Underguild down on me, and at a time when I needed to move about the city freely. I had to proceed cautiously.

"What will you do with him if I tell you?"

The Guilder grinned, revealing a bit of blood that had seeped between his yellowed teeth. "Show him a traitor's punishment."

Cutting off the offender's hands was the traditional reprimand for the Underguild, but I suspected Kalindi wouldn't stop there. I wondered what Talan had done to warrant the threat.

"I'll consider it," I said finally, reviling the necessary lie.

"Don't take long. The Undermaster is not a patient man. And you wouldn't want to give him a reason to show his displeasure."

With one final leer, the Guilder turned down the alley and disappeared.

The vagrants who had been with us had all melted away, leaving me alone in the alley. On the main street, the dusk mob had passed on to cause destruction elsewhere. I heaved a sigh of relief at the near escape.

But I wasn't safe yet. Cautiously taking to the street again, I kept my knife out as I ran to the Laurel Palace gates.

CHAPTER NINE

EYES IN THE NIGHT

Agmon Brandheart, Foremost of the First Wardens, quickly arose as the leader. A commander and a soldier, he embraced Tyurn's Gift and gathered the other wardens of humanity scattered across Telae to his side. Boldly, they went out to meet their enemy.

Famine had gathered legions of his own to his banner, both human and daemon, for many longed for the power he promised. Many more filled the daemon god's war tents than Agmon Brandheart had managed to marshal.

Even still, they met on the battlefield. Wearing the form of a great scaled beast, Famine flew over the armies, and wherever the daemon-god went, no warden could stand before him.

Agmon Brandheart, most noble of humanity, called a challenge to Famine. But the daemon only laughed and continued his slaughter elsewhere. And no matter how Agmon challenged him, Famine would not face him.

- The Seeds of Famine, a translation from the Lighted-tongue; by Oracle Kalene of deme Hull; 881 SLP

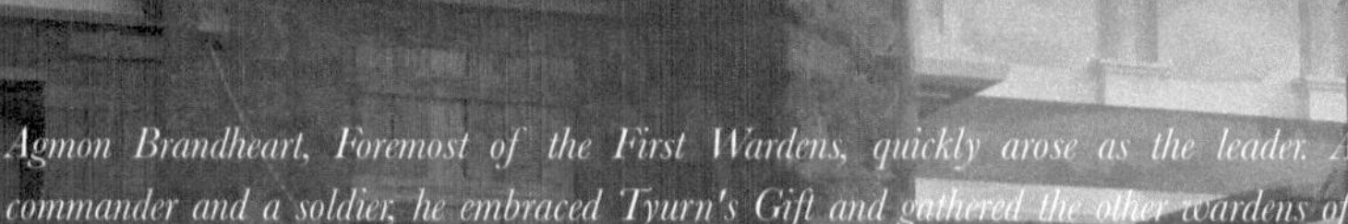

Sleep took a long while to come.

Foremost on my mind was the Guilder's threat. I worried less about myself than Talan, though I knew the threat meant he was thus far safe. Still, how long would he remain that way with Kalindi bent on revenge and the reach of the Underguild at his disposal?

But even that threat felt almost insignificant when I contemplated the one rising, hidden, for all of us. Famine sought to break into our world, into Telae. And Eltris believed he would do so when Vusu's control inevitably slipped. I wondered if I'd done the right thing now, putting a quarrel in his side. Yet how could I have done any less? Unchecked, Vusu would destroy Oedija just as surely as Famine.

But there remained Eltris's belief that Vusu somehow held Famine in check. How a man, even a powerful warden, could leash a god defied my comprehension.

But I couldn't think about any of that. Not Famine, not Vusu, and especially not Talan. Though I didn't know what danger I posed to the city by straying into the Pyrthae, it was warning enough for me to try not to dream.

But not enough to stop from trying to channel.

I pushed the worries from my mind and set into Eltris's exercises. My body gathered a warm energy as I rolled my awareness through every limb and digit, even to the thin skin of my scalp, imagining my focus like a ball of light wherever it traveled. But the warmth was not the thrumming heat of radiance, and when I tried to open myself to the Pyrthae, my locus remained stubbornly closed.

I sighed and set into the mental exercises, trying to clear my mind of my lingering worries. But no matter how I insisted on emptiness, thoughts clung to me like barnacles to a ship's hull. If Talan was safe from Kalindi's henchmen. If I dared Oedija's streets again when riots and thieves ruled them by day and Guilders, Seekers, and Silks haunted them by night. If the stubborn old Master Augur would ever tell me everything I needed to know to stop Vusu and Famine. If we had a prayer of a chance of stopping the daemon god at all.

Sometime in the midst of my worries, I was carried into an uneasy oblivion.

I blinked my eyes open to daylight, surprised I'd fallen asleep. It felt as though I'd just lain down. No dreams of soaring through the Pyrthae greeted me, nor glimpses of Talan as a flame or otherwise. Perhaps the augur's exercises had worked. Even knowing it was for the best, I couldn't help but feel disappointed.

Rising, I looked in my wardrobe and found, to my pleasant surprise, that Hyrol had found the note I'd left for him and had supplied me a full closet of chitons, trousers, and tunics, as well as an oil-treated cloak. I didn't hesitate in grabbing a pair of tunic and trousers and, after securing my knife, I put them on.

But when reaching for a chiton to pull over them, I paused. Seeker wardens, Guilders, and Silks haunted Oedija's streets, to say nothing of the common cutthroats and cutpurses. If I was to wander the city by myself, I had to give myself the best chance to run.

Tightening my jaw, I took only the cloak and closed the wardrobe.

Walking downstairs, I entered the atrium and found my days were gathering a pattern. Galene the clerk waited to take my account once more.

"First Verifier," she greeted me as she cast a disdainful glance at my clothes.

"Galene," I said pleasantly. "You look as well as could be expected."

After exchanging several more biting sentences, I dispensed of her with flippant haste, then set off for the Laurel bridge. Though fear crawled up my throat and tightened it, I knew I had to go out into Oedija once again. I had to read more of my ancient texts, then do my due diligence to the Order by rooting out corruption. I wasn't sure either would pan out. But trying was better than cowering in my room.

Filled with nervous energy, eager to ease the guilt I felt toward Nomusa, I settled on attending to my Verifier task. But though the command ultimately came from Orhan, I wouldn't do as the Preservist leader desired and find some scapegoat for his corruption charges. I aimed to investigate where the rotten heart of Oedija actually pulsed.

Orhan's estate was located in the center of the Petaled Fence, the richest part of deme Iris. The community was sprawled over a hill that afforded views of both the ocean and the distant mountains, and it was separated from the rest of the inner city by an intricately carved stone wall and guards posted at its gates. Ordinary residents were not permitted access unless they had received invitations.

But as I reached the gates, I thrust my Verifier medallion at the guards, hoping my position would be enough. After exchanging a look, they grudgingly admitted me, and I entered the Petaled Fence for the first time. Walking a little ways down the wide street paved with a black-veined white marble, I tried to repress my awe as I craned my neck to spy Orhan's manor near the peak of the hill, which rose nearly as high as the Laurel Palace to the west. Though it wasn't as grand or opulent as the Wreath's homestead, which stretched over half a mile with its interior gardens, it said much of Orhan's sense of his place in the world that he made the attempt.

I took pains to ascend to it by covert ways, or as covert as I could manage in an unfamiliar place. Available alleyways to sneak through were lacking in a district of manors and the reputable shops that serviced them. So instead, I opted for taking a wide arc through the district, avoiding the main thoroughfare on which Orhan would no doubt have eyes posted, and I approached from the back of the estate. There, I found a perfect stake-out spot, a conveniently located Eidolan sanctuary with a balcony facing out toward the Low Consul's estate and an open view of his back gate. After stopping by a shop to pick up a peering glass, I made for the balcony, and through frequent and generous donations to the offering plate, the oracle and his acolytes let me be.

Yet for all my troubles, I was little rewarded. Though I watched those coming and going from the estate, I didn't see anyone suspicious enough to follow when they left. Not even Valemish priests came to the Low Consul's manor. Though I wasn't surprised that Orhan was discreet, particularly in broad daylight, I had hoped to see more.

In the frequent pauses between Orhan's visitors, I practiced Eltris's techniques, telling myself that there was little use in wasting time while I waited. A flimsy excuse; I couldn't deny that I burned to channel as easily as Xaron and Talan did. Had not duty and guilt called, my desire would have shut me indoors all day to work at it.

But as the grains in the sandglass slowly counted the afternoon away, I left off both of my pursuits with a heavy heart. A day with nothing accomplished was a sore blow at this stage. Yet I couldn't think of what else I could do. With evening approaching, I stole back to the Aviary for the night.

I began the next day much the same way. Though the oracle and acolytes cast me odd looks, they didn't complain when I put another handful of cullets in the offering plate. Morning came and went. Though I watched Orhan's entrance with rapt attention, not even permitting myself to stray into Eltris's exercises, I found no visitor worthy of pursuit.

As the noon bell rang in the sanctuary tower, I turned from my vantage point and left. Mulling over the problem, I could think of no better way to catch Orhan in his corruption that wouldn't be reckless. No doubt I could convince Xaron to sneak into the estate, but I had only vague ideas of what I'd have him look for. There was little point in risking it until I did.

Little knowing what else I could do, I made for Tomes and pushed guilty thoughts of Linos aside. With Platon as my usual accomplice, I read *The Seeds of Famine*. The book had, however, wandered into the territory of aggravating. For reasons beyond my understanding, it now strayed through the minutiae of the Hunger War, detailing the number of troops on each side, which notables joined which army, where the important battles took place, and the like. Dutifully, I waded through the mundane events, searching for useful scraps and coming up short.

Only one detail stood apart from the rest, the same question that bothered Agmon Brandheart: why Famine avoided confronting him. I dared to hope that, whatever the reason, it would be the key to defeating him once more.

But the hope of that answer couldn't keep me down there forever. Turns later, with an aching back and neck, I left the library. Blinking as I stepped back into the sunlight, it took me several moments before I spotted the man walking down the cobblestones in coarse, brown robes too poor for even an Acadian.

"Hilarion, do a tumble!" I called to him.

Xaron turned and, recognizing me, grinned.

"You're rather pleased with yourself," he observed with a wry smile as I approached. "Yet a jape comes to mind when I see you as well."

I glanced down at myself. I'd almost forgotten that I'd forgone the chiton that day, and my tunic and trousers were visible beneath my cloak. "I'm going through a wardrobe adjustment at the moment," I said dismissively.

"I can see that. I can't say it's flattering, but at least it suits you." He gave me a wink.

I ignored his words and pulled him into a hug to whisper in his ear. "Are you here for what I think you are?"

He hesitated and glanced around as he pulled away, then nodded slightly.

"I want to come with."

"No!" He scanned the area nervously again. Though no one was nearby, he continued in a quieter voice. "Airene, you can't. You're too prominent. You'd draw the wrong attention."

"And *you* don't draw attention?"

"A different kind. I'm a laughingstock. No one really pays attention to where Hilarion goes. But a Verifier means serious business. You only go where there's something to be sniffed out."

"I suppose," I admitted grudgingly. "Fine. I'll leave you to it for now. But it won't be long before I force the issue."

His lips tightened, but he didn't deny it. We both knew the dangers we faced. Once I gained control over my channeling, Xaron couldn't object any longer to my learning to protect myself.

I squeezed his hand briefly. "Come to the Aviary soon. You haven't seen what a dump they've put us up in."

"Nomusa says it's a ruby in the rough, once you carve the crud off it." Xaron grinned. "I can't wait to see it."

"Then come tonight. We can make an evening of it. Since I'm stuck behind walls then anyway."

He shrugged. "Can't argue with that. I'll see you then."

With that, he turned and went to his warden training, leaving me to carry on my own way.

My predicaments rolled round and round in my head as I slipped down the streets back to the Laurel Palace gates. A steady drizzle, barely more than mist, had quickly covered the city and obscured the roads. I pulled up the hood of my cloak and peered around, more on edge than usual, as I could only see people a dozen feet away from me. Yet I was growing adept at avoiding troublesome spots in this new cityscape, circumventing the places where I'd seen or heard of thieves frequenting. Rumors, which had always made my ears perk up, now took on a greater interest. The wrong warning could leave me sprawled in an alley, never to rise again.

Even so, I doubted I could have avoided Guilders if they sought me. Why they might be quiet put me ill at ease. My fears whispered that they'd caught Talan and had no more use for me. But reason asserted itself; more likely, they'd seen no signs of communication between us and had no orders to push the issue further.

Still, I couldn't help but want to search for him, and not only to make sure he was safe. I missed his voice, his warm touch. I missed the safety I felt in his presence. But I wouldn't endanger him by seeking him out, not for those reasons. I sighed and forced the desire to recede to the back of my mind.

Reaching the gates of the Wreath grounds, I mulled over where to go. It felt like a long time since I'd last spoken with Jaxas, but I didn't have anything in particular to report. True that I'd learned more of Famine; but that the daemon god sought to come to our world to consume it was hardly news. Everyone who had heard the tales of the Hunger War knew that was Famine's desire. There was little point in wasting the Archon's time, especially when I wasn't sure how welcome I'd be.

Instead, I turned to the bridge and made my way across. But at the turn to the Aviary, I kept going straight, and headed instead for the broken dome looming out of the mist.

Entering inside the Conclave, I found the place transformed by the showers. Water slicked the stone steps and filmed the benches. The few Servants still present huddled miserably within the few unbroken alcoves, while the honors wore flat expressions as they hurried to and fro, droplets trickling down their shaven heads.

I stood for a moment just inside the doors, staring at the small portal behind the Archon's dais. I couldn't recall if the Demos Council door was kept closed in times when they weren't in session. But I hadn't been studying it for more than a minute before the door opened, and the Low Consuls began to file out. Feiyan left first, the rest of the Equalists with her, while Orhan and the Preservists followed after.

Not wishing for any trying interactions just then, I pulled my hood down further and stepped into an alcove. I found myself watching Orhan. The middle-aged, portly man took each step slowly, careful on the slick stone, but his resolute smile never left his face. A thought began to itch in the back of my head, then whittled away into an idea. A smile found my lips. Orhan's eyes darted toward me, and I looked away, hoping he hadn't recognized me. I didn't look back until he and the others had filed out of the great double doors.

Nomusa and Jaxas came last, lingering behind the rest and speaking in a low conference. I wondered what they spoke about and if Nomusa would later keep it secret. I hadn't forgotten about the figure in the red cloak in the Laurel gardens.

Stepping from the shadows, I caught both of their gazes and strode toward them. "Evening."

"First Verifier Airene." Jaxas's eyes were flat and unreadable as he gave me a respectful nod. "You just missed the session."

"And a lively one at that," Nomusa added. She looked tired but still elated. I recognized it as how I'd often felt in the midst of a fine hunt. A glimmer of envy wormed its way inside me.

"How's that?" I asked lightly.

"Daelya and Berker were at each others' throats over the organization of the defenses. How much to requisition there, how to organize the supplies, and the like."

"I thought those details were left to the Stratechons."

"For the most part, they are," Jaxas replied. "Which was precisely the Preservist point. But Daelya felt that a more active role might be necessary considering the circumstances."

I kept my doubts to myself. If any defense Oedija could muster would make a difference, I'd be amazed. But saying so wouldn't help anyone.

"Archon, if you wouldn't mind, could I have a private word with Nomusa?"

"Of course." He gave a brief bow, then turned away. Just before he left through the doors, a hooded man I hadn't seen standing there turned out to walk next to him. I studied him with skepticism.

"Who's that with Jaxas?"

Nomusa turned to look. "The new Tribune acting as the handler of the Shepherds — or what remains of them, anyway. He's taken it upon himself to be a guard of sorts. But enough about him. What did you want to discuss? Or should it wait until we're back at the Aviary?"

I glanced around and saw no one near. But after the Tribune had appeared from nowhere, even whispered words didn't feel safe.

"It can wait," I decided.

We hurried across the Conclave grounds, our cloaks pulled tight about us. The rain hadn't relented, but only fell harder. By the time we reached the Aviary's doors, even the oily skin of my cloak couldn't prevent the rain soaking through. Stepping inside, I shivered and peeled the wet fabric off, then slumped into a seat.

"Tea or coffee?" Nomusa offered, already headed toward the kitchen.

"Is mulled wine on offer?"

She rolled her eyes and disappeared inside the kitchen, reappearing a few minutes later with two mugs of steaming tea. I accepted the cup, folding my hands around it and breathing in the pleasantly spicy scent of cinnamon and cloves.

Nomusa sipped her tea. "So, what was it you wanted to talk about?"

I set the mug down. "The Low Consuls. They have solars within the Conclave, don't they? Where they compose letters and keep documents?"

She nodded. "The Servants do as well, though they're often shared rooms." Her gaze grew sharp. "Why do you ask?"

I flashed a rueful smile. "Sounds like you've already guessed why. I staked out Orhan's estate this morning and saw nothing. Unless you'd rather Xaron risk a house-break, his Conclave solar is our only option for evidence of corruption."

She was already shaking her head. "You're not seeing the whole painting, Airene. We can't go after Orhan for corruption, period. He has too much power — in the Council, in the Conclave, and from his own money and influence. Even if we find evidence that he's plotting something, what could we do with it?"

"Act on whatever we learn. Thwart his plans. Anything is better than looking aside from the fact that he might very well be undermining Oedija's defense for his own gain."

"And what if you're caught? Orhan would disband the Order in a heartbeat. Verchlesa and Tychon would side with the Preservists for certain; even the Equalists might affirm the decision. No one wants Finches digging up their secrets."

I'd feared her reacting this way and had hoped for better. "Then what do you think we should do?" I demanded. "Nomusa, unless you have a better path forward, I think we have to do this. We need Orhan and his lackeys out of the way, for Oedija's sake. And this is the only step I've found as to how we might begin unseating him."

Nomusa cast her gaze down at the table, taking a sip of her tea. After a long minute, she sighed and met my gaze. "I'm just afraid, Aire. Afraid of losing all we've gained."

I reached over and took her hand. "So am I. But as Talan would say, it's time to throw in the spokes and pray."

She snorted lightly and squeezed my hand. "You'd do better not to take advice from him."

The front door burst open. Nomusa and I jumped to our feet, my shins bruising on the table as my hand went to the knife under my tunic. But as the man stepped in and threw off his hood, I let my hand fall away. Xaron grinned at both of our expressions.

"Did I startle you?" he asked innocently.

"Next time, knock," I said drily as I collapsed back onto the bench. "Now sit."

"Someone's in good humor tonight." He obliged by sitting next to Nomusa and looked around. "So, this is the place. Ruby in the rough indeed."

"She'll get there," Nomusa said reproachfully.

"You can get a tour later," I said. "We have something else to discuss first."

His eyebrows shot up. "Do we?"

I shared a look with Nomusa. Despite her earlier opinion, she obliged me with a small smile.

I turned back to Xaron. "How would you like to do another house-break?"

———

"It's late enough," Xaron insisted for the third time. "The moons are hidden. It's raining. No one will be out, and the guards will be inattentive, if they're watching inside the grounds at all."

"Just a little longer." I took a sip of my second cup of tea, feigning patience. But he was right; the time had come. From where he, Nomusa, and I waited in the dining hall of the Aviary, we could see the night had grown as dark as Oedija ever saw. Even the radiant winds were lost amid the drizzling gloom. The patter of rain and the distant tide of the ocean muffled any other sounds. The light from the pyr lamps mounted periodically throughout the grounds seemed subdued. It was as good a night for a house-break as we could have hoped for.

Xaron slumped against the table. "No one tells you the end of a nation involves so much waiting."

"This isn't the end of Oedija," I said without conviction.

"We used to wait this long for house-breaks all the time," Nomusa reminded us.

Xaron gave us a baleful glare. "But then it had been to break in somewhere that would be a challenge. This is a job for a street urchin."

I hoped he was right. Conclave guards only patrolled the fence around the grounds, not around the Conclave chambers. With Xaron by my side, locked doors would pose no issue. Nomusa had talked us through where Orhan's solar was located; all that remained was to break in and rifle the messages. We could be done with the whole task in a turn of the sandglass if all went as expected.

"At least you get to wear normal clothes for a change."

"Normal for you," he muttered. "A fine wardrobe change you've made."

"They're practical," I said stiffly.

"And stylish," Nomusa added with a smirk.

He suddenly stood. "Let's go. Nomusa, you said the clerk locks up at the second turn after sundown. That was two turns ago. The only thing that will come of us waiting longer is less sleep."

I sighed and rose with him. "Fine. But if we get caught because we left too early, I'll expect you to get us out of it."

He grinned and opened the door. A chill monsoon wind swept in. "Why don't you take care of it? After all, you're like me now."

"Not quite," Nomusa said from the table. "She can't channel."

Her words pricked me, but I pretended otherwise as I glanced back. "Wish us luck."

Her expression had grown serious. "'Thae's blessings."

I gave her a tight smile, then followed Xaron out the door.

"You'll channel soon," he murmured as he closed it. "Don't worry."

I nodded and led the way into the rain. It couldn't come soon enough.

As we crossed the grounds, I saw no one within sight, as the border fence and the guards that patrolled it were hidden from view by numerous groves. Yet as Xaron and I made our way toward the cobblestone road before the Conclave doors, we kept a careful watch and both ears open for footsteps in the rain. The grounds appeared empty of any other travelers.

We reached the Conclave doors. "Alright, house-breaker," I whispered to Xaron as I scanned the darkness behind us. "Time to show your worth."

Xaron kneeled next to the keyhole and peered through it. It was many times the size of a regular keyhole; the key to turn it must have been as big as one of my hands. Brow creased in concentration, he wriggled his fingers inside it and felt around for a moment before drawing them out with a smile.

"Simple. All I will need to do is press in the tumblers with some gentle kinesis."

I hoped he was right. "Work your magic then."

Flashing me a wry grin, he put his fingers back inside the keyhole. His brow creased, his smile faded, and his eyes drifted close as his fingers worked inside the lock for a few moments. I looked away and scanned the area again. Though no one should have any reason to be here so late, I couldn't shake the feeling we were being watched.

I heard a series of clicks, then a satisfied grunt from Xaron. The door rumbled as he pulled one open. "There you are," he said with satisfaction. "Simple, didn't I say?"

"Gloat inside." I pushed him in and heaved the thick door shut behind us.

The thin light that came through the broken shell of the dome did little to remit the deeper darkness around us. Yet relief washed over me at the idea of the doors being between us and any unseen watchers.

I could feel Xaron's eyes on me. "Are you alright?" he asked. "You seem on edge."

I shook my head. "Just feel like something's watching. Can you lock the door behind us?"

"Of course. We'll only be in here a short time though. Is it necessary?"

"Please. For my sanity."

He shrugged and kneeled back before the keyhole. A few moments later, I heard the tumblers shifting, then the click of the lock turning back into place.

"Thank you. Now, a little light would be nice."

"Channel it yourself," Xaron complained, but he obliged with a large flame flaring up from his fingertips. "Would you like me to lead the way?"

I winced at the echo his words produced in the cavernous building. "Quiet now. Our voices carry too much for talking."

We ghosted along the edge of the chamber toward the hallway that held the Servants' solars. From Nomusa's directions, I knew they were situated along a corridor that curved around one side of the Conclave. The Low Consuls' solars were at the far end, positioning them closer to the small chamber at the back of the building where they most often congregated. As the doors were unlabeled and the darkness conspired to confound us, we had to backtrack twice before I was sure we stood before Orhan's door.

"You sure you don't want to check again?" Xaron teased softly as he crouched before the door. Even his slender fingers could fit no more than one at a time in this keyhole, and he seemed to be having an issue with it.

"You can open it, right?"

"Give me a moment."

I glanced up and down the corridor. The feeling of being watched had returned, though I still saw nothing. But seeing as how Xaron had extinguished his flame, that didn't mean much.

"Sorry," he muttered. "I need to concentrate."

I kneeled next to him, staring wide-eyed into the darkness. Blood pounded in my ears. "Hurry," I breathed. "I think someone else is here."

A puff of air caught my cheek as the door clicked. "Aha!" Xaron announced too loudly for comfort. "There we are."

The flame reappeared, showing that Xaron now stood. As light again shown down the hallway, I thought I saw a shadow fleeing into the gloom. A trick of the light, I told myself, as chills crept up my spine.

"Inside, quickly," I urged, following my own advice and slipping inside the solar. "And lock the door behind."

"Again?" he complained. But he shut us in the room and bent to comply. As his flame disappeared, the faint glow of covered pyr lamps cast the room in pallid illumination.

I tried to use Eltris's practice to relax my nerves as he worked on the lock, but it was no use. "Is it me, or are Eltris's exercises worthless?" I griped.

"They're worthless," Xaron readily agreed. "You should try the Shifting Sands meditation."

"The what?"

"Something Isi showed me. You imagine yourself walking through a desert, more or less. It focuses me every time."

I stared at where I knew he crouched in the darkness. "Isi," I muttered to myself.

The lock clicked, then a flame flared back to life to reveal his shame-faced look. "What?" he demanded at my smirk.

"Nothing. We have searching to do, don't we?"

Locating two of the pyr lamps, we began to roam Orhan's solar, which turned out to be a series of three rooms. One hosted nothing more than a washing basin and a clean chamberpot. The other, I guessed, was for the use of the clerks and honors within Orhan's employ from the scattering of quills and small desks. Returning to the main chamber, which I hoped was Orhan's own workspace, I began to peruse the parchments scattered across the much larger desk. I'd assumed Orhan would be a neat and organized person from the way he conducted himself, but found myself sorely mistaken. Papers were in disorderly stacks all across the surface and piled into cubby holes with seemingly no rhyme or reason. I wondered bitterly if he'd done so just to make searching his papers difficult as I scanned one document after another.

I quickly abandoned the larger papers in favor of the smaller finch scrolls. The sort of evidence I sought wouldn't be in formal documentation, but communications between the Preservist leader and any entity in opposition to the Council's stated goals. Yet even his missives contained little of import. One was from a proprietor giving a brief account of the losses to Orhan's estate this past harvest. His lands, like the others around Oedija, seemed to have been sorely affected by the droughts. Another was a letter from his daughter, who was apparently lodging in his manor outside the city. Perhaps it was significant that he didn't wish her to be in

Oedija city. But with the Avvadin Imperium marching up from the south, anyone with the means might do the same. My own family was on a Wreath estate in the countryside, after all.

"Airene," Xaron hissed from next to me. He, too, had been rifling through finch messages, and he offered one to me. "Read this one. It's in the ash-tongue."

With skepticism born of the weary slog, I accepted it from him. I was only just proficient in the Avvadin script and had to struggle to decipher the words:

You grow heretical as the end draws near, Sakin. Take care you do not discard your only friends at the turning of the tide. You will have your reward, in this life and the next. So long as you do not displease either of your masters.

More arks pass through the gates everyday. Soon will come our time to rise.

Be sure you rise with us.

My chest fluttered, though I couldn't tell whether it was from excitement or fear. The missive was unsigned, but it didn't need to be. From the language used, this had to come from a Valemish priest, a Kul.

I told Xaron what it said. "Good work," I whispered to him. "This is exactly what we need."

He nodded, but his brow was creased with concern. "But what does it mean? 'Soon will come our time to rise' — Will the Valemish attack from within Oedija's walls? And what is within the arks they're smuggling in?"

"Weapons? Money?" I shrugged. "We suspected the Valemish conspired against Oedija. Now we have proof of it, and against Orhan as well."

"Proof, yes. But will it be enough to remove him from power? I doubt it. The rest of his faction would never turn on him. And even if the other five and Jaxas voted to remove him, would he defer to their decision? Or would it just rouse rebellion sooner rather than later?" Xaron shook his head. "This is why I've stayed away from politics. It becomes muddled too quickly."

"It's a bit late to stay out of politics. You've stepped right into them."

"You don't have to tell me that," Xaron muttered. "Its stink is all I can smell. Come on. We can at least tell Nomusa what we found and see what she says."

After we'd put Orhan's solar back together as much as we remembered it, we returned to the door, and Xaron set once more to unlocking it. I neatly rolled up the scroll and tucked it into a subtle pocket in my cloak. Only then did my thoughts turn back to the watcher I'd imagined outside the door. I hoped it was just my imagination getting the better of me. Either way, we had no choice now but to leave as swiftly as we could.

The door clicked open, and I followed after Xaron as we exited back into the hall. As he channeled radiance, the hall flared into light.

A silhouette fled down the hall away from us.

This time, I knew I wasn't mistaken. "There!" I yelled as I pointed. "After him!"

Xaron needed no prodding, but charged forward. I hurried behind, endeavoring to keep up, if only to remain in the light. The figure fled before us, footsteps echoing in the empty hall. Who were they? What had they heard? And worst of all, who might they report back to? Breath hissed in my throat as I sprinted faster.

Reaching the end of the corridor, the figure didn't turn toward the door, but into the main chamber. I stuttered to a halt near the doors, but didn't stare in confusion for long as they leaped impossibly high to grab hold of the jagged edge of a broken wall and haul themselves up.

"They're a warden!" I cried to Xaron. "Be careful!"

With typical rashness, Xaron followed, leaping dozens of feet into the air to land on the same broken wall. The figure leaped outside, and as my friend gave chase, I lost sight of them both. Meaning to follow, I ran to the great double doors when a terrible realization occurred to me. Xaron had locked the doors. As I tried to push them open, I found I was trapped inside.

I stepped back, trying to think of a way out. Fear and frustration clouded my thoughts. I stared into the darkness behind me, trying desperately to detect any movement. The watcher might not have been alone; perhaps, even now, I was being stalked by his companions. I ground my teeth and pressed my back against the solid door. There was nothing I could do but wait and hope it was Xaron who returned for me.

As I waited, I tried desperately to open myself to the Pyrthae. Channeling was my only protection if the other warden returned. Channeling might even get me out of here, if I could use kinesis to trip the lock. But once again, Eltris's exercises failed me. I couldn't stop my constant searching of the darkness to clear my mind nor relax my body. I exhaled in frustration. None of the wardens I'd seen had any trouble channeling on command. But I knew of no other way than Eltris's.

A scuffle of sandals on stone sounded from where Xaron and the warden had exited. My breath caught as I listened in terror to the sounds of someone coming closer. Was it Xaron returning? Or had the errant warden doubled back?

"Airene," Xaron called softly.

I let out my breath and sagged against the door. A moment later, I saw him drop into the chamber and look around.

"Here," I called back to him.

He ran lightly over to meet me. "I lost him," he said, voice tight with frustration. "He slipped over the fence, and I knew I couldn't leave you in here."

"You should have followed him," I said without conviction.

Xaron laughed and pulled me in with an arm over my shoulders. "I knew you'd be scared of the dark."

I didn't dignify his teasing with a response.

"But anyway," he continued, "we at least know something about them. Seeing as he was a warden, he was most likely a Seeker."

"Most likely. But we don't know."

"No. But everything Finches do is guesswork, isn't it? Now, assuming it *was* a Seeker, what did he want? Was he watching us, or here for something else? I doubt he meant us harm — the Manifest would have sent more men otherwise."

I nodded. "Either way, it seems an awful coincidence, doesn't it? That the Seeker would be here the same night we were?"

Xaron was silent for a moment. "Unless they're always watching," he muttered.

I'd thought the same thing. "How would you feel about running the perimeter at night? Of the Conclave as well as the Laurel Palace. You'll get to channel all you want for a turn or two."

He grinned. "You know just how to manipulate me. Of course I'll do it. I have precious few duties as it is."

I drew him into a tighter embrace. "Thank you. Now, if you could get us out of here—"

A rattle began in the lock of the great doors. Xaron and I froze, staring, before reality set in.

"Guards!" I hissed.

Xaron looked around frantically. "There's nowhere to go. Only a warden could escape without the doors."

A wild idea entered my head. "Carry me! Can you lift me up there?"

The key was turning in the lock, the tumblers sliding into place. Time was running out. Xaron stared at the distance, brow creased.

"I don't know," he whispered. "I could hurt you!"

I pushed him to the wall as the door began to creak open. "No time!"

We reached the base of the broken wall as whoever was outside began to enter. The light from the torches they carried gleamed off their helms, showing them to be Conclave guards, and shone on the tips of their spears.

"Show yourselves!" one of them called, sweeping the torch around. Its light fell over the ruined chamber.

I jumped into Xaron's arms. "Just do it!" I hissed.

The motion caught the guards' attention. "Thieves! Stop right there!"

Xaron didn't hesitate any longer. His wiry frame held surprising strength, for he held me easily in his arms. "Hold on," he muttered, dropping into a crouch.

Then, with a sudden lurch, we were flying. I heard kinesis pounding against the floor as Xaron launched us upward to the narrow ledge. For a moment, it looked like we wouldn't reach the rocky ledge — then his feet almost floated to land on the stone. He swayed back and forth for balance for a moment, then said, "Brace yourself," before leaping down on the other side.

I saw the rubble littering the base of the wall a moment before it was underfoot. Xaron's feet scrabbled against it, then he slipped, sliding down it with a curse. Stone banged against my clothing, ripping and bruising. But as we slid to a halt, me half hanging from Xaron's arms, I knew we were lucky to still be alive.

I scrambled to my feet. "The Aviary!" I hissed, then set off at a run. My knee hurt where I'd knocked it against a rock. Xaron lagged behind me. I hoped I hadn't pushed him to his limits, but I couldn't stop to reconsider things now.

The guards were not quick in following. By the time we slipped inside the Aviary doors, their torches were still near the entrance of the Conclave. Perhaps Xaron revealing that he was a warden had deterred their pursuit. Whatever the reason, I was grateful to slide into a chair and catch my breath.

"That seemed like it ended well."

I startled upright and stared wide-eyed at the figure in the corner. Only a moment later did I recognize Nomusa's voice. "Don't do that," I snapped, fear sharpening my words.

She uncovered a pyrkin lamp, revealing her amused smile. "Why were those guards after you? Did you make that much noise?"

I explained everything while Xaron was hunched over, still breathing hard. I interrupted the telling halfway through to ask if he needed anything, but he just waved a hand. I kept an eye on him all the same. Hopefully all he needed was rest.

Nomusa held out a hand. "Let me see the note."

I gave it over, unable to hide my surprise. "You can read ash-tongue?"

"I was the heiress to my ishaka," she said with wry amusement. "I was tutored in all of the languages of the Four Realms, though my sand-tongue is poor. I thought you knew that."

As she finished, she looked up with her brow creased. "I agree with you — this must be from the Valemish. But there are still a lot of questions."

"But it's enough to cast suspicion on him. The rest of the Council should see it."

Nomusa bit her lip. "Maybe. But we should sleep on it. I have a feeling all of this will move swifter than we like, and we need to be prepared for it."

I reached over and shook Xaron's shoulder, as he'd slumped onto the table. "Can you make it back up to your tower?"

"Don't make me," he said without lifting his head.

I grinned, realizing he'd be fine. "I'm sure we can make you up a pallet. Come on. I guess it's my turn to carry you."

CHAPTER TEN

THE YORANDU HEIR

Clepsammia appeared to Agmon Brandheart. Clad in a cloak of night, she was invisible to all eyes but his.

'Why does this daemon flee before me?' Agmon thundered. 'Can he not match my power?'

'More than match it,' the Maiden of the Sands said. 'Famine's power grows with each passing day. It is his destiny to swallow the whole of the world.'

Agmon Brandheart, bravest of all men, paled at this prophecy. 'Then we must fail. He cannot be defeated.'

'No. In the end, all must perish, swallowed by the God of Hunger. But all things end, Brandheart. It is not the end that measures the life, but the purpose fulfilled.'

She thought of her father, gone from this world, but did not impart his passing. For even the wardens, gifted with her father's dying strength, did not know the Ruler of All Realms no longer reigned.

Agmon stood straighter. 'Then I shall fulfill mine, so long as it ends in glory. If I can but force my enemy to face me!'

— The Seeds of Famine, a translation from the Lighted-tongue; by Oracle Kalene of deme Hull; 881 SLP

The summons came early the next morning.

Nomusa shook me awake. "The Council wishes to see us," she said quietly. "Now."

I sat up, immediately alert. "Orhan knows we broke in," I guessed.

"Probably. The guards must have reported the intruders to him." Her brow was creased. "This is moving faster than I thought. And until we know how this will play out, I think we should keep Orhan's missive secret for now."

"Why bother?" I rose and clambered over Xaron, who snored on a makeshift pallet on the floor, and pulled out a tunic and trousers from my wardrobe.

Nomusa gave me a look. I sighed and pulled down a chiton as well. Best not to ruffle the Council's feathers just now.

"Feiyan must be the one to reveal this. We lack the authority to accomplish anything. Well, anything except the Order's dissolution."

I looked sharply at her. "Feiyan? Since when is she our friend?"

Nomusa bit her lip. "Airene, I meant to tell you sooner. But Feiyan… she's allied with us now."

The mystery that had surrounded my friend suddenly came into painful clarity. "The stranger in the red cloak the day I awoke. That was Feiyan?"

"Kako, actually."

"So Feiyan is on our side, is she?" I asked sarcastically. "From what I've seen, she's only ever been on her own side."

"She helped confirm both of us as First Verifiers, if you remember."

"Reluctantly."

"And she gave us the Thulu pyrkin before the Despoina's trial."

"Because she didn't believe in its usefulness." I threw up my hands. "None of this makes me trust her, Nomusa. I doubt anything will."

"But you must. She has authority and resources that we don't. And she grows closer to Jaxas everyday."

"To Jaxas? I thought she was the Despoina's pet."

"Not anymore. Ever since the trial, her flattery has been directed toward a different Wreath."

I frowned. It wasn't unlike Feiyan to shift loyalties, but I didn't like Jaxas accepting her confidences. Though, of course, Nomusa had as well. Feiyan was a parasite I'd never be rid of, it seemed.

"She'll not betray us," Nomusa pressed. "Not in this, anyway. We both want to keep the city in one piece."

I bit back further words. We had no choice in this matter, I knew, but it didn't make me like it any better. I wiped at the sleep lingering around my eyes.

"I'm sorry. I know you're making the best of a tough situation."

Nomusa nodded stiffly, not looking at me. "Thank you. Now, if you're ready, we'd better go."

"Where are we going?" Xaron asked sleepily from the floor.

"Nowhere with you," I told him. "Sleep."

With a grunt of assent, he turned on his side and curled back up into his blankets.

After a brisk walk, Nomusa and I arrived at the Conclave doors. I felt for Orhan's stolen message, which I'd secured in a small scroll case under my chiton. Though I didn't plan to reveal it, I couldn't trust it to remain anywhere but on my person.

As if there hadn't been a break-in the night before, the guards waved us through as normal. Though, I reflected, they'd hardly accuse one of their own of the deed. The gloomy day peeked in through the broken dome, drizzling rain onto the floor. Few Servants and their staff milled about, their proceedings for the day not yet begun. My own short rest was already catching up with me, my mind groggy and my body stiff. I pushed my discomforts from mind as Nomusa led us down to the Council chamber door. Giving me a final significant look, she spoke to the honor waiting by the door, and moments later, we were escorted inside.

The Council chamber was emptier than usual. Most of the Low Consuls were not yet there, only the five of the Preservist faction. Orhan smiled heartily at us, flanked by his fellows. Berker, sitting at Orhan's right, leaned forward, the smile on his face like a wolf staring at a pair of lambs.

"First Verifiers," Orhan greeted us. "Good morn to you both."

Nomusa and I bowed, mine more perfunctory than hers.

"Good morn, Low Consuls," Nomusa said, her tone nothing but gracious. "To what do we owe the pleasure of your summons?"

Orhan motioned for us to move further inside, and we reluctantly complied.

"An unusual circumstance, to be sure," he said. "It seems that the recent devastation to our chambers here in the Conclave has left us vulnerable to thieves. Last night, guards reported two wardens fleeing the premises."

I kept my face carefully composed. "Sounds like Seeker wardens. Did they disturb anything?"

Orhan's gaze settled on me, a slight smile playing on his lips. "Why, yes they did. I entered my solar this morning only to find my papers in a great disarray. I must confess, I am a rather suspicious man. Thus, I give my things the appearance of disorganization so that rifling hands will be less cautious."

My throat went dry, but Nomusa said smoothly, "A wise approach, and one that has now served us well."

The Preservist leader smiled in acknowledgement, then looked at me. I said nothing, but stared back, hoping my silence wouldn't seem culpability. It couldn't make him more suspicious than he already was.

Nomusa glanced at me, then looked back at Orhan. "Low Consul, if we might ask, did they take anything from your papers?"

"Nothing of import — merely a friendly correspondence. But those unfamiliar with our relationship may read too much into it." His gaze slowly panned from Nomusa to me again. I met it steadily. I'd show no signs of guilt. I couldn't be guilty before a man trying to sell us to a foreign empire.

"I assume you wish us to investigate?" Nomusa inquired.

"No, no, that is quite alright. I don't know what you could discover. The thieves were quite adept. I just wanted to pass on word of it to you, and a reminder to remain cautious."

The way he smiled made my skin crawl.

"We'll keep that in mind," Nomusa promised.

Orhan nodded. "Good. Now, I need not remind you that the Yorandu delegation arrives tonight. I trust we will see you both there?"

Nomusa's smile stiffened. "Of course," was all she could manage.

"Very well. You are dismissed."

We thanked them, bowed, and left the room as swiftly as we dared.

"We have to move quickly," Nomusa said in a low voice when we were outside the Conclave chambers. "It's only a matter of time before Orhan has us searched. He might have even sent someone to the Aviary while we were gone."

I sighed. "Then we'd best speak with Feiyan soon."

Nomusa cast me a sideways glance. "I'll handle it. I know you'd prefer to stay far away from her."

"What tipped you off to that?"

A smile tugged at her lips, but her expression smoothed a moment later. "I suppose we should discuss the Yorandu delegation arriving tonight."

I winced, knowing the depth of the emotions behind her words. I tried to imagine how such an encounter would feel. Something akin to running into Vusu in the midst of a festival, perhaps. But though Vusu had killed or maimed my brothers, he hadn't robbed me of my home, family, and inheritance in the same stroke, and all at a young age. I suspected such wounds didn't heal, but only scarred over, prone to breaking open at the first reminder. Mine certainly promised to never fade.

"I can speak with them," I offered. "Perhaps you don't even have to come."

She shook her head. "As Firsts of the new Order of Verifiers, we are to be presented before the Yorandu Heir. The Council believes we should do our utmost to convince the Yorandu delegation that Oedija is taking active steps to overcome its significant challenges. We are part of that. They may also expect us to report in brief to the Yorandu Heir on the progress we've made on rooting out corruption within the upper echelons of our society. Besides, this will be the first time since the trial that all the most powerful in Oedija have gathered together. If Vusu has been waiting for an opportunity to strike, he may get no better one. I have to attend."

Her jaw stiffened, and I quickly changed the subject. "What time should we meet?"

"The fourth turn of the afternoon. You need a bath and plenty of time to prepare."

I rolled my eyes, but didn't deny it. Nearly a span's worth of grime clung to me, and my hair had been reduced to a frizzy mess.

"Oedija is breaking, and we're spending time bathing." I shook my head. "What a strange world we live in."

"But it's the way things are, so no point in moaning about it. Now come on. I think I have a comb that won't break on those tangles of yours…"

———

The Laurel Palace, resplendent as it was, needed no additional decoration. Yet as Nomusa and I entered inside, we found it had been furnished with further marvels. Braziers, burning with golden flames, lined the walkway through the atrium. As we passed between them, heat pouring over us and sweat beading on my skin, I wondered if it was channeling or alchemy behind them. When I was a true warden, I hoped I'd be able to tell the difference.

Nomusa muttered complaints about the braziers as she wiped at her brow with a hand cloth. Even shining with sweat, she looked as stunning as I'd expected, though in the simple way she'd adopted since becoming a First Verifier. A deep violet peplos of a supple, flowing material flattered her curvaceous figure. She'd curled her hair neatly against her head. Her only jewelry was the Verifier medallion and a bracelet of emerald-colored glass. When I saw a sparkle within them that went beyond reflected sunlight, I'd known she'd been to visit Maesos; no one else used pyrkin to set their works aflame.

I knew I must look plain beside her in my borrowed, pale green peplos. Nomusa claimed the color accentuated my eyes, but I was more concerned with the necessity of leaving both tunic and knife behind. Though trouble from the Seekers was possible, I could see no way to keep either one without it being blatantly apparent. Not that I could do much against other wardens at the moment. But it was reassuring all the same to have a blade close at hand.

We followed the people before us, Servants by their line of conversation, down the carpeted walk to the feast hall. Room after room, the braziers continued.

"The guests must be the feast," I observed drily. "I can't see any other reason to bake us all before arriving."

Nomusa shrugged. "Intimidation. Perhaps Asileia wishes to show her suitor that while Oedija suffers, it isn't weak."

"Only a fool would fall for that." I left the last part of my thought unspoken: that I hoped the Yorandu Heir was a fool, for all of our sakes.

As we arrived at the feast hall, we found it transformed since our last visit. Pyr lamps, glowing the gold and green of the Wreaths, floated around the room, powerful magnets holding them aloft. Banners had been unfurled along the walls, depicting scenes of conquest against fearsome beasts as well as stories of the Eidola and the Lighted Passage. An array of food as vast as I'd ever seen spread before us in a spectacle of color, texture, and shape. My mouth began watering as I saw chocolate, a rare delicacy, adorning a number of desserts that I had no names for. Drinks, too, were more plentiful than I'd ever seen, with honors serving them to guests from platters.

But though the feast invited me to indulge, a sharp guilt needled me. Many starved on the streets of Oedija. Perhaps a show of plenty was one of the necessary frivolities of ceremony, but it did little to ease my conscience.

Forgoing food for the moment, I turned my attention to the dais that had been raised at the far end of the room, a wooden scaffold painted gold that rose half a man's height and creaked with the weight of the people walking across it. Upon the platform, Despoina Asileia Wreath sat in a throne made of wicker wood, the ends fanning out several cubits above her, fashioned like a peacock's feathers. The Despoina had not turned herself gold or bared her breasts as she had for her Ascension, but wore a sober violet chiton, even if the fold across the front did open coquettishly, hinting at what lay beneath. Her face had been painted to exaggerate her features, serving now only to emphasize the bored expression with which she stared over the proceedings.

Next to the Despoina stood one of the few female laurel guards I'd seen: First Laurel Synne, Nomusa had told me earlier. Her face was all hard planes as she stared at the people milling around her, daring any to approach. A hard woman she must be indeed to fill Lykos's boots.

My gaze caught on the four manacled men surrounding her. Fear and loathing struck through me. The Shepherds' faces were hidden within aqua hoods, but I knew they stared out with dead eyes. Loyalty to Oedija they might claim, but that didn't make them my allies. Especially not with the secret I kept hidden. I didn't know if they could detect attunement just by a looking at a person, and I didn't want to find out. I spotted their Tribune handler lurking around the edges of the dais. He scowled as he stared around him, his head of thinning hair shining with perspiration, his maroon robes billowing loose about his shoulders. A nervous sort, I suspected. Best not to run into him either.

I averted my eyes and sought friendlier faces. Xaron was easiest to spot, and not only because of his Hilarion clothes. As I watched, he spouted a fountain of flames into the air from his mouth, to the amazement of the onlookers. I shook my head. The breadth of his tricks astonished me, particularly now that I was a warden myself. He was clearly reveling in having an audience to perform in front of.

Jaxas was almost as easy to find, if only because of the company he kept. He was absorbed in conversation with a pair of Bali dressed in as strange a fashion as I'd ever seen. The older man wore a robe patterned of a variety of bright colors, and a stole made of a leopard's hide draped around his neck. His peppered hair was braided tightly against his head.

The boy was more extravagantly dressed. Though he was slightly shorter than myself, his feather crown rose high above my head, the yellow and blue quills plucked from a bird I didn't know. Across his chest hung a broad collar of bronze, etched in fine detail with a hundred images, and from the collar hung ribbons of woven silk dyed in as many colors as his older escort's robes. His stomach was bare, revealing a young man's lithe figure, and his arms were revealed as well but for the many bracelets jangling about his forearms and wrists. He wore a skirt of bronze plates, and the sandals on his feet were painted gold.

The Yorandu Heir, Komo. I had known Komo was young, but I hadn't expected him to look no more than fourteen years old. I doubted he even grew hair over his lip. The older man would be an advisor — I doubted a warrior would wear those robes.

I felt Nomusa stiffen by me, no doubt glimpsing the Yorandu visitors as well. "I'm going to mingle," she muttered. "Keep an ear out for anything of interest." She headed in the opposite direction of the delegation.

I sighed and examined them again only to find Jaxas had spotted me. Our eyes met for a moment before he turned away to respond to something Komo had said. I turned away as well. If he wanted something from me, he could find me.

Dozens of patricians, Servants, and other notables of Oedija had grouped together. Most conversed in hushed tones, though from one or two erupted boisterous laughter. Yet in these times, most conversations would be of trade and commerce, of soldiers and strongholds. Between the knots of important and prosperous folk, honors flitted back and forth. I spotted Nikias in one corner scowling over it all. No doubt even this flaw-less affair wasn't up to the steward's standards.

As I scanned the room, I searched for a quarry oblivious enough to allow a Finch to eavesdrop. The wine in my hand called to me. Though it smelled too sweet, I wanted to lose myself in it and leave behind my worries for a time. Instead, I only drank it in sips. The threat of a Manifest attack weighed heavily on my mind, and I found myself glancing often at the windows and doors.

"A frown at a celebration sticks out like a finch among terns."

I startled and turned to the speaker, who had approached from behind. My mood soured further still at the sight of the richly dressed honor. "Kako."

The man wore a smile that didn't touch his eyes. In flattery of the Wreaths, he wore boldly green robes with a golden stole draped around his neck. Silver chains adorned his neck as well as his wrists, perhaps in mockery of his caste, though he still sported the tin spiral earrings and shaved head of his fellow honors.

"If you can't enjoy yourself at a party of such great expense," he continued, "I don't know what would please you, First Verifier."

"Perhaps I'm displeased *because* of the great expense."

"Ah, you think it wasteful. But is it not more wasteful to attend and not delight in it?"

I was in no mood to mince words with the silver-tongued fool. "What does your mistress want?"

"Why would you assume she wants for anything? No, Airene. The Low Consul has all she desires of you for the moment."

Even knowing he was baiting me, I couldn't help but ask, "What do you mean?"

The honor's eyes glimmered with the light of a nearby pyr lamp. "But that is half the fun, isn't it? My knowing, your wondering."

I shrugged, playing for nonchalant. "You've said nothing to wonder about."

"No, perhaps I haven't." A smile lingered about the corners of his lips. "Perhaps it isn't me you should ask after, but your closest allies. Perhaps you don't keep them as close as you think."

Chills prickled up my spine, but I forced a smile. "If you mean your arrangement with Nomusa, I know all about it."

Despite my hopes otherwise, Kako's smile didn't slip. "Oh, I thought you might. But you have more friends than her."

With that last barb, the honor turned and melded back into the crowd.

Kako had a gift for mischief. I spite of myself, his words stuck in my mind like a sliver under a fingernail. The honor was many things, but he rarely told a lie that did not contain a kernel of truth. But who else could he mean but Nomusa?

Seeking to distract myself, I ghosted near a group who seemed intent enough in their discussion not to notice me. But as soon as I drifted within earshot, one of them cast me a scowl and gestured to the others. I moved on as if I hadn't noticed. But as I approached my second group of targets, I was noticed again and rebuffed, forced to drift further on.

It wasn't long before I realized what I needed. And I knew just the person to help me obtain it.

I found Xaron in one corner of the room entertaining four young women, likely patrician daughters. I stood just behind them and crossed my arms, unable to decide if I was amused or annoyed at how avidly he sought to charm them.

"But what is this?" he declared as he reached toward the ear of one of the girls. She giggled and moved out of the way, then gasped as his hand blossomed in a vision of shifting colored light. It seemed a streaked painting, and I thought I detected images in it — a butterfly settling on a flower, the sun shining golden through waving grass…

One of the girls gasped, and I blinked. The vision had felt like a nudge on my mind, like when Kyros had sent the message to the librarian from his tower. I looked at my friend with fresh eyes. Xaron had just channeled quintessence, I was sure of it. And I was equally sure he had no idea he had.

His gaze slid over to me, and he closed his fist, making the pastoral scene disappear. "Alas, but I require a respite from my service," he said with a deep bow. "If you fine ladies would excuse me…"

"You're not dismissed yet!" one of the girls objected. "You have to entertain us when we ask. Show us more!"

I moved around the patricians and looped my arm though Xaron's. "Hilarion is going to entertain me now," I said firmly, meeting the eye of the spoiled girl. "If you'll excuse us."

As I led Xaron away, I heard the girl whisper loudly, "I know what kind of entertainment *she's* after," and she and her companions burst into giggles. I ignored them as well as Xaron, for he grinned as I led him to as private an alcove as could be found in the bustling feast hall.

"Growing jealous?" he teased me as he stole my cup of wine and drained it.

"Very." I waved over an honor and received two goblets more. "Xaron, I need your help."

"Oh? Not the kind that girl was insinuating, surely?"

I gave him a flat stare, but he just grinned at me. "Teasing, Aire. What did you need?"

"Cover. We need to pretend to have a conversation while I listen in on people around the room. No one will let me get close enough."

"You *are* wearing a rather intimidating scowl," he pointed out. "But I'm sure it doesn't help that you're one of the leaders of an organization who used to put people like them in the stockyards."

"Exactly my point. So can you help me?"

"Help you?" He wore a mischievous look. "I can do you one better. Put down your wine."

Confused, I obliged, setting my glass next to his. I grew even more perplexed as Xaron raised his hands to my temples.

"What are you doing?"

"Helping you hear." He closed his eyes, his face clearing of emotion. "You may want to brace yourself."

I discovered what he meant a moment later. Without preamble, the room shifted around me, then a wave of sound crashed over me. I reeled under the weight of it. The score of conversations had crescendoed until they filled my head, too loud and overwhelming to distinguish from one another. I would have cried out were I not afraid my own yell would provoke further pain.

As abruptly as it had come, the deluge subsided. "Airene?" I heard Xaron's voice so clearly it seemed as if he spoke in my head. "Did I hurt you?"

"What did you just do?" My own voice reverberated in my head, and I winced. While not quite painful, it wasn't a pleasant sensation.

"I amplified the sound around you. Remember when I told you sound is merely vibrations? Just as any Hilarion amplifies the vibrations in speakers' throats, I can amplify the sounds you hear. But are you sure you're not hurt? You're scrunching up your face like you've eaten a lemon — seeds, rind, and all."

"I'm fine," I lied. With the discomfort of speaking, I wanted to avoid explanations as much as possible. But I couldn't help asking, "You're using kinesis then?"

"Yes. A variation of it."

It clicked then. Before, when Xaron had been channeling the light scene for the girls, I'd thought I felt quintessence pressing on my mind. As my present pain subsided, I again felt that same touch, surrounding me like a bubble. Xaron channeled quintessence though he didn't know it. He always had. As Eltris had said, quintessence was the tool that shaped energy. All channeling required quintessence; though some, like this trick, seemed to require more than simpler channels.

I tucked away my questions. Only one person might answer them for me, and I'd have to wait until tomorrow to ask her. "We may as well make use of this. Can you pick out a conversation for me?"

"Yes. Who would you like to hear?"

Only then did I realize I'd squeezed my eyes shut. Opening them, my vision swam as I scanned the room. I picked out the first interesting pairing I found. "Focus on the Despoina and the Bali man she's speaking with."

The sound whirled around me, and I closed my eyes again as the deluge filled my mind. Then, as the voices settled to a manageable level, two came to me clearer than the rest.

"I have heard you are the — what do you call it? The mouthpiece of a god." The man had a rich baritone with a timbre that made me suspect he was fully aware of it.

"A goddess," Asileia responded shortly. Her voice sounded reedy and thin compared to his. "I am the Hand of Clepsammia."

"Ah, my apologies, my lady. And Clepsammia — she is a powerful goddess, no?"

"She claims all the sands of time."

"Powerful indeed." I heard the rustle of the man's clothes as he moved — cloth scraping together, ornaments of some kind clinking. "A perfect matching for a powerful woman."

Suddenly, I realized with horror what this conversation was: the Bali was courting our Despoina. Yet I knew by the masculine voice it couldn't be the Yorandu Heir.

In my surprise, I missed Asileia's response, and the man was saying with irritation, "If the Despoina does not wish me near, I am sure she would tell you."

"Leave him," Asileia snapped. "I would hear his words."

The sound of sandals on wood faded away. Someone had come to intervene, I gathered; perhaps a guard or an advisor, or even Jaxas.

"Is it not wearying, all these people fretting over you, when you have no need to be cared for? Not a woman such as you."

"Yes. It is wearying."

"Why don't you send them away? Or perhaps we could go somewhere they will not bother you. Somewhere more… private."

A long silence fell, telling of Leia's deliberations over his words. "I will meet this prince of yours first," Asileia decided at length. "But you and I will speak again. I would hear more of what you see when you gaze upon me."

"Yes, divine queen of mine eye."

I reached out and touched Xaron, and he obliged by pulling me away from the conversation. "Well?" he whispered.

My head was starting to ache, but I didn't ask him to stop. The evening was only just getting started. "I'll tell you later. Do you see any Low Consuls? Or Kako — I can't get something he said earlier out of my head." The briefest doubt that Feiyan's henchman may have been alluding to Xaron flashed through my mind, but I dismissed it as quickly as it came. Questioning my trust in Xaron wasn't an option.

"No. But there is — Burning hells!"

My senses seared as Xaron's hand lifted from my temples. As the world righted under my feet, I put out a hand to the wall, gasping slightly. Queasiness assaulted me, and for a moment, it was hard to open my eyes.

"Aire." Xaron sounded as if he spoke through clenched teeth.

I opened my eyes. Coming toward us were two Shepherds, the crowd flinching away before them, their dead eyes never straying from us.

"Why approach now?" Xaron muttered. "I've been channeling all evening. I have a right to."

Sharp fingers needled through my gut, but it wasn't for Xaron that I feared. Remembering Eltris's unnaturally keen hearing, and understanding it now for what it was, I didn't dare respond. Shepherds might easily be enhancing their own senses.

The two manacled wardens stood before us, balefully looking out from under their hoods. For the moment, they stared at Xaron. "You have channeled, though you are forbidden," one told him.

"I'm Hilarion!" Xaron responded angrily. "I have every right to channel!"

"Only for the entertainment of others."

Though I quailed inside, I spoke up. "He was entertaining me. Surely that's not outside his bounds."

Icy water seemed to pour over me as both Shepherds turned their gazes on me. "This Hilarion was entertaining you," the Shepherd repeated.

His expression didn't shift. I had no idea if he believed me or not. "Yes," I said firmly. "He was."

"Don't worry about him!" a reedy voice snapped from behind them. Stepping between the Shepherds was the Tribune I'd seen before. "The boy has the right, as he said. Return to your posts!"

The Shepherds moved without hesitation back to where they had previously stood. The Tribune looked between Xaron and me. "Entertaining her, were you?" he asked with a leer.

"Yes," Xaron responded stiffly.

Unperturbed, the Tribune peered at me. "And who are you?" he barked. His eyes wandered down to my medallion. "Ah. One of the new Finches. Friends with Hilarion, are you?"

"I believe I'm the one who gets to ask questions," I said calmly. "You're the new handler of the Shepherds?"

The Tribune sneered. "And I thought you lot were supposed to be sharp. Why else would they obey me?"

"Pray you fare better than the last one. As I recall, I shot him with a crossbow."

The man only grinned wider. "We'll have to see if you get lucky twice." Without another word, he turned and stalked back through the crowd.

I found Xaron staring at me. "What?"

"With Tribune Timon just then, you were a bit… short.."

"You heard the way he talked to us. I can't stand men like him." But the truth became apparent even as I spoke. "I suppose he scares me," I admitted in a whisper. "Because of… you know."

Xaron smiled sympathetically. "Of course I know. But drawing his ire won't do you any favors."

He was right, of course. But I couldn't completely dispel the sudden anger that had filled me, and with my head beginning to ache again, I felt it simmering just below the surface.

"I suppose I'd better try to eavesdrop the usual way again," I said grudgingly. "And you have more tricks to perform."

A grin blossomed on his face. "And more young ladies to amuse."

I rolled my eyes as Xaron sauntered away to be immediately hailed for a performance. At least someone was enjoying their new position.

I hunted around half-heartedly for another group to pester, picking up my wine and sipping at it again. But before I could decide on a target, Nomusa emerged from the crowd. I knew what she'd say from her black look before she opened her mouth.

"It's time," she declared shortly, then turned toward the dais.

Quelling my dread, I followed.

Jaxas and Komo, still conversing at the base of the dais, turned as we approached. The young Bali Heir's face brightened like a boy anticipating a sweet.

"These are the Finches? And one of them Bali!" He spoke with the same accent as the man I'd heard speaking with the Despoina, and in the same sonorous manner, like he wasn't afraid of his words being heard.

"Yes," Jaxas responded, his eyes briefly meeting mine. I saw caution written there and wondered at its source. "Shaka-Heir Charatta Yorandu Komo, please meet First Verifier Nomusa and First Verifier Airene."

"Two Firsts?" the older Bali man standing next to them said. "That is unusual, is it not?"

"It is," Jaxas acknowledged. "But our First Verifiers work well together, and the times call for unprecedented actions."

"They do," Komo agreed easily. "I am glad to meet both of you. Particularly one of my countryfolk." He extended his hand to Nomusa, clearly seeking to give the usual Bali greeting.

Nomusa didn't look down at his hand, but gave a short, stiff bow, little more than a nod. She said nothing.

As the young Heir's brow knit in confusion, I rushed to say, "We're glad to meet you as well, Shaka-Heir Komo. And which of your warriors do we have the pleasure of meeting?"

The older man laughed, though I noticed the exchange hadn't escaped his attention. "A charming one, aren't you? I am no warrior, First Verifier, but the Heir's advisor. You may simply call me Nkosi. Long have I served his father, and so may I hope to serve him."

But though Komo had lowered his arm, he hadn't looked aside from Nomusa. "Why do you not greet me as tradition would bade?"

Dangerous waters, those. I tried to navigate the conversation away from them. "Nomusa has long since left her homeland, and I'm afraid she no longer practices—"

"Tradition." Nomusa cut through my rushed words, and to my consternation, the other three focused on her. "What do you know of tradition?"

Komo stared at her in astonishment. "I am young, but I have been well tutored, First Verifier. Yet I do not think this is what you mean."

Nkosi narrowed his eyes. "A Bali in Oedija, resentful of the Heir. I don't have to wonder long to know which ishaka you fled from."

"Nor should you wonder at who is my family," Nomusa shot back. "If you've served his father, their blood is on your hands as well."

"Blood on his hands?" Komo sounded astonished. "Nkosi is an honorable and loyal—"

"Peace, Heir Komo," the advisor interrupted him. His eyes did not leave Nomusa. "What she says is true. Her family's blood does stain my hands, and I am not ashamed to say so."

Hard lines deepened in Nomusa's face as she stared at Komo's advisor. I stood by, helpless to intervene. Jaxas was similarly silent, watching with hollowed eyes.

"Speak plainly," Komo demanded of Nkosi. "Who is she?"

"Nomusa, as she said before. Eshalo Yorandu Nomusa."

The Shaka-Heir's eyes widened. "Eshalo," he whispered, turning toward Nomusa. "But I was told all your family had died."

"No," the Bali advisor said. "Your father and I never conspired to deceive you, Komo. But we always knew the Eshalo scion lurked somewhere within the Four Realms."

Komo bowed his head. "Truly, I am sorry," he said with his gaze lowered. "Just because your family's death was necessary does not mean I do not regret it."

Jaxas looked as astonished at his words as I was. Nomusa's teeth bared in a snarl. "*Necessary*, was it?" she sneered. "You think to dismiss murder with words? To rob me of my homeland and make amends with apologies?" She turned her head aside, fists clenched and arms stiff at her sides.

Komo's head shot up. "No! Of course not! I merely wished to—"

"Heir Komo," Nkosi said, reprimand sharp in his voice. "We will speak of this later." He turned his angry gaze on Jaxas. "You bring us here to negotiate an alliance, yet flaunt this rebel in our face. You play a dangerous game, Archon."

"Nkosi," Jaxas started, but the advisor had already turned away.

"Heir Komo, I suggest we retire for the evening to ponder our future relationship with Oedija."

"As you wish," the boy said, his uncertainty plain. As he turned after his advisor, he cast one last lingering look back at Nomusa. I almost pitied the boy for the pain in his expression.

"Both of you will come with me. Now."

I turned toward Jaxas. Never had I seen anger on such open display from the Archon.

"Of course." I glanced at Nomusa.

She still looked aside, hands clenched in fists. When Jaxas began walking away, she finally spoke, her voice tight. "I will return to my quarters now."

As Jaxas turned back to answer her, she stalked past him and out of the banquet hall. The Archon shook his head sharply and beckoned me to follow him out.

Amid the stares and mounting murmurs around us, the Archon led me off the carpeted path and up the stairs. I breathed a sigh of relief. As terrible as that had been to witness, it had been worse with all those people watching. I'd already gained notoriety from the Despoina's trial. Finches could only operate effectively from the shadows, and the Order was attracting far too much light for my liking.

As we ascended the stairs and entered Jaxas's solar, his ire grew almost palpable. Sealing the door and sharply dismissing Nikias, who had scrambled after us during our hasty exit, he stalked over to stand before the cold hearth, facing away from me.

"Why," he began in a low voice, "in the burning depths of the 'Thae did you not tell me of this before?"

My cheeks burned. "It wasn't relevant before."

"And now?" He turned toward me, eyes catching the yellow light of the pyr lamps mounted along the walls. "Leia already walks a thin line.

Her recent trial, her erratic behavior, rumors of Myron's survival, to say nothing of both fronts that Oedija faces — all of these already conspire against this alliance with the Yorandu. And just when I believed we might be making progress, we're thwarted yet again."

I thought of the Bali man courting Asileia and decided now wasn't the best time to mention that additional wrinkle in his plans. "I'm sorry, Jaxas. Things have been moving fast."

"And you've not kept up." The hollowness of his face was made more prominent by the shadows. "You've not been the same since you woke, Airene. You haven't been to see me, and I've heard little of your activities. I need the woman who brought the plans of the Manifest grinding to a halt. I need the Finch who convinced me to put the fate of our city in her hands. Can you be her once again?"

I let his words wash past me as I stared into one of the lamps. I wished I could tell him the truth. But all I had was the same tired excuse.

"You must defend our nation," I said, quiet but firm. "I seek to defend the Four Realms from the threat no one else acknowledges."

His expression didn't shift. "You think I don't know the threat Vusu still poses?"

"Not Vusu. Famine."

We stared at each other for a long moment. The Archon looked away first.

"Famine," he repeated softly. "And what can we to do to stop a god?"

"I don't know. But we must try."

He straightened. "Be that as it may. I know I don't have authority over you anymore. So I ask you as a friend. Please, Airene. Don't forget about your home city in the throes of your pyr hunt."

Perhaps he didn't mean to dismiss my quest, but I couldn't think he truly understood if he put Oedija above dealing with Famine. All I could manage was a nod before I turned away.

As I touched a hand to the door, Jaxas spoke again. "Tell Nomusa to stay away from Komo. Please."

I only nodded again.

Escaping the palace, I didn't hail a carriage, not knowing which I was permitted to use, but walked back down to the Aviary. Night had fallen while we'd taken part in the revelry, and though the wind off the sea was cold and wet, and clouds crowded out the lights of the radiant winds and the moons, there was still a peacefulness in the air that I hadn't felt in a long time. Now that I couldn't safely wander Oedija's streets at night, only on Wreath and Conclave grounds could I find solace.

But I couldn't find peace tonight. Though it hadn't been completely my fault, I still felt responsible for what had happened. Somehow, I had to repair it.

But even as I made the resolution, I felt it wilting before my greater purpose. No matter how Jaxas pleaded, no matter how much I felt I was making a ruin of my responsibilities, I had to stay true to my course. Famine was the enemy of all. No other concern could come before him.

As the cold wind bit through my thin dress and whipped my hair into my face, I wondered bitterly how many relationships and people would fall to my quest.

I returned to the Aviary, tore off my borrowed peplos, and unwound my hair, replacing them with a tunic, trousers, and a simple plait. The chill of the oncoming wet season permeated the room, so I pulled on a cloak as well and clung it tight around me as I sat on my bed. I was restless, far too restless to sleep, yet I didn't know where to go. I was as good as a prisoner here at night, and the chains of safety and comfort were tight about me.

I tried to relax with Eltris's exercises once again, but found my mind drifting. Something nudged at the edge of my thoughts. It was the same feeling as if I'd forgotten something important, but couldn't for the life of me remember it. I turned restlessly in my bed, trying to quiet my mind for sleep.

My eyes fluttered open, then went wide. The glow of pyrkin from the cracked pot had reminded me of something. *The whisper finch.* The pyrkin had looked like the glowing patch of feathers on its chest.

They will come for him the night he arrives. The whisper finch's words came back to me now. In the intervening days, I'd neglected to puzzle them out, distracted by everything else that had occurred. Now, the knot began to unravel. *He fears the knowledge he brings to Oedija.* The events and players of the evening fresh in mind, the words suddenly took on new meaning.

What knowledge the Shaka-Heir brought to Oedija, and who feared it, I still didn't know. But Komo was in danger, and I was the only one who knew.

I only prayed I wasn't too late.

CHAPTER ELEVEN

RIFT

Clepsammia had known Agmon Brandheart would fight until his end. A knowing smile played on her lips, for she knew all that would come, and the destiny he would complete.

'I can help you face Famine,' said she. 'You must find the one who may endanger him most and beseech her aid.'

'How can any being, god or mortal, endanger one such as Famine?'

'Because she completes him. Go find the goddess Harvest. And then you will have the only ally you need.'

— The Seeds of Famine, a translation from the Lighted-tongue; by Oracle Kalene of deme Hull; 831 SLP

I ran back to the bridge through the pelting rain.

What I could do to stop anyone who sought to harm Komo, I had no idea. I still couldn't channel. I might alert Komo's warriors or the laurel guards, but if it were Seeker wardens after him, neither would be enough to stop them.

There was one person who could help, however.

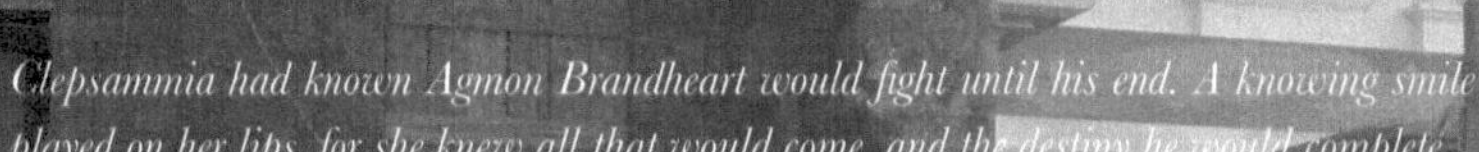

I arrived back at the palace doors, gasping and dripping. The amused guards looked me up and down, but glimpsing my medallion, they allowed me to pass. They didn't even check me for a weapon. What they would have done if they'd found my knife strapped against my back, I didn't know, but it didn't bode well for them to be lax if assassins were after Komo. I caught my breath as I slowed to a walk, ruining the carpet with every sodden step. I'd look mad enough entering the feast hall dressed as I was — no need to be panting like a lathered mule as well.

Reaching the feast hall, I entered within. Finely dressed patricians glanced at me, then looked away with offended expressions. I refrained from smoothing my frazzled hair and looked around. The Despoina no longer sat in her throne, perhaps having found a private moment with the Bali man. But it was Xaron, tucked away in a far corner with giggling girls, whom I sought.

My patience at its end, I wove my way to him, the task made easier by the rich and powerful stepping out of the way, as if afraid of the rainwater dripping from me. Reaching the corner, I pushed past the girls and grabbed my friend's arm.

"Come on. No time to lose."

The bouquet he'd formed of fiery radiance burned away into nothing. "What?" he objected. "What do you mean?"

"You're taking him again?" the same spoiled girl as before complained, then muttered, "Greedy hag."

I ignored her and dragged Xaron through the crowd.

Once we were outside the feast hall's doors, he pulled away. "What's going on?" he demanded, bewildered.

"I'll explain as we walk. Do you know where Komo's quarters are?"

"No. Why would I?"

I sifted through our contacts. "Nikias. Have you seen him?"

"He followed you and Jaxas out after you made that scene with Komo."

"Perhaps he's in Jaxas's solar," I murmured. We didn't have any better chance to find Komo, so I turned toward the stairs. "Let's go."

"He will not be there."

I whirled toward the unfamiliar voice. An honor stood not six paces away. From her position near the open doors, she'd been just out of sight before. Xaron looked between us curiously, as if we might know each other. Perhaps it was the familiarity with which she'd spoken to us. Honors tended to be deferential and to wait until they were spoken to.

"You know where Nikias is?" I asked.

"Yes. But you wish to know where Shaka-Heir Komo resides, do you not? I can take you to him."

Time was pressing; my questions for her would have to wait. I nodded. "As quickly as you can."

The honor quickly led us up the grand stairs, then up a second stair-case. Taking the hallway south, we entered the same wing of the Laurel Palace as the guest quarters located on the first floor. I could already tell this wing of rooms was fit for kings and queens. The walls were lined with lavish paintings of notable people and events in Oedija's history, and the floor was thick with golden carpets. The honor pointed at the most extravagant of the doors, which was inlaid with gold. It was also the only one with Bali soldiers outside it, dressed in a similar manner to their prince, though without all the feathers and silk. Curved swords were belted at their waists. Though one was a woman, her only adjustment was an additional black wrapping around her breasts under the broad, bronze collar.

"The Shaka-Heir is within," the honor said in a hushed voice, though Komo's guards had already noticed us.

"Thank you," I said, then began to brush past her.

The honor's voice arrested me. "Remember this, First Verifier. Remember that I aided you in your time of need."

It was my turn to look back, bewildered. But the honor only gave me a nod before turning and striding away.

"What was going on with her?" I asked Xaron.

"No idea."

No time to wonder. I drew in a breath and approached Komo's guards with as close to a smile as I could manage.

"Evening. I need to see the Heir as soon as possible."

The male guard, a veteran with a scar above one eye that partially closed it, looked me up and down. "I do not think you have the authority for that request. Who are you?"

Xaron broke in. "You should speak with more respect, man. This is the First Verifier of Oedija."

The man looked unfazed. "And you are the jester, no? Then perhaps this is why you tell me the First Verifier wishes to see the Shaka-na so soon after she and her companion offended him. To do so would seem a jest to me."

I wondered if this was the First of Komo's guard, as well-informed and confident as he appeared. But until I knew, I wasn't sure I wished to confide what I suspected was coming. "I apologize for that, and will be glad to apologize to the Shaka-Heir myself. But my errand is urgent, and I must see him. Will you tell him we wish to meet?"

The guard looked me over again, then spoke to his companion. "Go to the Shaka-na."

The woman nodded and turned to knock at the door. A call from within admitted her, and she slipped inside.

The veteran guard stared at us as we waited. I couldn't keep from shifting my feet. Xaron looked as if he might burst with questions, for I still hadn't explained what was happening.

"You are as nervous as a *taliga* — an asher, as you call it," Komo's guard noted. "I would wonder but that you do not have the white fingers."

Surprise compelled me to look at him. I could not tell if the man was joking or not, for his expression was as serious as before.

"What is your name?" I asked him.

"Zolani."

"Zolani. How long have you served Heir Komo?"

"All his life." He pointed at his scar with a sudden grin. "And I will serve him the rest of his life, spirits willing."

I wondered uncomfortably if he had gained that scar killing Nomusa's family. The thought made my favorable first impression of Zolani sour.

The door opened again, and the female guard stepped out. "Shaka-na Komo will see you now."

Xaron and I slipped between the guards to enter within. The decor inside almost made me wonder if we were still in the Laurel Palace and not transported to the Bali plateaus. The room was brightly lit with green pyr lamps. Vines crept along the walls, vibrant and alive, and leafy plants in great decorated pots filled the corners. As we were in the hosting room of the suite, there was a table and cupboard, likely holding liquors and other objects to entertain guests.

Komo stood in the middle of the room and watched as we approached, his young features drawn. He'd discarded the ceremonial garments from before and wore a simple white tunic and loose pants that cinched around his ankles above his bare feet.

"First Verifier Airene," he said gravely. "I am surprised that you visit me so soon after..." He shrugged. "Well, you were there."

Despite the urgency, I couldn't let things lie at that, especially when his advisor stepped into the room with a severe look. Before they'd believe the threat I needed to warn them of, I had to regain some measure of credibility.

"I apologize, Heir Komo. We meant no offense. Archon Jaxas was not aware of Nomusa's heritage, and I didn't think of what trouble it might cause." A quick look at Nkosi included him in the apology.

The advisor did not ease his hard demeanor. "And now you bring us your royal jester to salve the wound. Tell me, Airene the Finch. How many ways do you wish to insult us this day?"

Before I could think of a reply, Komo looked around at the advisor. "Peace, Nkosi. You have taught me to look at people and give time to judge them fairly. I do not think we have given the First Verifier a fair measure yet, nor time to explain herself."

A small smile softened Nkosi's features. "I have not judged her, Shaka-na. I meant to cut to the quick of the matter through sharp words. But perhaps even that was not yet necessary." He looked back to me. "Please, First Verifier. I will assume then you did not come idly."

My estimation of the young ruler-to-be had risen greatly. Even though I knew as Nomusa's friend I ought not to like him and his kin, I couldn't help a begrudging respect forming.

"Thank you Heir Komo, Advisor Nkosi. I do come tonight with urgent news." I paused, gathering the courage to say the words. "I fear your lives might be in danger."

They didn't react with the surprise I expected, but merely shared a look.

"And from whom do you expect this attack?" Nkosi asked calmly. His posture seemed to have shifted minutely, but suddenly, it he seemed as if he might spring forward at a moment's notice.

Time to throw the spokes, as Talan would have said.

"From Seekers, those who ascribe to the movement known as the Manifest. They have wardens among their numbers. And I believe they are coming after you tonight."

"Why so soon?" Komo wondered aloud as he looked again to his advisor. "Our negotiations may yet fail. Why attack before anything has even been decided?"

The advisor only nodded his head in acknowledgement. "Zolani," he called out.

The veteran guard peered in at once. "Yes, Nkosi-sa?"

But the advisor didn't have time to answer — for the room suddenly split with a shriek like from a great dying beast.

The floor shook under us, making me fall to my knees. Fighting for balance, I wrenched my head up and stared. The ceiling had ripped open — not in fragments of stone, but like the very seams of the world had been rent apart. Every color and light known to humankind assaulted my senses. I knew immediately what it meant as a familiar wave of nausea flooded through me.

Someone had cut open a path from the Pyrthae.

"Xaron!" I shouted.

Just as he looked up, our attackers emerged from the tear, clumsily turning about midair to fall gracelessly to the floor. Three at a time, they poured through, as much as the tear would allow. Violet tatu adorned their faces, and dark robes whipped about them.

Seeker wardens.

The room burst into a frenzy. Zolani whipped his sickle-shaped sword at the closest of the Seekers. The feral screamed and collapsed, but threw up his hands as he fell. A wave of kinesis barreled into the veteran guard, and he flew backward to land against the wall with a faint crash.

I narrowly avoided the erratic wave as I threw myself to the ground. Scrambling to my feet, I saw Xaron slam one into a wall so hard that his skull cracked with red lines, a grotesque parody of his spidery violet tatu. The moment after, Xaron cried out as a line of fire cut against his shoulder.

Nkosi, despite wearing cumbersome robes, fought with hands and feet, disabling and knocking one of the wardens flat to the ground before striking his throat with a savage jab.

Komo, though a boy, fought with as much prowess as the men, moving with the grace only hard years of practicing Ixolo could have afforded him. He knocked one Seeker to the ground with a sweep of his legs, then leaped and kicked a Seeker just emerging from the rent into the wall. I stared at the force behind the blow, then found my suspicions confirmed as, a moment later, another of the wardens threw kinesis at the boy. Komo turned and met it with open hands, then twisted his body around. The blast dispersed around him. I stared in amazement.

The boy was a warden.

But a Seeker had finally noticed me huddled on the ground and raised her hands toward me, sparks gathered at her fingertips. I desperately willed my locus to open, but I remained as closed to the Pyrthae as before.

The split second of hesitation was enough. Fire leaped toward me.

I turned aside too late. Flames caught my shoulder, searing where they touched. Tumbling to the ground, I gasped with the pain and scrambled away.

A glance back showed the warden readying a second attempt on my life. But before she could channel, someone barreled past me, steel flashing in their hands. As the second of Komo's guard attacked, the Seeker turned the fire on her, but missed. The guard flashed her sickle-blade across her opponent's throat, and the Seeker fell in a red spray.

Gasping with fear and pain, I fled for the door. Every movement of my right shoulder pulled at the scorched skin and sent waves of sickening agony through my body. Yet as I found the safety of the cool stone outside, I gritted my teeth, reached around under my back, and pulled free Nomusa's knife. I held it up in my left hand as the screams and rumbles of channeled energy sounded from within. I'd killed before, but I was no warrior. I was scared near witless just thinking about reentering the chamber. Even though I'd weathered the horrors of the Despoina's trial, I wasn't prepared for this.

But I never would be.

Gripping the dagger tight, I turned into the room again. Five Seekers still fought against Xaron, Komo, and Nkosi. Xaron and Komo often wove into each other's conflicts as they dodged and dispersed the attacks against them. Each had sustained wounds horrible to behold, but didn't seem to slow from them. Nkosi kept to the walls, only striking out when a Seeker came near. Zolani and the female guard lay motionless along the walls. The Pyrthaen tear still hovered above, flooding the room with a strange light. None seemed to notice my return. I ghosted along the edge of the room, the walls now pocketed from errant blasts of fire and force.

As Xaron flung one Seeker toward the wall six feet away from me, I buried my fear and leaped forward, raising my knife with both hands. The pain of my burn only fueled the fury with which I stabbed the knife down into the stunned man. The blade, clumsily aimed, entered between his neck and shoulder, tearing through the flesh with an ease that stunned me. The Seeker jerked his head up at me, horror and wrath and pain twisted together. As he raised a trembling hand toward me, I jerked away, leaving my knife in his shoulder. Before he could try for vengeance, his hand fell away, and his head fell forward.

"Back!" one of the Seekers shouted above the fray. "Back to the 'Thae, fools!" The warden followed her own advice and, with a kinesis-propelled jump, flew back into the rent above.

Her retreat broke the rest. The last three Seekers immediately followed, two crashing into each other in their haste to flee. Xaron gave one a parting burn on the leg before he sank against the wall, gasping.

I stood and watched dully as Nkosi stepped up next to the Shaka-Heir and placed a hand on his shoulder. They both looked up into the Pyrthaen tear, which had already begun to seal over. Though my ears were dull from the battle, I faintly heard the advisor's murmured words. "You did well, Komo. Very well. Now we must care for our fallen. See to Zolani. I will go to Sunto."

My gaze drifted down to my wet hands. The blood had begun to form a strange lattice as it streamed down my skin, the pattern reminding me of the violet tatu of the Manifest.

"They're both dead," Komo said quietly, but he did as his advisor asked, kneeling by the crumpled body of the veteran warrior. "He has no pulse, nor life in his eyes. He has joined our ancestors."

"Sunto as well." The advisor kneeled next to the female guard, who lay twisted on the ground on the other side, blood pooling under her head. "*Kwagati umya wako umgoda hlahla.* Would they had died under the boughs of the isikhayha."

"They will find their way rootward, I do not doubt. Their spirits were strong and their hearts true."

My gaze lingered on the veteran. He'd meant to serve Komo all his life. A bitter irony it had ceased this night.

But I had my own to attend to. Still feeling as if I walked in a dream, I kneeled next to Xaron, wiped my hands on my trousers, and put a hand to his head. Blood matted his hair.

"Xaron," I said softly. "Are you alright?"

He looked up with a pained grin. "They ruined my outfit."

A small smile crept over my own lips. "I'm sure we can find you another potato sack to wear. Let's get you to a healer."

Ignoring his protests that he could walk, and ignoring my own hurts, I pulled Xaron's arm over my good shoulder and helped him stand.

To my surprise, Komo stood at his other side. Though cuts and burns puckered up the skin of his arms and chest, and his white clothes were splattered with red, he didn't seem much wearied or injured from the battle. He met my eye without hesitation as he extended a hand with a bloody knife in it. I flinched as I recognized the weapon as my own.

"You spoke the truth, First Verifier Airene," he said. "I will remember your warning. Now, let me help you."

I stared at him, not accepting my dagger. "You're nearly as badly injured as he is."

He gave a small laugh. "My wounds will heal." He suddenly looked to Nkosi. "It feels wrong to laugh in the face of death."

His advisor shook his head. "If we cannot laugh now, then what good has laughter ever served? You do no injustice to their names, Shaka-na. The passed do not wish the living to linger, but to move on and be merry when they can."

Komo gave him a small nod, then turned back to Xaron and me. "I don't mean to delay. Let us be off. But do you not need your knife?"

Though my skin crawled, I finally accepted it and clutched the grip hard. If we weren't still in danger now, we would be eventually. I couldn't let the fear of hurting others stop me from protecting myself and my companions.

No matter how much I might wish it could be otherwise.

———

Several turns later, Xaron was settled into a bed, and I sat next to him. It was the same bed I'd occupied just under a span before. I sat in the same chair Corin had. I wondered if she'd discovered anything of her sister yet. At least she would be safer than us.

Just as she'd led me into the situation that landed me in that bed, so I'd done with Xaron. I glanced at him. He slept finally, though he'd moaned for the previous turn, complaining about being unable to lay on his side from his wounds. The healer had said his injuries were not serious and would heal, and had given him a poppy tincture to help him rest. Yet cracked ribs and seared skin were far more than I wished my friend to suffer because of me.

I stared down at the exposed knife in my lap, clean of blood now. It glinted dully with the green light that crept in through the windows. The storm had broken, and the radiant winds were out once more, pulsing as they streamed over the city. I didn't touch the blade, but studied the sharp edge of it. I had killed a man with it mere turns before. He was the second person I'd killed; third, if Vusu succumbed to my quarrel. It didn't have the shock of the first time, yet I doubted the great emptiness that welled up in its wake would ever depart. I wondered bleakly how many more I could kill before there was nothing left of me to drain away.

Despair covered me as a blanket, suffocating, with no escape. I didn't try to throw it off. I let it bear me down, down to an oblivion where it might ease away.

Only in the midst of that darkness did I see the glimmer of light. It pulsed gently like a star on a clear dusk. Instinctively, I reached toward it, the only light in this place. As I touched it, the light eased a little wider. I grasped eagerly at it, pulling for more. It readily complied. The star cast off a suffusing warmth, one that drove away the shadows. I allowed in more, letting it fill me until it threatened to burn.

I jolted awake, suddenly aware. Half of my fingertips, dug into my trousers, glowed with a dampened light. Trembling, I raised them.

Two fingertips on my left hand and three on my right glowed warmly.

Held in the midst of the comforting warmth, I didn't fear them. Radiance filled me to the brim, but I didn't overflow with it. Easing my tensed muscles, I relaxed and let the energy swirl inside me.

Nkosi had told Komo not to linger on the dead, but to move on and be merry. The guilt and horror of what I'd faced hadn't faded.

Yet, embraced by the power of the Pyrthae, living the culmination of fanciful childhood dreams, I allowed myself to smile and drift away on a river of light.

INTERLUDE I

SEDA

Seda balanced the tray in one hand as she slipped the key from her neck. She always carried it under her chiton, hanging cold against her skin, where no one might be tempted to steal it from her. It still made her uneasy, carrying the key to Master's room. She didn't want to fail his trust. But even more than that, it was unsettling that he needed a lock at all. Before his illness, he'd feared nothing, for nothing could harm him.

Now he had not the strength to leave his room.

She banished the traitorous thoughts as she fitted the key in the lock. Such thoughts could sink her into despair, and then she couldn't serve Master. And he needed her as he never had before.

Almost as soon as she entered, he called out to her. "Seda?" His voice was cracked and weak as if parched. Yet the ewers of water she brought to him were always empty when she returned.

"I am here, Master." She pulled the door closed and locked it, then turned too quickly and almost upended the tray. A bit of broth spilled from the bowl onto the crusty bread.

Stupid girl. Clumsy girl. She thought the insults, for Master wouldn't approve of her cursing herself. He had often told Seda that she, like every being, had a spark of divinity within her, and that if she couldn't respect herself as she was, she should at least treat herself well for that. She tried to obey. But when she acted so stupid, so clumsy, she knew she deserved to be punished. As Valem punished his children, as Seda's father had punished her with his fists, so Seda felt she should punish her failings.

She must, for she couldn't fail Master.

She was careful with the tray as she walked to him and set it down. His room was square — fourteen paces each way, she'd discovered during long turns of waiting. Only the light of a single, swinging pyr lamp illuminated the room. Master preferred torches, saying fire was cleansing while pyrkin was crowding, but even he admitted he was too weak to risk it now. And Seda worried even the small amount of smoke from a torch would weaken him further.

"I brought bread and broth, Master," she murmured as she kneeled and took the bowl and spoon in hand. Master was facing her, still dressed in the torn robe he'd worn since the night his illness began. Once it had been white; now, it was charred ashy and stained dark with blood. She wished he would let her bathe and clothe him. But it was his eyes that bothered her most. Always open, they stared past her into places that Seda couldn't see, and that she feared no man should ever look.

She stifled her worry and brought the spoon to his lips. "Drink, Master. It will make you feel better."

As soon as the spoon touched his lips, he lapped it up greedily. Seda smiled. A hungry day was a good day. Giving him a few more spoonfuls of broth, she asked, "Would you like softened bread, Master?" She didn't expect an answer, nor did she receive one. Tearing off a bit of the bread and dipping it in the bowl, she brought it to his lips. Master accepted it and chewed, his expression absent and blank.

As she dipped a second piece of bread, his hand snaked out and grabbed her arm, upsetting the bowl of broth. She bit back the curses at herself as she stared into Master's urgent stare.

"Yes, Master?"

"Seda," he said, voice gravelly but stronger than before. "You are still here."

Relief flooded her. This was him, truly him, returned to her at last. "Yes, Master," she said. "Always."

"No." He shook his head slowly. "Not always, loyal one. Soon, you must go to another." He closed his eyes. Seda wondered if he'd fallen asleep.

Then his eyelids fluttered open again. "He tries to claim me," he muttered, more to himself than Seda. "He has his claws in me. I don't know that I can let him go now."

The words stuck like barbs in her. Before she could decide on soothing words, Master spoke again. "Do you remember when you came to me, Seda?"

"Of course, Master."

"A girl nearly killed by her father." Seda was gratified at the fire that burned in his eyes. "You couldn't stay with him, that much was clear. And I saw in you the unbreakable honor it requires to remain a true servant."

"Yes, Master," she replied, and tried to believe it. But she couldn't shake the doubt that nothing in her was unbreakable. Nothing was even whole enough to break.

"And do you know how I knew this?"

"No, Master."

"I knew because no matter what your father did to you, no matter how bruised and bloody he left you, you refused to leave him. No amount of suffering would cause you to abandon those you had dedicated yourself to." His eyes seemed to reach behind her.

"Yes, Master." This at least she could agree with. She would never leave him. Not after all he had done for her. And she for him.

He sighed heavily. "I hope you do not blame me for taking you away from him and having him killed. He made it simple. A daemon in a man's skin, he was, and few were sad to see him go."

Seda kept very still. If only she could unhear words. But she could not.

"You never told me that before, Master," she said quietly. "That you were behind his sentencing and execution."

Master looked up at her, surprised. "Didn't I? Oh, Seda. I don't wish to give you pain. I… my mind wanders. I'm not as I was…"

Stupid, stupid girl. She had caused him anguish. Why must she always speak the wrong things?

"You should drink more broth, Master," she said, reaching for the spoon with her other hand — her shame-hand, against the teachings of her faith, but he still gripped her right arm too tightly to use. She was glad he had the strength to hold her so firmly.

"Seda, Seda. When will you let him go?"

She froze as the spoon dipped into the broth. She didn't dare look into Master's eyes. She knew by the harshness of the voice that it wasn't his mind she would see behind them.

"Other," she breathed.

"*Other*," the one who had stolen Master's tongue sneered. "Why must you call me that name, *Other?* I am no other but the servant to our true master."

"No one can be master but he who has mastered himself." She repeated it in her mind, the mantra Master had taught her in preparation for this day. When daemons would steal his tongue and tempt her from his service.

"But there is, Seda. If you would but open yourself to me, I could show you I have. But you know it all the same. You know your master serves not himself, but a greater lord, the same as I serve. The same as *you* serve."

"No. Master does not serve the Snake. The Snake serves him. The Snake is bound to him."

"The Snake is wound around his neck!" the Other mocked. "Or is it not his tongue I speak with?"

"Silence!" she hissed through clenched teeth. He held her so tightly she could feel the bruises starting to form. But she would not struggle. She would not leave. Master had barely eaten. He needed sustenance to recover his strength.

As if hearing her thoughts, the Other said, "He'll not rise again, Seda. Look at the wound in his side! See the foul corruption pouring from it, the tainted flesh that pulls back cracked and purple! See the shaft shot deep! That it missed his vitals was a disservice. It has prolonged his suffering, only made it longer before my master can claim him."

"He can heal," she murmured. "His wounds have always healed before."

She saw from the corner of her eye Master's face draw back in a rictus grin. "Ah, Seda. But he won't heal this time. Our true master won't let him."

The truth she'd long suspected hit her with a blow harder than her father had ever managed. She crumpled in on herself, breath coming fast and shallow. *Stupid girl. Stupid, stupid girl.* She should have done something before. She should have stopped the Other and the Snake before it came to this. It didn't matter that she couldn't think of what she could have done differently. All she knew was that she hadn't done enough.

"Seda?"

Relief flooded her. "Master!" She wanted to throw herself on him and burst into tears, but she couldn't burden him with her own sorrow. She had to be strong for him.

"I… lost myself for a moment. I think it would be best if you left me to rest again."

She looked down at the nearly untouched tray. She should have done something to help before he became so weak, it was true. But it wasn't too late to try to do all she could.

Seda drew in a deep breath.

"No, Master. You told me you took me in because I would never stop serving you. Let me show you it is true. I will not leave until you eat all this tray's contents."

Master wore his own smile now. "Seda. What would I do without you?"

You will never have to find out, she resolved as she brought the lukewarm liquid to his lips. She would never leave him.

No matter how much he hurt her.

CHAPTER TWELVE

A FINCH FOUND

Agmon Brandheart and his most loyal First Wardens left the battlefield in search of Harvest. They combed all the realms for the goddess. Yet nowhere could she be found.

'She has retreated beyond our pleas!' one despaired. 'She will not harken to our call!'

'We will find her,' Agmon boldly claimed, though his own courage faltered. 'If we have to search to the corners of Telae and the heights and depths of the Pyrthae, we will find her!'

- The Seeds of Famine, a translation from the Lighted-tongue, by Oracle Kalene of deme Hull; 881 SLP

I woke to a knock on the door.

Rubbing my eyes, I sat up. My back was stiff and sore, the night spent sleeping in a chair doing little to improve upon what the melee in Komo's quarters had started. As little as I'd contributed, I felt battered and bruised, and my seared skin pulled painfully as I shifted.

The knock came again. "Airene? Xaron?" Nomusa called through.

"Coming," I groaned in response.

Enough daylight peeked between the curtains that I had little trouble finding my way to the door and unlatching it. As the door opened, Nomusa slipped in, her face lined with worry.

"How is he?"

"I'm not sure," I admitted. "I only just woke up."

Locking the door, we walked together to his bedside. Nomusa had found us after the Seeker attack last night, so it wasn't the first time she saw the cuts and burns that ran patchwork over Xaron's skin. I winced as I noticed a spot over his right ear where radiance had burned his hair off. It could have been much worse, yet if I knew Xaron, he would fixate on how that hair would never grow back. Despite our scrutiny and hushed conversation, he didn't stir. I wondered if we should be worried by that.

"Kallias the Sculptor is coming to see him today after he visits the… Yorandu delegation. Jaxas sent for him last night, but the Acadian healer keeps his own schedule, even for princes." She wore a hint of a vindictive smile as she said it. Nomusa's attitude toward Komo seemed to have improved since he'd fought by Xaron and me, but every transformation had its limits.

I shrugged. "I doubt he'll need it. Komo told me his wounds would heal. Perhaps he has a similar gift as our Sculptor does."

She'd flinched at his name, then shook her head in disgust. "Magic abounds now," she muttered. "Our enemies, our friends… Even people I've known half my life." She gave me a sidelong look.

I held up my left hand silently, putting on display the two fingers that had glowed with radiance the night before. "They've appeared," I said quietly. "My shifts. I channeled last night and controlled it."

Her brow creasing, Nomusa took my hand and examined the fingertips closely. She inhaled sharply. "I see them moving." She met my eyes. "You really are a warden."

"Yes. I am." I drew my hand away.

"Did it happen during the fight?"

"No. After."

Only then did it occur to me how lucky that was. While Xaron was permitted to channel, and Komo possessed some measure of diplomatic immunity, I wouldn't be so fortunate if I were exposed as a warden. Even channeling in defense of Oedija's interests, I'd still be liable to the Tribunal's justice at the hands of Shepherds. And where channeling was done for harm, the only sentence I could expect was death.

"Airene?"

I realized Nomusa had said my name more than once. "I'm fine. Just thinking."

She suddenly pulled me into a firm hug, though mindful of my burn. "Your injuries are less visible, but I know they're there. I'm sorry you had to endure all that. Again."

I sighed and relaxed into her embrace. But almost as soon as I released the worries of the night before, the new day's concerns pressed in. "We have work to do." A moment later, I realized how callous that sounded and amended weakly, "That came out wrong."

"Don't apologize. A few rough words won't offend me." She released me and smiled. But I saw her own concerns weighing on her mind behind her eyes. "I wanted to delay telling you this, but the Council has called you to their session this morning. They demand an account of what occurred in Komo's chambers."

"Why? So they can squawk over it and do nothing?"

"I don't like it either, but you'd do better to find a softer side of your tongue. You'll make no friends among the Low Consuls chastising them, and we badly need friends."

"Fine. But I have some demands of my own. Coffee and food, to start."

Nomusa raised an eyebrow. "Setting your sights a little high, aren't you?"

"That's as high as I'd like to shoot as well," a sleepy voice spoke from next to us.

Nomusa and I whirled on Xaron.

"How are you feeling?" Nomusa asked.

"Feeling?" Xaron groaned as he tried to sit up, then abandoned the attempt. "All too much right now."

"If his humor has gotten this bad, I think he's close to joining the ancestors," I commented.

"How I'm feeling right now makes me wish it. 'Thae above, where did those Seekers learn to channel like that?"

"Vusu," Nomusa and I answered at once.

Xaron grinned weakly. "Right."

Mindful of the approaching Council meeting, Nomusa went to fetch my demands to bring back to the room. We broke our fast together, the meal almost strange with how easy and familiar it felt. How long had it been since we shared a simple meal? How long would it be until our next?

Too soon, Nomusa and I said goodbye to a morose Xaron, then made our way out of the palace and across the bridge. We were quiet much of the way, anticipation of the meeting silencing idle conversation. That there would be a reckoning for the attack, I had no doubt. I only hoped something good would come out of it for once. I snorted lightly. Things were getting desperate if I were hoping for something good from the Demos Council.

Nomusa cocked an eyebrow. "Something amusing?"

"Oh, just the usual irony. How little there is to hope for, and how I can't help but keep hoping."

She shrugged. "A failing of which we're all guilty. But it helps us face things, doesn't it?"

I flashed her a bitter smile. We'd need a good deal more than false hope to face this down.

Too soon, we were admitted into the inner chamber of the Conclave and stood before the Council. Of the Low Consuls, Feiyan was missing, as was Berker. But we had additional guests lining the wall: the five white-haired, red-caped Stratechons, leaders of Oedija's paltry defenses. I eyed them, wondering what their presence might mean for the Order.

Jaxas gave us a look that seemed a warning as we entered. Orhan spoke first. "First Verifiers. I hope you had a pleasant evening."

"I've not changed since then, so you can tell for yourself how pleasant mine was." The words were out of my mouth before I could stop them.

"Yes," Orhan replied lightly. "You do seem to have taken some injuries. But it is no more than one deserves for shirking their duties, is it?"

His disdain twisted my guts with fury, but I struggled to keep my tone even. "Perhaps you could clarify your meaning."

"Oh? But I thought it would be perfectly clear, when our esteemed guest was brutally attacked immediately after you arrived at his quarters."

Cold ran through me with the shock of a sea spray. The gazes on me suddenly seemed like those of a pack of hungry dogs, waiting for their chance to attack. It was all I could do to refrain from licking my dry lips.

"Are you implying I had something to do with the attack?" I asked carefully.

A sneer curled Orhan's lips. But before the Preservist leader could answer, Jaxas cut in. "I am sure Low Consul Orhan wouldn't imply that of our trusted Finches. After all, Airene and Nomusa orchestrated the trap that thwarted Vusumuzi's ambitions against the realm. Surely, such an action insulates them from any suspicion of collaboration."

Orhan didn't lose his smile, nor did he look aside from me. "Of course. Such an implication would be... ungenerous of me."

"Good. As Archon, it is my duty to facilitate, so I will do so now. The subject before us is now abundantly clear, I trust."

"Quite," Daelya said drily.

"The defense of our guests is paramount, particularly when the visitor is a prince and a potential suitor to our Despoina in a time of great need." Jaxas turned to the Stratechons. "Have you agreed upon your plans yet?"

The white-haired generals looked between themselves wearing a range of emotions — disgust, impatience, even boredom. "No, Archon," the middle one answered, a man with a thick mane impressive for a man of his age. "We are still determining the best course."

"Perhaps I'd better decide for you," Jaxas snapped.

I stared at him. Rarely had I seen him lose his temper, and now I'd witnessed it twice in a day's turn.

As the others in the chamber shared significant looks, and the Strate-chons huffed in affronted silence, Jaxas exhaled softly and continued in a quieter, if no less exasperated, tone. "Orhan, I believe you wished to ask our First Verifiers a few questions."

The patrician smiled, not bothering to hide his smugness. "Yes, indeed I would. The lack of information we've received from your Order is, if I may be frank, abysmal. Perhaps you were not involved in the Shaka-Heir's attack." He let the pause linger, leaving no doubt as to what he implied. "Yet it is apparent you received intelligence about it. Why did you not act sooner? And from whence did this information come?"

I didn't wait for Nomusa to answer, though I knew it would likely be wiser. "As soon as I heard the Seekers were coming for Heir Komo, I ran to him. I only had time to find—" Too late I realized my mistake, but I cut off all the same.

But the wily leader of the Preservists smiled like he'd led me right to where he'd wanted. "You only had time to find your friend Hilarion. So he could help kill those Seekers by using Tyurn's Gift, isn't that right?"

Someone gasped; I didn't see who. My eyes were leveled at Orhan. He met my gaze, knowing that I couldn't touch him. But that didn't mean I wouldn't try.

Nomusa cut in before I could reply. "If he channeled in defense of our guest, is that not something to be celebrated? When should magic be used, if not for the good of Oedija?"

Orhan leaned back. "But that is the wrong question, First Verifier. It's not what magic should be used for. It's if it should be used at all. And the answer to that, I think, is clear to all of us."

"No." Again, my tongue leaped before me, and I couldn't reign it in. "No, I don't think it's clear. You're comfortable allowing magic to proliferate north of the wall. You're fine with the Valemish training Tefra and keeping Silks within the depths of their temples. But when Xaron uses his power to save a person you very much need alive, you say it's a crime." I ignored Nomusa's pleading look and spoke over her as she tried to interrupt. "If you wanted to do something about the Manifest and prevent this from happening, Orhan, you would have invaded their compound long ago. You would have put an end to these Seekers before they ever truly started."

Orhan's eyes didn't shift, though the smile had finally faded. "First Verifier Airene, I believe you forget that I do not hold charge of Oedija's forces. The Stratechons do."

I glanced at the old soldiers. It didn't stretch the imagination to guess why they'd done nothing. The Preservists commanded much of the wealth of Oedija, and I suspected that a fair amount of that gold now lined the Stratechons' purses.

I gave a curt bow. "Excuse me, Low Consuls, Stratechons. But you can understand we are very busy at the moment. If you have no further questions, we'll make our departure." Not waiting for a response, I turned and left the chamber.

Nomusa didn't catch me until I'd almost reached the Aviary. She must have nearly run, for I hadn't slowed my pace even for my injuries. Whirling me around outside the door, she stared at me with a desperation I hadn't yet seen.

"Please, Airene. Don't do this."

My anger hadn't abated, and I found myself speaking sharply. "Do what?"

"Don't throw away what we've worked so long to gain. I know you may not feel so now, but we need this position. Without it, we'd be as insignificant as we were before. You wouldn't be admitted to the Acadium. You couldn't read those ancient tomes or see Eltris again."

I tried to deny her words, but knew I couldn't. So I said nothing.

"I know you must follow the hunt that calls you; your looking into the Despot's murder proved that. And I'll do my best not to let them stop you. Just… don't sabotage us in front of the Council. Please."

I'd never heard Nomusa so conciliatory. I could only nod.

Her furrowed brow smoothed. "Good. We both have things to do. But I want to make sure you're alright."

"I'm fine." I knew it was what she needed to hear.

I hoped it was true.

———

After I changed into clothes that weren't burned and bloodied, I made my way out into the city and headed for the Acadium library. As each day yielded less, it began to dawn on me how unlikely my quest was to bear fruit. Why would I find something in among the dusty books in a span when others had been reading them for decades?

But I'd visited the Pyrthae. I'd seen Famine with my own eyes. And Eltris, stubborn as she was, might fill in the other gaps in my knowledge. Perhaps there were secrets contained in those books that no other could recognize but I.

So I spent the rest of the morning and early afternoon with Platon down in Tomes, breathing in the slow decay of vellum, parchment, and paper. I'd left off in the middle of the depictions of the Hunger War, and wasn't eager to resume them.

Yet only half a turn into my reading, the text made an abrupt shift. From details of supply lines and regiment numbers, it honed in on Agmon Brandheart and a significant visit by Clepsammia.

'I can help you face Famine,' said she. 'You must find the one who may endanger him most and beseech her aid.'

'How can any being, god or mortal, endanger one such as Famine?'

'Because she completes him. Go find the goddess Harvest. And then you will have the only ally you need.'

I leaned back in my hard chair, pondering. The twist was unexpected, to say the least. Harvest was a minor Eidolan goddess, one worshipped by farmers and ranchers, who were most affected by her whimsies, real or believed. I'd never heard of her tied to Famine in any of the stories told during the Festival of Radiance. That she would be cited by Clepsammia as the one who could endanger Famine defied belief.

Because she completes him.

The words stuck fast in my mind. Famine's appetite was insatiable, or so the stories always said. Yet now that I thought on it, there was a certain logic to the thought that if anything could temper Famine's hunger, it was the Goddess of Bounty.

But if I were to rest my hopes on Harvest, I had to first know she truly existed.

I leaned forward to my reading again and found my hopes sinking. Agmon and his First Wardens, it seemed, had difficulty finding Harvest. They abandoned their war with Famine and his armies to set to it, but despite months of searching, they couldn't find her. As my reading time wound to an end, they seemed no closer to locating the goddess.

Then, just as I was about to shut the book, Clepsammia appeared to Agmon again. I absorbed the words, squinting as I tried to make sense of them.

'Harvest has sown seeds of herself among you,' she told them. 'To find her, you must find them.'

'But how will we know a Seed of Harvest?' demanded Agmon Brandheart.

Clepsammia, Seer of All, hid her smile. 'She will show herself to you. All you must do is hold to your patience.'

The book was named *The Seeds of Famine*, but it seemed he wasn't the only one to spread his seeds. Harvest, too, had sown of herself among humanity. And in lieu of the goddess herself, such a "Seed of Harvest" could apparently suffice in combatting Famine.

Questions swirled in my mind. What did it mean to be a Seed of Harvest, or a Seed of Famine for that matter? For the God of Hunger, it had earlier been implied it was a means of corruption, a way to sway the First Wardens to his side. What would it mean for Harvest?

Then there was the matter of Clepsammia's role in all this. Up until this reading session, I'd taken her role for granted. As the Maiden of the Sands, it made sense that she would help destiny along its course. But her continual interventions prodded me in a new way, invoking memories to turn a new face.

First, my dream, the night Famine almost took me: A woman in gray had intervened when Vusu couldn't stop Famine. Only, I'd sensed even then that she wasn't human. Her features had been strange and altered; human-like, but not quite. And clutched in her hand had been a sandglass.

I knew it couldn't be Clepsammia herself I'd seen. It was one thing to discover Famine was real. It was another to believe the Pyrthae was littered with the gods of legend. Besides, it had been a dream. I wasn't sure I could rely on anything I'd seen in it being real. I had probably imagined her because of my readings.

But then there was the other matter. Despoina Asileia had insisted often enough that she was the Hand of Clepsammia for the claim to become meaningless. But if Clepsammia were real, could it be the Despoina wasn't mad? Could there be a rhyme or reason to her erratic actions?

The answers would have to wait. With a measure of reluctance, I stood and stretched. Eltris's next lesson awaited that evening, and I had another task to handle before then, one I could no longer neglect. With Orhan on our trail and a government rife with treason, I had to help Nomusa and Jaxas set things right, insomuch as was possible. And since I couldn't leave off my hunt to do it, I'd have to call in an extra set of hands.

I ascended the many stairs to exit the library. But before I left, I convinced Platon to inquire as to when his master, the mysterious Master Librarian, might be available. If anyone could answer questions about legends and lore, it would be her. After sending the poor pupil back and forth several times, we agreed upon an appointment in two days. I was sure she only relented to it because I was a regular visitor now. From her aloof manner, I guessed the woman's only true love was for books.

The matter settled, I hurriedly left the Acadium and made my way toward Port. When I arrived at Zipho's, the aroma of roasting coffee instantly brightened my spirits. A smile tugged at my lips as I strolled in.

I was surprised and pleased to see Nomusa leaning against the counter running around the tree in the middle of the room. She seemed as startled to see me.

"Don't you have somewhere to be?" I teased her as I came around the counter.

"I could say the same for you. Grow tired of crossing your eyes in that tomb you call a library?"

"Nothing a mug of hot coffee won't fix."

Zipho slyly nodded and turned away to brew my drink. Leaning closer to Nomusa, I asked her, "But really, I didn't think you left the Conclave grounds these days. Zipho was just complaining you never visit her."

"I don't nearly enough. But there were a few things I wanted to... discuss. That only she would truly understand."

I looked away. Simple enough to guess her meaning by her tone. I couldn't fault her for wanting to speak to another about her predicament with Komo, especially as Zipho had also fled during the Yorandu coup. And I was too close to the situation, with too much stake, to offer the support she needed.

But a small ache remained in my chest all the same.

As Zipho and Nomusa bantered next to me, loneliness slowly crept up on me. I didn't want to be forced to sit and drink my coffee while making light conversation, but it was too late to avoid it. Suddenly, I badly wished Talan were here with us. No matter how dark the situation, he seemed able to persist through it. I'd never realized what a steady presence he was in my life until he went so conspicuously silent.

Then a memory of my dream in the Pyrthae surfaced from the depths of my mind. Zipho brought me my coffee, and I sipped it absently as she and Nomusa spoke. If what I'd seen in the dream were true, then Talan had been with someone else. It could have been anyone — a contact, an ally, even an enemy — yet I suddenly wondered if it wasn't another woman. After all, it had been in the dead of night, and the flames had shown them so close as to be intertwined...

A familiar cloak passed by the door. I stood abruptly, mouthing a silent prayer. My coffee was barely touched, and Zipho gave me a severe look, but Nomusa only waved me on. "Go hunt," she said, like an oracle bestowing a blessing.

I nodded gratefully and turned out of the cafe, another silver coin hidden under my mug.

I didn't go far, but turned into the usual alley in which I met Wisp. Once again, paupers littered the filthy ground. I stepped around them, repressing the fear that one of them would rise and hold a knife to my throat. Besides, I could channel now, at least part of the time. I told myself I didn't need to fear a vagrant's blade, and hoped it was true.

Wisp waited at the other end. A second hooded figure stood at her shoulder. Beneath the cloak, I couldn't see much of their face, and I kept a careful eye on them as I approached. I'd meant to push my offer of becoming a Verifier on Wisp again, but the stranger's presence threatened to infringe on that.

"We will meet in the narrow alley from now on," Wisp said, her nose wrinkled. Though she was a denizen of the streets, the reek of urine and nightsoil that permeated the air seemed to needle her.

"Fine." I nodded at the person behind her and asked bluntly, "And who is this?"

Wisp inclined her head slightly. "This is your new Verifier."

As I raised a skeptical eyebrow, the figure lowered their hood. My confusion only increased. For standing there was a female honor, complete with a bald scalp and ears flashing with tin spiral earrings.

"What do you mean, my new Verifier?" I demanded of Wisp. A joke; it had to be a strange joke from my even stranger contact. Surely she couldn't mean for an honor to be a Verifier.

Why not? a small voice whispered in my head. *If you were an honor, would you not still be a Finch?* The incongruity stunned me. Never had I thought about honors in such terms. I didn't like the light it put me in.

Wisp's mouth quirked in as wide of a smile as I'd seen from her. "You asked me to be your Verifier. I refused. You asked me to reconsider. I did not. But I did consider your plight. Now, I have provided you the ideal person to accomplish your tasks."

I looked again at the honor. The markings of her caste did not diminish her gentle, pretty features. Her dark cloak obscured the simple clothes I assumed she wore beneath. Most striking were her eyes, sharp-edged and the shade of light brown of the caramel treats sold in the finest bakeries in Bazaar.

"My apologies," I murmured to her. "I am First Verifier Airene. If Wisp speaks well of you, I don't mean to cast doubt on your skills."

The woman waited a breath after I finished. Though she was an honor, I didn't think it was out of hesitation.

"I am Kelena. Kelena of House Iason." Though her voice was soft, it had a quality that compelled me to listen closely.

I frowned. "House Iason. You don't mean—"

"The Low Consul? Yes."

My mind spun at the implications. Iason was one of the five Preservists on the Council. To have an honor of his house as a Verifier... Yet I shook my head. "Iason would never dismiss you. Not to become a Verifier."

For the first time, a flash of emotion passed over the honor's face. I wondered at it. Perhaps this was about freedom for her, an opportunity to escape her present conditions.

"Perhaps not," Kelena said evenly. "But perhaps I could persuade you to try all the same."

Considering my relationship with the Council at the moment, I doubted they would permit me so much as a drink of water in their presence if I asked. But she didn't need to know that.

I crossed my arms. "I'm listening."

"First of all, you've already seen a demonstration of the depth and breadth of my knowledge. Perhaps you remember an honor in the Laurel Palace who directed you toward the Yorandu Heir's rooms?"

She spoke with the air of a recited speech, but her words still captivated me. "That was you?" I tried to remember what the woman had looked like.

A smile quirked Kelena's lips, though it didn't reach her eyes. "Do we honors look so similar to you?"

"No, no, I—"

"She was but one of my hands," Kelena continued smoothly over my fumbling, while Wisp grinned outright. "One of the many I can call upon should the need arise. My network spans all of Oedija, even into places I suspect you have a difficult time reaching."

Honors. I had considered the possibility so often before that her web was immediately clear to me. Honors were the perfect network of spies. They were in every major household, every arm of the demotism, throughout the whole of the polis. And many of them were in the Manifest as well, if Wisp had spoken true when we'd last met. I'd never known how to tap into such a network. And now here it was, served on a platter before me.

I pretended to consider it, not wishing the full measure of my eagerness to show through. I knew I should feel more hesitant. Despite Wisp's commendation and Kelena's apparent show of usefulness, I still didn't know her and couldn't be certain of her intentions.

"If I'm to initiate you, I'd like to know some things first. How far does your network reach? What new information can you bring the Order?"

The honor raised an eyebrow slightly. "You wish to know from whom the Manifest receives funding. You wish to know their movements, their defenses, their plans. You wish to know where they have hidden away Myron Wreath, and what the Visage Vusumuzi has been doing since the Despoina's trial. All this and more, I can provide you, if you give me the time and resources."

It was a simple decision. Even if Kelena was serving on someone else's behalf, the promise of all that was worth the risk. And Nomusa had, after all, said we'd have to take risks on whom we trusted.

I would just have to hold my own secrets close.

I clasped my hands together, taking care to keep my fingertips hidden. "Very well, Kelena of House Iason. I must talk this over with my fellow First Verifier, but I'm sure we can come to an agreement. Meet me here tomorrow at the same time and I'll have your answer."

Kelena bowed slightly, though not nearly enough to befit her caste. I was glad for it. Seeing beyond the markings now, I felt a great sense of shame that I'd ever expected such a gesture from her. What made her any less than me, after all?

"I will await your answer tomorrow," she said as neutrally as before. With a nod at Wisp, she turned and walked down the alley.

I looked after her with some concern. "Is she alright traveling Oedija by herself?"

Wisp gave me a sly look. "Safer than you have been."

I turned my face aside, heat flushing my cheeks. The woman was far too omniscient for her own good.

"Thank you for bringing her," I said quickly. "She promises much."

"And will deliver on it." Wisp looked abruptly up and down the alley. "Now do you wish for news or not?"

"Of course." I handed over a full silver. "I want to hear it all."

CHAPTER THIRTEEN

THE WATCHERS

Clepsammia knew of the First Wardens' despair, and appeared to them again.

'Harvest has sown seeds of herself among you,' she told them. 'To find her, you must find them.'

'But how will we know a Seed of Harvest?' demanded Agmon Brandheart.

Clepsammia, Seer of All, hid her smile. 'She will show herself to you. All you must do is hold to your patience.'

'The hardest command of all,' the Hero of Man said bitterly. But at her behest, he waited.

The Seeds of Famine, a translation from the Lighted-tongue; by Oracle Kalene of deme Hull; 881 SLP

After Wisp informed me of the goings-on of Oedija, I checked in at Zipho's to see if Nomusa was still there, but arrived too late. Catching sight of the sandglass in the cafe, I found I was running behind for my lesson with Eltris. Cursing, I set off at a jog, leaving Zipho calling after me.

Despite Nomusa's warning, I would have flagged down a cartman had I come across one, but they seemed few and far between these days. Perhaps they'd all converted into Seekers, I mused sourly as my breath rattled in my lungs and passersby cast distrustful glances in my direction.

Half a turn after the bells had tolled my appointment's allowed time, I reached Eltris's tower with several stitches in my sides. Gasping to catch my breath, I knocked sharply on the door. "Eltris! I'm sorry I'm late!"

"Not Eltris!" a voice responded sharply from the other side. "What are you to call me?"

My blood up from the exercise, I had to close my eyes and will myself patience for a moment before stiffly replying, "I'm sorry I'm late, master."

The door swung open, revealing the augur's face flushed with anger. "If you wish to be a warden, then you must be here for your instruction. Don't make me wait again."

I pushed down my rearing rebelliousness and followed her as she turned to the stairs. It wasn't an auspicious start to the lesson.

As I mounted the last step, she called back without looking around. "Have you made progress since our last meeting?"

"Yes. I channeled last night."

"I thought you might." Reaching the other side of the room, Eltris turned swiftly. Her eyes glinted in the bright lamplight. "Need seems to bring out the best in you."

She knew of the attack on Komo, then; how, I couldn't say. Considering how little she seemed to socialize, I doubted she'd gotten it by hearsay. More likely, she'd seen the Seekers traveling through the Pyrthae, or divined it by some way of channeling quintessence I knew nothing of. Though if she had, I didn't like to think what it said of her that she hadn't come to our aid.

"I didn't channel during the attack. It happened later that night."

I explained in brief what had occurred, smoothing over the anguish it had cost me. Somehow, I doubted Eltris would be sympathetic to despair. As I spoke, the augur didn't shift, but nodded sharply as I finished.

"Radiance and quintessence. Very well. We shall focus on these."

"Because I channeled them first?"

"Call me master," Eltris reminded me sternly. "You show an affinity for both, girl. Even more, you show you can control one while you endanger yourself with the other. Perhaps with time you won't be kindling awaiting the spark to burn everyone around you."

I bit back the words searing my tongue.

The augur smiled thinly. "Good. Perhaps you are still capable of being trained. Now show me what you remember of our exercises."

We practiced body awareness first. When performing it while lying down became simple enough, she varied the positions, having me stand, then walk around the room. With each iteration, it grew harder to maintain true awareness throughout my body. I suspected the exercise would only grow more complicated as I mastered each step.

After a long time, she moved to the mental exercises. As tedious as the previous practice had been, this was worse. My thoughts madly struggled against dismissal. It felt as if letting them go completely would scatter everything I'd worked so hard to gather into my mind, never to be reassembled. And no matter how I tried, I couldn't overcome the unreasonable fear.

Eltris seemed to sense it. "If you cannot control your mind, how can you hope to control the Pyrthae?" she snapped, rising from where she'd been sitting crosslegged before me.

"I'll try to do better, master." I gave the words more bite than I intended. As always seemed to happen, the exercises had brought on a headache, and my mood had soured as Eltris pushed me harder.

"You must do more than try!" Exhaling hard like a mule, Eltris turned away and whistled, holding out her arm. To my surprise, one of the finches landed on it, then began to peck at her. Only then did I see the augur had laid seeds along her forearm.

I watched as the colorful bird ate for a moment, then was pushed aside as a larger one alighted next to it. Two more joined the fray, until Eltris shooed them off and spread seed on the ground. Dozens of finches swooped down to feast.

As I watched the birds, I realized my thoughts had come together of their own accord, coalescing into a long-simmering question. "What beings will I draw by channeling quintessence?"

"I have already told you — beings who mean you danger." Her voice did not have as much rebuke as before. She, too, watched the birds peck at the floor.

"Daemons?"

Eltris snorted. "Daemons no more exist than gods do."

I hid a smile. The augur had wandered into my trap. "Who other than daemons would prey on humans from the Pyrthae?"

The augur met my gaze with a hard smile of her own. "Don't think you can lure me into revealing more than I wish to, girl. I'll tell you all you need to know, no more."

I wanted to rail against her stubbornness, but Eltris didn't respond to coercion. I had to tease out her knowledge slowly.

"Very well. No more tricks. But I should know what might harm me by channeling quintessence. Just in case it happens by accident."

"From what I've seen of you, it's more likely to happen by intention. But if it will quiet your incessant questions for a time, I'll feed you a little." She paused, yellow eyes narrowing as she studied the finches hopping about our feet. "Pyr and Quintyr are the primary beings drawn to quintessence."

I vaguely remembered her using that word, "Quintyr," before. "Didn't you say Famine was a Quintyr?"

Eltris startled, looking around at me. "Damned depths of 'Thae," she muttered. "I suppose I did."

Somehow, I had scored a mark, but I was more irked than triumphant. Why must she intentionally keep information from me? But once more, I held back my annoyance. "Why would pyr and Quintyr pose us wardens a threat? What is it about channeling quintessence that makes them dangerous?"

The augur sighed. "It's because they *are* quintessence. As our minds are composed of quintessence, their whole beings are formed from it. It is their animating substance, and it gives them the ability to form the other energies into bodies that suit them. And as our bodies and minds decay from the years, so do they. Unless they halt senescence by gaining more quintessence."

"They remain whole by taking others' quintessence? But wouldn't that kill those they steal from?"

"Don't we also kill to stay alive?" A small smile played on the Master Augur's lips. "Don't condemn them for doing what they must. It's the way of things, not something you can change. But that doesn't mean we must give them what they desire."

I thought uneasily of the presence that had attacked me through Linos's touch. Had it been a pyr seeking to steal my quintessence? And what might it already have done to Linos? I almost asked Eltris, but stayed my tongue at the last moment. It was not only that I desired to keep my secrets as she kept hers. The woman had a coldness about her that made me wonder if she saw me as anything more than a tool. I didn't want to put Linos in her power. Perhaps it was a question I'd ask Kallias the Sculptor, if I could catch him.

I turned to another idea nagging me. "Famine. You said that quintessence is what he hungers for, too. But he's Quintyr, a god, not a pyr?"

Her smile was gone as quick as it had come. "The Quintyr are not gods," Eltris snapped. "Don't confuse them for each other. Gods are the inventions of small-minded scoria, while the Quintyr are a reality."

Though I bristled at her dismissal of "scoria" — those who could not channel — it was her other point that snagged my thoughts.

There are no gods.

"Then what are the Quintyr?" I pressed.

"They're older than humanity, far older — for they were already ancient when our world was young. They are the original occupants of the Pyrthae, and thereby rule it. Their minds do not work as ours do. While ours flit about to this intent and that, theirs are fixed upon a single purpose, and bend all of their significant wills toward that purpose."

Chills made chicken-flesh of my skin. "And Famine's purpose is consuming our world."

"Consuming all quintessence. But yes, our world included."

Not wanting to consider that again, my mind flitted back to my reading. "But Famine isn't the only one? There are more Quintyr than him?"

"No, Famine is not the only one."

I waited for her to say more, but when it was clear she'd keep her lips sealed, I opted for a more straightforward tactic. "Does Harvest exist?"

Her surprise was gratifying, her mouth opening and closing before she found a response. "Why would you ask that?" she snapped. "Where did you hear that name?"

I shrugged. "She's the Eidolan Goddess of Bounty. It might be handy for her to exist when droughts are afflicting the Four Realms."

"Would it?" Eltris mocked me. "How unfortunate, then, that Harvest is dead."

All my smug satisfaction vanished instantly. "Dead?" I repeated.

For once, Eltris seemed solemn and sincere. "Yes. From all I've observed, from a lifetime of searching, Harvest long ago succumbed to her enemy. The one most bent on her destruction."

"Famine," I murmured.

"Yes. She was supposed to be able to complete him. And for a time, it seemed she had. The Hunger War ended with Harvest binding Famine. But a thousand years later, Famine has reemerged, while Harvest has not."

In one stroke, she had all but robbed the meaning from everything I'd read in *The Seeds of Famine*. Even if I didn't yet know the end of the story, I knew its results.

I shook my head. "There has to be more to it than that. Perhaps she's just hiding somewhere. Like Famine was all this time."

"I doubt it, girl. I've been to what may as well be her grave marker. I don't think we can rely on Harvest to bind Famine for us again."

"Then what of the other Quintyr?" I insisted. "Which others exist? Surely one of them will intervene. If Quintyr can kill each other, they must want to save themselves from Famine."

Eltris was shaking her head before I'd finished. "They won't intervene. Those who still exist have long ago retreated deep into the Pyrthae, beyond human grasp, or settled so firmly into our world that they have begun losing sight of what they once were. The few who don't sleep and haven't forgotten have no concern for Famine or are too weak to challenge him." The augur suddenly seemed old, her shoulders slumping forward as she stared at the birds still hopping about the stone, searching for any remaining seeds. "We're on our own, girl. We have to find our own way this time."

My head throbbed, and my mind spun. But I couldn't let things lie there. I couldn't give up hope.

"Vusu. He's held Famine captive for years — decades, if he's really Yama from the stories. He's the most powerful warden I've heard of. But if he can do it, perhaps others can."

"He's as strongly attuned as he is *because* of Famine, girl. And he only holds Famine because Famine wills it."

I looked up from the birds to stare at her. "Why? Why would he let himself be held?"

As I watched her, I sensed her teetering on the balance of whether or not to tell me. I waited in silence, knowing a nudge would likely send her in the wrong direction.

Finally, she sighed, long and slow. "Because Famine knows that, should his opportunity arise, he can use Vusu as a conduit into our world."

I listened to the tweeting of the birds, so at odds with the cold dread twisting my stomach into knots.

"So when Vusu dies…" I said faintly.

"Perhaps Famine breaks into our world. Or perhaps not." Eltris shrugged. "But I would hope for Vusu to hold on, so we don't have to find out."

Another thought cut even deeper. "It's my fault. I forced the confrontation with Vusu. I shot him through with a crossbow."

"Yes. You did."

After a moment of somber quiet, she turned away. "I think that's all for today. Come back in three days. And mind my warning, girl. Do not stray into the Pyrthae."

I nodded, numb with all I had learned, and turned toward the stairs. But a sudden thought gave me pause, and I found myself turning back.

"You said before I could endanger all of Oedija by entering the Pyrthae. But I don't understand why. Can Famine use me as a conduit as well? Can he use any warden?"

Eltris didn't look at me for a long moment. When she did, her eyes were impassive, her mouth set in a firm line. "Any warden who channels quintessence or enters the Pyrthae is endangered by Famine and hungry pyr. But you are right; most wardens are not a danger to more than themselves. Famine cannot use any warden to break into Telae."

"Then why is it different for me?"

The Master Augur stared at me, and this time she didn't answer. As the silence dragged on, a realization welled up in my gut, cold and hard. I'd neglected the mystery that had plagued me when I first awoke. Now, I could no longer ignore it.

"How did I become attuned?" I asked quietly.

Eltris shook her head. "And you imagine yourself a Finch. There's only one way you could have become a warden, girl."

With that, she turned and walked down the stairs.

I watched her descend into the gloom below, unmoving, consciously forcing myself to take deep breaths. Only once she'd gone out of sight did I descend the stairs myself. In the dim yellow light below, Eltris was a shadow moving among the books and other scholarly implements. She didn't look as I rattled open the door and exited.

Outside, the cool air of the season drove the cold deeper into me. I left the alley and wandered aimlessly about the Acadium campus. As I passed by Acadians and pupils going about their business, traveling between the modest halls and well-tended towers, Eltris's parting words circled in my mind.

There's only one way you could have become a warden.

Talan believed the Buyujinn, or greater spirits in Avvad, were responsible for attuning wardens. Here in Oedija, the Eidolans believed their gods were behind it. But if Eltris was right, there were no gods, only Quintyr and pyr. Yet at least one of the Eidolan gods of old was Quintyr. Perhaps others existed as well — or had, before they disappeared. And if gods were Quintyr, then it stood to reason that the Quintyr must be attuning wardens.

And I knew of only one Quintyr in Oedija.

No. I increased my pace and turned onto less populated paths. I couldn't accept it. Yet I couldn't deny it must be what Eltris believed. Why else would she look at me with pity, with revulsion? Why else would I endanger the city by entering the Pyrthae?

But though logic herded me toward that one conclusion, I grasped for other explanations. Only two seemed vaguely promising. The boy who had spoken through the whisper finch — he had visited me twice before my attunement. Perhaps he was behind it. Or perhaps the gray woman from the Pyrthae, the Clepsammia pyr — perhaps she was the goddess in truth.

The Seeds of Famine. I'd read the book for days, read that Famine had corrupted Tyurn's Gift and meant to use it for his own gain. But I'd never stopped to think what it meant.

Now it seemed all too obvious.

As I entered a courtyard, my gaze happened on a familiar figure walking quickly ahead. Relief flooded through me. *Xaron.* If anyone could distract me from these thoughts, it was him.

I hurried over to fall in step with him.

He glanced over, not seeming surprised. As before, he wore Hilarion's garb, though a cloak covered much, the drawn hood even hiding some of the wheat-crown on his brow. He didn't seem much the worse for wear after what had occurred the night before.

"I'm surprised to see you up," I remarked.

"Kallias saw to me." He shrugged. "Apparently my wounds were simple to fix."

Looking him up and down, his gait seemed slightly unsteady. "Maybe so, but he can't make you well in a morning, Xaron," I reprimanded. "Even if he healed your wounds, you still need rest."

"I'll be fine." He glanced at me. "You're probably worse off. You haven't had your burn seen to."

I shrugged. My clothes had irritated the raw shoulder all day, but it was it the least thing bothering me at that moment. "I'll be fine. Where are we headed?"

His eyes flickered to either side, watchful and wary. I knew of only one place that might draw out such hesitation.

"Don't say I can't come. I'll follow if you try to forbid me."

"It's too dangerous," he said in a low voice. "What if you get us all caught?"

Doubt almost made me give it up. But as my recent revelation burned inside me, I felt a reckless desire to do something, *anything.* Desperation overcame the doubt.

"Any of you might be followed and caught," I pointed out. "I won't change that. I need to learn, Xaron. *Actually* learn."

"You *are* learning! Or isn't Eltris putting you through those body and mind exercises?"

"Yes. But it's more than that. I..."

The confession was on the tip of my tongue. But, with the knowledge still fresh and raw, I couldn't bring myself to say it. I didn't want to see the horror I felt reflected back in his eyes.

"She holds back most of her secrets," I said instead. "She knows what's out there, what's breaking free — but still, she keeps them."

"Have patience with Eltris. She's not easy, and it may not feel like you're learning anything. But she has a method to her mad ways. You'll learn everything you need to. Eventually." He gave me a sympathetic smile.

"I have a feeling our definitions of what I need to know are different."

We walked in silence for some time. When I glimpsed the same fountain twice, I glanced at Xaron. "So are you going to take me there, or are we just going to walk in circles?"

He at least had the decency to look sheepish. "Sorry. It's just... I don't think you should channel in front of anyone we can't trust, Airene. You could lose everything if the wrong person sees you."

"You don't think you can trust everyone training with Isidora?"

"I do trust them," he amended hurriedly. "But I'm not risking as much as you are. I'm already known as a warden, even as a warden who has channeled in a fight. It might not even impact me to be discovered here. But you put your life on the line. Is it worth it?"

As much as I hated to admit it, he had a point. And part of me wondered if I should be channeling at all. "You're right. It would be stupid to expose myself." As his expression began to grow hopeful, I hurried to say, "So I'll just watch everyone else. I won't give any indication that I'm a warden. Isidora already knows I'm aware of your group and that I know the danger Vusu poses. I'll just say I'm there to see what we have to fight against the Manifest."

His obstinacy melted away, and he shook his head with a rueful grin. "You always could talk me into things against my better judgment."

I shrugged. "What are friends for if not to get you into trouble?"

Xaron set our path straight now, taking us off the main road and into a rundown section on the south side of the campus. The sky had clouded over, and the alleys we traveled through were dark and shadowed. I took care to peer around each corner. We ought to have been safe behind the Acadium fence; even a determined and clever vagabond would be hard-pressed to circumvent the barbed tops of the metal wall. But it wasn't common thieves that worried me. Seeker wardens knew no boundaries, and I doubted the Imperium's Silks did either. Even Guilders could make their way in if they wanted to. With all the adversaries populating the city, it paid to always remain cautious.

Finally, Xaron stopped midway through a moldy alley in front of a plain wooden door with a greeting hole. The building was made of lime-stone that looked a century unwashed. Its mortar suffered from neglect, and several sections of its walls seemed liable to fall at any moment. Yet it was large enough for its intended purpose, and far enough from the usual paths of Acadians to avoid casual notice.

Xaron knocked three times. A moment later, the door opened.

"About time," Isidora said, a hand resting on her hip. Unlike the last time I'd seen her, she now wore a homespun tunic and trousers. They did as little to accentuate her figure as the Acadian robes before, yet she wore them without any evident self-consciousness. I envied her that. Despite wearing a similar set of clothes, there was still part of me that wished to pull my cloak tight about me so others couldn't see.

As the Acadian's gaze slid over to me, her smile faltered. "Ah. And you came as well."

"I hope that's alright," Xaron said in a low voice. "Seeing as how she already knows about, you know..."

"Of course. Come in — we can discuss this more freely inside."

Isidora stepped aside, and I followed Xaron in. The atrium was gloomy and poorly lit by a few scattered torches. I could barely see the high ceiling in the flickering light. Something soft pressed beneath my sandals: carpet, an odd luxury for the poor conditions of the place. The air was thick with mildew, and dust streamed through the light.

We were not alone. Fourteen silhouetted figures stood among the stone columns, watching as Xaron and I entered.

"Hello, Watchers!" Xaron called cheerily as he approached them.

A few answered back, their voices friendly. "Ho, Hilarion!" a young man's voice called above the rest.

Xaron just grinned in response. He seemed comfortable here, which helped put me further at ease.

"Good. We're all here then." Isidora strode past us into the center of the columns. "Watchers, we have a guest tonight. Meet First Verifier Airene."

The shadowed Acadians muttered among themselves. I shifted, suddenly nervous. I would have preferred to have kept my identity hidden in this dark room, but it was evidently too late for that now.

"If you don't recognize her name, you may know her title," Isidora continued. "That might alarm some of you. But rest assured, she's on our side. Even if Xaron didn't already attest to her good faith, even if she didn't already know what we do and make no moves to oust us, then shooting a crossbow through the Visage of the Wyvern should be proof enough that she's one of us."

The murmurs seemed to take on a different note. I glimpsed a few nods and smiles from the shadowed faces. I nodded back, glad for the darkness as my face flushed with pride. For, no matter the ramifications of my shooting Vusu, part of me was still glad I had.

"She wanted to see what we Watchers have to fight the Seekers, so let's show her. We're starting with the usual — the Shifting Sands meditation."

One or two Acadians groaned, and Isidora shot them a look. "You need the practice most of all, Heron. An eight-year-old boy could put your focus to shame."

"Bring one and we'll see," Heron retorted. But he folded down onto the floor with the rest, crossing his legs and sitting with his back straight. Xaron joined them. It left me alone standing, unsure of what to do.

Isidora seemed to sense my discomfort. "You may join us for this first exercise, Airene, if you wish."

I nodded and quickly sat, though more meditation was the last thing I wanted after my lesson with Eltris. But it was better than standing and watching.

"Close your eyes and clear your mind," the Acadian began, her tone softening. "Listen to my words and feel as I feel."

The experience was entirely different from Eltris's mediation. Instead of attempting to empty our thoughts, Isidora filled them with a vividly described scene. At her prompting, a wide desert expanded across my mind's eye. Waves of sands poured over the crests of dunes. The hot sun beat down on our heads. Dry air filled my lungs with every breath. There was no end to the horizon before me. I followed an unseen path toward a destination I'd never reach.

"All may shift around you," she prompted us several times. "You alone are still."

And I was, for a time. When Isidora told us to dismiss the scene and we stood and stretched, I marveled at how much more effective it had been for me than Eltris's stubborn repetition for me to stop thinking. Perhaps I'd have to paint my own scene during my next lesson, no matter what the Master Augur instructed, though I doubted I'd manage it was well on my own without Isidora's guidance.

The Watchers, as they referred to themselves, then moved into the next phase of their training, one that I could also participate in. Mirroring Eltris's exercises, this was intended to prepare our bodies. We moved in ways I hadn't since I was a child, pushing ourselves off the floor, running in place, and circling our arms until our muscles were warm and limber. Despite sweat beading on my forehead, I found my tension easing and my headache dissipating. Again, I found it superior to Eltris's method. I was beginning to wonder if the augur knew what she was about at all.

Then began exercises I couldn't participate in. Leaning against a column, I watched as Isidora led the gathered Acadians through the intentional channeling of each of the elements. This, at least, wasn't unlike what Eltris had made Xaron do during the lesson I'd witnessed. Isidora instructed them in the steps for making their radiance a single stream so it had no seams that an opponent could use to pull it apart, then how to sharpen your kinesis to ward against dispersion.

When they arrived at magnesis, I was surprised to see Xaron step up next to her and instruct them in polar charges and magnetic fields. True, he'd successfully channeled lightning against Vusu. But to see my friend as an authority on the subject meant seeing him in a new light. Talented and strong as he might be in his attunement, he had barely a season of training. It went to show how novice all these Acadians were in their magic.

I tried not to think about my own inability as they channeled, but found it impossible. My hands flexed and relaxed as the Acadians practiced each energetic element. A longing to join them ached in my chest. I watched their every gesture and hung onto every word of Isidora and

Xaron's instructions. Never had I listened closer to my friend. Though I'd heard much of it during Xaron's lesson with Eltris, it took on a different aspect now. I wanted to test my own mettle. I wanted to know if I could channel at will yet, and where my five shifts would rank among the others. If I had this gift, I wanted to know how I measured.

No matter who had given it to me.

My anxiousness only increased as Isidora moved them into what seemed the most anticipated part of the practice: sparring. Xaron paired off with Heron and beat the joking young man a dozen times in a row. Other pairs were more evenly matched. Two on the opposite end of the room were barely able to muster flickers of magic against each other. Isidora moved from pair to pair, supervising as best she could. I paid particular attention to the intense matches. My fingertips itched with anticipation as blows were turned aside or met. Even in their Acadian robes, many of the men and women moved nimbly as they wove in and out of their channeling.

But even in practice, channeling was far from safe. A cry filled the room as an errant beam of radiance clipped a woman's shoulder and sent her spiraling to the ground. Isidora was by her side immediately, and the sparring died down for a moment. But as she crouched next to the young woman, Isidora snapped at the others, "Why are you standing around and staring? You're supposed to be sparring! You think Seekers will stop fighting if one of us gets hurt?"

The cold reality of what they trained for sprang the room back into action. The Acadians took to the practice with new abandon. It inflamed me as well. My toes had begun to itch along with my fingertips. I rubbed my hands against my trousers as I watched Xaron send Heron tumbling through the columns, wincing as the young man hit the floor again and again, clouds of dust rising around him. Xaron looked about, but his gaze didn't settle on me. Isidora watched him and nodded approvingly, at which my friend grinned. I looked between them and wondered at the uncomfortable feeling in my gut.

Only then did I realize what had been building up inside me without my realizing it. As if a dam broke, radiance suddenly flooded my body, filling me with a warm elation unparalleled by anything else I'd experienced. The energy coursing through me tried to burn away my sudden anxiety, but I clung desperately to it. If I let go of that worry, I knew I would channel outright. Already I could feel the heat pressing against my fingers and toes. With horror, I looked down and saw light seeping through the skin. I curled my toes into my sandals and balled my hands, squeezing shut my eyes as I did. I couldn't channel here. I wouldn't allow it.

But the more I tensed, the more the energy intensified. I couldn't close off my locus to the Pyrthae, not this time. More radiance crowded into me with every moment. It felt as if my very organs must burn from it. I couldn't hold anymore, but I couldn't release it. Fear clawed through me. I'd die if I didn't release it now. I had to.

NO!

The denial surged out of me in a rush. Dimly, I was aware I'd collapsed to my knees, and my body trembled with sustained tension. But though something had escaped me, I found some of the radiance pressing back through the opening inside me. Strained but emboldened, I mustered my will and pressed against it further. The warmth and peacefulness of radiance leeched away as I pushed it back into the higher plane. Exhaustion rushed into its place, but I didn't relent. I pushed the last of the energy back through the locus, then blocked it off. I didn't know how to seal the gap in me, but I meant to dam it for as long as I could.

"Airene? Airene!"

Slowly, I opened my eyes. Xaron and Isidora kneeled next to me. Even the flickering torchlight pained my sensitive eyes. But I didn't relax. If I let up my concentration even for a moment, I knew radiance would flood through me again. And this time, I wouldn't be able to stop it from escaping.

"I'm fine," I said through clenched teeth.

"Whatever that was seems to have affected her most," Isidora commented. She looked in pain as well, eyes squinted and her brow creased. "I suppose it makes sense. She wouldn't have any defenses against it."

Xaron didn't say anything, but his eyes betrayed his suspicions. "I'll escort her home," he offered as he slid an arm around my waist. "Airene, can you stand?"

"Yes." I wouldn't have been able to without his support. My legs were wobbly from my struggle with radiance as if my very bones had melted. Step by step, Xaron led me from the room, the rest of the Acadians watching me.

But I couldn't worry about that. Breath hissing through my teeth, I walked out, hunched over like an old woman, fighting every moment to keep from burning them all alive.

CHAPTER FOURTEEN

TWIN FLAMES

As with all of Clepsammia's prophecies, this one came to pass, and swifter than expected. Eleven days after the Goddess of Fate came to them, as Agmon Brandheart sat at his war council, a girl boldly entered.

'What is this?' Agmon demanded. 'Who are you?'

'I am Aika of the Green,' the girl said. Her voice spoke of the country folk living in the hills, a poor and uncivilized people.

Agmon grew enraged. 'We return to war in the morn. Why have you disturbed us at such a dire time?'

'Because I am the one you have been seeking. I dreamed of a snake devouring fruit from a great tree and woke to fire in my veins.'

'So did it happen to many of us,' Agmon replied. 'But though we possess godly power, none of us have the seed of a god within us. How are we to know the Seed of Harvest has planted within you?'

'No words can tell; only my actions will. Take me before Famine and I will show you.'

Her courage swayed even the iron will of Agmon Brandheart. 'Very well,' the Hero of Man said. 'When we ride on the morrow, you will ride at the fore   and may Harvest keep you safe.'

— *The Seeds of Famine, a translation from the Lighted-tongue; by Oracle Kalene of deme Hull; 881 SLP*

The walk home was long and hard, my locus not closing until we'd already stepped through the Laurel Palace gates. Xaron had to support me the entire way. From the smirks and coarse words of the laurel guards, I knew they thought me drunk.

"Even you can do better than a drowned Finch, Hilarion," one of them japed.

"Very funny," Xaron replied wearily. The journey home had been no easier on him, and we had to go a ways to the Aviary yet.

But as my connection to the Pyrthae severed, I found I was able to walk. My legs still wobbled, and my head hurt worse than it had since I'd woken from my three-day sleep, but at least I could remain upright.

As we mounted the bridge and the wind hid our words from any eavesdroppers, he finally asked, "Were you damming your locus?"

I nodded, too weary for words.

He smiled sympathetically. "I told you about when I had to do that as a kid. It was a brief phase for me; you shouldn't have to do it for long. And who knows, maybe as an adult, you'll master it faster. That you didn't channel tonight was a marvel itself. I had three accidents before I managed to put a lid on it."

I nodded to his compliment and kept my eyes on my feet. Though the bridge had sides high enough to stop me from tipping over, I didn't fancy falling to the stone all the same. My knees hurt enough from collapsing in the Acadium earlier, and that had been on carpet.

"Don't worry about Isi and the others guessing," he continued. "They seemed to think that whatever you did came from somewhere else, and that scoria would be more vulnerable to it."

"Good," I murmured. At least that much had been achieved from my efforts.

He looked sidelong at me. "What *did* you do, anyway? Was that quintessence?"

"Don't know."

He shrugged. "I guess it doesn't matter."

We lapsed into silence for a few tottering steps.

"I shouldn't have brought you," he mused aloud. "I should have known it was too early, that it would be too taxing."

"You think you should have known that seeing other people channel would make me channel too?" I asked sarcastically.

"But you didn't just watch, Airene. Isi put you through the beginning exercises. Your body and mind were made as ready to channel as any of ours. Besides, there's something about being around other wardens that makes it come easier. Feeling the energy coursing through the air... It brings it out of you."

I didn't regret attending, no matter what had happened. I'd learned more in those turns than I had in my two lessons with Eltris. But my mind clung to another thought.

"Are you close with Isidora?"

He glanced at me. "We work well together," he said carefully.

"Apparently you're her authority on magnesis."

"I guess. Airene, is everything alright?"

"Everything's fine." My head hurt, my body was sore and weak, and what was supposed to be a gift was barely under my control. But none of that had to do with Xaron. It wasn't fair to take out my frustration on him.

Xaron knew me well enough to let things lie. We walked the rest of the way to the Aviary in silence. He bid me a brief farewell when we arrived at its weather-worn door, and I managed to paste on a weary smile before turning inside. It had only just grown dark, but after I ate a brief supper of the cold food Sizani had left out for me, I trudged upstairs to my room, intending to tuck in. I'd just have to make an early start of the next day.

But when I reached my room, I found Nomusa's door cracked open and yellow light streaming out from within. Since she was awake, I knew I should talk to her about our potential new Verifier. And, if I were up to it, my new revelation. Sighing inwardly, I knocked lightly on her door and pressed in.

Nomusa looked up from a series of finch scrolls scattered on the floor around her. She seemed as much at ease curled up on the floor as standing straight among a group of Servants. "You're cutting it close to dark," she observed, then narrowed her eyes. "You look awful. Did you get mugged again?"

"Worse — I ran into Xaron."

I slumped onto her bed and reported the evening to her, though I had a feeling I wouldn't like her response. Sure enough, it followed the lines I'd feared.

"You shouldn't have gone," she said reproachfully. "Not only was it risky for all of them, but look what happened to you."

It annoyed me how closely her response mirrored Xaron's. "I had to go. Not only is it good to know which wardens are on our side, but I need to learn to channel. Didn't you say we have to take risks?"

"That's not what I meant, and you know it."

I knew I wouldn't keep my temper much longer and quickly changed the subject. "But that's not what I wanted to talk to you about. I think we should take on a new Verifier."

"Oh?" Nomusa arched an eyebrow. "And who has gained your trust?"

"She hasn't gained my trust yet. But what she offers is enticing."

"You have my attention."

I drew in a breath. "Her name is Kelena. And she's an honor to Iason."

"An honor? To Iason?" She looked dumbfounded. "Why would she be a good Verifier? And where did you even find her?"

"Wisp brought her to me. I know it's strange, but I think we should give her a chance. She's already aided us once. You remember last night, when that honor led Xaron and me up to Komo's rooms?" I flinched as I said the Shaka-Heir's name. Nomusa's face had gone carefully blank, and I pressed quickly on. "She said to remember that she helped us. Then Kelena brought up the incident and said she was responsible for the honor's aid."

Nomusa's brow creased. "Are you saying this Kelena was able to contact an honor within the Laurel Palace to help you at the drop of a copper?"

Now that she mentioned it, it didn't seem likely. "I guess I don't know. Maybe this is another time we're being set up to be betrayed, like with Vusu. Maybe we shouldn't make her a Verifier after all."

"Perhaps. But if she's telling the truth, if she's able to make use of other honors so quickly... that could be invaluable. And you said she presently serves Iason? Think of the information and access she could provide. We might even be able to make headway on the Council's mandate to find corruption. Though not the way they'd like us to." Wicked humor lit her eyes.

"All true. And Vusu did help us as well as manipulate us. Even if she isn't on our side, we still might get some use out of her." I put my head in my hands and kneaded my temples. Hard enough to make a decision like this, much less when I felt as I did just then.

Nomusa spared me the burden. "Let's bring her on. I don't see how she could put us more at risk than we already are. And I doubt the Council will confirm her anyway. But if we try, it will prove we're serious about working with her."

"Fine." I rose, my body screaming in protest. "Now I'm going to collapse in bed."

She rose smoothly and gave me a hug, sniffing as she did. "Make time to wash tomorrow. You haven't gone since the fight last night, have you?"

"I didn't have the time," I said, slightly affronted. But I quailed at the suggestion. Time wasn't the only reason I hadn't ventured to the baths. With the city in turmoil, bathing was a risk I didn't like to take.

Nomusa sensed my reservation. "We have baths here at the Conclave, you know. I can show them to you tomorrow if you like. Who knows, it might be good for your wounds as well."

"If you insist."

"I do." She looked at me with her head cocked like bird. "Your hygiene is growing almost as poor as our old Guilder friend's."

I smiled at the thought of Talan, even as a sudden ache woke inside me at his absence. "Please let me never get that bad."

"You won't while I'm around. Now go; get some sleep. Tomorrow will come soon enough."

———

I woke with Talan's flame in mind.

Nomusa's reminder of him seemed to have wormed its way into my thoughts, and likely my dreams. I smiled to myself for a moment as I remembered his roguish smile and knowing eyes, the soft touch from his rough hands. Wherever he was, I hoped he was keeping himself safe, though I knew it was a vain hope.

Then I remembered the last I'd heard of him.

I sat bolt upright. How many days had it been since the Guilder had passed on Kalindi's threat? In the whirl of activity, I hadn't given more than a thought to warning Talan. But would it be better to warn him, or would seeking him only further endanger him?

Only when I rose and thought of what the rest of the day held for me did I realize how impractical the idea to find him was. Once I bathed, I knew I should squeeze in what I could of my research in Tomes, then give Kelena the news with enough time for the Council meeting that evening, and finally attend the meeting. I wished I could skip the latter, but if I wanted to be taken seriously as a First Verifier, I had to appear before the Low Consuls.

But if I truly valued my friend, something had to give. I decided to take off the morning and hunt him out. As he'd said his hiding holes were compromised, I knew visiting his old places would get me nowhere. If I assumed he wasn't still in Hull, where I'd seen him in the Pyrthae-dream, that left just one place to check. Failing that, I'd could only hope he'd show up soon.

I readied myself as quickly as I could, rushing the clerk Galene through her accounting and dragging Nomusa from her bed to the Conclave baths. My being in a hurry wasn't a new development, and she didn't question where I rushed off to. I barely noticed the fluted columns and finely carved pediments around us as I sloughed off the olive oil from my hair and skin.

As soon as I'd cleaned and dressed, I bound up my damp hair and hurried off toward Port. With crowds still gathered about the Conclave gates, as they had been except for the few turns when the Conclave guards had driven them away, I had to take the long way around from the lesser-known gate Corin had shown me. This time, the guards didn't taunt me, but eyed me apprehensively as I, a lone woman, went out into the city. I was growing more comfortable with navigating this new Oedija, but a lump of fear always sat in my gut.

I hurried through Iris's streets toward my home deme, keeping an eye over my shoulder the whole way. Instead of turning inward toward Zipho's, Maesos's, and Canopy, I turned toward the Lighted Sea. My destination was at the far end of the harbor and took several turns to reach. I hoped I wasn't wasting my time.

Remembering from my last trip the safest route down the cliffside, I took one last look around before descending the slippery rocks. That I'd traveled it successfully before made it little easier. Every foot- and hand-hold I sought carefully, and my limbs trembled with more than exertion. But it was no more than a quarter-turn before I lowered myself to the edge of the cave's mouth and carefully folded my way inside.

As my eyes adjusted to the dimness, I found an unkempt man facing me, a knife bared in his hand. Dark stubble layered his chin, and his hair, bound back in a tail, was shiny with grease. His eyes were narrowed in suspicion, their golden color almost hidden in shadow.

Upon seeing me, though, the man sheathed the knife with a flourish and a half-cocked grin. "I wondered when you'd find me."

"Hope the delay didn't disappoint." A smile found its way onto my own lips as I stepped toward him. Filthy or no, Talan was a sight for sore eyes. "I have so much to tell you."

"As do I." His eyes flickered back deeper into the cave, where the faint glow of firelight came from.

"What? Are you burning breakfast?" I teased, stepping within reach of him. Nomusa was right; the man's hygiene was appalling. But still, I reached out to embrace him. The things I had to tell him were bursting to get out. But for a little while at least, all I wanted was to hold him.

Just as I was about to touch him, he stepped away. I flinched, then lowered my arms. There was apology in his eyes, but it didn't lessen the hurt suddenly rising inside me.

"Airene," Talan said quickly, "there's something I should tell you—"

"Is this the Airene I've been hearing so much about?"

My hand went to my knife as a figure emerged from the darkness of the cave — a woman, nearly as tall as Talan and darker of skin than Nomusa. The part of myself that wasn't dumb with surprise wondered if she were Bali or from the southern provinces of Avvad. Her sharp features were scored by many scars, but her beauty and air of confidence were unmarred by them. She wore a rough-spun tunic, fraying trousers, and well-worn boots, and carried them with all the confidence of Feiyan in her fine robes. Her dark, round eyes studied me with a hint of amusement.

I remembered the other flame I'd seen with Talan in my dream and cursed myself for a fool.

"Hello." The word came out half-choked.

"I've startled you," the woman said. "My apologies."

"Airene, this is Sule. Sule and I have known each for a long time." Talan had lost his usual self-possession. His eyes looked anywhere but at mine.

"A very long time," the woman agreed.

"I see." I looked back toward the mouth of the cave and out over the sea. I wondered if I should leave before I gave vent to the anger suddenly roiling inside me.

"Sule, could you give us a moment?" His gaze found me, but I didn't meet it.

"Of course," the woman said easily, retreating back into the cave. Her eyes gleamed as the rest of her was lost in shadow. Even retreated, with the echo and the size of the cave, she would likely hear everything we said.

I lowered my voice anyway. "I didn't mean to surprise you."

"Let me explain," Talan said, barely softening his voice. "It's not what it looks like."

I finally met his eyes. "I'm listening."

He ran a hand over his greasy hair, as if attempting to tame it. "It's as I said. I've known Sule for a long time. She and I were… childhood friends."

"You're not making this sound any better."

"I know, I know. But the tale is far stranger than I know how to tell you." He drew a breath. "Here's the short of it. You remember how I lived for some years in Erimis?"

I nodded.

"My home is actually some ways south of there, in one of the provinces long ago conquered by the Imperium. Sule and I knew each other from our hometown. We were in a cabal and—"

"A cabal?" I interrupted.

Talan waved his hand. "Just a group of children, really, who thought we were hard and worldly. Anyway, for a while, we were close. But… a situation came up. She made one decision, I made another. When we parted, I never expected to see her again. I moved to Erimis then, for a fresh start, and made a name for myself."

"I'll say. Wraithsbane, isn't that the one?"

He groaned. "Not exactly what I meant. But after a number of bad turns and foolish decisions, I found myself in a poor way, and taking on a job I knew I shouldn't. Just then, Sule showed up again."

"And you made up and were friends again."

He gave me a wry grin. "Not as I remember it. Though I wouldn't say we parted enemies…" He shrugged. "Again, I never thought I'd see her again."

"Yet here she is."

"She showed up here in Oedija soon after the Despoina's trial and came to me. At the time, the situation with Kalindi was particularly precarious, and I judged it best to take her in to keep an eye on her."

"Why?" I demanded, not caring that I spoke louder. "Why couldn't you just wave and pass by?"

Talan closed his eyes. "Because she can find me no matter where I am."

It took a moment for that to sink in. "Why?" I asked in a hushed voice. "Is she a warden?"

He nodded. "Not only that, but she — She isn't the Sule I knew before." Talan glanced back at the woman, who crouched next to the fire in the back of the cave. "She's different."

"Different how?"

"Perhaps it would be easier for me to explain."

Sule stood and turned back toward us. Annoyance spiked through me, but I held my tongue.

"I am both Sule and another," she continued. "It has been a long time since we thought of ourselves as separate, but I suppose you would see us as jinni and human in one body."

Cold realization dawned on me. My hand strayed back to my knife. "This is the Damask Esir who tried to kill you back in Erimis?" I demanded of Talan, though I kept my eyes on the woman. "The one possessed by a Qarin?"

"Yes. She won't harm you, Airene. I told you, we have an understanding."

"I don't see how you could come to an understanding after that."

Sule, or the one who called herself that, took a step forward. "Then perhaps you've never had to band with an enemy in the face of a greater threat."

Despite myself, I thought of Feiyan. I shook my head free of her face. It wasn't at all the same as lying down next to her at night, next to this… *thing*. This abomination that was what the daemon sought to make of Linos.

"You're evil and twisted." I nearly spat out the words. "You stole that woman's body for your own."

"Not quite. She who was once Sule was broken. I cared for her body as I mended her, and she sustained me and brought me back my memories.

Yes, I benefit as well, I don't deny it. But now neither of us can exist without the other."

I wanted to look away from the woman. The very sight of her repulsed me. I felt I could almost see the daemon that prowled behind the human eyes. But I could do nothing against her. Not only was she not human, but she was trained as a Damask Esir, one of the elite soldiers of Avvad enslaved to loyalty by the pyr known as Qarin. And she was a warden. My knife would be of little use against her, and though I tried to open myself to the Pyrthae, my locus now remained stubbornly closed. I could only hope I could pull the wool from Talan's eyes.

"She's manipulating you," I told him. "She's still Esir, can't you see that? The Qarin controls her. How can you trust anything she says?"

"I can't." Though he looked tense, he didn't seem wary of Sule. "But I have no choice. She can find me, Airene, no matter where I am. Unless I keep her close, I endanger myself."

"Then kill her."

Talan's head shot up, his eyes wide. Behind him, a rueful smile twisted onto the woman's face.

"That would be difficult," he admitted weakly. "But even if I could, I don't want to, Airene. Sule is a valuable ally."

I could scarcely believe what he was saying. "She's not an ally, Talan! She's our enemy!"

"No," the Esir interjected. "Our enemy is Avvad. The Kahin-Shah bound Sule and I together. I was enslaved as much as she was at the hands of the Tefra. Now we wish to take our revenge."

"Then take it elsewhere," I shot back. "Anywhere but here."

"Airene." Talan's tone was almost pleading. "Avvad's armies advance on Oedija. Vusu and his Seekers grow stronger with every passing day. Kalindi and his minions spread like a disease throughout the city — thieving, coercing, murdering. We need allies, any we can get. Sule has agreed to aid me in preparing to meet Avvad. I'll not cut her loose."

I felt something tear inside me.

"Then keep her," I snapped. "You're welcome to each other. Just don't expect me to save you when she stabs you in your sleep."

I backed toward the entrance, feeling for the wall behind me. Talan didn't follow. His bright, honey-hued eyes watched me, brow furrowed. Sule, standing behind him, shook her head with a small smile.

But as angry as I was with him, I knew I had to warn him. "Oh, by the way, a Guilder found me. They're searching for you, Talan. Don't let them find you."

His eyes widened, and he took a step forward. "Airene, wait. It's not safe—"

"Nowhere is safe," I cut him off bitterly.

I'd reached the cave entrance and reluctantly released my knife. My hand trembled as I seized the stone wall, but my grip held. I looked back once more at Talan, wishing there were words to show him the depth of his mistake. But anger sealed my lips shut.

Without another word, I turned and started the slow climb up from the cave.

CHAPTER FIFTEEN

HONORARY VERIFIER

Just before the two armies clashed in what promised to be the final battle, Clepsammia again appeared before Agmon Brandheart as he sought to read the stars.

'Your Seed of Harvest has appeared,' he told the goddess. 'Now we will see if you have spoken the truth.'

'I have,' Clepsammia replied, 'but I have not spoken all of it.' Her smile grew wide with anticipation.

'Tell me,' Agmon demanded.

'The gift given to you by my father, the power for a mortal to wield a god's power, was his last act. Tyurn Sky-Sea, Ruler of All Realms, is dead.'

Agmon Brandheart felt hope grow cold in his breast. 'What can tame Famine's appetite if not the Lord of All? We are doomed!'

'You have not yet heard everything, noblest of mortals. There is an uglier truth still to behold.'

'Then speak it and leave me to despair!'

'Despair… do you believe that to be your destiny, Agmon Brandheart?' Clepsammia drew nearer still.

'The truth, bravest of men, is that even as Tyurn Sky-Sea bestowed his last gift upon you, Famine was in him. Your skill in wielding the elements of my world is as much of the God of Hunger as my father.'

Agmon's heart wrenched in his chest so that he thought he would collapse. 'Our enemy is in me? In all of us?'

'All of the First Wardens are Seeds of Famine. Other gods have touched your kind and opened you to the Higher and Lower Realms. But you, Agmon Brandheart, are born of my father's guilt and your enemy's gluttony.'

The Hero of Man sank to his knees. 'He will turn us to his cause. That is why he has not destroyed us.'

Clepsammia did not hide her smile. 'Perhaps. But this flaw cuts both ways. Famine does not stay away only to make you an ally. He cannot deny one born of his seed. Within your heart, Agmon Brandheart, lies the power to restrain a god.

'But to restrain Famine, you must offer him something in kind. A sacrifice of spirit, or an offering of blood...'

- The Seeds of Famine, a translation from the Lighted-tongue; by Oracle Kalene of deme Hull; 881 SLP

R eaching Zipho's cafe a half-turn before Kelena was due, I sat and brooded over a cup of coffee. The cafe owner, sensing I was in no mood for gossip, left me alone after she'd served me.

As I stared into the dark, steaming liquid, regret slowly seeped through me like a stain into wood. Yet as soon as I thought of that strange, beautiful woman huddled next to Talan at night, my blood began to boil anew. Each sip tasted more bitter than the last. We needed allies, true. But we didn't need abominations like her.

Abomination. Did that make Linos an abomination as well?

I remembered the harsh words that had come from his tongue, the presence that had tried to take me. Was he even now yoked, as Sule was by the Qarin? Had I saved Linos only to doom him to a life as a daemon's slave?

Draining the rest of my coffee, I bade my farewells to Zipho, left the cafe, and made for the narrow alley.

Coming to the end of the alley, I peered in and saw a hooded figure standing midway through. So full of misery and self-loathing, I almost didn't care if it was a Guilder or thief waiting to waylay me rather than my contact. Turning sideways, I sidled through the narrow space toward the figure.

When I was a few paces away, Kelena pulled back her hood. "First Verifier Airene," the honor greeted me. Despite her impassive tone, she twitched with nervous energy.

"Hello, Kelena." I paused, awkward suddenly. I'd been aloof and suspicious when we'd first met, but now we were intending to throw in our lots together. I'd have to start acting much warmer toward her. "Is your day going well?" I asked her tentatively.

She seemed surprised by the question. "Fine," she said shortly. "And yours?"

"Not well."

We lapsed into silence again. So much for friendly sentiment. I ignored the flush rising along my neck and said quickly, "Nomusa and I have decided to take you on. So long as you're still interested."

As I regained my composure, Kelena regained hers. "I am," she said, drawing herself up straight.

"Good. Before it can be official, we need the Demos Council to confirm you. Nomusa is setting an appointment with them for the sixth turn this evening. Can you be there?"

She seemed startled by the mention of the Council. I wondered how much hell Iason would raise.

"Yes," she answered stiffly.

"I'll see you at the Conclave gates then." I began to slide back the way I'd come before I remembered something else. "There's a side-gate on the north end of the Conclave grounds. I'd suggest making your way there rather than the main gates."

Kelena nodded and turned away. I glimpsed a small smile playing on her lips before she pulled her hood back on.

When I exited the alley, I let out a long sigh. I hoped Nomusa and I could make good on our promise. Despite myself, I found I was beginning to trust the woman.

Yet if we were to work together, we had a hard battle ahead of us yet.

———

Though there was too little time before the Council meeting for my usual activities, I still made for the Acadium campus. If I hurried, I had just enough time to make it there and back. The daemon-possessed woman still haunted me so that despite days of ignoring Linos while visiting Tomes, I suddenly felt the urge to visit him.

Already wearied from the day's walking and my climb to the children's cave, my legs and lungs were burning by the time I reached the Ward. The same clerk as before sat in attendance, and she eyed me as I approached.

"Are you seeking healing?" she asked with false sweetness.

I brushed back a stray hair that had come out of its braid. "No, thanks. I'm here to see Linos. Ward three, bed sixty-four."

After the clerk confirmed it, she let me find my own way in, though I felt her eyes follow me. She wasn't the only one to cast looks my way. A disheveled woman in tunic and trousers wasn't the usual visitor here. I tightened my jaw and stared straight forward, refusing to acknowledge their stares.

Reaching Linos's room, I found a healer's assistant attending to my brother. She bowed out as soon as I explained who I was, though not without a wary look of her own. I ignored her and looked down at Linos.

He seemed in much the same condition as last time and lay flat on his back, eyes set in their webs of violet lines and staring at the ceiling. I didn't come close. I hated that I feared even to touch him.

"Linos," I murmured. "What has been done to us?"

He didn't answer, as I'd known he wouldn't. As I'd hoped he wouldn't. If he had, I knew it wouldn't be him speaking.

"I think I understand more about how you've become the way you are," I continued. "You've been hollowed out by him, haven't you? By Famine. But I don't know why. I wish you could tell me."

My little brother had always pretended to know more than he did, but I was sure he knew things that might help me now. If he could only rouse and tell me.

"Linos," I whispered. "Little Lion, can you hear me?"

His head snapped toward me so quickly that I jumped.

"He can't," the daemon that seized his tongue crowed. "But I can, sweet nectar to my soul."

My chest tightened so it became hard to breathe. "You don't have a soul," I hissed.

"I'm nothing *but* soul," the daemon corrected me. "But soon, *very* soon, I'll be more. I'll have a body of my own."

I wanted to shake the daemon from my brother. "Leave him alone!"

"Oh, no, Airene. I don't mean to leave him. As you well know." The daemon stretched Linos's mouth into a wide smile.

I wanted to scream and strike at him. I wondered desperately if channeling quintessence could harm the pyr, or at least dislodge him. But even if it might, I couldn't channel at will. I was helpless.

"You won't have him," I warned as I backed toward the door. "I won't let you."

"I'll be waiting!" the harsh voice called as I fled from the room.

Putting the door between my brother and me, I stood panting behind it for a moment. Healers and assistants passed by, casting odd looks my way. When one actually stopped to inquire if I was well, I decided I had to move on. Time was already short as it was.

But I couldn't leave my brother like this without doing anything.

I stormed up to the clerk at the front. Someone had arrived there before me, so I waited impatiently for them to finish before walking up to her. Rather than smug and superior, the woman looked frightened at my expression. I tried to soften my scowl, but it was etched into my face.

"When was the last time Kallias visited my brother?" I demanded.

The clerk blinked. "Kallias the Sculptor?"

"Who else?"

Lines formed on her brow, but she flipped open her heavy book and began to search through, her finger scanning the lines. "Sixty-three, sixty-four…" Her finger stopped, and after a moment, she glanced up nervously. "It seems the Sculptor hasn't visited your brother since he was first admitted."

The cold fury of an ocean's swell swept through me. I had another appointment to make. "Thank you," I said, then began to turn away. But something under the entry caught my eye. The clerk had begun to close the book, so I thrust a hand out to stop it. "Wait. Who visited him there?"

The clerk stared at me with a scandalized expression, but she obliged by folding the book back open. "Master Augur Eltris. Is that whom you're referring to?"

I stared at the name in the book. Eltris had been to visit my brother and hadn't told me. How much did she know? What did she plan for him?

"Thank you," I said woodenly, then turned away.

Outside, I stepped to the side of the entrance. My vision tilted drunkenly. Even within the Acadium, my brother was in danger. I shook my head and set off at a fast walk, knowing I had no more time to stand around and consider it. All I knew was that somehow, someway, I had to protect my brother.

Especially from my supposed allies.

———

My mind was in as bad a way as my appearance when I arrived at the Conclave north gate. Kelena already awaited me. Her expression was carefully blank, but I was sure she saw every errant hair and mud splatter up my trousers. I put it from mind. If the Council put me out for a rough appearance, they were even pettier than I'd thought.

"You ready?" I asked as I drew out my Finch medallion for the guards, who were less reticent about expressing their skepticism of my dress.

She nodded and followed.

Nomusa met us at the Conclave doors. "Hello, Kelena," she said, nodding as the honor bowed her greeting to her. Then she turned to me. "You're racing the sandglass to the last speck. I was about to hunt you out myself if you didn't show up soon. What happened?"

"A long day. Weren't you saying we're running short on time? Let's go recommend a Verifier." I gave Kelena an encouraging smile, but she didn't return it as she stared around the Conclave. Even as an honor to Iason, she'd likely never seen the grand seat of the demotism before. And she had a big trial before her. She couldn't be blamed for missing a few things. My smile slipped away.

We hurried down the Conclave steps to the Council's small door. As we neared, the same male honor as before stepped forward. "The Council awaits you, First Verifiers," he said, rebuke plain in his voice.

"We know," I said, my forced good humor evaporating.

Nomusa halted me with a touch to the arm. "Remember what we discussed before," she warned softly. "Let me do the talking."

She was right. I was in no condition to speak to the Council. I pushed down the mutinous feelings that rose in me and nodded.

Her smile formed a thin line. "A good start. Kelena, if you'll follow me."

We entered the Council chamber. All ten of the Low Consuls were gathered along with Jaxas. No one smiled or spoke as we filed inside. I met Jaxas's gaze and was surprised to see cold consideration there. I lowered my gaze to the floor. The room had a chill feel to it that had nothing to do with the monsoon winds spiraling through the open windows.

"Demos Council," Nomusa began with a bow. "Thank you for your time. I'll be brief. We bring before you one we hope to be the first to join the new Order of Verifiers. This is Kelena of Iris. By all accounts, she is—"

"Kelena of Iason, you mean!" Iason, usually stuttering and uncertain, was neither now. His fury made him tremble as he stared at Kelena. "I assume I will return to a sooty kitchen this night, won't I, honor?"

Kelena flushed, but didn't flinch away from his stare. "Perhaps," she said in a quiet voice nearly swallowed by a sudden gust. "But that will no longer be my concern if you confirm me."

"If!" Iason sputtered, looking around with wide eyes. "There's no question of i-it!"

"I would not say that, old man." Feiyan leaned back in her chair, amusement dancing in her eyes. "Some of us are more open to equal opportunities for all."

Berker leaned on the table, his face growing purple with rage. "She's an honor!" he snarled. "She can no more be a Finch than a dog can be a Servant!"

"Peace, please," Orhan interjected. A mocking smile played on his lips, and I wondered what he had in store for us. "We have not heard out the First Verifiers."

"Thank you, Orhan," Nomusa said graciously, though her eyes betrayed her unease. "It's plain that Kelena is an honor. But this is her advantage. She's established a network of honors that span the whole of Oedija, giving us eyes and ears into places we hadn't previously." She paused, letting the suspense build.

As with most things, Berker was deaf to it. "Like what?"

"Like the Manifest compound," Nomusa said smoothly. "And the

Laurel Palace. Thanks to Kelena's foresight, an honor was waiting to bring Airene up to the Yorandu delegation's quarters the night the Seeker wardens attacked. With her aid, we may know well before the next attack and be able to prepare for it."

The Low Consuls exchanged looks, and Orhan's smile grew. Too late, I realized why. These ten people, the most influential in all of Oedija, had more secrets between them than the rest of the city combined. To be told the honors of their households might double as spies only weakened our case. Even those among the Council who wished the Order success wouldn't sacrifice their own privacy. Nomusa seemed to sense the same thing, while Kelena's expression remained impassive.

"For the good of Oedija," Nomusa continued hurriedly, "we should elect Kelena of Iris as a Verifier of the Conclave." She fell silent, neck darkening with a blush as she stared stonily at the opposite wall.

Jaxas moved minutely. "We are called to a vote," he said in a soft voice. "Those in favor of electing Kelena to the position of Verifier?"

Feiyan immediately raised her hand. I gave her a grudging nod, and she smiled sweetly in return. But it seemed our accordance was in vain. Daelya raised her hand hesitantly, and Zehaar only followed suit after her two fellow Equalists stared at her. Yet no other hands ascended. My hopes sank.

"All opposed?"

Iason's hand was up first, with the rest of the Preservists following. I waited for the last two hands to raise, and inevitably, they did. Verchlesa of Thys and Tychon of Hull didn't seem as vindicated like Orhan and his faction, only resolutely determined. Too much risk, too much change. I glanced at Kelena, but she was a statue in her stillness.

"The honor Kelena's appointment is denied," Jaxas said. "Thank you, First Verifiers. You are dismissed."

I felt his eyes on me, but I didn't meet them. I could guess what the Archon meant by his gaze.

"J-just a moment!" Iason cried. The old man stood shakily to his feet and pointed an accusing finger at Nomusa. "You t-try to steal my honor, make her one of your F-Finches, and expect there to be no c-c-consequences? Kelena was my most reliable girl! Yet in light of this betrayal, I am f-forced to dismiss her. Now that I am sh-short-handed, you will have to supply someone in her p-p-place." He smiled wickedly at this idea of vindication.

Nomusa bowed stiffly. "Very well. We will find an honor to replace Kelena in your household. Anything else, Low Consul Iason?"

He had already sunk back down, the smug smile still on his wizened face. "N-no. That is all."

Nomusa bowed again, and I followed after. The bow Kelena gave was stiff but to the exact angle required. It seemed that the more fate beat her back into the role decreed for her, the less human she became.

We didn't speak until we were outside the Conclave doors. "Come with us," Nomusa said, then turned toward the Aviary.

Though Kelena gave no indication she'd heard, she followed her after a moment. I trailed behind.

A short while later, we were inside the Aviary's atrium, and Nomusa invited us to sit as she slid onto one of the tables. She picked up a slice of mango from the platter next to her and thoughtfully bit into it.

"Kelena," she said after a moment, "I'm sorry."

"You presented it poorly. You made it seem threatening to them." Kelena didn't look at either of us as the bitter words spilled forth. "You didn't think through the barriers being an honor to one of the Low Consuls would pose. You didn't think how resistant they would be to change. You should have let me speak. If they'd heard me speak, they would have known I'm not a silent maid with a shaved head and tin earrings. They would have heard what I am. They would know how I could help them." Tears glistened in her eyes, but she resolutely stared straight ahead.

Nomusa looked surprised. "You could have spoken if you wished. Neither of us prevented you."

Kelena finally looked over at her. "It would have been unseemly!" she hissed.

I gave a sardonic laugh. "The Order is nothing if not unseemly."

The honor turned her hateful eyes on me. "You haven't been told all your life to remain silent until spoken to. You haven't been taught to give the utmost respect to authority, or risk a slap across the face. You move through the world with assumptions that it will give as you require, and it complies. You think it must be this way for all." She jerked her head away. "It is not."

I listened in astonishment. She was right. I'd expected the same treatment for her as for myself. It was no more than she deserved. But that didn't mean it was what others would give her.

Yet as I exchanged a worried glance with Nomusa, it wasn't for this gap in our vision. We both knew that if we didn't act quickly, we'd lose her.

Looking back to Kelena, I said the only thing I could. "You're right. And I'm sorry we weren't able to initiate you into the Order."

Kelena's eyes narrowed, and her mouth parted, but no words came out. An apology was likely the last thing she'd expected.

"But that doesn't mean you can't be a Finch," Nomusa quickly followed up. "For most of our lives, Airene and I have acted as Verifiers without official recognition. I wish we could have given it to you, but we don't have to let it stand in the way of working together as if you were one of our own."

The honor's eyes slid over to Nomusa now. "You would still take me on as a Finch?" she asked slowly. "You would risk the Order's dissolution to bring on an honor?"

"It's not charity," I admitted. "We need you. You have access, contacts, and knowledge that we sorely require."

After looking between us for a moment, Kelena nodded. "I have no other place now. If you'll have me still, I'll join you. But I'll need food and shelter."

"And coin," I stated firmly. "Nomusa, can we tap the remaining five silvers to our daily allowance?"

"Galene will question it. It would be safer to give her coins out of our own allowances. Perhaps one and a half each?"

I nodded. "Is that sufficient, Kelena? Three scions per day?"

Her eyes were wide. "What would I use them for?" she asked in a small voice.

I realized with a start that she may never have possessed money of her own before. Some honors worked at the banks sorting money, but no honor was permitted possessions of their own. Any money she'd spent before had been Iason's.

"Whatever the work requires," I said. "Surely even honors take bribes."

She shook her head. "Not coin. Favors we exchange, and small items we cannot obtain except through barter. What use could an honor have for coin?"

"To stash it," I suggested. "To save up enough to escape to another life, or to at least have the choice."

Yet again Kelena shook her head. "Where would they go? Oedija is home. Our families and friends are here. Our lives are here. We don't know the world beyond the polis's walls, except for those of us who have lived on the estates. We'd be more slaves than here, for our masters would be the hateful Fates."

I closed my eyes. I didn't know the Fates she referenced, but the rest made all too much sense. Every man, woman, and child wanted the freedom to do with their life as they would. But not at any cost.

"Very well," I ceded. "But you will get the coin nevertheless. If you must say you're spending it on another's behalf, so be it. But it's yours to use how you see fit."

"Just don't buy clothes like Airene's," Nomusa suggested. "Get something a bit more fashionable."

As I shot her a dirty look, a smile slowly crept onto Kelena's face. It brought out a smile of my own. Perhaps we'd gained a new Finch after all.

Nomusa grew serious again. "We'll need a cover story. But I can think of only one that's suitable."

"I'll do it," Kelena said abruptly. At Nomusa's surprise, she clarified, "You wish me to be the Order's honor, do you not?"

Nomusa nodded slowly. "Only for appearances. In all other ways, you'll be a Finch, with full rights and responsibilities. But you'll have to keep that from everyone, including Hyrol, the Aviary's current honor."

To my surprise, Kelena smiled. "No need to worry about that. Hyrol is part of my network."

Chills prickled my skin. Though some part of me was gratified to be vindicated in my suspicion of Hyrol, most of me wondered at what we'd gotten ourselves into.

Nomusa masked her own reaction. "That's settled then. Now we have to assign duties. Airene, I assume our responsibilities remain the same?"

I nodded and said nothing. Until I knew how our recent inductee would take the news of Famine, I didn't want to risk ruining my credibility with her.

Nomusa looked to Kelena. "Then that leaves your duties. We have a glaring gap of knowledge where it concerns the Manifest. Our top priority is to anticipate when the Seekers will make their next attack, and where. Any additional news you can gain of the Despot's whereabouts and Vusu's doings would also be invaluable."

Kelena nodded, though her eyes darted between us, clearly wondering what we'd kept for ourselves. I resolutely looked away, not meeting her gaze. There would be time enough to tell her later.

"Good. Then I have one last piece of news." Nomusa cast me a look. "The Archon approached me earlier today. He informed me that the Council has deemed it necessary to elect the last Low Consul. As the typical manner of doing so — by consensus — has left it open, it will require a simple majority among the remaining unrepresented eleven Servants to win."

I listened, stunned. Was this why Jaxas had stared so intently at me? I grasped immediately what it meant for him. So long as the eleventh seat of the Council was empty, Jaxas had the power to break ties. Once it was filled, he returned to little more than a glorified moderator. It was the way our demotism was supposed to function, true. The Servants were of the citizens of Oedija, elected to power rather than inheriting it as the Wreaths did. Yet despite all those lofty ideals, I knew Jaxas was who we needed in that position right now.

"Is there no way to delay it?"

Nomusa shook her head. "The date is set. Three days from now, the last Low Consul will be elected. With times as desperate as they are, nothing is likely to change that. I'm working with the Equalists to find a suitable candidate, as well as with Tychon and Verchlesa, if they're willing. We won't allow Orhan and his Preservists to determine the course of Oedija."

I hoped she was right. For if they elected one of Preservist leanings, I feared Oedija would already be lost.

CHAPTER SIXTEEN

A SUMMONS AT DUSK

Clepsammia released Agmon Brandheart from his vision. 'It is for you to decide, Hero of Man. You must make your choice soon.'

Agmon opened his eyes and found they'd arrived at the battlefront. The enemy soared before them in the form of a great serpent. All trembled as Famine's eye, black as a stormy night, fell upon them.

But one stepped before the others: a girl, of no great height or import. Only as he saw her did Agmon Brandheart remember Aika of the Green riding in his vanguard.

Fearless, the girl challenged the God of Hunger soaring above. 'Daemon! I offer you a chance to sate your ravenous desire! I will tame the hunger that commands you, if you but dare to come near!'

Famine immediately dove at the girl like a hawk at a mouse, his jaws opening wide. Agmon, staring inside his gaping maw, saw the end of all times within. He quailed and waited for the girl to be consumed.

But Aika of the Green stood her ground. 'Famine!' she called again. 'I offer myself as Sacrifice! My blood and my spirit are yours!' And upon these words, she raised a knife as white as bone, then plunged it through her own chest.

— The Seeds of Famine, a translation from the Lighted-tongue; by Oracle Kalene of deme Hull; 881 SLP

I lay in bed, sleepless, Isidora's mind-painting exercises faltering in my mind. Despite night having settled over Oedija, Nomusa and Kelena had gone out to sway the upcoming election, insomuch as they could. The honor, knowing many secrets of the Servants, promised to be useful if it came to coercion. It left me alone to think over the day — or avoid thinking about it, as I'd opted to do.

Yet after my thoughts became so distracted that I couldn't remember if I was supposed to be imagining a desert or a sandy beach, I sighed and sat up. Images of what was happening to Linos kept asserting themselves every time I tried to focus. The barbs of Eltris keeping information from me and Kallias the Sculptor being too important to treat my brother followed quickly behind.

But imaginings of Talan with Sule were what stirred me to anger. How the man could be foolish enough to trust a daemon, I couldn't understand. If he wouldn't listen to reason, I didn't know what could sway him.

Helplessness and frustration conspired to keep me from sleep as well. Finally, I relented to their tide. Rising, I bound my sandals and threw on my cloak, then left.

I only made it to the tower before something drew my eye. In the low light of the pyr lamps, among the many finches settling down for night, I glimpsed a tightly bound scroll attached to the leg of a green-plumed bird. Ascending nearer the top of the tower, I took some seed from a nearby trough and cooed softly, trying to coax the bird toward me. Eventually, I succeeded. The finch ate contentedly as I untied the scroll, then withdrew my knife to cut the unfamiliar seal, a tree with its branches formed into a sphere — the shape of the Bali isikhayha trees, if I wasn't mistaken. The script was strange to me as well, written in large, flowing letters barely recognizable as Oedija's sea-tongue.

First Verifier Airene,
*   The Shaka-Heir bids you visit his quarters this night, if you are able. If this missive arrives too late, he wishes you to come at your earliest convenience.*

~ Faluwa Yorandu Nkosi, Advisor to Charratta Yorandu Komo, Shaka-Heir of the Yorandu

I lowered the small scroll, considering. When this message had arrived was critical to know. Though Nomusa made liberal use of our finches, I'd found little reason to, and I hadn't been watching for scrolls. Either way, I could ill afford to delay. The turn wasn't too late as to attempt a visit, and I clearly wasn't going to fall asleep.

Finally having a purpose, I hurried toward the Laurel Palace. The green radiant winds streamed across the cloud-dappled night sky, lighting my way as I crossed the bridge and ascended the hill to the golden Wreath estate. Though I didn't recognize the guards, they admitted me at a flash of my medallion. Recalling my steps from two nights before, I found my way back up to Komo's quarters.

But as I traveled down the hallways of the opulent wing, I found the Bali guards stood in front of a different door. I froze as I realized why. Memories of the fleeting battle crashed through my mind. Screams filled the air. Blood splattered the floor. Bodies slammed into stone walls with sickening squelches. The perfumes of burned flesh and fresh death filled my nose.

I nearly doubled over. It must have only been a moment before the panic passed and I was able to draw in a ragged breath, yet the moment dragged on and on. But eventually, my eyes again saw the hallways before me. The unfamiliar guards watched me. They could have been carved from wood for all their expressions shifted.

Feeling as if I walked in a dream, I put one foot in front of the other until I stood before them, grasping for words. "Heir Komo summoned me."

One of the guards raised an eyebrow. "And you are?"

Recognition of his voice startled me from my daze. Incredulous, I stared at the man, words completely escaping me now. Without having to search, the traitor guard who competed for the Despoina's affections stood before me.

It was easy to see why he thought he stood a chance, even with royalty. In addition to his honey baritone voice, he had strong features and bright, lively eyes. The hardened muscles of his arms and stomach were on fine display in his warrior's garb. He looked dangerous and alluring all at once. A smile played at the corners of his lips even as his eyes narrowed at me. Yet scorn didn't diminish his beauty, but somehow enhanced it.

"What do you think?" the would-be seducer asked his fellow guard. "Which of the sea-city herbs did this one take?"

He clearly intended offense by speaking in my own tongue. Yet still, I found myself tongue-tied.

The other guard didn't answer either. A taller, thinner man already balding despite his youth, his brow knitted together as he studied me. "Are you well?" he asked, his words heavily accented.

I finally rallied. "Yes. I just… I was remembering what happened here before."

The guards exchanged a look. The younger man said something in a low, excited voice in the Yorandu tree-tongue, but the traitor guard just shook his head, amusement plain in his expression.

"My friend believes that you remember this as the Shaka-Heir remembers," he informed me, speaking with exaggerated slowness. "That you feel the violence of places."

I knew he mocked me, yet in my stunned state, anger couldn't reach me. "Remembering as *I* do is enough," I told him. "I was there with Heir Komo when the Seekers came."

The traitor guard's smile slipped, and his eyes flickered to the medallion at my chest. "First Verifier Airene?"

My name and title returned some semblance of my dignity. "Yes. Now will you admit me?"

The traitor guard spoke rapidly to his companion, and the younger man shot me an inscrutable look before knocking on the door, then entering within. The traitor and I were left in silence. With each passing moment, I felt more myself. If the memories hadn't faded, they'd lost some of their cutting edge.

"What's your name?" I asked him flatly.

The traitor guard seemed to have recovered his mocking confidence. "Why? Do you wish to report me for my suspicions?"

"What's your name?" I repeated.

"Bhaka." He said it as if it were of no importance.

I didn't respond, but waited until the door opened again. The younger guard stepped out and motioned to me. "Shaka-Heir will see you."

As he held the door open, I stepped inside. I felt Bhaka's gaze on me as I passed him, but I didn't look over as his fellow closed the door behind me.

"First Verifier Airene."

Komo wore a loose white tunic and short trousers, similar to what he'd worn the night of the attack. The Shaka-Heir's boyish voice had none of the buoyancy from when I'd first met him at the feast. I wondered if his "feeling the violence of places" was taking its toll.

"Heir Komo." I bowed and approached. The room was not as richly adorned as his initial quarters had been, lacking the vines covering the walls. Komo's advisor Nkosi stood in one corner of the room next to a bookshelf. He didn't look up at my entrance, seeming engrossed in a small book cradled in his hands.

Komo noticed my study of the room and shrugged. "Do not fear — we are comfortable here. I am more worried about you. How do you fare? I saw the man they call Hilarion up and walking."

"I'm fine. My wounds were not so dire. And yes, Xaron was healed without complications, thankfully. I see you're well yourself."

Komo nodded absently. "Yes. As I said, it does not take my body long to heal. I had feared I would call you from your bed with the note, but I could not wait."

"You needn't have worried. What did you wish to speak of?"

The boy glanced back at his advisor, but Nkosi continued to ignore us. "Asileia Wreath," he said with some reluctance.

I tried to hide my surprise. How strange that the topic should come up now, with the Shaka-Heir's traitor standing outside his door. But as I considered telling him, I realized I couldn't. We needed the Yorandu as allies, and the surest way to tie the bonds was through marriage. To confess our Despoina might have a dalliance with his guard could only serve to undermine our burgeoning relationship.

I tried to ignore the guilt that assailed me as I stowed the admittance away. "What would you like to know about the Despoina?" I asked lightly.

Komo's brow creased. "You seem reluctant to discuss her, as do most Oedijans I have encountered. Is it considered rude in your customs to speak of your leaders?"

I thought quickly. "It isn't offensive exactly. But people might be reticent because they don't know her personally. She's a figurehead, and most recognize her as little more than that."

"And you?" the boy pressed. "You have spoken with her, have you not? What has been your impression?"

I strained to think of which of her qualities might be put in a positive light. "I have only spoken directly with her once, and she hasn't worn the Evergreen Wreath long. But she seems a driven woman, and one intent on making Oedija strong."

"So I have heard. Yet what others tell me and what I see do not match." He shifted, his gaze wandering from me. "She seems… distracted. And she often speaks of being the Hand of Clepsammia. Is this a title of some importance to your people?"

His mentioning her self-proclaimed title stirred an idea that sent cold fingers crawling down my spine, and for a moment, I lost the line of my thoughts. But now wasn't the time to consider it.

I scrambled for a way to spin this hiccup. "She means that, as the Despoina, she is the ambassador of the Eidolan gods. A recently adopted title, but one steeped in tradition."

Nkosi's book snapped closed. "Enough," he said, his tone halfway between annoyance and amusement. "Enough dancing around the truth. The Shaka-Heir wishes to know whether or not he courts a madwoman."

My tact was nearly banished before the bold question, but I clung resolutely to it. "Some might be offended by that question."

"But I do not think you take offense easily. Tell us, First Verifier Airene. Is the Despoina god-touched?"

"Nkosi," Komo said nervously. His eyes darted between us.

"It is under control, Shaka-na. The question, Finch."

Nkosi knew. If I was to salvage our relationship, I had no other choice but to confess the truth. "I don't know. But once, I believed her mad enough to attempt to murder her father."

The two exchanged glances.

"I wondered when you would speak of your missing Despot." Satisfaction warmed Nkosi's tone. "Myron Wreath is alive, is he not?"

My mind spun. Who would have told him that? This game raced ahead of me. Until I found a way to get ahead of it, the truth was the safest route. "We believe so."

"Yet you have not recovered him."

I saw my chance then and seized it. "We haven't the strength. The Manifest hold Myron Wreath captive. There's been no demand for ransom, so freeing him by force has become the only option. We need you, Heir Komo, to rid the traitors of our city."

"But if Myron Wreath is freed, does he not resume his position as the Despot?" Nkosi pressed. "Would not Asileia be forced to cede the crown back to her father?"

Curses ran through my mind. I hadn't considered that angle before. "I don't know. You'd have to pose the question to the Archon."

"Jaxas Wreath. The man in line after Asileia, is he not? I wonder if there are not other reasons Myron has yet to be recovered."

For a moment, I could do nothing but stare. The implication was an insult to the man who had sacrificed so much for Oedija.

"I would not fear that," I said coolly.

"Please, Nkosi," Komo urged. "Do not repel everyone in Oedija. We may yet make this alliance."

"When we have been met with little but lies and deceit? I do not see what we would have to gain, Shaka-na."

The boy turned to his advisor. "We have not been honest either. Tell her. Tell her what only one of the Bali would know."

Nkosi seemed taken aback, his night-dark skin flushing darker. My curiosity grew as I looked between them.

"You are right," the man admitted. Then he approached me and held out the small book he'd been reading.

I hesitated a moment before accepting it. Though it seemed well-cared for, the cover was time-worn, the words and images faded beyond recognition. "What's this?" I asked.

"*Tales of the Desolate,* you would call it in the sea-tongue."

Everything fell into place. I knew what they thought they withheld. "The story of how the eleventh ishaka became the Unnamed. The story of Yama and Lophe and their Serpent God."

They stared at me, eyes wide. "Then you know?" Komo pressed.

I nodded slowly. Yet the weight of the admittance held back the words. If they didn't suspect what I suspected they did — what I hoped they did — I might still drive them away. But as it was, they hesitated over the marriage and alliance. They might leave us. I suddenly resolved that if they did, it would be knowing the full extent of the threat that Oedija and the entirety of the Four Realms faced.

"Heir Komo, the Serpent God that assailed the Bali ishakas didn't leave this world. And Yama didn't die in obscurity. He came to another place and continued to serve his god. He came here, to Oedija." I drew in a breath for the final confession. "The former Tribune Vusumuzi is Yama in another guise, and the Dragon he and the Manifest revere is the Serpent God returned."

Komo stared at me, features lifted almost in awe. "You knew. All this time, you've known. And yet you do not fear to face him."

Nkosi seemed to have aged. "It is as I feared then. The world again buckles beneath the tightening coils."

I held the book out to him, but the advisor pressed it back into my hands. "No. You are familiar with the stories, but you have not read all. This is an older version than the one you will have seen. After Yama and Lophe fell, the Shakas agreed that the Twins' words were too dangerous for any to hear. So a copy in our tree-tongue was disseminated that stripped their speeches away, leaving only the history and the warnings against the Serpent God. The book you hold now is the original, written from firsthand accounts in your sea-tongue, in case it fell into the wrong hands of our countrymen. It contains the very words spoken by Yama and Lophe."

The tome suddenly felt heavy in my hands. I considered what this might mean. "How do you know it's accurate? How do you know this additional material wasn't an author's invention?"

"This book has been handed down through the line of the Shaka's family, unblemished by history's workings, that was written by the advisor to the Yorandu Shaka at that time," Nkosi said. "It is uncorrupted."

I looked the advisor in the eye. The time for half-truths was over. "But you broke that bloodline. You murdered Nomusa's family."

Nkosi didn't flinch as I expected him to. "Madness does not prey only on Oedija's rulers," he said softly. "My Shaka did what had to be done."

I looked aside. The man spoke with far too much belief to be comfortable. Could he speak the truth in this as well? Had Nomusa's father been as mad as Asileia was becoming?

"I need to think this through," I found myself saying. I bowed stiffly, not meeting their eyes. "Thank you for the book."

"Keep it safe, First Verifier Airene," Nkosi responded. "Read it. And when you have, we will speak of this further."

I nodded, then turned from the room.

THE SAME COIN

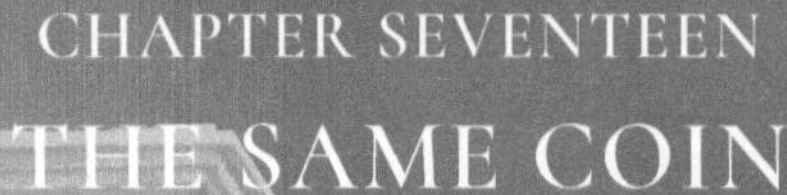

As Aika of the Green fell to the earth, unmoving, Agmon Brandheart found his courage. Calling the charge, the First Wardens surged forward to meet the enemy.

But as Famine swooped down to accept the girl's body, the ground suddenly trembled. A tree, as shining and brilliant as the sun, grew where none had stood before. As all stared in awe, they saw the God of Hunger plunge onto its branches.

Famine screamed, and raged, and lashed his great serpentine body back and forth, but he could not break free of the white limbs thrust through him. Slowly, his movements grew sluggish; then he ceased to move at all.

Agmon Brandheart stared into his enemy's black eyes, but could not tell if he lived or had died, for he had never seen life behind them before. 'Is it over?' he whispered. 'Is it done?'

The Hero of Man sank to his knees and wept. For all they had lost. For the girl who had saved them. And for the coward he had shown himself to be.

— *The Seeds of Famine*, a translation from the Lighted-tongue, by Oracle Kalene of deme Hull, 881 SLP

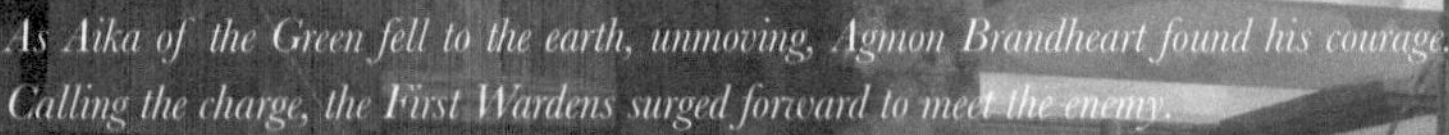

I read through the night.

The previous copy of *Tales of the Desolate* that Nomusa had lent me had been intriguing and vivid enough to haunt my dreams. This original was utterly engrossing. Now that I knew Yama and his Serpent God for what they were, everything took on new meaning. The will that drove the Twins to conquest their fellow people, the hunger for power and vengeance, were all too familiar.

Yet there was more still in this first edition. Yama and Lophe's own words were littered across every page, and when Yama spoke, it was as if I heard the words from Vusu's own lips. *All that is great comes with sacrifice,* he whispered into the still air. I had to look around to ensure he wasn't there.

Though most of what I read made my skin crawl, one revelation comforted me. Again and again, Vusu spoke of being haunted by Famine — by his hunger, by his promises of power, by his thirst for violence and blood. I'd felt none of these things since my own attunement. Surely, it could mean only one thing.

I wasn't a Seed of Famine.

The earlier suspicion I'd held loosened and relaxed inside me. Despite the heaviness of the rest of the text and the sleepless night, I felt almost light as I closed the fraying cover and sat up. Another Quintyr must have opened me to the Pyrthae. No matter who was responsible, it couldn't be worse than the God of Hunger.

As for the rest… I had to think over what I'd read and pick apart the sentences. Almost, I could understand Vusu's motivations, his purpose. What was written here, in a century-old book, both corroborated and undermined what I knew of Vusu.

I pitied him.

I shook my head of the strange feeling. There wasn't a man in Telae less worthy of pity, that I knew well. I rose from bed, a nervous vigor coursing through me. Sleep was impossible now, and I had a full day ahead of me. Despite all I'd learned, there were too many gaps in my understanding. The meeting with the Master Librarian might fill those in.

Yet I could face anything now that I knew I was uncorrupted.

Tucking the book protectively under my arm, I donned my cloak and, still in my clothes from the night before, quickly left the Aviary. I drifted along, nearly dizzy with the lack of sleep and food, but I didn't take the time to stop. Answers were the true sustenance I needed.

When I reached the Yorandu wing, I approached Komo's door, where a different pair of guards now kept watch. At my request, one inquired within, then soon ushered me inside.

Komo rose from a chair to stand with his hands clasped behind his back, a boy trying to appear a man. Heavy-lidded eyes and slumped shoulders told me he'd claimed as little sleep as myself. His advisor was nowhere to be seen.

I bowed briefly and produced the book from beneath my cloak. "I read it last night."

"Then you have done more than I." The boy tried on a smile that failed to reach his eyes. "I know the stories of the Unnamed, of course. But I've not received close instruction."

"Perhaps you'd like to." I held out the book.

The Heir hesitated before stepping forward to receive it. "Nkosi might want you to keep it," he said dubiously.

It struck me then how much of a child he still was. The sympathy that filled me cut with its sharp edges. Too closely it mirrored the guilt I felt for not being able to protect Linos.

"You take it for now," I said gently. "It's safer here with you. If I want to read it again or Nkosi wants me to have it, I can always return."

Komo nodded wearily and turned to set it on the shelf in the corner. "Nkosi has already gone to the Conclave this morning, or so I have been told. I have only just risen. If you wish to speak to him, perhaps you should seek him there."

I contemplated it briefly. "I'll visit later. I don't wish to be caught in the web of politics at the moment."

"A bit late for that."

"Far too late."

We shared a fleeting smile.

"I'd better be on my way." I bowed again. "But I'll return this evening if you're available."

"They have a walk planned for me in your Laurel Groves with the Despoina." Komo tried to keep his voice composed, but dread seeped between his words. "But perhaps after."

"Just as long as it isn't as late as last night's meeting. I must sleep sometime."

His brow knit together. "Of course. Forgive me — you must sleep then."

I smiled. "Only teasing, Heir Komo. I doubt any of us will rest much anymore."

———

The sun had crept into the sky by the time I left the Wreath grounds, its low angle casting the alleys in shadow. Despite my thoughts conspiring to distract my weary mind, I tried to keep watch. In daylight, I was safer out on the main streets, but nowhere was truly secure in Oedija these days.

Luck was with me, and I made it to the Acadium without incident. First, I went to the Ward. Linos was much the same as when I'd visited the day before, still staring up at the ceiling. I didn't venture close but sat in the corner of the room, watching him. Now more than ever I wished him to rise and flash his mischievous grin, to give some sign I hadn't completely failed him. I'd glimpsed the depth of Vusu's madness and had some inkling of what he was capable of. Fear for my brother grew further still as I wondered what he'd gone through.

And why. Despite all I'd read, I still had no answers as to why both of my brothers had been targeted by Vusu. I wondered if I ever would.

Leaving without disturbing him, I found my way to Tomes. My appointment with the Master Librarian wasn't until that afternoon, but I knew I was getting close to finishing *The Seeds of Famine*, and was eager to be done with it, even if deciphering the ancient words sounded interminably tedious. Platon had learned to leave me to my studies as he wandered the great library, humming to himself and playing small games that he dashed aside at the slightest sound, fearing his master was coming down to chastise him.

But if I'd feared the words would be dull, I was wrong. I hadn't squinted long in the yellow light of the pyr lamps before my heart began to thump hard in my chest. A girl, Aika of the Green, had appeared before Agmon Brandheart and proclaimed herself to be the Seed of Harvest he'd been looking for. Despite his doubts, Agmon sent her to the front lines to prove her worth against Famine.

Then Clepsammia once again appeared before the First of Firsts, and made yet another revelation: that the First Wardens were all Seeds of Famine as well as of Tyurn Sky-Sea, Tyurn's Gift corrupted even as it was given. But it was her next words that made my breath catch:

> *The Hero of Man sank to his knees. 'He will turn us to his cause. That is why he has not destroyed us.'*
>
> *Clepsammia did not hide her smile. 'Perhaps. But this flaw cuts both ways. Famine does not stay away only to make you an ally. He cannot deny one born of his seed. Within your heart, Agmon Brandheart, lies the power to restrain a god.*
>
> *'But to restrain Famine, you must offer him something in kind. A sacrifice of spirit, or an offering of blood...'*

Blood pounded in my ears as I read the lines again. *He cannot deny one born of his blood. Within your heart lies the power to restrain a god.* They were true; I'd seen they were true. I'd wondered how Vusu was able to hold Famine to his will; now, I had the barest shadow of an answer. Being a Seed of Famine, it gave him the power to restrain the God of Hunger. Why and how that could be, I didn't yet know. Eltris clearly thought she understood, believing Famine stayed of his own will, seeking to break into Telae. But now, I wondered if there wasn't more to it.

And Clepsammia's last words — "*But to restrain Famine, you must offer him something in kind. A sacrifice of spirit, or an offering of blood.*" I had seen that, too, proved true. At the Despoina's trial, Vusu had cut Linos's arm, spilled his blood, and declared it a sacrifice for Famine. Then Famine had come, opening a path into the Pyrthae, and I'd followed.

I leaned back and rubbed my eyes. If these things written in the ancient text were true, what else that it declared might be? Had Tyurn Sky-Sea existed, and died to attune the First Wardens? And Clepsammia — was she real as well? Had it truly been her I'd seen in the Pyrthae, who had protected me from Famine? Was it she who hounded the Despoina into madness? *The Smile of Fate*, Clepsammia's expression was called. And so it had felt when I'd looked upon it, even when I'd not believed her to be more than a dream.

And Harvest, and the Seeds of Harvest — this book said they could complete Famine. Could they be what we needed? But if that were true, if Aika of the Green were a Seed of Harvest, then why had Famine returned when he'd been restrained?

My appointment drawing to a close, I bent back to the book and kept reading, hoping the answers would be in the text.

The battle came, and Aika rode at the front of the army. She encountered Famine, and her called words to him burned into my mind:

'Daemon! I offer you a chance to sate your ravenous desire! I will tame the hunger that commands you, if you but dare to come near!'

Famine dove at the girl like a hawk at a mouse, his jaws opening wide. Agmon, staring inside his gaping maw, saw the end of all times within. He quailed and waited for the girl to be consumed.

But Aika of the Green stood her ground. 'Famine!' she called again. 'I offer myself as Sacrifice! My blood and my spirit are yours!' And upon these words, she raised a knife as white as bone, then plunged it through her own chest.

Breathless, I continued on, seeking what her sacrifice would bring:

But as Famine swooped down to accept the girl's body, the ground suddenly trembled. A tree, as shining and brilliant as the sun, grew where none had stood before. As all stared in awe, they saw the God of Hunger plunge onto its branches.

Famine screamed, and raged, and lashed his great serpentine body back and forth, but he could not break free of the white limbs thrust through him. Slowly, his movements grew sluggish; then he ceased to move at all.

I scanned the words after, but little else was written. The Hunger War ended there. The land fell into ruin from the battles, and the people were forced into exile. They began a journey across the sea, led by their remaining gods, Clepsammia among them. And so my ancestors embarked on the Lighted Passage and came to found Oedija.

I returned to Famine's defeat, mulling over the words. Now that I'd reached the conclusion, instead of the elation of discovery, I found myself filled with a vague disappointment. Perhaps these passages held clues to defeating Famine once more, but the answers it offered were riddled with holes. What was this "knife as white as bone" with which Aika sacrificed herself? Why did a white tree grow in her place, and why did Famine die on its branches? And if Famine *did* die, if the Seed of Harvest completed him, how had he returned?

Scooting back my chair with a screech, I stood and began to pace. One question after another filtered through my mind, and one by one, they unfolded into a widening fear. I didn't push them away, but let each blossom inside me. My chest felt full of them; my gut ached. My palms sweated with the effort of holding them in.

Realization suddenly dawned on me. *My locus* — it opened inside me and the Pyrthae's energy filled me. Once again, I'd managed to channel when I least meant to.

In a fit of abandon, I let it suffuse me, unable to release the soothing warmth. Radiance, I recognized it, as my head began to grow light, and the pains of reading faded to buzzing numbness.

But as the energy urged me to draw more, the comfort drained away. I couldn't channel; not radiance, not here. A thousand years or more of literature was housed in this library. All it would take was a stray ray of radiance for it to all go up in flames.

Remembering my training, I unclenched my fists and sat back in my chair, forcing myself to relax. My limbs went slack and heavy, and the muscles of my abdomen released.

For a moment, nothing changed. Then slowly, ever so slowly, the warmth of radiance drained away, until at last my locus sealed itself shut again.

A weary smile crept onto my face. I'd stopped myself from channeling.

"First Finch Airene?"

I startled, then relaxed as I saw the library's boy coming cautiously down the hall. "You don't have to use a title, Platon. Especially not one you made up."

The boy grinned. He knew me well enough to realize I wouldn't press my authority on him. I was glad for the familiarity, though it made me remember how ornery Linos had been at his age. My chest gathered a different ache.

"Sorry." The unrepentant boy bowed mockingly and grinned even wider. "I thought maybe you'd want to go up. I think it's time for the appointment."

I rubbed at my sore neck. "Has it been that long?"

"Has to be! You were napping for a while."

"I wasn't napping."

"Uh huh." The boy rolled his eyes. "Anyway, it's my job to get you there on time, or Master Hagne will have a fit."

We ascended back to the main floor of the library. In the wake of the near accident, my questions upon finishing *The Seeds of Famine* had fled me. But as Platon prattled on and my weary legs mounted stair after endless stair, they found me again. At least I might soon have someone to discuss them with.

Platon led me to the Master Librarian's solar, a tiny room that seemed built from the wall as an afterthought. Entering within, I found the space crammed full of books. There was barely room for me to stand. A single pyr lamp hung above us, leaving the corners of the small solar in shadow. Master Hagne herself sat among the stacks, a hood pulled over her face. When it slipped back, I saw what Xaron had mercilessly poked fun at. Her skin was pocked with what looked like scales, and her eyes glittered yellow from the shadows like a rabid animal. Though pity rose in me for her mistreatment, I kept my distance, hoping whatever ailment had struck her as a child was long gone.

As we began to haltingly converse, I quickly realized my hopes for the meeting were unfounded. Master Hagne dismissed my interest in legends and, speaking rapidly, tried to divert my interest to areas that held her concern more, particularly Qao Fu poetry of the eighth century — which, if she was to be believed, was the premiere art of any civilization that had existed. I nodded and agreed until I could work her back around to my own area of interest, each time in vain. If the woman knew anything of Famine, Harvest, and the rest of the story, she wasn't likely to turn to the topic soon.

But the meeting wasn't entirely in vain. After the fifth time I turned back to the topic, the Master Librarian irritably suggested I go speak with the Master Historian, or as she put it, "that hack who pretends to know history." I sensed a rivalry between the two and hoped it was one-sided. If the Master Historian was as petty as this Acadian, an entire afternoon would be wasted.

Thanking her, I beat a hasty retreat, only to be intercepted by Platon. "Well?" he asked eagerly. "Did she get you the answers you needed?"

"Closer," I hedged, not wanting to hurt the boy's feelings. I gathered that ascertaining a meeting with Master Hagne was no mean feat. "Thanks for all your help."

The pupil beamed. "I'll see you tomorrow!"

After I extracted directions from the boy, I made straight for the Master Historian. Acadian Helene — she allegedly didn't like to use the title "master" — lived near the front of the Acadium in a square limestone house. Glancing up at the second-story windows, I glimpsed a head bent to work, and dared to hope she'd pause to admit a visitor.

I wasn't disappointed. After one of her apprentices inquired upstairs, Acadian Helene came down to greet me. She was just past middle-aged and had black hair streaked with gray, a round face with plain features, and a smile that warmed me immediately.

"First Verifier Airene, I understand?" she said with a respectful bow. "It's a pleasure to welcome you."

"Thank you." I bowed in return. "I was told you prefer to be called Acadian Helene?"

"Just Helene is fine. Come. From what I've heard, you have some questions that may take a long while to answer."

Mystified, I followed her upstairs. Her solar was nearly as small as Master Hagne's, but lacked the same cramped feeling. Where the librarian's room had been dank and dark, Helene's was light and airy, with open windows admitting a cool breeze. Books were neatly aligned on shelves except for two open on her desk. A pen and ink sat ready to be used, and a leaf of parchment was filled halfway down with neat lines of letters.

Helene requested tea from her apprentice, then sat us down in a corner opposite of her desk. "Now. I'll let you ask what it is you need."

"Thank you for your time, Helene."

"Not at all! My hand was just beginning to cramp, and I always smear the ink when I don't let it rest."

I nodded, smiling in spite of my heavy thoughts. "You may have heard already, but I'm looking into legends surrounding Famine from before the Lighted Passage."

"Yes, I did hear." The Acadian studied me, a shrewd look coming into her eyes. "But as to why you're pursuing it, I'm not yet certain."

Something stayed the admittance on my tongue. The historian seemed an open-minded woman, but I wasn't sure if she'd take me seriously if I told her the truth. "A persistent curiosity, let's say."

"An odd time for an odd curiosity." Helene lightened her words with a smile. "Particularly for a First Verifier."

"Perhaps. Is it the wrong time to ask?"

"Not at all. I wouldn't discourage interest in history at any time. Please, ask your questions, and I'll do my best to answer them."

I considered where to start. Which query would be the least likely to arouse derision? And what did I most need to know?

"How was Famine defeated before the Lighted Passage?"

She tilted her head to the side, like a finch considering seed spread before it. "'Defeated' is not the word I would use — 'repressed' is more like it. According to the writings we have — *The Seeds of Famine* being the foremost source — the phenomenon our forebears labeled as 'Famine' was suppressed through the ritual of Sacrifice."

"Sacrifice?" I imagined Aika of the Green plunging the dagger into her chest. "What does it mean, to offer oneself as Sacrifice?"

Helene smiled. "You speak as one familiar with the text. You've read *The Seeds of Famine?*"

"I just finished it, actually."

"A persistent curiosity to carry you through all that cramped script! But to answer your question, no one truly knows what it means to be a Sacrifice. But as those who acted as Sacrifices were written thereafter as if dead, I believe it must involve suicide."

"It seemed that way with Aika of the Green."

"Ah, yes, the girl from the hills. It is a common motif in Oedijan stories, the ordinary child coming from nowhere and nothing to save the kingdom. I doubt *The Seeds of Famine* was the first to use it."

"Could you tell me of its particular rendition?"

She nodded with an easy smile. "We know little of Aika of the Green but that she was born in the hills of the western lands to a poor farmer's family who was forced to move to the city when their lands became fallow. There, she lost her parents to disease and violence, leaving her alone in a dangerous city. Aika was hungry, thirsty, with no home but a muddy alley, when she sank down to sleep for what she thought would be the last time. Then she dreamed of a snake.

"In this dream, the snake was wound around a tree branch, gnawing at the orange fruit hanging heavy there. As Aika approached it, it didn't seem to notice, but finished the first piece of fruit before starting in on the next. Its long tail swung down far enough that it hung just before the girl.

"Approaching it, Aika stretched out a hand to touch the snake's tail. As her finger made contact, the snake immediately left off the fruit and swung its head around to face her. The girl fell back, staring wide-eyed at the serpent. It was large enough that it could swallow her whole. Just before it struck, Aika startled awake, only to find her hands were glowing with fire. Somehow, during the course of the dream, she had become attuned to the Pyrthae.

"Aika claimed that the snake was Famine himself, and that she became attuned by drawing close to his presence. Though none of the First Wardens seemed to believe this, her startling beginning is the only characteristic that sets her apart. Her channeling was not very strong, nor did she seem gifted as a warrior, healer, or crafter. Yet when she offered herself as Sacrifice to him, it was enough to tame Famine and drive him from this world."

I found my brow had furrowed and tried to smooth it. "I don't under-stand. I thought Aika was a Seed of Harvest. But what you say makes it sound like Famine attuned her."

Acadian Helene cocked her head. "So it does. But it's a matter of some debate as to whether or not Famine and Harvest are separate beings, or two sides of the same coin. The theory makes a certain sense — many cultures' deities occupy dichotomous roles within their pantheons. The merciful judge. The trickster champion of the people. The bloodthirsty savior."

Despite myself, I found disappointment churning in my gut. "You think this is nothing but stories. Tales told to children."

The Master Historian laughed. "Well, I wouldn't tell this one to my children, if I had any! But yes, of course I do."

She seemed to sense my disquiet, for she continued kindly, "I under-stand the hope, First Verifier. With drought and war coming, it's only natural to seek comfort in stories. But I would caution you against taking these legends as anything more than tales told to explain the troubles that the world brings."

I looked out the window. Acadian Helene was a warden herself; she wouldn't be in the Acadium otherwise. If she could reach into the Pyrthae, she'd know how very real the enemy we faced was. But how long had it been since she channeled? She was an Acadian through and through, skeptical of all she could not see. I wouldn't convince her of the truth when I had but scraps of it.

Glancing back toward her, I put on a strained smile. "Of course. As I said, it's no more than a passing fancy."

Helene smiled in return. "Of course. Now, I apologize, but I have a treatise that I should return to. The events around us will one day be noted in history, and I mean to be the hand that writes them."

I rose and bowed. "I'm sure you will be," I said, though I wasn't sure of it at all. "Thank you for your time, Acadian Helene."

The Master Historian finally stood. "It was a diverting discussion, First Verifier. Do visit again."

———

The day grew golden as I left the Acadium. I still had a couple of turns until night took hold, but I'd have to hurry unless I wished to encounter the dusk mobs once more. My attention wandered as I walked. All I'd learned over the past day and night swirled in my tired mind. Almost, I felt I had the answer to the problems before me, if I could only have a clear moment to think. But nothing was clear; I walked as if in a fog, the sleepless night finally catching up to me.

I was halfway back to the Laurel Palace, the sun sunk behind the roofs, when I noticed the street around me had emptied. Alertness cut through the mind-fog. I tried to be furtive as I glanced behind me.

Two men walked on either side of the street, keeping a dozen paces away. Hoods were pulled over their faces, but I felt their watching eyes on me.

My limbs went weak, but I quickened my step. My breath came swift and shallow. I couldn't help looking behind me, though it would betray my awareness of them. They didn't close the distance between us, but kept pace with me. I didn't dare run.

After glancing back yet again, I found before me two more figures had materialized. Breath stuck in my throat. Terror robbed the strength from my limbs. I stumbled to a halt. Four men surrounded me, with no help in sight. I hoped it was only coin they wanted.

But when they closed in around me and I glimpsed the glowing, blue eye inked into their wrists, I couldn't fool myself any longer.

One of the Guilders grinned as he neared. "Hello, Finch. Remember me?"

I didn't have the wits to respond. I knew I should reach for my knife. I knew I should try to channel. But both seemed impossibly out of reach. I'd never channeled upon command. I couldn't manage it now. The anticipation of what they'd do to me filled my head, fear pushing out all else.

"Ah, she has gone silent. And I was hoping she'd struggle." The Guilder, the one whose nose I'd bloodied, grinned at his companions. They let out low chuckles.

"What do you want?" The words came out as a plea.

"What do I want? A dangerous question." I could see the hairs on his chin, he was so close. "I want to pay you back for breaking my nose. I want to make you scream. And I want to make sure you know that crossing the Undermaster when he makes you a deal has one end." The grin stretched wider. "But I'm not going to make it quick."

At that, the men surged forward.

Only as they moved did I spring back to myself. Desperate animal rage suffused me as I reached for my knife. But as I tugged at it, it stuck in its scabbard, and before I could wrench it loose, hands seized me and crushed me to the ground.

The Guilder got his wish as I screamed. The smell of unwashed men's bodies filled my nose, and dust filled my mouth as they pressed me against the cobblestones. Shrieks, barely recognizable as my own, erupted from me until a hand pressed my head down hard. Sudden pain; my forehead wet;

dizziness washing over me. I ceased to struggle, my limbs grown too heavy to move.

"You know," the Guilder said over me, "your lover thought that you'd put up a better fight. He *screamed* that you wouldn't let us take you alive when we put him under the knife. Yet here you are. A ripe fruit for the plucking."

Helpless rage seized me again, and I bucked and struggled anew. Someone wrenched my hair, then stars flooded my vision as something hit me. Sickening pain washed down me. Head blazing, I gasped, fresh blood dripping down my face.

"That's better," the Guilder crooned. "Nice and quiet while we put you in your place. If there is an afterlife, I hope your Talan is watching from it."

I felt a tug on my trousers, but my belt kept them in place. Groggily, I batted at their hands, but my fingers had grown too clumsy to pry them off.

"Not here!" the first Guilder snapped. "What if those damned mobs come? Pull her into the alley."

"I wasn't having a go!" a gruffer voice protested. "Keep your damned britches on."

"Quick!" a whiny voice cried. "Someone's coming!"

The street lifted away, and I didn't fight as the Guilders dragged me along. I glimpsed a streak of red splattered on the stones before shadows closed around me. As the shock began to wear off, pain assaulted my head and ribs in a steady, pounding throb.

Disorientation didn't stay anger flooding back in once more. I thrashed suddenly, dislodging one man with an errant kick. But there were too many. As soon as we were in the alley, they pressed me against the ground again. The choking stink of nightsoil and urine filled my nostrils, and though I tried to cry out, they seized my hair again and pressed my face into the grime.

"Flip her over!" the first Guilder commanded. "I'll have the first turn."

"Why?" the gruff voice responded. "Because you were stupid enough to let her hit you in the nose?"

"Because Kalindi would have you flayed and hung up if I let him know all the dirt I have on you. Now get her pants off — I don't want to smell this shit any longer than I have to."

"Do it yourself. I'm not going to undress your whores for you."

I clawed back my wits and tried to focus on my gut. With pain radiating from my side, it was the last thing I wanted to think about, but I strained to open myself to the Pyrthae. It was no use. I couldn't call upon the exercises of Eltris or Isidora. Magic remained as aloof as it always had.

The Guilders must have sorted out their problems, for I was flipped over and my belt pulled open. I thought I would pass out from fear, almost hoped I would. My trousers were just beginning to follow when the Guilders exclaimed again.

"Burning riot's passing!" the whiny voice called.

"Don't bloody call them over!" the gruff voice hissed. "They'll leave us be if we don't call attention to ourselves."

I knew then what I had to do. Hoping a broken rib wouldn't puncture my lungs, I drew in as deep of a breath as I could. But before more than a screech could come out, a gloved hand clapped over my mouth.

"I don't think so," the first Guilder whispered in my ear, words dripping with venomous satisfaction. "No one's coming to save you."

I clamped my jaws down on his hand, but the leather of the glove was too thick to bite through. In vain, I wished desperately for someone to come. *Talan* — would he know? Was he watching out for me as he'd done before? *Eltris* — would she sense something was wrong and appear from nowhere?

But no matter who I thought of, I knew there was no chance of them finding me. I was out in the city on my own. The Guilder was right.

No one was coming to save me.

INTERLUDE II

CORIN

Corin sat in the dimly lit storefront, staring into the vase's shifting light. The smooth curve of the glass was dappled blue, the pyrkin inside shifting their hues and vibrance with each passing moment. Her sister might have seen something in the patterns, Kari having the gift for reading the signs. Corin had never envied her sister the ability, as it had always been as much a curse as a gift. But now she wished she could see as Kari did. She wished something, someone, could show her the right path forward.

It had been a full span since she'd betrayed Airene to keep Kari alive. A full span during which anything might have happened to her sister for her failure to complete her betrayal.

And what had Corin done to save her?

The old anger, ever simmering below her stony facade, bubbled up once more. Only now, it had nowhere to go. She couldn't push a cart until she was dragging with exhaustion. She couldn't spar with the other outriders of her company and thrash her rage away. She'd spent full spans in the freezing rain when training with her comrades, accepting abuse from the gods and the Forerider of their band without complaint. She'd endured starvation, thirst, and every hurt known to woman. But there'd always been a path to follow, an enemy to fight, an objective to accomplish.

It was the waiting that drove her mad. The waiting, and not knowing what she waited for.

Corin stood, fists clenched at her sides. She longed to reach out and dash the vase against the wall. But she was better than that. However much time passed didn't change what she was. She was an outrider, one of the *yaendul*. She didn't cede control to anger — not in the heat of battle, not in the middle of a glass shop. Picturing an icy cave, she found the frost's calm. For a time, she stood and imagined water dripping from the icicles that hung like teeth from the caves of Jolduun.

Calm slipped away as she realized which cave she'd imagined. The cave she'd hidden her sister and mother in before leaving.

The anger rushed back in with acid words. *Fool woman.* Why had she trusted the chief's word? Why had she believed his fear and honor would be enough to leave Kari and Mother alone? Why was she so stupid as to ruin everything she'd ever touched? She'd failed her fellow outriders when she refused to kill her sister for the sorceress she was. She'd failed her sister when, after two years, she couldn't raise the funds to bring her and their mother over. She'd failed Airene, who had given her a home when she'd had no other in this foreign city.

Corin blinked, eyes burning. She wouldn't shame herself even in private. She wouldn't let tears fall. *If saltwater is to fall, let it fall as sweat,* her Forerider had often said. Right he'd been then, and right it was now. She didn't deserve to weep. She didn't deserve pity, especially not from herself.

She had warning of Maesos's approach by the creak of his forge door opening.

"Corin? Are you still sitting out there? Come in, you'll catch a chill!"

The old glassblower emerged into the room. He'd been laboring in his forge down the hall as he often did, and his ragged work shirt was stained with sweat.

Even after three years in the city, she struggled to find the right words in the sea-tongue. "No, thank you. I'm going out."

"Out? The streets aren't safe now, my girl, not with evening fast fading. Even for you — or perhaps especially. Outlanders aren't especially well-loved, you know."

"I'll be fine."

Maesos squinted at her. "Very well. I can't stop you. But where are you off to so late?"

Corin looked aside and held her tongue.

After several long moments, the glassblower sighed. "I suppose it's none of my business. But take care of yourself, Corin. Anything can happen these days. I gave Airene my promise to watch over you, and I mean to keep it as much as I can."

She nodded, not meeting his gaze. She hoped he'd go away. She had one thing left to handle before she left.

But instead of turning away, he reached into his soot-smeared apron and began scooting around the displays of his glassware toward her. Corin fought down the anxiety that reared at his approach and made herself stand still.

Maesos pulled his hand out, holding up a stoppered vial. "Here. Take this."

Corin didn't reach out to take it, but only eyed the green, swirling mixture suspiciously. "Pyrkin?"

"Not just any pyrkin. Do you remember the special bolts you carted for me the day of the Despoina's trial? This is the last of that strain. I've sent for more, of course, but that may not arrive for full spans yet. Perhaps not before the Imperium does."

She stared at it, uncomprehending. "Why give it to me?"

The glassblower took her hand. Corin flinched, but didn't pull away.

If Maesos noticed her reaction, he didn't comment on it as he placed the vial in her hand. "For protection, Corin," he said gently. "Should you run into anything out there like we encountered in Vusumuzi."

Despite herself, Corin held up the vial. The green pyrkin pulsed with light, the patterns mesmerizing. Almost, she felt she could read what they tried to tell her. *Fool woman.* She covered the light with her hand and slipped it into the pocket inside her trousers.

"Thank you," she said quietly.

"Of course. Now come back safely. I'll need your help shouldering a delivery to Bazaar in the morn." His smile widened, but his eyes watched her carefully.

Corin looked away. The emotion behind his eyes was far too much like pity. "I will."

After a moment, he retreated back to his workshop. Corin waited until she heard the creak of his door closing before kneeling and reaching behind the counter. Her hand closed upon a bundled item. Drawing it out, she loosened the ties on the long knife, but didn't withdraw it from the bag. Should she be stopped by the city guard, concealing the weapon might save her from detainment. Not that she intended to let anyone detain her.

Clutching it, Corin swept her gaze around the shop, knowing she only delayed the inevitable. If this was the last time she was in this place, the last time she saw the glassblower, so be it. He'd shown her kindness, but her first loyalty was not to him.

She opened the door and strode out onto the evening streets.

———

Corin padded softly through the growing shadows. She wasn't a small woman, and years had passed since she'd thrown aside her wolf-skin cloak. But still, she remembered the long instruction in stealth and misdirection. Then it had been for shadowed forests and frost-gnawed hills in the twilit winter. Here in the city of Oedija, surrounded by worn stone and rotting wood, one lesson remained.

If you must expose yourself to an enemy, never let them know you see them.

She didn't shift her gait when she detected her pursuers. They gave themselves away with small sounds: pebbles scuffed and sent tumbling from roofs; the swish of their clothes; hushed pants of exertion. Among the nearly empty streets, fleeing before the coming dusk mobs, even small sounds stood out. Perhaps they meant her harm. Perhaps they wondered what an outlander woman was up to walking the streets so late in the day.

It didn't matter. She couldn't afford to be tracked now. Corin feigned interest in something on the other side of the street and crossed, moving away from her pursuers. As soon as she came to a street crossing where they couldn't follow on rooftop, she took an alley off the wider road. Unless they were more skilled than she knew, she'd lost them for a time.

As a cartwoman, she knew only the main thoroughfares of Oedija that were wide enough to allow a cart through. But with the Pillars rising high from every deme, she didn't fear getting lost. It was who might find her that concerned her. She gripped her hidden knife tightly and strained her senses.

In the alleys, noises came from the destitute who had made their homes there. The mutters between huddled figures. Small scuffles for prized alcoves. Grunts of people taking comfort where they could. All of it set her nerves further on edge, for they disguised the noise any tails might be making. And, she admitted to herself, she feared these people themselves. She remembered all too keenly her helpless rage as the five boys had robbed her and Airene of all the coins they'd had. Had she then possessed a weapon, she might have killed them all, or attempted to. Even for an outrider against untrained lads, those odds were long.

A woman's muffled scream suddenly sounded from the alley she passed. Corin's hair stood on end. Despite herself, she glanced over. Four figures pressed down someone struggling in the dirt.

Her back tightened, her hands bunching into fists. But four on one — long odds, too long, when those men looked armed and dangerous. And she wasn't here for a stranger in an alley. It wasn't worth the risk.

Corin tightened her jaw and looked aside, pushing down the guilt and self-loathing. A bitter drink she was used to swallowing.

It wasn't long before the temple square came into view. Corin remained out of sight in the alley and scanned the area. Dusk had fully arrived. Two city guards stood at their post at the temple stairs. Corin crouched down to wait.

She didn't have to wait long. An acolyte exited the temple and, with an anxious look either way, scurried down the steps. As he neared the guards, they turned with stony expressions toward him. One extended a hand. The acolyte fished inside his robes for a moment before producing a bag. The guard took it with a grin and pocketed it. With a cursory look around, they sauntered away.

It was the same routine they'd followed the other two nights she'd staked out the temple. If the rest of the routine held, she had less than a quarter-turn before four acolytes arrived with a covered ark. Corin found the frost's calm. She was hard and cold as the age-old ice high upon Jolduun's mountainsides. When her worries had stilled and her focus had sharpened to a fine edge, she stood and strode toward the temple entrance.

No one stepped out to stop her. Sweeping her gaze behind, she found no watchers. Yet in an exposed square of this size, there were many places from which she could be watched. Corin lengthened her stride and took the stairs to the entrance two at a time. Reaching the doors, she looked around once more, then slipped inside.

The corridors within were oppressive, especially for a woman of her height. Corin stifled her usual panic inside closed spaces and continued forward. Of the three passages, she took the left one, then followed it around a bend and down to the level below.

After a narrow stairway, a square, unlit room opened up. Corin backtracked for a torch, then returned and looked about. The room had been used for moneylending when she'd last visited; now, it lay abandoned. Misgivings rose in her, but Corin pressed on, moving aside the curtains that hung at the back of the room and slipping into the narrow passage beyond.

This corridor was lined with doors, and Corin moved slowly as she passed them. While she'd been to the prior room three times, she'd never been back here before. Always an acolyte had sat before the curtains, attending the ledgers for the debtors coming in. Corin had never been desperate enough to see what was beyond. Her pulse quickened. Would there be gold enough here to buy her sister's freedom?

A door behind her opened.

Corin whirled, ripping the knife free of its concealing bag and holding the torch up behind her. Her face was cast in shadow, while the stocky man in robes she faced was blinded. He cried out and flung up a warding hand.

"Who's there?" he demanded.

Corin considered him for a moment. Though he was not in his red robes, she recognized the priest who had given her the order to betray Airene. The same as who threatened her sister's safety. The frost's calm thawing before her anger, she drew herself up to her full height.

"Corin. A debtor."

"A debtor? Come back in the morning then." The priest's eyes darted to the steel glinting in her hand.

She released the blade and let it fall. As the priest watched it clatter to the floor, Corin stepped forward, seized him by the robes, and shoved him roughly against the wall.

The priest barely resisted, the futility of it plain in her strong grip. "What?" he sneered, his eyes wide. "Do you think to intimidate me?"

"Tell me where you keep my sister, and I will not kill you."

The priest's eyes widened and his mouth twisted. She could smell the fear in his sweat. "Kill me? If you do, you'll never recover your witch sister!"

She slammed him against the wall so hard his head bounced against the stone. His eyes rolled once, and a groan escaped him. Corin held him pinned there with one arm, the torch held close to his face, the heat uncomfortable and the light half-blinding.

"Tell me where you keep my sister," she repeated slowly.

"I don't know!" The priest's voice had grown shrill. "I never knew! I was just to deliver you the messages. I never knew their plans for her—"

"I need more information," Corin informed him. "Or I do not need you alive."

The priest blinked rapidly, his eyes wandering. She wondered if she'd shoved him too hard.

"I — The high priest! He will know. We must ask the high priest!"

"Where is the high priest?"

"In the sanctum."

Corin considered it. It was likely to be a trap. The acolytes with the ark could even now be entering the temple. Others might be guarding the sanctum. Yet she'd come this far. She couldn't leave without knowing how to get to her sister.

She stared hard at the priest. His eyes shifted away from hers. He wasn't telling her all, she was sure of that. She wondered if she should kill him even if he told the truth. But as much as she wished to make him pay for the wrongs he'd dealt her sister, for the wrongs he'd made Corin perform, he was more useful as a hostage. For now.

Using the weight of her body, she heaved him to the ground. The graceless man barely caught himself as he tumbled. While he scrambled to his feet, she retrieved her knife and swiftly stood over him again.

"Lead the way," she commanded him. "And remain silent."

The priest went before her, ascending up the narrow stairway and back to where the passages met. There they took the center passage, the hallway only a little wider than the last. The priest seemed to regain more of his injured pride with every passing moment. Corin considered reminding him why he'd lost it in the first place, but decided it wasn't worth the noise. They continued forward in silence, the priest only stopping to give spare directions. Her nerves were on end as she gazed into each shadowy corridor they passed. Nothing was ever there, yet she felt watched, as if invisible eyes peered out from the walls.

The passage slowly widened, then opened into a tall chamber. Cool, almost fresh air rushed around her as she entered. Corin shot rapid glances around the room. There were too many places a crossbowman could hide.

The priest suddenly burst into a run, dashing away from her. "Intruder!" he yelled. "Murderer!"

Corin cursed in her own tongue as she heeled in pursuit. "Stop!" she shouted. "Or I'll kill you!"

He ran slowly across the circle chamber, and she sprinted after him, thinking to catch him before he entered the next doorway. Before she could reach him, however, something moved out of the corner of her eye. Crouching and whirling around, Corin let the priest go as she took full stock of her new opponent.

Her blood ran cold as her eyes fell upon it.

It wasn't human. She wasn't even sure it was a spirit. It seemed little more than two long bands of shimmering cloth, crossed and intersecting as if around an invisible body, drifting slowly through the air as if gliding through water.

A Silk of Avvad, she realized. A daemon made manifest. One of the bound pyr that made the Imperium feared across the world.

An unfamiliar lust reared inside her. She suddenly wanted to throw herself upon the Silk. She wanted to be consumed in its folds. Before she realized it, she'd taken several steps toward it, the torch and knife fallen from her hands as she reached out. She wondered how soft it would be when she touched it.

The outrider in her reared, and she jerked back.

The Silk quivered, seeming to sense her resistance, then drifted forward quicker. The desire redoubled inside her, almost overwhelming her tenuous control.

Gasping for breath, she thrust a hand into her trouser's pocket. Her fingers closed around the vial secreted there. But even as she pulled it loose, she didn't know what to do with it. The pyrkin could dampen a warden's channeling. But what could it do against a daemon?

She was barely aware of pulling at the vial's stopper, her hands numb and weak. The Silk was mere paces away, the ends of its strands reaching toward her. Her skin shivered with anticipation.

Then it touched her, and her skin began to peel away.

CHAPTER EIGHTEEN
NO ONE

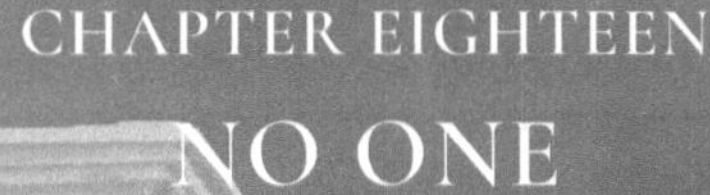

As they finally pulled off my trousers, the cold, wet mud on my bare skin awoke a new depth of terror, vast and numbing.

Even as I squeezed my legs closed, I knew the futility of it, and was confirmed as their rough hands forced them apart again. My cries went unheard, their leader still having his hand clamped tight over my mouth. The dusk mob passed by the alley entrance. Enraptured with rage, none of them noticed the four figures hunched over in the alley. Or perhaps none of them cared.

I felt the fight dying inside me as a man kneeled between my held-open legs. My mind fled my broken body, seeking any escape it could from its ending. And it would be the end, I had no doubt. I'd crossed Kalindi. I'd visited Talan and hadn't told the Undermaster of his location.

Now I'd pay the price.

I watched as if from a distance as the man untied his pants, his three companions standing around him. Time slowed, drawing out the pain of the moment so thinly I fooled myself into thinking I no longer felt it. It was all I could do to stare at the scene. I was a warden. Yet I couldn't stop the rape and death that were swiftly closing in on me.

I pulled further away. The man moved as slowly as if through honey. *Why prolong it?* I despaired at my thinning sanity. *Why make this moment linger?* I wanted it over with. I wanted all the pain to stop. I deserved at least that dignity, didn't I? I deserved to become nothing, no one.

I deserved not to exist.

I wrenched my gaze away, no longer able to watch. As I looked up, surprise dampened the despair. Around me, Oedija had become mirrored, a thin layer of emptiness filling the gaps between them. I glanced down again at the scene below. The Guilder kneeling before me had still not fully taken off his trousers. On the street next to us, the dusk mob flowed like a river of molasses.

I'd fled into the Pyrthae, and time had slowed. I'd channeled quintessence.

But I couldn't wrestle with what that meant now. My body was still below. I had to do *something*.

But if I was going to do anything, I'd have to work quickly. I stared at the men surrounding my body. What quintessence could do to them, I didn't know. I'd just have to try.

I threw my Pyrthaen self down at my assaulters, heedless of what the speed might do to me. I aimed first for the man kneeling before me, his pants halfway down his thighs, his desire open for all to see. Screaming soundlessly, I reached my ghostly hands forward as I crashed against him with all the force I could muster.

I lost myself.

Flashes of scenes filled me as I dove inside his mind. A boy skipping down a muddy street. A man beating a woman into the dirt floor of a house while a boy cried in the corner. A boy winning his first fistfight and feeling the glow of victory as the other boys clapped him on the back. The first whimpering girl he took in a dark, dirty alleyway.

Rage brought me back to myself. I wrenched myself apart and felt the Guilder's pain briefly, then awareness ceased as I broke the connection. Soaring back into the sky, I glanced down to see the man collapsed over my legs, senseless, even as my body lay prone, eyes staring into nothing.

I had to struggle hard to keep myself together. The foray into the man's mind had left me weak and strained. I didn't know if I could survive another attack. But seeing as I had no other weapons to fight with, I braced myself for a second dive.

Cold as I'd never experienced before pierced my arm.

Shocked, I tried wrenching myself away from whatever had seized me as I looked around. An amorphous cloud of flickering light hovered next to me. Only the hand thrust from it was distinguishable as human. But as its presence flooded me, I knew it was far from mortal.

I've been waiting, the daemon gloated. *Waiting for when your foolishness brought you here again. Now you are in* my *plane, human. You can't escape!*

I cried out wordlessly and tried to resist. To my horror, I was losing my shape. My feet and hands began to grow indistinct, melting into glowing mist. Memories leaked from me in wisps of light. I began to forget as they trailed away from me. *Who am I?* I thought desperately. *Who am I supposed to be?*

You are mine. That is all you ever need be again.

NO!

Denial surged within me, shutting out the comfort of the lie. I pressed against the pyr's foreign presence. Bit by bit, I forced it out of my awareness until I reached the boundaries of my body.

Then I wrenched my arm away and floated to the side.

The daemon didn't follow, perhaps stunned by what I'd done. I didn't wait to see if it would attack again but looked down, desperate for a way out. My body still lay prone beneath the Guilder I'd knocked unconscious, but no one else surrounded us. Not sparing a moment to wonder, I dove toward my body. I felt the pyr stirring behind me, but didn't turn as the world below rushed closer. Even as I neared, I didn't dare slow.

I crashed into my body.

As my mind melded with it, returning to its natural form, a flood of sensations washed through me. Everywhere hurt. I gasped and fought to keep above the pain. A ringing filled my ears, and my vision blurred.

But as strong as the agony was, my revulsion for the man draped over me was stronger. Summoning the last of my willpower, I heaved the limp man off of me and snatched up my trousers as I scampered back. My body shook as I pulled them back on, emotions twisting with searing heat inside me. I shoved the feelings down and dressed as quickly as I could, the mud smeared over my legs making the trousers stick and catch.

I kept a fearful watch as I dressed, expecting at any moment to see three hooded figures running down the alley toward me. Why the Guilders had left, I couldn't tell. Perhaps they thought both their companion and myself dead and didn't care enough to check. Or perhaps they feared something — magic, or a daemon — had gotten to us and feared for their own lives. It didn't matter. Either way, I had to flee before they gathered their courage and returned.

I turned toward the street. The dusk mob had passed, leaving the road clear for me to travel upon. But something made me hesitate. I glanced back down at the unconscious Guilder. He still lived. I sensed I'd have felt it if I'd killed him by entering his mind, or whatever I'd done.

Before I could consider it further, my vision suddenly doubled. I reeled as the world tilted beneath me. As my eyes fluttered open, I saw the mirrored Oedija again hung down above me.

The daemon — he must have done something, pulled me out of my body! But as I looked around, I didn't see him, and I felt myself anchored firmly to the ground.

But *someone* watched me. Spinning around, I saw a shape floating in the strange light of the spirit realm. Eleven strands of gray cloth trailed from her robes, and her tilted eyes watched me with avid interest.

"Clepsammia," I muttered aloud, the name reverberating in my mind.

The gray spirit smiled at me. Something in her expression made me uneasy, as if she knew something I had yet to discover.

I stared up at her, waiting, expecting something to happen. My skin prickled with the danger. I knew Clepsammia, or whatever pyr took her form, might mean me harm. But I couldn't summon the will to flee. With my head craned back, I felt so tired all I could do was stare up at the Goddess of Fate and wait.

Clepsammia drifted closer. Still wearing her eerie smile, she gestured, twisting around her hand with a finger extended like a spoon stirring a mug. I could only watch dumbly. Whatever she meant to say was beyond me.

When she rushed forward, I was barely conscious enough to startle. Yet I couldn't escape. Clepsammia neared too rapidly.

She crashed into me.

I stumbled backward, but felt myself lifting up. Exhaustion fled before the invigorating fire that filled me. The pain in my ribs and head eased.

A moment later, the heat faded, but some of its effects lingered. Though pain crept back in, I had the strength to remain standing, and my ribs didn't threaten to bend me over. The double-vision lingered, though, and I looked up again at the gray woman floating through the Pyrthae.

Clepsammia put a finger to her smiling lips. Then the Pyrthae shredded once more out of existence.

I blinked as my vision returned to normal, and my mind returned to the present. The Guilder still lay at my feet. Dusk had taken hold, the afterglow of the sun fast fading. I'd escaped one trouble, but I had many others to evade. And though Clepsammia, or whoever that pyr was, had bolstered my strength, I felt it once more fast fading.

Yet despite the urgency, I looked down at the Guilder. Part of me wished to finish what I'd started. Fear, pain, and anger were a caustic solution burning as it wound its way through me. The knife Nomusa had given me still pressed against my back.

It would only take a moment, part of me whispered. *Just a quick slit across the throat. You've killed before. Why not end this despicable man's life? He would have raped and murdered you. Why leave him alive? He'll only do it to someone else.*

I wrenched myself away, sick at the hate roiling inside me. I couldn't do it. I'd never wanted to kill before, but then I hadn't had the choice. Now I did.

Besides, it was a small mercy. With the state that Oedija was in, another might easily kill him if they passed by. Or perhaps he'd never wake from the slumber I'd thrust upon him.

Before I could convince myself otherwise, I limped away and left the man to his fate.

———

I didn't collapse until I reached the bridge.

Amid the other hurts holding me in a half-conscious daze, the pain of my knees hitting the stone was barely noticeable. I'd only made it halfway across. Perhaps I was within a quarter-turn walk of the Aviary, but it felt like miles away. Terror and Clepsammia's gift of strength had driven me past the Laurel Palace's gate, but since I'd entered the Wreath grounds, I'd been losing the battle to exhaustion. My fight with the Guilders and the daemon had left me nauseous and weak. The ringing in my ears had faded to a whine, and my vision blurred around the edges. My ribs hurt with each breath. If the Guilders hadn't broken them, I guessed they were sorely bruised. My hair was matted with dried blood, and my head ached. That was the last time someone would yank me by my hair, I promised myself, though there was little fire in it. A deeper exhaustion assaulted me. Channeling quintessence had a cost, Eltris had said. Now I was paying it.

I clutched the stone railing to remain upright and stared through the balusters over the gently lit sea. The cloud moon glowed with violet light just below the clouds, while the two white orbs were lost somewhere above. Flashes of green showed where the radiant winds struggled to break free of the overcast sky. It would have been beautiful were I not drowning in pain.

The turning of my stomach suddenly became too much. I pulled myself above the railing and heaved out the little left in my stomach. My ribs were aflame with each retch. When it passed, I was nearly too tired to wipe at my mouth. I wanted to lie down where I was and fall into a deep sleep.

Only by berating myself did I stay upright. *Stupid woman. Stupid, stupid woman.* Why had I remained out so late? I'd known the dangers and ignored them. I'd grown careless, and it had nearly cost me my life. Sobs suddenly rose and choked me. The truth of how close a call it had been finally settled in. Never had I felt so alone. Before, others had intervened before I came to any real harm. Xaron, Nomusa, Corin, Talan — my friends had always been there to save me when I needed it most.

But this time, I'd been on my own. And now it was up to me to get myself home.

I forced myself back to my feet. *Just one more step*, I bargained with my weary body. *One more, then you can rest.* Slowly, painfully, the distance between me and the Aviary closed. When the moldy, lopsided building loomed from the darkness, tears of relief trickled down my face. Warmth and comfort were close. I was almost safe.

Reaching the door, I limped inside and looked around. A lone pyr lamp illuminated the room. Taking it in hand, I staggered down the hallway, dragged myself up the finch tower steps, and approached my room at the end. I wanted nothing more than to lie on my bed and lose myself in a long, deep sleep.

But as I cracked open my door, I saw a figure hunched on my bed and froze. It was too late. The person within, noticing the squeal of the door, stood swiftly and walked over to it. I made a pathetic attempt at yanking out my knife before the man's face came into the light.

"Talan," I murmured. My knees gave way to my sudden relief.

"Airene? Airene, are you alright?"

Talan hurried forward, wrapping an arm around my waist. I cried out as he squeezed my injured side and weakly pulled at his arm. "Ribs," I gasped.

He cringed, then shifted his grip under my arms. Taking the lamp from me, he helped me inside. Once I'd settled onto the bed and lay down, he thrust the light next to my head, examining my wounds. I winced as he trailed the light down me, taking in every detail. Part of me was mortified for him to see me in this condition. The greater part would rather it be no one else.

When he finished, he set the lamp down and shut the door, then strode over and glanced out the window. At length, he returned and crouched beside my bed.

"Who did this?" he asked, voice stripped of emotion.

I hesitated. I recognized that tone. Men had died the last time Talan had spoken like that.

But I couldn't lie to him. The word came out in a whisper. "Guilders."

He suddenly looked away, his fists clenching so tightly his knuckles popped. Before I knew what I was doing, I shrank away from him. It was all I could do to sit there, dazed, as he faced whatever boiled inside him.

It took him a long time to turn back to me. A haunted look lingered in his eyes. "How can you ever forgive me?" he asked in a low, choked voice.

"Forgive you?" A laugh forced its way out from my raw throat. "It's not your fault."

He bowed his head. "It is, Airene. It is."

We sat in silence for a long time before he spoke again. "I've been waiting since it started to get dark. Ever since you visited the cave, something nagged at me. I didn't think of it at the time, considering everything else happening. But finally, I realized the danger you might be in. I came as soon as it was safe and waited. And when you didn't return, I began to worry."

"My fault," I mumbled. "It was my fault. I shouldn't have gone. I exposed you."

He just shook his head. "If you hadn't come to me, I would have gone to you. I couldn't have stayed away much longer."

The world suddenly lurched. Talan cursed under his breath as he steadied me, then gripped my hand. "How can I make you comfortable?"

My throat was dry, and my stomach settled enough to feel ravenous. But the thought of sending him away terrified me. I imagined Guilders climbing in through the window to finish what their fellows had started. I imagined invisible fingers clawing at my mind.

I clung to his hand. "Stay."

He took my hands and kissed them, heedless of the grime that covered them.

"As long as you like," he murmured.

———

When I awoke the next morning, Talan was gone.

Cool, gray daylight pressed in around me. I stared up at the ceiling, absently tracing the shapes of the lichen. Countless times I'd awoken throughout the night and only fallen back into an uneasy slumber once I'd seen Talan standing or sitting at the window, staring out into the darkness. Once, he hadn't been there, and I'd sat up despite my ribs, panic making it impossible to breathe. But he'd returned moments later, reassuring me he'd just been to the outhouse, that he was only gone for a moment. Still, sleep had been longer in coming.

But now that it was light, the mysterious man had once again disappeared, like a pyr that only haunted the night. As I stared up at the ceiling, I wondered if I'd imagined the entire sequence. I'd heard of people hitting their head and seeing things. If I hadn't imagined him, it was an odd coincidence that he'd been waiting for me, even with his explanations.

But when I glanced at the door, I saw a small scroll tied to the handle. My ribs spread fire through my body, and a moan escaped me as I sat up, but I resolutely rose to my feet and tottered to the door. Clumsy fingers, abused during the fight, fumbled to untie the string, then unrolled it and stared. The letters swam, and I had to squint to read the text.

I didn't want to leave you. But you won't be safe so long as Kalindi lives. I'll do what I must to protect you.

We shared far too little time. I should have moved sooner. But always, I have treasured what moments we had.

Care for yourself, my Finch.

The parchment trembled in my hand as I stared at it, torn between tearing it to shreds and carefully tucking it away for safekeeping. It was unsigned, but I knew which idiotic man had written it. *I'll do what I must to protect you.* The damned fool thought he could kill Kalindi. Never mind that the new Undermaster of Oedija had all of the Underguild's resources at his disposal. Hundreds were in his employ, many of them hardened killers. Even a warden like Talan couldn't overcome those odds.

I returned to the bed and gingerly lowered myself back onto it. Talan had to be stopped before he got himself killed. But who could find him in time? The only person I knew with that significant of reach was Wisp. But how might I reach her quickly?

The answer came a moment later. *Kelena* — she might have a way. I had to find our honorary Finch. Then, I promised myself, when Talan was safe, I could rest.

With a groan, I pushed myself from the bed once more and fetched my sandals. I still wore the dirty clothes from the day before, but I felt soiled by more than that. Stripping them away, I cleaned off what I could in my washing basin and put on a fresh tunic and trousers. Every movement sent pain cascading through my limbs. My ribs weren't the only thing to hurt — the burn on my shoulder had been rubbed bloody from the scuffle, and several of my toes were red and swollen from kicking the Guilders. My jaw ached and my head throbbed, particularly where they'd hit my skull against the ground. I was lucky to be alive, much less walking. Yet I couldn't help the frustration that it would all slow me down.

As I limped out of my room, though, pride slowly welled up in my chest. I'd survived. I'd survived four Guilders, and a daemon as well. A small smile crept onto my face. Perhaps I wasn't such a terrible warden after all. I didn't even care how god-struck that pleasure might make me seem.

But the smile faded as I remembered the helplessness, the pain. The man wrenching down my trousers and placing himself before me. I staggered and caught against the wall, overcome for a moment. I'd never felt so unclean. Even if I had time to visit the baths, even the secluded Conclave baths, I doubted I could undress. I wondered if I would ever feel comfortable naked again.

But Talan needed to be saved from his damned foolishness, and I was the only one who knew it. I heaved a sigh, girded myself against my ailments, and descended the stairs of the tower.

———

It didn't take me long to reason out that Kelena would be in the Conclave. With the eleventh Low Consul to be elected tomorrow, I knew she'd be there, politicking beside Nomusa. Ignoring the stares of the guards, I limped into the vast Conclave chamber and scanned the people scattered across it. It was far busier than I'd seen it since the trial, with nearly half of the Servants in attendance. The hushed conversations hummed with tension, like a hive of hornets stirring. I ignored it. At the moment, the election wasn't my concern.

I spotted Nomusa at the edge of a knot of Low Consuls. *The three Equalists*, I realized as I studied them. Feiyan's honor Kako stood at his mistress's shoulder in bright yellow robes. Even at this distance, he seemed to be smirking. Feiyan herself looked to be in intense conversation with my fellow First Verifier. I saw many other honors in the Conclave, but of Kelena, there was no sign. I rubbed at my eyes as my vision started to swim again.

"First Verifier."

I startled before I could catch myself, then turned to the voice at my shoulder. Kelena stood in a plain white robe, her face impassive.

"Kelena," I greeted her with relief. "I was just looking for you. I expected you to be with Nomusa."

"I cannot be. I've been deemed offensive to my former master's eyes, and a risk to our task." She didn't bother hiding her bitterness.

I needed to turn that around. I wracked my aching head for a way, but nothing would come to me.

Then Kelena seemed to notice my appearance. "Have you been attacked?" she asked, brow creasing as she looked me up and down.

I grimaced. "Is it that obvious?"

"There is blood in your hair. Are you well, First Verifier? I can send for a healer."

I tried not to think of what it said about my state of mind that I'd missed blood crusted in my hair. "Never mind that. I need you to find someone. He'll get himself killed if I don't stop him."

Kelena stared at me without answering. I had the uncomfortable feeling she was trying to decide if I was delirious or not. She glanced aside and made a small motion with her hand. I followed her gaze and saw an honor approaching.

Before I could say anything, Kelena asked, "Who?"

"Talan Wraithsbane." I winced at saying his epithet, but it was my best hope for identifying him. "Formerly a Guilder."

She nodded, her expression blank. "And if I find him, what message am I to convey?"

"Just tell me where he is. I'll deliver any message in person."

The honor stood by Kelena, and she leaned over to whisper in his ear. When she leaned away, he nodded and departed, making for the main doors. I watched his progress. "Is it that simple?" I asked in amazement. "You have but to whisper to an honor here, and word will spread?"

"No. He has gone for a healer. First Verifier, I will look into your missing Guilder myself, but you must rest with someone watching over you. Who can I call to look after you?"

It took me a moment to understand. "Rest? I don't need rest. We need to go after Talan."

"You're hurt, First Verifier. You need to wash those wounds before they corrupt, and you need rest. I won't hunt down Talan Wraithsbane until you return to your bed."

It was mutinous behavior, and I opened my mouth to lambast her for it, but stopped myself just in time. I swayed on my feet. Mud and who knew what else still crusted up my legs. My stomach turned uncomfortably, and my head pounded so that it was hard to think. I would have ground my teeth if my jaw didn't hurt too.

"Fine," I relented. "Maybe I do need to rest."

She nodded, a crease wrinkling in her brow. "Good. I will send someone to escort you to the baths first—"

"*No.* No baths."

Kelena looked exasperated. "You must clean yourself, First Verifier."

I looked down, unable to find the words to explain. "Please. No baths."

Her voice was gentle when she spoke. "Let me walk with you. But whom should I send for to stay with you while you rest? I will need to go after your former Guilder."

I turned my mind back into gear. Nomusa was too busy right now. Talan was obviously not an option. "Xaron. The Wreaths' Hilarion, if you didn't know."

She nodded. "Very well. He'll be sent for. Now come; walk with me."

After she pulled aside another honor with whispered instructions, we followed her out of the door. I suspected Kelena still meant to bring me to the baths, and I wasn't sure what I would do when we arrived. I knew I should clean myself. But to expose myself again... It seemed beyond what I could endure.

We were quiet until we'd left the guards behind and walked along the promenade. Only the wind and the calls of seabirds surrounded us.

Kelena didn't look at me as she spoke. "Honors are considered property by some of their masters, and we are often used as property. Our labor doesn't belong to us, nor the fruits of it. And some masters even take away the rights of our own bodies."

My stomach turned. I risked a glance at her, and saw her expression had grown stony.

"Did Iason...?" I hesitated, unable to ask the question.

"Rape me? No. His sons did."

Dizziness passed over me again. She said it matter-of-factly, as if it were an ordinary occurrence. For her, I supposed it was. I suddenly felt like I'd been false. I hadn't actually been violated. Even now, could I imagine what that was truly like?

"I'm sorry," I said lamely.

"I don't mention it for pity, First Verifier. I tell you to say that I have felt what you feel, many times before. And in the end, you must take the bath."

"They didn't rape me. They didn't get that far."

From her expression, I wasn't sure she believed me. "All the more reason to bathe and be rid of their filth. Will you wash it away, First Verifier?"

I almost felt silly. The feeling didn't lessen the discomfort, but it made it somewhat more bearable. "Yes. I'll wash it away."

Kelena smiled a smile that went no deeper than her skin, then led me into the baths.

CHAPTER NINETEEN

ELECTION

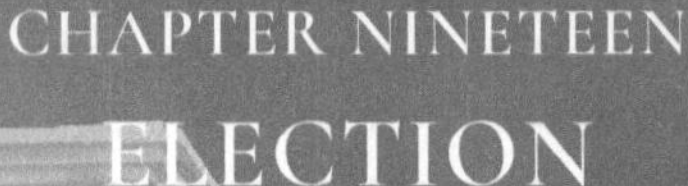

Kelena saw me through my bath, then escorted me back to the Aviary. Guilt wracked me for keeping her from hunting down Talan, but I couldn't form the words to send her away. It was bad enough to sit on a bench and let her fellow honors rub olive oil into my skin and wash my wounds. I couldn't send away the one person who brought me some comfort in that moment.

Xaron waited at the Aviary's door. Upon seeing us, he ran over and immediately began to fret over me. "The healer's inside. Airene, what happened? Who did this? And when?"

I answered his flurry of questions as best I could, though my tongue and mind were growing sluggish. The pain, kept at bay by urgency and awkwardness, swept back in. I took shallow breaths and told him everything — all except how near I'd come to being violated. He was enraged enough as it was, and I had no wish to recount it.

Kelena left us at the door, and after I'd thanked her as sincerely as I could, she set off toward the Conclave gates. Xaron helped me to my bed, where the healer met us and began her examination of my wounds. I was grateful it was a woman inspecting me. A stranger touching my bare skin was bad enough; I doubted I could stand it if the healer had been male. The healer made me breathe in deeply with my tunic raised while she watched. Running her hands over my wounds, she determined my ribs weren't broken, but only bruised.

"There will be pain, but you must not breathe shallowly," she told me. "That will only foul your humors further."

My head seemed as fine as it could be, considering the circumstances, though the healer warned me I might feel strange for four spans still. For the pain, she provided a poppy tincture and instructed me to drink it that very moment. At first, I refused. Part of me wished to keep my wits about me. Another part feared Guilders coming to seek revenge. But at her and Xaron's insistence, and as my pain continued to wear on me, I relented. The healer left Xaron and me then, promising to check back later that day.

I settled down and blinked blearily. Sleep already had a grip on me. But I couldn't rest yet.

"Xaron."

He kneeled next to my bed. "Yes?"

"Talan is in danger. He…" I closed my eyes, fighting off a wave of drowsiness. "He's going after Kalindi. Fool man. He's going to try to kill him."

"Bold," Xaron breathed. "But after what they did to you, I almost want to follow him."

"You can't." I took his hand in mine, my sense of touch already half-numbed. "You have to stay and watch over me."

He clasped my hand with both of his. "Gladly."

Oblivion edged in, but once again I fought it off. "Xaron?"

"Yes?"

"Are you in love with Isidora?"

His grip tightened on my hand, then loosened as he let out a laugh. "Maybe," he admitted, almost sounding surprised at his own admittance.

I gave a soft snort. "Only you wouldn't know."

"Oh? Then you know if you love Talan Wraithsbane, do you?"

A smile found its way onto my face. "Perhaps."

"You're impossible. Go to sleep."

Releasing my resistance, I did.

———

I didn't fully awaken until the next morning, though I rose several times throughout the evening and night to take care of necessities. Xaron stayed by me the entire time. Once when I awoke, he was humming to himself and channeling a line of flames into a circle. Another, he was pacing the room.

"You can go," I'd told him groggily.

He'd stared disdainfully at me. "Go to sleep."

Once more, I obeyed him.

When I awoke the final time, birds called outside. The sky was overcast, but bright enough to dazzle my eyes. Xaron sat slumped in a chair he'd dragged in from downstairs, his chin to his chest. I winced at the crick in his neck he'd no doubt wake up with.

For a moment, I was content to lay back. Pain needled my sides and head, though it was still dulled by the poppy tincture. I feared it would return when I rose. But suddenly, I remembered what today portended, and couldn't stop from sitting up with a groan.

Xaron awoke at the sound, sitting bolt upright and staring around in alarm. "What's going on?"

"The election. When is it?"

He blinked at me. "Election?"

"For the Low Consul, cotton-head."

He rubbed a hand over his eyes. "Ah. Right. I think it's at the fourth turn of the morning."

"Fourth?" I stared out the window. "It has to be nearing the third, don't you think?"

He shrugged. "Either way, I guarantee Nomusa has tied herself in a knot by now. You didn't wake during her visit yesterday. She's worse off than you in some ways."

"She stopped by?" Sympathy and guilt rose in me at the thought of my friend. I'd seen little of Nomusa of late, and done nothing to ease the burdens she carried for our Order.

"Briefly. She rested for a few turns, then rose to work again, writing finch messages to send come morning. I've never seen her work so hard, Aire. She's almost a different person."

"No, not different. Just the person she was always meant to be." I glanced at him. "Before your corrupting influence, that is."

He cocked a smile. "If anything, *she* corrupted *me*."

I swung my legs off the bed. I'd slept in my clothes, so only the sandals remained to don. But I stared at them balefully across the room. Bending over to lash them to my feet didn't promise to be a pleasant task with my ribs.

Xaron saw my look and rose. "I can get them."

"I can put on my own sandals," I protested.

"But not helping would be like neglecting to flip over an upturned turtle. Allow me."

When we'd finished readying ourselves, we walked across the grounds to the Conclave. The hubbub could be heard from outside the great cracked doors. I clung to Xaron's arm as we entered and stared around us.

Once again, around half of the Servants were in attendance, along with their staffs of clerks. With honors moving between them and providing refreshments, it almost seemed the Conclave of old, but for the ruined dome above. I tried to find heart in it. But I knew a functioning demotism wouldn't be enough to save us from Famine, nor Avvad. I doubted it could even save us from ourselves.

We spotted Nomusa, but as she appeared in the midst of an animated argument, we didn't venture closer. The thin man near her, however, looked up and saw us, then began to ascend the curved stairs around the outside of the Conclave chamber toward us.

"I'm glad to see you up, First Verifier," Jaxas said as he neared. "I'd feared the worst when I heard what happened." He was dressed in plain robes today, and his eyes seemed on the verge of disappearing within the dark circles around them.

I let go of Xaron's arm to stand on my own, even though it taxed my paltry strength. "I couldn't stay in bed for this. How are we doing?"

"I'm not allowed to take sides," the Archon reminded me with a wry smile. "But if I were, I'd be happier to be an Equalist. The contest is close, but your fellow First Verifier seems to have swayed the critical vote. If only the election could occur now."

I studied him and his bowed weariness. "And you. Are you content to return to being a moderator rather than a voice on the Council?"

All traces of humor disappeared from his expression. "Do I have a choice?"

I shrugged. "You always have a choice."

He studied me for a long moment. "Have you had any word of the Despoina?"

I blinked, taken aback by the abrupt change in conversation. "I've been resting in the Aviary. I'm not liable to hear many whispers when I'm unconscious."

He bowed his head and stepped closer. "It's a vain hope. Still, I must ask. Airene, if you know anything of her, please, tell me. I've not had word of her since last night."

"Last night?" I dredged up a vague memory. "Wasn't she with Komo last night?"

He nodded gravely. "They met in the Laurel Groves. I attended as well."

"Very romantic," I observed wryly.

"Leia did not appear pleased either. She stared away from the Heir much of the time, often ignoring his words to make some idle comment of her own." He shook his head. "I don't know my cousin anymore, Airene. I fear we're losing her to whatever inner daemons plague her."

He spoke with the familiarity we'd gained before the trial. That familiarity, and the things I knew that he didn't, emboldened me to speak.

"I don't think we'll gain her back, Jaxas. I think we have to move forward anyway, and act in spite of it."

"Act in spite of it," he murmured. "What do you mean?"

I considered my next words. "Komo's advisor gave me a book two nights ago. I stayed up all that night to read it."

The Archon studied me silently, waiting.

"It was called *Tales of the Desolate*. I'd read another version of it, but that one had been censored. It didn't have the words of Yama himself in it."

Xaron shifted next to me, but it was Jaxas who muttered softly, "Vusu's words. From when he first began serving Famine."

"Exactly. And what it says… I don't know how he's lasted this long. Famine eats at his mind, Jaxas. Between that and the wound I dealt him, he won't have the strength to hold on much longer."

"I'm afraid I don't understand. Why would we want him to?"

"Because even though he's using Famine for his own gains, Vusu is also holding him back from the world. If he stops, then we will have the daemon god himself to contend with, unbridled."

The Archon rubbed at his temples. When he pulled his hands away, he looked older and more tired than I'd yet seen him. "First we wish to defeat him, now we wish to keep him alive. What's the right course, Airene? What can we do against this threat?"

I little knew myself. But I answered the only way I could. "What we have been doing. Preparing. Learning what we can. Struggling on."

He shook his head. "It's not enough. How could it ever have been enough?"

"It has to be." Another thought occurred to me. "Jaxas, if the ruling Wreath somehow becomes unfit for service to the demotism, what happens? Does another take over?"

He didn't seem surprised by the question. "They serve until death, Airene. Taking the Evergreen Wreath before then is insurrection."

The gargantuan bell tolled from the dais. Even broken, the deep sound resonated throughout the chamber. Jaxas looked toward it.

"The fourth turn of the morning," he murmured. "It's time." He glanced back at me, then walked away without another word.

"Cheery conversation," Xaron observed.

"You'd think you'd be more worried about the end of Oedija."

"What's the use?" The smile slipped from his face as we watched Jaxas and the Low Consuls enter the small, cave-like room behind the dais. "Those gray-heads decide our fates, don't they?"

The eleven Servants voting for the new Low Consul had lined up at the door. The first of them filed through.

"Only if we let them," I said. "Come with me. I need to talk to someone else."

Komo and Nkosi stood in the far corner of the chamber, silently observing the proceedings. Except for Nomusa, they were the only Bali there, and their dark olive skin and ornamentations made them stand out like toucans among pigeons.

Xaron and I approached and bowed. "Heir Komo. Advisor Nkosi," I greeted them.

"First Verifier Airene." Komo smiled genuinely, though it remained small. The worried creases between his brow didn't smooth. "Or may I abandon your title?"

I returned the smile. "Call me what you like."

"'Little finch' is what she prefers," Xaron said confidentially.

Komo laughed softly as I arched an eyebrow at my friend.

"I think I'll stick with Airene," the Heir said. "What can I do for you?"

"I wanted to speak with you about your meeting with the Despoina last night."

His expression fell. "Ah. What do you wish to know?"

From his reaction, it seemed Jaxas had been accurate in his account. "Did it go well?" I asked lightly.

"No," Nkosi broke in. "It did not. As you well know, First Verifier."

"Nkosi," Komo rebuked him. "But he does have a point. It is no more than we expected after our earlier discussions."

I felt Xaron looking at me questioningly, but I ignored him, only half-feigning a wince from a stab of pain in my side. "Did she seem distracted by anything in particular?" I pressed.

"Not by any one thing, but by everything. The only time she carried a real conversation was with one of my guards."

My stomach sank. "Do you mind if I ask which one?"

Nkosi looked at me sharply, but Komo just cocked his head. "His name is Bhaka. I believe he stood guard when you visited the other night. Why do you ask?"

"First Verifier," Nkosi said, his tone edged with reprimand, "if you know something, it would be better to tell us now."

I'd been too direct. But I knew I couldn't reveal what I suspected yet, even if it damaged the trust we'd built. "I don't know anything. But if I find something out, I'll be sure to tell you."

The advisor eyed me suspiciously, but Komo, good-hearted lad that he was, just nodded. "I trust you will," he said.

The dais bell tolled again. As the gathered crowd quieted, I glanced down at the platform and saw Jaxas leading the Low Consuls up its crumbling steps. My stomach lurched. I found Nomusa standing behind the platform, her expression stony. I felt her nervousness as if it were my own. Behind the Low Consuls followed two unfamiliar Servants. When they moved to stand slightly before the Council, I assumed they were the candidates for the office.

As Jaxas stepped forth, the bow in his shoulders even more pronounced than before, my stomach sank. I already knew what was coming.

"In a vote of six to five, the eleventh seat of the Demos Council has finally been filled," he spoke, only audible from the echo of the chamber. "Rusen of Bazaar, if you will speak the oaths and accept the responsibility, we welcome you as a Low Consul of Oedija."

Most of the gathered people clapped loudly, while the rest remained silent. The man who stepped forward nodded solemnly. He was tall, thin, and obviously Avvadin from the cloth wound around his head.

I stared, scarcely able to believe it. We'd lost. The Preservists controlled the Demos Council.

My gaze wandered to Nomusa and found her leaning against the wall, looking dazed. The sight of her pained me more than the results. I knew how she'd struggled to win this, and still, she'd failed.

As Jaxas finished taking Rusen's oaths of fealty to Oedija, Orhan stepped forward from the others. "As the Council is finally complete, we have many things to decide in these tumultuous times," he declared. "You may expect our pronouncements soon."

Dread filled me at the words. What new obstacles would Orhan put before us? Suddenly, I felt the same weight Jaxas had shown to feel earlier pressing down on me. At every turn, a new challenge presented itself. When would they stop? When could Oedija face its enemies with its full strength and not rip itself apart?

Xaron gripped my arm. "Airene. The honor, Kelena. She looks frenzied."

All concern for the election swept from my mind as I followed Xaron's gaze. Kelena hurried toward us, much of the composure she typically bore cast away. Fear made me almost dizzy. I knew what news she must bring, given the task I'd set before her. I almost turned away, not wishing to hear the words, but her address arrested me.

"First Verifier," she said, panting slightly as she stopped before us.

"There's been an attack. Seekers at the Acadium, in the Archmaster's tower."

"The Manifest attacked Kyros?" I asked blankly. Despite the direness of the news, I thought only of one thing: this wasn't about Talan; he wasn't dead, not yet. Relief washed through me.

Kelena's eyes were wide and panicked. "I didn't know this was coming. I didn't notice any increase in activity. Perhaps they know not to trust the honors."

I thought over it quickly. "If Ariston leads the Manifest, he likely would know. We'll look into it. But did you hear anything of Talan?"

"No, not yet." Kelena's expression made it evident which she thought was the more important of the tasks. I had to bite my tongue as my temper flared up. Even knowing that she was probably right, it didn't change the fact that I wished I could hunt him down myself.

"We'd better go," Xaron said. "I'll fetch Nomusa."

I worried still for Talan, but I had no choice but to nod. There was nothing more I could do for him. Considering all of our other concerns, I had to accept that. Xaron slipped through the crowd toward Nomusa.

"Kelena, come with me," I said. "I have to tell someone else the news before we go to the Acadium."

We found our way through the crowd up to the dais. The Low Consuls had begun to file back into the chamber, and we had to hurry the last steps to catch Jaxas before he entered after them. I hissed at the pain in my ribs as we jostled people out of the way, but didn't slow as we neared.

"Archon Jaxas!" I called out breathlessly, hoping my words weren't lost in the hubbub of the Servants. The noise had increased following Orhan's announcement. "Wait a moment!"

Jaxas slowly turned back. His eyes were flat and cold. "Yes, First Verifier?"

I leaned forward, hoping others wouldn't overhear. But there was no time to find a more private place.

"There's been an attack at the Acadium. If Kelena is correct, Kyros's tower has been assaulted by Seeker wardens. I'm going over there to see into it now."

He didn't show any surprise or horror, but considered me with the same flat stare. "They've attacked again," he repeated. "And we didn't anticipate it."

I winced. "Yes. But we are still—"

"I'm not chastising you. I'm seeing a piece to a puzzle I've long stared at, but never known how to place. It is coming together now, whether I will it or not." He stared at me with sudden sharpness. "We must do what we must. Is that not what you said to me, Airene?"

"Yes, it is," I answered uneasily.

He nodded as if to himself. "Go. Learn what you can. Anticipate what must be done next. I'll meet you at my solar when the Council is finished here." He turned to Kelena. "Kelena, can you send an honor to Tribune Timon? Tell him to bring his charges here to see me."

As Kelena nodded, I looked between them with confusion. Jaxas seemed familiar with Kelena's network. Had it just been what we'd told him when we'd tried to make her a Verifier? Or had Nomusa informed him of Kelena's informal status as part of the Order? Even though he was our ally, I would have thought she would run such a decision by me first.

Jaxas looked back to me. "I'll see you soon," he said, then abruptly turned away.

"Jaxas, wait."

The Archon paused, then turned back expectantly. "Quickly, now."

The words spilled forth. "I think I know where the Despoina is. Or rather, whom she's with." I nervously scanned the crowd until I found Komo and Nkosi standing out of earshot. "I fear one of Komo's guards has seduced her. There have been signs of it. I thought you should know in case this danger spreads wider than we know and she needs protection."

Jaxas stared at me for a long moment in the midst of the hubbub. In that motionless gaze, I saw anger flaring to life. The smile that pulled at his lips was more fearsome than a snarl.

"Protection?" Acid dripped from the word. "But she's already accompanied by a guard."

Without another word, he turned into the Council room.

I stared after him. But as Xaron and Nomusa approached, I turned from the closing door and put it from mind. Time enough to think on it later.

Seeing the defeat in Nomusa's posture, I winced. "You alright?"

She stared woodenly at me. "If there's been an attack at the Acadium, we'd best look into it. After all, we're not much use here, are we?"

Not knowing what else to do, I nodded, then led the way out of the Conclave, one limping step at a time.

CHAPTER TWENTY

THE BROKEN TOWER

Yet if I thirst for their blood, if I hunger for their spirit, does that stain the righteousness of our task?

- Tales of the Desolate, uncensored; 1092 SLP

"They came in broad daylight?" Xaron asked with eyebrows raised. "Bold, I know."

My answer was weary. We'd only just left the Conclave gates, but already, I felt my body tiring. As the morning went on, each breath came more painful than the last. But I was determined not to return to bed, nor to let fear stop me from leaving the Conclave grounds. I'd wasted too much time already.

I glanced at Kelena and Nomusa, but both were silent. "What do you think?" I asked Nomusa.

She shrugged, offering nothing else. I let it be. All she needed was some time to nurse her pride; she'd be back to normal soon, I was sure.

The walk to the Acadium was tense and quiet. It couldn't be anything else with Seeker wardens at large again. If they dared to attack Kyros in broad daylight, who knew where they might appear next. The shadow of the Underguild lay over me as well, and I peered into every passing alley, expecting to see blue tatu glowing in the darkness. If the Guilders didn't already know I was alive, it wouldn't be long before word spread. And Kalindi wasn't one to leave loose threads, to hear Talan tell it.

Talan. I took as deep of a breath as I could manage as a different sort of pain spread through me. That damned fool had better take care of himself.

A touch on my arm. I glanced over to see Xaron's brow creased with concern. "Are you alright?"

"Fine. Just a moment of weakness."

His gaze lingered, but he looked away without another word.

By the time we reached the Acadium gates, my misery had augmented. Agony crawled up both legs and pounded in my head, to say nothing of how each labored breath burned in my chest. I feared even the journey back to the Laurel Palace might prove too much for me. If only Clepsammia, or whoever wore her guise, could bolster my strength now.

As the Acadium gates came into sight, the changes there jolted me back to alertness. The guards at the gate had tripled, and some of them wore no armor, but only leather and heavy cloth. *Those trained to fight wardens,* I assumed. By wielding no metal, they insulated themselves against the devastating effects of magnesis upon ordinary soldiers. I'd rarely seen the Acadium's premier guards. Usually, they only emerged if there was an incident with a warden on the campus, and that was a rare enough occasion to warrant few sightings. They eyed us mistrustfully as we approached, particularly Xaron, upon observing his Hilarion clothes. Yet when Nomusa and I showed our Finch medallions, they waved us through.

The campus was more disorderly. Acadians milled about the paths, walking in knots and muttering among themselves. They, too, looked upon our group with suspicion and passed quickly by. These were the same people who would have held a pleasant conversation with a stranger only a few days before. I shook my head and continued on.

We saw signs of damage from the Archmaster's tower long before arriving. The tall spire, black against the gray sky, spouted dark smoke. Kyros's rooms had burned; perhaps they still did. I wondered how our quarrelsome warden had fared. Little as I liked him, we could ill afford his death.

Seeing the tower again awoke a new dread in me. Twenty-two floors it rose, if memory served. I didn't know if I could manage them in my condition. But I knew I had to try.

A small crowd had formed at the base of the tower. I only recognized one among them.

"Isi!" Xaron called. He pushed through the crowd to embrace the Acadian. She returned it with a weary smile. Some small, protective part of me found it strange to see another woman being so familiar with him, but I pushed it down as Nomusa, Kelena, and I followed after him.

"You came," Isidora said as we reached her.

"Of course." He looked her up and down, and I saw what he must have: dust and soot coated her clothes. "Did you fight them?" Xaron asked apprehensively.

She shook her head. "I arrived afterward and helped put out the fire."

"Was anyone killed? Anything in particular damaged or taken?" I broke in.

"It's hard to say. It's still a mess up there. You're welcome to see for yourselves." She eyed me with a skeptical look.

Was my weakness so obvious? But I didn't need her doubts on top of my own. I nodded at Isidora and walked inside unassisted. Behind, Xaron made his farewells as Kelena and Nomusa followed me.

As I set my foot onto the first stair, Nomusa stopped me with a touch. "You don't have to go up."

"I do," I responded. "I visited his quarters before. I might notice something amiss."

"Not likely from one visit. And look at you. You're barely standing, and this tower is twenty-two circles tall."

I was uncomfortably aware of Kelena watching us and pulled Nomusa closer. "What else am I going to do? Ariston and Vusu aren't going to be content with biding their time much longer. If they're confident enough to attack Kyros, who knows where they'll strike next. I have to know why they came here. It might help us anticipate what they'll do next."

"Even still, you have limits, Airene. Don't push past them."

I closed my eyes, trying not to sway as I did. I was exhausted to the bone. I wasn't at all sure I could make it. If only I'd mastered channeling, I might be more assured. Then I'd be able to bolster my strength with kinesis, as Xaron sometimes did. Or perhaps I could will my body to heal, as Komo was able to do, and as I'd done during my first, long sleep.

But there was no use in wishing for rain. I had to make the decision and stick with it.

I drew in a deep breath and winced. "I'm going. I'll take it slow. I'll rest at every circle. But I'm going up."

Nomusa looked at me with a mixture of bemusement and fondness. "You always keep going," she said quietly. "How do you do it?"

I shrugged, a flush creeping up my neck. "I can't rest when something needs doing, that's all."

She wrapped an arm around me, gingerly avoiding my ribs as best she could. "At least let me help."

It took a full turn to reach the top of Kyros's tower. Xaron and Kelena went ahead to confirm we could enter inside, though I wasn't about to wait for permission after the torment I endured ascending. True to my word, I rested at each circle, and not of my own volition. Pain unlike anything I'd experienced before cascaded through me, and I was drenched in sweat. I hoped I wasn't doing permanent damage to my body. But I couldn't turn back. I had to see the Archmaster's chambers.

Finally, with Nomusa supporting me every step of the way, we arrived. I tried to hide my wheezing breaths as we entered within the scorched doorway.

The scene soon made me forget my suffering. Isidora had been right; it was difficult to tell if anything had been targeted, as the whole room was a wreck. The expensive carpets were burned and smeared with soot. The seared tapestries curled in on themselves like sun-withered grass, still trailing smoke. The pyr lamps, once levitating, were overturned on the floor, white pyrkin gleaming where it was strewn over carpet and stone. Bookshelves were broken, smashed in as if by a gigantic hammer. Books were scattered and torn all across the room. Four Acadians moved about the chamber and picked these up, carefully flipping through the pages as they evaluated them for damage.

Despite the open rent in the ceiling that admitted the cool air outside, the room was as hot as Maesos's forge. Red coals still smoked near the opening. I tried not to cough, fearing the pain it would bring.

Xaron and Kelena stepped from the corner where they'd been waiting. "Pretty bad, huh?" he murmured.

I nodded distractedly. My gaze moved to the cabinets of strange trophies Kyros held and saw the glass smashed in and the items missing. I tried to remember what had been there before. *An empty glass orb. A red mask with the aspect of a daemon. A white, wooden dagger—*

I drew in a sharp breath, then hissed it out painfully.

Nomusa took my hand. "What is it? Is it the smoke?"

I shook my head, wondering if I should say what I suspected in front of Kelena. I decided to risk it. "I think I know what they were after. What they took."

My companions' eyes widened.

"What is it then?" Xaron exclaimed.

"A wooden knife as white as bone. It would look like a child's toy."

Nomusa raised an eyebrow. "A wooden knife?"

"Just help me search for it, in case I'm wrong, or they missed it. I'll explain later."

"Perhaps we should ask him first." Kelena nodded to the figure standing in the center of the room.

Kyros Brighteyed, clad in soot-smeared bed robes, glared about his chambers, his eyes once again filled with Pyrthaen light. "Leave that one!" he snapped at an Acadian as she picked up a book.

The young woman startled and dropped it, then scurried to the next one.

Kyros seemed to notice us as our gaze fell on him. His eyes lingered on me. "What are you doing here?" he growled. "Just can't keep your beak out of anything, eh?"

Nomusa spoke first. "It's our duty to investigate, Archmaster Kyros."

The man snorted. "Then figure this out. Seven of those 'Thae-damned Seekers showed up, tried to kill me, then left. Why'd they do that?"

I swept my gaze over the room. "They did a fair deal more than that." I pointed at the smashed display wall. "What did they take?"

The Archmaster' scowl deepened. "Everything they didn't break. As they should — that was a valuable collection of artifacts." He waved a hand. "Now get out. We're trying to clean up around here."

"I think I need a short rest from the climb," I said lightly. With a parting smile that felt more like a grimace, Nomusa helped me over to sit on a trunk, Xaron and Kelena following.

Kyros's eyes stayed on us for a moment before he turned to bark at another Acadian. I didn't doubt he could eavesdrop if he wanted to, but I wouldn't be saying anything he didn't already know.

"He's not telling the full truth," Kelena said quietly. "I think he knows what they wanted."

Xaron nodded. "According to what Kyros told Isi, the Seekers seemed surprised the Archmaster was in. Kyros thought it had to do with him being up and about again — they probably didn't expect him to still be in his room late in the morning. She also said that he didn't understand why they'd taken what they had."

"Did she say what that was?"

He shrugged. "She didn't know. Maybe it was that knife."

"But why the knife?" Nomusa asked. "What use is it?"

I glanced at Kyros, but I was thinking about Kelena. Perhaps it was past time she knew the truth.

"I think it has something to do with Famine," I said quietly.

All three of them stared at me. I thought I saw Kyros startle as well.

"I read about it in an ancient tome, *The Seeds of Famine*, written just after the Lighted Passage. To defeat Famine, a knife like that was used to… sacrifice someone."

"Sacrifice someone?" Nomusa's brow furrowed. "Like kill them?"

I nodded.

She shook her head. "What good would killing them do?"

"Perhaps it was an artifact with some latent power. Talan spoke of a chalice once that could pour any substance from it. And there are stories of other magical artifacts."

"But that's just it — they're stories."

"And so was Famine, until he wasn't."

"Airene might be right," Xaron broke in. "I know the Qao Fu wear veils that are made partly by channeling to keep out the sand."

"The *ikoz* are bound by a certain cloth," Kelena spoke softly. "And there are legends among our people of items that brought men and women in contact with the Fates."

"The Fates?" Xaron queried.

"The spirits of death among my people, the Kalthuae." She smiled thinly. "We honors have become well-acquainted with the Fates ever since our enslavement."

An uncomfortable silence fell between us, broken only by the shuffling of the Acadians around the room and Kyros's reprimands.

"We should head back down," Nomusa said, her expression neutral. She glanced at me. "Are you well enough to try?"

I nodded, though I felt far from well. The thought of all those stairs sent chills of dread through my body.

But before I could rise, another figure emerged from the stairwell and threw back her hood. I stared in astonishment as Eltris irritably brushed back the wispy gray hairs that sprang into her face and strode toward Kyros.

The Archmaster looked surprised as well as displeased. "My rooms have become a spectacle, have they? Birds and bird-watchers settling the place! What are you doing here, Eltris?"

"What did they take?" The Master Augur spoke as if Kyros were her subordinate, rather than the reverse.

His face purpled with rage. "What gives you the right to—?"

"It's far past time for that, Kyros. Time is of the essence. Did they take it?"

The Archmaster's glowing eyes flickered toward us. Eltris looked around for the first time and visibly startled. Her expression darkened as she saw me sitting behind the other three.

"What are you doing here?" she demanded.

Xaron stammered a greeting, but I spoke over him. "What do you suspect they took?"

"Never mind," Eltris snapped. She looked back to Kyros. "I expect an answer momentarily. Don't block me out as before or I'll break down your barriers. And that won't be pleasant for either of us."

Turning on her heels, the augur made swiftly for the door.

My head spun. *The bone-white dagger* — that had to be what Eltris meant. But did that mean she knew what it was used for? And if she knew, who else might have knowledge of it?

"Eltris, wait!" I rose and lurched after her, my legs nearly buckling beneath me. Xaron and Nomusa caught me and held me upright.

The Master Augur whirled back. "Stop this now, girl! Are you still so blind? Don't you see what will result from your foolish pride?"

"Pride?" I could scarcely believe her words. "You think I act out of *pride?*"

"Of course it's pride! And pride will be your undoing." She turned abruptly to leave.

"I'm not done with you!" I said angrily. My ribs ached, but I pushed through the pain. "Why did you visit Linos and not tell me?"

Eltris paused and glanced back. "It's none of your concern."

"Damned if it's not! He's my brother!"

"Not anymore. He's empty, girl. He's what Vusu called him — a vessel. A shell waiting to be filled." The flickering light of the dying coals caught in her eyes. "You know who Vusu intends to fill him with."

My breath caught. All the knowledge I'd gathered suddenly spun together.

He cannot deny one born of his seed...

Within your heart lies the power to restrain a god...

A sacrifice of spirit, or an offering of blood...

She raised a knife white as bone, then plunged it through her own chest...

My knees went weak. I would have fallen but for Xaron and Nomusa's support. Yet though I struggled to deny Eltris's words and my conclusions, I could only whisper it. "Liar."

The Master Augur shook her head and turned back down the stairs. The slapping of her sandals faded as she descended the stairs.

I drew in a shaky breath and recovered my balance, then extricated myself from my friends. "We'd better go."

Xaron hovered at my shoulder. "Airene, about Linos... I'm sure she didn't mean that."

I closed my eyes and felt myself sway, exhaustion threatening to claim me. "She meant it, Xaron. I don't think Eltris is the wise woman you hoped she was. I think she's a recluse so used to keeping her secrets that she won't reveal them until it's too late."

I opened my eyes and found my vision swimming. "We have to meet Jaxas. I don't want to keep him waiting." I glanced at Kelena. "Will you come too?"

The honor nodded. "My network watches the Manifest. And for your

Guilder," she added with a look at me. "I can do no more than wait until I receive word back."

Xaron and Nomusa exchanged looks across me, but I ignored them and turned for the door. "Fine. Then we'll wait."

"We may hear back by the time we get down this tower," Xaron noted lightly.

Even his levity could do little to lighten my mood. Yet I took his arm all the same as we began the long descent.

———

Xaron and Nomusa took turns supporting me as we walked back through Oedija's streets to the Laurel Palace. Dark, overcast skies added to the uneasy feeling in the air. Brawls and robberies broke out in alleys as we passed. Along most streets, shop windows were broken in, and carts and stalls lay abandoned.

All around us, the city was tearing itself apart.

My heart hammered from more than exertion. At any moment, I expected Guilders to emerge from the shadows and surround us. A knot of four men drifted by, leering and calling jeers after us. But when Xaron flared fire to life in his hands, they scampered back the way they'd come, cursing "damned daemons" until their angry shouts faded away.

It seemed a miracle that we reached the Laurel Palace unscathed. The guard at the gates had doubled, and they shouted and pushed back at the crowd as they admitted us. More than one of the gathered people received a hard crack from their spears. I winced and hurried past to ascend the hill to the palace.

The last of my strength was fast fading. My anger with Eltris had only sustained me through the descent of Kyros's tower; ever since, it had been a losing battle. Each step became less steady than the last. A haze had settled over my thoughts. I barely heard Xaron and Nomusa as they spoke. Only the worry and fear cut through the cloud and kept me moving forward.

We pushed on until we reached Jaxas's solar. Wits dulled, I barely recognized Nikias standing before us as Nomusa and Xaron led me into the room and to a chair by the hearth. I didn't notice Jaxas until he moved into the firelight and sat next to me.

"Rest," he said as he leaned forward in his chair. "All you must do is rest."

I had no choice but to obey. My head lolled back on the chair, and my eyes closed.

When I opened them again, pain greeted me. My ribs seemed truly broken this time, fire radiating from them through the whole of my midriff. My neck had joined the rest of my body in stiff discomfort. Someone had draped a heavy blanket over me and propped up my feet with a stool. I groaned as I sat up and gingerly stretched my sore limbs.

"You're awake."

I tweaked my ribs as I startled and looked around. Jaxas stood before the glass balcony doors, hands clasped behind his back. He glanced at me, then looked back out over the metropolis. His posture was erect, his chin held high.

I tried to sit up straighter with little success. "Where are the others?"

"They'll return soon."

There seemed more unsaid in his words. I waited.

He glanced over after several long moments. "Do you believe in fate, Airene?"

I blinked, my sleep-fogged mind trying to follow. "I believe we forge our own fates. I believe what happens to us is the result of cause and effect. It's not written in stone, nor threaded by divine hands."

Even as I spoke, I thought of Clepsammia and wondered if I still believed that.

"Perhaps it is both," Jaxas said. "For every action and every event seems to have been drawing me in one direction. I've seen this juncture arriving for a time, yet always I thought, 'There is time, there is still time.' But the sieve has narrowed. There is no other choice now but the one before me. One choice that will change the course of my life, and of everyone in Oedija."

"I'm sure you'll make the right decision." I hoped I sounded more confident than I felt. His vague words seeded disquiet in me.

He turned and smiled, skin tight against his skull. "I hope I already have. But enough philosophizing. The fully formed Demos Council has met, as you know. The Low Consuls have issued a number of decrees. The first was the dissolution of the Order of Verifiers, on account of insubordination and ineffectiveness of its Finches."

I stared at him, my mind turning in slow circles.

"I'm no longer First Verifier," I said slowly. "Or even a common Verifier."

"No longer."

It didn't matter. With enemies closing in on all sides, the title didn't matter. But though I told myself that again and again, it still hurt. I'd striven my whole life to become a true Verifier. I couldn't cut away that childhood dream with logic. I could only imagine how Nomusa must be feeling.

"There's more," Jaxas continued. "The Low Consuls also decided that, with enemies besetting us from both within and without, they require every resource and shred of authority. Thus, the power of the Laurel Palace has been curbed, its resources staunched. We Wreaths will lose all staff but the minimum required to support our family and lands, and the guard will be stripped as well. All of our funds in the banks will be confiscated. Only the small coffers kept within the Laurel Palace remain to us. And as the Archon, I no longer possess any right to voice my opinion, but am relegated purely to a role of moderation."

I stared at him. I had at least known the disbandment of the Order was possible. But this went far beyond that. "Orhan is boxing us in. He's taking away any tool we have for resistance." I slumped in the cushioned chair. "You have no soldiers or resources. I have no access or authority. What are we going to do, Jaxas? How can we fight anyone like this? The Avvadin Imperium? Vusu? Famine?"

The Archon was wreathed in the soft evening light that glowed from his balcony doors. "We make the one choice remaining to us," he said quietly. "We act as you so recently advised. We do everything in our power, no matter what others might think of us. No matter the consequences we might suffer."

Cold fingers crawled up my spine. "What do you mean?"

He didn't answer, but shifted his gaze back over the city. "Hilarion Xaron has gone to fetch the Watchers. First Verifier Nomusa inquires into the glassblower Maesos, to see if he possesses more pyrkin bolts such as we used at Leia's trial. Verifier Kelena goes to Heir Komo to see if he will lend his strength to ours." He glanced at me. "Shall we join their gathering at the Laurel Groves?"

My unease grew greater still. "Why are they gathering?"

"We cannot allow Vusu to command the battle anymore. We cannot wait for the Council to take action. Avvad marches north within the span; we must be ready when they arrive. The Manifest must no longer plague us when they begin the siege." He stared into my eyes, seeming to search for something behind them. "We shall strike now, before the Seekers can take the next step in their plans. We will cut the head from the snake and hope it kills the body."

His intentions hit me, sudden as a bird crashing into a window. "You mean to kill Vusu."

Jaxas nodded slowly. "Kelena's honors report of his continued weakness since the trial. If he is killed, the Manifest will lose its Visage. Perhaps it will lose its will to resist as well. But more than that, we cannot afford them to keep Myron Wreath hostage any longer. It has tied our hands for too long. With his safety secured, action against the Seekers may proceed unhindered."

I was stunned. Boldness was not what I'd come to expect of Jaxas Wreath. Hearing his plans, I wondered if I knew the man at all.

"But how can we do this? We don't have the strength."

"Watcher Isidora informs me that her wardens are ready for this. I have no choice but to believe her. With help from the laurel guard and Heir Komo, I hope it will be enough."

Watcher Isidora. I hadn't realized Jaxas was in communication with the Acadian, much less close enough to command her. And he'd clearly been communicating with Kelena at length. I had the creeping suspicion that I was missing something right before my eyes.

"Vusu is in the heart of the Wyvern's Claw, and you don't know where the Despot is," I pointed out.

"Kelena's contacts inform us of this as well — that Myron Wreath is held in a warehouse in Brinecoast."

I couldn't believe I hadn't heard it from Kelena herself. Still, I struggled to mask my annoyance. "If you want to do both, you'll have to split your forces."

"We will. And in the middle of the enemy compound, no less. Yet we must do these two things at the same time, or we will lose both opportunities." He considered me for a moment. "I don't think it's as impossible as you seem to believe. The Seekers are not an army. They post sentries, but are untrained and ill organized. And our forces will have a significant distraction to use as cover."

When had the foundations for these plans been laid? As I studied the unshifting determination on the Archon's face, I couldn't say. Perhaps, locked away in the depths of Tomes for many long turns, I'd missed far more than I knew.

"You seem to have thought this through." The words sounded vapid even to my own ears, and I continued quickly, "I suppose we'd better go to the Laurel Groves then."

Though I made to rise, Jaxas arrested me when he spoke again. "Airene. I didn't mean to exclude you from my plans. But you have been..." He searched for the word.

"Distracted," I supplied. I wondered why he felt the need to apologize to me. He owed me nothing.

Knowing we could delay no longer, I pressed out of the chair, a groan escaping me. My chest, the pain of which had been a slow burn with each breath in the chair, spiked, but I fought it down.

"Not distracted," he said at length. "You strive against a greater problem. I didn't wish to pull you away from it with my own concerns."

I turned to look at him with watering eyes. What was he thinking behind that calm demeanor? What other plans did he keep hidden even now?

"We'd better go while I'm still standing," I advised.

Jaxas nodded, his gaze not leaving me. "The carriage is waiting out front. It's not far."

I suppressed a grim smile. Not far, perhaps, if every breath weren't agony. But I let him believe the comforting lie, and tried to believe it myself, as we began our slow descent.

CHAPTER TWENTY-ONE

BURN

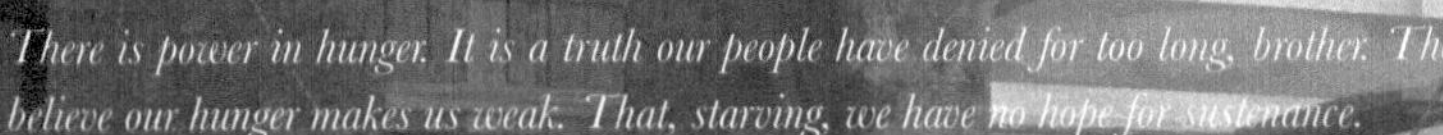

There is power in hunger. It is a truth our people have denied for too long, brother. They believe our hunger makes us weak. That, starving, we have no hope for sustenance.

But we know they are wrong, brother. In our God, we have glimpsed power only we can grasp. And I know you hunger for it as much as I…

— Tales of the Desolate, uncensored; 1092 SLP

The others appeared from the gray twilight as Jaxas and I rolled into the Laurel Groves.

At every lurch of the carriage, I had to hold back a gasp, my ribs seeming to puncture new holes inside me. But I forgot my pain when rows of dark figures emerged from the dusky light. For a moment, I couldn't help but doubt those silhouettes were on our side, but rather Seekers or Guilders waiting in ambush, though none of them moved toward us.

"Our army," Jaxas said softly next to me.

I glanced at him. With a single pyr lamp lighting the carriage, shadows obscured his features. *Our army* — an odd thing to call them, an army. And if this were an army, it was his, not ours.

I exited as soon as the carriage rolled to a stop, leaning heavily on the hand of the driver to set foot on the ground. Every breath burned in my chest, but I tried to not let it show. These were our defenders against the Seekers. I wanted to be strong for them, or as strong as I could manage. I walked between the rows of figures, then stopped to look at those who had gathered.

To one side, the fourteen Watchers stood silently under the boughs of olive trees. Isidora stood before them, and Xaron next to her. They seemed to be holding hands, but when I looked again, their arms hung by their sides. Xaron had changed from his Hilarion clothes to as simple a tunic and trousers as I'd seen him wear, and a hood and cloak were pulled over his shoulders. The Acadians had disguised themselves similarly. With the dark cloaks on, I was uneasily reminded of the Seekers we'd fought in Komo's quarters.

This is different, I reminded myself. We were fighting for the right side. Even if we also used our forbidden magic for violence.

The laurel guards had gathered as well. I vaguely recognized the woman who stood before them: Synne of Gate, the First Laurel. She possessed a calm confidence and met my gaze with cool consideration. A score of armored warriors stood behind her, their armor gleaming dully from the pyr lamps mounted periodically along the garden road. They bore spears and bucklers, and short stabbing swords at their hips, like a taxos ready for war.

The group of warriors Komo stood before starkly contrasted with the laurel guards. His Yorandu soldiers wore peculiar armor of feathers, tassels, bones, and brass. All of them, Komo included, had one side of their faces painted green, which seemed almost to glow in the low light, so they appeared as otherworldly spirits more than soldiers. I nodded at the Shaka-Heir, and the boy nodded solemnly in return. My heart wrenched for him. He was so young, yet he didn't flinch from this, even though it would likely require him to kill again. I hoped he could endure it.

All of them would go, and I would stay. It pained me to admit it, but I knew better than to imagine I might go with them. I'd be more of a burden than help. I couldn't reliably channel, or even walk far at the moment.

Yet the relief that flooded through me brought with it the heat of shame to my face. I was glad for the darkness to hide it.

Nomusa stood next to Kelena, still clothed in the fine, simple robes she'd worn to the Conclave. I'd hoped to see Corin with her, bearing a cart of Maesos's goods, but my hopes were in vain. My friend glanced my way with hooded eyes, then looked away. I feared to think what that look meant. Kelena wore a dark cloak, the hood hiding her shaven head and tin spiral earrings. Her eyes were pools of darkness as she stared at me.

"Good. We are gathered." Jaxas stopped next to me and surveyed the small army, then glanced at me. Without saying a word, he strode over to speak with Komo.

Not knowing what to make of the Archon's behavior, I put him from mind and approached Nomusa and Kelena.

Nomusa watched me, her brow creased with concern. "I don't think you should be up and walking. I worried when we left you asleep in Jaxas's solar, but now I wish you'd stayed."

"Glad to hear I'm welcome." I grimaced as a fresh wave of pain washed over me and hoped she took it for a smile. "Are Maesos's goods still coming?"

She shook her head. "No. He had no more of the pyrkin strain. And unless he can find someone to smuggle more from the Thulu ishaka, we won't have those bolts again."

The disappointment was sharp, but I tried to push it from mind. "And Corin? I expected her to be here."

Nomusa shrugged. "Maesos hadn't seen her for two days. I suppose she's found some other place to stay."

"Perhaps," I managed, and tried not to think about it further. There was nothing I could do for her now. Just as there was nothing I could do for Talan. Cold fear clawed through my gut. How many friends would I lose before this war was over?

I stepped forward and wrapped my arms around Nomusa, drawing her in as close as my ribs allowed. "You'll be safe at least," I whispered.

She returned the embrace as carefully. "Perhaps. But I'll be in the lion's den. Someone has to watch the Council and make sure they don't interfere."

"You're the bravest of us all then." Releasing her, I turned to Kelena and took a breath to compose myself. "You seem to be in close contact with Jaxas."

The honor's expression remained blank. "I believe you attached yourself to Archon Jaxas as well when you wished to be involved in events of importance. I had resources that could be of value to him, and so I offered them."

That took me aback. She thought I'd tried to reprimand her. And perhaps I had, I realized too late.

"I don't fault you for it," I amended. "In fact, I'm grateful. We need anything to strike a blow against the Manifest."

She smiled thinly. "This will be more than a blow, Airene."

I was surprised at how thin my name sounded without my recently acquired title. It didn't matter, I reminded myself. Before Kelena could see the effect of her words, I turned and made my slow way toward Xaron and Isidora.

My friend flashed me a cocky smile as I approached, but it was too wide to be believable. Isidora looked a little more certain, though her fingers danced against her legs. But I'd seen her kill without hesitation during the trial. I trusted she'd keep her wits about her in a fight.

"You're awake," Xaron observed. "I thought that climb might have done you in."

"Not yet." I looked him up and down. "You look good out of Hilarion clothes. More yourself."

"I *feel* more myself. You have no idea how scratchy sackcloth is. Especially when it's rubbing against your—"

"Glad to see you'll be watching over him," I interrupted quickly, addressing Isidora. "Make sure he comes out alive, will you?"

She flashed me a thin smile. "I will. I want him to stick around, for some reason beyond me."

Xaron shrugged. "It's no mystery. You're in love with me."

The Watcher leader flushed, while Xaron grinned at her.

I smiled too, then seized his hand. "Don't do anything stupid."

He pulled me into an embrace. "Unlike your own clandestine love," he murmured into my hair.

I nodded wearily, letting him take some of my weight. But as he was the one going into danger, I knew I couldn't lean on his strength. Reluctantly, I pulled away and glanced over at Komo and his warriors. "I should thank him for being here."

"Then go. We'll come back, never fear."

I tried not to think about it as I turned toward the Bali regiment. The boy watched my slow approach, his expression brittle. Even his sense of control, incredible in his youth, couldn't hide the fear behind his painted face.

I stopped a respectful distance before him. "You didn't have to come."

"I did," the boy replied heavily. "You showed me that. Even Nkosi said honor compelled me to go."

"Nkosi did? It's hard to believe that old root came around."

A smile flitted across Komo's lips. "I am glad he knew better than to try and come with us. He can be too stubborn for his own good."

"I know the kind. Take care, Heir Komo."

"And you, Finch Airene."

I turned away, not having the heart to correct him, and found Jaxas standing not far behind me. But the man next to him, and the four hooded strangers behind them, made me stop in my tracks. Even in the dim light, the aqua color of the cowls made their identity clear.

"What are they doing here?" The words came out as a demand.

"Tribune Timon has come at my request," Jaxas said, his tone neutral.

The Tribune leered at him, his pinched features only worsened by the heavy shadows clinging to his hollowed eyes. "Hello again, Finch. Or should I even call you that now?"

I barely hid my distaste. "Why?" I asked Jaxas bluntly.

The Archon studied me for a moment. "You'll understand soon."

He turned from me to the rest of those gathered, and I stared at his back. I didn't like how mysteries were piling up around the man, the one Wreath I thought I could trust. I hoped I still could, no matter the secrets he kept from me.

"Thank you all for harking to my call tonight," Jaxas began, his voice loud and strong, almost reminiscent of Myron. "I know it is on short notice and the message was vague. But we must act quickly if we are to take advantage and get ahead of our foes."

"You mean the Manifest." Isidora posed it as a question.

Jaxas nodded. "And others. The Avvadin Imperium marches on our city. We cannot hope to prevail if Oedija stands divided against its armies. We must strike at the heart of the Manifest now and hope it is enough to begin its unraveling."

"What is our quarry?" First Laurel Synne asked, her words precise and clipped.

Jaxas swept his gaze slowly over his audience. "The head of the dragon," he said, quiet but carrying in the silence. "We strike for Vusumuzi himself."

As murmurs bubbled up around us, I feared the news would break this tenuous fellowship. But even though they shifted their feet and glanced nervously at their compatriots, no one backed away. A warm glow of pride began in my chest. I stood among Oedija's bravest, I knew that now. I tried to ignore the squirm of guilt that I wouldn't have to put my own courage to the test tonight.

Jaxas gestured to Kelena, who still stood next to Nomusa. "Kelena has eyes and ears among the Seekers, and has learned of the traitor's location. She has also heard continual reports that he remains in a room at the heart of the Wyvern's Claw, the wooden amphitheater off the shores of Lake Thys. By all accounts, he remains ill from the bolt Airene shot through him."

My face flushed as all eyes turned toward me. I struggled to remain properly dignified, though Xaron's grin didn't help.

"Isidora, Xaron, and the other Watchers will enter by stealth into the Claw," Jaxas continued. "Following Kelena's instructions, you will navigate your way to where Vusu lays ill, then execute him in the name of Oedija's justice. When you are finished, you are to go to the lake's shore, where Kelena has planned an escape."

Some of the Watchers visibly shivered. Even having shot Vusu once, my skin broke out into chicken flesh. *Execute him.* The order sounded cold, military. The command of a king.

Xaron spoke up. "What is this escape? Always best to know your escape when you house-break."

The Archon nodded at Kelena, and she cleared her throat. "There are boats on Lake Thys that none will expect to aid us," she said, a slight shake in her voice. "The honors on these boats will direct them to the shore at the appointed signal: the waving of a torch at the landing point."

"What kind of boats?" Xaron pressed. "Fishing vessels?"

Kelena hesitated. "Lotus Ships."

Xaron's eyes widened, then he let out a laugh. "This isn't the way I expected to spend my first night on a Lotus Ship!"

Isidora cast him a bemused look, then asked, "Why would these honors risk their lives for us?"

"Because they are whores." Kelena seemed to have gained back her bite. "And no one is more despised and mistreated than an honor-whore."

I cringed, imagining how true that must be.

"In exchange," Jaxas said, unperturbed by Kelena's vehemence, "I have promised them freedom from their class and profession, with both financial support and the opportunity to learn another trade."

I turned my gaze to the Archon, eyes narrowed. Considering how significantly the Council had clipped his power, he had no way of making good on such promises. Perhaps it was necessary, but the lie didn't sit easily.

Yet Jaxas gave no sign of guilt as he turned to the last of the gathered. "First Laurel Synne, Heir Komo and his guards have agreed to accompany you on a separate mission. There's a warehouse in Brinecoast where Vusumuzi keeps an important hostage, someone you might believe to be dead — Despot Myron Wreath."

The First Laurel's stiff expression broke as her brow creased. Yet she only gave a nod in acknowledgement before turning to Komo. "I have developed a strategy for entering the warehouse, Heir Komo. We may discuss this before we embark."

The Bali prince nodded, his face drawn. "That would be good." His words were only undermined slightly by a boyish crack in his voice.

Jaxas bowed deeply to each gathered group. By their astonished expressions, I knew all comprehended what it meant. It was a singular honor for any Wreath to bow to anyone, much less foreign soldiers, outlaw wardens, and common plebeians.

"Thank you all for your unbelievable faith and courage," he said as he straightened. "These are dangerous tasks I ask of you. Many of you are not trained for battle. Yet to a one, you have borne the burdens I've laid at your feet. Whatever the results tonight, each one of you will be remembered as heroes, your deeds forever memorialized."

"You save Oedija," I suddenly interjected. As all eyes turned to me, I fought down a flush and continued softer, "You save her when she most needs it."

Nomusa arched an amused eyebrow, while Xaron smiled openly. I let out a breath and smiled back. Whatever embarrassment I might have cost myself, it was worth it see a little levity from my friends.

Jaxas glanced up at the dark sky. "The sands are running low. Go while we still have time."

At his words, they dispersed. I hugged Xaron one last time before he and the other Watchers swept after the Yorandu soldiers and laurel guards. Nomusa came to stand by me as we watched them disappear into the gloom. Soon, only Jaxas, Tribune Timon, and the four Shepherds were left, their manacles clinking softly as they shifted. I glanced at them mistrustfully, but looked away as Jaxas bent toward the Tribune to speak.

"He didn't name their task," I muttered to Nomusa.

"I wondered at that as well."

We waited in silence until their conversation finished. Timon, noticing our gazes, grinned wickedly at us before turning down the cobblestone path, the four Shepherds following silently behind. I suddenly wondered how he managed to control them. It made sense that Vusu had been able to. But Timon? He seemed little more than a small, spiteful man.

"They have perhaps the most important task tonight," Jaxas said as he walked up next to us.

Before I could ask what he meant, he continued. "Come. Airene, we will drop you off at the Laurel Palace on our way to the Conclave."

My jaw nearly dropped. "What? I should come with you."

"No," he said firmly. "You're still unwell. The safest place for you is in my solar tonight. Rest there and trust that we'll do our parts."

I felt the truth of his words. My limbs shook with the simple act of standing, and my pain worsened with every passing moment. Yet I couldn't let it go at that.

"There must be something I can do. I wouldn't rest tonight even if I were stepping over death's threshold."

The hard lines in the Archon's face softened. "I'm sorry, Airene. It is what's best for you."

Nomusa's expression spasmed, clearly torn, yet she remained silent. I couldn't find a good excuse to delay them any longer. At a motion from Jaxas, Nomusa and I piled into the carriage and soon rumbled down the garden path.

Someone had lit the hearth in Jaxas's solar, and the room had filled with a suffusing warmth. Yet I couldn't find comfort in it as I let the door swing shut behind me with a heavy thud. My heart hammered painfully in my chest, and each labored breath sent waves of pain throughout my body. The guilt was worse still. I staggered over to a chair by the fire and slumped into it, closing my eyes and resting my head back.

Everyone had a role in this night, the night we would tear down the Manifest. Everyone — except for me. It showed just how little consequence I was. What had I done this past span but muddle through old books and speak with batty spinsters? I'd thrown away the Order and a lifelong dream. I'd failed to discover how to defeat Famine and learned little enough besides. I could barely channel to save my life, as I'd found out.

Now it was clear why I had no role. There was none I could perform without bungling it.

Wallowing in self-misery and pain, I considered calling for a poppy tincture. *If I can do nothing but rest, let me rest like the dead,* I thought. But something held me back. I'd told Jaxas I couldn't rest while the others risked their lives. I'd stand by that, no matter how futile the gesture.

Yet as time dragged on and the warmth from the fire seeped into my bones, I found my eyelids drifting closed. Visions of the horrible things befalling my friends couldn't stay the exhaustion. Even as I despised myself, even as I sat upright to try to stay awake, gasping at the pain from my ribs, I could barely keep my eyes open.

Then something boomed like thunder outside.

My eyes flew wide open. A moment later, the windows and doors rattled, and vibrations pulsed through the stone under my feet. Fear and vigor flooded me, compelling me to stand and hurry to the balcony doors.

It took but a moment to find the source of the eruption. Over the wall, across the dark lake in the deme beyond, a conflagration greater than any I'd seen blazed and spread. I stared as the flames and smoke billowed up. *We have no volcanoes in Oedija* — it was all that I could think in the daze.

The truth hit me a moment afterward.

My knees buckled as I saw it was true. The wooden amphitheater, the one I'd once feared would catch flame, finally had.

The Wyvern's Claw burned.

INTERLUDE III
TALAN

A knife in the back. A hand clasped over the gasping mouth. Warm life spilling over his skin.

Talan held his breath as the man jerked his last in his arms. So long as he didn't breathe, he could keep calm. So long as he didn't smell the bitter, coppery stench, his stomach wouldn't purge itself clean.

His lips twisted into a bitter smile as the man grew still and heavy in his arms. If only he could believe his own lies.

He released the limp man to the ground. As he sucked in a breath, the stink of blood filled his nostrils. *The perfume of a killer,* he thought, and coughed as bile hit the back of his throat.

He didn't startle as someone came up next to him in the darkness, moving on silent feet, but acknowledged his companion with a nod.

"You've changed," noted Sule, or the one who wore her skin. She glanced at the body lying still on the ground. "You're more like how Sule remembers you."

He tried to ignore her words and looked down the tunnel. He didn't see any silhouettes against the dim pyr lamp at the far end, but that didn't mean much. The Underguild's network of tunnels, caves, and forgotten caverns was riddled with holes in which an enterprising street urchin or malevolent dwarf could listen.

"The quieter we are, the less chance of discovery," he reminded his companion softly, then motioned for her to follow. He pretended not to notice the small smile the Qarin-possessed woman wore as he turned from her and set off down the tunnel.

His footsteps were nearly silent, a steady flow of kinesis cushioning his footfalls. Behind him, Sule did the same; he could only hear her following by the soft rustle of her clothes. All else was silent but for a slow drip of water somewhere ahead.

He heard them before he saw them — a sudden patter of feet approaching from either end.

Talan whirled and channeled, sending seven sharp darts of kinesis hurtling down the hall. From the cries, a few found their marks. On his other side, metal sang softly as Sule drew her sword from its cloth-wrapped scabbard and charged at the men approaching from behind. The cries echoing down the tunnel told of her blade finding its mark.

Talan barreled toward the three figures limned with lamplight ahead of him and threw forward radiance. Yellow flames surged from his fingertips and leaped up to embrace his attackers. Their screams crescendoed to join those of the men Sule cut down, then abruptly stopped as Talan sent out another round of kinetic darts. The three figures collapsed, silent but for the crackle of their burning flesh.

Sule sauntered up behind him, no longer bothering to cushion her steps. "They know we're here."

Talan flexed his hands, fingers numb from the quick channeling. "We'd best hurry then."

But he hesitated. He could taste the foul aroma of blood and burned meat. The smoke made his head light and dizzy. He tried not to think of how it must feel to burn, or for pure force to rip through your gut.

Find your center, he reminded himself. The words of his long-ago mentor came to mind after: *If all the world is whirling, what can you do but turn with it?*

He took in a shallow breath, then leaped over the flaming corpses with a kinetic push. He didn't look back as he set into a jog.

The necessity for silence gone, they moved more quickly. They were close now. He knew these catacombs as well as any part of the city. He'd held an audience with the Guildmasters on dozens of occasions and could have followed the winding paths with his eyes closed — had he ever trusted his fellow Guilders enough to attempt it. It would all be settled soon. He couldn't keep a self-loathing smile from his lips.

No one waited before the great doors to the final chamber. The entryway stood wide open. Talan halted and raised a hand, and Sule heeded his warning. A line of torches implied a path toward the open doors. He scanned the rest of the greeting chamber, squinting into the shadows that gathered around the edges, but saw no one. Unless Guilders hung like bats from the black ceiling above, this room was empty.

He turned halfway back to his companion and studied her from the corner of his eye. The Qarin had given him its word that it would cooperate and help him undermine the Underguild. But Talan could only rely upon it hating Avvad. Beyond that, he wasn't sure what the jinni possessing his childhood flame desired, much less if it aligned with his own goals and well-being.

"Perhaps they wait in ambush beyond," he whispered to Sule. "Will you continue?"

He could almost see the spirit gazing out from the woman's eyes. "I gave you my word, and it is binding. Let's meet this ambush together, Talan Wraithsbane."

Talan closed his eyes. Despite all he'd seen and done, the fear had never gone away. He didn't want to die. Least of all to scum like Kalindi; least of all now. But he'd made a promise to Airene, and he meant to stick to it.

He'd keep her safe.

Yet he couldn't help but wonder at himself. When had he become so resolved to protect her? In some ways, he barely knew her. They'd spoken little of their childhoods, of their fears and hopes and dreams. Most often, it had been business that brought them together.

But there was a spark in her that he'd seen in no one else. It was a gamble to throw away his life to save hers, a gamble that the spark was real. A gamble that they would have the chance to fan it into flame.

He'd always been too much of a gambler for his own good.

"Let's," he said softly. Then, standing, he walked into plain view and crossed the chamber to the door. Sule's footsteps echoed softly behind him.

As he entered the grand chamber at the heart of the Underguild, he saw the five thrones of the Guildmasters were filled. The putrid smell of decay told him who occupied them. His smile curled into a snarl as he witnessed what had become of his former leaders.

In the center slouched Hax, the man who had brought about an unprecedented period of order and civility to crime in Oedija. He'd survived dozens of attempts on his life. He hadn't survived Kalindi.

On the left sat what remained of the woman responsible for Talan's induction into the Underguild. Peralda had been one of the most fascinating women he'd met, able to manipulate the worst of humanity into doing her bidding — including Talan, as it turned out. He suspected she had wanted him to take her place as Guildmaster after her. He'd never know now, nor if he would have accepted the dubious honor.

The figure in the rightmost seat shifted in the shadows. Sheltered from the lamplight, he couldn't make out the man's features. But Talan remembered who had always sat in that seat.

"Kalindi."

"*Undermaster* Kalindi," the hidden man corrected him softly. As he leaned forward, his face came slowly into the light. A sweep of black hair fell over features that might have been handsome, had Talan not known what lay beneath them.

"I wondered when you'd try for me, Wraithsbane. Everyone said you were unpredictable. But I knew you'd come slithering to me." His lips curled into a sneer. "All I had to do was threaten your little Finch to ensure it."

His heart hammered in his throat. "Predictable or unpredictable," he said with forced calm. "Either way, this ends the same."

"Does it? And how is that, Wraithsbane?"

Talan ignored him. The conversation was a ruse, meant to do nothing more than buy time as he observed the corners of the room for assailants lying in wait. Unless they hung from the ceiling high above, he saw none. Kalindi's arrogance had no limits. The fool still didn't know what Talan was capable of. But he couldn't rely on the man's stupidity for his own safety.

Opening his locus wider, he spread his awareness around him. It strained his mind to do so for long, but for a moment, he glimpsed every living thing around him, including the two dozen men creeping toward them from the former chamber. Guilders had been lying in wait after all.

But they weren't what made his blood run cold. Something else lurked beyond them.

A familiar desire suddenly suffused him. *Come,* four voices whispered in his mind. *Come. Become one with us.*

He sealed his locus, cutting off the connection with a gasp. The edges of his mind felt torn and frayed, but the fear cut worse. *Ikoz,* Silks — here, among the Guilders. He'd long suspected the Valemish harbored them within the city limits. But he hadn't thought to find them in league with the Underguild. Avvad's reach was greater than any of them had realized.

Kalindi's grin grew wide, and he leaned forward as if to loom over them. "Is something wrong, Wraithsbane?"

"Silks," Sule breathed next to him, the Qarin having sensed them as well.

Talan nodded and risked a glance behind. Without his awareness spread, he had no idea how close the men creeping up on them were. Tentatively, he opened himself to Valem's power again, allowing in trickles of radiance and kinesis. Without spreading his awareness, the spirits would be hard-pressed to assault his mind. Even if they could find a way, he had to channel regardless; otherwise, he'd be nothing to the score of men closing in.

"Now, now, Talan," Kalindi suddenly addressed them. "It does not have to end like this." His tone had changed, from sneering to conciliatory.

Talan trusted this side of Kalindi even less. Yet he found himself looking up at the self-proclaimed Undermaster and asking flatly, "What?"

"I don't throw away good tools. I could make use of you. If you agree to my terms, I'll spare your life."

Anger suddenly flared back to life within him. "And what terms are those?"

"You have connections in many places. The Laurel Palace. The Conclave, through the new Order of Verifiers. Eyes and ears in these places would serve me well. So here's my proposal, Wraithsbane. You spy for me, and I swear to let you and your companion here go free, and to never touch your Finch again. I think that's more than fair, don't you?"

Talan closed his eyes and bowed his head. The tendons in his jaw felt like they'd snap. Veins pulsed in his forehead. For a moment, he couldn't breathe for the hatred that poured through him. The image of the Guilders kicking and throwing Airene to the ground, of ripping her clothes off, filled his mind with a force so that he could think of nothing else. Only his revulsion that he considered Kalindi's offer for a moment cut through it, that his fear of death and killing would give him pause.

But he knew better. If he'd learned one thing in Avvad, it was that the best way to kill a snake was to chop off its head.

Opening his eyes, he raised a hand. He opened his locus wider and pulled on the stream of energy that poured in. Kinesis formed at his fingertips, honed until it reached a fine, narrow point.

Kalindi's eyes grew wide, and he scrambled out of his chair. But he couldn't avoid the bolt of force that sped from Talan's fingertips and caught him in the temple. A red spray fanned out from where it entered. The Undermaster spun from the dais, landing headfirst on the stone floor below with a sickening crunch, and his limp body fell after.

Talan watched impassively as Kalindi twitched, then stopped moving. This corpse didn't fill him with revulsion as the others had, but an ugly pleasure. *What have you made of me?* he thought to the dead Undermaster. *What did this place make of us all?*

"They're coming." Sule faced the doors behind them, her curved sword held aloft, and slowly backed away.

Talan turned as well, feeling strangely disconnected from his body. He heard them now in the chamber beyond, their stealthy approach abandoned. His hand moved into his pocket and drew out a long shard of obsidian, then channeled radiance into it. It began to glow.

"We may die here." His voice sounded far away. A strange, sardonic smile tugged at his lips. He didn't bother to hide it.

Sule stared at him. As he met her eyes, he saw the Qarin there again.

"Hold yourself together," she commanded. "I'm not ready to leave this world again."

He nodded even as the odd mood clung to him and grasped for the urgency that had driven him before. *The spark. Remember the spark. Remember what this gamble was taken for.*

As the first of the Guilders slipped through the doors, Talan raised the glowing shard and channeled. Radiance, gathered in a blinding beam, blazed forward, burning and cutting through shadowed figures. Screams from the doorway told of others dying in the chamber beyond.

But some had slipped through and spread out around them, knives and crossbows coming up. Talan cut off the stream, nearly staggering with the exertion. Exhaustion pulled at him. The long route in and the effort of continuous channeling had drained him. But he pulled for more still, gathering kinesis and throwing it up before him. Waves of pure force caught and turned aside the bolts and knives that hurtled their way, then knocked the Guilders roughly against the wall. Not enough force to hurt them, but hopefully enough to daze.

Tucking away his obsidian shard, he drew out a long, curved knife and sprinted forward. Behind him, Sule screamed as she ran to engage Guilders on their flank. He threw small waves of kinesis before him until he reached the first of them. The man, off-balance from his relentless magic, had time for his eyes to widen just before Talan whipped his knife across his throat.

The other Guilders were scrambling to flee from him, heading for the door where their fellows had gathered but didn't dare enter. No doubt Kalindi's corpse and two wardens gave them pause. Weariness dulled his mind, but Talan moved his leaden legs after them and forced a wide grin onto his face.

"Come on, friends!" he called to them. "I have a red smile for each of you!"

They broke. Like a herd of panicked cattle, they rammed against each other in their eagerness to escape. Sule was the herd-dog driving them on, her sword cutting down those too slow or stupid to run. She stopped just shy of the entrance, breathing heavily, but still firm and upright.

"They're still coming," he reminded her.

Sule met his eyes and nodded, then quickly backed away from the clearing entrance.

He felt them before they drifted through the doorway. Desire seeped into him, so subtly that, even though he was aware of what would happen, he almost took a step toward them. They looked like little more than strands of shimmering cloth floating through the air. But Talan had felt their touch before. As they came nearer, he struggled to keep his mind straight. The desire to go to them, to lose himself in their oblivion, nearly overwhelmed his weary will. *Rest,* their voices whispered in his head. *Rest, and worry no more. Struggle no more. Feel no more.*

He wrenched his mind from their grasp and was dimly aware of falling to his knees. Reaching desperately back into his memory, he tried to recall how he'd warded himself against them before. But his head felt full of cotton. The fire of Valem that had burned inside him had dampened so that it was little more than coals.

Sule had backed away to the Guildmasters' thrones. "Talan!" she cried, her voice shrill with fear. "You must fight them! They'll destroy me!"

He forced himself to rise. The knife dropped from his numb fingers, and he fumbled in his pocket for the obsidian shard. *It begins with the spin,* he thought he remembered. Or was it the hook? It didn't matter that he'd practiced the banishing technique countless times since leaving Erimis. With the weight of four Silks bearing down on him, he couldn't wake the cleansing fire to free them from their bonds.

Talan sank to his knees and closed his eyes as the Silks drifted closer.

CHAPTER TWENTY-TWO

SEEDS OF FAMINE

Can any man survive this endless hunger?

- Tales of the Desolate, uncensored; 1092 SLP

I stared at the burning amphitheater, thoughts floating through my numb mind.

Xaron, Isidora, and the Watchers had been tasked with entering the Wyvern's Claw. They'd sought Vusu's room at the heart of it. They'd meant to kill Vusu.

But I couldn't put the thoughts in any order that made sense of the sight before me. I wanted to believe they meant nothing.

Yet the haze cleared, and the truth asserted itself. I couldn't fool myself any longer. I sank to my knees. It didn't matter what had started the fire. Perhaps it had been stray radiance from one of the Watchers, inexperienced as they were. Perhaps it was a trap set by Vusu's minions. Or perhaps Vusu had been undiminished in his power and paid his would-be assassins in kind. But it didn't matter.

No matter what had happened, it didn't change the fact that Xaron was likely now burning within.

Sobs wracked my tormented body, but I fought them off as I crawled to the chair by the fire. I had to see for myself. I had to know if Xaron was still alive.

Dragging myself into the chair, I closed my eyes and tried to slow my hysterical breathing. Focus, Eltris had reminded me during our lessons, was only possible when your mind was not controlled by other things.

But I couldn't wrest back control. Fear and shame and guilt twined inside me and pulled my thoughts into terrible imaginings. I saw each of my loved ones — Xaron, Talan, Nomusa, my family — tortured and killed at the hands of hooded shadows.

Only my anger was stronger. I ceded to it, let it fill me. I cut away the nightmares and squeezed my eyes shut tighter. I could do nothing if I couldn't focus.

I had to enter the Pyrthae. Even if I couldn't save them, I had to see.

I abandoned Eltris's techniques and tried Isidora's. I painted a desert in my mind, brushing in dunes and a clear blue sky in broad strokes. Almost as soon as I'd visualized the rough sketch, the scene carried me aloft like a leaf on a strong gust, as if it had been waiting for me all along.

I found myself ascending a dune. The pains of my body disappeared, and a thin strength returned to my limbs. Hot wind whipped dust into my face. My throat was parched with thirst, eyes gritty and dry. The sands slipped beneath my bare feet, each step losing ground.

But I carried on. Dusty air wheezed in my lungs, but with each passing moment, breathing grew easier. I tilted my head back and saw nothing but the sharp edge of the dune above me. I scrambled up the last few steps to the crest.

As soon as my foot touched the top, I felt myself lift away, the ground losing its grip on me. Panic rising, I bent down to the sand, desperate to grab hold. It was too late. The sky took me with greater force with each passing moment, its weight having reversed. I fell upward into nothing. Barely able to breathe, I closed my eyes and let it take me.

All may shift around you. You alone are still. Isidora's words as she led us through the scene came back to me. I held them tight in my mind. All shifted around me. But I was still. My fear could not touch me.

Opening my eyes, I looked above me, only to see there wasn't sky, but a desert, seen as if I looked down from a tall tower. *All may shift around me, but I am still,* I told the panic that tried to wrest back control. My ascent — or descent, it seemed now — slowed as I repeated the mantra in my head. As I came to a halt, hovering midair, I gazed down at the landscape below me, blinking in sudden recognition.

Oedija had become a wasteland.

I barely recognized it in the dull light that suffused the barren city. But I knew the shape of its shoreline and the circle of the city wall too well to deceive myself. Tall dunes of ashy gray sand had built up around the inner city as high as the wall itself. The Half-Wall on the south side was nothing more than a long, tall mound of sand. The Lighted Sea was drained, the cliffs at the edge of Oedija marking where it had once been. Only an endless brown basin remained of it now. The Pillars were strange here, melding with their mirror images into seamless bars of dark gray stone. The Laurel Palace below me was still recognizable upon its hill away from the consuming sand, though its towers were broken and its walls eroded. The Conclave's dome had almost completely caved in.

Movement drew my gaze eastward, to where a huge storm of sand turned above the city. Stretching the size of an entire deme, sand billowed slowly from it, yet I felt sure the force of its winds could tear the skin from my body. The twister reached into the mirror Oedija above as well, forming a shape like a spinning top that swayed back and forth from its connecting points. The center of the tornado seemed to project the light that filled this place, for the further away from it the land was, the more it fell into shadow.

Fear ran through me as I recognized what it meant. When I'd dreamed my way into the Pyrthae before, Famine had appeared as an inferno. I guessed that I now gazed upon the daemon god's new form.

I glanced down at myself and startled at the form I'd taken. I didn't have a body, but was a vague figure of spinning sand and wind. Seeing my form, I felt, too, the boundaries I put around it to keep it to that shape.

I tore my gaze away and studied the landscape again. Now that I knew what form wardens might take, I saw the other swirling patches dotting Oedija. Three hovered around Famine. Dozens of others fluttered to the northeast. Fear and exhilaration gripped me as I recognized who those must be, and what they must mean.

I willed myself toward Xaron and the Watchers, trapped deep in the Claw, but somehow still alive.

As I neared, I sensed the danger they were in. Xaron, whom I intuitively knew as I'd known Talan's flame before, seemed barely able to keep turning. I descended fast toward him, though I didn't know what I could do. Xaron I might recognize, but I couldn't distinguish between the Watchers and the Seeker wardens among the other shapes that spun against each other. If I threw myself at any of them, attacking them the only way I knew how, I might as easily harm an ally as an enemy, and leave my allies and friends worse off than before.

I halted a couple of dozen feet above and watched Xaron's life fading, urgency hammering through my form and threatening to break it apart. Ideas spun through my head, but I dismissed each of them in turn. Just as I'd suspected and feared, I could do nothing more than watch.

Then I felt something pressing against the boundaries of myself, and I startled and looked behind. The gray, twisted face of Clepsammia smiled her mocking smile at me as she gripped my sandy shoulder. Somehow, it became more solid under her touch. I felt I could almost hear her thoughts this way, for all the good it did — her thoughts were in no tongue that I understood.

I didn't try to pull away. Now that she was here, I remembered the last time the Maiden of the Sands had appeared before me. When I'd struggled even to stand after the Guilders' attack, she had done something, something that gave me the strength to make it all the way back to the Aviary.

As if sensing my thoughts, Clepsammia's smile tugged unnaturally wider. She twisted her hand through my shoulder, and the sand where she'd touched spun faster. A warm glow of energy suffused me from the spot.

For a moment, I didn't understand; then realization hit me like a crashing wave. I stared, dumbstruck, at the thought of a goddess aiding me. But remembering Xaron's plight below me, I didn't waste a moment longer, but turned and dove for him.

Strength flowing through me, I rushed at Xaron. I barely knew what I did, but as I reached him, I summoned forth my energy and *pushed* it into him, spinning his wind into a fury as I flew by. Passing, I looked back, and for a moment, I feared I'd dispersed his slowly swirling sand.

Then his spiral reared up and surged, his twister growing stronger and more distinct.

Exhilaration surged through me. I'd given Xaron back his strength! I sent a silent thanks to Clepsammia, then turned my gaze to the other fluttering gales below me. Some of those would be Watchers, some of them Seekers. For Xaron's sake, I didn't dare give any others wind. I glanced back at where Clepsammia had floated, wondering if she might guide me again, but the goddess had disappeared. Hoping I'd done enough, I reluctantly ascended back into the sky.

Famine again drew my gaze. I couldn't tell if it was my imagination, but his twister seemed to be growing larger, its winds stronger, with every passing moment. Only then did I wonder why Famine, bound as he was by Vusu, wasn't in the Wyvern's Claw as well. Wincing, I considered Famine's sandstorm closer. Near its base rose a Pillar; but if it was Bazaar's, Iris's, or the Acadium's Pillar, I couldn't tell. It was too hard to distinguish among the force of his winds.

Another thought jolted me back to myself. Xaron wasn't the only one in danger. I scanned Oedija, searching for more signs of wardens. To the northwest, one twister still spun strongly: Komo at Brinecoast, attempting to save Myron, I guessed. As he didn't seem in danger of fading, I continued my search, moving in a wide berth around Famine back toward the Laurel Palace, then onward until I hovered near the Conclave's Pillar.

Finally, I spotted him. To the southeast, small, fluttering sands, little more than a gust, were about to sputter out.

Talan.

As I threw myself toward him, I recognized Sule and her Qarin, a thin spiral reaching up to the mirrored Oedija. Its connection seemed so thin a small breeze might sever it. I ignored it. The daemon would have to take care of itself. I wouldn't assist it, no matter whose side it claimed to be on.

Talan's winds stirred, then faltered, stilling and falling to the ground. Fear flooding through me, I didn't slow my fast descent as I neared. Where before I'd breathed energy into Xaron, I now thrust it into Talan, throwing the whole of my being into him and filling him like wind in sails.

A storm of emotions flooded through me. Senses flashed through my mind. The putrid stench of rotting corpses. Exhaustion heavy in my limbs. But something else pulled at me strongest, an intense desire to lose myself and finally find peace...

NO!

They — whatever they were — flowed like gentle zephyrs into Talan's sputtering wind, sapping his strength and will. I moved to block them, their whispers only tantalizing to me, the separation provided by the Pyrthae enough to resist them. And though I'd given of myself to both Xaron and Talan, my will seemed to have only grown stronger.

As I sheltered Talan from whatever assaulted him, I stirred him back to life. His being still flowing through mine, I knew he'd pushed himself too hard. Maybe beyond what I could repair. I suffocated my fears and pressed more of myself into him.

He suddenly grasped toward me, touching my mind roughly like a blind man gripping my face. *Do I know you?* He flung the question around him clumsily, not knowing how to direct it at me.

Rise, I told him. *Kill Kalindi. Then return to me.*

I felt his amazement and recognition. *Airene?*

My heart soared, but I knew I couldn't keep him longer. The Silks — as I'd identified his foes from his mind — battered against my wall, but I knew it was only he who could contend with them.

Go! With the command, I lifted away, giving him one last burst of wind before I disentangled our spirits. One last glance showed Talan rising once more, his sands billowing with strength.

I reluctantly turned my attention away from him and back north. Famine had grown ever greater. The middle of the tornado extended out, bloated with lazily rolling dust. But I could see how the winds whipped fast near the ends of it. Whatever was happening, Famine was gaining power — and quickly.

I had to go to him. I had to see what was causing Famine's rapid rise in strength. Did Vusu grow with him? Or had Famine already broken free? And what did the source of the storm mean, that it was not within the Claw?

Maintaining a careful distance, I brought myself closer to the daemon god. I could feel the pull of his winds from far outside the storm's bounds. I studied the area from which it came. The Laurel Palace was to the west of it, the Conclave southwest. Now that I was closer, I could barely pick out Bazaar's Pillar beyond, showing me the storm rose from—

The Acadium.

Heedless of the danger, I threw myself toward the storm. I didn't know what Vusu and Famine were after, or what was augmenting their power. But they'd claimed Linos once before.

I wouldn't let them have what was left of him.

I flew through the desolate city. Famine's pull on my mind became stronger as I neared, threatening to split it asunder. I had to fight every moment to keep myself together. The ethereal light within the twister pulsed brighter, like the beating heart of the sun. I dove low, dipping below the burgeoning middle of the tornado, and soared within the channels of sand covering the city.

Reaching the base of the twister, I halted, trying to make sense of the scene before me. Famine was weaker here at the base, for he rose from another spiraling wind — Vusu, I guessed. Two other winds contended with Vusu, diving into him again and again, each time weakening him a little more. One other held back a small distance. Vaguely I recognized these, but I couldn't place who they were.

Then I saw the small, fluttering breeze flowing around Vusu, and I froze, caught between fear and hope. I knew who that tiny squall was.

Linos!

I cried out to him, unable to stop myself from drifting forward. I hadn't known that any part of my brother was still alive. To see him, to know him, brought me more strength and hope than I'd had in a long time.

LINOS!

I felt him stir in response, and my hopes soared. There were no words to his reaching, no conscious thought. But recognition was enough. My brother was still alive, and some part of him still knew me.

But he was in danger. His slow squall seemed to depend on Vusu's winds to continue swirling, and again and again, the two other gales attacked Vusu. Anger surged through me. There were too many unknowns, too much to consider.

But I had no time. Linos was in danger.

Gathering the errant winds of myself and tightening them so that a tempest roared within me, I threw myself toward the melee. I flew faster than I'd dared let myself before, gathering speed and force. The others noticed me as I approached, but couldn't leave off their fighting.

Suddenly, the gale that had held back lashed toward me and twisted into me.

Airene! Eltris's voice boomed into me, nearly enough to tear me apart. *Stop, STOP! Before you ruin us all!*

Her tendrils pulled at me, tilting me from my course. I struggled to shake her loose, but couldn't manage it.

Let me go! I snarled, flinging my rage at her.

She flinched, but didn't release me. *You don't understand what you do!*

How could I? You never told me!

Inexorably, I pulled her toward Linos and the others. Before, when I'd first strayed into the Pyrthae, Eltris had been able to collapse me into unconsciousness. But either she'd weakened or I'd grown stronger; now, she couldn't resist my efforts.

Release me! I commanded her. *Let me go to him! I'll save my brother!*

Your brother is dead! His spirit is fragmented. He's gone, Airene! Now you must let him fulfill his purpose. You cannot interfere!

I pried her consciousness from me one strand at a time. *So you've plotted with Vusu this whole time!* I threw at her. *You always meant to kill my brother!*

Her anger stirred and strengthened her, and she clung so tightly that I couldn't pry her loose. *Vusumuzi means to seal away Famine, fool girl! He's sought to end Famine for decades. As a young man, he foolishly accepted the Quintyr into his being in exchange for power. But since then, he has seen his folly and the ruin Famine would bring if loosed upon the world. He seeks to be rid of him forever!*

As much as I wanted to, I couldn't deny the truth of her words. With our minds entwined, the force of her conviction filled me. It didn't help that I'd begun to suspect as much since I'd read Nkosi's book.

Even as Vusu and my brother were attacked again and again by the two opposing spirits, I knew I had to ask. *Why destroy Oedija then? Why kill hundreds of innocents? Why mutilate and maim two of my brothers?*

It would take too long for you to understand. You must trust me, Airene. Do not interfere!

Rage suddenly flared up in me again. *Trust you? You've done nothing to earn my trust!*

Summoning all the force of my disdain, I threw Eltris off with a mighty gust. I felt the augur's surprise just before our connection severed and she was tossed away like a cast-off rag.

Not wasting a moment, I soared forward. But as I neared the struggling gales, I slowed, then stopped. Vusu seemed to be protecting Linos from the other two. But he'd been too long my enemy to trust his intentions now. Knowing Eltris was just behind, I knew I had to make a choice.

Diving, I threw myself into the fray.

I tangled with the winds, fighting and pushing back as they tried to toss me and shred me. But I had only struggled a moment before something like a strong gale swept over me, and the turbulent scene shifted.

Suddenly, the sands began to drain away below me, revealing figures caught in a struggle.

Vusu emerged from the sands first, his arms raised, something slender and white clasped in his hands. He was even thinner than before, so skeletal that it seemed the barest blow must shatter him. He wore the same peplos as the day of the Despoina's trial, only now the white fabric was soiled and stained with crusted blood. The source of his weakness was plain, the broken bolt still emerging from between his ribs.

The arms of another man parted from the sands after, holding Vusu's wrists. Kyros Brighteyed, I recognized him, as his balding head, loose jowls, and glowing eyes came into view. The Archmaster was clad in rich robes and purpling in the face from exertion. Strange as it seemed, the thick man was barely able to match Vusu's strength, though the traitor looked halfway a corpse.

Then the last of the sands parted, revealing a prone figure lying on the bed beneath the uplifted arms of the men. Vusu and Kyros struggled over my brother's bed as he stared, unseeing, up at them.

I hovered, entranced with horror, as I watched their struggle. I felt their wills clash, over and over, each weakening, neither breaking. The other presence I'd sensed was nowhere to be seen, though I felt it still, searching for an opening in their defenses. Staring down at Linos's scarred face, I guessed who it must be. The daemon who had seized Linos's tongue now sought to fully claim my brother.

What I had to do crystallized in my mind. I pooled all the hate, the fear, the fury surging inside me and drew on its fire. I'd do whatever I had to, not knowing the cost.

I would save Linos.

Drawing myself away, sand flooded the scene again, all three swallowed within them. Back in the Pyrthae, I searched the ruins of Oedija. Eltris still hovered above, watching, waiting. But it wasn't her I was looking for. Just above me, staying at the perimeters of the whipping winds of Famine's sandstorm, lingered the swirling sand of Linos's daemon.

Anger pulsing through me, I threw myself after it.

Sensing its danger, the pyr fled into the blighted buildings. I pursued, speeding far faster than I could have run, faster than a diving hawk. But as the buildings opened into a desolate forum, the daemon was nowhere to be seen.

I swore loudly as I looked for it, even knowing it was futile. Here, it was in its element. I'd have to settle that score another time. Turning, I threw myself back toward my brother and the contending wardens.

Though I felt Eltris's focus on me, she didn't try to stop me, perhaps knowing she could no longer match me. I gathered speed and force as I dove toward Vusu and Kyros struggling over my brother. Famine's fell light pulsed above, as if in delight of the struggle. I didn't slow, didn't let myself think of what might happen when I collided. I formed myself into force and fury and threw myself into the fray.

My aim was true. As I collided, I managed to avoid Linos and Kyros and cut through Vusu's winds alone, carving through to the center of them. I felt the pain ripping through his awareness as if it were my own, deep and wide enough that I almost lost myself in it. But momentum drove me deeper still, until finally, something gave way.

I felt him break.

Some part of me became aware of Kyros throwing Vusu back against the wall in the real world, and Vusu's head hitting against the stone, his arm flopping out at an unnatural angle. The Visage of the Wyvern didn't rise, but stirred sluggishly to look down at the item in his hand. *The white-wood knife*, I suddenly recognized. The one the Seekers had stolen from Kyros, that Eltris had called the sacrificial knife. The same as Aika of the Green had thrust into her own breast. Kyros strode around Linos toward the traitor. I watched, unable to look away, eager to see him make an end of my enemy.

But I'd lingered too long — for suddenly, I felt Vusu seize me. Even broken and dying, his grip was too strong for me to flee. Panicking, I struggled, but still he bore me up.

Up into the the storm above.

As Famine loomed around me, I stilled, like a hare spotted in the open streets. A dark storm of sand and wind walled us in. Above, a heavenly sphere, the source of the strange light, glowed like the sun and pulsed like a beating heart.

Hunger and hate suddenly burst through me. I felt myself draining away into the abyss of the daemon god. There seemed no end to his horrible desire. But Vusu still held me.

You. The word was resonant with bitter irony. *Again, it is you who stops me.*

I had too little of myself for speech, my will draining into the ravenous hunger around me.

Keep hold of yourself, Airene of Port. Listen well. There will be only two Seeds of Famine when I am gone. Only your brother, and you. One of you must become the Sacri-

fice, then descend stoneward. Only this can contain the Serpent, and only for a time. Do you understand?

Horror brought me back to myself for a brief moment. *No!* I cried out, as much in answer as denial.

I felt his bitter laugh echo through me. *You doom us and do not even know how. Seek my honor, Seda. She possesses all that I could tell you. You must do this, Airene, if you wish to stop Famine. I cannot hold him for much longer.*

The sphere of light above pulsed violently, as if it were a grotesque, enormous egg, and what was contained inside struggled to break free. Dread washed over me anew.

Go! Vusu commanded me, both weakness and strength in the word. *Go, and do what I could not.*

He ripped me free and sent me tumbling away from the tempest. Dazed, I struggled to find myself, my winds scattered about me. Only one thought, stubbornly clung to, forced myself back together.

Linos. I had to make sure he was safe.

Though my awareness strained at the seams of my form, like a skin too full of water, I cobbled my consciousness back together and looked around. Famine's storm raged stronger still, the wind and sand whipping at me and eroding my strength. Pulling back further, I saw at the base of the storm Vusu's winds faltering, but still spinning. Linos had begun to spiral wider, free finally of his master. Kyros swirled strong.

As I dove at them again, the sands parted just in time to see Kyros closing the last of the distance to Vusu, lightning sparking on his fingertips. Vusu glanced up at where I watched, as if he could see me, then raised the wooden knife in his unbroken arm. His body trembled as he positioned the knife above his chest.

His whisper cut through me. *"Famine, I give myself to you as Sacrifice."*

Then Vusu plunged the dagger into his chest.

The Pyrthae vibrated for a moment, the tremor rattling me. Then the tempest that had raged above us disappeared without a trace. The orb of unholy light dissipated as well, and the Pyrthae fell into sudden darkness. I was lost in the black, yet I couldn't move, shock and disbelief rooting me in place.

Famine was gone, truly gone. I couldn't feel him at all.

I roused myself to take stock of the situation. Vusu, too, had vanished. Giving himself as Sacrifice had killed him, or taken him somewhere I couldn't follow. The daemon that had plagued Linos had long since fled. Kyros was melding away as he returned to our world. I felt myself fading as well. Suddenly, all that I'd done caught up with me. I couldn't even muster the energy to fear for myself.

But I wasn't allowed to slip into oblivion. Someone seized me, anger burning me awake.

Idiot girl! Eltris raged against me. *You damned fool! What have you done? You've ruined us!*

They're gone, I thought wearily. *Famine and Vusu both.*

You don't understand! You never will!

She let me slip through her fingers, and I didn't resist as I melded with the darkness.

CHAPTER TWENTY-THREE

THE DESPOT OF OEDIJA

Every man has the chance to remake himself, but few do. To be reforged is to be melted down to the essence of what you are, the impurities burned away, so you may be made stronger.

You and I may be reforged again, brother, should we have the daring to seize this moment, and the courage to face the pain of being born again…

— Tales of the Desolate, uncensored; 1092 SLP

I woke with a head stuffed full of wool. Blinking through the stars in my vision, I stared around me. A moment later, I recognized where I was. *Jaxas's solar.*

Yet I had the distinct feeling I'd been somewhere else entirely a moment before.

Footsteps scuffled behind me. I started, sitting up in the chair I'd been slumped in and groaning with my body's protests. A pair of familiar beady eyes stared down at me, a look of rebuke plastered on his pinched features. Yet with my head in a fog, I found myself uncertain.

"Nikias?" I asked tentatively.

The steward sniffed. "Good, you're awake. Come. The Despot has summoned you."

His words were nonsense to me. *The Despot?* I searched my memory, hoping to make sense of things.

The Claw had burst into flame. Xaron had been in danger.

And I'd gone to him.

I'd entered the Pyrthae. I'd saved him and Talan by channeling quintessence as Clepsammia showed me. I'd felt powerful there, more so with each passing moment.

But then I remembered the rest. The cavernous hunger permeating me as Vusu held me in the midst of Famine's storm. I remembered the traitor's words. *There will be only two Seeds of Famine when I am gone. Only your brother, and you.*

Seeds of Famine.

Eltris's despising words after our last lesson came back to me. *And you imagine yourself a Finch. There's only one way you could have become a warden, girl.*

The suspicion I'd held and dismissed was true.

As I sat, numb with the realization, more pieces fell into place. In *The Seeds of Famine*, Aika of the Green had awoken as a warden after a dream of Famine. *A Seed of Harvest*, she had claimed to be. But I suspected now whose Seed she had truly been.

I slumped down in my seat, all strength leaving my body.

"First Verifier Airene. Are you listening?"

I barely heard Nikias through the tempest of my thoughts. What did it mean? What did it mean that Famine had opened me to the Pyrthae? Was I tainted? Were his fate and mine now bound together? Did he even now worm his way into my mind and spirit, hollowing me, turning me to his cause? Linos, too, had been attuned by Famine — I believed Vusu that far. Perhaps I was doomed to become what he had, little more than a scrap of spirit left to me, little more than an empty vessel, waiting to be filled.

"Airene!"

I dragged myself up from my heavy thoughts. "Yes, Nikias. I hear you."

Nikias didn't bother hiding his disapproval. "His Radiance wishes for your presence immediately. If you are not well enough to stand, I shall order you an invalid's litter."

The strangeness of Nikias's words drew me further from my stupor. *His Radiance?* Even for the Wreaths, the address went too far, particularly when the Laurel Palace had lost even more power by Council decree.

But oddity aside, it was welcome news. It must mean that Komo and First Laurel Synne had succeeded in recovering Despot Myron Wreath. I could only hope Xaron and the Watchers had returned as well. But what had Myron done to earn so much respect upon his return?

I turned through the possibilities. There was another explanation: that this was all a charade put on by Orhan and the Preservists to disguise their crimes. But I didn't see why Nikias would comply, unless Jaxas had ordered him to.

The steward turned from me, a disgusted look on his face. "I will send an honor for a litter then."

"Wait — I can stand."

Not sure if I actually could, I lifted myself from the chair and turned to face him. Pain didn't drown me as I'd expected. My ribs still throbbed dully, but it barely hurt to breathe anymore. The back of my head, tender from where the Guilders had struck it against the ground, only smarted. I smiled grimly. My body had healed itself once again, at least partially.

But any pleasure I took in it was tainted by the knowledge that it was only by Famine's gift — or curse — that it was possible.

My legs still unsteady, I leaned on the chair. "Where are we going?"

Nikias watched me as if he expected me to collapse at any moment. "As I said, we go to meet the Despot. He waits before the palace to make a pronouncement to his people."

That seemed like Myron at least. He'd always basked in the attention of the people at ceremonies. Though why he would care about me attending him, I hadn't the slightest clue.

But I was more interested in other things at the moment. "Nikias, I'm sorry, but I have other places to be. My brother — I must see to him."

Displeasure gleamed in his eyes. "You serve at the Despot's pleasure now, First Verifier Airene. It won't do to stir his displeasure."

His words gave me pause yet again. *First Verifier? I serve at the Despot's pleasure?* Had the Laurel Palace taken up the Order of Verifiers after the Conclave cast us off? There were too many questions, too many things I didn't know. Much as I wished to check on my brother and friends, I needed to attend to these mysteries. Linos wouldn't be in danger for the moment now that Vusu had given himself as Sacrifice. And if Xaron, Nomusa, and Talan weren't safe, there was nothing more I could do.

Besides, I didn't think Nikias meant to give me a choice.

My throat dry, I managed to keep my tone light. "By all means, Steward, lead the way."

———

Though sunlight barely pierced the gray of the overcast morning, the crowds had already gathered for Myron's announcement. As Nikias and I emerged from the Laurel Palace doors, we were assaulted by the tumultuous sound they made, cascading up the hill from below. Even outside the gates a quarter-mile down, the noise was astounding. And the swell of the crowd — there seemed no end to the gathered people. I felt dizzy standing above them all, as if I were the focus of their attention. Fear, too, was part of it. Since I'd seen what the Manifest and dusk mobs were capable of, I didn't trust crowds. I wondered if this one had gathered merely to greet their returning Despot, or for a more nefarious purpose.

"I'm glad to see you up and walking," said a soft voice by my side.

I glanced over, recognizing Jaxas's voice, but I had to look twice to be sure it was he. The Archon stood as tall and proud as I'd ever seen him. No longer did he seem sickly or bowed by life or duty. The thinness of his features held strength, like a slender tree standing strong after a storm. His robes were rich but simple, decorated in the green and gold that signified the royal family. He wore a golden chain studded with emeralds, and rings glittered upon his fingers. I'd never seen him so ornamented, nor ever expected to.

"Jaxas," I started, but a scowl from Nikias silenced me. My confusion only increased as the steward bowed nearly level with the ground.

"Your Radiance, I have brought the First Verifier," the man said, his tone subdued and formal. "If you will excuse me, I must be about other arrangements for the announcement."

"Of course. Do what you must, and with my thanks, Nikias." Jaxas inclined his head to the steward.

Nikias seemed to take it as a great honor, for he walked away with his chin upright.

I turned back to the Archon. "When did you earn that respect? *Your Radiance*, I mean."

Jaxas smiled, but his eyes remained untouched. For the first time, I wondered if I'd spoken too familiarly.

"I wanted you to be here," he finally said. "You most of all, Airene of Oedija."

I wondered at that curious epithet, but it was the least of the abounding riddles. "What for? What's going on, Jaxas?"

He turned his gaze toward the roaring crowd below. "A change in the tides, I hope. A new dawn for our realm, and not our last."

I stared, at a loss for words.

He looked again at me. "All will be made clear soon. Did you rest well? Nikias said you slept for a long time. I don't fault you for it," he continued quickly at my expression. "You're severely injured, Airene. You need rest."

"I wasn't resting."

The truth suddenly played on the tip of my tongue. I knew what it meant if I told him what I was. I'd have to live with the consequences, for good or for ill. I thought I knew Jaxas. But he'd surprised me many times in the past span, and he kept many more secrets than I'd suspected. Did I know him well enough to entrust him with my life?

As I opened my mouth to speak, I realized I did.

"I channeled. I walked the Pyrthae in a dream, Jaxas. I saw some of what happened at the Claw and Brinecoast. And I was there at the Acadium with Vusu, Kyros, and Eltris, when…" I struggled to put what

I'd seen, what I'd done, into words. "When Vusu died," I finished lamely.

Even trusting him, I couldn't meet his eyes, dreading what I'd see. Revulsion? Fear? But when I finally met Jaxas's gaze, I saw a fierce joy there, deep in his dark, recessed eyes. I nearly flinched back from the bluntness of it.

"Thank you," he said quietly. "Thank you for you trusting me as few others would. You cannot know what it means to me."

My mouth opened, then closed. "You knew?" was all I could manage to say.

He nodded. "There were many signs. The circumstances of how you suddenly fell ill. The conferences with Eltris and Isidora's Watchers. But it was the burns in your blankets seen by your honor, Hyrol, that confirmed it."

Anger stirred me from my shock. "You were spying on me? I suspected Hyrol might be watching for someone else. I didn't think it'd be you."

The Archon held me in his gaze until the anger flickered uncertainly in me.

"I watched for your protection," he said, so quietly his words were almost lost in the tumult of the crowd. "You thwarted Vusu's plans, Airene. The Manifest might still decide to kill you at any moment. I couldn't let you go to the Conclave, knowing they couldn't protect you."

I stared at him, trying to see the truth in his eyes, desperately hoping it was as he spoke it. That Jaxas had sought to protect me, not keep track of my movements. But even after my confession, I'd never felt less certain of him.

An honor walked from behind a column, startling me. Without hesitation, she approached and whispered in Jaxas's ear. Though his eyes didn't leave me, Jaxas nodded once, and the honor hurried away.

"The time has come," he said to me. "I'd appreciate if you stood nearby, Airene. As close as is courteous." He paused. "Can you project voices yet?"

I flinched and glanced over my shoulder to be sure the honor was out of earshot. "I don't think so," I muttered. "And I don't want everyone to know what I am besides."

He nodded slowly. "I'll respect your wishes. Just know that the time for secrets may soon be over."

I doubted he would ever be past keeping his. But I nodded all the same.

"It's nearly time for the speech," he said, turning. "We should be heading down."

"Just one question," I said hurriedly. "Xaron, Nomusa, Komo — where are they? They must have returned with Myron Wreath if he's to make an announcement." I looked around. "Where is he, anyway? Is he set to make a grand entrance as usual?"

The amusement in Jaxas's eyes irked me beyond measure, but his words set me at ease. "They are safe, never fear. Nomusa is doing me a favor at the moment, and Xaron has need of rest. The Watchers didn't fair well in the Wyvern's Claw, as you have probably surmised from your... dream-walk. Just over half of them survived, Isidora among them."

I nearly folded over with the wave of relief that washed over me. They were alive and safe. Tears burned at my eyes. "High heights of the 'Thae, but I'm relieved to hear you say that."

"Heir Komo and First Laurel Synne also survived and completed their task."

"I figured they, at least, had succeeded." I gestured at the crowd below us.

Jaxas gave a thin smile that didn't reach his eyes. Again, I wondered what I was missing.

He turned. "We must go. The people are waiting."

I had no choice but to follow.

As Jaxas emerged from the columns and started down the main stairwell from the Laurel Palace, the crowd suddenly roared even louder. Jaxas nodded and smiled. Despite being a Wreath, he showed none of the showmanship of Myron, nor the gaudy ostentatiousness of the Despot's daughter. He was a soft-spoken man, and presented himself as nothing else. Yet there was no denying his regality as he walked slowly ahead of me.

I followed at a distance. Laurel guards lined the way, and two Shepherds had taken up post at the next landing. Tribune Timon waited there too, his slithering gaze finding me as I approached. I looked aside, remembering Jaxas's private words with the Tribune. Why was he here with his Shepherds? What task had Jaxas previously set them to? I hadn't noticed them during my dream-walk, but I hadn't been searching for them.

My gaze wandered to the person standing next to him. First Laurel Synne's stare was cool as she nodded to me after bowing low to Jaxas. She looked somewhat the worse for wear from her journey into Brinecoast, a dark cut still trickling red down her forehead, her armor crusted with dried blood. Yet her posture only slightly sagged from the night's expedition.

Jaxas stepped down next to the Tribune and leaned toward him. I stared hard, wishing my head wasn't pounding so I could make sense of the situation.

"Airene."

Recognizing the voice, I turned with a relieved smile. "Heir Komo. I—"

The smile froze on my lips at the sight of him. The boy had fared far worse than the First Laurel. Bruises and cuts littered his skin, visible from his ceremonial warrior's garb. In places, his flesh had turned ashy. The eye set in the midst of the flaking green paint was purpled and swelled almost shut. His bottom lip was puffy on one side, making his smile look more like a grimace. His nose was bent and trickled blood.

"It will heal," he said hurriedly at my horrified expression. "Nothing is permanently broken."

"That's good. But still…"

It wasn't just his wounds. Only a boy of fourteen, and he suffered as a man. No — he *was* a man, with all the responsibilities and maturity of one. Despite myself, I felt a glow of pride for the Bali prince. I hoped Linos would act as well as Komo when he came out of his stupor. Perhaps without Vusu, Famine, and the daemon plaguing him, he would even soon rise.

Nkosi, two steps behind the boy, nodded to me. "Our *Shaka-na* is strong, as his father and mother raised him to be. He has done our ishaka proud with his actions tonight."

I nodded in agreement. "But where is the Despot? I was told he'd be making an announcement soon."

Komo and Nkosi exchanged glances. "He is," the boy said, seeming confused.

Before I could ask anything further, silence dropped behind me. Turning, I saw Jaxas stood at the edge of the dais, one of the Shepherd's hands touching his throat, and flinched as his voice crashed over the gathering.

"People of Oedija! You will have heard many rumors why we gather here today. You have heard my uncle, Myron Wreath, is not dead. You have heard my cousin, Asileia Wreath, has fled the city. You have heard the Wyvern's Claw of Thys burns to the ground, and that a battle has taken place north of the wall. Perhaps you have even heard that Shepherds have visited the Conclave." He paused, letting the words sink in. "I come now to tell you all of this is true. The Claw burned at the hands of wardens I sent to kill the traitor Vusumuzi."

For a moment, I stopped breathing. The crowd stirred, but the noise was conflicted and confused. Some shouted angrily, but most seemed uneasy. *How else had the Wreaths used wardens?* they must be thinking. *How else have they played with fire?* I couldn't believe Jaxas would throw this brand onto the tinder of the crowd's temper.

Jaxas continued as if he hadn't noticed the commotion. "Vusumuzi, who called himself the Visage of the Wyvern and led the rebel faction the Manifest, was the most powerful warden of our time. Yet he fled before our Watchers, wardens of the Acadium who were trained to defend us against him. Vusumuzi burned his base of operations as he left, but the Watchers escaped. Vusumuzi, in the end, did not. Though he fled to the Acadium, he died there with a knife in his chest."

Scattered cheers pierced the uneasiness, but not nearly as many as I'd hoped for. A century and a half of distrust of magic couldn't be undone with a single action. Even if they had seen Vusu as a great threat, taking him on with any wardens other than the Shepherds was too much to swallow. I wondered if Jaxas knew what a grave error he was committing. But there was no stopping it now as he continued.

"With Vusumuzi's death, we hope to dismantle the Manifest. To any of you who know those who followed him, tell them: their leader is dead. They should disperse and return to their lives, so that we may prepare for the other threats against Oedija.

"But the traitor's justice is not all we gained last night. Myron Wreath, my uncle, has been recovered from the clutches of the Manifest. However, to our great sadness, he has suffered horrible mistreatment at their hands. For now, he deems himself too ill to serve as your Despot, and has asked another to Ascend in his place. Yet further tragedy finds us. Asileia Wreath, your erstwhile Despoina, has fled the city. So it falls to the last member of our family to take up the Evergreen Wreath."

Suddenly, Nikias bustled past me. I stared down at his hands to see a vibrantly green crown of leaves and twigs. He passed the Evergreen Wreath to Tribune Timon. The Tribune, with an inappropriate grin plastered over his face, raised the crown aloft. Jaxas turned and bowed his head so that the shorter man could set it atop his brow. He turned back to the almost completely silent crowd, a quiet echoed in myself.

"I stand before you as your new Despot, people of Oedija, to act on your behalf, and to protect you from the many enemies who threaten us."

He paused. If he expected applause, he was disappointed. Too much had happened too quickly for them to know how to react. I myself could only stare.

"And already I do so," Jaxas continued relentlessly. "As my reign begins, I have put necessary decrees in place. Beginning with the Demos Council. In ordinary times, their laggardly way of conducting the nation's business might suffice. In war, it does not. Henceforth, I have disbanded the Council and suspended the power of the Conclave. All such power will return to the Laurel Palace as was done in the days of our ancestors."

Finally, the crowd roared. I watched the gates below rattle as people pressed against them, shouting and screaming. A few even started climbing them before laurel guards jabbed them back with the blunt end of their spears. This was a cauldron ready to boil over, and Jaxas only fed the fire.

"Avvad marches on our city!" Jaxas called above the noise, his voice thundering down the hill. "We must prepare for war! I will lead us through this trial. With your help, people of Oedija, we will turn aside the Imperium!"

I doubted the renewed cries were from enthusiasm. I could do nothing but stare at our newly Ascended Despot. He'd done it. He'd done what some part of me had hoped he would do. And from what he'd said earlier, he'd done it in part because of my words and influence.

But now that he'd finally acted, I couldn't help but wish he had not. Rather than unite Oedija, it promised to break it in a way that could never be mended.

Famine might be suppressed, but the tremors of his arrival still wracked the city apart.

His pronouncements finished, Jaxas turned away, and his gaze found and held me. I returned it, though I was sure he could read the fear behind my eyes.

His expression didn't shift as he approached me. "Wait for me in my solar," he instructed, then started up the stairs. I cast one last look back at the roiling crowd, then obeyed my new Despot's command.

———

I stared out through the balcony doors of Jaxas's solar. Watching. Waiting.

Nikias had filled me in on some of the vaguer details of Jaxas's speech. Myron had indeed been recovered and was in critical condition. Presently, he was under bed-watch by order of the Wreath healers. As for if he was sick enough to serve as Despot, the steward professed belief that Jaxas spoke truly. I kept my doubts to myself.

As for his daughter, Asileia had officially fled the city with Bhaka, Komo's traitorous guard. In some sense, this was true. Both had left the city — but not together. The former Despoina was now being kept at the same Wreath manor in the northern prefectures as my family. As for Bhaka, Komo had sent him back home with three of his guards to accept Yorandu justice.

Now Jaxas met with his new circle of advisors. Among them were, to my dismay, Feiyan and Timon. The former Tribune was now acting as the High Tribune, and Feiyan moved to occupy the premier counselor position of old, First Consul, which made her authority second only to Jaxas's. My blood boiled every time I imagined her smug smile at achieving such a high level of power. I hoped our new Despot knew what he was doing. Feiyan might be a useful tool, but only so long as her interests aligned with our own.

I tried to deny the last of my feelings toward it, but I was too weary to lie, even to myself. That he had chosen Feiyan for such a position over me smarted, even as I knew it was preposterous to feel that way. I was no counselor, no second-in-command. I was injured and a liability as a warden, among a host of other reasons.

Yet I couldn't drown the jealousy and resentment.

More aggravating still was that I couldn't reach Linos, nor had I heard more from Xaron and Nomusa, or anything from Talan. Corin, too, was still missing from before the night's action had begun. My weakness was only one part of the reason for not leaving to find information for myself. Despite watching for several turns as I absently ate from the array of food laid out in Jaxas's solar, the crowds around the Laurel Palace hadn't dispersed. In fact, they only seemed to swell greater, as if the spreading word brought more curious eyes to glimpse the Despot who had taken back his family's ancestral power. I could only hope all my friends were safe, and that Linos was out of the hands of those who wished him harm. I even dared to hope he'd awakened at last.

A creak sounded from the far side of the room, and I turned to see the door opening. But it wasn't Jaxas who walked through. Worries momentarily forgotten, I crossed the short distance and wrapped Xaron and Nomusa in a tight embrace.

"You're late," I chastised them, not letting go.

"Come off it," Xaron complained. "You weren't worried about us. You knew we'd make it out."

Nomusa pried me off with a small smile. "I'm sorry to keep you waiting. Jaxas gave us a task to immediately attend to."

My spirits sank further. Yet two more people had been given priority over me. That they were my friends only made it worse. "And that duty was?"

They exchanged a glance. "Establishing the Watchers as an official order of Oedija," Nomusa admitted with reluctance.

I blinked. So much was changing, and all at once. Suddenly, I wanted to hear nothing more of it. "Never mind that. Tell me what happened last night."

They exchanged another look, no doubt surprised at my lack of curiosity, but obliged. Xaron began with what I suspected was an exaggerated account of his foray into the Wyvern's Claw. According to him, they'd had to overcome Seeker wardens at every turn until they finally arrived at the center room in the tallest part of the amphitheater, where Vusu was supposed to be lying ill in bed. Instead, they'd encountered a room empty but for an intricate trap that shattered dozens of pots filled with oil on the wooden floor, then set them to flames. They'd been forced to flee to avoid being swallowed by the chasing inferno. To make matters worse, Seeker wardens closed in behind them, and they'd had to fight their way out. Six of the Watchers hadn't returned. Recounting this finally seemed to dampen Xaron's mood. He morosely confessed that they hadn't even killed Vusu for their troubles.

Nomusa's story was no less eventful. Having gone to the Conclave at Jaxas's behest, she'd stood in the great chamber and borne witness to the overthrow of the Demos Council. Tribune Timon had marched his four Shepherds down the stairs to the small door behind the dais and entered without invitation. Nomusa hadn't seen everything that occurred, but it wasn't long after that the Low Consuls were marched out. Only Feiyan had been missing — for, as usual, she was ahead of the game. They'd come out quietly for the most part, but only after Berker had been made an example of. One of the Shepherds burned his arm badly when he resisted, and none of the others risked it. I felt some small measure of vindication at Berker's punishment, but it was tainted with the realization that Shepherds were free to use their magic against even the elected officials of our demotism. Even if the Low Consul was an ass, it was a dangerous precedent. The Conclave guards, having witnessed the devastation wardens were capable of during the Despoina's trial, didn't resist either, but let the Demos Council be led away.

At their urging, I reluctantly revealed that, despite being chair-bound, I'd had my own notable night. They stared at me in incredulity as I described entering the Pyrthae and the Oedijan wasteland. Xaron's eyes widened as I confessed I'd uplifted his flagging spirit. He pulled me into a tight embrace.

"You saved me, Airene. I was tamping down flames so that others behind me could escape and thought I would fall on the spot. Then suddenly, I felt energy sweep through me. And to think that was you!" He shook his head. "You've grown into your gift so quickly. It's amazing."

I flushed. "I can't really claim the credit. Clepsammia showed me how."

"Clepsammia?" Nomusa cut in. "The Eidolan goddess?"

I nodded and explained my encounters with her, my suspicions of her role in Asileia's madness, and that, perhaps, other Eidolan gods were not all myths.

Nomusa shook her head slowly. "Gods and daemons among us. You can't have anything more incredible to say."

"Just wait."

It was then I told them of how I'd hopefully saved Talan, then turned to face Famine and saw the conflict beneath him, and what I'd done about it. I told them Vusu's words and actions, and how he'd taken his own life with the white-wood knife, and how immediately Famine had disappeared.

Only his words concerning me and Linos as Seeds of Famine did I hold back.

"Just like that, he contained a god," Xaron breathed. "I can't believe his power."

"But why?" Nomusa demanded. "Why would he break apart our city, then sacrifice himself to save it?"

"I know some answers." I had yet to tell them all I'd learned from my readings, but it would have to wait. "And we might discover the rest if we find his honor Seda."

Xaron frowned. "If she's still alive. She might have burned with the Claw."

"I doubt Vusu would have been that shortsighted. No, I bet she's somewhere safe in the Manifest compound, waiting for her master's return."

Before we could continue, the door creaked open. Seeing who it was, all three of us quickly stood. Jaxas — *Despot* Jaxas — stood in the doorway. As we began to bow, he motioned irritably.

"Please, sit down. I've enough of that bowing and scraping from everyone else."

We slowly sat again. I watched him warily. He'd caught me off-guard many times in the course of a day's turning and might hold further surprises still.

Jaxas paced over to stand in front of the fire. For a minute, he did nothing but stare into it. We didn't resume our conversation, too conscious of the potency of our subject. We couldn't discuss Famine before I reported to Jaxas, and I didn't know when that might occur. But then, it was my duty to tell him when I had something to report.

I steeled myself. "Despot Jax— Your Radiance, I mean—"

"Didn't I say enough of that?" His voice was soft, and he didn't turn around, but it somehow made the words more threatening. I swallowed and waited. I had a warden's gift burgeoning inside me, yet this unattuned man could still put the fear of the gods in me.

He suddenly turned. "Xaron. Nomusa. Thank you for your work earlier. Is all well in establishing the Order of Watchers? Have you discussed with Nikias the establishment of living quarters for them in the palace garrison?"

"We have... sir." Her words fell flat as she searched for the proper address.

The Despot's hooded eyes fell on her. "Call me Jaxas if you must call me anything. But that is good. The Watchers will be of utter importance in keeping my rule. I shall call on them soon to discuss their duties." His gaze turned on Xaron. "And you shall pass on my orders to them."

Xaron looked startled. "Me?"

"Who else, but the First Warden to the Despot?" He smiled slightly as Xaron's eyes widened. "You may keep Hilarion's tower, Xaron — but I would discard the robes. They can't have been comfortable."

"You have no idea," my friend muttered. "I mean, thank you, Jaxas. I hope I will — That is, I'll do my best to serve you."

Jaxas nodded absently, his gaze turning to Nomusa. "And you, Nomusa. I may have suspended the powers of the Conclave, but I will still need their bureaucratic expertise in governing the city and state. As my Archon, it will be your obligation to persuade them to perform their duties. Will you help me?"

She accepted her new position with more grace than Xaron had managed. "Thank you, Jaxas. I will do all I can."

Anticipation filled me as Jaxas's gaze turned finally to me. "I will speak further with both of you in a short while. But now, if you would grant me a private moment with Airene."

My friends glanced at me, questions in their eyes, but they swiftly complied.

As the door closed behind them, I wasn't sure what to feel. What could he have to say that he would wish to keep secret from Xaron and Nomusa? Or perhaps, I mused, the privacy was for my sake — to save me from embarrassment.

Jaxas stared at me for a long moment, silhouetted by the firelight. "I mean to make Kelena my new First Verifier."

I blinked rapidly. My throat had gone completely dry. It had been the one position left that I could imagine him giving me. "Very well," was all I could think to say.

"I need you to know, Airene, it's not because I think you incapable. But the last span has shown me Kelena's value. I need her and the connections she possesses. She's hungry to prove herself. Deny her this chance, and I fear I'll lose all she has access to."

"I understand." I did. I couldn't have admitted it before, but this turn of events forced me to stare the truth in the eye: Kelena was a far better Finch than I'd ever been. I felt adrift. What did that mean for the past decade? What had I been striving for?

"But I have another task for you, Airene," he continued. "One I would trust only to you. You must find the way to stop Famine, if one exists."

A laugh escaped me, and Jaxas stared at me in surprise.

"You're well-informed, but not well enough," I told him. "Famine is gone, Jaxas. Vusu made a Sacrifice of himself to lock him away, as was done of old."

The Despot stared at me until I shifted uncomfortably, then turned his gaze out over the city.

"You're sure?" he asked quietly.

"I saw it happen. Though… Vusu said he wouldn't be able to hold him long. I don't know how long that means. The last Sacrifice trapped Famine for a thousand years as far as I know. Perhaps only a little while may give us a year, or a decade."

"Perhaps. I will set you to the watch all the same. But if it is in vain, then I will give you another impossible task beside it." He turned a sudden wry smile on me. "After all, you work miracles, do you not?"

I shrugged uncomfortably. "What is your wish now?"

The smile disappeared as swiftly as it had come. "I wish you to stop an empire, Airene. I wish you to find the way to defeat soldiers who cannot be seen or killed. I wish you to dispense of the Silks before they pour over our walls and end our defense before it's begun. And I wish you to counter the Tefra who command them."

I stared at him. Another impossible task, indeed. "As easily ask for the moons," I muttered.

"Only this. Will you try?"

"Of course." I knew no other answer to give.

He nodded grimly. "Of titles, I know of none to give such a position."

I thought for a moment, then startled at a realization. "Give me none. I don't need any, so long as I have access to where I need to go and the requisite resources. In fact, it's probably better I have no title. Perhaps I can escape the attention of prying eyes."

Jaxas considered me for a moment. "Chaos becomes you," he murmured.

He spared me the need to respond by stepping quickly toward the door. "If your report of the night can wait, I have much other business to attend to. As do you."

"Yes," I said, still somewhat flustered by his enigmatic words. "But I must see my brother first."

"Of course. Ask Synne — she will grant you an escort to the Acadium. And if you feel your brother's accommodations are not adequate, you have my permission to bring him here."

The Despot didn't give me time to thank him before he turned from his solar and departed.

CHAPTER TWENTY-FOUR

REBORN

— Tales of the Desolate, uncensored; 1092 SLP

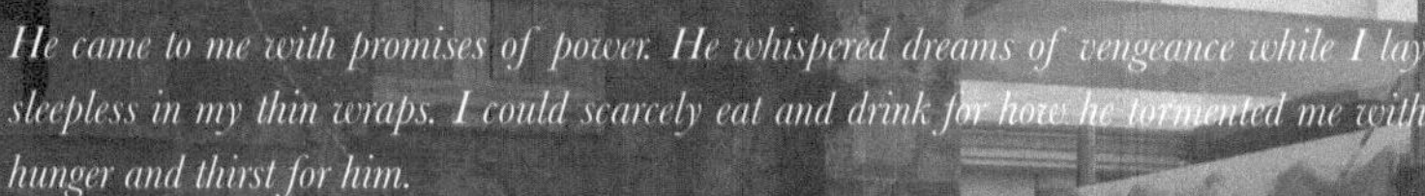

I contemplated my rapid changes in fortunes as I rode alone in a carriage to the Acadium. Before, in Jaxas's solar, I had despaired of ever reaching Linos. Little had I known that, in a few turns, I would have access to a carriage and armored guard at a moment's notice.

It was the least of the things stirring about me. With Xaron and Nomusa about their new duties, I had no one to distract me. I looked outside in an effort to escape my worries, but Jaxas Ascending had not stopped Oedija's degradation; if anything, it had accelerated it. The number of houses I saw with busted shutters and doors hanging off of their hinges made chills run up my skin. The dusk mobs would be out tonight, I was sure, and in greater numbers than before. People crouched along the street, staring up with unbridled resentment at my passing carriage. I let the window drape fall closed again and sat back, wondering what I would do if they charged. They wouldn't dare do so with three guards riding with me. Or so I hoped.

Arrival at the Acadium came as a relief. After a brief pause, the Acadium guards waved us through, and the carriage rolled up the hill onto the campus. I couldn't hear how the guards explained who I was. Refusing a title had seemed a noble thing before. Now I wondered if it was simply impractical. But unless I wished to go crawling back to Jaxas, I'd have to live with my choice.

A short time later, we pulled up in front of the Ward, and I stepped out of the carriage. My ribs were still sore and my skin bruised, but I felt surprisingly hale otherwise. Yet I couldn't help a rueful smile imagining what a sight I looked, with my dark clothes and hair falling just above my shoulders.

Then I thought of whom I went to, and all humor faded.

My step quickened as I entered and found Linos's room, ignoring the clerk who called after me. I found his door hung slightly ajar. Only then did I wonder if danger might not linger here. My fingertips suddenly itched, and I rubbed them on my trousers as I stepped toward the door and eased it open.

Two people waited within, standing over the bed in the center where Linos lay, staring unseeing up.

"Finally she comes," Kyros Brighteyed growled as he turned. "I'd have thought you cared more for your brother, Finch." The Archmaster's remaining hair was tousled and his robes rumpled. From the looks of him, he'd been here all night.

"I do," I replied calmly. I turned my gaze to Eltris, who also stood silently by Linos's bed. "What are you two still doing here?"

Eltris's eyes flashed with an emotion too quick to read. *Anger? Disgust?* I wondered why I even cared anymore.

"Watching," the augur replied at length. "Waiting."

"Something at which you're well-practiced." The sneering words were out of my mouth before I could second-guess them.

Kyros laughed hollowly. "She's finally found her bite, has she? Calm yourself, Finch. Vusumuzi died trying to get to this boy, so we have stood guard in case his pet Seekers come to finish the job. Better to thank us than strike out. It's clear we're all on the same side."

"I wouldn't say that." My gaze stayed on Eltris. "You would have let him sacrifice my brother. You would have let him die."

The Master Augur said nothing, but only returned my stare coolly.

"That's in the past now," Kyros said impatiently. "First Verifier Airene, we have questions for you. First, when did you become attuned to the Pyrthae? And how? I only detected hints of it a span ago when you visited, but that has certainly changed. Did you keep it hidden before?"

Cringing at how brazenly Kyros announced my secret, I quickly closed the door and glanced at Eltris. It wouldn't have surprised me if she'd exposed me simply from spite. "I didn't hide it. I wasn't sure I was a warden when I saw you."

"You weren't sure? Do you mean to say you've only just become attuned?" He snorted. "Impossible! You wrestled this old augur and won!"

"I did," I agreed, hoping I hid the vindictive pleasure warming my chest. "But nevertheless, I'm still fresh to this. Channeling on command still comes with difficulty."

"A rare talent then." There was a new note in the man's tone. Not admiration or respect, exactly, but the hunger of a collector staring at a prized find.

"Or a singular Quintyr sparked her," Eltris said quietly.

Fire built inside me as I stared at the augur. Kyros looked between us, a scowl deepening his face.

"What does that mean?" he demanded. "How would you know which it was?"

Anger seized my tongue. "Are you so sore that I bested you that you would resort to this?" I railed against Eltris. "Are you that upset the pupil so quickly eclipsed the master?"

Her eyes widened. "Fool girl! Did you not wonder why your power had augmented? *It was because you were near him!* He was close to breaking free, and stronger than ever before! Look at your shifts now — see if they have not spread!"

"Who?" Kyros demanded again. "You can't mean—?" His eyes widened. "But that daemon can't attune wardens! Can he?"

My temples throbbed so that I couldn't think straight, couldn't hold the biting words back. "At least I'm not a bitter old woman sacrificing young boys so she doesn't have to risk her own pathetic life!"

I looked away, unable to stand the sight of the crone. Silence fell between us. My chest heaved as I struggled to master myself. I regretted the words as soon as they'd left my mouth, but I couldn't deny them. Every word had been true, as far as I believed.

But no matter how I might wish to, I couldn't afford to drive her away. At length, I looked up to find the augur still staring at me.

"I can't trust you," I said, my voice pitched soft but firm. "Not after what you meant to do. But I need you. Vusu said he couldn't hold Famine for long. When he returns, we need to be ready."

Eltris studied me without blinking, her yellow eyes like a raptor's. Kyros's, meanwhile, blazed with Pyrthaen light as he looked between us. I wished he hadn't heard everything. Yet perhaps it was for the best. We'd need everyone we could muster if we were to survive Famine's return.

"Fine," the augur said shortly. Without another word, she strode past me and out of the door.

I stood completely still until I was sure she was gone. Even then, it was hard to let my fury slip away. I shook my head. What a pair we made, my tutor and me.

The Archmaster stepped toward the door, but hesitated at the entrance. "It is true, then? You were attuned by Famine?"

There seemed little point in denying it now. "Yes. As far as I know."

Kyros laughed like a man before the gallows. "I didn't believe the old augur when she told me he was here in Oedija. Famine, returned to the world. It was the stuff of children's stories! But last night, I felt Vusu approaching the Acadium. And when I moved to stop him, I sensed a vast presence behind him, thwarting my every attempt to defeat the old Bali. I knew it then. I knew the Quintyr had returned to meddle in men's affairs."

"So it appears."

He moved once more for the door, but stopped and said gruffly, "Your brother is still in there. I felt him when I fought Vusu." He lingered a moment longer before nodding and briskly departing.

I watched him go, mute with surprise. Perhaps there was a heart in the irascible warden after all.

Heartened by the Archmaster's words, I moved next to Linos, but stood just out of reach. Too well I remembered what had happened the last time I'd touched him. Though I'd driven away the daemon that had plagued him, still I hesitated. I drew in a breath. I couldn't live in fear of my brother forever.

Slowly, I stepped forward and reached toward him. My finger brushed the skin of his arm.

Nothing.

I smiled in relief. My brother was free of that horror at least. For now. But the joy was fleeting. I raised my hand to smooth the hair from his brow. I wished I could close his staring eyes. I wished I could wash away the violet scars around them. But wishing would gain me nothing. I had to learn more to be able to help him. Even from a woman who would have let Vusu kill both of my brothers.

Did you not wonder why your power had augmented?

Eltris's words in mind, I turned my hands over and peered at my fingertips. Breath caught in my throat. All ten of my fingerprints shifted now, the skin moving like ripples on a pond's surface. I was *shur*, a ten-shift warden, with as much potential for channeling as Xaron.

I dropped my hands and took Linos's hand in my own, clutching it as if it were a line thrown out to a drowning sailor. A thought struck me. I turned his hand over to expose his fingertips.

All five prints on the hand I held shifted.

I flipped his hand back over. "Let's get you out of here," I murmured, hating the tremble in my voice. "I'll keep you safe, Little Lion. Trust your big sister."

Almost, I fooled myself into thinking his eyelid twitched at my words. But, despite what Kyros had said, I knew it was nothing more than my imagination. Linos clung to his body, but just barely. He likely wouldn't wake until I figured out a way to help him.

I sighed and, turning from him, summoned the healers.

———

Once Linos was secured inside the carriage, we made our way back to the Laurel Palace. I tried to ignore the world outside for a few moments of peace. I held Linos's hand for the trip and tried not to listen to the shouting and sounds of struggle interspersed by the creaking of the carriage. My mind lost itself in a sea of vague fears and worries.

I woke from my uneasy rest to the squeaking of the palace gates. Sitting up straight, I waited for the carriage to ascend the long way up the hillside.

But before we had gone far, the carriage rolled to a halt.

If we hadn't been inside Wreath grounds, I might have been worried rather than curious. Just as I was about to poke my head out and see what was the matter, a knock came at the door. I opened it to a laurel guard standing stiffly at attention.

"Lady, there's a man here who says he must deliver a message. He told me to tell you that he bears, ah, 'a chalice of unrequited intoxication'—"

I pushed past the guard before he'd finished and saw him standing just beyond. His hair was ragged and singed, his clothes torn and stiff with dried blood.

It didn't matter. He was here.

He was alive.

Talan flashed me his half-grin as he pulled me gently into his arms.

"Not too gentle," I told him as I squeezed him harder. "My ribs are healed."

"They healed?" He chuckled into my hair. "Ah, Airene. You never cease to amaze me."

I was barely conscious of the guards and driver watching as I held onto him. He reeked of smoke and blood and grime, but I didn't care.

"How did you survive?" I whispered into his chest. "You were so weak. I thought you'd never rise again."

I felt him nod. "Four Silks bore down on me. I was already drained from fighting my way into the Underguild. Dismissing one *ikoz* is difficult. I've never dismissed more. I thought I was dead; I'll admit, I'd given up. I'd done what I'd set out to do. I thought to myself that, as long as I saved her life, that might balance out the scales of my life."

I pulled back and tilted my head back to look into his amber eyes, shimmering with emotion. My eyes burned as well. I opened my mouth to speak, but I couldn't find the right words.

"But then someone came," he continued quietly. "Someone rushed into my being and demanded I rise. You didn't speak with words, but bared the secrets of your life to me. Of a childhood fraught with death and disappointment. Of an unsettled youth searching for something more than an ordinary life could offer. Of the loneliness you never dared show to anyone lest they think you weak."

My knees felt as if they couldn't support me any longer. "I showed you all that?" I asked faintly.

"And more. You left nothing of yourself hidden. Every part of your being, Airene, wished me to rise again." The smile crept onto his lips again. "So I must reveal my little secret in recompense. I never could refuse you."

Fire filled my body, a very different kind than I'd experienced recently. For the moment, I didn't care that the world teetered on the balance. All I wanted was for this moment to go on.

I leaned up and kissed him.

Our lips lingered on each other's. Underneath the sweat and stench of battle, something earthy and wholesome and entirely of him filled my lungs. I didn't want to stop breathing him in.

He pulled away first, clearing his throat lightly as he glanced behind me. A flush crept up my neck as I followed his glance. The driver was busy pretending not to notice, but all three of the guards were openly grinning and watching.

"I'll find you later," he offered. "For a walk," he added pointedly as the guards began to snicker.

"I'd love that." My smile was beginning to make my cheeks ache.

How I found the strength to turn from him and enter back inside the carriage, I didn't know. As the driver cracked the reins and the mules began to pull us away, I watched out the window until Talan disappeared around the hill's bend.

———

The rest of the day passed in a blur of activity. Arriving with Linos, I tracked down Nikias, settled my brother into a room, and secured proper care for him. The steward irritably reminded me that there were guards injured from the foray into the Manifest, but I didn't stop pestering him until he promised he would send a healer by as soon as one was available.

By the time I returned to the room I'd taken as my own, I found a message waiting for me.

Meet me at the Silvencrest. Eighth turn. I'll be waiting.

I marveled at Talan's quick sleuthing in discovering my quarters even as I wondered at the location of our rendezvous. The Silvencrest on the Conclave grounds was where the largest wave on the Oedijan coast crashed into a breakwater on evenings when the three moons were aligned in the sky. By some fortune, it seemed such an event was happening tonight. But that was the least thing that excited me. I smiled to myself, but knew there wasn't time to indulge in fantasies at the moment.

Quickly heading to the dining hall, I found Nomusa and Xaron there. As I ate a hasty meal, I divulged all I could of the afternoon's events.

"That rogue," Xaron groaned. "I always thought that whole thing between you two would just blow over. You just kissed him on the cheek, surely?"

"That's not how I remember it." I winked at him.

Xaron received his own share of teasing when Isidora came up behind him and wrapped him a hug. Nomusa and I grinned at each other.

But having finished the meal, I was eager to be away. Just before I could escape, Nomusa stood and wrapped me in an embrace. "I'm glad you both can find some happiness amid all this," she said, the smile fading from her expression. "Don't be your usual self and feel guilty about it."

"I hadn't until you said something. But now…"

She snorted and turned me toward the door. "Just go."

I took her advice and pushed worry from my mind as I headed for the exit. Avvad marched on Oedija. People starved in the streets. Famine lurked somewhere out of sight, restrained for the moment by Vusu's fading strength. But, I told myself, I couldn't always delay my happiness for the world's problems. Jaxas had charged me with two impossible tasks. One night away wouldn't harm my prospects of accomplishing them.

As my walk went on, passing down the hill of the Laurel Palace to the bridge across to the Conclave, my rationalizations grew thinner. Yet I clung resolutely to them. *One night of rest,* I begged myself. *One night with Talan.* Yet I couldn't dislodge the feeling. Worry had planted a seed in me and taken root. And though I struggled against it, it pressed on my mind, growing and stretching and making my head ache.

As the pain spiked, I suddenly realized this wasn't just a guilty conscience. *Something* had started to run rampant through my mind, beyond my control. My head felt heavy and full as a melon. My vision fuzzed. I stumbled forward a few steps, then lost my balance, scraping my hands as I fell to the rough stones of the bridge. Wild thoughts raced through my head. Had I channeled too much quintessence? It felt as if the agony couldn't possibly grow. My senses faded before it. Panic rose in my chest, and my breaths came quick and shallow. I thought I would faint.

My mind split open.

Colors and lights flashed around me. I spun around and around, disoriented. Only as my turning slowed did I see that I floated apart from my body.

I was now in a different Oedija.

I tried gathering my wits as I looked wildly around. The Pyrthae appeared the same desert as it had before; only now, it had gained a new feature. In the center of it, a huge, black chasm yawned open, leaking motes of light and shifting waves of iridescent colors. I stared at it with dread and a slow understanding. The worry had not left my mind, but swelled further by the second. It grew and grew until it became a drive I'd neglected, a desire I'd never fulfilled, a thirst I'd never slaked. To my horror, I found myself drifting closer to the pit, the hunger that roared inside me directing all of its attention toward it, as if I might be satiated by whatever lay within. A horrible suspicion seized me. I knew what this was.

Then he emerged.

His head came into view first, as large as a dozen palaces stacked on top of one another. His black, pitted eye seemed to see everything and nothing at once. His maw, gaping impossibly wide, showed long, sharp teeth nearly as dark as his eyes. His body came slithering out after, covered in dark, great scales oscillating between the deep purple of thunderclouds and the scarlet of blood. Two pairs of powerful legs were attached to the lithe, snake-like body, bowed like a lizard's and ending in wickedly curved claws. His long form stretched nearly the length of the ruined Oedija below as his tail emerged, sparking with lightning and fire.

The dragon's sinuous body curled and undulated across the sky. From his dance, Famine seemed to enjoy his newfound freedom. I drifted ever closer, unable to help myself. The hunger had wholly seized me. I felt nothing but the desire to lose myself in the daemon god. To be consumed.

Take me! I flung toward the dragon. *Come take me! I offer myself to you!*

He didn't even turn his head toward me, but froze. Like a predator suddenly smelling prey, Famine jerked his head to the side and stared east.

I didn't care what he looked at. *Here!* I thought desperately, then launched myself up at him.

But the Quintyr had his sights set on something greater. His yearning suddenly poured out from him so that I nearly drowned in it. His serpentine body writhed and began to slither through the air with impossible speed. I stared in despair after him as he faded into the distance, finally drifting to a halt. The hunger inside me ached, then suddenly abated.

With it returned reason and horror. Only with the desire's release did I understand what I'd witnessed. I would have collapsed had I been in the real world.

Vusu had already failed. Famine had returned. And there was no one to save us from him now.

No one, if Vusu was to be believed, but Linos and me.

I drifted through the desolate, mirrored world, staring after the daemon god. For several long moments, I could do nothing but watch, expecting at any moment for him to rush back and seize me in his jaws. But he was gone. For now, there was no sign of his return.

I drifted back down to myself. Though the bridge was broken in this version of Oedija, I knew my body waited just below. And if the end of the world had come, I couldn't lie in the middle of the bridge and wait for it. For what little good it would do, I had work to attend to.

And no time for even a night of reprieve.

I descended into my bruised body and, as pain washed over me afresh, rose shakily to my feet. I almost turned toward the Conclave grounds and Talan waiting at the Silvencrest. But I imagined the disappointment on his face when I told him all that could not be. And in this moment, I couldn't bear it.

Despair sapping my strength, I turned and walked heavily back the way I had come.

Eazal stared at the endless expanse laid out before him.

Perched atop a dune, the desert stretched for miles in every direction. The world had been leeched of color. Gray dominated the landscape, the strange sands of the Wumofu seeming the ashes from a great conflagration that had long ago swept over the land. Nothing but twisted trees survived here now. Neither men nor spirits walked this place, the sand and air undisturbed by the passage of even the wind.

His were the only footprints on the still dunes as he pushed ever further into the wasteland's heart.

As if sensing his mood, Azhi spoke into his mind. *I am with you. Do not fear. I have walked this path before, long ago. Would you like me to tell you of it?*

Eazal bowed his head. Being comforted by a child — was this what he'd come to? "I'm fine, lad," he responded aloud. "But I would hear that tale still. I should know what is to come."

Despite his words, as the boy spirit began to speak and Eazal continued his long walk, he barely listened. The loneliness of the desert pressed in around him, no matter his constant companion. Azhi, the spirit who had first brought Valem's curse of magic to him, had been with him ever since his hasty departure from Oedija. When he'd failed the Valemish and was most at risk, the boy had appeared to him through a whisper finch and led him safely from their grasp. And after, when he'd begun wandering as he had in the years before his return to Oedija, Azhi appeared again, this time to give him purpose. Eazal had listened, though he hadn't believed him. The words the boy had spoken were impossible. Taozu the Corrupted

— or Famine, as Oedija knew the God of Hunger — was not only real, but reborn. Even coming from a spirit, it was too far beyond his experience to comprehend. What did he know of gods and the higher and lower realms? He'd failed to retain the religion of his ancestors. How could he now believe the gods not only existed, but that one had awoken to bring chaos and ruin to the world?

But Azhi hadn't given up. How he'd convinced him in the end, Eazal couldn't explain. He'd ignored the boy's first urgent warnings, dwelling on his own losses. His wife and daughter had slipped fully from his grasp. It had been one thing to be pursued by the Finch girl, Airene, and her companions. It was another to stand against the whole of the Valemish. Despair had made the days of walking meld into one another, numbing him to any sense of purpose.

Yet all the while, Azhi stayed by him. At night, he watched over him while he slept, and had saved Eazal's life from beasts and highwaymen by waking him with a sharp peck. Eazal had come to trust the boy, and with trust came a listening ear.

Slowly, the emptiness of his life filled with the spirit's unwavering resolve, and he'd taken Azhi's task as his own.

Only when he'd accepted the call had Azhi given him the visions. He showed him the things he'd seen of Taozu's past comings: the great rent in the earth south of Avvad's provinces; the lake that had once been filled with blood in the Bali highlands; the vast, wasted empire of the Wumofu Desert. All, Azhi had claimed, had the Corrupted to thank for their destruction. And the same ancient spirit who would inevitably claim the whole of the world — unless something was done to stop him.

Then he'd told Eazal what he meant to do, and how he needed Eazal to do it.

And so Eazal had traveled northeast to the far reaches of the Four Realms, where the Qao Fu cavern-cities marked the edge of civilization. Then they'd pushed past even that boundary, out into the Wumofu Desert, despite all the warnings they'd received. *Only the Yusishu could walk the path,* they'd told him, *before the last went and never returned.* Eazal had his own misgivings looking at the forbidding desert. But Azhi had told him not to fear. He'd walked this path before and would lead Eazal true. Trusting him as he'd trusted him many times before on their sojourn, Eazal had packed water and supplies for five days, then walked into the desert with only the spirit to guide him through it.

All was calm and quiet around him as he walked. But Azhi spoke of a different time in his mind. *The wind never ceased,* he was saying. *Only by wearing veils woven by a lost art could one travel the desert. An endless storm, deep at the heart of the old empire, drove those gales howling through the rest of the Wumofu.*

Eazal listened as he walked without replying. The spirit's voice had grown stronger as they continued their journey. When they'd reached the Qao Fu caverns, he had spoken to Eazal directly for the first time rather than through the whisper finch. Why he could suddenly speak into his mind, the boy didn't have an answer. Yet they had been through much together. To doubt him now would be folly. He had to trust that the spirit would bring him through this task alive, as he had done through the rest of this journey.

This hidden road was called the Ancestor's Path in those times, Azhi was saying. *The spirits of our dead kin would sing the path to the one who walked it, if they had ears to hear. I kept my mind open to their calls for days as I walked, for to shut out the ancestors would be to lose your way, and to become lost meant certain death.*

Azhi went quiet for a moment. Eazal wished he had found another point in his tale to cease speaking. The reminder of death was the last thing he needed in this forsaken place. He sighed and rolled his aching shoulders. He was far too old to be plodding up dune after dune, taking two steps where one would have served on firmer ground. He wondered what he was even doing here, traveling this desolation. Why had he let the boy convince him this was necessary?

Look, the boy said suddenly. *Look to the horizon ahead, and tell me what you see.*

Eazal obliged, though without interest. As he'd expected, he saw nothing. The air was hazy with heat. Mirages were commonplace; he'd seen enough false watering holes now to know that much. Perhaps even a spirit's eyes could be fooled.

He began to tell Azhi as much when the words died on his lips. At the top of his vision, something projected from the blue sky. It was faint with haze, but it didn't disappear as Eazal blinked. The mirages had always been near the desert floor where the heat's movement was greatest. And this was no watering hole. It looked like a multitude of pale fingers scratching against the sky.

"What is that?" he asked, his dry tongue moving thickly around his mouth.

Our destination. The place where we will recover what was lost long ago. And, by it, we will seal Famine away once more.

———

It took all the rest of that day to reach it. Eazal had watched with unceasing awe as what looked like an impossibly gargantuan tree emerged from the sky. Its bark was gray, though Azhi claimed it had once been white as fresh-fallen snow.

My ancestors bound Famine in this place. For a thousand years, the one named the Yusishu would walk the Ancestor's Path to here, the Chains, and sacrifice themselves in order for him to remain bound. The Yusishu were lauded and praised, so much so that it was an honor every child dreamed of attaining themselves. Children cannot comprehend the end of their lives. They only saw the glory in it, the offerings left to them before their journey, and the statues carved of them afterward. They didn't understand what the sacrifice truly meant.

Eazal listened, thinking it strange that the boy spoke as if he were not himself a child. But then again, the spirit had no doubt existed for years. He was likely older than Eazal, though he'd not said so one way or another. The way he spoke of events in a distant past betrayed his age. By now, Azhi was much less a child than Eazal himself, no matter the youthfulness of the voice in his head.

Finally, their long walk came to an end. Reaching the base of the Chains, Eazal stared at it. The trunk was as thick around as the Ten-Tiered Bazaar, the greatest of Oedija's markets. Its bark, if it were truly bark, was as smooth as stone and as textureless as still water. For some reason, Eazal was loathe to come nearer to it. Something about the structure seemed strange and malevolent. This was as much a product of magic as anything he'd seen. Surely, only the gods themselves could grow such a tree.

Suddenly, a wind whipped up from the ground next to him, swirling the sand into a small squall. Eazal flinched and stepped away. There'd been no wind in all the desert; why would a gust rise now? The wind didn't die away, but seemed to lazily float through the air, resolving into a strangely human form. Lips formed of gray sand smiled at Eazal. A chill ran down his spine as he stared at the desert spirit.

"Hello, Eazal," a familiar boy's voice said. It had a strange echo to it, but Eazal couldn't mistake its owner.

"Azhi?"

The figure twisted his sand-shaped head to look at the great tree. "Our worlds are closer here. The Chains anchors them together. Here, I can almost be as I was in life." The spirit looked back to him with swirling gray eyes. "I admit, sometimes, I miss it."

Eazal couldn't explain the fear that stirred in his stomach. He wished they could be away from this strange tree. "This place makes me uneasy. Where is this thing we must retrieve?"

Azhi didn't respond for a long moment. Then he turned and floated over the gray to the base of the mammoth tree. "It is somewhere here, buried under the sands. But if the storm died after Famine departed, it shouldn't be buried deep. Stand back and cover your eyes."

Eazal obeyed, putting both hands over his face. A moment later, sediment whipped against him, the force of it stinging the exposed skin on the back of his hands.

"Here," Azhi said softly. "Come see it."

He dropped his hands and reluctantly walked up to stand next to the sand spirit. At the bottom of a small pit, the smooth, white shaft of a scepter was exposed. It looked like the femur of a long-dead creature. Though it didn't appear notable to his eyes, it was apparently the object of their quest.

Still, Eazal hesitated to reach for it. "That is the Binding Ruyi?"

"Yes. The scepter that once kept Famine sealed away for a millennium, and may do so once again. Will you take it, Eazal? Will you do what I, a spirit with no mortal hands, cannot? Will you help stop Taozu from consuming the rest of the world?"

Eazal sighed out heavily. He'd trusted Azhi this far. No matter his discomfort, he had to see this through. And why else had he come here? He hadn't walked a thousand miles to turn aside from his duty.

Or from his redemption.

"I'll do what I can," he spoke, almost to himself.

He eased his aching body down into the pit, sliding along it and barely avoiding stepping on the scepter at the bottom. Clinging to the eroding walls around him, he reached out and gripped the scepter, then pulled. It came free easily, as if the sand wished to be rid of it. Eazal lifted it before his eyes. The haft was smooth, and all of it was as white as bone. The end curved into the head of a threatening snake, its mouth open wide to strike, four long fangs protruding forth. As eerie as it had seemed above, it now seemed a small, delicate thing for such a large task. Could this elegant scepter possibly do what Azhi claimed?

"I have it," he said. "I'm bringing it back out."

He turned back to climb out of the pit. He didn't see Azhi standing above and wondered where he'd gone as he studied his escape. The walls eroded before his touch, but the pit wasn't very deep. If he scrambled quickly, he could ascend it. He set his exhausted limbs to the task, taking care not to crush the scepter as he climbed.

It struck his mind, quick and deadly as a viper.

Agony as he'd never known burst through him. For a moment, he lost hold of his senses. He couldn't tell if he screamed or if his limbs writhed. All his mind was filled with it. Desperately, he sought an end, but wave after wave washed over him.

Why? he cried out. *Why must I suffer more?*

As abruptly as it had come, the pain eased. Eazal slowly came back to his senses. But something felt wrong. Though he could feel the rough touch of the sand against his face, the breath rattling in his lungs, the exhaustion in his limbs, something felt broken.

For no matter how he commanded his body, he couldn't even twitch his eyelid.

Then his body moved of its own power, rising onto one elbow. "This body is heavier than I would have thought," Eazal's own lips muttered as he awkwardly pulled at the sand. His body moved as if for the first time. As if it had forgotten how.

The truth struck him as hard and sudden as the pain had. He tried to scream, but he couldn't form the words. He felt the muscles of his face tighten, but it wasn't his words that came out.

"I am sorry," his mouth spoke. He felt the other presence move his tongue even as he heard the words. "I did not wish to do this, Eazal. You must believe me. But time is too short to hesitate."

Every part of him roared against this intrusion. His own body, taken and controlled against his will! Like an animal in a cage, he battered what was left of himself against the invisible walls that penned him in— or tried to. But as he sought his boundaries, he found he couldn't understand his prison. There seemed nothing binding him, yet no way free. His anger melded into horror as he ceased to struggle.

A daemon possessed him. Azhi, whose purpose he had taken as his own, whom he'd trusted with his life, had seized his body.

Eazal's lips again spoke unbidden words. "Once, long ago, another spirit sought to do to me what I have done to you. She failed, and in doing so, allowed Famine to break free." His head bowed forward against the sand. "No. That is denying my part in it. I let her whispers of glory manipulate me into believing I was something I knew I was not. I let myself believe that I had a greater part to play in the world, one only I could perform. In a way, she was right. I did have a part to play, great and terrible. For it was I who let Famine loose. And in doing so, it was I who doomed the Lower and Higher Planes both.

"So it must be I who rectifies this, Eazal. And to do so, I must have a body. I hope you will come to understand. I won't harm you, nor your body, as much as I can prevent it. And when the task is complete, I will give it back to you so that you may live out your days in peace. Trust me as you have trusted me this whole journey. I did not lie when I spoke of the importance of this task. The danger to both of our worlds is the same. Taozu, Famine — he has come again, and will consume everything if he is not stopped. I ask no more sacrifice of you than I have given myself."

Eazal had ceased to struggle. It was futile. The daemon had an iron hold on him now. He could do nothing but listen to the boy's lies, trapped in his own flesh.

"I can feel him, Eazal. Can you? He has broken free of the Yusishu who yoked him. Vusumuzi, a man of more strength than I have ever seen before, has finally succumbed to his struggle. And in doing so, he has fed the Dragon enough so that he can once again hunt. His presence cuts across the Higher Plane as he seeks worthy prey. It will not be long before he grows powerful enough to break free into your world. And when he does, I fear it will be for the final time."

Eazal's arm raised the Binding Ruyi before his eyes. His gaze traveled up its length. "We must find the Corrupted before that happens," Azhi spoke through him softly. "We must seal him away, forever if we can. I hope we will do it together, Eazal."

Eazal didn't try to reply. If he was trapped, he wouldn't assuage the daemon's conscience, if one could exist in such a creature. He tucked himself small into the dark corners of his body where he remained. He'd watch and wait for his moment.

Then he'd take back what was his, no matter the cost.

Azhi made him sigh. "Brace yourself, my friend. I have shown you much. But now you will see all."

Eazal had channeled before, when Valem's curse first manifested in him. He had felt the power of the Molten God run through his veins to burn at the single toe that showed his mark. But what he had felt then was but a fraction of the power that filled him now. As energy carved its way into him, he thought he would burn away before it.

Azhi raised Eazal's arm with the scepter in it, then cut it sharply down in front of him. A tear appeared in the air before them. Eazal stared at it, numb with fear, wondering at what he witnessed.

The daemon hauled his body up, reaching for the tear in the world. It swirled with shifting colors and light like a pool formed of pyrkin. He extended Eazal's hand toward it.

It was too much. Eazal threw himself at his cage again, begging Azhi not to touch it. He knew such magic must destroy him.

As his finger brushed the substance of the other realm, it seized him. Eazal felt himself pull away, then leave the world behind.

REQUIEM OF SILENCE

THE FAMINE CYCLE
BOOK III

PROLOGUE

Secrets have governed my life. As surely as the tides of fate, my hunt for them has molded me, become my identity. Their allure drove me into a long-dead profession, and their capriciousness haunted me with the tragedies of my brothers. The pursuit of them has endangered my life more times than I can count.

I have always believed in the power of secrets. But I could never have known they would hold the key to caging a god.

Famine is real. It took me a long time to accept what that means. But now I must.

He will consume my world. I alone stand in his way.

Why me? — the self-pitying question has occurred to me many times during this ruinous journey. *Why must I bear this burden?* I have mulled over the matter during many sleepless nights, listening to the monsoon rains patter on the windows of the Laurel Palace.

There are a few answers. In part, influences beyond my control put me here. In part, my own actions and mistakes were responsible.

But there is no doubt that it is true, that I must be the one to stop the daemon god. If only for the secrets I alone understand.

The true power in secrets has always been in how they are wielded. I must use mine perfectly if I am to succeed.

I will be the Sacrifice.

This dragon, this daemon god — he has plagued us for too long. I will end the cycle if I can. But even if all I can do is delay his return, it will be enough.

Famine must be stopped. No matter the cost. No matter the sacrifice I must make.

Even if there is little of the world left to save.

CHAPTER ONE

ASSASSIN

I drifted into the Pyrthae.

If anything could have focused my mind, it was the Council's discussion playing out in high drama before me. Tempers had long since flown out the window. Kyros had bellowed his piece and stood in the corner of Jaxas's solar, stewing and staring over the cityscape, though the view was obscured by rain and smoke. Feiyan looked at each of us, a small smile turning her lips even now, waiting for her moment to claw still more power to herself. Jaxas, wan with dark circles under his eyes, and wearing a green crown that seemed to weigh as heavily as gold, leaned onto the table and stared at his steepled hands, as if hoping to find answers between them.

I blinked away my double-vision of the city and sat up in my chair. Nomusa glanced at me from where she sat at Jaxas's left, and Xaron's brow creased with concern as he watched me from across the round table.

I gave a small shake of my head. My problems could wait. These were proceedings I wouldn't interrupt if I could help it.

"And the casualties were high," Kelena was saying. "Scores died, perhaps hundreds."

"How many were guards?" asked Feiyan, smug as a fed cat.

Kelena's jaw worked silently for a moment. I could guess what she was thinking. Being an honor herself, she was keenly aware of how little the loss of her people's lives mattered to the First Consul.

"Three," she said at last.

Feiyan smiled and leaned back. "Well, that's more than a fair trade, wouldn't you say? Three lives for a hundred traitors dead."

Silence filled Jaxas's solar. I stared around the room, hoping someone would speak out. Nomusa, the new Archon. Xaron, the First Warden. Isidora, the First Watcher, leader of the new division of battle wardens under Jaxas's command. Kyros, of course, remained the Archmaster. Kelena was now the sole First Verifier. Even Shaka-Heir Komo, though not an official part of the Council, had the right to speak, for he and his people were critical allies of Oedija.

And then there was Feiyan. The sly minx had worked her way into Jaxas's good graces to become his First Consul, his closest advisor and second-in-command. Only Jaxas, the Despot of Oedija and sole ruler of the nation, possessed more power.

All present had titles, had the right to make their opinions heard. All except for me, as Feiyan reminded me at every meeting.

Two spans before, it had seemed reasonable, even noble, to refuse a formal position from Jaxas. Then, I'd been sick of failing my duties as a First Verifier. I'd thought I could best oppose Famine by having no distractions and operating from the shadows. A good part of me still believed that. But in these Council meetings, though Jaxas continued to invite me, my words carried no more weight than a finch's chirp.

At times like these, I sorely regretted that decision.

The Manifest Massacre, people were already calling it. So many dead in a riot that had emerged from nowhere and accomplished nothing. It had begun with a simple gathering. Then, as city guards flooded the scene, they fanned the sparks into flame. Even an angry mob stood little chance against trained and armed men.

For all the titles at this Council, none here knew how to deal with the issue before them. I couldn't remain silent any longer.

I felt dizzy from my 'Thae-drift, yet still, I stood. "Jaxas, if I may speak."

His hollowed eyes found mine. "Yes, Airene. Of course."

I looked around the room. "We all know what's coming. Who's at our doorstep. The reports have the Avvadin vanguard arriving within the span, with the rest of the armies following a span after. We cannot still be waging war on another front when they arrive."

"Are we at war with the Manifest?" Feiyan asked with a small smile. "I believe we just slaughtered their followers, or so the people say."

"But that's just it. The city guard didn't just kill Seekers; they killed our own citizens. The very people we need to support Oedija if we're to come through this."

"The very people who now support the Manifest!" Kyros broke in. "They're traitors! Unquestionably traitors!"

I clenched my jaw and held my tongue. There was no winning a shouting match with the Archmaster.

Jaxas turned from Kyros to me. "I believe a proposal was forthcoming."

The rest of the Council looked back to me as well, their expressions a mix of apprehension, scorn, and hope. I wondered which was predominant, if my idea was doomed to flounder from the start.

"Yes," I said, "there is. I propose we strike at the heart of the Manifest. If we gut their leadership, we can unravel them from within."

"Assassination." Feiyan's lips curled. "We've discussed and dismissed this before. We have no assassins, nor can we spare any Watchers to pretend to be one. Where, then, would this killer come from?"

I took a breath, wondering if I'd really thought this plan through, if it didn't spawn from the same madness that tightened its grip on me each day. Nomusa and Xaron stared at me, horror quickly settling in.

Unwilling to meet their eyes, I looked at Jaxas. "I believe I have someone, Your Radiance. If I have your permission to proceed, I will inform them of it."

Jaxas's dark eyes had become as hard as flint. The Council fell silent as he considered my words, though Xaron looked as if he might burst forth at any moment.

"Yes," the Despot said at length. "You have my permission. When will it be done?"

I pushed down my fear long enough to speak. "Tomorrow night."

———

When the Council session broke shortly after, Nomusa and Xaron pulled me aside in the hallway outside Jaxas's solar. Isidora lingered just out of earshot as she waited for Xaron, their romance somehow continuing to flourish even as the world came to an end.

"You can't mean what I think you did," Xaron muttered.

"I did."

"You'd better be planning to send Talan." Nomusa looked me up and down. "Because *you* would be dead at the entrance."

I chose to play it coy. "Maybe."

Neither of them were fooled. Xaron shook his head. "Aire, I know

Avvad is almost here, and the Manifest Massacre just happened at the worst of times. I know you feel Famine feasting and growing more powerful by the day. But this... this is throwing your life away."

"It's not, Xaron. It's doing what must be done." I leaned in closer. "Ariston the Dishonored holds information, information I need. Vusu told me to find his honor, Seda, to understand all he's done, and Ariston has Seda. Go to him, and I can finally reach her."

Nomusa straightened. "You can't be sure she's in the Brinecoast compound. Ariston might be, but he may keep Seda somewhere else entirely."

"But I do know. I saw her there."

They shared a look. I knew what they were thinking even before they spoke.

"'Thae-drifting again?" Xaron asked quietly. "Airene, you shouldn't. You've not even been a warden for a season."

"And yet I'm doing things you've never attempted."

Nomusa seized my arm. "Because you're reckless!" she hissed. "Don't do this, Airene. Please!"

I almost gave in. Seeing their looks, the desperate love in them, I almost said the words they wanted so badly to hear. Instead, I lowered my head and spoke to the floor.

"I have to. Or Famine wins."

The hallway fell silent when the door to Jaxas's solar opened, revealing Feiyan. Her violet robes lined with silver swished as she strode toward us.

"So here's our little assassin. Trying to talk her out of it? I wouldn't bother." She reached out and put a hand to my cheek. I flinched from her clammy touch, but just managed not to draw away.

"You always were a finch flying too close to the sun," she cooed softly. "Always destined to destroy yourself."

I acted without thinking. My locus opened; the power of the Pyrthae came within reach.

I channeled.

Feiyan yelped and withdrew her hand, staring at it. The skin on it had reddened as if burned. When she looked up, her smile was gone.

Only then did I realize the significance of what I'd done. It was more than that I'd used radiance without channeling it through the shifts on my fingertips and toes, though that was extraordinary enough. Feiyan was the First Consul now. She could order me killed if she wanted to. I didn't think Jaxas would allow it, but what if he didn't find out in time?

Still, as Nomusa had noted, I'd always been reckless. Instead of apologizing, I pasted on a smile of my own. "I almost hope this is goodbye."

"It will be, if you dare to use magic against me again." Feiyan swept down the stairs without a backwards glance.

Xaron and Nomusa stared at me. "Did you just—?" Xaron started.

"Yes. I did." I closed my locus and felt weariness seep into my bones.

Nomusa shook her head. "Airene, I love you; you know I do. Which is why you should listen when I say you're not well."

"No one is well. Our city is about to be under siege."

"But not everyone is losing their minds."

I looked her squarely in the eyes, a touch of my temper returning. "I'm not mad, Nomu. Not yet. Believe it or not, but I've thought this through. It's the only way I can get what we need. The only way to help Oedija."

Jaxas's door opened again, but this time, it was the Despot himself who stepped out. He walked with renewed vigor these days, ever since he'd overthrown the Conclave and seized power exclusively for the Laurel Palace. Though all the cares of the realm weighed on his thin shoulders, though the circles under his eyes darkened with each passing night, he'd never seemed so full of life. As if this were what he'd been born to do.

I wished I felt half as prepared for my tasks.

He nodded to us, and we gave deep bows in return. I wondered if we ought to kneel, as had been the custom of old, but Jaxas — or, more to the point, Nikias — hadn't yet demanded it.

The Despot's gaze found and held me. "Airene. Do you still mean to do this?"

I hesitated, but there was little point in denying it. He knew whom I meant to be the assassin. "I must."

His eyes flickered to my friends. "And will anyone accompany you?"

"No." I said it firmly before either of my friends could speak up.

"We'll see about that," Xaron amended with a rebellious look.

"No, First Warden Xaron; I agree with her. This is not your task. I need you for the war to come." The Despot looked back at me. "Airene walks a different path."

I looked away, unable to meet his gaze. If anyone knew the road I traveled now, it was Jaxas.

"But don't go alone," he continued. "Find that Guilder friend of yours — Talan Wraithsbane. From what I have heard, he sounds like the right man for the job."

I winced. "He is." *Or was.* I wondered if he would be now, but kept my expression blank. Xaron and Nomusa didn't bother hiding their doubts.

If Jaxas noticed, he didn't show it. "Then it's settled. Eleven blessings, Airene. Our hopes go with you."

With that, the Despot and his ever-present shadow of Nikias walked past us, the steward with a lingering skeptical look.

Nomusa waited until they were out of earshot before speaking. "The Manifest aren't supposed to be your concern, Airene. Not even Oedija can be, no matter what Jaxas says."

"You're a Seed of Famine, right?" Xaron's eyes darted around to make sure no one but Isidora was near enough to overhear, though the words would be gibberish to most. "Just you and Linos. You two are the only ones who can stop that daemon god. And at the moment, I don't think your brother is up to the task."

"Not stop him," I said softly. "Repress him. And only for a little while."

They exchanged glances. All of us knew what that meant for me.

"Still" — Nomusa's voice trembled, then steadied — "still, you cannot throw your life away on some pyr hunt. We'll sort out the Manifest another way."

I shook my head. "It's not about that. I need Seda, remember? She's my key to defeating Famine." Or so I hoped. Part of me wondered if I went down this road just to delay the inevitable. If this was, as Nomusa put it, a pyr hunt.

She sighed. "Fine. But at least do as Jaxas asked and bring Talan."

A bitter laugh escaped me. "I doubt he'll want to go."

"Try. He might surprise you."

Xaron snorted. "I wouldn't go that far. But even if he's an ass, he's loyal and competent."

I looked down the staircase, hiding the emotions I couldn't repress. "Even after the Silvencrest?"

An awkward silence fell, punctuated by the bustling steps of honors hurrying past.

Nomusa's answer came in a murmur. "It was a panicked decision. And you've been busy since, understandably so. He can't expect you to make time for dalliances."

"Especially when even *you* haven't," Xaron said with a sly look.

"Not now, Xaron," she snapped. "Airene, he's a grown man. He'll understand if you just go talk to him."

"Maybe," I hedged. "Maybe not."

Either way, I had little choice. Without Talan, this excursion stood an even scanter chance of success, and there wasn't much hope for it to begin with.

But, despite my wishes otherwise, I didn't know that the Talan I needed was still with us.

CHAPTER TWO

BLOOD AND WINE

"Above all else, two appetites infect our men: one for spilling blood, and the second for overflowing wine."

- Father Tarik, a priest of Valem; date unknown

I fell to brooding as I left through the northern Laurel gate and traveled through Sandglass. I'd had brief contact with Talan since that day I'd left him at the Silvencrest two spans before, the same evening as Famine's return from wherever Vusu had briefly imprisoned him. Only one note had found me — a few lines devoid of affection telling where I could find him, ending with a barb: *In case you have time for me.*

I hadn't had the stomach to visit.

With an effort, I pushed the gloomy thoughts from my mind and focused on my surroundings. Oedija was suffering a calm after the storm for the moment, but danger still abounded. The massacre at Brinecoast had come as a shock, but I doubted it would tamp down the violence permanently. Too much fear and anger filled the air. Death was on the horizon, and Avvad's armies brought it ever closer.

But though vagrants lurked in most of the alleys I passed, their eyes glimmering as they watched me, none tried to assault me. Perhaps it was the bald confidence with which I walked, even if half of that confidence was faked. I could channel well for my limited experience, but even wardens were vulnerable to knives and arrows.

The place I sought was close to the border along Bazaar. Muttering

Talan's directions to myself under my breath, I strolled along the street until I found it. A cellar door to a butcher shop, tucked just inside a shadowed alcove. No one lingered nearby, and I wondered if that was coincidence or if knowledge of its inhabitants kept people away.

Shrugging off my fear, I approached the door and, finding it unlatched, hauled it open. The stench of rotting flesh wafted up from the dark entrance, and I gagged, swallowing back bile as it hit the back of my throat. Bitterly, I wondered if Talan pointed me to this entrance for petty revenge as I climbed down into the reeking cellar, closing the hatch behind me.

The darkness became nearly complete, and my heart hammered in my chest. I hadn't brought a pyr lamp, yet I was loath to channel my own light. Even here, at the beginning of what should be an abandoned tunnel, I didn't want to risk someone finding me. But it was the least of the risks I'd taken lately.

Opening my locus, a pleasant heat swelled in my belly and spread throughout my body. Holding up a hand, I allowed a sliver of the energy to flare onto my fingertips. I held the potential for an inferno inside me, and part of me ached to release it, but I pushed the wild desire down and pressed on through the cellar.

After some searching, I found a rotting animal skin that hid a damp tunnel, moisture from the monsoons finding their way into it. Each splashing footfall echoed down the path. There'd be no disguising my approach.

But as I exited the tunnel into a wider cavern, no one appeared. I brightened my light and looked around the chamber. Its walls were covered in mud, but I glimpsed underneath the muck faded etchings, masterful works lost to time. This wasn't just some smuggler's den; this had once been an important building, either to my ancestors or those of the honors. *We're always looking to the Pyrthae and sky above for great things, and forget the hidden wonders lying below,* Talan had once said to me. The truth was spread out before me.

I walked across the chamber to a broad entrance that led to a larger corridor, this one immune from the damp. There, I paused. The glow of pyrkin lay ahead, escaping from a small door along the side of the tunnel. I extinguished my light and crept forward. I couldn't yet soften my footsteps like Xaron, but I'd had enough practice sneaking around in my Finching days that my approach was nearly silent. Reaching the edge of the doorway, I peered around.

And found the point of a knife leveled at my eye.

A strangled gasp escaped me as I flooded my body with radiance and kinesis. I barely kept from striking out, even as I looked beyond the knife to the man who held it. Power birthed of the god who had attuned me raged within.

"You," the man growled. He withdrew the knife, tucked it into his ragged clothes, then turned away without another word.

I hesitated at the doorway, breath still coming quick and heart pounding. With an effort, I dismissed my magic and closed my locus. The tunnels seemed especially dun and dank without the Pyrthae's touch upon me. Or perhaps the cold came from Talan's expression.

I set my jaw. Time to set aside the past and do what had to be done. Feelings didn't matter in the face of Telae's destruction.

Not much did, when it came to it.

I followed him into a dark hall. On the other side opened up a small chamber. Perhaps, in another time, it had been a gathering room, a place to entertain guests. Stone benches ran along the curved walls, likely set before tables that had long ago rotted away and never been replaced. The flickering light illuminating the room came from the far end. There, Talan's silhouette crouched, his back to me. I put one foot in front of the other, forcing myself to approach.

Even when I stood behind him, he didn't turn around. I stared into his small fire burning on the stone floor. On top of what looked to be broken timbers, strips of cloth twisted as they burned. It was the only fuel he could find in the Underguild's old haunts, I guessed.

I worked myself up to ask the question. "Is Sule here?"

"Was she the reason?" Talan half-turned toward me, unkempt hair falling before his eyes. In his hand, he clutched a flask.

I averted my gaze. "My request is sensitive. I just wanted to be sure we were alone."

Abruptly, he stood and faced me, breath hot against my face, the sickly sweet stench of wine wafting over me. "I have to know, Airene. It's been two spans since you left me at the Silvencrest. I've tried to talk to you and you've refused me. So answer me now: why didn't you come that night?"

I couldn't meet his eyes, afraid of what I'd find in them. Of what he would see in mine. "I told you. Famine" — I winced, the name burning on my tongue — "he returned as I crossed the bridge. I couldn't go to our rendezvous after that."

"Yes, you could have."

He reached for my hand, and I didn't have the strength to refuse him. Even grimy and stinking of liquor, his touch sent fire racing through me with far more urgency than radiance ever did.

"You could have," he repeated. "We could have faced that bastard together, could have stolen a little piece of happiness to spite him. After the moment we shared, I thought we were finally getting our chance. But then..."

His gaze was hard on me, amber eyes glinting in the firelight, and suddenly, I couldn't take it any longer. I swallowed back the sobs threatening to rise in my throat, swallowed all the bitter disappointment and rage at the unfairness of it all. Only when I had felt the caustic solution settle back in my stomach did I turn my gaze up to his.

"I promised Jaxas I'd kill Ariston the Dishonored."

Talan blinked. "What?"

"I need to find the honor with him," I plowed on. "Seda, Vusu's personal honor. Vusu said before his death that she has everything I need to know. I saw her with him in... in the Pyrthae." Better to say that than a dream, though these days, the two were increasingly intertwined in my experience. "I will do what must be done."

His eyes grew harder with every word. Almost, I could have believed him sober, but for the slight sway in his stance.

"You want me to come with," he said quietly. "That's why you came here."

I clenched my jaw, then forced out the only word I could. "Yes."

He closed his eyes for a moment, then opened them again. I almost flinched at the fire in them.

"You say you'll kill Ariston. But you're no killer, Airene. You've only killed two people, and both in self-defense. You can't murder someone in cold blood."

Ice crept through my veins. I spoke through numb lips. "I have to. Someone has to."

Talan barked a harsh laugh. "I've struck down so many men and women I can't count them all. I didn't even see their faces, most of them. I've murdered with a knife, and Valem's curse. Even with my bare hands." He leaned toward me. "Who better than I to kill this unruly honor?"

I knew Talan, knew him down to his bones. I saw behind the fury to the drowning pain, the guilt at all that blood on his hands. He wasn't a murderer either, no matter what he said. A soldier, yes, but always on the right side of the fight. A good man, down at his core, who did the best thing in the worst of situations.

But I still couldn't help a shiver of fear running through me at his stare.

"I'm not asking you to kill him," I muttered. "I'm asking you to help me get to him. That's all."

He broke eye contact first, turning to look into the dying flames. I stepped up beside him, wanting to put a hand on his shoulder, to lean into him, hold him, kiss him. But I couldn't, not now. Maybe not ever.

"When do we go?" he asked without turning around.

I felt something loosen inside me, knowing I wouldn't have to do this alone. Even as another part tightened with guilt that I'd roped him into danger once again.

"Tomorrow night. We'll meet at the Sandglass gate."

He nodded, then took a long pull from his flask. "If that's all, you can see I have a busy night to get back to." He spoke without turning around, wiping his mouth as he did.

I stared at him a moment longer, but he didn't glance back. I lowered my gaze. It was for the best. If he'd met my eyes, my resolve and better judgment would have crumbled.

"That's all," I murmured, then made my way back through the gloom.

At the end of the passage, I lifted the cellar door and stepped out into the dark alley. Instead of the roiling tumult in my belly settling after speaking with Talan, it had grown worse. I stiffened my trembling lips, latched the cellar door, and exited onto the main street.

Few people were around, but I spotted a knot of men loitering in an alcove. As I passed under a mounted pyr lamp, their eyes turned toward me.

"Oi, wench!" one of them called across the street. "Come here a moment! Come give Atlan a kiss!"

The others cackled, shadowed faces turned toward me, eyes glinting in the thin light.

I should have kept walking. Most likely, they would have left me be. I should have given them the chance.

But at their leers, something snapped in me. I spun toward them, body coursing with energy, fingers burning.

"Come here then," I said, my voice not seeming my own. "Come claim it."

The men shuffled back, faces startled in a sudden red glow. I looked down and saw flames crawling out from the tips of my gloves and over my hands. Even then, I couldn't hold back.

"Well?" I taunted. "I'm waiting!"

I could barely hear their responses as they backed away, though I picked up a few curses and mentions of "daemon." I smiled, cold and brittle, as they disappeared into the darkness.

As I released my hold on radiance and closed my locus, I felt even more deadened than before. Slapping my hands to dampen the lingering tongues of fire, I closed my eyes and tilted my head back, breathing in and out. I pictured Isidora's desert in my mind, hoping it would center me, that it would bring me back to myself again and out of the boiling rage that always seemed to be with me now.

When I opened my eyes, I found that, instead of clouds and the dull light of the moons, buildings hung overhead. I swiveled my gaze up and down the street and saw a mirror image of it above.

A spike of pleasure ran through me. Somewhere, far in the distance, Famine had feasted well, and felt for a moment his hunger abate.

But only for a moment.

I pulled myself back from the 'Thae-drift and into my shivering body. As the vision of the mirror Oedija blew away like smoke, I gasped and doubled forward.

I'm losing it. Famine is growing stronger, and I'm losing myself.

Standing upright so quickly my vision fuzzed for a moment, I let out a low laugh. If I was our only hope, we had no hope at all.

But I'd never been one to give in. My legs wobbly beneath me, I made my way down the dark street back to the Laurel Palace.

CHAPTER THREE
RECKLESS

I stared at the building across the canal and wondered if I'd already gone mad.

The warehouse rose from the gloomy night like a cliff, just as tall and impassable. Once, during the height of Brinecoast's wealth a century back, it had housed the salt for which the deme was named. Since then, it was slowly abandoned, its senescence mirroring the district's own. Vagrants and rats became more common than trading goods.

Now, the Manifest infested it.

Even with the cloud moon's violet light and the green radiant winds illuminating the cityscape, I couldn't see anyone standing watch. Yet Seekers had never been lax, nor had Ariston fallen so far as to lose all his followers. Much as I wished otherwise, there would be sentinels to reckon with.

I hoped they wouldn't spot us in return. Talan and I wore dark clothes, a hooded cloak thrown over to ward off the rain. Gloves covered my hands, and not only for the warmth. My shifts had continued to advance.

Not content to remain at my fingers, all the skin up to my wrists moved in mesmerizing patterns now. I wore gloves as often as I could get away with it, and never showed my hands without good reason.

Soon, however, I would have to remove them. Channeling was required this night, and I'd already burned through one pair the night before.

I glanced at Talan, crouched beside me behind the canal wall opposite to the Manifest hideout. I was grateful for the salt stinging my nose from the incessant wind off the sea, for otherwise I would have smelled the stench of alcohol hanging about the former Guilder. Still, he reeked less than he had the previous night. Considering what I'd put him through, and what I expected of him now, I could hardly ask for more.

"See anyone?" I whispered, pitching my voice low though the gale would disguise any noise we made.

He shook his head. "Not see; sense." His lopsided smile materialized as his eyes slid over to me. "Can you not feel them?"

I only shrugged. Talan had always displayed a preternatural awareness of his surroundings. I suspected it was something to do with an unconscious use of quintessence, but if so, it was another of his secrets I had yet to uncover.

Yet I had my own methods. Trusting him to keep watch, I closed my eyes, opened my locus to the Pyrthae, and channeled.

The world changed around me as I drifted into the spirit realm. Though my eyes remained closed, I gained a different sort of vision as my soul peeled away from my body. The strange, shifting landscape of the Pyrthae was disorienting for a moment. The colors, kaleidoscopic and ever-changing, made my head spin if I studied them overlong, and distances fluctuated, the warehouse seeming within reach one moment, then far away the next. I quickly adjusted, having spent enough time in the pyr's plane to be used to the shift.

Refocusing, I confirmed Talan's declaration, counting the glowing flames that signified those attuned to the Pyrthae. There were eight Seekers in total: two on the warehouse roof, six within. *Only eight?* It was far fewer than I had expected and much fewer than I'd dared hope for. Xaron, Isidora, and their Watchers had whittled away their numbers, and Vusu's fall lost even more, but this force showed that desertion had become widespread within the Manifest.

But though eight made for better odds, Talan and I still numbered just two. We had to proceed carefully, lest we be the ones with knives in our backs.

I eased back out of the Pyrthae, but did not entirely reenter the material plane. Instead, I employed a trick I'd discovered in the spans since

Famine's liberation: I hovered halfway between. Enough of me occupied my body to speak, hear, and even move if needed, yet I still saw within the Pyrthae. It was useful for keeping track of wardens.

I spoke to Talan, following the Seekers' flames as I did. "I see eight. Two above, six within."

"I sensed the same."

In his silence, I heard his unspoken question. I didn't offer an explanation; he didn't ask.

"Our approach then. From above?"

I balked at the idea. "And how do we reach the roof?"

I heard the smile in his voice. "Oh, my Finch. You're a warden now. Do you forget you can fly, if you only try?"

Ordinarily, his mockery would not have bothered me, for Talan had always been gentle. Now, however, there was a bitter edge to it that could cut.

With little other recourse, I ignored the gibe. "I'm still clumsy with kinesis. I doubt I could make that leap."

"I could send down a rope. Or did you miss that I'd brought one?"

I had noticed it, but being treated like I was still unattuned was not something I wanted to perpetuate. I struggled to remain neutral. "Fine. You'll lower the rope. But let me ease the way."

"And how do you propose to do that from down here?"

It was my turn to smile. "Wait and see. But don't be surprised when the watchers no longer watch."

Leaving him with a taste of his own potion, I fully entered the Pyrthae once more. Instead of hovering above my body, I ventured forth, soaring through the law-defying realm. I drew close to the warehouse roof to the nearest of the two Seekers until I felt the heat of his flame. It was not the warmth of fire, but the strength of his quintessence. How brightly it burned in the Pyrthae was a sign of how much of his spirit entered this realm, and thus the depth of his attunement.

This Seeker appeared to be a four-shift. I debated attempting to snuff him out entirely, but quickly rejected the thought. Though I presently fashioned myself as an assassin, and these Seekers had chosen a faction opposing mine, I had no desire to sow more death than I had to.

I kept my approach slow but inexorable as I neared the Seeker. Pieces of his soul leaked out and threaded through my own the closer I came. I saw his thoughts and memories in fragments, a puzzle I did not try to piece together. Through them, I glimpsed his face, his friends, his family. I saw moments of hunger and despair. He was a thin man, desperate to survive as drought and war impoverished the realm.

I stifled my pity. When I had channeled quintessence before, I had used it clumsily and incompetently. These past few spans, I had trained myself hard to change that. When not poring over the tomes that might clue me into how to defeat Famine or searching for Vusu's servant Seda, I had devoted every free moment to comprehending and honing my newfound abilities. At the outset of my attunement, such time spent seemed an indulgence, a pastime unlikely to yield results, and every warden I knew reinforced this view. Now, however, I was a ten-shift and growing stronger every day. As Famine swelled in power, so did I.

If I was to be the Sacrifice and ensnare a dragon, I had to be as strong as possible.

During my training, I had learned more than one new skill. Now I used another of them as I pressed my quintessence into the Seeker's. He registered something was wrong at once and instinctively fought against my presence. I didn't resist, but instead emitted calming thoughts and words, backing them with the power my amplified spirit wielded.

Sleep, I told the sentinel. *Rest your eyes, only for a moment. Nothing moves through the dark.*

His resistance ceased. His spirit-flame dimmed. Like a cup set over a candle, the Seeker sputtered into unconsciousness.

I withdrew and waited. When he did not rouse, I smiled and moved to the next watcher on the opposite side of the roof. She resisted more than the first, her five-shift connection lending her increased strength, but it wasn't long before I'd lulled her into unawareness as well.

Had I been able to ambush the other six Seekers in the same way, I would have continued. But grouped as they were, even if I brought one down, the others would be alerted to our presence. We would have to handle them in a different way.

I returned to Telae. The world seemed to tremble beneath my feet, and for a moment, I thought I would sprawl on my rear. But a steadying hand on the canal wall proved sufficient to suffer through the vertigo until it dissipated.

"Back?" Talan muttered. He bent in close so that his breath puffed over me in a cloud of sour wine.

I leaned away. "The Seekers atop the roof are out cold. The others below are still alert, though."

By the faint illumination, I detected the smile curling his lips. "You astound me, Airene, truly. I would ask how you did it, but I have a feeling you'll withhold your secret."

I jerked my head toward the wall and the warehouse beyond it. "You'll just have to trust me."

The amusement faded from his expression, and I regretted my choice of words at once.

"Would that I could," he muttered. Before I could respond, he was rising and darting off toward the short bridge across the canal, then to the warehouse beyond it.

I watched him go, a shadow in the gloom, and tried to stifle the despondency welling up in me. *You had no choice,* I lectured my guilt. *Famine had returned. There's no time for anything between you and him.*

Yet none of the placations seemed to stick.

Talan reached the base of the nearest warehouse wall, then paused. A moment later, he flew up from the ground. Though it did not seem possible, he sailed smoothly to the top of the warehouse, then reached out and hauled himself over in one fluid motion.

But his kinesis-fueled leap was not entirely discreet, for a crack accompanied it that was audible even from where I crouched three dozen paces away. I winced and channeled quintessence to keep tabs on the Seekers within the warehouse. There was movement; they seemed to be heading toward where Talan had leaped from.

Profanities tumbled through my mind as I tried to figure out what to do. Talan decided for me, tossing down his heavy length of rope so the end dangled a few cubits above the ground. Muttering curses aloud now, I rose and sprinted toward it, ignoring the groaning in my legs, stiff from crouching for so long.

Breath rasped in my throat as I reached for the rope and hauled myself up. My mind flashed back to when I'd done a similar thing when entering the Wyvern's Claw. Though I was now a warden, I hadn't learned to channel kinesis to fuel my body as Xaron and Talan could. My efforts were all my own, and it wasn't long before my arms and shoulders burned.

It seemed a long time later when I dragged myself over the lip and onto the flat roof. No sooner had I tumbled over than Talan hauled up the rope, grunting softly with each motion. The rope was thick and heavy, its kind typically used for hoisting sails on ships, and even for a warden who could channel kinesis effectively, it was an arduous task. Yet in moments, he had accomplished it and coiled the rope before crouching next to me.

"You alright?" he asked. He sounded more like himself than he had in a long while.

I nodded, but could spare no more thought for a response, for I channeled quintessence again. The situation was as I feared. The Seekers had noticed something, whether it was the flare of Talan's channeling or the sounds of our arrival. Their footsteps echoed up to us from below, as did their hushed, urgent voices.

"Damn," Talan muttered, peering at the edge of the roof as if expecting one of our enemies to come soaring over it at any moment. "Think they're coming?"

"Best not to wait and find out."

The former Guilder seemed to consider it for a moment before shaking his head. "Best *you* don't. You'll have a tricky time infiltrating while they hunt you, so I'll draw them off." A shadow of a smile touched his mouth. "I have a few ideas for how to make sure they can't ignore me."

I gripped his arm, fear causing me to squeeze harder than I intended. "Don't be a fool, Talan Wraithsbane."

His eyes found mine. "The same to you, Airene the Finch."

Then he was tearing free of my grasp and vaulting over the edge to a drop that should have broken his legs. The cries of surprise and pain that wafted up moments later told me his descent hadn't gone unnoticed.

I shook my head in disbelief. The man never did listen to me.

But I had my own task to be about. Praying for his safety to gods I only halfway believed in, I pressed on.

CHAPTER FOUR

DISHONORABLE

The Kalthuae were an accomplished people before the landing of the Lighted Passage. They raised marvelous temples of innovative architecture, designed to celebrate their many foreign gods. Some of these structures stretched toward the Pyrthae, while others dove deep underground.

The city is a mausoleum for these empty sanctuaries now, though many were torn down or lost to the centuries. We no longer know the names of these gods, nor what forms they took, for no records of them were kept. If they did once exist, they seem to have ceased to touch our world…

- Oedija: A History; by Acadian Helene, Master Historian; 1167 LP

A brief check on the two Seekers atop the warehouse assured me they remained unconscious. A proper assassin would have slit their throats; I indulged in mercy instead, creeping away from their prone bodies and hoping it wouldn't prove to be a fatal mistake.

The sounds of the clash below had faded away, the Seekers taking off in pursuit of Talan. Trying to forget that he was running or fighting for his life, I set to searching for a way inside. The warehouse had fallen into disrepair along with Brinecoast, and in several locations, the timber had rotted and folded in. A drizzle pattered on my hood and the surrounding roof, a testament to where the building's ruin had originated.

Gingerly, I tested the boards with my foot, but dared not venture farther. If I fell, I doubted I'd be able to catch myself, magic notwithstanding.

So I tied Talan's heavy rope through a gap in the low wall edging the roof, tugged on it to see if it would hold, then began lowering myself down. The aperture was about twice as wide as my shoulders, but reaching splinters of wood snagged at my hair and clothes and scratched my skin as I went through. I gritted my teeth and endured it. With the ground far below and my feet scrabbling for a hold on the writhing rope, a few cuts and scrapes were the least of my concerns.

My stomach clenched tight the entire drop, until at last, my sandals touched the ground. Stifling a sigh of relief, I studied my surroundings. Illumination was scant, with little more than the light of the moons and radiant winds filtering in through the holes in the roof. Dark piles of refuse and abandoned crates huddled throughout the warehouse. The air had a thick scent of dust and disuse. Had someone stumbled upon this place, they would see few signs that it was occupied.

Yet this had to be where the Dishonored hid. For Talan's sake, I hoped I wasn't wrong.

I crouched behind the nearest pile of debris and channeled quintessence. A brief check ensured that the two Seekers above were the only attuned around. That did not, of course, guarantee there weren't unattuned guards posted throughout the warehouse, but I'd been listening and had heard nothing. Considering I had to see to search for my target, I would just have to take a gamble on light.

Exiting the Pyrthae and enduring the transition, I rose a moment later and pulled at radiance. Its warmth unfurled in my body as it streamed toward the shifts on my fingers. There, I gathered it into a small, glowing orb and lifted it to look at my surroundings.

The warehouse's size was intimidating. Mounds upon mounds of refuse littered the ground. I stepped over rusted nails, moldy boards, and smashed crates in my search, and more always lay ahead.

One area seemed to be where the Seekers had stationed themselves. It was marginally cleaner and boasted a small fire pit in its center, still smoking from recent use, as well as blanket rolls around it. I explored the area around the camp more thoroughly, but saw no sign of other occupants. If Ariston and Seda were here, they were likely secured underneath a hidden hatch somewhere.

Pausing at the Seeker camp, I reassessed my approach. I could search all night and still not find them in the chaotic, sprawling chamber. I had to be more focused. And I knew how I could do it.

Dismissing my hold on radiance, I closed my eyes, then dredged up from my memories a particular instance, when Xaron had sharpened my hearing to eavesdrop on distant conversations. I dissected the moment, trying to remember each thing he had done to augment my senses. It was little enough; his magic had mostly been beyond my awareness then. I cursed myself for not asking him about it and his other tricks since I'd begun to understand my attunement, but there'd been too little time, and I hadn't yet had a need for them. I'd been more focused on my own discoveries than anything other wardens might have to share.

I would just have to uncover this on my own as well.

I focused my hearing. On another occasion, Xaron had explained that sound was just a natural variant of kinesis. Seeing this as a starting point, I drew in the element through my locus. My body buzzed with the fresh energy, but my hearing grew no more acute.

But it had not been kinesis alone that enabled this. Xaron had channeled quintessence, though he did not know it. Drawing on it now, part of my mind extended into the Pyrthae, but did not fully enter it. In that halfway space, I could both feel the kinesis in me and perceive it in my spirit-flame. If I could sense it, I reasoned, perhaps I could manipulate it.

I reached out with invisible hands and began to mold it. Kinesis was everywhere in the Pyrthae. If I changed it so that kinesis did not flow away from me, but *toward*...

Sound burst into my ears.

Before, it had been all but silent in the warehouse, only the occasional scratching to be heard, likely from a rodent or bird that had taken refuge here. Now, every noise clawed into my skull. I steadied myself against the ground and heard the scraping of my palms on the dust. If it had not been so excruciating to endure, I would have been fascinated.

But I still had a task ahead of me. Opening my eyes, I squinted and peered with hazy vision around the warehouse. As on the occasion with Xaron, wherever I looked, my hearing also honed in. I hoped that, by scanning the warehouse, I might locate a hatch beneath which Ariston and Seda hid.

Before I'd scanned half the chamber, an ache began throbbing in my head. I ground my teeth, then stopped as the noise irritated my ears further. I just had to press on. A little more, and—

My thoughts silenced as I heard something. It was not the shifting of debris or the scuttling of rats, but a swish that could only come from the movement of cloth, and the *pat-pat-pat* of feet on stone.

I noted the area, then released my grip on the elements and sighed with relief. My suffering had yielded results.

I rose, swayed for a moment as the disorientation seized me, then stumbled through it, weaving my way toward the place where I'd heard the promising sounds. As my balance returned, I slowed my approach, prudence winning out over urgency. I summoned radiance again to illuminate the rubbish. There were signs that objects had been moved in this area, the dust trampled by feet, and of something being dragged. A crate lay conspicuously at the end of these tracks.

A smile alighted on my lips. 'Thae above, I had them.

Being silent now would be nigh impossible, so I settled for swiftness. Gripping the edges of the crate, I heaved at it, grunting with the effort. Even empty and partially broken, the box was almost beyond my strength to move. I debated channeling kinesis to blast it out of the way, but settled for dragging it away myself. No need to stretch my abilities further than I had to.

At last, I moved the crate, then stepped back to wipe the sweat from my brow as I took in the result. As I'd hoped, a trapdoor lay beneath. A thrill went through me, intoxicating and terrifying. All that was left to do was open it and find out if my quarries truly were within.

I took a moment to settle my nerves, then drew in kinesis and radiance. I'd never used them to much effect in a fight, but even my clumsy wielding, backed by the power of my attunement, should be more than sufficient to take care of any opponent before me. So I hoped.

Drawing in a deep breath, I called fire to the fingertips of my right hand, then reached out for the leather strap serving as a handle on the hatch. Heaving it open, I saw a shadow moving below me and thrust my hand forward.

"Stop there!"

As the illumination from the flames leaking from my shift caught on the figure, however, I knew I was outmatched. An object pointed at me — a crossbow, loaded and drawn, and aimed at my chest.

I didn't lower my hand, though magic would not save me now. Vusu had eventually died in part because of the quarrel I had shot into him. Even wardens were not invulnerable to weapons, and I was mere feet from this bolt.

I looked at the face beyond the weapon and startled. The changes that had come over Ariston were shocking. His head, before shaved bald, had grown a layer of dark stubble. His face had been thin, but now verged upon skeletal, approaching how Vusu had appeared near the end of his life, or like Jaxas before he'd taken the Evergreen Wreath for his own.

The Dishonored seemed alarmed at seeing me as well, though a smile spoiled his lips a moment later. "Of course," he rasped, his rich voice flatter than the last time I'd heard him. "It would be you who found us."

I didn't move. Though the standoff wasn't in my favor, I couldn't risk trying to find a new balance, lest the former honor allow his hand to slip on the lever. All I could do was talk.

So I spoke.

"Ariston the Dishonored. I've been searching for you."

A laugh escaped his lips. "And you have found me. What will you do now, Airene the Finch? Or is it First Verifier these days? Perhaps 'murderer' would be more to the point."

That last title rankled me. How many times had I wondered it of myself? I tried not to let my guilt show, but kept my outstretched hand steady and my voice calm.

"We don't have to do this, Ariston. I just want to talk. Lower your weapon, and I won't harm you."

The crossbow, a heavy wooden piece that looked made for a laurel guard, shook slightly in the man's emaciated arms, but Ariston did not otherwise shift. "You kill my protectors, but merely wish to speak with me. Why, Finch, do I not believe you?"

Truth had a power that lies often did not. I searched for the slivers I could safely share with Ariston.

"I didn't kill those Seekers. Some, we drew off, while others are unconscious." All true, though if Talan still survived, I doubted all of them would live through the night.

The former honor frowned. "Even if that is true, I must assume you came here to kill me. I am what remains of the Manifest. While I live, I pose a threat."

I skirted around the issue. "Perhaps so. But my fight is with someone far more dangerous than you, Ariston. One who is enemy to us both."

His eyes flickered to the ceiling, and I knew he looked to the sky beyond. "You do not mean Avvad, do you?"

"You know I don't."

Ariston's gaze settled back on me. "Still, it does not answer why you are *here.*"

I couldn't tell the full truth, so I settled for half. "I've come for Seda."

"Seda?" His eyebrows flew up. "Why her?"

"Despite being Avvadin, she acted as an honor to Vusu, as I'm sure you're aware. She knows what I require. The key to defeating Famine."

"Is that so?" Despite the skepticism in his voice, to my eye, the crossbow lowered a fraction. "Why should she?"

My hand trembled, yet I took the final leap. "Because Vusu told me she did."

Part of me expected Ariston to laugh. Instead, he grew graver. I couldn't tell if fear manipulated my senses, or if the crossbow raised once again.

"Vusu is dead, Finch. He has been for spans. He could not have told you anything, even if I believed he had."

My chest felt as if rope had been wound and pulled tight about it. I was losing him and coming closer to a confrontation I couldn't hope to survive. Words alone would not influence him. Ariston had suffered too much at my hands to believe me now.

So I drew upon the only resource left to me.

I channeled. It was not the radiance burning at my fingertips that I reached for, but quintessence. My soul split between the planes, material and spirit, and I stretched it blindly toward the man before me. He was no warden. He lacked attunement to the Pyrthae. By all rights, I should not be able to influence him.

My only hope was that, somehow, everything I had been taught about being a warden was wrong.

Where before, I had always used quintessence within the Pyrthae, now I tried to wield it in Telae. It pushed forward through my body to my fingertips, but there abruptly halted. My hopes faltered. In this realm, my spirit was trapped in my body. I couldn't do it.

I racked my head for other possibilities. If it could not reach beyond my flesh, was there another way it could spread? While I schemed, Ariston's eyes narrowed, and his body tightened, showing all the signs of preparing to fire.

Then it came to me: quintessence could be melded with other elements. I had just done so to augment my hearing, and how often had I seen Xaron manipulate radiance into illusions? It was quintessence made manifest — or so I hoped.

Drawing kinesis into my body, I spoke, this time projecting with both elements. "Ariston. Do not shoot. Our only hope of defeating Famine is by working together. Let me speak with Seda and discover what she knows. Then I will leave you to your fate, and I will go to mine."

It was nothing I hadn't said before, though I spoke now with finality. I could only hope the quintessence lacing the kinesis held the influence I tried to infuse into it.

The former honor's eyes crossed for a moment, then he blinked rapidly. As he shifted the crossbow, I flinched, braced for the deadly impact of the bolt tearing through my flesh.

It never came. Instead, Ariston opened his mouth and spoke.

"I do not think I should believe you, Finch. Yet I find I do."

He raised the crossbow so the quarrel no longer aimed at me. My chest loosened a fraction. I repressed the radiance flickering at my fingertips and brushed back the sweat dripping into my eyes.

"Thank you, Ariston. You won't regret this."

The Dishonored's mouth twisted as he turned from the hatch door and stepped deeper within, allowing room for me to clamber down the short ladder. "If I do, I doubt I will be alive to regret it long."

I hid my expression by turning away and setting a foot to the top rung. That, at least, we agreed upon.

CHAPTER FIVE

HIS MOST LOYAL SERVANT

We were not always honors, we Kalthuae. Once, before the Lighted Passage that upended our world, to act as an honor was considered noble, the suppression of pride for the good of all. Many of the notable men and women of the old world could only accomplish what they did through the service of their honors.

Then Oedija's ancestors came across the water and conquered our people. They named us "honors," for it was a more palatable label than "slaves." Peaceful as we Kalthuae were then, we accepted our fate.

But it is not honorable to be what we are; it is unjust. And I dedicate my life to righting these wrongs, for our people now and forevermore.

- A Nation's Sins; by Ariston the Dishonored; date unknown

As I entered Ariston's cellar, I was reminded of Talan's many disreputable hideouts spread throughout Oedija. It had the same mildewy stench, though underlaid with urine, as well as similar cramped walls and the claustrophobia that accompanied them. Violet pyrkin was smeared over the dirt walls, casting the single chamber in an ethereal light not unlike the Pyrthae. Little occupied the space: two makeshift cots, a spattering of satchels, and in one corner, a small kitchen entailing a pot and a sparse collection of half-spoiled foodstuffs.

One of the sleeping areas was a neat rectangle of blankets. The other was occupied. Even in the odd light, I recognized Seda. Her head was bare, though scarred and pocked from clumsy shaves. Her face was down-cast, seemingly disinterested in my appearance, as if she had given up on caring even about her own well-being. Like Ariston, she looked much thinner than the first time I'd seen her, a flower wilted from lack of sun and rain. As I watched, she gently rocked back and forth, her thin arms curled around her knees, her lips mouthing silent sentences. By all looks, she was madder than our former Despoina.

I couldn't help but pity her.

"She has become like this in the past span," Ariston spoke from behind me. "Barely eats. Barely sleeps. I do not know how much longer she will survive."

Privately, I agreed with his assessment. I had traveled the streets of Oedija all my life and seen my fair share of starving souls. They had that same skeletal frame, that feverish look in the eyes. Foreboding grew in me. I wanted to flee this scene of encroaching death. Only my purpose forced me to stay.

"Does she speak?" I asked in a hushed voice, partly afraid of her over-hearing me, though it seemed like she paid us no heed.

"Yes. But only on her terms, and never for long."

It was troubling to put my back to Ariston, but I did so, maintaining a pretense of trust. As I looked upon Seda, I tried to harden myself to her plight. She had dedicated herself to serving the man who had caused the city so much anguish, the man who had hollowed out my brother's mind. As pathetic as she appeared now, she had chosen her fate.

Yet no matter how I had tried, mercy refused to die in me. So I adopted a different tact: wielding compassion as a weapon.

As I had once done with Asileia in her gardens, I put myself on level with Seda, sitting cross-legged on the ground before her. My hands rested on my knees, showing them to be empty. For several moments, I sat quietly, observing her while pretending to look elsewhere. I hoped to give her time to adjust to my presence.

If it made any difference, she didn't show it. Seda continued to rock back and forth, back and forth, as endless in her self-comforting movement as waves against a shore. My wariness outwore my patience, for I was keenly aware Ariston might still change his mind and shoot me in the back. Last that I'd looked, the crossbow remained drawn and loaded. Though urgency pulsed inside me, I kept my voice low and calm.

"Seda. Do you remember me?"

At her name, Seda paused. Her eyes did not lift from their spot on the ground, but her lips stopped moving. I took it as progress.

I placed a hand against my chest and forced a smile. "I'm Airene. We met once, spans ago. Your master sent me, Seda. Vusumuzi wanted me to find you."

The mention of Vusu was the key I'd searched for. Seda's head jerked up, her dark eyes chasms as they bore into my face. My expression grew rigid, the smile false, so I let it slip away and waited.

"My master?" Seda murmured at length, her words little more than a whisper.

I nodded. "I saw him before he… passed. He told me to find you, said you were the secret to defeating the enemy we hold in common. Famine — or Taozu, he might have called him. Do you know anything of this?"

Seda was shaking her head before I'd finished speaking. "The Other," she muttered. "The Corruptor. The Serpent."

By those titles, I knew we spoke of the same adversary. My gut tightened at the thought of Famine as I'd last seen him, and my violent desire to be consumed by him. With an effort, I pushed away the memory. I needed no more fear just then.

"Yes," I continued. "Though your master is gone, you can still be loyal to him. You can still serve."

My gut twisted as I uttered the words. Their relationship revolted me. I couldn't understand the willing subjugation of oneself to another, as Seda had done, nor the acceptance on Vusu's part. But I had to set my own biases aside to succeed here. Again, I forced myself to calm and spoke.

"Will you help me, Seda? Will you help me achieve your master's aim?"

The honor seemed to return somewhat to her senses. There was a spark in her eyes that had nothing to do with the lavender light of the pyrkin as she stared unblinkingly at me.

"How?" she asked quietly. "How did he ask this of you?"

My mind whirred. I hadn't expected her to question anything that came from her master. But I'd gambled this far. I had to believe what I could reveal of the truth would prove sufficient.

"As he lay dying, I was there with him, Seda." I raised my hand slowly, holding it palm up, fingertips extended. "I'm a warden, just like your master. We were in the Pyrthae together when Famine was breaking free of him. He caged him a little longer, though his strength was nearly at its end. I've never seen such power before."

That much was true. Though I reviled the man, I couldn't help but admire Vusu's fortitude.

"But before he descended," I continued, "he told me I would have to be the one to defeat the daemon god now. And that I must find you to do it."

A lump formed in my throat. Not from sorrow, no — I wasn't sorry to see the end of Vusu. It was terror at what his expiry meant for me. It was the impossible burden of my task, resting on my shoulders alone.

The weight of the world — I couldn't bear it all. Yet I had to.

Seda hadn't looked away from me the entire time I spoke, unnerving in her focus. I tried not to let it show while I listened for any sign of Ariston's betrayal.

Then she moved. I flinched as Seda reached under her pile of fraying blankets, but didn't shift away as she extracted her hands to reveal what she sought. My shoulders lowered as my curiosity was piqued. She didn't hold a knife, but a small, leather-bound book. Its face was plain and dyed a deep scarlet, and the ends of the pages looked worn and frayed. Though I burned to know what it portended, I kept my hands still.

Her voice was scratchy and quiet when she spoke, but Seda seemed to have found some hidden measure of resolve, for fresh certainty underlay her words. "This is my master's journal. He asked me to keep it safe before he left. I know little of the daemon that haunted him, and I would never reveal his secrets. Never." Her eyes drifted down to the book. "But he told me one would come seeking it after he was gone. I did not know what he meant. Now I do." Her gaze lifted, and there seemed a desperate hunger in her as she lifted the book toward me. "Take it. Fight the *sheytin*. My master was a good man, a very good man... Let his death not be in vain."

On our sentiments toward her master, we couldn't be further from agreement. But I nodded as I took Vusu's journal in hand. "I'll do all I can," I said, knowing it was all I could promise.

I longed to open the diary then and there and discover the secrets of my enemy within its pages, but I wasn't yet out of danger. Murmuring thanks to Seda, I stood and turned back to Ariston. He still cradled the crossbow in his arms, but he didn't look inclined to raise it, his posture weary as he slumped against one of the dilapidated walls. His eyes, tracing the purple pyrkin on the wall opposite him, lazily came back to rest on mine.

"I hope you do as you say," he said. "This is not a nemesis who allows mistakes."

"I know."

Both of us seemed to be waiting for something. My stated purpose in coming accomplished, there was little reason for me to stay. But I hadn't forgotten my promise to Jaxas. Nor had I forgiven Ariston's hand in Linos's ruination. He was lax and unprepared, and apparently coming to trust me.

I could kill him.

And yet, I couldn't. I could not raise my hand or draw on the elements to do it. I'd claimed to be an assassin, but I was wrong. There was good in Ariston; I'd glimpsed that this night. Even for his sins, I could not stamp that out.

"Go," I told him. "Leave the city. Don't return."

He stiffened, and seeming to become more alert. The Dishonored glanced toward the exit, perhaps wondering if my intentions were as honest as they had first appeared.

"What do you mean?" he asked slowly.

"Leave now — you won't have another chance. The Manifest is all but dismantled, but the Despot will not overlook your hand in creating it. He will hunt you down if you remain in Oedija."

I must have instilled more into my words than I meant. Ariston's next words captured and held me.

"You came here to kill me."

I stiffened. How could I answer that? If I lied, would he know? If I told the truth, would he strike before I could explain?

Before I could decide, the hatch was wrenched open. At once, I drew upon my magic and whirled toward it with hands raised. Ariston reacted, too — by pointing his crossbow at me.

"Dishonored!" an unfamiliar voice shouted through the portal. "Are you hurt?"

Curses jostled in my head. My heart seemed to beat against my temples. I had delayed too long, and Seekers had come. Now, I would pay dearly for the mistake.

Before anyone could speak or move, a shriek came from behind me.

"Do not harm her!"

I was as startled by Seda's outburst as Ariston. His eyes darted toward the Avvadin honor for a moment before settling back on me. I didn't dare move, though my skin crawled as I stared down the tip of the crossbow.

Once more, Ariston lowered it, the quarrel aiming at the ground.

Breath whooshed back in my lungs, and relief made my knees weak. I lowered my hands, but not my guard as I waited for Ariston to speak.

"Seda is right," he said. "You should not be harmed. If everything I suspect about you is true, you must survive. You have a purpose to fulfill, do you not?"

I nodded, my throat gone too dry for words.

Ariston cocked his head slightly. "I will heed your words, Finch. Though once my ancestors ruled these lands, I, their descendant and heir, am forced to flee them. Yet we all must make sacrifices, must we not?"

Was that use of the word "sacrifice" intentional, or mere coincidence? Did he know my purpose? Now was not the time to inquire further. I had to take my exit and hope he wouldn't change his mind.

"Yes," I muttered. "We must."

The Dishonored smiled, the expression ghastly on his thin face. "Let her pass," he commanded the Seekers above. "And as Seda bids, do not harm her."

"Dishonored—"

"Do not," Ariston pressed, and received grudging assents.

At the incline of his head, I made for the ladder. My palms were sweaty on the rungs, and not only from the radiance still pouring through me. It went against every instinct I had to leave myself so vulnerable as I climbed out of the cellar past the Seekers. Yet I was lucky just to be alive; I didn't push it further.

The Seekers cast me hard glares as I rose to my feet between them. Despite their leader's command, their hands were raised toward me, distortions around their fingers telling of the energetic elements held at the ready. I only glanced at each, then strode quickly for where I saw the door cracked open at the far end of the warehouse.

I didn't slow until long after their stares left my back.

CHAPTER SIX

SECRETS OF THE SERPENT

*Power was to be paid for in blood. Though no words were spoken, Lophe and I under-
stood the bargain. If we accepted the Serpent's offer, we would sacrifice unto it souls in
return.*

It was an exchange I made gladly, great spirits help me.

- The journal of Vusumuzi; date unknown

Talan found me as I reached the edge of Brinecoast.

I kept a careful watch as I hurried away from the Manifest bastion, even occasionally flitting into the Pyrthae to keep tabs on any nearby wardens. Still, he managed to surprise me. Flames flickered at my fingertips before I recognized him emerging from a nearby alley. I lowered my arm with a relieved sigh.

"Talan. You survived."

He flashed a smile as he closed the distance between us. "Takes more than a few half-trained ferals to kill me."

"Not much more." I looked him up and down. Burns blackened his vest and tunic, and blood stained his trousers. Even in the shrouded night, I detected purpling on his face telling of fresh bruises. Unkempt to start with, he appeared little better than a beggar now, and one who had recently received a beating. I wondered if any had survived his retribution, then decided it was better not to ask.

Talan shrugged. "One or two got a hit in." He gestured to the burden I carried. "Your mission was successful?"

I glanced down at Vusu's journal, which I'd compulsively checked to be sure I still had throughout the walk. Even clutched in my hands, its importance made it seem as if it might slip away at any moment.

"Mostly. I found Seda. She gave me this."

"This?"

"Vusu's journal."

He raised an eyebrow at that. "Perhaps this was worth it then."

"We'll see." I thought again of those he'd likely killed and struggled not to picture him doing it. My gut churned anew.

Talan seemed to see something was wrong, for he bent forward to peer into my downcast eyes. "But you said you were 'mostly' successful. What happened?"

I couldn't say what made it hard to confess. Part of me felt ashamed I couldn't kill, even when it might be for the best, especially when Talan seemed to do it so easily. Another part was angry at my shame. But I had always been honest with Talan. I didn't want that to change now.

"It's Ariston… I couldn't do it, Talan. I let him go, told him to flee."

His expression made me regret ever doubting him. Talan reached toward me, then seemed to notice how grimy his hands were and only lowered them again. His eyes caught mine.

"You're not an assassin, Airene — and that's a good thing. I wouldn't want you to be. Besides, things might be better this way. The Manifest aren't much of a threat anymore."

"No. Not much."

"Put it from your mind." But as Talan smiled, he must have remembered what lay between us, for it slipped away. "But we should get you back. With Avvad nearing, you need all the sleep you can get."

"And you?" The words came out like a challenge.

The smile was back, but it failed to touch his eyes. "I have my own appointments to keep."

I suspected those would be the same wine bottles keeping him company — and perhaps Sule and her Qarin. I turned away, trying to hide the envy and disgust I couldn't repress.

"Then let's go." I walked away without seeing if he followed.

We parted at the Laurel Palace with barely a farewell. I spoke greetings to the guards on watch, but ignored their raised eyebrows as I strode between them and up to the golden castle. It took the entire walk to the doors to pull my stewing thoughts away from the former Guilder. My head throbbed with exhaustion, for dawn was not far off now, yet I could not sleep. Secrets simmered beneath my fingertips, secrets I needed to learn if I was to have any chance against Famine.

Instead of my bed, I sought the kitchens. There, a drowsy servant brewed me a carafe of coffee, which I took to the feast hall to drink along with yesterday's bread while I read. My stomach roiled, upset by the long night, yet I was always ravenous. Famine's touch pressed on me, body and soul.

I forgot my discomforts as I examined the journal open before me. I'd feared it would be written in Vusu's native language, but instead found it in our modern sea-tongue. I wondered why. Almost, it seemed he had expected an Oedijan to one day read it. Perhaps that was why he kept the journal in the first place.

His words were sometimes difficult to read, jotted down with splashed ink and in a cramped and hurried scrawl, and my eyes strained with the effort. Yet I managed it, and soon, the mind of the man who had brought so much turmoil to Oedija unfolded before me.

He began with his first encounter with Famine. I suspected he had composed this journal after he had already come to Oedija, for its perspective was of an older man regretting his younger self's actions. He told of his ishaka, the Zakale, and how he and his brother had sought divine intervention when his tribe suffered during a terrible drought. A great spirit found him, one taking the form of a vast serpent, and offered them the sorcery to save their people.

> *Power was to be paid for in blood. Though no words were spoken, Lophe and I understood the bargain. If we accepted the Serpent's offer, we would sacrifice unto it souls in return.*
>
> *It was an exchange I made gladly, great spirits help me.*

My skin erupted into gooseflesh. It was an arrangement I would never make, yet having seen Oedija suffer, I could all too easily understand how Vusu had. *Tales of the Desolate*, which recounted these same events from a different perspective, had made Vusu — Yama, he'd been then — and his brother Lophe seem monsters in service of their Serpent God. Now, I wondered if they'd had much of a choice in the matter.

I had felt Famine's hunger. If I thought about it, I could feel it then. How much worse would it be when the dragon god was bound to them, starving and insistent, not free to feast on his own?

Could Vusu have been less of a villain than I suspected?

I pushed the uncomfortable thought away and kept reading, paging through Vusu's account of the Bali war. He kept it brief, shame lacing each word, and only made minimal mentions of the atrocities for which he was responsible. Instead, he focused on how Famine feasted on those they slew, and their corresponding growth in power.

We believed ourselves immortal, for a time. That we had ascended to become gods. Foolish, when we served a god ourselves. But we were young, lusting for blood, yearning for justice. And power fueled our arrogance.

Then came the day I lost my brother.

My resolve broke with his soul's departure, my belief in our cause breaking with it. The loss of him, by my side since birth... For a time, I believe I truly went mad. I did not know how to understand his absence. And so I refused to believe it.

I spoke to him all throughout the day for longer than I care to admit. I confided in him, commiserated with his troubles, joked and laughed.

But I was alone. It was only to the ghost in my head that I spoke.

Grief was not the only thing responsible for my madness, I think. With my brother gone and our followers scattered, the Serpent's focus fell entirely on me. His hunger tormented me no matter how much I ate, nor how much I fed him. Lophe had shouldered more of that burden than I knew, and my mind buckled beneath it.

How he came out of his madness, Vusu didn't specify. I detected dark depths into which he refused to delve.

Soon, he moved on to his realizations around his relationship with Famine.

I had made a deal with a daemon, and now I understood what that meant. So awakened my resolve to win free of it.

I searched the Four Realms for answers. For decades, this hunt consumed me. I stole into the archives of the Kahin-Shah in Erimis, defying soul-stealing spirits and mind-yoked guards to do so. I pored over the knowledge there, the greatest collected in the known world.

And I discovered nothing.

Slowly, I puzzled out why. Avvad had never suffered an attack by the Serpent. I had to search in places that had. So I returned to where I had first encountered the god: my home ishaka. And there, I followed its trail to the Qao Fu jaitin.

Finally, my search bore fruit. Much of what I learned was too warped in myth to be of use, but there were some treasures. I discovered that an empire had once sprawled across the Wumofu Desert, an empire whose descendants became the Qao Fu people. I learned of a ritual just over a century faded that involved sending a child as a "savior" to a white tree whose boughs pierced the sky itself — the Chains, it was known.

And I heard of the terrible spirit — Taozu the Corrupted — once trapped within that tree, but who had been freed when the ritual was sabotaged.

Tradition muddled the meanings, but I parsed out the truth. My Serpent — Taozu, Famine — had once been caged, but won his freedom a hundred and twenty years before.

What he had done in the intervening time before finding me, I could only speculate, though I guessed by his hunger it was to hunt and grow stronger. But even more than discovering his immediate origins, I reveled in one other fact.

If the Serpent had been imprisoned once, he could be imprisoned again.

The means by which this could occur, too, revealed itself. Involved in the ritual was a scepter, what they called a "ruyi," one as white as the vast tree. But it had been lost to the sands when the ritual failed.

This scepter seemed key in defying my god. So I set out into the wasteland to find it.

My heart beat a little faster at that. It was a matching description to Aika's knife, the artifact the ancient girl had used to become a Sacrifice. Aika had speared Famine upon the branches of a tree in the Hunger War my ancestors fought long ago across the Lighted Sea.

Pressing aside my horror at the ritual that would sacrifice children, I read on.

For how large the tree was said to be, it was difficult to find, for it was distant, and the sky was often obscured by dust. Yet at last, I saw it looming out of the distance, as tall and thick-limbed as the Qao Fu had spoken, though gray where it was said to be white. It would have been a wonder had it not failed in its purpose, to the ruin of my life and the world.

I tried to imagine such a tree and failed. The Pillars scattered about Oedija were the tallest things I knew, and they did not come close to such a height. I decided to reserve judgment until I'd read further.

I poured more coffee, careful not to splash on the pages, intending to press on. But the feast hall had populated during my reading, and noise rose with others' arrival. Dawn must have broken and gone. Eyes gritty, mood sour, I tried to concentrate through the conversations springing up around me. Eventually, I would have to go someplace else, but I couldn't yet muster the energy to move.

I soon regretted it when a familiar voice spoke. "Airene."

Curbing my impatience, I looked up at Corin, readying a weary explanation for why I couldn't chat, but the words stuck in my throat. The former cartwoman wasn't alone. A young woman stood beside her, with pale skin and blonde hair that marked her as an outlander of Jolduun, as did her strange clothes, all fur and coarse leather and pilled wool.

Clues abounded as to the newcomer's identity, yet I couldn't turn the tired cogs of my mind to come to a conclusion. Corin provided the answer a moment later as she held up one of her calloused hands to gesture toward the young woman.

"This is my sister, Kari."

Her sister — the resemblance was unmistakable once she pointed it out. Though Corin's features were blunter and rounder, and her brow more pronounced, their noses possessed the same petiteness, and their ears were inordinately small.

And there was the matter that the entirety of Corin's life had been bent toward bringing this very sister to Oedija to escape the persecution back in their homeland.

"Kari." My voice came out faint, so I cleared my throat and tried again. "It's good to meet you after all these years."

Only after I'd spoken did I wonder if she understood the sea-tongue. Corin had possessed only a rudimentary grasp of Oedija's language when she first moved to the mainland. Kari's response, however, put my mind at ease. Though her words were heavily accented, her diction was clear enough to understand.

"I thank you, Airene Finch. For taking care of Sister." Kari grinned. She had a toothy smile, one that seemed almost childish in its exuberance.

I returned it hesitantly. "She's taken care of me as well."

Corin nodded gravely. "We are family. We watch out for one another."

Family. That she would apply that word to me when her sister stood next to her, the sister for whom she had sacrificed all other happiness, caught me by the throat. I blinked rapidly to keep my eyes dry.

"Thank you, Corin. Of course we are."

Kari startled me by reaching across the table and seizing my hand. "We are sisters!"

But as soon as we touched, Corin's sister froze. Her eyes seemed to grow distant, and she clutched my hand tightly enough to hurt. I tried to hide my wince as I wondered what was happening.

Then I remembered.

Corin had named her sister a witch. Likely, it meant she was attuned. As her trance went on, a horrible suspicion rose in me. I tried to pull away, but she held fast. Only by slipping off my glove could I escape her, and I would thereby expose my expanding shifts. Fortunately, Corin intervened before I was forced to.

"Kari! *Seska!*" The former cartwoman seized her sister by the shoulders and brought her upright. Kari spasmed, her eyelids fluttering, before she seemed to come to. Her eyes traveled to the ceiling for a long moment before they settled back on me. No hint of a smile remained, but only a haggard stare.

"You are *pilsaam*," she said. "Tainted. Beware the bone, Airene Finch; it traps you."

The hairs rose on the nape of my neck. I couldn't precisely understand her words, yet they didn't seem idle ravings. They flirted around ideas I

had been reading about, secrets which I desperately needed to know —
and those I wished to hide.

I tried to disguise my feelings behind a kindly smile. "Thank you, Kari.
I'll take your words to heart."

I had no desire to remain in the feast hall then. Gathering my possessions as hurriedly as I dared, I rose from the table. Corin watched me
silently, her sister still held close with one hand.

"You are going?" my former loftmate asked quietly.

"Afraid so. This book — I have to keep reading it. I'm sorry, I don't
mean to rush off, I just..."

My words trailed off. We both knew the true reason I fled. Yet I saw
only acceptance in my friend's eyes.

"If you need anything, Airene," Corin said, "ask. I will do it."

My throat tightened again, so I merely nodded, then turned and fled,
Kari's words chasing me to my room.

CHAPTER SEVEN

SUMMONS

Daemon possessions have long been a tradition among our people. How often it has actu-
ally occurred, I cannot say, yet I suspect it is less frequent than claimed. For some, it has
provided a convenient excuse for improper behavior. A dalliance done under a spirit's
influence, after all, can hardly be one's own fault.

But there is undoubtedly some truth behind the more reputable claims. Avvad is
suspected of knowingly possessing their own people. Incidents in Oedija have no expla-
nation as well. Persons whose personalities change overnight. Deeds done with seemingly
no rationale.

Maybe there is another explanation. But for want of one, we must fear the pyr who
might wish us harm.

- Tales of Wardens: A brief study of Oedijan folk stories; by Acadian Helene, Master
Historian; 1160 SLP

With Vusu's journal clutched in one hand and my heel of stale bread in the other, I sought Linos's room.

Perhaps it was Corin's reminder of family, or seeing her with her sister, but when I was forced from the feast hall, the urge to visit him arose in me.

My younger brother had shown no will in the spans since his harrowing escape from the end of Vusu's knife. Still, I made it a point to visit him each day and spend a little time with him. I hoped my presence might eventually coax out the part of his spirit that lingered.

Kyros Brighteyed had said something remained of Linos, though tenuously connected. I had to believe there was enough that he would once again be the life-filled young man I remembered.

The healing ward was at the opposite end of the palace from the feast hall. Linos's room was one of four available. Plain, almost austere in its adornment, it boasted little more than a bed, a washing basin, and a small cabinet.

My brother lay in the bed, never seeming to blink as he stared up at the ceiling. I could only look at him for a moment before I turned back to fetch one of the honors monitoring the sick ward, asking them for a tray of food and broth. Though Linos sometimes fed himself, when he was in his more apathetic states, broth was the simplest for me to give him. It wasn't necessary; his attendants took good care of all his needs. Yet the elder sister in me always felt the inclination to look after him.

I fetched a chair and dragged it next to his bed, then sat heavily in it while I waited for the food. Vusu's journal hung unopened in my hand as I stared out the window over my brother's bed. I often found it difficult to look directly at him. The mauve scars around his eyes, resembling the last clawing of the damned, reminded me too much of what he'd suffered.

I entered briefly into the Pyrthae. Each time I indulged the inclination, I hoped I would see a change in his spirit, but there was only a glimmer of a flame, and I felt no recognition from it as I neared.

Returning to my body, I leaned back and finally cracked open the book. It took my weary eyes a long while to focus, then longer still to find where I'd left off. At last, I picked it up: Vusu was drawing conclusions for his visit to the Qao Fu.

> *This substance, whether it was stone or bark or something not of this world, I could not tell, even having touched the trunk of the Chains. But that it had held Famine once, and only failed when the wrong sacrificial boy was sent for the duty, was too tantalizing an idea to dismiss.*

The idea, with its echoes to Aika and her tale, intrigued me as well. My interest hooked once more, I began to read faster.

> *Having learned all I could among the Qao Fu, I ventured southwest to a different land. From the jaitin's elders, I had heard rumors of another appearance of the Serpent, long ago and in a land far across the western seas. I set out for Oedija, hoping to hear more of the "Hunger War" that led to their immigration to these lands.*
>
> *Through forests and across plains, around the mountains guarding the nation's northern front, I finally arrived at the so-called "Pearl of the Four Realms," and found the title to be only slightly aggrandized. Oedija was a true city, with all its flaws and marvels. The poor littered the streets, while the rich lived in palatial manors. Merchants*

flung every good imaginable from across the known world at me, each slavering for a bit of coin.

Yet there were rumblings of unease. Despoina Zalfene was building what would become known as the Half-Wall, an incomplete defense against Avvad to the south. And word of the conflict among my people, the war I had begun, had long ago traveled across the miles. I hid my identity with magic, pretending to belong to a neighboring ishaka, the Yorandu, and changed my name to the one I bear now. Though forty years had passed since my uprising, I feared someone might guess I was the Yama who had spilled so much blood.

The names and events Vusu referenced were strange to see, for it was still difficult to imagine the length of his life. He had seen over a century, and yet had still possessed a vitality befitting a man of Xaron's years.

I wondered if I would inherit Famine's strength as well. I doubted I would live long enough to find out.

Without my name and station, the knowledge I sought was barred to me. But for a warden of my power, nothing was beyond my reach for long. In the dead of night, I stole into the library at the heart of the Acadium and delved into the depths of its lore. I learned of their absent gods, the Eidola, and the name by which they knew my Serpent: Famine. I read of the Hunger War, the conflict between the deities, and how it had ended with a girl, who had killed the daemon god upon the branches of a white tree.

No doubt the scholars believed it to be myth, as I once would have. But I suspected the stories were quite real, at least at their core. The tree in the Wumofu was proof alone. But for all I learned of the Serpent's nature, and how I saw patterns emerging as to how I might one day be rid of him, no immediate solution revealed itself.

The two god-binding trees, Aika's knife and the Qao Fu scepter — there were connections that I could not yet untangle, clues that might help me in my present quandary if I could only understand them. Too tired for speculation, I resolved to finish my reading before I attempted to draw any conclusions. *And get sleep,* I amended as I turned back to the pages.

Like myself, Vusu wondered about Harvest and her role in Aika's story:

In the years that followed, I questioned the truth of the Oedijan stories. What was real and what was not? Was this Harvest any more material than the other absent gods? Yet Famine exists, and though he is a god confined by my blood and flesh, he seems too immortal and pervasive to be named anything else.

I required the scepter or the knife, but knew not where either lay. Yet even with them, I was beginning to understand that, if I wished to truly be rid of the daemon plaguing me, and to rid the world of him besides, it would require more than myself.

I needed a sacrifice; better yet, the right sacrifice. It seemed likely a child would be required, or a youth, for both stories had involved the young. They likely had to have some influence of a god, of Harvest or Famine. But it would take years to discover what would do.

So I realized I must establish myself here in Oedija, become more than a pathetic vagrant living among paupers. I needed influence, resources, access. And, most important of all, I needed people upon which to experiment.

For only with all the world behind me could anyone hope to survive. And survival is worth any sacrifice.

At this, I leaned in, wondering if, at last, I might discover the secrets to my brother's condition. But before I could read further, the door to Linos's room opened. The honor had returned, balancing a heavy tray of food as she came over to the bed. I thanked her, then looked away until she'd gone. After Kelena's revelations of what an honor's life was like, I hadn't felt comfortable requesting their services. Still, my task was too urgent to do otherwise.

Still famished, I scarfed down half the tray before I attended to Linos. Broth dribbled out of the corners of his mouth and down his chin as I unsuccessfully tried to feed him. Making him sit up worked better, but he failed to rouse and take the spoon himself. I fought down my disappointment, but soon grew too discouraged to continue. I finished the meal myself.

Satiated for the moment, I set the tray on Linos's side table and settled back into my chair. The need for sleep was catching up to me. I opened the journal to where I'd last read, but at once began nodding off. I leaned on Linos's bed, trying to prop myself up and persist a little longer.

As my head rested on the covers, my resolve melted away.

It wasn't a restful sleep. I dreamed of my mother, slinking off into the night when she thought no one else was awake, to attend one of her various liaisons throughout the years. In the dream, I was a child again, listening to her footsteps. She'd always believed herself stealthy, yet I'd heard her every departure. Not for the first time, I wondered if my brothers and I shared the same father. If the man I called father was, in truth, my own blood.

But I didn't mull over the memory for long. As often happened since Famine's reemergence, I drifted into the Pyrthae.

The landscape was not the parallel mirrorscape I was used to seeing while awake, but the sandy wasteland it had been when I fought against Vusu. I was sand in a gale, spinning in a torrent through the dusky sky. A glow settled over the city, as if the very buildings themselves emitted light. I roamed, looking over Oedija, this city I called home, and how it had been ravaged.

Was this what it would soon be reduced to? I feared the dangers facing it were too great to overcome. Famine, Avvad, rioting from our own people — the Manifest's fall was a minor victory. I still had only the slightest idea of how to deal with the daemon god. I feared I would only gain days of reprieve for Telae. Vusu had only held on for a few turns, and even half-dead, he'd been far stronger. As I looked down, it seemed the winds in that phantasmal place would pull me apart, grain by grain, until there was nothing left.

A part of me thought that might not be so bad. Then, at least, I wouldn't have to struggle any longer.

It is not the only way.

I gathered the strands of myself as I flinched away from the voice. A moment later, I recognized it, even as I saw the stray swirl of sand filtering toward me like a serpent through water.

The boy in the whisper finch, I thought back.

Yes. The boy moved closer, then reshaped himself, the sand coalescing into the approximation of a child. With dun lips, he formed a smile. I found it more haunting than reassuring, yet the boy had helped me often enough that I didn't flee.

You're a pyr? I queried him.

He nodded, the movement not quite natural to his sandy flesh. *As you have long suspected.*

Why are you helping me? It was the question that had always kept me from fully trusting him. Motivations were far more telling than oaths.

The boy gestured with one hand, his fingers fraying even as they flexed. *To right old wrongs. To mend the world. To stop Taozu.*

Taozu. An old Qao Fu name, and one I now recognized well. *Famine.*

The boy drifted closer. *The Corrupted stole everything from me. My life. My honor. My family. I will not let him take my world. So I intend to aid you, Airene the Finch, if you let me. I will help you cage him once again.*

How do you know my name? Why won't you tell me yours? My frustration mounted. Though I appreciated allies, I liked ones I could rely upon more.

His shoulders rose and fell. *My name is no secret. I am Azhi; Xian Azhi, once.*

Azhi. A Qao Fu name, too. How have you survived? You're only a boy.

The pyr smiled again. *Though young, before I died, I was a talented weaver, as we called our attuned, one of the best in my jaitin. My ability made me reckless. I craved eternal honor and earned immortal shame. So I have endured, hoping to right my wrongs.*

His words didn't add up in my mind. *Your wrongs… what wrong could a boy have done?*

The sand spirit slowly spun, tendrils of his body breaking off to curl around him, like the strands of a Silk's bonds.

I appear as a child to you, Airene, but I am older than any alive. My existence reaches back centuries, and my sins as well. The boy bowed his head and continued to turn. *I am to blame for Taozu's return. I am the one who freed him.*

My thoughts were frozen for a moment. Then, as the pieces fell into place, my mind raced.

How? When? Why?

They were only the first of the many questions assaulting me. Answers tried to crowd in next to them. Hadn't I just read something of the like in Vusu's journal? Could it possibly be referencing the boy before me?

Azhi stopped his revolution and raised his hands as if in surrender. *I will tell you all, Airene. I will guide you as best I can. But to explain the rest, you must meet me.*

That threw me off-kilter. *What do you mean? We can talk now.*

No. He shook his head. *In the flesh. In Telae.*

But you're a pyr!

In part, yes. But I wear a face you will recognize. Do not fear me, Airene. And remember: I am ever your friend. If we are to defeat Famine, we must do so together.

Those claiming to be friends had tricked me before, and I wasn't trusting to begin with. Yet Azhi had assisted me many times and never asked for anything in return. Without his interventions, I doubted I would still be breathing.

I made my decision.

Where will we meet?

The pyr's relief washed out from him. Apparently, he hadn't been sure what I would do, either. *The Pillar in the Conclave. I will be there as soon as the sun has set this night.*

How will you enter? I wondered whose face he would wear. Then it occurred to me how a pyr might wear any face, and fear struck through me. *Wait! Will you—?*

At dusk!

Azhi fled. His body splintered, bursting out in a hundred different directions, and I watched as the Pyrthaen winds carried him away. Foreboding filled me as surely as the plane's energy, and I hadn't shrugged it off when I emerged from sleep's clutches.

Awake, I raised my head and clutched it with a groan. My neck was horribly sore, my skull pounded, and my limbs dragged with exhaustion. Yet a feverish energy filled me as well. I didn't know if it was born of the need for answers or Famine's connection to me, augmenting my attunement and flooding me with power. I wouldn't get any more rest now, not until after the meeting this evening.

I would go. Against my better judgment, despite the knowledge of what Azhi likely was, I would go to the Conclave Pillar. The pyr held back many secrets, but I believed him when he said he had information I required to cage Famine.

No matter how foolish and desperate it seemed, I had to grasp at every chance. There was little hope of success as it was. If it took a few risks to further it, then I would gladly accept them.

I rose, stretched, and stared out the window. The sun was already falling toward the horizon past the Lighted Sea. I had to go now if I meant to meet Azhi in time. My stomach, grumbling already, would have to wait.

My gaze fell to my brother, still lying in the same position. I was racked by guilt again, but I hardened myself to it.

"This is the only way, Linos," I whispered to him and pressed his hand. "Azhi might be a Qarin, but he has the answers I need."

I feared that the pyr was the kind of abomination I hated most, a spirit who occupied a human body to once again exist in Telae. It was the same kind as had haunted Linos and sometimes possessed him.

But I would go. I would overcome my prejudice and listen. I had no other choice.

I straightened, adjusted my disheveled clothes, still the same as I'd worn to infiltrate the Manifest warehouse. Then I strode down the hallway toward the Conclave.

CHAPTER EIGHT

OLD ENEMIES

There is comfort in seeing the face of an enemy. When they stand there before you, you know they do not plot behind your back.

- The journal of Vusumuzi; date unknown

I reached the Conclave Pillar as the sun touched the horizon.

I absently followed the sunset's progression as my mind sorted through what to expect from the coming conversation. The clouds crowding the sky caught the light, glowing crimson for miles in either direction. It would have made me smile under other circumstances.

Now, all I could see was the angry color of blood, waiting to be spilled.

Though my eyes were distracted, I kept watch in the Pyrthae. As a pyr — and Qarin, I suspected — Azhi would leave a mark I could not miss. Yet for all my caution, I saw no sign of him coming.

The Conclave had often been bustling during previous visits, but now, the courtyard lay quiet. Even if its authority had been stripped with Jaxas's seizure of the city, its offices remained open to conduct the administrative affairs of the city. Oedija needed its bureaucracy, with its expertise and competence, now more than ever. Stability was sorely lacking in our nation.

With the courtyard empty, it would be impossible for Azhi to evade me no matter the body he wore. Yet still, I remained uneasy. I didn't have to reach far to realize why.

I wear a face you will recognize.

Which face? Whose body had he seized? I feared for my friends. I knew little of how daemons took their hosts, but Talan had once said they must be attuned to become so. Nomusa would be safe, as would my family far away on the Wreath estate. But Xaron and Talan were at risk, as were Isidora and her Watchers.

And so was Linos.

My heart raced. Could he be the one Azhi occupied? Vusu had once named him Vessel. A daemon had already possessed him before. Why not again? He had little resistance to offer.

No sooner had I resolved to run back to my brother than the Pillar began to change.

I stared as the dull gray stone swiftly gathered light of its own making. I channeled quintessence on instinct and sensed it was not just a trick of reflections. Something was channeling through the stone.

Something — or someone.

A further baffling sight appeared. Where no one had stood before, a man took shape. The Pillar in the Pyrthae vibrated, and a flame with a long tether emerged. In Telae, the light coalesced into a man's shape, then slowly stripped away, like the unrolling of a tapestry. Underneath, the man looked very much real, his flesh unblemished by his peculiar method of travel.

So bewildered was I by this entrance that, for a moment, I did not recognize him. When I did, I flinched back, an arm raised as animal fear flooded through me.

Eazal smiled at me, the corners of his eyes crinkling.

"Hello, Airene. I am sorry to startle you."

I couldn't respond. My heart battered at my chest. I wanted to run, run anywhere, even off the edge of the cliff. My terror was irrational; part of me remained dispassionate enough to realize that. I was ten times the warden Eazal had revealed himself to be before he fled.

But he'd nearly killed me. And now he'd returned to finish the job.

I lowered my arm and clenched my hands into fists. My fingertips burned with radiance against my palms, blistering the skin, but I couldn't stop it.

"Don't come near me." My voice came out strained and weaker than I wanted, but my intent was clear. After how we'd parted, he had to know I was a warden.

The man raised his hands. As he had once been an apothecary, they were calloused and marred from contact with hazardous elements. He was gaunt, his eyes hollowed and his lips thin, and aged years beyond when I'd last seen him. Yet there burned in his eyes a vitality he lacked before.

"Airene," he spoke in a low voice. "I warned you I would come bearing a familiar face."

His words rang in my head, and I stared at him in disbelief. They too closely matched Azhi's earlier statement. But it was possible Eazal had been spying on us in the Pyrthae. He could know which words to say to gain my trust.

I channeled quintessence and peered into the realm above, and there saw the telltale connection of a Qarin and their host, as I'd viewed with Talan's companion Sule several times before. Eazal was not alone in his body any longer.

Though the man had tried to murder me, it still repulsed me.

"Tell me your name," I demanded.

"Xian Azhi. As I told you in the Higher Plane."

I could barely relax my jaw enough to speak. It was all the confirmation I could hope for, yet it wasn't enough. I needed answers.

"How?" There were too many questions to sort through. "How did you come through the Pillar? How did you possess *him*?"

Eazal — or rather, Azhi — shrugged. "I know you believe him evil, Airene. But remember him when you first met. Eazal of Sandglass was a wretched man, not a wicked one. He tried to kill you because his wife and daughter were threatened by a Valemish priest. When he failed, he was desperate enough to entrust his life to me."

"So he chose this, did he?" I shot back. "He wanted to be possessed?"

"Of course not. But, in time, he will grow to understand." Azhi's expression darkened. "So I must hope."

It seemed an honest answer, but I found little reassurance in it. "And how did you come to be here?"

"To explain that would take more time than we can spare. I will say this: matter and energy are two sides of a coin. They share more in common than you might think. How did you suppose you first entered the Pyrthae, a realm of pure energy, then returned in the flesh?"

It was a fair question, and one which I'd had too little time to consider. But doubt would show a fissure in my armor; I intended to keep as strong a defense as I could.

"And what does that have to do with the Pillar?"

"They are not mere stone, Airene. The Pillars are connected; not in this world, but in the other. Have you never noticed how their points bend toward one another, as if to touch? They are passages, ways of traveling quickly about the city. I suspect they were once commonly used, before magic became seen here as wicked."

I looked up in the Pyrthae and saw on that point, at least, he spoke truly. The Pillars arced like the talons of the Wyvern's Claw, back before it had burned down. The very tips of their peaks touched together.

Passages? I wondered how such a thing could be constructed, and to span both Telae and the Pyrthae. Another reminder of just how little I knew of my powers.

In the flesh, my gaze remained steady on Azhi. "Fine. I'll take your word on it. But I cannot trust you now, Azhi. Not while you wear his face."

Azhi grimaced. "I must keep it. To do what must be done, I must have a body. But if you cannot trust me, Airene, at least listen. We have precious little time, and there is much to be done."

I knew that as well as he, felt the urgency throbbing in my bones. I refused to let it rush me into a fatal decision.

"Speak, then. I will listen, but I don't promise to believe."

Azhi nodded. "That is all I ask. But if I might sit. This body… I am still unused to how it tires."

His words made my skin crawl, yet I nodded and skirted out of the way as he went to a nearby stone bench. A sigh escaped his lips as he sat, and he stretched and rolled his limbs as if to relieve lingering pains.

"Some things, I have missed," Azhi murmured, almost to himself. "Others, I have not."

He seemed to come back to himself a moment later, for his eyes found me as I moved to stand in front of him, a dozen cubits away.

"I will start, briefly, at the beginning of my knowledge," he said. "A thousand years ago, my people claimed, the god we named Taozu was confined within a cage called *Liantao* — the Chains, in your sea-tongue. This prison, deep within the Wumofu Desert, manifested as an impossibly large tree with bark as hard as stone and as white as the sun. Its branches reached to the stars themselves, and through all the planes spiritual and material."

The Chains. Vusu had written of the large tree in his journal, though it had been gray when he visited it. Having heard of it from two sources, I no longer doubted it existed.

"Every generation, a child was chosen from among the jaitin to go to the Chains and renew the bonds." Azhi's eyes fell to his hands, clutching at each other as if they wrestled. "We knew it as walking the Ancestors' Path, for their spirits sang the way to us, their bones buried deep beneath the sands to guide the chosen child. Anyone who walked it would not return, for the only way to strengthen the cage was through sacrifice."

This story, too, Vusu had addressed. I tried to hide my distaste and suspected I did it poorly. Azhi had only to glance up to see it.

"I know — it must seem strange and barbaric to you. But among my people, it was a great honor, one envied by all the other children. I was the most jealous of all, so much so that I did what no other had done before: I stole the duty for myself."

"You what?" I could scarcely believe it. Not only had children been sacrificed decade after decade, but they *longed* to be killed?

Azhi smiled, his expression drenched in regret. "A foolish act with a foolish end. I was tricked into believing I was truly the one who must go by a spirit. Afterward, I came to understand they longed only to consume my soul for their own survival. But at the time, I thought it another sign that I was blessed, that I must go on my journey."

His head fell again, and he stared at the ground. "But excuses grow flimsier each year. Suffice it to say, I failed in my mission. Instead of feeding my spirit to the Chains, I gave Taozu my blood. And thus, at last, he broke free of his bonds."

Something about his story didn't add up. "But Famine was bound by Vusu. He hasn't been free since… when did you free him?"

Azhi met my eyes. "Two centuries ago."

Two hundred years. I tried to imagine such an existence. Azhi had seen generations born and buried while he lived on. Was it for this purpose alone? For the day he knew Famine would threaten the world once more? Or was he now like the greedy spirit he'd once been tricked by?

He seemed to sense the war inside my head. "Considering all that Taozu has wrought in the past season, I can understand why you would be skeptical. But you must understand that when the Corrupted first won free of his cage, he was shriveled and weak, starved of the spirit for which he hungered. It took him years to harvest and grow to a vestige of his former might, and then he could only prey upon those spirits he could catch. I watched him on his hunt for years before he found a new way to obtain the essence he craved."

I guessed what he alluded to, but remained silent. No need to give him words to twist to his own purpose.

Azhi confirmed my suspicions aloud. "He sought those reckless enough to accept his bargain: the power of the Higher Plane in exchange for souls sacrificed to him. He bonded himself with two young Bali men from an outcast ishaka, and by them harvested the essence of humans and animals common to the Mortal Plane. And thus he grew and grew, biding his time until he could break free."

"Yama and Lophe," I murmured, lulled into speaking. "But Vusu didn't let him break free for decades after their crusade failed. He held him."

Azhi flashed me a wan smile. "He did, for far longer than I thought possible. I began to believe he would find a way to imprison the great spirit, as the Chains once had. But as every Seed before him, his strength eventually faded, and his despair grew."

A realization struck me. "You knew what he did," I said slowly. "Yet you didn't intervene. You didn't stop him from..."

I couldn't say it; fury choked out the rest of my words.

Azhi winced and looked away. "I did not have the power to. Only through other beings was I able to assist you, Airene, and then only at great risk. Taozu is a jealous being. He always watched for prey, and on several occasions, he nearly caught me. Only now that he has gone am I safe here — or, at least, safer than before."

I shook my head. My eyes felt swollen in their sockets. I badly needed sleep, but even more, I needed answers. Not daring to let the Qarin and his host out of my sight for a moment, I tried to reason through what else I needed to know.

"You hoped Vusu had a way to contain him," I said. "To cage Famine. That must mean you don't know how yourself."

Azhi sighed and stretched again. Evidently, his body was chafing at him once more, aged joints and muscles aching. When he finished, he leaned his elbows onto his knees.

"In one sense, you are correct: I do not know precisely how it is done. With a few exceptions, no being in existence has witnessed Taozu's capture, for a millennia is a long time for even a spirit to survive."

My thoughts caught on his words. "Exceptions? What exceptions?"

His eyebrows drew together. "Surely, you know. Their influence lingers upon you. They have intervened in your life and Oedija's fate more thoroughly than I have."

Only then did it occur to me. "Clepsammia," I breathed.

"Yes. She and some of the other great spirits have always interacted with the Mortal Plane. Too few remain now. Yet though they cannot, or will not, tell their secrets, I believe they are the key to defeating our enemy."

I wanted to tear Azhi's knowledge from Eazal's head, yet I tried to hide my eagerness. Though the daemon seemed to speak truthfully, I didn't want to introduce any sign of weakness, lest he take advantage.

So I only cocked an eyebrow. "Go on."

Azhi glanced toward the horizon. The sun's glow was fading, leaving the sky blue with touches of green from the radiant winds. "There are items in Telae that relate to the great spirits," he said, eyes sliding back to me. "Artifacts forged by or from their essence. One of these was used in the ritual that caged Taozu for hundreds of years. We called it the Binding Ruyi, and it appeared to be made of the same substance as the Chains."

The possessed man straightened, then reached a hand down to his waist. At once, I raised a hand, radiance flickering at the tips of my fingers. Azhi did not startle, but only looked up with a small smile.

"Still, you do not trust me," he murmured. "Yet you must, Airene, if we are to defeat our enemy."

I was in no mood for a lecture. "What were you reaching for?"

"The thing of which I spoke. The Binding Ruyi."

My breath caught. Though he hadn't said a false word that I knew of, I couldn't believe him.

"The Quintyr artifact. You have it here?"

"Yes. Would you like to see it?"

It shamed me, but I nodded. Even if it exposed a vulnerability, I had to see.

Azhi gave me another smile, then reached again for the cloth-wrapped object hanging from the sash wound around his middle. It seemed a peculiar shape, now that I looked closer at it. He slipped it free, unwrapped it, then held it up.

The artifact was a short scepter, no longer than my arm. Its shape was of a snake or a dragon, the head of it open-mouthed as if it meant to lash out. It appeared smooth in texture, and from top to bottom, it was as white as bone.

It had been mentioned in Vusu's journal, this scepter, or one very much like it. Even more, it was not the only object I'd seen of its kind. Though I'd held neither item, I knew it would be the same material as Aika's knife, which Vusu had used to become a Sacrifice and bind Famine for those brief turns.

Artifacts of the Quintyr. My head spun to think of what it might mean.

Azhi watched me carefully, judging my reactions. As silence stretched on, he finally broke it. "You recognize something in this ruyi, do you not?"

I debated the wisdom of revealing anything, then nodded. The pyr had extended a measure of trust to me. I could give that much back.

"It resembles an object I've seen, one Vusu used to end his life, and another I've heard tell of. But tell me, daemon — what do you plan to do with it?"

He laid the ruyi on his lap. "As I said, I do not know precisely how to use the Binding Ruyi to ensnare Taozu once again. But we will not discover it here, away from him." His eyes rose to meet mine once more. "We must go to him, Airene. We must pursue Taozu and bind him. He grows stronger by the day, by the turn. Already, he can again consume the other great spirits. Soon, he will challenge the mightiest among them. I have seen what has happened through his supremacy. The wastelands across the breadth of the world. Only here, in the Four Realms, and a few pockets in other lands remain. Only here does civilization remain intact."

Azhi looked aside, and I couldn't deny the passion in his voice. Hadn't Eltris once said the same of the world? But to think that only in the Four

Realms life remained, especially when we warred among ourselves... It was a terrible, bitter truth to swallow.

"If the other gods fall," he continued, softer now, "nothing will stand in the way of these lands becoming every bit as desolate as the Wumofu. All life will be consumed."

I remembered Oedija as I'd seen it in my dream, a sandy wasteland, and knew how close that vision was coming to pass. It struck terror through me that made my legs feel like straw and my head faint. Only by force of will did I remain upright.

"You would have me abandon Oedija?" I had to force out the words, for my throat tried to clamp shut. "Leave my friends and family to face Avvad on their own?"

Even as I said it, I wondered what I could do by remaining behind. I was no warrior. I had a unique capacity for channeling quintessence, but it would do little good against an army. And what use would it be to defeat the Imperium if Famine still destroyed Telae?

Still, I couldn't go. Not on Azhi's word and my suspicions alone. This was too much for my weary mind. I needed to think things over. I needed time.

Though I had none to spare.

Azhi seemed to weigh his words before responding. "I realize this must seem like a great gamble, trusting me. Leaving behind everything you know to venture into the unknown. But you can sense Taozu, can you not? You feel how he grows; your connection to the Pyrthae grows with him. I see it, even if I did not already know it."

His words struck too close to the mark. "What do you mean?"

Eazal's eyes contained the centuries of Azhi's life within them. "You are the last of the Seeds, Airene, now that Vusumuzi is dead. You are the only one who can bind him now."

It wasn't anything I didn't already know. Still, it broke me. I stumbled back a step, staring at the possessed man like he'd struck me. My mind was numb with panic.

"I must go," I managed to say before turning away.

"We must leave soon, Airene!" Azhi shouted after me. "I will return here tomorrow. Be ready, or we may be too late."

I only stumbled away from him, then nearly ran back to the Laurel Palace.

It wasn't fast enough to outrun the thoughts that haunted me.

CHAPTER NINE

SACRIFICE

The night pressed in thick by the time I returned to my room. Golden pyr lamps illuminated the palace halls, and I flitted from one pool of light to the next. Though I was as safe as I could be within the Laurel Palace walls, it felt as if a specter stalked me and would seize me the moment I stopped moving.

I reached my room without incident, shut the door, and leaned against it. My eyelids drifted closed. For a moment, it was all I could do to simply breathe. I felt too tired to stand, yet too anxious to lie down. My head was full to bursting with all the knowledge I had gained and all I must do.

Yet my immediate duty was clear: I couldn't make any decision before I finished reading Vusu's journal. Already, a confluence between his thoughts and Azhi's proclamations had appeared, and I was only halfway through. I still hoped to discover the answers that plagued me, greatest of all how one committed oneself as a Sacrifice to Famine.

Only, didn't I already know how? I'd witnessed Vusu doing it, saw its results. Perhaps there were nuances I'd missed in the rush of the moment, but I suspected fear was what truly held me back. Fear, and a desperate hope that I might not have to die, no matter all the evidence mounting to the contrary.

I knew the truth. The best I could do was become a Sacrifice and hold Famine at bay. If we were lucky, I would imprison him for centuries. If we weren't… I couldn't consider what would happen then.

So I read, though my eyes crossed and my head ached and my neck sent shooting pains into my shoulders. I read as Vusu detailed his experiments in how he might more permanently confine the daemon god.

A vessel, a human vessel, is what is required. I have served as such for decades, but perhaps it is not necessary for me to be the Sacrifice. Perhaps another might be used in my place, and thus become a permanent prison.

My skin crawled, though I could muster little more reaction than that. Here was where the idea had begun for what he had done to Linos. What he had attempted on Thero and failed. Painful as it was to follow the man's twisted thoughts, I forced myself to read on. It was the only way I could make my brothers' sacrifices mean something.

After failing to make ready many for the Serpent, I have noticed a pattern in those who seem more suitable. This tendency runs in families, in bloodlines, as if it is a trait passed down. What it might be, I cannot say, yet it is my best lead yet.

And there, at last, it had come from nowhere: the explanation I'd long been searching for. I stared at the words, my mind slow to unravel their portent. What had happened to Linos hadn't been an accident. He'd been targeted as Thero's younger brother, who must have been more promising than most.

It also meant Vusu's interest in me hadn't stopped at how my profession as a Finch might benefit him. He'd been interested in my entire family and something in our blood, something that made us ideal for his experiments.

I'd been pacing my room in order to stay awake while I read, but now I collapsed onto the bed. My body felt numb, my mind empty. I wondered what it meant, this trait that ran through my family. It had brought us so much pain and misery. How could it be anything but evil?

I buried my face in my hands. My eyes felt feverish against my palms. I would have cried had I had the tears, but I was dry, empty. There was no venting the misery that filled me.

Yet only a few moments passed before a glimmering thought lifted it, if slightly. I raised my head and stared at the journal on my desk, my mind slowly chewing through the realization.

Perhaps whatever ran in my family's blood could be used for good. Perhaps it was a certain kind of fate that this duty of ensnaring Famine should fall to me. For if the trait made us ideal cages for the daemon god, I might be the perfect Sacrifice.

Maybe I would stop him for good. Maybe I could be enough — if I could catch him.

But Famine was far to the east; I could feel him, as I always could, feasting and reveling in it. It would take spans, if not seasons, to reach him, and that was only if he didn't move farther away. Besides, Avvad could arrive any day at Oedija's walls, and their scouts no doubt patrolled the surrounding lands. Then there would be no departure for anyone.

I covered the pyr lamp I'd been reading by and lay again on my bed with a soft groan. I would rest and decide come morning. For now, it was all I could do.

My mind wasn't content to stop just yet. Even as I drifted into sleep's clutches, a remembered fragment from an old tome floated through my mind:

How are we to know the Seed of Harvest has planted within you? Agmon Brandheart, the First of the Wardens, had asked Aika of the Green.

No words can tell; only my actions will, she'd responded. *Take me before Famine and I will show you.*

The thought lingered for a moment, caught by idle curiosity — then it passed on, and I fell away.

————

I startled awake, only realizing after I'd sat up that a knock had awoken me.

Combing my fingers through my tangled hair, I stumbled over to the door, then hesitated. I was dressed, a precaution against just such rude awakenings, though my appearance was still far from presentable. But it wasn't that thought that stopped me but of Shepherds, who had once come calling on Xaron and forced him to flee for his life. I doubted such a thing would happen to me, but caution bade me to crack open the door and peer out at my visitor.

Then I saw who it was. I hastily pulled the door open and bowed.

The Despot of Oedija was not to be kept waiting.

Jaxas was as thin as ever, yet stood more erect and with more vigor than I'd ever seen before he wore the Evergreen Wreath. His robes were the deep green of winter moss, and a golden stole hung about his neck. A few steps behind, Nikias and two guards waited, the steward staring at me with a baleful glare.

"Even for a man of my resources," Jaxas said in his mild manner, "you are a difficult woman to track down, Airene."

Had I not still been so weary, I might have flushed. "Sorry. I didn't mean to evade you."

"I'm sure." Without waiting for an invitation, he strode inside, forcing me to back out of his way. The Despot scanned my room, his expression hiding what he made of its disarray, before turning back to me. Nikias and the guards remained in the hall.

"You have missed my council two evenings in a row," Jaxas said, as dispassionate as if observing the weather.

I wasn't fooled. This was a reprimand, and I would take it as such. It was safer to take a monarch too seriously than not at all — even a man with whom I'd shared much.

I bowed again. "I apologize once more. My duties have kept me away."

"Duties." Jaxas spoke the word as if it were new to him. "Such as reporting your mission's results, you mean."

I winced. "That is one."

Jaxas did not smile; he rarely smiled these days. Ruling had changed him, molded him into the man Oedija needed him to be. I wasn't sure I preferred the Despot to who he had been before.

"Well then," he prompted after a moment's silence. "Tell me: were you successful?"

I debated how to answer that. But as hesitation might be interpreted poorly, I didn't pause long.

"Ariston has been taken care of. And I found Seda, Vusu's honor. After some convincing, she gave me his journal. Reading it has been preoccupying me since."

None of it was an outright lie, though the truth was certainly veiled. Yet I'd told Jaxas I would assassinate Ariston, and I had not. The man I'd known before would understand.

But the Despot he was now? His reaction, I couldn't predict.

Jaxas's hooded eyes were unshifting on me for a long moment. When he spoke, his tone hadn't shifted, yet his words chilled me through.

"Kelena's network gave me an interesting report. That a man of Ariston's description fled north from the city, and a bald Avvadin woman traveled with him. Unless they saw a ghost, I cannot see how this aligns with your story."

My heart pounded hard in my chest. I kept my chin high. I could only hope that the soundness of our partnership thus far would keep me safe. Since he knew the truth, my best policy now was to abandon all deceit.

"I didn't say I killed him, Jaxas. The Manifest is all but dismantled, and with him gone, it lacks a leader. Killing him would have done no good, and perhaps cost me my chance to get the journal from Seda."

"Seda," Jaxas repeated. "Vusu's honor."

I nodded. "I have to think about our greater enemy. It was a gamble I don't regret."

The Despot stared at me a moment longer, then turned and began to pace my chamber. I watched him, his movements making me nervous. Yet with as uncertain of ground as I stood upon, I held my tongue.

At last, he turned back to me. "I had hoped it might be otherwise. Now I see the truth plain before me. You are no assassin, Airene. Yet you must harden your heart all the same. An army is at our doorstep, an army we cannot hope to defeat without substantial losses. But no war is ever won without sacrifice."

I couldn't help it; a bitter smile worked its way onto my lips. "You think I don't know that? That I haven't already made sacrifices to get as far as we have?"

He cut me off before my self-pity could carry on further. "We all have. I betrayed ideals I have believed in my entire life to do what must be done. I betrayed my uncle and my cousin and seized a crown that was not mine. Yet I accepted my burden of guilt, and I bear it, just as you must carry yours."

Yours does not require you to die!

I wanted to shout the words at him and barely bit them back. Turning my head aside, I hid the resentment that boiled inside me. It surprised me with its vehemence. I had mourned all that occurred, yet I hadn't known the sense of injustice I felt until Jaxas unlocked it.

Perhaps he sensed it, for the Despot pivoted the conversation. "You say you recovered Vusu's journal. Does it have the answers you seek? The key to stopping Famine?"

Since he'd made a concession, I had no choice but to do the same. "I'm not sure. It explains much of his motivations and actions, but I've found little that will turn the tide. I'm only part of the way through, however. The last pages will likely reveal the most."

Jaxas nodded and turned to the door. He paused before exiting, his gaze tilting back toward me.

"Read. That is your only duty, Airene. The Four Realms have little time — and Oedija even less."

With that, the Despot strode from my room and shut my door behind him.

I stared at the wood, but my thoughts had already flitted back to my last thought before sleep. I'd remembered a passage, one from my days spent down in the Acadium's archives. It had seemed significant when suspended halfway between consciousness, but now...

How are we to know the Seed of Harvest has planted within you?

I shook my head. *Harvest.* Perhaps some version of Clepsammia existed, and Famine as well, but it didn't mean all of the Eidolan deities existed. And if she did, what of it? Harvest was a minor goddess of no import. She bore no relevance in this war.

But why, then, did both Aika and Agmon believe her to be so crucial?

With no ready conclusion, I pushed the thought from my mind. I had to dress, eat, and fetch coffee, then finish Vusu's journal. Then I had to decide if I would take up Azhi on his offer. I had no time for stray fantasies.

Yet I'd never been good at letting go of curiosities. Even as I went about my tasks, I knew the thought would linger.

CHAPTER TEN

THE RIGHT MOMENT

All has changed in a moment. Oedija, the Four Realms — perhaps even lands beyond ours will feel the reverberations of what happens here.

A moment was all it took. But perhaps all it will take is one more moment, the right one, to change things for the better.

- A Modern History of Oedija (in composition); by Acadian Helene, Master Historian; 1171 LP

As Jaxas commanded, I finished Vusu's journal that morning. I had fewer pages to read than I'd initially thought, for many of the leaves, almost a quarter of the journal, were left blank. Even those filled held few revelations. Vusu detailed the reasons for his actions, for fomenting unrest and founding the Manifest. He'd believed the only way to defeat Famine was to rally the entire world, to produce such a state of alarm that everyone in the Four Realms would rise against him and the daemon god within him.

But it seemed a madman's plan. Why foment divisions rather than forge alliances? He could have sought help instead of enemies to destroy him, and the threat could have been overcome without such bloodshed.

Yet from all I'd seen of Vusu, I thought I understood his reasoning. Long ago, as a young man of a fading ishaka, he'd chosen to make war on his kinsmen. Conflict had long simmered within Vusu, and Famine's inhabitance of his soul likely expanded it.

Understanding brought no further notion of how to proceed, however.

Journal clutched in my hands, I paced my room for so long it seemed I must wear a line into the stone floor. I had to make a move, but I didn't know which way to go. Each trail branching before me led to the same result, one I couldn't accept.

Only one avenue had opened before me that held even a chance of defeating Famine. Yet how could I trust Azhi, a Qarin occupying the body of my would-be assassin?

So I paced, racking my brain for another way, and each time coming up short.

Half a turn into my fretting, I realized I wouldn't be able to decide on my own. But who could I turn to? Nomusa and Xaron were needed here in Oedija; their positions were too important to vacate. And I guessed at the first insinuation of trusting Azhi, they'd tie me up to keep me from acting rashly. Talan was likely too deep into his cups for me to trust his judgment.

The next person I thought of surprised me. *Eltris*. The spans had cooled my anger toward her, though I hadn't recovered my opinion of the Master Augur. She'd been willing to let Vusu make Linos his Sacrifice; after that, I doubted I could ever trust her again. Still, either she or Kyros had taken Aika's knife, and if Azhi had spoken the truth, I would need the artifact no matter which path I traveled.

So it was that I set off for the Acadium.

The air was oppressive as I strode down the streets, and the guards who let me out of the gate stared at me like I were mad. Perhaps I was. The city guard had all but abandoned control over the revolting population, marshaling the walls' defenses against Avvad instead. Likewise, the taxoi Jaxas had ordered into being were occupied with drilling intensely so they wouldn't fold at the first charge — though that seemed a distinctive possibility regardless, considering the Avvadin forces had been trained from the cradle.

But I wasn't defenseless any longer. When a group of three men leered at me, I scared them off with a flare of radiance. It was unwise to advertise my attunement, yet I doubted word would reach back to anyone who would move against me. Jaxas knew and let me roam free. Of those in power, only Feiyan was vindictive enough to attempt something, but she seemed too distracted by her newfound position to mind me much.

The Acadium was near to the Laurel Palace, and I returned without further incident. The guards hesitated to admit me, for I had no official authority, but I had only to remind them I had the Despot's ear for them to relent. I went quickly through before they changed their minds.

The city's mania had infected the campus as well. Acadians bustled to and fro, heads bowed and eyes darting, constantly watching for threats. I ignored the passersby and headed straight for the squat tower where the old augur resided. If I knew Eltris, she wouldn't have vacated her decrepit accommodations even now.

Reaching her door, I pounded thrice on the weathered wood. Several minutes passed before I grew suspicious. The Master Augur had always been fond of petty retribution. After the way I'd left things between us, it was no surprise she sought to punish me now.

Just as I thought I might actually attempt to climb through her window, as I'd once fantasized doing, she opened the door. Her yellow eyes peered out from the gloom beyond the cracked door, like a cat ready to pounce.

"You," was all she said.

I forced a smile. "Hello, Eltris. Mind letting me in?"

The augur scoffed. "I doubt you'd give me a choice."

The aged woman turned and shuffled back inside. I kept my temper leashed and followed her in, sealing the door behind me and trying not to be uneasy at the darkness. Whatever the conflicts between us, Eltris meant me no harm.

Or so I hoped.

"Up here," she ordered from ahead, and I saw her ascending the stairs. I meekly trailed behind, a firm hold on my tongue.

The chamber upstairs was much the same as I remembered it. Finches fluttered among the rafters, their feathers red and yellow and green, chirping to each other as they danced. The same musty carpet was rolled out over the length of stone floor, pocked with stray radiant flares. Flames burned high in the braziers, filling the place with stifling heat.

Eltris stalked to the middle of the room before turning to face me. Her face, always wrinkled, seemed to have gathered a few more lines, and her gray hair was turning white. In just a season, Eltris had gained years.

But aging did nothing to moderate her temper.

"Well?" she snapped when I didn't immediately speak. "Say what you want, or do you have the time for social visits?"

Despite my better judgment, my muscles tightened, readying for an assault. I'd come to mend bridges, but my resolve was quickly fading.

"I won't be long," I said. "I came for the knife." I didn't explain which one; there was no need.

If my request surprised the augur, she didn't show it. "And what would you want that for?"

"It's Aika's knife, an artifact used to cage Famine. And I'm the one who must imprison him now."

I longed to shake answers out of the aged woman. My fists clenched and my fingernails dug into my palms as I stared at her, daring her to deny me. As the silence stretched, I told myself I would wait her out.

As usual, impatience won the argument.

"Will you always stand by and watch the world burn?" I demanded, taking a step forward. "Will you let Famine consume everything before you act? I don't ask you to risk your neck — Eidola know you won't do that. All I ask is that you give me the knife. Then we never need see each other again."

The old woman sneered, and my fury grew to towering heights. Before I could invent a proper insult that would slap the amusement from her face, however, the Master Augur responded.

"You believe doing anything is better than nothing. But that is how we've come to where we are now. Vusu dead. Famine free—"

I interrupted her. "And that's my fault, is that right?"

"Yes," Eltris answered at once. "Undoubtedly."

I could barely think through the haze over my thoughts. Part of me wanted to tear her apart and burn her to the bones. Yet even if I could have managed it, I never would. If she infuriated me, it was only because I knew how much more Eltris could accomplish if she acted. That she did nothing but wait was a stance I couldn't sympathize with.

"When?" My tone was measured, my fury cold. "When will you act?"

"When it is time."

I smiled, but there was no joy in it. "By then, it will be too late."

I had little hope I would convince her. Eltris was the most stubborn woman I had met, and that included Nomusa, Feiyan, and my mother. Yet I couldn't leave without that knife. That was how I would offer myself as Famine's Sacrifice. Without it, there was no point in pursuing the dragon.

There would be little I could do at all.

So I took a deep breath and imagined the desert Isidora had once illustrated for me in a meditation practice, and I found calm there. When my heart slowed, I looked up at the aged woman, whose eyes had never shifted from me, and held her gaze.

"I must be the Sacrifice, Eltris. I am the only Seed of Famine—"

"Not the only one," she interrupted.

I held my anger in check this time. Linos was another reason I couldn't leave without taking Aika's knife. If Eltris had been willing to sacrifice him once, I doubted she'd hesitate again.

"I am the only one still awake," I amended. "If Linos was..." The suggestion was too painful to consider, so I skipped past it. "We don't know what would happen. Would he contain Famine without his will behind it? Or would he only be consumed?" I swallowed, again pushing away images of that occurrence. "I know which possibility I think is more likely, and which I would rely upon."

I expected Eltris to have a snippy reply, perhaps how I was the least reliable woman in Oedija. If she had, I might not have been able to contain myself any longer.

She didn't speak for several long moments. As I stared into her eyes, I was surprised to find shrewd evaluation there instead of the usual disdain.

"You've learned," she said at last. "You've gained some control over that temper of yours."

I gave no reply. Her observation irritated me, but I refused to show it, knowing she goaded me. So I waited.

Eltris nodded sharply, then approached. I stiffened as she did. It wasn't that I feared an attack. Eltris had only ever touched me in the Pyrthae, first when she'd saved me, and then when she'd tried to obstruct me. Her nearness made me nervous in a way I didn't entirely understand.

She stopped several paces away and put her hands to her waist. Her fingers pressed through her billow of robes for several moments before appearing again, a cubit-long wrapped object in her hands.

My breath caught. I didn't dare speak, hardly daring breathe lest it change her mind.

"You are wrong about many things," the augur said. "Most things, in fact. But in this, you are right. You are the Sacrifice. It will be by your hand that Famine is trapped, or not. Much as I wish it otherwise, I cannot change that it will be your decision when and where to use this. Just swear to me, girl, that you will choose the right moment."

Eltris held out the wrapped parcel. I advanced slowly and took it, then unfurled it enough to glimpse the bone-white material beneath.

Aika's knife. She'd given it to me after all.

I replaced the cloth. "Thank you," I murmured, my anger abruptly gone. "I will use it correctly. I will choose the right moment."

The augur snorted and turned her back on me. "Don't you have some other place to be?" she said pointedly over her shoulder.

Just like that, all my dislike returned. But I'd done what I'd come to do. Firming my jaw, I turned and left without a farewell.

As I closed the tower door behind me and made for the end of the alley, part of me wondered if I would ever see the old woman again.

CHAPTER ELEVEN

A CHOICE

I must make a choice. I have come to many crossroads in my unnatural lifespan. I have not always made the right turn. But this is the most damning.

How can I choose between paths when both end in my death?

- The journal of Vusumuzi; date unknown

I almost made it back to the Laurel Palace without trouble.

With my channeling dissuading likely assailants, I fled along the main roads from the Acadium. I witnessed several fights breaking out: once between the city watch and commoners, another among drunken scoundrels. All ended with blood spraying and yells filling the hazy air. I increased my pace, nearly running, breath rattling and heart pumping at the violence.

I was in a state by the time the bastion came into sight. So as someone stepped out from the alley next to me, I whipped up both hands and drew on radiance until it burned.

Talan held up his hands, his smile never shifting.

Exhaling shakily, I lowered mine. "Do you have to do that?"

"How else would you have me approach? Waving my hands and shouting?" The former Guilder looked around with raised eyebrows. "Subtlety suits me, and I believe our surroundings call for it."

Though I repressed the radiance back through my locus, I kept a watchful eye on Talan. He seemed to stand straighter than before, though he'd always moved with a slouch, and to swagger more than sway.

Standing a couple of paces apart, I couldn't detect the stench of stale wine about him.

Almost, I dared to hope the man I'd once known might be returning to me. But I didn't push my good fortune that far.

He smiled wider at my scrutiny and spread his arms. "Do I have pyrkin in my hair?"

A sigh escaped me, and with it left the tension I'd been clinging to. "It's good to see you out and about, even considering the times."

He advanced slowly, arms falling back to his sides. Every movement was deliberate, like I were a cat he might scare off.

"I had to find you," he spoke softly. His eyes flitted about us for a moment before they settled back on me. "The journal. Have you read it?"

I nodded.

"And?"

What could I say? "It explained much about Vusu. But…"

"…it didn't give the answers you sought," Talan finished.

The truth escaped me then. "I have a path forward, Talan. But I'm afraid to take it. That it's not what I hope it is. That I won't return."

I looked aside, my eyes burning, when Talan surprised me by seizing my hands. His skin was warm to the touch, as it always had been before. I didn't pull away.

"Is it the right path?" he murmured.

"I think so."

He squeezed my hands. "Then you'll have the courage to take it. Trust me — courage is one thing you've never lacked. Common sense, on the other hand…"

A laugh burst from me, half-choked by a sob. I hadn't thought I could laugh then, and it took me by surprise. I extracted one of my hands to wipe across my eyes and nose. Talan smiled all the while, but amusement faded from his eyes.

"Airene, if you plan to do something rash, I only ask one thing: don't exclude me. Always, you have asked my aid before. Don't change that now."

My throat was dry, the words the wrong shape to fit through it, so I nodded and smiled. Given the circumstances, it was as close to an apology as I could have hoped for.

"I will," I finally managed.

He flashed me a lopsided grin, and again looked like the man I'd once known. "You know where to find me."

As suddenly as he'd appeared, Talan dissolved back into the shadows.

———

I paced the length of Linos's room. Window, door, window, door — they were the guideposts of my walking. I wished I had such signs for my path. A choice lay before me, yet I did not know how to make it. It was a gamble to stay, an even greater one to leave.

Which was worth taking?

My gaze fell to my brother, lying on his side. His back was turned toward me, but I had seen his eyes open and unblinking. Leaving would mean abandoning him. I wouldn't be able to protect him from Eltris's designs.

At the thought of the augur, I drew out the enwrapped knife and held it in both hands before me. Aika's knife. If Azhi was telling the truth, between the two of us, we now possessed the two artifacts that could entrap Famine. It was as good a chance as we'd ever had.

I'd rarely hesitated to act before. Yet now, I couldn't make the only decision that seemed possible.

The door opened. Startled, I hid the dagger behind my back and readied magic in my other hand. As the visitors revealed themselves, however, I hastily closed my locus. My face burned, but I met Nomusa and Xaron's curious gazes straight on. By the flickering of their eyes, my reaction hadn't gone unnoticed.

"Airene?" Xaron said cautiously. "Are you well?"

I dredged up a smile. "Sorry. It's been a long couple of days."

He gave me a sympathetic look. "We figured as much. That's why we came."

Nomusa gestured toward the door. "All of us."

I tried not to startle again as Corin and Kari came through the doorway. "You two as well?" I said before I could rethink my words.

The former cartwoman nodded slowly. "We thought we would find you here," she said, her words soft as if speaking to spooked livestock.

I looked between my friends, trying to read in their expressions what was behind this appearance. "Well," I said at last. "You found me. But don't you have other things to do?"

Nomusa exchanged a glance with Xaron before speaking. "I wish we were only here for a visit. But the truth is we're worried, Airene. Worried about you."

It shouldn't have come as a surprise, yet it did.

"Worried?" A laugh bubbled up from me. "What is there to be worried about?"

Xaron grimaced as he edged forward. "If I wasn't before, I would be now. Aire, we've barely seen you the past few days. And the last time we did, you said you were going to, ah, kill someone."

"We want to know what you've been up to." Nomusa crossed her arms over her chest. "And what you're planning to do next."

I took them in with fresh eyes. Each was wearing the garb of their respective offices. Nomusa's peplos was the light green of the ocean's froth, in flattery of the royal family's colors. Xaron's clothes were just as fine, if more practical, jacket and trousers, both of dark violet and loose for effortless movement. Corin was in the plain but well-made clothes suitable for an Oedijan man, a tan tunic and dark pants, while Kari wore the bright clothes of her outlandish people, aqua and red and tan in reeling patterns.

My former Finches, at least, had places here. Responsibilities. If I told them what I'd learned and what I intended to do, was I afraid they would try to talk me out of it?

Or that they'd leave behind all they'd worked so hard to gain and join my foolhardy quest?

Corin had just as much to lose, if not more. She'd recovered her sister after years of separation, and with Kari under threat the entire time. Surely, she could least afford to come with me. Surely, she would not want to.

Yet I had long ago learned to trust my instincts. I didn't want them to sacrifice everything, but I feared I could not do this alone. If I was to succeed, I would need them, if only to carry me to my final destination.

I sighed, then spoke. "I have to leave Oedija. I have to hunt Famine."

CHAPTER TWELVE

DESERTERS

"To flee the defense of one's homeland in its time of need is a contemptible crime. Hence, the penalty for desertion, death, is well deserved."

- On the formation of a standing army; by Stratechon Bion, 1086 SLP

Deserters?" Xaron asked the same question he'd spoken twice already. "You'd have us be deserters?"

"And to follow the apothecary." Nomusa's nose wrinkled. Her carriage had become more erect with each of my conclusions. "Need I remind you that Eazal tried to kill you?"

"I know, I know. But can you see another way?" Exasperated as I was, I tried to hold back my temper. I'd expected every one of these objections as soon as I'd begun my confession, and I knew they were reasonable. It didn't change how wearisome it was to answer them not once, but repeatedly, as our arguments circled back over the same points.

"Many." Nomusa wore a heavy frown. "Of which we've already told you."

"Jaxas will never allow it." Xaron paced, plainly agitated. "We'd never get past the city gates. They're closed to all traffic, you know. Fear of spies and deserters, I suppose — and apparently it's not unwarranted!"

"We're not deserters." I spoke the words through gritted teeth. Friends they might be, but I was coming dangerously close to wanting to strangle the both of them. "We're the damned opposite of deserters — martyrs, more like."

Xaron snorted a laugh, while Nomusa shook her head. Neither had budged an inch in all the time we'd spoken. Our discussion had lasted through the afternoon. I kept a watchful eye for the sun's fall, knowing we had only so long to argue. If they weren't convinced by the time I had to meet Eazal, I would have to leave alone.

Alone with a Qarin and my would-be murderer. The thought sent a thrill of fear running through me. I hoped it wouldn't come to that.

Corin, who had remained silent beside her sister, now straightened from the wall she'd been leaning on. "Kari. What have you to say?"

All eyes turned to the young woman. She'd proved remarkably apt at sitting and waiting, but seemed as content to speak as well. Her gaze turned upon me, and I tried not to flinch before its intensity.

"He has his claws in you," she murmured.

The hair on my arms raised at her words, so similar to ones Azhi had once spoken to me. Did she know? How could she? The others seemed at as much of a loss as me, looking between each other.

Corin broke the silence. "Where Airene goes, I will too. If my sister is willing." She looked at Kari, who nodded at once.

I gave them both a grateful smile, then glanced at Xaron and Nomusa. Our former loftmate's words seemed to shame them, and they shared a look that told volumes. But still, I held my breath until they spoke.

"Of course we're with you, Airene," Xaron said. "We know what's at stake."

"We just wanted to make sure you're right." One of Nomusa's eyelids flickered, but she covered it well. "It's a big risk."

I wasn't irritated by their hesitancy now, only grateful they would come at all. "I know," I replied. "But we'll never be certain, not with how much time we have left. I think this is our best shot."

They hesitated a moment longer, then each nodded. I smiled at them, then included Corin and Kari in it.

"Thank you, everyone. I'm lucky to have friends like you. If I didn't..."

I was surprised as tears pricked my eyes. I turned my head aside. Someone reached out and squeezed my shoulder; Nomusa, I saw out of the corner of my eye.

"We're here with you, Airene. All the way."

All the way. I nodded, too choked up for words.

Xaron cleared his throat and sniffed. "Avvad is at our doorstep," he said, voice gruff with emotion. "If we leave now, I suppose we could be killed for it."

My tears dried at the stark reminder. Looking up, I saw my fear reflected in my friends' eyes.

"We must keep this from Jaxas." I glanced at the door. "And Kelena. And Feiyan, of course," I added as an afterthought.

Xaron looked aghast. "As if any of us would tell *her*."

The others nodded along.

"We'll begin gathering supplies," Nomusa offered. "Subtly."

"I will assist," Corin spoke up. "I know what is needed for traveling."

I nodded. "That's settled then. Guess I'd better let Talan know."

Xaron's eyebrows rose. "You two patch things up, then?"

"Enough." I withheld a grimace. "If not as much as I'd like."

Nomusa reached out and pressed my arm, but her smile was more teasing than sympathetic. "Don't worry. I'm sure it's a long way to wherever we're going. Plenty of time to become... reacquainted."

As the others laughed, I turned away to hide my flush and all but fled to the palace aviary.

———

Before we left, I returned to Linos's bedside.

I'd finished packing. Soon, dusk would fall and we would need to leave, but I couldn't do so without visiting my brother one last time. I stared at his still face, his open eyes, his too-thin body, its sharp angles apparent beneath his robe. Gently, I brushed a hand over his hair. It had lost much of its golden sheen, as if mirroring his soul's fading.

"They'll care for you here," I murmured. "Even if I don't come back, Jaxas will look after you. And Famine... I won't let anything happen to you, hear me? Your sister is still watching over you, Little Lion."

I waited for an answer, but of course, none came. There'd be no moment of closure, no strengthening of familial bonds. Pressing his hand one last time, I stood and left.

I met with the others outside my room. Isidora had joined us, too loyal to Xaron to not go. Talan would meet us where Azhi waited.

Once I gathered my pack from within my room, my friends and I went together to the Laurel bridge. We were burdened with what supplies we thought we might need. Nomusa guided this process, having once crossed the Four Realms to flee her ishaka, but Corin had given a surprising amount of input. I wondered at all I still didn't know of her past, even after all we'd shared together.

Though a pack animal would have been useful, we were gathering suspicion enough by readying for travel that we decided not to risk it. Judging from the strain on my shoulders and how my feet already ached with the weight, it was going to be a long journey.

Everything had gone smoothly to that point. I almost hoped we would escape unnoticed. But at the sight of the figures standing at the foot of the bridge, my hopes plummeted.

Feiyan and Kelena, surrounded by a contingent of soldiers, waited for us.

My gut tightened. I glanced at Xaron and Isidora and detected their attunements opened, their magic at the ready. A fight among Oedija's own was the last thing I wanted, yet I followed suit. Radiance burned brightly in me, making my skin itch.

As we neared, I saw Feiyan wore an infuriating smile. Kelena, on the other hand, was as somber as if she attended a funeral.

"My dear Finches!" Feiyan called out when we came within earshot. "I *am* so glad you came. I was beginning to think you'd disappoint me!"

It had started to rain, and the patter of water on the pavers made it so I almost had to shout to make myself heard. "We don't want trouble, Feiyan. Let us pass."

Her upper lip curled. "You are familiar with Oedijan law, are you not? Surely, you've skirted it often enough to know. What is the penalty for desertion, Airene?"

I knew. My hands clenched into fists. "Let us pass," I repeated, hoping she might relent, knowing she wouldn't.

But before Feiyan could speak again, Kelena took a step forward.

"Why?" she called across the cubits between us. "Why leave? I did not think you were cowards!"

Her words cut deeper than I'd expected. Nomusa answered before I could.

"We're not, Kelena. We're not fleeing. It's just that we're needed more elsewhere."

My friend glanced at me, as if unsure of how much more she should say. My thoughts had settled, however. I knew what must be said.

"We're facing Famine." I looked at Kelena first, then Feiyan. "He must be stopped at any cost."

"Even if your home will burn and your people become enslaved?" Feiyan mocked.

I didn't rise to the bait, but met her gaze with a steady one of my own. "Let us pass, Feiyan. You know you cannot stop us. And we shouldn't fight among ourselves. Tyurn knows we have enough enemies as it is."

The First Consul showed no sign of being swayed. The guards glanced at her. Their faces remained impassive, but their fear was clear. They knew they wouldn't stand long before wardens. Kelena, too, looked to Feiyan.

"If they wish to leave, let them," the First Verifier said. "We will find others to take their places."

Feiyan's lips twisted. "Very well. It shouldn't be difficult; they were never vitally important."

The comment stung. Hadn't I also wondered what I was doing in the Council? Yet there was nothing for it but to push down the shame along with the rest.

At a gesture from the First Consul, the laurel guards parted. I led my company forward, trying not to hunch over with my burdens before their watchful gaze. Feiyan's was hard to ignore; Kelena's was harder. Though she'd given her blessing, there was too much hurt in her eyes for my comfort.

I breathed easier when we were past, but only a little. It was just the first hurdle in fleeing the city.

I watched for Azhi as we approached the Conclave Pillar, but saw no sign of him. Worry gnawed at my belly. Had he played us false? I didn't know why he would do so, yet I couldn't banish my mistrust. Any delay cost us. I had little confidence Jaxas would allow us to leave as easily as his councilors had.

By their expressions, my companions felt the same pressure. "Where is he?" Nomusa asked as she looked around. "No place to hide here."

Isidora stared at Xaron, as if to say *What did I tell you?* Xaron wore a grimace, his hands clenching and unclenching as he peered around.

Then I noticed someone approaching from the nearest grove. I tensed, waiting to see who it was, but relaxed a moment later as Talan's features came into view.

"You," Xaron sneered. "Lurking in the shadows, as usual."

Talan looked at him sidelong. "I'm surprised. You've abandoned your usual garish outfits for a sensible one."

I intervened before things could get out of hand. "Thanks for coming, Talan."

His gaze traveled back to me. "Of course," he muttered, though he looked aside.

I tried to think of something else to say, but nothing came, so I contented myself with keeping watch for Azhi. When I saw no sign of the possessed apothecary, I invented a new plan for finding him. I channeled quintessence, and the world I knew became overlaid by the Pyrthae. Those of my companions who were wardens were dancing flames there in the gloom.

But no sooner had I entered than the Pillar glowed in both planes. I stared, suspecting who was coming, yet unsure if I was ready for his arrival.

I knew him by his Qarin's connection even before I released my hold on quintessence and saw him with my own eyes. Blinking away the

Pyrthae, I stared at the face of my would-be murderer once more. My fear must have crossed my expression, for the apothecary winced.

"I did not mean to startle you," Azhi offered.

I shook my head and tried to even my breathing. The daemon-possessed man was certainly dressed for travel. He carried a smaller pack than ours, and it seemed better secured as well, hugging his back while the rest of ours dragged toward the pavers. He stood tall and seemed invigorated.

I knew that stance. He had purpose and direction once more. I hoped his was the same as ours.

I didn't make introductions; there would be time enough for it later, and I couldn't find any pleasantries in me. Instead, I asked him bluntly, "Why did we meet here? Every city exit is far."

Azhi gave me a tight smile. "We will not leave by a gate. Did you think we would spend spans on foot traveling through Oedija's wilderness?"

I kept my silence. What else could I have expected? But unless my intuition had dulled, I guessed another plan was forthcoming.

By the widening of Xaron's eyes, he'd divined it. "Gods," he breathed. "You mean for us to travel through the Pyrthae?"

It had come to me as soon as Xaron started speaking. I stared at Azhi, just as dumbfounded.

"How are we to know this isn't a trap?" I demanded. "That you don't mean to lure us to where you can take our quintessence?"

"How would those of us unattuned even reach it?" Nomusa wondered.

Azhi cast me a guarded look. "This is not a trick, Airene. I have dedicated my existence to rectifying my mistakes. If you still do not trust me, why did you come?" Without waiting for an answer, he turned to Nomusa. "And our means of travel are open to any, warden or not. After all, Airene entered the Pyrthae before she became attuned."

Amid everything else that had happened, I'd almost forgotten that had been my first experience with the Pyrthae. What had occurred because of that experience did little to settle my fears.

Isidora spoke up, her eyes settled on me. "Even if it is a trap, we aren't helpless. Wardens have power in the Pyrthae. We can protect ourselves."

The resolve of the former Acadian decided me. I gave her a tight smile and a nod, then faced Azhi again.

"Fine. We'll do this your way. But if you betray us..."

"I know." For a moment, the apothecary looked as old as the pyr inhabiting him. "Watch as I open a portal. Then you can enter and leave the Pyrthae as you will."

I hardened myself to pity and observed him, channeling quintessence to be sure I missed nothing. Though my mistrust wounded the daemon, I wouldn't allow it to make me any less cautious.

Reaching to his belt, he withdrew an object there, white and long. The Binding Ruyi — I recognized the scepter from when he'd shown it to me before. Extending it before him, he reached up into the air. I was aware of him channeling — was it quintessence?

Suddenly, he ripped down his arm, and the fabric of the world split apart.

I stared at the tear. It had opened as wide as my forearm, just enough that we might sidle through. Within, light shifted in ever-changing colors, as many and varied as any rainbow. The touch of every element I knew and more reached toward me, affecting both my body and being. The warmth of radiance; the vibrance of kinesis; the elation of magnesis.

As I looked into its depths, I tried to master my fear. I would enter it. I had to. It wasn't a rash error, not this time.

I hoped.

"Quickly!" Azhi urged.

I took a step forward and reached up. The others followed me a step afterward, as reluctant as I to travel this way. But before any of us could take the last step, a familiar sound blared through the air.

As it swelled in the sky and cascaded down to us in the courtyard, I looked north toward its source. I could have died happy never hearing it again, but I wasn't that fortunate.

The shell horns of the Laurel Palace called once more.

I knew how many times they would blow. There were no signs of fire, and Jaxas wouldn't have died so soon after leaving him. And this was news we'd been expecting all season.

The horns trumpeted once, then twice. *War*, it meant. War had come to our walls.

Avvad had arrived at last. And we were fleeing.

Deserters, Feiyan had named us. Despite how I rationalized it before, I wasn't sure she was wrong. As much as I feared facing Famine, I had a method by which to battle him. Against the Imperium, I had no such comfort.

My city would fall, and I wouldn't be there to protect it.

"Now, Airene!"

I glanced at Azhi, then at the rest of my companions. Their faces mirrored all that I felt, yet determination was etched into every taut muscle.

I hardened my will and nodded, then stepped forward. Pushing aside my doubts and fears, I stepped up to the tear.

Extending a hand, I touched the Pyrthae, and it seized me and dragged me in.

THE TARNISHED PEARL

DESPOINA: Accuse me of what you will! But you must acknowledge this; never did I allow the Pearl of the Four Realms to be tarnished!

- The Trial of Zalfene Wreath, from the records of the Confessionary Tribunal; 1087 SLP

The world shifted and multiplied.

I hadn't fully inhabited the Pyrthae since I'd first become attuned. It was a different experience than channeling quintessence. I felt light and weightless then, like I could fly, and the landscape took on a different aspect than the real world. Now it was as a mirror image of the world we had left, albeit twisted and malformed. While I didn't carry the same burdens as I had back in Telae, and the rucksack lightened considerably, I didn't think I could lift off and soar as in my dreams.

We stood on solid ground exactly like the paving stones we had left behind, but for how the light distorted and changed hues. Looking up, I could see the mirror image of the Conclave above me, impossibly hanging upside down. Around me, the whole of Oedija spread out, almost claustrophobic in how it crowded out the sky. The air shifted with color and movement. Energy buzzed through me, urgent and dangerous.

I looked at my companions and found they'd also changed. Their bodies had lost their boundaries, their essence trailing away from them in thin mist. Their coloring, too, faded to shades of gray. Xaron was the light gray of morning fog, while Nomusa was the dark gray of storm clouds. The others were somewhere in between, each as distinctive in their tint as they were different in the material world. Though their bodies were amorphous, I found I could make out their facial features, though I knew their emotions by how they emanated from them.

Azhi took a similar shape as the others, but with a critical difference. Around Eazal's shadowed figure, the daemon appeared as a white glow. If I stared hard enough, I thought I could detect the boy he'd once been, lingering just beneath the man's face. I didn't look overlong; I needed no more reason to doubt him.

I looked down at myself and found I had become a shade as well. It was my body, and yet not. It was like looking at my reflection in a fountain's surface: the same, yet malleable. I tried to suck in a breath, but what is breathing without air?

That was not the sole change. I had the feeling that my present form was not the only possible shape I could take. That if I but imagined hard enough, I might become…

I shook my head, or what I thought of as my head. No — it *was* my head. I clung tightly to my belief.

Think otherwise, and I feared where it might lead.

As I drew out of my musings, I became aware that we weren't alone in this strange plane. Other beings flitted above us, as weightless as I was when I channeled quintessence. Their shapes weren't limited by what was possible, but by their imaginations and willpower. Pyr, I knew them to be; yet I hadn't realized how thickly they thronged the city. Their presence heightened my unease further still.

After exchanging looks with each member of my party, I turned to Azhi. "Where to now?"

Azhi glanced at me, then looked past. "Can you not feel him?"

With the mention, Famine's presence reasserted itself. The hunger pulled stronger now, an aching that began in my middle and spread through my limbs to touch every pore. I couldn't hide from it or distract myself with food here in the Pyrthae. I tried not to let show how deeply his influence had seeped.

"I do. He's still to the east. The Bali ishakas."

"Yes." Azhi's voice dropped to a murmur, yet it remained resonant in this uncanny plane. "He feasts now. Another spirit falls to his appetite."

I felt that, too. A wash of pleasure and satiation passed through me, so intense I almost smiled. But it didn't ease the hunger, only caused it to grow. I felt on the verge of tears with its agony, though I wasn't sure if I could cry here.

"Let's go," I spoke to the others, tone sharp. If anyone noticed, their shadowy faces gave no sign as they followed.

We made for the Conclave gate and exited onto the promenade. A glance up showed that, though time seemed to proceed at a normal pace here, it had slowed in the world suspended above us, which represented Telae. The few people we saw on the streets walked as if through honey, though their urgency was still apparent in their movements. They were ragged and thin and worn. I shifted my gaze back to my immediate surroundings. Spans of travel would take days in this realm with its peculiar sense of time. I had to keep that in mind, that enduring this would be worth it, in the end.

We proceeded through the city, heading for deme Gate. Though the journey was safer than traveling in Telae, particularly with the Avvadin army having arrived, anxiety threaded through me. I kept an eye out for the pyr flitting through the sky, wondering which were daemons and which were not. Was that distinction even relevant? Azhi had been helpful to me before inhabiting Eazal. Perhaps pyr weren't separate kinds after all, but only differentiated by their actions.

I wasn't alone in my wariness. I caught my companions glancing up, and though their expressions were lost on me, their auras provided signs of their thoughts. Xaron even seemed to channel, and I paused in astonishment at the sight. In the material world, I couldn't see when he exerted his will over the energetic elements, only feel it through my quintessence, or see the results. But here, I watched his quintessence as it molded radiance, kinesis, and magnesis into weapons. It was like liquid light, like fire turned to water, flowing around his body in an undulating swirl.

If he thought to deter the pyr, he was disappointed. A dozen of the nearest spirits drifted closer at this display. I braced myself, wondering if they were more like fish curious about something dropped in their pond, or hawks spying prey.

Azhi decided for me. "Cease!" he called to Xaron, worry pulsating from him. "Channeling attracts them. It shows them the essence they crave."

That you crave as well. I kept the thought to myself.

Xaron startled and released his hold on his magic, glancing at our guide before watching the daemons again. Despite this concession, they circled closer, ringing just a score of cubits overhead. I had to fight hard to keep from following Xaron's lead.

"They're too close," I called to Azhi. "We need to drive them off!"

"Leave them, and they may depart. If you attack—"

But the pyr's hopes were dashed as soon as he expressed them. As if on a signal, the spirits dove, all making for Xaron.

I shouted and reached for the elements. It was a similar mechanism as channeling in Telae, with my locus providing the anchor point for directing the magic, but the quintessence radiating from my skin told me it was a very different experience than expected.

But there was no time to dwell upon it. As the daemons reached my friends, I channeled radiance and kinesis. They shot forward in a roaring plume, fire churning in the battering waves of force. A handful of the pyr were caught in my assault and went spiraling away.

I didn't strike alone. Xaron and Isidora both channeled as well, their onslaught sending half a dozen more flying upward. Talan whirled bizarrely, yet he emitted a torrent of magic that scattered the rest of the pyr momentarily. Corin and Nomusa, devoid of magic, cowered before the phantoms. Kari might have helped, but she seemed lost in a daze as she stared up at the pyr. Azhi, too, didn't fight, but kept a wary distance.

I shoved down my thoughts. It didn't matter; we didn't need their help. We could handle these on our own.

Recovering from the initial assaults, three of the spirits turned midair and dove for me, while the others opted to attack against my attuned companions. They spread out so that I couldn't repeat the same tactic as before. Instead, I opened my hands before me and arced my magic. It only caught one of them, the other two spinning lithely out of the way.

I scrambled for a follow-up, sweeping my hands above me and sending a wave of kinesis cascading upward. This buffeted the pyr, delaying but not stopping them.

My frustration and fear mounted, and they weren't contained to my body. I felt them vibrating from me, infecting the surrounding air like a miasma.

Then it occurred to me. If energy didn't deter them, perhaps something else would.

I channeled quintessence, taking the shimmering white substance of my soul and forming it into a different shape. I finished my work just as the pyr reached me. They lacked bodies, but from their amorphous shapes reached appendages eerily similar to arms and hands.

But I had a weapon now. I'd formed my quintessence into a spear, one pulsating with light and infused with all my bleak emotions. I stabbed upward and pierced through one. Though its body seemed as insubstantial as a cloud, I felt resistance to the spearhead. A scream rent the air, and the pyr fled.

Two more remained. One, caught by my first attack, stayed at a distance, but the second caught me in its grip. It was my turn to shriek. A flood of fragmented emotions and memories poured through me, most of them not my own. I struggled to keep ahold of myself and raised my spear before I brought it stabbing down.

This pyr lasted no longer than the first. At the touch of the spear's point, the spirit released its hold and fled.

There was no time to celebrate, for the third remained undeterred. Before it could catch me, I stabbed upward and caught it like a fish on a harpoon. The sharp point cut into its substance, and it took off after the others, wailing without words.

My enemies driven off, I staggered back and let my spear fall to my side. My companions had all fared well; Talan was helping Xaron and Isidora drive off the last three. He, too, appeared to be channeling quintessence, but in a twister that banished rather than harmed the spirits. As the final pyr fled, the former Guilder glanced back at me and grinned. I returned the smile, wondering if he could see my gratitude wafting around me.

Then I remembered that not all had fought so valiantly to protect us. Turning, I faced Azhi. The apothecary still glowed with his possession. His face appeared blank to me.

"Next time," I said, "I'd like to see you fight with us."

He nodded, though I wasn't sure it was the answer I was looking for. My anger grew tighter. Before I could think of what to say, however, our guide walked past me.

"Come quickly," he said. "We must flee the city before more find us."

Though I didn't breathe air in the Pyrthae, I exhaled my frustration. He was right; we needed to go, and not just to leave before the daemons regained their courage. Famine roared in the distant east. Though he was hundreds of miles away, I heard it and felt it in the pit of my stomach.

Grimacing, I followed our guide, hoping once more he wasn't leading us astray.

The buildings crowded close and dark around us. We hurried, as if thieves waited in every alley. I kept an eye on the world above us, watching for both daemons and for what occurred in the city we'd left behind. Some commonfolk appeared to be running, though with time slowed, every stride took several of ours to complete. I wondered what they sought to escape and feared for them.

The walls appeared ahead and above us as we reached the end of deme Gate. As expected, the portcullis was closed.

"What now?" I asked pointedly of Azhi. My temper hadn't cooled.

He didn't answer, but crouched slightly, then leaped into the air. Defying all natural laws, he kept ascending until he fell lightly on the top of the wall. There, he turned back and glanced down at us.

"You must learn how to move here if we are to make good time," he called. "Will yourself into the air. Believe, and it will be so."

My anger flared again. "And what about those who cannot channel?"

"Even they may defy their bodies' limitations."

I realized that must be true. Hadn't I done exactly that when I first came here through a rift? Yet now that I knew more of the Pyrthae and channeling, ignorance could no longer lend me a helping hand. I closed my eyes, forced away my doubts, and tried to believe as Azhi had instructed.

I can reach the top of the wall. I am weightless. I will rise.

I crouched, following our guide's example. I ignored the cries of dismay and joy from my companions, concentrating only on my own thoughts. Then, when my belief was ironclad in my mind, I leaped.

When my feet had not touched the ground for several moments, I opened my eyes.

Oedija hung below as well as above me. I drifted upward, though with every passing second, my momentum slowed. The top of the wall was a dozen cubits below me and a score ahead.

My chest seized. I felt myself begin to drop as my belief in my buoyancy crumbled. Desperate, I tried to cling to it, but it had eroded too far.

I crashed to the ground.

The landing was painful, but much less than it would have been in Telae. I heard my companions crying out to me, but I couldn't attend to them. Clenching my jaw, I stood. My legs weren't broken; they didn't even seem capable of breaking here. If anything, it was my quintessence that had taken a hit, the glow emanating from my form dampened.

I waved to the others, some of who had already reached the wall, then readied a second attempt. Talan, Xaron, and Kari had achieved it, so I knew I could as well.

The belief came to me easier now. When I was ready, I made another leap, my eyes open all the while. I set my gaze upon the wall and willed myself toward it. To my surprise, I drifted upward — until my shock again began eroding my will. Ready for it, I managed to repair it enough to float toward the wall until, at last, I touched down.

Talan and Xaron were on either side of me as soon as I landed. "Are you hurt?" the former Guilder asked, even as Xaron exclaimed, "I'm surprised your legs aren't snapped in half!"

"I don't think we really have legs here," I noted wryly, then reached out to press Talan's hand. "I'm fine. Don't worry."

Touch was strange here in the Pyrthae, I now discovered. Just as the boundaries of our bodies had eroded, so had the distance between our souls. I was tempted to delve into him, as I once had. To see his memories, his thoughts, his feelings…

I jerked back and saw he looked as startled as me. We both turned our heads aside. I wondered if he had been as curious as I at that sharing. If a part of him had wanted to let down his guard and merge.

Azhi spoke, drawing my attention back to him. "The Pyrthae is not like your world. The material has been made spiritual; your flesh has become like your soul. They share more alike than you know." He paused, cocking his head to one side, then shook it and continued. "I will explain more later. For now, we must go, before we are attacked again."

I looked to the others to find them nodding before I inclined my own head. Nomusa and Corin were just reaching the top, both opting to climb rather than try to fly. For now, it seemed sufficient.

As Azhi turned away, I followed him and didn't look back at the city. We'd already abandoned Oedija to its fate. This was only the last step.

I couldn't cry here; my form had no tears or moisture. I was glad for it. I held my chin high as we headed east, the call of Famine's hunger pulsating ever within me, beckoning me onward to my inevitable end.

INTERLUDE I
JAXAS

Jaxas Wreath, the Despot of Oedija, gazed over his city to those beyond the walls who would destroy it.

The fields had come alive with soldiers, blackening the landscape like an infestation of rats. It was only the vanguard of the Avvadin armies, yet already they were impressive to behold. Two thousand cavalry had led the way and begun cutting off trade routes and harrying any who had dared to remain outside the walls. The sky darkened with the smoke from the farmhouses they burned.

More intimidating still was the smaller regiment leading the horsemen. The Damask Esir, evident from their blood-red garb, had already proven their prowess in a skirmish with an Oedijan taxoi, killing two militiamen for every one of theirs who fell, even though they'd been outnumbered. They fought like devils possessed them — and if his intelligence was correct, they did.

But the worst was still to come.

The infantry. The siege weapons. The Silks and the Tefra. Enemies numerous as the stars in the sky. Jaxas had marshaled a force of eight thousand, but it wasn't nearly enough, nor were they trained half as well as the meanest member of the Kahin-Shah's military. And what could he do against spirits who couldn't be killed, who had magnetic allure and stole souls with a touch? Even his small battalion of Watchers possessed no weapon that could harm them.

He closed his skeletal hands into fists and shut his eyes. *We cannot match them.* He'd always known it. Yet, with the desperate optimism that had carried him through life, that had allowed him to believe in Asileia long after she'd gone mad, to seize the Evergreen Wreath without believing himself evil — still, he'd carried on. Though he would never say it aloud, Jaxas knew he was clever, even devious when need called for it. He'd hoped the seeds he'd planted in the people near him might bear fruit.

But now, Kelena reported they had abandoned him.

Airene. Nomusa. Xaron. Isidora. Four he had welcomed onto his Council, who had shown nothing but stout hearts and sound minds. Who had sacrificed everything to do what was right.

Or so he'd thought.

Now, he wondered if it had only been a desperate bid for their own gain. They'd been penniless and on the run when he swept them up. Xaron had been a feral warden evading the Shepherds, destined for execution. He'd thought being their savior would bind them to him.

It seemed he, however, had been the one taken advantage of.

Jaxas turned from the balcony and went inside his solar. He ignored Feiyan, who tried to engage him in a discussion, and strode down the hall toward a worn door at the end. Without knocking, he turned the key and stepped inside, closing the door behind him as he entered.

Myron Wreath looked over from where he'd been staring out the window.

Jaxas studied the changes in his uncle. He'd always had a generous head of hair, but now it thinned at his pate. His eyes, once incisive, were unfocused and wandering. He wondered what thoughts the former monarch had now, if he cursed his nephew in his moments of clarity. Though, to his knowledge, Myron had never come awake enough to comprehend the switch in stations.

"Uncle. How are you?"

Myron stared at Jaxas as he spoke, but turned away before replying. The aging man's gaze fell to his hands, which twitched now. That more than anything else placed a hard pit in Jaxas's stomach.

He walked up to stand next to his uncle. The man had all but raised him as a son.

Yet you betrayed him.

Jaxas tried not to listen to the whisper in the back of his head. What choice had he had? It was foolish to regret necessary actions.

"We're losing, Uncle," he murmured. "I am failing. How did you stand up under this burden?"

Even as he asked the question, he knew even the Myron of old would have no answers. He'd been the Despot in name only, never wielded the power and responsibility Jaxas did now.

He'd never faced their nation's annihilation.

"Oedija will starve, then be butchered. The people whose souls are not stolen will be enslaved. Our realm will fall."

He hadn't expected a response, and so was surprised when Myron looked up at him. Almost, the Despot's eyes seemed like they had of old.

"Do you believe that to be your destiny, Jaxas?" Myron's voice was pilled and worn now, but it retained some of the richness he had been known for. "Reach, and perhaps you will grasp what you seek. Clepsammia gives to those who strive."

The pit in Jaxas's gut grew larger. He was tired of hearing about Clepsammia, or any of the Eidola, for that matter.

"Of course, Uncle."

He left soon after. Yet as he closed Myron's door, Jaxas paused there, struck by a thought. Though the words had been flippant and disconnected from reality, they had contained a kernel of wisdom.

Reach.

Perhaps Oedija's fate was inevitable. Perhaps he would be the last Despot to fail their nation. But he refused to stop trying to save it until every avenue had been exhausted. No — he wouldn't stop even then.

Only death could conquer his will.

A grim smile stole over his lips as he entered back into his solar. Feiyan, who was bent over a correspondence, jerked her head up at his entrance, then seemed to notice his change in demeanor.

"Shall we continue?" she asked with an arched eyebrow.

Jaxas nodded, then set back to work.

CHAPTER FOURTEEN

THROUGH FOREIGN LANDS

When traveling through foreign provinces, I am reminded of the comforts of home, and all the things taken for granted. From fare, to formalities, to even the flavor of the pests, there is much lost of one's native land.

Yet much is also gained. Wonder only exists in the foreign. I seek to claim it for my own.

- An Oedijan's Account of the Bali Ishakas; by Manenes of Gate, an itinerant scholar; 1140 SLP

We continued long into the night, only stopping when the glow of the Avvadin army's fires faded from view.

I was too burdened with emotion to be thankful when Azhi cut another rift out of the Pyrthae. My head felt numb; my body ached. My companions looked in much the same condition. The few conversations that started up had only to do with the logistics of setting up camp, and those were kept brief.

We had walked above the countless enemies facing our homeland. We knew how little hope our people had of prevailing against them.

I at least had the comfort that most of my family was safe on a Wreath estate. Zipho, as good as kin to Nomusa, remained behind, as did Xaron's parents. I didn't know of Isidora's kin. For my part, Linos's fate weighed heavily on my mind.

I told myself we would return in time to help. It wasn't entirely out of the realm of possibility. We gained much time by traveling through the

Pyrthae. If we only had to go to the Bali highlands and back, the siege might last long enough that we could return.

I tried not to think of how unlikely it was that I'd return at all.

Adding to my discomfiture was my lack of knowledge of the outdoors. I'd never spent a day outside of Oedija. A hum of anxiety threaded through me at the darkness that pressed in around us. Though Corin reassured us that wild animals would not disturb a party so large as ours, and Azhi suspected pyr wouldn't be an issue outside of Oedija, I still had the sense of being watched.

Making matters worse was the continual hunger filtering into me from my connection with Famine. As we ate our sparse meal of hardtack and salted fish, I kept my dissatisfaction to myself. I no longer dined at the Laurel Palace, able to feast any time of day that I wished.

Trying not to wallow in misery, I went to Azhi. The man didn't make for the best of conversationalists, yet there were many things left to discuss between us. The strangeness of the Pyrthae and the somberness of the siege had repressed my questions for a moment, but in the idleness of camp, they reemerged.

Our guide, however, evaded my queries once more. "We will discuss it in the morning," he begged off, and I reluctantly relented. His shoulders were slumped and his eyes hooded. Eazal was not a young man, nor had he ever looked strong. Whatever energy Azhi infused in him could not ward off his host's need for rest.

I volunteered for the first watch, knowing I would catch little sleep in my present mood. Soon I sat alone at the banked campfire, staring into the darkness. All three moons were out, but a layer of clouds, no doubt driven in by the monsoon winds, muted their light. I was swaddled in my chilling fears. My body throbbed from carrying my pack, and my head hurt from traveling through the Pyrthae.

The nightly sounds were foreign to me. The city was never quiet, but this was a different sort of cacophony. Bugs and birds called. Leaves and grasses shifted in the wind. I huddled my knees close to my chest and became marginally warmer. Perhaps they weren't malevolent sounds, but unfamiliar as they were, they might as well have been.

As much for a distraction as out of curiosity, I drew out the wrapped object I kept at my hip. Unwinding the cloth, I gripped Aika's knife by the hilt and held it up. Though it appeared orange from the dampened firelight, its glow betrayed how white it was. I tested its edge and found it sharp, gaining a slight cut on my finger for my interest. It was not as honed as steel, but felt more like bone, or perhaps wood.

I bent over it, examining it closer. Its texture was slightly porous and rough, like coral. What it was made of, I couldn't tell. A strange wood or stone from across the Lighted Sea? Or was it formed of the bones of some creature?

I let the knife fall back to my lap. I would not guess the answer. Perhaps it didn't even matter. I was grasping at straws, hoping one might be a rope that could enable me to escape the trap I found myself in.

Yet I had one avenue still left to explore. My locus was already open in case I needed to defend the camp, so it was simple enough to draw on quintessence. I emerged halfway into the Pyrthae again and marveled at the difference. When my body didn't enter it, but only my spirit, it was not nearly as disorienting, nor did I have the same strictures. Yet, remembering Azhi's earlier lesson on belief, I wondered how much of those differences were in my mind.

But that wasn't my concern now; I concentrated back on the task at hand. Staring down at the knife with Pyrthaen-vision, I nearly dropped it. A brilliant glow emanated from it, and while light could act peculiarly in the spirit realm, this was different.

Aika's knife gleamed like it contained quintessence. Like it was, in some way, alive.

I narrowed my focus, aware that I bent closer in the physical world. My grasp on the nuances of quintessence was still elementary, knowing just enough to identify those wardens familiar to me by their distinct patterns. Yet there was something to peering at the knife's quintessence that felt like staring at the surface of a well. I couldn't see beyond the surface, yet there seemed hidden depths to it… and something familiar glimmering at the bottom.

"You make for a poor sentry, my Finch. Your eyes aren't even up."

I jerked upright and shut my locus as I whirled around. The abrupt changes disoriented me for a moment, but I already knew by the voice who had surprised me in the night.

"Talan," I greeted him softly.

The former Guilder folded with his easy grace onto the ground next to me, then leaned over to peer down at the artifact cradled in my hands. "The knife again?"

"With everything going on, I haven't really had a chance to look at it."

His smile told me he knew just how much that had grated on me. "And now?"

"Now, I was interrupted just as I found that chance."

Talan let out a low laugh. "Ah, Airene. You ever were a prickly rose."

My cheeks betrayed me, warming despite the chilly night. I ran a hand through my hair, suddenly aware of how disheveled it had become from our travels.

"You don't usually compare me to flowers," I said. The words sounded inane to my own ears.

For once, he didn't tease me about them. As I met his shadowed gaze, I found a stirring inside me I hadn't dared hope for again.

His words killed it.

"When you left me at the Silvencrest," said Talan, his voice gravelly and soft, "I thought you didn't want the same thing as I did. No, not thought — I *felt* it. My head knew your reasons were fair. My heart had different opinions. And with everything that happened in the Underguild…" He turned his head aside, and I saw by the firelight his jaw was clenched tight.

I repressed my fears and reached out to touch his hand, wrapping my fingers about it. I wished I didn't hold the knife just then, but I couldn't think of where else to put it. His gaze meeting mine pushed the distraction away.

Just when I needed them, words failed me. Then I realized I didn't need them after all.

I leaned forward and, closing my eyes, my lips found his.

We lingered there for several long moments, softly appreciating one another. I was suddenly warmed through. I longed to wrap my arms around him and kiss him deeper still.

He pulled away first, cupping my cheek with one hand. His callouses rubbed against my skin. I didn't mind.

"One of us must keep watch," Talan murmured. "And I fear I shall not be able to sleep now."

A laugh bubbled out of me. "And you think I will?"

For once, his smirk became a full-lipped grin. He jerked his head toward the shelter where I was to sleep with Nomusa. "Best go, or neither of us will."

Heart pattering, I rose before I lacked the strength to. Words swelled in my chest, but I could not say them.

"Good night," was all I murmured before fleeing, the artifact clutched in my hand all but forgotten.

CHAPTER FIFTEEN

HOMECOMING

Though the Bali peoples are largely peaceful, they are not without their conflicts. Dynasties rise and fall with surprising regularity. As recently as ten years ago, the Yondali ishaka endured such an event, where all of the previous leader's family was killed, as is the tradition for such uprisings. Famously, half a century ago, the Zakale, now known as the Unnamed, also suffered such a change in leadership, when the twin brothers Yama and Lophe attempted to conquer all the highlands.

- An Oedijan's Account of the Bali Ishakas; by Manenes of Gate, an itinerant scholar; 1140 SLP

We entered the Pyrthae before dawn struck, and thus began our daily cycle.

The days blurred together, as did the dual planes of matter and spirit. After transitioning between Telae and Pyrthae repeatedly, I anticipated it would become easier. Once more, my hopes were thwarted. Every evening was spent in weary dissolution, vaguely ill from the day's travel. Our spirits dragged through deeper mires than those we were forced to camp in. Our appearances matched our internal states, becoming increasingly disheveled the longer we went without baths.

Yet there were brighter angles. Talan and I regained our warmth of the past, and added to it a fresh closeness. Sometimes, I felt like an adolescent again, burning with self-conscious desire. We had little time to make good on it, nor privacy.

But the kisses were all the sweeter for being stolen.

I tried not to think about what would come after we reached our desti-nation. Tried not to feel the guilt I knew I should. I went to my death; no one had any delusions about that. Talan knew as well as anyone. He could make his own decisions.

But does he know it?

I tried to remember if I'd told him of my fate and couldn't recall any particular instance. Though I tried to dismiss the worry, it wouldn't keep quiet.

Shouldn't you protect him, if you can?

I had no answers. All I knew was I couldn't resist our daily dalliances, nor did I wish to.

A more ambiguous boon also affected me. Famine's hunger was growing stronger; whether from the closing distance or his waxing strength, I couldn't tell. Yet with it came an escalation of my vitality. The pack, which had cut into my shoulders and set my back aching, seemed lighter with each day. Even after the long marches, I could barely keep still, filled with an anxious energy like I were about to make a speech before a crowd. By the darting glances from the others, they noticed my agitation, but no one commented on it. Likely, they suspected the cause.

The landscapes of both planes shifted around us with our progress. Our route took us south of the Askorpi Range and through the Pagore Wilderness, places I'd seen on maps but never imagined I would visit. We reached a river, and I guessed it to be the source of the Walano River, which ran past Oedija, many miles away.

The more familiar land features shifted as we continued. The foliage grew thicker, the ground wetter, the land rising in cliffs and falling in canyons. Green dominated the world, though colors shifted in the Pyrthae. Water became almost a constant sound, whether from rain, rivers, or waterfalls. Though it seemed to flow, a touch revealed it to be nothing more than an imitation.

On the seventh day of our journey, we emerged from a dense thicket to see a rise in the land. At last, our destination was at hand. As we were in the Pyrthae, the landscape doubled and became even more impressive for it. I had always known great plateaus dominated the Bali highlands, but it was entirely different to experience it. Even more than the snow-capped mountains of the Askorpi had, they stole my breath away — or would have, had I the need to breathe in the spirit realm. Something about the domineering cliffs and the verdant landscape spoke of a paradise I'd never known existed.

I looked at Nomusa, and I saw in her expression my own feelings amplified. Underlying them was a deep sorrow, the fear and nostalgia of an exile's return. I ached for her, my Pyrthaen body almost vibrating with it.

"Home," she whispered.

I think our entire party heard, and most had the decency not to respond. Azhi, however, proved to be the exception.

"We will exit here and plan our approach. I trust we will have to go in secret." He looked at Nomusa now, not disguising his irritation.

His casual cruelty made me burn. While our guide tolerated everyone in our party, he'd never truly accepted them as necessary, believing they slowed us. Nomusa's situation, in his eyes, was evidence to support this belief.

But I knew better. Without my friends surrounding and supporting me, I wouldn't be able to do what I must. If the price was being a friend in return to them, it was one I would willingly pay.

"We will," I said shortly, then cut a path back to Telae. I'd practiced the technique as often as I could, enough to achieve a tear on the first attempt.

Exiting the Pyrthae always came as a relief. The moistness in the air surprised me, immediately beading on my skin. The day was bright even though there was a thin layer of clouds overhead. The weather and the sky had almost become strangers; I was growing used to having the ground doubled and suspended overhead.

We settled into our routines for setting up camp. I tried to ignore the small spats that inevitably started up. Though we mostly got along, Xaron and Talan often took issue with each other, and Nomusa was liable to be annoyed at anyone who got in her way.

Under other circumstances, I didn't doubt I would have joined in. But concerns about who carried their fair share of work seemed petty with death awaiting me.

When we gathered again and munched on our lackluster rations, I spoke. "He still lies eastward. North somewhat, too."

Azhi nodded. "That is what I sense as well. The distance is still significant, though closing. But I do not think he is on the Yorandu plateau."

"So we will bypass it." Nomusa's tone was carefully composed, a fact not lost on the others. Despite snapping at her earlier, Xaron cast her a sympathetic look. Even Talan's callous amusement seemed to lessen.

Azhi, on the other hand, remained merciless. "Yes. We will rest here, then travel until we reach the end of the plateau. It may take a full day's walk, but we cannot risk being delayed by being captured."

No one disagreed, and so the plan was set. The sun hung in the sky, yet under the thick canopy, it was almost dark. I lay down next to Nomusa, eyes drifting closed and thoughts dozing, when she spoke.

"I miss it. Home."

Sleepily, I reached out and took her hand. "I know."
We fell asleep that way, neither of us letting go.

———

When a deeper gloom fell over our camp, Azhi woke us. Once more, we packed and entered the Pyrthae.

I was drowsy when I tottered under my pack through the rent in the material world. But as soon as I emerged into the Pyrthae, my body buzzed with fresh energy. Some of it was the mere feeling of the place. The greater part was the stronger pull of Famine. He was feasting again, and with each soul he consumed, a shiver of pleasure ran through me. I felt soiled for experiencing joy at such a horrid thing, though I knew the sin wasn't mine.

We hurried on, ascending the landscape in a way we never could have in Telae. Even those unattuned in our party formed their belief strong enough to at least scramble up the side of the cliffs. Corin struggled the most, her straightforward mind having difficulty contradicting the rules of Telae.

Nomusa had her own troubles. I tried to disguise my smugness at this, for much came easily to her in our former lives. By her sharp look my way, I did a poor job of hiding it.

True to Azhi's word, the journey went through the night and into the day. I wondered how much further the plateau could stretch when I saw signs of the trees thinning. Hopeful at any change, knowing the plateau beyond should be barren and arid, I peered closer at the sky to see what lay ahead and was surprised to find a city emerging from the wilderness. We had seen the occasional domicile, but nothing more.

Mtani, it was, the capital of the Yorandu ishaka, telling by our direction and its size. A glance at Nomusa showed her homesickness had worsened. I reached out to her, but in the Pyrthae, touch didn't hold the same comfort. I withdrew almost as soon as we made contact; her memories cut too deeply.

We traveled through the city, and I stared at the strange buildings surrounding us. They simultaneously seemed to battle against nature and integrate with it. Vines crept over thatched roofs and around circular walls, their leaves mostly green, but some in startling shades of red and violet. Most homes were single-storied chambers, but the larger ones sprawled in a series of connecting circles. The streets were paved with boards more often than stones. Feathers, horns, and beads hung from the eaves in homemade ornamentation.

A glance above showed the people to whom the city belonged. They thronged the streets, many laughing as they passed one another. Almost, it seemed like a village rather than a city. I smiled at the sight. If most were like Komo and Nomusa, I would have been glad to meet more of the Yorandu.

What could only be the Shaka's manor rose from the center of the city, the view of it clear from anywhere we walked. It sat atop a hill, and its compound sprawled across it. At the bottom, a fence with jagged metal atop it warned against intruders. I caught Nomusa's gaze drifting toward it often. When she didn't mention it, I judged it best to keep my peace. Some things were easiest to endure when kept unspoken.

Beyond the manor, we came to a fenced grove. As I observed the plants within it, I thought I understood what we looked upon. They were trees, but of a variety I'd never seen before. Their trunks split low upon them into a sphere of branches, and each was thorny like the stem of a rose, but at such a large scale that each thorn was the size of a dagger. If they were what I thought they were, they made for a curious thing to consider holy.

I turned to Nomusa to confirm my suspicions, but paused at her expression. "What? What is it?"

The others had stopped and looked at her as well. Nomusa shook her head. "This is an *isikhayha* grove… but they're all dead."

Looking at the strange trees again, I saw at once what she meant. Their limbs were dun and leafless, mere replicas of our world. They had no magic of their own.

"They're supposed to be partly spirit, aren't they?" I asked. "That's why their pyrkin have such strange properties. Like stopping a warden from channeling."

Nomusa nodded, still seeming in a daze. "I don't understand how this happened."

"You know who is behind it."

Azhi had come up on us. I skirted a step away, never wanting to be too near to him.

"Famine," Talan murmured.

The daemon nodded. "He is strong now, strong enough to overcome their defenses. He has feasted on this grove and grown stronger still. I would be surprised if any of the *isikhayhas* have survived."

Nomusa stared at the dead holy trees a moment longer, then turned her head aside. "We should continue," she muttered, then set off without waiting for a reply.

I stared at my friend's back, helpless to understand what this meant to her. It was a loss that I had no similar experience to. But I hated to see her in pain. If my presence was all the comfort I could offer, so be it.

I caught up with her, and we walked side by side in silence.

—————

The light was fading by the time we passed through the other side of Mtani, and our party's energy flagged. But we hadn't yet reached the end of the plateau, so we pressed on, walking by the ethereal light that permeated the spirit realm.

Kari seemed most exhausted, sometimes stumbling so her sister had to catch her. Even Azhi showed signs of strain. Sometimes, I wondered if Eazal fought against his daemon host, as the man twitched in unnatural ways. I was the freshest of our company, though I found little solace in it, knowing the reason for it.

At last, we reached a long bridge that spanned the final divide. At first appearance, it seemed a precariously built thing, composed of taut ropes and boards that swayed with the Pyrthae's mimicry of wind. We approached it cautiously and tested each board before putting our weight on it. A silly precaution, perhaps; in theory, we had only to believe we could float to stop a fall. Yet as I peered over the ropes suspended as railings into the dark chasm below, I couldn't quite kill my natural fear.

I sighed in relief when we made it to the other end. But though we'd reached the Zakale plateau, where I assumed Famine must be, the march was not yet done. So close to the bridge, we risked discovery by Yorandu patrols, or even those from the neighboring ishakas, Yondali and Masu. We had to venture in deeper, beyond the reach of the jungle, to be protected.

The next day had long risen by the time we found the end of the foliage. The changes had come upon the land swifter than I'd expected. Within a mile, it transitioned from thick forest to barren desert, with scarcely a tree to be seen. A deep sense of unease threaded through me as I looked around at the endless expanse. I knew what was behind it — or rather, who.

Then I saw him.

Distances had a way of shifting in the Pyrthae. My vision saw nothing but blank horizon one moment; the next, it seemed to have lengthened so even far-off objects appeared much closer than they should have. Famine had been nothing more than a speck floating through the air before the shift occurred. He seemed more defined even than the last time I'd seen him, and almost bloated in his middle, like he'd swallowed an entire herd of cattle at once. I wondered what source of quintessence he'd possibly found to feast on in this forbidding land. I wondered if I truly wanted to know.

But, whether or not I willed it, I would discover it soon.

I didn't mention what I'd seen as we stepped out of the Pyrthae and into the blinding sunlight. Though the whole of the spirit realm was filled with light, the sun bothered my eyes. In stark contrast to when we'd exited before, the air was hot and dry.

Between the light and heat, sleep seemed impossible, yet we set up camp all the same. I lay down next to Nomusa atop my bedroll and sweated through my clothes under the canvas tent. A nervous energy coursed through me, and my mind circled back to the deed I must soon perform.

The deed. I would have laughed if not for Nomusa sleeping. The term was wholly inadequate for what I would soon have to do.

Neither fear nor self-pity kept me up for long. I had drifted off to a dreamless sleep when a sound hooked me and dragged me back out. Groggy, it took me a moment to register what it meant. But as Nomusa shot upright and darted a startled look at me, it finally registered.

A man had shouted, and not in a tongue I knew.

"He says to come out," Nomusa whispered. Her eyes were wide, her nostrils flared. "Be ready."

I had no need for the warning; my locus was already open, and Pyrthaen energies pressed against my fingertips.

The man yelled again, and we heard the shuffling noises of our companions leaving their shelters.

"Let's go see," I said to Nomusa, then led the way out into the blinding sunlight.

CHAPTER SIXTEEN

AN EXILE'S WELCOME

"Never leave a rival alive, or you will forever be known as a usurper. Death is not fair, least of all for the innocent and the young. But blood on the father's hands is passed to the daughter. The price must be paid."

- Charratta Yorandu Ibubesi, Shaka of the Yorandu; 1162 SLP

I wasn't surprised to see Bali warriors surrounding our camp. Even less so that they had us entirely at their mercy.

As they glowered at us, I observed them in turn. Their features and the cerulean tatu on their arms resembled Nomusa's, but there, the similarities ended. Like Shaka-Heir Komo and his retinue had worn, bronze collars covered most of their chests, though their bellies were left bare, and leather skirts hung just above their knees. Each had half their face painted green; war paint, as I understood the custom. Most carried spears, and knives were secured at their hips. A few held no weapons at all, and these I feared most. If Komo represented the prowess of Bali wardens, they would be difficult to overcome, especially when we were outnumbered four to one.

It didn't help that we had chosen a poor location for a battle. Hoping to evade detection, Corin had advised that we take refuge at the bottom of a basin, a sandstone cliff sheltering our tents. That ridge was now occupied by archers, their arrows nocked, points trained at our hearts.

I glanced at Nomusa. Her face had transformed into hard planes as she stared up at her kinsmen, yet it seemed a shallow mask. I trembled to think about what lay beneath it. If she feared them, what chance did we have?

One of the Bali warriors spoke, and I realized I understood him. Though his sea-tongue was heavily accented, his meaning was clear.

"You are a strange group." He scanned us with a baleful gaze, his thick beard making his expression even more severe. "Oedijans, are you not?"

A moment of silence passed as we looked at each other. I expected Nomusa to answer, but when she only continued to stare, I spoke up.

"Yes. We're from Oedija."

The warrior didn't answer for a long moment, but only continued to study us. "And yet you are here," he said at last.

I opened my mouth, then hesitated. How much should I admit of our purpose? But the Yorandu were allied with Oedija now, and secrets wouldn't get us far. And Famine feasted; I felt it in my bones as his satiation fluttered through me. We couldn't afford any delay.

I swallowed before speaking. "We don't mean to intrude, but our mission is urgent. We're hunting something dangerous. A… daemon." *A god* seemed too grandiose to win us anything but laughter. "He's near, on this very plateau. We were going to reach him today to… handle him."

The warrior's expression did not change for all my farfetched words. His followers, however, exchanged looks with raised eyebrows. I kept my eyes on the leader, willing him to believe, wishing I could channel to convince him. But with their wardens possibly able to sense it, I didn't dare.

When the silence prolonged, and my companions glanced at me with increasing alarm, I spoke again. "What is your name?"

I didn't expect the warrior to answer and was surprised when he did.

"Khoda Yorandu Ayize."

Nomusa stirred. "Ayize," she murmured, as if in recognition.

Ayize looked at her again, eyes narrowed. I decided to head off any inconvenient questions. "Well met, Ayize. I'm Airene of Port." I wondered if I should introduce my party, then thought better of it. Best to avoid the matter than be forced to lie about Nomusa's identity. "We understand we are trespassing, and regret that we were forced to, but—"

Ayize cut off my babbling. "How did you come here? Our borders are guarded and patrolled, the bridge watched. If you are headed into the Desolate, you cannot have come from that way."

He waited, expectant. I wished someone would help me. It was perplexing that he deigned to speak to me at all. My experience with Bali showed them to speak to their kinsmen when present instead of addressing foreigners. But it was growing difficult to answer his questions. My gaze drifted to Talan, but he only shrugged.

Repressing a sigh, I resigned myself to the truth. "We came through the Pyrthae."

That finally provoked a reaction. Ayize's bushy eyebrows rose, and murmurs erupted from his followers. As the leader raised a hand, I flinched, fearing the worst, but it was only a gesture for silence.

"Oedija does not have wardens," the warrior said slowly. "Not ones without chains."

"It does." Talan finally came to my rescue, though I wasn't sure I wanted more attention drawn to his smirk. "Most of us before you are wardens, having hidden under the Shepherds' noses for years. But that has changed." The former Guilder jerked his head in Xaron and Isidora's direction. "They're both part of the warden division the new Despot's established. Even part of his inner Council, so I hear."

It took an effort not to chew my lip as I waited for Ayize's response. He looked over each of us again, as if hoping to see one of us break and expose what we'd said as a lie.

Then his eyes settled on Nomusa, and my stomach sank.

"You are familiar," he said. "You seem a kinswoman. You know our tongue. Yet you speak like an Oedijan."

Nomusa flinched. I knew how it must hurt to be seen as an outsider among her own people. Still, I pleaded silently for her to lie. *Don't make your stand. Not here. Not now.*

Her chin lifted high, and I knew what she would say before the words left her mouth.

"I am Eshalo Yorandu Nomusa. My father was the Shaka of our people before he was betrayed and murdered. I am the rightful Heir."

No one was silent then. Some warriors shouted, their weapons bristling. My locus had been open, and now I flooded my body with radiance and kinesis. Violence seemed inevitable now, little as any of us could afford it.

"*Silence!*" Ayize bellowed, and all fell quiet at once.

The leader gave his warriors one last hard look, then gazed back down on Nomusa. "So. You survived."

My friend was like a drawn bow herself, every muscle taut. "I alone did."

He nodded, as if it was the answer he expected. "I supported your father, Nomusa-sha. I grieved to see your family slain."

"And yet you serve the usurper."

I couldn't keep silent, not while she struck aside his concession. "Of course he does, Nomusa. What would you have him do, die? Go into exile?"

She cast me as furious a glare as I'd ever seen from her. But I preferred her rage be directed at me than those who might kill us — or so I told myself, as I withered with hurt.

"No," said Ayize. "You are right to be angry, Heir Exile. You have been wronged by all Yorandu, even by those who do not wish it."

My surprise was almost sufficient for me to forget Nomusa's anger. Nomusa seemed just as astonished, her mouth parted as she stared up at the warrior.

The Bali muttered again, and more than one wore mutinous looks. Yet Ayize's authority had not eroded so much that they didn't fall silent at a gesture.

"But past wrongs do not change present duty. I must take you before Shaka Ibubesi to face his judgment. He rules the Yorandu and has for nearly two decades. I will not risk another war of succession."

"*Fareshi* coward," Nomusa hissed through clenched teeth.

Ayize flinched, but didn't rise to the goad. "But… for a time, our goals may align. You say you hunt a daemon."

My pulse quickened. "We do."

"In a sense, so do we. And as our quarry lies in the same direction as yours, I wonder if our enemies are not the same." Ayize turned his gaze aside then — toward Famine, I recognized.

My companions looked as confused as I was on this point. Then Kari murmured, just loud enough to catch, "The trees…"

The realization struck me. "The *isikhayhas*. You hunt the one responsible for their wilting."

Fresh mutters started up again, though of a different timbre than following Nomusa's revelation. My friend turned back to look at me, her stare a warning without the need for words. I only spared her a glance. I still held hope that the gamble would pay off.

Ayize frowned now. "How could you know this? It happened two days ago, and the news was kept quiet."

We had come this far, and the warrior seemed as reasonable a man as we could expect to get. I pressed further.

"It is as I said before: we came here through the Pyrthae. We saw the trees, dead and brown, as we passed. And we knew the daemon we hunt must be behind it."

The warriors had begun to yell in their tongue to Ayize, and by Nomusa's expression, they were not words of support. They did not entirely quiet as the leader gestured again for them to cease.

"This daemon," he said to me, the word seeming unfamiliar in his mouth. "Is it named?"

I swallowed and nodded. "Taozu, he is known to the Qao Fu. Famine, we call him. But here, he was once known as the Serpent God."

Pandemonium broke out. I braced to channel as Bali warriors shouted — to protest my assertions, I was certain. My companions flinched as well, and I sensed their readiness to fight by their stances: the flexing of their fingers and hands, the reaching for weapons.

"Quiet, all of you!"

I didn't think they would listen this time. As it was, it took them a lot longer to comply than duty dictated. But as each fell under their leader's glower, they lapsed into sullen silence.

"They speak the truth!" said Ayize, and relief flooded through me so powerfully my knees went weak. He continued speaking in our sea-tongue, though he addressed his warriors. "Their story stretches my understanding, yet I cannot fault a word. Are we so confident as to spurn allies? Do we know our enemy so well as to deafen our ears?"

Logic seemed to suffice where authority had floundered. The warriors looked no happier, but most seemed placated, at least for the moment.

Ayize turned back to stare down at Nomusa. "We will join your hunt, for it is the same as ours." As we reeled from this inexplicable change of heart, he continued. "When it is finished, however, you must settle our other business. Nomusa-sha, you will come with us to be presented to Shaka Ibubesi and await his verdict."

I almost couldn't bring myself to look at Nomusa. Our lives and our mission were in her hands now, and she had shown little inclination to cooperate. I only breathed again as she nodded.

"Fine."

Ayize studied her a moment longer, then turned away. "Come. The hunt continues."

My head spun, but no more than the warriors' must. I firmed my will and looked at my companions, bafflement and relief battling for supremacy over their faces. I could only shrug.

"Guess we'd better follow," I said, and with that, we did.

CHAPTER SEVENTEEN

THE RED LAKE

Our hands trembled, yet we made the cuts. Every man, woman, and child sent before us, we put to the knife.

How could we do otherwise? Our God demanded it. His thirst is slaked by blood; his hunger, by spirit.

He must be fed, lest he feasts upon us.

- Tales of the Desolate, uncensored; 1092 SLP

So it was that our strange company grew stranger as we joined forces with the Yorandu warriors.

We packed up our camp, but left our rucksacks there in the basin. Famine was not far ahead, and with the war party almost unladen, it was the only way we could keep up and be ready for a fight. Ayize waited until we came after him, then wordlessly turned away.

I puzzled over the warrior's decision for a long time before I mustered the courage to ask. Ignoring my companions' hushed questions, I wove between his scowling fighters and found my way to the man's side.

Ayize didn't seem one prone to preambles, so I gave him none. "What changed your mind?"

He glanced at me sidelong, but didn't answer until we began descending the next rocky slope. The land grew more foreboding with each step into it. I readily believed the fearsome reputation the Wumofu had gained for being entirely inhospitable to life.

"You know of the Serpent God," he said. "Do you know of its worshippers?"

I shrugged. "Some." A moment later, it occurred to me what he was saying. "But I thought they existed during the civil war."

"They have always existed in the shadows. Lophe and Yama showed that the" — Ayize struggled to find the right word — "the great spirit could confer great power, if it wished. Others have craved that, especially the desperate."

"But Famine has been caged since then. He..." I struggled to find a concise way to explain all I knew, then abandoned the attempt. "I don't think he's given many others power since."

"No," Ayize agreed. "But it does not keep the foolish from madness. And now that he reigns again, those who have clung to the beliefs have flocked back."

He paused, his jaw spasming. Knowing a hard confession when I saw one, I contented myself with waiting.

At last, he spoke. "They have been stealing people. Women and children mostly, but men as well. All who are vulnerable."

My stomach churned. "Why? You can't force people to believe in..." I trailed off, remembering something I had read in the book on the Bali civil war. "Tyurn's balls. They're sacrificing them, aren't they?"

Ayize's expression resembled a thundercloud. "We do not know; none have returned. But if they live, we will retrieve them."

Children. He'd said they took children. I had to swallow to keep the contents of my belly down, even as anger flared through me.

"How many cultists are there?"

"Not many. By their tracks, two dozen at most."

"Are they wardens?"

Ayize didn't answer, by which I guessed he didn't know this, either.

"The *isikhayhas* were the final sign," he said at last. "We knew it must be connected, for they have survived beyond our history." He paused, and I saw he was choked with emotion. I realized then just how little I understood of the Bali's relationship with their sacred trees. Their deaths were worse than their people's, as hard as it was for me to believe.

"We will make them pay," I said, hoping it was true.

I fell back soon after, though not before Ayize questioned me in turn. I explained what I could. That one who had kept Famine at bay had failed. That we had ways to stop the daemon god, if we could get to him before he broke into our world. Ayize didn't indicate if he believed me, but only nodded, a man taking in information to make his own judgments. I could respect that, as it had always been my practice as well. I only hoped our conclusions would align.

After filtering back through his warriors, who still had not warmed to me, I fell in line beside my companions. Nomusa, who kept as far from her kinsmen as she could, drifted close enough to hear, though not without a resentful look at the backs ahead of her.

In brief, I caught them up on what I'd gleaned. They had a dozen questions I couldn't answer: Were the cultists attuned to the Pyrthae? How were they armed? Would we attack with the Yorandu? When I threw up my hands time and again, they finally relented.

"Glad we're walking into a fight blind," Xaron muttered, loud enough for all to hear. I didn't rise to the bait, seeing his nervousness by the fluttering of his fingers, and Isidora's reassuring hand intertwining with his.

Talan sidled up next to me. "Stay close to me," he muttered. "Don't enter the fight unless you have to. Promise me, Airene."

I nodded, knowing he wouldn't be dissuaded, even as I churned with guilt. Only then did my part in the mission come back to me.

As if summoned by my thoughts, Azhi came up on my other side. Talan frowned, but moved away at my request. I glanced at the possessed man and felt I could almost see the boy spirit peering out of his eyes. I looked away again.

"It is almost time."

I didn't ask what he meant. We both knew.

"Yes," I whispered.

"You will still do it? Offer him your spirit and body, and so bind him?"

"Yes."

The word trembled as it left my lips. When the time had been far off, I'd kept the fear at bay. There had always been another leg of our journey to tackle, another distraction. Almost, I'd let myself forget the fate that awaited me when, at last, we caught up to Famine.

I couldn't forget it now.

Azhi's gaze was hard on me though, so I willed my expression to smoothness. "Just…" I didn't know quite what I wanted to say, only that I needed something, some assurance, from this ally I still did not entirely trust. "Don't make it a waste."

"I won't."

I glanced down at the sash around his middle, and the scepter tucked into it. How he would use it, I still didn't know. But I didn't even understand Aika's knife and how to be a Sacrifice with certainty. We were all flailing in the dark, hoping our attacks would land against the monster stalking us.

I forced my mind to other thoughts, lest my courage fail.

"Take care of them. Make sure they return home. And when it's over, you'll release Eazal, won't you?"

"Of course. I have always intended to."

Did he answer one question and not the other? I didn't have the heart to ask. With a tight nod, I branched my path from his.

Xaron swiftly closed in. "What does he want?"

"The same as all of us: to cage Famine."

I couldn't meet his eyes. Xaron knew, just as Nomusa and Azhi did. For once, he didn't speak, but only put an arm around my back.

It was enough to keep me going.

One of the scouts who had gone ahead returned, his expression grave.

The time had come.

Ayize ordered his warriors into formation, then turned to our company. "Nomusa-sha, I trust you and your companions know best how to use your strengths." His eyes slid over to me, then the others. "Be sure not to cross our line of fire, or I cannot protect you."

Nomusa answered something in their tongue, and Ayize's eyes narrowed. Suspecting her words to be less than kind, I hastened to say, "We won't interfere. We'll have our hands full with the Serpent."

The Bali warrior scrutinized me, no doubt wondering what we possibly intended to do to stop a deity. "Trees' blessing," was all he said before turning away.

Their warriors led the way. Daylight had begun to fail, so it was simple enough to identify where the cultists lay by the glow of their campfires. I opened myself to the Pyrthae and filled myself with the energetic elements, if only for the comfort of them. My companions might have been miles away for all the reassurance they brought me. I shivered, though I couldn't truly be cold when filled with radiance.

"Airene?"

So absorbed was I with my misery, I hadn't noticed Talan come close. I tried to muster a smile and failed.

He took my arm and pulled me to a stop, looking into my eyes one at a time. I was reminded of the intimacy we had shared and ached knowing we never would again. It made me want to turn aside from him, but stopped short, not wishing to arouse his suspicion.

Then he said the words I'd long feared. "You've told me everything, haven't you? About Famine?"

I desperately wanted to swallow, but he would notice the nervous gesture. My voice croaked as I spoke. "Yes. I'm just… afraid."

That much was true. His gaze softened, and he pulled me into a tight embrace.

"I won't let anything happen to you," he murmured, so certain I almost believed him.

The others had halted with us, and as Azhi neared, I knew we had to continue. "We're coming," I said, avoiding his studying gaze and following the war party.

Then all conversation ceased, for by a signal from one of the forward warriors, the final ridge was at hand. We passed by a still body; a cultist on watch, I guessed. A hint of blood lingered in the dry air, too pungent to belong to only one corpse. In complete silence, Ayize directed his warriors to line the ridge and ready their weapons. Over the hammering of my heart, I heard the people below, some laughing, others crying.

With my throat closed almost too much to breathe, I peered over the cliff to the basin below.

A rudimentary camp sprawled across the sandy ground. Tents nestled against the foot of the cliff and around it to where the ridge descended toward the basin in a crescent shape. There was a score of the shelters, and though the hour was growing late, their occupants appeared to all be outside of them.

The cultists were dressed like Ayize's warriors, but with horrifying changes. Some had barely healed scars and fresh cuts that seemed too measured to be accidentally accrued. Others had red tatu of serpents, dragons, and other terrifying creatures overlaying those of their original ishakas. Bones poked through their flesh in places, even on their faces, giving the sense that they were barely human at all. They leaped and danced and swayed, the many campfires at their backs casting dancing shadows across their bodies to make them appear more alien still.

But it was the pit around which they danced that terrified me most of all.

Bodies hung head-first off the edges of the pit. Their necks seemed to have been cut, for scarlet streaks leaked from them into the pit. Enough blood had collected to fill the bottom, the pool dark and still.

Dozens, maybe even a hundred, all dead and drained.

My stomach bucked and churned, and I had to swallow back my bile. What kind of people could do this? What evil possessed them? I felt Famine's influence; I was his gods-damned Seed. But never had I had an inclination to do *this*.

I hadn't come here to kill cultists. But if it came to that, I found myself more than willing.

Another feeling pulled at my attention. There was something else, something more than the horrors of the cultists below. A hidden presence that reveled in the atrocities.

I channeled quintessence and peered into the Pyrthae. And there he was.

Famine filled the sky, brilliant and pearlescent in his ink-dark, sinuous body. He seemed more distinct than before, the features sharper, like a painting twice drawn over. He had grown as well, swelling to double his size, and he'd never been small. If left to his own designs, he would soon stretch across all the city of Oedija.

He didn't seem to notice me, for he writhed around a thin, chalky cloud that filtered around him. *Quintessence.* I sensed it with the same revulsion that I'd smelled the blood. This was not only death, but eradication. Nothing would exist of those sacrificed once he consumed their spirits.

The thought awoke the anger I needed.

Though he didn't pay me heed, I felt him. His hunger and satiation wracked me, body and soul. The elation it filled me with sickened me. At least I didn't feel the wild abandon to give myself to him I had before.

A scream split the air.

As I oriented back to Telae, I saw the first arrow fly. More yells followed, both of pain and rage. Silhouettes seethed in the night all around me.

The violence had begun.

The end approached.

CHAPTER EIGHTEEN

AN OFFERING OF BLOOD

I must give to him what he seeks, but also the agent by which to bind him. Spirit, to placate his endless hunger; blood, to anchor him in our world; body, by which I gain power over him.

- The journal of Vusumuzi; date unknown

Radiance filled the sky.

I flinched as one of the nearby Yorandu warriors was blasted back, able to do nothing but watch as he fell to the ground, screaming and burning. Some of our enemies, at least, were wardens.

But this wasn't my fight. I had to live long enough to fulfill my purpose.

My companions shouted at me, but I ignored them and scampered along the ridge. I had to get closer, as close as I could to where Famine loomed, before I did what I had to do. I had to draw his attention. Or did I only have to say his name?

Do it! part of myself screamed. *Why do you wait?*

I ignored the voice and raced down the rise, tripping and only just keeping my feet under me. With kinesis at my toes, every step sprang me forward farther, and soon I neared the bottom.

Four figures emerged from around boulders before me; cultists, I saw at once. Their target was plain, for I'd left the Yorandu warriors behind. I barely had time to ready my sorcery before they struck.

I spun as flames scorched the air where I'd been. Gaining my feet, I threw up kinesis in a wave. I'd underestimated how much my strength had grown. The deluge crumbled the stone as it barreled forth and sent the cultists flying backwards a dozen paces. They screamed in the air, then fell abruptly silent as they landed with bone-crunching force on the hard ground.

I didn't wait to see if any would rise, but kept running, only glancing over my shoulder to ensure no one followed.

"*Airene!*"

Talan's cry cut through me. I staggered, then kept moving forward without looking back. My vision blurred as tears stung my eyes. I couldn't stop, couldn't hesitate, or I might never start again.

Fighting spread all around me. Wardens squared off against those attuned in Ayize's company. The cultists seemed to hold their own. There were more than Ayize had reported, many more — maybe fifty at a glance. But the Yorandu were well-armed and trained, and the cultists fell before their sorcery, spears, and arrows.

I weaved around the clashes where I could and buffeted back any who attempted to come after me. Twice, flying missiles nearly caught me, and I barely knocked them aside in time. I rounded the descent and came into the basin — and there it spread before me, sickening to behold.

The blood lake.

I gagged as I stumbled toward the bodies ringing its edge. Cultists swarmed here. They lunged at me as I neared, eyes wide and bloodshot. Something possessed them, be it daemon or drug, for they acted with no regard for their safety.

I screamed and blasted them back.

The cultists sailed away, blackened and smoking. It was as mighty an offensive as I'd ever put forth, yet I barely felt the strain. I was intoxicated, drunk on violence and sorrow. My balance pitched as I turned my head up to the sky.

Death choked me with its putrid stench. Death filled my ears with shrieks and sobs. Death was everywhere I looked.

Yet as I opened my eyes to the Pyrthae, I saw a more terrifying sight.

Famine cavorted in the sky, twisting and slithering in what could only be called ecstasy. Through our connection, his pleasure became my own. I fought down a smile as he sucked in the souls of those dying around me. I tried to deny my growing invigoration as the battle raged on.

He did not see or notice me, even now. I bared my teeth, then let the word tear free of my throat.

"*FAMINE!*"

In this plane, my command became something else, a white wave that cascaded from me. As it touched the daemon god, his movements jerked to a halt, and his vast head swiveled around to peer at me with one eye.

I'd forgotten how black and cold his gaze was until it settled on me. There was no end to the darkness in those eyes, their own brand of oblivion.

I fought not to be lost, blinking and shaking my head. The words — what were the words I was supposed to say?

But though my mind had gone blank, my hand hadn't forgotten its duty. Instinctively, I'd drawn Aika's knife and now clutched it in both hands. I held it out, the blade pointing toward my chest. It had never seemed so sharp as it did then.

Something about this drew Famine's interest, for he turned fully toward me. His mouth still hung open, and in that chasm, I saw the glimmer of souls being forever consumed.

He'll devour the world. All you love. All you hate. Everything.

It was the last push I needed. I drew in a breath, then shouted out the words.

"Famine, I offer myself as Sacri—"

Before I could finish, I fell crashing to the ground.

The Pyrthae faded from my vision as I fought against the one restraining me. They were strong; a warden, with kinesis-strengthened limbs. I swelled with force to counter theirs, but stopped just short of releasing as I glimpsed their face.

"Don't!" Talan grunted with the effort of holding me. My knife had scored a cut on his shoulder, red staining the white. As I watched, the dagger absorbed the blood, leaving it as untouched as before.

Then I snapped out of my daze and let my magic flow back out of me.

Talan collapsed atop me, but he didn't allow himself time to rest. Stumbling to his feet, I watched him disperse one kinetic attack, then shred a radiant plume. The battle sounded as if it waned, but still it limped on.

I came to my feet, barely feeling as if I were there. I was supposed to be dead. I'd come here to die.

Why am I still alive?

But though Talan had interrupted me, I still had a chance. He was distracted. Perhaps now—

His hand closed over my hand, then he pried Aika's knife away.

"Talan!" I grabbed at his arm, but I didn't fight him for it. I couldn't take it back from him without hurting him. Even amid the battle, words were my best weapon. "I have to, don't you see? I have to die!"

He shoved me away, countering another attack. Against all reason, his lips curved upward.

"If you think I'll allow that," he yelled as he spun around me, blocking another blow, "you don't know me at all, my Finch!"

I stared at him, trying to sort through what I should do. Part of me knew I should help keep him alive, and myself for that matter. I was going to die anyway, but I had to die in the right way.

Yet I felt a curious lack of concern for my own well-being. Death was death, in some ways. It was difficult to accept it, only now to push it away.

But slowly, the stupor faded. As a kinetic wave charged toward Talan, I channeled to counter it, meeting it with greater force.

I whirled to ward against other attacks, but found that the battle had abruptly ceased. Those cultists who weren't dead either lay too injured to fight or had surrendered and were being tied up by Yorandu warriors. We had won, and better still, survived. Even those of us who weren't supposed to.

Turning, I channeled quintessence and stared up again, only to lurch to a halt.

Famine soared away. The cloud of quintessence he'd feasted on had thinned to almost nothing, too thin to hold his attention, especially since he'd grown. His satiation was already fading; it was time to seek the next feast. The daemon god's long, sinuous body undulated as he sped off through the air, back toward the ishakas.

I could do nothing but watch him leave.

"No." My knees gave way. I barely noticed the pain of the impact as I stared after Famine, already obscured by the rise in the land.

We'd come close, so close to ending it.

But once more, I had failed.

I felt Talan nearby, and the others gathering around, for their quintessence blazed in my senses. All the wardens, at least, had survived. I couldn't look at them, couldn't bear to see the horror, the disappointment, the anger. It would only amplify the feelings simmering inside me.

"Airene."

I squeezed my eyes shut, releasing my hold on quintessence and trying not to tremble. I couldn't kneel forever. Eventually, I had to face this.

Face him.

I opened my eyes and found him crouched before me. His mouth smiled; his eyes did anything but. He looked as if he were shivering.

"Why?" It came out as a whisper. "Why did you…?"

I shook my head, then tried to rise to my feet. Nomusa and Xaron were there to help me, and I gave each of them a grateful look before turning back to Talan. The former Guilder stood as well, looking as if he were trying to stand before an angry ocean, wave after wave crashing against him.

"I'll explain it all," I murmured. "But we have other messes to clean up first."

With that, I numbed myself to pain and carried on.

INTERLUDE II
JIHU

She had just set the flask to boil when the knock came at the door.

Jihu stiffened. Nearly three decades of hiding, and still she had never grown used to it. But her nerves quickly hardened again, and she quickly set to hiding any evidence of her work: peeling off the heavy leather gloves, dampening the fires, ensuring nothing would explode in her absence.

Closing the door behind her, she peered into a looking glass, hung next to the laboratory for just such an occasion as this. And a good thing — as usual, ash dotted her hair. She combed it out with her fingers, grimacing as she pulled hair loose from its tight bun.

There was no time to fix it. The knock came again, polite but insistent. If it was whom she suspected, they would not soon turn away.

She eyed the front door. Her husband was out, scrounging up any food he could find to purchase with the last of their savings. She was aged and scarred, and though she hated to acknowledge it, becoming frailer by the year.

Yet Jihu had never been defenseless. More than a few men had discovered that to their regret.

Smoothing her expression, she approached the door, took in a breath, then opened it.

Armored guards stood there. Worse, a quick glance showed them to be from the Laurel Palace, telling by the insignia engraved into their helms and breastplates. Behind them stood aqua cowls and shadowed faces, undeniable signs of Shepherds.

Jihu felt too warm, and in a way that had nothing to do with aging.

The soldier who had knocked stepped aside, speaking as she did. "You have been graced by a visit from the Despot himself, His Radiance Jaxas Wreath. Bow before your ruler."

Jihu's eyes flickered past the woman, and only then did she see him. She didn't know his face, but she would have known him for the Despot by his clothes and appearance. Jaxas Wreath was as thin as everyone said; "a skeleton in robes," her crassest neighbors called him. His gold-and-green robes were voluminous around his spare frame. He had a slight hunch to his posture, though his head was held high. The Evergreen Wreath, eternally verdant, sat atop his brow.

Seeing him, she didn't hesitate longer, but bent her protesting body over itself.

"Thank you, but that is not necessary. Please, Jihu, rise and speak with me. Time is not a luxury we can waste."

His voice had a whispering quality to it, like he was confiding a secret in her, just between the two of them. Even more ensnaring were his eyes, burning like coals with an inner fire. That fire was familiar, for a similar one fueled herself.

"Please, Your Radiance, be welcome," she said, picking up the address from the guard. "My home is humble, but—"

"No apologies necessary." The Despot was already sweeping forward, and Jihu had to step hastily aside to make way for him. The soldier who had spoken looked annoyed, perhaps at her charge entering a house without her first inspecting it, but she only wordlessly followed. To Jihu's relief, the other laurel guards and the Shepherds remained on her stoop.

Jihu's back trickled with sweat, but she kept her expression stony. They wouldn't suspect her of any misdoings. The Despot of Oedija didn't make house visits for arrests. And though she hadn't expected him personally, she *had* expected someone to come knocking.

It was inevitable after her son's request at the beginning of the season.

She took the opportunity to calm herself by offering tea, which the Despot politely accepted. Fetching the last of the oolong leaves from her home jaitin, Jihu set a pot to boil and sprinkled the dried leaves in the cups. When she could delay no longer, she turned back to the monarch and waited.

The Despot studied her with his feverish eyes for a long moment. She wondered if he'd taken ill, or if the stress of all he faced was overcoming him. She hoped not. However illegitimate the way he'd claimed power, Oedija needed a leader now if it was to survive the army knocking at its gates.

Jaxas Wreath shifted in his chair, but before she could apologize for its meanness, he spoke. "I assume you know why I have come here, Jihu."

She decided to play it safe. "I am sorry, Your Radiance. But I do not."

A slight crease appeared on his brow, and a thrill of fear shot through her. Displeasing this man was not likely to end well if half the things spoken about him were true.

"First Watcher Xaron said he'd spoken with you. Though you refused, you must know my request."

There it was; the truth, baldly stated. Terror rattled through her as she realized the power he possessed over her. But instead of weakening, Jihu found her resolve set. She'd always thrived under adversity.

"Ah." She gave a perfunctory bow. "Of course, Your Radiance. You mean my experiments."

"They are more than experiments, by your son's report. 'Catalysm' — that is what you call it, your brand of magic?"

Jihu tilted her chin up. "Yes, Your Radiance. It is my invention."

To her surprise, the Despot sniffed the air. "Unless I am mistaken, we have just interrupted you."

That rocked her back. What had he smelled? Her nose was growing dull if she'd missed that. Rumors had put Jaxas Wreath as being devious, but he was even sharper than she'd counted on.

She gave a stiff nod. "It is no concern, Your Radiance. Nothing that will endanger you."

"And here I was hoping it would." Jaxas leaned forward on her rickety table, the wood creaking as it bore his weight. "Danger to myself is not my concern, Jihu. I have a nation to protect."

Before she could answer, the Despot nodded at the fireplace. "But it seems our water is boiling?"

She scrambled after the excuse. By the time she had poured the water to allow the tea to steep, Jihu had collected and calmed herself again. She turned to face her unusual guest.

"With the humblest respect, Your Radiance, I am not sure you understand what you ask. Catalysm is volatile and dangerous. It is not a thing to be trifled with."

Jaxas Wreath scrutinized her in silence, long enough to make her want to squirm. When he spoke, it seemed an abrupt change in topic.

"Have you seen the Avvadin army outside our walls, Jihu?"

She shook her head, though she'd dreamed of it often enough that it seemed like she had.

"It is vast, unassailable. They are as numerous as fish in the Lighted Sea. They have warden priests, enslaved spirits, and the deadly Damask

Esir. And what do we have?" The Despot spread his arms, eyebrows quirked, as if to show her. "A few groups of militiamen, a small collection of wardens, my palace guard. Hardly enough to withstand a siege."

Jihu knew what he was asking. Knew she should deny him if she could. But with each fresh reminder of how doomed Oedija was, she felt herself drawn into his plight. Her resolve, built over decades, crumbled further, just as it had when her son had made the request.

But she'd always been able to say no to Xaron. The Despot was another matter entirely.

Jaxas Wreath smiled, but it was a sad, limp thing. "We need you, Jihu. We cannot hope to last a day without your expertise. If what Xaron has said is true, you could give Oedija a fighting chance."

She should say no. Explain how many it could kill. How it could harm their own soldiers as easily as the enemy. She opened her mouth to say just that.

Her tongue betrayed her.

"I have already begun the concoctions, Your Radiance."

His eyes widened. "Then you did not refuse your son."

"I did." She grimaced, then wondered if such an expression was appropriate before one as high as him. "But I have always believed in caution, Your Radiance. I thought this request possible and prepared for it."

"If you were ready for a visit from the Ruling Wreath, then you are just the woman I've been looking for."

With a wry smile, Jaxas Wreath rose. It might have been her imagination, but he seemed to stand a fraction taller.

"First Laurel Synne here will discuss the details with you. I'm afraid I must depart myself. But know, Jihu, that anything you need is at your disposal. Anything at all."

She meant to let him depart as he strode toward the door. But she had been a mother too long to allow that, even of her monarch.

"Protect Xaron," she said to his back. "Please, Your Radiance. Protect my son."

Jaxas Wreath turned back, and she flinched at the sadness in his eyes.

"I'm not sure I can protect anyone. But I promise to try."

With that, the Despot of Oedija swept from her home.

Jihu stared after him, but the female guard had remained behind, so she shook out of her stupor and went to the cups of steeping tea, abandoned before she could serve them.

"Drink," she told the guard as she set the cup before her. "Then we may proceed."

First Laurel Synne eyed her with something like respect, then took a sip.

Jihu repressed a sigh. She had always known it would come back to this. Magic could not be long suppressed. It hadn't worked for Xaron, nor for herself.

Now, it was time to embrace it, and hope it was not too late.

THE THIRD FOLD

The bold witch becomes lost
If she rises too high
Or falls too low
They are not places for mortals
The gods guard their claim
Beware, beware

- A scribestone of Jolduun; estimated 300 SLP

W e fled before Ayize could stop us.
Though my spirits were low, I brimmed with power spilled over from my enemy, and it was a simple matter of cutting open a rift into the Pyrthae and stepping through. I caught a last glimpse of Ayize's resigned expression before sealing it closed behind my party.

"What was that?" Talan hovered near me, anger radiating from him in a scarlet cloud. "Airene, what in the 'Thae's depths happened back there? Why were you—?"

"We have to go," I interrupted, turning my back on him. I doubted my shame was hidden, exposed as we all were in the spirit realm. "We have to reach our camp and figure out our next steps before we can stop and chat."

"If you think I'll let you— "

"Guilder," Xaron interjected, "she's right. We're not exactly safe yet."

I turned back to watch as Talan rounded on my former loftmate. But our companions stood firm beside Xaron, and after a moment, the former Guilder sighed and took a step back.

"Fine," he conceded. "I'll wait for now. But once we're through this…"

I only began walking away. That was one conversation I would happily put off forever if I could. But as long as he held Aika's knife, there was little chance of finding an end beforehand. I'd seen the way he clutched it, like he was afraid it would stab me of its own accord if he let it go.

As our party set off, I took stock of my companions' conditions. We'd sustained blessedly few injuries. Nomusa had a burned shoulder from a stray ray of radiance. Kari had a bruised lip, though I couldn't figure out how she'd received it. Talan was in worse shape. Having thrown himself into the fighting to pursue me, he'd received cuts and burns that left his coat in tatters, but seemed to hurt little. A pack, however, would make the injuries more uncomfortable.

I wanted to thank him for saving my life, but considering what still lay ahead, the words felt too ironic to utter.

By traveling through the Pyrthae, we easily reached our camp before Ayize could, loaded up our packs again, and reentered the spirit realm. Only when we were safely away did we turn to one another and realize the obvious.

"What do we do now?" Xaron took off his pack and set it down on the shimmering ground. A smile quirked his lips, though by how his eyes flared, I could tell it wasn't from humor.

I felt Talan's stare and avoided looking at him. "We follow."

"No. We must move ahead of Taozu."

Only as Azhi spoke did I realize what a state he was in. His fury was palpable, radiating off him in an orange mist. It didn't take much effort to guess why.

"I'm sorry." My head fell, shame making it feel too heavy to keep upright.

"Sorry?" Talan barked a bitter laugh and turned away.

Azhi turned his glare on him, while the rest of my companions wore various expressions ranging from sorrowful to confused. None spoke up before our guide continued.

"As you no doubt sense, Airene, our quarry moves southwest. I have a guess where he is headed, and why."

Nomusa answered before I could. "Avvad."

"Avvad?" Isidora frowned. "What is there for him?"

Azhi spoke in a sigh. "Valem."

A shiver ran through me. The others seemed to feel it as well.

"*Valem?*" Xaron shook his head. "Don't tell me he exists, too."

The daemon-possessed man smiled, and I saw more than a shimmer of the pyr around him. "He does. Long has Valem slumbered, as have many of his fellow great spirits. But he has always exerted influence over the world. Part of his essence resides in the volcano that bears his name, feeding the rage he craves."

Even knowing of the existence of the Quintyr, it was a shock to hear of yet another god who was more than myth. But the epiphany that came after was more troubling still.

"Has he grown so powerful as to challenge him?" I said. "A fellow Quintyr?"

Azhi looked back at me. "You know he has. This was our best chance to stop him while he was distracted by feeding. Now he flies to war, to finish the slaughter of his fellow gods he started long ago."

I'd been so focused on keeping Famine from our world I'd forgotten the damage he could do in his. "Eidola above..."

"They won't save us." Azhi smiled then, and I found I preferred his scowl. "Some have tried. But none have ever been as powerful as Famine after he has feasted so much."

"How can we do anything?" Nomusa demanded. "Even gods are inept! We're just human." Her arms pressed tight against her belly. I guessed she was still on edge from her encounters with her kinsmen.

"We are. But we have Airene." Azhi looked at me, and I read more in his eyes: *If she will do as she should have done.*

I turned away. My own shame was a heavy enough burden to bear without adding his.

No one responded to that. They had an inkling of the methods upon which we relied to defeat our enemy, but they had never truly understood. I wouldn't have been able to in their position, either. I scarcely believed myself, and I'd witnessed Vusu use them.

But he didn't truly succeed, a part of me whispered, *nor has anyone before him. Famine always comes back. The cycle continues.*

I hugged my arms about me, wishing I wasn't filled to the brim with Famine-born energy. I wanted to feel too tired to go on. As it was, I tried to focus back on what we knew and could do, not all that we could not.

"Whether or not he's challenging Valem, he's going in that direction." I turned my gaze over my small party, looking each of them in the eye — except for Talan. "Azhi's right; we need to get ahead. But how?"

Kari spoke, surprising us all. "The third fold."

We stared at her.

"What's that?" I asked, wondering if it was worth the bother. She had rarely given straight answers before, and I doubted that would change now.

The witch glanced from one of us to another, her brow drawn. "The world above." She gestured with a hand to the mirror image of Telae hanging above us.

Corin laid a hand on her sister's shoulder, their images shimmering with the contact. "You must explain, Sister. We do not know this third fold."

Kari stared at Corin for a moment longer before a smile blossomed on her face. "Ah. Then I shall—"

Before she finished speaking, a silvery cloud erupted from her form. I flinched, but couldn't avoid it as it passed over me.

Images exploded into my mind.

They passed by swiftly, a whirlwind of the senses. I smelled vinegar and saltwater, peered into a depthless cave and then the bright sun; then a woman appeared, and she felt familiar and warm. Enough of my wits remained to recognize her as an outlander, and that her features were etched in Kari's face, and Corin's. Blonde hair. Kind eyes. Strong jaw.

Their mother.

No sooner had I figured it out than the woman spoke. "Listen, Kari, and listen well. Long ago, the gods sundered the spirit world to protect witches who visited it. We call these sections 'folds,' like wrinkles in fabric, for they are but pieces of the same cloth."

As she spoke, the scene around the woman filled out, adding texture and detail. It was a fine summer day, judging by the sun and warmth. The grass of the fields surrounding us was yellow, and bird calls filled the air. Kari was remembering more, I guessed, and thus strengthening the memory's picture.

"The first fold," her mother continued, "is a reflection of our world, a place humans can understand. Have you seen it in your dreams, sweet-blossom? It looks as if a second world hangs above you, but neither is truly there. They are created, and never to be trusted — yet as long as you stay within these reflections, you will not be lost.

"But there are folds above and below. The second fold is under your feet, through the ground. Never go there, sweet-blossom — you must promise me! Time is fickle in the spirit world. In the second fold, years will seem moments to you. I may be gone by the time you return. Would you want that?"

Kari, as she remembered herself, gave a muddled response. I couldn't see her clearly, perhaps because she didn't see herself in that moment. Yet she remembered well the touch of her mother's hand on her head, stroking her hair to counter the frightening words.

"There is also a world above the first fold, through the hanging world — the third fold. This is a safer place to go, sweet-blossom, but nowhere in the spirit world is safe. Time slows the higher you go, so spans would be only days in our world, and distance warps as well. But it lacks the familiar surroundings of the first fold, and many witches have become lost there.

"If you find yourself in the spirit world, and need to escape the first fold, ascend to the third fold. All that is needed to break through it is to believe. Wraiths who have forgotten themselves will not follow you there. So long as you do not wander, you will be safe."

The scenes dissolved into mist. I blinked, and the Pyrthae reasserted itself.

So Kari hadn't been the first witch in her family. My mind drifted past the thought to what I'd learned from the visions. *The first fold*, I thought as I gazed around me. The words echoed things Eltris had told me long ago, but were conveyed in a clearer way than the augur had ever bothered with."Stoneward" and "skyward" had been the most she explained of the places beyond the initial staging ground of the Pyrthae. But it seemed they were as distinctive of realms as that which now surrounded us.

"Tyurn's balls, what *was* that?" Xaron shook his head as if to clear it.

Kari looked puzzled again, so I spoke up. "Her memories. She shared them with quintessence."

Isidora nodded, while Xaron grimaced. "Why not just say it," he grumbled.

I smiled at that. But with Talan still glowering my way, my amusement didn't last long.

"So this third fold is dangerous, but will make travel even quicker." I glanced at Azhi. "Will it work?"

He nodded, the motion blurring his image for a moment. "It is our only choice."

I was tired of ultimatums, yet I muttered my agreement.

"And how will we get up there?" Nomusa pointed out.

I craned back my neck to look up. Hundreds of cubits stretched between us and the hanging world. *All that is needed to break through is belief,* Kari's mother had said. Belief had carried us far before; it had allowed us to defy the natural laws, to weigh less and jump higher. Perhaps, if we believed hard enough, we could even soar.

Kari was already demonstrating this. Her chin tilted up, a smile on her lips, she began to float, her feet leaving the ground. Corin stepped toward her, seeming about to pull her back down, but she stopped short and watched with the rest of us as the witch ascended higher and higher. My stomach clenched when she went high enough for a fall to kill her. I suspected it wouldn't, but I'd too often followed my instincts to silence them now.

"We should follow her," Azhi said. Then he, too, started to drift upward. "Believe, and you can," he added before he picked up speed and went out of earshot.

I found my gaze falling to Talan. His silhouette, all shades of darkness, still shimmered with anger. Yet he said nothing as he glided upward.

"*Fareshi* wardens," Nomusa muttered. She shot me a look. "And what are Corin and I supposed to do?"

"The same thing," I countered. "This doesn't have to do with channeling. It's force of will."

Xaron suddenly grinned and spread his arms. "Exactly! See? All in your head, so to speak!"

I saw then that he ascended with the others. A moment later, Isidora followed suit, a wondering smile on her lips.

That left Corin, Nomusa, and me. I was certain I could follow, having more experience than most in the Pyrthae, but I was reluctant to attempt it until the other two had succeeded. Corin looked even more dubious than Nomusa. I wondered if she was too grounded in good sense to be able to believe in anything not of the material world.

I approached her. "If it's easier, pretend that you believe it. It might work the same way."

The cartwoman's brow was still furrowed, but she nodded, trusting me as she always had. Yet a minute passed, and still nothing changed.

"Airene!"

I looked over and found Nomusa floating above the ground, a mixture of bafflement and delight making her expression childlike. A laugh bubbled out of me, taking me by surprise. I hadn't thought I could laugh after what we had just witnessed.

I looked back to Corin, hoping she had also succeeded, but her feet remained firmly on the ground. The smile slipped away as I contemplated what to do.

Then an idea came to me.

"Hold my hands. I want to try something."

We clasped hands, and a feeling like channeling magnesis buzzed through me. I *felt* Corin in a way that went beyond words or senses. It was like how Kari had shared her memory. Our quintessences touched; I delved inside her, and she inside me.

With an effort, I reinforced the boundaries of myself, and the feeling faded. Looking into Corin's shadowy face, I saw I was not the only one disturbed by it.

"Hold tight," I muttered, then closed my eyes and focused all my mind on one thing:

The sky weighs nothing. I weigh nothing. I am weightless.

I repeated the phrases, again and again, binding and reinforcing them.

Each time doubts seeded in, memories of how heavy the sky pressed down on us to keep mortals to the ground, I let them drift past and away. They could only weigh me down.

I almost spoiled it as the feeling of the ground beneath my shoes disappeared, my natural skepticism reasserting itself. But doing it only served to reinforce my belief rather than undermine it. Opening my eyes, I saw Corin still hadn't succeeded herself. A smile played on my lips as I floated to the edge of her reach, then became anchored down by her.

But I knew I didn't have to be.

Corin weighs nothing, I thought, and barely a moment passed before she, too, lifted off the ground. I wanted to laugh. I'd flown in the Pyrthae when visiting as a spirit, but in my actual body, it had seemed impossible. Now, all boundaries had been broken.

What could hold us down?

Corin's hands were tight on my own, though I knew she wouldn't fall so long as I believed for both of us. The ground fell away, and the reflected world above grew nearer. I saw Kari reach it and press her hands against it, then look down. After a moment, she lifted her head again, and before my eyes, she sank into it.

I blinked, this feat stretching the limits of my belief. Then I took it as inspiration.

The sky is not solid. I can pass through it. Corin can pass through it.

By the time we reached the edge of the first fold, almost all my companions had passed through. Nomusa still pressed her hands against it, wearing a look of consternation. I took pity on her.

"Come here — I think I can help."

I tried prying loose one hand free of Corin's panicked grasp, but she clung on until I gave her an exasperated look. When at last she released me, only to hold with both hands to my other one, I reached out to my fellow Finch. Nomusa looked skeptical, but she took hold of it just as my head brushed the suspended ground. I closed my eyes and added to my belief, then dragged my friends up into the world above.

Darkness for a moment, then light pressed on my eyelids. I felt the differences of the third fold even before I saw them. A cold, incessant wind blew, piercing my spirit and sapping my strength. I wondered how long I could endure it. Opening my eyes, I noticed it looked much different from the first fold. The world was cast in a dusky blue light that seemed to come from everywhere and nowhere. A thin mist slithered through the sky, and I resolved to stay away from it, for it reminded me too much of pyr. Below our feet was an unnaturally flat surface that resembled tiles, but lacked the texture to make them real. They seemed more like the concept of floor rather than floor itself.

Already, I didn't much care for the third fold.

Yet there was nothing for it. I set my jaw, firmed my belief, and released my friends' hands. "Stay close, and we'll be alright," I said.

They both nodded, fear shining from their shimmering forms. I hoped they couldn't see my own as I tried to bury it deep inside me.

"Come," Azhi called from ahead. "Keep your feet on the floor, and you will not become lost." The two halves of him, human and pyr, seemed on the verge of splitting apart up here. Light and shadow leaned away from each other. I wondered if it was due to ascending higher in the Pyrthae, or if Eazal strove against his captor.

Though it disturbed me to think about it, I put it from my mind. We'd trusted him this far. We could do it a little longer.

The daemon led, and we followed.

THE FINAL SOLUTION

How long have I searched for another solution? But there is no other way. Death, blood, and sacrifice are what he craves, and they are what will bind him.

But it is not death of only the body that I will suffer, but the soul. Annihilation…
If I accept this burden, never again will I fly through the forest. Never again will I see my brother, if he has lingered all these long cycles.

Condemn myself, or condemn all… Men were not made for such dilemmas.

- The journal of Vusumuzi; date unknown

Not long into our journey through the third fold of the Pyrthae, Talan fell in beside me.

By silent consent, Nomusa and Corin drifted away, granting us privacy. I wasn't sure that I wanted it. In the journey since the battle at the blood lake, I had dreaded this moment, and would have put it off longer if I could have.

But Talan deserved the truth. No matter how much it hurt us both.

He didn't speak for several strides, yet I heard murmurs of his thoughts. I tried to hold my own close, afraid of what he would sense from me.

"Why?"

I closed my eyes, wishing I could drift up and become lost in the endless blue space above us. *Why.* The only question he needed answered. The very one I wished I didn't have to.

"It's the only way to stop Famine," I answered at last.

"By suicide?"

I winced. "By sacrifice. I don't want to die, Talan."

"Then don't."

His obstinacy was beginning to grate on me. "I told you, it's the only way."

Our features had become murkier this high in the Pyrthae, but I knew he wore his usual smirk as he responded. "How do you know that? Because a few dusty old tomes said so?"

Now I plainly radiated my frustration. It drew glances from the others, but no one intervened. I wondered if they could hear every word we spoke. Sound didn't always work as expected here. Even whispers might be heard over miles.

"Vusu held Famine at bay by acting as a Sacrifice. Aika, whose knife you stole from me, did the same during the first Hunger War. It's how Seeds of Famine have always caged him. It's the *only* way. He's a 'Thae-cursed god, Talan. We're fortunate there's any way to defy him at all."

He was shaking his head even before I'd finished speaking. "Vusu stopped him for a day. Even this Aika only held him for so long before he returned. It doesn't last, Airene. Why not search for a different way? Why die, when he'll only return years or days later?"

I burned with fury, and in response, the radiance in my form gathered heat. He didn't mean to insult me by implying I could only hold Famine for days, but I couldn't help but take it that way.

Still, I needed him, and not only for the artifact. Talan had always been there for me. He'd saved my life more times than I could count. That he might turn his back on me now, when I needed him more than ever, was a thought I could not bear.

So I took the only avenue left to me. I seized his arm and spliced our souls.

We'd done it before, when Talan was dying to Silks in the Underguild tunnels, and I'd given him the strength to live. This time, I pushed not energy into him, but knowledge. I held all the memories I had of learning how to defeat Famine, the certitude with which I held them, and thrust them into his mind. He resisted, trying to twist out of my grasp, but I was the stronger one here. I didn't let him go until he sagged, all that I could share with him exhausted.

When I released him, Talan backed away a step and stared at me. I felt it more than saw it, for his body had become murkier, and his eyes were nothing more than shadowed pits. Still, I held his gaze, willing him to believe, to understand, to support me as I needed him to.

He took another step back, shook his head, then walked away. I stared after him, trying not to shatter.

———

We continued on.

Our company grew morose. Morale had already been low after the fight with the cultists, but Talan and my falling out lowered it further still. Perhaps even more impactful was the third fold itself. The wind never ceased to blow, and our strength and resolve were carried away on its current. Each step became laborious, and no matter how I told myself I was weightless, my legs felt like anvils.

But I still sensed Famine. His hunger pulled me forward.

Mostly, we were silent. All that needed to be discussed had been. We had hopes more than plans, yet could make nothing more concrete until we found Famine again.

Yet in the changeless landscape, something shifted. Where only cold had reigned, an inkling of warmth seeped through me, like the first touch of dawn reaching over the horizon. I thought I imagined it, but it grew with each passing moment, the effect rapidly amplifying.

"Something is coming," Azhi said. "Something is here…"

I barely heeded him, for another thing caught my attention. The directionless light had turned from blue to darker hues. From yellow to red, then to angry violet.

Before I could feel alarmed, the Pyrthae split apart.

Lightning flashed. I screamed as I threw myself flat to the tiled floor. Around me, my companions sank through it, fleeing the third fold for the safety below: Xaron, Isidora, Azhi, Talan. I would have fled as well, but I couldn't abandon the others. Corin and Nomusa needed me.

Kari had taken hold of her sister and rapidly passed through, so I lunged toward Nomusa. Her features had almost entirely dissipated, leaving an amorphous spirit trembling with terror. I was so close to her, mere inches away, my fingers reaching—

A tidal wave crashed over me.

Pain and emotion rode the lightning that ravaged my spirit. Rage, it seemed, but of a particular kind. Like when I saw Feiyan succeed and wished for it myself.

An envious anger, but without bounds or control.

I fought to stay above it, but how could I fight a feeling? I pulsed quintessence, but if it had any effect, I couldn't detect it.

The magnetic attack didn't last forever, though; perhaps it was only a moment. As it released me, I sagged against the tile, exhausted and in agony. Nomusa was speaking beside me, but I couldn't understand her words. The booming presence had filled my mind and scoured it clean of willpower.

But self-preservation is difficult to kill. As Nomusa seized my hand, I knew what to do. *It is not real,* I thought, then sank through the floor.

Then we were falling.

Weightless, I thought, but the first measure of belief had sapped my scant strength. Nomusa clung to me, winding around me with all of her being. Without meaning to, she seeped into me as well. Fragments of memories bit at me, all the times she'd been afraid. Hearing her family murdered when she hid in a cupboard. Fleeing into the jungle, afraid of the dark and all it held. Entering Oedija's gates and quailing at all the foreign humanity amassing around her.

Each wound provoked my protective instincts, honed over years of employing them on Linos. I wrapped myself around Nomusa and thought, *The sky weighs nothing.*

Our fall abruptly slowed.

We hovered there for a long time as I recovered enough to control our descent. When we finally touched down on the ground of the first fold, Nomusa and I fell apart and sprawled upon it. Our companions were there around us, worry in all their voices. But I could only heed one.

"Airene." Talan cupped my neck, supporting my head. "Are you hurt?"

I shook my head. I was in pain, but it didn't feel permanent. "Just need to rest," I murmured.

But already, I felt better. I closed my eyes, knowing I should not fall asleep in the Pyrthae, unable to help it.

He cared for me still. He would never stop caring. It was all the comfort I needed.

I felt my friends pull me out of the Pyrthae and reenter Telae just before darkness entirely claimed me.

CHAPTER TWENTY-ONE

PRINCIPLE

Gods are no more free than men. They are bound by themselves, the rules by which they dictate their lives. Each possesses a calling to which they dedicate their existence — some for the good of humanity, some for evil.

Understand these principles well, and know how they can be exploited, and you may survive your encounter with them.

- Scroll fragment; origin unknown; estimated 31 PLP

What in the Lighted hells happened up there?"

I opened my eyes to Isidora's question. Shadowed greenery surrounded me, solid and natural in its appearance. A forest.

We're in Telae.

Only then did I remember exiting the Pyrthae just before I fell unconscious. How long had it been? Not long enough for them to discover the answer to what had just occurred.

A groan escaped me as I sat up.

Talan was by my side in a moment, as was Nomusa. "Easy," my fellow Finch muttered. "You were struck hard up there."

The former Guilder spoke at the same time. "You're certain you're not hurt?"

"I'm fine." I wasn't, but it felt better to not have them hovering over me like hens about a chick. Easing them back, I breathed through the nausea that stole over me, then looked up at Isidora. She wore a frown until she noticed my gaze, then smoothed it away.

"It wasn't just a storm," I said. "When the lightning hit me, I felt something behind it. Emotion undiluted. It was anger, but there was more to it." I reached for the hazy memories, trying to capture the right words to describe the feeling. "Like the anger at seeing someone with something you want to have."

"Envy?" Xaron guessed.

"Does it matter?" Isidora had always had a great capacity for patience, but it seemed to finally be depleted. "It doesn't answer *what* that was."

"It does matter." Azhi leaned against a nearby tree. "If the storm was sentient, that makes it a very different thing."

"Sentient." I met his gaze. "You think it was… a pyr?"

He shook his head. "A great spirit. A Quintyr."

My skin rose in gooseflesh. It made a certain sense. The storm had been implacable and single-minded, yet there had been something conscious behind it. And simple pyr were never that powerful.

"Another one?" Xaron shook his head. "They're sprouting all around us!"

"Not precisely," Azhi said. "This one has likely wandered the third fold for millennia, not touching the mortal realm or its inhabitants. After all, how many have entered the Pyrthae, much less the level above the first?"

I sat with the thought. The daemon was right once more; there was so much we didn't know of the Pyrthae, despite traveling through it for many days. Could far more Quintyr exist than we knew, just beyond our reach? Were there more stoneward or skyward?

Isidora spoke up again. "If there are more up there, then we cannot travel through it. It's too great a risk."

Azhi frowned, but didn't respond. No one else objected. I grimaced, knowing I had to speak.

"Famine's still ahead of us. If anything, he's gained ground. I don't know that we have a choice."

"No." Talan put his hand on my shoulder, softening the denial. "Better we reach him whole than not at all."

I suspected his ulterior motives, but only sighed. My body felt heavy with all I'd put it through. Traveling the Pyrthae already took its toll; being attacked by a savage Quintyr only made matters worse.

Yet even as I sat there, vitality swept through me. My spirits lifted, and my apprehension grew in proportion. Famine had found a fresh source of quintessence to feast on. I hoped we weren't already too late.

I stood, surprising everyone. "We should keep going. Famine has arrived wherever he was headed. I don't think he's far. If we can reach him before we rest, we might still stand a chance."

The others nodded, though most with heavy resignation. Isidora's frustration had not abated, telling from her scowl, but she only sighed without further protest. I wondered if they knew the reason behind my sudden revival. Talan, at least, watched me with narrowed eyes and a sharp smirk.

I bent and retrieved my pack from where they'd lain it next to me and shouldered it once more. Then, as Azhi cut into the spirit realm, I followed the others in.

———

"The great spirits," Azhi said a short way into our walk, "or the Quintyr, if you prefer, are governed by their driving principles. They are different beings than mortals, with their own brands of reason and logic. In some ways, their minds are more limited than ours; in other ways, they are unimaginably expansive."

The daemon had begun the lecture at a prompting question from Xaron as he mulled aloud over the magnetic storm. I remained silent, content to listen. Eltris had spoken of this once, but she had always kept secrets. And there was the likelihood that this spirit had learned something in his two centuries of existence that the augur had not.

"Famine," he continued, "is driven by hunger — a desire for quintessence, specifically. This is partly what makes him so powerful; it is in his nature to accumulate it and destroy any who could challenge him."

Xaron frowned. Though Eazal had once been familiar to him, he'd grown used to Azhi in a way I could never manage. "And Valem? He's powerful as well. What's his principle?"

"Rage," Talan answered before Azhi could.

The daemon turned back and eyed him thoughtfully. "Yes. That is why he imbued part of himself in the volcano. I believe it fuels him in a similar way as Famine's feasting. That is why he remains perhaps the most powerful spirit in either world."

A thought occurred to me. "Quintyr can influence the material world, even if they cannot enter it."

My words drew Azhi's eye to me now. "Yes. They cannot help but radiate their principle, and no being with quintessence is entirely separate from the spirit realm."

I nodded, wondering how it had never occurred to me before. "Maybe that's how Vusu created the Manifest so swiftly, and why it dismantled so soon after Famine left Oedija. Their hunger for more — it was born of him."

Azhi drifted back to walk next to me, and though I preferred to keep my distance, I allowed it.

"Not born," he corrected gently. "Amplified. Those drawn to the movement were the worst off. The poor. The hungry. The daemonized." He glanced at Xaron, who only shrugged.

My thoughts turned inward again as I contemplated my own actions. I'd been driven by a hunger of my own, hadn't I? The desire to understand, to pull the secrets surrounding me into the light, and thus achieve fame and fortune. Had that been Famine's influence all along?

Was he why I'd sacrificed everything to come to this point?

I didn't know, and I wasn't sure I wanted to know. If it was Famine, it would make me his pawn. But it somehow would be worse if it was solely my own. If it was my hubris and ambition that had brought ruin to so many I loved.

Linos. I hoped he still lived, that Oedija stood against Avvad. But just as before, I could do nothing for him. Nothing at all to protect my little brother.

"Avvad," Talan spoke up again. "My people are also influenced. Valem seeds hate in their hearts…"

As he trailed off, something in his voice drew me from my misery. I stared at him, puzzled for several moments before I recognized the emotions vibrating from his spirit. *Relief.*

Only then did I understand. For as long as I'd known him, Talan had resented his home country. The Avvadin Imperium had taken everything from him, ground him down to a shadow, until he had to leave or lose himself entirely.

But it was still his home, his people. He wanted to love them. Now, he'd found a way to rationalize why he still did.

I smiled at him, and he returned it. For once, the interaction was devoid of irony.

"What of Clepsammia?" Nomusa asked into the silence that had fallen.

I glanced at her, curious why she had thought about it. She only shrugged in response.

Azhi, too, seemed intrigued by her question, head cocked to one side. "As with many of the Eidolan gods, the answer is in her stories. Fate is her principle, Nomusa. The guiding of mortals along the paths she has determined to be best, or correct, or inevitable." He shook his head. "I have never known her intentions, if they are helpful or harmful to those of the material plane. Only what drives her."

Fate. I thought over my interactions with the Quintyr, or at least the spirit I believed to be her. She seemed to have been well-intentioned; she had saved me twice, after all. But none of the Quintyr seemed good or evil on their face. They fulfilled their principles; that was that. Just as a storm or natural disaster couldn't be moral in their actions, neither could they.

Not even Famine was truly evil. Though that fact didn't change what we had to do.

"And Harvest… she is growth? Or perhaps life?"

This came again from Talan, once more surprising me. I wondered how he even knew to ask of her when I remembered how I'd pushed my memories onto him. His smile had faded, and the impressions of his eyes narrowed. I mulled over what he might have in mind.

Azhi smiled, and there seemed something knowing in it. "Yes — vitality is how I think of it. She is, or was, Famine's antithesis, for her principle was to help quintessence flourish. But she is dead, consumed by her enemy in the last Hunger War. Life cannot triumph over death, in the end."

That put an end to the conversation. But as we carried on our journey, I glanced often at Talan. He seemed to mull over something, and come to conclusions that didn't altogether displease him.

I only stopped when he caught me looking and flashed me a smirk. It didn't stop me from wondering what he was planning.

CHAPTER TWENTY-TWO

WHIRLING WORLD

The light was fading when the first signs of civilization came into view. I'd long ago felt that we neared our destination. Famine's presence pulled at me strongly now, and his hunger had waxed. I guessed that his present feast was running thin. But it didn't feel as if he was leaving. Something kept him tethered in place.

As homesteads appeared, then a city and volcano beyond, I saw my enemy and understood.

The volcano named for Valem rose above the city of Erimis. Lava trickled down its sides, and smoke billowed out of its top in a thin black plume. Impressive as it was, it was the Quintyr curled around its sides that caught my attention.

Famine was now long and large enough that he encircled the volcano's peak twice. The dragon god had his teeth sunk into the rock, and by the working of his jaw, he was trying to gnaw his way in. Around where he chewed, more lava spewed out, and Famine flinched back as it splashed on his snout. As he shook his great head free of it, I wondered if it was lava we actually saw. We were in the Pyrthae, and whatever it was had hurt a

Quintyr. More likely Valem fought back against the intrusion, though lazily.

"Valem still sleeps," Azhi murmured.

"Not for long, by the look of it," Nomusa noted.

I wondered what would happen if Valem awakened. The thought drew my attention to the city sprawled below. Erimis was fortunate to have survived this long at the foot of an active volcano. I'd heard of eruptions occurring in the past, lava flooding the streets and killing people by the thousands. Yet the Avvadin considered this a holy and powerful place. No matter how many times Valem drove them out, they always came crawling back.

We were still outside Erimis's walls when Azhi turned back to face us. "We must agree this time," he said. I knew his words were meant for me, though he didn't look my way. "I believe our best chance is to awaken Valem and provoke battle between him and Taozu. Then, while he is distracted, Airene will cage him."

Everyone glanced at me — or past me. Condemning a friend to death could not be an easy thing.

I nodded, trying not to let my fear show. "Yes. I will."

Talan shifted as if about to speak, and I braced myself for his objections. But none came.

"We should rest before the attempt," the former Guilder said. "I know a man who will grant us shelter, no matter how many years have passed since I last saw him." He gestured, and when Azhi followed, the others filed behind the men.

I stared at Talan's back, unable to move. He'd been willing to doom Telae to save me before. Had that changed? Was he now ready to let me die? I was glad I brought up the rear of our party, for I was sure I did a poor job of hiding my feelings.

In the Pyrthaen version of Erimis, the outer gates were open, so we entered the city without issue. Its foreign buildings rose around us. I wasn't unused to Avvadin architecture, Oedija being plenty influenced by it, but it still felt strange to be surrounded by it.

Sandstone and volcanic rock adorned the domiciles and walkways. As we traveled the main promenade, I looked up to see people thronging the streets. Resentment twisted in my gut. They looked almost normal here, their lives unaffected by war, while my people suffered.

But it wouldn't be long before they knew Oedija's pain. We would make sure of that.

I only caught myself for the nasty thought afterward. Was it Valem's influence or my anger that spawned it? I hated doubting even my own mind. Not knowing which was the source, I tried numbing emotion altogether and focusing on putting one foot before the other.

We came ever nearer to Valem's base. Famine's hunger hollowed me out so I felt as empty as a cloud, drifting through the streets. *Eat*, the nagging thoughts came. *Drink*. Unable to do anything for it, I tried my best to ignore it.

At last, we stopped before a building that could only be a temple. It was large and formed of sandstone, with a dome in the middle and wings extending out from it. Its bricks and gilding were aged, but seemed to have once been built at great expense. I wondered if a Kahin-Shah had once favored it, and when it had fallen out of the ruling family's good graces.

Talan turned, conflicting emotions radiating from him. "My home," he said with a twist of his lips. "The temple of the Hortum Kor."

How odd, to see the place he'd so often spoken of. My gaze lingered on the facade as I followed Talan and the others around to the alley next to it. Hidden there, Talan cut a rift back into Telae, then led the way through. I exited last. My natural senses reemerged in a flood, the stenches in particular overwhelming. It was quieter than I expected, though the crowds had been fading above us in the Pyrthae as we traveled.

The disorientation only took a moment to adjust to, but I was glad when Talan reached out a hand to steady me. My eyes alighted on his, then darted away. Doubt still seeped through me. His brow creased slightly, but he said nothing before drawing back.

"This way," he said. "We shouldn't linger outdoors past nightfall. The Silks enforce the curfew."

He led us to the front of the temple. Passing through the doors, I saw we weren't alone. The foyer was dark, but ahead of us was a rotunda illuminated by the fading sunlight and the rising moons. A single figure occupied the space between the columns, an older man by his graying hair. I was astonished to see him occupied by the strangest practice.

The man was spinning.

He whirled in place, around and around, with such balance and grace I wouldn't have believed it possible was it not before my eyes. I'd heard Talan describe the dances of the temple he'd once been part of, and the effect to which he'd employed them against Silks. But to see one play out before me was another matter altogether.

As we approached, the man stopped turning and faced us. He had thick and wild hair, grayed with dark strands throughout. Deep furrows worked into his skin, and many of them seemed to be lines from smiles and laughter. His eyes were arresting, the color of honey, and his skin was a deep bronze.

He seemed to have been aware of us, for he didn't startle. Yet his eyes widened as his gaze fell upon Talan.

"I would think you a ghost, had you come alone," the grizzled man murmured in the ash-tongue.

Talan grinned as fully as I'd ever witnessed. "I'm here in the flesh, you old lion."

Then they were striding toward each other and embracing, laughing and smiling all the while. Tears were in the older man's eyes; I couldn't see Talan as he faced away, but I guessed he was in much the same state. My chest felt full at the sight. Until I saw him so happy, I'd never known how lonely Talan must have always felt in Oedija. The thought brought a tinge of bittersweet with it.

After several moments, they broke apart, and the priest wiped at his eyes before smiling apologetically. "It's been five years," he said by way of explanation. "But don't leave your companions as strangers, Talan. All are welcome here."

Corin and Kari's brows were furrowed, unable to follow along in the Avvadin language. I spoke in the sea-tongue instead. "Do you know Oedijan speech?"

The priest started, then chuckled as he responded in the same tongue. "I do. My apologies — I should have known where you were from."

"Some of them are," Talan conceded. "But if you don't mind, Osman, we have urgent business here. Perhaps we might make introductions while having refreshments…?"

The priest, Osman, loosed another laugh. "You never were shy about asking for food!"

We followed the grizzled man and Talan deeper into the temple, where they turned into a cozy room just large enough to fit us all. It boasted a thin mattress, full bookshelves, and a merrily burning hearth that warmed the space. A glass window looked out over Erimis and let in a little more illumination.

Once we were all settled on the bed and the few chairs available, Osman sent Talan to fetch the food, and to my amazement, the former Guilder complied with a single quip. The two had fallen back into roles of mentor and mentee so easily I wondered if I'd underestimated just how close they were. It was more like how a father and son interacted.

As Talan's footsteps faded, the priest peered at each of us. Though he still wore a friendly smile, a hint of shrewdness entered his eyes.

"Now," he said, still speaking in the sea-tongue, "why don't you tell me who all I've just allowed into my temple."

We gave brief introductions, and Osman returned the favor. He was apparently called the "Hodja" here — a head priest, I gathered from his description. A silence fell for a moment, then the priest asked the inevitable question.

"Why are you here? What trouble have you dragged Talan into?"

I looked at Azhi, and he looked at me. As the others turned to one of the two of us, Osman did the same. I was quickly discovering where Talan had gathered much of his mannerisms and his sharp wit. The priest's stare was difficult to endure.

I was on the verge of admitting our mission when Talan returned. He bore platters filled with pita bread, hard cheese that had a ripe stench and was tinged green, and plump, purple grapes. A veritable feast; reports had been of drought in Avvad as well as Oedija, and I was grateful we wouldn't starve here.

We set to soothing our aching bellies while Talan took charge of the explanations. He painted in broad, bold strokes all we battled against: the Manifest, Avvad, and even Famine. The Hodja didn't seem to begrudge us for the war our leaders had brought us to; to the contrary, he seemed against war entirely and sympathetic to the Oedijan cause. I also thought he would balk at the insinuation that the dragon god existed in actuality, but he only nodded. Only after did it occur to me that he *was* a priest; belief was his expertise.

When Talan finished, I dared to hope the interrogation was over. Then Osman smiled and said quietly, "So you have pursued Famine here to Erimis. Now what do you mean to do?"

A knife could have cut the silence. My companions all glanced at me, so Osman followed suit. His eyes narrowed minutely, even as the smile never left his lips.

"Airene, wasn't it?"

I nodded. "Airene the Finch, to some."

He smiled wider. "It seems my answer lies with you, by how your friends are trying not to look at you."

I glanced at Talan, but no aid was forthcoming from him. He seemed almost amused as he watched me flail with the decision of how much to reveal. He clearly trusted this priest, and we had put our lives in his hands already. Yet it remained that he was Avvadin, and a worshipper of Valem. I doubted I could ever fully trust him.

But the truth had long been my best weapon. I employed it now.

"We mean to awaken Valem and challenge Famine — to cage him, if we can."

Osman stiffened. His eyes shifted to Talan, who showed no amusement of his own.

"Is this true?" the priest asked quietly. "You want to awaken him?"

Talan's shoulders bowed. "It's the only way."

"It's the wrong way." I saw now why Talan called the Hodja an "old lion" as he leaned his elbows onto his knees, his eyes bright with the firelight. "When Valem awakens, he erupts. You know this. Would you kill thousands, Talan? Thousands of your kinsmen?"

I flinched, though I'd known the price all along. But to put it in such bald terms placed it in a new and disturbing light.

Talan bowed his head and spoke to the floor. "If we do not, hundreds of thousands more will die. The whole of the Four Realms, and the world besides."

Osman stared at him, then turned his eyes across the others around the room. "You all believe this?" He sounded incredulous. "That you must do this, or the world will end?"

"We *know* this, Hodja Osman," Azhi said, as calm and composed as ever. "It is in Famine's nature to devour, and he will do so until there is nothing left."

The priest seemed slow to anger, but his temper was rising now, telling by the scowl stealing over it. I gripped my seat, half a loaf abandoned on my lap, hoping that coming to the temple hadn't been a mistake.

"I would not hear massacre preached by you, *Qarin*," Osman all but spat. "You, who steals the body of another!"

All of us startled at the accusation, all but Talan and Azhi himself. The daemon only gave a small smile, while the former Guilder shook his head, as if he'd been expecting this.

Perhaps he had. In a rush, I realized Talan had set a trap for us to stop my sacrifice. A trap for *me*. Anger flared within me, and when he glanced my way, I didn't bother hiding it. Talan grimaced and looked away again.

"Yes," Azhi spoke into the silence. "This body is not my own, as my companions know. But I do it only out of necessity, Hodja Osman. I will go to any lengths to stop Taozu, for his tyranny is the guilt I have borne for far longer than you have been alive. Telae must survive, and for that to happen, a sacrifice must be made."

With unerring intuition, Osman looked at me. My temper sputtered out as quickly as it had come, cold fear replacing it.

"Blood and spirit," he muttered. "The same cost, I expect."

Though my feelings of hurt toward Talan had not changed, I looked at him then. How could Osman know this? The priest was far more knowledgeable in these matters than I'd thought possible. By Talan's expression, he wasn't surprised.

The Hodja calmed as he looked at me again. "You do not need to awaken Valem, Airene and company; not yet. As my onetime pupil no doubt believes by bringing you here." He cast a sidelong glance at Talan, who flashed an innocent smile, before continuing. "Even Buyujinn have always been enticed and susceptible to sacrifice. Perhaps, if we work together, we can come up with a different plan."

A different plan. One that did not involve me dying. It sounded too good to be true.

It *was* too good to be true. If it wasn't, someone across the ages would have discovered it before now, and Famine's cycle would have been broken.

But they hadn't. This was the way. The only way.

My hands had tightened into fists. As Talan's eyes flickered down to them, I loosened my muscles and smoothed my face. Neither of us was deceived.

Osman watched the exchange, but he only rose with a sigh. "Stay here the night; rest and think over it. We'll speak more in the morning." He addressed Talan then. "The north dormitory is open. We've had fewer recruits than normal in recent years."

Talan nodded and gestured us out. We thanked our host, but as I met his eyes, I could tell neither of us trusted the other.

Just as well. I already knew I wouldn't be relying on his hospitality for long.

CHAPTER TWENTY-THREE

THE ONLY WAY

I have betrayed many. I will betray many more. But is it truly betrayal when I do so for the greater good?

- The journal of Vusumuzi; date unknown

While I waited for my companions' breathing to even out in sleep, I drifted into the Pyrthae.

My thoughts had been circling it, so I wasn't surprised to find myself there. The landscape always appeared differently than when I entered the spirit realm in the flesh, and this occasion proved no different.

Erimis had turned into a volcanic wasteland. Lava flowed through the city streets. I could tell where wardens lay by concentrated swirls of cinders, a variation on the cyclones and flames they'd appeared as before. The heat was intense and uncomfortable; radiance dominated the energetic elements here.

It was no mystery why. My gaze traveled to the volcano in which Valem slumbered, ablaze with fire and lava and so bright it hurt to look at. More frightening still was the beast entwining its peak, from whom I felt a hunger that hollowed out my soul.

Famine had a similar form as upon my company's arrival, except he was now wreathed in flames. He'd made progress gnawing through the stone, his head disappearing into the mountainside.

How far did he have to go to feast on Valem's quintessence? I feared it wouldn't be long. Perhaps this new form of his protected him from the volcano's defenses; perhaps it was just a feature of this variant of the Pyrthae. Either way, it didn't bode well for my party's present plans.

I hadn't entered the Pyrthae with any particular intention, but now that I laid eyes on my enemy once more, I felt one crystalize in my mind.

We couldn't afford to delay. If I had to die, I didn't want to live with the fear of it any longer.

Facing the heat below, I dove back into my body. The world turned dark and cool as I opened my eyes in Telae, gasping for air. For a moment, it had seemed I breathed in the fumes exuded by Valem, but in truth, it was only the scent of hot stone. I waited until I'd calmed, then gazed around at my companions.

And froze. A silhouette stood in the open doorway.

As it approached, I opened my locus wide and sucked in energy. This close to Famine, my abilities were as great as they ever were, far surpassing anything another warden could amass. But I couldn't unleash it all without hurting my companions. I had to be careful.

Then a dim glow appeared on the figure's fingers, illuminating their face. I stifled a groan as I repressed my magic and frowned. It was only Talan.

He wore a smirk as he neared, though it lacked some of its usual bite. Maybe it was how shadowed his eyes looked, almost malevolent in the darkness, if I didn't know better.

"Sorry to startle you," he murmured as he kneeled next to my cot.

"Who says you did?"

His smile widened briefly, then disappeared. "Can we talk?"

I nodded, then rose and followed him from the dormitory. I was still dressed, being in the habit from our journey. He had found clean clothes himself, and much more in the Avvadin style than I was used to seeing him wear, with a sash instead of a belt and shoes with pointed toes. Somehow, they suited him.

Talan led me to the rotunda where we'd first seen Osman spinning. When he reached its center, he looked up at the ceiling.

"This is where it happened," he said, his back still to me. "Where I became attuned."

I nodded. He'd told me the story before, though it hit differently to see the place where it had occurred. "When the Buyujinni visited you."

Talan turned to look at me over his shoulder. "The Shrouded Mother, patroness of the Hortum Kor. I thought it a gift. But it turns out she only wanted to steal my soul."

A prickling ran through me. "What did you really want to talk about, Talan?"

He fully faced me then, his stance set like he readied for me to charge him. Seeing him like that, even suspecting his ulterior motives, I wanted to fold him into my arms and be enveloped in his. We'd never had a proper courtship like either of us wanted or deserved. Of all my regrets for my life, it ranked high on the list.

But he was going to try convincing me why Osman was right; I was sure of it. I hardened myself and waited for the attack.

He drew in a breath, then exhaled it slowly. "I've been thinking about all you shared with me, up there. About what you have to do. And there are some things that are just beginning to line up."

"Like?" My interest was piqued, but I tried not to show it, sure he would take advantage of any vulnerability he could.

"That tree in the Wumofu, that Azhi showed you — the Chains. And the one you read about, the one that grew from Aika of the Green."

I nodded, letting the silence draw him out.

One corner of his lips quirked. He wasn't fooled, but he continued all the same. "You've talked about being a Seed of Famine. But Aika also claimed to be a Seed of Harvest. What if that's the important piece, Airene? A tree as a symbol for the Goddess of Bounty — what could be better suited?"

I frowned. It wasn't a poor point; its logic intrigued me. But I didn't see how it would support his argument.

"That doesn't change what I have to do, Talan. The sacrifice I have to make."

He took several steps closer, but stopped just beyond reach. "The temple that Buyujinni lured me to — do you remember how I described it?"

I played along with the tangent, though I remained cautious. "It was like an underground city, all of white stone."

"But it wasn't stone; they were souls, solidified and manifest. I have never forgotten how the city felt alive, and I finally realized that's why this felt so familiar."

Talan's hand went to his waist, and he withdrew the bone-white knife to hold it out before him. I stared at it with fresh eyes, then raised my gaze to meet his.

"You think this knife is made of quintessence as well. The quintessence of Harvest."

He nodded, eyes bright in the moon-lifted darkness. "And not only that. I've been studying that scepter Azhi carries. It looks to be made of the same material as this dagger. And since it was used for a similar purpose, to bind Famine—"

"—maybe it's Harvest's soul."

My head reeled. As with most epiphanies, I found a smile claiming my lips.

Talan grinned as he drew nearer still. "We feared that she was dead, but she's not. Harvest still lives and has for thousands of years. There's hope, Airene. We just have to figure out how to reach her."

My smile faded as I took his assumptions to their conclusion. "I know how to reach her, Talan. It's like Osman says: 'spirit and blood.' Only through sacrifice—"

"*Airene.*" He tucked the knife back into his sash and took my hands in his. "You're thinking too narrowly. What if there's a different way, one that doesn't kill you? What if… I don't know, we sacrificed pigs instead? Every animal has quintessence, right? Maybe that would be enough."

I didn't pull away, but only just. Objections brimmed on my tongue. *It has to be a Seed of Famine*, I wanted to say. *It has to be me.*

But I couldn't speak the words, couldn't extinguish this spark flaring in him. Talan, once made bitter and cynical by the world, had found a reason to hope.

His eyes darted between each of my own, searching for something. "We're close to understanding this. Too close to throw it away by doing the same thing that's been done before and perpetuating the cycle. Swear to me, Airene. Swear to me you won't do anything until we figure this out."

I hesitated. Then I whispered, "I promise."

He seemed taken aback for a moment, then his lopsided smile returned. I ached to see it, for soon it would slip away entirely.

Talan asked for time, but time was precisely what we didn't have. He had meant to convince me of his way of thinking, but the revelations only solidified my own resolutions. It provided rationale to the ritual that would take my life. It helped me make peace with it.

I gazed into his eyes, those belonging to a man I'd come to care deeply for over these past three years, and my old resolve reemerged. I would do anything to save him. To protect him.

I would die, since that was what it would take.

I freed my hands, wrapped them around the back of his neck, and drew him closer. His breath was warm on my face.

"I love you," I murmured, then channeled as our lips touched.

Quintessence had always had a stronger influence when I touched my target. I was at the height of my power, with Famine having grown strong and being nearby.

Even Talan, as clever and talented as he was, stood no chance.

Sleep, I commanded him, and his eyes widened for a moment. The next, his eyelids drooped closed, and his body went slack. I clung to him, making sure he would not come to harm in the fall. But he surprised me by struggling back upright.

"Airene…" he said thickly, his eyelids fluttering as he tried to focus on my face.

I smiled sadly back at him. *Sleep,* I repeated the command, more forcefully.

He sagged in my arms, dragging me to the floor as I cradled his limp body.

I lingered for a moment after he fell unconscious, loathe to leave him. But he would be safe there, even sprawled in the middle of the floor. Our companions or Osman would discover him come morning, or perhaps before that, if I succeeded in my aim.

I abandoned him for his own safety.

I took Aika's knife from him and clutched it as I stood. I would need nothing else. Not with what I intended.

Only my grasp on quintessence alerted me to the presence of someone behind me.

Spinning around, I readied myself to fight, but saw it was again unnecessary. Osman stood there, his hair wilder than usual so it truly resembled a lion's mane. I was surprised he was a warden, but only just. It made a certain sense, considering his bond with Talan. But it was his expression that made me truly wary.

"He cares for you," the Hodja said. "As he has cared for no one else."

I clenched my jaw. He knew precisely where to strike, this priest.

"That's why I'm doing this."

"Is it? Or do you want revenge on my country for what it has done to yours?"

The accusation startled me. I opened my mouth to deny it, then paused. Could that be part of why I sought to awaken Valem? For revenge? It bothered me that I couldn't fully say.

But I couldn't show doubt before him, not now. "It's the only way. Please move aside, Osman."

He shook his head. "Don't do this, Airene the Finch. Please. You will kill innocents, thousands of them. I know you must hate my people, but there is much good among us, too. Do not destroy it all."

I tried shutting out the words. What choice did I have? It was one city or the world. I'd already surrendered my home; what was my enemy's capital next to that?

Yet my response came out in a whisper. "I have to."

I didn't hesitate any longer. Calling upon quintessence, I cut a rift into the Pyrthae with the white knife, then leaped inside. Osman's wide eyes were the last I saw of the world.

CHAPTER TWENTY-FOUR

THE FIRES BELOW

The young are plentiful, their knowledge is shallow, and their desire for glory is great. Send forth one, no younger than fourteen, to the Chains each generation, and name them Yusishu, Savior. Heap honor upon them even after their passing, for thus will children crave to be chosen.

It is not a barbaric practice, as foreigners claim. It is the Savior's duty, and one of the utmost importance. What better purpose for one's life, what greater glory, than to give oneself to save one's people?

- The Ancestors' Path; by Matriarch Yin Shengton of Daodo-Yuan; estimated 900 SLP

The world burned around me.

I almost stepped back into the rift as the heat rolled over my being. Radiance shimmered violet in the air, unbalancing the energies and throwing them into chaos. I had no flesh here, but I was pained as if I did.

But Famine had made me strong enough to endure. Hardening the borders of my soul, I closed the portal between the planes, then exited the temple. Erimis now reflected the true one I'd left behind in Telae, but for the searing air.

My gaze was drawn upward, and there my quarry lay still: Famine, burrowing into the volcano. He was not aflame now, and as lava flowed around his head, his scales blackened beneath it. Still, if it caused him injury, it wasn't enough to stop him.

I looked down at my hand, still clutching the impression of Aika's knife. I didn't know precisely what I had to do, but I knew where it ended.

I walked toward the volcano and the dragon atop it.

Maybe I could have flown to him, freed of Telae's natural laws as I was, but there was a comfort in walking. It delayed the inevitable, and I treasured that small luxury.

I barely noticed the city as I moved through it. My chest was heavy with regret. I would never say goodbye to Linos or the rest of my family. My last act toward Jaxas was to abandon him and his city, my home. And there were my friends, of course: Nomusa, Xaron, Corin. Talan. I had to put them from my mind before I fled back the way I'd come.

But maybe I would see Thero soon, after so many years apart. I smiled and hoped it was true.

Before I knew it, I'd passed beyond the city walls and begun ascending the side of the mountain. In Telae, such exercise would have left me out of breath before I'd taken a dozen steps. Here, with Famine's power fueling me and his hunger driving me on, I was relentless.

The heat increased with every step. Radiance dominated the air, almost to the exclusion of any other element. It was all I could do to endure it.

Yet it was better than what simmered under my feet. This also resembled heat, but one that bludgeoned my spirit. Pressure built inside me as I fought against the intrusion. My resolve weakened, and something else leaked in.

Rage roared to life in my chest.

I stopped where I was, struck by the force of it. I should not have to sacrifice everything! Why should I die when no one else did? It wasn't *fair*, wasn't *right*. So I wouldn't do it. They could damn well save themselves if they wanted to! I would show them, show all of them—

I mended my fragile walls and collapsed onto the searing ground.

The sudden wrath that had swept over me still pressed at my mind, undiminished in its strength, but it no longer dominated me. The force of it left me trembling. In a moment, I'd almost abandoned everything I'd been working toward.

But Valem would not be put off for long.

I would have wept for fear and frustration had I been able to. As it was, there was only one thing I could do. I drew upon the deep reservoirs of vigor Famine had connected me to, rose to my feet, and kept climbing.

The caldera atop the volcano drew near. Lava flowed around me now, rivers of fire that would eat through skin and bone in seconds. Famine was close as well. In Telae, it might have been only a hundred cubits before me that his first coil lay; here, distance was more fickle, less easy to pin down. I stared at his scaled body, twenty times my height and dark as a moonless night, and tried unsuccessfully to banish my fear.

At fifty paces away, I stopped. It was close enough; it had to be, for I could make myself go no farther. Now came the first of my uncertainties.

How would I awaken Valem?

I raised Aika's knife again, wondering if it was up to the task. Did it only work to cage Famine because I was his Seed? Or because Harvest was his antithesis? Or perhaps there was another reason I didn't know.

But it wasn't to cage the Avvadin god that I acted now, but only to awaken him. For that, all I needed was within me: spirit and blood.

Blood required a body, however, and that meant returning to Telae. I didn't know what Valem's sides would be like so high up, but judging by the lava spilling around me, it would be far from hospitable. Hoping I would live long enough for the task, I lifted my hand to cut open the rift.

"Airene, *wait!*"

I startled and spun around to see someone hurrying up the mountain behind me. I barely recognized him, for his shape was cloudy and amorphous under the strain of withstanding the Quintyr. But as I saw two spirits separating from each other, I knew who it was.

"What are you doing here?" I demanded of Azhi. I wanted to ask if Eazal was breaking free, but didn't. Part of me hoped he would manage it. Even though he'd tried to kill me, his enslavement had never sat easy with me.

Azhi stopped and crumpled to the ground. But though he looked spent, his voice reverberated within me.

"Aiding you. You should have told me you were going. I would have come."

I ignored the reprimand. There was no time for it. "How can you help? You're barely staying together."

"I am sufficient for this." His blurred form rose a little, as if he straightened on his knees, while the half of him I guessed to be Eazal strained back down the slope. "I have brought the Binding Ruyi to awaken Valem."

That finally piqued my interest. "We don't want to cage him, just awaken him."

"It will. Through it, I will give of myself to him. A sacrifice of spirit."

Spirit and blood, Osman had said. But I decided Azhi stood as good a chance of knowing what would work as the priest did.

"Fine. Can you do it here, in the Pyrthae?"

"Yes. If I let go…"

Before I could ask what he meant, Azhi split apart.

I took a step toward him, hand outstretched, shock shivering through me. I'd seen it coming, yet still, I wasn't ready for it. As the front half of his spirit collapsed, the back half flowed swiftly down the volcano. The farther away they went, the more solidified their form became, until I could clearly see it was Eazal who fled his captor.

In a single smooth motion, Azhi rose to hover in the air. Once again, he wore the form of the Qao Fu boy he'd been before he'd died. Free from chaining Eazal, his poise had returned and his force multiplied.

"He will survive," the pyr said at my lingering look. His voice was a boy's too, higher-pitched and prone to cracking. "He knows many of my tricks now."

I hoped he was right. Eazal had tried to kill me, but only because he was under duress. I'd forgiven Corin for her betrayal under the same circumstances. Could I do any less for the apothecary?

But he couldn't be my concern now. I turned back to look uphill, at the massive, sinuous body, and the gouts of flame and smoke beyond. I was ready.

Ready to die.

"Awaken him."

I felt Azhi comply before I saw it. His quintessence was like a cool breeze amid the fiery terrain. I glanced back and saw him slowly walking on the slope behind me, the scepter dragging along the stone. A trail of white mist billowed out from behind it to settle on the black rock. The boy spirit wore a solemn expression, and I wondered at how young he must have been when he first set out to do this. No older than thirteen, by his look.

But he was a child no longer. He had a right to make his own sacrifices.

Azhi channeled his spirit into the mountain, and the stone lapped it up like a thirsty hound. He wandered away from my position, making a revolution of the volcano, never moving the scepter's head from the stone. I began to follow, the need to bear witness too strong to ignore. It wouldn't take me away from Famine, for he was always just above, writhing in antic-ipation. Besides, I had to know if he faded before Valem awakened, in case I needed to finish the job.

Erimis disappeared from view as we went around the far side of the volcano. Where lava flowed in our path, Azhi hovered above it, dragging the scepter through, while I hopped with unnatural buoyancy. My daemon guide was being worn down, but he kept moving and channeling, never stopping for more than a moment. Despite myself, I wanted to reach out and help him, but I knew what his answer would be, the only answer it could be.

This was his burden to bear. My own would come soon.

As I walked, my mind wandered into dangerous fantasies. Talan charging up the mountainside and dissuading me from this course of action, having found a different way to deal with Famine. Xaron and Nomusa restraining me and convincing me to run far away from all of this. Corin still attempting to repay the debt she felt she owed me by offering to be the Sacrifice in my stead. Even Eazal, running back up the mountain and throwing himself at Azhi to stop him from waking Valem.

But none of them came; I'd evaded or subdued them too well. I was alone with the daemon.

Azhi tripped and fell to one knee, and I startled out of my daydreams. Before I could speak, he used the scepter to pry himself up and limp on. Only then did I wonder what the cost of this act would be for him. If he gave of himself as fully as I soon would.

Only then did I trust him, and was sorry that it had taken me so long.

Had nothing happened thus far, I would have stopped him. But the volcano below us, always alive, became increasingly violent. Radiance was not the only thing to burn now. From deep in the ground, a distant presence welled up, building with every passing moment. I knew it was sentient just as I felt Azhi to be, its quintessence resonating with mine. But this was a foreign mind, strange in its workings, both too simple and too vast to comprehend. I could barely focus on it, or even endure it, for it was painful to behold.

Valem was awakening.

My heart ached for Azhi, stumbling now with each step, but I turned my face skyward. Famine had noticed the rousing of the Quintyr he meant to feast upon, judging by the savage vibrations of his folds. Whether he would fight or flee, I couldn't tell. I had to be ready to act swiftly, to see the moment he was weakest and take advantage of it.

The ground rumbled beneath me, and a new feeling roused in me.

Though it seemed like little time had passed, we had nearly completed a circuit around the volcano, and Erimis came back into view. As the lava gushed from the top and sides of Valem, I thought of all the people Talan and Osman had pleaded on behalf of. This god would not come gently; he would wipe out half the city before they rose from their beds. Perhaps even my friends would be caught in the destruction.

I'd known this would happen, all of it. But until that moment, I hadn't felt it.

This was what Vusu would do, what he *had* done. Spending lives like coins.

I would willingly give my life to defeat Famine. But I had to do it without becoming the man who stole my brothers from me.

"*Azhi!*" I shouted in a way beyond words. "*Stop! We cannot do this!*"

The spirit boy paused, turned back. He barely kept his shape anymore, his essence leaking in a cloud around him, so I couldn't tell if he met my eyes or not. Yet I sensed something in him understood me.

"*All those people!*" I continued. "*They'll die, Azhi! They won't escape!*"

His head fell so his gaze was on the scepter, still touching the stone. As he looked back up at me, I mimed lifting my arm, then realized I might have to do it for him; he didn't seem to have the strength anymore. I lurched into a fast walk, though it was difficult even to move.

I was half a dozen strides away when lava spewed up from beneath his feet.

"*No!*"

I fell to my knees as I stared at where the boy had been. The lava blinded me, yet I couldn't look away.

The volcano had swallowed him whole.

Once more, I was too late.

Valem rumbled alive, and fresh lava spilled up from behind. I began to fear the same fate awaited me. I couldn't stop what Azhi had begun. Now, I had to press forward. If I wasn't to waste Azhi and Erimis's sacrifices, I had to act now.

I looked up at Famine, muttered a half-hearted prayer, and cut back into Telae.

Then stopped and stared.

The eruption was not just happening in the Pyrthae. In my plane as well, Valem spilled forth lava. Through the rift, I saw it flowing beneath where I would step out, as well as for a score of paces to either side. And telling from what was happening in the spiritual plane, the entire mountainside might explode at any moment.

I sealed the rift shut, but I didn't relent. This was my last chance. I ran up the volcano, rivers of fire drawing ever nearer on either side. When I judged I'd moved to a clear spot from my brief glimpse, I cut a rift again. Lava lay before me still, but I was closer. I almost didn't bother sealing it, but I was trying to mend the world, not break it further. I braved ever nearer the lava and tried again.

Stone, as hot as all the hells, lay before me.

I didn't stop for doubt — I threw myself out of the rift. And was nearly knocked flat by the heat.

A scream worked free of my throat, but I couldn't hear it. Roaring filled my ears. My flesh felt aflame; perhaps it was. I was dying, and not slowly.

I had to do it now.

Somehow, I mustered the concentration to channel quintessence. The Pyrthae came back into view, as did Famine. To my surprise and horror, the daemon god no longer tried to feast on the volcanic Quintyr, but had drawn out. His dragon countenance was marred with oozing burns, and his size had lessened. His quintessence shone half as bright.

He was injured and diminished. So far, the plan was working.

Valem rumbled, and fresh lava spurted up, splashing over Famine, weakening him further.

This was my chance. My last chance.

"Famine!" I shouted in both realms. My body was failing, but my soul clung on.

The daemon god swiveled his immense head to stare at me, death-black eyes set among the charred scales.

I held up Aika's knife trembling before my chest. *"I offer myself as Sacrifice!"*

I drove the knife toward my flesh.

I waited for the pain. The cold. The darkness.

But there was nothing.

With my vision in the Pyrthae, it took me a long time to realize why. Only as I opened my real eyes did I discover I'd been knocked off my feet. I looked at my hands, red and blistered, only to find they were empty. I looked around me; only black stone and orange, sweltering air.

Then I saw the knife. Burning in lava.

I didn't even have the breath to scream. I watched as the only thing that could bind Famine swiftly smoldered into ashes. Did I imagine the shriek as Harvest's soul disappeared into the aether? Perhaps it was only in my head.

I raised my gaze and found Famine had turned away from me, my hold over him lost. Then, with Valem still lashing after him, he turned and flew away.

I watched him go, my body dying, my soul fractured. Perhaps I would have stayed there, but for what happened next.

The volcano erupted.

CHAPTER TWENTY-FIVE

RAGE, HOPE, DESPAIR

Rage, hope, despair
The Lord laments, the Lord laments
Fear, awe, prepare
The worthy ascend, the worthy ascend

- Prayer to Valem, origin unknown

As the sky rained stone and fire, I fled.

Instinct saved me. I didn't will myself upright; my body acted on its own initiative. I didn't consciously cut into the Pyrthae; my hand and mind conspired against me.

I didn't want to live, but I couldn't help but keep on doing just that.

Even as I escaped into the spirit realm, I found little relief. Radiance churned all around me, as dangerous as the lava in Telae. The need to survive numbed all else, so I easily imposed beliefs on my mind.

The sky is weightless, I thought, and lifted from the ground to float over the volcano.

I didn't look down until the heat had begun to fade. When I finally did, the sight that greeted me was too bizarre to understand. The mountain was red and black, smoke and fire billowing out of it like a sea of daemons. I felt Valem, too, and his earth-shaking rage. The city suffered for it; the ground cracked, the lava flowed, and the stones fell upon the rooftops.

My fault, I reminded myself, then descended.

I didn't care about my life, but I still cared for my friends. Already, I feared I was too late. With dangerous speed, I dove toward the temple of the Hortum Kor, too near the feet of the volcano. Horror grew as the heat of Valem's fury blazed about me again. *I cannot be hurt*, I willed to myself, and as I crashed into the rotunda, it was so.

Slipping in a window and falling to the floor, I finally cut my way back into the material world. Stepping free, the injuries I had suffered announced themselves with screaming urgency. I gasped and choked, noxious gases having nearly suffocated me upon Valem's slope. My skin was in agony, and more with each movement as it pulled and tore. I lumbered forward, feeling a corpse somehow still standing, and went to the dormitory where I'd left them.

There they were, shouting and pulling together their things, arguing over something that my mind couldn't parse.

Then they saw me.

At once, they collapsed about me, touching me until I flinched back in pain. Did they know the emergency? I tried to tell them, yet couldn't form coherent words. But I could show them with my actions, and I did, cutting back into the Pyrthae and gesturing them inside.

Though hesitant, Xaron obeyed first, dragging Isidora with him into the rift. Corin ushered Kari in next, and Nomusa came after. They all looked at me, but I could barely meet their gazes. My vision was hazy, yet I could still read what was behind their eyes.

Talan shouldered my pack along with his own, but he didn't follow the others. His eyes smoldered on me; there was no hint of a smile now.

I gestured to the portal, hoping he would understand. He glanced to the side, toward Osman's chamber, then hung his head as he strode forward into the Pyrthae.

I entered last, sealing the tear behind me. Only then did I realize I hadn't done so atop Valem. I wondered what the consequences of that would be. Surely no worse than what had already befallen Erimis.

No sooner had I turned back to my companions than did Talan seize my arm. With the touch came all he wished to convey to me, and I reeled under the onslaught: the anger, the betrayal, the fear.

He released me a moment later, but the knowledge lingered, burning in a different way than my wounds. Talan turned his back on me and faced the others.

"We head for the outside of the city," he announced, then led the way.

The others looked at me, but the situation was clear. Escape first; questions later. I shambled after them, bringing up the rear.

We didn't make it far into Erimis's streets before we had to will ourselves into the air. In this realm, at least, lava flowed in rivers down the stones. We'd seen the path of past fire rivers on our way in, but Valem didn't content himself to that avenue this time. It was everywhere, destroying and all-consuming. None of his worshippers were spared his fury.

In the air, we were safe. I found it easiest to move, for I kept few of my beliefs now, and my mind latched onto any I provided it. Almost, I flew as I did when I entered the Pyrthae as spirit alone. The others floated to the reflection and entered the third fold, coming out again ahead of me from the bend in time. I could have followed, but something in me didn't allow it.

When Erimis's walls lay behind us, Talan gestured to descend. I followed, though fear had returned, seeping through my stupefaction. We landed in a forest clearing, then Talan opened a path back into Telae.

No sooner had I set foot on real earth did I collapse. My body shrieked in protest, but I couldn't muster up the will to care as I sprawled on the grass. The sky glowed red above, Valem's fires lighting up the night. I wanted to sleep and never wake, but my companions crowded around me, hounding me with questions.

"Airene, oh Airene… How did you get those burns?" Nomusa reached out a hand, but stopped short of touching me.

"How can we help?" Xaron wrung his hands. He kept glancing at Isidora, but the First Watcher only frowned.

"Where is Azhi?" she asked.

I only shook my head. I couldn't muster any other answer.

Corin watched on with evident concern, while Kari looked curious. And Talan… My gaze wandered up to him, willing him to look at me, but he only scowled off into the woods. My head fell, unable to keep upright any longer.

After silence fell, I tried speaking and found I could whisper. "I'm sorry."

Xaron and Nomusa leaned in close. "Sorry?" Xaron queried. He gave Nomusa a look. "For what, Airene?"

"For killing all those people." Talan didn't look around as he spoke the damning words.

I tried to speak, but couldn't again. My throat had swelled up, and not only from inhaling smoke.

"Did you…?" Isidora's eyes widened. "You did, didn't you?"

I nodded, unable to look at her.

"Did what?" Xaron threw a hand toward the fire-wreathed mountain. Even miles away, ash rained down on us from Valem. "You're saying she did *this*?"

"Yes," I whispered. "Azhi, too."

My companions shared a silent conversation. When they turned back to me, I saw their consensus was not falling in my favor.

"Airene…" Nomusa bit her lip. "You cannot be serious."

I cleared my throat, to no avail. "I am."

"*That?* How could you do that? Tyurn's balls, it's a volcano! You can't make a volcano erupt on your own!"

"But he's not just a volcano," Talan interjected. "He's a god. And she made a sacrifice to him."

I shook my head. "Azhi did. He gave his life. I wanted to…" *Stop him*, I almost said, but cut myself short. Excuses didn't matter now; I was complicit, and all knew it.

"And Famine?" Isidora watched me with narrowed eyes. "Did you stop him?"

"No." I held up my empty, scarred hands. "I lost them. The knife. The scepter. They're gone."

Everyone went still as the implications set in.

"The scepter *and* the knife…" Xaron let loose a joyless laugh. "But Airene, those were the tools we needed to—"

"I know." An edge had returned to my voice, though he didn't deserve it.

Isidora looked between the others. "Those were to be used to cage Famine, weren't they? So it's impossible now?"

I nodded, but couldn't speak the affirmation. It was too terrible to utter aloud.

My companions reeled, each in their own way. Xaron laughed. Nomusa stalked off to the edge of the clearing. Isidora kneeled where she stood. Corin frowned, reacting so little I wondered if she understood. Talan didn't move a muscle.

Yet Kari's response was most curious of all, for she smiled with what seemed genuine amusement.

"It is not," she said. "The same is in you, Airene. In all of us, but you most of all."

I stared dully at her, not bothering to try and understand. She was mad; no one else could be undeterred by what I'd just confessed.

Without warning, Talan turned and brought the focus of the group on him. His eyes were only for me, though.

"She's right. It's not done. Not yet."

His words were cold, but fire blazed within them. I found it hard to meet his gaze, but forced myself to all the same.

"What do you mean?" I asked, voice rasping.

No warmth radiated from him as he spoke. "You shared all you knew with me, Airene. And I believe I've figured out something that you overlooked. As I would have done eventually, had you given me more time."

I winced, but didn't look away. I'd done too much of that lately.

"Don't leave us in suspense." Xaron crossed his arms.

Talan glanced at him, then turned back to me. "Those items — the knife, the scepter. We guessed them to be shards of Harvest, her soul made material."

I nodded. The others stared, surprise written into their expressions. He didn't pause to explain, but only continued.

"But there's a reason they felt familiar to you." His eyes bore into me. "A reason Vusu targeted your family. And I think a part of you has known why for a while."

I stilled but for the shivering brought about by my burns. I couldn't have turned away from him had I tried. My silence drew him out.

"Harvest lives in you, Airene. You carry a piece of her spirit. You're her 'seed,' just as surely as you're Famine's."

The declaration fell upon me like a droplet in still water. It rippled through my being, changing everywhere it touched. I didn't know what to make of it, but I felt the resonance of the truth.

"Like Aika," I muttered. "A Seed of Harvest and Famine."

Talan nodded. His smile had returned, but I wish it hadn't. It was bitter and cold and biting, and all for my benefit.

"I felt her when you surrendered your memories. I didn't know what she was, but she is a distinct part of you." His voice fell softer. Our companions were frozen around us, transfixed by what he said. "Hope isn't lost. Not as long as Harvest lives within you."

Hope. Did I still have hope after all I'd witnessed, all I'd done? I hung my head. Though I felt dry of all moisture, tears squeezed from my eyes.

A hand touched my shoulder, then a second. Next I knew, my companions surrounded me, comforting, mourning. I looked up and stared at them through blurred vision, and though every touch was agony, the consolation was greater.

Only Talan remained apart. I looked at him and knew what lay between us couldn't be ignored.

"I'm sorry, Talan. Sorry I woke Valem. Sorry I betrayed you. Is… is Osman alright? His priests, and the children?"

As if they were the words he'd been waiting to hear, Talan deflated with a sigh. "They should be fine. Osman has places to hide, and no small power of his own. He'll protect them."

I tried to smile, but my lips wouldn't comply. As soon as Talan saw it, his face hardened again, even as he kneeled behind the others.

"But Airene, if we're to do this, to defeat Famine, you must trust us, all of us. We won't let you fail. We all need this to succeed. You aren't fighting this war alone."

Before, I wouldn't have believed him. I thought that since I had to die, I alone carried the burden of the world.

But I wasn't the only one to have made sacrifices. All of them had lost something or someone. And Azhi's absence was a reminder that some might even have to give their own lives.

I wiped gingerly at my tears and nodded. "I know that now."

Quiet reigned for a time before Xaron broke it.

"So… what now? Do we chase after Famine again?" His expression turned sour. "What are we supposed to do when we find him this time?"

"That depends on her." Talan scooted closer to sit cross-legged before me. "You said before that the knife was the only way to access Harvest. But I don't think that's true. I touched her through your spirit. Perhaps, if you try, you can as well." He paused, his eyes flickering around our group before settling back on me. "Reach for Harvest, Airene. You must be able to touch her. I suspect you already have, on some level. We need you to now. Reach for her."

I didn't protest or ask how. I'd made catastrophic mistakes and betrayed his trust; now was my chance to atone. Closing my eyes, I cleared my mind, then let her name fill it.

Harvest?

No response. I didn't give up. Talan had felt her within me, within my spirit. Perhaps by accessing it, I could reach her.

I opened my locus, channeled quintessence, and drifted halfway into the Pyrthae. Valem's awakening buffeted me from his distant mountain, while Famine's hunger pulled me in the opposite direction. I tried to ignore both as I reached not outward with my spirit, but within. Was there a similar presence to the other Quintyr there? I couldn't detect anything. Doubt seeded through me. Yet Talan was right: I had to trust him, or I would fail once more.

Harvest. I fixed her name in my mind. Perhaps it wasn't her true name, but on this plane, it was never about words. Intention, will, and belief were the organizing principles here, the laws by which the spirit realm was formed. Those would have to be enough.

Harvest, I called again. *Hear me, Harvest. Do you sleep in me? Have you been with me my entire life?*

I thought of the ways she might have impacted me. Perhaps she had insulated me from my childhood; the loss of my brother and the scorn of my mother could have easily scarred me, as they had Linos. Perhaps it hadn't been Famine or Clepsammia who spawned my ambition, but the sliver of Harvest's soul living within me. After all, the need to strive for ever greater things could be more than a hunger; it could be growth as well.

But there were other events where I could infer her direct interference. I hadn't perished when Famine struck me and made me his own, opening my locus to channeling, nor when fire blossomed from me during Eazal's attempted assassination. I had healed.

Was that you, Harvest? Did you heal me?

All those days and nights of seeking the truth about Famine — something had sustained me and kept me going. Though I suffered failure again and again, I didn't yield. There was a well within me, depthless, that had never yet run out.

Are you that well? Answer me, Harvest, please!

I delved into myself, memories manifesting around me, then fading in turn. I sifted through them, but could never find more than a trace of the goddess. If Harvest had to do with any of those events, there was no explicit link.

Then an idea occurred to me. If Harvest had ever appeared, it had been in my time of need. Where Famine desired the sacrifice of others, Harvest longed to sacrifice herself.

I hesitated, then took the plunge. I broke down the walls I'd erected to keep at bay all the hurts, fears, and doubts that plagued me and let them inundate my mind, filling it to the exclusion of all else. It felt as if I would die, floundering among them, drowning in the flood of despair. I treaded water, while the Pyrthae twisted around me, molding to the onslaught of emotion so it became a waking nightmare.

Harvest, please… I need you…

Something changed.

At first, it was a gentle warmth, like morning sunlight grazing an eyelid. With that first contact, my awareness expanded, the feeling spreading throughout my mind, then my body. She didn't force her way anywhere, but gently touched until I invited her further in. I didn't resist or fight back. I didn't give in to the apprehension at what I attempted. I trusted her as I trusted Talan, and Nomusa and Xaron, and all the friends and allies I'd gathered along the way. And with it came a blossoming that didn't banish my fears, but filled me with hope and invigoration so no room remained for them.

Harvest. Her name filled my mind as her presence filled my soul. She pulsed in recognition, and I smiled.

"Airene!"

I didn't want to leave her, but with my needs fulfilled, she was already departing. Reluctantly, I felt her glow fade, her warmth cool, until I almost shivered in her absence.

But I didn't, not quite. For now, I held the truth. She *was* in me; she always had been.

Harvest was alive in my soul.

I ceased to channel, closed my locus, and opened my eyes. And found my companions crowded around me, squawking in amazement.

As I comprehended what had caught their fascination, I looked down at my hands and blinked. My hands had been red and chapped before, burned by the nearness of the lava and heat in the air. Now, they were whole, my skin beige and unblemished. I lifted my sleeves and found the same; looked at my sandaled feet and it was no different. I touched my face, and all was as if the events of the night had never occurred.

"What happened?" I expected the question to come out as a croak, but my throat had mended as well.

"You healed." Nomusa tentatively brushed her fingertips over my cheek, her eyes wide. "You were burned, then you started to heal."

"Like before," Corin added. She leaned over the others. "After you became a warden."

Kari glanced up at her sister, her brow scrunched. "Of course she did. Why would she not?"

Corin only shook her head.

"Was it her?" The question came from Talan, who kneeled next to Nomusa. "Was it Harvest?"

I nodded. Then, though it seemed impossible after everything that had occurred, I smiled.

"You were right, Talan. She *was* within me. She is still. And I know how to reach her. She'll come when I need her."

Thinking of Famine and the coming confrontation dampened my elation, but it didn't smother it. She'd driven away too many of my fears for that now.

He nodded, and even gave me a small smile. But no more. I didn't begrudge him that. I still owed him much, and was prepared to continue to pay my debt for as long as I could.

"Time to go." Talan paused, looking at me. "Which way did he fly?"

At his words, the others seemed to rouse from their reveries, and they looked to me for an answer. I didn't need to ask whom he meant.

"Due north."

"North." Xaron frowned as he looked north. "Only one thing lies in that direction."

I'd guessed the same thing. "Yes. He's returning to Oedija."

Silence descended once more, suspended for a long moment.

"Why?" Nomusa's voice was heavy with resignation. "After traveling the length of the Four Realms, why return now?"

I think she knew even as she asked. But I spoke the conclusion aloud.

"There is war there, which means souls to devour. But I think it's more. I think he feels it's time. Time to break through."

Despite the gift Harvest had given me, fresh horror awoke in me then. *Linos.* I didn't know how Famine could force his way into Telae, but I suspected my brother had something to do with it. I'd failed him too much already to allow that to happen.

"To Oedija, then." Talan sounded almost wistful.

To Oedija. It was far from the homecoming any of us wished for.

But still, we were homeward bound.

CHAPTER TWENTY-SIX

THE ENDLESS STAIR

They watch from great heights. They wait, though we know not for what. Sometimes, they grow restless…

Dare not venture near, lest you are lost to their whims.

- Scroll fragment; origin unknown; estimated 84 SLP

With our path clear before us, we wasted no time in setting upon it.

Everyone was tired. Hungry. Exhausted in both spirit and body. But no one complained as I opened a rift back into the Pyrthae, nor faltered as I instructed everyone to lift themselves up to the reflected world hanging overhead.

We had hope again. And after so long without it, it sustained us as nothing else could.

I alone felt truly revitalized. Harvest had cleansed me of many of the ills plaguing me; not entirely, but enough to gift me strength. Famine fed me more. Through our ill-fated connection, I felt small spurts of pleasure. He was feasting, which likely meant he had already reached our city. The sands were running out, and we were still so far away.

"We have to rise," I called to the others. "To the third fold."

They stared back at me, terror plain in their expressions and in the color emanating from their spirits. I understood it and shared it. This was a desperate act. But now I knew I was strong enough for it.

"The storm!" Nomusa objected. "What if it finds us again?"

"Then we'll flee it. But we have to try, Nomusa. It's our only chance of arriving in time. Famine will use Linos if he can; I know he will. I cannot allow it, nor can the world afford it."

She stared at me for a long moment, then nodded. With her capitulation, the others began to fall. I looked last at Talan, willing him to understand. Then I realized it wasn't resistance I saw in him, but determination. He would stay with me to the last.

Gratitude washed through me, and as I smiled at him, he returned it with one of his own.

The feeling was short-lived as we ascended. Kari had the presence of mind to assist her sister this time. I went to Nomusa, but she lifted off the ground of her own will, scowling as she stared at the reflected world above.

As we rose through the air, Valem and Erimis came into clearer view. The city had become a wasteland. Its streets were orange and bright with the molten fire flowing through them. Yet there was something beautiful to it, if I forgot the suffering of those within. Something that inspired awe and humbled me.

I looked away as the reflected land above drew nearer. With trees hanging upside down around me, I pressed my hands against the grass and dirt, then willed myself through.

I'd hoped the third fold of the Pyrthae would feel warmer than the last time, but as I emerged and stood on the featureless tile floor, the chilling winds proved to be unabated. Girding myself against them, I waited for my companions to gather around.

"We have to go as high as we can!" I had to shout to be heard over the gale. "I'll build a staircase so we don't get lost!"

"Build a staircase?" Xaron narrowed his eyes, and from more than the knifing wind. "Out of what?"

I only closed my eyes in answer and imagined it. There was a resonance to the Pyrthae, and all the more in the relative emptiness of the third fold. I knew my will had been enacted even before I opened my eyes.

The mist that swirled and danced through the sky had coalesced into stairs, rising as far as I could see. I smiled. The sight of them doubly reinforced my belief; they would hold during our flight.

Looking back at Xaron, I found him emanating amazement as he stared up at it. The others were in much the same state. I suspected their belief would also work to maintain the stairs.

A sliver of doubt remained. If this didn't work, we'd be lost in the Pyrthae, perhaps for good. But now wasn't the moment for hesitation.

"No time to waste," I called to my companions, then set my foot on the misty staircase. The first step held, as did the second. Soon, the tiled floor was falling away below me, and all my companions followed behind.

We climbed. The third fold was never-changing. The wind blew; the mist swirled; the light shone with cool, diffused light. Only the disappearance of the floor below showed any sign of progress, and then for only a moment.

I only just kept my doubts at bay. My belief had to be absolute if we were to make it through. I resolved to climb as high as we could, then build the stairs back down. No use in questioning whether it would build the right way down, or lose our sense of direction entirely. Belief was our salvation now.

We climbed, and climbed, and climbed, and the others soon wearied. Not in limb or body, for they had none; their souls themselves were eroded by the numbing winds. I felt much the same, though whenever I tired, I thought of Harvest slumbering within me and took heart in her. I wouldn't falter so long as she was with me.

"Should we turn back?"

I didn't look around at Talan, worried staring down at the staircase fading into the mist would break my belief. "Soon."

No sooner had I spoken than I felt them.

They appeared as light, glowing like distant suns above. The sensation came closer with each step, crowding in like the heat of a lit hearth. I almost felt I could reach out and touch it; then I tried, stretching my arms overhead.

Something brushed my hands.

I should have been startled, but the presence behind that touch was calm, reassuring. I knew they meant me no harm, not when their assurances whispered in my head. They didn't speak in words, but in feelings.

They promised an unchanging existence. They promised solace, respite. Oblivion, the final rest.

Why fight against that?

"Airene, I feel something." Talan spoke again, as if from a great distance. It was difficult for me to focus on his words. "There's a change in the air."

I paused in my questing after the vast minds above. Only then did I sense it: a distant agitation that jangled through me like I'd drank one cup of coffee too many.

The realization struck me just as Talan announced it: "Another storm!"

I withdrew from whatever beings I'd touched souls with. I didn't want to; I longed to throw myself after them, to accept all they offered. But my companions needed me, as did everyone else remaining in the world below. I couldn't rest yet.

"We'll descend as quickly as we can." I adjusted my will, and the stairs rearranged themselves. Opening my eyes, I saw the staircase now went down, fading into the mist. I felt off balance for a moment. How did I know it would lead back to Telae and the first fold? That the direction truly was down?

I shook my head, then stepped forward, holding to hope.

The storm was coming, and quickly. Magnesis resonated within me, the elements that my soul had gathered around it sparking. Yet it was not the only unfamiliar sensation. A slight pressure came from above, like the weight of the sky in the material plane, but a fraction of its strength. Sensations stirred inside me, like a churning in my belly, one thing spawning another in a chain of energy. I couldn't associate these elements with anything I'd felt before. Were they different combinations, or entirely new energies, like the catalysm Xaron's mother used?

But such ideas wouldn't save us from the storm. I pressed the notions away, firmed my will, and hurried my pace.

We ran down the steps, taking them two at a time. I contemplated leaping off and attempting to fall back to Telae. But it was too risky; there was no sensation for orientation up here but for the staircase and the mild sky-weight, and both would disappear as soon as we drew away from them.

We had to stay the course. It was the only sure way.

The storm overtook us, as I'd known it would. But it wasn't above us like the previous time; now, it surged to life all around. My companions cried out as the air became charged. I felt my soul shriek its terror. But the staircase held, and our descent continued. If we could keep going, could only endure…

The first strike boomed behind me.

Stopping mid-stride, I whirled around and saw a body falling slowly into the mist by the stairs.

"*Talan!*"

I threw myself after him.

Propelled by terror, I caught Talan in moments and wrapped myself around him. Belief was sufficient to rise back to the staircase, still faintly above us. I reached it and collapsed upon it, setting him down roughly. The stairs were only so wide, so his body, as much as it still resembled one, dangled off either end. Our companions were nowhere to be seen.

"Airene, Talan! Where are you?"

Their cries came from above; the fools must have stopped. Growling in frustration, I lifted Talan onto my shoulders, then set back up. I wouldn't have been able to carry him in Telae, but here, my strength was sufficient. The air had turned violet. I could see the impressions of lightning all around me, just waiting to be unleashed.

But what if I believed they couldn't hurt us? A desperate gambit perhaps, but it was worth a shot. It was our only possible defense.

The rest of our party came into view above. As soon as they saw me laden with Talan, they hurried down. I waited, trying not to expect lightning to strike, but denying it instead. Doubt would get us killed.

They reached us, but even as they babbled questions, I turned with barely an acknowledgement and ran downward. *It cannot hurt us*, I thought, I hoped, I pleaded. *The lightning will not strike me.*

A bolt flashed down three stairs below. I flinched, then scolded myself for it. Belief couldn't be a shield if it cracked. I firmed it.

Then the world shattered.

I was falling, a thousand shards of glass tinkling to the ground. But there was no ground — only pain and air and endless wind. I was lost among it.

It was some time before I could see. Even as my vision cleared, the pain stayed. I bore it as I took in my surroundings. Nothing but blue air all around. I'd fallen free of the storm, at least.

Then I noticed I wasn't alone; somehow, I still clung to Talan. *Magnesis*, I realized; we'd been charged to stick to one another. A lucky stroke.

But there, our luck ran out. The stairs were gone from sight. We could not know up from down. In every direction hovered the same mist, the same blue light, the same chilling wind.

We were lost in the third fold.

"Talan?" I reached for him in a way beyond words. Our spirits were touching, so I could feel his lack of awareness. I could only hope it wasn't a permanent state.

I would have to get out of this on my own.

I racked my mind. I delved into my senses for any change in the environment. There was nothing, nothing at all. Harvest couldn't save me here.

Then I realized another Quintyr could.

Famine's hunger had become so much a part of me I had forgotten it for a moment. Still, it tugged, pulling me toward the daemon god who had connected me to this world. I smiled and willed myself after it.

The irony of my salvation was too rich.

Assured Talan and I would survive, I turned my thoughts to the others. It was possible that, even without me there, the stairs would hold, for all had believed in them. My fears that it wouldn't could only hurt their chances. I pushed them from my mind, concentrating instead on reaching safety ourselves.

Talan stirred before I saw any sign of progress. "Airene..." he muttered, or I thought he did. With our souls intertwined, he could have thought my name and I would have known.

"You're safe." I pressed feelings of warmth and home upon him, hoping to reassure him. Memories of Canopy, I recognized them afterward. "We'll reach the floor soon."

"Lightning...?"

"It struck you twice."

Muddled surprise at that. "Damn... The others?"

I didn't want to answer, but knew I had to. "We lost them. Hopefully, they're still descending by the stairs."

He went quiet, but we couldn't conceal our fears from one another.

At last, the tiled floor loomed into view. I slowed our free fall to land lightly upon it. We hadn't come straight down; drawn by Famine, our drop had been angled. Part of me had hoped to find the bottom of the staircase, but that was just as improbable now as before. We could only trust our friends would find their own way out.

A shudder of pleasure ran through me. I tried not to take satisfaction in it, knowing what it meant. The daemon god felt near now, very near.

"I think we're there," I said. "I think we're above Oedija."

Talan's spirit still felt ravaged, his form nebulous and torn. But I felt his assent. "So we must go," he whispered.

I made to move through the floor and back into the first fold, but Talan seized my arm. I waited, feeling he had something to say.

"Remember," he said at last, his voice stronger than it had been a moment before. "What you've learned of Harvest. What you know of Famine. Use that knowledge. And if you can..."

"...I'll come back to you."

He nodded. I tried to hide the feelings roiling through me and knew I did a poor job of it. Even if I succeeded, I doubted this was a mission I could come back from. Talan was too practical to have delusions about it either.

For a moment, we were silent together, sharing a quiet union. It spoke loudly enough.

"Are you ready?" he asked at length.

"Yes." And I was. Ready as I ever would be.

"Then we go."

Hand in hand, we descended through the tiled floor.

And emerged into chaos.

Figures swarmed around us, marching and fighting and dying as they hung upside down from the reflected world. A storm was raging, for radiance fell upward like rain upon the scene. I jerked down, away from what I realized was a battle.

And if there was battle, then this could only be…

I looked below, and Oedija spread beneath us, burning and broken.

And soaring between the mirror lands, swallowing the souls pouring into the Pyrthae, was Famine.

CHAPTER TWENTY-SEVEN
CATALYST

We do not know all the energies that flow through the gods' realms. Witches may use some, yet others resist manipulation. Perhaps they are not for mortals, but reserved for the gods.

Yet I wonder what has been locked away. What heavenly powers we might still touch...

- A scribestone of Jolduun; estimated 300 SLP

For a long moment, I hovered above Famine, watching his long, dark form slither through the quintessence, thick as fog from men and women dying on the battlefield. Already, he had grown since attacking Valem, though not as great as he had been before Erimis. We had gained ground, but were quickly losing it.

Talan jerked my arm, rousing me from my stupor.

"We have to leave!" he cried, pulling me toward the city walls. "Famine will take us!"

I wanted this to end here and now, but I knew he was right. I'd reached Harvest midway between the worlds before; reason dictated I had to be at least partially within Telae to reach her again. And here, with a battle underway and Famine growing fat on dead souls, it would be just as foolish as when I'd collapsed upon Valem's slope.

So we headed for Oedija's walls, or what remained of them. The stone had shattered under the barrage of Avvadin artillery, the gate pounded inward into a mess of shattered wood. Soldiers fought at the entrance, but even my untrained eyes could see my countrymen were swiftly folding. As we watched, Avvadin cavalry charged in, and even slowed by our view from the Pyrthae, they seemed a deadly wave of hooves, swords, and spears.

Death was everywhere around us. Even when their bodies fell, their spirits wouldn't find peace. I wished I could close my eyes to it, but each killing was like a barb in my soul.

"Airene!" Talan urged, and I peeled my eyes away.

We willed ourselves forward with renewed speed. As we entered Oedija, we dipped lower, for while Famine remained over the battle outside the walls, it was safe to do so. Midway between the mirror cities, I couldn't help but see how we fared again.

There was fighting in the streets. In Port, red-clothed soldiers fought against those set against them. Damask Esir; I knew them by the Qarin that controlled them and were visible to me here in the Pyrthae. They were supposed to be the supreme warriors of Avvad, yet those they faced seemed to match them. I understood why as I took in the strangeness of their battle garb, feathers and bone and bronze, and the styles of fighting I'd seen Nomusa practice in Canopy.

Komo and his warriors fought down there. I was glad they still held their own.

Other areas were less contested. Spirits lurked in Bazaar: Silks, sweeping upon any soldier they found and enwrapping them. No trace of quintessence rose from them, for their souls were devoured by the bound pyr. I wondered what could be done to stop them.

Not all the fighting was between Oedija and Avvad. Dirty, thin men stormed a granary in deme Hull, though I doubted much food remained inside it. Just outside the Laurel Palace, there looked to be riots at the gates, people only just held back by the laurel guards. I hadn't thought my heart could break further. Here we were, losing and dying to invaders, and we still couldn't unite against them.

Talan's next words pulled my attention back. "Where to?"

I tried to focus. *Famine.* As badly as the battle proceeded, he remained a worse threat. I could feel how powerful he'd become; his presence was distorting even this layer of the Pyrthae, a wasteland spreading across the fields where he soared. It wouldn't be long before he resolved to break free.

I needed to be ready.

The answer came to me. "Linos. We have to find Linos."

Famine would come for my brother before me; I knew it as I knew the daemon god's nature. Linos was defenseless, yet could likely still serve as a conduit into Telae. I had to find him and protect him.

Talan didn't argue. "Where is he?"

Only then did I realize I didn't know. At a calmer time, I might have been able to sense him by his connection to the Pyrthae. But amid this chaos, there was little prospect of that happening.

One spot remained likely, however. "The Laurel Palace — we'll check there first."

Talan clasped my hand, sending strength and hope into me, though he could ill afford to lose any. I expressed my gratitude back, then we sped down to the palace. I aimed for Jaxas's solar, which faced out over the city. If I knew the Despot, that was where he would be, commanding the defenses where the Stratechons fell short.

As we approached, I found Jaxas wasn't on the balcony as I had supposed, but on the broad stairs leading up to the Laurel Palace. Wondering what he was thinking by exposing himself unnecessarily to danger, I directed Talan down. We landed around where I could see the Despot and his followers milling.

I exchanged a look with Talan, then cut open a rift.

As we stepped out into the real world, pain pelted my face, and lightning flashed, blinding me. Shouts sounded around us, and I recovered my vision in time to see spears bristling toward us. Kinesis sprang to my fingertips and pulsed outward. Vaguely, I noticed the pillars rising around me crack and scatter dust, but my eyes were set on the man surrounded by his staggering guards.

Jaxas held up one bony hand. "Stand down. You know these two."

The laurel guards, one of them First Laurel Synne, the other one I didn't know, obeyed at once. Synne wore a scowl, not bothering to disguise her hate. I could hardly blame her. She probably thought me a deserter still.

The Despot's eyes were no less difficult to meet. His robes were drenched, revealing just how thin he'd become under them, yet he stood taller than when I'd left him. Jaxas thrived during conflict; it was the anticipation that made him wilt away.

"So," he spoke into the tumult. "You return at the fall."

I hardened my expression, blinking against the rain running into my eyes. "Famine is here."

His facial muscles twitched, and his frown deepened. "Then you have failed."

"Not yet," Talan said. He slouched, exhausted from our journey to this point, and looked miserable as rain plastered his clothes to his lithe frame. Yet, impossibly, a smile curled his lips. "Help us, and Airene can still succeed."

"To what end?" The Despot's eyes drifted over my shoulder to the burning city beyond. "Will there be anything left to save?"

"Jaxas." The word came out sharp enough that Synne took a threatening step forward. I didn't spare her a look; there wasn't time. "You've never lost hope before. Don't lose it now. Help me, and we might still help Oedija."

For a moment, I thought he'd refuse. The Despot's face was furrowed with sorrow and anger. Yet he nodded.

"Tell me what you need, and I will do what I can."

I flashed him a grateful smile. "Linos — I need to find him."

"Your brother?" Jaxas frowned again, but he didn't question me. "He's not here."

My chest grew tight. "What? Where is he?"

"The Master Augur came and took him. Said she could help him."

I stared in disbelief. Then red-hot anger blossomed through me. *Eltris.* She'd stolen my brother. I knew what she intended for him. She'd nearly let him become a Sacrifice to Famine before.

She would doom us all if she had her way.

I took a step forward, and the laurel guards' spears lowered a fraction. I didn't care. "Where did she take him?" I demanded. "Where is that 'Thae-damned woman?"

Jaxas didn't quail before my anger, but drew up straighter. "I do not know, Airene. I would tell you if I did."

Talan gripped my arm, and though his touch seemed to burn, I didn't shake him off. "The Acadium!" he said, a thunderclap almost drowning him out. "Perhaps she took him to her tower!"

Before I could respond, I felt a tear in the world open at my back.

I whirled around in time to see five figures emerge from the Pyrthae. My chest leaped with recognition. Xaron, Nomusa, Corin, Kari, Isidora. They'd survived the storm of the third fold.

I threw my arms around my fellow Finches, and they embraced me tightly back. "We thought you died," Xaron said, his voice choked. "When Talan fell and you jumped after him…"

"I didn't." I pulled back and flashed a grin. "And neither did you."

Nomusa held me by the back of my neck, staring intently into my eyes. "You'll have to explain yourself later."

I shrugged. "There will have to be a later for that."

The joy of our reunion was short-lived. Jaxas stepped forward and, in a hoarse but commanding voice, said, "I am glad you've returned, but we have dire need of you now, First Watcher and First Warden."

Xaron and Isidora straightened at the Despot's address. "Yes, Your Radiance," Isidora said formally. "We will fight wherever we're needed." Xaron nodded, though a bit of his apprehension of old had returned.

"Good." Jaxas looked to the demes to the east, and my stomach sank as I suspected what he had in mind. His words a moment later confirmed it.

"Silks run rampant through Bazaar. I know you do not know how to stop them, but if they can be delayed…"

"We'll try, Your Radiance." The First Watcher didn't show the least bit of hesitancy. Glancing at Xaron, she gave him a small smile, and he seemed to take heart in it.

"Perhaps burying them in rubble?" Xaron suggested. "If they're chained by the fabric, perhaps obstructing it will restrict their movements."

Talan shrugged. "Worth a try. But be warned: their most potent weapon is against your mind. They will tempt you to go to their embrace. Resist it at all costs." He paused, then continued. "If you have to fight them, try to use quintessence. It's the only thing I've found effective against them."

The two nodded, though I didn't know either of them to have consciously used quintessence before. As they glanced at the Despot, Jaxas waved a dismissal. "May the Eidola watch over you," he murmured.

Xaron looked at me, and I tried for a smile. He failed to return one.

Corin surprised me by kneeling at Jaxas's feet. "I would fight for you, Your Radiance. Send me where I am needed."

Nomusa did not kneel, but stepped forward as well. "And me. I can fight as my people do."

I longed to tell them to stay, that it was too dangerous. But with the risks I would soon take, how could I speak against theirs?

Jaxas looked from one woman to the other, then nodded. "The fighting will find us soon enough. Stay by my side and you will have your moment."

Jaxas's eyes flickered to me, and I suspected he had placed them purposefully. Gratitude flooded me. But before I could find the words to express it, something boomed from afar.

Whirling around, I stared toward the noise, not knowing what to expect. A part of me feared it was Famine, already breaking through the veil between the realms.

The sight that greeted me was stranger still.

Between the broken doors of the eastern gate, green flames rose in a plume, almost too bright to look at directly. Even as I watched, the flames spread in a tsunami that crested the walls. The resulting crashes thundered in my ears even across the distance, and the ground shook beneath my feet. I grabbed for a column, and stone crumbled beneath my fingertips as I fought for balance.

Blinking against the flashing afterimages, I stared at the black smoke that rose from the fey fires, then turned back to the Despot. Jaxas wore a grim smile now. Almost, I felt I could see the flames in his eyes.

"Catalysm!" he answered my unspoken question. "Our last defense!"

"Mother came through!" Xaron sounded dazed, as if it was the last thing he had expected. From all I had heard of his mother, I wouldn't have blamed him if it was.

"Not quite your last!" Talan called, and I looked where he pointed. In Port, flashes of what could only be radiance flared against the invaders, who looked like little more than red smudges in the distance. Wardens, *our* wardens, were fighting back. I'd feared them all dead.

"Did you think Kyros would yield so easily?" Jaxas nodded to Bazaar, and I saw a wall of violet flames burn down the street. The Archmaster had always been prodigious in his strength; I hoped that, with Xaron and Isidora's aid, it would be enough to overcome even Silks. By Talan's pursed lips, he kept his doubts.

But I couldn't be distracted; none of this was my immediate concern. I had to find Linos.

I turned to Jaxas again, meaning to say something, when a second roar sounded behind me. But this was not an explosion, but human voices raised in challenge.

I whirled back to see red-clad people surging up the steps of the Laurel Palace, steel flashing in their hands. There were two dozen, and each with a snarl on their lips. As I watched, one soared through the air, leaping twenty cubits in the air before landing on a step above and continuing their sprint up. Others followed his lead. At their pace, they would be upon us in moments.

Yet for a split second, I could only stare, unable to believe it. But my eyes knew the truth.

The Damask Esir had found us.

CHAPTER TWENTY-EIGHT

TO THE LAST BREATH

"Foreign states are like chickens: chop off the head, and the body will continue to flail. But eventually, both must fall.

To kill the heads of state, send the Damask Esir to clear a path, then the priests and their leashed spirits to finish it."

- Aasjuqal Kahin-Shah, the First Prophet King of the Avvadin Imperium; date unknown

Shouting rang around me, but I ignored it, pulling on the energetic elements until they stormed inside me, then loosing it upon the advancing enemies.

Fire erupted from my fingers, growing and forming into a wall a dozen cubits high, then flying down the wide stairs. Rain sizzled in the heat as it pattered against it, but it blazed too hot to be dampened. I trembled with the force of it, yet with Famine so near and at the height of his power, I could endure the pressure.

As the fiery avalanche crashed upon the Damask Esir, I maintained it a moment longer, then released, blinking through the black spots left on my vision to see the results of my attack. Expecting to see mangled black corpses lying prone on the stairs, it took me a moment to understand what the oncoming shapes were.

The attack had barely slowed the Esir. Except for one fallen to the ground, screaming and writhing as he burned, the others had repelled the flames.

Wardens. In the confusion, I had forgotten every one of them could channel, and had been trained in its use their entire lives.

I had no time for a follow-up, for in mere strides, they were upon us. My companions and Jaxas's guards met the charge.

I stumbled back a step, conjuring kinesis and throwing it at the two closest to me in a desperate ploy. They shredded through it, whirling and bringing about their curved swords to slice at me in perfect coordination. I screamed a denial, but even as I summoned radiance to blast at them, I feared it was too little.

Mid-swing, one of the enemy soldiers collapsed, while the other went flying as Talan crashed into him.

There was a flurry of motion, then Talan was staggering back, a line in his shirt dripping red as rain washed the blood away. Whipping his head up, he caught my gaze and yelled, "The Qarin! Sever their connections!"

I nodded, cursing myself for not remembering earlier, and channeled quintessence. As magic laid their spirits bare, so were the connections to the beings by which Avvad leashed them, resembling long candle wicks, flames burning at the top.

As another Esir lunged at me, I lashed out with an invisible weapon of my own, and the connection frayed under it like string. The woman collapsed with a bloodcurdling cry, then lay twitching on the stairs.

Skirting farther back, I tripped over a stair and fell on my rump. I scrambled back to my feet, jaw clenched, resolve tight, then found my next targets: two Esir sparring against Corin. The former cartwoman proved as handy with a blade as she always claimed, and though outnumbered and bleeding, she had so far defended her sister cowering behind her.

I struck at one Esir, and as the Qarin's connection frayed, the woman toppled. But before I could reach the second, the soldier found a gap in the cartwoman's defenses. A blade slashed across Corin's chest, and she jerked back, a surprised look on her face.

"CORIN!"

I was running toward her, heedless of my safety, slipping and sliding on the rain-slicked stones and knowing I was already too late. I cut the Esir free of his daemon, then ignored him as I skidded to a halt before my fallen friend. Kari was already there, cradling her sister's head and rocking back and forth. She looked up at me, eyes wide and pleading.

"Heal her!" she cried. "You must heal her!"

"I don't know how!" My thoughts raced as I kneeled and hovered my hands over the wound. It spurted forth blood, faster than I had ever seen before. "Corin, Eidola above, Corin..."

I knew no way to stop it. But I had to try.

Harvest! Harvest, please help her!

I was halfway between realms, just as I had been before. I pressed my need inward, resonating through my soul.

The goddess did not rise within me.

Bracing myself, I placed my hands on Corin's chest like I could stem the wound, gagged as blood poured through my fingers, warm and reeking.

"Harvest, *please!*" I begged aloud.

Corin's heart was beating too fast. I looked into my friend's eyes and saw the life fading. It would not be long now.

Still, Harvest did not come.

"I'm sorry." I withdrew my hands and sat back on my feet, shoulders sagging. "I'm so sorry."

Corin wasn't a warden, so I couldn't feel her quintessence in the Pyrthae. Yet I still knew the moment she left.

Kari wailed into the battle surrounding us. "*CORINNA!*"

"Airene!"

A hand tugged on my arm, heaving me to my feet. Mind numb, I looked around and saw it was Xaron, long hair plastered against his face, shallow wounds bleeding across his body. He shook me, and I abruptly came back to my senses.

"More are coming!" He turned me to face down the palace stairs, pointing. "Silks!"

I saw them at once. There were about ten of them, each little more than knotted bands of silken cloth, twisted around a body invisible to my eyes. But they were not hidden in the Pyrthae. There, they blazed, their quintessence bright and powerful.

They glided across the ground, the ends of the cloth reaching like an ant's antennae, feeling the air for their next victims. The blood of those they had already claimed soaked the silk so it was dyed pink, blood dripping from the ends as rain poured down.

Behind the bound spirits came their masters, the Tefra, priests of Valem. They wore the gold-and-jade masks I had glimpsed before, hiding the burns inflicted upon them in a demonstration of their faith. Red cowls covered their heads, and black robes their bodies. Chains hung from their arms as they held them up, commanding the daemons before them.

I looked back to the Silks sweeping up the stairs, and only then did I notice the feeling rising in me. Having experienced the spirits' allure through Talan's memories, it felt familiar, and the desire was not unlike the hunger Famine awoke in me. I had yearned to be consumed by the daemon god when he first broke free of Vusu. The feeling stirring in me now paled in comparison.

Yet they could kill us with an embrace. And unlike the Damask Esir, I knew no effective way to deal with them.

"Airene, we need to go!" Talan was by my side, shouting in my ear, a hand protectively on my shoulder. "We must face Famine!"

I looked up to see the dragon god swooping through the Pyrthae over the field. His wounds looked to have healed, and he was close to the size he had been before Valem. I gritted my teeth, knowing Talan was right, wishing he was wrong.

Still, I pleaded. "I can't leave them! The Silks will take them all!" I glanced at Corin, and a surge of emotion lapped at me, trying to swallow me down. "I won't let them die!"

"Go, Airene!" Xaron spoke now, eyes shining, fear etched into his face, though he tried not to show it. "We'll make it through!"

I stared at him, then looked to find my other companions. Isidora had just cut down a Damask Esir with a well-timed slash of kinesis, and she retreated to put her back to Xaron, panting and sagging with exhaustion. Nomusa, pressed against one of the Laurel Palace's columns, looked mostly unharmed, yet she huddled on the ground, clutching at the stone and staring down at the Silks with wide eyes. Their influence must be worst for her, and unattuned as she was, she had no defenses against them. Kari still huddled by her sister's body near the front of the fighting, ignoring the advancing spirits and priests as if they couldn't harm her. Jaxas had retreated within the palace with his messengers and some of his protectors, while a dozen laurel guards fought against the Damask Esir still standing.

They might die here, just as Corin had. If I stayed, I might save them. But if Famine broke free of the Pyrthae, we would all die.

There was only one choice.

I looked back at Talan, then, with teeth clenched together, I nodded.

He smiled bitterly, then glanced at Xaron. "Keep them alive. Remember to use quintessence."

Xaron grimaced and nodded. I knew as well as he did that he'd never been a deft hand at it. I had to hope he would learn quickly.

I tried to say a goodbye, but the words stuck in my throat. "Don't be a hero," was all I could think to say. My eyes stung with more than the rain splashing into them.

Xaron tried to smile and failed. "Could say the same for you."

Talan cut us short by slashing down. I felt him channel quintessence as he split the fabric of reality open.

"No more delays," he said, directing me toward the tear.

With one last look at the friends I was abandoning, I turned to the rift and stepped in. The strangeness seized me at once, then I shuddered and adjusted. Talan came through a moment afterward, then turned and sealed it behind us.

I looked around at the scene, now distorted with the Pyrthaen touch: colors eschew and shifting, the very air seeming to shimmer with the energies coursing through it. The quintessence of the wardens and spirits shone, while a glance up revealed their corporeal bodies hanging from the reflected world overhead.

"Airene."

At Talan's urging, I moved forward and left them behind.

CHAPTER TWENTY-NINE

CHAOS

Each battle is controlled chaos. Wars are won by small measures of will.

- On the formation of a standing army; by Stratechon Bion, 1086 SLP

We ran past our enemies — the remaining Damask Esir, the Tefra, the Silks — leaving them to overrun our friends, then threw off the sky to launch into the air. I wished I could as easily shed my guilt, but it remained a heavy weight within me.

The Acadium was not far, especially when soaring, and soon, its sprawl of buildings appeared below us. But Famine had drifted closer, consuming the souls that drifted up from the city now. As he spiraled through the air, his presence pulled at me, beckoning toward him, a dozen times the strength of the clothbound spirits. Between his influence and my burning guilt, I had to fight hard to concentrate on the matter at hand.

Swooping down to the world below, I searched for signs of my brother or Eltris. I looked to her tower first, but it lay dark and empty. Panic rising in me, I swept my gaze over the rest of the campus. Could she be hiding somewhere here? Perhaps she'd returned Linos to the Ward, where he'd spent several spans before. Would that mean he'd taken a turn for the worse? Would they have a bed for him amid a war?

But even as I studied the building, I sensed something beyond it. My gaze was drawn to the tower of Kyros Brighteyed, then up to the very top of it. There, at its broken apex, stood two wardens. Could it be Eltris and

Linos? It seemed impossible that she could have brought my brother so high, but it was the best lead I had.

I ascended to the top of the black tower, Talan by my side. Famine was drawing dangerously near now. I tried to ignore him and sped toward my destination.

We had almost reached the tower's peak when a figure materialized before us, arresting our path. I braced myself to fight and almost bowled through before I recognized them. For a moment, I could only stare.

Against all odds, Clepsammia had appeared.

The Maiden of the Sands looked much the same as I'd seen her before. Her shape was the approximation of a woman's, but with distorted proportions: legs and arms of different lengths, her face oddly asymmetrical. Her coloring was as flat and gray as the ocean at night. Her silver hair and tattered robes streamed about her. A wide smile dominated her face, and even her angled eyes seemed to share in it.

I reached out to Talan, warning him with a touch. His soul bunched tight beneath my hand, but he refrained from an attack.

"Who is she?" he whispered.

I didn't answer him, my eyes glued to her lips. Why did she smile? What plan did she have for us, for me?

But it wasn't her lips that moved, but her hand. The one that didn't hold the sandglass pointed upward, toward the Oedija hanging above us.

I frowned, uncomprehending. "What?" I shouted at her. "What do you want?"

The gray ribbons of her robe trailed lazily about her, unaffected by the movements of the massive dragon nearby or the war below. She only turned her head upward, as if to emphasize the direction of her hand.

"Why up?" I tried to think of what she could intend. "What does that mean?"

Clepsammia gave no answer. With one last amused glance, the goddess turned and dissolved into mist.

Talan tugged at my hand as he rose. "Airene!"

He was right. Putting the enigma from my mind, I followed him up to the top of the tower. It appeared much as I remembered it, the room burned and the ceiling broken from the Seekers who had stolen Aika's knife from the Archmaster. The two wardens appeared to be in the center of the chamber, judging by the swirling flames of their Pyrthaen connection.

I glanced at Talan, and he shrugged. Then something loomed behind him.

Shouting wordlessly, I grabbed at the former Guilder and drew him back, staring up in horror at the one approaching.

Famine had seen me. Famine was coming.

I didn't hesitate to wonder why, but fled at once. Talan flew with me, darting for the tower to land on the uneven floor. Famine was fast, slicing through the air as if it took no effort. His mouth gaped wide behind us, and an endless, dark chasm showed within.

Temptation stole over me to fling myself toward him, but I'd been ready for it and fought it down. With an agonized cry, I cut open a rift, then lurched through it.

My entrance was far from graceful as I fell to the rain-slicked stones. Talan was a step behind me, though he remained on his feet. While I failed to rise, he kept the presence of mind to pivot and run his fingertips along the seams between the realities. Through the shifting light, I saw the darkness closing in as Famine sought still to swallow us. Fear choked me. Could he escape through the rift? Did he even need a conduit?

Talan yelped as he mended the last of the rift — yet even then, I feared it wasn't enough. The air distorted, the shape of the daemon god's teeth impressed upon it for a moment.

But the next, they faded, and reality resolved as it was supposed to be.

I had no time to breathe a sigh of relief, for fire blazed toward me. On instinct, I whirled toward it and channeled kinesis. Famine's presence roared into me at the opening of my locus, and I rebuffed the flames with a mighty blast as I borrowed his power.

The woman who had attacked me stumbled a step back, but no farther. Only then did I catch a glimpse of her face and recognize her.

"Eltris!" I shouted, and the Master Augur paused in her assault to squint at me from beneath a drenched hood. I could see from her yellow eyes that she recognized me, but her posture remained as tense as before.

"You," was all the greeting I received.

My anger, tightly coiled about me, snapped free. "Where is he?" I demanded. "What have you done with my brother?"

But even as I spoke, my eyes alighted on him. Linos stood a little ways behind her. His head was tilted back, his mouth ajar. A memory darted through my mind: he and I, young and as innocent as we'd ever been, running through Riverport's streets catching raindrops on our tongues.

I shook free of it and heaved a sigh. My little brother was still alive, at least. She hadn't killed him.

As Eltris stalked toward me, her expression said she had a fight in mind. Yet instead of attacking, she only said, "About time you came, girl! He'll find him soon!"

Animosity fled before the declaration. No need to ask whom she meant; I felt his presence swelling within me in a way it never had before.

With an effort, I closed my locus, but it only brought a small measure of relief. Famine was too strong now.

Fear trembled through me. I'd hoped that Linos and I would be beyond the daemon god's reach in Telae. But he had attuned us; that was a connection that couldn't be denied. Soon, he would take advantage of it.

Eltris was shouting something at me, but I ignored her, spinning through my thoughts. She was out of her depth now and had nothing to offer. All the while, Famine's presence grew, a sense of bloating around my locus underlying the hunger I was used to.

There was only one thing to do — the final thing.

I closed my eyes, held close my hopes, and opened my locus. But before I could channel, my connection to sorcery burst wide.

My soul split in two as Famine poured through.

REQUIEM

My spirit broke; my mind split apart. Yet enough of me remained to bear witness.

I drifted apart from my body, yet looked into both planes. In the Pyrthae, Famine, as long as Oedija was wide and as thick around as the tower I lay upon, dove at me, then *into* me. My locus had been corrupted into a portal, and he exploited it.

As he traveled through me, I felt his agony. He was a being unnatural to Telae, not meant for the material world, and his substance was far more difficult to transmute than my own.

But I watched in my world, too, as he burst free of me, reformed and nearly as massive as when he'd entered, then soared into the sky. As his length slithered through, it corkscrewed in the air above the tower. Still, he defied the natural laws, the sky's weight lifting for him alone.

A far corner of myself screamed at me to stop him, to call upon Harvest and trap him, but it was too small to have effect. I was helpless to impede Famine, lacking even the power to move, to think.

If Harvest remained within me, she was silent and offered no help. I waited for a final splitting, the death that must come after such a ravaging.

His tail, layered with impenetrable dark plates and wicked spines, tore free into the air, and then he was gone. I heard his triumphant roar as if from a distance, though I knew it must make my ears bleed with its volume. My spirit settled back into my body, and I saw with dimmed eyes as my enemy unfurled to undulate through the air.

Famine loosed his booming cry again, then dove out of sight.

Figures flitted above me, but I couldn't follow or identify them. Too little of me remained to even close my eyes, yet I was still there. That part of me that had never died fought for control, though it was a battle she couldn't hope to win.

A face neared my own. I knew him as much by his soul as his features. *Talan.* He shone in my mind, brighter than the light that remained to me. He was speaking, but my hearing was lost. Words of encouragement, perhaps, or mourning; I took comfort in them either way.

Here, at the end, I wouldn't die alone.

With that resignation came an exhalation, of body and soul. My vision dimmed to darkness. A strange warmth rose around me. Death was gentle; I hadn't expected it, and was grateful.

Then, silence.

But even in that quiet, there was a song. A requiem for the departed, to carry them to a place beyond. There was no melody or harmony, yet it moved with a music of its own tempo. I listened and was content to pass down its current and into the dark depths at its core.

Yet the warmth grew, and grew, then swelled greater still. Suddenly, I knew it wasn't heat at all, but a soul within my own. The soul I'd been aware of; the soul that had been with me all along. And where it spread its influence, the last night lifted, and the song faded away.

Slowly, inevitably, Harvest pieced me back together.

In a cradle composed of her essence, the goddess healed me. The silence gave way to an incessant clanging, the beating of my heart, then the distinct sounds of the world. I tasted blood from biting my tongue and oily smoke on the air. My nose filled with the nauseating, overpowering stench of a reptile long confined.

Then my vision returned, and Talan's face appeared above me.

"Airene?" His hand cupped my cheek, while tears trailed down his. I reached up to wipe them away before I realized I could move my arms again.

A wondering smile came to Talan's lips. I returned it. But both were fleeting. Harvest remained vital in me, reminding me that my duty had not ceased with my small death.

I was not his. I never could be.

"I'm alive," I murmured, rising from the erratic pavers of the tower floor. "But I must still cage him, Talan. Please, help me."

It was like knives stabbed into me, again and again, as the joy crumpled on his face. A sliver of the smile remained, but only enough to curl one corner.

"Of course," he answered, and though his voice was soft, his eyes screamed.

I ignored it. I had to. "Linos. You must get him away from here. And Eltris, too, if she tries to stay." I couldn't see the aged augur, but suspected she was just out of sight.

Talan's mouth parted, hesitant. "I'm sorry, Airene. Eltris didn't survive."

I stared at him, startled from my purpose for a moment. "What?"

"She saved us. When Famine emerged, his magic would have torn us apart but for her. She shielded us at the cost of her own life."

He looked over, and I followed his gaze to her body. She was on her back, eyes staring sightlessly above. Violet burns ran jagged along her body, too similar to the scars around Linos's eyes. She seemed smaller now, the force of her personality having made her seem larger.

I was surprised by the tears prickling my eyes. I had never gotten along with the woman, nor even much liked her. But she had been my teacher once, and she and I had shared the same goal, and sacrificed everything to reach it.

In the end, she had hesitated to give up my brother, and saved his life as well as Talan's.

"Rest at last, Eltris," I muttered, lowering my gaze.

A trumpeting that shook the very tower stones blared through the sky, pulling me from my thoughts. I knew what I would see even before I turned to look.

Famine.

His exultation at this greatest feast sent sickening pleasure through my soul. Our connection felt stronger than ever since his passage through me. In making me his conduit into Telae, he had bound us tighter together.

I looked back at Talan and pushed away my fresh grief for Eltris. I wished I could comfort him, knew that I couldn't. Yet I'd always found that as powerful as truth obscured could be, truth revealed was still more potent.

"I love you, Talan. I have for a long time now. I only wish I'd told you sooner."

His expression softened. His hands found mine and clung to them. I almost felt his quintessence through the touching of our shifts.

"I've never kept my feelings a secret." He bit his lip, eyes darting away, then drawing back to mine. "Must you die now? When we finally have what we always should have?"

"Talan." I closed my eyes. I was strong again, but it was a fragile strength. I couldn't continue to refuse him. "I need you to help me. In every way."

I felt his answer through our hands. Then his lips brushed upon my forehead. I opened my eyes to see him rising, our fingers falling away from one another.

"I'll save your brother," he said. "Make sure you save yourself."

I nodded. It was the only answer I could give.

Another cry crashed against my ears. Talan held my gaze a moment longer, then grimaced and turned back to the other two. I rose to my feet, still vaguely surprised to find myself whole, and tottered to an opening in the chamber's walls.

There, I looked upon Famine.

I hadn't thought he could appear more terrifying than he had in the Pyrthae, but the sight of him now proved me wrong. With his powerful body made flesh, it gathered a weight that was apparent with every turn through the air. Dark clouds obscured the sky, yet his aubergine scales seemed to gather an unholy light. Horns curled from his head, and spines bristled from his mane and along his back. But his eyes remained the same, dark pits that swallowed souls.

His physical embodiment, however, posed the least of the danger. Sorcery crackled around him, the mastery and use of it as inherent to him as breathing to mortals. Storms formed and broke as he dove into the dark ranks of the Avvadin army, blue lightning killing the soldiers as surely as his crushing jaws. Magnesis was not the only element running amok; kinesis blasted men, horses, and siege machines to the ground, leaving them in pieces. Radiance blossomed into angry plumes, spinning through yet more of the dissolving troops.

At other passes, energies of which I understood nothing activated. Some made men rise into the air, as if freed of that force that kept them to the ground. When it released them, they fell and didn't rise again. I thought I recognized catalysm, however, when a tide of explosions erupted in violet light.

In the short time since he'd broken free, Famine had devastated the armies of our enemy. Yet I couldn't find any celebration in my heart.

He was my only enemy now. Impossible as it promised to be, I had to try to defeat him.

I closed my eyes, holding both my awareness of Famine and Harvest in my mind. They were there, both of them. I was their Seed, and now I would unveil the promise that held.

I opened my locus to the Pyrthae and flung my challenge through both planes.

"Famine!"

If he heard me, he didn't show it. The daemon god swooped down to decimate another phalanx before rising again.

I sought after our connection, that thing that had lodged in my spirit and twisted our fates together. Holding it firmly in my grasp, I shouted again, directing all my force of thought at it.

"Famine, heed me!"

This time, my cry reached him. The great dragon writhed around so his head faced me. His dark eyes found me at once, and all my doubts flooded through me again. I clung to my courage and pressed on.

"Come, Devourer! I am your weakness, your final flaw! Come and kill me and be free!"

He didn't know speech, but he must have felt some level of my truth. Famine surged into the sky, cutting through the cloud layer, and Telae fractured at his passage. Lightning rippled across the bellies of the clouds, charging the air so my hair stood on end.

He wasn't fleeing. He'd tasted what this world offered, and he wasn't capable of stopping until he'd consumed all of it. Such was his nature.

I had mere moments.

From the corner of my eye, I saw Talan drag Linos, as mindlessly compliant as before, into a Pyrthaen rift. I put them from my mind. They were safe, as much as they could be, and I needed all of my wherewithal for what came next.

Famine was rapidly nearing, but I ignored him, reaching instead after that other celestial being who lodged in my soul. *Harvest,* I thought, and she glowed brighter in response.

I didn't know if it would work. But it was the only thing I had.

I need of you again. We all do. But I won't ask and not give something in return. Perhaps it's what you need.

In my fear, I'd begun rambling. Famine's presence grew urgent. Even Harvest seemed to radiate alarm.

I tried again. *Save us as you saved us before. I don't have the knife, but I must have the tree. So I give to you my life to grow it. Harvest, I am your Sacrifice. Please—*

But the time for words, even unspoken, came to a sudden end. The sky split open, and Famine ripped free of it. He was a blur overhead as he dove toward me. His mouth open, I almost believed he could swallow the world.

I braced myself, waiting for the end.

CHAPTER THIRTY-ONE

ZENITH

The gods wait at death's gates. They hold in their hands potential without end.

- Scroll fragment; origin unknown; estimated 212 PLP

Before Famine could reach the tower, Harvest and I grew together as one.

The boundaries between myself and the goddess eroded so I didn't know where she ended and I began. It didn't matter. Our mission was the same, and together, we found the strength to do it.

We grew, and grew, and grew, and we stood strong against our enemy's charge.

My limbs were no longer limited to arms and legs. A tree, the mortal part of my mind recognized, yet that fragment which touched divinity knew this to be only an interpretation. Our trunk used the stone tower to spread and broaden. Our roots pressed through the rock and dove deep into the earth below. Our branches reached up, but not for the rain and light. They were weapons, sharp and stalwart, and a thousand rose to greet our enemy with a killing embrace.

Yet Famine was no feeble adversary. He'd grown fat on souls, and he commanded the Pyrthae even in this realm. Fire blistered our branches, and pure force broke them. His hard scales repelled our attacks, and his teeth gnawed through us. Harvest screamed at the destruction, but death had always been part of growth's cycle. It did not dissuade her.

Yet it wasn't enough. Miraculous as her emergence had been, Harvest couldn't match her ancient foe.

But maybe she didn't have to.

Though I'd merged with Harvest, I kept my connection to Famine. It had made me feel his hunger, but also his satiation. I'd detested the link and never plumbed its depths before, yet it had always lent me power.

What prevented me from reaching for more?

I followed the ravenous appetite now and dove into it. In my mortal mind, I saw myself entering his mouth and plunging down his throat. Even entwined with a deity, I wasn't prepared for what awaited me.

There was no end to Famine's hunger, and in that moment, I felt all of it. It threatened to devour me.

I fought for sanity and sensed something more. Famine was not his drive alone; he was also the substance that fueled his body. It was the same as every spirit was made of, what filled humans and elevated our intellects.

I reached forward, and quintessence met my touch, silken and warm.

I had to push down my revulsion. These were the souls of those he'd consumed, people robbed even of an afterlife. I hated touching them, using them.

But to save them, I had to do just that.

I reached for the quintessence and channeled it. I hadn't known if it would respond, and yet it did. What was Famine's was mine to command, now that I seized it.

So I pulled it into myself, then funneled it into Harvest. Even in the dragon's gullet, I felt the goddess weave it into herself. Our tree grew again, and Famine's assault slowed.

Then the daemon god roared, and I became lost to the world.

Next I knew, I was vomited up and flung back into my tree-body. When I recovered, I reached again for Famine's quintessence and found myself blocked. He roared a warning; he knew my trick and would not fall for it again.

But it had been enough. Harvest no longer faltered before the dragon's attacks, but rebuffed them and pushed him back. It was Famine on the defensive now, lashing and biting at branches grown sharp enough to pierce his scales. Harvest had a hundred spears, a thousand arrows, and they all sought our enemy's heart.

The first snuck through his counteroffensive, then a second. Famine roared, but it was too late. He hung impaled on our branches, and we were pitiless.

A dozen more branches broke through his armor, but even that wasn't enough. I knew it with Harvest's knowing: Famine would not die, not truly. Just as the goddess had survived for millennia, her seeds scattered across the world, he was ever-encompassing as well. Hunger could never be vanquished, but only kept at bay, in an ever-renewing cycle.

He has consumed too much. I pressed my assertion on Harvest, and she grew a score more branches in agreement. If he couldn't be killed, we would do everything in our power to bring him as close to death as we could. So we struck him, ensnaring him, staking him with bark and branch. And we grew higher still.

Famine! I threw out the challenge, sending it vibrating down our connection and humming in our blood-strewn branches. *I am your cage now!*

My awareness of Oedija had faded, but I could sense the city falling away with our deep-set roots as our canopy ascended. I smothered the doubt that arose at that and pressed on. I couldn't think of what I was leaving behind. All I had was needed for the fight.

Famine was ailing, but he struggled against us every cubit we rose, breaking our branches and screaming his protests. But for every spine he escaped, we skewered him with three more. Neither Harvest nor I would yield.

I didn't think of where we brought him until I remembered Clepsammia's final, enigmatic suggestion. Up, she'd pointed — skyward, not stoneward. It was contrary to what Vusu had believed we must do to cage Famine, opposite of Eltris's understanding and Aika's actions. But as we took Famine into the sky, I thought I understood. The years passed slowly in the fold below, but those who went there slumbered. Above the third fold, beings still roamed, and I suspected what manner of creatures they were now.

Only then did I realize we weren't fully in Telae anymore, but also the Pyrthae. Had we pierced the layer above to rise among the radiant winds, where we mortals had always believed the Pyrthae existed? Or had Harvest's nature taken us back into the realm she was born of and ruled?

Yet it didn't matter; it felt right. Famine was both spirit and material now. To detain him for good, his chains had to be in both realms as well. He wouldn't fully die, but spread across Telae and the Pyrthae, the dragon would be weak enough to hold for the length of existence.

I felt when we broke free of the first fold and into the third, for even with Harvest's nurturing warmth coursing through my substance, the icy winds seeped in. Famine's resistance grew weaker, and I wondered if the cold sapped his dwindling strength. The goddess, on the other hand, was relentless. Her growth slowed, but only fractionally, and we continued our race ever upward.

Time bent. Before I knew it, we had risen beyond the cold and broken into the place above. Serenity stole over me, as it had before, even as I endeavored with Harvest to keep Famine confined. Yet the daemon god had ceased to writhe. Had he given up, conceded he could not win?

Yet I was joined with him still, and by it sensed this was something different. Famine couldn't violate his drive anymore than the other Quintyr. But what we brought him to was part of that: oblivion, the cessation of substance. An end to hunger. Nothing but silence surrounded us — then the air filled with them.

The gods had descended.

Some were warm to my mind's touch, and some burned. Others were frigid, chilling me even from afar. With them came a plethora of sensations, each of their drives made manifest.

The storm that had been violent with envy was Odaon. Clepsammia was there, with her touch of inevitability. Other Eidola existed, too: Caradon Night-Veil, cold as the darkness he claimed; Lavvash, electric and whimsical in her moods; Cendaur, steadier in his temperament. Some, I had no names for; perhaps the deities of forgotten lands, robbed of life by Famine long ago.

All gathered around the dragon impaled upon Harvest's branches, and he roused again, but not to fight. Was it the greeting of kin? No, nothing quite so warm. But there was recognition and familiarity. Perhaps that was as close as divine beings came to welcoming their own.

They reached out, not with hands, but the essence of themselves, and enwrapped him. This, I thought, must provoke him, but still he did not struggle. Our branches impaled him, yet they wound around to touch every part of him. He was like a worm in a cocoon, and I wondered if it was a chrysalis or a cage.

Then they melded away, and it was like they had stripped the flesh from the bones. The skeleton of the daemon god remained, but a third part of him had been split off. Divided, he couldn't return to his full power. He would be forever imprisoned.

Their quarry lashed to themselves, the Quintyr ascended, then disappeared.

As suddenly as they'd come, their presence departed. Only Harvest and I remained, along with the inert parts of Famine. I waited, content with my goddess. I knew the moment must pass to another, but as I did not know what that would be, I only listened to the silence. It stirred through my awareness. Death is a silence, yet so is anticipation. The moment before a vital change.

Harvest felt as my thoughts turned ahead, and something changed between us. A gulf had grown, for as things grow together, they also grow apart. We had always been two separate beings, she and I, even as we'd merged as one. She didn't need me any longer; her seed had matured and become its own vessel.

And I — I was the offshoot that must be pruned.

I didn't resent it as she gently but firmly pried me away from herself, then sent me afloat in the void. I knew it was her nature to do so. And what was I now, apart from her?

Was I Airene still?

I didn't know; almost, I didn't care. Yet some things remained, anchoring me to existence. I had left behind people I cared for, tasks left undone.

For them, I held the fraying parts of myself together. I stayed me, Airene.

Then I descended.

CHAPTER THIRTY-TWO
BEAUTY IN THE BROKEN

I crave the end, when there are no battles to wage, no people to save, no gods to cage. Then, at last, I will close my eyes, and I will rest.

- The journal of Vusumuzi; date unknown

I fell slowly, inevitably. The fated return.

Yet as I passed through the third fold and into the first, I saw nothing was as I'd hoped it would be.

Oedija lay destroyed, but the first sight that caught my attention was the tree. It dominated the middle of the city, far taller than Kyros's tower, from which it had spawned. Its bark was smooth and a brilliant white, nearly shining amid the smoky haze. It spanned both cityscapes, above and below, the trunk breaking into the third fold and leaving only a few branches behind.

For a moment, I could only look upon what I had, for a moment, become. I marveled at the goddess that had lived within me.

Eventually, my eyes were drawn to one of the lower branches. Something hung there, a dark shape against the shining tree. A premonition struck me as I neared. I knew what I would find, perhaps by the threadbare connection remaining between it and my spirit. Yet still, I had to see.

I hovered there and looked at my body.

The branch had grown through me, centered on my locus. Had it speared me when Harvest first grew, or in the battle afterward?

But it didn't matter. The truth was evident and had been ever since I gave my life to the goddess.

I had died.

I gazed upon my still eyes, my limp hands, my slightly parted mouth. They were all too waxen and pale now. There was no blood, but that made me seem no less a corpse.

I had become the Sacrifice in the end — not to Famine, but to Harvest. That made the difference.

It made facing my death bearable. Only just.

I lingered, but even with it being my own body, it seemed macabre to look overlong. And this was not the reason I'd returned. Other tasks awaited me.

I drifted away, turning my gaze to Oedija. My home, so utterly destroyed: walls toppled, gates twisted, buildings burned, people butchered. It should have crippled me with despair, yet it didn't. A seed of something else had been planted among the ruin, a seed which, I had to hope, would flower and grow.

Oedija would rebuild. My home would be restored. Not soon, nor as it was before. But it would grow.

For me, here and now, that was enough.

I honed my focus, searching for those I sought. It wasn't long before I found them at the Laurel Palace, together and alive. Mostly.

It tore me apart and sewed me together, that sight. I flew to them, yearning to be as near as I could, knowing it wouldn't be near enough.

I went to the reflected cityscape above, for there they all appeared, pictured in that mirror of the material world. My friends stood at the entrance to the palace, on the stairs where Jaxas had announced himself Despot, where the Damask Esir had cut down Corin. As they gazed over the shattered city, I floated, invisible among them, taking them in one by one.

Xaron leaned on Isidora, lines etched into his face that had nothing to do with laughter. He'd been injured, both in body and spirit, and only stood by his lover's support. Yet he had survived. He, along with the other wardens, had succeeded in driving off the Silks. I wondered if I'd ever been prouder of him.

Isidora had fared better, though a haunted look dominated her eyes. Yet they had each other; my friend would be cared for and loved. I hoped he would soon laugh again.

With a last touch upon Xaron's face, I turned away.

I went to Nomusa next, standing not far from them. Her face was hard, her eyes wide, yet I recognized the set of her jaw. She wasn't broken, nor would she be. Would she stay in Oedija, or return to reclaim her ishaka? Whatever future awaited her, I trusted her determination would see her through it.

I reached out and pressed her hand, hoping some part of her could feel it.

Then I drifted to Kari. She sat by her sister's body, cradling Corin's head, her eyes distant and dry. She did not smile now, but frowned toward the ruined city; her view of the future, perhaps. I could only hope that with time, she would find her smile again, and a place to belong here in Oedija.

My friends weren't alone; Jaxas, Feiyan, and Komo stood among them. I looked over them, wondering if they had been more ally or adversary. For Jaxas, at least, fondness won over. All he'd done, I believed, was in service of the demotism. I hoped he would not become the tyrant I feared, especially with Feiyan as his advisor. But even she, for all her malevolence, had shown she would fight for Oedija, so long as it aligned with her own self-interest. I hoped it would be so, for everyone's sake. Komo, at least, would be a good ruler, so long as the horrors he saw in this war didn't scar him too deeply.

Two others stood with them. I delayed my approach. I feared I might never leave their sides once I looked. Yet still, I drifted closer to hover before them.

Talan and Linos stood side by side. The former Guilder had an arm held out, as if ready to catch Linos at any moment, yet my brother looked steady on his feet. His eyes were as vacant as before, his mouth slack, and the whole of my being cried out for him. Famine and Vusu were gone, yet he carried the scars they'd inflicted upon him. At least he was beyond their reach now.

I cupped his face in both my hands, as I often had when we were children, and planted an insubstantial kiss upon his forehead.

Then I turned to Talan. Fear stirred within me at his expression. I saw little of the hope the others carried. Each of them had a purpose before them; Talan lacked that. Perhaps, had I remained behind…

But that, too, was a future Harvest had pruned away. There was little point in dwelling on it.

I touched his hands, his face, then wrapped myself around him. I willed him to feel me, to hold me, but of course he didn't. He was beyond my reach now, in Telae, while I remained in the Pyrthae.

Then it occurred to me: pyr had crossed the barrier between worlds before. Perhaps, even now, I could as well.

I dove to the Telae reflected below. Though my friends would not appear in image, those attuned I could feel, even though none of them were channeling at the moment. I knew each, and I brushed by Xaron before stopping before Linos. Other than Kari, he was most present on this plane, for his spirit drifted while the others were anchored in their bodies. I wrapped myself around him, and had I been able to, I would have wept.

He was there, my brother, still there. I pressed my thoughts upon him.

Wake, Little Lion. It's time to awaken.

Perhaps he made some small response; perhaps I imagined it. Still, I didn't give up. Time and determination were all I had now.

Clinging to him, I gathered all the memories we'd shared, the person I knew him to be, and in the same way I'd passed knowledge onto Talan before, I tried to do so with Linos. Perhaps because he wasn't fully in the Pyrthae, there was a barrier to my attempts. I pushed harder against it, made my intentions firm and vivid.

Wake up, Linos! I shouted into the void.

Then the dam broke. Suddenly, he was all around me, and it was *him.*

There were no words, barely fully formed thoughts, yet I knew my brother's mind and treasured every moment. I shared my understanding of him, and he drank greedily of it. A moment later, I became aware what this drained: my quintessence, my soul.

I didn't stop. I was afraid, but my love for him was stronger.

When at last I had no more to give, I separated myself and looked upon him with dimmed senses. His spirit seemed stronger, more anchored. Would it be enough? I could only hope.

There was so little of me left, nothing more than wisps of a cloud. I wouldn't be able to see everyone I'd wished to. My mother, father, and elder sister. Maesos. Other friends and allies, both old and new.

Yet I held onto existence a little longer as I drifted back to Talan. He was even harder to reach than Linos, yet I tried with all the strength I had left. He was too far; I wouldn't reach him. I felt myself slipping away.

Then he cut into the Pyrthae, and suddenly he was there, all of him.

"Airene!" He held me close, and I curled into his embrace. My ability to speak had faded, but my memories remained, so I pressed these upon him. He flinched at first, defying my attempts, then opened up entirely.

I flowed into his soul, and his into mine. Like two rivers joining waters.

Yet a part of me resisted, stubbornly retaining itself. The part that had always lain in the dark, the quiet, the secret places of my soul. Secrets had been the baubles I chased after, that drove me near to madness in their pursuit. They were what allowed me to protect Telae from Famine. Had I not sought after them so ruthlessly, every plane of existence would have been reaped barren.

This wasn't how I imagined my life would turn, when I dreamed of being a Finch as a little girl. It wasn't how I hoped it would end. And so I clung a moment longer to those treasured dreams.

But though there is beauty in cycles, it is also in their breaking.

Nestled into Talan's being, I finally let go of myself. Would Thero be waiting for me in whatever existed beyond? Would I join the gods? Or would I be part of the man I loved for however long he lived, and perhaps even in the time after?

I did not know. Perhaps they were secrets I would discover. But at least Talan and I would keep one last secret between ourselves.

I closed my eyes, listened, and welcomed the song that swallowed me down.

CHAPTER THIRTY-THREE
FROM A SEED

He hovered in the Pyrthae until her presence faded. Only when his soul grew cold did Talan retreat into his own world.

As he set foot onto the steps leading up to the Laurel Palace, the others that had been standing nearby crowded around with questions. Talan ignored them, lost in himself. He had felt her, tugging at him, and had opened the way. He'd thought to find her there, whole and as he'd known her. But there'd been so little of her remaining, a ghost of herself.

She'd folded into him — then, like that, she was gone.

But Airene had left him with more than her absence. Just as she'd shared of her memories before, she had again. He saw her final battle with Famine, her sacrifice to Harvest. He saw the dragon impaled upon the white branches, then lifted away by the gods above. He saw as the goddess that had so sorely used her cut her loose, like a shriveled leaf shed in autumn.

He was filled with anger and love and pride. But most of all, he floundered in pain.

"Are you there?" he muttered, not caring that he spoke aloud, that he must seem mad to the others. "Are you sleeping inside me?"

But Talan had sensed the manner of slumber she entered. Airene was gone, and all that remained of her, he carried inside him.

Am I worthy of it? He knew the answer all too well.

"Talan. Please, answer me."

Talan roused from his stupor to meet Xaron's eyes. They'd never gotten along, the jester having been protective of Airene and distrusting of him — as well he should have. But Talan liked to think he'd earned his trust now, as Xaron gripped him by the shoulders and gazed into his eyes with unspoken emotion.

"What did you ask?" he murmured.

"What just happened? You entered the Pyrthae, then—" Xaron broke off, turning away for a moment. But he'd found steel inside him over the past season, and he glanced back up. "Was it her?" he continued, quieter. "Did she…?"

Talan hesitated, then stepped back, breaking Xaron's grip. The others crowded around them to hear his answer.

It came out as a sigh. "Yes. It was her. And she did. Famine is gone for good."

They began babbling among each other and asking more of him, but Talan turned away. He didn't want to speak of it, didn't even want to think of it. Airene was as close now as she'd ever been.

Then why does she feel so far away?

He made to leave, intending to find some proprietor of a drinking hole brave or stupid enough to be operating at a time like this. But when he faced the youth standing behind him, all thoughts of it left his mind.

Linos stared at him. But for once, his bright blue eyes were not glazed over.

He *saw* Talan.

Airene's brother blinked, his lips quivering for a moment before words escaped them. "Who are you?" He slowly turned and looked around him, a bit of the daze returning at the sight. "Where am I? Is this… Oedija?"

Talan stared for a moment, baffled. But he'd always been good at thinking on his feet. Setting his mind, he stepped forward and commanded the youth's attention.

"Yes. You're Linos, right? Linos of Riverport?"

He spoke it as a reminder. Linos hesitated, perhaps trying to decide if it was true, then nodded. "Suppose I am."

Talan smiled, hoping it came off as reassuring. "You've been sick, Linos. A lot of things have changed. There've been tragedies and miracles. I think you being better now is one of them."

Only then did he realize what had truly happened. *Airene.* All of this had started with her trying to save her brother. He doubted she would have rested until she'd given everything to do so.

He looked away as his eyes pricked with moisture.

"Alright." Linos's speech returned stronger with each word. "How do you know me? Why have you been looking after me?"

Talan noticed the others had seen the change in Linos and froze in surprise — all except the Despot and his First Consul, who had returned to governing their broken city. A flurry of messengers, laurel guards, and militiamen streamed up and down the stairs now, none of them unblemished by war.

He ignored them, focusing his attention on Linos. "I'm Talan, a friend of your sister's. There's a lot to catch you up on, but just know, Airene did it all for you..."

Then he told her tale. And as his chest grew warm, Talan wanted to believe some part of her remained to take comfort in her deeds.

But he had never been one to indulge in delusion.

———

Talan told Linos all there was to tell. In the course of the telling, they went to the kitchens of the Laurel Palace and scrounged whatever food they could find there. The staff, unsure of what else to do in the face of tragedy, had prepared their usual fare. It always felt odd to eat after a day of death, but Talan had endured enough of them to know that memories didn't provide nourishment.

After he'd finished, with embellishments from Nomusa and especially Xaron, who had come along with them, Linos had sat quietly, then excused himself, claiming to be tired. Talan suspected the truth. His sister had just died and his home been destroyed. It was a lot to take in, and not something he wanted to think through in the company of near strangers.

Talan had slunk off himself then, feeling much the same way. He wandered through the Laurel Palace, then beyond it. The guards seemed to know who he was, for they nodded as he passed and didn't stop him. He only smiled back, letting all that burned inside him show through.

He hadn't known where he headed, but he wasn't surprised when he approached the towering white tree. The streets were strewn with bodies and refuse. The fighting had ended, but the wounded and dying still cried out for help. He passed them by, unable to aid them even if he'd had the skill to. Yet others were there, providing comfort and necessities. As much as could be done would be.

At last, he reached the first of the giant roots, then craned his neck back. The tree rose as high as the Chains Azhi had once described, its branches extending into the sky beyond sight, fading to hazy shadows, then nothing at all. He wondered if they reached into the Pyrthae itself, then remembered from Airene's memories that they did, and even beyond that.

Memories, he thought, directing it at Airene like a prayer. *Is that all I have left?*

He kneeled before the root and pressed both hands to it. The bark was smooth and porous, just like the knife Airene had once borne. Like bone. It held an unnatural warmth, a sense of aliveness the knife had lacked. But he couldn't feel Airene, nor any distinct presence.

He opened his locus and channeled quintessence. The aliveness of the tree came into starker view; it was spirit, through and through, a soul grown so great it spanned both worlds. *And binds them,* he mused, wondering what that meant for the future.

With his senses wide open, he noticed the approach of the three others before he faced them. When at last he could ignore them no longer, Talan sighed, closed himself to his gift, then rose and turned.

Nomusa, Xaron, and Linos stood there. Talan wondered for a moment where the others had gone, then let the thought go. There were a dozen things that might occupy them with Oedija in a smoldering ruin and a scattered army on the retreat.

"Figured we'd find you here." Nomusa placed a hand on one hip and tried to smile, but fell short.

Talan shrugged, not caring to respond.

"It's hard to believe." Linos looked up, just as Talan had. "That a goddess lived inside her."

She also lived in you. But Talan couldn't find the energy to form the words.

Nomusa stepped closer. "We should do something. Something to honor her."

Honor her? He couldn't repress a smirk. What did it matter to her, their honor? He'd felt her spirit fade into him. There was nothing left of her separate from himself. Yet at the wariness in their expressions, he sighed and relented. If they needed this, he wouldn't deny it to them.

They each spoke words, recalling loving memories and wishing a good fate upon her. "You never gave up," Nomusa said. "Never lost hope. Even when the rest of us did." Her eyes were dry, but there was a hollowness in her voice and a heaviness in her shoulders that had never been there before.

"All will know your name," Xaron said, smiling as tears trickled down his cheeks. "I think that would make you happy. You always did hanker for attention. Eidola above, I'll miss that."

Linos's eyes were red and shadowed as it came his turn. "You saved me," he murmured. "Saved all of us. You always watched out for others. For me. It's just like you to give your life for the world."

As the youth finished, all three looked to Talan, so he bowed his head and muttered his piece to the ground. "Hope you know what you did. Hope it brought you peace."

They were quiet for several minutes, then Nomusa turned to him. "What do you mean to do now?"

Talan looked up. They waited expectantly; for what, he couldn't say. He shrugged again, and when that didn't seem sufficient, said, "You three make plans then?"

Linos barked a short, bitter laugh. "Find my family, I suppose. And then…" He punctuated it with a shrug.

"You've your life ahead of you." Talan didn't know why he bothered saying the words. *Though I'd be lying if I didn't see myself in him.*

"You'll find a purpose," he continued. "It'll keep you going. Just like with your sister."

"If you say so." The youth looked equally apprehensive and afraid. Talan wondered how quickly he would return to his former ways, the debauchery that had landed him in the Manifest's clutches.

Unless I can stop the slide. He thought he might even have the will to try. It would be like a redemption for his own lost years, if he succeeded.

For Airene's sake, he had to try.

Nomusa broke into his thoughts. "Xaron and I will help Jaxas in his plans, at least for now. To rebuild, and be stronger than before."

Talan snorted a laugh. "Politicians…"

"There was substance there, too," Xaron hurried to say. "He freed the honors, Talan. All of them."

That cut his amusement short. Talan scrutinized the jester, trying to detect any hint of a joke, but he looked utterly serious. A different sort of smile came to Talan then.

"Well," he muttered. "That should be interesting to see."

"There's more." Xaron licked his lips. "Wardens like you and Linos, outside of his employ… he freed you as well. Being attuned is no longer a crime."

For a long moment, the words didn't settle in. When they did, all Talan could do was laugh.

"There won't be much of Oedija left soon, will there?" he said bitingly.

"Probably not." Xaron gave a strained grin. "But it's progress."

Linos snorted a laugh. "I'll make the most of it while it lasts."

Nomusa gave the youth a resigned look, then turned back to Talan. "Jaxas might do some good. You could, too, if you tried."

Talan closed his eyes, letting the laughter slip back into the emptiness that filled him. *Try.* He didn't want to try any longer. But he'd experienced this cycle before; he knew where it ended.

"He claims Oedija is not dead, but will regrow," Nomusa said. "Just like the tree that saved us from Famine."

Talan cracked open his eyes again, sieving his thoughts. He was free: free of the Underguild, of Avvad, of Oedija and its Shepherds. It had been so long since he'd not been hunted for merely existing that he could scarcely comprehend it.

Maybe he didn't have to hide any longer. Maybe he could step out of the shadows and live in the light.

And live without her.

He looked up at the great white tree behind him. "The Harvest Tree," he'd already heard it called, and had no doubt the name would stick.

I won't think of the goddess when I see it, he thought to it. *Only you.*

Then a thought stuck in his mind, and he froze.

"Goddess," Talan murmured before looking at Linos. The youth eyed him strangely, but did not flinch from his stare.

Nomusa frowned at each of them. "What'd you say?"

"Goddess," Linos clarified. "What I want to know is why he said it."

Instead of answering, Talan opened his locus and channeled. His vision doubled, layering upon his eyes the world lit up with glowing quintessence, and he stared at Linos. He didn't know the youth well, but he knew Airene. And when he saw traces of her burning through her brother's soul along with another, his smile grew wide.

Closing his locus, he blinked and adjusted to normality, then spoke to Linos. "They're both in you."

"Both." Linos looked as if he wanted to bolt, but his feet remained rooted where he was. "Who do you mean?"

"Your sister didn't just die for you. She gave the last of her soul to you. And she didn't disappear, but is still within you."

"But she's dead." Linos craned back his neck to stare at her body far above. "What does it matter, if she's still not with us?"

Talan stepped closer to him. "Because she's not the only one alive in your soul. Harvest is, too."

For a moment, none of them moved. Then all three of his companions burst out at once.

"They are?" Nomusa demanded. "You can see them when you channel, can't you?"

"Just like you," Xaron exclaimed, "to only just be mentioning this! If only I could see them, too..."

"What are you saying?" Linos's voice cracked with emotion. "That we can... save her?"

Talan's smile had faded, and something harder remained behind. "I don't know. But if you're willing, I'd like to try something."

Linos had been intractable before being taken by the Manifest, at least in the few instances Talan had met him. Now, however, he moved quickly to Talan's instructions, as eager to help his sister as Talan was. Nomusa and Xaron watched as Talan and Linos stepped closer to the Harvest Tree and placed their hands on it.

"Is there anything we can do?" Nomusa asked tentatively.

"Put your hands on our shoulders," Talan said after a moment's speculation, more to keep them occupied than out of any hope it would help. "You can share your memories of her as well."

After exchanging a glance, Xaron and Nomusa followed his lead, their hands warm against his shoulders. As they became still behind, Talan closed his eyes and concentrated first on the feeling of the smooth bark beneath his palms, then the spirit that inhabited it. This tree was one part of Famine's prison. It stood to reason that not all of Harvest had departed it.

It will work. It must.

I need you.

He couldn't have admitted it aloud, but neither could he deny the truth. Airene had believed in him, helped make him a better man. When he envisioned a brighter future, she was always foremost in it.

He didn't want to guess what he would become otherwise.

So he gathered all the memories they had shared, all the moments both intimate and hard, and he channeled. His spirit quickly found Linos and Xaron's, Nomusa's beyond the sorcery, and with a recklessness that surprised himself, he broke their boundaries to touch upon their souls. Both flinched, but neither recoiled, and soon, their thoughts threaded across the gaps.

Joined, Talan delved both deeper into the tree and into Linos. *Harvest,* he called into the aether, reaching after that presence he had first sensed in Airene; so small, yet so impossibly vast. *Harvest, I need you. Airene needs you!*

The great being still slept.

He didn't relent, but pressed all their recollections upon the goddess. Airene traveling the rooftops with him. The kiss they shared before the Laurel Palace, then the many on the path to the Bali highlands. One of Linos's memories snuck in as well: when she ruffled her little brother's hair and said to him, *I'll always look after you, Little Lion.*

Still, nothing. Minutes carried on. Talan felt the resolve of the other two men waver, but he didn't let them give in. He carried on, dragging them with him, calling for the goddess with mind and memory, pleading for her life.

She needs to be alive! She can't go this way!

Desperate, he reached for another presence, the one that had settled inside him after working her miracle.

Airene, it's time to wake up. No more resting. Come back to us; come back to me.

He wasn't sure any of her was left, yet he felt something stir, little more than a feeble flame. He blew on it, coaxing it to life with his thoughts and emotions, hoping, needing it to be her.

Like a key turning in a lock, Harvest suddenly roared through them.

It was pain and promise as the goddess seized hold of his soul. Talan couldn't have let go if he wanted to now. Ruthlessly, Harvest combed through his being, turning over every memory, both of himself and Airene. He didn't know what she searched for, if it was to judge his worthiness, or Airene's, or something else entirely.

But he endured it. It was the only way.

As swiftly as she came, Harvest departed, and Talan sagged against the tree with her retreat. The others broke off, and he heard their voices from a distance, but he couldn't pay them heed. As the goddess faded into the tree, Talan tried to follow. He wasn't swift or strong enough. Within moments, she evaded his grasp, then was gone.

Gone.

She'd left. He'd failed, failed her again.

I'm sorry, Airene. I tried.

Despair dragged him down, but Xaron's call roused him. "Talan, look! Look up!"

Hope flared back to life as Talan opened his eyes and craned back his neck, looking where the jester pointed to a branch high above them. *Airene's branch.* Only, it looked different from before, shorter, and with the body upon it less obvious.

"It's retreating," Nomusa said, awe in her voice. "She's going into the tree."

"A seed," Linos whispered, and with that word, Talan understood.

He surged back into the Pyrthae, pressing against the tree, expectant now. He didn't have to wait long. Before them, the bark warmed with quintessence, building faster with every moment. He felt Harvest grow in her presence, but within her, something else was evolving.

His eyes had drifted closed again, but as the second presence in the tree moved forward, he opened them. A seam was splitting up the side of the trunk. But instead of darkness beyond it, a person, clad in ragged clothes, was emerging.

Talan staggered to his feet as he left the Pyrthae. His head pounded, but a grin split his face, emotion choking him so he could barely utter her name.

"Airene."

She stepped free of the tree and looked around, eyes glassy. Her gaze slid over each of their faces, then settled on Linos's. She blinked, and her stare sharpened. A smile slowly grew, and she raised her arms.

"Brother."

The youth bolted forward, wrapping his long limbs around her, holding her tight. Talan grinned the wider to see it.

When the siblings released each other, Airene turned and saw him next. Her smile faltered, but she held out her hands to him. He took them, running his hands over her skin. They felt the same as before: smooth but for calloused patches.

Her eyes brought his back up and held them.

"Harvest's seed was in Linos," she murmured, "but you brought me back. Thank you, Talan. You did what I couldn't."

Before he could think of a response, Xaron and Nomusa were there, crowding around and holding her. Talan released her hands, missing her touch as soon as it left. But it wasn't long before her friends stepped back, and Airene reached for him again. He pushed his fingers through hers and wondered if he'd ever felt more complete.

Airene looked around at each of them, then smiled sheepishly. "I feel a bit like Xaron, but I have to say, I'm starving. Think Jaxas's kitchens are still open to us?"

They shared a laugh, then their small group turned toward the Laurel Palace. Talan kept close to Airene's side.

Ash and ruin surrounded them still. Many had suffered, and many more would in the days to come.

But for himself, Talan had never seen a brighter future.

EPILOGUE

I live.

It is not the ending I expected when I set off in pursuit of Famine. Perhaps not even what I deserve.

Each day, I remember this, and I am grateful.

With Harvest, I defeated Famine. But the cost… that is a specter that haunts me everywhere I look.

The season has turned back to summer, but Oedija still lies in ruin. Between the God of Hunger's feasting and the siege by Avvad's armies, there is much to recover from.

Yet Famine is gone and the Avvadin fled back home, their numbers decimated. And by Kelena's reports, the Kahin-Shah was one of those killed in Valem's fires.

Avvad is another devastated empire. Only this was one I had a hand in razing.

But its fall means our world is safer, and each day, we become a little stronger. The rubble has been cleared from the streets. The fields flourish this season, as if to make up for lost time. Trade and commerce are invigorated, and the ports are busy even at night.

We have suffered. Many lost their lives. But like the great tree at our city's center, we will grow, and someday become again the Pearl of the Four Realms.

As for myself… I have come to know a secret so plain, yet elusive for so many years, I wonder that I have even claimed it.

I am happy.

I shouldn't be; I know that. Blood stains my hands and soul. Many friends and allies are dead — Corin, Eltris, Azhi. Yet though I often weep for remembering them and all they lost, I cannot deny it. I have too much good in my life not to find joy in it.

My brother is returned to me, whole and as full of trouble as before — or as close as could be expected. Often I catch him staring at nothing, a look in his eyes I recognize well. He catches me doing the same sometimes.

But we are together, and together bear our scars.

The rest of my family rejoined us in Oedija, though reluctantly. Their home destroyed, my mother preferred the fineries of the Wreath estate. Yet even Jaxas's generosity can only be depended on so far, and at my insistence, and that of my father, weak as he's become, they returned. Like the rest of us, they rebuild, and for the first time in my lifespan they are free of their debts, vanished with the Valemish. It is as promising a start as I could hope for them.

My family has, in a way, grown to include others. Kari is now involved in my daily routine. With her sister gone, I felt an obligation to look after her and found her employment suitable to her odd disposition. She is melancholy, but resilient, considering all she lost. I think she will find joy again, given time. With each passing day, I understand her more, and we grow closer.

Nomusa, too, has proven strong, though that is nothing more than I expected. Remaining as Jaxas's Archon, she heads up the rebuilding of the Conclave into a proper governing body, hoping one day, it will rule again without the Despot's supervision. When time allows, we even share a drink or two at Zipho's cafe, which fortunately survived the calamity, and it's like we're back in Canopy, high above the city, our lives full of promise.

But sometimes, she speaks of the home she left behind. I wonder if she will leave us someday to reclaim it, and what that will mean for Komo should she do so.

Xaron and Isidora are receiving a fresh start here in Oedija, for our First Watcher has become pregnant. Everyday, he smiles more with anticipation, and he dotes on Isidora, to her infinite annoyance. I could almost believe him ready to be a father, though it seems like only yesterday he was guzzling down wine, not a care in the world.

And his family has grown in more than one way. Following her miraculous defense of Oedija with catalysm, Jihu reached out to her son, and amends were made between them. Every time I hear of them, they seem to grow closer.

And then there is Talan.

The piece of happiness we found while tailing after Famine? We have reclaimed it in full and more. Finally, we have our chance.

We will not squander it.

But family and friends are not my only preoccupation. Now I have a new purpose. Famine won't return; of that, I am certain. But other threats, be they pyr, Quintyr, or human, might yet assail us.

We can no longer deny our gifts, no longer shun our wardens. We must embrace them, harness them… and protect against them.

And there are more wardens than ever. With Harvest's return came a proliferation of attunements, so now a tenth of Oedija's population manifests magic to some extent. It is a transition that requires a firm hand to not let matters devolve into chaos, one guided by a person who has experience in such matters.

Or two persons, as it happens.

Jaxas appointed me as the First Attuner to oversee this, with Talan as my Second. Though I have my reservations about Jaxas remaining as the Despot of Oedija, the work is too urgent to ignore. Linos and Kari aid the effort as well, as much as their dispositions allow. I finally have a seat at Jaxas's Council — though I make as infrequent use of it as I can. Yet it is the position I require to effect the change I wish to see.

The work is unceasing and thankless. It is not what I imagined myself doing when growing up. Yet I am tired of living in the shadows, and I would only be in Kelena's way as a Verifier.

But once a Finch, a part of me will always remain one. There are those among the fledgling wardens who do not wish to be guided, whom we must seek and convince to come under our sway. Talan in particular is talented at this persuasion.

But in the seeking is where I thrive.

So Famine's cycle came to an end, and a new one was born. One of Harvest, perhaps. Or of humanity.

Only the seasons will tell, and the actions of each one of us. All I know is that I will never cease shaping it.

What can we not grow from a seed?

THE END OF THE CYCLE

The main trilogy of The Famine Cycle ends with *Requiem of Silence*. But three stories remain in this omnibus edition.

The first is the prequel novella *Secret Seller*, which follows Airene and her fellow Finches as they seek the murderer of a nobleman and stumble upon plots that are expanded on in the main trilogy.

The second is another novella, *The Phantom Heist*, which follows Talan Wraithsbane in his semi-humorous escapades before the events of the trilogy.

The third is the short story "The Caged God," which was the original prologue to *Whispers of Ruin* and gives more background to both Azhi and Famine.

May you enjoy them all.

~ J.D.L. Rosell

SECRET SELLER

A FAMINE CYCLE
NOVELLA

A FINCH IN THE STORM

It wasn't the first time I had watched Xaron drink an entire skin of wine at once, but it was the fastest.

With lifted eyebrows and a reluctant smile, I shook my head as he wriggled the sack to drain the last drops, then threw it aside with a satisfied sigh.

"How's that?" he asked, grinning lopsidedly at me. "All in one go!"

I mustered up every bit of lackluster in me. "*Very* impressive."

"You've been practicing," Nomusa observed from next to me on our patched divan. "Why wasn't I invited?"

I shook my head and looked out the large bay window before us. Oedija, our home city, spread out before us in a shimmering sea of lights. Canopy, our loft, provided a fine vantage point, even if the derelict tower was drafty, leaky, and often chilly. In the daytime, we could see all the way to the western seafront where the ocean extended ever outward, far and away to the lands from which my ancestors had come.

Xaron belched, drawing my gaze back inside, and I shook my head. He often acted the fool as well as dressed like one in bright coats and fine trousers, but Xaron was far more than his appearance. Barely taller than Nomusa and willow-lean, he possessed a lithe strength suited to a man who often visited the gymnasiums. His position as our tracker and house-breaker kept him fit, even if his lifestyle tended him toward slothfulness. But most surprising was the secret gift he hid from all but us, his accomplices. For if it were known, we could all be killed for it.

He chuckled as I glanced at him. He didn't have the decency to look ashamed. "You're always invited, Nomu, you know that," he said to our third companion. "Airene, on the other hand, has to work on her constitution before I can be seen with her." He couldn't resist lightening the gibe with a smile.

"Pardon me for practicing moderation," I said drily. "A foreign concept for you two, I know."

"Don't listen to her." Nomusa waved a hand as if to disperse a foul odor. "It's not our fault she doesn't know how to relax."

I nearly rolled my eyes. Nomusa knew far too well how to relax in my opinion. She liked to indulge what Oedijan society deemed "vices" — drinking to excess and finding different strangers with whom to spend the night — though her own Bali culture didn't frown upon such behavior. She easily managed it, too, blessed as she was with a fullness of figure, natural charisma, and a finely featured face to leave a woman jealous — including me, in my weaker moments. While I had inherited a certain prettiness from my mother, I was but a candle to Nomusa's beauty. She used her talents to keen advantage in our work, manipulating those who had valuable information into tipping their hand, whether by guile or charm. She, too, bore a hidden past, if a less dangerous one. For if her parents hadn't been killed and herself exiled from her homeland eleven years before, she would be the ruler of her home chiefdom.

I didn't protest, but smiled thinly. "I just don't celebrate every small job we complete." Supposedly, this was what my companions' revelry was all about: satisfying another client in our line of work as Finches, surveyors of whispers and rumors, who turned happenstance and hunted knowledge into a profit. Yet after seven years of running down common mysteries, I found little reason to celebrate.

I continued. "Even a city guard could have discovered that it was a disgruntled apprentice breaking that potter's wares. Give me something significant, and I'll be happy to drink myself silly afterward."

"I doubt you would even then," Nomusa said snidely.

Xaron studied me for a long moment. Or perhaps he squinted because his vision was starting to swim. "I think the monsoons have you down again," he concluded. "Happens every year, doesn't it? It was bound to come again."

I kept my expression carefully neutral and looked out the bay window again. Now, I didn't see the lights of the city as a sea blending together, but as islands. Whole demes — Iris and Bazaar most notable among them — were wreathed in light; pyr lamps filled with bioluminescent pyrkin lined their cobblestone streets and lit their alleys. But other districts like our Port only half-shone, the local government only allocating funds enough to illuminate street crossings. Still others, like those located outside the walls, were nearly dark. And it was never darker than now, in the midst of the monsoon season, when the moons shone dully through the cover of clouds and the radiant winds, green rivers of light cast off from the spirit realm of the Pyrthae that encircled the world, were reduced to ghostly wisps.

"Airene?" Xaron broke the silence, looking at me with growing concern.

"Maybe," I murmured.

Nomusa's eyes suddenly lit with understanding. "Ah. I had almost forgotten it was nearing."

Xaron's brow crinkled. "Nearing? What's nearing?"

Nomusa looked at me, and I grudgingly nodded my consent. "The day her brother died," she explained softly.

The swift change in mood was palpable. I cringed at how I'd precipitated it, but there was no help for it now.

"Oh," Xaron said. His eyes searched me, seeking some sign of how to proceed. "I didn't know."

I let out a long sigh. "No reason you would. It happened eleven years ago. Long enough that I shouldn't let it get me down every time the anniversary comes around."

"Yes, but still…" Xaron hedged. "I feel bad."

"Don't. You couldn't have known, and it doesn't mean you shouldn't enjoy yourself when we succeed." I lowered my eyes. "I really didn't mean to rain on your celebration."

Xaron knelt next to me and pressed my hand. His sour breath filled my nostrils. "You don't have to apologize," he said fiercely.

I smiled and squeezed his hand back, his fingers burning against my skin, the heat emanating from them a quirk of his hidden talents. But kind as he was being, I suddenly wanted nothing more than to be alone.

I stood. "I think I'll get a breath of fresh air."

Xaron stood as well. "I'll go with you."

Nomusa pulled him down next to her. "Not you, you sweet fool. She wants a moment alone."

"Oh." Xaron looked at me with a sheep's innocence, or maybe the dumbness of a drunk.

I fondly patted his cheek. "I'll be right back. Save some wine for me?"

He brightened and nodded. "Sure we will."

Nomusa snorted. "No, we won't. Not if I have anything to do with it."

Xaron shrugged helplessly. "I'll do what I can," he amended.

"That's all I could ask." With a lingering smile, I turned to the door and exited onto the balcony.

The twittering of birds greeted me as well as the cold, wet night. I closed the door behind, shivering and drawing my arms around me. Even clad in a chiton thick enough for the chill that the monsoons brought, it was nowhere near sufficient to keep out the steady drizzle and the cold gusts of wind that drove against our loft. Yet I didn't retreat inside, but approached the finch cage that hung beneath a small sheltered alcove.

Finches had long been the preferred messenger birds of Oedija. Trained to recognize locations by scent when their beaks were dipped in jars of perfume that matched their destination, they were perfect for delivering messages across a sprawling city within a turn of the sandglass. On a clear day, one could see the colorful birds flitting to and fro above the rooftops, delivering thousands of messages each day. In Xaron, Nomusa, and my work as merchants of rumors, quick access to information was critical to our success, and it wasn't without reason that we were called Finches. We hosted a healthy population of the birds within the cage of every color and pattern.

I liked to take care of them, despite the hassle of hauling seed up the eleven circles of stairs to the top of our tower, and the messy chore of cleaning out the bottom of their cage. My fondness extended beyond their usefulness though. In the few idle moments I allowed myself in our daily work, I liked to watch the birds and admire their delicate beauty. So small, yet their impact was often great.

Ignoring my body's shivering protests, I cooed to the finches and refilled their trough with fresh seed. Two immediately hopped over and began pecking at it, and I smiled as I watched them eat.

Abruptly, a cascade of violet lightning curled across the sky, followed by the booming crash of thunder. I flinched. It was not fear of the lightning; it rarely hit the city itself. Rather it was the way the lighting had curled together, arcing in towards a center point like silk in a spider's web. Without warning, my last memory of Thero seized me.

He'd been dead for days by the time the city guard found him. My older brother, seventeen years old, had seemed invincible and utterly in control to my eleven-year-old self. Yet Thero had ended up like Mother had always warned he would: tangled up with nefarious activities among bad folks, and unable to extricate himself from it before it was too late.

I had worshipped him growing up. As Mother was far from a nurturing parent and distracted with our youngest brother and simple oldest sister, and Father was constantly working as a shipwright, it was Thero who often looked after me. Yet rare was the time that I felt like a burden. Instead he took me out into the Oedijan streets he loved, showing me his favorite rooftop perches, and instructing me in navigating the streets safely. He showed me the best times and places to eavesdrop on conversations, and how to get those who looked at you with ill intent to disregard you and leave you alone. Reckless he might have been, and most might have frowned upon the places he took me. But at the time, I knew he would always protect me, no matter what happened.

Whoever killed him had dumped him into the canal, likely hoping he'd be washed out to sea before anyone found him. His flesh bloated, horribly disfiguring the handsome face I remembered. My parents had warned me and my siblings not to look, yet I'd never been able to contain my curiosity. Even more, I couldn't shake the feeling that this was all a mistake, that this wasn't Thero, but some other young man caught in the wrong situation at the wrong time. But when I saw his face, even distorted as it was, I knew it was him.

His green eyes had always been laughing in life, but now they were glassy still and discolored with blood. His skin was marbled and puffy. Yet the thing I found strangest was the jagged lines around his eyes. Thin and violet, they were inked into his skin like tatu, but without a discernible pattern or shape. A mess of scars, like lighting in a storm cloud.

Horrified and distraught, I couldn't look away, and Father had to pull me back so they could take him to the furnace and release his spirit to the Pyrthae above. Yet the sight had stayed with me all of these years, as had the lingering mystery of his death. At one point in my self-deluded youth, I had believed I would find his murderer and bring them to justice. I never had, nor even discovered a trace of what had happened. One boy's murder in this polis was too unremarkable to be much noted. Yet still, eleven years later, it sometimes haunted me.

I shook my head and turned to go back inside. But as I did, something flitted by in the corner of my eye. Another finch had alighted on our railing and announced its displeasure at such a wet voyage with a flurry of high-pitched protests. My curiosity was aroused. A bird in the rain promised an urgent message. And a distraction from my morose thoughts.

I murmured to the finch as I drew it under the sheltered alcove and gave it seed. While it ate, I fumbled to untie the wet twine wrapped about its leg, then extricate the case that held a tightly wound scroll. I recognized the seal, a vase set in the wax: Maesos.

The glimmer of excitement faded. Maesos had been my first employer when I'd started this line of work at fifteen. At that time, no one had taken me seriously as a Finch, scoffing either at the profession as a child's invention with no practical value, or simply at my youthful age and lofty sense of self-worth. Yet Maesos had seen something in me. After he hired me on as his shop's clerk, he soon set me loose to gather my whispers, and together we made him the most successful glass smith in Port. Since that time seven years ago, he had remained mine and my companions' most loyal client.

While I always liked to hear from him, it was unlikely he could provide the sort of distraction I craved. Though, with this bird coming in the rain, who knew what he had to say. I cut it open and unraveled it. The message inside was brief and splotchy with moisture, but I could still make out Maesos' scrawl:

My Finch,
> *Visit tomorrow, the earlier the better. I might have the job you've been waiting for.*
> *~Your Gaffer*

My breath caught. With our long history, Maesos wouldn't say he had such a job lightly. For he knew I'd always waited for a hunt to come along where I'd be proud to call myself a Verifier like those of the Order of old. The Order of Verifiers had been a governmental body from over a hundred years ago that had routed out corruption in Oedija. The Conclave disbanded them after just three years of existence, as the Verifiers had been so competent at their jobs that every wealthy patrician and politician feared for their positions. Someday, I wished to have that sort of notoriety, that purity of purpose.

If Maesos' promise held true, it looked like tomorrow would not be the restful day Xaron and Nomusa craved. I smiled and turned back inside. The season was finally starting to look up.

CHAPTER TWO

A FRAGILE SITUATION

Nomusa and Xaron didn't take well to the change of plans. "But we just finished a job," Xaron complained as he lay back on the divan. "Can't it wait a day? I had big plans to stuff myself and practice my juggling."

Nomusa snorted. "You think that's important? I was going to see what I could catch at the taverns. If this is what it sounds like, I might not have another chance for a span — *faresh*, perhaps even longer!"

I crossed my arms. "He said the earlier the better. I'll be waking you both before dawn."

Xaron sat bolt upright. "Before dawn?" he exclaimed, sloshing wine over the already much-stained divan in his violent protest. "That's preposterous!"

I only smiled in response.

True to my word, I roused my wine-logged companions in the gray light before dawn, and with much cajoling and promising, managed to herd them to Maesos' shop within the turn of the sandglass. It was gray and drizzling outside, but my mood was better than it had been all during the season. Xaron, on the other hand, gazed out miserably from the hood of his cloak. "Did it have to be so early?" he complained for the tenth time. "It was supposed to be a day off."

"If you don't want to feel bad," I chided, "you shouldn't drink a barrel of wine at a time. You're not Nomusa."

"I wanted the record," he muttered as Nomusa smirked at him. Unlike

Xaron, she was as alert and ken as ever. As far as a night of wine and revelry went, last night had been a tame occasion for her.

I raised my hand to knock again, but it opened and revealed a familiar grinning face. "Well, if it isn't my favorite Finches!"

"Your only Finches, I hope," I said with a smile, entering as he stepped aside. I would have hugged him, but he had on his glass smithing gear, and I wasn't keen on smearing ash and sweat over myself. As Xaron and Nomusa entered after me, I studied my old friend. His white hair stuck out at odd angles, seared gray at the ends where he hadn't been careful with hot tongs. His shirt, ragged and ridden with holes, hung loosely from his thick body under a dirty apron. But his kindly eyes had always been his best feature and made all the rest endearing.

"Sit down, sit down." Maesos gestured to a few chairs he had out for customers. Xaron gratefully complied, and I politely followed suit, while Nomusa continued to stand. Maesos shook his head with a small smile at her. "Always so stubborn. But no matter — I know you're allergic to small talk when there's interesting business about, Airene."

"Yet here you are, chattering away," I said with an arched eyebrow.

Maesos bellowed a laugh. "Guilty indeed! Well then, here's what I have." He cleared his throat and leaned forward. "Late yesterday, I received word from an acquaintance that a certain patrician, one Agmon of Iris, fell dead in the middle of the evening worship."

"That doesn't mean anything," Xaron protested. "People fall dead all the time. Especially old people." He raised his eyebrows irreverently at Maesos.

The glass smith chuckled. "Indeed they do, though don't expect it of me yet! But it was the manner in which he died that made this curious." He cleared his throat again. "It appears that his, ah, stomach burst open."

"Burst open?" Nomusa said with a frown.

"That's right. And what's more… Red pyrkin spilled out."

I narrowed my eyes. "Hold on. Agmon of Iris… Wasn't he portly, liked styling his beard, particularly fond of red robes lined with gold?"

Maesos nodded. "The very one."

"He owned a glass shop himself, didn't he?" I pressed. "Was it the glassblower who warned you?" Before Maesos could answer, my mind galloped ahead to its own conclusions. "Oh, Eidola above. He's worried that people will think it was you? Some kind of sick way of trying to get ahead of the competition?"

The glass smith laughed nervously. "Sharp as usual, Airene. My dabbling in pyrkin seems to be causing me issues once again."

I glanced around at the man's pieces of glass on display around us. He enhanced the look of his glass through the use of pyrkin, organisms that were like moss but glowed with their own light. It was this feature that gave them their name, as it was assumed pyrkin somehow drew the energy for their luminescence from the Pyrthae. Most Oedijans used pyrkin cultures to light their homes, as it was much cheaper than wood or candles.

But though they were widely used for illumination, pyrkin weren't supposed to be used in other ways. Even including them in glass was skirting the laws that forbade any meddling into the Pyrthaen elements, which had been put in place a century and a half earlier after a period of rule by wardens — as those who channeled magic were called — when a certain group of them had used their powers to brutally rule over the polis. Since their overthrow, wardens had either been confined to the Acadium, which amounted to a prison masquerading as a place of learning, or they were hunted down as feral beasts. Like Xaron would be if he were ever discovered.

Playing with pyrkin wasn't on the same level as being a warden. But if something came along to draw attention to it, it could be just as dangerous.

He cleared his throat. "It was not the glassblower who told me, but another commercial associate of Agmon's. I may not have mentioned him before, as… well. His practices are even more suspect than my own."

I was taken aback by that, and I studied Maesos in this new light. It was disconcerting to hear he kept secrets from me. Yet as little as I liked it, I supposed he was allowed to hold back whatever he liked. "We'd best hear of them now at least."

"Ah, yes." Maesos wrung his hands. "You see, his trade is… tinctures. With its primary ingredient being pyrkin."

That set my mind spinning. Before I could decide which question I wanted to ask, Xaron said incredulously, "Tinctures? He makes drinks with pyrkin? And people actually buy this stuff?"

"There are many strange properties to pyrkin, Xaron," Maesos said, his brow drawing down. "It has the appearance of moss, yet moves as if it were a creature. Most strains emit light constantly and need only water to survive for many years. To say nothing of the unique qualities that each individual variety possesses. So yes, Xaron, people buy and drink his tinctures. And many say they've seen the changes they've desired from them." He touched the balding pate on his head. "By the Eleven, but I could use one for hair growth myself."

Xaron held up his hands. "Fine, fine. But that still has to be illegal."

The glass smith nodded. "Indeed. Which is why I've kept it hidden from you all this time." He glanced at me, an apology in his eyes now. I nodded to him. When he kept a secret to protect a friend, I couldn't hold it against him.

As the moment started to stretch, I asked, "What is the name of this apothecary?"

Maesos hesitated a moment. "Eazal," he said finally. "Eazal of Sandglass."

"Wait," Xaron said, his eyes scrunched up. "Eazal… I know that name." His eyes widened. "Oh. That explains a lot."

"What?" I demanded.

My fellow Finch looked at me. "I've actually met Eazal before."

"That seems unlikely," Nomusa observed drily.

Xaron ignored her. "You know how my mother used to dabble in mixtures herself, right? Well, before her accident, she would meet with apothecaries and other people who created mixtures from around Oedija. One of the few she actually respected for his craft was Eazal." He shook his head. "He didn't strike me as a criminal sort, but I guess I was twelve at the time and wouldn't have known."

I frowned. "I don't suppose you know where he lives?"

Even as Xaron shook his head, Maesos spoke. "Even if you did, he doesn't reside there any longer. In his message, Eazal informed me that he was going to flee in light of everything, as he would be held in the highest suspicion by the Tribunal should his association with Agmon come to light."

I mulled over that. If the Tribunal, the branch of government responsible for administering justice, was already on his trail — as well as, perhaps, whoever had killed Agmon — maybe Xaron's acquaintance with our mysterious apothecary could come in useful. If we could find him.

"While we discover where he's hiding, we may as well visit the sanctuary he died in," I reasoned. "Can you point us in the right direction?"

CHAPTER THREE

AT SANCTUARY DOORS

The Eidolan sanctuary in deme Iris was better preserved than most I'd visited and retained much of its former glory. Its worn pediment rose on six thick columns smeared with a gray patina from their long watch. Etched into the stonework were the eleven Eidola, with the World-Father, Tyurn Sky-Sea, in the center. But the worn faces of the gods said much of how the religion had fallen out of fashion with many Oedijans. Fiery Valemism, a religion centered around an angry, volcanic god from the southern empire of Avvad, had taken the place of Eidolan as the primary religion of Oedija. But despite having some Avvadin cultural inheritance from my father's side, it had never much spoken to me. When I had a craving for the divine or a philosophical itch, I came to the oracles and their sanctuaries for satisfaction.

As Nomusa, Xaron, and I filed through the great doors, an acolyte quickly approached. Glancing down the center aisle over the acolyte's shoulder, I saw a ring of candles in the middle of the floor. Familiar as I was with Eidolan rituals, I knew what this one was erected for: a ward against daemons, the malevolent pyr said to reside in the Pyrthae. They were often blamed for ill happenings, yet I had a feeling such spirits were more myth than reality. I kept my skepticism to myself.

"Welcome, children of Tyurn," the acolyte said hurriedly. "If you would excuse us, some odd happenings have forced us to be less than hospitable. Perhaps we can foster your prayers later—"

Little as I wanted to, I saw I was going to have to bull over this poor acolyte. "We haven't come for prayer," I interrupted him. "We've come about the man who died."

The young man wrung his hands, glancing back towards the candles, or perhaps to the oracle's rooms behind the altar. "I'm afraid I can't speak to you about that. Please, I must insist that you leave."

Nomusa stepped forward. "At least let us speak with the oracle," she said as if it were so reasonable a request he could hardly refuse.

The acolyte's tongue moistened his lips. "Please, my ladies, my sir, I can't—"

"Look!" Xaron pointed back at the candles, and we all turned to see the flickering flames roar up in a dozen conflagrations. It was all I could do not to laugh at how the acolyte jumped and cowered away, even as another part of me groaned at Xaron's recklessness.

"That's a sign we should continue, right?" Xaron continued to string the boy along. "I'm going to take that as a sign." He led the way down the aisle before the acolyte could respond. When it became apparent that the poor boy, shaking and still staring at the candles, wasn't going to stop us, Nomusa and I followed on his heels.

I walked up next to Xaron. "You shouldn't be so blatant with your talents."

He rolled his eyes. "That dullard doesn't know the difference between divinity and divine gifts."

"And you don't know the difference between wisdom and wisecracks," Nomusa said, flanking his other side. "Caution would not be the worst thing to practice from time to time."

Xaron shrugged. "I'll consider it next time you don't need me to save your investigation."

We stopped at the end of the aisle by the circle of candles. I stared at the empty space, as if trying to summon back the image of Agmon's body when he died there. Yet now that Xaron wasn't channeling and scaring acolytes, there was nothing out of the ordinary about the space. Then I saw it: a hint of red glow tucked under one of the front pews. A bit of pyrkin from our unfortunate patrician, I did not doubt. I gestured us on, and my companions and I moved behind the altar to the heavy, blue curtains that guarded the back room, ignoring the acolyte's weak protests for us to stop.

I pushed the curtains aside to reveal a small, circular room with a wizened, bald man in ash-gray robes in the middle of it. The man didn't look up from the book before him as we entered. It was a mammoth thing, half the length of his person, and so heavy it had to be mounted on a pedestal to be handled. We waited for a minute, then two, for him to acknowledge us. In the end, Xaron's impatience won, and he cleared his throat loudly.

"You are the intruders here." The oracle still didn't look up. "Perhaps it would be polite if you first announced your intentions before barging into sanctums."

I shot a glance at Xaron, but he only shrugged. "Our apologies, Father," I said, "but our errand is a hasty one. We were hoping you could—"

"Death is not always a hasty affair," the oracle interrupted, his voice echoing off the close stone walls. "Sometimes, it is slow, ever so slow, almost too slow to bear." He finally looked up at us, a man with petite, shriveled features and watery blue eyes. I thought I saw a twinkle of humor in his expression, though I didn't understand the jape. "So, too, with errands. Perhaps this rush is all of your imagination, would you not agree?"

"If we might, sir," Nomusa said. Her upbringing in her homeland tended to make her polite towards elders. "But the circumstances of this death bring about our urgency. We fear—"

"I know what you fear," the oracle interrupted again, and I couldn't control my mouth twitching. He didn't seem to share Nomusa's penchant for respect. "I know," he repeated, "for it has been echoed by another who has since come."

"Another?" I stepped forward. "Father, if you could tell us, it would be of immeasurable help."

"To whom? Your own selfish aims? Or the glory of the Eleven?" The oracle studied each of us in turn, and I flinched as his eyes lingered on me. "A man's death is nothing to profit from."

A flicker of doubt passed through my mind. It was true enough that I was eager to pursue this case. True also that we would likely profit if we solved it, whether in reputation or monetary gain or, hopefully, both. But that didn't change that we would be bringing justice to a murder. Surely solving such a crime could justify somewhat impure motivations.

But I also knew my history. When I first became a Finch at fifteen, I at least thought then that my intentions were pure. But what fifteen-year-old doesn't dream of glory? And had it truly gone away, even seven years later?

But even if it was my motivation, he couldn't know that. "Of course not," I said briskly. "We're here to see that no one else does. Which is why, Father, it would be helpful if you could tell us who else has inquired after Agmon of Iris."

The oracle raised an eyebrow. "I do not divulge sanctuary secrets to strangers. And you have yet to introduce yourselves."

Xaron gave a cursory bow. "Xaron," he said brightly. "A pleasure to meet you."

Nomusa and I shared a glance, and she rolled her eyes. But when she faced the oracle, she had composed herself and bowed deeply. "Nomusa of Port."

"And I'm Airene of Port," I said with my own bow. "We fashion ourselves Verifiers like those of old."

The oracle squinted at us. "Finches, are you?" His expression lightened, and he gave a short laugh. "I never thought to see Finches flitting about in my lifetime. Not acting with the authority of the Conclave, I trust, but the mission remains the same."

All the coercion, sneaking, and lying we did on a daily basis flashed through my mind. "It does," I said, wanting to believe it. "Can I ask your name, Father?"

The oracle waved his hand impatiently. "I'm an old priest; my name is of no consequence. Call me Father if you must call me anything." He peered at Nomusa with a queer expression. "Or 'sir' — I rather like that one."

A hint of pink colored Nomusa's olive cheeks.

"Well then." The oracle parted through us and pushed aside the curtains. "Let's go take a look."

Sharing glances with each other, Nomusa, Xaron, and I followed him back into the main chamber, where he led us to the ring of candles. "It was in the middle of the interpretation yesterday," the oracle explained, pacing the perimeter. "He scrambled into the aisle and fell to the floor, screaming and clutching at his gut." The oracle shook his head. "A horrible sight. It was worse still when the red glow began in his middle, and then it suddenly—" The oracle spread his hands apart like a fountain.

"He burst," Xaron said with a knowing nod.

The oracle glanced with a sad smile at the acolyte standing at the doors, who watched us warily. "It was not a pleasant mess to clean up."

"Pardon, sir — Father," Nomusa said. "But did Agmon have anyone who bore him a grudge?"

"A jilted lover? An estranged brother? A disappointed mother?" Xaron hazarded guesses.

The oracle shook his head. "None that I know of. I cannot tell you of his confessions, for those are between the gods and him. But of what I know... no, I know of no enemies." He paused, his eyes seeming to search about his sanctuary. "However... a woman visited here who indicated an interest in his passing."

I kept my expression carefully neutral. "What did she say?"

"Little enough, yet she left a distinct impression. She wished to know how he died, which I, of course, did not divulge. After all, I don't go around spreading gossip."

Xaron snorted.

"Then she said some strange things, all regarding the importance that I not spread what happened here to anyone." The oracle flashed a brief smile. "I always was a rebellious man, Tyurn forgive me."

I wondered who this woman was. "What did she look like?"

The oracle shook his head. "When you live as long as I do, faces start to blend together. But what I can tell you is that the woman had hair like fresh ice."

I frowned. Outlanders from the western seas had light-colored hair, but blue was a sight I had yet to see. "Thank you," I said to the oracle with another bow. "If we discover who was behind Agmon's death, we'll be sure to bring them to justice."

The old man smiled at each of us in turn, and to my surprise, bowed deeply. "Nothing would please me more. None was more generous to the sanctuary than Agmon. But be careful. Death can come to the young as well as the old." With one last significant glance, he returned behind his thick curtains.

———

"Where do you get hair like that?" Xaron wondered as we exited the sanctuary. "I could go for some orange hair myself."

"I would have thought we'd have heard of hair of that color before," Nomusa mused.

I shrugged. "Oedija hides all sorts of characters. Maybe she lives in one of the outer demes—"

I stopped mid-sentence as a man stepped out from around one of the columns not six paces away from us. The man, Avvadin by the look of him, leaned against the column and stared at us with a lazy smile. He wore a fez half tilted off his long greasy hair, and though it was cool outside, his stained shirt was unlaced down to his chest and his sky-blue vest flapped open. His trousers were smudged and dirty as if it had been years since they'd seen a wash, much less a good scrubbing. The straps of his sandals seemed wont to snap at any moment. Yet for all that, he had bright, honey-brown eyes that seemed to pierce through my clean garments, as if to see all the dirty secrets I hid behind them. I tried not to notice the tone of his muscles beneath his vest, nor the strong line of his jaw beneath the suspiciously clean jaw.

"Hanim," the Avvadin said. His eyes flickered to Xaron briefly but seemed content to settle on Nomusa and me. "If it pleases you to pause a moment…"

"We don't want to buy anything," Xaron said, starting to walk past him, but I held Xaron back. The man's arm was turned towards us so that I could plainly see that on the inside of his left wrist was the unmistakable glow of the shrouded eye tatu. Nomusa hissed, indicating she'd seen it as well.

The man's smile thinned. "I see we understand each other now."

Xaron followed our gazes, and his eyes widened. "A Guilder?"

I was just as surprised. The Underguild, the syndicate of thieves and organized crime in Oedija and elsewhere across the Four Realms, had its agents in many places. But here at an Eidolan sanctuary was not where I expected to find one. We knew he was a Guilder from his mark, a tatu formed from a glowing blue ink that was said to be impossible to falsify.

The Guilder shrugged. "Is it such a surprise considering what you've just discovered? My masters are very interested in the death of Agmon of Iris. Would we not be interested, too, in anyone else so pressed to investigate it?"

"I'd rather you leave us out of it," Xaron muttered.

I took his arm and gently squeezed, hoping he would understand the need for silence. The Underguild was not an organization to be taken lightly.

The man saw my gesture, and his leer widened. "She keeps you on a tight leash, does she not, Xaron of Port?"

Xaron flinched at his name, and Nomusa spoke in his defense. "How do you know him?"

"I know all of you." His gaze slid over us, greasy as a skewer of street stand meat. "Nomusa, a fugitive from her own ishaka. Her family, once the rulers of the chiefdom, were overthrown by usurpers, and her parents killed in the process. Forced into exile, she came to live with — what do you Bali call that relation again, the wife of your uncle? A bond-sister? Ah, but it doesn't matter now, for she's been dead for, how long now, six years?"

Nomusa hissed, but she couldn't deny the truth of it. I stared in growing fear at this man, and all the more as he turned towards me.

"And you," the Guilder said. "Airene of Port now, but you grew up in Riverport. Oedijan your whole life. However…" He held up a finger. "Your parentage is, regrettably, questionable. But not all women stay faithful when they tire of their husbands, hm?"

I tried to deny the holes his words bore into me. I was curious about most mysteries I came across. But my mother's dalliances was one I never wanted to know anything more of, much less hear mentioned casually to me by a stranger. "And who are you?" I asked, hating the way my voice trembled.

"It's only fair for me to tell you, isn't it?" He paced back across the steps of the sanctuary. "Talan, you can call me. But it's not all of my name. If you wish to know the rest, you'll have to discover it yourselves."

"Well, Talan," Nomusa said in a tight voice, "are you going to tell us your reason for revealing our life stories in the middle of the streets or not?"

Talan smirked. "Indeed I will. Now that you are impressed by the depth of my knowledge and are convinced of my prescience, you will believe me when I tell you the location of the man you seek."

I gave a short laugh, but didn't say anything. I didn't want to reveal that it wasn't a man we sought now, but a woman.

The Guilder looked at me. "Ah, you must think I've forgotten the silver-haired woman who visited here." He shook his head with another infuriating smile. "But it is not her I mean, but a man with more accessible information. One Eazal of Sandglass."

The humor drained from me, and fear began creeping up in its place. Though he offered us honey, I did not like the flavor of his extensive knowledge, and trusted him with it less.

"What do you know of him?" Xaron demanded.

"His location, as I said. Or are you not interested?"

"Don't play coy with us, Guilder." Nomusa put her hands on her hips. "If you mean to tell us what you know, then be out with it."

"As you wish," Talan said, studying his nails. "Go to an inn in Bazaar called the Weeping Hills. There, you will find your man."

Even though I didn't trust this Guilder, I knew I would set off for Bazaar at once. But I wasn't yet satisfied. "Why tell us this?" I demanded. "Why not go yourself if you're so interested?"

The smile was back, wider than before. "I come as a sort of benefactor. Your spiritual guide, perhaps. A pyr made flesh."

Xaron snorted next to me, and Talan nodded appreciatively.

I crossed my arms. "That's not an answer."

"Then perhaps you should ask a better question." Talan gave a mocking bow, then turned and walked away. I watched until he slipped into an alley and out of sight.

We three Finches were left to stare at each other, until Xaron threw up his hands. "What in the dark depths of the 'Thae was that? Was he waiting the whole time we were in the sanctuary to put on that performance?"

"He does have a flair for the dramatic," I observed drily.

Nomusa adjusted her hair. "I like him. He's certainly more amusing than other Guilders we've met."

I shook my head. "Please. Take any other man to bed. Just not him."

She gave me an amused look. "What? Do you have eyes for him then?"

Xaron looked between us with amazement. "Him? He had half a year's mud on him!"

"I think we have more important things to do," I said loudly. "Like maybe visit that inn?" I set off in the direction of Bazaar before either of them could protest. But as little as I wished to talk about Talan, I couldn't help but look for our enigmatic Guilder in every shadow we passed.

CHAPTER FOUR

THE PYRTHAEN APOTHECARY

Half a turn later, we entered the weather-stained door of the Weeping Hills. It wasn't situated on the finest of Bazaar streets, but it was a clean and well-maintained establishment. Decorated in the dreary Avvadin style, its ceiling was composed of slats of nearly black wood, and red tapestries hung from its walls. The clientele was similarly Avvadin, with fezzes, turbans, and beads adorning the heads of men and women, as well as a number of beards. The plates were chipped, the utensils tarnished, and while the visitors didn't appear to be paupers, the wear of their clothes left much to be desired. An out-of-the-way inn, perfect for a man to hide unnoticed.

I cast a look around, but as expected, I didn't see our apothecary in the main living area. Time for a bit of investigation, then. I glanced at Nomusa. "You ready?" I muttered.

"When am I not?" she whispered back.

We approached the innkeeper's counter, where a portly man with red and silver beads hanging from his mustache sat scratching in a ledger. He glanced up at us without much interest — until, that is, Nomusa leaned over the counter. While she hadn't worn robes any more licentious than usual, her usual left enough skin exposed to draw the eye of most men, and a number of women as well.

"Hello there," Nomusa said in a low voice, her eyes locked onto the innkeeper.

The man ogled her, his eyes traveling up and down her figure almost reluctantly. "Yes?" he asked uncertainly.

Her hand traced over the countertop, inching closer to where he sat on the other side. "I have something I need."

The innkeeper swallowed. "And what would that be? A room, perhaps?"

"Aren't you a forward one?" Nomusa arched an eyebrow at him.

The man flushed and spluttered, "But I didn't mean—"

"I am teasing, of course," Nomusa interrupted smoothly. "I am, however, here to seek the company of another man. One of your patrons, Eazal, sent a bird for me. Apparently, he is in need of some… comfort."

The innkeeper's eyes wandered to myself and Xaron standing behind her. "Ah. But what are your companions here for?"

"To safeguard my virtue," Nomusa said in a lightly barbed tone. "If you could but tell me which room he is staying in, we'll leave you to your… ledgers."

Innkeeper looked from one of us to the other, finally landing on Nomusa. "I'm afraid I cannot do that," he said, the words seeming to cost him. "Without permission, I do not give out the location of my guests. My apologies, hanim."

But he had told us more than he knew. I hid a smile. The Guilder had told the truth. Our apothecary was here.

Nomusa sighed dramatically. "Come, then," she said to Xaron and me, and she swept across the common room. I felt the eyes of the innkeeper as well as many of his patrons upon us as we crossed the floor to the stairs. I expected the various strongmen across the room to stop us, but not one of them shifted as we ascended the stairs. Whether it was because of Nomusa's lingering influence on the innkeeper or a lax security, I could not tell.

Once we were on the floor above, we stared down the cramped hallway that continued in either direction, dingy doors lining the walls. Stairs led up to a third floor with assumedly even more rooms. I sighed. We were so close to Eazal, yet locating him among these rooms — and convincing him to open the door — might prove more difficult than the first step.

"I did my part," Nomusa said, crossing her arms. "Someone else will have to figure out how to find him."

Xaron screwed up his eyes in concentration for a moment before a smile spread across his face. "Wait. I know something I could try."

I had a feeling I knew what it would relate to. "Not in the middle of an inn," I hissed.

But Xaron had gotten the idea in his head now, and he wasn't going to let go. Always eager to use his abilities no matter if they would help or not, it was a wonder he hadn't been caught yet. "Look," he said, kneeling in the middle of the hallway. "This is all it is." He pressed his fingertips to the floorboards and closed his eyes. I knew he'd begun to channel.

I sighed and nodded at the stairs. "Can you watch there?" I said to Nomusa. "I'll watch the doors."

Nomusa nodded and took up her position.

"Quiet," Xaron hissed. "I can't hear."

I crouched down next to him. "What are you doing?" I whispered.

He cracked an eye open. "Trying to listen. And you keep interrupting me."

I gave him an incredulous look. "Listening? I thought you were channeling."

Xaron sighed. "Sound is no more than vibrations, Airene. And vibrations use the same energy as kinesis. If I concentrate very hard, I might be able to feel the movements of the guests and know which rooms are occupied." He jerked upright. "Or I guess I can feel that," he muttered.

I shared a look with Nomusa. "Feel what?"

Xaron stood and pointed down the hall. "There. Whatever Eazal has done with pyrkin, it's left behind a… trace." He shrugged. "I don't know how else to explain it. It's like hot oil left in a pan. When I open myself up to it, it burns and makes it pretty obvious where it's splashing from."

As usual, talk of the Pyrthaen awoke both curiosity and uneasiness in me. Knowing I would never fully understand what Xaron was talking about would drive me mad if I thought too long on it. "We'll take your word for it. Quietly, now."

We crept down the hallway towards the door Xaron had pointed to. I winced at every creak, but nothing could be done for it. Finally, Xaron indicated we were in front of the door, and I took a deep breath and knocked.

There was no reply for a long moment. "Yes?" a hoarse voice said from within.

"Eazal of Sandglass," I called through the thick wood. "We need to speak with you. If you could open up for a moment—"

"I'm sorry," the apothecary cut me off. "I have suffered from a long illness and need to rest. If you'll return another time…"

Xaron leaned into the doorway. "Eazal? This is Xaron, the son of Jihu. Do you remember her?"

There was a long pause on the other side of the door. "Yes, I remember," Eazal replied softly. "We haven't spoken since her accident."

"It's actually about her that we need to speak," Xaron continued spinning out the lie. "Can you open up for us?"

Another long pause. "Thank you for visiting, Xaron. But I must refuse.

As I said, you've caught me at a poor time. Please, if you would leave me alone."

Xaron shrugged helplessly at us, but I had an idea. "That's actually why we're here, Eazal," I said, pressing close to the door. "Jihu heard what happened, and she wanted us to help you."

I held my breath as we waited for his reply. Suddenly, I heard the bolt on the door sliding, and the door creaked open. "Come in," came the hoarse reply. "I must trust that Jihu wouldn't send her son to murder me."

With that foreboding greeting, I pressed inside. The room was dark and lit by a single pot of violet pyrkin in the far corner. By the low light, I saw the furnishings were even more modest than the common room down-stairs, with a single narrow bed pressed against the wall, a table that held the pyrkin pot, and a chair by the shuttered window. In the middle of the floor on a small, shabby rug stood our apothecary. His features were shad-owed, but from the way the darkness fell on him, I could tell he was gaunt. As he turned his face towards us and the light hit him, I also saw he was middle-aged, just old enough to have a child around our age.

"Come in," Eazal said. "I have trusted you this far. I may as well see what help it is you offer."

As we stepped inside and closed the door, I hoped we weren't misplacing our trust as well.

The door shut. We all stood in silence for a moment, examining each other, until Xaron broke it. "You look older than the last time I saw you," he said cheerfully.

The apothecary turned his hollowed eyes towards him, and I squirmed with discomfort. But rather than take offense, the shadow of a smile appeared on his thin lips. "Yes," he agreed, "I do. As do you, Xaron, though I still recognize your voice."

Xaron gave a brief bow. "Jihu sends you her greetings. She would have come herself, but as you may know, she doesn't leave the house much since her accident."

"Yes. I remember this. It's been many years since I've seen or heard from her." Eazal bowed his head.

We lapsed into silence. I thought of how to best approach the subject at hand, but it was Eazal who spoke next. "So. You claim to have come to my aid. Yet I know of nothing you could do."

I couldn't hold my tongue any longer. "We should start by you setting our facts straight. We know the basics of your predicament, but if we're going to help, we need to know everything."

Xaron and Nomusa both cast me disapproving looks, while Eazal stared at me with his expression carefully composed. "Of course," he answered slowly. "Ask your questions, and I will answer them as I can."

"Your partner was murdered," I stated bluntly. "Agmon of Iris. Do you know who did it?"

Eazal hesitated, then nodded. "Yes."

My pulse quickened, and I only barely held my tongue, waiting. But the apothecary offered no further information.

"Could you tell us?" Xaron probed gently.

Another breath, then a shake of his head. "Not yet," Eazal murmured. "But please, ask your other questions."

So he didn't completely trust us yet. I couldn't blame him, though I found I had to rein in my patience all the same. "Did you know he was going to be murdered?"

Eazal's eyes flickered, then he shook his head. "No. Not exactly. There were… disagreements. Hesitations. And other arrangements had been made. But I did not believe it would come to that."

"You must say more than that, Eazal," Xaron chided. "You're barely telling us anything."

The apothecary looked to him. "These aren't people to cross, Xaron. I only speak as much as I believe safe for you to know. If you were to learn too much… I do not doubt they would do the same to you as they did to Agmon." He bowed his head. "As they have done, I believe, to many other people."

I stared at the man. I had thought he spoke vaguely to protect himself. Now I saw him in a new light: he was trying to protect us. I thought also of who might inspire such fear. One organization came to mind, particular considering the mysterious visitor who had waited for us outside the Eidolan sanctuary. But this — widespread murder, from the sound of it — wasn't the Underguild I knew. True, they made examples of those who broke their shadow-rules. But this was brutal coercion, not subtle enforcement. It had to be some other group I didn't yet know of.

"Can you tell us of these other victims?" Nomusa asked, glancing at the door. I suddenly understood why. We hadn't been exactly discreet in our inquiries after him. And if these people had the influence to scare Eazal this much, we might be in increasing danger the longer we stayed.

Predictably, Eazal shook his head. "I'm sorry. Perhaps this wasn't a good idea after all."

"Please, Eazal," Xaron pleaded, extending a hand towards him. "Let us help you."

The man shrank back from his touch, fading into the corner where his bed was tucked against. "No, Xaron. I think it is best that you leave now."

I felt the sands of time streaming away from us, measured in the quick beat of my heart. We didn't have time for any more delays. "Eazal," I said severely. "Your partner was murdered yesterday. And from what you say, more people will be killed soon. We might be able to prevent that. But if you keep what you know secret, you'll be just as responsible for their deaths as whoever is doing this."

The apothecary seemed to really look at me for the first time. "Who are you people?" he asked in a low voice.

"Finches," Xaron replied easily with a shrug. "So will you help us or not?"

Eazal looked at him, then Nomusa, finally resting on me. He breathed out a heavy sigh. "I suppose this was bound to come crashing down sooner rather than later," he muttered. Louder, he said, "At the tenth turn of the night, our contact will arrive at the manor of a recently elected Servant, one Feiyan of Port."

Feiyan — my mouth twisted in disgust, an expression mirrored by my companions. We had all heard rumors of the way that spider had obtained her power and position. Yet all the bribery, extortion, and framing she had conducted to make her commercial ventures successful had been done with such a light touch that we had never had enough solid whispers to put an end to her illicit activities. I wasn't surprised to hear she was tangled up in this, yet another shady business dealing.

"Be there," Eazal continued, "and you will know the face I know of the one whom you seek." He paused. "And perhaps you will discover why you should abandon your questioning into this. Think of your mother, Xaron."

Xaron shook his head with mock mournfulness. "A low trick, my long-ago uncle, and one to which I've been long immune." He bowed to the apothecary. "But thank you for what you've given us so far. And if you have more to confess, you can find us at—"

"Send a bird to Port's aviary," I interrupted him. The last thing we needed was to be giving out Canopy's location. "We'll arrange a meeting via finch."

Eazal met my eyes. From his look, I suspected we would not be hearing from him again.

"Now," the apothecary murmured, "I am sorry to appear rude, but you three should leave."

Nomusa opened the door with a furtive glance into the hallway. "You might consider a new location," she said back to the apothecary. "Too many people know where you are."

He gave a thin smile. "There isn't a place in Oedija I could hide. But I appreciate the advice."

With one last look back, we exited the apothecary's room, closing the door behind us. As we walked back down the hallway, the bolt clicked back in place. I hoped it wouldn't be the last time we saw him alive.

"Well then," Xaron said. "I guess we have a rendezvous to catch?"

I nodded. "We should take carts or we'll miss it."

"If you're willing to spending the coin for carts," Nomusa said drily, "it must be desperate."

Our squabbling cut off as we entered the common room again. Suddenly, the patrons I had assumed to be innocent now seemed to be watching us, while the licentious innkeeper seemed to have a malicious glint to his eyes. With a shiver of paranoia, I shuffled us quickly out of the inn and onto the street.

CHAPTER FIVE

THE SERVANT OF PORT

Our three cartmen bore us across the city in a turn and a half. As we dismounted and paid them, they wheeled off, shining with sweat and their purses jingling with nickel magnes. As for my companions and I, we had to straighten our hair and beat the dust off our clothes. We'd paid the men well for the quick ride, but no amount of tip could keep the trip from being an uncomfortable and dirty one. But in a city where people were in a greater supply than beasts of burden, we used what transportation we had.

Having had the cartmen let us off a little ways from Servant Feiyan's compound, we walked the last bit on foot, keeping under the overhanging apartments and hoping the shadows and night would hide us from any watching eyes. Soon, her manor came into view. Pressing against the wall of a shop, we peered around the corner at it. Xaron whistled as we looked over the sprawling compound. "You don't see that everyday in Port."

It wasn't the richest estate we'd ever seen, certainly not more than many in Iris and Bazaar, two of the richer demes of Oedija. Yet rising on a hill from the row of other houses and shops, it was practically a palace here in Port. Composed of an estate that stretched out towards a cliff, it encompassed a dozen times more space than any of its neighbors. Small gestures towards opulence had also been made in its decorations, but it seemed to me a performance more than a genuine display of extravagance. Feiyan's rise may have been meteoric, but her coffers — and power — weren't without their limits.

I pressed back against the shop wall. "Now I suppose we wait."

"Not for long," Nomusa murmured. "The glass mounted in the last forum read nine and a half turns. Eazal's intermediary could be here at any moment."

She was quickly proven correct. Barely a quarter-turn after we'd arrived, there was movement out of the darkness. I squinted at the figure approaching the manor gate, but it wasn't until it stood before the two mounted pyr lamps that I saw the flash of silver. My breath caught. "It's her. The woman from the sanctuary."

"You'd think they'd send a less distinctive emissary," Nomusa muttered.

"Well, here she is." Xaron looked between Nomusa and me. "Do you have any bright ideas, or can I do what I'm best at now?"

I shared a look with Nomusa. We'd briefly discussed what to do once we saw the contact earlier, but hadn't come to any consensus. Just seeing her in association with the Servant wasn't enough to get us very far in finding out who was behind Agmon's murder. To locate our next lead, we had to actually overhear the conversation between Feiyan and this intermediary. Which called for a house-break.

It was exactly the last thing we wanted to do.

Five years before, near the beginning of when Nomusa and I started working together as Finches, we didn't have many rules in our quest to succeed. Only one: no house-breaks. If we couldn't hear the whispers by other means, we figured we weren't worth our salt as Verifiers.

Of course, we only made this rule after Nomusa convinced me to break into a whorehouse owner's private solar, and I was nearly caught by the burliest woman I have ever seen. Needless to say, the experience was bruising enough to keep both Nomusa and me adherent to the rule.

Until, that is, Xaron came along two years ago and turned everything upside. We met Xaron when he broke into a house that we had been staking out to find out who had stolen a pair of trousers, an incident more significant than it sounds on its face. After a series of misunderstandings, he ended up moving into Canopy with us and becoming a Finch.

I had tried my best to ensure all of us stuck to our rule of no house-breaks. But as a warden, Xaron's gifts sometimes made it too easy to consider breaking it when options became limited. Like now, for instance.

I didn't want Xaron to do it. I didn't want him to feel eager like he always did when he had a chance to use his magic beyond the simple parlor tricks he practiced in Canopy. If he was caught, it wouldn't just mean imprisonment like it would for Nomusa and I. Living as a feral warden outside the confines of the Acadium warranted death. And with the law enforced by Shepherds, battle-trained wardens who were indoctrinated into the rules of the demotism, it was no mean risk. But I saw no other option than to give up, and resign ourselves to potentially more people dying at the hands of this woman's master.

Nomusa nodded her assent, and I sighed. "Fine. You can do it."

Xaron immediately started to head away, but I arrested him with a hand on his arm. "But if you run into trouble, give us the signal. All right?"

He flashed a grin. "I won't need to." The next moment, he had taken off at a lope, sticking to shadows on the opposite side of the compound. No doubt he searched the perimeter for the best entry point.

I watched him disappear into the darkness. Suddenly, I found myself wishing we'd taken the time to stop by Canopy. There, I had a Finch mask and a Tribunal medallion I might have used in case he did need our aid. Even if he gave the signal, at this moment, I had no idea what we could to do help.

Then an idea occurred to me.

"I have to go somewhere," I told Nomusa hurriedly.

"What?" she hissed, eyes narrowing. "Where are you going? We have to make sure Xaron makes it out safely."

"That's what I intend to do." I quickly told her my plan before I hurried off into the dark alleys of Oedija.

CHAPTER SIX

HOUSE-BREAK

XARON

It wasn't the first cliff Xaron had climbed, but it was certainly the tallest. Strolling towards the dock so that he was nearly at the base of the cliff, he craned his neck back. The cliff was exposed for the most part, but if he continued further into the inlet, the opposite stone face leaned closer and cast part of the ascent in shadow. He smiled, thinking that Feiyan must enjoy this private view often during the day. At night, it was Xaron's to claim.

Having circled the Servant's compound, he'd determined that his best bet for infiltrating the estate would be to ascend the cliff. At seventy spans high, that was no mean feat. But Xaron just smiled to look at it. If he knew himself at all, he was up to the task.

And he was itching to channel.

Glancing around to make sure no one watched or followed, he made his way over the boulders towards the cove. He could have launched himself over the rough terrain with a burst of kinesis, but even he wasn't so foolish as to waste his strength on convenience. Still, as he hopped from stone to stone, his hands and feet itched, the energy of the Pyrthae pressing at his fingertips and toes. It had been too long since he'd had a chance to properly channel beyond the little that Airene and Nomusa allowed him within Canopy.

And the things he could do if he were allowed. He'd scaled walls in a single jump. He'd performed acrobatics every bit as complicated as the men at the gymnasiums. Once, when a Shepherd had tailed him, he'd vaulted over rooftops to escape. And the tricks with radiance he could perform — juggling fire, casting simple illusions, bursts of light as distractions. He was gifted with this power, yet was told by everyone around him that he couldn't use it.

Once, he'd lived in a place where he wasn't restricted. After he'd left his home at seventeen for refusing to stop channeling, he'd found a commune of other feral wardens, and Graz, their leader, took him under his wing. Like Xaron himself, Graz and the others had believed that those with an attunement to the Pyrthae shouldn't be treated as the detritus of the polis, either shooed into the Acadium to live out their days in repression and among dusty books, or made into the brutal Shepherds who forced other wardens into the same choice. No, they believed they had a right to be exactly who they were, and lived following that shared belief. For two glorious years, Xaron had seen a different future than had been promised for his whole life up until that point.

And then the Shepherds had come.

He had been out purchasing food for the coming span when they came. When he returned, two satchels of bread and fruit slung over his shoulders, he found their home blackened and smoldering. He wanted to run inside, to see if they'd died in the flames or had been taken away, but he hadn't had the courage. Everyone in the vicinity would know that house had been blighted with the daemonic presence of feral wardens. If he was associated with it, he, too, could meet their same fate.

So instead, he ran, never to know for sure what had happened to his friends.

But even two years later, he still carried on their belief as best he could. Sure, he was cautious, or as cautious as he could compel himself to be. But he still channeled everyday, even if it was just a little. He wouldn't let the world around press him into forgetting who he truly was. He would carry on their small rebellion for them. And hopefully, their deaths would someday not be in vain.

Xaron slipped down a large, slick stone and found where he would begin his climb: a recess in the rock that crawled up most of the cliff and was spiderwebbed with cracks perfect for toe and finger grips. Wiping his sweaty palms, he forced himself to breathe through the sudden gurgling in his stomach. He was just excited, he told himself.

He reached the lowest cracks and gingerly put his fingers in them, testing how they held his weight. He'd always known he had long fingers and toes, but suddenly they seemed far too fragile for this task. He breathed in, then out. Only one way to fix that.

He channeled. It was a test, just a few small streams of kinesis to his digits to reinforce their strength, but he felt the difference as he gripped the stone and lifted himself up. He easily clung to the handholds now. It didn't, however, strengthen his arms and legs. He had to be careful, or he'd wear himself out. That, or he'd tear his limbs off with an erratic burst. Just as his magic conferred power, it came with inherent risks as well. But there was little point in dwelling on those possibilities now.

Before he began the climb, he studied the wall again. When he'd first had this idea, he'd humored himself with the fantasy of clearing the cliff in three jumps. Now he saw how foolish that plan had been. It was far too risky and noisy. He'd have to go the long, slow, boring way. With a sigh, he began to climb.

It was easy going at first, and the cracks were plentiful and easily within reach. But a third of the way up, Xaron realized he was headed towards trouble. Not only were his arms quickly tiring, but as he looked ahead in the low light for his next handholds, he saw they grew thinner and further apart. It should have scared him, and his upset stomach told him it probably did. But mostly, he felt the itch of anticipation. Energy flowed through him. He could do this, would do this. After all, what kind of warden was he if he couldn't?

He picked his way up the wall until he couldn't find the next firm handhold, a little less than two-thirds of the way up, then braced himself. He checked the flow of the elements inside him and allowed in a bit more kinesis. He felt the rock groan beneath his fingers as the pressure from the magic increased. He looked up again for the spot he was aiming for. From where he was, it'd be a long leap. But he didn't stop to let doubt seep in. Bracing his legs and flexing his arms, he channeled kinesis in a huge burst and threw himself up the cliff.

He flew. Lifting off the rock face, his old handholds crumbled as he exploded kinesis into them and propelled himself towards the sky. He was twenty spans from the top, ten spans, five — but he was slowing. At the moment of suspension, still a few spans from the top, the horrible realization that he wasn't going to make it slammed into him. He reached out, his hand shy of the cliff's lip. Panic reared inside him, and he began flailing about him as if something might appear out of nowhere for him to grab. But he was too far away. There was nothing around him but air.

Xaron began to fall.

But he wasn't out of ideas yet. Thrusting his legs out beneath him, he pulled at every bit of magic he had access to and directed kinesis towards his feet. Pure force rippled behind him as he tried to use the very air to propel him forward. His gut ached as his locus, the center point of his connection the Pyrthae, strained from channeling so much energy, and his limbs burned from directing it. But he wasn't falling anymore, and bit by bit, he moved closer to the cliff's edge. Xaron gritted his teeth and pushed harder, engaging his hands in it as well. An arm's length away, a hand's breadth—

He reached out and grabbed the stone lip of the edge of the cliff and clung to it like a drowning sailor to a rope. Fully aware of the sear from too much channeling, Xaron cut the streams off abruptly and let his body fall against the cliff. He was pouring sweat, but as he pulled himself to safety, he grinned. He'd done it. Close call regardless, he'd done it.

He flipped onto his back and looked up at the cloudy sky laced with green tendrils from the radiant winds when his breath caught at a thought. When he'd leaped that final distance, he'd channeled enough kinesis to break stone. How much noise had he made? He didn't hear any alarms sounding or footsteps approaching, but he knew he couldn't lie in repose for long.

Ignoring his leaden limbs, Xaron sat upright and crawled to the low stone barrier that ran along the cliff's edge. Listening, he detected a faint whisper on the other side, perhaps two guards in quiet conversation. Xaron risked a peek over the wall. Shadowy forms littered the courtyard, but he quickly saw they were not guards, but statues and fountains and other ornamentation. Only a lone guard stood with a pyr lamp in the whole the courtyard, and he shone his beam into the darkness toward the docks. Either he hadn't made as much noise as he'd thought, or this guard was deafer than stone.

Ducking back down, Xaron took a deep breath, then once more opened himself up to the Pyrthae. Power streamed through him, starting in his belly and spreading to his limbs. Though it hurt as it flowed, he sighed with relief. He never felt more alive than when he channeled; the rest of existence without it seemed drab and dull-edged. Sitting up and peering over once more, he saw the guard still staring out over the dock and took his chance. Slipping over the wall, he slinked across the courtyard in a crouch. By channeling a small stream of kinesis to soften his footfalls, he barely made a whisper as he passed. He moved around the curves of fountains, around the edges of gardens, behind benches and chairs so that he was soon ten paces behind the guard, the man's mutterings plain to hear.

"Every damn night…" the man said. "Every damn night she goes out. And what's she have to say for it? 'What would you have me do, Eg? Stay in the house all the time?' Like that's a punishment. Like I don't work every night for her to do just that. What I wouldn't give to be home right now…"

Stifling a chuckle, Xaron slipped past the guard to the door. Opening it without the guard hearing or seeing would be difficult, but Xaron had just the trick for it. Channeling radiance, he repressed its shining properties, and instead let it spread in a thin sheet before him, covering his way to the door. If it worked as he'd practiced in Canopy — employed then to steal the last mango without his fellow Finches noticing — he'd be reflecting back a similar environment as was around him. It would look strange to the guard if he looked too closely at it, but Xaron hoped it would at least disguise his movement. As for sound, Xaron would have to trust to fate and hope that Feiyan was one of those masters who wouldn't tolerate a squeaky hinge.

Placing his hand on the handle, Xaron held his breath as he gently pulled. It swung silently open a crack. Just a little wider, and he'd be able to slip through with the guard none the wiser—

The hinge screeched.

The guard spun, his lamp shining straight at where Xaron crouched. Xaron froze, natural instincts urging him to hide, even though he had no better cover around than his shield of radiance. With the light on his illusion, he didn't know whether it was better to move out of the way or not, so he froze in indecision.

"What in the high heights of the 'Thae...?" the guard muttered, walking forward and staring at where Xaron crouched. What he saw, Xaron didn't know. Perhaps it looked like a piece of wall floating disembodied from it. Or perhaps he couldn't see the door at all. The shield drew its images from the environment around, but what exactly it drew, Xaron hadn't refined his magic enough to know.

The guard was only six paces away, his hand outstretched toward Xaron's radiance shield, when Xaron finally willed himself to move. Just as he did, the guard flinched. Xaron cringed; the wall must have moved in the guard's eyes. There was nothing for it but to move quickly and slip through the door, then quickly close it behind. Blessedly, as he escaped while the guard still stared in confusion, the hinges were quiet this time. Just before the door shut, he heard the final gasp from the guard as the illusion shifted once again, then the sealed door shut out all sound.

Walking quickly, Xaron dispelled the radiance shield and slunk his way through the nearly complete darkness. If the guard decided to come through, casting another radiance shield would likely only provoke further curiosity. Xaron needed to truly disappear. He blindly felt his way along the wall, his pounding blood the only thing he could hear. His fingers drifted along an open doorframe, and Xaron, breathing a prayer to any god who would listen, moved behind it.

No sooner had he done so than the outside door opened. "Hello?" the guard called softly. Xaron heard him take one step in, then two. Light flickered on the doorframe. His stomach churned, and he waited for the guard to step through and spot him. But after a few quick breaths, the man just muttered to himself, and his retreating steps echoed in the room. The door closed once again.

He let out a heavy sigh. He was inside and undiscovered. But the worst was still to come. Now he had to sneak through the grounds — and get out — without being detected.

Nothing for it but to keep moving.

Channeling a tiny tongue of fire for light, Xaron navigated his way through the dark rooms, half-bent over just in case he needed to hide or bolt. Twice he nearly bumped into a fragile vase or other decoration, but he corrected himself just in time. He had no idea where he was, or even where he was trying to go. As this thought rattled around his head, he became more and more uncertain of what he was even trying to do here. Had he infiltrated her compound just to prove to he could do it? Was this about upholding what Graz and the others had believed, or just making himself look good before his accomplices?

Xaron shook his head and focused back on his current predicament. There'd be time enough to contemplate his motivations later if he made it back out. He had nearly reached another closed doorway through a room that looked to be an entertainment hall when the door opened. Xaron immediately extinguished his light and ducked behind a table. He didn't have much cover. All it would take was a glance from the guard to be caught.

But it wasn't a guard who walked through. The woman who entered the room looked to be little older than Xaron was, and though her eyes were shadowed, Xaron thought they had the distinctive narrow shape of his people, the Qao Fu. From the way she strode across the room, walking in front of the man who was with her, he knew this must be the matron of the estate, Servant Feiyan herself.

"It seems like common sense," Feiyan observed mildly to her companion. "I didn't think I needed to tell her explicitly that making sculptures of other people's ponds is rude."

Sculptures from ponds? Xaron didn't know what to make of that. He kept listening as they were hidden from view behind the table.

"Perhaps she believes she did you a service," the man next to her offered. "After all, it is quite a nice sculpture."

They stepped around the table, and Xaron was almost as surprised at the flippant tone he used with the Servant as he was at his appearance. From his shaved head and tin spiral earrings, this man was an honor, one of the caste in Oedija relegated to servitude. This honor, however, wore rich robes far beyond his station, and had none of the submissiveness of other honors Xaron had met. He knew little what to make of it all.

"Quite," Feiyan replied sourly. "Just what I wanted: a feral sculpting her image in my garden."

Now his heart was pumping. Feral, she'd said. He had a strong suspicion he knew who they were referring to as well. Suddenly, his unease doubled at the task before him.

"Truly, who does she think she is?" the Servant continued to gripe. "Coming with her commands, as if I were nothing but a common honor."

"Ouch," the honor said mildly.

The smile she shared with him seemed that of friends. Bewildered, Xaron wondered just who this honor was.

Feiyan faced forward again and exhaled noisily. "Time to be the Servant again. Try not to let me say something that might get myself killed."

"Isn't that why you keep me around?"

They entered through another doorway.

Xaron knew he had to hear more of this feral. Summoning his courage, he darted forward on silent feet and caught the door just before it closed. He held his breath, waiting for either the honor or his mistress to notice. But they must have been too absorbed in their conversation, for neither raised an alarm. When he thought enough time had passed, he exhaled and slowly, ever so slowly, opened the door to peer in.

A hallway lined with pyr lamps extended for several dozen spans. From it came a steady, cool breeze. It had to lead outside, he reasoned. Xaron smiled at that. Outside he'd have a much easier time moving around, and less chance of being surprised. He itched to bolt down the hall at that moment, but the receding figures at the end of the hall pressed caution on him once more. He slipped through and softly let the door close behind.

Xaron kept low as he slunk down the hall after Feiyan and the honor. Though his back ached and his legs cramped and he could barely refrain from panting, he knew how easy it would be for them to look back and catch him. Not that crouching would hide him, but it couldn't hurt his chances.

They moved around a bend, and Xaron took a quick moment to stand and stretch his abused muscles, then peered around the corner after them. The entrance to a garden between sections of the estate lay beyond, but so did Feiyan and the honor, who had stopped at the exit. Xaron silently cursed and pulled back, and listened as their conversation drifted down the hall.

"She has no respect at all," Feiyan hissed. "Sitting atop a statue of herself in my garden. Unrefined arrogance, it is."

"Perhaps we should reconsider this relationship," the honor observed.

"You speak as if I have a choice." Bitterness tinged the Servant's words now. In sharp clarity, Xaron suddenly saw how vulnerable Feiyan felt before this woman. "I tell you, Kako. These people... I fear very little in my life, as you know. Fear has always been the tool I've best employed, but never had used against me. But her and her master — these, I fear. For all the power and influence I've gathered, nothing I can do could touch them."

"I know," the honor named Kako said simply. "Let us never forget that then, and not let them use our fear against us."

Xaron heard them proceed further into the garden and followed after. Ducking behind a row of manicured laurel shrugs, he glimpsed between the leaves the statue the Servant had referred to, and blinked in surprise. A statue of ice rose from the pond in the middle of the garden, a woman's features formed into it with unnatural smoothness, as if the water had frozen in exactly that shape rather than been carved. Perched atop it was a silver-haired woman in a dark tunic and trousers. Xaron stared at her, wondering at what she had wrought. He thought he knew much of channeling, yet he had not the first idea of how he would create such a thing, as he knew she must have. Magic was supposed to work by using the energies of the Pyrthae to create effects. Radiance, kinesis, magnesis — these were the tools a warden had to work with. And none of these could create ice that Xaron knew of. A creeping sense of awe came over him.

"You're late." Her silvery blue hair flashed through the darkness like broken ice bobbing down a mountain river as she leaped down from her statue to approach the Servant and her honor.

"My apologies," Feiyan said as the woman stalked up to stand before her. "What a beautiful sculpture you formed for me." Her tone had utterly changed, from barbs to oily placation. Xaron liked this side of Feiyan even less.

The silver-haired woman smirked. "Yes, it is beautiful, isn't it? And just like beauty, its existence will be fleeting."

The Servant inclined her head a fraction. "Just as swiftly opportunities come and go. I understand you have news of our arrangement."

"Yes." The silver-haired woman turned away to trace a finger along the statue. "Our apothecary has fled, it seems. Until we discover where he has gone, we cannot proceed with our plans. Any assistance you might provide in this area would be of great appreciation to my master."

Feiyan bowed her head. "It would be my pleasure."

"Once he is found, and I'm sure he will be soon, then I trust you remain capable of delivering the expected concoctions from the apothecary. My master is eager to have his designs move forward. He has been waiting a very long time for results, and feels he is growing very near to them now."

The Servant bowed again. "Of course. Though I must admit, my confidence has been somewhat shaken following the unfortunate death of Agmon of Iris. It is strange that he should die so soon after breaking off his relationship with your master."

The silver-haired woman smiled a cold smile. "Yes. It is."

"But of course you have nothing to fear of that from me, Iela," Feiyan continued smoothly. "I remain at your master's disposal."

Xaron wracked his memory for any mention of an 'Iela' before when he'd lived in the feral commune, but came up with nothing. While he thought, he shifted his feet to relieve his aching muscles.

A twig snapped beneath his foot.

He froze as Iela whipped her head towards his hiding spot. "What's that?"

His heart hammered in his ears so that he couldn't make out Feiyan's response. But it didn't matter. Whatever she said, Iela didn't listen, but slowly began to walk toward his hiding spot.

Xaron thought highly of his abilities, but he'd never fought with them. This Iela, on the other hand, looked like she knew her way around a fight. But there was nothing he could do. If he tried a radiance shield, she'd see through it in an instant.

Xaron closed his eyes. There was only one thing he could do. He reached into his pocket and gave the signal, only hoping that his companions' aid wouldn't come too late.

CHAPTER SEVEN

LODESTONES

Just as I returned to Nomusa from my last-minute visit, I received the signal.

I froze mid-step as I felt it, hoping it had been my imagination. But there it came again: a twitch of the lodestone in my pocket. A year before, Xaron had managed to bond a pair of iron ore pieces with his magic. Ever since, we'd used them to send a signal if one of us needed aid. I had only needed to do so once, and then only to extricate myself from an awkward situation with a jeweler we were investigating happening upon me eavesdropping. Nothing like the life-and-death situation he faced now.

Heart hammering in my ears, I took the last few steps to Nomusa and said in a rush, "He gave the signal. I have to go in." Then I whirled by her, setting off for the front gate of Feiyan's estate.

"What are you going to do?" my companion called quietly after me. I didn't turn to respond, but quickened my pace. We had no time to waste.

The guards at the gate gave me a strange look as I gave my fake name, Jaxale, and the title of acolyte, but they admitted me into the courtyard, and one went to fetch their mistress. I wasn't surprised they so readily accepted my disguise. After all, my errand had been to retrieve the gray robes and the eleven-pointed star pendant that Eidolan acolytes wore. I looked the part; now I just had to play it.

It was all I could do not to shuffle my feet as the door guard stared steadily at me, chewing over and over what looked to be mushed brown leaves. After avoiding his gaze for a while, I stared back at him until he grew bored and looked down the street.

The gate guard came back alone. "The mistress is busy. You can leave a message if you want."

I sweated a little more wondering what that meant. "Thank you for trying," I said, bowing politely, meek and sweet as a kind-hearted acolyte. I hoped it would be a jarring enough contrast with my next words. "Please tell her that my master bids that she visit him soon. He has been faithful to his word and spoken of what happened to no one, nor of her part in it." I bowed again. "We will continue to practice discretion, despite all who inquire into it."

The guard blinked. "I'll tell her that." He began to close the door then hesitated. "Hold on. Just wait here a minute."

I nodded and smiled graciously as the man closed the door. If he knew anything of what she was up to lately, I didn't doubt that he dashed to give Feiyan word of what I'd said. The door guard stared at me again with renewed interest.

In half the time as the first wait, the door opened again, this time revealing a woman I immediately recognized from sketches on the announcements of the elections. It helped that Feiyan was Qao Fu, rare enough among Oedijan officials. She was young still, little more than a decade older than me, and had acquired a measure of the healthy weight that often came with wealth. Her robes looked expensive, and though she wore gold and silver, they lacked for jewels. Her eyes were what held me, though: cold, curious, and calculating beyond even what I'd expected from her reputation.

"Ah, an Eidolan acolyte," she said with a thin smile. "I am always pleased to host one of the faith."

Her calm reaction put me off-balance, no doubt as it was intended to do. I tried to recover my wits, giving myself time to compose myself by bowing low. "Mistress, I am sorry to disturb you so late—"

"Indeed, it is quite late," Feiyan interrupted in a pleasant tone. "Yet when you say such interesting things, I cannot help but make time for you. So tell me, Acolyte Jaxale. What did you mean by your words?"

As the full realization of how much power Feiyan commanded here, with three of her guards in close reach and the late night shielding us from many prying eyes, I did not have to try for my voice to quiver with fear. "Please, Mistress Feiyan," I said, my voice high with distress. "Do not be angry with me. I was only sent to tell you we keep faith after..." I trailed off.

The Servant studied me for a long, unshifting moment. "We. Who do you mean by that?"

"The sanctuary, of course, my Servant." I bowed quickly once more. "And the oracle. He wishes to—"

"I believe your master is mistaken," Feiyan interrupted again. "I do not know of what you speak, nor what secret he means to keep of mine." To my surprise, she gave me the slightest bow, which was a sign of respect for one of so low a station as an acolyte. Hoping I looked properly flustered, I bowed one last time and thanked her profusely, then left down the walkway with unfeigned haste. Once the guard at the gate had let me out with a leer, I hurried away down the street and out of sight until I returned to the alley where Nomusa waited.

As soon as I had ducked behind the corner again, she seized me and stared me in the eyes. "What is going on, Airene?"

I exhaled and let my shoulders drop from around my ears. "I don't know yet. But I hope it was enough."

———

Xaron held his breath as Iela continued to approach his hiding spot behind the laurel bushes.

"Might I ask what you're looking at?" Feiyan said mildly.

"Is there anyone else in these gardens?" Iela asked without turning towards the Servant. "Guards who patrol it, or perhaps a gardener?"

"They wouldn't be here while I have a meeting. I am sure it's just a pigeon; they like to eat the berries off the bushes."

"Then when I look, I suppose I'll see a pigeon."

"Please, Iela," Feiyan said, annoyance starting to show in her voice. "I serve at your master's leisure, but I am a busy woman. If you do not have anything more to say…"

Iela was halfway towards Xaron before she stopped and turned. "Yes. I suppose you are right. I am busy as well."

Xaron let out a slow exhale of relief as she walked back to where the Servant and the honor Kako waited. He wasn't in the clear yet, but he looked to be out of immediate danger. He hoped Airene wouldn't do anything rash now that he'd given the signal, though.

"As I was saying," Iela said, "if you hear anything of Eazal of Sand-glass, do tell us. Our arrangement cannot proceed without him."

Xaron couldn't decide if the Servant's expression shifted or not. "Indeed, that would be most unfortunate," she said neutrally. "I will have my best men out searching for him."

Iela frowned at that. "As long as it is done discreetly. Now, as you say, we are both busy, and I have other calls to pay this night." She began to turn away.

"If I may, emissary," the honor Kako spoke up. "It is not my place, but I compelled to inquire all the same as to what these potions will be used for. The methods by which we are administering them is… suspect, to say the least. Are they poison?"

Iela turned slowly back towards him. "No, they are not poison," she said softly. "They are the antidote. A new world is coming, one without these mistruths plaguing it. Where those who deserve to rule are doing so."

Xaron had an uncomfortable feeling that she thought those who "deserved to rule" were wardens like her. And himself. Once wardens had ruled; all in Oedija knew of the Tyrant Wardens from over a century before, whose cruel reign and denigration of those without an attunement to the Pyrthae had spurred all the rules that governed wardens in their own age. He found himself strangely both repulsed and intrigued by her suggestion.

Iela shook her head. "Beyond that, I cannot say. But just as the cure is often as deadly as the disease, it is true that many will die from these tinctures." A pause. "But I trust that will not be an issue for you."

Feiyan hesitated just a moment too long before smiling. "Of course not."

"Good. If that's settled then—"

"Mistress!"

Xaron startled as a guard entered from the entryway behind him and hurried towards the three standing under the steadily melting sculpture. In his haste, the guard had missed him crouching in the shrubbery. Xaron breathed out a sigh of relief as he passed, but he didn't know that he could risk another chance at discovery like that. He had to flee. Yet he couldn't help but eavesdrop on a few last words.

"Yes?" Feiyan said to her guard. "What is it?"

"Mistress, there is a girl here for you," the guard huffed as he came up to her. "An acolyte, apparently."

"What in the eleven hells could an Eidolan acolyte be doing here?" Feiyan wondered aloud.

"Mistress, I do not know. Shall I inquire?"

"What do you think you should do?" the honor Kako said sarcastically. "Do you think you should divine the purpose of her visit before bothering our mistress with her presence?"

Xaron didn't wait to hear an answer. Considering the timing, he had a feeling he knew exactly who this Eidolan acolyte was. Slinking from the laurel bush and back through the entryway, Xaron went back inside to take the long way back out of the Servant's estate.

CHAPTER EIGHT

THE GUILDMASTERS

When Xaron finally arrived back at the alley where Nomusa and I waited, I drew him into an embrace, grime and sweat and all. "You damned fool," I muttered into his shoulder.

"Let him breathe a moment." Nomusa gently pried me off, while Xaron had an embarrassed but pleased grin plastered on his face.

I poked him in the chest. "I pretended to be an acolyte for you. Had to play the demure, chaste girl to that she-devil Feiyan's face."

His grin widened. "I figured it was you. Thanks again, though to be honest, I was practically escaping by then anyway."

I rolled my eyes. "You could have stopped with thanks."

"Perhaps you had best tell us what you learned," Nomusa interjected.

Xaron took a deep breath, then launched into his tale. He recounted how he'd scaled the cliff in a single leap, crossed the courtyard under the guard's nose without being detected once, then how he'd traveled the rooms without light and didn't bump into a single thing.

Nomusa and I exchanged glances. We knew better than to believe a word of it.

Finally, he arrived at the important points: how the silver-haired woman's name was Iela, and that she was a feral warden who could do things with channeling — like creating ice sculptures — that Xaron could not. And he told of how this feral frightened Feiyan enough that she didn't think her power was anything compared to the power Iela's master wielded. Apprehension prickled my skin. I understood how she felt that way from just Xaron's description. If this mysterious man had a feral warden working for him, who knew what other resources he might have at his disposal.

After Xaron had finished his telling, Nomusa said in an awed voice, "Another feral warden." She shook her head. "I do not like the idea of crossing her."

I remained silent. I didn't like it any better than she, but I also knew we couldn't abandon this hunt now. Too many lives could be at stake. Not to mention the opportunity this represented for us.

"But what do you think they are really administering the pyrkin potions for?" Xaron wondered aloud. "It doesn't make any sense. If it's not meant to kill these people, what is it meant to do?"

I shrugged. "I suppose Eazal would be able tell us if we could convince him. But beyond that, I don't know of any other leads." I screwed up my eyes in concentration. "I feel like we almost know enough of the picture for this to be something substantial, something of value to someone. But we still need evidence, tangible evidence."

"Or allies who only require rumors," a voice said from further down the alley.

We whirled, looking for the speaker. His voice seemed familiar. When the man stepped from the shadows a moment later, I instantly recognized who it was. "Talan the Guilder," I greeted him grimly. "Still lurking about?" I wondered how much he had overheard.

He bowed slightly. "It's what I'm paid to do. You, however, seem to lack some skill in what you're paid to do. Or did none of you observe me listening to your conversation?"

"Perhaps not," Nomusa said, sidling a step closer and falling into a balanced stance. I recognized it as one from her homeland's martial art of Ixolo, which allowed for immediate offensive action. "But that's not our only skill."

Next to me, Xaron had his fists clenched like he might try striking at the Guilder as well. I knew I had to handle the situation quickly, or things could get out of hand. Guilders were not a defenseless sort of people, and I didn't want either of my friends to be in danger.

"What do you want?" I said. "You must want something if you're announcing yourself."

Talan inclined his head towards me, a half-sneer plastered over his face. He seemed to take little note of Nomusa and Xaron's aggression. "How very astute of you. Yes, I want something. What you've learned through your—" His lips twitched. "—brave endeavors promises to be precisely the information I could use."

"Could it," Nomusa said dryly. Her stance hadn't shifted. "Well, now you have it."

"Ah, but I need the Finches as well as the scroll." Talan spread his arms. "The tale is not the same without its embellishments."

Xaron flushed, so I spoke before he could. "I'm assuming this is a two-way offer?"

"Of course." The Guilder lowered his arms, and the smile faded as well. "You wish to achieve justice, no? For a man's murder not to go unpunished, and to prevent the deaths of others? This is what I can offer. So long as you can stomach its flavor."

Justice by the Underguild — my stomach turned at the thought. But I didn't see how we could have the conventional kind through the Tribunal. Reporting the silver-haired as a feral warden might draw too much scrutiny on ourselves — more specifically, on Xaron — for me to risk, as well as bring the scrutiny of whoever her master was upon us. If Feiyan was scared of this mysterious man, I certainly didn't want to cross him before we were prepared with the proper allies.

I looked at Nomusa, and though her brow was drawn, she nodded, apparently having arrived at the same conclusion. Xaron still stared distrustfully at Talan, but I nodded at the Guilder all the same. "I suppose we'll take it."

Xaron's eyebrows shot up, glancing between Nomusa and I, but I kept my eyes on Talan. He grinned. "Fantastic. Shall we be on our way then?"

"On our way?" I asked cautiously.

His grin turned sly. "You can't make a deal with daemons without meeting them in their dark depths, can you?"

———

Two turns of the sandglass later, we found ourselves in another alley and another deme, accepting blindfolds from Talan.

"I can't believe we're doing this," Xaron muttered for the tenth time.

"I can't believe you are, either," Talan taunted as he pulled Xaron's blindfold tighter. Xaron yelped in surprise and tried striking the Guilder, but the man easily dodged him and smiled wider.

I was the last to be blindfolded and stood nervously as Talan came up behind me. His arms moved about on either side, encircling me as he brought up the blindfold. "You knew this was standard practice," I said to Xaron as my vision disappeared, trying to ignore the closeness of the Guilder. Contrary to my expectation, he didn't smell at all dirty, but had an almost pleasant earthiness to his scent. I pushed it out of mind. "This is all part of the plan." I didn't mention how nervous I was myself to put ourselves wholly at the mercy of this Guilder. By all I'd seen of him, Talan was self-serving, self-centered, and far too smug. Hardly the most trustworthy of allies. But desperation calls for foolish gestures, as it's said.

Blind as newborn mice, we held hands as Talan led us forward. Assumedly, we went to the secret entry point into the Underguild's underground network. I was in the middle of our line, with Nomusa in front holding Talan's hand, and Xaron coming last holding mine. He squeezed it at one point, and I squeezed back, glad that at least I went with friends.

We stumbled along a stony path for a while. The ground underneath eventually changed to dirt, then wooden planks some time after that. I felt the cool pressure of being underground settle around us and shivered. I wondered if, even now, people lined the edges of our passage watching us and weighing our merits. Or perhaps they eagerly awaited our condemnation; it seemed as if walking the passages of the Underguild might warrant such a measure. But no knives pierced us, and no harsh words called out. The phantoms were in my imagination, but it didn't make them any less real.

Barely half a turn must have passed before we halted, but it felt much longer. "Here is fine," Talan said, and I heard Nomusa's murmur of relief as her blindfold was removed. My own followed soon after, and I held back a sigh as I looked around, blinking. A vast cavern rose up around us, the edges of it lit by long scars filled with glowing pyrkin. But it wasn't all a crude cave. Pillars carved an indeterminably long time ago rose to form the edges of the rough walls. On every surface were colors and patterns worn down and weathered by time. It looked like a cathedral to some forgotten god more ancient than the Eidola. I couldn't imagine where we were under the city to have so much space around us.

"What is this place?" I whispered to no one in particular.

Talan stopped next to me. "The legacy of our forebears, built by the ancestors of those whom Oedijans call honors. We're always looking to the Pyrthae and sky above for great things, and forget the hidden wonders lying below."

I looked over at him, startled to hear almost poetic words from the rogue's lips. I recognized also that I knew very little of the history behind the honors indeed. "I suppose you don't forget."

For once, he didn't smirk. "Not yet."

I pondered that as my eyes lingered on his shaved chin, thoughts aimlessly wandering over his inconsistencies when the door we waited before suddenly opened. A herald that could have passed for a cutpurse slouched in. "Well, don't leave the masters waiting!" he snapped. "In you go!"

My companions and I looked at each other, but we'd come this far. No turning back now.

We entered a chamber even grander than the one before. More ruined pillars rose to unplumbable blackness, and only ghostly smears of pyrkin along the stone kept the darkness at bay.

We approached the far end of the hall, where five chairs rose upon a naturally formed dais occupied by three men and two women. These were the Guildmasters. Their number, it was said, was in mocking salute to the five Stratechons, the elected military officials in charge of the nation's defense. As above, so below — the old Eidolan saying that directed its followers to adhere to the ways of the Pyrthae ironically came to mind.

I knew their names, or at least the names they went by, as did everyone else with half an ear in Oedija. Peralda, Xalfar, Hax, Lae, and Kalindi — the puppeteers behind so many of the workings of the city, both ill and good. Perhaps they were permitted certain liberties that weren't completely legal, but they also provided many services, such as finding and punishing perpetrators of violent crimes, or those who didn't pay the requisite taxes for petty crimes like pickpocketing and burglary. Such measures went a long way. After all, there's no better way to limit an activity than to tax it.

We were twenty paces away when Talan gestured for us to halt. "Efendi and hanims—" the Guilder said smoothly.

"Leave your Avvadin formalities out of this, Wraithsbane!" a big man clad in rough leathers boomed. Xalfar, unless I was mistaken. He had the ruddy complexion of those long familiar with the allures of drink. "You've taken a great burning gamble with your well-being by bringing these three down here."

Wraithsbane? I glanced over at Talan, whose smile was twitching. I wondered what that odd moniker signified about him.

"Master Xalfar," Talan said, his tone no longer dulcet, "I fully appreciate the risks. But I assure you, your suspicions are ill-founded in this instance." His eyes flickered to me. "I have been watching them for some time now, and I know they can be trusted as much as any one of our organization."

I kept my face composed. A lie? Or had he truly been tailing us before this? If he had, it evoked the question of what had brought him to it. And it made me wonder who else's attention we of Canopy might have attracted.

"You know this, do you?" a tall, bowed Guildmaster said — Lae, I believed. She had such long proportions that I suspected she'd spent a good deal of time on the rack at some point in her nefarious career. "Tell me, Guilder Talan: how is it that you can see the intentions in another's heart?"

"All such secrets are laid bare to one who has studied hearts all their life." Suddenly, a knife flicked up from the Guilder into the air, and everyone flinched. Everyone except Talan — he snatched it and secreted it away again in a flash. The two Guildmasters who had spoken thus far frowned deeper.

I wondered how Talan maintained his precarious position here when he antagonized, even threatened, his superiors. But a tinkling bell of laughter from the chair on the far left promised to clear up the mystery. A plump woman in robes the blue of the summer sea leaned forward, a smile still playing on her lips. The generous amount of gray in her curled hair told her age, yet she had a mischievous youthful expression in her eyes. It seemed Guildmaster Peralda had a special liking for our Wraithsbane.

"Now, now, my Avvadin hound," she cooed. "We can't go barking at every hare, can we?"

Talan's expression went carefully neutral as he regarded Peralda. "Yes, hanim," he said, his tone subdued.

I stared. For all his attitude, he had practically rolled over and shown her his belly. I wondered what the story was behind that as well. So many mysteries surrounding this man, and I'd trusted him enough to blindfold me and my companions and lead us down to the Eleven only knew where. For a Finch like me, his secrets had an almost irresistible allure. I itched to uncover them then and there, before I remembered the more salient mystery of murder before me.

"Enough," the fourth Guildmaster said in a hoarse whisper that, despite being soft, distinctly carried through the large chamber. He sat in the middle of the five and spoke with an authority of a master among masters. This must be Hax, the longest-serving Guildmaster and de facto head of the Underguild, insomuch as was possible for the syndicate. From what I'd heard, he had survived multiple assassination attempts in the two decades he'd held his position, and his wasted body — the pitted skin, the sunken eyes, the hoarse voice — showed that the tales were likely accurate.

"No more of this squabbling," Hax continued. "We know why these Finches are here." He didn't stumble over the term, nor did his expression shift when he said it. He at least did not mock us for owning the label. Despite the precarious situation, my chest warmed with pride.

"Someone has challenged our reputation." He paused, his tongue wetting his lips. I cringed; even at a glimpse, I could see it was purpled and bloated. "This cannot pass unacknowledged. To do so would be to deny what the Underguild is."

I glanced at Xaron and Nomusa and saw my restrained hope reflected in their expressions.

"However," Hax continued, "I have not built the Underguild through hasty and rash punishment. We will hear what you have to say, Airene, Nomusa, and Xaron of Port. But the measure of our justice will be our own decision." He made a small gesture, and Talan nodded at me to speak.

I glanced at Nomusa and Xaron, then turned to the leaders of the Underguild. "Guildmasters, my companions and I have been investigating the death of the patrician Agmon of Iris for this past day and night." I hesitated, wondering how much of the whole truth I should tell. "We were concerned about justice for Agmon, as well as what the mysterious nature of his death might portend."

"And what would that be?" Lae interrupted.

"Agmon had a hand in an illicit business with his partner, Eazal of Sandglass. They—" Once again, I paused. Revealing Eazal's trade might endanger him, depending on whether or not he was sanctioned by the Underguild.

"Yes?" Xalfar prompted impatiently.

I kept my eyes on Hax, who stared at me without blinking. "They brewed tinctures using pyrkin and distributed them for a variety of effects to their clients. Allegedly, they were safe. Then a woman named Iela came as an emissary to her master, and that all changed."

The Guildmasters looked among themselves with raised eyebrows. "Iela," Hax said in his hoarse voice. "A woman with hair of silver and blue?"

I nodded, and the Guildmasters began muttering. Then they knew her. It wasn't so surprising, considering how rare such a hair color was.

Hax waved a hand. "Tell us the rest, Finch."

So I did. I told of how Iela had them change the potions into ones that could harm, for a reason we had not been able to yet uncover. I also told of how Agmon balked at doing this and sought a way out, which was when Iela had him murdered with one of their own creations. I recounted how we followed the trail at Eazal's suggestion to Feiyan's estate, as she was to be the new distributor, and how Iela seemed to be forcing the newly raised Servant as much as she had the other two.

Once I'd finished, Hax leaned back. "Is there anything else?"

Xaron glanced at me, a question in his eyes. I wondered myself how much he should tell, but we'd already committed ourselves this far. I nodded.

Xaron cleared his throat. "This Iela is a warden."

The last Guildmaster, who had been shrouded in shadow, leaned forward so quickly that I flinched, almost expecting him to jump at us. Kalindi stared balefully from beneath long, black bangs. His dark features might have been handsome were not they not accompanied by a pair of gleaming, cold eyes, that almost seemed to catch the meager light of the hall. "How did you overhear a private conversation between a mistress and her servant? How did you, of all people, discover Feiyan was dealing with a feral warden?" A wicked grin grew on the Guildmaster's face as he watched Xaron squirm.

My mind spun for explanations while Xaron spluttered a reply. But to my surprise, it was Talan who interceded. "Xaron is a house-breaker, Master Kalindi. Perhaps you are familiar with the specialty?"

The Guildmaster turned his wolfish gaze on the Guilder. "Perhaps I am. But the estate of Servant Feiyan is inaccessible to those of… ordinary skill."

Talan shrugged. "I myself would not have an issue with it, though admittedly I am not of ordinary skill. However, I have seen Xaron at work. He is quite capable of the task."

Fear suddenly struck me. If Talan had truly seen Xaron at work, he would also have seen him channeling. I studied the Guilder, but I couldn't detect anything behind his mask of bemused contempt. A mask — that was exactly what his expressions came to. If only I could see beneath. But here he was, standing up for Xaron before his superiors, who might kill him for lying to them. Either he didn't know, or he wasn't revealing it for his own reasons. Yet it put me ill at ease to have to trust Xaron's secret to a Guilder's good intentions.

Kalindi melted back into his chair and said nothing, but the grin had dissipated, and he looked away, apparently bored again.

Hax studied his fellow Guildmaster for a moment, then turned back to us. "We have heard your accusation and your evidence. Now we will hear what reward you seek for this information."

That was one thing you had to appreciate about the Underguild — dishonest work earned honest pay. But I swallowed hard and said, "We don't need a reward."

Nomusa and Xaron shot bewildered looks my way, but I didn't meet their eyes. "Nothing?" Xalfar scoffed. "And we're supposed to believe that!"

Lae looked similarly skeptical. "'Surely there must be something."

Hax seemed to be waiting for an answer, just as I'd hoped. After pausing a long moment so that I would appear hesitant, I said tentatively, "If we might be granted a boon, then it would simply be this. First, that Eazal not be harmed. I do not believe he should be held responsible for Agmon's death, nor the others his tinctures may have harmed."

When Xaron flashed a look of gratefulness at me, I knew I'd done the right thing.

"Of course, my dear," Peralda said soothingly. "We don't punish innocents here, surely."

"Second," I continued, "that the glass smith Maesos of Port be protected from any retribution. He fears he might become framed for Agmon's death, an event in which he had no part, as you now know."

"Is that all?" Hax wheezed.

I spoke again before I lost my nerve, "Lastly, that my companions and I be granted amnesty for our activities as Finches. I don't want to have to worry about getting a knife in the back for looking into the wrong thing. I don't ask permission to pursue anything we wish — just that you give us a warning if we happen to cross paths."

Hax studied me for a moment, then gave a slight nod. "These terms are acceptable. Now, you have given us much to discuss. You will be told our decision on the morrow." The Guildmaster made another small gesture. Talan touched my arm, and I understood our conversation was at an end.

"Thank you for hearing us, Guildmasters," I said, bowing to them before Talan escorted us out of the cavern.

CHAPTER NINE

A KNOCK ON THE DOOR

Our business with the Guildmasters concluded, Talan blindfolded us again and led us above ground. As soon as we emerged into the open air, I breathed it in hungrily. I'd never join the Under-guild if only because they spent too much time in stale tunnels.

After the Guilder removed our blinds, I touched his arm lightly. "Thank you. None of this could be happening had you not taken a wager on us."

Talan smiled ruefully. "This? It is so assured it is hardly a bet. I'd gamble the shirt off my back for less."

Nomusa stood at my shoulder. "Time to go. We'd best try and get some sleep with the little night left to us."

I nodded and looked at Xaron. He was strangely withdrawn, not even casting spiteful glances at Talan like he had the whole time we'd been with him. Kalindi's accusations must have really shaken him. I slid an arm around his waist, and he startled, so I kept the hug brief. "Let's go," I said. "I think we all need sleep."

Talan gave a sweeping bow. "Until tomorrow then, hanims." The Guilder passed us and turned the corner. Before he was out of sight, he gave me one lingering look, then he was gone. As we set off on our own walk back to Canopy, I tried not to think about it. I had plenty of distrac-tions already — my stomach was rumbling, having missed dinner from all our running about, and I was dragging with exhaustion. Good thing the walk was short.

As we neared our tower, though, I grew more alert, and felt Nomusa and Xaron tense as well. By silent agreement, we went slowly up the stairs of the tower, glancing in at every circle to ensure there weren't hidden assassins waiting for us. Finally, we reached our door, which looked thankfully undisturbed. Nomusa set to unlocking it while Xaron and I watched down the stairs, expecting at any moment to see the shadows of approaching enemies appear on the walls.

Nomusa opened the door, and we quickly stepped inside, locking it behind. A collective sigh of relief rose from all three of us. Xaron slid down the door to sit, looking more exhausted than I'd seen him. He must have channeled much during his house-break.

"You should get some rest," I told him. "We'll need you sharp tomorrow."

Xaron's eyes flickered up. "I think he knows."

I shared a look with Nomusa. "Who?" I asked, though I thought I knew.

His expression twisted into a sneer. "Talan *Wraithsbane.*"

His contempt for the Guilder came from fear now, I could see. Crouching next to him, I said softly, "Xaron, what happened to Graz and your friends isn't going to happen to you. Talan didn't turn you in. Even if he does know, I don't think he ever will."

Nomusa crouched on his other side, gently rubbing his back. "We'll keep a close eye on him. If we see any signs that he'll betray us—" Her jaw flexed. "We'll see that he won't."

Xaron straightened up, then slowly rose to his feet. His cheeks were flushed. "I appreciate you two trying to look after me," he said softly. "But you don't know what it's like. Knowing that you could be hunted at any moment, at this very moment. Knowing that one little slip up could give someone the power of life or death over you." He shook his head. "I need to sleep. I'll see you in the morning."

He went into his room, not even lingering for dinner. It was so unlike him to forgo any meal that I couldn't help but feel worried for him. Nomusa and I looked at each other, but we said nothing. He was right; we didn't know what his life was like. We weren't hunted like he was.

But I knew one thing. The dark depths of the 'Thae would swallow us before I let Talan Wraithsbane harm him.

———

I slept fitfully that night. Every moment, I expected the door to creak open, or perhaps splinter at a sudden blow, and cloaked figures to rush in with knives raised. A storm had started up, contributing to my unease.

Licks of lightning crawled across the sky followed by window-rattling booms.

I rose before the sun, too restless to pretend to sleep any longer. I checked on our finches for messages, then when nothing had come, I set to cleaning our loft. With our busy schedules, Canopy was in a persistent state of disarray. As I straightened up and wiped down, I thought of all that had happened and reviewed my own actions. I turned them this way and that, questioning my reasons, straining to discover the flaws. They weren't hard to find. In a game of whispers and murder, every move was precarious, and many of mine in this hunt had been downright reckless.

Three sharp knocks rapped on the door, and I stiffened halfway through scrubbing a pot. I was dressed in just the tunic and trousers that I typically wore beneath my robes. No one else was awake, nor likely would be for another turn. I considered waking them, but decided to take a look through the greeting hole first to see who I was dealing with. No need to disturb them if it wasn't anything to worry about.

Despite my forced nonchalance, my heart was pounding as I flipped open the cover to the greeting hole. I waited a moment before I put my eye to it; it wasn't unheard of for assassins to blow poisoned darts into the hole, and I didn't want to risk it. But when nothing happened for five breaths, I finally lowered my head to look through.

Eazal's dark eyes stared back from the other side. "Airene," he said in a cracked voice.

For a moment, I didn't know what to say. I hadn't honestly expected to see the apothecary again. "Eazal," I greeted him. "What are you doing here?" I made no move to open the door. My mind whirled. How had he found us?

"Airene, listen to me," Eazal said, desperation clear in his voice. He sounded as if he'd been up since the night before. I wondered if he'd slept at all in the two days since his friend died. "What I am going to tell you might sound mad, but I need you to listen."

My breath came fast, but I whispered, "Tell me."

"I… I need you to come with me. Now. Alone."

I was shaking my head even before he'd finished. "You know I can't do that. Now of all times I cannot do that." It chilled me that he would even ask.

"Please, Airene." All the fragile pride the man had possessed before was broken. He leaned against the door, his eye pressed so close to the greeting hole he almost blocked out the light from the stairwell lamps. "She has my family. She says she'll kill them if you don't come with me."

Shivers ran up my skin. No need to ask who she was. "How do you know Iela is telling the truth? She could be bluffing."

A shake of his head. "Do you know what she is, what she can do? Do you know the resources she can access?" He broke off with a sob, and only continued a moment later. "I believe her. She'll do it."

I chewed my lip. I still wasn't convinced that this wasn't a bluff. But either way, it was obvious it was a trap. Iela must have heard that we were looking into her affairs. Perhaps Eazal himself had told her when she caught up to him, as she clearly had. Even with his family's lives potentially under threat, I knew too little to heedlessly put my life in his hands.

I shook my head. "I am sorry if that's true, Eazal. But I cannot go with you."

He pressed his eye against the hole again so only a glimmer of his eye showed. "She thought you might say that," he growled, his voice changed. "She said it wouldn't be enough. And she has a solution for that, too."

"What solution?" I asked calmly.

He began to laugh like a man before the gallows. "That she knows your family, Airene of Riverport. That she knows where they live. Tryphon. Melitta. Sophene. Linos."

As he named each of my family members, my blood ran cold. "No," I breathed. In that moment, I believed it was true. How they had been discovered, I didn't yet know. But somehow, this warden knew where my family was and could kill them at any moment.

"Now," Eazal said slowly. "Come with me. We must meet her within the turn."

For a moment, even though he told me what I needed to do, I couldn't move. I was frozen in place. It was my greatest fear, my work endangering my family. I had always known it was a possibility. But I'd never believed it would actually come to pass.

"Come," the apothecary whispered.

I backed away from the door, my body hardly feeling my own. Almost without thought, I began moving to the kitchen, to the bin of dishes and utensils I'd stacked after washing. From them, I drew out a sharp knife we'd used two days before to cut open fruit.

My hands numb, I wrapped it in a cloth, then tucked it into the back of my trousers with my tunic bunched under it to keep it from falling. It stayed for the moment. It would have to do.

I knew I could not hesitate any longer. Not if my family was going to survive.

I went to the door and slowly opened it, then said to the phantom of a man before me, "Lead the way."

CHAPTER TEN

ALLEY SECRETS

She waited for us in a nearby alley.

As I approached the feral warden, a kitchen knife pressing into the small of my back, the blue light of pre-dawn only vaguely making anything visible, I knew I was likely walking to my death. It gave an unreal sense to everything, as if I hadn't actually awoken, but was stuck in a dream, a dream in which everything I had feared and everything I had worked toward came crumbling down around me. Yet I knew it wasn't so. This was the reality I had made. The sum of my mistakes.

"Airene," Iela greeted me. Even her voice made me grow cold. She looked much the same as she had when I'd seen her enter Feiyan's estate the night before.

"Iela," I said through numb lips.

"I suppose we are beyond introductions." She smiled thinly. "We both know so much about each other already, and yet we're only just meeting. Isn't it odd?"

I could think of no other response than the one question that had hounded me since Eazal had led me from Canopy's door. "Why did you bring me here?"

Her eyes widened in mock surprise. "Why? If you haven't figured that much out, Airene, you are not the Finch I thought you were."

That struck a spark of anger back in me, a hint of warmth amidst the cold of fear. I grasped at it, trying to fan it into further flames. I had a feeling I would need it to survive this.

"But I do have one more selfish purpose," she continued in a soft voice.

"You see, Airene, I do not like people who meddle in my affairs. Particularly when they bring the eye of the Underguild upon me." She shook her head. "Perhaps I could have forgiven you if you had not reached that far. But this will cause many problems for me. It cannot stand."

I stared at her in sullen silence, trying to hold onto my anger. My hand itched to reach for the knife prodding my back, but I restrained myself. It was foolish to reach for it now when she could kill me with a flick of her hand. I had to wait for an opportunity, if one would ever come.

"And so," the silver-haired woman continued, "before I kill you, I want you to see how thoroughly you've failed your family." Her smile grew wider. "I want you to know that the person responsible for your brother's disappearance all those years ago is standing before you."

I stared at her, uncomprehending for a moment. The barrage of revelations in the situation — and her admission of her intentions for me — left me dazed and weak. "Thero?" I asked uncertainly.

"Ah, how slowly you recall him," she mocked. "Thero! Or do you not remember discovering him dead in the canal, horrible marks etched across his face?"

I could not speak, but stared at her as the anger burned brighter.

"He seemed so promising too," Iela said with a mocking smile. "Full of potential, like tinder ready to ignite. But like so many before him, my master could not tap that power inside him. And so he…" She shrugged. "He fizzled out."

Quivering with the rage I held inside, it was all I could to do stay in place.

She glanced at Eazal, who cowered against the wall, shrinking into himself as if the feral warden might forget he was there. "But now that I have the apothecary, I think our progress will come more swiftly. And my dream — and my master's dream — will finally come to pass."

I took a step toward her. I knew it was foolish and utter idiocy to consider making a move against her when she was fully aware. Yet the hatred burning inside me was like nothing I'd felt before. In my work, I had always been cool and distant and maintained a level head. But she had told me that she and her master had killed Thero. He had been subject to their experiments. And I couldn't help but picture myself pulling out the knife and stabbing it through her chest.

Iela must have seen something of the rage in my eyes, for she smiled widely. "Ah, there it is. What I've been waiting for." She raised her hand. "Now, I think I'll get some satisfaction out of your death."

Not waiting for her to channel, I dashed forward and drew out the knife. Iela looked surprised for a moment, then the smile returned, and something emitted from her hand. A frigid gale hit me with a force that knocked the breath out of me, and though I had been running, I found my limbs wearying and slowing. I sank to my knees, shivering, the knife nearly falling from my nerveless grip. Never before had I been so cold. I could barely think through it.

"Release the knife now, Airene," Iela chided, continuing to channel a flurry of frozen air around me. "I have enjoyed your struggles, but it's time to let it end."

In defiance of my screaming body, I looked up at her through frosted eyelashes. I would not die on my knees and bowing before her. If I had to die, I would be staring her in the eyes. It was this last spark of defiance that I clung to as my mind began to shut down.

Something moved behind her. For a moment, I thought I had begun to hallucinate. Then I saw it again. From the rooftops above, a dark figure jumped down toward the feral warden, something blazing white-hot in its hand.

As the figure leaped onto Iela and thrust its glowing hand at her, the cold surrounding me dissipated with a scream of the feral warden's surprise. She fell and rolled with the other figure, writhing and screaming as they fought like alley cats. My joints stiff with cold and my muscles leaden with it, I forced myself to stand, the kitchen knife still somehow in my grip. My vision swam, but slowly I started to make out who it was that struggled against the feral warden with what looked like a stake in its hand. I blinked. Against all reason, I suddenly saw it was Talan.

The thought stuck, as frozen in my mind as my body. That stake glowed with radiance. Which meant Talan was a warden.

But I didn't take time to consider it. Stumbling forward, I took an account of the fight. Talan and Iela were locked in a deadly embrace. His stake had pierced her gut, and a glow pulsed around it. But Iela, her face a mask of rage and pain, had her hands on his arms, and where her fingers touched, patches of ice blossomed over his clothes. From Talan's pained expression, her channeling reached beyond the fabric.

I moved my stiff legs closer as they continued to struggle on the ground, fire and ice battling for dominance. I limped up next to the strug-gling pair and stood over them, gripping the knife as hard as I could. Iela's bloodshot eyes found me, going wide when she realized my intentions. She tried ripping one off of Talan's arm, but she'd sealed her own fate — the ice locked her in for a moment too long.

With a scream that came from somewhere deep inside me, I raised the knife and stabbed it down into her throat.

CHAPTER ELEVEN

THE CITY OF WHISPERS

The events afterward blurred together. I remember staring down at my hands still curled around the knife's hilt, heat and cold still washing over me in feverish waves, while blood pooled around the blade in Iela's neck. I watched until the life went out of the woman's eyes. I remember kneeling there until Talan, shivering and blue-lipped, led me out of the alley, frost still tinging the ugly purple bruises on his arms.

We walked from the alley as dawn began to light the day. The intense cold that had seized me faded, but another weakness still lingered. My hands were wet. I knew I shouldn't look down as the Guilder led me away, but I couldn't help it, and my gaze inexorably fell to them.

Blood. I'd never had so much blood on me, had barely seen so much blood at once. Only once at the shipyard where my father worked, when a mast collapsed on a man and crushed his chest. But this blood I had spilled. Her blood. I'd killed her. And we'd left her body in the alley for someone else to discover, just as the city guards had discovered Thero.

But no. That wasn't the same. She had killed Thero for insane, incomprehensible reasons, while I had killed to save myself and Talan. I closed my eyes and wished I could believe it was so simple.

Even though she would have killed me and my family, and likely Talan, Nomusa, and Xaron as well. Even though she had murdered Thero, and had likely murdered many more. It still broke some part of me that I had taken her life away. In my own eyes at least, it didn't make me any less of a murderer.

Talan bent his head close. "Breathe," he told me. I tried to obey.

gulping in long, deep breaths. But even as the guilt wracked me worse than the pain in my limbs, my hands shaking, my teeth chattering, I knew I would survive this. Perhaps it would take me a while to get over it, to stop seeing the red on my hands, but eventually, the color would wash away. Perhaps that was what scared me most, that forgetting that would inevitably come, and obscure my ugly deeds even from myself.

In the way the Guilder held me, unflinching and steady, I sensed I wasn't alone in my guilt. That at some point in the past, he, too, had felt as I did now. I wondered again about that shadowed past of his. It wasn't exactly a comforting realization, but somehow, it made a difference.

After I had calmed, I pushed away from Talan and walked unsteadily on my own. "We must hurry," I said faintly. "We can't be seen like this."

Talan nodded. "I have a place nearby I can change at. But I can return you to your tower."

I considered him for a moment. How long had the Guilder watched us before he stepped out from the shadows? Somehow, I couldn't summon up the unease I knew I should feel at that. The unease I did feel was that it felt comforting instead. So he was a Guilder, and a feral warden. None of that matter. When I had been in danger, he had come and saved me.

"Come with me," I said. Reaching out, I took his bloody hand in mine. And after a moment's hesitation, he nodded and let me lead him along the street and back to Canopy.

———

The reunion in Canopy went as well as could be expected. Xaron and Nomusa were in a panic and rushed to the door as soon as I knocked. I couldn't help but notice the red mark I left on the wood. As soon as it opened, Xaron jumped to conclusions and nearly started a fight with Talan then and there, and I was only just able to talk him out of it.

Once we'd both cleaned up and wore new clothes — Talan looking comical in one of Xaron's bright tunics — they sat me down on the divan and managed to pry the tale out of me. Both were wide-eyed by the end of it.

"Airene," Nomusa said in a hushed voice, her hand squeezing mine.

Xaron looked stricken as he stood before the bay window. "I can't believe we weren't there," he muttered. He cast a sulky look over at the Guilder, who leaned next to the balcony door, his head bowed. Yet I thought I detected the hint of a smile at my friend's look.

I shook my head. "I'll be okay," I said, my voice breaking as I said it. Nomusa folded me into her arms anew.

A little while later, though, I pushed away again. "I really will be," I told my companions. "I just need some time to think things through."

The rest of that day, I allowed my friends to comfort me, and give me food and water, with promises of coffee at Zipho's cafe later. Even as a quiet resolution for a further hunt formed in the back of my mind, I let myself relax. I thought Thero would have liked that. He'd always loved having a good time, always had a smile on his face. I closed my eyes and, for the first time in my living memory, felt hope for someday understanding who had done this to him. And for the first time in a long time since his death, the guilt eased a bit.

————

Before he left Canopy, Talan informed me that before he had come to my aid, he had alerted a fellow Guilder of Iela's intentions, and that they would have recovered the body. I couldn't help but wonder what they'd do with it. Burn it? Throw it out to sea? Or leave it in some deep, dark tunnel below the city? I didn't have the nerve to ask.

Instead, I turned the conversation to the apothecary. "Will Eazal have gotten away?"

Talan shrugged. "It's likely, at least for the moment. But the Underguild has an extensive network. We'll catch him before he can go anywhere."

I wondered when I'd see Talan next. True, it seemed I had a new working relationship with the Underguild, one which I expected I'd need to find out who this powerful, mysterious man was behind Iela and her operations. But if I was to avoid their business, that didn't exactly indicate I'd be working often with a Guilder. "I think I owe you a thank you."

A softness settled over his expression unlike anything I'd seen him wear yet. "You don't owe me anything," he said quietly.

My heartbeat sounded louder in my ears. "Thank you all the same."

I don't know who looked away first, but the moment passed as our gazes broke. Talan looked down the stairs of my tower, then leaned conspiratorially forward. "If you should ever need me again," he said in a low voice, "go to the tavern the Ignorant Ignoble in Bazaar, and ask the barkeeper for 'a chalice of unrequited intoxication.'"

I nodded. It was a curious passphrase, but I'd heard stranger. "I'll keep that in mind."

He leaned back once more, his usual smile returning. "And even if you don't need me…"

I cocked an eyebrow. "Don't push your luck."

Talan bowed sarcastically. "Take care of yourself, my Finch," he said. Then he slipped down the stairs without a backward glance.

I stood there a moment, thinking again of the passphrase he'd given me. I knew myself well enough that I wouldn't call after him unless I did need him for information or a job. But I hoped it wouldn't be long.

———

The next day, Maesos sent a bird begging for me to visit, so us three Finches stopped by his glass shop. As soon as I'd entered, he folded me into his arms. "Oh, Airene," he said, and for a time, he just held me. I didn't even mind the ash he spread all over my clothes.

When I managed to gently pry him away, he looked at me with watery eyes. "Your friends told me everything. I feel responsible," he admitted. "I set you onto this hunt. If I hadn't mentioned anything—"

"Maesos," I said severely. "None of this is your fault. Xaron, Nomusa, and I knew what we were getting ourselves into." I took a deep breath. "And if you ever hear anything like this again, I want you to tell us first thing. Okay?"

He shook his head with a look of amazement. "You're one strong girl." The glass blower cleared his throat. "I'm proud of you, little Finch."

"Stop that, Maesos. You'll embarrass her," Xaron observed with a smirk.

My old friend's face grew serious. "I have heard of strains of pyrkin that might help against those like that silver-haired woman," he said in a low voice. "I promise you, Airene, I will do my best to find them if they exist. And if you ever need them…"

"I'm sure we'll be fine," I said, hoping it was true. "But thank you, Maesos. Truly."

Soon after, we said our farewells to the glass smith, then set out for another day of leisure around the city that my friends had forced on me. I supposed there were worse fates to bear.

———

When we returned that evening, I found two messages waiting for me.

The first was from a hand I didn't recognize, though I knew the name signed on it from Xaron's recent house-break. Kako, Feiyan's righthand honor.

Airene of Port,
> *My mistress has come to the understanding that you recently paid a visit to her*

estate, and learned something of her business dealings that puts her in a compromising light. I trust this information will remain undisclosed. For if it is revealed, I can assure you, one of your companions will be unable to infiltrate manors with their remarkable gifts any longer.

My heart was in my throat as I read it a second time. She knew. Somehow, Feiyan knew either Nomusa or Xaron was a feral warden. Perhaps she had that much confidence in her compound security. Or perhaps she'd had reports from other sources. I pushed away doubts of Talan immediately; after what we'd been through, I doubted he would betray us. But the mystery didn't change one thing: Feiyan was even less a woman that we wanted to cross.

The second finch was from someone I'd been looking forward to hearing from, yet it was no more pleasant. The message inside was simple: *The apothecary fled the city. Little I can do now, but I'll still try. I am sorry.* Talan hadn't signed it, but I knew it was him all the same.

I slumped against the railing and looked out over the drizzling city. Eazal had been my main hope for finding out who Iela's master was, yet I hadn't even tried looking for him myself, but instead indulged in two full days of leisure. Now, with Feiyan making threats against my accomplices, I had only the Underguild as a lead. But if Talan had not already told me anything, I had little confidence that would bear fruit.

I should have felt angry at the apothecary, or at least at myself, but I was too empty for rage at the moment. I hoped he had saved his family, if he had ever had family threatened in the first place. But I hoped even more that one day, he would think himself safe to return.

I would be waiting.

THE
PHANTOM
HEIST

A FAMINE CYCLE
NOVELLA

CHAPTER ONE

A DUSK FOR DEFAULTS

On the first evening of my last job, I stared at my cracked ceiling and wondered how it had come to this.

It was chilly thinking, wrapped in my last blanket on the thin mat that was my final furnishing, and with the cool night air finding its way through the many openings in the walls. The room was growing dark with dusk, and all the lamps, candles, and pyrkin — the glowing fungus-like plant that people often smeared on the walls for light — had gone with the rest of my worldly possessions.

All I owned was on my person: a wine-red fez, a sky-blue vest, a fine, white silk tunic, and a worn pair of trousers. Secreted within my trousers' pocket was my obsidian shard, one of the secrets to my success, and the one thing I'd never sell.

Apparently, all the rest was dispensable.

I sighed and stretched, but there was little point in trying to find a more comfortable position. Soon I'd be away, off to meet the only fools in Erimis, capital of the Avvadin Imperium, who would risk hiring me. My luck that they were rich fools.

But with foolish men came foolish ideas, and I feared to hear why Bazaad wanted my particular skills. Vault-breaking was hardly an innocuous profession. And the vault-breaking I performed often crossed people of the highest stations.

But my more immediate concern was the people I'd already crossed. My debts to them were so deep I didn't know why I bothered trying to climb out. Here in my quarters, it'd be easy to find me — the Underguild had more than enough resources to sniff me out wherever I hid. My only chance was to try to pay my debts and hope they didn't want to collect before I finished the job.

How had it come to this — as if I didn't already know. The gambling and the drinking had done their part, but it'd been the peacock that had finally done me in.

I'd broken into a wealthy pasha's manor and slipped away with his wife's box of jewels. I'd infiltrated a silk merchant's shop even when the Tefra, elite priests who could channel the power of Valem, had set jinn to guard the place. I'd traversed all over Obsidian Heights, the richest district of Erimis, infiltrating the best-guarded manors.

Yet all it had taken was one corpulent bird for my career to come crashing down.

My pitying thoughts were interrupted by a subtle shift in the air. It wasn't a sound or sight, but an intuition, and one I knew to trust. Rising quickly, I peered between the slats of my shuttered window at the court-yard outside. Nothing. Still, I backed away and kept out of sight. Whether I saw them or not, I knew there was someone out there, and I had no doubt who it was.

The Guilders had come for their silver.

My quarters, leased from a landlord with little tolerance for mischief, had no ready escape routes, but I'd been in enough tight spots to know my way around. Staying out of sight, I slunk over to the far end of the room where a high window awaited me. Once, a table had assisted me in getting up to it. Now, I had to do it the way I did all of my impossible feats for vault-breaking: using a gift — or curse — that I wasn't supposed to have, and for which I would pay the red price if it were discovered.

Closing my eyes and centering myself, I coaxed my connection to the Underneath, the world ruled by the Molten God Valem, back into flame. Anxiety fueled and propelled the process, and in moments, lines of heat were spreading from my gut, the central point of my connection, throughout my body until they pressed at my fingertips and toes.

I had seven shifts, which meant I had the potential to be relatively powerful among the Branded, those who could channel Valem's power. I'd never been able to learn much about my Branding other than what was commonly known: that Valem, or one of his great spirits, had formed in me a connection with that other world that allowed me to draw on its power. Why Valem had chosen me, I hadn't the slightest clue. But I'd always figured that, since I had it, I might as well put it to good use.

Channeling energy to my feet, I expelled it as force and leaped the ten feet up to the window. Grabbing hold of the windowsill, I hung on with one hand while the other worked the shutters off. It was no mean feat, especially while trying to be quiet, but I managed. Prying it off, I dropped back to the floor and placed it gently down so it wouldn't clatter. Then it was back up to the window, this time to slip through and haul myself onto the flat rooftop.

Once I was hidden behind the small lip running around the roof's edge, I risked glancing down. No one on the far side of the tenement. I slipped to the part of the roof facing the courtyard and looked again. A man edged along a wall three stories down, scanning around him. Had I been in my quarters, it would have been impossible to see him coming. These Guilders were no amateurs.

I silently crept along the roof toward the entrance to my quarters. My door went out to an alcove at the top of the stairs, so I'd be able to hear if they approached that way. I only had to wait a few minutes before my patience was rewarded with the first visitor.

For being an agent of the night, his steps clomped up the stairs like the giant white-skinned elephants rumored to live to the south. I heard him rap on my door.

"Talan!" the Guilder shouted in. "Talan Wraithsbane!"

I cringed at the name. Though I was sure no one knew just how accurate 'Wraithsbane' was, all traders of debauchery in Erimis knew the man who didn't fear to walk the streets at night in defiance of the Silks that patrolled them. Still, it was a bit dramatic, even for my tastes.

"We both know why I'm here. Have you the silver or not?" the Guilder demanded.

Silence. I wondered how they'd enter. Break down the door and try to detain me in a show of force? Come in through the windows and take me by stealth? And my punishment — would it be the usual severing of fingers or hands, or were my substantial debts enough to warrant a more stringent penalty? Let it be the latter, I thought; better death than losing my fingers. A Branded vault-breaker without fingers was no more than a beggar.

At the entrance, I heard whispered commands. By stealth then — I should have assumed as much. I listened to their boots shuffling along the landing below, then scraping against the side of the building. But did I detect some of the scrambling coming closer—?

His head appeared over the lip, and with his Guilder training, he spotted me in moments, his lips pulling back in a snarl.

I kicked the man in the nose, sending him tumbling backward. A moment later, his yell cut off as he hit the landing below. Barely a story down, he had probably survived the fall.

I ignored my souring stomach and the shouts of alarm below as I planned my next move. There was no use in fighting all the Guilders. To overcome them, I would be forced to use Valem's power in blatant ways, and likely someone in the building would bear witness to it. That would bring people down on me even more dangerous than the Underguild. There was only one option: I had to flee.

Still moving at a crouch, I looked at the next building over. A small street ran between, and the distance had to be twenty cubits across. If I channeled a burst of force, I could make it. Probably. Feeling inward, I kindled my inner fire back to life and braced my legs for the jump.

I heard a scrape behind me and dove to one side. Just in time — a knife clinked against the roof, sending chips of clay flying about me.

Gaining my feet and looking back, I saw the Guilder who had thrown the knife charging. Now or never. I hopped onto the lip of the roof, and before I could doubt myself, I channeled and leaped.

For a moment, I hung in the air, weightless and untethered, almost like I was flying. Then I reached the top of my arc and began to fall, and wished I'd flown a little longer. The opposite roof was close, but not close enough.

I wasn't going to make it.

I flailed for a handhold, but missed the lip of the roof, then the window beneath it. Channeling force, I desperately scrabbled at the side of the building, trying to find a purchase to slow my descent. I was halfway down the building before my fingers crashed into a small lip between the first and second stories. Strengthened with Valem's power, I broke through it, but my momentum had slowed enough that when I landed on my feet moments later, the impact didn't leave me crippled.

I didn't look around to see if my pursuers followed, but limped away as fast as I could, heading for my clandestine meeting, and hoping it came soon enough.

CHAPTER TWO

A MIDNIGHT TO MISREMEMBER

Dusty and sweaty, I hurried through the streets as the last of the sunlight faded. The Underguild had agents all over Erimis, and there was no telling where they might be hiding. Yet if they watched, they did not intervene, for I made it to the street corner where I was to meet my contact without anyone stopping me.

My contact was easy to identify among the last of the rabble packing up their stands. An agha of noble birth and standing, he wore rich red robes and had a thick peppered beard. But it was his countenance of disapproval that truly gave him away. Bazaad was not a fellow easily impressed, a fact I'd quickly found out when a former friend of a former friend put us in contact.

He caught sight of me as I approached, his expression souring as he took in my appearance. I'd acquired a new rip in my trousers from my fall, and dust layered my clothes. My fez tilted wildly off my long, messy hair. I fixed the hat at least. This was my last chance, after all.

"Talan," Bazaad said with the slightest bow that politeness would allow.

"Bazaad." I made mine deeper. It was appropriate for his rank, but I thought he knew the mockery I infused into it from his sharp look.

"You're late." His eyes wandered over me, as if to say he suspected why I had been tardy.

I gestured us onward. "Best not to delay then. We both know we can't linger."

The agha relented and began leading us down the street in the opposite direction I'd indicated. "Perhaps so. Unless the rumors are true, and the night holds no threat for you." He glanced at me from under his bushy eyebrows. "Wraithsbane."

I hid my grimace. "True enough," I said lightly. "But not all my companions are so fearless."

Bazaad raised an eyebrow, but he said nothing. I resolved to keep my tongue on a tighter leash, though I doubted I'd manage it.

I followed my companion down two more turns, then into a moldy alley. The red afterglow of the sun illuminated a roof full of feathers, hollow bones, and too-intelligent tongues that sat atop the house we'd arrived at. Parrots — apparently, my new employer had a fondness for feeding the birds that infested Erimis. One of the avian shingles cawed at us as we skirted past the front entrance to a back door. Another parrot called, "Rah! Where's the pita? Where's the pita?"

I stared, wondering if this was what passed for discreet among these men who sought to hire me. This was a last-ditch job for fools, and no mistake. I couldn't help a rueful grin. I'd come to the right place.

"Talan." Bazaad directed his substantial belly at me. "There is one other matter. It might be best not to mention the, ah, peacock. You are good at what you do from what I've heard, and they are not to think otherwise."

I bristled. That damn peacock again. "I am good at what I do."

"You are good at what you do," the agha sighed. "Valem help us all."

Letting it go, I waited as Bazaad knocked in a specific sequence. A moment later, a call-window slid open, and a pair of full, nut-brown eyes behind round spectacles peered out, escorted by the plucks of an ouk and a cloud of smoke.

"Sweet Mother below!" the glasses and eyes exclaimed. "Pour the port — Bazaad's back, and he's brought the boy!"

Wondering why twenty-six wasn't sufficient to escape being called 'boy,' I allowed Bazaad to usher me through the door into a bright, homey room. The smell of sweet smoke and sickly-sweet alcohol just added to the comfort, as did the various bottles of wine and spirits on a crooked wooden table. Around it were seated three men, all with cup and pipe in hand and staring at me. In the corner was the source of the strained music: a woman cradling the string-and-wood ouk as if it were her babe.

"Wraithsbane — Talan Wraithsbane, isn't that right?" The doorkeeper turned out to be quite a little man, and nearly as wide as he was tall. His belly put Bazaad's own to shame, proportionally speaking, and the rest of his features were nearly as plump.

"That depends on what's said about him," I said with an obligatory smile.

"Only the best! Our agha has nothing but golden words for you, dear boy, and the only gold typically in his mouth are his teeth. Welcome, welcome!" He bowed so vigorously that I was afraid he might topple over.

"Talan, this is Semih," Bazaad said. "My apologies, but we use no family names in the Firewater Den. Just know him as our gracious host."

"Speak nothing of it," Semih said with a pleased smile, waving a hand before his face. "The aloe is made to soothe the burn, as they say. I am your servant quite by compulsion of my conscience!"

Bazaad ignored him and moved me on to the table. "Comrades, may I present Talan, our honored guest this evening."

The men at the table stood to bow and shake hands. Quicker than the rest was a stolid-looking fellow, a man my senior by no more than a decade, who eclipsed my height and doubled my shoulders' width. His splotchy complexion and bloodshot eyes suggested a stringent habit of imbibing potent liquors.

"Wraithsbane," he said gruffly as we shook, then clapped me on the shoulder with his shame-hand and gave it a painful squeeze. I wasn't sure if I was to take it as a surprising display of intimacy or aggression, so I dodged with a smile. "The name's Erkan," the man continued. "Some of your exploits would make my wife's ears bleed, and I owe you a drink if even half are true."

"For your wife's sake, let's hope not," I said with another small smile.

The next man was even taller than Erkan, though his bent back disguised it. As he gripped my hand, I could almost feel every tendon and bone in his. For his worn-down manner, he struck me as young for these old-timers, with bright, moist eyes, a chin nearly unblemished by a beard, and thin, black hair cascading from beneath a tall fur hat.

"Lovely," he said in a soft, almost lyrical voice.

I plastered a smile on, even as he continued holding my hand. "Well met. And what was your name?"

"Cemal."

Funny — he looked like a camel.

He glanced at my hand, then back at my face, and mumbled something I couldn't quite catch.

"Sorry?"

Cemal leaned closer. "Flames burn deep within you," he murmured.

My hand felt as if it had been stung, and I quickly extricated it from his long fingers. "No deeper than the rest of Valem's subjugated," I said, smiling over the unease stirring in my stomach. I'd worked hard to cull information about my Branding. If I wasn't outright killed upon being discovered, I had no doubt I'd be forced to become one of the Tefra, my face scarred by fire and hidden by a jade mask.

This Cemal couldn't know of my Branding, I was sure of it. Perhaps it was just an oddly timed recitation of poetry. But if he *was* attuned to Brandings, I hoped he would keep it to himself.

Moving on quickly, I approached the final man. He was a short and slight fellow, with an oddly bent ear peeking out from beneath an ocean-blue fez. From the sly smile and knowing look in his eyes, you might have thought we were long-time accomplices. But with his broad, misshapen mouth and pitted skin, such a face would be burned in my mind.

"Haluk," he said. "I have heard so much about you, yet you remain to me an…" He winked. "An enigma. I must ask: is it true what you did in Pasha Zulfikar's manor?"

"You might not believe me, but snipping his wife's robes the first time was the simple part. It was the four times after that became tricky."

Haluk shook his head and turned away, that knowing smile still playing across his lips while he tugged at his bent ear.

"Well, if that's done with…" Bazaad impatiently ushered me to the table.

"Please, Efendi Wraithsbane, let me pour you something!" Semih exclaimed as I sat. "Our hot summer days leave parched throats, they do indeed. What may I serve you?"

I was near salivating at the prospect of spirits, a too-rare treat in the officially dry Imperium. "Surprise me. Perhaps something with a shake of sweet to start and a hint of zest to finish."

"We are of one mind!" Semih cried, and began shuffling through the bottles.

"Not that one!" Erkan bellowed as Semih reached for one bottle. "He said 'zest and sweet,' not 'take my burned tongue off'! Try that new Oedijan import — no, *no*, the green bottle, you ash-headed twit!"

"That would, perhaps, do," Haluk said mildly, "but you might try an orange rum."

"He *might*," Erkan said as he loomed over him, "but he *might* be looking for something to mix things up. Eh, Wraithsbane?"

"It's been so long since I've had a proper drink, I've probably lost any discernment. Either will have my unending thanks."

But Semih, hovering between the two recommendations, couldn't make a decision — so Erkan made it for him, snatching the green bottle and pouring it into my glass. "So we don't wait 'til ashes blow over us all," he muttered. "Now, can we get this damn thing started?"

"Nonsense!" Semih said, recovered from Erkan's slight. "You mustn't rush business, Efendi Erkan, no indeed. You would pass up all the things worth knowing!"

Haluk leaned forward with curled lips. "I have many things worth knowing. I suppose you haven't heard of our Grand Vizier's peacock?"

I sputtered my wine, only half on purpose, but it didn't divert the conversation. Cemal nodded with what passed for eagerness and said softly, "It fluttered from the window, a candle dancing in the wind."

"It was burning *pushed* out, you mean," Erkan declared.

"Ah, indeed," Haluk said with an uplifted finger, "but by who?"

All the blood in my body rushed to my head, but Bazaad swooped in to rescue me. "Do not discuss such groundless rumors," he scolded them. "It is unseemly of people of our station."

Erkan held up his cup and glared at him. "And this is seemly? We're beyond manners here, Bazaad."

Haluk, looking displeased that his moment of revelation was being stolen, tried again. "But *who* would do such a thing to our Grand Vizier's beloved pet?"

He can't know, I told myself, but that sly smile of his persisted. I needed this money to survive the span. But just when my silver tongue needed to earn its keep, it lay limp in my mouth.

"Who indeed?" Semih obliged his companion, leaning forward.

The small man met our eyes, then leaned forward himself. "It is said a Silk drove it out."

"A Silk?" Erkan snorted. "That's the most ash-burnt thing I've heard yet. You think a jinni gives a caw about a bird?"

"Then how," Haluk retorted, "did the creature fly from the window, and only the coral clothes of a Silk were visible? Or, I suppose, men fly like birds?"

Cemal, looking pained with the need to speak, finally blurted, "But the Harem saw!"

"Saw what?" Erkan demanded, pouring something amber into his cup. "Speak your damned mind, Cemal, it won't burning kill you."

Haluk looked as eager to hear what Cemal had to say, though he tried to hide it behind another smile, while Bazaad watched the proceedings with a shepherd's fond and resigned expression. I suppressed a sigh and watched with him.

"A man," Cemal said, eyes wide. "Descending from a rope, in the robes of those who are kept behind."

"A Silk's robes," Haluk said thoughtfully. "I suppose that makes sense."

"How does that make sense?" Erkan spat. "Where would he get them? It's not like people go around stealing Silks' clothes — more likely his own skin would be torn off." As tough as he acted, the man shivered visibly at the thought.

The others looked stricken as well. I would have laughed had they not been discussing my recent shame.

Semih recovered first. "A Tefra would have access to them," he piped up.

This rallied Erkan. "Of course they would — but what would a burning Tefra do running around the Grand Vizier's quarters, throwing peacocks out windows, then parading about the Harem's chambers? That'd be his head, yoking Silks for the Prophet King or not."

The Tefra — another one of my favorite topics to discuss. I swallowed the rest of the wine down and stood. No man deserved this kind of torture, but especially not when he was riding the gentle waves of intoxication for the first time in weeks. "I fawn over rumors as much as the next washer-woman, but I'd appreciate if we could get back on track here."

Bazaad pulled at his pipe and slowly exhaled. "Yes, let us. I have informed Talan of our task's basic premise, but the details remain to be divulged."

"Don't blame you," Erkan snorted. "Trap him here so he can't get away when he hears." He took yet another hearty swig.

Bazaad turned the whole of his agha-importance on the man now. "Erkan, you had best shut that flapping curtain you call a mouth, or we shan't have ourselves the best vault-breaker to ever walk this city. Is that what you want?"

"Fine then," Erkan muttered, staring into his wine. "Tell him your burning idea already."

"And what idea would that be?" I pressed.

The agha's gaze returned to me, considering.

"Better give him a refill first," Erkan blared again, apparently not chastised into complete silence. Semih rushed to comply with the green bottle. My head buzzing pleasantly, I nodded my gratitude to the host, and he beamed in return.

Bazaad cleared his throat, looking at everyone before his gaze settled back on me. "You have heard of the Mausoleum of Glass?"

I was taken aback. "Agha, I break into guarded places. How would I not know of the most perilous of the Imperium's treasuries?"

"Just so. Though 'treasury' is a curious term to assign it. It did not start that way if the tales tell true — Aasjuqal built it as a temple to our Molten Lord. It was thought that, if such a worshipful place were close to his fiery roots, those who dared to tempt fate would gain Valem's respect and be rewarded with terrible power. That was when he was more active, of course, and a Lament occurred every other year. But when malevolent jinn drove out or killed the last of the zealots, Ayberk Kahin-Shah fitted it for this other purpose."

Bazaad frowned and shook his head. "In any case," he continued, "it happens that a possession was taken away from our forebears some decades ago, during the first of the Purity Purges. Nehir's Chalice, it is now called."

"Then I suppose you'll tell him the story," Erkan muttered.

Bazaad glared at him. "Perhaps I shall, Erkan, if it is not too much bother for you." He turned back to me. "It is named after the enchantress who made it and died by it. Whether she deserved that punishment, no one can say; yet her king had been murdered by it and someone had to take the blame."

"A cursed cup. I fail to see how that serves your purposes." Or, indeed, what their use for it could be.

Bazaad raised an eyebrow. "You know our reputation as suppliers of spirits?"

"Of course. But I assume there's more to it if I'm breaking into an Imperial vault."

"Astute as ever, Talan. The liquor business is only the veneer of our operations, and the means by which we fund our true goals."

He paused, and studied me for a long moment, like a bear eyeing its next meal. "Do you love the Avvadin Imperium, Talan?"

"I can't say I've ever harbored warm feelings for it."

"I thought not. But I wished to ensure it, for we..." Bazaad looked around at the others, and received nods of confirmation in return, then looked back at me. "We seek to overthrow the Prophet King's regime. For good."

I liked this plan better all the time. "Overthrow the Imperium. Sounds very reasonable and attainable." I had to swallow down the panicked laughter threatening to bubble up. "But I'm a bit unclear as to how a cup will help that."

"Nehir's Chalice," Bazaad corrected severely. "But yes, we are meandering off the point." He cleared his throat. "Recently, I was informed that the artifact is kept in the Mausoleum."

"In the Vacant City, then." That was the heart of the Mausoleum. Not only did Aasjuqal, our Imperium's founder, see it fit to build the pyramidic temple out of black granite and volcanic glass from the side of Valem, but he carved out a cluster of empty buildings inside of it, supposedly to house his enslaved jinn. Silks were its only occupants, floating between the piles of gilded whips, jeweled underwraps, and other nonsense that the titled rich and religious elite, the Foremost, concocted.

"Quite so," Haluk said, giving me another knowing smile.

"And what exactly is this Chalice?" I inquired. "I mean, two people died from it. Is it laced with poison?"

Bazaad frowned, Erkan snorted, Haluk smirked, Semih wiped at his forehead with a handkerchief of silk. All smoked in ouk-stricken silence — all except for Cemal, who peered at me with wide, watery eyes, seeming more like his namesake animal all the time. "A poisoned cup, yes," he said, wrapping his fingers as if around an invisible version of it. "But also a panacea."

I tried to keep my face smooth. "I'm afraid I don't quite understand." How anyone could understand the man was beyond me.

But I understood one thing: It was a cup that I was about to risk my life for. A Valem-seared, damnable cup. It was at that moment that I realized just how far I'd fallen this past week, and all from one peacock. Mostly.

I turned to Bazaad. "Tell me there's more, or I won't need this drink for my head to spin."

Erkan leaned forward with a smile that looked savage among these respectable, plotting drunks. "Didn't I tell you!" he said, gesticulating wildly with his shame-hand, the other too busy nursing his goblet. "He's going to run! And can you blame him?"

"But — ah, Erkan," Semih stumbled. "Was it not your idea—?"

"A *jest*, I said it in jest! Can't you ash-filled dunces understand a simple jest?" He slammed a hand down on the table, rattling the bottles and making Cemal jump.

"Quiet," Bazaad demanded. His eyes hadn't left me. "Let me explain, Talan. This cup — it is no ordinary cup."

"I would never dream to claim that. I'm sure sentimentality counts for much. The lives of six men, apparently."

"It has certain properties," the agha continued stubbornly. "Properties that are useful to our cause."

"Copper pays the way, as they say."

"For one burned moment, *will you listen to me?*"

My mouth may not know when to quit flapping, but my ears had more sense. I shut up and listened.

Bazaad harrumphed. "It is said never to run dry of liquors."

"Our cause will spread," Haluk said sagely.

"We'll fill the streets with drunks," Erkan snorted.

Cemal nodded solemnly.

I was speechless — but only for a moment. "You... really believe that's true." I looked to the ouk player for confirmation of their madness, but she placidly played on, her fingers never faltering in their plucking.

"Why not?" Haluk objected. "Do we not have eternal flames in the temples? And spirits clad in mortal coil? And the wonder of the Thunder

Below Our Feet?" He smiled, and this time it came off as the condescension of a zealot.

We also had Branded like me leeching off of the Underearth's power, since we were naming wonders of the world. But that was a far cry from a magical fountain of spirits. "If it *is* some unending font of sots," I hedged, "what does that do for you?"

Bazaad leaned forward. "Talan, ask yourself: what is the worst the Prophet King has done to us?"

I didn't have to think long to come up with a few answers. "Conquering dozens of independent peoples and slaughtering any who oppose? Forbidding all religions other than the worship of Valem? Enslaving the spirits of any who dare to rebel into Silks?"

He shook his head. "No, Talan. These are terrible, indeed they are. But to rob a man of doing what he wants with his own body? That is the worst crime of all."

"Ah." I drained the rest of my wine in silence, suddenly realizing how matters stood. I was learning a valuable lesson that I already should have known: You can't reason with madmen, and least of all drunk ones.

Bazaad sat back, satisfied, as if I'd confirmed his assertion. "We will have pimars of gold and silver to spare. And once they discover they can have the comfort of liquor for free, they will flock to our front, never fear. Men are inebriated on noble causes."

Letting go of all resistance, I held out my cup. "Fine. A chalice of an unrequited intoxication — surely worth risking death for."

"He understands!" Semih said happily, clapping Erkan on the shoulder, though he quickly flinched back at his glare.

"Good," Bazaad said. "Now, what say you, Talan? Are you our man?"

Everyone stopped for a moment, even the ouk player, though she just had an itch on her nose. Semih, nervously bustling as he always seemed to be, stopped midway through filling my glass.

"Well now," I hedged. "Some of the finer points of this job could be clarified first."

"Of course," Bazaad said quickly. Even he seemed nervous that I might decline, despite knowing my predicament. "What would you like to know?"

The mind boggled at all the things I wanted to know, but I knew an understanding of the turns my life had just taken was too great of a wish. "First off," I started, "do you have any leads into the Mausoleum?"

"A simple answer!" Semih chirped with an uplifted finger. "Essentially, no. But this is your expertise, is it not, Efendi Wraithsbane?"

I wanted to tear at my hair in frustration. "It is indeed," I said graciously. "And I shall provide marvelously for it, never fear. But are there, say, any other assets I should be aware of?"

"Ah," Haluk said, leaning forward. "But we have not yet mentioned your… accomplices."

My mind started going through my former acquaintances, wondering who they'd possibly gotten to agree to this foolhardy mission. Parrot? Muckdeck? Irontoe? "I'm utterly mystified. Might you illuminate me?"

Haluk smiled slightly, but before he could speak, Erkan stole his thunder once again. "It's us three, or couldn't you tell we're burning thieves from the look of us?" He punctuated the statement with a bitter laugh.

I hadn't thought my stomach could sink lower. "Ah. Which three, exactly?"

Cemal pointed — first at himself, then Erkan, and last at Haluk.

"I'm sorry," Semih rushed to say, "but Bazaad and I are much too recognizable to manage such antics. We'd be more hindrance than help, I fear."

And this triad of sops was supposed to be better? I smiled all the wider. "You are too kind. Three companions are far more than I could have hoped for."

Haluk leaned back, looking pleased, while Erkan squinted suspiciously at me. Bazaad seemed to catch my mood, but he didn't speak.

Even still, I could tell my response had been less than they'd hoped for. Burn it all — if it was my last opportunity, I might as well make the most of it. I grabbed the orange rum I'd been eyeing all night, filled my cup, and raised it.

"You asked me if I'm your man. If I'll agree to lead you to a wellspring of middling sweetness and a lifetime of misremembered nights. To joy unrelenting and unceasing, and happiness in every drop. What can a man say, but to damn those who stand between him and his friends' prize?" I shook my cup for emphasis, sloshing a bit of the rum onto my hand, but I didn't let that slow me. "I say yes! Let us steal back your chalice, and let the Imperium rot from its very core!"

The cheer was pathetic at best, but the rum was reassuring as it burned down my throat. When I looked back up, I saw why they were so silent. To a man, they were draining their glasses.

How could I have doubted they were my kind of lowlifes?

———

As the evening dragged on and the talk turned back to peacocks splattered in the Obsidian Palace courtyard, even the drink wasn't worth staying for. I pushed to my feet, only just managing to keep upright. "Well, good efendi," I said as coherently as I could, "this has made for a very pleashant — ah, pleasant evening, thanks to you all. I hope to bring you many more shoon — soon."

The rest stood up as abruptly and unsteadily. "What?" Erkan exclaimed. "You're leaving?"

"Quite," I said with a debonair air. "Why, is that a problem?"

"He loves to show off, our Wraithsbane," Bazaad said with lowered eyebrows. "That he does not fear to tread where other men dare not. As long as you bring that confidence to the Mausoleum, Talan, and do not get yourself killed before then, I admire the quality."

"You have my assurances, Bazaad — I'll wait until your hallowed job is through to let death take me."

As I exchanged bows and handshakes all around again, Bazaad said, "We do not usually meet more than once a week, but such an occasion can shift our routine, I am sure. When would suit you best, Talan?"

"That depends. Will there be more of this at our next meeting?" I gestured to the bottles scattered across the table.

"Of course!" Semih cried. "We wouldn't be the Firewater Den without them!"

"In that case, I'll have a preliminary plan by tomorrow evening."

"Good." Bazaad ushered me to the door, blocking the others from following with his great frame, and we escaped outside. When the cool evening air and three moons' light settled over our shoulders, the agha shivered and looked about nervously. I almost laughed to see such an important man unsettled. Aghas, after all, could have conferences with the Kahin-Shah himself if need commanded it.

"Never fear," I said. "They won't come where I am."

"I do hope so," he muttered. But he shook it off admirably fast for one still vulnerable. "But you have questions, I'm sure."

"Maybe a few. Say, one for each of my alleged accomplices."

Bazaad sighed. "Yes, there is that bit of trouble. I am not sure you could dissuade them even if they will be a hindrance, so you had best use them any way you can."

"But why?" I insisted. "Who in their right mind wants to do the task before me?" At a look from Bazaad, I amended, "Anyone who isn't a fabulously renowned breaker, that is."

"They each have their reasons. Cemal, I believe, is purely driven by interest — it *is* a historical monument, practically alive with jinn, and those sorts of mysteries fascinate him. Haluk..." Bazaad folded his hands before him and bowed his head a moment. "At this point, it is fervor that drives him most, though perhaps he hopes for something more... material. He had a rather unfortunate habit until recently, and he seems to have replaced it with an unblinking belief in our cause. But you know how these addictions come and go."

"Don't tell me — cinderlung, wasn't it?"

Bazaad looked at me in mild astonishment. "The fingertips," I explained. "They're still bleached."

"Ah… Well, yes. But it is sorted out now. As for Erkan, I would warrant he wishes for an escape of some sort."

"There are hot springs out east — wouldn't he prefer that sort of vacation?"

"Unfortunately, no." Bazaad looked out back towards the street, looking as if fear was again threatening to take hold. "If you are truly leaving, best to do it before too long."

I shook his hand and bowed once more. "Thank you," I said simply. "For the chance."

He started to turn away, then paused. "Just do not make me regret it." He hurried back inside.

Alone, I stumbled onto the sprawling, dark streets of Erimis, hoping beyond hope to find some soft place to sleep.

CHAPTER THREE

A DAWN TO RUE

The next morning, I woke to find I had two problems on my hands. Or rather, in my head, as the pounding first went, and in my gut, like the stewing second. It was one of those times I was caught between two undesirable choices: sitting up or staying down, upchucking or choking. In such cases, inertia almost always wins out.

But I'd been sleeping in an alley, and it was not the most comfortable of beds. So after a bit of recuperation — the head-between-the-knees kind — I managed to gain my feet with a steadying hand on the wall. Somehow, I found it in me to laugh. No matter how drunk I'd been in the past, I'd never found myself passed out in an alley. I was at least glad I'd kept the presence of mind to set wards, or I might never have woken.

My choice of beds hadn't been all inebriation-induced. Even in last night's state, I'd remembered I couldn't return to my quarters without the Underguild knowing. Where else was there to go, really, when you didn't have a coin to your name? I didn't even have a decent place to piss now — so I relieved myself in the alley, like any common pauper.

But as I emerged from between the buildings, combing back my hair to fit again under my red fez, I realized there was one place I could go, which I'd unconsciously drifted to last night. Just across the way sat a large stone building, with a dome in the center and four wings extending off the sides. It had a stately grace, as many old, well-kept buildings do, though decadence was evident in its mossy bricks and the dull gild of its molding. This one was built in the time of Ayberk Kahin-Shah two hundred years ago in honor of the Buyujinn, the Shrouded Mother, as well as to show his favor towards the religious sect the Hortum Kor, or Those Who Dance with Whirling Embers. This was their temple still, I knew all too well.

My growling stomach demanded that I enter, so I soon found myself through the doors and inside the foyer. Familiar things take on a strange aspect when your head is muddled; you notice things you never would have noticed before. Like the corner a pupil had been sweeping all the temple's dust into — 'cutting corners,' you might say. Or the bronze flaking around the slot of the collection vat. Or the film of jade patina on the facade of the Shrouded Mother, one of the Lost Mother's many manifestations, coating the veil behind which her eyes were hidden, forever mourning the sons and daughters she lost to Valem's rage. Each were a reminder that time doesn't stop when you leave a place. It's always gnawing away.

The foyer blended into the eaves of a sunlit rotunda, and served as a place for the poor to stand and watch the performances that often took place there. I stepped between the columns of the rotunda and into the whirling circle they formed around and glimpsed a hint of the temple's former glory. The polished floor sparkled with sunlight from the high windows by the clever placement of silver between and around balconies, and enough light was reflected to set the whole room ablaze. The marble lining on the balconies was a clean and bright white, while the wooden trims were waxed and dark. On a full day, two hundred watchers could look upon the Kor spinning below, sky blue skirts spread, turning around the point of their conical red caps like tops turned the wrong way.

It felt right, proper, to turn as they did — as I had, once. For when your head is spinning — and everything else for that matter — what else can you do but spin with it?

Standing in the middle of the circle, I set my feet, straightened and relaxed my body, and set my arms into position: left low, right high, palms splayed skyward. My chin went level with the floor, my eyes found a stable spot on a column, and I tightened my core. My feet shifted closer, one just before the other.

Then I began to turn.

I moved slowly to start, like a waterwheel in the dry season, always to the left around the heart. The heart is the center of our bodies, and as such it was the hub of my turn. My gaze lingered on a column, and I caught it as I turned back around, keeping the creeping dizziness at bay. I imagined I heard the great heart-drums that lined the floor during a performance thumping the beat, one for each turn, vibrating the whole of my body with each booming hit.

I turned faster and closed my eyes, and the sunlight flashed over my eyelids. I felt my balance shifting, but I kept the pace, kept turning. My body had caught the rhythm, and my head was catching on. As I balanced out, I could almost picture the mammoth red finger of Valem pressing down on my head, keeping my erect body rooted as it spun round and round.

Nausea almost stopped me as I spun faster, imaginary drums still thrumming, but I knew I was getting close. Close to that moment when spinning seemed more natural than staying still. When I would understand in my very body that we were made to spin; that we, at our very core, are nothing but spinning parts, mimicking the astrological bodies, the world itself. When I would feel that my body had joined them, and in their simultaneous movements, become one.

But the thing about spinning is that it always eventually stops. The peace dissipates, the truth falls flat on its face, and the tilting world reasserts itself. I stopped whirling and looked up at the crossing sunbeams, wondering how to untangle the knots I'd tied myself into.

———

After grabbing a loaf of pita from the kitchens, I walked down one of the temple's wings toward a closed door. For all the ornate decor in the rotunda, this one was as plain as a newly felled tree. But that was just the way the temple's Hodja wanted it; the temple's general richness was often the subject of his scathing comments. Of course, he was entitled to say what he wanted of his place of worship so long as he continued to maintain it. Though he could have attended to the discipline of his duster a little bit more.

Chewing on a warm bite of bread, I knocked on the door. It was still early, but Osman usually rose before dawn. If he was on his usual schedule, he would be pacing and reading a book. If it was *truly* a standard day, that book would be *Meditations by Turns*, by the Original Twister himself, who was said to have spun and charmed the Shrouded Mother into stopping the Prophet King from annihilating a rebelling colony. My colony, actually — it might have been why I sought this temple in particular when I first came to Erimis, those ten years ago. A hungry, lonely adolescent with nowhere to go. I was feeling all too much like that boy these days.

I barely heard the slaps of feet on stone before the door swung open to reveal a familiar face framed by a cloud of black and gray hair. Just like him — utterly in command of himself in every aspect, but he allowed the mane to do what it would.

"Talan. Or... what do they call you these days? Ghost-wrestler? Phantom-kicker?"

"Ha, ha, haven't heard those before. Neglecting your reading to think of cheap gibes?"

"Of course not — they come to me like breathing. Besides, some of us don't go out of our way to sin."

"Because it comes naturally, I suppose."

He gave me a grin and stepped aside. As I brushed past, I smelled fresh sweat on him. It wasn't reading this morning, but spinning. I could sympathize with feeling unbalanced, though I wondered what had him feeling so.

His chambers hadn't changed much since the last time I'd visited. In one corner, a mattress thinner than a feather and harder than a stone. Along the opposite wall, several bookshelves, sparsely occupied, though not from lack of trying. And on the last wall, a wide, bright window, with a soft cushion for guests and a tough one for himself. In the center was a desk with a few stacks of paper and some letters half-composed.

Osman himself was eternal as ever. Though strands of his wild mane were leeched of color, the lines had furrowed deeper into his skin, and his deeply bronze skin had turned slightly more ashen, he remained a lithe, vigorous man, with a sense of weightlessness about his stride. His eyes, the hue of wildflower honey, seemed to laugh and empathize all at once, though I knew from experience they could petrify if the situation called for it.

"So," Osman said, closing the door, "ask for money first. I'd like to get that part out of the way."

I took a big bite of pita and chewed it long and well before answering. "Now, Os, when have I ever asked for money?"

"You have a point. Typically, you propose a scheme, then request... what was it? Ah, yes — *financing*."

"So you do see the difference. I'm glad to hear it, as—"

"Wait," he said, holding up a hand. "No need to say."

"What they say of a master's perception must be true: you read my mind's movements like a Tefra does the stars."

I chewed another bite and took a turn about the room. Os's eyes followed me closely; not suspicious, not curious, just with his usual engaged attention.

"If it's true that I have a scheme," I continued, "explanations are wind; my need ought to be clear."

"As an ash-blown day."

We exchanged smiles. Nothing had changed, of course. There was no ford for this issue. But between us, that had never mattered.

"Just out of curiosity," he said, "though I'm sure I won't want to know once I've asked — but who's the victim now?"

"You should ask where. And it's the Mausoleum — where else?"

Osman gave me a serious look now, trying to see if I was bluffing, but I let nothing on. "Consider your proposal heartily rejected," he said. "Now that we're done with that nonsense… have you kept up your practice?"

"Every day that I don't drink or throw spokes."

He stared at me, and I almost felt ashamed at the profound disappointment in his eyes. "My best student and he doesn't even keep the turns. What legacy do I leave behind?"

"A bit early to worry about that, don't you think? But never fear — none of your progeny could match your own skills."

"One might," he said, crossing his arms and leaning against the desk, "if he practiced."

I took another bite. "I might have time to practice if I didn't have to search for financing."

Osman suddenly leaned forward and looked at me. I could imagine all the things he saw: dusty, unkempt hair peeking out from my tilted fez; bloodshot eyes, foul breath, stained and wrinkled clothes. He didn't comment on anything, though, but leaned back and said, "It does look like you've been busy."

"Then we've reached a switchback? Perhaps we can come to an understanding."

But he waved his hand, and I knew it wasn't the time to push. I took my last bite regretfully.

"Any new victims to the temple?" I asked him, licking the crumbs from my fingers.

He smiled, if a lion smiling could be called that. "Two came last Threefall. One lost his lunch the first day. I'm still trying to break the other. Hundred spins a session until it happens."

"You are the paragon of puking; if anyone can manage it, you will. Or, if you're lucky, you'll have another promising pupil."

"The Mother knows my luck isn't good enough for that."

There was another moment of silence, and I walked over to the window. Valem's side was smoky today, the sun barely piercing through the haze of his breath. Though I knew it didn't necessarily mean a Lament, there was always the chance it might. Thirty-eight years ago, the last time that the Father mourned his wife's sacrifice of herself in order to birth humanity, half of Erimis was caught in a river of molten lava as it cut straight down the middle of the city, killing hundreds and displacing thousands.

And that had been a gentle Lament.

But that was my people in a nutshell: drawn to power like parrots to pita, the inevitable and deadly consequences be damned. And I was nothing if not a man of my people.

Osman joined me at the window, putting his foot up on the bench and leaning into it like a dandy posing for a lady. "An active day. Let us hope his servants don't have an active night."

It seemed the Hodja had a different fear. The Silks, though for the most part calm and adherent to their routes, seemed to roam more on nights when Valem was rousing.

Suddenly, a memory half-forgotten came to mind. Perhaps it was the dull edge of anxiety from Valem's activity; perhaps it was just hearing about a Silk here, in the Kor temple. All at once, I lived again my first close pass with a Silk, and blinked with the force of the memory.

I wet my lips as I studied Osman looking out the window. I had always wanted to ask him about that incident, and had before, but it was a dangerous topic to broach. If he didn't coldly ignore me, he would demand I choose another subject or leave his solar. But if I couldn't ask it now, a man in my own right and far removed from his tutelage, I'd never understand what had happened.

Besides, what was ever gained without a bit of danger?

"Os, do you remember the night I left?"

There was the slightest stiffening in his jaw that would have been imperceptible to anyone who didn't know him. But he at least responded, even if it was with a terse, "Yes."

I pressed on, asking the question I'd never been able to figure out. "What was that Silk doing inside the temple?"

———

The memory was still visceral and clear. It began with my returning to the temple right after I'd thought I'd left it for the last time. I had stormed out in a rage, one of the many times I railed against Osman for his stringent rules, and had resolved never to return. But I'd left so quickly I hadn't taken my possessions, and now I was back to steal them. The curtains up front didn't keep anyone out; who would take from one of the faith, especially the pauper Hortum Kor? What did they have worth stealing? Yet there I was, stealing into the foyer, and meaning to take more besides.

I was almost to my wing when I noticed it.

Silks were named for the two slowly waving bands of cloth that chained them, as it was all you could see of them. What their invisible bodies really looked like, and how they employed them to kill people, no one could say — but everyone had a guess. Some thought it used its cloth manacles to slice men apart. Others thought they had claws and teeth we couldn't see, that they were some sort of harpy half-held in this world. From what I'd seen — and I'd seen a lot of Silks — neither of these were quite right. But I didn't go around spouting my theories on it. Some knowledge you didn't spread if you valued your neck and its attachment to your shoulders.

This Silk was spinning, unusual for the spirits, right in the middle of the rotunda. I froze, hoping it hadn't already detected me, and slowly backed away. Too late — it abruptly turned to face me with what seemed its front. The four ends of the bands, curled about its invisible body like vines on a tree, waved gently in the air as if suspended in water.

Then it glided forward, and the desire awakened inside me.

How can I explain it? It seeped into my very spirit, crystallized my blood so that I was no more the master of my body than I was of the wind. I became a moth to the flame, yearning to be consumed. I surrendered to it.

Yet as great as my yen was, some part of my reason was still awake, recognizing that I moved not away from the Silk as I should have been, but toward it. I screamed as my body revolted in lust and rushed to embrace what could only prove to be my death.

The Silk was mere paces away when it slowed, and I shuddered to a stop as well. Its ribbons reached out like the tendrils of a newly born plant, or the tentacles of a fabled sea monster. I reached forward as well despite my better judgment. I'd never wanted to touch something so much as then. I wondered if the cloth was as soft as the rumors claimed.

My finger brushed the fabric, and my skin *rippled*. It pulled towards the jinn in folds, straining and stretching to get free. Like the Silk wished to clothe itself in my skin.

But before any tears appeared, a change swept over me, like a wall of fire burning through a forest, purifying and inescapable. I felt another presence pulsing inside me. It didn't feel intrusive like a parasite, but was like the memory of my mother embracing me as a child and the warmth in her arms. This other presence reassured me without words, calmed me, let me know I would not be harmed.

Then came the second change. An inferno blazed to life within my gut and spread to the tips of every limb. It suffused me more thoroughly than the presence, burning away my will, burning away even my sense of body. I was little more than a forge with no way to tamp down the flames as they seared and purified.

Just when I thought it would envelop me, the fire died down, and I could think and sense the world again. When I came to, I found that many strange things had happened. For some reason, I was slowly spinning. Even more incomprehensible, the Silk that had just been trying to kill me hovered at some paces away. And lastly, when I brought my hands up, they were glowing with trailing wisps of light. I stared at them. My sense of wonder had burned to cinders, and I could do little more than that.

Slowly, I began to understand. I had heard of this even in legends, but never thought it anything more than stories told to children, or that of empires to their unwitting subjects. But light and fire at my fingertips — there was only one explanation that I knew of for that.

Somehow, inexplicably, I had become Branded.

Kill it.

I startled, stumbling out of my slow spin. A reedy, woman's voice had suddenly spoken in my ear. "Hello?" I said aloud with a raw throat, though I didn't see where the voice could have come from.

Reach out, it spoke again. *Touch it. You no longer have anything to fear.*

I eyed the Silk floating before me. The voice had to mean it. "Why?" I demanded.

It will kill you, my son.

Without warning, the Silk's tendrils shot out toward me. I reflexively threw out my hands to catch them, though fear ran through me. But as my skin touched the cloth, it didn't rip off. Instead, it was the jinni who tried to pull away, violently tugging away, though it had been the one to surge forward. Somehow, I felt I shouldn't let go. I feared it would do as the voice said if I let it free.

Something flared deep inside me, and I felt warmth spread through me anew. Without knowing why, I started to whirl, and the Silk began to wrap around me. We turned, once, twice, thrice, around and around. I nestled into it, and it pressed close about me. I tasted it on my tongue; I almost seemed to remember who it was, its — her — past, this jinni that was once human. I began to forget which memories were hers and which were mine.

Then the cloth beneath my fingers began to grow hot. I brought it up, and, disbelieving, saw more of the impossible: fire emerged from my hand, spreading fast across the cloth. It was not red or orange or yellow, but the pale violet of a late sunset sky just before the dark of night settles in. It burned crisp and clear and spread fast, and did not consume as it went, but danced atop the fabric.

As the Silk wrapped about me, and I into her, I slowly felt her memories, my memories, fade into forgetfulness.

I stood there for a long time, wrapped in those silk bands. Osman found me like that, still turning in place, staring at nothing but my hand and the unburned cloth running from it. It felt just as soft as everyone had always imagined.

The memory is not as strong as it was before; years and other experiences have left it wan in comparison. But even so, I remember how I embraced the woman that had been chained into a Silk. How I burned her away. And of the other woman's voice I hadn't heard since.

———

"What was it doing here?" I asked Osman again. I had been standing there silent for a moment too long. But then again, so had he.

"I don't know," he responded quietly.

"Don't you? Even when they wander, it's nearly unheard of that they would enter a building unless they were under orders." I paused, not sure if I wanted to voice my long-held suspicions, for the uncertain implications they might bear. "Were they… here for me?"

"What?" He sounded genuinely surprised as he turned toward me, then barked a laugh. "No, they weren't here for you."

"Is that so ridiculous?" I demanded. "Maybe they found out I was Branded—"

"*You* didn't even know you were Branded until that night," Osman cut me off. "How could anyone else have known? Was somebody peering at your fingers or toes on a regular basis?"

I fought back a flush. "No, but—"

"Let it go. Count it as a blessing of the Shrouded Mother." He turned away. "Now, if you don't mind, I have classes to lead."

"No," I repeated stubbornly, walking around in front of him. "I'm not going to let you brush it off this time. Of all the things you've told me, why hold this back?"

The Hodja — my Hodja — leaned in close enough for me to smell the licorice tea on his breath. "You don't need to steal every damn thing in sight," he growled. "Especially not something in another man's past."

That went too far. "Another man's past? I almost died that night. If anything, that night belongs to me."

He pushed past me, and even in my annoyance, I allowed him, though not without a small shove. "Well," I called after him, "how about at least giving me that loan?"

What he said was unbefitting a priest's mouth. But it was as good a balm as I could hope for. Even without my answers, I relaxed. At least nothing between us had changed.

CHAPTER FOUR

A MORNING FOR FLEEING

With my head somewhat clearer, my belly somewhat fuller, and my appearance just as disheveled, I decided it was past time to act professional and perform some reconnaissance.

I headed down to the canal docks, passing the usual sights, smells, and sounds along the way. Men and women at stalls harked their wares, and the aromas of citrus fruits, savory meats, and fragrant spices sent my stomach rumbling all over again. Most corners hosted some kind of beggar, whether they were musicians plucking ouks, banging drums, and trilling on flutes, or cripples made during the Prophet King's many wars. There were, of course, the usual stinks of any city, but the latrines were at least covered and a few feet deep here, and washed out frequently enough to take the bite out of their pungency.

Soon enough, I reached the Jade Docks, which were built off the city's main canal, the Crimson. Stepping to its edge, I looked along its red-lichen walls, down the docked boats and market stalls to the broad base of the Mausoleum of Glass. A moat branched about the pyramid to dissuade any perpetrators, and dissuaded I felt, though more for all the excrement, urine, and unknowable other filth in the water.

I lifted my gaze to the Mausoleum itself. It leaned off of one sheer side of volcanic Valem, shaped in the traditional stepped pyramid of the Foremost. But since half of it was a cave, only the front facade protruded, a building composed of blocks of black and scarlet granite. It was not entirely made of stone, though; fireglass ornamented its sides in significant shapes for the faith and imperium. Here the crescent flame, the symbol of the Tefra. There the spread-feather peacock, the icon of the religious and political elite the Foremost. And on the other side, the five interlocking circles, the fingertips of Aasjuqal, holy mark of the first Prophet King of Avvad. They weren't his actual fingerprints, of course; as Branded, his prints would have constantly shifted. Just as mine do.

As I stared at the Mausoleum from the middle of the street, dock workers irritably pushing past me, I plumbed my thoughts for some plan to save me from my sodden fate. But it wasn't until my gaze happened upon some unstopped barrels next to me that I felt an idea latch on like a barnacle inside my skull.

We'd float in by barrel. Yes, a man to a barrel, and we'd drift right up to the Mausoleum, approaching it from the backside. Then we'd scale the pyramid's sides, maybe with grappling hooks, bound with cloth to dampen the clatter. We'd ascend, right to the very top, where the only entrance lay, and…

And…

Sneak past the guards, into the thick double doors locked with keys only they held, and past the other guards that no doubt waited within?

The plan unraveled as reason returned. Floating in barrels on the Crimson — how would we breathe, or direct ourselves toward our destination, or not tip over? And using grappling hooks to climb the Mausoleum? There were no purchases for them, not with walls slippery with lichen, and they'd clang like prisoners on the work lines, cloth around them or no. Then, of course, there were all those yayas waiting for us at the top.

I'd never had such an idiotic plan.

But such is the way of vault-breaking: the first scheme is always bad. But scrape away the scum, and something will show up beneath.

Usually.

With the sun beating down hard, and my schemes coming up dry, I was getting two kinds of thirst. So I tucked the plans away to let them fester and sought out a game of spokes with some liquor to wash it down.

Dodging around deeply tanned sailors with even deeper scowls, I crossed Cobbler Bridge and headed down a narrow, crud-crusted flight of stairs on the other side. A few old women were down at the water, bent low in a vain attempt to scrub stained laundry clean in the dirty water. I squeezed behind them, trying not to get my own clothes dirty. I continued along until I reached an opening with a reek of nightsoil and piss.

But the smell alone didn't make me hesitate. As chills crawled up my spine, I glanced at the walkways around the canal above me. Nothing. But I wasn't usually wrong about these things. And there were plenty of people who would have reason to watch me.

I quickly walked along the thin ledge inside, hoping I was escaping any following eyes.

It wasn't far until I saw the soft, moss-green glow of pyr lamps from within a caved-in wall, accompanied by the serious sounds of grunts and one strand of intermittent, desperate laughter. My stomach sank as I recognized that tittering snicker. Its owner, Parrot, had one hell of a shrewd eye on him. Or his pet parrot did. Still, considering the circumstances, I was going to have to risk it.

Twisting my lucky shard in my pocket, I turned the corner to see four men crouched around a makeshift rug of someone's turban and a small stack of obsidian spokes. One had a parrot perched on top of his tall, fur hat. As I watched, the spokes settled, and the man leaned back and cackled, hitting high registers I'd previously thought only flutes could reach, while his bird cawed with him. Parrot's bony hands snatched at a small pile of coppers as he continued to laugh.

The second man, a rotund fellow, huffed and puffed, his face flushing red. I didn't recognize him and pinned him as another merchant recently fallen from lofty aspirations into this stinking pit. His clothes were too fine for him to have been here long, though he was here to stay, if the way he leaked coppers was any indication.

The last two men I didn't recognize, and I saw why from the blue markings along their arms, denoting their families and tribes and other, more obscure symbols. Bali, traders or travelers from the eastern plateaus. Their hair was shorn short, but I realized my error a moment later; one of them wasn't a man at all, but a woman. I had never been a discriminatory type, but women in Avvad weren't typically found in the slums unless they were the whoring kind of wench. But that was what you had to love about scraping the underbelly of Erimis: you never knew what sort of grime you were going to get.

"Efendi!" I said, withdrawing my shard. "Is there room for one more lost soul in this morass of sin?"

Parrot eyed me shrewdly, fingers still full of coins, while his parrot — let's call it Shrewd — cawed, "Rah! Cat got the crook!"

"Never been so right, my friend," Parrot said, stretching up to stroke his pet while one eye leered at me from beneath his fur hat. "What are you doing here, Wraithsbane? Don't you have a" — he looked around with exaggerated pronouncement — "a *bird* to steal?"

Keeping my expression flat, I studied the others' reactions. The fat man showed eagerness, perhaps thinking a new player might change his luck. The two Bali, known for their stoicism around strangers, could have been made of obsidian for all they reacted. "Birds are off-limits, Parrot —

I'm not an iconoclast. I'm just here to lose my shirt, the same as any of you scoundrels."

I shrugged off my jacket, ran the silk regretfully through my fingers for a moment, then tossed it over the spokes. "There's my starting wager. Got to be worth something even to you plebeian lot."

Parrot watched me a moment longer, face hard, then burst out laughing. "Sit, sit! Or crouch, as it were."

"Rah!" Shrewd cawed. "Dole the damn wager!"

"All business, my friend! But first, introductions. Everyone, meet Wraithsbane, the premier house-breaker of pashas and Silk-guarded vaults alike." Parrot eyed me, letting me know there were words left unspoken, and it was a favor owed. As if I needed another debt.

He made the introductions, and I pretended to listen. "The pleasure is mine," I said and gave an exaggerated bow to each of them. Then I waggled my shard over the pile. "Now, if you wouldn't mind…"

But Parrot wasn't ready to release his advantage. He looked me up and down the chest, and my guts twisted like a Hortum Kor.

"Dole the damn wager!" Shrewd cried. "Dole the damn wager!"

"Yes, I think he shall," Parrot said, the green glint in his eyes not only from the pyr lamps. "These are warm days, don't you think, Wraithsbane? Too warm for that shirt of yours."

I stared hard at him, but we both knew I was full of peacock defecations. "All right," I finally said. Slowly, I pulled off my last, soft, beautiful shirt, and tossed it in with my jacket. "Can I keep my trousers and underwraps, or would you like to see it all?"

"Not yet," Parrot cackled, then pushed my clothes aside to gather up the spokes, including my own. But then he stopped and stared.

I shivered and wrapped my arms around me as the other three also stared. I knew what they must see: it wasn't just the whipping scars from my youthful thieving crisscrossing my back and ribs; faint, violet veins extended from my stomach over my birth-scar, faintly glowing in the dim light.

"Well?" I demanded. "Did we come here to watch me shiver, or are we going to make a toss?"

Parrot bent down to straighten up the pile of spokes without another word, and the others quickly looked aside as well. I exhaled in temporary relief, and let my hands fall. My eyes lingered on the old wound though, tracing each arm of the star-shaped scar. Sometimes, even these years later, it still seems to reverberate with remembered pain.

But the others were throwing in wagers now, thirty or so coppers, worth a hundredth of the cost of those clothes. But I had little fear. I knew that soon, I'd win them both back, and have that comfortable jingle back about my waist. I waited as Parrot, having arranged the small stack of obsidian, handed it to the merchant for his toss.

In the game of Bonfire, one tries to form a "bonfire" from the spokes by propping up as many as possible. There are a couple of complicating factors, however. First, you must pitch them onto the playing surface, and refrain from touching them afterward; if you do, you forfeit the round and, depending on your fellow players, your literal hand. But before you pitch, you have three tosses to rearrange in midair how the spokes are collected in your hands. No cupping your palms or any other nonsense; just one, two, three tosses, then a pitch two feet off the ground, and see how the spokes stand.

So the merchant, his face going red with not breathing, made his tosses — terrible, ineffective little things — then went for the pitch. A horrible affair, with not a single spoke remotely upright. The man stood himself up as if to compensate and stared down furiously.

Next up was the Bali man. He made a valiant attempt, but his hands, thick and clumsy things, just made a mess of it, and he returned similar results as the merchant.

But then it went to the Bali woman and my — how she managed to manipulate those spokes! But in the end, she couldn't manage the bonfire: only two, with the support of the other four spokes, qualified as standing.

From my place in the circle, it should have been my turn, but I handed them along to Parrot. "I need to remember how it's done," I said. "Can I learn from the best?"

The man laughed. Still, he accepted the spokes and made a go of it, long fingers wrapping around the six pieces of black stone. He adjusted once, somehow flipping one; then twice, and another flipped sideways; thrice, and the traditional triangle was between his hands; and the pitch—

—Landed with a perfect bonfire. The three he'd put in the triangle braced the butts of the three standing, which leaned on each other in that mutually supporting, balanced way. Parrot and his parrot laughed manically while gathering up the spokes, raking them in like they were the coins he was about to collect.

But my luck wasn't quite up. Before accepting the spokes, I closed my eyes for a second and pretended the world was revolving around me, in the disorienting, reassuring way of the whirl. It centered me and helped me remember. Warm energy entered my body from my locus, filled my chest, spread down my arms. When heat pushed against my fingertips like I was pressing them to hot coals, I opened my eyes and accepted the pile to Parrot's strange stare.

Almost without thinking, in the same state of mind that I whirled, I made the adjustments, one two three. My hands were splayed with a two-spoke base, a risky move. But I didn't hesitate. I went for the pitch—

—And four spokes landed upright. I leaped up in celebration.

But then something happened. Perhaps I moved the turban, though I remember being as careful as I always am. More likely, one of those other bastards sabotaged my perfect landing. But I was standing there, fists thrust in the air when, one by one, the spokes collapsed onto themselves.

Parrot laughed harder than I'd ever seen before, and I was about to strangle him right then and there.

"Mine!" crowed Shrewd. "Mine!"

"Ours, my greedy friend," Parrot cooed, hands reaching out for the small pile of coins nestled into my beautiful shirt and the sky blue jacket. I stared. I'd given those spokes a bit of *push* to stay upright, but still, they'd fallen. Even if someone had pulled the whole turban out from underneath, that shouldn't have happened.

I wasn't the only one in denial. The merchant leaped up, face redder than ever. "This game is rigged!" he yelled. "Utterly rigged! No — I'm *not* losing again to you, you damn rat!"

The two Bali stood as well, long knives of dark iron drawn, sporting wary, hard expressions.

Parrot haughtily gained his feet. "Now, efendi — and hanim — we wouldn't want to bloody Wraithsbane's clothes, would we? Former clothes, rather." He cackled, but there was no humor in it. "Oh, and it might be a good idea to respect the game. There are certain people that guarantee these events, after all. We wouldn't want to find your bodies in the canal — or not find them at all."

The other three probably didn't know the truth of his words, but I did. And those men weren't ones I'd willingly cross. Well, any more than I already had.

The merchant's eyes were about to bulge out of his head, and I thought he'd jump my fellow crook at any moment. But no — it wasn't rage on his face, but fear. I couldn't understand why until I realized he wasn't looking at Parrot, but beyond him.

I turned, and my heart stopped. There, arms crossed, weight shifted casually to one side, was a Damask Esir. A female, province-bred Damask Esir — and a bey at that, in charge of a battalion, from the silver, multi-layered belt winding around her waist.

If you don't know the Damask Esir, you can't understand why my heart suddenly decided to take up residence in my throat. It wasn't just that their order reported directly to the Kahin-Shah himself, or that they acted in his name to rout corruption in his Imperium and fight his enemies, or even that they were frighteningly efficient in both capacities. It was how they had become who they were. Though they looked like ordinary men and women, they were said to be the product of demonic rituals that robbed them of who they once were, and turned them completely to the Prophet King's employment. Unlike ordinary guards, they were incorruptible and implacable in their goals.

And here one had discovered my fellow gamblers and me blatantly breaking one of the Kahin-Shah's cardinal laws.

She watched us contemptuously, running her eyes over the pile of black stone on the floor, then over us players, one by one. Her forehead and hair were wrapped in white cloth, contrasting the umber of her skin, with a loose red wrap about her head and shoulders. A jagged, pink scar ran over her left eyebrow, and numerous other small markings were on her broad, provincial face. The rest was the typical Damask Esir uniform: short jacket, trousers, and shoes, all in various shades of red, with steel mail barely visible under the cuffs.

Her eyes settled on me, trailing down to the violet starburst on my abdomen. "Quite the game," she said, her voice the slightest bit hoarse as if she'd been screaming recently. "May I try?"

Her manner was strange for an Esir, but her confidence certainly fit. She didn't even flinch at the Bali sailors' bared knives; she just walked briskly over, picked up the pile of obsidian spokes, then dashed them against the crumbled wall. I winced and hoped the strengthening on my shard remained. The others, at least, were dashed to pieces.

"Very fun," she said, dusting her hands. "Did I win?"

She walked in the middle of us, mere feet from two drawn daggers, her back turned. Then she bent down, scooped up my jacket, then snatched my shirt from Parrot's limp hands. The coins tittered to the ground.

But though she seemed vulnerable, the Bali don't move, and neither did I, even as she straightened and grinned at me. That seemed friendly enough, but I watched her eyes, how they never flickered from their cold consideration, nor from the hard resolve to perform any action. Any at all.

She tossed my shirt and jacket to me, and I barely caught them, clumsy in my uneasiness. "Come, Talan of Duman," she said and walked past. I shivered at hearing my name attached to my home province. However she knew where I was from, it didn't bode well for me.

She looked back. "Before I decide to turn you all in instead."

Without a backward look at my recent companions, I darted to the wall and snatched up my shard, then ran to catch up to the Esir bey. Somehow, I'd ended that game poorer than I could have possibly imagined.

———

I tried not to be obvious in studying her as we exited into daylight. There was something familiar about her, especially when she'd grinned, but I couldn't place it. Before I could wrack my brains too thoroughly, though, she looked over and caught me staring.

"You still don't know?" she asked quietly. A familiar voice, too, though distorted; my mind spun faster, and not in the focused whirling I was used to.

"I'm sorry, Esir, but what should I know?" I asked, mustering up politeness for its final stand.

She looked at me, and I studied her features in full. Her irises were the pale pink of a Silk's robes, a feature all Damask Esir seemed to share. But the other parts were more familiar: wide, high-set cheekbones, a slightly dimpled chin, lips more luscious and feminine than the rest of her combined. If she knew my province, then perhaps… it was her home too.

I almost gasped with the force of recognition. "Sule?"

Her expression seemed almost pained for a moment, and she turned away. "Yanara," she said softly, "My redname is Yanara."

She looked changed from the last time I saw her — just over a decade ago, now. Perhaps it was the uniform, perhaps the scars, but she looked hardened and dangerous. And those eyes — maybe it was just the color, but they smoldered with an angry fire that seemed to have long been burning.

Sule, here before me; not only alive but one of the Kahin-Shah's bloodback beys. "Yanara." It felt strange in my mouth, like an ill-fitting shoe you keep trying to pull on. Before I could help myself, I asked, "And what if I call you Sule anyway?"

She stared at me again. "Then," she said slowly, "I'll have to cut your tongue off for impudence."

I shivered. A demon-ritual and ten years of blood and sweat can change a woman. But then another thought set a sweat to accompany the chill. If she knew why she'd been forced into the prison and the Damask Esir, she might be inclined to cut off a lot more than just my tongue.

We ascended from the canal in uneasy silence but stopped at Cobbler Bridge. I was still shirtless, my clothes crumpled in my hand, unable to act on my own initiative from fear of her capriciousness.

She stopped and swiveled stiffly as a rusty joint, and I followed. The bustle of the city was burbling with the constant stream of people, and the air almost smelled clean compared to the sewers. Most didn't even spare me a glance, even though it was against the Grey Dictums to be undressed as I was. Sule — Yanara — was the one to draw any attention directed our way.

I reached for a question that had been bothering me and gathered up all my feeble courage. "How did you find me?"

She didn't even glance over. "By chance. I am recently stationed here, and was surveying the local sights when I saw you sneaking down into that tunnel."

"Ah." That explained the feeling of being watched before.

For all the bustle about us, the silence grew tense between us. I shrugged my naked shoulders, wondering if I should wait for her explicit permission to dress or not. Or maybe she had the thought that iron would better suit me. If so, it was the strangest arrest I'd heard of.

But could it be she was caught in indecision? Their ritual was supposed to take away their past selves, which was why they often used provincials instead of proper Avvadin citizens. Could it be that it hadn't fully worked on her?

I'm nothing if not a gambler. So I hedged my bets, figuring I had little and less to lose. "You look good," I said as suavely as I could.

Maybe there was more to why I said that. Because of the way we'd last seen each other. Because I didn't know how much she knew of why she and the others landed in the dungeons, while I galavanted off to Erimis. Maybe there was a bit of an apology in that vague compliment.

Especially since she'd once told me I was the only person in the world who cared for her, ten long years ago.

She finally looked at me, taut as a cranked crossbow, and I braced myself for harsh words or worse. But she only cocked her head to the side as if listening. Silence returned for a long minute. I looked away, barely refraining from fidgeting with my shard. When I dared to look back, all the tension had fallen from her. I exhaled as silently as I could. My gamble seemed to pay off — even if the sudden change was eerie.

"Meet me here on this bridge tonight," she said softly, eyes darting about as if to watch for eavesdroppers. "Just as the sun sets, no later."

My stomach sunk. It wasn't freedom I'd won with the toss — it was just a different sort of bondage. Still, better than rotting in a cell. "Of course."

She started turning away. "And," she added, "don't think about not showing up. I'll find you again."

I couldn't think to do anything other than stand there while her confident strides bore her further away, and the past closer than it had been in years. Too close.

I finally put my shirt and jacket back on, letting them remain undone, and walked the other way. But even though I'd seen her turn away, I felt the creeping sensation of watching eyes return. I didn't turn back to see if she was watching, though I suspected she did not. Maybe it was one of the other people to whom I was indebted tailing me.

Or maybe it was simply the past come back to haunt me.

A TWILIGHT FOR BRUTALITY

With such a taxing morning, I resolved to spend my afternoon in leisure. Water and shade were my primary callings, but staying out of the way of yayas — those spineless guards that go "yah yah" to every demand of the Foremost — remained a top priority. Still, even as I skirted kicks from the city guards and glares from the women standing by the wells, my mind was occupied with what the evening would bring. What did Sule — Yanara — want from me? Could she know what I'd done? And if she did, why didn't she kill me right away?

While the high sun and the heavy thoughts beat down on my fez-trapped head, I was tempted many times to return to my quarters. I'd risk whatever menaces my collectors had waiting for me if only to wear clean clothes again, wash my face in water that didn't smell foul, and spend a few hours dozing on my mattress. But it couldn't be so, not until I'd paid what the Underguild was due.

When evening came around, I bowed my respect to the Father and adoration to the Mother, then centered myself with a whirl in an abandoned alley. I was in a bit more of a bind than I'd initially thought. Sule — Yanara, burn it all — had asked me to meet her at the bridge at sundown. But the Firewater Den expected me to appear at nearly the same time.

I decided to drop by Semih's early. Those Denizens seemed the better people to displease. Even if they pulled the purse strings, it was better to lose coins than my hands.

I traveled through Lavabed back to Semih's house. The road still portrayed remnants of its namesake, for beneath the fireglass paving stones was the igneous crust left after the lava flow. It had once covered this whole span, a league thick and a dozen leagues long. It could easily happen again, *would* happen again. Great prophet or no, Aasjuqal was a fool to settle here, and we were fools for staying.

It was that hour of the day when the air turned to gold and the heat finally subsided to a temperature approaching pleasant. I looked up the mountainside to the grand buildings of Obsidian Heights. The sprawling palace of the Prophet King loomed over the district like a dragon jealously guarding its hoard. The spindly towers its spines; the pyramids its great clawed feet; the doors the mouth ready to douse us all in flames.

Before its columns, two enormous stone statues, the height of some of the shorter towers, loomed and watched over the city. One bore the visage of Aasjuqal Kahin-Shah; the other, the snarling, snouted visage of Valem, a wyvern's head on a man's body. They might have struck a foreigner as intimidating, but we in Erimis knew their bite. It was like the gnawing of a dog on your leg, unnoticeable until one day, your foot fell off.

I recognized Semih's house easily enough from the lazy rainbow of parrots across his roof. Lightly swatting away the pesky birds, I walked down the side alley to the door and knocked at random, not knowing their code. Still, before long, the call-window slid open, and Semih's face emerged, the angriest expression beneath his spectacles I'd yet seen on him. I stepped back in surprise, but the scowl disappeared as soon as he recognized me.

"Talan Wraithsbane!" He closed the call-window and opened the door. "You are quite early for the agreed time, no?"

"Sorry to intrude," I said, "but an opportunity for our plan has arisen, and I can't come later. You'll forgive my absence, I'm sure."

"Of course! Anything for the" — His eyebrows wiggled — "*the plan.*"

"Yes." I cleared my throat. "If you don't mind me asking… You looked a bit put off just now. Are you sure this is all right?"

"Ah." The eyebrows fell. "I thought… but think nothing of it, it's nothing to mind."

"Semih. We're risking our lives together. We should tell each other the truth." I just wanted to itch my insatiable curiosity.

"Well…" From his indecisiveness, Semih seemed as afflicted of a gossip as I was. "All right, then. It's Erkan."

"Erkan?"

He sighed. "He just left before you came, taking a few of our bottles with him. I feared he was — Valem forbid it — already back for more, using your name to get through the door."

My hand fingered my shard as I thought. The burly man's vice was no surprise, but still... I leaned in close and asked softly, "Is that going to be an issue for our plan?"

"Oh, no! He hasn't that little sense. Though I do fear for his wife... But where are my manners — here I am, leaving you at the door! Please, please, come in! And take wet refreshment, if you wish."

Tempted as I was, I declined. Yanara hadn't made trouble about my trying to escape her, but I didn't want to give her any excuses to change her mind. Instead, Semih sent a servant girl for food, then poured a generous glass of wine that, if his cheeks told the story true, wasn't his first.

Once seated, we chatted lightly until the food came, at which point I let his words wash over me as I devoured what must have been a whole lamb, three loaves of pita, and a jug of water. Semih showed nothing but approval and held his own during our impromptu feast. He hadn't happened upon his plump figure by happenstance.

When I was satisfied and a bit sleepy, I moved to more pressing matters. "I stopped by the Mausoleum earlier to scope things out."

"Did you?" Semih, always attentive, perked up even more. "And one of your usual brilliant plans is already in motion, no doubt!"

The back of my throat itched. "One is in development. This morning, though, I simply observed what I could, of the layout of the vault and all that."

"Indeed you did! And what can you tell me of it?" Semih leaned forward, the smile on his face a touch more sly than I expected from him.

"The Crimson leads straight to the Mausoleum, did you know that?"

"Unfortunately, I've not been around it much. Right to the foot, is it?"

"Soaking the feet. And there's a moat."

"A moat indeed! Around the whole of it? Or the three sides, I mean?"

"Yes." I wracked my head for more, but it just rang like an empty barrel.

Easygoing Semih seemed at a loss as well. "I see. But there is a moat, is there?"

I let the words tumble forth, hoping they would lead somewhere. "There's only one bridge, leading to the one stairway. The other sides are almost unnavigable, what with how high each steppe is."

"So... there's only one way in?" Semih ventured.

"There's only one way guarded." I stopped, for suddenly I saw where I was headed. That damn discarded plan from before — had I really been about to propose that to my employer?

But Semih had its thread now, and he was eagerly unraveling it. "I see, I *see*! One way guarded, but we won't go that way, will we? *Almost* unnavigable, indeed — approach from the back, that's our way in!"

"Well, I don't—"

"Barrels! Approach by barrels! Then, when you get along the backside, then you — I don't know — *toss* a line of rope up, with a hook on the end, what are they called? Ah, yes, *grappling* hooks — toss one, then climb up the side, and enter in without being seen! That's the plan, is it not?"

The irony of the situation swung me like a pendulum between bemusement and annoyance. "Well, no," I said as gently as I could. "There is only one path, the one by the stairs. All that stuff with the barrels and hooks — that won't work."

Semih scrunched his brow. "But — was that not your plan, efendi?"

I shook my head. "That? Just part of the scheming process — get the bad ones out there to show the obstacles and available avenues. Now we know: we have to go in the front door."

He paled. "That… how can we, Talan Wraithsbane? Why would they let in a… well, to be frank, a pack of thieves?"

I ripped off another piece of pita, folded it around a chunk of lamb, and ripped into it, beginning to chew it slowly. "We won't be a pack of thieves," I said around the mouthful. "I've got a contact I'm working on now, a bloodback. She—"

"A— a—" Semih looked as if a Silk had suddenly appeared behind me. "Damask Esir?" he finally finished, incredulity propelling his voice to high registers.

"Yes. And she's female, and a bey to boot. Fascinating, no? In any case, she's the one I'm meeting tonight. Right now, actually." I took one last bite and rose. "Thanks for your hospitality — and help."

"Help?" His face flushed as he bowed. "I have helped the great Wraithsbane — the pleasure is all mine, dear efendi!"

"Until tomorrow night," I said with a flourishing bow back, then headed out the door.

———

My spirits were badly flagging by the time I approached Cobbler Bridge, and they sunk even further when I saw Yanara was already waiting. She'd lost the scarlet uniform in favor of masculine clothes so unassuming they could have been a peasant boy's garb. It made her look more familiar, closer to how I remembered her: the leader of our cabal, stupidly fearless, utterly resentful of gender norms, and, most of all, confident in every step.

But as much as she made me nervous, I felt even more so looking at the nearby Mausoleum. It still seemed to loom, even though I was far enough away I could cover it with a hand. My skin crawled with that same watched feeling, and I couldn't help a foolish thought that maybe the vault, knowing the Firewater Den's plans, watched and waited for us, for the moment when we all descended into its belly and forfeited our lives. How I would come up with any other plan than that, I had not the slightest inkling.

When I set foot on the bridge, she said, "So they call you Wraithsbane now?"

I couldn't tell if she was sneering or not, but either way, it made me uneasy to hear my street title. She'd been looking into my reputation, which meant she probably also knew of my debts. "Titles tend to come from exaggerated stories."

"Then there is a story?"

"There's always a story. But some aren't worth telling."

I stopped five paces away, but she surprised me by stepping so close that our faces were barely a hand apart. In contrast to the stink of the city, there was a faint scent of roses about her. I wondered if all Damask Esir took roses so seriously.

"Well," she said softly, "you'd better think of the good stories to tell. We have a lot of catching up to do."

If only she knew how much.

"By all means," I said, starting to edge back. "Perhaps we can walk until—"

"There's time for that later," she interrupted. "I'll be stationed here a while longer, I think. Perhaps permanently." She stepped forward again and suddenly put a hand possessively on the back of my neck. "But right now, I want a taste of what we had."

Holding me in place, she leaned in and — well, *latched* onto my mouth. It wasn't passionate or tender or messy; it was just damned determined. Of course, I returned it as best as I could manage, not being in a position to deny it.

When she let me pull away, she wore a small, satisfied smile. "Not what I meant, but I didn't mind it. Though you're a bit stiff, Talan. I may be Esir, but I'm not going to kill you."

I was a bit stiff?

She continued. "What I meant was… Remember our old tactics, back in Dumanabad? We used to run those soft bastards into the mud."

"Yes. We were fairly brutal."

She stared at me, then burst out laughing. It was strange to think I hadn't heard that laugh in ten years, but I found I wasn't too nostalgic for it. "Brutal," she snorted. "Right."

I noticed again the scar on her brow and wondered how many others had been cut into her body over that decade. Perhaps our old antics seemed like child's play after what she'd been through.

"I'm thinking a little brutality is just what I need now. And—" She abruptly cut off and tilted her head to the side, her eyes growing unfocused like had happened at our last meeting. I wondered how long ago she'd picked the tic up.

She snapped out of whatever trance she was in, then growled. Yes, growled. "I agree," she said softly. "Yes, let's do it."

I hesitated, not wanting to rile her up, but I had to ask. "Do what, exactly?"

"A bruiser."

Oh. My stomach twisted into a knot even sailors would be hard-put to unravel. "Yanara, I — I don't really feel up for that."

She cocked her head. "Why not?" she asked slowly.

"That's not — I don't really do that anymore. It's just a bit—"

"Brutal?" She smiled savagely. "You're above such common violence now, is that it?" She leaned in close, roses filling my nose again. "You didn't used to be. You used to crave it."

I swallowed, trying not to remember. "That was years ago." Long enough that the memories of it didn't sear, but not long enough to cool the burning guilt. "We can change. We don't have to do that anymore. We can be better."

"Better." She moved the word around in her mouth as if tasting it. "You're right — we are better. But we always were, Talan — always better than everyone around us." She leaned forward, and her eyes gleamed with the light from a pyr lamp behind me. "You need to remember that."

Could she still believe our youthful delusions? "We were insane," I said, but she grabbed my arm and pulled me behind. Unless I wanted to make an enemy of the Imperium itself, I had no choice but to let her.

"Sometimes," she said, almost singing the word, "you're better with a little insanity."

———

We watched the man load up the last of his pottery from the shadows along a lonely road in Lavabed. The man's stand was small and forlorn now that its wares were packed away. The little cart he'd loaded hardly looked better, though the vases, bowls, and cups at least looked well-formed and durable.

"Too easy," Yanara crowed softly. Her mood had grown ever more jubilant as we watched, and was now about as high as the Prophet King's palace. She slapped my arm lightly. "Let's go."

I followed, my gut clenched tight, but I put on a scowl all the same —

no good could come if I didn't play my part convincingly. I couldn't do a thing to save this man now.

At least, that's what I kept telling myself.

"Wait!" she called, waving a hand and striding forward.

The man, a heavily bearded fellow with wisps of hair peeking out from a small, cream-colored cap, looked up, eyes darting back and forth between us.

"Please," I said, but it didn't sound polite. "You'd better wait up."

He left the stand's curtains furled in his rush to get behind his cart. "Sorry," he muttered as he started to wheel away. "Not open for business."

Yanara kicked the wheel with a crack, and the cart jerked to the side, sending a bowl sliding to the ground. I winced as it shattered on the stones. "Do you have time now?" she asked sweetly.

My throat was too tight to breathe at the terror on his face. "Please," he muttered, letting go of his cart and backing away. "I have a family to feed. Please."

Yanara looked back to me. I swallowed and tried finding the words. "We have empty bellies ourselves," I lied. "Now where's the copper?"

"Please…"

Civilian clothes or no, Yanara moved with every bit of Damask Esir arrogance around the cart and backhanded the man across the face, and I flinched as he fell to the ground. "Where is it?" Yanara spat down at him.

"I—"

"*Where is it?*"

"I — in my robe. Here, take it, but please, spare me…" With a shaking hand, he drew out a purse from within his clothes and held it up, its contents clinking together with pathetic irregularity.

"Well, well, Wraithsbane," a voice said from not far behind me. "I never thought to find you stealing from potters to pay your debts. A far fall from aghas and Grand Vizier's peacocks, isn't it?"

Cursing, I spun, the fire igniting in my center and my fingertips hot with energy. But there wasn't just one speaker — three men stood there, faces hooded and silhouetted by dusk's red light. And that wasn't all of them — two other pairs came up the road on either side, their hands glinting with sharp implements. My throat swelled near closed. Seven Guilders, here to collect my debt — in whatever measure they could, no doubt.

Yanara moved to stand by me. Anger and eagerness flared in equal measures in her coral eyes. "You've made a lot of friends here," she said in a low voice. "Which burning ones are these?"

"Collectors." I wished I had carried a knife on me, the Kahin-Shah's ban be damned. Instead, I grabbed my lucky shard. With Valem's fire burning within, flames rushing through my veins and pushing at my fingertips, it would serve me even better.

"That's right," said the man who had spoken before. "See, there's a certain price if a man can't pay his debts among our folk. Especially when those debts are a thousand silver pimars."

"Well, you know. Peacocks happened."

The man laughed. "Peacocks indeed. I hope the sight of that peacock's feathered ass flying from the balcony was worth every last one of your fingers."

The cowled men beside the speaker drew out their knives.

My fingers — it was no better than I'd expected. So I was to be a testament to how the Underguild treated those who didn't pay their debts.

But I couldn't lose my fingers. They were how I wielded the fire. They were how I'd become the vault-breaker I was. Without them, I was nothing.

They just might be worth dying for.

"Sorry, efendi," I said. "These lads aren't for sale. Perhaps you'll take steel to your gut instead?"

Yanara laughed, and I was flooded with gratefulness, even if I couldn't understand why she'd stand by me against such odds. Still, I'd take being backed by a half-mad bloodback than no aid at all.

"Fine, Wraithsbane," the leading man said. "We'll take the blood fare then. Men?" He nodded to each of the Underguild agents around him.

They advanced.

"If I get out of this," I muttered as I backed away, "I'm going to sear the tail feathers off every last peacock."

"Concentrate," Yanara admonished. "Ready yourself."

But I wasn't ready, especially not for when the cart-man started to run. He made it two steps before a knife blossomed in his back, and he fell with a sickening squelch to the stone.

I clenched my jaw, Brands and anger both burning now. If nothing else, I'd make the Guilders pay for that man's life.

The seven fanned out before us. There was just the cart and the stall between, and some stone buildings at our backs. No escape.

The first two dashed forward. Coward that I am, I scrambled back, putting the cart between me and their gleaming knives. My hand slipped out of my pocket, and the shard, glowing with energy, spilled light on the cart in front of me and over the flatware. Suddenly, I saw them for what they were: ammunition. I scooped up a pot in my shame-hand and crouched back, hiding my shard and watching for my first assailants.

I could see from around the corner of the cart that Yanara had already started the fight, leaping at the men on our left and cutting down the first, all while drawing most of them away from me. Four others uncertainly circled her, feinting moves that never committed. She only encouraged it — with bared teeth and flashing knife, she looked more rabid than any starving mongrel and twice as dangerous.

If she had four, that just left the two still standing for me. Just two — who was I kidding. One was more than enough to kill me. I prayed to the Lost Mother that she was here with my luck.

To the right, I saw one edging closer to the cart. As for the other—

Something hissed through the air, and I instinctively threw my hands up before me. Flames burned from my fingers, flowing around the shard and shattering the pot in my hand. But the projectile — a dart most likely — puffed into ashes against my face, doing no more damage than blinding me for a moment. I wiped at my eyes, desperately trying to keep track of my first stalker.

Seeing me distracted, the man rapidly closed in, rushing around the cart with a bellow. I managed to grab a stray pot from the ground and narrowly knocked his knife away twice, but he kept working to find an opening. I was lucky that we were between the stand and cart, allowing only a narrow pathway to get at me. But if he found his opening, all it would take was one mistake for the knife to find some part of me I wasn't ready to lose.

I didn't give him the chance. Leaping back from a sudden charge, I pointed my shard at him, and while he continued forward, his face scrunched up in confusion. But he must have still thought it his opportunity, for he lunged forward with the knife.

In the precious seconds I had left, I pushed all the searing energy in my body through my fingers and into the shard, then I unleashed.

The air sizzled in front of me, and darkness fled from the flash of light. Through my spotty vision, I saw his dark form fly away. Pottery shattered — I must have sent him into the cart — but all the world was fuzzy and gray. I staggered behind the stall, hoping beyond hope that the man was dead.

Crouching behind the stand, I waited for my vision to return, terrified that the man with the darts was even now creeping up on me. Then came the shivering — it felt like all the heat in my body had drained away. I forced myself to peer above the stall for any further assailants, but all I saw was a second body near Yanara and the bloodback still furiously twisting and slashing among the other three men.

Then I saw the dart man, his blow stick pointing at me from behind the upturned cart. I yelped and ducked. The dart hit the stucco behind and pattered lightly to the ground.

Bravery decided to rear its ugly head. I stood and rushed around the stall, running at the place where the man had just been. He wasn't there. This side of the street was empty but for scattered pieces of pottery and two limp bodies. I whirled about, trying to find where he'd gone. Suddenly, there he was, lunging from behind the stall where I had just been, a knife aimed at my chest. Desperate, I fell to the ground and reached out for anything to save me.

Two things happened that almost made me believe the Lost Mother really did watch over me. First, my hand found an unbroken vase. Second, I swung, and even though I could barely see the flashing knife, the vase managed to connect. It shattered in my hand, leaving behind several shallow gashes, but it also sent the blade flying from the man's grip.

Then there was a third thing: a bright light flashed from over by Yanara, and a wave of heat billowed against my face.

I glanced over, expecting the worst, but all I could see was Yanara driving back two men now with no sign of where the heat had come from. But I had my own problems to deal with. The dart man, having scrambled and collected his knife, was advancing once more.

"You have a lot of damn nerve, Wraithsbane," he said through gritted teeth. "You're a dead man now. If it's not me, it'll be one of my brothers. You can't escape the Underguild."

I leaped to my feet and waved my shard before me. It still glowed from the fire I'd channeled into it. "Now remember what just happened to your companion. Wouldn't it be better to forget this whole thing, and keep your miserable life?" I wasn't sure I had it in me to make good on the warning, but I hoped he wouldn't see that from my shaking arms and legs.

"Damn daemon," the man muttered. He advanced steadily, only a dozen feet away now, and I couldn't scoot back fast enough. Still, I tried to back away faster—

—And tripped over something behind me. The cart-man's body, I saw as I tumbled to the street. The man had taken some measure of revenge after all.

I managed not to completely sprawl and staggered back to my feet. But my assailant, seeing the opportunity, rushed at me, dagger ready to thrust again. It was too late to run.

My chest lurched with a sudden tug of desire.

I saw it emerge from an alley on the opposite side of the street, coming up behind the dart-man, and I could tell from his sudden jerk that he felt it too. He started shaking as he stumbled to a halt a few paces from me and slowly turned, face twisted in a mixture of terror and love. I fared a bit better; practice helped me keep control, even if the feeling was just as terribly strong. I had focus enough to move forward and give him a timely kick in the small of the back, propelling him toward the Silk drifting down the road. The man's arms lifted, maybe to catch himself, maybe to reach out in an embrace.

The Silk enveloped its long cloth arms about him, and I watched the man's skin. Because I knew what was about to happen. I'd seen it all before.

The skin rippled, pulling, straining, tearing.

Then it burst.

I threw an arm up, but there was no stopping the spray, even at this distance. Blood splattered across my face and in my mouth, and I gagged at the metallic taste. But nothing more erupted; the Silk had fully embraced the man. The would-be assassin still writhed in the empty folds, as if in ecstasy, and the stains slowly spread. I couldn't look away; my skin itched; the craving carved out my innards, hollowing me. I felt a promise echoing from the jinni that only one thing could fill.

The Silk dropped its inert victim to the ground, discarding the man like no more than a fruit peel. Then it floated towards me.

I could have just warded it off, but what of Yanara? She would have been helpless to a Silk's attack, especially if caught unawares.

But…

Wouldn't that solve my problems? Perhaps the Underguild would think their agents died to a Damask Esir and forgotten all about me. And she wouldn't have her insidious hold on me, making me come out on insane nostalgic trips into our savage past. I could go free to my old life, or at least have a chance at it.

But I didn't ward. I let it come on. Because somewhere in me, I'd always felt guilty for betraying her once, and I couldn't do it twice. Not when she had already saved me.

I took a deep breath, trembling to hold the desire at bay, and called to mind the steps that had given me the name Wraithsbane.

As the Silk came, two paces away, I engaged the first: the lure. I performed a slow half-turn, inviting. My arms drifted up, the shard in my right, held back. The jinn's cloth billowed forward with yearning.

Next, the snare. As I clenched my jaw against the rebellion of my skin, I whirled another turn, this time quick. My shard caught on a piece of the Silk's bonds and quickly gathered it in folds.

Third, the embrace. I whirled it in, around me, coral cloth covering me like a chrysalis. My body reveled and revolted at its touch. I could feel the Silk vibrating with anticipation. It knew consumption was coming soon. It craved it.

But then came the sear. I stoked the little fire left in me and released. The energy streamed from my fingers, down the shard, and spread all about me. Pale violet flames spread across the cloth, rushing to every available piece of fabric. I felt the Silk jerk, suddenly aware that something was wrong, terribly wrong, and it pulled at my hold. But the fire soothed as it burned, numbed as it killed, and the creature soon stopped struggling, hanging limply as if it was nothing but cloth.

But the flames weren't just on the specter — they were all over my skin too. Burning, searing pain spread throughout me, and I gritted my teeth against it. I bore it because I had to, bore it though I was so weak I could hardly stand.

The fire inside me extinguished, and I felt myself letting go. After all, what was I holding on for? Maybe I'd just let it burn. It didn't feel so bad now. It was almost gentle as it danced across my skin. Maybe I'd close my eyes for a moment, and let it do its work. I'd go away, just for a moment, just until it was done.

I closed my eyes, and let the world lapse into blessed darkness.

———

"Talan! Talan, you searing fool, snap out of it and peel those rags off. We've got to burn them, and I'm sure you'd rather not burn with them."

I blinked. I'd been standing there, numb and unthinking while clutching at two strands of blood-stained cloth wrapped around me. I shuddered — the fabric, whatever it was, was too damn soft on my hands.

My hands — I looked at them. Unburnt, whole — alive. I was still alive.

Once I'd torn off the garments, I slumped to the ground, panting. I thought back over the whole fight, trying to come to terms with all that had just happened.

For one, how furiously Yanara had fought. "You killed five men by yourself?"

She smiled, but her eyes remained cold. "I would guess their only training was flailing about with clubs in the sewers."

"And murdering debtors." I shuddered again at the close call.

Even Yanara, a bloodback bey, hadn't escaped unscathed. Her knees were torn and bloody, and there were several red lines in her tunic. There was also a cut over her right eyebrow, mirroring the scar on her left.

She toed the pile of pink cloth. "You killed a man with light. I assume you can set these on fire. No one can know you freed a Silk."

I thought about trying to summon the energy inside of me and shook my head. "It'd be dangerous for me to do that right now." And besides, I wondered why she even cared what happened to me. Shouldn't she be turning me in?

She nodded, accepting it like she might evaluate a military situation.

Then she knelt next to me and grabbed my hand. I flinched at her touch, but it was no worse than our earlier kiss. She turned my hand over, palm up, and peered at my fingertips. I wished I could pull away. I knew what she was doing: she wanted to see the signs of my Branding for herself, tracing my shifting prints. In the low light, the change must have been hard to see, but it wasn't long before she leaned away, satisfied. "Does it hurt?" she asked quietly. "Feeling Valem's power inside of you?"

As little as I wished to, I forced the words out. "It burns, but not much, if you only channel a bit."

It was a lie. There was nothing as intoxicating as channeling. But I wasn't about to let her know that, especially when I could barely admit it to myself.

She nodded as if it was what she'd expected. "How did you escape the Tefra's examinations? I would have thought they checked for it in the dungeons."

My heart started beating hard. I stuttered, trying to come up with a plausible lie. "I guess it just came late enough that they missed me. I got lucky."

Yanara stared at me. "Lucky," she repeated softly. I didn't like the way she said it.

But then she rose to her feet. "We have to get rid of these now," she said, nudging the Silk's bonds again. "We'll weigh them down in the Crimson."

Then she walked off, leaving me to pick up the cloths, struggle to my feet, and limp as fast as I could after her.

No one peered out from their shuttered windows at us, though if they had, they would have seen a curious sight. People didn't just wander about at night, not with Silks floating around. Well, normal folks didn't. But we made it to the canal and, with a bit of rubble tied up in it, tossed the Silk's remains into the dirty depths.

I bent over double again, exhausted with just the effort of standing. I couldn't contain my questions any longer. "Yanara," I panted, "why are we here tonight? Why did all this happen?"

"Sounds like you owe some debts."

"You know what I mean. Why were we even out here?"

She looked down at me, chin uplifted, looking as proud as an Oedijan goddess. "Orders," she said.

I wondered what the hell kind of orders would call for this. I didn't like things I didn't understand, especially not when they could land me in eternal bondage.

"Same time tomorrow," she continued, now looking over the water, "in the same place. Don't make me wait."

"What for? Another mistimed bruiser? I'm sorry, Yanara, but I think if I'm out at night like this again, I really might get—"

"Just be there," she interrupted. Then she left me, exhausted and hunted as I was, and with Silks prowling every street.

So much for old flames. But since I'd burned her in the past, my time was about due.

I was at a loss for where to go for a moment. My quarters were more out of the question than ever before, and the sewers, which Guilders used as passageways, even more so.

So I went home.

I saw a few Silks along the way, but they stuck to their routes on the main road and left me and the rats to scurry away. Only carrier parrots seemed to notice my passage, and these called after me whatever phrases their masters had taught them. "Rah! Derya is a dirty whore! Rah!" Everyone else was asleep in their beds or listening anxiously to my passing, fearing anyone mad enough to dare the dark streets.

I made it to my destination exhausted but alive. I looked up, and the familiar dome was more inviting than a cool bath with one of the Harem attending it.

Entering, I saw I wasn't the only one still up. In the middle of the rotunda, cast in ethereal light, was a slowly turning man. His eyes were closed, his head relaxed, and his arms were raised. He looked so at peace, I couldn't help but love him for it. And perhaps envy him a bit, too.

I didn't make any noise, but he startled, seeming to know he'd gathered a spectator. When he saw it was me, though, a smile, genuine and happy, spread across his face.

"Well," Osman said, "I figured you'd come crawling back here."

I hesitated. It could be dangerous for him if I stayed here. I hadn't let myself think that during my walk, not wanting to believe I truly had nowhere to go. But suddenly, it pressed in with a certainty that I couldn't ignore. "Never mind," I said, turning away. "I shouldn't have come here."

"Talan, wait, wait — I was only teasing." I heard his footsteps tap up to me, and I waited, not yet having the strength to leave. He stood next to me and put a hand on my shoulder. "You know you're always welcome. More than welcome. I wish you'd come back and stay."

"You know I can't do that," I said, my voice strangely breaking. "That I shouldn't be here. That you put your life, your students' lives, at risk when I do."

"Talan."

He gathered me into his arms, and I let him, releasing all my ashen resolve. To his folly and mine.

"You are worth the risk. You've always been worth the risk. Whenever you need a home — if you ever decide to stay — we're here for you. I'll always be here."

I couldn't fight it. "Fine," I said, trying to pretend not to care. "If you insist."

We drew apart, and he smiled. Then he realized what he was hugging, and looked down at his robes in disgust. "I only insist that you change clothes. Now come on — we should at least get some sleep tonight."

CHAPTER SIX

A DAYSPRING
FOR WHIRLING

I woke with a clear head and my back supported by a comfortable, if firm, bed. A sliver of morning mist shimmered with the first rays of morning through a narrow window above. I exhaled a sigh of relief, perfectly at rest, perfectly at peace.

Then I started to remember.

First, I remembered that I was hunted by people that had as damned-far a reach as any could in this city of our Kahin-Shah's. And I had no way to stop them — now that it had come to blood, there was no chance that paying off my debts would resolve anything. In Erimis, we repaid fire with fire.

Second, I had an insane Damask Esir drawing me into her… insanity. What was she going to want me to do now?

Third, I had a job to do — and, blood and ashes, I *had* to do it. Why? I didn't even really know. But I suspected it had to do with that soot-filled excuse of a peacock I threw out the Grand Vizier's window.

And last… there was a man dead. Because of me. Perhaps the seven assassins who died last night were my fault as well, but I only felt guilt for the cart-man's death. It turned my stomach sour and filled my head with buzzing anxiety to know an innocent man was murdered on behalf of my sins.

I sat up, shivering, intending to leave the bed and my thoughts behind, but still they came: How he was someone's son, and someone's brother, some child's father, the poor kid staying up waiting for his father to come back, asking his mother over and over where he was…

But in the end, if it were between him or me, I'd always choose to stay alive. Once I realized that, any grief seemed hollow and falsified, a lie I told myself to think I was still a reasonably good person.

There was no staying in bed now; I shirked over to the clean clothes Osman had given me the night before. They were nowhere near as elegant as my former ones, but more serviceable than I deserved. He'd even managed to find trousers and a tunic instead of the typical Hortum Kor conical robe. Designed to spread out in a perfect circle when one whirled, it wasn't ideal for inconspicuousness on the streets.

Dressed, my stomach sent me straight for the kitchens. It was poor fare, eating bread day after day, with the barest supplement of meat, vegetables, or even fruit, and my belly knew it. Or perhaps it was still sour for another reason.

My feet carried me next to Osman's quarters. It was light enough that he ought to be awake, so I rapped on the door three times and waited. When it opened, his face looked long and haggard, shadows bunched under his eyes, and his hair was even more rebellious than usual.

"And I thought I slept poorly," I observed.

He frowned and let me in. "Bring me any?" he said, indicating my pita.

"You don't eat until after you've had your morning whirl, and from your state, it seems you haven't even done that yet."

"Caught." He mockingly held out his wrists as if to be manacled. "Come in. Sit."

Sit? It was our custom to stand. Still, I obliged, folding onto his window seat with a bit of apprehension. "Am I to undergo some cultic ritual?"

"That's not far off," he said as he turned his desk chair around to straddle it the wrong way. "I have a suggestion."

For a moment, curious as I should have been, all I wanted to talk about was my guilt. But I sensed he was struggling with something as well, and I pushed my own needs down. "All right. Let's hear it."

He stared at the floor for a long moment before speaking. "You asked what the Silk was doing here that night you… left."

I swallowed. I wasn't expecting that. "Yes."

"And I said it wasn't coming for you."

"Right." My chest tightened like the skin of a drumhead.

"Well… that was only partially true."

I smiled, despite what it meant. "You think I didn't know that? It was the night I discovered I was Branded. How could it have been something else?"

He raised an eyebrow. "Slow down. I said partially."

"Right. Go on."

"The other half of the reason… well, it's because of… because of me."

For once, I held my tongue as I waited.

Osman sighed, leaning further into the back of his chair. "You're not the only one who is Father-Branded, Talan."

It took me a moment to understand. "You?"

"Me."

My head spun. "But if they've known since then, and they know where you are, how come you've been left alone? Had they just found out when they discovered me?"

He absently twisted his beard together. "Things are complicated among the Tefra. They've sworn an oath only to guard and protect and never seize power for themselves. Yet they're on all of the Imperium's battlefronts, managing the regiments of Silks, as well as ensuring that Avvadins maintain a certain rigor of religiosity. Occupying such positions is hard to do without any corruption in their mission. They're pulled in too many directions, and that means their methods don't strictly match up with their oaths."

That I knew all too well. True, the Tefra didn't engage in violence themselves. But it had always seemed to me that the worst men this world had to offer never dirtied their hands, but let others do it for them. The Tefra were more of the same. "What's that to do with anything?"

"I'm getting there. They knew about me long before you came along; in fact, they've known since I took over the Hortum Kor. But though they tried swaying me to their side, enticing me with luxuries and exclamations of duty and offers of power, they couldn't win me over. And I was in too prestigious of a position for them to force me to accept the burns without consequences." Osman looked at me hard. "But if they had one of my initiates to hold captive, or perhaps even to convert… You were a bargaining chip. For me."

"And since I was your favorite student, that would have been a signifi-cant chip indeed."

He cocked an eyebrow again. "That's why I kicked you out of the temple, Talan. It wasn't because I was afraid of your criminal activities, or embarrassed by your misconduct, or never thought you'd amount to anything."

I flinched at his accusations from that night. Even now, so many years later, they weren't easy to hear. He saw it was so and sighed. "I've never given up on you, and I never will. I just had to drive you away until I knew it was safe for you to return."

But I thought of something, and a vein throbbed in my neck. "Why didn't you just tell me the truth? Why say all those lies? Valem's burned name, I was seventeen. I could have handled it."

"You could have handled it for yourself, certainly." His lips curled slightly. "But I had reasons. For one, I never received any proof of the truth of it; the Tefra never claimed to have done it. As for the other reason… perhaps I was wrong, but I mostly did it so you wouldn't do something stupid. For me."

I saw it ever so clearly. "No," I said softly, a slight burning in my chest even now from the suggestion of it. "You weren't wrong."

He cleared his throat and sat up straighter. "Well, I say all that for context. For what I'm about to suggest." He paused again. "To help with your heist."

I blinked, uncomprehending. "What does—?"

"These men you work for — the Firewater Den. They weren't always called that. Their most famous name, which you might recognize, is the Rosewater Resistance."

I did recognize it — any boy in Erimis, in the whole of the Avvadin Imperium, would recognize it. The tales of their rebellion nearly a hundred years ago were whispered at night by parents, mostly as warnings of disobedience. But, from other accounts, they almost succeeded in taking down the Prophet King and his Tefra.

"But even if you know their name, you might not know what they became after they were rounded up and put in chains, their leaders thrown to the Father's fires. There's even a hint of their original name in it: the Damask Esir."

I had to stand; it was too much. "You're kidding. How does that make any sense? The Damask Esir are the Kahin-Shah's *personal* guard. They're utterly loyal. How do you get that from rebels?"

"You don't know what they're subjected to, Talan. It's not exactly the daemon rituals like most people think, but they're not called Esir — thralls — for no reason." Osman stared at the floor. "You've heard of the Qarin?"

"I didn't know there'd be an examination when I came here. Yes, I know them — the two little jinn in our heads, voices of conscience and sin."

"That's not exactly correct. Most of us don't have Qarin, and they're not so simple as spouting good or evil thoughts. As far as I know, the only people who have Qarin are the Damask Esir. That's what makes them loyal to death. They don't have a choice about it; they're slaves to their emperor, and Qarin are the yokes."

I heard him, but couldn't quite comprehend as I tried making sense of how this affected my most recent interactions with a bloodback. If Yanara was controlled by a Qarin, how could she go around robbing craftsmen with me? Killing assailants wasn't too out of line for an Esir, but assaulting citizens? Still, I remembered the way she had paused and cocked her head, as if listening…

"Bloody ashes," I muttered. "Sear me straight to the Underearth."

"Is it that much of a shock?"

I couldn't decide whether or not to tell him about Yanara, though I wasn't sure why I hesitated. I had confessed more important things to him before, things that could have landed me in the dungeons for the rest of my life, if not a one-way trip to Valem's fires. What was one more piece of damning information between us?

But considering what he had just told me, the answer revealed itself: he'd worry. He might intervene. If the Damask Esir were truly loyal no matter what, then Yanara wasn't straying from her duties; she was spinning me into a trap. At this point, that seemed most likely, even if it made her the best damn mummer I'd ever come across. I wouldn't think a person could fake the bloodlust she showed, nor her erraticism. She seemed more like someone unwinding than a spider spinning a web.

But either way, if I told Osman, he might do something stupid. And he'd risked enough for me already with the Underguild trying to collect my blood fare. I had to keep him in the dark on this one. For his own good.

The irony of the role reversal was bittersweet.

"Yes, a shock," I said. "Just a lot I didn't know all at once."

He stood as well and touched my shoulder. "I don't know if I can approve of you throwing in your lot with the Firewater Den, even with their decorated past. I'm not fond of the Imperium—" His voice fell to a whisper. "—but the Den isn't like they used to be."

I thought back to severe Bazaad, jolly Semih, sour Erkan, strange Cemal, sneaky Haluk… and I was inclined to agree.

"Still," he continued, hand falling away, "if you insist on it, I may as well give you a good excuse to be there." He turned away and picked up a sack, then opened it so I could peer in.

I did and blinked. "Are they just getting ragged, or are you expecting me to launder them?"

He laughed. "No, no, none of that. These Kor robes are your key to the Mausoleum."

"Another joke. You just want to see me and my accomplices get thrown into the canal, robes floating about us, baring our underparts to whatever nibbling fish manage to live in the damn Crimson."

"Listen, will you?" He tried giving me the bag, but when I threw up my hands, he set it at my feet. "Remember the Span of Calming?"

"Yes. How could I forget those painful days?" I only partly jested. It was the most boring and embarrassing part of being a whirler, spinning on all corners of the city to supposedly calm wandering jinn. The only thing that really came of it was harassment by every passing girl and boy.

"Something you didn't know is that we don't just spin in public. We go everywhere there are jinn. Especially Silks."

It clicked. "You go inside the Vacant City for the Calming?"

"Of course — the Shrouded Mother is our Buyujinn, is she not? You can go right down the lift and into its belly with no guards accompanying. Of course, they search you afterward — you'll have to figure out that part yourself. But this will at least get you in."

It seemed almost too good to be true, even with that part about the lift. Then I frowned, remembering. "But the Span isn't for another month." Far too long to wait at the rate things were progressing.

"Of course not. But the jinn are getting restless, and the Silks roam further off their paths. Perhaps I informed the Tefra it's necessary for an early Calming to keep things in order."

Suddenly, the impossible had come within my grasp. I hadn't realized how much I'd been running on false hope until that moment. Coughing to loose my suddenly tight throat, I croaked, "Thank you, Os. Really, thank you."

He smiled, but it was tinged with sadness. "Just make sure you do this properly. Don't make it another peacock incident."

My eyes nearly popped out of my head. "Even you know about that?"

He snorted. "I know a lot you don't." But the joviality quickly drained from him. "In particular, there's one thing you should know before you're sure you want to enter."

"I'm not sure anything can keep my wounded pride from the job — but please, enlighten me."

He caught my gaze and held it. "This is serious, Talan. I don't know what it means, but I think it a bad sign." He paused and tipped his chair dangerously forward. "The last few years, the Vacant City has seemed different. It's been… shifting."

"Shifting?"

"We don't go among the buildings as a rule, or even go far from the lift — too much of a risk for anyone not Tefra. Still, even from there, it seems like the buildings are different each visit. I thought it just a fault in my memory the first couple times, but the third… As I said, I don't know what it might portend, but it's best to be wary."

"Well, if the buildings come alive and attack me, I've been duly warned."

He gave me a glare intending to burn, but his ire had lost more than a bit of its fire over the years. I smiled pleasantly back, trying not to let him see my nervousness. No point in making him worry more.

"Fine," he growled. "If you want to be a fool about this, that's on you. But know this: jinn down there aren't like Silks. They're wild. Untamed."

"Jinn before they're leashed?" I swallowed. Would my methods for dealing with Silks hold up against jinn with no bonds?

"Possibly. But I have a feeling the Tefra haven't told me everything about the place. Each time I descend, I feel… a presence. Pressing on me, into me. Perhaps so great as to be Buyujinn, I don't know. But if it is, it falls to the natural order of things — the pressure always eases after the Calming."

I didn't know what to make of that, and I knew better than to dismiss Os's fears except in jest. "Good to know. But even if there are strange jinn down there, I know how to take care of myself."

My Hodja looked up again, and his hard teacher eyes softened for once. "Yes, I suppose you do," he said quietly.

Then he cleared his throat and stood. "I have classes to teach. But walk with me, and I'll tell you a few more things you should know about the Mausoleum…"

———

With the bag of robes in hand and new knowledge in my head, I set off for the exit, only stopping for a quick snack. But when I reached the doors, I halted. All the problems I hadn't resolved washed over me. The Underguild, the heist, Yanara — and now, it was even more complicated than before. I couldn't walk the streets, not unless I wanted to risk a knife in my back at any moment.

I stood there trembling before I thought of it. A disguise — how parrot-brained I was! I was holding a bag full of Kor robes, hats, and sandals, and I hadn't thought to put them on. It didn't bode well for the rest of the day.

But after I slipped on the clothes, I felt a bit better and brave enough to go outside. It didn't go much for hiding my face, but religious robes provide a certain kind of anonymity. Even though we all know initiates and priests can sin — and often do — we still assume their innocence. After all, at least they're trying.

But still, I couldn't help but feel as if eyes followed me throughout the whole walk.

I made it all the way back to Lavabed, even past the spot where crimson now stained the stones. The bodies, though, were gone, cleared away by yayas or the Underguild — who can say. Still, I tried not to look around and strode through as fast as I could without attracting attention.

One thing did arrest my attention though. A tall, stooped figure walked down the street before me, easily visible through the crowd — Cemal. Before him walked two adolescent girls, a thin woman holding each of their hands. They walked some ten paces in front, but their frequent, impatient glances back confirmed their affiliation. Cemal, for his part, hardly seemed to notice; his eyes were down, his lips moving in murmurs, his thoughts in some distant land. For his sake, I hoped it was a friendlier place than this.

When I reached Semih's house, I stripped off the Kor robes and stuffed them back in the bag, then proceeded to the back door. I didn't expect to find anyone else there. But after my exchange with the servant-girl — this time, with even more incredulity emanating through the call-window — I entered to find not only Semih sitting with a glass and decanter of purple wine but Bazaad as well. Semih rushed over, bowing and shaking my hand, but Bazaad remained seated.

"Well," the agha said. "Our thief does still honor the contract."

"What do you expect?" I snapped. "It's been three days." My annoyance surprised everyone in the room, myself most of all — I was more on edge than I knew. "I'm sorry," I muttered, tossing the bag of clothes to the floor and taking Semih's offered seat. "There have been... complications."

Bazaad stared at me, cold and unflinching. "I see. I don't suppose you care to divulge these complications?"

I delayed the inevitable by picking a liquor. Not able to concentrate, I went for what I now knew to be dependable: the orange rum from the first night. "All right. But so you don't suddenly believe me inadequate, let me share my plan first."

"Yes!" Semih said, leaning forward. "*Your* plan." He winked, and it took me a moment to understand why.

"Our plan, then," I said reluctantly, though I supposed it was Osman's plan most of all. Then I explained about the Calming, and the Kor practices, and what access that granted us.

"Once the two yayas at the door wave us inside, we come into the main chamber," I said. "Four guards operate the winches to the lift, while one Tefra watches over them. We step into the cage, they lower us — and just like that, we're inside, free to roam and steal as we like."

"Marvelous!" Semih exclaimed. "A stupendous plan!"

Bazaad was less enthusiastic. "It sounds... simple."

"Simple is good in this line of work," I said. "Simple is very, very good. Especially if you don't have to rely on any single person to get the job done."

Bazaad nodded, but still seemed unconvinced. "And you expect to simply walk out with Nehir's Chalice in hand?

I still didn't quite have that figured out, but I wasn't about to let the old bear know that. "They don't typically check the Kor," I lied.

One eyebrow raised. "And if they happen to this time?"

I shrugged casually while my mind wove together some haphazard story. "Can't hurt to be safe, I suppose. There's a certain item in my trade that will do the trick — a thief's slip, it's called. You can put items in it, but they don't change the size of the bag. The yayas can pat us down to their hearts' desire, and they'll never feel it."

"And such an item — I suppose it costs." Bazaad watched me very carefully.

The sudden urge to lick my lips almost overwhelmed me. I'd hoped my thoughts weren't as transparent as that. "Not so much as you might think," I said, hedging my bets. "Ten silver pimars, fifteen at most. They're not supposed to be hard to enchant, and there's a liberal supply from the Bali chiefdoms."

"The Bali?" Semih asked with wonder. "Such an unexpected place!"

"Well, they wear so few clothes, they need to put their stone knives somewhere."

Semih snorted in appreciation, while Bazaad somehow looked even more severe at the inappropriate remark. However, he just said, "I can arrange for twenty silver before you leave here. Consider the extra an advance. So then, what of these complications?"

"Yes, well." I couldn't help licking my lips now. "There are two things, mostly. Kind of one thing, in a way." I took a steadying breath, nerves fluttering. "The Underguild came to collect."

Semih looked confused, but Bazaad groaned and began rubbing his temples. "Talan," he said in a low, deflated voice.

"That would have been the end of me, but for the other matter. It seems a certain — ah, person from my past has reemerged."

"And they fought off Underguild assassins?" Bazaad said from behind his hand. "Must be a singular person."

"Well… she's Damask Esir."

The agha became still as Erimis at night, and Semih looked more confused than ever. "What?" he asked. "What is it, Bazaad? A Damask Esir — a good friend to have, yes, I should think?"

"No," the old bear growled. "Exactly the *wrong* kind of friend to have." From the way he looked at me, I thought he must know the bloodbacks' history was intertwined with his and his Den's. And perhaps even how the old Rosewater Resistance members were kept in line.

"How many dead?" Bazaad asked quietly.

"Seven. Plus an innocent." I ignored my stomach souring at that — now wasn't the time for guilt.

"All her?"

"No," I said, somewhat defensive. "Surely you don't think so little of me. Two I can claim, and neither of them the cart-man."

"Well," he said. "We will just have to keep you here then until the heist and pray to the Mother that her husband's not feeling vengeful."

"Uh, actually — I can't stay."

Bazaad's look nearly boiled the blood out of me, so I quickly continued. "The Esir expects me again tonight. I have to go, or chance making it worse." I smiled weakly. "You understand, I'm sure."

I downed my rum and reached to pour more, but the fuming agha grabbed my wrist. "Son," he growled, leaning forward, "I'm putting a lot of trust in you right now. The whole of our cause is in your hands. If you fail us, we don't just lose a chance at a cup. We lose our lives and any hope of freedom from a tyrannical and unjust government." The corner of his mouth twitched, and not in a smile. "My life's work, and my life, depend on you. Do not char it black by getting drunk before seeing a Damask Esir."

I let go of the bottle, and he let go of me. It took a few moments to catch my breath; I wasn't sure if I felt more angry or ashamed.

Semih, who had been nervously looking back and forth, suddenly jumped up, his chair scooting back with a squeal. "Food, food, food — we all need food!" Then he bustled from the place like a chastised serving girl.

Bazaad and I sat in silence, during which I absently scrubbed at the sticky crud on the table, no doubt from long-spilled drinks. It wasn't much of a distraction from the pounding thirst in my throat and the throbbing veins in my forehead, but it was better than looking at Bazaad. Especially when I felt his eyes still on me.

Finally, the agha sighed, and leaned forward to pick up the bottle of rum, then splashed a bit in my cup. I stared, not quite believing the gesture. Sure enough, he followed it up with water.

"I may have been… harsh," Bazaad managed, pushing the glass towards me. "Please, accept my apology."

I took up the glass and lifted it with a small smile. "Men of the Den can't hold grudges against each other." Then I took a drink, savoring the burn, weak as it was.

"Yes… yes, you are one of us now, aren't you?"

I looked up suspiciously. "Well, it was a joke. But I guess that depends on what it entails."

"Thankless resistance. Long nights with few results. Many imbibed spirits."

"In." I raised my glass in toast.

Bazaad chuckled. "You will do fine, Talan. You will do us just fine."

I wished I had half his confidence.

———

I hid the morning away in Semih's house. Bazaad left after a time to attend to other business, saying he'd be back that night with the rest of the Fire-water Denizens. Without anyone to shame us, Semih and I devoured half a cow, then a nap seemed in order to settle our gluttony.

I woke in a panic.

The room Semih had settled me in — which was small but comfortable, and furnished lavishly with exotic rugs and wall-hangings — was greatly darkened since I'd lain down. Too dark. I bolted upright and whipped aside the curtains to see the sun already kissing the horizon. And I was to be at the docks already! With images of Yanara tearing apart those five men all too clear in my mind, I hurried and arranged my clothes, pulled on my boots, and set out the door. Semih caught me just as I crossed the threshold.

"Will you be back, Wraithsbane?" he called. Then, bustling closer, he said softer, "For the gathering?"

"The Damask Esir will keep me, regrettably. But tell them: be ready tomorrow, just before noon." My smile hung a bit loosely on my face; Semih and I may have also dipped into the liquor during our feast. "It's all happening at noon."

All the usual ruddiness to Semih's cheeks drained away. "Tomorrow? B-but... isn't it too soon? Aren't there preparations? Your thief's slip, for one..."

I laughed, too loudly. A bit of caution came back to me when I remembered the men likely lurking in the dark, but not near enough of it. "Evening is the *only* time to buy one. And if we wait any longer, I'm afraid one of your lads might bow out of the whole thing." I took Semih's hand and patted him familiarly with my shame-hand. "It will be fine, Semih. Trust me."

I turned to depart but remembered one last thing. "Oh, and Semih? Tell them to practice their spinning."

"Spinning?" He sounded skeptical.

I laughed. "Think of it as intentional reeling — you ought to be good at that."

I waved and disappeared into the growing darkness.

CHAPTER SEVEN

AN EVENTIDE TO DISROBE

Once I was alone, night pressed down and all confidence washed away as sudden as a monsoon rain. Every shadow seemed to glint with hidden knives, every curious face malignant with murder. Sometimes, I even thought I saw the pale visage of the man I'd burned come back to haunt — and hurt.

What people must have thought, to see me flitting from one street to another, as if pursued by a flock of mad parrots. I wished not for the first time that the Hortum Kor wore hoods instead of hats. But wishing is wanton wanting, as the saying goes — there was nothing for it but to keep walking.

Somehow, despite all the wrath Valem should have hurled at me, I saw the bridge come into view without incident and exhaled a sigh of relief — though why I should have felt relief was beyond any rationalization. Yanara was standing there, bringing me a whole host of problems. Like what we had slated for tonight. And what she'd think of me reeking of alcohol.

And if she was enslaved by a Qarin that was even now pulling me into a trap.

Still, unless I wanted two homicidal powers after me rather than just one, I had to move forward. And besides, she'd recognized me — did she already know of my gig with Those Who Dance with Whirling Embers? And the more I thought about it, it was a stupid move to dress like this; what if she mentioned it and word spread to the yayas guarding the Mausoleum tomorrow?

I stared at that huge pyramid as I meandered through the docks. The fireglass was a dark scarlet from the setting sun, the color of congealed blood.

Tearing my gaze away, I approached under Yanara's unrelenting stare. She was back in her bloodback uniform. It seemed we wouldn't be performing another bruiser, at least. What she thought of me in my own uniform, she didn't say.

"So," I broke the silence. "Glad to see you're still alive."

She remained cold in stark contrast to the lingering balmy heat. "Did you expect less?"

"Well, no. But I also didn't expect myself to make it through the city not once, but twice, after a run-in with the Underguild." I peered into the long shadows formed by the canal's walls, and by the various shipping equipment spread about the docks. "And speaking of which, it's nigh their hours… shall we get going?"

"Don't worry about them anymore."

I looked at her sharply, thinking her truly mad, Qarin or no. "Not worry? The damned lawless breed like blossom fowls, and aren't half as charming up close. Or maybe you don't remember last night?"

"Enough." Her tone bore every manner and expectation of a bey now. "If you'll stop babbling like a searing idiot for a moment, I'll explain." She breathed in deeply. "Mother and Father, you didn't used to talk like this."

I held my tongue.

"While you were boozing" — her nostrils flared — "I was flushing out those ants. They will be long in returning, and perhaps with a shorter memory."

Only then did I notice the fresh gash on her cheek, almost a continuance of the scar above her eyebrow. And how she stood: though still bolt upright, she leaned like a woman heavy with birth looking for the next chair to collapse into. "Burn me..." I marveled. "You attacked the Underguild."

"Yes," she snapped. "You'll be safe, for a time. And they know none died by your hand — I made it clear that you cowered in a corner while my men and I did the butchering."

I wasn't terribly fond of the story, but the results were nice enough. Still, I'd never known the syndicate to act the kicked cur. But I was a branch in a strong gust; she could toss me however she wished, and I had no option but to bend.

"Well," I ventured, "where would you like to enjoy our newfound freedom?"

She didn't snap this time but put her arm through mine. For the first time since our reunion, I remembered she was shorter than me. With all her authority and strength, she seemed to loom like the stone giants of the Obsidian Palace, or Valem and his Wife before they descended into the Underearth. Sule had never seemed that way; rough as she'd always been, Sule had ever been a girl to me.

And now, as she set us to walking, she'd become a girl again. It might have been reassuring, were it not so sudden a change, and in stark contrast to her appearance.

"Tell me about home," she said softly. I swiftly complied.

———

We talked for a long while, wandering the moon-fired stones of sleeping Erimis. Or rather, I talked — she was content to hold my arm and listen. Even when I asked for input and confirmation, I barely received back a word or nod. Which set me to wondering with my current suspicions: perhaps the Qarin stole more than just her ability to know what was right and wrong, and who she should be loyal to. Perhaps it stole her very memories, so she remembered nothing but being Damask Esir, nothing before enthrallment. At least until the Qarin tried to trick a certain thief into believing his old comrade had returned to his side.

But for my suspicions, those moments of us walking would have almost felt familiar. But for her silence, she would have almost been the old Sule.

Sometime after the sun set and the moons brightened the sky, Yanara suddenly took the lead again, yanking my arm. "Where are we going?" I asked as I followed, hiding my anxiety behind a bantering tone. While reminiscing was all well and good, not knowing my Esir companion's designs for me was quite the opposite.

"Someplace to talk."

As if we hadn't already had ample opportunity.

We left the Jade Docks, through the narrow strip of Lavabed, and started venturing near Obsidian Heights. The wall that separated the district reserved for the Foremost from the common sinners loomed just above when she turned us toward a merrily lit inn. It was like a spectral hand squeezed my throat as we walked to its door. I suddenly realized what we were doing here. Panic, which had subsided while walking the peaceful streets, rose up again and set me to quivering, no matter how I resisted it. If Yanara noticed, she didn't show it, but pulled me through the door under a sign declaring the inn's name as "The Dance of Peacocks."

The inn opened into a series of galleries so richly adorned they seemed better suited to an Obsidian Heights establishment. Bright, red fireglass ran across the ceiling, gently glowing with the light of gold-hued pyr lamps. The walls were also gold, but tinted a dusky obsidian, while the floors were a dark hardwood with soft but well-worn rugs.

The clientele seemed educated as well as rich. Those not sitting in groups — and even some who were — had papers or books before them, and were quietly perusing them over cups of tea. Their clothes, too, showed their classes: here a priest of another order than the Hortum Kor, there a bejeweled merchant, and there a group of landed efendi, by their uplifted chins and arrogant airs.

And there in the corner, a certain someone I knew: Haluk sat at a table with a taller, simply dressed man. There was something about the way they sat that struck me; perhaps it was the angry expression on the man's face, or Haluk's own sorrowful but firm one. Even in the midst of my own predicament, I wondered what argument they were having.

They looked up with the rest of the inn at the sight of an Esir and a Kor entering together. Startled looks spread like wildfire across the rooms. I wondered what exactly was the cause of their surprise. The odd combination? A powerful woman clad in men's clothes? Or did they know about the Qarin, their being well-educated and all, and could not contain their revulsion?

I particularly sympathized with this last point.

Yanara's lip slightly curled, but she only strode over to the woman standing behind the desk and asked after a room. The woman, possessing all the composure her guests lacked, promptly led us upstairs. Perhaps Yanara just wanted a quiet place to talk. Perhaps.

My robe had become incredibly hot.

The innkeeper led us to a room that was more modest than the galleries downstairs. There was little more than a chair, a side table with a wicker lamp, and a bed, with barely a dozen paces between. Hardly a proper place to… talk.

The innkeeper bowed out, and Yanara shut the door behind her, while I took station near the window. I wasn't there long. As the door clicked shut, she spun on her heels with military precision, stalked over to me, and hauled me onto the bed. Partly surprised, mostly spineless, I flopped on to it like a handless hand-puppet.

I leaned up on my elbows, warily waiting for what came next. When my eyes fell on her, they went wide. Her uniform had started to unravel.

Before, when she'd been clad in men's clothes, I'd thought her wild beauty faded since our youth. Now I saw how very wrong I'd been. First, the head wrap and handkerchief were shed, releasing a sprig of springy black hair. Then, the long jacket shrugged from her shoulders, the belts unbuckled, and the tunic went over her head, leaving her torso bare but for her underwraps. As much as my eyes traced her figure, I stumbled over her many healed wounds, the most prominent of which ran red and raised across her belly, from under the wraps down past her navel.

The wraps didn't stay on long; they unraveled before my eyes, round and round, until they fell to the floor, and left behind nothing but two plump and bare breasts. I couldn't take my eyes from them, even as something clawed at the back of my mind not to look, not to trust what was happening. But my libido compelled my appreciation.

Now the boots were kicked off, the trousers fell, and the lower underwraps formed a messy pile on the floor. Her legs were strong and her hips wide, but there was no extra flesh anywhere on her body; she was soldier-lean. My eyes followed up her legs, to a patch of hair leading down between them.

She watched my eyes with no smile; her expression was as hard as it had been during the bruiser. She walked towards me, hips slightly swaying with the movement, and put one knee, then the other, about my legs. Her straddle gave me a new angle of appreciation.

My throat felt like it would never fully open again. "Yanara," I choked out, but she suddenly fell to her hands, her face bare inches from mine, her breath hot on my face.

"Sule," she whispered harshly. "Call me Sule."

"Sule, then. Just wait a moment—"

"What?" She saw my eyes falling to her chest, tracing the curves along it. "You still find me attractive." Then she ran a hand over the front of my robe to show exactly what she meant.

It was true, undeniably true: she was a beautiful woman, almost statuesque in it. Here in the heart of Avvad, others derided the territorial woman as possessing a crude sort of beauty, or only found her so in fetishes. But I was from the territories as well. She was my kind of beauty.

But still, even with desire burning in her eyes, I knew it was not what I wanted. I thought it might fill me, but it was like a coin dropping in a dry well, the echo sounding back up the long shaft. There was nothing here, no true connection; and with Sule, I couldn't indulge simple lust. My chest wrenched with the long-seated guilt rising once more.

I pushed her hand away. "You know I do," I agreed, "but this is not the time."

She rose again, looming over me. "Not the time?" she said, voice dripping with bitterness. "Would you have me wait another ten years? Fight a thousand battles again? How long would you have me wait, to reclaim what was once mine?"

The possessiveness made my nerves clatter and clang. "It can't be, Sule. Not ever. I am… sorry."

For a moment, she didn't react, and panic rather than lust threatened to choke me. I found myself telling the first story I could think of. "While I've lived here in Erimis, I met someone. A woman. But she didn't feel the same way as I did. I don't want to go into it, but... it didn't end pleasantly."

There was a dangerous glint in those pink eyes. "But she's gone. She's nothing to us."

"Well..." I tried to sit up, though it was awkward with her still over me. "I mean that she got in my head, and now I can't help thinking that every woman that... well, that they want something other than... this." I waved indiscriminately at us and swallowed, amazed that I was actually going to keep on with this farce. "So I... go to whores. At least with them, I know what it is they want in return. It's a clean deal."

She leaned down again, slowly, and made me stare into her eyes. "Then pay me."

"What?" But I knew where this was going.

"Pay me," she repeated. "Then you can trust me, right? You trust whores, so give me coppers. Then you don't have to think I'm twisting you for something else. Pay me."

"I — You don't mean that—"

"I want you, and you want to pay me. What's the harm?" She smiled, but suddenly in the shadowed dark, it looked more like a snarl. "I'll be your little *whore*."

I tried to slide out from underneath her, but she clamped her legs over mine. Then she started moving her hands over the robe, tugging it off with the violence of a warrior in battle. Underneath, I was still fully clothed, but she didn't pause before she began tearing these off as well.

"Sule, stop—"

"Pay me after." Her tone was acid on parchment, eating through. "I'm not a picky whore."

My jacket was off, my tunic untucked, and my trousers were unlaced. Her fingertips burned like the sun where they touched my skin.

Then I snapped out of whatever shock I'd lapsed into and pushed on her shoulders, shoving her back. "Stop, Sule, *stop*!"

And, amazingly, she did. Sitting up over me, breasts heaving with every breath, she looked a living statue in her naked fury.

"How did you escape?" she asked quietly.

"What?"

"Our whole cabal was captured that night. We saw glimpses of each other in the dungeons before I got taken away. But you — I never saw you. I thought they'd killed you, or worse."

Or made you a Silk, she must have thought. But I thought her own fate was worse than that.

"I…" But I had no lie prepared this time. I thought I'd never see any of the Duman cabal again, hoped I wouldn't. I had been captured before they had. But instead of staying true to my cabal, I had given them up for a quick pass to freedom. I'd told myself that people were getting hurt, and I could stop it, and that was true enough. But truly, I was a coward, and afraid, and looking out for only myself.

I doubted there was any room for forgiveness in her heart, and I didn't blame her.

My silence was answer enough. I couldn't decide if she looked closer to crying or grinding her thumbs in my eyes. Maybe both were as natural to a Damask Esir.

I slid out from beneath her. "I'm sorry," I muttered, reaching for my clothes. "I'm sorry."

The silence pressed in sharp while I redressed. I didn't even hear her move once her breathing settled. All I could hear was a small murmur from downstairs. "I'm sorry," I repeated and put a hand on the door.

"If I see you again," she started. And didn't finish.

"Sorry," I muttered again and slipped out. Back downstairs, I ducked my head, so I wouldn't see the knowing gazes of every patron of the galleries, and practically fell out into the chilling night.

My feet took me to Osman's temple. But looking up at the lofty dome and the wings that splayed out like a dragonfly, I knew this was not my home for the night. I had no home this night.

I thought about going to Semih's, to beg a night off of him, but then I remembered I had coin enough for a room, thanks to the "thief slip" I was supposed to buy. Perhaps not my ideal use of it, but the prospect of inter-action sounded beyond me.

Gambling the night away, too, was beyond me — it held none of the sweet anticipation it did before. Anticipation requires hope for something better than you had before.

Perhaps it was because I was unmoored, but I drifted to the thing most occupying my thoughts, the thing on which all my hopes rested, and stared at it by the light of the three moons. The Mausoleum's glass seemed composed of shadows and white glares, none of the pink visible but from the cloudy moon's violet glow. There were two sets of pyr lamps mounted by the watchful yayas, and the guards peered out into the night for anyone stupid enough to try stealing from within.

I tried to smile at the idiocy of it all, but alone and lonely, I couldn't muster it. It was a hard thing to stare at what my life had come to, to stare it in the face and realize all my efforts had come to naught. That no one, or next to no one, would care for my passing when it soon came. That this was all a race that inevitably would end with me collapsing as a bloody corpse, my soul ripped away by a silk-garbed phantom.

Then again, who knew. Valem favors those who forge their own way. He Branded me — perhaps that was sign enough that I could make it through all this.

But underneath all the placating fabrications, I doubted it.

CHAPTER EIGHT

A FORENOON FOR REMAINING CALM

For all my doom and gloom the evening before and my restless, anxious sleep during the night, I woke with a strange sort of clairvoyance. It was the first time in a long time that I'd slept without dreams. I hadn't seen Yanara chasing me down, nor assassins in the shadows, nor the recurring nightmare of a jinni's smiling face looming over me, hand squeezing my heart to pulp. Tired, but restful, peace.

And just in time. Today was the day.

In my room at a cheap inn, I took the time to do my morning necessaries — eating, relieving, paying respects to Valem, whirling for myself — then I was out the door, clad again in my Hortum Kor robe. The day being Dini, those few people who were out meandered slowly toward their destinations. Dini was a day of contemplation and rest; even mighty Valem did not storm his displeasure every day, but took his rest today, so it followed that Avvadin warriors should do the same. The patrolling yayas seemed dull-eyed and lackadaisical; they barely nodded at me as they passed, even politeness for supposed religious figures too much for such a day.

A perfect day for a Calming.

I reached Semih's house when the sun was mid-rise, but though it would be completely proper to enter through the front, by habit, I went to the back. The flocking parrots didn't even annoy me when they landed on my hat and shoulders, croaking words they'd picked up but just missed the point, like "Payday?" and "Flute?" and "I rant a rum!" That last bit might have seemed a bit risky of a phrase, but yayas knew better than to pay attention to the burned birds.

I shrugged them off. "No pita, fruit, or rum today, my friends—but when I come back, you can have all of the last you'd like."

Like they knew what I was saying, they all started cawing at once, and fluttered into a kaleidoscopic twister. I laughed; it was a good omen for whirling.

This time, my knock was answered with Bazaad's shrewd eyes and bristling eyebrows peering out the call-window. "I had begun to wonder if you would show up."

"With my reputation on the line? Please, Bazaad — I'm nothing if not self-preserving."

"I should hope so." He swung open the door and held it for me. "This is the day for it like no other."

I patted his shoulder with my shame-hand and smiled at his twitching cheek. "Relax, agha — all will be well."

The rest of our merry troupe was gathered around the usual pitted, sticky table. What I was not so pleased to see was the green bottle clutched in Erkan's hands.

"What in the searing Underearth is he doing with that?" I demanded of Bazaad.

"Efendi Talan — ah, Wraithsbane," Semih stuttered, while Erkan glowered at me and took a long, defiant swig. "Truly, we have no excuse, but… Erkan claims it grants him, ah, courage."

"A coward's courage!" I was close to shouting. I shook my head, trying to rein my temper back in; when that failed, I paced to do *something*. Erkan wasn't truly necessary, though I'd begun counting on him in my mind if it came to a scrap. And four men searching down in a cavernous pyramid was better than three. But if he walked in there reeking of alcohol, our charade wouldn't last long.

I squared off against Erkan, who now had his legs kicked up onto the table and was slouched back in his chair like he didn't have a care in the world. "Fine, Erkan. You're staying."

He apparently wasn't expecting that, for he glared up at me with all the fire of an eruption. "Blood and ashes to you, *Wraithsbane*," he growled. "Treating me like my *wife*. I'll drink when I please and still do anything twice as good as you."

"You're slurring your words, so there's the first thing that's inadequate," I pointed out. "You won't be able to whirl, much less walk in — or out — of the Mausoleum."

He swished another mouthful of the stuff and sputtered around it,

"Burn this whole burning plan. Hasn't got a runny turd of a chance of working anyway."

Glancing at the others, they seemed unsettled. Cemal was bent nearly double over the table, his eyes level with a pair of knots in the wood, studying them with the intensity another man might a pair of bare breasts. Haluk still had a smug smile, but his eyes were scrunched and lined, and he was staring off into space rather than maintaining his usual shrewd exterior. Semih was a sweaty wreck, and even Bazaad couldn't help but fidget.

"It has," I said, a fire starting to burn in my belly and rise through my chest. "It has a chance, better than a chance. It has to work, and it will. But — but even if it doesn't, burn it all, we have to try."

They were all watching now, vacillating between hope and hopelessness, like parrots unable to decide which hand they wanted to eat from.

"Don't you remember what you are?" I demanded. "Not the Firewater Den — before. The Rosewater Resistance. You were the hope of all of Avvad — the only hope, and you came damned close to fulfilling on that. Are we going to let ourselves continue to be slaves to the whims of a few? Slaves in our very bodies?"

"No," whispered Haluk. All artifice had drained away, and he looked haggard as an unstuffed scarecrow.

"No, we will not. Not when they enslave thousands — hundreds of thousands — all across the world. Not when they leash even the jinn and enslave our spirits if we defy them. Can we stand for such crimes to continue?"

"No," Erkan croaked. The bottle was still in his hand, but at least it sat on the table, unmoving.

"No. Now, we have a chance to turn the tide. We have a trick up our sleeves, and a narrow opportunity to make good on it. Are we going to turn cowards at the last moment, or walk boldly ahead, as our Father taught us to do?"

Cemal looked up, his head still horizontal with the table. "The parrots," he said softly. "Prisms soaring."

"Ah, yes — we shall be soaring prisms when we're through." To be honest, the speech's momentum seemed to break an axle at that point, but I'd made my point. "Well, let's get to it, then, shall we?"

It was an even less hearty cheer than the first night — but at least they didn't say no.

We were all silent for a moment, all thinking of what lay ahead. Then Haluk said, "You have the thief's slip, no?"

Oh yes. We were prepared.

———

After too many minutes of deflections, assurances, and a bit of bullying, I managed to get them off the thief's slip and onto our mission. "Bazaad and Semih told you the plan, no?" I asked my cabal of three, ignoring the two portly men not coming along.

"Indeed," Haluk said. "You might say we have studied it quite assiduously, and are as expert in its details as yourself."

If only they knew how expert I was on my plan. "We could all use a review. First, what are we — four Hortum Kor — doing at the Mausoleum?"

"Burning spinning around," Erkan growled. "What else do Kor do?"

He still had the bottle in his hand, but I tried not to look at it. The veins in my temples would start pounding if I did. "We're here for a Calming. We're holding one earlier this year because—"

"Ah, if I may," Haluk interrupted with far too much eagerness. "Because the Silks have been wandering off course, and we are concerned for the public's safety."

"Right, to calm the jinn. So we keep telling this to the yayas until we're down the lift. And then?"

"We…" Haluk started, but his eyes scrunched together. He started pulling at his deformed ear in agitation.

"A sojourn for the cup," Cemal said softly.

"A sojourn, sure. We split into pairs and search the buildings for the Chalice. The faster we go, the less suspicious the guards will be."

Haluk answered again. "Then you put the Chalice in your thief's slip — which I'd still like to see, efendi, if you wouldn't mind? — we call up, they bring us up the lift, and pat us down. And when they find nothing, they let us go free, and in possession of the artifact."

"It is, as Bazaad called it" — I glanced at the agha, but he was staring down at his folded hands — "a simple plan. Just stick to it and we might get out of this alive."

A short while later, I managed to get my ragged band of thieves in costume and filed out the door. We looked the sorriest pocket of whirlers I'd ever seen, not fit to pacify a sleeping baby, much less Silks out for our souls. But we were showing up, and that was more than I'd expected from the start. I fingered my obsidian shard, which was stowed in the single deep pocket on the front of the robe, and wished I could spin it across my fingers and give my nervous energy some outlet. But it doesn't do to show uncertainty as a leader. I'd just have to keep it in for the moment.

Erkan looked especially comical with his shoulders back, head upright, and feet finding every crack in the road. I should have had him practice a spin before we left, but I'd been too afraid he'd let loose all the rotten contents of his stomach. We'd stuffed him full of pita and water at least; hopefully, everything would keep down.

Cemal and Haluk were two more visions of oddity. I could only imagine what it would look like for such a tall, bowed man to spin, and if he could keep his balance hunched over like that. Not to mention that the robe didn't fit him, flapping well above his ankles. Haluk had the opposite problem. Robe bunched in his hands, he looked like a girl pretending at being a woman.

Doubts rose in my mind again, but I couldn't think about those now. This was my last chance to get things right. I was going to get that damned Chalice. I'd get the money, pay off the Underguild, and get back my old reputation. I would, so long as last night with Yanara didn't blast everything to the searing skies like Valem in a temper tantrum.

We went first to the Jade Docks, where most of the movement was by the parrots cawing from atop closed stands. Selling on Dini is prohibited, as such a base activity was no fit way to contemplate the Molten God and the Lost Mother.

Neither was stealing, but Valem hadn't erupted over it so far.

The Mausoleum was positively shining. The red undertones in the fire-glass glowed, making it seem as if the Vacant City inside were aflame. Any other day, it would look marvelous; today, it looked more than vaguely threatening, like a jewel set to lure you into a trap. The men behind me sensed it, too; Erkan was shaking so much that I felt the barest glimmer of sympathy for him.

As we approached the base of the pyramid, I was able to make out the positions of its guards. Four yayas were stationed at the bottom of the stairs, warding away would-be loiterers with harsh glares. Only two more were stationed outside a pair of midnight-black double doors to a room at the very top, some two hundred or so feet up. Already hot as we were, I wasn't looking forward to the hike up and was even more concerned that Erkan wouldn't manage it.

But first, we had to convince the yayas we were supposed to be here.

"Look alive," I whispered back to my companions. "And act saintly."

"Quit your commanding," Erkan growled back.

I arched an eyebrow at him more casually than I felt. Then, with a deep breath, I turned to the four guards leering at me with patronizing glares and approached. "Good Dini to you, efendi."

The bastards didn't even nod back, much less bow. "Look at that," one said to another. "Our whirlers did show up."

A shiver of fear went through me. "You were expecting us." I tried to make it a statement rather than a question.

"Of course," the second yaya said. "Hodja Osman always informs us before a Calming."

Informed they were, but it didn't incline them to move out of the way.

"Of course," I said with forced steadiness. "And I'm sure he pressed how vital it is that we perform our task as soon as possible. What with the Silks starting to wander."

"Of course." The first yaya smirked, and shifted about as much as a boulder in a breeze.

"Alright, we get it," Erkan suddenly spoke up from behind me, and my stomach dropped like I'd stumbled down a hole. "You could still deny us, but you won't. So move out of the burning way."

My head seemed empty of blood. Lightheaded, my hand hovered above my deep pocket, ready to grab my shard at the first sign of trouble. To my surprise and relief, however, the four yayas glanced at each other, then laughed and parted to reveal the door.

"You may want to calm your man first, spinner," the first guard said to me as we passed. "He seems a bit… unbalanced."

I gritted my teeth and wondered what in the searing Underearth was going on. If we were caught, we were caught already. To try walking away now would only result in a quick arrest and sentence to rot in the dungeons for life. There was no way now but up.

I set my foot on the first step and started the long climb up the stairs.

As I'd suspected, the stairs were no easy feat, and I was panting by a third of the way up, and my thighs were burning. The other three were having a tougher time of it, Haluk in particular. As the stairs were twice the height of what they should have been, the shorter man had to practically haul himself up each one. And Semih had thought we could scale this from the far side from the canal… As little amusement as I should have felt right then, I chuckled. I needed a good laugh.

We eventually made it to the top, our sky-blue robes somewhat darker about the armpits and our throats ragged as a convict's whipped back. The two yayas stationed there smirked at us. At least they didn't hold us up, but stepped up to the huge doors — which rose some three or four times our height — and slowly pulled them open just enough for us to slip through. Madmen that we were, we did, Erkan nearly stumbling with the effort.

As we stepped through, it felt as if we'd entered another era. The whole square chamber glittered with jade: jade column settings, fluted jade chandeliers, jade insets in the stone walls and ceiling. Not a pyr lamp was to be seen, nor the reds and violets so popular today. And the columns' carvings — they were grandiose and blatant in their praise of Valem, not the subtle symbols artisans now preferred.

Again, the place seemed largely understaffed, with only four guards in the whole place, all standing around what looked like a cage barely large enough to fit a lion. But in the far corner stood a red-cowled, gold-masked figure, chains hanging from his arms, watching us with sightless jade eyes. I couldn't help a shiver as I felt the Tefra's gaze on me as distinctly as being doused with cold water, knowing that his horribly burned face lingered just below the facade.

The Tefra didn't shift as we approached, while the yayas haughtily stared at our ragtag band. I saw it was not just a cage they surrounded, but a cage on a platform, suspended by four thick chains and cranks. Though I'd been forewarned about the lift, I still felt a jolt at seeing that our only way in and out was being operated by four burly guards with bad attitudes, and that a Tefra watched over them to ensure good behavior.

It has to work was the only thing I could think, over and over, until I wasn't sure if I believed it or not. As if it mattered at this point.

"Good Dini, efendi," I said pleasantly as we approached, breath labored from the climb. "You were told of our coming, I assume?"

"Ah, the whirlers," one said up front, the burliest of the four. "We were just thinking you wouldn't make it."

"We nearly didn't — those stairs are no mere feat."

The men chuckled, and not in a pleasant way. "Best not be too exhausted," the big one rumbled. "'Cause it's time for a little preview of what's going on down below."

"What's that?" I tried not to make it sound like a demand — or whining, for that matter.

The yaya indicated what he meant with his pinky finger, twirling it about like he was stirring tea. "Time to spin, titter-toes. Show us how you're going to pacify all the city's spirits. Might make us feel as relaxed as if our heads were resting on a wench's bosom."

The other three snickered, and I felt their sneering expectations bearing down on us. "All right, then. Initiates of the Hortum Kor," I said, turning to my three companions. "These fine guards wish to commune with Valem by witnessing our whirling."

The guards snickered again, but nobody made any further crude remarks. It says much of a god when even irreverent men fear to blaspheme his name directly.

The sour expressions I received back from my fellow "Kor" seemed as if they'd like to do a good deal more than blaspheme. But they followed my lead, and as I began my first turn, they moved with me.

What started as almost solemn quickly unraveled with a thud, a yelp, and a burst of laughter. I kept turning, already knowing I could do nothing for its cause: Erkan, unable to bear the sky's weight any longer, sprawled across the stone floor. I gritted my teeth, wondering why none of these guards stopped a man so flagrantly defying the Grey Dictums with drunk-enness. Perhaps discipline wasn't as tight as I'd thought among their ranks.

Or perhaps they were playing with us, like hawks with hares.

"Alright," the big yaya said through his chuckles. "I've seen churned butter spin better, but that'll do."

I stopped, a vague nausea eating at my stomach, and faced them again. The cage door was now open. I heard Erkan grunting to get on his feet behind me. "Well?" the guard said, face once again stony. "Time to twirl where it counts."

For once, the words didn't come. The cage, barely six feet tall, would have forced Cemal to crouch was he not already. But it wasn't just that: it was the yawning abyss below it, peering through the cracks around the edges, its deep darkness obscuring anything below.

"In we go," I said as heartily as I could and led them in. Somehow, the men kept true and followed me. We shivered as one, though, when the door latched shut behind us. Behind the guards, I saw the Tefra's mask still steadily on us, and my shiver worsened.

"That's not locked," the guard said, "but I wouldn't open it 'til you get to the bottom."

"Just don't get us there too fast," I replied.

The man didn't respond but moved into position. Then they turned their wheels, and let go.

The cage fell, and my feet left the floor as it hurtled through the fath-omless darkness.

CHAPTER NINE

A NOON FOR GLOOM

For a moment, I flew.

The next instant, the cage stopped, and my cheek slammed flat against the cold, iron floor. Better than the stone below, I supposed; at least I was whole and alive.

The yayas laughed above, and the four of us in the cage, toppled and tangled into each other, could only groan. It promised to be a long trip down, or too short of one.

"We made it," Haluk whispered as we stood, keeping quiet since the guards were not far above. "Just as I knew we would." I could only just make out a vague smirk in the darkness.

Erkan's response was to hurl, most of it making it off the edge of the platform. "Burn you," he spluttered. "Burn you all."

"If this is what you call making it," I observed to Haluk, ignoring Erkan. "Keep up that bravado — big help it'll be when you're up against jinn and magic treasures and yayas that probably won't let us out."

If Cemal was touched by any fear or consternation, he didn't show it. His only response was to grasp at the bars and peer through them, his head looking this way and that, studying the wonders about him. His interest gave me courage somehow, enough to take a look myself.

Though it was darker down inside the Vacant City, it was far from lightless. The walls, both the pyramid and the cave, glowed with a soft, pale luminescence that faded into darkness above. The light came from below. Sure enough, as I looked down at the buildings and streets, I could see that the city itself glowed like the moons. I wondered if pyrkin lived in the very stone. There was no flickering, waxing, or waning; every wall was visible, softly glowing like stars.

The architecture of the city was also strange. The hard lines that were typical to the buildings of Erimis had been replaced by curves. Domes, arches, vaults, tapered columns — it was as if Valem had molded them from salt with one sweep of his great hand. And yet, though the collection of hundreds of buildings expanded below us, there was not a thing to be seen among them. I expected — with creeping bumps along my skin — to at least see spectral Silks floating through the streets. But even these were absent. It truly was the Vacant City.

What we were supposed to be Calming, I couldn't say. But I thought back to what Osman said, of the presence he'd felt growing each time he visited, and I shivered. Yet if one of the Buyujinn was here with us, I didn't feel them yet.

The cage just kept creaking down, and a thick heat began pressing in as if Valem himself were breathing down on us. As we descended, further details came into view: the uneven lighting among buildings, and signs of abandoned life — a boot tossed into a corner, a dirty handkerchief…

…And a skeleton so white it looked as if it had been treated with lye.

While I decided whether or not to mention it, Haluk wandered over next to me and saw it lying there. "Oh." All the bluster in the slight man went out quick as a puffed candle, and he suddenly sagged like an unstrung ouk.

I patted his shoulder. "Damn fool, that one. Had no plan coming in most likely. But we've got one, solid through. And the Silks won't bother us." I winked at him, but I couldn't kindle the secret smile back in him. The gloom was pressing in too thickly now.

With another jarring halt, the cage clunked down on the ground. "All out!" came the echoing shout from above. "Out, out, out!"

"Keep your searing trousers on," I muttered as we filed out. My team looked even more threadbare than when we'd entered: Erkan a foul-mouthed mess, Haluk pale as a ghost, and my own nerves a tattered mess. At least Cemal didn't look afraid.

Just as I closed the door behind us, the metal jerked out from beneath my hand, and fear sprung up in me. "Ho!" I yelled up after the rising cage. I almost leaped up onto it, but I fought the urge down. "Leave that down here!"

All I heard back was a faint, echoing laughter.

They were just having a jape, I reassured myself. They would let us up when the time came. Muttering under my breath, I turned to see not three men, but two. Panic seized me. "Firewater Denizens! Where's your third?"

Haluk and Erkan looked about, confused, perhaps at being referenced by that name. I didn't have time to worry about that — Cemal could already be stripped more naked than the day he was born if an unbound jinni had gotten to him. "Just follow me!" I ran past them, heart beating fast, and into the white, rounded buildings and — perhaps unwisely — began shouting Cemal's name.

The hunchback hadn't gone far. I found him standing in front of a hovel that was little more than half a sphere with an arched entrance half a man's height. "Sear it all, Cemal," I panted as I jogged up to him, "if you don't stay with me, I can't keep the spirits from flaying you."

"…and this the farmer's shed…" Cemal was muttering, completely oblivious to me or his life's endangerment. What in the searing hell was he talking about a farmer for?

I looked back at the sound of footsteps and was relieved to see it was Haluk and Erkan approaching. "Mother's good graces," I said. "I don't know how you've gotten by so far, Cemal. You're as lost as a parrot in pita."

But Haluk, hearing Cemal's muttering, suddenly became more animated than I'd ever seen him and rushed up to the bowed man. "Ah!" he cried, the sound billowing through the open cavern. "I believe he understands!"

"Understands?" I looked to Erkan for lack of anyone else. But with orange spittle drying on his chin and his hair a sweat-curled mess, he wasn't exactly a saint of sanity himself.

"Of course! He knows where to go!" Haluk put his ear close Cemal's lips, trying to pick up every word. It was all gibberish, stuff like "The watchman's tower" and "the seamstress's sons" and the like. "He always did have an affinity for patterns," Haluk said softly. "Let him work it out."

I had no idea how else to find Nehir's Chalice in this underground city, so I left them to it and concentrated on setting wards. Not that we needed them. I'd expected the place to be thick with Silks, to feel their insatiable pull from every corner — but there was nothing, not even a prickle of desire. It seemed as vacant as the name promised.

Could the Imperium rely on reputation alone to protect this place? And if there were no Silks, why hadn't Osman mentioned this along with everything else? He'd said they were wild, not completely absent. To my shame, I felt a flicker of doubt for the Hodja's loyalty — but with all he'd done for me, it seemed rather unlikely that he'd betray me now. Which meant this was a new development, beyond even what he'd noticed before.

I felt the caress of watching eyes on me every moment I was there, and maybe even a hint of a presence beyond them. But it didn't feel oppressive, just… familiar. Creeping like eyes watching me, but less malevolent. Still, I had trouble believing that, if some Buyujinn loomed, it was not waiting for us to walk into some web they'd spun.

That was unless I imagined the whole thing and was more insane than Cemal.

Still, if anyone was equipped to deal with jinn, it was me. I couldn't worry about that now. "We need to get moving," I said. "Haluk, can you get him to lead us?"

"I do have a certain... pull with him," the slight man said, returning to his usual demeanor. He took Cemal by the arm and started walking him down the street, whispering to him all the while. But Cemal suddenly pulled away, looking about wildly before heading in the opposite direction.

"Pull indeed," I muttered to Haluk as the pair walked by, and he suddenly became very attentive of his charge.

"Searing hell," Erkan said, lumbering up next to me. "Valem's sure laughing now. Lost, and following a pair of idiots."

"We're all idiots," I reminded him.

Before my eyes, the hard exterior unwound. His jaw slackened, and his eyes seemed to shrink back into his skull. "Yes," he said hollowly. "We are."

We followed behind in silence for a moment, both looking around before he continued. "I wish I'd told the family that."

"That we're idiots?"

"That I'm sorry."

"Sorry?" I was too busy peering into each building's doorway to pay much attention to him. So far, each was as bare and clean as a tenantless manor for all I could tell.

"Yes. For all the... They haven't had it easy. I haven't made it easy."

He hung his head. One hand on my shard, I put my shame-hand on his shoulder in a familiar touch, as he'd done to me before. "I'm sure they know how you feel."

"Sure as hell said sorry enough." His eyes were doused coals. "But apologies didn't mean much when I always gave them another bruise later."

I wasn't looking for Silks anymore. My hand rested uncomfortably on his shoulder. "We all..." *Make mistakes* is how that phrase goes, but I didn't think it applied here.

"They always bothered me," he growled, the coals sparking back to life. "Always clawed at my back, complaining that I pissed away my inheritance and made mincemeat of my father's commerce. So what? Are they starving or unclothed? Burning ungrateful, the whole lot." His body shook.

I withdrew my hand, myself close to shaking. "Well," I said in measured tones, "maybe you'll be better to them, when we return." There was more I wanted to say, much more. But the middle of a vault-break wasn't the time to have it out.

He looked at me, and I was surprised to see pity in his eyes. "Yes," he said, roughly clapping me on the back. "Perhaps."

It took all my self-control not to lay him low then and there. I pulled away from his touch and put several paces between us.

We were a couple of streets away from the lift, about halfway to the edge of the pyramid, when Haluk called from around a corner ahead. "Come quickly! We've found something in here!"

Eager to leave my companion behind, I pushed down my anger and hustled ahead to find our other two companions standing before a singular building. In a white alcove shaped like the arc of a rainbow, four tapered columns came down like teeth. The building rose behind it, oddly familiar in the dome's shape and the wings extending out from it.

"What did you find?" I asked.

"Cemal believes he has worked it out," Haluk started, but Cemal suddenly came to life.

"Yes," he said in that oddly lilting voice of his. "I know the skeleton now, where the bones are scattered and the skull has fallen."

"That's fine. Is this the skull holding all our liquor, then?"

The tears in Cemal's eyes had a light like the moons on a lake's stirring surface. "Yes. The Chalice is within."

"Great." I looked around us one last time, down the new street we'd just turned on, but it only continued to glow faintly. "Let's go find it."

I led the way in, cringing away from all the glowing surfaces. Seeing them up close, I could see they weren't smooth, but rough and pocketed like freshly cooled lava on Valem's seaside face. Somehow — in a way I couldn't quite describe — the walls felt alive, like these buildings were the bones of a spectral giant that could at any moment rise from its slumber and shrug us mortals off like specks of dirt.

I was nearly trembling as I entered the building, and what I saw only made it worse. The place was even more familiar than outside: a foyer wrapped around a round, smooth floor under a three-story rotunda. Among the upper stories were balconies where spectators might watch what occurred below. Like people whirling.

I stood in a calcified version of the Hortum Kor temple.

"What in Valem's forty-one names is this?" I muttered, looking around and trying not to let the rising panic in my chest take over.

But I hadn't seen the strangest part. Floating in the middle of the room was a dented, tarnished silver goblet that faintly gleamed as it turned. Encrusted with jade stones, it sported a flared lip and base. Nothing held it up, nor was it hanging from anything I could see.

Sure as the searing Underearth, a cup that floated had to be our Chalice of Unrequited Intoxication. Nehir's Chalice. What other decrepit cup would someone go to all that work to suspend?

I took a small step forward and squinted at it, trying to detect what mechanism held it aloft. Magnets and their strange effects on metal were the Foremost's latest infatuation, but I'd never seen anything like this. I checked the columns for devices when I saw it.

It appeared before my darting eyes, something in their movement bringing it into visibility. Before, there'd seemed only dust idly spinning about the Chalice through the dim glow. But as my eyes slid over the empty space, a floating shape took a familiar form. It seemed a human body loosely clad in eight strands of starry cloth, the ends loose and slowly moving as if suspended in water. Where the head should have been was only a veil shallowly indented where there should be a mouth, a nose, two eyes.

I recognized her. I'd seen her statue displayed before the temple rotunda countless times before. For this was the Kor's matron spirit. The Shrouded Mother. Not a legend as I'd always believed, but a true Buyujinn. A hand of Valem.

My heart tried leaping out of my chest as I jumped back. When I tried to focus on her, my eyes stopped flickering, and she disappeared from view.

"Welcome home, my son." A woman's voice, strong and worn as a beaten reed mat, spoke loudly in my ear.

I yelped and jumped back further.

"What are you about, Wraithsbane?" Erkan barked.

"Talan, are you well?" Haluk chimed in.

But I saw Cemal had noticed the Buyujinn as well, his eyes darting back and forth, his face twisting in dawning horror.

I flickered my eyes to keep her in sight. "Who are you?"

"Do you not already know? Does a child not recognize his mother?" The voice spoke in my other ear.

"I don't know what you're talking about." Blood rushed from my head, leaving me feeling faint and queasy.

"Not of flesh, dear boy. I would not concern myself with such... profanity. But I am your mother. I have raised you. Cared for you. Trained you to be what you are, and what you were meant to be."

I could feel the others staring at me, but I didn't draw my focus from the Shrouded Mother. "I'm sure. Though it is odd that you accomplished all this when we've only just met."

"You have felt my hand in many ways, even if you did not recognize it."

"Name one."

The phantom woman sighed, her breath a child breeze. "Do you remember our first meeting? I wanted to touch the moonlight, and your temple was so beautiful a spot wreathed in moonlight. Then I saw you, embraced you, burned you…"

The spinning Silk, the night I left the Hortum Kor when the strange voice had spoken. The night I was Branded. "You?"

"My voice, my hands — I have many. And is it not strange that a long, lost friend — if you would consider her a friend — would suddenly find you? Particularly one of the Damask Esir."

I could have been thrown atop the Lost Mother's cold peak from the shudder that ran through me. "That was all you?"

"Me, Talan. And does it not seem strange your Hodja, so disapproving of your schemes, finally relents and tells you how to enter my Mausoleum? To come to me?" She laughed, and it sounded like echoes in a cold cave. "Even stubborn men are vulnerable in their dreams."

Sweat joined the chills, mixing in an unpleasant war of hot against cold. "Why? Why do any of this?"

I could almost feel her smile. "You are my son, Talan. I have made you what you are, given to you all you possess. And you have worshipped me in my temple, though you did not believe me real. Now, you must serve me more directly. You alone could come to me in this prison of mine, and you alone can help me. Only you can free me."

I tried to swallow, but something was damming it nearly closed. "Free you?"

Her laugh gained a sharp edge. "Look at me!" Her bands of cloth billowed into the air. "They think to control me, but they do not know the depth of their folly. I will not be enslaved."

From the corner of my eyes, I could see my companions, who apparently couldn't hear any of the Shrouded Mother's words, shifting uneasily toward the door.

"But you must understand." The Shrouded Mother drifted closer. "I will tell you a story, my son. A story of myself, and you, and your strange, sad companions. A story of our people."

I rubbed my temples with one hand, the other gripping my obsidian shard, eyes still bouncing back and forth. "I'm listening."

The Mother's voice sang in both my ears. "Before the Imperium, our people lived on this land. The People of the Firewaters, we called ourselves, for this mighty volcano was our god, and I its avatar. They basked in life-giving and life-taking rivers and worshipped me. Does the name sound familiar, child?"

The Firewater Den. And I'd thought the name simply referred to the burn of liquor.

"My people lived here first. They had deep roots. Then when the land ripped apart before the Serpent in the south, invaders came and tore every last one of them away from Valem's feet."

Osman had sometimes referenced a people before the Avvadin, especially in relation to the Hortum Kor, but I'd not paid much attention. I'd never had a mind for things not immediately present. "You're trying to say I'm one of those natives? But I'm from a province. My family never lived near Erimis."

"When our home was taken, where do you think we fled? Some forgot, and mixed blood with the invaders. But some of my children remembered. They nursed their wounds, until they were strong enough to rise, and almost topple the marauders from within their hideous empire."

"You're not... you helped the Rosewater Resistance?"

I'd kept sight of her, but suddenly her image jumped forward right between the columns. I yelped and backed hard into the wall behind me. The rough stone clung to my robe and hat.

"So it has been called. But with the children of those brave men and women enslaved and serving the so-called Prophet King, it does seem a thing of the past." I almost felt the Buyujinn smiling behind her shroud. "But the People of the Firewaters did not die. We lived on."

"You mean in the Damask Esir?" All of those involved in the Rosewater Resistance had been killed or enslaved as Damask Esir as far as I recalled.

"There are few of your kin among those thralls now, but my children remain many. They are all around you." She swept the shimmering cloths before her. "They who serve as my eyes and hands."

We hadn't seen anything down here other than her. I wondered uneasily where they were hiding. As for her "hands"... "The Silks?"

A low, bitter laugh filled my ears. "They didn't want to enthrall us only in life, but made us serve even in death. But they do not have power enough to contain me."

It was always said Silks were the spirits of our conquered enemies. Could this be what was meant? But how would they find those particular jinn? It didn't add up. Yet I knew too little to question her.

Though, if she had so few followers as to try and claim me, she must be pretty desperate.

"All right, I understand." With an ache gathering behind my flickering eyes, I wanted nothing more than for this to be over. "So the Firewater People gave birth to the Rosewater Revolution, who gave birth to the Firewater Den, which brings us here, with you enslaved." I nodded over at the three men quaking in their petite whirling shoes. "You really want to claim them as your children, too?"

"They are, whether I will it so or not. And they have served their role. They have brought you to me. Perhaps they do not realize still why they felt so strongly they must recover this cup." Then the shrouded specter upturned the Chalice, and liquid started pouring from it. The liquid kept changing color, going from dawn-red to dusk-violet to water-clear.

And it kept pouring. It was the real treasure, and it was exactly what was claimed to be — for whatever that was worth to me now.

Time to make our escape then. "Glad to meet you, but we can't stay too long. Guards waiting above and all that. So if we could just take that Chalice off your hands…"

The following laughter burrowed into my ears and dug about my brain. "This thing? It is nothing, Talan — a fruit to lure the parrot." The cup went flying through the air, and my heart lodged in my throat. As no one was close enough to catch it, I cringed as it banged on the ground. It landed near my Firewater companions, and they, despite their fear, dove to keep it from rolling far.

"No, Talan. I have sacrificed for your well-being, given of my children to further your learning and welfare. Now it is time you help your mother in return."

"I don't—" I started to protest, but I was interrupted by sudden shouts.

"Wraithsbane!" Haluk cried. "The lift!"

Sidling away from the Buyujinn, I backed out through the arches again. She let me go; I had the sense that she was smiling behind her veil. I was outside in the stifling air again when I heard it: the whine of turning wheels, the clanging of chain links, the creak of metal shifting. The rattle of bars.

I risked turning around and looking up. There was the cage, a quarter of the way down, and quickly being lowered.

It wasn't empty. A woman in a coal and fire uniform stared down at me, descending into the heart of the pyramid, coming ever closer. A thought raced around my mind: How did she know?

"This is your sacrifice for me, my son."

CHAPTER TEN

A NOON FOR DOOM

Yanara was barely more than a dim outline, but I knew it was her. Some part of me had known this had all happened too easily: the yayas letting us in, including drunk Erkan, without questioning the untimely Calming; Yanara knowing what I was and resenting me, but no ramifications coming from it; searing hell, even the Underguild situation had resolved too easily. Now it was all coming together: not the old luck, but a noose slowly tightening, and a Buyujinn was pulling the knot. All so I could somehow free her.

I stood dumb, unable to move, while my companions panicked. "Damn this whole mission," Erkan cursed, turning back and forth, torn over which direction to run. "Damn this swine slop!"

Haluk fidgeted in place, eyes darting between our phantom adversary and our very solid one. "Well," he said, clearing his throat over and over. He was the one holding the Chalice, and he rubbed it between his palms, leaving a sheen of sweat on its dull metal surface.

Cemal seemed to be the only one with any composure. Unfortunately, whatever he was concentrating on wasn't much help to us.

Shivers crept up my spine as I realized I'd turned my back on the Shrouded Mother. But when I spun back around, she was still behind the columns. "Do not worry," she said in my left ear, making me jump again. "She will come to you; she will find you. All you must do is stay here next to me."

"Burn that." I pulled out my shard and spun it across my fingers.

Yanara was halfway down. That whole descent, I didn't think she had taken her eyes from me once.

"Ho!" I shouted at the others. "There have to be artifacts in here, and maybe weapons. We have five minutes to find one that's useful."

I looked at Cemal, hoping he'd set his mind to it, but his gaze hadn't left Yanara. "She has changed the lock," he said dreamily. "She, or the other who lives within."

More gooseflesh broke out along my neck, but I didn't have time to be spooked. "Haluk, Erkan — let's go!"

But Erkan had other plans. Wresting the Chalice, from Haluk's grasp, he threw back his head and tilted the cup into his open mouth. Out flowed a pure, sparkling, amber liquid, the reek of alcohol pungent even several paces away.

I grabbed Haluk's arm. "Leave him. We have to find something now."

Haluk nodded, his cheek twitching. I checked the lift's position again and saw it had dipped below the white tops of the buildings. She was almost to the ground.

We ran into each of the buildings along the lane, one by one. I tried to ignore how many of them looked familiar, rationalizing to myself that I couldn't possibly be seeing them correctly. Of course, that house wasn't one I'd robbed. Or that one wasn't a replica of my quarters; mine were smaller than these. But when my childhood home cropped up, complete with carvings of Father's ouk leaning in the corner and Mother's slingshot on the windowsill, it was a bit harder to swallow.

Despite our searching, nothing was usable. What objects weren't composed of the white material of the buildings were useless treasures: piles of gold coins, jeweled scepters, ornamental chests. Any other time, they would have made our fortune, but now, all they looked to do was seal our fate. And our five minutes must have been nearing a close, for the cage had started to lift back into the air, empty. Yanara was no doubt hunting us even now.

That was when I spotted the tuft of hair. Reaching into a cabinet, I pulled out a strand of coarse hair to reveal a long, leathery line. Or three lines, as it turned out, all composed of supple corded leather, all with hair tufts at the end. The cords led back to a handle of bone set with jade and inlaid with silver. A three-tailed yak's whip; I couldn't believe I was holding one. They were said to be the preferred weapon of the kings of Avvad before it had become Avvad. This one might be two thousand years old, yet it was perfectly intact.

Haluk jumped back as I snapped it forward with a satisfying crack. I just had to hope it would be enough against an elite armored warrior.

"Come on." I led the way to the door and out into the street. The last place I wanted to be when I found her was inside, cornered and waiting to be hunted down.

There was no time for any other preparations. As soon as we stepped out, there she was, standing at the other end of the street, curved shamshir extending from one hand, gaze pointed straight at us. Straight at me.

Barely a dozen paces away, Erkan and Cemal were still standing before the temple, if it could be called standing. Erkan was about as bent over as Cemal by this point and leaning against a nearby arch to stay upright, while Cemal hadn't come out of his catatonic trance. Yanara ignored them, though. She had eyes only for me.

"Sentence reduced," she called, her voice reverberating. "From service to time."

"What are you talking about?" I called back.

"A reduced sentence. That's what I expected to see when I looked up our criminal records. That you had sold me out for a better cut. Which I could understand."

"Sule—"

"*Don't call me that!*" The scream sounded like what every child expects to hear from ash-jinn during a Lament, a scream full of hate and burning pain. "*Sule* died when she was thrown into battle and had to kill or be killed. *Sule* died when she received fifty lashes for trying to escape that miserable hell. *Sule* died when my conscience — Ah, Valem—" She grabbed her head with her shame-hand, gritting her teeth and squeezing her eyes shut.

But just as I began to hope her headache was bad enough to be debilitating, she furiously shook it off and kept going. "And if she didn't die then, she sure as searing hell died when she found that the one thing that kept her going, the one person that she thought still waited somewhere for her, turned her in for coppers."

I couldn't find the words for a reply. She was coming close. My body was wound tight with fear. "Yanara, I was—"

"The same burning person you are now. Up to the same games, with the same silver tongue trying to snake your way out of it. Maybe I ought to cut out that damned tongue. Then we'll see how you slither away."

My head was foggy. Just when I needed it clear. How she knew I would be here, I could only guess. Perhaps the unusual request for a Calming had been reported to her. Maybe the Shrouded Mother had a more direct method of communication. But that knowledge wouldn't help me now. The Buyujinn's intentions for me were clear. Why I had to die to free her was a mystery I didn't seem likely to solve.

I tried summoning up the hot energy in my belly, to channel and burn her away like I had the Guilder before, but I couldn't feel it. I was too drained and wound up and guilty as all Valem's fires. But I wasn't giving up. I gripped the whip in my shame-hand and the obsidian shard in my other and tried to keep my shaking legs firm and strong.

"You were becoming dangerous, Yanara. Not only to our victims — to us, your cabal. Burned Valem, you killed a man for a golden pocket watch!"

Yanara suddenly laughed, the sound sharp as a jackal's, her eyes never leaving me. "Oh — it's my fault, is it? You're not guilty — you never were." She smiled wildly, and at only twenty paces off she looked ever more like a prowling tiger. "Doesn't matter — you'll get your sentence anyway. It always comes, sooner or later." The grin widened into a snarl.

Haluk backed away, and I ground my teeth. Four men I had brought down here, and I was the only one willing to fight. What were they going to do, run away while she hunted them down? There was no other way; I had to tap into my Branding and kindle it to flame. Otherwise, this would be a very short fight.

She stopped just ten paces off. "Come, Talan." Her shamshir leaned on her shoulder. "What can you do against an Esir?"

Just as all hope seemed cut loose, I saw someone creeping up behind Yanara. Erkan, nearly on all fours, clutched a rock in his hand, and his wild eyes were set on Yanara's back. It might be enough if she didn't notice.

Shard useless at the moment, I struck out with the whip, managing to get all three lines snapping more or less at my target. But Yanara hopped back, smile fading as concentration settled over her face. She didn't think it would be as easy a fight as she had been acting.

I drew the whip back for another lash, trying to keep her attention when I found myself backpedaling as she suddenly rushed forward. I struck weakly at her at the last moment, but it glanced off her leather uniform while her sword still came on. I narrowly jumped back from a stab, then to the side from a slash. Her strikes were passing so close they nearly cut the breath out of my lungs.

Then I saw Erkan stumbling to his feet and trying to get a good position behind her. I had to give him the chance. So I made one last-ditch effort: I threw my Kor hat. It was made of stiff linen, and I got a good shot at her face so that Yanara missed a swing and had to bat a hand at it to see again. It was long enough. I lashed out with the whip, and this time, it wasn't just a glancing blow. Though the two outside cords whacked against her vambraces, the third struck hard against her cheek, knocking her head back and drawing blood.

Erkan saw his opportunity and leaped forward, roaring as he lifted a sizable rock above his head and brought it down on her. It looked so certain a victory I allowed myself to hope. She had to be thoroughly disoriented, surely enough for him to get the hit in.

Yanara didn't even look. Spinning, her blade leading, it ended with a flash of steel and a speckling of red on the bone-white stone. Erkan fell to one knee, clutching his thigh, screaming, stone spinning from his hand to the ground. But Yanara hadn't stopped moving. In the same fluid motion, she whipped her blade around and leveled it at the screaming man. I didn't have time for anything but to watch in horror.

His head jerked forward with the impact, and he sunk nervelessly to the ground. His hands twitched horribly as the Damask Esir drew her sword from the back of his neck. Blood gushed from the deep wound. As the red liquid flowed onto the white ground, the stone steamed as if eager to taste it.

I swallowed back bile as I squared off again. There was no hope. I couldn't get out of this now, not alone. With how easily she'd killed him, I was surprised I was still alive. But this was it. End of the line.

Without warning or preamble, the energy flared up in my belly, spreading like wildfire. I didn't hesitate, didn't wonder, but channeled as rage and power flowed through me.

Wordlessly screaming, I pointed my shard at Yanara. Though she must have known what that meant, she just stood and watched as the obsidian started to glow, then blaze. The fire raced through my veins, filling every muscle, bone, and nerve along the way, making my hair stand up like when lightning strikes near. Then it was pressing on my fingertips, pushing, violently shoving, aching to be released. So I did — I directed it into the obsidian shard, expelling it forward straight at her.

It all happened in a moment. My arm snapped back, throwing me off balance. My vision flashed white then black. Heat billowed over my skin. There was a sound like the very air catching fire.

After the impact — I could hear the breaking of stone, the silence after — I was still backing away from the sizzling heat and the smoke. I expected to smell the horrible stench of the burned, mangled body of the person I used to love in my youth. Tears were already burning my eyes; guilt burned in my stomach, and my knees were weak. She would have killed me, her and the Shrouded Mother. Yet I couldn't help thinking I'd betrayed her again.

A peal of woman's laughter broke through the miasma of my guilt.

I opened my eyes and peered through the flashing afterimage. There she stood, whole and unharmed, staring back at me with a savage grin. Black rings fanned out from her over the streets and buildings, signs of the waves of scorching flames that must have come off of her. I remembered the billow of heat at my back that night we fought the Guilder assassins, and suddenly it clicked into place.

"You too?" I choked out, disbelieving.

"Training brought out the best in me." Her pale pink eyes were dead of anything but amusement.

I, however, suspected a different source. If the Shrouded Mother had Branded me, why wouldn't she Brand Yanara as well? Though it begged the question: why would she Brand both of us if we were to fight?

But it didn't matter at the moment as Yanara stepped forward to finish me off.

I stumbled to my feet, ready to give it one last, desperate effort, when I saw her suddenly jerk to the side and clutch at her head, eyes going wide. Her sword fell from her hand, and she was barely breathing, little gasps coming out. Her sword hand clutched at her throat.

Yanara fell to her knees and started screaming her throat bloody.

"Mother!" she managed to gargle out. "Mother, I came, I came! You called, and I came! Why would you—?" Another scream overwhelmed any intelligible words.

Bewildered, my eyes flitted over the scene, trying to make sense of it — and that was when I saw her. The Shrouded Mother loomed over Yanara, just barely visible cloths twisted around the Damask Esir. I didn't even have to flit my eyes to see her now — the phantom had become more solid, and even if she was still little more than a thin mist, the sight chilled me to my core.

Something spectral and luminescent emerged from Yanara, who groaned and screamed by turns, twitching with every savage jerk by the Mother. Bit by bit, I made out the details of the emerging figure: a bulbous head, a neck too small to support it, a tiny chest, small arms with rolls of fat. From it extended what looked like roots, or a web of mother-cords like a baby has on its belly at birth. Its face, though, had nothing of a tree or babe. Though scrunched with pain, its pale eyes, all too human, seemed to know exactly what was occurring. It even looked scared, pleading, as it stared at me.

The Shrouded Mother's whisper was in my ear again, and now I could see curling fingers of mist from the corner of my eye. "You see that I care for you, now, my son. I sacrifice my daughter to save you once more. I will never let you die if you but serve me."

She tugged savagely at the spectral creature that she'd pulled from Yanara, and the Esir's screams began anew. "The time has come to prove your loyalty. You must sacrifice for me." Her ice-cold breath, in such contrast to the hot air, funneled down my ear canal. "Take up her sword, Talan. Kill her."

CHAPTER ELEVEN

AN AFTERNOON TOO SOON

I straightened with my heart thundering inside my skull and stared down at Yanara. Once a girl, if a brutal, feral one. Once my friend, my lover — and still longed to be if her recent actions were any indication.

I dropped the whip and clutched my shard as I stepped forward. Though I looked at Yanara, I kept track of the now visible phantom from the corner of my eye. The Shrouded Mother clutched what must be the Qarin in her hands, the glowing creature writhing in anguish.

I knelt down next to Yanara, who moaned and stared with dull eyes at the ground as her fingers dug into her face. Carefully, I picked up the shamshir with my shame-hand. Its hilt was slick with blood. I felt the Buyujinn smiling behind me, felt her anticipation as I rose and stood over my victim. I tightened my grip.

She'd been enslaved in her very mind. And I was a large part of the reason why that happened.

I glanced around at the Shrouded Mother. "Why? Why do you want me to kill her?"

Her displeasure at being questioned was palpable: a bitter taste on my tongue, a stabbing pain in my head, a pressure in my ears. "For me, my son. Sacrifice her, and I can finally break these bonds."

Kill Yanara, and the Buyujinn would be freed. I shuddered. Yet would it be so wrong to free her? She was my temple's patron spirit, a supposedly good-hearted jinni from the days of yore. If I believed her, she'd contributed to the Rosewater Resistance and had taken control of some of the Silks away from the Tefra. Freeing her would destabilize the Imperium in some measurable way, certainly more than a cup ever could. Wasn't that worth sacrificing one who should be my enemy?

But she had manipulated me and everyone around me to get what she wanted. She'd made shambles of my life through her gifts and subtle influences, and killed more than one innocent man. She could, even now, be pulling my thoughts to get her way — and how would I ever know?

I swallowed. I knew my decision.

I willed the fire inside me back into being, and the heat welled up in my belly to race along both arms to the tips of my seven Branded fingers. Then I let it stream along both the shamshir and shard in my hands.

"Talan, my son," the Shrouded Mother whispered. Her voice cut, sharp as glass. "Why do you call on your gift?"

I had to move fast, for I could feel her presence bearing down on me. In one clumsy motion, I swung the sword around and through the glowing roots extending into Yanara's head. They fell like dead worms as I severed them.

The twin screams that followed were like nothing I had heard before.

I didn't let it stop me, but whirled with the motion of the swing and threw aside the sword as I moved. Through the blur of motion, I felt the Mother's fury like fire lashing at me. "You burning fool! I said kill her, not free her! Now—"

I didn't let her finish. Whirling close, I buried the shard deep in the furrows of her eight, long strips of cloth. She hissed, writhing to pull free, but she was mine now. I whirled closer, her cloths wrapping around me, drawing her closer, and myself further within her folds.

"Ah — you wish to be my sacrifice? But you were to be my servant, my prophet." She hummed, and I felt the sudden desire flare up inside me as it might with an ordinary Silk. But this — it was powerful, overwhelming, intoxicating with such potency I lost all intentions for a moment. I stopped spinning, numbly staring before me as she wound about me like a snake.

My mind slipped further and further away as the Shrouded Mother purred in my ear. "You will do. Yes, you will do." Her honey tones were soothing as a mother to her newborn. I felt her run her hand beneath my clothes and against my bare skin, and even vacant as I was, I shivered with delight. "Your sacrifice will do very nicely…" My bonds tightened, her silken body constricting.

She began to draw me out of my body.

My skin chilled to ice. My blood ran cold. The fire inside me, the Shrouded Mother's horrid gift, had almost extinguished.

But it hadn't quite.

The last piece of my broken self surged forward through the cold tangle of my mind, seizing the energy of the Underearth and flaring it outward like festival fireworks. Violet burned my eyes as the flames burst from my body, untamed and untempered, carelessly consuming wherever it went. My skin, before cold as a corpse, now burned like the stones of a stoked kiln.

The Mother, realizing her mistake, tried to pull away. "You cannot!" she hissed, her voice rising. "You cannot! I gave this power to you — you cannot use it against me! You are my child, my sacrifice. I am eternal! I have been here five hundred years, and will exist five hundred more, until all the Imperium joins me or falls to the fires! *You cannot stop ME, Talan! I WILL PERSIST—*"

Her final scream cut off suddenly, leaving only echoes in its wake. My silken bonds fell slack, and the body of the Shrouded Mother fell about me. I sank to my knees among the limp strands, eyelids flickering as I tried to open my eyes. I longed to see what had become of my enemy. But I couldn't fight the encroaching darkness. I felt myself falling forward, and even the blunt punch of the stone wasn't enough to keep me conscious.

———

The taste of salty metal like I'd licked the knife serving a seasoned boar. I moved my thick tongue around, trying to sense where it was coming from. The pain of the wound guided me. Blood.

I groaned as I rolled onto my back. The half of my face that had been pressed to the stone floor was wet with blood, and I knew not all of it was my own. The reminder of violence was enough to hasten my rising, though I only managed to get to my hands and knees.

I opened my eyes and saw a pair of boots before me.

My gaze panned upwards to Yanara standing over me. One shoulder was raised higher than the other, almost kissing her ear, while one knee turned inwards. She looked as if she'd forgotten how to stand properly.

I stared up at her. I was too tired to stand; every limb felt like ingots of iron, and not just from tiredness. I hadn't counted on Yanara recovering while I turned on the Buyujinn, and now I was at her mercy. And yet, though I didn't want to die, I found myself feeling strangely calm as I looked up the Esir soldier. Death had already embraced me once. Now that I knew its touch, I no longer feared it.

"Are you going to kill me now?" I asked her quietly.

She stared down at me. "Ingar."

I blinked. "What?'

Suddenly, she shuddered, then coughed and spat up on the ground. "Ai..."

I shuffled back on my knees, too exhausted still to rise. Her threat might not have scared me, but this strangeness did. "Yanara?"

She looked up sharply. "Shu-lee."

It took me a moment to understand. "Sule," I repeated slowly. "All right. Sule, then."

Yanara — Sule — shook her head, or so I assumed from how it flopped from shoulder to shoulder. "Isham… I sham hut she hash leff. Fah now."

I slowly rose to my feet, trying not to groan as my knotted muscles protested and my head spun to interpret the strange words. "Sule, I really can't understand — "

Then you must hear me here, a deep, male voice spoke in my mind.

I yelped and stumbled back, glancing around me, but there was no one close enough to have spoken. Sule continued to stare at me, and slowly, it dawned on me. "Was that…?"

You brought this on yourself, the voice admonished.

I still couldn't believe it. "Valem below… Are you the Qarin? Yanara's Qarin?"

Sule — or rather, Sule's body — nodded. *I was. But no longer. To be Qarin is to be a slavemaster even as you are a thrall yourself. Forcing her to the Kahin-Shah's will was never my desire. After all, the resistance that ended with the Damask Esir wasn't just a human affair.* Sule stared, the intricacies of emotion lost in her twitching features. *I, too, paid for my rebellion.*

"The Rosewater Resistance… Both humans and jinn rebelled together."

Together and united. We were strong in our bonds and worked for the benefit of both. But since then, I have been used over and over to serve the Imperium and its tyrant leader. So when this old companion offered me a chance to escape… I could not see it as a worse option, even if I became nearly as enslaved to her. But now I have my freedom. Now I need not enslave Sule any longer.

My latent suspicion flared up. "But you're still—"

Sule would drown on her own spit if I left her right now. Sule's eyes stared reproach at me, voice and body acting in as much concert as the Qarin's poor control over her body would allow. *What I do now, I do to preserve.*

"Then about the whole killing me thing…"

Perhaps Sule still wishes you dead. A shiver of fear struck me, and I instinctively tightened my hand on my shard, still unconsciously gripped despite all I'd gone through. But the Qarin continued. *And perhaps she considers you sparing her life a debt repaid. Not knowing her will, I shall leave you alive.*

That was a small relief, at least. Looking past her, I saw Haluk lurking in a doorway, a stone clutched in his trembling hand. All around me rose the strange, glowing buildings. And high above us was the cage that could bring us out. My — our — predicament was all about us. But the answer to it was before me if only she — he — *they* would comply.

"What about helping us escape? You're Damask Esir as far as the yayas above know. They'll allow you up, won't they?"

Sule's head bobbed up and down. *There is a message I can send them, yes.* As the Qarin spoke in my mind, Sule's lips mouthed along.

I looked at Haluk. Despite my annoyance at his lack of assistance earlier, I nodded at him, and he shuffled towards us. I turned to look at Sule again, trying to ignore her unnatural posture, to see past it to the jinni caring for her instead of traveling free to the Underearth or wherever it wanted to go. "Let's get the searing hell out of here."

I could have done without seeing their grotesque grin back.

———

We took a minute to organize ourselves, gathering Cemal from the temple where he had stood clutching the Chalice to his bony chest. The Chalice — ah yes, the thing that had started this whole damn business. Though it wasn't truly to blame — the Shrouded Mother had that dubious honor — the tarnished, dented cup made a good enough scapegoat for me. Yet as I walked toward him, Cemal looked down at the cup, then held it out to me.

I took it, surprised. "You don't want to keep ahold of it?"

He shook his head, his moist eyes seeming even closer to weeping than usual. "I have a body to bear," he said softly.

The pit returned to my stomach as I looked back at Erkan. Suddenly, the Chalice seemed an even more paltry prize. Even if the man had turned out to be even more of a bastard than I'd first suspected, he didn't deserve this.

While I held it — and the whip I'd found, for good measure — Cemal and Haluk lifted Erkan's body, then wrapped him up in the Buyujinn's garments. I cringed to see it, yet I knew it was mere superstition that bothered me. A death shroud was a death shroud when it came down to it, and what was more appropriate than the armaments of your enemy?

All with our respective loads, our strange company made its way through the Vacant City, Qarin-Sule in the lead, while Erkan's body left a dotted, red trail behind on the white stone. I kept my eyes forward as the walk was a struggle. I felt much worse than even after the assassins had attacked. Then, it had just been a normal Silk I'd dispelled. The Shrouded Mother was something different altogether, and it had consequently drained that much more of my mental and physical stores. Even though I knew her to be gone, her presence had been so strong that I still thought I felt echoes of her all about us, like she couldn't quite let go. I imagined her invisible hands grasping at my every footstep, reaching out from the very stone itself. I walked faster.

We made it back to the clearing and the lift platform at its center. Qarin-Sule shambled up to the silver wire hanging down from the hole far above, and after she'd managed to grab it, she yanked it in a series of pulls. The message must have been true, for soon, we heard the cranks leap to life, and the rattling cage began its descent. Hope sang again in me, even if it was a muted song.

"Let's hope they don't ask too many questions," I noted as I watched the lift. "Or any, preferably. I don't think you'd stand up to scrutiny just now."

Qarin-Sule looked over at me, and suddenly I realized her shoulders were even. "I am thlearning," she said, voice strained but intelligible.

"Valem's forty-one names," I muttered. "I guess you are." I wondered if the Qarin had ever wanted a body of its own. How much harder to leave if it had.

The cage clanged to the ground. Haluk and Cemal loaded Erkan's body inside, and Qarin-Sule and I followed after. Swinging the door closed, the Qarin used Sule's arm to pull the silver wire once more, and soon after the cage lurched into the air.

I relaxed slightly now that we were in the air. The Shrouded Mother's influence would soon be left behind.

Then about a quarter of the way through our uneasy ride up, something began stirring below. A rumbling, like the grind of stone on stone. Wearily exasperated and wondering what last trap the Mother laid for us, I leaned my head through the bars.

The buildings were steaming, or so it seemed. White vapor rose from their roofs, curling lazily into the air. Then the single strands began to form together into thicker smokestacks, and more of it streamed from every surface: the streets, the sides of the pyramid itself. The stone was becoming smoke.

The buildings started to crumble, the ghostly mortar seeming to have been the only thing holding it together. Great chunks of stone began to crack off and fall into themselves. The streets cracked, and to the distress of us in the cage, the whole of the Mausoleum began to rumble in protest. We looked at the walls and the ceiling above, suddenly aware how high up in the air we were, and how vulnerable to falling stone.

But my eyes were on the mist. It had coalesced into one streaming sea as it rose toward us, it dawned on me what this must be. It should have been obvious, considering all things that hadn't added up. The Vacant City was supposed to have been occupied by Silks, but we had only seen the Shrouded Mother. It seemed to have lived up to its name after all. Now I saw that wasn't the case. The jinn had been all around us. They were in the buildings; they were the buildings themselves.

And now, they were freed.

Summoning energy I didn't know I had, I hauled myself up and stepped over Erkan's body to get to the middle of the cage. "Step back from the edges! They're jinn! Don't let them touch you!"

The others, distracted by the crumbling ceiling, were slow to comply, but I couldn't worry about them now. I began to turn, feeling inside myself for the spark to start the flames. I dropped the whip as I whirled faster and drew out my shard, though I kept hold of the Chalice in my other hand. Still, I didn't think of it as I turned into a proper whirl now, prying away my doubts so I could get at the core inside me. Slowly, I coaxed the flames to life, and I willed the streams of energy through my fingers and the shard to produce the violet warding fires.

I only had several rings of wards stacked by the time the sea of jinn caught up to us and began to press in. Only a couple ventured near at first, becoming distinct as they pulled away from their fellows to test my strength. I saw it play out in flashes as I continued to whirl. The fires flicked at them if they came too close, warning them away. Seemingly discouraged, the jinn melded back into the mist.

Just as it was beginning to look hopeful, the cage jerked to a halt, so suddenly I almost lost my balance. I couldn't take in much around me, but I could tell we hadn't reached the top yet, which meant the first of the spirits must have reached the yayas and overwhelmed or drove them away. I gritted my teeth as my companions yelled and panicked and got in my way, but there was nothing I could do but to keep pulling at the paltry stream of fire inside me.

The true onslaught began. I'd stacked more wards around the cage, but it was far from a complete seal when the sea of jinn crashed in. I gasped, the wards pulling for even more fire for me to maintain them, fire I didn't have. Despite the heat of the energy coursing through my body, I felt shivers setting in as cold spread throughout my body. There were too many. The fires grew thin in some places, and a few jinn began to wriggle through, wisps of smoke grasping for my companions. I tried to protect them, but I was too exhausted to give more. All I could do as I turned was watch as the holes multiplied and grew larger, and more and more of the spirits began pressing through.

Then someone threw their arms around me, disrupting my whirl and nearly making me stumble to the ground. I gave a guttural yell, my chattering teeth allowing no more than that. Whoever had embraced me had their hands splayed over my belly. I glanced down. A woman's hands.

Take her power if you can, the Qarin said in my mind. *Feed your strength with hers.*

I wanted to ask if it would kill her, but it didn't matter. I didn't know how to draw on another person's fire. It was all I could do to keep turning.

The Qarin seemed to think I hesitated for another reason. *She is stronger than you know. And she has me to help. Draw her power, Talan!*

I had no other choice but to try. Jinn reached in at every point, some waving strands mere fingers away from Haluk and Cemal cowering away from them. I couldn't last without another source of energy. Not knowing what to do, I focused on Sule's hands on my belly and was surprised to find I immediately sensed the four fiery channels from her hands. Though I'd never done it before, it was easy to draw on them once I felt them, as natural as a babe sucking at the nip. Fire trickled, then flowed, then cascaded through me. Rivers of fire coursed up my arms and out of my fingers and the shard again. As my wards strengthened and tightened, the wriggling white arms jerked back. Soon, a shimmering globe of violet light surrounded the cage.

But as soon as I'd secured it, I felt Qarin-Sule sag against my back, upsetting my balance once more. My legs became tangled in hers as she collapsed at my feet, and I tumbled against the bars of the cage, making it tilt dangerously back and forth. As soon as I stopped whirling, the shimmering sphere around us began to break apart, and the jinn pressed in again.

I staggered back to the middle, barely able to stand myself, but still I tried stoking the fire inside me to bolster the wards. But without the added energy from Sule and the Qarin, it wasn't enough. All I could manage was a candle to the furnace I needed to keep them out. I stared up as the sphere became ragged and broken. A jinni plunged through, breaking for me, and it was all I could do but wait.

"The Chalice!"

Haluk's sudden shout jolted me from my apathy, and I rallied the ward just I time to push back the jinni. "What?" I managed to tear from my throat.

"Use Nehir's Chalice!" the fanatic said again urgently. "It can produce any substance! Make your flames with it!"

I almost stopped spinning from the shock of it. But could it be true? Only one way to find out. Concentrating on the goblet in my hand, I willed it to make the violet ward flames. The sphere was little more than a skeleton now, the flames thin as knives. If this didn't work, the jinn would have us.

But the flames sprang up from the mouth of the Chalice as eager as young stallions and spread outward, pushing back with one sweep the jinn that reached in. I stared in wonder as I turned and bolstered the wards, strengthening them beyond what Qarin-Sule and I had managed. But I didn't stop when we were fully insulated — I pushed the flames from the Chalice outward, pushing into the jinn and driving them back. I couldn't see it, but I felt the pressure of their presence ease on the wards as they recoiled from them. I pushed further and further out until I could see the top of the Vacant City once again above us.

As my turns slowed, feeling more assured in our safety, I saw my companions more clearly. "It's working!" Haluk sang, still turning with me, his all-knowing facade crumbled in his joy. "It's working!"

Cemal stared at the sphere, his eyes wide and his hands clasped together and trembling.

Sule was sitting up on one elbow, the Qarin apparently back in control. She stared up at me as I continued to send out the flames, but I could feel the jinn leaving, or perhaps dissipating in the wards. I knew we'd be safe soon.

I let the flames die from the Chalice's mouth as I came to a halt. The world spun around and around, and my stomach lurched with it. I grimaced. It hadn't been a well-executed whirl and would leave me woozy for hours, but we were alive. I could hardly ask for more.

Haluk's sly smile was back. "Did I not tell you?"

"A little sooner would have been preferred." My exhaustion suddenly slumped me to the ground next to the bloodback. I met Sule's eyes, and once again tried seeing the jinni behind them. "Thank you," I muttered.

The Qarin nodded Sule's head in acknowledgment.

Now that we were safe, I set my tired mind to our last task. I craned my head back to look through the bars. The ward sphere, which had pushed out well beyond the cage, was starting to dissipate enough to see the exit from the Vacant City, a mere ten cubits away. Not far to climb, but we were all in varying states of exhaustion and had Erkan's body to bear.

"How do we get out?" I asked aloud.

"If I may, my friends…" Haluk started, stepping forward.

"Out with it."

"I am far from incapable in my ability to climb. Perhaps I shall scamper up the chain and lift us up, one wheel at a time?"

My heart beat harder just at the thought of it, but it we didn't seem to have another choice. "It's up to you. But consider: we'll be eternally licking your boots afterward if you do."

Haluk smirked and bowed, then gingerly opened the cage door, the hinges creaking as it swung out. As he leaned out over the long drop below, my stomach lurched. But the short man was able to easily reach on top and hauled himself up, showing surprising strength.

But now he had to climb the chain. I craned my head back to watch, but as soon as he stepped directly overhead, I saw through the bars and right up his Kor robe. Even the anticipation of rescue wasn't worth that sight.

So I listened with head bowed to every rattle of the chain, every grunt of exertion, with rising trepidation. Only when I heard the final whoop from the top did I take a deep breath.

But the cheer was followed by a hiss. "What is it?" I called, foreboding quickly returning. "What do you see?"

"Give me but a moment," Haluk called down between pants. "I will raise you up."

It took a good deal longer than a moment. Since it took four men to operate the lift usually, with one man to each crank, Haluk had to move from crank to crank in an attempt to keep us somewhat balanced in the cage. The better part of a turn must have gone by before the man managed to raise us up far enough to swing open the door again. Chalice and shard both tucked away in pockets, I took my turn bearing Erkan's body, bending down to lift his legs.

But as Cemal and I swung Erkan out of the cage and stepped out ourselves, I saw what Haluk had hissed at before. Red dotted every column and wall and streaked the floors in striated patterns. The four flayed bodies of the guards weren't far away.

In the corner, I saw the Tefra's corpse as well. But he hadn't been killed by jinn; from head to toe, he'd been split apart like a log with an axe. No jinn had done that. I glanced uneasily at Sule shambling ahead of Cemal and me and wondered what else this Qarin was capable of. Even if it claimed to have been enslaved before, what had been enslaving it?

I averted my gaze from the corpses and found Cemal's watery eyes, which seemed even wider than usual. I gave him a firm nod. "We'll be out of here soon. Help me with him?" The tall, bent man nodded in return, and we bent to our load. Haluk stepped next to Cemal and grabbed one of their companion's arms, looking down sadly at his prone form. And next to me, Qarin-Sule knelt and took up a leg.

We carried him toward the two huge doors that led out of the Mausoleum of Glass. The doors were now cracked in the middle as a testament to the massive force of jinn behind the blow. Cemal and Haluk shouldered them open wide enough to pass, then we staggered out onto the steps. I looked up from our load to see the new Erimis we had forged.

Fires burned in every section of the city, indiscriminate of class and race: Lavabed, Sin's Citadel, the Jade Docks, even Obsidian Heights. The air was grey with smoke, obscuring even the high noon sun, and turning a clear blue sky into the hue of stormy seas. Shouts and screams welled up from the buildings to cascade over the rooftops, sometimes piercing the rest of the din. Fighting, fleeing, hiding — there was a thick flavor of smoke and ash on my tongue. The taste of a city falling apart.

Haluk pulled us to the steps, but at that moment, the ground trembled, worse even than when we were still in the Vacant City. True fear shot through me, knowing its portent. I could almost picture the red eyes opening from the peak and the lava flowing down the volcano to envelop the city.

Valem was awakening. Whether it would be a day, a span, a season, who could tell how long he would take. But whenever the Father fully came awake, another Lament would be upon us.

The ground settled after a moment. "Well," I said, looking to each of my companions, "whether we meant to or not, it looks like we've started our revolution."

They stared back at me and each other. None of us could say this was what we wanted.

A DAY FOR PASSING ON
EPILOGUE

In the face of tragedy, a choice must be made. Either you knit with the people around you, or you tear loose to find some other place to call home. It's not a matter of nobility or bravery or loyalty. Instinct, pure self-preservation, drives us toward what we need, and we can do little but accept that outcome.

For their part, the Firewater Denizens became an inseparable cabal after Erkan's body was brought back. That first night, they drank themselves half to death with the Chalice, even as the city continued to shudder itself apart. The morning after, they vowed never to drink of it again — a vow they broke the very next night.

I drank with them, but when the others collapsed into slumber, I snuck away. At my core, I was a thief. I'd taken the silver I'd wanted from them, and now I left, no matter what proclamations I'd made on behalf of their cause. I was as exhausted as they, and could have hardly protected myself had a feral jinni happened upon me. But I'd made the opposite choice of them, intentionally or otherwise. One loose string in a city frayed to the very center of its weave was nothing much to comment on.

They would weave their tapestry back together eventually. The Firewater Resistance bloomed into being, and with a constant stream of liquid courage, it promised to be a long-lasting affair. A whole generation of tipsy young men and women formed the hive of its operations around the core members: Haluk and Cemal, Semih and Bazaad. I believed they would come through in the end if the alcohol didn't do them in first.

Another of our survivors made a similar choice as me. Once we returned Erkan's body, the Qarin departed, still in full possession of Sule's body. Where they would go, and whether the jinni would release control eventually, I couldn't know. But lacking the power to stop it and unwilling to kill her, I watched them limp off into the night, wondering all the while if I'd doomed Sule to a worse fate than even what the Shrouded Mother planned.

As for me... That night, I went to the place I once called home and made it my refuge for the final time.

———

It was afternoon before I dragged myself out of bed and found Osman. At that time of day, he was in the whirling rotunda, instructing young initiates on one of the Hortum Kor worships: Love in Strife, reunification with our world and ourselves in the midst of turmoil. With the remnants of smoke trailing about them, catching the rays of sunlight, there was something vaguely haunting and hallowed about them. As I leaned against a pillar and watched, I couldn't help a hard pit forming in my stomach. I remembered the times when simply whirling seemed to bring the world back into focus. How I wished those times could return.

I approached my old teacher during the first break in the lesson. "Osman. If you have a moment?"

The Hodja, walking toward me from the center of the rotunda, smiled his lion smile. "Sure, Talan. Never mind all these students eager to grow closer with the Underearth and our Molten God. We all revolve around your time, after all."

"Fine," I snapped. I was worn too thin to feel chagrined. "I'll come back later."

But Osman quickly caught me by the arm and began leading me away. "Keep practicing those steps until I return," he called over his shoulder to the dozen or so small whirlers. "And don't think I won't know if you stop!"

We were silent until we were halfway to his solar. "Your mood is infectious, Talan. Especially among children. Especially at a time like this."

"I know." I wished I could slink back to bed. "I don't mean to be a plague."

He nodded, then gently shoved me through his door and closed it behind. Once inside, he moved past me and knelt to light a fire and put on a pot of water. When we were seated across from each other, me in the window seat and him backward on his chair, we just stared past one another, until the water boiled and he rose to brew the tea.

"So," he said as he poured water into two cups full of dry, brown leaves, his back to me. "Where are you fleeing to now?"

My face flushed hot. "How did you know?"

One glinting eye peered back at me for a moment. "Talan," he said with an air of resignation.

"Ah. I guess I usually run away, don't I?"

His silence was answer enough.

"Well, this time is different."

"It always is."

"Then what do you suggest?" I pulled out my shard and started vigorously twirling it through my fingers. "Shall I just wait around until someone puts the pieces together and comes after me?"

There was only the clinking of a spoon against the cups for a moment. He sure was taking his time with that burning tea.

"Sule — Yanara — is missing, and her fellow bloodbacks won't know why. How long before someone comes forward and identifies me as the person she was with last? It could be someone at the docks, or a yaya still alive that knew about the Calming, or someone at that inn we went to, or the Tefra she dismissed. There are too many loose ends. Once those red priests — or Damask Esir, or *someone* high up in the Imperium — find and follow one of those threads, it's only a matter of time before the only whirling I'm doing is in chains in a dungeon cell. Is that what I should be doing?"

Osman turned back to me, the two steaming cups in hand. "You're right. I apologize."

"Thanks." I accepted the cup and breathed in the steam. Cinnamon and cloves wafted into my nose and began settling my roiling stomach. "I guess I'm just a bit worried. For you, maybe even more than myself. You're the one who recommended the Calming."

He looked surprised, then smiled ruefully. "For me? Don't worry about me, Talan. If anything, what happened would only confirm I was right about needing a Calming."

I nodded, unconvinced, but I could do nothing but accept him at his word.

Osman's brow crinkled again. "When I criticize you, it's not because I think poorly of you. I don't. I think you're an amazing young man, with many talents and much potential. I just want to see you use it for something good, Talan. More than stealing peacocks from fat pashas."

I gave him a small smile. At this point, after everything else I'd endured, that embarrassment didn't much sting anymore.

"Maybe this isn't your cause, even if you started all this. Maybe it is, just not here. But wherever you go, try and find something you believe in, will you? Because when you do…" He paused to take a sip of tea. "All this whirling and connecting to the universe — it takes on another layer."

For once, I didn't deride his philosophizing. There seemed something to it.

"Where are you planning to go?" he asked again after another long pause.

"Oedija. If it's the cosmopolitan place it claims to be, it could be the home Erimis never managed to become." I couldn't quite meet Osman's eyes, knowing how the words must pain him.

His smile was a bit strained, but I could see he agreed. "I hope so, too."

"I'll need a couple of days to get my things together, then I promise I'll stop infecting your temple with my attitude. But before I go, promise me one thing."

My Hodja raised an eyebrow, though I could see his eyes were shining. "I'd say anything, but I know you'd take advantage of me."

I mustered all the good spirits left to me. When that was all I had left, I had to make the best of it. "If you run across the High Vizier's next peacock, promise me you'll give it a kick in the feathers, will you?"

THE
CAGED
GOD

A FAMINE CYCLE STORY

As Azhi stared up at the Chains, he found there was an awful, mind-numbing grandeur to standing before the cage of a god.

The Chains rose out of the gray land, its branches spreading across the sky like pale lichen over an immense boulder. The only trees Azhi had seen in his twelve years were the stunted plants that could survive the brutal desert of the Wumofu. Never had he seen a tree grow so tall that the top of its branches disappeared into the swirling sands above.

But few had seen the cage of the Corrupted, and none had returned to tell the tale.

The storm spinning around the Chains was so thick and furious it was a wonder that any of it remained visible. Even with his veil, Azhi had to raise a sheltering arm to feel as if the wind would not peel the skin from his face. He wondered if the Chains reached the edge of the Higher Realm itself, which the elders said existed even above the infrequent desert clouds.

Sand suddenly twisted together next to him, and Azhi flinched as a figure took form. The being was exquisitely detailed, so much so he could discern its shape was a girl's, slighter and shorter than himself. Warmth and serenity radiated from the desert spirit. Though he had never seen her corporeal form before, Azhi recognized her at once.

"Imoan," he breathed. "Are you truly here?"

He felt her smile as much as saw it. "Not yet," she spoke, her voice echoing as if coming from a distance.

"Then you will be soon?"

She did not answer him, but only turned her gaze toward the smooth, white tree rising high above them. "Do you feel it?" she whispered. "He thrashes against the ties that bind him. *Taozu*."

The name split through Azhi's mind.

"Don't say his name here!" he cried, anger and fear sharpening his words.

The sand spirit did not seem to notice. "We must perform the Calming, and quickly. Or I fear he will break loose."

He looked to the Chains and felt what Imoan had described. A presence pulsed from the tree, contained within its huge trunk and sky-spanning branches. Without meaning to, he felt himself reach out with his gift to plumb the depths of the trapped being. It was like peering into an endless chasm. Azhi faced something far vaster and greater than anything he had felt before. He wondered how any bindings, even chains as great as these, could hold it.

"The Corrupted," he whispered, beginning to understand what that name truly meant.

Imoan placed a swirling hand on his shoulder, her touch uncomfortably warm. "I would not have selected you for the task if I did not think you capable. You can do this, Azhi. You must. You are the only one who can."

Her words stirred him, his faltering resolve hardening once more. Azhi had stolen this honor for himself. Now he had to prove himself deserving of it.

He took one step forward, then another. This close to the Chains, he did not need Imoan to know he walked the Evershifting Path. The ancestors sang with each step, affirming his journey as he drew close to his final destination. As he stepped close to the trunk, the winds abruptly died. But the world was far from silent. Behind him, the storm raged on, howling with all the fury the Wumofu could muster. And all around him, the ancestors sang, the chorus dissident and beautiful in a way that made Azhi tremble.

"Continue," Imoan urged him, her voice reedy and thin among the others. "Continue before it is too late."

Azhi could not hurry; it took all his strength just to put one foot before the other. As any other child of the desert, he had run the dunes of the Wumofu for many turns of the sandglass in their endless games. But the continuous march, with scant food and water, had weighed even his buoyant spirit down. Only the song of the ancestors kept it aloft now.

Reaching the base of the trunk, he paused. The path, ever one road before, had split around the Chains. The one curving to the right wound up around the trunk like a vine, while the one to the left dove into the earth like one of the tree's great roots. Yet though Azhi could perceive them by the strength of their songs, he could not follow either.

"What am I to do?" he called to Imoan.

The girl of sand drifted next to him. The swirling of her body faltered, spinning slower than before. "Follow the path," she murmured.

"Which one?"

The girl looked up. "Whichever you feel is right."

Azhi followed her gaze. Here next to the trunk, he could see the Chains extending ever up, past the dust storm around it, past any measure the human eye could see. Now he *knew* it reached the Higher Realm, for he saw no end to the pale branches. He strained to remember all he knew of the journey of the Yusishu, the savior who took on the Calming at risk of his own life. Azhi's journey, now. Always, the elders spoke of the Yusishu claiming their place in the Higher Realm once their task was complete, to live among the ancestors in peace and wealth of spirit.

By that clue, Azhi guessed which path he must take.

"Ancestors guide me," he murmured, then stepped onto the ascending path.

He expected to step through the path his gift sensed. Instead, his foot stopped a finger's width above the sands. Awed, Azhi took another step, then another. As if he climbed an invisible stairwell, each step carried him farther from the ground. *It's true,* he thought. The tales of the Yusishu ascending skyward were true. His burden felt light as he continued up the steps.

The further up he went, the more present Imoan grew beside him. Sand trickled away from her body, and the faint glow of the spirit beneath began to form. Her presence comforted and emboldened him. Azhi knew her to be an Elder One, one of the guardian spirits said to aid the Yusishu in their task. He knew it, just as he knew this was what he had been born to do. Azhi had been born the true Yusishu. That he had stolen both scepter and the opportunity to act as his people's savior was out of necessity. He did this to save his people.

"Take out the Binding Ruyi," Imoan spoke next to him. "Draw it along the trunk as you ascend and give of yourself as it demands, though sparingly. Your essence must last the sojourn."

Azhi did as she instructed, untying the scepter from his belt and placing the tip against the trunk. As soon as the end made contact, Azhi felt a jolt of awareness. The vast being trapped within the Chains, silent before, thrashed like a creature caught in a hidden trap. The Corrupted roared soundlessly, vibrating through Azhi so that, unprepared, he almost lost his footing. The ruyi strayed from the trunk, and as it lost contact, his awareness of the caged god fell away.

He stood trembling for a moment before Imoan placed a hand on his shoulder. "He is more a force of destruction than a sentient being," she murmured. "One that knows only hunger and how to sate it. The Corrupted is one of the oldest inhabitants of the Far Realms, and he will remain long after all else perishes. But by your hand, he will be trapped until dust is all he may scour. Rise, Yusishu. You must perform your duty."

What else could he do? His Elder One was urging him on. Azhi climbed to his feet, anchoring down the scepter for support. His legs trembled, and he swayed as he straightened. He *was* the true Yusishu. Only *he* could tame the Corrupted.

As his eyes sought the next step, he saw again nothing below him, nothing but empty air and the sands framed by the circle of wind. Panic rose in him, instinct battling against belief. His head flushed with fear. He felt his leg give out under him. In that splintered moment, he knew his faltering belief had not been enough.

Azhi pitched from the path and fell to the sands far below.

He sank like a stone through water. The white trunk of the Chains blurred by. Terror rose to swallow him. His head hit first, splitting like a cactus fruit dropped on stone, the sand hard from the force of his long fall. His neck buckled next, bending and cracking as his body followed fast after. Limbs splayed out and lashed against the ground, bones snapping so that he lay like cloth on a windless day. Blood leaked from his wounds, seeping into the sands.

The excruciating pain that should have flooded him had been ripped away, replaced by numbness. Azhi tried to move his arms and legs, but they did not respond. He could not see. He could not smell. He could not *feel*. Panic filled him, throbbing in the vacuum of himself. He had become nothing.

Then, without warning, the pain returned. *Something* fed on him. Like a desert cat gnawing on a bone, another presence feasted on the being he had become like he were nothing more than carrion.

A foul spirit had found him.

Stop! he tried to cry out. *Wait!*

But the foul spirit paid him no heed. It was a predator, and he was nothing more than sustenance to it.

Azhi abandoned his futile attempts to move his body and pushed instead with his gift. That, at least, seemed to remain with him, for as he made his essence hard and sharp, he provoked a response from his devourer. The great being almost seemed surprised as it drew back. Azhi tried to wrench himself away, but something bound him down, anchoring him in place.

My body. The memory of what had just happened — of his failure and his death — seeped into his awareness. *My body, broken and bleeding into the sands.*

The shock made him pause long enough that the evil spirit seized him again. This time, it chewed furiously, knowing he would not go quietly.

Azhi cried out as his essence was rapidly torn apart. *Imoan!* His Elder One had guided him this far. She would save him. But why hadn't she come already? *Imoan, please! He has his claws in me!*

Her answer was like a breath on the wind. *I am sorry, Azhi. For deceiving you. For what I have brought upon the world.*

She peeled her mind away from his, leaving him to his fate.

Azhi screamed as the vast being gnawed into him. Suddenly, he realized just what it was. *Taozu.* Taozu consumed him. Taozu, the Worldeater, worked his way free of his prison. And Azhi was to be his key.

The Corrupted pulsed at the recognition, as if gratified to be known again to the world. He did not pause in his feast.

No matter how he struggled, Azhi could not break free. The overwhelming emptiness behind Taozu's mind sucked him further in, into depths from which he knew he could not return. But before he could fade completely, he latched onto something else.

Chanting filled his mind.

The chanting rose all about Azhi, twisting and looping around him and Taozu like a noose. The Corrupted roared with rage and surprise. For a moment, his attention was pulled from Azhi.

He seized his chance. Ripping free of the last frail bonds of his body, Azhi gathered his remaining essence close to him and fled into the vast, unknowable plane about him.

Slowly, senses returned to him, though they were not the same as when he had been alive. Energy pulsed in this world, heat radiating through and around him. *He* was nothing more than energy and heat himself, or near enough. Azhi trembled at the sudden shift. He feared he would lose himself if he did not hold his essence tightly together in this strange, shifting world.

Taozu roared behind him once more, reminding Azhi of his lingering danger. He sensed the Corrupted now as a rising inferno, raging and seething against the glowing white rope that sought to contain him. As the chanting grew ever louder, Azhi suddenly understood. *The Evershifting Path.* Formed of the faded essence of the ancestors, it had risen in one last effort to contain its prisoner.

But as rope before fire, the ancestors were quickly thinning and fading, their song growing fainter. Despair froze Azhi in place as he realized the truth. Taozu would tear free. As he had destroyed the empires of old, so he would destroy the Four Realms, the last civilizations in the world.

And it had been Azhi who had freed him.

As Taozu's fury grew, so did his presence. Azhi felt his hunger for essence as if the hunger were his own. He quavered in terror once again. He felt the desire to consume fill him.

But he did not indulge it, but instead fled. Azhi left behind the thrashing demon and the fading ancestors. Only then did he realize the awful truth.

He had never been the Yusishu. He had been a stupid boy following a glorious mirage, believing an evil spirit to be an Elder One. Imoan had deceived him, but only because he had let her.

He was the boy who had doomed the world.

Azhi soared fast and far through the Higher Realm and left the Worldeater to break loose for his last, great feast.

ACKNOWLEDGMENTS

I owe a humongous round of thanks to the many people who left their mark on a Famine Cycle book:

Nick, who did the initial proofreading for *Whispers of Ruin*.

Sylvia Cottrell, the first editor of *Whispers of Ruin*.

Kaitlyn, my wife and first reader, who has always actively supported my writing career.

Shawn Sharrah, who excels with his proofreading.

Ömer Burak Önal, for the gorgeous new illustration for the omnibus.

Rachel St. Clair, for expanding on Ömer's art and designing it into its stupendous cover. Thank you also for the lovely series logo.

René Aigner and *Rebekah Teller*, for their wonderful original cover illustrations, included here as interior art.

My constantly kind *Patreon supporters*: Debbie, Tarris & Ruth, Larry, Don, Tony, Ben, and Nick.

And finally, thank you, *dear reader*, for seeing this series of mine through to its end.

~ *J.D.L. Rosell*

GLOSSARY

Acadians - The scholarly residents of the Acadium; often, they are wardens. While not all Acadians are wardens, any warden caught are forced to become an Acadian, or face the penalty of death.

The Acadium - Nominally, the center of learning and education within Oedija. The Acadium serves a dual purpose, however: the reeducation and containment of wardens.

Archon - The representative of the Despot or Despoina within the People's Conclave and Demos Council. Their powers are primarily limited to moderation, except when a member is missing on the Demos Council or a tie vote must be broken.

Avvad, or the Avvadin Imperium - The ever-expanding empire that lies to the south of Oedija.

Bali - The people who reside among the plateaus to the east of Oedija.

Buyujinn - The great spirits of the Avvadin people.

The Confessionary Tribunal, or the Tribunal - The judicial branch of Oedija's government, they are responsible for enforcing the rule of law, including the containment and punishment of rogue wardens. They are not elected, but are recruited by their own.

Daemons - Spirits who are considered evil or mean-spirited; also a derogatory term for wardens.

Damask Esir - The elite warriors of Avvad; said to be controlled by daemons called Qarin.

Demes - Districts of the city of Oedija.

Demos Council - The ruling council within the People's Conclave. Traditionally, it numbers eleven Low Consuls, with the Archon acting as a moderator, though often, the eleventh seat is disputed. Their responsibilities largely lie in determining the agenda within the larger Conclave. In times of strife, however, they are granted powers of military action and broad budgetary powers.

Demotism - A system of democratic republicanism in which representative officials are elected by citizens, or landowners, into a legislative ruling body.

The Despot/Despoina - The Ruling Wreath; a symbolic ruler who acts as a figurehead for Oedija. Small powers as the official emissary of Oedija and the nominal leader of Oedija's militia (when marshaled).

Eidola - The gods of the Eidolan religion.

Eidolanism - The religion of the original settlers of Oedija, in Airene's time, it is a fading religion, with many of its beliefs considered antiquated.

Energetic elements - The forms of energy present in the Pyrthae. Three energetic elements are commonly known: radiance, or heat and light; kinesis, or force; and magnesis, or the fields of magnetism. A fourth form of energy, catalysm, is also known to manifest in rare individuals. Other energetic elements are believed to exist, but are unconfirmed.

Finches (as a title) - Hunters and peddlers of secrets. While in purpose, their mission is to expose wrongdoing and uncover hidden truths, in practice they often perform small jobs recovering and threatening others with incriminating information for those who will pay.

First Laurel - The leader of the laurel guard, the soldiers defending the Laurel Palace and other Wreath properties.

The Four Realms - Considered the last bastions of civilization in a backwards world, four nations are united in peace by a concordance. These nations are: Oedija, the Bali ishakas, the Qao Fu jaitin, and the Avvadin Imperium.

Guilders - People who work on behalf of the Underguild.

Hilarion - The jester to the Despot or Despoina. Hilarion is always chosen from among Oedija's male wardens. Traditionally, he wears a crown of wheat, sackcloth clothes, and sandals bound with rope. Hilarion's nominal purpose is to entertain at the whim of the Ruling Wreath, but his true purpose is understood to be to diminish fear that people hold for wardens by making him an object of laughter and ridicule.

Honors - The lowest caste of Oedijan society. They are not permitted to own property, including money, nor choose their own employment, and are often housed and work within the estates of patricians. Honors are the descendants of the Kalthuae, the native inhabitants of the lands Oedija now claims, before settlers sailed from the west to found the nation.

Ishakas - The tribal kingdoms of the Bali people.

Jaitin - The matriarchal groups of the Qao Fu people; grouped by the caves in which they reside.

Low Consuls - The members of the Demos Council. Low Consuls are elected from the Conclave, requiring the support of ten of their fellow Servants to gain a seat.

Oedija - The "Pearl of the Four Realms"; the primary location of the story. A republican society undergoing significant turmoil, with threats from within and without.

Order of Verifiers - A branch of Oedija government tasked with routing out corruption. It was disbanded a few years after its founding, and a century before Airene of Port fashions herself after them.

The People's Conclave, or the Conclave - The legislative body of Oedija. Within their parameters lies the making and governance of laws, the taxing and determination of the treasury, the governance of commerce, and the defense of the nation.

The Peninsula - A rural area of Oedija to the north of the city of Oedija.

Prefectures - Areas of governance across Oedija's countryside.

Pyr - Spirits who are considered either benevolent or innocuous.

Pyrkin - A moss-like substance that is considered somewhere between plant and animal, it is supposed to have a connection to the Pyrthae, on account of its bioluminescence.

The Pyrthae - The plane of spirits, which is said to run parallel to the material plane, Telae.

Qao Fu - The people who reside among the desert caves to the northeast of Oedija.

Quintessence - The soul when it is used by channeling as an energetic element.

Servants - The elected leaders of Oedija, with semi-proportional representation from across Oedija's ten demes. They number one-hundred and twenty-one, minus those Servants who are elected to the Demos Council. They are responsible for legislative actions.

Shepherds - Members of the Confessionary Tribunal, they act under the guidance of a Tribune to contain or punish any rogue warden.

Stratechons - The five permanent military leaders of Oedija. Responsible for the city guard and the taxoi (when they are gathered).

Taxoi (s. taxos) - The militia of Oedija. As Oedija has no standing army, the taxoi are organized and financed by patrician households whenever the need arises.

Tefra - Priests of Avvad who use Silks, or bound spirits, to fight on their behalf.

Telae - The material plane; or, the world as it is known, including The Four Realms.

Tribunes - Members of the Confessionary Tribunal, they act as arbiters of Oedija's justice.

The Underguild - A semi-legitimized criminal organization. Overseen by five Guildmasters, the Underguild has a great hold over criminal activity in Oedija, and is largely responsible for its relatively low crime.

Verifiers of Truth, or Verifiers - Members of the Order of Verifiers, who were tasked with routing out corruption in Oedija's government, and were met with often violent resistance.

Wardens - People who are attuned to the Pyrthae and are able to manipulate forms of energy as magic. Across the Four Realms, they are forced into hiding, killed, lauded, and enslaved, depending on the nation. In Oedija, they are feared and kept to specific roles, such as Acadians or Shepherds, that suppresses their freedom and use of their abilities.

The Wreaths - The royal family of Oedija, formerly the true rulers of the nation when it was a monarchy.

Valemism / The Valemish - Worshippers of the volcanic god Valem, the religion of Valemism began in Avvad. It is considered a strict religion with a heavy emphasis on subjugation and obedience to authority, and the punishments for disobedience.

BOOKS BY J.D.L. ROSELL

Sign up for future releases at jdlrosell.com.

THE FAMINE CYCLE

1. Whispers of Ruin
2. Echoes of Chaos
3. Requiem of Silence

Secret Seller *(Prequel)*

The Phantom Heist *(Novella)*

———

RANGER OF THE TITAN WILDS

1. The Last Ranger
2. The First Ancestor
3. The Hidden Guardian
4. The Wilds Exile

———

LEGEND OF TAL

1. A King's Bargain
2. A Queen's Command
3. An Emperor's Gamble
4. A God's Plea

A Battle Between Blood *(Novella)*

———

THE RUNEWAR SAGA

1. The Throne of Ice & Ash
2. The Crown of Fire & Fury
3. The Stone of Iron & Omen

———

ABOUT THE AUTHOR

J.D.L. Rosell was swept away on a journey when he stepped foot outside his door and into The Hobbit. He hasn't stopped wandering since.

In his writing, he tries to recapture the wonder, adventure, and poignancy that captivated him as a child. His explorations have taken him to worlds set in over a dozen novels and five series, which include Ranger of the Titan Wilds, Legend of Tal, The Runewar Saga, and The Famine Cycle.

When he's not off on a quest, Rosell enjoys his newfound hobby of archery and older pastimes of hiking and landscape photography. But every hobbit returns home, and if you step softly and mind the potatoes, you may glimpse him curled up with his wife and two cats, Zelda and Abenthy, reading a good book or replaying his favorite video games.

To check out his writing for free, pick up his series starter story bundle at jdlrosell.com or contact him at josiah@jdlrosell.com.

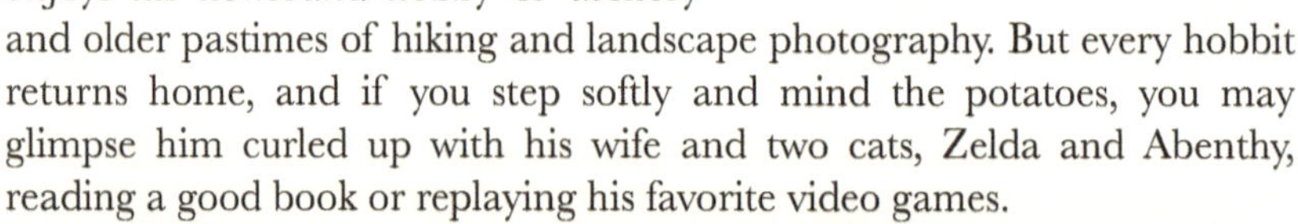